THE A B C MURDERS

ALSO BY AGATHA CHRISTIE

Mysteries
The Man in the Brown Suit
The Secret of Chimneys
The Seven Dials Mystery
The Mysterious Mr Quin
The Sittaford Mystery
The Hound of Death
The Listerdale Mystery
Why Didn't They Ask Evans?
Parker Pyne Investigates
Murder Is Easy
And Then There Were None
Death Comes as the End
Sparkling Cyanide
Crooked House
They Came to Baghdad
Destination Unknown
Spider's Web*
The Unexpected Guest*
Ordeal by Innocence
The Pale Horse
Endless Night
Passenger to Frankfurt

Poirot
The Mysterious Affair at Styles
The Murder on the Links
Poirot Investigates
The Murder of Roger Ackroyd
The Big Four
The Mystery of the Blue Train
Black Coffee*
Peril at End House
Lord Edgware Dies
Murder on the Orient Express
Three Act Tragedy
Death in the Clouds
The ABC Murders
Murder in Mesopotamia
Cards on the Table
Murder in the Mews
Dumb Witness
Death on the Nile
Appointment With Death
Hercule Poirot's Christmas
Sad Cypress
One, Two, Buckle My Shoe
Evil Under the Sun
Five Little Pigs
The Hollow
The Labours of Hercules
Taken at the Flood
Mrs McGinty's Dead
After the Funeral
Hickory Dickory Dock
Dead Man's Folly
Cat Among the Pigeons
The Adventure of the Christmas Pudding
The Clocks
Third Girl
Hallowe'en Party
Elephants Can Remember
Poirot's Early Cases
Curtain: Poirot's Last Case

Marple
The Murder at the Vicarage
The Thirteen Problems
The Body in the Library
The Moving Finger
A Murder is Announced
They Do It With Mirrors
A Pocket Full of Rye
4.50 from Paddington
The Mirror Crack'd from Side to Side
A Caribbean Mystery
At Bertram's Hotel
Nemesis
Sleeping Murder
Miss Marple's Final Cases

Tommy & Tuppence
The Secret Adversary
Partners in Crime
N or M?
By the Pricking of My Thumbs
Postern of Fate

Published as Mary Westmacott
Giant's Bread
Unfinished Portrait
Absent in the Spring
The Rose and the Yew Tree
A Daughter's a Daughter
The Burden

Memoirs
An Autobiography
Come, Tell Me How You Live
The Grand Tour

Plays and Stories
Akhnaton
The Mousetrap and Other Plays
The Floating Admiral (contributor)
Star Over Bethlehem

* novelized by Charles Osborne

Agatha Christie

The A B C Murders

HarperCollins*Publishers*

HarperCollins*Publishers* Ltd
1 London Bridge Street
London SE1 9GF
www.harpercollins.co.uk

This paperback edition 2013
8

First published in Great Britain by
Collins 1936

Agatha Christie® Poirot® The A B C Murders™
Copyright © 1936 Agatha Christie Limited. All rights reserved.
www.agathachristie.com

A catalogue record for this book is
available from the British Library

ISBN 978-0-00-752753-3 (PB)
ISBN 978-0-00-825567-1 (POD PB)

Set in Sabon by FMG using Atomik ePublisher from Easypress
Printed and bound by
CPI Group (UK) Ltd, Croydon, CR0 4YY

All rights reserved. No part of this publication may be
reproduced, stored in a retrieval system, or transmitted,
in any form or by any means, electronic, mechanical,
photocopying, recording or otherwise, without the prior
written permission of the publishers.

This book is sold subject to the condition that it shall not,
by way of trade or otherwise, be lent, re-sold, hired out or
otherwise circulated without the publisher's prior consent
in any form of binding or cover other than that in which it
is published and without a similar condition including this
condition being imposed on the subsequent purchaser.

MIX
Paper from
responsible sources
FSC
www.fsc.org
FSC C007454

FSC™ is a non-profit international organisation established to promote
the responsible management of the world's forests. Products carrying the
FSC label are independently certified to assure consumers that they come
from forests that are managed to meet the social, economic and
ecological needs of present and future generations,
and other controlled sources.

Find out more about HarperCollins and the environment at
www.harpercollins.co.uk/green

To James Watts
One of my most sympathetic readers

Contents

1. The Letter — 1
2. (Not from Captain Hastings' Personal Narrative) — 9
3. Andover — 10
4. Mrs Ascher — 18
5. Mary Drower — 25
6. The Scene of the Crime — 33
7. Mr Partridge and Mr Riddell — 45
8. The Second Letter — 51
9. The Bexhill-on-Sea Murder — 61
10. The Barnards — 72
11. Megan Barnard — 79
12. Donald Fraser — 86
13. A Conference — 91
14. The Third Letter — 100
15. Sir Carmichael Clarke — 108
16. (Not from Captain Hastings' Personal Narrative) — 119
17. Marking Time — 123
18. Poirot Makes a Speech — 131
19. By Way of Sweden — 144
20. Lady Clarke — 149
21. Description of a Murderer — 161
22. (Not from Captain Hastings' Personal Narrative) — 168
23. September 11th. Doncaster — 175
24. (Not from Captain Hastings' Personal Narrative) — 185
25. (Not from Captain Hastings' Personal Narrative) — 188
26. (Not from Captain Hastings' Personal Narrative) — 191
27. The Doncaster Murder — 194
28. (Not from Captain Hastings' Personal Narrative) — 202
29. At Scotland Yard — 212
30. (Not from Captain Hastings' Personal Narrative) — 217
31. Hercule Poirot Asks Questions — 219
32. And Catch a Fox — 227
33. Alexander Bonaparte Cust — 235
34. Poirot Explains — 243
35. Finale — 264

FOREWORD
BY
Captain Arthur Hastings, O. B. E.

In this narrative of mine I have departed from my usual practice of relating only those incidents and scenes at which I myself was present. Certain chapters, therefore, were written in the third person.

I wish to assure my readers that I can vouch for the occurences related in these chapters. If I have taken a certain poetic licence in describing the thoughts and feelings of various persons, it is because I believe I have set them down with a reasonable amount of accuracy. I may add that they have been "vetted" by my friend Hercule Poirot himself.

In conclusion, I will say that if I have described at too great lenght some of the secondary personal relationships which arose as a consequence of this strange series of crimes, it is because the human and personal element can never be ignored. Hercule Poirot once taught me in a very dramatic manner that romance can be a by-product of crime.

As to the solving of the A B C mystery, I can only say that in my opinion Poirot showed real genius in the way he tackled a problem entirely unlike any which had previously come his way.

CHAPTER 1

The Letter

It was in June of 1935 that I came home from my ranch in South America for a stay of about six months. It had been a difficult time for us out there. Like everyone else, we had suffered from world depression. I had various affairs to see to in England that I felt could only be successful if a personal touch was introduced. My wife remained to manage the ranch.

I need hardly say that one of my first actions on reaching England was to look up my old friend, Hercule Poirot.

I found him installed in one of the newest type of service flats in London. I accused him (and he admitted the fact) of having chosen this particular building entirely on account of its strictly geometrical appearance and proportions.

'But yes, my friend, it is of a most pleasing symmetry, do you not find it so?'

I said that I thought there could be too much squareness and, alluding to an old joke, I asked if in this super-modern hostelry they managed to induce hens to lay square eggs.

Poirot laughed heartily.

Agatha Christie

'Ah, you remember that? Alas! no—science has not yet induced the hens to conform to modern tastes, they still lay eggs of different sizes and colours!'

I examined my old friend with an affectionate eye. He was looking wonderfully well—hardly a day older than when I had last seen him.

'You're looking in fine fettle, Poirot,' I said. 'You've hardly aged at all. In fact, if it were possible, I should say that you had fewer grey hairs than when I saw you last.'

Poirot beamed on me.

'And why is that not possible? It is quite true.'

'Do you mean your hair is turning from grey to black instead of from black to grey?'

'Precisely.'

'But surely that's a scientific impossibility!'

'Not at all.'

'But that's very extraordinary. It seems against nature.'

'As usual, Hastings, you have the beautiful and unsuspicious mind. Years do not change that in you! You perceive a fact and mention the solution of it in the same breath without noticing that you are doing so!'

I stared at him, puzzled.

Without a word he walked into his bedroom and returned with a bottle in his hand which he handed to me.

I took it, for the moment uncomprehending.

It bore the words:

Revivit.—To bring back the natural tone of the hair. *Revivit* is *not* a dye. In five shades, Ash, Chestnut, Titian, Brown, Black.

'Poirot,' I cried. 'You have dyed your hair!'

'Ah, the comprehension comes to you!'

'So *that's* why your hair looks so much blacker than it did last time I was back.'

'Exactly.'

'Dear me,' I said, recovering from the shock. 'I suppose next time I come home I shall find you wearing false moustaches—or are you doing so now?'

Poirot winced. His moustaches had always been his sensitive point. He was inordinately proud of them. My words touched him on the raw.

'No, no, indeed, *mon ami*. That day, I pray the good God, is still far off. The false moustache! *Quel horreur!*'

He tugged at them vigorously to assure me of their genuine character.

'Well, they are very luxuriant still,' I said.

'*N'est ce pas?* Never, in the whole of London, have I seen a pair of moustaches to equal mine.'

A good job too, I thought privately. But I would not for the world have hurt Poirot's feelings by saying so.

Instead I asked if he still practised his profession on occasion.

'I know,' I said, 'that you actually retired years ago—'

'*C'est vrai*. To grow the vegetable marrows! And immediately a murder occurs—and I send the vegetable marrows to promenade themselves to the devil. And since then—I know very well what you will say—I am like the prima donna who makes positively the farewell performance! That farewell performance, it repeats itself an indefinite number of times!'

Agatha Christie

I laughed.

'In truth, it has been very like that. Each time I say: this is the end. But no, something else arises! And I will admit it, my friend, the retirement I care for it not at all. If the little grey cells are not exercised, they grow the rust.'

'I see,' I said. 'You exercise them in moderation.'

'Precisely. I pick and choose. For Hercule Poirot nowadays only the cream of crime.'

'Has there been much cream about?'

'*Pas mal*. Not long ago I had a narrow escape.'

'Of failure?'

'No, no.' Poirot looked shocked. 'But I—I, *Hercule Poirot*, was nearly exterminated.'

I whistled.

'An enterprising murderer!'

'Not so much enterprising as careless,' said Poirot. 'Precisely that—careless. But let us not talk of it. You know, Hastings, in many ways I regard you as my mascot.'

'Indeed?' I said. 'In what ways?'

Poirot did not answer my question directly. He went on:

'As soon as I heard you were coming over I said to myself: something will arise. As in former days we will hunt together, we two. But if so it must be no common affair. It must be something'—he waved his hands excitedly—'something *recherché*—delicate—*fine*...' He gave the last untranslatable word its full flavour.

'Upon my word, Poirot,' I said. 'Anyone would think you were ordering a dinner at the Ritz.'

'Whereas one cannot command a crime to order? Very true.' He sighed. 'But I believe in luck—in destiny, if you will. It is your destiny to stand beside me and prevent me from committing the unforgivable error.'

'What do you call the unforgivable error?'

'Overlooking the obvious.'

I turned this over in my mind without quite seeing the point.

'Well,' I said presently, smiling, 'has this super crime turned up yet?'

'*Pas encore*. At least—that is—'

He paused. A frown of perplexity creased his forehead. His hands automatically straightened an object or two that I had inadvertently pushed awry.

'I am not sure,' he said slowly.

There was something so odd about his tone that I looked at him in surprise.

The frown still lingered.

Suddenly with a brief decisive nod of the head he crossed the room to a desk near the window. Its contents, I need hardly say, were all neatly docketed and pigeon-holed so that he was able at once to lay his hand upon the paper he wanted.

He came slowly across to me, an open letter in his hand. He read it through himself, then passed it to me.

'Tell me, *mon ami*,' he said. 'What do you make of this?'

I took it from him with some interest.

It was written on thickish white notepaper in printed characters:

Agatha Christie

Mr Hercule Poirot,—You fancy yourself, don't you, at solving mysteries that are too difficult for our poor thick-headed British police? Let us see, Mr Clever Poirot, just how clever you can be. Perhaps you'll find this nut too hard to crack. Look out for Andover, on the 21st of the month.

    Yours, etc.,
    A B C.

I glanced at the envelope. That also was printed.
'Postmarked WC1,' said Poirot as I turned my attention to the postmark. 'Well, what is your opinion?'
I shrugged my shoulders as I handed it back to him.
'Some madman or other, I suppose.'
'That is all you have to say?'
'Well—doesn't it sound like a madman to you?'
'Yes, my friend, it does.'
His tone was grave. I looked at him curiously.
'You take this very seriously, Poirot.'
'A madman, *mon ami*, is to be taken seriously. A madman is a very dangerous thing.'
'Yes, of course, that is true... I hadn't considered that point... But what I meant was, it sounds more like a rather idiotic kind of hoax. Perhaps some convivial idiot who had had one over the eight.'
'*Comment?* Nine? Nine what?'
'Nothing—just an expression. I meant a fellow who was tight. No, damn it, a fellow who had had a spot too much to drink.'

'*Merci*, Hastings—the expression "tight" I *am* acquainted with it. As you say, there may be nothing more to it than that...'

'But you think there is?' I asked, struck by the dissatisfaction of his tone.

Poirot shook his head doubtfully, but he did not speak.

'What have you done about it?' I inquired.

'What can one do? I showed it to Japp. He was of the same opinion as you—a stupid hoax—that was the expression he used. They get these things every day at Scotland Yard. I, too, have had my share...'

'But you take this one seriously?'

Poirot replied slowly.

'There is something about that letter, Hastings, that I do not like...'

In spite of myself, his tone impressed me.

'You think—what?'

He shook his head, and picking up the letter, put it away again in the desk.

'If you really take it seriously, can't you do something?' I asked.

'As always, the man of action! But what is there to do? The county police have seen the letter but they, too, do not take it seriously. There are no fingerprints on it. There are no local clues as to the possible writer.'

'In fact there is only your own instinct?'

'Not instinct, Hastings. Instinct is a bad word. It is my *knowledge*—my *experience*—that tells me that something about that letter is wrong—'

He gesticulated as words failed him, then shook his head again.

'I may be making the mountain out of the anthill. In any case there is nothing to be done but wait.'

'Well, the 21st is Friday. If a whacking great robbery takes place near Andover then—'

'Ah, what a comfort that would be—!'

'*A comfort?*' I stared. The word seemed to be a very extraordinary one to use.

'A robbery may be a *thrill* but it can hardly be a comfort!' I protested.

Poirot shook his head energetically.

'You are in error, my friend. You do not understand my meaning. A robbery would be a relief since it would dispossess my mind of the fear of something else.'

'Of what?'

'*Murder*,' said Hercule Poirot.

CHAPTER 2

(Not from Captain Hastings' Personal Narrative)

Mr Alexander Bonaparte Cust rose from his seat and peered near-sightedly round the shabby bedroom. His back was stiff from sitting in a cramped position and as he stretched himself to his full height an onlooker would have realized that he was, in reality, quite a tall man. His stoop and his near-sighted peering gave a delusive impression.

Going to a well-worn overcoat hanging on the back of the door, he took from the pocket a packet of cheap cigarettes and some matches. He lit a cigarette and then returned to the table at which he had been sitting. He picked up a railway guide and consulted it, then he returned to the consideration of a typewritten list of names. With a pen, he made a tick against one of the first names on the list.

It was Thursday, June 20th.

CHAPTER 3

Andover

I had been impressed at the time by Poirot's forebodings about the anonymous letter he had received, but I must admit that the matter had passed from my mind when the 21st actually arrived and the first reminder of it came with a visit paid to my friend by Chief Inspector Japp of Scotland Yard. The CID inspector had been known to us for many years and he gave me a hearty welcome.

'Well, I never,' he exclaimed. 'If it isn't Captain Hastings back from the wilds of the what do you call it! Quite like old days seeing you here with Monsieur Poirot. You're looking well, too. Just a little bit thin on top, eh? Well, that's what we're all coming to. I'm the same.'

I winced slightly. I was under the impression that owing to the careful way I brushed my hair across the top of my head the thinness referred to by Japp was quite unnoticeable. However, Japp had never been remarkable for tact where I was concerned, so I put a good face upon it and agreed that we were none of us getting any younger.

'Except Monsieur Poirot here,' said Japp. 'Quite a good advertisement for a hair tonic, he'd be. Face fungus sprouting finer than ever. Coming out into the limelight, too, in his old age. Mixed up in all the celebrated cases of the day. Train mysteries, air mysteries, high society deaths—oh, he's here, there and everywhere. Never been so celebrated as since he retired.'

'I have already told Hastings that I am like the prima donna who makes always one more appearance,' said Poirot, smiling.

'I shouldn't wonder if you ended by detecting your own death,' said Japp, laughing heartily. 'That's an idea, that is. Ought to be put in a book.'

'It will be Hastings who will have to do that,' said Poirot, twinkling at me.

'Ha ha! That would be a joke, that would,' laughed Japp.

I failed to see why the idea was so extremely amusing, and in any case I thought the joke was in poor taste. Poirot, poor old chap, is getting on. Jokes about his approaching demise can hardly be agreeable to him.

Perhaps my manner showed my feelings, for Japp changed the subject.

'Have you heard about Monsieur Poirot's anonymous letter?'

'I showed it to Hastings the other day,' said my friend.

'Of course,' I exclaimed. 'It had quite slipped my memory. Let me see, what was the date mentioned?'

'The 21st,' said Japp. 'That's what I dropped in about. Yesterday was the 21st and just out of curiosity I rang up

Agatha Christie

Andover last night. It was a hoax all right. Nothing doing. One broken shop window—kid throwing stones—and a couple of drunk and disorderlies. So just for once our Belgian friend was barking up the wrong tree.'

'I am relieved, I must confess,' acknowledged Poirot.

'You'd quite got the wind up about it, hadn't you?' said Japp affectionately. 'Bless you, we get dozens of letters like that coming in every day! People with nothing better to do and a bit weak in the top storey sit down and write 'em. They don't mean any harm! Just a kind of excitement.'

'I have indeed been foolish to take the matter so seriously,' said Poirot. 'It is the nest of the horse that I put my nose into there.'

'You're mixing up mares and wasps,' said Japp.

'*Pardon?*'

'Just a couple of proverbs. Well, I must be off. Got a little business in the next street to see to—receiving stolen jewellery. I thought I'd just drop in on my way and put your mind at rest. Pity to let those grey cells function unnecessarily.'

With which words and a hearty laugh, Japp departed.

'He does not change much, the good Japp, eh?' asked Poirot.

'He looks much older,' I said. 'Getting as grey as a badger,' I added vindictively.

Poirot coughed and said:

'You know, Hastings, there is a little device—my hairdresser is a man of great ingenuity—one attaches it to the scalp and brushes one's own hair over it—it is not a wig, you comprehend—but—'

'Poirot,' I roared. 'Once and for all I will have nothing to do with the beastly inventions of your confounded hairdresser. What's the matter with the top of my head?'

'Nothing—nothing at all.'

'It's not as though I were going *bald*.'

'Of course not! Of course not!'

'The hot summers out there naturally cause the hair to fall out a bit. I shall take back a really good hair tonic.'

'*Précisément*.'

'And, anyway, what business is it of Japp's? He always was an offensive kind of devil. And no sense of humour. The kind of man who laughs when a chair is pulled away just as a man is about to sit down.'

'A great many people would laugh at that.'

'It's utterly senseless.'

'From the point of view of the man about to sit, certainly it is.'

'Well,' I said, slightly recovering my temper. (I admit that I am touchy about the thinness of my hair.) 'I'm sorry that anonymous letter business came to nothing.'

'I have indeed been in the wrong over that. About that letter, there was, I thought, the odour of the fish. Instead a mere stupidity. Alas, I grow old and suspicious like the blind watch-dog who growls when there is nothing there.'

'If I'm going to co-operate with you, we must look about for some other "creamy" crime,' I said with a laugh.

'You remember your remark of the other day? If you could order a crime as one orders a dinner, what would you choose?'

Agatha Christie

I fell in with his humour.

'Let me see now. Let's review the menu. Robbery? Forgery? No, I think not. Rather too vegetarian. It must be murder—red-blooded murder—with trimmings, of course.'

'Naturally. The *hors d'oeuvres*.'

'Who shall the victim be—man or woman? Man, I think. Some big-wig. American millionaire. Prime Minister. Newspaper proprietor. Scene of the crime—well, what's wrong with the good old library? Nothing like it for atmosphere. As for the weapon—well, it might be a curiously twisted dagger—or some blunt instrument—a carved stone idol—'

Poirot sighed.

'Or, of course,' I said, 'there's poison—but that's always so technical. Or a revolver shot echoing in the night. Then there must be a beautiful girl or two—'

'With auburn hair,' murmured my friend.

'Your same old joke. One of the beautiful girls, of course, must be unjustly suspected—and there's some misunderstanding between her and the young man. And then, of course, there must be some other suspects—an older woman—dark, dangerous type—and some friend or rival of the dead man's—and a quiet secretary—dark horse—and a hearty man with a bluff manner—and a couple of discharged servants or gamekeepers or somethings—and a damn fool of a detective rather like Japp—and well—that's about all.'

'That is your idea of the cream, eh?'

'I gather you don't agree.'

Poirot looked at me sadly.

'You have made there a very pretty résumé of nearly all the detective stories that have ever been written.'

'Well,' I said. 'What would *you* order?'

Poirot closed his eyes and leaned back in his chair. His voice came purringly from between his lips.

'A very simple crime. A crime with no complications. A crime of quiet domestic life... very unimpassioned—very *intime*.'

'How can a crime be *intime*?'

'Supposing,' murmured Poirot, 'that four people sit down to play bridge and one, the odd man out, sits in a chair by the fire. At the end of the evening the man by the fire is found dead. One of the four, while he is dummy, has gone over and killed him, and intent on the play of the hand, the other three have not noticed. Ah, there would be a crime for you! *Which of the four was it?*'

'Well,' I said. 'I can't see *any* excitement in that!'

Poirot threw me a glance of reproof.

'No, because there are no curiously twisted daggers, no blackmail, no emerald that is the stolen eye of a god, no untraceable Eastern poisons. You have the melodramatic soul, Hastings. You would like, not one murder, but a series of murders.'

'I admit,' I said, 'that a second murder in a book often cheers things up. If the murder happens in the first chapter, and you have to follow up everybody's alibi until the last page but one—well, it does get a bit tedious.'

The telephone rang and Poirot rose to answer.

Agatha Christie

''Allo,' he said. ''Allo. Yes, it is Hercule Poirot speaking.'

He listened for a minute or two and then I saw his face change.

His own side of the conversation was short and disjointed.

'*Mais oui*...'

'Yes, of course...'

'But yes, we will come...'

'Naturally...'

'It may be as you say...'

'Yes, I will bring it. *A tout à l'heure* then.'

He replaced the receiver and came across the room to me.

'That was Japp speaking, Hastings.'

'Yes?'

'He had just got back to the Yard. There was a message from Andover...'

'Andover?' I cried excitedly.

Poirot said slowly:

'An old woman of the name of Ascher who keeps a little tobacco and newspaper shop has been found murdered.'

I think I felt ever so slightly damped. My interest, quickened by the sound of Andover, suffered a faint check. I had expected something fantastic—out of the way! The murder of an old woman who kept a little tobacco shop seemed, somehow, sordid and uninteresting.

Poirot continued in the same slow, grave voice:

'The Andover police believe they can put their hand on the man who did it—'

I felt a second throb of disappointment.

'It seems the woman was on bad terms with her husband.

He drinks and is by way of being rather a nasty customer. He's threatened to take her life more than once.

'Nevertheless,' continued Poirot, 'in view of what has happened, the police there would like to have another look at the anonymous letter I received. I have said that you and I will go down to Andover at once.'

My spirits revived a little. After all, sordid as this crime seemed to be, it was a *crime*, and it was a long time since I had had any association with crime and criminals.

I hardly listened to the next words Poirot said. But they were to come back to me with significance later.

'This is the beginning,' said Hercule Poirot.

CHAPTER 4

Mrs Ascher

We were received at Andover by Inspector Glen, a tall fair-haired man with a pleasant smile.

For the sake of conciseness I think I had better give a brief résumé of the bare facts of the case.

The crime was discovered by Police Constable Dover at 1 am on the morning of the 22nd. When on his round he tried the door of the shop and found it unfastened, he entered and at first thought the place was empty. Directing his torch over the counter, however, he caught sight of the huddled-up body of the old woman. When the police surgeon arrived on the spot it was elicited that the woman had been struck down by a heavy blow on the back of the head, probably while she was reaching down a packet of cigarettes from the shelf behind the counter. Death must have occurred about nine to seven hours previously.

'But we've been able to get it down a bit nearer than that,' explained the inspector. 'We've found a man who went in and bought some tobacco at 5.30. And a second man went in and found the shop empty, as he thought, at five minutes past six. That puts the time at between 5.30 and 6.5. So far I haven't been able to find anyone who saw this man Ascher in the neighbourhood, but, of course, it's early as yet. He was in the Three Crowns at nine o'clock pretty far gone in drink. When we get hold of him he'll be detained on suspicion.'

'Not a very desirable character, inspector?' asked Poirot.

'Unpleasant bit of goods.'

'He didn't live with his wife?'

'No, they separated some years ago. Ascher's a German. He was a waiter at one time, but he took to drink and gradually became unemployable. His wife went into service for a bit. Her last place was as cook-housekeeper to an old lady, Miss Rose. She allowed her husband so much out of her wages to keep himself, but he was always getting drunk and coming round and making scenes at the places where she was employed. That's why she took the post with Miss Rose at The Grange. It's three miles out of Andover, dead in the country. He couldn't get at her there so well. When Miss Rose died, she left Mrs Ascher a small legacy, and the woman started this tobacco and newsagent business—quite a tiny place—just cheap cigarettes and a few newspapers—that sort of thing. She just about managed to keep going. Ascher used to come round and abuse her now and again and she used to give him a bit to get rid of him. She allowed him fifteen shillings a week regular.'

'Had they any children?' asked Poirot.

'No. There's a niece. She's in service near Overton. Very superior, steady young woman.'

'And you say this man Ascher used to threaten his wife?'

'That's right. He was a terror when he was in drink—cursing and swearing that he'd bash her head in. She had a hard time, did Mrs Ascher.'

'What age of woman was she?'

'Close on sixty—respectable and hard-working.'

Poirot said gravely:

'It is your opinion, inspector, that this man Ascher committed the crime?'

The inspector coughed cautiously.

'It's a bit early to say that, Mr Poirot, but I'd like to hear Franz Ascher's own account of how he spent yesterday evening. If he can give a satisfactory account of himself, well and good—if not—'

His pause was a pregnant one.

'Nothing was missing from the shop?'

'Nothing. Money in the till quite undisturbed. No signs of robbery.'

'You think that this man Ascher came into the shop drunk, started abusing his wife and finally struck her down?'

'It seems the most likely solution. But I must confess, sir, I'd like to have another look at that very odd letter you received. I was wondering if it was just possible that it came from this man Ascher.'

Poirot handed over the letter and the inspector read it with a frown.

'It doesn't read like Ascher,' he said at last. 'I doubt if Ascher would use the term "our" British police—not unless he was trying to be extra cunning—and I doubt if he's got the wits for that. Then the man's a wreck—all to pieces. His hand's too shaky to print letters clearly like this. It's good quality notepaper and ink, too. It's odd that the letter should mention the 21st of the month. Of course it *might* be coincidence.'

'That is possible—yes.'

'But I don't like this kind of coincidence, Mr Poirot. It's a bit too pat.'

He was silent for a minute or two—a frown creasing his forehead.

'A B C. Who the devil could A B C be? We'll see if Mary Drower (that's the niece) can give us any help. It's an odd business. But for this letter I'd have put my money on Franz Ascher for a certainty.'

'Do you know anything of Mrs Ascher's past?'

'She's a Hampshire woman. Went into service as a girl up in London—that's where she met Ascher and married him. Things must have been difficult for them during the war. She actually left him for good in 1922. They were in London then. She came back here to get away from him, but he got wind of where she was and followed her down here, pestering her for money—' A constable came in. 'Yes, Briggs, what is it?'

'It's the man Ascher, sir. We've brought him in.'

'Right. Bring him in here. Where was he?'

'Hiding in a truck on the railway siding.'

'He was, was he? Bring him along.'

Franz Ascher was indeed a miserable and unprepossessing specimen. He was blubbering and cringing and blustering alternately. His bleary eyes moved shiftily from one face to another.

'What do you want with me? I have not done nothing. It is a shame and a scandal to bring me here! You are swine, how dare you?' His manner changed suddenly. 'No, no, I do not mean that—you would not hurt a poor old man—not be hard on him. Everyone is hard on poor old Franz. Poor old Franz.'

Mr Ascher started to weep.

'That'll do, Ascher,' said the inspector. 'Pull yourself together. I'm not charging you with anything—yet. And you're not bound to make a statement unless you like. On the other hand, if you're *not* concerned in the murder of your wife—'

Ascher interrupted him—his voice rising to a scream.

'I did not kill her! I did not kill her! It is all lies! You are goddamned English pigs—all against me. I never kill her—never.'

'You threatened to often enough, Ascher.'

'No, no. You do not understand. That was just a joke—a good joke between me and Alice. She understood.'

'Funny kind of joke! Do you care to say where you were yesterday evening, Ascher?'

'Yes, yes—I tell you everything. I did not go near Alice. I am with friends—good friends. We are at the Seven Stars—and then we are at the Red Dog—'

He hurried on, his words stumbling over each other.

'Dick Willows—he was with me—and old Curdie—and George—and Platt and lots of the boys. I tell you I do not never go near Alice. Ach Gott, it is the truth I am telling you.'

His voice rose to a scream. The inspector nodded to his underling.

'Take him away. Detained on suspicion.'

'I don't know what to think,' he said as the unpleasant, shaking old man with the malevolent, mouthing jaw was removed. 'If it wasn't for the letter, I'd say he did it.'

'What about the men he mentions?'

'A bad crowd—not one of them would stick at perjury. I've no doubt he *was* with them the greater part of the evening. A lot depends on whether any one saw him near the shop between half-past five and six.'

Poirot shook his head thoughtfully.

'You are sure nothing was taken from the shop?'

The inspector shrugged his shoulders.

'That depends. A packet or two of cigarettes might have been taken—but you'd hardly commit murder for that.'

'And there was nothing—how shall I put it—introduced into the shop? Nothing that was odd there—incongruous?'

'There was a railway guide,' said the inspector.

'A railway guide?'

'Yes. It was open and turned face downward on the counter. Looked as though someone had been looking up the trains from Andover. Either the old woman or a customer.'

'Did she sell that type of thing?'

The inspector shook his head.

'She sold penny time-tables. This was a big one—kind of thing only Smith's or a big stationer would keep.'

Agatha Christie

A light came into Poirot's eyes. He leant forward.
A light came into the inspector's eye also.
'A railway guide, you say. A Bradshaw—*or an ABC?*'
'By the lord,' he said. 'It *was* an A B C.'

CHAPTER 5

Mary Drower

I think that I can date my interest in the case from that first mention of the A B C railway guide. Up till then I had not been able to raise much enthusiasm. This sordid murder of an old woman in a back-street shop was so like the usual type of crime reported in the newspapers that it failed to strike a significant note. In my own mind I had put down the anonymous letter with its mention of the 21st as a mere coincidence. Mrs Ascher, I felt reasonably sure, had been the victim of her drunken brute of a husband. But now the mention of the railway guide (so familiarly known by its abbreviation of A B C, listing as it did all railway stations in their alphabetical order) sent a quiver of excitement through me. Surely—surely this could not be a second coincidence?

The sordid crime took on a new aspect.

Who was the mysterious individual who had killed Mrs Ascher and left an A B C railway guide behind him?

When we left the police station our first visit was to the

mortuary to see the body of the dead woman. A strange feeling came over me as I gazed down on that wrinkled old face with the scanty grey hair drawn back tightly from the temples. It looked so peaceful, so incredibly remote from violence.

'Never knew who or what struck her,' observed the sergeant. 'That's what Dr Kerr says. I'm glad it was that way, poor old soul. A decent woman she was.'

'She must have been beautiful once,' said Poirot.

'Really?' I murmured incredulously.

'But yes, look at the line of the jaw, the bones, the moulding of the head.'

He sighed as he replaced the sheet and we left the mortuary.

Our next move was a brief interview with the police surgeon.

Dr Kerr was a competent-looking middle-aged man. He spoke briskly and with decision.

'The weapon wasn't found,' he said. 'Impossible to say what it may have been. A weighted stick, a club, a form of sandbag—any of those would fit the case.'

'Would much force be needed to strike such a blow?'

The doctor shot a keen glance at Poirot.

'Meaning, I suppose, could a shaky old man of seventy do it? Oh, yes, it's perfectly possible—given sufficient weight in the head of the weapon, quite a feeble person could achieve the desired result.'

'Then the murderer could just as well be a woman as a man?'

The suggestion took the doctor somewhat aback.

'A woman, eh? Well, I confess it never occurred to me to connect a woman with this type of crime. But of course it's possible—perfectly possible. Only, psychologically speaking, I shouldn't say this was a woman's crime.'

Poirot nodded his head in eager agreement.

'Perfectly, perfectly. On the face of it, highly improbable. But one must take all possibilities into account. The body was lying—how?'

The doctor gave us a careful description of the position of the victim. It was his opinion that she had been standing with her back to the counter (and therefore to her assailant) when the blow had been struck. She had slipped down in a heap behind the counter quite out of sight of anyone entering the shop casually.

When we had thanked Dr Kerr and taken our leave, Poirot said:

'You perceive, Hastings, that we have already one further point in favour of Ascher's innocence. If he had been abusing his wife and threatening her, she would have been *facing* him over the counter. Instead she had her *back* to her assailant—obviously she is reaching down tobacco or cigarettes for a *customer*.'

I gave a little shiver.

'Pretty gruesome.'

Poirot shook his head gravely.

'*Pauvre femme*,' he murmured.

Then he glanced at his watch.

'Overton is not, I think, many miles from here. Shall we

Agatha Christie

run over there and have an interview with the niece of the dead woman?'

'Surely you will go first to the shop where the crime took place?'

'I prefer to do that later. I have a reason.'

He did not explain further, and a few minutes later we were driving on the London road in the direction of Overton.

The address which the inspector had given us was that of a good-sized house about a mile on the London side of the village.

Our ring at the bell was answered by a pretty dark-haired girl whose eyes were red with recent weeping.

Poirot said gently:

'Ah! I think it is you who are Miss Mary Drower, the parlourmaid here?'

'Yes, sir, that's right. I'm Mary, sir.'

'Then perhaps I can talk to you for a few minutes if your mistress will not object. It is about your aunt, Mrs Ascher.'

'The mistress is out, sir. She wouldn't mind, I'm sure, if you came in here.'

She opened the door of a small morning-room. We entered and Poirot, seating himself on a chair by the window, looked up keenly into the girl's face.

'You have heard of your aunt's death, of course?'

The girl nodded, tears coming once more into her eyes.

'This morning, sir. The police came over. Oh! it's terrible! Poor auntie! Such a hard life as she'd had, too. And now this—it's too awful.'

'The police did not suggest your returning to Andover?'

'They said I must come to the inquest—that's on Monday, sir. But I've nowhere to go there—I couldn't fancy being over the shop—now—and what with the housemaid being away, I didn't want to put the mistress out more than may be.'

'You were fond of your aunt, Mary?' said Poirot gently.

'Indeed I was, sir. Very good she's been to me always, auntie has. I went to her in London when I was eleven years old, after mother died. I started in service when I was sixteen, but I usually went along to auntie's on my day out. A lot of trouble she went through with that German fellow. "My old devil," she used to call him. He'd never let her be in peace anywhere. Sponging, cadging old beast.'

The girl spoke with vehemence.

'Your aunt never thought of freeing herself by legal means from this persecution?'

'Well, you see, he was her husband, sir, you couldn't get away from that.'

The girl spoke simply but with finality.

'Tell me, Mary, he threatened her, did he not?'

'Oh, yes, sir, it was awful the things he used to say. That he'd cut her throat, and such like. Cursing and swearing too—both in German and in English. And yet auntie says he was a fine handsome figure of a man when she married him. It's dreadful to think, sir, what people come to.'

'Yes, indeed. And so, I suppose, Mary, having actually heard these threats, you were not so very surprised when you learnt what had happened?'

'Oh, but I was, sir. You see, sir, I never thought for one moment that he meant it. I thought it was just nasty talk and nothing more to it. And it isn't as though auntie was afraid of him. Why, I've seen him slink away like a dog with its tail between its legs when she turned on him. *He* was afraid of *her* if you like.'

'And yet she gave him money?'

'Well, he was her husband, you see, sir.'

'Yes, so you said before.' He paused for a minute or two. Then he said: 'Suppose that, after all, he did *not* kill her.'

'Didn't kill her?'

She stared.

'That is what I said. Supposing someone else killed her... Have you any idea who that someone else could be?'

She stared at him with even more amazement.

'I've no idea, sir. It doesn't seem likely, though, does it?'

'There was no one your aunt was afraid of?'

Mary shook her head.

'Auntie wasn't afraid of people. She'd a sharp tongue and she'd stand up to anybody.'

'You never heard her mention anyone who had a grudge against her?'

'No, indeed, sir.'

'Did she ever get anonymous letters?'

'What kind of letters did you say, sir?'

'Letters that weren't signed—or only signed by something like A B C.' He watched her narrowly, but plainly she was at a loss. She shook her head wonderingly.

'Has your aunt any relations except you?'

'Not now, sir. One of ten she was, but only three lived to grow up. My Uncle Tom was killed in the war, and my Uncle Harry went to South America and no one's heard of him since, and mother's dead, of course, so there's only me.'

'Had your aunt any savings? Any money put by?'

'She'd a little in the Savings Bank, sir—enough to bury her proper, that's what she always said. Otherwise she didn't more than just make ends meet—what with her old devil and all.'

Poirot nodded thoughtfully. He said—perhaps more to himself than to her:

'At present one is in the dark—there is no direction—if things get clearer—' He got up. 'If I want you at any time, Mary, I will write to you here.'

'As a matter of fact, sir, I'm giving in my notice. I don't like the country. I stayed here because I fancied it was a comfort to auntie to have me near by. But now'—again the tears rose in her eyes—'there's no reason I should stay, and so I'll go back to London. It's gayer for a girl there.'

'I wish that, when you do go, you would give me your address. Here is my card.'

He handed it to her. She looked at it with a puzzled frown.

'Then you're not—anything to do with the police, sir?'

'I am a private detective.'

She stood there looking at him for some moments in silence.

She said at last:

'Is there anything—queer going on, sir?'

'Yes, my child. There is—something queer going on. Later you may be able to help me.'

'I—I'll do anything, sir. It—it wasn't *right*, sir, auntie being killed.'

A strange way of putting it—but deeply moving.

A few seconds later we were driving back to Andover.

CHAPTER 6

The Scene of the Crime

The street in which the tragedy had occurred was a turning off the main street. Mrs Ascher's shop was situated about halfway down it on the right-hand side.

As we turned into the street Poirot glanced at his watch and I realized why he had delayed his visit to the scene of the crime until now. It was just on half-past five. He had wished to reproduce yesterday's atmosphere as closely as possible.

But if that had been his purpose it was defeated. Certainly at this moment the road bore very little likeness to its appearance on the previous evening. There were a certain number of small shops interspersed between private houses of the poorer class. I judged that ordinarily there would be a fair number of people passing up and down—mostly people of the poorer classes, with a good sprinkling of children playing on the pavements and in the road.

At this moment there was a solid mass of people standing staring at one particular house or shop and it took little perspicuity to guess which that was. What we saw was a mass of average human beings looking with intense interest at the spot where another human being had been done to death.

As we drew nearer this proved to be indeed the case. In front of a small dingy-looking shop with its shutters now closed stood a harassed-looking young policeman who was stolidly adjuring the crowd to 'pass along there.' By the help of a colleague, displacements took place—a certain number of people grudgingly sighed and betook themselves to their ordinary vocations, and almost immediately other persons came along and took up their stand to gaze their fill on the spot where murder had been committed.

Poirot stopped a little distance from the main body of the crowd. From where we stood the legend painted over the door could be read plainly enough. Poirot repeated it under his breath.

'A. Ascher. *Oui, c'est peut-être là—*'

He broke off.

'Come, let us go inside, Hastings.'

I was only too ready.

We made our way through the crowd and accosted the young policeman. Poirot produced the credentials which the inspector had given him. The constable nodded, and unlocked the door to let us pass within. We did so and entered to the intense interest of the lookers-on.

Inside it was very dark owing to the shutters being closed. The constable found and switched on the electric light. The bulb was a low-powered one so that the interior was still dimly lit.

I looked about me.

A dingy little place. A few cheap magazines strewn about, and yesterday's newspapers—all with a day's dust on them. Behind the counter a row of shelves reaching to the ceiling and packed with tobacco and packets of cigarettes. There were also a couple of jars of peppermint humbugs and barley sugar. A commonplace little shop, one of many thousand such others.

The constable in his slow Hampshire voice was explaining the *mise en scène*.

'Down in a heap behind the counter, that's where she was. Doctor says as how she never knew what hit her. Must have been reaching up to one of the shelves.'

'There was nothing in her hand?'

'No, sir, but there was a packet of Player's down beside her.'

Poirot nodded. His eyes swept round the small space observing—noting.

'And the railway guide was—where?'

'Here, sir.' The constable pointed out the spot on the counter. 'It was open at the right page for Andover and lying face down. Seems as though he must have been looking up the trains to London. If so, it mightn't have been an Andover man at all. But then, of course, the railway guide might have belonged to someone else what had nothing to do with the murder at all, but just forgot it here.'

'Fingerprints?' I suggested.

The man shook his head.

'The whole place was examined straight away, sir. There weren't none.'

Agatha Christie

'Not on the counter itself?' asked Poirot.

'A long sight too many, sir! All confused and jumbled up.'

'Any of Ascher's among them?'

'Too soon to say, sir.'

Poirot nodded, then asked if the dead woman lived over the shop.

'Yes, sir, you go through that door at the back, sir. You'll excuse me not coming with you, but I've got to stay—'

Poirot passed through the door in question and I followed him. Behind the shop was a microscopic sort of parlour and kitchen combined—it was neat and clean but very dreary looking and scantily furnished. On the mantelpiece were a few photographs. I went up and looked at them and Poirot joined me.

The photographs were three in all. One was a cheap portrait of the girl we had been with that afternoon, Mary Drower. She was obviously wearing her best clothes and had the self-conscious, wooden smile on her face that so often disfigures the expression in posed photography, and makes a snapshot preferable.

The second was a more expensive type of picture—an artistically blurred reproduction of an elderly woman with white hair. A high fur collar stood up round the neck.

I guessed that this was probably the Miss Rose who had left Mrs Ascher the small legacy which had enabled her to start in business.

The third photograph was a very old one, now faded and yellow. It represented a young man and woman in somewhat old-fashioned clothes standing arm in arm. The man had a button-hole and there was an air of bygone festivity about the whole pose.

'Probably a wedding picture,' said Poirot. 'Regard, Hastings, did I not tell you that she had been a beautiful woman?'

He was right. Disfigured by old-fashioned hairdressing and weird clothes, there was no disguising the handsomeness of the girl in the picture with her clear-cut features and spirited bearing. I looked closely at the second figure. It was almost impossible to recognise the seedy Ascher in this smart young man with the military bearing.

I recalled the leering drunken old man, and the toilworn face of the dead woman—and I shivered a little at the remorselessness of time...

From the parlour a stair led to two upstairs rooms. One was empty and unfurnished, the other had evidently been the dead woman's bedroom. After being searched by the police it had been left as it was. A couple of old worn blankets on the bed—a little stock of well-darned underwear in a drawer—cookery recipes in another—a paper-backed novel entitled *The Green Oasis*—a pair of new stockings—pathetic in their cheap shininess—a couple of china ornaments—a Dresden shepherd much broken, and a blue and yellow spotted dog—a black raincoat and a woolly jumper hanging on pegs—such were the worldly possessions of the late Alice Ascher.

If there had been any personal papers, the police had taken them.

'*Pauvre femme*,' murmured Poirot. 'Come, Hastings, there is nothing for us here.'

Agatha Christie

When we were once more in the street, he hesitated for a minute or two, then crossed the road. Almost exactly opposite Mrs Ascher's was a greengrocer's shop—of the type that has most of its stock outside rather than inside.

In a low voice Poirot gave me certain instructions. Then he himself entered the shop. After waiting a minute or two I followed him in. He was at the moment negotiating for a lettuce. I myself bought a pound of strawberries.

Poirot was talking animatedly to the stout lady who was serving him.

'It was just opposite you, was it not, that this murder occurred? What an affair! What a sensation it must have caused you!'

The stout lady was obviously tired of talking about the murder. She must have had a long day of it. She observed:

'It would be as well if some of that gaping crowd cleared off. What is there to look at, I'd like to know?'

'It must have been very different last night,' said Poirot. 'Possibly you even observed the murderer enter the shop—a tall, fair man with a beard, was he not? A Russian, so I have heard.'

'What's that?' The woman looked up sharply. 'A Russian did it, you say?'

'I understand that the police have arrested him.'

'Did you ever know?' The woman was excited, voluble. 'A foreigner.'

'*Mais oui*. I thought perhaps you might have noticed him last night?'

'Well, I don't get much chance of noticing, and that's a

fact. The evening's our busy time and there's always a fair few passing along and getting home after their work. A tall, fair man with a beard—no, I can't say I saw anyone of that description anywhere about.'

I broke in on my cue.

'Excuse me, sir,' I said to Poirot. 'I think you have been misinformed. A short *dark* man I was told.'

An interested discussion intervened in which the stout lady, her lank husband and a hoarse-voiced shop-boy all participated. No less than four short dark men had been observed, and the hoarse boy had seen a tall fair one, 'but he hadn't got no beard,' he added regretfully.

Finally, our purchases made, we left the establishment, leaving our falsehoods uncorrected.

'And what was the point of all that, Poirot?' I demanded somewhat reproachfully.

'*Parbleu*, I wanted to estimate the chances of a stranger being noticed entering the shop opposite.'

'Couldn't you simply have asked—without all that tissue of lies?'

'No, *mon ami*. If I had "simply asked", as you put it, I should have got no answer at all to my questions. You yourself are English and yet you do not seem to appreciate the quality of the English reaction to a direct question. It is invariably one of suspicion and the natural result is reticence. If I had asked those people for information they would have shut up like oysters. But by making a statement (and a somewhat out of the way and preposterous one) and by your contradiction of it, tongues are immediately loosened. We know also that that particular time was a "busy time"—that is, that everyone would be intent on their own concerns and that there would be a fair number of people passing along the pavements. Our murderer chose his time well, Hastings.'

He paused and then added on a deep note of reproach:

'Is it that you have not in any degree the common sense, Hastings? I say to you: "Make a purchase *quelconque*"—and you deliberately choose the strawberries! Already they commence to creep through their bag and endanger your good suit.'

With some dismay, I perceived that this was indeed the case.

I hastily presented the strawberries to a small boy who seemed highly astonished and faintly suspicious.

Poirot added the lettuce, thus setting the seal on the child's bewilderment.

He continued to drive the moral home.

'At a cheap greengrocer's—*not* strawberries. A strawberry, unless fresh picked, is bound to exude juice. A banana—some apples—even a cabbage—but *strawberries*—'

'It was the first thing I thought of,' I explained by way of excuse.

'That is unworthy of your imagination,' returned Poirot sternly.

He paused on the sidewalk.

The house and shop on the right of Mrs Ascher's was empty. A 'To Let' sign appeared in the windows. On the other side was a house with somewhat grimy muslin curtains.

To this house Poirot betook himself and, there being no bell, executed a series of sharp flourishes with the knocker.

The door was opened after some delay by a very dirty child with a nose that needed attention.

'Good evening,' said Poirot. 'Is your mother within?'

'Ay?' said the child.

It stared at us with disfavour and deep suspicion.

'Your mother,' said Poirot.

This took some twelve seconds to sink in, then the child turned and, bawling up the stairs 'Mum, you're wanted,' retreated to some fastness in the dim interior.

A sharp-faced woman looked over the balusters and began to descend.

'No good you wasting your time—' she began, but Poirot interrupted her.

He took off his hat and bowed magnificently.

'Good evening, madame. I am on the staff of the *Evening Flicker*. I want to persuade you to accept a fee of five pounds and let us have an article on your late neighbour, Mrs Ascher.'

The irate words arrested on her lips, the woman came down the stairs smoothing her hair and hitching at her skirt.

'Come inside, please—on the left there. Won't you sit down, sir.'

The tiny room was heavily over-crowded with a massive pseudo-Jacobean suite, but we managed to squeeze ourselves in and on to a hard-seated sofa.

'You must excuse me,' the woman was saying. 'I am sure I'm sorry I spoke so sharp just now, but you'd hardly

Agatha Christie

believe the worry one has to put up with—fellows coming along selling this, that and the other—vacuum cleaners, stockings, lavender bags and such-like foolery—and all so plausible and civil spoken. Got your name, too, pat they have. It's Mrs Fowler this, that and the other.'

Seizing adroitly on the name, Poirot said:

'Well, Mrs Fowler, I hope you're going to do what I ask.'

'I don't know, I'm sure.' The five pounds hung alluringly before Mrs Fowler's eyes. 'I *knew* Mrs Ascher, of course, but as to *writing* anything.'

Hastily Poirot reassured her. No labour on her part was required. He would elicit the facts from her and the interview would be written up.

Thus encouraged, Mrs Fowler plunged willingly into reminiscence, conjecture and hearsay.

Kept herself to herself, Mrs Ascher had. Not what you'd call really *friendly*, but there, she'd had a lot of trouble, poor soul, everyone knew that. And by rights Franz Ascher ought to have been locked up years ago. Not that Mrs Ascher had been afraid of him—real tartar she could be when roused! Give as good as she got any day. But there it was—the pitcher could go to the well once too often. Again and again, she, Mrs Fowler, had said to her: 'One of these days that man will do for you. Mark my words.' And he had done, hadn't he? And there had she, Mrs Fowler, been right next door and never heard a sound.

In a pause Poirot managed to insert a question.

Had Mrs Ascher ever received any peculiar letters—letters without a proper signature—just something like A B C?

Regretfully, Mrs Fowler returned a negative answer.

'I know the kind of thing you mean—anonymous letters they call them—mostly full of words you'd blush to say out loud. Well, I don't know, I'm sure, if Franz Ascher ever took to writing those. Mrs Ascher never let on to me if he did. What's that? A railway guide, an A B C? No, I never saw such a thing about—and I'm sure if Mrs Ascher had been sent one I'd have heard about it. I declare you could have knocked me down with a feather when I heard about this whole business. It was my girl Edie what came to me. "Mum," she says, "there's ever so many policemen next door." Gave me quite a turn, it did. "Well," I said, when I heard about it, "it does show that she ought never to have been alone in the house—that niece of hers ought to have been with her. A man in drink can be like a ravening wolf," I said, "and in my opinion a wild beast is neither more nor less than what that old devil of a husband of hers is. I've warned her," I said, "many times and now my words have come true. He'll do for you," I said. And he has done for her! You can't rightly estimate what a man will do when he's in drink and this murder's a proof of it.'

She wound up with a deep gasp.

'Nobody saw this man Ascher go into the shop, I believe?' said Poirot.

Mrs Fowler sniffed scornfully.

'Naturally he wasn't going to show himself,' she said.

How Mr Ascher had got there without showing himself she did not deign to explain.

She agreed that there was no back way into the house

Agatha Christie

and that Ascher was quite well known by sight in the district.

'But he didn't want to swing for it and he kept himself well hid.'

Poirot kept the conversational ball rolling some little time longer, but when it seemed certain that Mrs Fowler had told all that she knew not once but many times over, he terminated the interview, first paying out the promised sum.

'Rather a dear five pounds' worth, Poirot,' I ventured to remark when we were once more in the street.

'So far, yes.'

'You think she knows more than she has told?'

'My friend, we are in the peculiar position of *not knowing what questions to ask*. We are like little children playing *cache-cache* in the dark. We stretch out our hands and grope about. Mrs Fowler has told us all that she *thinks* she knows—and has thrown in several conjectures for good measure! In the future, however, her evidence may be useful. It is for the future that I have invested that sum of five pounds.'

I did not quite understand the point, but at this moment we ran into Inspector Glen.

CHAPTER 7

Mr Partridge and Mr Riddell

Inspector Glen was looking rather gloomy. He had, I gathered, spent the afternoon trying to get a complete list of persons who had been noticed entering the tobacco shop.

'And nobody has seen anyone?' Poirot inquired.

'Oh, yes, they have. Three tall men with furtive expressions—four short men with black moustaches—two beards—three fat men—all strangers—and all, if I'm to believe witnesses, with sinister expressions! I wonder somebody didn't see a gang of masked men with revolvers while they were about it!'

Poirot smiled sympathetically.

'Does anybody claim to have seen the man Ascher?'

'No, they don't. And that's another point in his favour. I've just told the Chief Constable that I think this is a job for Scotland Yard. I don't believe it's a local crime.'

Poirot said gravely:

'I agree with you.'

The inspector said:

'You know, Monsieur Poirot, it's a nasty business—a nasty business... I don't like it...'

We had two more interviews before returning to London.

The first was with Mr James Partridge. Mr Partridge was the last person known to have seen Mrs Ascher alive. He had made a purchase from her at 5.30.

Mr Partridge was a small man, a bank clerk by profession. He wore pince-nez, was very dry and spare-looking and extremely precise in all his utterances. He lived in a small house as neat and trim as himself.

'Mr—er—Poirot,' he said, glancing at the card my friend had handed to him. 'From Inspector Glen? What can I do for you, Mr Poirot?'

'I understand, Mr Partridge, that you were the last person to see Mrs Ascher alive.'

Mr Partridge placed his finger-tips together and looked at Poirot as though he were a doubtful cheque.

'That is a very debatable point, Mr Poirot,' he said. 'Many people may have made purchases from Mrs Ascher after I did so.'

'If so, they have not come forward to say so.'

Mr Partridge coughed.

'Some people, Mr Poirot, have no sense of public duty.'

He looked at us owlishly through his spectacles.

'Exceedingly true,' murmured Poirot. 'You, I understand, went to the police of your own accord?'

'Certainly I did. As soon as I heard of the shocking occurrence I perceived that my statement might be helpful and came forward accordingly.'

'A very proper spirit,' said Poirot solemnly. 'Perhaps you will be so kind as to repeat your story to me.'

'By all means. I was returning to this house and at 5.30 precisely—'

'Pardon, how was it that you knew the time so accurately?'

Mr Partridge looked a little annoyed at being interrupted.

'The church clock chimed. I looked at my watch and found I was a minute slow. That was just before I entered Mrs Ascher's shop.'

'Were you in the habit of making purchases there?'

'Fairly frequently. It was on my way home. About once or twice a week I was in the habit of purchasing two ounces of John Cotton mild.'

'Did you know Mrs Ascher at all? Anything of her circumstances or her history?'

'Nothing whatever. Beyond my purchase and an occasional remark as to the state of the weather, I had never spoken to her.'

'Did you know she had a drunken husband who was in the habit of threatening her life?'

'No, I knew nothing whatever about her.'

'You knew her by sight, however. Did anything about her appearance strike you as unusual yesterday evening? Did she appear flurried or put out in any way?'

Mr Partridge considered.

'As far as I noticed, she seemed exactly as usual,' he said.

Poirot rose.

'Thank you, Mr Partridge, for answering these questions. Have you, by any chance, an A B C in the house? I want to look up my return train to London.'

Agatha Christie

'On the shelf just behind you,' said Mr Partridge.

On the shelf in question were an A B C, a Bradshaw, the Stock Exchange Year Book, Kelly's Directory, a Who's Who and a local directory.

Poirot took down the A B C, pretended to look up a train, then thanked Mr Partridge and took his leave.

Our next interview was with Mr Albert Riddell and was of a highly different character. Mr Albert Riddell was a platelayer and our conversation took place to the accompaniment of the clattering of plates and dishes by Mr Riddell's obviously nervous wife, the growling of Mr Riddell's dog and the undisguised hostility of Mr Riddell himself.

He was a big clumsy giant of a man with a broad face and small suspicious eyes. He was in the act of eating meat-pie, washed down by exceedingly black tea. He peered at us angrily over the rim of his cup.

'Told all I've got to tell once, haven't I?' he growled. 'What's it to do with me, anyway? Told it to the blarsted police, I 'ave, and now I've got to spit it all out again to a couple of blarsted foreigners.'

Poirot gave a quick, amused glance in my direction and then said:

'In truth I sympathize with you, but what will you? It is a question of murder, is it not? One has to be very, very careful.'

'Best tell the gentleman what he wants, Bert,' said the woman nervously.

'You shut your blarsted mouth,' roared the giant.

'You did not, I think, go to the police of your own accord.' Poirot slipped the remark in neatly.

'Why the hell should I? It were no business of mine.'

'A matter of opinion,' said Poirot indifferently. 'There has been a murder—the police want to know who has been in the shop—I myself think it would have—what shall I say?—looked more natural if you had come forward.'

'I've got my work to do. Don't say I shouldn't have come forward in my own time—'

'But as it was, the police were given your name as that of a person seen to go into Mrs Ascher's and they had to come to you. Were they satisfied with your account?'

'Why shouldn't they be?' demanded Bert truculently.

Poirot merely shrugged his shoulders.

'What are you getting at, mister? Nobody's got anything against me? Everyone knows who did the old girl in, that b— of a husband of hers.'

'But he was not in the street that evening and you were.'

'Trying to fasten it on me, are you? Well, you won't succeed. What reason had I got to do a thing like that? Think I wanted to pinch a tin of her bloody tobacco? Think I'm a bloody homicidal maniac as they call it? Think I—?'

He rose threateningly from his seat. His wife bleated out:

'Bert, Bert—don't say such things. Bert—they'll think—'

'Calm yourself, monsieur,' said Poirot. 'I demand only your account of your visit. That you refuse it seems to me—what shall we say—a little odd?'

'Who said I refused anything?' Mr Riddell sank back again into his seat. 'I don't mind.'

'It was six o'clock when you entered the shop?'

'That's right—a minute or two after, as a matter of fact. Wanted a packet of Gold Flake. I pushed open the door—'

'It was closed, then?'

'That's right. I thought shop was shut, maybe. But it wasn't. I went in, there wasn't anyone about. I hammered on the counter and waited a bit. Nobody came, so I went out again. That's all, and you can put it in your pipe and smoke it.'

'You didn't see the body fallen down behind the counter?'

'No, no more would you have done—unless you was looking for it, maybe.'

'Was there a railway guide lying about?'

'Yes, there was—face downwards. It crossed my mind like that the old woman might have had to go off sudden by train and forgot to lock shop up.'

'Perhaps you picked up the railway guide or moved it along the counter?'

'Didn't touch the b— thing. I did just what I said.'

'And you did not see anyone leaving the shop before you yourself got there?'

'Didn't see any such thing. What I say is, why pitch on me—?'

Poirot rose.

'Nobody is pitching upon you—yet. Bonsoir, monsieur.'

He left the man with his mouth open and I followed him. In the street he consulted his watch.

'With great haste, my friend, we might manage to catch the 7.02. Let us despatch ourselves quickly.'

CHAPTER 8

The Second Letter

'Well?' I demanded eagerly.

We were seated in a first-class carriage which we had to ourselves. The train, an express, had just drawn out of Andover.

'The crime,' said Poirot, 'was committed by a man of medium height with red hair and a cast in the left eye. He limps slightly on the right foot and has a mole just below the shoulder-blade.'

'Poirot?' I cried.

For the moment I was completely taken in. Then the twinkle in my friend's eye undeceived me.

'Poirot!' I said again, this time in reproach.

'*Mon ami*, what will you? You fix upon me a look of doglike devotion and demand of me a pronouncement à la Sherlock Holmes! Now for the truth—*I do not know what the murderer looks like, nor where he lives, nor how to set hands upon him.*'

'If only he had left some clue,' I murmured.

Agatha Christie

'Yes, the clue—it is always the clue that attracts you. Alas that he did not smoke the cigarette and leave the ash, and then step in it with a shoe that has nails of a curious pattern. No—he is not so obliging. But at least, my friend, you have the *railway guide*. The A B C, that is a clue for you!'

'Do you think he left it by mistake then?'

'Of course not. He left it on purpose. The fingerprints tell us that.'

'But there weren't any on it.'

'That is what I mean. What was yesterday evening? A warm June night. Does a man stroll about on such an evening in *gloves*? Such a man would certainly have attracted attention. Therefore since there are no fingerprints on the A B C, it must have been carefully wiped. An innocent man would have left prints—a guilty man would not. So our murderer left it there for a purpose—but for all that it is none the less a clue. That A B C was bought by someone—it was carried by someone—there is a possibility there.'

'You think we may learn something that way?'

'Frankly, Hastings, I am not particularly hopeful. This man, this unknown X, obviously prides himself on his abilities. He is not likely to blaze a trail that can be followed straight away.'

'So that really the ABC isn't helpful at all.'

'Not in the sense you mean.'

'In any sense?'

Poirot did not answer at once. Then he said slowly:

'The answer to that is yes. We are confronted here by an

unknown personage. He is in the dark and seeks to remain in the dark. But in the very nature of things *he cannot help throwing light upon himself*. In one sense we know nothing about him—in another sense we know already a good deal. I see his figure dimly taking shape—a man who prints clearly and well—who buys good-quality paper—who is at great needs to express his personality. I see him as a child possibly ignored and passed over—I see him growing up with an inward sense of inferiority—warring with a sense of injustice... I see that inner urge—to assert himself—to focus attention on himself ever becoming stronger, and events, circumstances—crushing it down—heaping, perhaps, more humiliations on him. And inwardly the match is set to the powder train...'

'That's all pure conjecture,' I objected. 'It doesn't give you any practical help.'

'You prefer the match end, the cigarette ash, the nailed boots! You always have. But at least we can ask ourselves some practical questions. Why the A B C? Why Mrs Ascher? Why Andover?'

'The woman's past life seems simple enough,' I mused. 'The interviews with those two men were disappointing. They couldn't tell us anything more than we knew already.'

'To tell the truth, I did not expect much in that line. But we could not neglect two possible candidates for the murder.'

'Surely you don't think—'

'There is at least a possibility that the murderer lives in or near Andover. That is a possible answer to our question: "Why Andover?" Well, here were two men known to have been in the shop at the requisite time of day. Either of them *might* be the murderer. And there is nothing as yet to show that one or other of them is *not* the murderer.'

'That great hulking brute, Riddell, perhaps,' I admitted.

'Oh, I am inclined to acquit Riddell off-hand. He was nervous, blustering, obviously uneasy—'

'But surely that just shows—'

'A nature diametrically opposed to that which penned the A B C letter. Conceit and self-confidence are the characteristics that we must look for.'

'Someone who throws his weight about?'

'Possibly. But some people, under a nervous and self-effacing manner, conceal a great deal of vanity and self-satisfaction.'

'You don't think that little Mr Partridge—'

'He is more *le type*. One cannot say more than that. He acts as the writer of the letter would act—goes at once to the police—pushes himself to the fore—enjoys his position.'

'Do you really think—?'

'No, Hastings. Personally I believe that the murderer came from outside Andover, but we must neglect no avenue of research. And although I say "he" all the time, we must not exclude the possibility of a woman being concerned.'

'Surely not!'

'The method of attack is that of a man, I agree. But anonymous letters are written by women rather than by men. We must bear that in mind.'

I was silent for a few minutes, then I said:

'What do we do next?'

'My energetic Hastings,' Poirot said and smiled at me.

'No, but what do we do?'

'Nothing.'

'Nothing?' My disappointment rang out clearly.

'Am I the magician? The sorcerer? What would you have me do?'

Turning the matter over in my mind I found it difficult to give an answer. Nevertheless I felt convinced that something ought to be done and that we should not allow the grass to grow under our feet.

I said:

'There is the A B C—and the notepaper and envelope—'

'Naturally everything is being done in that line. The police have all the means at their disposal for that kind of inquiry. If anything is to be discovered on those lines have no fear but that they will discover it.'

With that I was forced to rest content.

In the days that followed I found Poirot curiously disinclined to discuss the case. When I tried to reopen the subject he waved it aside with an impatient hand.

In my own mind I was afraid that I fathomed his motive. Over the murder of Mrs Ascher, Poirot had sustained a defeat. A B C had challenged him—and A B C had won. My friend, accustomed to an unbroken line of successes, was sensitive to his failure—so much so that he could not even endure discussion of the subject. It was, perhaps, a sign of pettiness in so great a man, but even the most sober of us is liable to have his head turned by success.

In Poirot's case the head-turning process had been going on for years. Small wonder if its effects became noticeable at long last.

Understanding, I respected my friend's weakness and I made no further reference to the case. I read in the paper the account of the inquest. It was very brief, no mention was made of the A B C letter, and a verdict was returned of murder by some person or persons unknown. The crime attracted very little attention in the press. It had no popular or spectacular features. The murder of an old woman in a side street was soon passed over in the press for more thrilling topics.

Truth to tell, the affair was fading from my mind also, partly, I think, because I disliked to think of Poirot as being in any way associated with a failure, when on July 25th it was suddenly revived.

I had not seen Poirot for a couple of days as I had been away in Yorkshire for the weekend. I arrived back on Monday afternoon and the letter came by the six o'clock post. I remember the sudden, sharp intake of breath that Poirot gave as he slit open that particular envelope.

'It has come,' he said.

I stared at him—not understanding.

'What has come?'

'The second chapter of the A B C business.'

For a minute I looked at him uncomprehendingly. The matter had really passed from my memory.

'Read,' said Poirot and passed me over the letter.

As before, it was printed on good-quality paper.

Dear Mr Poirot,—Well, what about it? First game to me, I think. The Andover business went with a swing, didn't it?

But the fun's only just beginning. Let me draw your attention to Bexhill-on-Sea. Date, the 25th inst.

What a merry time we are having! Yours etc.

A B C

'Good God, Poirot,' I cried. 'Does this mean that this fiend is going to attempt another crime?'

'Naturally, Hastings. What else did you expect? Did you think that the Andover business was an isolated case? Do you not remember my saying: "This is the beginning"?'

'But this is horrible!'

'Yes, it is horrible.'

'We're up against a homicidal maniac.'

'Yes.'

His quietness was more impressive than any heroics could have been. I handed back the letter with a shudder.

The following morning saw us at a conference of powers. The Chief Constable of Sussex, the Assistant Commissioner of the CID, Inspector Glen from Andover, Superintendent Carter of the Sussex police, Japp and a younger inspector called Crome, and Dr Thompson, the famous alienist, were all assembled together. The postmark on this letter was Hampstead, but in Poirot's opinion little importance could be attached to this fact.

The matter was discussed fully. Dr Thompson was a pleasant middle-aged man who, in spite of his learning, contented himself with homely language, avoiding the technicalities of his profession.

'There's no doubt,' said the Assistant Commissioner, 'that the two letters are in the same hand. Both were written by the same person.'

'And we can fairly assume that that person was responsible for the Andover murder.'

'Quite. We've now got definite warning of a second crime scheduled to take place on the 25th—the day after tomorrow—at Bexhill. What steps can be taken?'

The Sussex Chief Constable looked at his superintendent.

'Well, Carter, what about it?'

The superintendent shook his head gravely.

'It's difficult, sir. There's not the least clue towards whom the victim may be. Speaking fair and square, what steps *can* we take?'

'A suggestion,' murmured Poirot.

Their faces turned to him.

'I think it possible that the surname of the intended victim will begin with the letter B.'

'That would be something,' said the superintendent doubtfully.

'An alphabetical complex,' said Dr Thompson thoughtfully.

'I suggest it as a possibility—no more. It came into my mind when I saw the name Ascher clearly written over the shop door of the unfortunate woman who was murdered last month. When I got the letter naming Bexhill it occurred to me as a possibility that the victim as well as the place might be selected by an alphabetical system.'

'It's possible,' said the doctor. 'On the other hand, it may be that the name Ascher was a coincidence—that the victim this time, no matter what her name is, will again be an old woman who keeps a shop. We're dealing, remember, with a madman. So far he hasn't given us any clue as to motive.'

'Has a madman any motive, sir?' asked the superintendent sceptically.

'Of course he has, man. A deadly logic is one of the special characteristics of acute mania. A man may believe himself divinely appointed to kill clergymen—or doctors—or old women in tobacco shops—and there's always some perfectly coherent reason behind it. We mustn't let the alphabetical business run away with us. Bexhill succeeding to Andover *may* be a mere coincidence.'

'We can at least take certain precautions, Carter, and make a special note of the B's, especially small shopkeepers, and keep a watch on all small tobacconists and newsagents looked after by a single person. I don't think there's anything more we can do than that. Naturally, keep tabs on all strangers as far as possible.'

The superintendent uttered a groan.

'With the schools breaking up and the holidays beginning? People are fairly flooding into the place this week.'

'We must do what we can,' the Chief Constable said sharply.

Inspector Glen spoke in his turn.

'I'll have a watch kept on anyone connected with the Ascher business. Those two witnesses, Partridge and Riddell, and of course Ascher himself. If they show any sign of leaving Andover they'll be followed.'

Agatha Christie

The conference broke up after a few more suggestions and a little desultory conversation.

'Poirot,' I said as we walked along by the river. 'Surely this crime can be prevented?'

He turned a haggard face to me.

'The sanity of a city full of men against the insanity of one man? I fear, Hastings—I very much fear. Remember the long-continued successes of Jack the Ripper.'

'It's horrible,' I said.

'Madness, Hastings, is a terrible thing… *I am afraid… I am very much afraid…*'

CHAPTER 9

The Bexhill-on-Sea Murder

I still remember my awakening on the morning of the 25th of July. It must have been about seven-thirty.

Poirot was standing by my bedside gently shaking me by the shoulder. One glance at his face brought me from semi-consciousness into the full possession of my faculties.

'What is it?' I demanded, sitting up rapidly.

His answer came quite simply, but a wealth of emotion lay behind the three words he uttered.

'It has happened.'

'What?' I cried. 'You mean—but *today* is the 25th.'

'It took place last night—or rather in the early hours of this morning.'

As I sprang from bed and made a rapid toilet, he recounted briefly what he had just learnt over the telephone.

'The body of a young girl has been found on the beach at Bexhill. She has been identified as Elizabeth Barnard, a waitress in one of the cafés, who lived with her parents in a little recently built bungalow. Medical evidence gave the time of death as between 11.30 and 1 am.'

'They're quite sure that this is *the* crime?' I asked, as I hastily lathered my face.

'*An A B C open at the trains to Bexhill was found actually under the body.*'

I shivered.

'This is horrible!'

'*Faites attention*, Hastings. I do not want a second tragedy in my rooms!'

I wiped the blood from my chin rather ruefully.

'What is our plan of campaign?' I asked.

'The car will call for us in a few moments' time. I will bring you a cup of coffee here so that there will be no delay in starting.'

Twenty minutes later we were in a fast police car crossing the Thames on our way out of London.

With us was Inspector Crome, who had been present at the conference the other day, and who was officially in charge of the case.

Crome was a very different type of officer from Japp. A much younger man, he was the silent, superior type. Well educated and well read, he was, for my taste, several shades too pleased with himself. He had lately gained kudos over a series of child murders, having patiently tracked down the criminal who was now in Broadmoor.

He was obviously a suitable person to undertake the present case, but I thought that he was just a little too aware of the fact himself. His manner to Poirot was a shade patronising. He deferred to him as a younger man to an older one—in a rather self-conscious, 'public school' way.

'I've had a good long talk with Dr Thompson,' he said. 'He's very interested in the "chain" or "series" type of murder. It's the product of a particular distorted type of mentality. As a layman one can't, of course, appreciate the finer points as they present themselves to a medical point of view.' He coughed. 'As a matter of fact—my last case—I don't know whether you read about it—the Mabel Homer case, the Muswell Hill schoolgirl, you know—that man Capper was extraordinary. Amazingly difficult to pin the crime on to him—it was his third, too! Looked as sane as you or I. But there are various tests—verbal traps, you know—quite modern, of course, there was nothing of that kind in your day. Once you can induce a man to give himself away, you've got him! He knows that you know and his nerve goes. He starts giving himself away right and left.'

'Even in my day that happened sometimes,' said Poirot.

Inspector Crome looked at him and murmured conversationally:

'Oh, yes?'

There was silence between us for some time. As we passed New Cross Station, Crome said:

'If there's anything you want to ask me about the case, pray do so.'

'You have not, I presume, a description of the dead girl?'

'She was twenty-three years of age, engaged as a waitress at the Ginger Cat café—'

'*Pas ça*. I wondered—if she were pretty?'

'As to that I've no information,' said Inspector Crome with a hint of withdrawal. His manner said: 'Really—these foreigners! All the same!'

A faint look of amusement came into Poirot's eyes.

'It does not seem to you important, that? Yet, *pour une femme*, it is of the first importance. Often it decides her destiny!'

Another silence fell.

It was not until we were nearing Sevenoaks that Poirot opened the conversation again.

'Were you informed, by any chance, how and with what the girl was strangled?'

Inspector Crome replied briefly.

'Strangled with her own belt—a thick, knitted affair, I gather.'

Poirot's eyes opened very wide.

'Aha,' he said. 'At last we have a piece of information that is very definite. That tells one something, does it not?'

'I haven't seen it yet,' said Inspector Crome coldly.

I felt impatient with the man's caution and lack of imagination.

'It gives us the hallmark of the murderer,' I said. 'The girl's own belt. It shows the particular beastliness of his mind!'

Poirot shot me a glance I could not fathom. On the face of it it conveyed humorous impatience. I thought that perhaps it was a warning not to be too outspoken in front of the inspector.

I relapsed into silence.

At Bexhill we were greeted by Superintendent Carter. He

had with him a pleasant-faced, intelligent-looking young inspector called Kelsey. The latter was detailed to work in with Crome over the case.

'You'll want to make your own inquiries, Crome,' said the superintendent. 'So I'll just give you the main heads of the matter and then you can get busy right away.'

'Thank you, sir,' said Crome.

'We've broken the news to her father and mother,' said the superintendent. 'Terrible shock to them, of course. I left them to recover a bit before questioning them, so you can start from the beginning there.'

'There are other members of the family—yes?' asked Poirot.

'There's a sister—a typist in London. She's been communicated with. And there's a young man—in fact, the girl was supposed to be out with him last night, I gather.'

'Any help from the A B C guide?' asked Crome.

'It's there,' the superintendent nodded towards the table. 'No fingerprints. Open at the page for Bexhill. A new copy, I should say—doesn't seem to have been opened much. Not bought anywhere round here. I've tried all the likely stationers.'

'Who discovered the body, sir?'

'One of these fresh-air, early-morning colonels. Colonel Jerome. He was out with his dog about 6 am. Went along the front in the direction of Cooden, and down on to the beach. Dog went off and sniffed at something. Colonel called it. Dog didn't come. Colonel had a look and thought something queer was up. Went over and looked. Behaved very properly. Didn't touch her at all and rang us up immediately.'

'And the time of death was round about midnight last night?'

'Between midnight and 1 am—that's pretty certain. Our homicidal joker is a man of his word. If he says the 25th, it is the 25th—though it may have been only by a few minutes.'

Crome nodded.

'Yes, that's his mentality all right. There's nothing else? Nobody saw anything helpful?'

'Not as far as we know. But it's early yet. Everyone who saw a girl in white walking with a man last night will be along to tell us about it soon, and as I imagine there were about four or five hundred girls in white walking with young men last night, it ought to be a nice business.'

'Well, sir, I'd better get down to it,' said Crome. 'There's the café and there's the girl's home. I'd better go to both of them. Kelsey can come with me.'

'And Mr Poirot?' asked the superintendent.

'I will accompany you,' said Poirot to Crome with a little bow.

Crome, I thought, looked slightly annoyed. Kelsey, who had not seen Poirot before, grinned broadly.

It was an unfortunate circumstance that the first time people saw my friend they were always disposed to consider him as a joke of the first water.

'What about this belt she was strangled with?' asked Crome. 'Mr Poirot is inclined to think it's a valuable clue. I expect he'd like to see it.'

'*Du tout*,' said Poirot quickly. 'You misunderstood me.'

'You'll get nothing from that,' said Carter. 'It wasn't a leather belt—might have got fingerprints if it had been. Just a thick sort of knitted silk—ideal for the purpose.'

I gave a shiver.

'Well,' said Crome, 'we'd better be getting along.'

We set out forthwith.

Our first visit was to the Ginger Cat. Situated on the sea front, this was the usual type of small tearoom. It had little tables covered with orange-checked cloths and basket-work chairs of exceeding discomfort with orange cushions on them. It was the kind of place that specialized in morning coffee, five different kinds of teas (Devonshire, Farmhouse, Fruit, Carlton and Plain), and a few sparing lunch dishes for females such as scrambled eggs and shrimps and macaroni au gratin.

The morning coffees were just getting under way. The manageress ushered us hastily into a very untidy back sanctum.

'Miss—eh—Merrion?' inquired Crome.

Miss Merrion bleated out in a high, distressed-gentlewoman voice:

'That is my name. This is a most distressing business. Most distressing. How it will affect our business I really cannot *think*!'

Miss Merrion was a very thin woman of forty with wispy orange hair (indeed she was astonishingly like a ginger cat herself). She played nervously with various fichus and frills that were part of her official costume.

'You'll have a boom,' said Inspector Kelsey encouragingly.

'You'll see! You won't be able to serve teas fast enough!'

'Disgusting,' said Miss Merrion. 'Truly disgusting. It makes one despair of human nature.'

But her eyes brightened nevertheless.

'What can you tell me about the dead girl, Miss Merrion?'

'Nothing,' said Miss Merrion positively. 'Absolutely nothing!'

'How long had she been working here?'

'This was the second summer.'

'You were satisfied with her?'

'She was a good waitress—quick and obliging.'

'She was pretty, yes?' inquired Poirot.

Miss Merrion, in her turn, gave him an 'Oh, these foreigners' look.

'She was a nice, clean-looking girl,' she said distantly.

'What time did she go off duty last night?' asked Crome.

'Eight o'clock. We close at eight. We do not serve dinners. There is no demand for them. Scrambled eggs and tea (Poirot shuddered) people come in for up to seven o'clock and sometimes after, but our rush is over by 6.30.'

'Did she mention to you how she proposed to spend her evening?'

'Certainly not,' said Miss Merrion emphatically. 'We were not on those terms.'

'No one came in and called for her? Anything like that?'

'No.'

'Did she seem quite her ordinary self? Not excited or depressed?'

'Really I could not say,' said Miss Merrion aloofly.

'How many waitresses do you employ?'

'Two normally, and an extra two after the 20th July until the end of August.'

'But Elizabeth Barnard was not one of the extras?'

'Miss Barnard was one of the regulars.'

'What about the other one?'

'Miss Higley? She is a very nice young lady.'

'Were she and Miss Barnard friends?'

'Really I could not say.'

'Perhaps we'd better have a word with her.'

'Now?'

'If you please.'

'I will send her to you,' said Miss Merrion, rising. 'Please keep her as short a time as possible. This is the morning coffee rush hour.'

The feline and gingery Miss Merrion left the room.

'Very refined,' remarked Inspector Kelsey. He mimicked the lady's mincing tone. *'Really I could not say.'*

A plump girl, slightly out of breath, with dark hair, rosy cheeks and dark eyes goggling with excitement, bounced in.

'Miss Merrion sent me,' she announced breathlessly.

'Miss Higley?'

'Yes, that's me.'

'You knew Elizabeth Barnard?'

'Oh, yes, I knew Betty. Isn't it *awful*? It's just too awful! I can't believe it's true. I've been saying to the girls all the morning I just *can't* believe it! "You know, girls," I said, "it just doesn't seem *real*. Betty! I mean, Betty Barnard, who's been here all along, *murdered*! I just can't believe it,"

I said. Five or six times I've pinched myself just to see if I wouldn't wake up. Betty murdered... It's—well, you know what I mean—it doesn't seem *real*.'

'You knew the dead girl well?' asked Crome.

'Well, she's worked here longer than I have. I only came this March. She was here last year. She was rather quiet, if you know what I mean. She wasn't one to joke or laugh a lot. I don't mean that she was exactly *quiet*—she'd plenty of fun in her and all that—but she didn't—well, she was quiet and she wasn't quiet, if you know what I mean.'

I will say for Inspector Crome that he was exceedingly patient. As a witness the buxom Miss Higley was persistently maddening. Every statement she made was repeated and qualified half a dozen times. The net result was meagre in the extreme.

She had not been on terms of intimacy with the dead girl. Elizabeth Barnard, it could be guessed, had considered herself a cut above Miss Higley. She had been friendly in working hours, but the girls had not seen much of her out of them. Elizabeth Barnard had had a 'friend' who worked at the estate agents near the station. Court & Brunskill. No, he wasn't Mr Court nor Mr Brunskill. He was a clerk there. She didn't know his name. But she knew him by sight well. Good-looking—oh, very good-looking, and always so nicely dressed. Clearly, there was a tinge of jealousy in Miss Higley's heart.

In the end it boiled down to this. Elizabeth Barnard had not confided in anyone in the café as to her plans for the evening, but in Miss Higley's opinion she had been going to meet her 'friend'. She had had on a new white dress, 'ever so sweet with one of the new necks.'

We had a word with each of the other two girls but with no further results. Betty Barnard had not said anything as to her plans and no one had noticed her in Bexhill during the course of the evening.

CHAPTER 10

The Barnards

Elizabeth Barnard's parents lived in a minute bungalow, one of fifty or so recently run up by a speculative builder on the confines of the town. The name of it was Llandudno.

Mr Barnard, a stout, bewildered-looking man of fifty-five or so, had noticed our approach and was standing waiting in the doorway.

'Come in, gentlemen,' he said.

Inspector Kelsey took the initiative.

'This is Inspector Crome of Scotland Yard, sir,' he said. 'He's come down to help us over this business.'

'Scotland Yard?' said Mr Barnard hopefully. 'That's good. This murdering villain's got to be laid by the heels. My poor little girl—' His face was distorted by a spasm of grief.

'And this is Mr Hercule Poirot, also from London, and er—'

'Captain Hastings,' said Poirot.

'Pleased to meet you, gentlemen,' said Mr Barnard mechanically. 'Come into the snuggery. I don't know that my poor wife's up to seeing you. All broken up, she is.'

However, by the time that we were ensconced in the living room of the bungalow, Mrs Barnard had made her appearance. She had evidently been crying bitterly, her eyes were reddened and she walked with the uncertain gait of a person who had had a great shock.

'Why, Mother, that's fine,' said Mr Barnard. 'You're sure you're all right—eh?'

He patted her shoulder and drew her down into a chair.

'The superintendent was very kind,' said Mr Barnard. 'After he'd broken the news to us, he said he'd leave any questions till later when we'd got over the first shock.'

'It is too cruel. Oh, it is too cruel,' cried Mrs Barnard tearfully. 'The cruellest thing that ever was, it is.'

Her voice had a faintly sing-song intonation that I thought for a moment was foreign till I remembered the name on the gate and realized that the 'effer wass' of her speech was in reality proof of her Welsh origin.

'It's very painful, madam, I know,' said Inspector Crome. 'And we've every sympathy for you, but we want to know all the facts we can so as to get to work as quick as possible.'

'That's sense, that is,' said Mr Barnard, nodding approval.

'Your daughter was twenty-three, I understand. She lived here with you and worked at the Ginger Cat café, is that right?'

'That's it.'

'This is a new place, isn't it? Where did you live before?'

'I was in the ironmongery business in Kennington. Retired two years ago. Always meant to live near the sea.'

Agatha Christie

'You have two daughters?'

'Yes. My elder daughter works in an office in London.'

'Weren't you alarmed when your daughter didn't come home last night?'

'We didn't know she hadn't,' said Mrs Barnard tearfully. 'Dad and I always go to bed early. Nine o'clock's our time. We never knew Betty hadn't come home till the police officer came and said—and said—'

She broke down.

'Was your daughter in the habit of—er—returning home late?'

'You know what girls are nowadays, inspector,' said Barnard. 'Independent, that's what they are. These summer evenings they're not going to rush home. All the same, Betty was usually in by eleven.'

'How did she get in? Was the door open?'

'Left the key under the mat—that's what we always did.'

'There is some rumour, I believe, that your daughter was engaged to be married?'

'They don't put it as formally as that nowadays,' said Mr Barnard.

'Donald Fraser his name is, and I liked him. I liked him very much,' said Mrs Barnard. 'Poor fellow, it'll be trouble for him—this news. Does he know yet, I wonder?'

'He works in Court & Brunskill's, I understand?'

'Yes, they're the estate agents.'

'Was he in the habit of meeting your daughter most evenings after her work?'

'Not every evening. Once or twice a week would be nearer.'

'Do you know if she was going to meet him yesterday?'

'She didn't say. Betty never said much about what she was doing or where she was going. But she was a good girl, Betty was. Oh, I can't believe—'

Mrs Barnard started sobbing again.

'Pull yourself together, old lady. Try to hold up, Mother,' urged her husband. 'We've got to get to the bottom of this.'

'I'm sure Donald would never—would never—' sobbed Mrs Barnard.

'Now just you pull yourself together,' repeated Mr Barnard.

'I wish to God I could give you some help—but the plain fact is I know nothing—nothing at all that can help you to find the dastardly scoundrel who did this. Betty was just a merry, happy girl—with a decent young fellow that she was—well, we'd have called it walking out with in my young days. Why anyone should want to murder her simply beats me—it doesn't make sense.'

'You're very near the truth there, Mr Barnard,' said Crome. 'I tell you what I'd like to do—have a look over Miss Barnard's room. There may be something—letters—or a diary.'

'Look over it and welcome,' said Mr Barnard, rising.

He led the way. Crome followed him, then Poirot, then Kelsey, and I brought up the rear.

I stopped for a minute to retie my shoelaces, and as I did so a taxi drew up outside and a girl jumped out of it. She paid the driver and hurried up the path to the house, carrying a small suitcase. As she entered the door she saw me and stopped dead.

There was something so arresting in her pose that it intrigued me.

'Who are you?' she said.

I came down a few steps. I felt embarrassed as to how exactly to reply. Should I give my name? Or mention that I had come here with the police? The girl, however, gave me no time to make a decision.

'Oh, well,' she said, 'I can guess.'

She pulled off the little white woollen cap she was wearing and threw it on the ground. I could see her better now as she turned a little so that the light fell on her.

My first impression was of the Dutch dolls that my sisters used to play with in my childhood. Her hair was black and cut in a straight bob and a bang across the forehead. Her cheek-bones were high and her whole figure had a queer modern angularity that was not, somehow, unattractive. She was not good-looking—plain rather—but there was an intensity about her, a forcefulness that made her a person quite impossible to overlook.

'You are Miss Barnard?' I asked.

'I am Megan Barnard. You belong to the police, I suppose?'

'Well,' I said. 'Not exactly—'

She interrupted me.

'I don't think I've got anything to say to you. My sister was a nice bright girl with no men friends. Good morning.'

She gave me a short laugh as she spoke and regarded me challengingly.

'That's the correct phrase, I believe?' she said.

'I'm not a reporter, if that's what you're getting at.'

'Well, what are you?' She looked around. 'Where's mum and dad?'

'Your father is showing the police your sister's bedroom. Your mother's in there. She's very upset.'

The girl seemed to make a decision.

'Come in here,' she said.

She pulled open a door and passed through. I followed her and found myself in a small, neat kitchen.

I was about to shut the door behind me—but found an unexpected resistance. The next moment Poirot had slipped quietly into the room and shut the door behind him.

'Mademoiselle Barnard?' he said with a quick bow.

'This is M. Hercule Poirot,' I said.

Megan Barnard gave him a quick, appraising glance.

'I've heard of you,' she said. 'You're the fashionable private sleuth, aren't you?'

'Not a pretty description—but it suffices,' said Poirot.

The girl sat down on the edge of the kitchen table. She felt in her bag for a cigarette. She placed it between her lips, lighted it, and then said in between two puffs of smoke:

'Somehow, I don't see what M. Hercule Poirot is doing in our humble little crime.'

'Mademoiselle,' said Poirot. 'What you do not see and what I do not see would probably fill a volume. But all that is of no practical importance. What *is* of practical importance is something that will not be easy to find.'

'What's that?'

Agatha Christie

'Death, mademoiselle, unfortunately creates a *prejudice*. A prejudice in favour of the deceased. I heard what you said just now to my friend Hastings. "A nice bright girl with no men friends." You said that in mockery of the newspapers. And it is very true—when a young girl is dead, that is the kind of thing that is said. She was bright. She was happy. She was sweet-tempered. She had not a care in the world. She had no undesirable acquaintances. There is a great charity always to the dead. Do you know what I should like this minute? I should like to find someone who knew Elizabeth Barnard *and who does not know she is dead*! Then, perhaps, I should hear what is useful to me—the truth.'

Megan Barnard looked at him for a few minutes in silence whilst she smoked. Then, at last, she spoke. Her words made me jump.

'Betty,' she said, 'was an unmitigated little ass!'

CHAPTER 11

Megan Barnard

As I said, Megan Barnard's words, and still more the crisp business-like tone in which they were uttered, made me jump.

Poirot, however, merely bowed his head gravely.

'*A la bonne heure*,' he said. 'You are intelligent, mademoiselle.'

Megan Barnard said, still in the same detached tone:

'I was extremely fond of Betty. But my fondness didn't blind me from seeing exactly the kind of silly little fool she was—and even telling her so upon occasions! Sisters are like that.'

'And did she pay any attention to your advice?'

'Probably not,' said Megan cynically.

'Will you, mademoiselle, be precise.'

The girl hesitated for a minute or two.

Poirot said with a slight smile:

'I will help you. I heard what you said to Hastings. That your sister was a bright, happy girl with no men friends. It was—*un peu*—the *opposite* that was true, was it not?'

Megan said slowly:

'There wasn't any harm in Betty. I want you to understand that. She'd always go straight. She's not the weekending kind. Nothing of that sort. But she liked being taken out and dancing and—oh, cheap flattery and compliments and all that sort of thing.'

'And she was pretty—yes?'

This question, the third time I had heard it, met this time with a practical response.

Megan slipped off the table, went to her suitcase, snapped it open and extracted something which she handed to Poirot.

In a leather frame was a head and shoulders of a fair-haired, smiling girl. Her hair had evidently recently been permed, it stood out from her head in a mass of rather frizzy curls. The smile was arch and artificial. It was certainly not a face that you could call beautiful, but it had an obvious and cheap prettiness.

Poirot handed it back, saying:

'You and she do not resemble each other, mademoiselle.'

'Oh! I'm the plain one of the family. I've always known that.' She seemed to brush aside the fact as unimportant.

'In what way exactly do you consider your sister was behaving foolishly? Do you mean, perhaps, in relation to Mr Donald Fraser?'

'That's it, exactly. Don's a very quiet sort of person—but he—well, naturally he'd resent certain things—and then—'

'And then what, mademoiselle?'

His eyes were on her very steadily.

It may have been my fancy but it seemed to me that she hesitated a second before answering.

'I was afraid that he might—chuck her altogether. And that would have been a pity. He's a very steady and hard-working man and would have made her a good husband.'

Poirot continued to gaze at her. She did not flush under his glance but returned it with one of her own equally steady and with something else in it—something that reminded me of her first defiant, disdainful manner.

'So it is like that,' he said at last. 'We do not speak the truth any longer.'

She shrugged her shoulders and turned towards the door.

'Well,' she said. 'I've done what I could to help you.'

Poirot's voice arrested her.

'Wait, mademoiselle. I have something to tell you. Come back.'

Rather unwillingly, I thought, she obeyed.

Somewhat to my surprise, Poirot plunged into the whole story of the A B C letters, the murder of Andover, and the railway guide found by the bodies.

He had no reason to complain of any lack of interest on her part. Her lips parted, her eyes gleaming, she hung on his words.

'Is this all true, M. Poirot?'

'Yes, it is true.'

'You really mean that my sister was killed by some horrible homicidal maniac?'

'Precisely?'

She drew a deep breath.

'Oh! Betty—Betty—how—how *ghastly*!'

'You see, mademoiselle, that the information for which I ask you can give freely without wondering whether or not it will hurt anyone.'

'Yes, I see that now.'

'Then let us continue our conversation. I have formed the idea that this Donald Fraser has, perhaps, a violent and jealous temper, is that right?'

Megan Barnard said quietly:

'I'm trusting you now, M. Poirot. I'm going to give you the absolute truth. Don is, as I say, a very quiet person—a bottled-up person, if you know what I mean. He can't always express what he feels in words. But underneath it all he minds things terribly. And he's got a jealous nature. He was always jealous of Betty. He was devoted to her—and of course she was very fond of him, but it wasn't in Betty to be fond of one person and not notice anybody else. She wasn't made that way. She'd got a—well, an eye for any nice-looking man who'd pass the time of day with her. And of course, working in the Ginger Cat, she was always running up against men—especially in the summer holidays. She was always very pat with her tongue and if they chaffed her she'd chaff back again. And then perhaps she'd meet them and go to the pictures or something like that. Nothing serious—never anything of that kind—but she just liked her fun. She used to say that as she'd got to settle down with Don one day she might as well have her fun now while she could.'

Megan paused and Poirot said:

The A B C Murders

'I understand. Continue.'

'It was just that attitude of mind of hers that Don couldn't understand. If she was really keen on him he couldn't see why she wanted to go out with other people. And once or twice they had flaming big rows about it.'

'M. Don, he was no longer quiet?'

'It's like all those quiet people, when they do lose their tempers they lose them with a vengeance. Don was so violent that Betty was frightened.'

'When was this?'

'There was one row nearly a year ago and another—a worse one—just over a month ago. I was home for the weekend—and I got them to patch it up again, and it was then I tried to knock a little sense into Betty—told her she was a little fool. All she would say was that there hadn't been any harm in it. Well, that was true enough, but all the same she was riding for a fall. You see, after the row a year ago, she'd got into the habit of telling a few useful lies on the principle that what the mind doesn't know the heart doesn't grieve over. This last flare-up came because she'd told Don she was going to Hastings to see a girl pal—and he found out that she'd really been over to Eastbourne with some man. He was a married man, as it happened, and he'd been a bit secretive about the business anyway—and so that made it worse. They had an awful scene—Betty saying that she wasn't married to him yet and she had a right to go about with whom she pleased and Don all white and shaking and saying that one day—one day—'

'Yes?'

83

'He'd commit murder—' said Megan in a lowered voice. She stopped and stared at Poirot.

He nodded his head gravely several times.

'And so, naturally, you were afraid...'

'I didn't think he'd actually done it—not for a minute! But I was afraid it might be brought up—the quarrel and all that he'd said—several people knew about it.'

Again Poirot nodded his head gravely.

'Just so. And I may say, mademoiselle, that but for the egoistical vanity of a killer, that is just what would have happened. If Donald Fraser escapes suspicion, it will be thanks to A B C's maniacal boasting.'

He was silent for a minute or two, then he said:

'Do you know if your sister met this married man, or any other man, lately?'

Megan shook her head.

'I don't know. I've been away, you see.'

'But what do you think?'

'She mayn't have met that particular man again. He'd probably sheer off if he thought there was a chance of a row, but it wouldn't surprise me if Betty had—well, been telling Don a few lies again. You see, she did so enjoy dancing and the pictures, and of course, Don couldn't afford to take her all the time.'

'If so, is she likely to have confided in anyone? The girl at the café, for instance?'

'I don't think that's likely. Betty couldn't bear the Higley girl. She thought her common. And the others would be new. Betty wasn't the confiding sort anyway.'

An electric bell trilled sharply above the girl's head.

She went to the window and leaned out. She drew back her head sharply.

'It's Don...'

'Bring him in here,' said Poirot quickly. 'I would like a word with him before our good inspector takes him in hand.'

Like a flash Megan Barnard was out of the kitchen, and a couple of seconds later she was back again leading Donald Fraser by the hand.

CHAPTER 12

Donald Fraser

I felt sorry at once for the young man. His white haggard face and bewildered eyes showed how great a shock he had had.

He was a well-made, fine-looking young fellow, standing close on six foot, not good-looking, but with a pleasant, freckled face, high cheek-bones and flaming red hair.

'What's this, Megan?' he said. 'Why in here? For God's sake, tell me—I've only just heard—Betty...'

His voice trailed away.

Poirot pushed forward a chair and he sank down on it.

My friend then extracted a small flask from his pocket, poured some of its contents into a convenient cup which was hanging on the dresser and said:

'Drink some of this, Mr Fraser. It will do you good.'

The young man obeyed. The brandy brought a little colour back into his face. He sat up straighter and turned once more to the girl. His manner was quite quiet and self-controlled.

The A B C Murders

'It's true, I suppose?' he said. 'Betty is—dead—killed?'

'It's true, Don.'

He said as though mechanically:

'Have you just come down from London?'

'Yes. Dad phoned me.'

'By the 9.30, I suppose?' said Donald Fraser.

His mind, shrinking from reality, ran for safety along these unimportant details.

'Yes.'

There was silence for a minute or two, then Fraser said:

'The police? Are they doing anything?'

'They're upstairs now. Looking through Betty's things, I suppose.'

'They've no idea who—? They don't know—?'

He stopped.

He had all a sensitive, shy person's dislike of putting violent facts into words.

Poirot moved forward a little and asked a question. He spoke in a businesslike, matter-of-fact voice as though what he asked was an unimportant detail.

'Did Miss Barnard tell you where she was going last night?'

Fraser replied to the question. He seemed to be speaking mechanically:

'She told me she was going with a girl friend to St Leonards.'

'Did you believe her?'

'I—' Suddenly the automaton came to life. 'What the devil do you mean?'

His face then, menacing, convulsed by sudden passion, made me understand that a girl might well be afraid of rousing his anger.

Poirot said crisply:

'Betty Barnard was killed by a homicidal murderer. Only by speaking the exact truth can you help us to get on his track.'

His glance for a minute turned to Megan.

'That's right, Don,' she said. 'It isn't a time for considering one's own feelings or anyone else's. You've got to come clean.'

Donald Fraser looked suspiciously at Poirot.

'Who are you? You don't belong to the police?'

'I am better than the police,' said Poirot. He said it without conscious arrogance. It was, to him, a simple statement of fact.

'Tell him,' said Megan.

Donald Fraser capitulated.

'I—wasn't sure,' he said. 'I believed her when she said it. Never thought of doing anything else. Afterwards—perhaps it was something in her manner. I—I, well, I began to wonder.'

'Yes?' said Poirot.

He had sat down opposite Donald Fraser. His eyes, fixed on the other man's, seemed to be exercising a mesmeric spell.

'I was ashamed of myself for being so suspicious. But—but I *was* suspicious… I thought of going to the front and watching her when she left the café. I actually went there. Then I felt I couldn't do that. Betty would see me and she'd be angry. She'd realize at once that I was watching her.'

'What did you do?'

'I went over to St Leonards. Got over there by eight o'clock. Then I watched the buses—to see if she were in them... But there was no sign of her...'

'And then?'

'I—I lost my head rather. I was convinced she was with some man. I thought it probable he had taken her in his car to Hastings. I went on there—looked in hotels and restaurants, hung round cinemas—went on the pier. All damn foolishness. Even if she was there I was unlikely to find her, and anyway, there were heaps of other places he might have taken her to instead of Hastings.'

He stopped. Precise as his tone had remained, I caught an undertone of that blind, bewildering misery and anger that had possessed him at the time he described.

'In the end I gave it up—came back.'

'At what time?'

'I don't know. I walked. It must have been midnight or after when I got home.'

'Then—'

The kitchen door opened.

'Oh, there you are,' said Inspector Kelsey.

Inspector Crome pushed past him, shot a glance at Poirot and a glance at the two strangers.

'Miss Megan Barnard and Mr Donald Fraser,' said Poirot, introducing them.

'This is Inspector Crome from London,' he explained.

Turning to the inspector, he said:

'While you pursued your investigations upstairs I have

been conversing with Miss Barnard and Mr Fraser, endeavouring if I could to find something that will throw light upon the matter.'

'Oh, yes?' said Inspector Crome, his thoughts not upon Poirot but upon the two newcomers.

Poirot retreated to the hall. Inspector Kelsey said kindly as he passed:

'Get anything?'

But his attention was distracted by his colleague and he did not wait for a reply.

I joined Poirot in the hall.

'Did anything strike you, Poirot?' I inquired.

'Only the amazing magnanimity of the murderer, Hastings.'

I had not the courage to say that I had not the least idea what he meant.

CHAPTER 13

A Conference

Conferences!

Much of my memories of the A B C case seem to be of conferences.

Conferences at Scotland Yard. At Poirot's rooms. Official conferences. Unofficial conferences.

This particular conference was to decide whether or not the facts relative to the anonymous letters should or should not be made public in the press.

The Bexhill murder had attracted much more attention than the Andover one.

It had, of course, far more elements of popularity. To begin with the victim was a young and good-looking girl. Also, it had taken place at a popular seaside resort.

All the details of the crime were reported fully and rehashed daily in thin disguises. The A B C railway guide came in for its share of attention. The favourite theory was that it had been bought locally by the murderer and that it was a valuable clue to his identity. It also seemed to show that he had come to the place by train and was intending to leave for London.

The railway guide had not figured at all in the meagre accounts of the Andover murder, so there seemed at present little likelihood of the two crimes being connected in the public eye.

'We've got to decide upon a policy,' said the Assistant Commissioner. 'The thing is—which way will give us the best results? Shall we give the public the facts—enlist their co-operation—after all, it'll be the co-operation of several million people, looking out for a madman—'

'He won't look like a madman,' interjected Dr Thompson.

'—looking out for sales of A B C's—and so on. Against that I suppose there's the advantage of working in the dark—not letting our man know what we're up to, but then there's the fact that *he knows very well that we know.* He's drawn attention to himself deliberately by his letters. Eh, Crome, what's your opinion?'

'I look at it this way, sir. If you make it public, *you're playing A B C's game*. That's what he wants—publicity—notoriety. That's what he's out after. I'm right, aren't I, doctor? He wants to make a splash.'

Thompson nodded.

The Assistant Commissioner said thoughtfully:

'So you're for balking him. Refusing him the publicity he's hankering after. What about you, M. Poirot?'

Poirot did not speak for a minute. When he did it was with an air of choosing his words carefully.

'It is difficult for me, Sir Lionel,' he said. 'I am, as you might say, an interested party. The challenge was sent to me. If I say "Suppress that fact—do not make it public," may it not be thought that it is my vanity that speaks? That I am afraid for my reputation? It is difficult! To speak out—to tell all—that has its advantages. It is, at least, a warning... On the other hand, I am as convinced as Inspector Crome *that it is what the murderer wants us to do.*'

'H'm!' said the Assistant Commissioner, rubbing his chin. He looked across at Dr Thompson. 'Suppose we refuse our lunatic the satisfaction of the publicity he craves. What's he likely to do?'

'Commit another crime,' said the doctor promptly.

'Force your hand.'

'And if we splash the thing about in headlines. Then what's his reaction?'

'Same answer. One way you *feed* his megalomania, the other you *balk* it. The result's the same. Another crime.'

'What do you say, M. Poirot?'

'I agree with Dr Thompson.'

'A cleft stick—eh? How many crimes do you think this—lunatic has in mind?'

Dr Thompson looked across at Poirot.

'Looks like A to Z,' he said cheerfully.

'Of course,' he went on, 'he won't get there. Not nearly. You'll have him by the heels long before that. Interesting to know how he'd have dealt with the letter X.' He recalled himself guiltily from this purely enjoyable speculation. 'But you'll have him long before that. G or H, let's say.'

The Assistant Commissioner struck the table with his fist.

'My God, are you telling me we're going to have five more murders?'

'It won't be as much as that, sir,' said Inspector Crome. 'Trust me.'

He spoke with confidence.

'Which letter of the alphabet do you place it at, inspector?' asked Poirot.

There was a slight ironic note in his voice. Crome, I thought, looked at him with a tinge of dislike adulterating the usual calm superiority.

'Might get him next time, M. Poirot. At any rate, I'd guarantee to get him by the time he gets to F.'

He turned to the Assistant Commissioner.

'I think I've got the psychology of the case fairly clear. Dr Thompson will correct me if I'm wrong. I take it that every time A B C brings a crime off, his self-confidence increases about a hundred per cent. Every time he feels "I'm clever—they can't catch me!" he becomes so over-weeningly confident that he also becomes careless. He exaggerates his own cleverness and everyone else's stupidity. Very soon he'd be hardly bothering to take any precautions at all. That's right, isn't it, doctor?'

Thompson nodded.

'That's usually the case. In non-medical terms it couldn't have been put better. You know something about such things, M. Poirot. Don't you agree?'

I don't think that Crome liked Thompson's appeal to Poirot. He considered that he and he only was the expert on this subject.

'It is as Inspector Crome says,' agreed Poirot.

'Paranoia,' murmured the doctor.

Poirot turned to Crome.

'Are there any material facts of interest in the Bexhill case?'

'Nothing very definite. A waiter at the Splendide at Eastbourne recognizes the dead girl's photograph as that of a young woman who dined there on the evening of the 24th in company with a middle-aged man in spectacles. It's also been recognized at a roadhouse place called the Scarlet Runner halfway between Bexhill and London. They say she was there about 9 pm on the 24th with a man who looked like a naval officer. They can't both be right, but either of them's probable. Of course, there's a host of other identifications, but most of them not good for much. We haven't been able to trace the A B C.'

'Well, you seem to be doing all that can be done, Crome,' said the Assistant Commissioner. 'What do you say, M. Poirot? Does any line of inquiry suggest itself to you?'

Poirot said slowly:

'It seems to me that there is one very important clue—the discovery of the motive.'

'Isn't that pretty obvious? An alphabetical complex. Isn't that what you called it, doctor?'

'Ça, oui,' said Poirot. 'There is an alphabetical complex. But why an alphabetical complex? A madman in particular has always a very strong reason for the crimes he commits.'

'Come, come, M. Poirot,' said Crome. 'Look at Stoneman in 1929. He ended by trying to do away with anyone who annoyed him in the slightest degree.'

Poirot turned to him.

Agatha Christie

'Quite so. But if you are a sufficiently great and important person, it is necessary that you should be spared small annoyances. If a fly settles on your forehead again and again, maddening you by its tickling—what do you do? You endeavour to kill that fly. You have no qualms about it. *You* are important—the fly is not. You kill the fly and the annoyance ceases. Your action appears to you sane and justifiable. Another reason for killing a fly is if you have a strong passion for hygiene. The fly is a potential source of danger to the community—the fly must go. So works the mind of the mentally deranged criminal. But consider now this case—*if the victims are alphabetically selected, then they are not being removed because they are a source of annoyance to the murderer personally*. It would be too much of a coincidence to combine the two.'

'That's a point,' said Dr Thompson. 'I remember a case where a woman's husband was condemned to death. She started killing the members of the jury one by one. Quite a time before the crimes were connected up. They seemed entirely haphazard. But as M. Poirot says, there isn't such a thing as a murderer who commits crimes at *random*. Either he removes people who stand (however insignificantly) in his path, or else he kills by *conviction*. He removes clergymen, or policemen, or prostitutes because he firmly believes that they *should* be removed. That doesn't apply here either as far as I can see. Mrs Ascher and Betty Barnard cannot be linked as members of the same class. Of course, it's possible that there is a sex complex. Both victims have been women. We can tell better, of course, after the next crime—'

'For God's sake, Thompson, don't speak so glibly of the next crime,' said Sir Lionel irritably. 'We're going to do all we can to prevent another crime.'

Dr Thompson held his peace and blew his nose with some violence.

'Have it your own way,' the noise seemed to say. 'If you won't face facts—'

The Assistant Commissioner turned to Poirot.

'I see what you're driving at, but I'm not quite clear yet.'

'I ask myself,' said Poirot, 'what passes exactly in the mind of the murderer? He kills, it would seem from his letters, *pour le sport*—to amuse himself. Can that really be true? And even if it is true, on what principle does he select his victims *apart from the merely alphabetical one*? If he kills merely to amuse himself he would not advertise the fact, since, otherwise, he could kill with impunity. But no, he seeks, as we all agree, to make the splash in the public eye—to assert his personality. In what way has his personality been suppressed that one can connect with the two victims he has so far selected? A final suggestion: Is his motive direct personal hatred of *me*, of Hercule Poirot? Does he challenge me in public because I have (unknown to myself) vanquished him somewhere in the course of my career? Or is his animosity impersonal—directed against a *foreigner*? And if so, what again has led to that? What injury has he suffered at a foreigner's hand?'

'All very suggestive questions,' said Dr Thompson.

Inspector Crome cleared his throat.

'Oh, yes? A little unanswerable at present, perhaps.'

'Nevertheless, my friend,' said Poirot, looking straight at him, '*it is there, in those questions, that the solution lies*. If we knew the exact reason—fantastic, perhaps, to us—but logical to him—of *why* our madman commits these crimes, we should know, perhaps, who the next victim is likely to be.'

Crome shook his head.

'He selects them haphazard—that's my opinion.'

'The magnanimous murderer,' said Poirot.

'What's that you say?'

'I said—the magnanimous murderer! Franz Ascher would have been arrested for the murder of his wife—Donald Fraser might have been arrested for the murder of Betty Barnard—if it had not been for the warning letters of A B C. Is he, then, so soft-hearted that he cannot bear others to suffer for something they did not do?'

'I've known stranger things happen,' said Dr Thompson. 'I've known men who've killed half a dozen victims all broken up because one of their victims didn't die instantaneously and suffered pain. All the same, I don't think that that is our fellow's reason. He wants the credit of these crimes for his own honour and glory. That's the explanation that fits best.'

'We've come to no decision about the publicity business,' said the Assistant Commissioner.

'If I may make a suggestion, sir,' said Crome. 'Why not wait till the receipt of the next letter? Make it public then—special editions, etc. It will make a bit of a panic in the particular town named, but it will put everyone whose name begins with C on their guard, and it'll put A B C on his mettle. He'll be determined to succeed. And that's when we'll get him.'

How little we knew what the future held.

CHAPTER 14

The Third Letter

I well remember the arrival of A B C's third letter.

I may say that all precautions had been taken so that when A B C resumed his campaign there should be no unnecessary delays. A young sergeant from Scotland Yard was attached to the house and if Poirot and I were out it was his duty to open anything that came so as to be able to communicate with headquarters without loss of time.

As the days succeeded each other we had all grown more and more on edge. Inspector Crome's aloof and superior manner grew more and more aloof and superior as one by one his more hopeful clues petered out. The vague descriptions of men said to have been seen with Betty Barnard proved useless. Various cars noticed in the vicinity of Bexhill and Cooden were either accounted for or could not be traced. The investigation of purchases of A B C railway guides caused inconvenience and trouble to heaps of innocent people.

As for ourselves, each time the postman's familiar rat-tat

sounded on the door, our hearts beat faster with apprehension. At least that was true for me, and I cannot but believe that Poirot experienced the same sensation.

He was, I knew, deeply unhappy over the case. He refused to leave London, preferring to be on the spot in case of emergency. In those hot dog days even his moustaches drooped—neglected for once by their owner.

It was on a Friday that A B C's third letter came. The evening post arrived about ten o'clock.

When we heard the familiar step and the brisk rat-tat, I rose and went along to the box. There were four or five letters, I remember. The last one I looked at was addressed in printed characters.

'Poirot,' I cried... My voice died away.

'It has come? Open it, Hastings. Quickly. Every moment may be needed. We must make our plans.'

I tore open the letter (Poirot for once did not reproach me with untidiness) and extracted the printed sheet.

'Read it,' said Poirot.

I read aloud:

Poor Mr Poirot,—Not so good at these little criminal matters as you thought yourself, are you? Rather past your prime, perhaps? Let us see if you can do any better this time. This time it's an easy one. Churston on the 30th. Do try and do something about it! It's a bit dull having it all my own way, you know!

Good hunting. Ever yours,
A B C.

Agatha Christie

'Churston,' I said, jumping to our own copy of an A B C. 'Let's see where it is.'

'Hastings,' Poirot's voice came sharply and interrupted me. 'When was that letter written? Is there a date on it?'

I glanced at the letter in my hand.

'Written on the 27th,' I announced.

'Did I hear you aright, Hastings? Did he give the date of the murder as the *30th*?'

'That's right. Let me see, that's—'

'*Bon Dieu*, Hastings—do you not realise? *Today is the 30th.*'

His eloquent hand pointed to the calendar on the wall. I caught up the daily paper to confirm it.

'But why—how—' I stammered.

Poirot caught up the torn envelope from the floor. Something unusual about the address had registered itself vaguely in my brain, but I had been too anxious to get at the contents of the letter to pay more than fleeting attention to it.

Poirot was at the time living in Whitehaven Mansions. The address ran: *M. Hercule Poirot, Whitehorse Mansions*, across the corner was scrawled: '*Not known at Whitehorse Mansions, EC1, nor at Whitehorse Court—try Whitehaven Mansions.*'

'*Mon Dieu!*' murmured Poirot. 'Does even chance aid this madman? *Vite—vite*—we must get on to Scotland Yard.'

A minute or two later we were speaking to Crome over the wire. For once the self-controlled inspector did not reply 'Oh, yes?' Instead a quickly stifled curse came to his lips.

He heard what we had to say, then rang off in order to get a trunk connection to Churston as rapidly as possible.

'*C'est trop tard*,' murmured Poirot.

'You can't be sure of that,' I argued, though without any great hope.

He glanced at the clock.

'Twenty minutes past ten? An hour and forty minutes to go. Is it likely that A B C will have held his hand so long?'

I opened the railway guide I had previously taken from its shelf.

'Churston, Devon,' I read, 'from Paddington 204¾ miles. Population 656. It sounds a fairly small place. Surely our man will be bound to be noticed there.'

'Even so, another life will have been taken,' murmured Poirot. 'What are the trains? I imagine train will be quicker than car.'

'There's a midnight train—sleeping car to Newton Abbot—gets there 6.08 am, and then Churston at 7.15.'

'That is from Paddington?'

'Paddington, yes.'

'We will take that, Hastings.'

'You'll hardly have time to get news before we start.'

'If we receive bad news tonight or tomorrow morning does it matter which?'

'There's something in that.'

I put a few things together in a suitcase while Poirot once more rang up Scotland Yard.

A few minutes later he came into the bedroom and demanded:

'*Mais qu'est ce que vous faites là?*'

'I was packing for you. I thought it would save time.'

'*Vous éprouvez trop d'émotion, Hastings*. It affects your hands and your wits. Is that a way to fold a coat? And regard what you have done to my pyjamas. If the hairwash breaks what will befall them?'

'Good heavens, Poirot,' I cried, 'this is a matter of life and death. What does it matter what happens to our clothes?'

'You have no sense of proportion, Hastings. We cannot catch a train earlier than the time that it leaves, and to ruin one's clothes will not be the least helpful in preventing a murder.'

Taking his suitcase from me firmly, he took the packing into his own hands.

He explained that we were to take the letter and envelope to Paddington with us. Someone from Scotland Yard would meet us there.

When we arrived on the platform the first person we saw was Inspector Crome.

He answered Poirot's look of inquiry.

'No news as yet. All men available are on the lookout. All persons whose name begins with C are being warned by phone when possible. There's just a chance. Where's the letter?'

Poirot gave it to him.

He examined it, swearing softly under his breath.

'Of all the damned luck. The stars in their courses fight for the fellow.'

'You don't think,' I suggested, 'that it was done on purpose?'

Crome shook his head.

'No. He's got his rules—crazy rules—and abides by them. Fair warning. He makes a point of that. That's where his boastfulness comes in. I wonder now—I'd almost bet the chap drinks White Horse whisky.'

'*Ah, c'est ingénieux, ça!*' said Poirot, driven to admiration in spite of himself. 'He prints the letter and the bottle is in front of him.'

'That's the way of it,' said Crome. 'We've all of us done much the same thing one time or another, unconsciously copied something that's just under the eye. He started off White and went on horse instead of haven...'

The inspector, we found, was also travelling by the train.

'Even if by some unbelievable luck nothing happened, Churston is the place to be. Our murderer is there, or has been there today. One of my men is on the phone here up to the last minute in case anything comes through.'

Just as the train was leaving the station we saw a man running down the platform. He reached the inspector's window and called up something.

As the train drew out of the station Poirot and I hurried along the corridor and tapped on the door of the inspector's sleeper.

'You have news—yes?' demanded Poirot.

Crome said quietly:

'It's about as bad as it can be. Sir Carmichael Clarke has been found with his head bashed in.'

Sir Carmichael Clarke, although his name was not very well known to the general public, was a man of some eminence. He had been in his time a very well-known throat specialist. Retiring from his profession very comfortably off, he had been able to indulge what had been one of the chief passions of his life—a collection of Chinese pottery and porcelain. A few years later, inheriting a considerable fortune from an elderly uncle, he had been able to indulge his passion to the full, and he was now the possessor of one of the best-known collections of Chinese art. He was married but had no children and lived in a house he had built for himself near the Devon coast, only coming to London on rare occasions such as when some important sale was on.

It did not require much reflection to realize that his death, following that of the young and pretty Betty Barnard, would provide the best newspaper sensation for years. The fact that it was August and that the papers were hard up for subject matter would make matters worse.

'*Eh bien*,' said Poirot. 'It is possible that publicity may do what private efforts have failed to do. The whole country now will be looking for A B C.'

'Unfortunately,' I said, 'that's what he wants.'

'True. But it may, all the same, be his undoing. Gratified by success, he may become careless… That is what I hope—that he may be drunk with his own cleverness.'

'How odd all this is, Poirot,' I exclaimed, struck suddenly by an idea. 'Do you know, this is the first crime of this kind that you and I have worked on together? All our murders have been—well, private murders, so to speak.'

'You are quite right, my friend. Always, up to now, it has fallen to our lot to work from the *inside*. It has been the history of the *victim* that was important. The important points have been: "Who benefited by the death? What opportunities had those round him to commit the crime?" It has always been the "*crime intime*". Here, for the first time in our association, it is cold-blooded, impersonal murder. Murder from the *outside*.'

I shivered.

'It's rather horrible...'

'Yes. I felt from the first, when I read the original letter, that there was something wrong—misshapen...'

He made an impatient gesture.

'One must not give way to the nerves... *This is no worse than any ordinary crime...*'

'It is... It is...'

'Is it worse to take the life or lives of strangers than to take the life of someone near and dear to you—someone who trusts and believes in you, perhaps?'

'It's worse because it's *mad*...'

'No, Hastings. It is not *worse*. It is only more *difficult*.'

'No, no, I do not agree with you. It's infinitely more frightening.'

Hercule Poirot said thoughtfully:

'It should be easier to discover because it is mad. A crime committed by someone shrewd and sane would be far more complicated. Here, if one could but hit on the *idea*... This alphabetical business, it has discrepancies. If I could once see the *idea*—then everything would be clear and simple...'

He sighed and shook his head.

'These crimes must not go on. Soon, soon, I must see the truth... Go, Hastings. Get some sleep. There will be much to do tomorrow.'

CHAPTER 15

Sir Carmichael Clarke

Churston, lying as it does between Brixham on the one side and Paignton and Torquay on the other, occupies a position about halfway round the curve of Torbay. Until about ten years ago it was merely a golf links and below the links a green sweep of countryside dropping down to the sea with only a farmhouse or two in the way of human occupation. But of late years there had been big building developments between Churston and Paignton and the coastline is now dotted with small houses and bungalows, new roads, etc.

Sir Carmichael Clarke had purchased a site of some two acres commanding an uninterrupted view of the sea. The house he had built was of modern design—a white rectangle that was not unpleasing to the eye. Apart from two big galleries that housed his collection it was not a large house.

Our arrival there took place about 8 am. A local police officer had met us at the station and had put us *au courant* of the situation.

Sir Carmichael Clarke, it seemed, had been in the habit of

The A B C Murders

taking a stroll after dinner every evening. When the police rang up—at some time after eleven—it was ascertained that he had not returned. Since his stroll usually followed the same course, it was not long before a search-party discovered his body. Death was due to a crashing blow with some heavy instrument on the back of the head. *An open A B C had been placed face downwards on the dead body.*

We arrived at Combeside (as the house was called) at about eight o'clock. The door was opened by an elderly butler whose shaking hands and disturbed face showed how much the tragedy had affected him.

'Good morning, Deveril,' said the police officer.

'Good morning, Mr Wells.'

'These are the gentlemen from London, Deveril.'

'This way, gentlemen.' He ushered us into a long dining-room where breakfast was laid. 'I'll get Mr Franklin.'

A minute or two later a big fair-haired man with a sunburnt face entered the room.

This was Franklin Clarke, the dead man's only brother.

He had the resolute competent manner of a man accustomed to meeting with emergencies.

'Good morning, gentlemen.'

Inspector Wells made the introductions.

'This is Inspector Crome of the CID, Mr Hercule Poirot and—er—Captain Hayter.'

'Hastings,' I corrected coldly.

Franklin Clarke shook hands with each of us in turn and in each case the handshake was accompanied by a piercing look.

Agatha Christie

'Let me offer you some breakfast,' he said. 'We can discuss the position as we eat.'

There were no dissentient voices and we were soon doing justice to excellent eggs and bacon and coffee.

'Now for it,' said Franklin Clarke. 'Inspector Wells gave me a rough idea of the position last night—though I may say it seemed one of the wildest tales I have ever heard. Am I really to believe, Inspector Crome, that my poor brother is the victim of a homicidal maniac, that this is the third murder that has occurred and that *in each case an A B C railway guide has been deposited beside the body*?'

'That is substantially the position, Mr Clarke.'

'But *why*? What earthly benefit can accrue from such a crime—even in the most diseased imagination?'

Poirot nodded his head in approval.

'You go straight to the point, Mr Franklin,' he said.

'It's not much good looking for motives at this stage, Mr Clarke,' said Inspector Crome. 'That's a matter for an alienist—though I may say that I've had a certain experience of criminal lunacy and that the motives are usually grossly inadequate. There is a desire to assert one's personality, to make a splash in the public eye—in fact, to be a somebody instead of a nonentity.'

'Is that true, M. Poirot?'

Clarke seemed incredulous. His appeal to the older man was not too well received by Inspector Crome, who frowned.

'Absolutely true,' replied my friend.

'At any rate such a man cannot escape detection long,' said Clarke thoughtfully.

'*Vous croyez?* Ah, but they are cunning—*ces gens là*! And you must remember *such a type has usually all the outer signs of insignificance*—he belongs to the class of person who is usually passed over and ignored or even laughed at!'

'Will you let me have a few facts, please, Mr Clarke,' said Crome, breaking in on the conversation.

'Certainly.'

'Your brother, I take it, was in his usual health and spirits yesterday? He received no unexpected letters? Nothing to upset him?'

'No. I should say he was quite his usual self.'

'Not upset and worried in any way.'

'Excuse me, inspector. I didn't say that. To be upset and worried was my poor brother's normal condition.'

'Why was that?'

'You may not know that my sister-in-law, Lady Clarke, is in very bad health. Frankly, between ourselves, she is suffering from an incurable cancer, and cannot live very much longer. Her illness has preyed terribly on my brother's mind. I myself returned from the East not long ago and I was shocked at the change in him.'

Poirot interpolated a question.

'Supposing, Mr Clarke, that your brother had been found shot at the foot of a cliff—or shot with a revolver beside him. What would have been your first thought?'

'Quite frankly, I should have jumped to the conclusion that it was suicide,' said Clarke.

'*Encore!*' said Poirot.

'What is that?'

Agatha Christie

'A fact that repeats itself. It is of no matter.'

'Anyway, it *wasn't* suicide,' said Crome with a touch of curtness. 'Now I believe, Mr Clarke, that it was your brother's habit to go for a stroll every evening?'

'Quite right. He always did.'

'Every night?'

'Well, not if it was pouring with rain, naturally.'

'And everyone in the house knew of this habit?'

'Of course.'

'And outside?'

'I don't quite know what you mean by outside. The gardener may have been aware of it or not, I don't know.'

'And in the village?'

'Strictly speaking, we haven't got a village. There's a post office and cottages at Churston Ferrers—but there's no village or shops.'

'I suppose a stranger hanging round the place would be fairly easily noticed?'

'On the contrary. In August all this part of the world is a seething mass of strangers. They come over every day from Brixham and Torquay and Paignton in cars and buses and on foot. Broadsands, which is down there (he pointed), is a very popular beach and so is Elbury Cove—it's a well-known beauty spot and people come there and picnic. I wish they didn't! You've no idea how beautiful and peaceful this part of the world is in June and the beginning of July.'

'So you don't think a stranger would be noticed?'

'Not unless he looked—well, off his head.'

'This man doesn't look off his head,' said Crome with certainty. 'You see what I'm getting at, Mr Clarke. This man must have been spying out the land beforehand and discovered your brother's habit of taking an evening stroll. I suppose, by the way, that no strange man came up to the house and asked to see Sir Carmichael yesterday?'

'Not that I know of—but we'll ask Deveril.'

He rang the bell and put the question to the butler.

'No, sir, no one came to see Sir Carmichael. And I didn't notice anyone hanging about the house either. No more did the maids, because I've asked them.'

The butler waited a moment, then inquired: 'Is that all, sir?'

'Yes, Deveril, you can go.'

The butler withdrew, drawing back in the doorway to let a young woman pass.

Franklin Clarke rose as she came in.

'This is Miss Grey, gentlemen. My brother's secretary.'

My attention was caught at once by the girl's extraordinary Scandinavian fairness. She had the almost colourless ash hair—light-grey eyes—and transparent glowing pallor that one finds amongst Norwegians and Swedes. She looked about twenty-seven and seemed to be as efficient as she was decorative.

'Can I help you in any way?' she asked as she sat down.

Clarke brought her a cup of coffee, but she refused any food.

'Did you deal with Sir Carmichael's correspondence?' asked Crome.

'Yes, all of it.'

'I suppose he never received a letter or letters signed ABC?'

'A B C?' She shook her head. 'No, I'm sure he didn't.'

'He didn't mention having seen anyone hanging about during his evening walks lately?'

'No. He never mentioned anything of the kind.'

'And you yourself have noticed no strangers?'

'Not exactly hanging about. Of course, there are a lot of people what you might call *wandering* about at this time of year. One often meets people strolling with an aimless look across the golf links or down the lanes to the sea. In the same way, practically everyone one sees this time of year is a stranger.'

Poirot nodded thoughtfully.

Inspector Crome asked to be taken over the ground of Sir Carmichael's nightly walk. Franklin Clarke led the way through the French window, and Miss Grey accompanied us.

She and I were a little behind the others.

'All this must have been a terrible shock to you all,' I said.

'It seems quite unbelievable. I had gone to bed last night when the police rang up. I heard voices downstairs and at last I came out and asked what was the matter. Deveril and Mr Clarke were just setting out with lanterns.'

'What time did Sir Carmichael usually come back from his walk?'

'About a quarter to ten. He used to let himself in by the side door and then sometimes he went straight to bed, sometimes to the gallery where his collections were. That is why, unless the police had rung up, he would probably not have been missed till they went to call him this morning.'

'It must have been a terrible shock to his wife?'

'Lady Clarke is kept under morphia a good deal. I think she is in too dazed a condition to appreciate what goes on round her.'

We had come out through a garden gate on to the golf links. Crossing a corner of them, we passed over a stile into a steep, winding lane.

'This leads down to Elbury Cove,' explained Franklin Clarke. 'But two years ago they made a new road leading from the main road to Broadsands and on to Elbury, so that now this lane is practically deserted.'

We went on down the lane. At the foot of it a path led between brambles and bracken down to the sea. Suddenly we came out on a grassy ridge overlooking the sea and a beach of glistening white stones. All round dark green trees ran down to the sea. It was an enchanting spot—white, deep green—and sapphire blue.

'How beautiful!' I exclaimed.

Clarke turned to me eagerly.

'Isn't it? Why people want to go abroad to the Riviera when they've got this! I've wandered all over the world in my time and, honest to God, I've never seen anything as beautiful.'

Then, as though ashamed of his eagerness, he said in a more matter-of-fact tone:

'This was my brother's evening walk. He came as far as here, then back up the path, and turning to the right

Agatha Christie

instead of the left, went past the farm and across the fields back to the house.'

We proceeded on our way till we came to a spot near the hedge, halfway across the field where the body had been found.

Crome nodded.

'Easy enough. The man stood here in the shadow. Your brother would have noticed nothing till the blow fell.'

The girl at my side gave a quick shiver.

Franklin Clarke said:

'Hold up, Thora. It's pretty beastly, but it's no use shirking facts.'

Thora Grey—the name suited her.

We went back to the house where the body had been taken after being photographed.

As we mounted the wide staircase the doctor came out of a room, black bag in hand.

'Anything to tell us, doctor?' inquired Clarke.

The doctor shook his head.

'Perfectly simple case. I'll keep the technicalities for the inquest. Anyway, he didn't suffer. Death must have been instantaneous.'

He moved away.

'I'll just go in and see Lady Clarke.'

A hospital nurse came out of a room farther along the corridor and the doctor joined her.

We went into the room out of which the doctor had come.

I came out again rather quickly. Thora Grey was still standing at the head of the stairs.

There was a queer scared expression on her face.

'Miss Grey—' I stopped. 'Is anything the matter?'

She looked at me.

'I was thinking,' she said, 'about D.'

'About D?' I stared at her stupidly.

'Yes. The next murder. Something must be done. It's got to be stopped.'

Clarke came out of the room behind me.

He said:

'What's got to be stopped, Thora?'

'These awful murders.'

'Yes.' His jaw thrust itself out aggressively. 'I want to talk to M. Poirot some time… Is Crome any good?' He shot the words out unexpectedly.

I replied that he was supposed to be a very clever officer.

My voice was perhaps not as enthusiastic as it might have been.

'He's got a damned offensive manner,' said Clarke. 'Looks as though he knows everything—and what *does* he know? Nothing at all as far as I can make out.'

He was silent for a minute or two. Then he said:

'M. Poirot's the man for my money. I've got a plan. But we'll talk of that later.'

He went along the passage and tapped at the same door as the doctor had entered.

I hesitated a moment. The girl was staring in front of her.

'What are you thinking of, Miss Grey?'

She turned her eyes towards me.

'I'm wondering *where he is now*… the murderer, I mean.

It's not twelve hours yet since it happened... Oh! aren't there any *real* clairvoyants who could see where he is now and what he is doing...'

'The police are searching—' I began.

My commonplace words broke the spell. Thora Grey pulled herself together.

'Yes,' she said. 'Of course.'

In her turn she descended the staircase. I stood there a moment longer conning her words over in my mind.

A B C...

Where was he now...?

CHAPTER 16

(Not from Captain Hastings' Personal Narrative)

Mr Alexander Bonaparte Cust came out with the rest of the audience from the Torquay Palladium, where he had been seeing and hearing that highly emotional film, *Not a Sparrow...*

He blinked a little as he came out into the afternoon sunshine and peered round him in that lost-dog fashion that was characteristic of him.

He murmured to himself: 'It's an idea...'

Newsboys passed along crying out:

'Latest... Homicidal Maniac at Churston...'

They carried placards on which was written:

CHURSTON MURDER. LATEST.

Mr Cust fumbled in his pocket, found a coin, and bought a paper. He did not open it at once.

Entering the Princess Gardens, he slowly made his way to a shelter facing Torquay harbour. He sat down and opened the paper.

There were big headlines:

SIR CARMICHAEL CLARKE MURDERED.
TERRIBLE TRAGEDY AT CHURSTON.
WORK OF A HOMICIDAL MANIAC.

And below them:

Only a month ago England was shocked and startled by the murder of a young girl, Elizabeth Barnard, at Bexhill. It may be remembered that an A B C railway guide figured in the case. An A B C was also found by the dead body of Sir Carmichael Clarke, and the police incline to the belief that both crimes were committed by the same person. Can it be possible that a homicidal murderer is going the round of our seaside resorts?…

A young man in flannel trousers and a bright blue Aertex shirt who was sitting beside Mr Cust remarked:

'Nasty business—eh?'

Mr Cust jumped.

'Oh, very—very—'

His hands, the young man noticed, were trembling so that he could hardly hold the paper.

'You never know with lunatics,' said the young man chattily. 'They don't always look barmy, you know. Often they seem just the same as you or me…'

'I suppose they do,' said Mr Cust.

'It's a fact. Sometimes it's the war what unhinged them—never been right since.'

'I—I expect you're right.'

'I don't hold with wars,' said the young man.

His companion turned on him.

'I don't hold with plague and sleeping sickness and famine and cancer... but they happen all the same!'

'War's preventable,' said the young man with assurance.

Mr Cust laughed. He laughed for some time.

The young man was slightly alarmed.

'He's a bit batty himself,' he thought.

Aloud he said:

'Sorry, sir, I expect you were in the war.'

'I was,' said Mr Cust. 'It—it—unsettled me. My head's never been right since. It aches, you know. Aches terribly.'

'Oh! I'm sorry about that,' said the young man awkwardly.

'Sometimes I hardly know what I'm doing...'

'Really? Well, I must be getting along,' said the young man and removed himself hurriedly. He knew what people were once they began to talk about their health.

Mr Cust remained with his paper.

He read and reread...

People passed to and fro in front of him.

Most of them were talking of the murder...

'Awful... do you think it was anything to do with the Chinese? Wasn't the waitress in a Chinese café...'

'Actually on the golf links...'

'I heard it was on the beach...'

'—but, darling, we took our tea to Elbury only *yesterday*...'

'—police are sure to get him...'

'—say he may be arrested any minute now...'

Agatha Christie

'—quite likely he's in Torquay... that other woman was who murdered the what do you call 'ems...'

Mr Cust folded up the paper very neatly and laid it on the seat. Then he rose and walked sedately along towards the town.

Girls passed him, girls in white and pink and blue, in summery frocks and pyjamas and shorts. They laughed and giggled. Their eyes appraised the men they passed.

Not once did their eyes linger for a second on Mr Cust...

He sat down at a little table and ordered tea and Devonshire cream...

CHAPTER 17

Marking Time

With the murder of Sir Carmichael Clarke the A B C mystery leaped into the fullest prominence.

The newspapers were full of nothing else. All sorts of 'clues' were reported to have been discovered. Arrests were announced to be imminent. There were photographs of every person or place remotely connected with the murder. There were interviews with anyone who would give interviews. There were questions asked in Parliament.

The Andover murder was now bracketed with the other two.

It was the belief of Scotland Yard that the fullest publicity was the best chance of laying the murderer by the heels. The population of Great Britain turned itself into an army of amateur sleuths.

The *Daily Flicker* had the grand inspiration of using the caption:

HE MAY BE IN *YOUR* TOWN!

Poirot, of course, was in the thick of things. The letters sent to him were published and facsimiled. He was abused wholesale for not having prevented the crimes and defended on the ground that he was on the point of naming the murderer.

Reporters incessantly badgered him for interviews.

What M. Poirot Says Today.

Which was usually followed by a half-column of imbecilities.

M. Poirot Takes Grave View of Situation.
M. Poirot on the Eve of Success.
Captain Hastings, the great friend of M. Poirot, told our Special Representative...

'Poirot,' I would cry. 'Pray believe me. I never said anything of the kind.'

My friend would reply kindly:

'I know, Hastings—I know. The spoken word and the written—there is an astonishing gulf between them. There is a way of turning sentences that completely reverses the original meaning.'

'I wouldn't like you to think I'd said—'

'But do not worry yourself. All this is of no importance. These imbecilities, even, may help.'

'How?'

'*Eh bien*,' said Poirot grimly. 'If our madman reads what I am supposed to have said to the *Daily Blague* today, he will lose all respect for me as an opponent!'

The A B C Murders

I am, perhaps, giving the impression that nothing practical was being done in the way of investigations. On the contrary, Scotland Yard and the local police of the various counties were indefatigable in following up the smallest clues.

Hotels, people who kept lodgings, boarding-houses—all those within a wide radius of the crimes were questioned minutely.

Hundreds of stories from imaginative people who had 'seen a man looking very queer and rolling his eyes', or 'noticed a man with a sinister face slinking along', were sifted to the last detail. No information, even of the vaguest character, was neglected. Trains, buses, trams, railway porters, conductors, bookstalls, stationers—there was an indefatigable round of questions and verifications.

At least a score of people were detained and questioned until they could satisfy the police as to their movements on the night in question.

The net result was not entirely a blank. Certain statements were borne in mind and noted down as of possible value, but without further evidence they led nowhere.

If Crome and his colleagues were indefatigable, Poirot seemed to me strangely supine. We argued now and again.

'But what is it that you would have me do, my friend? The routine inquiries, the police make them better than I do. Always—always you want me to run about like the dog.'

'Instead of which you sit at home like—like—'

'A sensible man! My force, Hastings, is in my *brain*, not in my *feet*! All the time, whilst I seem to you idle, I am reflecting.'

'Reflecting?' I cried. 'Is this a time for reflection?'

'Yes, a thousand times yes.'

'But what can you possibly gain by reflection? You know the facts of the three cases by heart.'

'It is not the facts I reflect upon—but the mind of the murderer.'

'The mind of a madman!'

'Precisely. And therefore not to be arrived at in a minute. *When I know what the murderer is like, I shall be able to find out who he is.* And all the time I learn more. After the Andover crime, what did we know about the murderer? Next to nothing at all. After the Bexhill crime? A little more. After the Churston murder? More still. I begin to see—not what *you* would like to see—the outlines of *a face and form* but the outlines of a *mind*. A mind that moves and works in certain definite directions. After the next crime—'

'Poirot!'

My friend looked at me dispassionately.

'But, yes, Hastings, I think it is almost certain there will be another. A lot depends on *la chance*. So far our *inconnu* has been lucky. This time the luck may turn against him. But in any case, after another crime, we shall know infinitely more. Crime is terribly revealing. Try and vary your methods as you will, your tastes, your habits, your attitude of mind, and your soul is revealed by your actions. There are confusing indications—sometimes it is as though there were two intelligences at work—but soon the outline will clear itself, *I shall know*.'

'Who it is?'

'No, Hastings, I shall not know his name and address! I shall know *what kind of a man he is*...'

'And then?...'

'*Et alors, je vais à la pêche.*'

As I looked rather bewildered, he went on:

'You comprehend, Hastings, an expert fisherman knows exactly what flies to offer to what fish. I shall offer the right kind of fly.'

'And then?'

'And then? And then? You are as bad as the superior Crome with his eternal "Oh, yes?" *Eh bien*, and then he will take the bait and the hook and we will reel in the line...'

'In the meantime people are dying right and left.'

'Three people. And there are, what is it—about 120—road deaths every week?'

'That is entirely different.'

'It is probably exactly the same to those who die. For the others, the relations, the friends—yes, there is a difference, but one thing at least rejoices me in this case.'

'By all means let us hear anything in the nature of rejoicing.'

'*Inutile* to be so sarcastic. It rejoices me that there is here no shadow of guilt to distress the innocent.'

'Isn't this worse?'

'No, no, a thousand times no! There is nothing so terrible as to live in an atmosphere of suspicion—to see eyes watching you and the love in them changing to fear—nothing so terrible as to suspect those near and dear to you—It is poisonous—a miasma. No, the poisoning of life for the innocent, that, at least, we cannot lay at A B C's door.'

Agatha Christie

'You'll soon be making excuses for the man!' I said bitterly.

'Why not? He may believe himself fully justified. We may, perhaps, end by having sympathy with his point of view.'

'Really, Poirot!'

'Alas! I have shocked you. First my inertia—and then my views.'

I shook my head without replying.

'All the same,' said Poirot after a minute or two. 'I have one project that will please you—since it is active and not passive. Also, it will entail a lot of conversation and practically no thought.'

I did not quite like his tone.

'What is it?' I asked cautiously.

'The extraction from the friends, relations and servants of the victims of all they know.'

'Do you suspect them of keeping things back, then?'

'Not intentionally. But telling everything you know always implies *selection*. If I were to say to you, recount me your day yesterday, you would perhaps reply: "I rose at nine, I breakfasted at half-past, I had eggs and bacon and coffee, I went to my club, etc." You would not include: "I tore my nail and had to cut it. I rang for shaving water. I spilt a little coffee on the tablecloth. I brushed my hat and put it on." One cannot tell *everything*. Therefore one *selects*. At the time of a murder people select what *they* think is important. But quite frequently they think wrong!'

'And how is one to get at the right things?'

'Simply, as I said just now, by conversation. By talking!

By discussing a certain happening, or a certain person, or a certain day, over and over again, extra details are bound to arise.'

'What kind of details?'

'Naturally that I do not know or I should not want to find out. But enough time has passed now for ordinary things to reassume their value. It is against all mathematical laws that in three cases of murder there is no single fact nor sentence with a bearing on the case. Some trivial happening, some trivial remark there *must* be which would be a pointer! It is looking for the needle in the haystack, I grant—*but in the haystack there is a needle*—of that I am convinced!'

It seemed to me extremely vague and hazy.

'You do not see it? Your wits are not so sharp as those of a mere servant girl.'

He tossed me over a letter. It was neatly written in a sloping board-school hand.

'Dear Sir,—I hope you will forgive the liberty I take in writing to you. I have been thinking a lot since these awful two murders like poor auntie's. It seems as though we're all in the same boat, as it were. I saw the young lady's picture in the paper, the young lady, I mean, that is the sister of the young lady that was killed at Bexhill. I made so bold as to write to her and tell her I was coming to London to get a place and asked if I could come to her or her mother as I said two heads might be better than one and I would not want much wages, but only to find out who this awful fiend is and perhaps we

might get at it better if we could say what we knew something might come of it.

'The young lady wrote very nicely and said as how she worked in an office and lived in a hostel, but she suggested I might write to you and she said she'd been thinking something of the same kind as I had. And she said we were in the same trouble and we ought to stand together. So I am writing, sir, to say I am coming to London and this is my address.

'Hoping I am not troubling you, Yours respectfully,
'Mary Drower.'

'Mary Drower,' said Poirot, 'is a very intelligent girl.'
He picked up another letter.
'Read this.'
It was a line from Franklin Clarke, saying that he was coming to London and would call upon Poirot the following day if not inconvenient.

'Do not despair, *mon ami*,' said Poirot. 'Action is about to begin.'

CHAPTER 18

Poirot Makes a Speech

Franklin Clarke arrived at three o'clock on the following afternoon and came straight to the point without beating about the bush.

'M. Poirot,' he said, 'I'm not satisfied.'

'No, Mr Clarke?'

'I've no doubt that Crome is a very efficient officer, but, frankly, he puts my back up. That air of his of knowing best! I hinted something of what I had in mind to your friend here when he was down at Churston, but I've had all my brother's affairs to settle up and I haven't been free until now. My idea is, M. Poirot, that we oughtn't to let the grass grow under our feet—'

'Just what Hastings is always saying!'

'—but go right ahead. We've got to get ready for the next crime.'

'So you think there will be a next crime?'

'Don't you?'

'Certainly.'

'Very well, then. I want to get organized.'

'Tell me your idea exactly?'

'I propose, M. Poirot, a kind of special legion—to work under your orders—composed of the friends and relatives of the murdered people.'

'*Une bonne idée.*'

'I'm glad you approve. By putting our heads together I feel we might get at something. Also, when the next warning comes, by being on the spot, one of us might—I don't say it's probable—but we might recognize some person as having been near the scene of a previous crime.'

'I see your idea, and I approve, but you must remember, Mr Clarke, the relations and friends of the other victims are hardly in your sphere of life. They are employed persons and though they might be given a short vacation—'

Franklin Clarke interrupted.

'That's just it. I'm the only person in a position to foot the bill. Not that I'm particularly well off myself, but my brother died a rich man and it will eventually come to me. I propose, as I say, to enrol a special legion, the members to be paid for their services at the same rate as they get habitually, with, of course, the additional expenses.'

'Who do you propose should form this legion?'

'I've been into that. As a matter of fact, I wrote to Miss Megan Barnard—indeed, this is partly her idea. I suggest myself, Miss Barnard, Mr Donald Fraser, who was engaged to the dead girl. Then there is a niece of the Andover woman—Miss Barnard knows her address. I don't think the husband would be of any use to us—I hear he's usually drunk. I also think the Barnards—the father and mother—are a bit old for active campaigning.'

'Nobody else?'

'Well—er—Miss Grey.'

He flushed slightly as he spoke the name.

'Oh! Miss Grey?'

Nobody in the world could put a gentle nuance of irony into a couple of words better than Poirot. About thirty-five years fell away from Franklin Clarke. He looked suddenly like a shy schoolboy.

'Yes. You see, Miss Grey was with my brother for over two years. She knows the countryside and the people round, and everything. I've been away for a year and a half.'

Poirot took pity on him and turned the conversation.

'You have been in the East? In China?'

'Yes. I had a kind of roving commission to purchase things for my brother.'

'Very interesting it must have been. *Eh bien*, Mr Clarke, I approve very highly of your idea. I was saying to Hastings only yesterday that a *rapprochement* of the people concerned was needed. It is necessary to pool reminiscences, to compare notes—*enfin* to talk the thing over—to talk—to talk—and again to talk. Out of some innocent phrase may come enlightenment.'

A few days later the 'Special Legion' met at Poirot's rooms.

As they sat round looking obediently towards Poirot, who had his place, like the chairman at a board meeting, at the head of the table, I myself passed them, as it were, in review, confirming or revising my first impressions of them.

Agatha Christie

The three girls were all of them striking-looking—the extraordinary fair beauty of Thora Grey, the dark intensity of Megan Barnard, with her strange Red Indian immobility of face—Mary Drower, neatly dressed in a black coat and skirt, with her pretty, intelligent face. Of the two men, Franklin Clarke, big, bronzed and talkative, Donald Fraser, self-contained and quiet, made an interesting contrast to each other.

Poirot, unable, of course, to resist the occasion, made a little speech.

'Mesdames and Messieurs, you know what we are here for. The police are doing their utmost to track down the criminal. I, too, in my different way. But it seems to me a reunion of those who have a personal interest in the matter—and also, I may say, a personal knowledge of the victims—might have results that an outside investigation cannot pretend to attain.

'Here we have three murders—an old woman, a young girl, an elderly man. Only one thing links these three people together—*the fact that the same person killed them*. That means that *the same person was present in three different localities* and was seen necessarily by a large number of people. That he is a madman in an advanced stage of mania goes without saying. That his appearance and behaviour give no suggestion of such a fact is equally certain. This person—and though I say *he*, remember it may be a man or a woman—has all the devilish cunning of insanity. He has succeeded so far in covering his traces completely. The police have certain vague indications but nothing upon which they can act.

'Nevertheless, there must exist indications which are not vague but certain. To take one particular point—this assassin, he did not arrive at Bexhill at midnight and find conveniently on the beach a young lady whose name began with B—'

'Must we go into that?'

It was Donald Fraser who spoke—the words wrung from him, it seemed, by some inner anguish.

'It is necessary to go into everything, monsieur,' said Poirot, turning to him. 'You are here, not to save your feelings by refusing to think of details, but if necessary to harrow them by going into the matter *au fond*. As I say, it was not *chance* that provided A B C with a victim in Betty Barnard. There must have been deliberate selection on his part—and therefore premeditation. That is to say, he must have reconnoitred the ground *beforehand*. There were facts of which he had informed himself—the best hour for the committing of the crime at Andover—the *mise en scène* at Bexhill—the habits of Sir Carmichael Clarke at Churston. Me, for one, I refuse to believe that there is *no* indication—no slightest hint—that might help to establish his identity.

'I make the assumption that one—or possibly *all* of you—*knows something that they do not know they know.*

'Sooner or later, by reason of your association with one another, something will come to light, will take on a significance as yet undreamed of. It is like the jig-saw puzzle—each of you may have *a piece apparently without meaning, but which when reunited may show a definite portion of the picture as a whole.*'

Agatha Christie

'Words!' said Megan Barnard.

'Eh?' Poirot looked at her inquiringly.

'What you've been saying. It's just words. It doesn't mean anything.'

She spoke with that kind of desperate intensity that I had come to associate with her personality.

'Words, mademoiselle, are only the outer clothing of ideas.'

'Well, I think it's sense,' said Mary Drower. 'I do really, miss. It's often when you're talking over things that you seem to see your way clear. Your mind gets made up for you sometimes without your knowing how it's happened. Talking leads to a lot of things one way and another.'

'If "least said is soonest mended", it's the converse we want here,' said Franklin Clarke.

'What do you say, Mr Fraser?'

'I rather doubt the practical applicability of what you say, M. Poirot.'

'What do you think, Thora?' asked Clarke.

'I think the principle of talking things over is always sound.'

'Suppose,' suggested Poirot, 'that you all go over your own remembrances of the time preceding the murder. Perhaps you'll start, Mr Clarke.'

'Let me see, on the morning of the day Car was killed I went off sailing. Caught eight mackerel. Lovely out there on the bay. Lunch at home. Irish stew, I remember. Slept in the hammock. Tea. Wrote some letters, missed the post, and drove into Paignton to post them. Then dinner and—I'm

The A B C Murders

not ashamed to say it—reread a book of E. Nesbit's that I used to love as a kid. Then the telephone rang—'

'No further. Now reflect, Mr Clarke, did you meet anyone on your way down to the sea in the morning?'

'Lots of people.'

'Can you remember anything about them?'

'Not a damned thing now.'

'Sure?'

'Well—let's see—I remember a remarkably fat woman—she wore a striped silk dress and I wondered why—had a couple of kids with her—two young men with a fox terrier on the beach throwing stones for it—Oh, yes, a girl with yellow hair squeaking as she bathed—funny how things come back—like a photograph developing.'

'You are a good subject. Now later in the day—the garden—going to the post—'

'The gardener watering... Going to the post? Nearly ran down a bicyclist—silly woman wobbling and shouting to a friend. That's all, I'm afraid.'

Poirot turned to Thora Grey.

'Miss Grey?'

Thora Grey replied in her clear, positive voice:

'I did correspondence with Sir Carmichael in the morning—saw the housekeeper. I wrote letters and did needlework in the afternoon, I fancy. It is difficult to remember. It was quite an ordinary day. I went to bed early.'

Rather to my surprise, Poirot asked no further. He said:

'Miss Barnard—can you bring back your remembrances of the last time you saw your sister?'

'It would be about a fortnight before her death. I was down for Saturday and Sunday. It was fine weather. We went to Hastings to the swimming pool.'

'What did you talk about most of the time?'

'I gave her a piece of my mind,' said Megan.

'And what else? She conversed of what?'

The girl frowned in an effort of memory.

'She talked about being hard up—of a hat and a couple of summer frocks she'd just bought. And a little of Don... She also said she disliked Milly Higley—that's the girl at the café—and we laughed about the Merrion woman who keeps the café... I don't remember anything else...'

'She didn't mention any man—forgive me, Mr Fraser—she might be meeting?'

'She wouldn't to me,' said Megan dryly.

Poirot turned to the red-haired young man with the square jaw.

'Mr Fraser—I want you to cast your mind back. You went, you said, to the café on the fatal evening. Your first intention was to wait there and watch for Betty Barnard to come out. Can you remember anyone at all whom you noticed whilst you were waiting there?'

'There were a large number of people walking along the front. I can't remember any of them.'

'Excuse me, but are you trying? However preoccupied the mind may be, the eye notices mechanically—unintelligently but accurately...'

The young man repeated doggedly:

'I don't remember anybody.'

Poirot sighed and turned to Mary Drower.

'I suppose you got letters from your aunt?'

'Oh, yes, sir.'

'When was the last?'

Mary thought a minute.

'Two days before the murder, sir.'

'What did it say?'

'She said the old devil had been round and that she'd sent him off with a flea in the ear—excuse the expression, sir—said she expected me over on the Wednesday—that's my day out, sir—and she said we'd go to the pictures. It was going to be my birthday, sir.'

Something—the thought of the little festivity perhaps—suddenly brought the tears to Mary's eyes. She gulped down a sob. Then apologized for it.

'You must forgive me, sir. I don't want to be silly. Crying's no good. It was just the thought of her—and me—looking forward to our treat. It upset me somehow, sir.'

'I know just what you feel like,' said Franklin Clarke. 'It's always the little things that get one—and especially anything like a treat or a present—something jolly and natural. I remember seeing a woman run over once. She'd just bought some new shoes. I saw her lying there—and the burst parcel with the ridiculous little high-heeled slippers peeping out—it gave me a turn—they looked so pathetic.'

Megan said with a sudden eager warmth:

'That's true—that's awfully true. The same thing happened after Betty—died. Mum had bought some stockings for her as a present—bought them the very day it happened. Poor mum, she was all broken up. I found her crying over them. She kept saying: "I bought them for Betty—I bought them for Betty—and she never even saw them."'

Her own voice quivered a little. She leaned forward, looking straight at Franklin Clarke. There was between them a sudden sympathy—a fraternity in trouble.

'I know,' he said. 'I know exactly. Those are just the sort of things that are hell to remember.'

Donald Fraser stirred uneasily.

Thora Grey diverted the conversation.

'Aren't we going to make any plans—for the future?' she asked.

'Of course.' Franklin Clarke resumed his ordinary manner. 'I think that when the moment comes—that is, when the fourth letter arrives—we ought to join forces. Until then, perhaps we might each try our luck on our own. I don't know whether there are any points M. Poirot thinks might repay investigation?'

'I could make some suggestions,' said Poirot.

'Good. I'll take them down.' He produced a notebook. 'Go ahead, M. Poirot. A—?'

'I consider it just possible that the waitress, Milly Higley, might know something useful.'

'A—Milly Higley,' wrote down Franklin Clarke.

'I suggest two methods of approach. You, Miss Barnard, might try what I call the offensive approach.'

'I suppose you think that suits my style?' said Megan dryly.

'Pick a quarrel with the girl—say you knew she never

liked your sister—and that your sister had told you all about *her*. If I do not err, that will provoke a flood of recrimination. She will tell you just what she thought of your sister! Some useful fact may emerge.'

'And the second method?'

'May I suggest, Mr Fraser, that you should show signs of interest in the girl?'

'Is that necessary.'

'No, it is not necessary. It is just a possible line of exploration.'

'Shall I try my hand?' asked Franklin. 'I've—er—a pretty wide experience, M. Poirot. Let me see what I can do with the young lady.'

'You've got your own part of the world to attend to,' said Thora Grey rather sharply.

Franklin's face fell just a little.

'Yes,' he said. 'I have.'

'*Tout de même*, I do not think there is much you can do down there for the present,' said Poirot. 'Mademoiselle Grey now, she is far more fitted—'

Thora Grey interrupted him.

'But you see, M. Poirot, I have left Devon for good.'

'Ah? I did not understand.'

'Miss Grey very kindly stayed on to help me clear up things,' said Franklin. 'But naturally she prefers a post in London.'

Poirot directed a sharp glance from one to the other.

'How is Lady Clarke?' he demanded.

I was admiring the faint colour in Thora Grey's cheeks and almost missed Clarke's reply.

'Pretty bad. By the way, M. Poirot, I wonder if you could see your way to running down to Devon and paying her a visit? She expressed a desire to see you before I left. Of course, she often can't see people for a couple of days at a time, but if you would risk that—at my expense, of course.'

'Certainly, Mr Clarke. Shall we say the day after tomorrow?'

'Good. I'll let nurse know and she'll arrange the dope accordingly.'

'For you, my child,' said Poirot, turning to Mary, 'I think you might perhaps do good work in Andover. Try the children.'

'The children?'

'Yes. Children will not chat readily to outsiders. But you are known in the street where your aunt lived. There were a good many children playing about. They may have noticed who went in and out of your aunt's shop.'

'What about Miss Grey and myself?' asked Clarke. 'That is, if I'm not to go to Bexhill.'

'M. Poirot,' said Thora Grey, 'what was the postmark on the third letter?'

'Putney, mademoiselle.'

She said thoughtfully: 'SW15, Putney, that is right, is it not?'

'For a wonder, the newspapers printed it correctly.'

'That seems to point to A B C being a Londoner.'

'On the face of it, yes.'

'One ought to be able to draw him,' said Clarke. 'M. Poirot, how would it be if I inserted an advertisement—something after these lines: *A B C. Urgent, H.P. close on your track. A hundred for my silence. X.Y.Z.* Nothing quite so crude as that—but you see the idea. It might draw him.'

'It is a possibility—yes.'

'Might induce him to try and have a shot at me.'

'I think it's very dangerous and silly,' said Thora Grey sharply.

'What about it, M. Poirot?'

'It can do no harm to try. I think myself that A B C will be too cunning to reply.' Poirot smiled a little. 'I see, Mr Clarke, that you are—if I may say so without being offensive—still a boy at heart.'

Franklin Clarke looked a little abashed.

'Well,' he said, consulting his notebook. 'We're making a start.

A—Miss Barnard and Milly Higley.
B—Mr Fraser and Miss Higley.
C—Children in Andover.
D—Advertisement.

'I don't feel any of it is much good, but it will be something to do whilst waiting.'

He got up and a few minutes later the meeting had dispersed.

CHAPTER 19

By Way of Sweden

Poirot returned to his seat and sat humming a little tune to himself.

'Unfortunate that she is so intelligent,' he murmured.

'Who?'

'Megan Barnard. Mademoiselle Megan. "Words," she snaps out. At once she perceives that what I am saying means nothing at all. Everybody else was taken in.'

'I thought it sounded very plausible.'

'Plausible, yes. It was just that she perceived.'

'Didn't you mean what you said, then?'

'What I said could have been comprised into one short sentence. Instead I repeated myself *ad lib* without anyone but Mademoiselle Megan being aware of the fact.'

'But why?'

'*Eh bien*—to get things going! To imbue everyone with the impression that there was work to be done! To start—shall we say—the conversations!'

'Don't you think any of these lines will lead to anything?'

The A B C Murders

'Oh, it is always possible.'

He chuckled.

'In the midst of tragedy we start the comedy. It is so, is it not?'

'What *do* you mean?'

'The human drama, Hastings! Reflect a little minute. Here are three sets of human beings brought together by a common tragedy. Immediately a second drama commences—*tout à fait à part*. Do you remember my first case in England? Oh, so many years ago now. I brought together two people who loved one another—by the simple method of having one of them arrested for murder! Nothing less would have done it! In the midst of death we are in life, Hastings... Murder, I have often noticed, is a great matchmaker.'

'Really, Poirot,' I cried scandalized. 'I'm sure none of those people was thinking of anything but—'

'Oh! my dear friend. And what about yourself?'

'I?'

'*Mais oui*, as they departed, did you not come back from the door humming a tune?'

'One may do that without being callous.'

'Certainly, but that tune told me your thoughts.'

'Indeed?'

'Yes. To hum a tune is extremely dangerous. It reveals the subconscious mind. The tune you hummed dates, I think, from the days of the war. *Comme ça*,' Poirot sang in an abominable falsetto voice:

'Some of the time I love a brunette,
Some of the time I love a blonde
(Who comes from Eden by way of Sweden).

'What could be more revealing? *Mais je crois que la blonde l'emporte sur la brunette!*'

'Really, Poirot,' I cried, blushing slightly.

'*C'est tout naturel*. Did you observe how Franklin Clarke was suddenly at one and in sympathy with Mademoiselle Megan? How he leaned forward and looked at her? And did you also notice how very much annoyed Mademoiselle Thora Grey was about it? And Mr Donald Fraser, he—'

'Poirot,' I said. 'Your mind is incurably sentimental.'

'That is the last thing my mind is. You are the sentimental one, Hastings.'

I was about to argue the point hotly, but at that moment the door opened.

To my astonishment it was Thora Grey who entered.

'Forgive me for coming back,' she said composedly. 'But there was something that I think I would like to tell you, M. Poirot.'

'Certainly, mademoiselle. Sit down, will you not?'

She took a seat and hesitated for just a minute as though choosing her words.

'It is just this, M. Poirot. Mr Clarke very generously gave you to understand just now that I had left Combeside by my own wish. He is a very kind and loyal person. But as a matter of fact, it is not quite like that. I was quite prepared to stay on—there is any amount of work to be done in

The A B C Murders

connection with the collections. It was Lady Clarke who wished me to leave! I can make allowances. She is a very ill woman, and her brain is somewhat muddled with the drugs they give her. It makes her suspicious and fanciful. She took an unreasoning dislike to me and insisted that I should leave the house.'

I could not but admire the girl's courage. She did not attempt to gloss over facts, as so many might have been tempted to do, but went straight to the point with an admirable candour. My heart went out to her in admiration and sympathy.

'I call it splendid of you to come and tell us this,' I said.

'It's always better to have the truth,' she said with a little smile. 'I don't want to shelter behind Mr Clarke's chivalry. He is a very chivalrous man.'

There was a warm glow in her words. She evidently admired Franklin Clarke enormously.

'You have been very honest, mademoiselle,' said Poirot.

'It is rather a blow to me,' said Thora ruefully. 'I had no idea Lady Clarke disliked me so much. In fact, I always thought she was rather fond of me.' She made a wry face. 'One lives and learns.'

She rose.

'That is all I came to say. Goodbye.'

I accompanied her downstairs.

'I call that very sporting of her,' I said as I returned to the room. 'She has courage, that girl.'

'And calculation.'

'What do you mean—calculation?'

'I mean that she has the power of looking ahead.'

I looked at him doubtfully.

'She really is a lovely girl,' I said.

'And wears very lovely clothes. That crêpe marocain and the silver fox collar—*dernier cri*.'

'You're a man milliner, Poirot. I never notice what people have on.'

'You should join a nudist colony.'

As I was about to make an indignant rejoinder, he said, with a sudden change of subject:

'Do you know, Hastings, I cannot rid my mind of the impression that already, in our conversations this afternoon, something was said that was significant. It is odd—I cannot pin down exactly what it was... Just an impression that passed through my mind... *That reminds me of something I have already heard or seen or noted...*'

'Something at Churston?'

'No—not at Churston... Before that... No matter, presently it will come to me...'

He looked at me (perhaps I had not been attending very closely), laughed and began once more to hum.

'She is an angel, is she not? From Eden, by way of Sweden...'

'Poirot,' I said. 'Go to the devil!'

CHAPTER 20

Lady Clarke

There was an air of deep and settled melancholy over Combeside when we saw it again for the second time. This may, perhaps, have been partly due to the weather—it was a moist September day with a hint of autumn in the air, and partly, no doubt, it was the semi-shut-up state of the house. The downstairs rooms were closed and shuttered, and the small room into which we were shown smelt damp and airless.

A capable-looking hospital nurse came to us there pulling down her starched cuffs.

'M. Poirot?' she said briskly. 'I am Nurse Capstick. I got Mr Clarke's letter saying you were coming.'

Poirot inquired after Lady Clarke's health.

'Not at all bad really, all things considered.'

'All things considered,' I presumed, meant considering she was under sentence of death.

'One can't hope for much improvement, of course, but some new treatment has made things a little easier for her. Dr Logan is quite pleased with her condition.'

Agatha Christie

'But it is true, is it not, that she can never recover?'

'Oh, we never actually *say* that,' said Nurse Capstick, a little shocked by this plain speaking.

'I suppose her husband's death was a terrible shock to her?'

'Well, M. Poirot, if you understand what I mean, it wasn't as much of a shock as it would have been to anyone in full possession of her health and faculties. Things are *dimmed* for Lady Clarke in her condition.'

'Pardon my asking, but was she deeply attached to her husband and he to her?'

'Oh, yes, they were a very happy couple. He was very worried and upset about her, poor man. It's always worse for a doctor, you know. They can't buoy themselves up with false hopes. I'm afraid it preyed on his mind very much to begin with.'

'To begin with? Not so much afterwards?'

'One gets used to everything, doesn't one? And then Sir Carmichael had his collection. A hobby is a great consolation to a man. He used to run up to sales occasionally, and then he and Miss Grey were busy recataloguing and rearranging the museum on a new system.'

'Oh, yes—Miss Grey. She has left, has she not?'

'Yes—I'm very sorry about it—but ladies do take these fancies sometimes when they're not well. And there's no arguing with them. It's better to give in. Miss Grey was very sensible about it.'

'Had Lady Clarke always disliked her?'

'No—that is to say, not *disliked*. As a matter of fact, I

think she rather liked her to begin with. But there, I mustn't keep you gossiping. My patient will be wondering what has become of us.'

She led us upstairs to a room on the first floor. What had at one time been a bedroom had been turned into a cheerful-looking sitting-room.

Lady Clarke was sitting in a big armchair near the window. She was painfully thin, and her face had the grey, haggard look of one who suffers much pain. She had a slightly faraway, dreamy look, and I noticed that the pupils of her eyes were mere pin-points.

'This is M. Poirot whom you wanted to see,' said Nurse Capstick in her high, cheerful voice.

'Oh, yes, M. Poirot,' said Lady Clarke vaguely.

She extended her hand.

'My friend Captain Hastings, Lady Clarke.'

'How do you do? So good of you both to come.'

We sat down as her vague gesture directed. There was a silence. Lady Clarke seemed to have lapsed into a dream.

Presently with a slight effort she roused herself.

'It was about Car, wasn't it? About Car's death. Oh, yes.'

She sighed, but still in a faraway manner, shaking her head.

'We never thought it would be that way round... I was so sure I should be the first to go...' She mused a minute or two. 'Car was very strong—wonderful for his age. He was never ill. He was nearly sixty—but he seemed more like fifty... Yes, very strong...'

She relapsed again into her dream. Poirot, who was well

acquainted with the effects of certain drugs and of how they give their taker the impression of endless time, said nothing.

Lady Clarke said suddenly:

'Yes—it was good of you to come. I told Franklin. He said he wouldn't forget to tell you. I hope Franklin isn't going to be foolish... he's so easily taken in, in spite of having knocked about the world so much. Men are like that... They remain boys... Franklin, in particular.'

'He has an impulsive nature,' said Poirot.

'Yes—yes... And very chivalrous. Men are so foolish that way. Even Car—' Her voice tailed off.

She shook her head with a febrile impatience.

'Everything's so dim... One's body is a nuisance, M. Poirot, especially when it gets the upper hand. One is conscious of nothing else—whether the pain will hold off or not—nothing else seems to matter.'

'I know, Lady Clarke. It is one of the tragedies of this life.'

'It makes me so stupid. I cannot even remember what it was I wanted to say to you.'

'Was it something about your husband's death?'

'Car's death? Yes, perhaps... Mad, poor creature—the murderer, I mean. It's all the noise and the speed nowadays—people can't stand it. I've always been sorry for mad people—their heads must feel so queer. And then, being shut up—it must be so terrible. But what else can one do? If they kill people...' She shook her head—gently pained. 'You haven't caught him yet?' she asked.

'No, not yet.'

'He must have been hanging round here that day.'

'There were so many strangers about, Lady Clarke. It is the holiday season.'

'Yes—I forgot... But they keep down by the beaches, they don't come up near the house.'

'No stranger came to the house that day.'

'Who says so?' demanded Lady Clarke, with a sudden vigour.

Poirot looked slightly taken aback.

'The servants,' he said. 'Miss Grey.'

Lady Clarke said very distinctly:

'That girl is a liar!'

I started on my chair. Poirot threw me a glance.

Lady Clarke was going on, speaking now rather feverishly.

'I didn't like her. I never liked her. Car thought all the world of her. Used to go on about her being an orphan and alone in the world. What's wrong with being an orphan? Sometimes it's a blessing in disguise. You might have a good-for-nothing father and a mother who drank—then you would have something to complain about. Said she was so brave and such a good worker. I dare say she did her work well! I don't know where all this bravery came in!'

'Now don't excite yourself, dear,' said Nurse Capstick, intervening. 'We mustn't have you getting tired.'

'I soon sent her packing! Franklin had the impertinence to suggest that she might be a comfort to me. Comfort to me indeed! The sooner I saw the last of her the better—that's what I said! Franklin's a fool! I didn't want him getting mixed up with her. He's a boy! No sense! "I'll give her three months' salary, if you like," I said. "But out she goes.

I don't want her in the house a day longer." There's one thing about being ill—men can't argue with you. He did what I said and she went. Went like a martyr, I expect—with more sweetness and bravery!'

'Now, dear, don't get so excited. It's bad for you.'

Lady Clarke waved Nurse Capstick away.

'You were as much of a fool about her as anyone else.'

'Oh! Lady Clarke, you mustn't say that. I did think Miss Grey a very nice girl—so romantic-looking, like someone out of a novel.'

'I've no patience with the lot of you,' said Lady Clarke feebly.

'Well, she's gone now, my dear. Gone right away.'

Lady Clarke shook her head with feeble impatience but she did not answer.

Poirot said:

'Why did you say that Miss Grey was a liar?'

'Because she is. She told you no strangers came to the house, didn't she?'

'Yes.'

'Very well, then. I saw her—with my own eyes—out of this window—talking to a perfectly strange man on the front doorstep.'

'When was this?'

'In the morning of the day Car died—about eleven o'clock.'

'What did this man look like?'

'An ordinary sort of man. Nothing special.'

'A gentleman—or a tradesman?'

'Not a tradesman. A shabby sort of person. I can't remember.'

A sudden quiver of pain shot across her face.

'Please—you must go now—I'm a little tired—Nurse.'

We obeyed the cue and took our departure.

'That's an extraordinary story,' I said to Poirot as we journeyed back to London. 'About Miss Grey and a strange man.'

'You see, Hastings? It is, as I tell you: *there is always something to be found out.*'

'Why did the girl lie about it and say she had seen no one?'

'I can think of seven separate reasons—one of them an extremely simple one.'

'Is that a snub?' I asked.

'It is, perhaps, an invitation to use your ingenuity. But there is no need for us to perturb ourselves. The easiest way to answer the question is to ask her.'

'And suppose she tells us another lie.'

'That would indeed be interesting—and highly suggestive.'

'It is monstrous to suppose that a girl like that could be in league with a madman.'

'Precisely—so I do not suppose it.'

I thought for some minutes longer.

'A good-looking girl has a hard time of it,' I said at last with a sigh.

'*Du tout.* Disabuse your mind of that idea.'

'It's true,' I insisted, 'everyone's hand is against her simply because she is good-looking.'

Agatha Christie

'You speak the *bêtises*, my friend. Whose hand was against her at Combeside? Sir Carmichael's? Franklin's? Nurse Capstick's?'

'Lady Clarke was down on her, all right.'

'*Mon ami*, you are full of charitable feeling towards beautiful young girls. Me, I feel charitable to sick old ladies. It may be that Lady Clarke was the clear-sighted one—and that her husband, Mr Franklin Clarke and Nurse Capstick were all as blind as bats—and Captain Hastings.'

'You've got a grudge against that girl, Poirot.'

To my surprise his eyes twinkled suddenly.

'Perhaps it is that I like to mount you on your romantic high horse, Hastings. You are always the true knight—ready to come to the rescue of damsels in distress—good-looking damsels, *bien entendu*.'

'How ridiculous you are, Poirot,' I said, unable to keep from laughing.

'Ah, well, one cannot be tragic all the time. More and more I interest myself in the human developments that arise out of this tragedy. It is three dramas of family life that we have there. First there is Andover—the whole tragic life of Mrs Ascher, her struggles, her support of her German husband, the devotion of her niece. That alone would make a novel. Then you have Bexhill—the happy, easy-going father and mother, the two daughters so widely differing from each other—the pretty fluffy fool, and the intense, strong-willed Megan with her clear intelligence and her ruthless passion for truth. And the other figure— the self-controlled young Scotsman with his passionate jealousy and his worship of the dead girl. Finally you have the Churston household—the dying wife, and the husband absorbed in his collections, but with a growing tenderness and sympathy for the beautiful girl who helps him so sympathetically, and then the younger brother, vigorous, attractive, interesting, with a romantic glamour about him from his long travels.

'Realize, Hastings, that in the ordinary course of events *those three separate dramas would never have touched each other*. They would have pursued their course uninfluenced by each other. The permutations and combinations of life, Hastings—I never cease to be fascinated by them.'

'This is Paddington,' was the only answer I made.

It was time, I felt, that someone pricked the bubble.

On our arrival at Whitehaven Mansions we were told that a gentleman was waiting to see Poirot.

I expected it to be Franklin, or perhaps Japp, but to my astonishment it turned out to be none other than Donald Fraser.

He seemed very embarrassed and his inarticulateness was more noticeable than ever.

Poirot did not press him to come to the point of his visit, but instead suggested sandwiches and a glass of wine.

Until these made their appearance he monopolized the conversation, explaining where we had been, and speaking with kindliness and feeling of the invalid woman.

Not until we had finished the sandwiches and sipped the wine did he give the conversation a personal turn.

'You have come from Bexhill, Mr Fraser?'

'Yes.'

Agatha Christie

'Any success with Milly Higley?'

'Milly Higley? Milly Higley?' Fraser repeated the name wonderingly. 'Oh, that girl! No, I haven't done anything there yet. It's—'

He stopped. His hands twisted themselves together nervously.

'I don't know why I've come to you,' he burst out.

'I know,' said Poirot.

'You can't. How can you?'

'You have come to me because there is something that you must tell to someone. You were quite right. I am the proper person. Speak!'

Poirot's air of assurance had its effect. Fraser looked at him with a queer air of grateful obedience.

'You think so?'

'*Parbleu*, I am sure of it.'

'M. Poirot, do you know anything about dreams?'

It was the last thing I had expected him to say.

Poirot, however, seemed in no wise surprised.

'I do,' he replied. 'You have been dreaming—?'

'Yes. I suppose you'll say it's only natural that I should—should dream about—It. But it isn't an ordinary dream.'

'No?'

'No?'

'I've dreamed it now three nights running, sir... I think I'm going mad...'

'Tell me—'

The man's face was livid. His eyes were staring out of his head. As a matter of fact, he *looked* mad.

'It's always the same. I'm on the beach. Looking for Betty. She's lost—only lost, you understand. I've got to find her. I've got to give her her belt. I'm carrying it in my hand. And then—'

'Yes?'

'The dream changes... I'm not looking any more. She's there in front of me—sitting on the beach. She doesn't see me coming—It's—oh, I can't—'

'Go on.'

Poirot's voice was authoritative—firm.

'I come up behind her... she doesn't hear me... I slip the belt round her neck and pull—oh—pull...'

The agony in his voice was frightful... I gripped the arms of my chair... The thing was too real.

'She's choking... she's dead... I've strangled her—and then her head falls back and I see her face... and it's *Megan*—not Betty!'

He leant back white and shaking. Poirot poured out another glass of wine and passed it over to him.

'What's the meaning of it, M. Poirot? Why does it come to me? Every night...?'

'Drink up your wine,' ordered Poirot.

The young man did so, then he asked in a calmer voice: 'What does it mean? I—I didn't kill her, did I?'

What Poirot answered I do not know, for at that minute I heard the postman's knock and automatically I left the room.

What I took out of the letter-box banished all my interest in Donald Fraser's extraordinary revelations.

I raced back into the sitting-room.

'Poirot,' I cried. 'It's come. The fourth letter.'

He sprang up, seized it from me, caught up his paper-knife and slit it open. He spread it out on the table.

The three of us read it together.

Still no success? Fie! Fie! What are you and the police doing? Well, well, isn't this fun? And where shall we go next for honey?

    Poor Mr Poirot. I'm quite sorry for you.

    If at first you don't succeed, try, try, try again.

    We've a long way to go still.

    Tipperary? No—that comes farther on. Letter T.

    The next little incident will take place at Doncaster on September 11th.

    So long.

    A B C.

CHAPTER 21

Description of a Murderer

It was at this moment, I think, that what Poirot called the human element began to fade out of the picture again. It was as though, the mind being unable to stand unadulterated horror, we had had an interval of normal human interests.

We had, one and all, felt the impossibility of doing anything until the fourth letter should come revealing the projected scene of the D murder. That atmosphere of waiting had brought a release of tension.

But now, with the printed words jeering from the white stiff paper, the hunt was up once more.

Inspector Crome had come round from the Yard, and while he was still there, Franklin Clarke and Megan Barnard came in.

The girl explained that she, too, had come up from Bexhill.

'I wanted to ask Mr Clarke something.'

She seemed rather anxious to excuse and explain her procedure. I just noted the fact without attaching much importance to it.

Agatha Christie

The letter naturally filled my mind to the exclusion of all else.

Crome was not, I think, any too pleased to see the various participants in the drama. He became extremely official and non-committal.

'I'll take this with me, M. Poirot. If you care to take a copy of it—'

'No, no, it is not necessary.'

'What are your plans, inspector?' asked Clarke.

'Fairly comprehensive ones, Mr Clarke.'

'This time we've got to get him,' said Clarke. 'I may tell you, inspector, that we've formed an association of our own to deal with the matter. A legion of interested parties.'

Inspector Crome said in his best manner:

'Oh, yes?'

'I gather you don't think much of amateurs, inspector?'

'You've hardly the same resources at your command, have you, Mr Clarke?'

'We've got a personal axe to grind—and that's something.'

'Oh, yes?'

'I fancy your own task isn't going to be too easy, inspector. In fact, I rather fancy old A B C has done you again.'

Crome, I noticed, could often be goaded into speech when other methods would have failed.

'I don't fancy the public will have much to criticize in our arrangements this time,' he said. 'The fool has given us ample warning. The 11th isn't till Wednesday of next week. That gives ample time for a publicity campaign in the press. Doncaster will be thoroughly warned. Every soul whose name begins with a D will be on his or her guard—that's so much to the good. Also, we'll draft police into the town on a fairly large scale. That's already been arranged for by consent of all the Chief Constables in England. The whole of Doncaster, police and civilians, will be out to catch one man—and with reasonable luck, we ought to get him!'

Clarke said quietly:

'It's easy to see you're not a sporting man, inspector.'

Crome stared at him.

'What do you mean, Mr Clarke?'

'Man alive, don't you realize that on *next Wednesday the St Leger is being run at Doncaster*?'

The inspector's jaw dropped. For the life of him he could not bring out the familiar 'Oh, yes?' Instead he said:

'That's true. Yes, that complicates matters…'

'A B C is no fool, even if he *is* a madman.'

We were all silent for a minute or two, taking in the situation. The crowds on the race-course—the passionate, sport-loving English public—the endless complications.

Poirot murmured:

'*C'est ingénieux. Tout de même c'est bien imaginé, ça.*'

'It's my belief,' said Clarke, 'that the murder will take place on the race-course—perhaps actually while the Leger is being run.'

For the moment his sporting instincts took a momentary pleasure in the thought…

Inspector Crome rose, taking the letter with him.

'The St Leger is a complication,' he allowed. 'It's unfortunate.'

He went out. We heard a murmur of voices in the hallway.

Agatha Christie

A minute later Thora Grey entered.

She said anxiously:

'The inspector told me there is another letter. Where this time?'

It was raining outside. Thora Grey was wearing a black coat and skirt and furs. A little black hat just perched itself on the side of her golden head.

It was to Franklin Clarke that she spoke and she came right up to him and, with a hand on his arm, waited for his answer.

'Doncaster—and on the day of the St Leger.'

We settled down to a discussion. It went without saying that we all intended to be present, but the race-meeting undoubtedly complicated the plans we had made tentatively beforehand.

A feeling of discouragement swept over me. What could this little band of six people do, after all, however strong their personal interest in the matter might be? There would be innumerable police, keen-eyed and alert, watching all likely spots. What could six more pairs of eyes do?

As though in answer to my thought, Poirot raised his voice. He spoke rather like a schoolmaster or a priest.

'*Mes enfants*,' he said. 'We must not disperse the strength. We must approach this matter with method and order in our thoughts. We must look within and not without for the truth. We must say to ourselves—each one of us—what do *I* know about the murderer? And so we must build up a composite picture of the man we are going to seek.'

'We know nothing about him,' sighed Thora Grey

helplessly.

'No, no, mademoiselle. That is not true. Each one of us knows something about him—*if we only knew what it is we know. I am convinced that the knowledge is there* if we could only get at it.'

Clarke shook his head.

'We don't know anything—whether he's old or young, fair or dark! None of us has ever seen him or spoken to him! We've gone over everything we all know again and again.'

'Not everything! For instance, Miss Grey here told us that she did not see or speak to any stranger on the day that Sir Carmichael Clarke was murdered.'

Thora Grey nodded.

'That's quite right.'

'Is it? *Lady Clarke told us, mademoiselle, that from her window she saw you standing on the front doorstep talking to a man.*'

'She saw *me* talking to a strange man?' The girl seemed genuinely astonished. Surely that pure, limpid look could not be anything but genuine.

She shook her head.

'Lady Clarke must have made a mistake. I never—Oh!'

The exclamation came suddenly—jerked out of her. A crimson wave flooded her cheeks.

'I remember now! How stupid! I'd forgotten all about it. But it wasn't important. Just one of those men who come round selling stockings—you know, ex-army people. They're very persistent. I had to get rid of him. I was just crossing the hall when he came to the door. He spoke to me instead of ringing but he was quite a harmless sort of person. I suppose that's why I forgot about him.'

Poirot was swaying to and fro, his hands clasped to his head. He was muttering to himself with such vehemence that nobody else said anything, but stared at him instead.

'Stockings,' he was murmuring. 'Stockings... stockings... stockings... *ça vient*... stockings... stockings... it is the *motif—yes*... three months ago... and the other day... and now. *Bon Dieu*, I have it!'

He sat upright and fixed me with an imperious eye.

'You remember, Hastings? Andover. The shop. We go upstairs. The bedroom. On a chair. *A pair of new silk stockings*. And now I know what it was that roused my attention two days ago. It was you, mademoiselle—' He turned on Megan. 'You spoke of your mother who wept *because she had bought your sister some new stockings on the very day of the murder*...'

He looked round on us all.

'You see? *It is the same motif* three times repeated. That cannot be coincidence. When mademoiselle spoke I had the feeling that what she said linked up with something. I know now with what. The words spoken by Mrs Ascher's next-door neighbour, Mrs Fowler. About people who were always trying to *sell* you things—and she mentioned *stockings*. Tell me, mademoiselle, it is true, is it not, that your mother bought those stockings, not at a shop, but from someone who came to the door?'

'Yes—yes—she did... I remember now. She said something about being sorry for these wretched men who go round and try to get orders.'

'But what's the connection?' cried Franklin. 'That a man came selling stockings proves nothing!'

'I tell you, my friends, it *cannot* be coincidence. Three crimes—and every time a man selling stockings and spying out the land.'

He wheeled round on Thora.

'*A vous la parole!* Describe this man.'

She looked at him blankly.

'I can't... I don't know how... He had glasses, I think—and a shabby overcoat...'

'*Mieux que ça, mademoiselle.*'

'He stooped... I don't know. I hardly looked at him. He wasn't the sort of man you'd notice...'

Poirot said gravely:

'You are quite right, mademoiselle. The whole secret of the murders lies there in your description of the murderer—for without a doubt he *was* the murderer! "*He wasn't the sort of man you'd notice.*" Yes—there is no doubt about it... You have described the murderer!'

CHAPTER 22

(Not from Captain Hastings' Personal Narrative)

Mr Alexander Bonaparte Cust sat very still. His breakfast lay cold and untasted on his plate. A newspaper was propped up against the teapot and it was this newspaper that Mr Cust was reading with avid interest.

Suddenly he got up, paced to and fro for a minute, then sank back into a chair by the window. He buried his head in his hands with a stifled groan.

He did not hear the sound of the opening door. His landlady, Mrs Marbury, stood in the doorway.

'I was wondering, Mr Cust, if you'd fancy a nice—why, whatever is it? Aren't you feeling well?'

Mr Cust raised his head from his hands.

'Nothing. It's nothing at all, Mrs Marbury. I'm not—feeling very well this morning.'

Mrs Marbury inspected the breakfast tray.

'So I see. You haven't touched your breakfast. Is it your head troubling you again?'

'No. At least, yes... I—I just feel a bit out of sorts.'

'Well, I'm sorry, I'm sure. You'll not be going away today, then?'

Mr Cust sprang up abruptly.

'No, no. I have to go. It's business. Important. Very important.'

His hands were shaking. Seeing him so agitated, Mrs Marbury tried to soothe him.

'Well, if you must—you must. Going far this time?'

'No. I'm going to'—he hesitated for a minute or two—'Cheltenham.'

There was something so peculiar about the tentative way he said the word that Mrs Marbury looked at him in surprise.

'Cheltenham's a nice place,' she said conversationally. 'I went there from Bristol one year. The shops are ever so nice.'

'I suppose so—yes.'

Mrs Marbury stooped rather stiffly—for stooping did not suit her figure—to pick up the paper that was lying crumpled on the floor.

'Nothing but this murdering business in the papers nowadays,' she said as she glanced at the headlines before putting it back on the table. 'Gives me the creeps, it does. I don't read it. It's like Jack the Ripper all over again.'

Mr Cust's lips moved, but no sound came from them.

'Doncaster—that's the place he's going to do his next murder,' said Mrs Marbury. 'And tomorrow! Fairly makes your flesh creep, doesn't it? If I lived in Doncaster and my name began with a D, I'd take the first train away, that I would. I'd run no risks. What did you say, Mr Cust?'

Agatha Christie

'Nothing, Mrs Marbury—nothing.'

'It's the races and all. No doubt he thinks he'll get his opportunity there. Hundreds of police, they say, they're drafting in and—Why, Mr Cust, you *do* look bad. Hadn't you better have a little drop of something? Really, now, you oughtn't to go travelling today.'

Mr Cust drew himself up.

'It is necessary, Mrs Marbury. I have always been punctual in my—engagements. People must have—must have confidence in you! When I have undertaken to do a thing, I carry it through. It is the only way to get on in—in—business.'

'But if you're ill?'

'I am not ill, Mrs Marbury. Just a little worried over— various personal matters. I slept badly. I am really quite all right.'

His manner was so firm that Mrs Marbury gathered up the breakfast things and reluctantly left the room.

Mr Cust dragged out a suitcase from under the bed and began to pack. Pyjamas, sponge-bag, spare collar, leather slippers. Then unlocking a cupboard, he transferred a dozen or so flattish cardboard boxes about ten inches by seven from a shelf to the suitcase.

He just glanced at the railway guide on the table and then left the room, suitcase in hand.

Setting it down in the hall, he put on his hat and overcoat. As he did so he sighed deeply, so deeply that the girl who came out from a room at the side looked at him in concern.

'Anything the matter, Mr Cust?'

'Nothing, Miss Lily.'

The A B C Murders

'You were sighing so!'

Mr Cust said abruptly:

'Are you at all subject to premonitions, Miss Lily? To presentiments?'

'Well, I don't know that I am, really... Of course, there are days when you just feel everything's going wrong, and days when you feel everything's going right.'

'Quite,' said Mr Cust.

He sighed again.

'Well, goodbye, Miss Lily. Goodbye. I'm sure you've been very kind to me always here.'

'Well, don't say goodbye as though you were going away for ever,' laughed Lily.

'No, no, of course not.'

'See you Friday,' laughed the girl. 'Where are you going this time? Seaside again.'

'No, no—er—Cheltenham.'

'Well, that's nice, too. But not quite as nice as Torquay. That must have been lovely. I want to go there for my holiday next year. By the way, you must have been quite near where the murder was—the A B C murder. It happened while you were down there, didn't it?'

'Er—yes. But Churston's six or seven miles away.'

'All the same, it must have been exciting! Why, you may have passed the murderer in the street! You may have been quite near to him!'

'Yes, I may, of course,' said Mr Cust with such a ghastly and contorted smile that Lily Marbury noticed it.

'Oh, Mr Cust, you *don't* look well.'

Agatha Christie

'I'm quite all right, quite all right. Goodbye, Miss Marbury.'

He fumbled to raise his hat, caught up his suitcase and fairly hastened out of the front door.

'Funny old thing,' said Lily Marbury indulgently. 'Looks half batty to my mind.'

Inspector Crome said to his subordinate:

'Get me out a list of all stocking manufacturing firms and circularize them. I want a list of all their agents—you know, fellows who sell on commission and tout for orders.'

'This the A B C case, sir?'

'Yes. One of Mr Hercule Poirot's ideas.' The inspector's tone was disdainful. 'Probably nothing in it, but it doesn't do to neglect any chance, however faint.'

'Right, sir. Mr Poirot's done some good stuff in his time, but I think he's a bit gaga now, sir.'

'He's a mountebank,' said Inspector Crome. 'Always posing. Takes in some people. It doesn't take in *me*. Now then, about the arrangement for Doncaster…'

Tom Hartigan said to Lily Marbury:

'Saw your old dugout this morning.'

'Who? Mr Cust?'

'Cust it was. At Euston. Looking like a lost hen, as usual. I think the fellow's half loony. He needs someone to look after him. First he dropped his paper and then he dropped his ticket. I picked that up—he hadn't the faintest idea he'd lost it. Thanked me in an agitated sort of manner, but I don't think he recognized me.'

'Oh, well,' said Lily. 'He's only seen you passing in the hall, and not very often at that.'

They danced once round the floor.

'You dance something beautiful,' said Tom.

'Go on,' said Lily and wriggled yet a little closer.

They danced round again.

'Did you say Euston or Paddington?' asked Lily abruptly. 'Where you saw old Cust, I mean?'

'Euston.'

'Are you sure?'

'Of course I'm sure. What do you think?'

'Funny. I thought you went to Cheltenham from Paddington.'

'So you do. But old Cust wasn't going to Cheltenham. He was going to Doncaster.'

'Cheltenham.'

'Doncaster. I know, my girl! After all, I picked up his ticket, didn't I?'

'Well, he told *me* he was going to Cheltenham. I'm sure he did.'

'Oh, you've got it wrong. He was going to Doncaster all right. Some people have all the luck. I've got a bit on Firefly for the Leger and I'd love to see it run.'

'I shouldn't think Mr Cust went to race-meetings, he doesn't look the kind. Oh, Tom, I hope he won't get murdered. It's Doncaster the A B C murder's going to be.'

'Cust'll be all right. His name doesn't begin with a D.'

'He might have been murdered last time. He was down near Churston at Torquay when the last murder happened.'

'Was he? That's a bit of a coincidence, isn't it?'

He laughed.

'He wasn't at Bexhill the time before, was he?'

Lily crinkled her brows.

'He was away… Yes, I remember he was away… because he forgot his bathing-dress. Mother was mending it for him. And she said: "There—Mr Cust went away yesterday without his bathing-dress after all," and I said: "Oh, never mind the old bathing-dress—there's been the most awful murder," I said, "a girl strangled at Bexhill."'

'Well, if he wanted his bathing-dress, he must have been going to the seaside. I say, Lily'—his face crinkled up with amusement. 'What price your old dugout being the murderer himself?'

'Poor Mr Cust? He wouldn't hurt a fly,' laughed Lily.

They danced on happily—in their conscious minds nothing but the pleasure of being together.

In their unconscious minds something stirred…

CHAPTER 23

September 11th. Doncaster

Doncaster!

I shall, I think, remember that 11th of September all my life.

Indeed, whenever I see a mention of the St Leger my mind flies automatically not to horse-racing but to murder.

When I recall my own sensations, the thing that stands out most is a sickening sense of insufficiency. We were here—on the spot—Poirot, myself, Clarke, Fraser, Megan Barnard, Thora Grey and Mary Drower, and in the last resort *what could any of us do?*

We were building on a forlorn hope—on the chance of recognizing amongst a crowd of thousands of people a face or figure imperfectly seen on an occasion one, two or three months back.

The odds were in reality greater than that. Of us all, the only person likely to make such a recognition was Thora Grey.

Some of her serenity had broken down under the strain.

Agatha Christie

Her calm, efficient manner was gone. She sat twisting her hands together, almost weeping, appealing incoherently to Poirot.

'I never really looked at him... Why didn't I? What a fool I was. You're depending on me, all of you... and I shall let you down. Because even if I did see him again I mightn't recognize him. I've got a bad memory for faces.'

Poirot, whatever he might say to me, and however harshly he might seem to criticize the girl, showed nothing but kindness now. His manner was tender in the extreme. It struck me that Poirot was no more indifferent to beauty in distress than I was.

He patted her shoulder kindly.

'Now then, *petite*, not the hysteria. We cannot have that. If you should see this man you would recognize him.'

'How do you know?'

'Oh, a great many reasons—for one, because the red succeeds the black.'

'What do you mean, Poirot?' I cried.

'I speak the language of the tables. At roulette there may be a long run on the black—but in the end *red must turn up*. It is the mathematical laws of chance.'

'You mean that luck turns?'

'Exactly, Hastings. And that is where the gambler (and the murderer, who is, after all, only a supreme kind of gambler since what he risks is not his money but his life) often lacks intelligent anticipation. Because he *has* won he thinks he will *continue* to win! He does not leave the tables in good time with his pocket full. So in crime the murderer who is successful *cannot conceive the possibility of not being successful*! He takes to *himself* all the credit for a successful performance—but I tell you, my friends, however carefully planned, no crime can be successful without luck!'

'Isn't that going rather far?' demurred Franklin Clarke.

Poirot waved his hands excitedly.

'No, no. It is an even chance, if you like, but it *must* be in your favour. Consider! It might have happened that someone enters Mrs Ascher's shop just as the murderer is leaving. That person might have thought of looking behind the counter, have seen the dead woman—and either laid hands on the murderer straight away or else been able to give such an accurate description of him to the police that he would have been arrested forthwith.'

'Yes, of course, that's possible,' admitted Clarke. 'What it comes to is that a murderer's got to take a chance.'

'Precisely. A murderer is always a gambler. And, like many gamblers, a murderer often does not know when to stop. With each crime his opinion of his own abilities is strengthened. His sense of proportion is warped. He does not say "I have been clever *and lucky*!" No, he says only "I have been clever!" And his opinion of his cleverness grows and then, *mes amis*, the ball spins, and the run of colour is over—it drops into a new number and the croupier calls out "*Rouge*."'

'You think that will happen in this case?' asked Megan, drawing her brows together in a frown.

'It *must* happen sooner or later! So far *the luck has been with the criminal*—sooner or later it must turn and be with us. I believe that it *has* turned! The clue of the stockings is the beginning. Now, instead of everything going *right* for him, everything will go *wrong* for him! And he, too, will begin to make mistakes...'

'I will say you're heartening,' said Franklin Clarke. 'We all need a bit of comfort. I've had a paralysing feeling of helplessness ever since I woke up.'

'It seems to me highly problematical that we can accomplish anything of practical value,' said Donald Fraser.

Megan rapped out:

'Don't be a defeatist, Don.'

Mary Drower, flushing up a little, said:

'What I say is, you never know. That wicked fiend's in this place, and so are we—and after all, you do run up against people in the funniest way sometimes.'

I fumed:

'If only we could do something more.'

'You must remember, Hastings, that the police are doing everything reasonably possible. Special constables have been enrolled. The good Inspector Crome may have the irritating manner, but he is a very able police officer, and Colonel Anderson, the Chief Constable, is a man of action. They have taken the fullest measures for watching and patrolling the town and the race-course. There will be plain-clothes men everywhere. There is also the press campaign. The public is fully warned.'

Donald Fraser shook his head.

'He'll never attempt it, I'm thinking,' he said more hopefully. 'The man would just be mad!'

'Unfortunately,' said Clarke dryly, 'he is mad! What do you think, M. Poirot? Will he give it up or will he try to carry it through?'

'In my opinion the strength of his obsession is such that he *must* attempt to carry out his promise! Not to do so would be to admit failure, and that his insane egoism would never allow. That, I may say, is also Dr Thompson's opinion. Our hope is that he may be caught in the attempt.'

Donald shook his head again.

'He'll be very cunning.'

Poirot glanced at his watch. We took the hint. It had been agreed that we were to make an all-day session of it, patrolling as many streets as possible in the morning, and later, stationing ourselves at various likely points on the race-course.

I say 'we'. Of course, in my own case such a patrol was of little avail since I was never likely to have set eyes on A B C. However, as the idea was to separate so as to cover as wide an area as possible I had suggested that I should act as escort to one of the ladies.

Poirot had agreed—I am afraid with somewhat of a twinkle in his eye.

The girls went off to get their hats on. Donald Fraser was standing by the window looking out, apparently lost in thought.

Franklin Clarke glanced over at him, then evidently deciding that the other was too abstracted to count as a listener, he lowered his voice a little and addressed Poirot.

'Look here, M. Poirot. You went down to Churston, I

know, and saw my sister-in-law. Did she say—or hint—I mean—did she suggest at all—?'

He stopped, embarrassed.

Poirot answered with a face of blank innocence that aroused my strongest suspicions.

'*Comment?* Did your sister-in-law say, hint, or suggest—what?'

Franklin Clarke got rather red.

'Perhaps you think this isn't a time for butting in with personal things—'

'*Du tout!*'

'But I feel I'd like to get things quite straight.'

'An admirable course.'

This time I think Clarke began to suspect Poirot's bland face of concealing some inner amusement. He ploughed on rather heavily.

'My sister-in-law's an awfully nice woman—I've been very fond of her always—but of course she's been ill some time—and in that kind of illness—being given drugs and all that—one tends to—well, to *fancy* things about people!'

'Ah?'

By now there was no mistaking the twinkle in Poirot's eye.

But Franklin Clarke, absorbed in his diplomatic task, was past noticing it.

'It's about Thora—Miss Grey,' he said.

'Oh, it is of Miss Grey you speak?' Poirot's tone held innocent surprise.

'Yes. Lady Clarke got certain ideas in her head. You see, Thora—Miss Grey is well, rather a good-looking girl—'

The A B C Murders

'Perhaps—yes,' conceded Poirot.

'And women, even the best of them, are a bit catty about other women. Of course, Thora was invaluable to my brother—he always said she was the best secretary he ever had—and he was very fond of her, too. But it was all perfectly straight and above-board. I mean, Thora isn't the sort of girl—'

'No?' said Poirot helpfully.

'But my sister-in-law got it into her head to be—well—jealous, I suppose. Not that she ever showed anything. But after Car's death, when there was a question of Miss Grey staying on—well, Charlotte cut up rough. Of course, it's partly the illness and the morphia and all that—Nurse Capstick says so—she says we mustn't blame Charlotte for getting these ideas into her head—'

He paused.

'Yes?'

'What I want you to understand, M. Poirot, is that there isn't anything in it at all. It's just a sick woman's imaginings. Look here'—he fumbled in his pocket—'here's a letter I received from my brother when I was in the Malay States. I'd like you to read it because it shows exactly what terms they were on.'

Poirot took it. Franklin came over beside him and with a pointing finger read some of the extracts out loud.

—things go on here much as usual. Charlotte is moderately free from pain. I wish one could say more. You may remember Thora Grey? She is a dear girl and a greater

comfort to me than I can tell you. I should not have known what to do through this bad time but for her. Her sympathy and interest are unfailing. She has an exquisite taste and flair for beautiful things and shares my passion for Chinese art. I was indeed lucky to find her. No daughter could be a closer or more sympathetic companion. Her life had been a difficult and not always a happy one, but I am glad to feel that here she has a home and true affection.

'You see,' said Franklin, *'that's* how my brother felt to her. He thought of her like a daughter. What I feel so unfair is the fact that the moment my brother is dead, his wife practically turns her out of the house! Women really are devils, M. Poirot.'

'Your sister-in-law is ill and in pain, remember.'

'I know. That's what I keep saying to myself. One mustn't judge her. All the same, I thought I'd show you this. I don't want you to get a false impression of Thora from anything Lady Clarke may have said.'

Poirot returned the letter.

'I can assure you,' he said, smiling, 'that I never permit myself to get false impressions from anything anyone tells me. I form my own judgments.'

'Well,' said Clarke, stowing away the letter. 'I'm glad I showed it to you anyway. Here come the girls. We'd better be off.'

As we left the room, Poirot called me back.

'You are determined to accompany the expedition, Hastings?'

'Oh, yes. I shouldn't be happy staying here inactive.'

'There is activity of mind as well as body, Hastings.'

'Well, you're better at it than I am,' I said.

'You are incontestably right, Hastings. Am I correct in supposing that you intend to be a cavalier to one of the ladies?'

'That was the idea.'

'And which lady did you propose to honour with your company?'

'Well—I—er—hadn't considered yet.'

'What about Miss Barnard?'

'She's rather the independent type,' I demurred.

'Miss Grey?'

'Yes. She's better.'

'I find you, Hastings, singularly though transparently dishonest! All along you had made up your mind to spend the day with your blonde angel!'

'Oh, really, Poirot!'

'I am sorry to upset your plans, but I must request you to give your escort elsewhere.'

'Oh, all right. I think you've got a weakness for that Dutch doll of a girl.'

'The person you are to escort is Mary Drower—and I must request you not to leave her.'

'But, Poirot, why?'

'Because, my dear friend, her name begins with a D. We must take no chances.'

I saw the justice of his remark. At first it seemed far-fetched, but then I realized that if A B C had a fanatical hatred of Poirot, he might very well be keeping himself informed of Poirot's movements. And in that case the elimination of Mary Drower might strike him as a very pat fourth stroke.

I promised to be faithful to my trust.

I went out leaving Poirot sitting in a chair near the window.

In front of him was a little roulette wheel. He spun it as I went out of the door and called after me:

'*Rouge*—that is a good omen, Hastings. The luck, it turns!'

CHAPTER 24

(Not from Captain Hastings' Personal Narrative)

Below his breath Mr Leadbetter uttered a grunt of impatience as his next-door neighbour got up and stumbled clumsily past him, dropping his hat over the seat in front, and leaning over to retrieve it.

All this at the culminating moment of *Not a Sparrow*, that all-star, thrilling drama of pathos and beauty that Mr Leadbetter had been looking forward to seeing for a whole week.

The golden-haired heroine, played by Katherine Royal (in Mr Leadbetter's opinion the leading film actress in the world), was just giving vent to a hoarse cry of indignation:

'Never. I would sooner starve. But I shan't starve. Remember those words: *not a sparrow falls—*'

Mr Leadbetter moved his head irritably from right to left. People! Why on earth people couldn't wait till the *end* of a film... And to leave at this soul-stirring moment.

Ah, that was better. The annoying gentleman had passed on and out. Mr Leadbetter had a full view of the screen

Agatha Christie

and of Katherine Royal standing by the window in the Van Schreiner Mansion in New York.

And now she was boarding the train—the child in her arms... What curious trains they had in America—not at all like English trains.

Ah, there was Steve again in his shack in the mountains...

The film pursued its course to its emotional and semi-religious end.

Mr Leadbetter breathed a sigh of satisfaction as the lights went up.

He rose slowly to his feet, blinking a little.

He never left the cinema very quickly. It always took him a moment or two to return to the prosaic reality of everyday life.

He glanced round. Not many people this afternoon—naturally. They were all at the races. Mr Leadbetter did not approve of racing nor of playing cards nor of drinking nor of smoking. This left him more energy to enjoy going to the pictures.

Everyone was hurrying towards the exit. Mr Leadbetter prepared to follow suit. The man in the seat in front of him was asleep—slumped down in his chair. Mr Leadbetter felt indignant to think that anyone could sleep with such a drama as *Not a Sparrow* going on.

An irate gentleman was saying to the sleeping man whose legs were stretched out blocking the way:

'Excuse *me*, sir.'

Mr Leadbetter reached the exit. He looked back.

There seemed to be some sort of commotion. A

commissionaire... a little knot of people... Perhaps that man in front of him was dead drunk and not asleep...

He hesitated and then passed out—and in so doing missed the sensation of the day—a greater sensation even than Not Half winning the St Leger at 85 to 1.

The commissionaire was saying:

'Believe you're right, sir... He's ill... Why—what's the matter, sir?'

The other had drawn away his hand with an exclamation and was examining a red sticky smear.

'Blood...'

The commissionaire gave a stifled exclamation.

He had caught sight of the corner of something yellow projecting from under the seat.

'Gor blimey!' he said. *'It's a b— A B C.'*

CHAPTER 25

(Not from Captain Hastings' Personal Narrative)

Mr Cust came out of the Regal Cinema and looked up at the sky.

A beautiful evening... A really beautiful evening...

A quotation from Browning came into his head.

'God's in His heaven. All's right with the world.'

He had always been fond of that quotation.

Only there were times, very often, when he had felt it wasn't true...

He trotted along the street smiling to himself until he came to the Black Swan where he was staying.

He climbed the stairs to his bedroom, a stuffy little room on the second floor, giving over a paved inner court and garage.

As he entered the room his smile faded suddenly. There was a stain on his sleeve near the cuff. He touched it tentatively—wet and red—blood...

His hand dipped into his pocket and brought out something—a long slender knife. The blade of that, too, was sticky and red...

Mr Cust sat there a long time.

Once his eyes shot round the room like those of a hunted animal.

His tongue passed feverishly over his lips...

'It isn't my fault,' said Mr Cust.

He sounded as though he were arguing with somebody—a schoolboy pleading to his headmaster.

He passed his tongue over his lips again...

Again, tentatively, he felt his coat sleeve.

His eyes crossed the room to the wash-basin.

A minute later he was pouring out water from the old-fashioned jug into the basin. Removing his coat, he rinsed the sleeve, carefully squeezing it out...

Ugh! The water was red now...

A tap on the door.

He stood there frozen into immobility—staring.

The door opened. A plump young woman—jug in hand.

'Oh, excuse me, sir. Your hot water, sir.'

He managed to speak then.

'Thank you... I've washed in cold...'

Why had he said that? Immediately her eyes went to the basin.

He said frenziedly: 'I—I've cut my hand...'

There was a pause—yes, surely a very long pause—before she said: 'Yes, sir.'

She went out, shutting the door.

Mr Cust stood as though turned to stone.

He listened.

It had come—at last...

Were there voices—exclamations—feet mounting the stairs?

He could hear nothing but the beating of his own heart...

Then, suddenly, from frozen immobility he leaped into activity.

He slipped on his coat, tiptoed to the door and opened it. No noises as yet except the familiar murmur arising from the bar. He crept down the stairs...

Still no one. That was luck. He paused at the foot of the stairs. Which way now?

He made up his mind, darted quickly along a passage and out by the door that gave into the yard. A couple of chauffeurs were there tinkering with cars and discussing winners and losers.

Mr Cust hurried across the yard and out into the street.

Round the first corner to the right—then to the left—right again...

Dare he risk the station?

Yes—there would be crowds there—special trains— if luck were on his side he would do it all right...

If only luck were with him...

CHAPTER 26

(Not from Captain Hastings' Personal Narrative)

Inspector Crome was listening to the excited utterances of Mr Leadbetter.

'I assure you, inspector, my heart misses a beat when I think of it. He must actually have been sitting beside me all through the programme!'

Inspector Crome, completely indifferent to the behaviour of Mr Leadbetter's heart, said:

'Just let me have it quite clear? This man went out towards the close of the big picture—'

'*Not a Sparrow*—Katherine Royal,' murmured Mr Leadbetter automatically.

'He passed you and in doing so stumbled—'

'He *pretended* to stumble, I see it now. Then he leaned over the seat in front to pick up his hat. He must have stabbed the poor fellow then.'

'You didn't hear anything? A cry? Or a groan?'

Mr Leadbetter had heard nothing but the loud, hoarse accents of Katherine Royal, but in the vividness of his

Agatha Christie

imagination he invented a groan.

Inspector Crome took the groan at its face value and bade him proceed.

'And then he went out—'

'Can you describe him?'

'He was a very big man. Six foot at least. A giant.'

'Fair or dark?'

'I—well—I'm not exactly sure. I think he was bald. A sinister-looking fellow.'

'He didn't limp, did he?' asked Inspector Crome.

'Yes—yes, now you come to speak of it I think he did limp. Very dark, he might have been some kind of half-caste.'

'Was he in his seat the last time the lights came up?'

'No. He came in after the big picture began.'

Inspector Crome nodded, handed Mr Leadbetter a statement to sign and got rid of him.

'That's about as bad a witness as you'll find,' he remarked pessimistically. 'He'd say anything with a little leading. It's perfectly clear that he hasn't the faintest idea what our man looks like. Let's have the commissionaire back.'

The commissionaire, very stiff and military, came in and stood to attention, his eyes fixed on Colonel Anderson.

'Now, then, Jameson, let's hear your story.'

Jameson saluted.

'Yes sir. Close of the performance, sir. I was told there was a gentleman taken ill, sir. Gentleman was in the two and fourpennies, slumped down in his seat like. Other gentlemen standing around. Gentleman looked bad to me, sir. One of the gentlemen standing by put his hand to the ill gentleman's coat and drew my attention. Blood, sir. It was clear the gentleman was dead—stabbed, sir. My attention was drawn to an A B C railway guide, sir, under the seat. Wishing to act correctly, I did not touch same, but reported to the police immediately that a tragedy had occurred.'

'Very good. Jameson, you acted very properly.'

'Thank you, sir.'

'Did you notice a man leaving the two and fourpennies about five minutes earlier?'

'There were several, sir.'

'Could you describe them?'

'Afraid not, sir. One was Mr Geoffrey Parnell. And there was a young fellow, Sam Baker, with his young lady. I didn't notice anybody else particular.'

'A pity. That'll do, Jameson.'

'Yes sir.'

The commissionaire saluted and departed.

'The medical details we've got,' said Colonel Anderson. 'We'd better have the fellow that found him next.'

A police constable came in and saluted.

'Mr Hercule Poirot's here, sir, and another gentleman.'

Inspector Crome frowned.

'Oh, well,' he said. 'Better have 'em in, I suppose.'

CHAPTER 27

The Doncaster Murder

Coming in hard on Poirot's heels, I just caught the fag end of Inspector Crome's remark.

Both he and the Chief Constable were looking worried and depressed.

Colonel Anderson greeted us with a nod of the head.

'Glad you've come, M. Poirot,' he said politely. I think he guessed that Crome's remark might have reached our ears. 'We've got it in the neck again, you see.'

'Another A B C murder?'

'Yes. Damned audacious bit of work. Man leaned over and stabbed the fellow in the back.'

'Stabbed this time?'

'Yes, varies his methods a bit, doesn't he? Biff on the head, strangled, now a knife. Versatile devil—what? Here are the medical details if you care to see 'em.'

He shoved a paper towards Poirot. 'A B C down on the floor between the dead man's feet,' he added.

'Has the dead man been identified?' asked Poirot.

'Yes. A B C's slipped up for once—if that's any satisfaction to us. Deceased's a man called Earlsfield—George Earlsfield. Barber by profession.'

'Curious,' commented Poirot.

'May have skipped a letter,' suggested the colonel.

My friend shook his head doubtfully.

'Shall we have in the next witness?' asked Crome. 'He's anxious to get home.'

'Yes, yes—let's get on.'

A middle-aged gentleman strongly resembling the frog footman in *Alice in Wonderland* was led in. He was highly excited and his voice was shrill with emotion.

'Most shocking experience I have ever known,' he squeaked. 'I have a weak heart, sir—a very weak heart, it might have been the death of me.'

'Your name, please,' said the inspector.

'Downes. Roger Emmanuel Downes.'

'Profession?'

'I am a master at Highfield School for boys.'

'Now, Mr Downes, will you tell us in your own words what happened.'

'I can tell you that very shortly, gentlemen. At the close of the performance I rose from my seat. The seat on my left was empty but in the one beyond a man was sitting, apparently asleep. I was unable to pass him to get out as his legs were stuck out in front of him. I asked him to allow me to pass. As he did not move I repeated my request in—a—er—slightly louder tone. He still made no response. I then took him by the shoulder to waken him. His body slumped down further and I became aware that he was either unconscious or seriously ill. I called out: "This gentleman is taken ill. Fetch the commissionaire." The commissionaire came. As I took my hand from the man's shoulder I found it was wet and red... I can assure you, gentlemen, the shock was terrific! Anything might have happened! For years I have suffered from cardiac weakness—'

Colonel Anderson was looking at Mr Downes with a very curious expression.

'You can consider that you're a lucky man, Mr Downes.'

'I do, sir. Not even a palpitation!'

'You don't quite take my meaning, Mr Downes. You were sitting two seats away, you say?'

'Actually I was sitting at first in the next seat to the murdered man—then I moved along so as to be behind an empty seat.'

'You're about the same height and build as the dead man, aren't you, and you were wearing a woollen scarf round your neck just as he was?'

'I fail to see—' began Mr Downes stiffly.

'I'm telling you, man,' said Colonel Anderson, 'just where your luck came in. Somehow or other, when the murderer followed you in, he got confused. *He picked on the wrong back*. I'll eat my hat, Mr Downes, if that knife wasn't meant for you!'

However well Mr Downes' heart had stood former tests, it was unable to stand up to this one. He sank on a chair, gasped, and turned purple in the face.

'Water,' he gasped. 'Water...'

A glass was brought him. He sipped it whilst his complexion gradually returned to the normal.

'Me?' he said. 'Why me?'

'It looks like it,' said Crome. 'In fact, it's the only explanation.'

'You mean that this man—this—this fiend incarnate—this bloodthirsty madman has been following *me* about waiting for an opportunity?'

'I should say that was the way of it.'

'But in heaven's name, why *me*?' demanded the outraged schoolmaster.

Inspector Crome struggled with the temptation to reply: 'Why not?' and said instead: 'I'm afraid it's no good expecting a lunatic to have reasons for what he does.'

'God bless my soul,' said Mr Downes, sobered into whispering.

He got up. He looked suddenly old and shaken.

'If you don't want me any more, gentlemen, I think I'll go home. I—I don't feel very well.'

'That's quite all right, Mr Downes. I'll send a constable with you—just to see you're all right.'

'Oh, no—no, thank you. That's not necessary.'

'Might as well,' said Colonel Anderson gruffly.

His eyes slid sideways, asking an imperceptible question of the inspector. The latter gave an equally imperceptible nod.

Mr Downes went out shakily.

'Just as well he didn't tumble to it,' said Colonel Anderson. 'There'll be a couple of them—eh?'

'Yes, sir. Your Inspector Rice has made arrangements. The house will be watched.'

'You think,' said Poirot, 'that when A B C finds out his mistake he might try again?'

Anderson nodded.

'It's a possibility,' he said. 'Seems a methodical sort of chap, A B C. It will upset him if things don't go according to programme.'

Poirot nodded thoughtfully.

'Wish we could get a description of the fellow,' said Colonel Anderson irritably. 'We're as much in the dark as ever.'

'It may come,' said Poirot.

'Think so? Well, it's possible. Damn it all, hasn't anyone got eyes in their head?'

'Have patience,' said Poirot.

'You seem very confident, M. Poirot. Got any reason for this optimism?'

'Yes, Colonel Anderson. Up to now, the murderer has not made a mistake. He is bound to make one soon.'

'If that's all you've got to go on,' began the Chief Constable with a snort, but he was interrupted.

'Mr Ball of the Black Swan is here with a young woman, sir. He reckons he's got summat to say might help you.'

'Bring them along. Bring them along. We can do with anything helpful.'

Mr Ball of the Black Swan was a large, slow-thinking, heavily moving man. He exhaled a strong odour of beer. With him was a plump young woman with round eyes clearly in a state of high excitement.

'Hope I'm not intruding or wasting valuable time,' said Mr Ball in a slow, thick voice. 'But this wench, Mary here, reckons she's got something to tell as you ought to know.'

Mary giggled in a half-hearted way.

'Well, my girl, what is it?' said Anderson. 'What's your name?'

'Mary, sir, Mary Stroud.'

'Well, Mary, out with it.'

Mary turned her round eyes on her master.

'It's her business to take up hot water to the gents' bedrooms,' said Mr Ball, coming to the rescue. 'About half a dozen gentlemen we'd got staying. Some for the races and some just commercials.'

'Yes, yes,' said Anderson impatiently.

'Get on, lass,' said Mr Ball. 'Tell your tale. Nowt to be afraid of.'

Mary gasped, groaned and plunged in a breathless voice into her narrative.

'I knocked on door and there wasn't no answer, otherwise I wouldn't have gone in least ways not unless the gentleman had said "Come in," and as he didn't say nothing I went in and he was there washing his hands.'

She paused and breathed deeply.

'Go on, my girl,' said Anderson.

Mary looked sideways at her master and as though receiving inspiration from his slow nod, plunged on again.

'"It's your hot water, sir," I said, "and I did knock," but "Oh," he says, "I've washed in cold," he said, and so, naturally, I looks in basin, and oh! God help me, sir, *it were all red!*'

Agatha Christie

'Red?' said Anderson sharply.

Ball struck in.

'The lass told me that he had his coat off and that he was holding the sleeve of it, and it was all wet—that's right, eh, lass?'

'Yes, sir, that's right, sir.'

She plunged on:

'And his face, sir, it looked queer, mortal queer it looked. Gave me quite a turn.'

'When was this?' asked Anderson sharply.

'About a quarter after five, so near as I can reckon.'

'Over three hours ago,' snapped Anderson. 'Why didn't you come at once?'

'Didn't hear about it at once,' said Ball. 'Not till news came along as there'd been another murder done. And then the lass she screams out as it might have been blood in the basin, and I asks her what she means, and she tells me. Well, it doesn't sound right to me and I went upstairs myself. Nobody in the room. I asks a few questions and one of the lads in courtyard says he saw a fellow sneaking out that way and by his description it was the right one. So I says to the missus as Mary here had best go to police. She doesn't like the idea, Mary doesn't, and I says I'll come along with her.'

Inspector Crome drew a sheet of paper towards him.

'Describe this man,' he said. 'As quick as you can. There's no time to be lost.'

'Medium-sized he were,' said Mary. 'And stooped and wore glasses.'

The A B C Murders

'His clothes?'

'A dark suit and a Homburg hat. Rather shabby-looking.'

She could add little to this description.

Inspector Crome did not insist unduly. The telephone wires were soon busy, but neither the inspector nor the Chief Constable were over-optimistic.

Crome elicited the fact that the man, when seen sneaking across the yard, had had no bag or suitcase.

'There's a chance there,' he said.

Two men were despatched to the Black Swan.

Mr Ball, swelling with pride and importance, and Mary, somewhat tearful, accompanied them.

The sergeant returned about ten minutes later.

'I've brought the register, sir,' he said. 'Here's the signature.'

We crowded round. The writing was small and cramped—not easy to read.

'A. B. Case—or is it Cash?' said the Chief Constable.

'A B C,' said Crome significantly.

'What about luggage?' asked Anderson.

'One good-sized suitcase, sir, full of small cardboard boxes.'

'Boxes? What was in 'em?'

'Stockings, sir. Silk stockings.'

Crome turned to Poirot.

'Congratulations,' he said. 'Your hunch was right.'

CHAPTER 28

(Not from Captain Hastings' Personal Narrative)

Inspector Crome was in his office at Scotland Yard.

The telephone on his desk gave a discreet buzz and he picked it up.

'Jacobs speaking, sir. There's a young fellow come in with a story that I think you ought to hear.'

Inspector Crome sighed. On an average twenty people a day turned up with so-called important information about the A B C case. Some of them were harmless lunatics, some of them were well-meaning persons who genuinely believed that their information was of value. It was the duty of Sergeant Jacobs to act as a human sieve—retaining the grosser matter and passing on the residue to his superior.

'Very well, Jacobs,' said Crome. 'Send him along.'

A few minutes later there was a tap on the inspector's door and Sergeant Jacobs appeared, ushering in a tall, moderately good-looking young man.

'This is Mr Tom Hartigan, sir. He's got something to tell us which may have a possible bearing on the A B C case.'

The inspector rose pleasantly and shook hands.

'Good morning, Mr Hartigan. Sit down, won't you? Smoke? Have a cigarette?'

Tom Hartigan sat down awkwardly and looked with some awe at what he called in his own mind 'One of the big-wigs.' The appearance of the inspector vaguely disappointed him. He looked quite an ordinary person!

'Now then,' said Crome. 'You've got something to tell us that you think may have a bearing on the case. Fire ahead.'

Tom began nervously.

'Of course it may be nothing at all. It's just an idea of mine. I may be wasting your time.'

Again Inspector Crome sighed imperceptibly. The amount of time he had to waste in reassuring people!

'We're the best judge of that. Let's have the facts, Mr Hartigan.'

'Well, it's like this, sir. I've got a young lady, you see, and her mother lets rooms. Up Camden Town way. Their second-floor back has been let for over a year to a man called Cust.'

'Cust—eh?'

'That's right, sir. A sort of middle-aged bloke what's rather vague and soft—and come down in the world a bit, I should say. Sort of creature who wouldn't hurt a fly you'd say—and I'd never of dreamed of anything being wrong if it hadn't been for something rather odd.'

In a somewhat confused manner and repeating himself once or twice, Tom described his encounter with Mr Cust at Euston Station and the incident of the dropped ticket.

Agatha Christie

'You see, sir, look at it how you will, it's funny like. Lily—that's my young lady, sir—she was quite positive that it was Cheltenham he said, and her mother says the same—says she remembers distinct talking about it the morning he went off. Of course, I didn't pay much attention to it at the time. Lily—my young lady—said as how she hoped he wouldn't cop it from this A B C fellow going to Doncaster—and then she says it's rather a coincidence because he was down Churston way at the time of the last crime. Laughing like, I asks her whether he was at Bexhill the time before, and she says she don't know where he was, but he was away at the seaside—that she does know. And then I said to her it would be odd if he was the A B C himself and she said poor Mr Cust wouldn't hurt a fly—and that was all at the time. We didn't think no more about it. At least, in a sort of way I did, sir, underneath like. I began wondering about this Cust fellow and thinking that, after all, harmless as he seemed, he might be a bit batty.'

Tom took a breath and then went on. Inspector Crome was listening intently now.

'And then after the Doncaster murder, sir, it was in all the papers that information was wanted as to the whereabouts of a certain A B Case or Cash, and it gave a description that fitted well enough. First evening off I had, I went round to Lily's and asked her what her Mr Cust's initials were. She couldn't remember at first, but her mother did. Said they were A B right enough. Then we got down to it and tried to figure out if Cust had been away at the time of the first murder at Andover. Well, as you know, sir, it isn't too easy to remember things three months back. We had a job of it, but we got it fixed down in the end, because Mrs Marbury had a brother come from Canada to see her on June 21st. He arrived unexpected like and she wanted to give him a bed, and Lily suggested that as Mr Cust was away Bert Smith might have his bed. But Mrs Marbury wouldn't agree, because she said it wasn't acting right by her lodger, and she always liked to act fair and square. But we fixed the date all right because of Bert Smith's ship docking at Southampton that day.'

Inspector Crome had listened very attentively, jotting down an occasional note.

'That's all?' he asked.

'That's all, sir. I hope you don't think I'm making a lot of nothing.'

Tom flushed slightly.

'Not at all. You were quite right to come here. Of course, it's very slight evidence—these dates may be mere coincidence and the likeness of the name, too. But it certainly warrants my having an interview with your Mr Cust. Is he at home now?'

'Yes, sir.'

'When did he return?'

'The evening of the Doncaster murder, sir.'

'What's he been doing since?'

'He's stayed in mostly, sir. And he's been looking very queer, Mrs Marbury says. He buys a lot of newspapers—goes out early and gets the morning ones, and then after dark he goes out and gets the evening ones. Mrs Marbury says he talks a lot to himself, too. She thinks he's getting queerer.'

'What is this Mrs Marbury's address?'

Tom gave it to him.

'Thank you. I shall probably be calling round in the course of the day. I need hardly tell you to be careful of your manner if you come across this Cust.'

He rose and shook hands.

'You may be quite satisfied you did the right thing in coming to us. Good morning, Mr Hartigan.'

'Well, sir?' asked Jacobs, re-entering the room a few minutes later. 'Think it's the goods?'

'It's promising,' said Inspector Crome. 'That is, if the facts are as the boy stated them. We've had no luck with the stocking manufacturers yet. It was time we got hold of something. By the way, give me that file of the Churston case.'

He spent some minutes looking for what he wanted.

'Ah, here it is. It's amongst the statements made to the Torquay police. Young man of the name of Hill. Deposes he was leaving the Torquay Palladium after the film *Not a Sparrow* and noticed a man behaving queerly. He was talking to himself. Hill heard him say "That's an idea." *Not a Sparrow*—that's the film that was on at the Regal in Doncaster?'

'Yes, sir.'

'There may be something in that. Nothing to it at the time—but it's possible that the idea of the *modus operandi* for his next crime occurred to our man then. We've got Hill's name and address, I see. His description of the man is vague but it links up well enough with the descriptions of Mary Stroud and this Tom Hartigan...'

He nodded thoughtfully.

'We're getting warm,' said Inspector Crome—rather inaccurately, for he himself was always slightly chilly.

'Any instructions, sir?'

'Put on a couple of men to watch this Camden Town address, but I don't want our bird frightened. I must have a word with the AC. Then I think it would be as well if Cust was brought along here and asked if he'd like to make a statement. It sounds as though he's quite ready to get rattled.'

Outside Tom Hartigan had rejoined Lily Marbury who was waiting for him on the Embankment.

'All right, Tom?'

Tom nodded.

'I saw Inspector Crome himself. The one who's in charge of the case.'

'What's he like?'

'A bit quiet and lah-di-dah—not my idea of a detective.'

'That's Lord Trenchard's new kind,' said Lily with respect. 'Some of them are ever so grand. Well, what did he say?'

Tom gave her a brief résumé of the interview.

'So they think as it really was him?'

'They think it might be. Anyway, they'll come along and ask him a question or two.'

'Poor Mr Cust.'

'It's no good saying poor Mr Cust, my girl. If he's A B C, he's committed four terrible murders.'

Lily sighed and shook her head.

'It does seem awful,' she observed.

'Well, now you're going to come and have a bite of lunch, my girl. Just you think that if we're right I expect my name will be in the papers!'

'Oh, Tom, will it?'

'Rather. And yours, too. *And* your mother's. And I dare say you'll have your picture in it, too.'

'Oh, Tom.' Lily squeezed his arm in an ecstasy.

'And in the meantime what do you say to a bite at the Corner House?'

Lily squeezed tighter.

'Come on then!'

'All right—half a minute. I must just telephone from the station.'

'Who to?'

'A girl I was going to meet.'

She slipped across the road, and rejoined him three minutes later, looking rather flushed.

'Now then, Tom.'

She slipped her arm in his.

'Tell me more about Scotland Yard. You didn't see the other one there?'

'What other one?'

'The Belgian gentleman. The one that A B C writes to always.'

'No. He wasn't there.'

'Well, tell me all about it. What happened when you got inside? Who did you speak to and what did you say?'

The A B C Murders

Mr Cust put the receiver back very gently on the hook.

He turned to where Mrs Marbury was standing in the doorway of the room, clearly devoured with curiosity.

'Not often you have a telephone call, Mr Cust?'

'No—er—no, Mrs Marbury. It isn't.'

'Not bad news, I trust?'

'No—no.' How persistent the woman was. His eyes caught the legend on the newspaper he was carrying.

Births—Marriages—Deaths...

'My sister's just had a little boy,' he blurted out.

He—who had never had a sister!

'Oh, dear! Now—well, that *is* nice, I am sure. ("And never once mentioned a sister all these years," was her inward thought. "If that isn't just like a man!") I was surprised, I'll tell you, when the lady asked to speak to Mr Cust. Just at first I fancied it was my Lily's voice—something like hers, it was—but haughtier if you know what I mean—sort of high up in the air. Well, Mr Cust, my congratulations, I'm sure. Is it the first one, or have you other little nephews and nieces?'

'It's the only one,' said Mr Cust. 'The only one I've ever had or likely to have, and—er—I think I must go off at once. They—they want me to come. I—I think I can just catch a train if I hurry.'

'Will you be away long, Mr Cust?' called Mrs Marbury as he ran up the stairs.

'Oh, no—two or three days—that's all.'

He disappeared into his bedroom. Mrs Marbury retired into the kitchen, thinking sentimentally of 'the dear little mite'.

Her conscience gave her a sudden twinge.

Agatha Christie

Last night Tom and Lily and all the hunting back over dates! Trying to make out that Mr Cust was that dreadful monster, A B C. Just because of his initials and because of a few coincidences.

'I don't suppose they meant it seriously,' she thought comfortably. 'And now I hope they'll be ashamed of themselves.'

In some obscure way that she could not have explained, Mr Cust's statement that his sister had had a baby had effectually removed any doubts Mrs Marbury might have had of her lodger's *bona fides*.

'I hope she didn't have too hard a time of it, poor dear,' thought Mrs Marbury, testing an iron against her cheek before beginning to iron out Lily's silk slip.

Her mind ran comfortably on a well-worn obstetric track.

Mr Cust came quietly down the stairs, a bag in his hand. His eyes rested a minute on the telephone.

That brief conversation re-echoed in his brain.

'Is that you, Mr Cust? I thought you might like to know there's an inspector from Scotland Yard may be coming to see you...'

What had he said? He couldn't remember.

'Thank you—thank you, my dear... very kind of you...'

Something like that.

Why had she telephoned to him? Could she possibly have guessed? Or did she just want to make sure he would stay in for the inspector's visit?

But how did she know the inspector was coming?

And her voice—she'd disguised her voice from her mother...

It looked—it looked—as though she *knew*...

But surely if she knew, she wouldn't...

She might, though. Women were very queer. Unexpectedly cruel and unexpectedly kind. He'd seen Lily once letting a mouse out of a mouse-trap.

A kind girl...

A kind, pretty girl...

He paused by the hall stand with its load of umbrellas and coats.

Should he...?

A slight noise from the kitchen decided him...

No, there wasn't time...

Mrs Marbury might come out...

He opened the front door, passed through and closed it behind him...

Where...?

CHAPTER 29

At Scotland Yard

Conference again.

The Assistant Commissioner, Inspector Crome, Poirot and myself.

The AC was saying:

'A good tip that of yours, M. Poirot, about checking a large sale of stockings.'

Poirot spread out his hands.

'It was indicated. This man could not be a regular agent. He sold outright instead of touting for orders.'

'Got everything clear so far, inspector?'

'I think so, sir.' Crome consulted a file. 'Shall I run over the position to date?'

'Yes, please.'

'I've checked up with Churston, Paignton and Torquay. Got a list of people where he went and offered stockings. I must say he did the thing thoroughly. Stayed at the Pitt, small hotel near Torre Station. Returned to the hotel at 10.30 on the night of the murder. Could have taken a train from Churston at 9.57, getting to Torre at 10.20. No one answering to his description noticed on train or at station, but that Friday was Dartmouth Regatta and the trains back from Kingswear were pretty full.

'Bexhill much the same. Stayed at the Globe under his own name. Offered stockings to about a dozen addresses, including Mrs Barnard and including the Ginger Cat. Left hotel early in the evening. Arrived back in London about 11.30 the following morning. As to Andover, same procedure. Stayed at the Feathers. Offered stockings to Mrs Fowler, next door to Mrs Ascher, and to half a dozen other people in the street. The pair Mrs Ascher had I got from the niece (name of Drower)—they're identical with Cust's supply.'

'So far, good,' said the AC.

'Acting on information received,' said the inspector, 'I went to the address given me by Hartigan, but found that Cust had left the house about half an hour previously. He received a telephone message, I'm told. First time such a thing had happened to him, so his landlady told me.'

'An accomplice?' suggested the Assistant Commissioner.

'Hardly,' said Poirot. 'It is odd that—unless—'

We all looked at him inquiringly as he paused.

He shook his head, however, and the inspector proceeded.

'I made a thorough search of the room he had occupied. That search puts the matter beyond doubt. I found a block of notepaper similar to that on which the letters were written, a large quantity of hosiery and—at the back of the cupboard where the hosiery was stored—a parcel much the same shape and size but which turned out to contain—not hosiery—*but eight new A B C railway guides!*'

'Proof positive,' said the Assistant Commissioner.

'I've found something else, too,' said the inspector—his voice becoming suddenly almost human with triumph. 'Only found it this morning, sir. Not had time to report yet. There was no sign of the knife in his room—'

'It would be the act of an imbecile to bring that back with him,' remarked Poirot.

'After all, he's not a reasonable human being,' remarked the inspector. 'Anway, it occurred to me that he might just possibly have brought it back to the house and then realized the danger of hiding it (as M. Poirot points out) in his room, and have looked about elsewhere. What place in the house would he be likely to select? I got it straight away. *The hall stand*—no one ever moves a hall stand. With a lot of trouble I got it moved out from the wall—and there it was!'

'The knife?'

'The knife. Not a doubt of it. The dried blood's still on it.'

'Good work, Crome,' said the AC approvingly. 'We only need one thing more now.'

'What's that?'

'The man himself.'

'We'll get him, sir. Never fear.'

The inspector's tone was confident.

'What do you say, M. Poirot?'

Poirot started out of a reverie.

'I beg your pardon?'

'We were saying that it was only a matter of time before we got our man. Do you agree?'

'Oh, that—yes. Without a doubt.'

His tone was so abstracted that the others looked at him curiously.

'Is there anything worrying you, M. Poirot?'

'There is something that worries me very much. It is the *why*? The *motive*.'

'But, my dear fellow, the man's crazy,' said the Assistant Commissioner impatiently.

'I understand what M. Poirot means,' said Crome, coming graciously to the rescue. 'He's quite right. There's got to be some definite obsession. I think we'll find the root of the matter in an intensified inferiority complex. There may be a persecution mania, too, and if so he may possibly associate M. Poirot with it. He may have the delusion that M. Poirot is a detective employed on purpose to hunt him down.'

'H'm,' said the AC. 'That's the jargon that's talked nowadays. In my day if a man was mad he was mad and we didn't look about for scientific terms to soften it down. I suppose a thoroughly up-to-date doctor would suggest putting a man like A B C in a nursing home, telling him what a fine fellow he was for forty-five days on end and then letting him out as a responsible member of society.'

Poirot smiled but did not answer.

The conference broke up.

'Well,' said the Assistant Commissioner. 'As you say, Crome, pulling him in is only a matter of time.'

Agatha Christie

'We'd have had him before now,' said the inspector, 'if he wasn't so ordinary-looking. We've worried enough perfectly inoffensive citizens as it is.'

'I wonder where he is at this minute,' said the Assistant Commissioner.

CHAPTER 30

(Not from Captain Hastings' Personal Narrative)

Mr Cust stood by a greengrocer's shop.
 He stared across the road.
 Yes, that was it.
 Mrs Ascher. Newsagent and Tobacconist...
 In the empty window was a sign.
 To Let.
 Empty...
 Lifeless...
 'Excuse me, sir.'
 The greengrocer's wife, trying to get at some lemons.
 He apologized, moved to one side.
 Slowly he shuffled away—back towards the main street of the town...
 It was difficult—very difficult—now that he hadn't any money left...
 Not having had anything to eat all day made one feel very queer and light-headed...
 He looked at a poster outside a newsagent's shop.

Agatha Christie

The A B C Case. Murderer Still at Large. Interviews with M. Hercule Poirot.

Mr Cust said to himself:

'Hercule Poirot. I wonder if *he* knows...'

He walked on again.

It wouldn't do to stand staring at that poster...

He thought:

'I can't go on much longer...'

Foot in front of foot... what an odd thing walking was...

Foot in front of foot—ridiculous.

Highly ridiculous...

But man was a ridiculous animal anyway...

And he, Alexander Bonaparte Cust, was particularly ridiculous.

He had always been...

People had always laughed at him...

He couldn't blame them...

Where was he going? He didn't know. He'd come to the end. He no longer looked anywhere but at his feet.

Foot in front of foot.

He looked up. Lights in front of him. And letters...

Police Station.

'That's funny,' said Mr Cust. He gave a little giggle.

Then he stepped inside. Suddenly, as he did so, he swayed and fell forward.

CHAPTER 31

Hercule Poirot Asks Questions

It was a clear November day. Dr Thompson and Chief Inspector Japp had come round to acquaint Poirot with the result of the police court proceedings in the case of Rex *v.* Alexander Bonaparte Cust.

Poirot himself had had a slight bronchial chill which had prevented his attending. Fortunately he had not insisted on having my company.

'Committed for trial,' said Japp. 'So that's that.'

'Isn't it unusual?' I asked, 'for a defence to be offered at this stage? I thought prisoners always reserved their defence.'

'It's the usual course,' said Japp. 'I suppose young Lucas thought he might rush it through. He's a trier, I will say. Insanity's the only defence possible.'

Poirot shrugged his shoulders.

'With insanity there can be no acquittal. Imprisonment during His Majesty's pleasure is hardly preferable to death.'

'I suppose Lucas thought there was a chance,' said Japp. 'With a first-class alibi for the Bexhill murder, the whole case might be weakened. I don't think he realized how strong our case is. Anyway, Lucas goes in for originality. He's a young man, and he wants to hit the public eye.'

Poirot turned to Thompson.

'What's your opinion, doctor?'

'Of Cust? Upon my soul, I don't know what to say. He's playing the sane man remarkably well. He's an epileptic, of course.'

'What an amazing dénouement that was,' I said.

'His falling into the Andover police station in a fit? Yes—it was a fitting dramatic curtain to the drama. A B C has always timed his effects well.'

'Is it possible to commit a crime and be unaware of it?' I asked. 'His denials seem to have a ring of truth in them.'

Dr Thompson smiled a little.

'You mustn't be taken in by that theatrical "I swear by God" pose. It's my opinion *that Cust knows perfectly well he committed* the murders.'

'When they're as fervent as that they usually do,' said Crome.

'As to your question,' went on Thompson, 'it's perfectly possible for an epileptic subject in a state of somnambulism to commit an action and be entirely unaware of having done so. But it is the general opinion that such an action must "not be contrary to the will of the person in the waking state".'

He went on discussing the matter, speaking of *grand mal* and *petit mal* and, to tell the truth, confusing me hopelessly as is often the case when a learned person holds forth on his own subject.

The A B C Murders

'However, I'm against the theory that Cust committed these crimes without knowing he'd done them. You might put that theory forward if it weren't for the letters. The letters knock the theory on the head. They show premeditation and a careful planning of the crime.'

'And of the letters we have still no explanation,' said Poirot.

'That interests you?'

'Naturally—since they were written to me. And on the subject of the letters Cust is persistently dumb. Until I get at the reason for those letters being written to me, I shall not feel that the case is solved.'

'Yes—I can understand that from your point of view. There doesn't seem to be any reason to believe that the man ever came up against you in any way?'

'None whatever.'

'I might make a suggestion. Your name!'

'My name?'

'Yes. Cust is saddled—apparently by the whim of his mother (Oedipus complex there, I shouldn't wonder!)—with two extremely bombastic Christian names: Alexander and Bonaparte. You see the implications? Alexander—the popularly supposed undefeatable who sighed for more worlds to conquer. Bonaparte—the great Emperor of the French. He wants an adversary—an adversary, one might say, in his class. Well—there you are—Hercules the strong.'

'Your words are very suggestive, doctor. They foster ideas...'

'Oh, it's only a suggestion. Well, I must be off.'

Agatha Christie

Dr Thompson went out. Japp remained.

'Does this alibi worry you?' Poirot asked.

'It does a little,' admitted the inspector. 'Mind you, I don't believe in it, because I know it isn't true. But it is going to be the deuce to break it. This man Strange is a tough character.'

'Describe him to me.'

'He's a man of forty. A tough, confident, self-opinionated mining engineer. It's my opinion that it was he who insisted on his evidence being taken now. He wants to get off to Chile. He hoped the thing might be settled out of hand.'

'He's one of the most positive people I've ever seen,' I said.

'The type of man who would not like to admit he was mistaken,' said Poirot thoughtfully.

'He sticks to his story and he's not one to be heckled. He swears by all that's blue that he picked up Cust in the Whitecross Hotel at Eastbourne on the evening of July 24th. He was lonely and wanted someone to talk to. As far as I can see, Cust made an ideal listener. He didn't interrupt! After dinner he and Cust played dominoes. It appears Strange was a whale on dominoes and to his surprise Cust was pretty hot stuff too. Queer game, dominoes. People go mad about it. They'll play for hours. That's what Strange and Cust did apparently. Cust wanted to go to bed but Strange wouldn't hear of it—swore they'd keep it up until midnight at least. And that's what they did do. They separated at ten minutes past midnight. And if Cust was in the Whitecross Hotel at Eastbourne at ten minutes past midnight on the morning of the 25th he couldn't very well be strangling Betty Barnard on the beach at Bexhill between midnight and one o'clock.'

The A B C Murders

'The problem certainly seems insuperable,' said Poirot thoughtfully. 'Decidedly, it gives one to think.'

'It's given Crome something to think about,' said Japp.

'This man Strange is very positive?'

'Yes. He's an obstinate devil. And it's difficult to see just where the flaw is. Supposing Strange is making a mistake and the man wasn't Cust—why on earth should he *say* his name is Cust? And the writing in the hotel register is his all right. You can't say he's an accomplice—homicidal lunatics don't have accomplices! Did the girl die later? The doctor was quite firm in his evidence, and anyway it would take some time for Cust to get out of the hotel at Eastbourne without being seen and get over to Bexhill—about fourteen miles away—'

'It is a problem—yes,' said Poirot.

'Of course, strictly speaking, it oughtn't to matter. We've got Cust on the Doncaster murder—the blood-stained coat, the knife—not a loophole there. You couldn't bounce any jury into acquitting him. But it spoils a pretty case. He did the Doncaster murder. He did the Churston murder. He did the Andover murder. Then, by hell, he *must* have done the Bexhill murder. But I don't see how!'

He shook his head and got up.

'Now's your chance, M. Poirot,' he said. 'Crome's in a fog. Exert those cellular arrangements of yours I used to hear so much about. Show us the way he did it.'

Japp departed.

'What about it, Poirot?' I said. 'Are the little grey cells equal to the task?'

Agatha Christie

Poirot answered my question by another.

'Tell me, Hastings, do you consider the case ended?'

'Well—yes, practically speaking. We've got the man. And we've got most of the evidence. It's only the trimmings that are needed.'

Poirot shook his head.

'The case is ended! The case! The case is the *man*, Hastings. Until we know all about the man, the mystery is as deep as ever. It is not victory because we have put him in the dock!'

'We know a fair amount about him.'

'We know nothing at all! We know where he was born. We know he fought in the war and received a slight wound in the head and that he was discharged from the army owing to epilepsy. We know that he lodged with Mrs Marbury for nearly two years. We know that he was quiet and retiring—the sort of man that nobody notices. We know that he invented and carried out an intensely clever scheme of systemized murder. We know that he made certain incredibly stupid blunders. We know that he killed without pity and quite ruthlessly. We know, too, that he was kindly enough not to let blame rest on any other person for the crimes he committed. If he wanted to kill unmolested—how easy to let other persons suffer for his crimes. Do you not see, Hastings, that the man is a mass of contradictions? Stupid and cunning, ruthless and magnanimous—*and that there must be some dominating factor that reconciles his two natures*.'

'Of course, if you treat him like a psychological study,' I began.

'What else has this case been since the beginning? All along I have been groping my way—trying *to get* to know the murderer. And now I realize, Hastings, *that I do not know him at all!* I am at sea.'

'The lust for power—' I began.

'Yes—that might explain a good deal... But it does not satisfy me. There are things I want to know. *Why* did he commit these murders? *Why* did he choose those particular people—?'

'Alphabetically—' I began.

'Was Betty Barnard the only person in Bexhill whose name began with a B? Betty Barnard—I had an idea there... It ought to be true—it must be true. But if so—'

He was silent for some time. I did not like to interrupt him.

As a matter of fact, I believe I fell asleep.

I woke to find Poirot's hand on my shoulder.

'*Mon cher Hastings*,' he said affectionately. 'My good genius.'

I was quite confused by this sudden mark of esteem.

'It is true,' Poirot insisted. 'Always—always—you help me—you bring me luck. You inspire me.'

'How have I inspired you this time?' I asked.

'While I was asking myself certain questions I remembered a remark of yours—a remark absolutely shimmering in its clear vision. Did I not say to you once that you had a genius for stating the obvious. It is the obvious that I have neglected.'

'What is this brilliant remark of mine?' I asked.

Agatha Christie

'It makes everything as clear as crystal. I see the answers to all my questions. The reason for Mrs Ascher (that, it is true, I glimpsed long ago), the reason for Sir Carmichael Clarke, the reason for the Doncaster murder, and finally and supremely important, *the reason for Hercule Poirot.*'

'Could you kindly explain?' I asked.

'Not at the moment. I require first a little more information. That I can get from our Special Legion. And then—then, *when I have got the answer to a certain question, I will go and see A B C.* We will be face to face at last—A B C and Hercule Poirot—the adversaries.'

'And then?' I asked.

'And then,' said Poirot. 'We will talk! *Je vous assure, Hastings*—there is nothing so dangerous *for anyone who has something to hide* as conversation! Speech, so a wise old Frenchman said to me once, is an invention of man's to prevent him from thinking. It is also an infallible means of discovering that which he wishes to hide. A human being, Hastings, cannot resist the opportunity to reveal himself and express his personality which conversation gives him. Every time he will give himself away.'

'What do you expect Cust to tell you?'

Hercule Poirot smiled.

'A lie,' he said. 'And by it, I shall know the truth!'

CHAPTER 32

And Catch a Fox

During the next few days Poirot was very busy. He made mysterious absences, talked very little, frowned to himself, and consistently refused to satisfy my natural curiosity as to the brilliance I had, according to him, displayed in the past.

I was not invited to accompany him on his mysterious comings and goings—a fact which I somewhat resented.

Towards the end of the week, however, he announced his intention of paying a visit to Bexhill and neighbourhood and suggested that I should come with him. Needless to say, I accepted with alacrity.

The invitation, I discovered, was not extended to me alone. The members of our Special Legion were also invited.

They were as intrigued by Poirot as I was. Nevertheless, by the end of the day, I had at any rate an idea as to the direction in which Poirot's thoughts were tending.

He first visited Mr and Mrs Barnard and got an exact account from her as to the hour at which Mr Cust had called on her and exactly what he had said. He then went to the hotel at which Cust had put up and extracted a minute description of that gentleman's departure. As far as I could judge, no new facts were elicited by his questions but he himself seemed quite satisfied.

Next he went to the beach—to the place where Betty Barnard's body had been discovered. Here he walked round in circles for some minutes studying the shingle attentively. I could see little point in this, since the tide covered the spot twice a day.

However I have learnt by this time that Poirot's actions are usually dictated by an idea—however meaningless they may seem.

He then walked from the beach to the nearest point at which a car could have been parked. From there again he went to the place where the Eastbourne buses waited before leaving Bexhill.

Finally he took us all to the Ginger Cat café, where we had a somewhat stale tea served by the plump waitress, Milly Higley.

Her he complimented in a flowing Gallic style on the shape of her ankles.

'The legs of the English—always they are too thin! But you, mademoiselle, have the perfect leg. It has shape—it has an ankle!'

Milly Higley giggled a good deal and told him not to go on so. She knew what French gentlemen were like.

Poirot did not trouble to contradict her mistake as to his nationality. He merely ogled her in such a way that I was startled and almost shocked.

'*Voilà*,' said Poirot, 'I have finished in Bexhill. Presently I go to Eastbourne. One little inquiry there—that is all. Unnecessary for you all to accompany me. In the meantime come back to the hotel and let us have a cocktail. That Carlton tea, it was abominable!'

As we were sipping our cocktails Franklin Clarke said curiously:

'I suppose we can guess what you are after? You're out to break that alibi. But I can't see what you're so pleased about. You haven't got a new fact of any kind.'

'No—that is true.'

'Well, then?'

'Patience. Everything arranges itself, given time.'

'You seem quite pleased with yourself anyway.'

'Nothing so far has contradicted my little idea—that is why.'

His face grew serious.

'My friend Hastings told me once that he had, as a young man, played a game called The Truth. It was a game where everyone in turn was asked three questions—two of which must be answered truthfully. The third one could be barred. The questions, naturally, were of the most indiscreet kind. But to begin with everyone had to swear that they would indeed speak the truth, and nothing but the truth.'

He paused.

'Well?' said Megan.

'*Eh bien*—me, I want to play that game. Only it is not necessary to have three questions. One will be enough. One question to each of you.'

Agatha Christie

'Of course,' said Clarke impatiently. 'We'll answer anything.'

'Ah, but I want it to be more serious than that. Do you all swear to speak the truth?'

He was so solemn about it that the others, puzzled, became solemn themselves. They all swore as he demanded.

'*Bon,*' said Poirot briskly. 'Let us begin—'

'I'm ready,' said Thora Grey.

'Ah, but ladies first—this time it would not be the politeness. We will start elsewhere.'

He turned to Franklin Clarke.

'What, *mon cher M. Clarke*, did you think of the hats the ladies wore at Ascot this year?'

Franklin Clarke stared at him.

'Is this a joke?'

'Certainly not.'

'Is that seriously your question?'

'It is.'

Clarke began to grin.

'Well, M. Poirot, I didn't actually go to Ascot, but from what I could see of them driving in cars, women's hats for Ascot were an even bigger joke than the hats they wear ordinarily.'

'Fantastic?'

'Quite fantastic.'

Poirot smiled and turned to Donald Fraser.

'When did you take your holiday this year, monsieur?'

It was Fraser's turn to stare.

'My holiday? The first two weeks in August.'

His face quivered suddenly. I guessed that the question had brought the loss of the girl he loved back to him.

Poirot, however, did not seem to pay much attention to the reply. He turned to Thora Grey and I heard the slight difference in his voice. It had tightened up. His question came sharp and clear.

'Mademoiselle, in the event of Lady Clarke's death, would you have married Sir Carmichael if he had asked you?'

The girl sprang up.

'How dare you ask me such a question. It's—it's insulting!'

'Perhaps. But you have sworn to speak the truth. *Eh bien*—Yes or no?'

'Sir Carmichael was wonderfully kind to me. He treated me almost like a daughter. And that's how I felt to him—just affectionate and grateful.'

'Pardon me, but that is not answering Yes or No, mademoiselle.'

She hesitated.

'The answer, of course, is no!'

He made no comment.

'Thank you, mademoiselle.'

He turned to Megan Barnard. The girl's face was very pale. She was breathing hard as though braced up for an ordeal.

Poirot's voice came out like the crack of a whiplash.

'Mademoiselle, what do you hope will be the result of my investigations? Do you want me to find out the truth—or not?'

Her head went back proudly. I was fairly sure of her answer. Megan, I knew, had a fanatical passion for truth.

Her answer came clearly—and it stupefied me.

'No!'

We all jumped. Poirot leant forward studying her face.

'Mademoiselle Megan,' he said, 'you may not want the truth but—*ma foi*—you can speak it!'

He turned towards the door, then, recollecting, went to Mary Drower.

'Tell me, *mon enfant*, have you a young man?'

Mary, who had been looking apprehensive, looked startled and blushed.

'Oh, Mr Poirot. I—I—well, I'm not sure.'

He smiled.

'*Alors c'est bien, mon enfant.*'

He looked round for me.

'Come, Hastings, we must start for Eastbourne.'

The car was waiting and soon we were driving along the coast road that leads through Pevensey to Eastbourne.

'Is it any use asking you anything, Poirot?'

'Not at this moment. Draw your own conclusions as to what I am doing.'

I relapsed into silence.

Poirot, who seemed pleased with himself, hummed a little tune. As we passed through Pevensey he suggested that we stop and have a look over the castle.

As we were returning towards the car, we paused a moment to watch a ring of children—Brownies, I guessed, by their get-up—who were singing a ditty in shrill, untuneful voices…

'What is it that they say, Hastings? I cannot catch the words.'

I listened—till I caught one refrain.

'—*And catch a fox*
And put him in a box
And never let him go.'

'And catch a fox and put him in a box and never let him go!' repeated Poirot.

His face had gone suddenly grave and stern.

'It is very terrible that, Hastings.' He was silent a minute. 'You hunt the fox here?'

'I don't. I've never been able to afford to hunt. And I don't think there's much hunting in this part of the world.'

'I meant in England generally. A strange sport. The waiting at the covert side—then they sound the tally-ho, do they not?—and the run begins—across the country—over the hedges and ditches—and the fox he runs—and sometimes he doubles back—but the dogs—'

'Hounds!'

'—hounds are on his trail, and at last they catch him and he dies—quickly and horribly.'

'I suppose it does sound cruel, but really—'

'The fox enjoys it? Do not say *les bêtises*, my friend. *Tout de même*—it is better that—the quick, cruel death—than what those children were singing...

'To be shut away—in a box—for ever... No, it is not good, that.'

He shook his head. Then he said, with a change of tone:

'Tomorrow, I am to visit the man Cust,' and he added to the chauffeur:

'Back to London.'

'Aren't you going to Eastbourne?' I cried.

'What need? I know—quite enough for my purpose.'

CHAPTER 33

Alexander Bonaparte Cust

I was not present at the interview that took place between Poirot and that strange man—Alexander Bonaparte Cust. Owing to his association with the police and the peculiar circumstances of the case, Poirot had no difficulty in obtaining a Home Office order—but that order did not extend to me, and in any case it was essential, from Poirot's point of view, that that interview should be absolutely private—the two men face to face.

He has given me, however, such a detailed account of what passed between them that I set it down with as much confidence on paper as though I had actually been present.

Mr Cust seemed to have shrunk. His stoop was more apparent. His fingers plucked vaguely at his coat.

For some time, I gather, Poirot did not speak.

He sat and looked at the man opposite him.

The atmosphere became restful—soothing—full of infinite leisure...

It must have been a dramatic moment—this meeting of

the two adversaries in the long drama. In Poirot's place I should have felt the dramatic thrill.

Poirot, however, is nothing if not matter-of-fact. He was absorbed in producing a certain effect upon the man opposite him.

At last he said gently:

'Do you know who I am?'

The other shook his head.

'No—no—I can't say I do. Unless you are Mr Lucas's—what do they call it?—junior. Or perhaps you come from Mr Maynard?'

(Maynard & Cole were the defending solicitors.)

His tone was polite but not very interested. He seemed absorbed in some inner abstraction.

'I am Hercule Poirot...'

Poirot said the words very gently... and watched for the effect.

Mr Cust raised his head a little.

'Oh, yes?'

He said it as naturally as Inspector Crome might have said it—but without the superciliousness.

Then, a minute later, he repeated his remark.

'Oh, yes?' he said, and this time his tone was different—it held an awakened interest. He raised his head and looked at Poirot.

Hercule Poirot met his gaze and nodded his own head gently once or twice.

'Yes,' he said. 'I am the man to whom you wrote the letters.'

At once the contact was broken. Mr Cust dropped his eyes and spoke irritably and fretfully.

'I never wrote to you. Those letters weren't written by me. I've said so again and again.'

'I know,' said Poirot. 'But if you did not write them, who did?'

'An enemy. I must have an enemy. They are all against me. The police—everyone—all against me. It's a gigantic conspiracy.'

Poirot did not reply.

Mr Cust said:

'Everyone's hand has been against me—always.'

'Even when you were a child?'

Mr Cust seemed to consider.

'No—no—not exactly then. My mother was very fond of me. But she was ambitious—terribly ambitious. That's why she gave me those ridiculous names. She had some absurd idea that I'd cut a figure in the world. She was always urging me to assert myself—talking about will-power... saying anyone could be master of his fate... she said I could do anything!'

He was silent for a minute.

'She was quite wrong, of course. I realized that myself quite soon. I wasn't the sort of person to get on in life. I was always doing foolish things—making myself look ridiculous. And I was timid—afraid of people. I had a bad time at school—the boys found out my Christian names—they used to tease me about them... I did very badly at school—in games and work and everything.'

He shook his head.

'Just as well poor mother died. She'd have been disappointed... Even when I was at the Commercial College I was stupid—it took me longer to learn typing and shorthand than anyone else. And yet I didn't *feel* stupid—if you know what I mean.'

He cast a sudden appealing look at the other man.

'I know what you mean,' said Poirot. 'Go on.'

'It was just the feeling that everybody else *thought* me stupid. Very paralysing. It was the same thing later in the office.'

'And later still in the war?' prompted Poirot.

Mr Cust's face lightened up suddenly.

'You know,' he said, 'I enjoyed the war. What I had of it, that was. I felt, for the first time, a man like anybody else. We were all in the same box. I was as good as anyone else.'

His smile faded.

'And then I got that wound on the head. Very slight. But they found out I had fits... I'd always known, of course, that there were times when I hadn't been quite sure what I was doing. Lapses, you know. And of course, once or twice I'd fallen down. But I don't really think they ought to have discharged me for that. No, I don't think it was right.'

'And afterwards?' asked Poirot.

'I got a place as a clerk. Of course there was good money to be got just then. And I didn't do so badly after the war. Of course, a smaller salary... And—I didn't seem to get on. I was always being passed over for promotion. I wasn't go-ahead enough. It grew very difficult—really very difficult.... Especially when the slump came. To tell you the truth, I'd got hardly enough to keep body and soul together (and you've got to look presentable as a clerk) when I got the offer of this stocking job. A salary and commission!'

Poirot said gently:

'But you are aware, are you not, that the firm whom you say employed you deny the fact?'

Mr Cust got excited again.

'That's because they're in the conspiracy—they must be in the conspiracy.'

He went on:

'I've got written evidence—written evidence. I've got their letters to me, giving me instructions as to what places to go to and a list of people to call on.'

'Not *written* evidence exactly—*typewritten* evidence.'

'It's the same thing. Naturally a big firm of wholesale manufacturers typewrite their letters.'

'Don't you know, Mr Cust, that a typewriter can be identified? All those letters were typed by one particular machine.'

'What of it?'

'And that machine was your own—the one found in your room.'

'It was sent me by the firm at the beginning of my job.'

'Yes, but these letters were received *afterwards*. So it looks, does it not, as though *you typed them yourself and posted them to yourself*?'

'No, no! It's all part of the plot against me!'

He added suddenly:

'Besides, their letters *would* be written on the same kind of machine.'

'The same *kind*, but not the same actual machine.'

Mr Cust repeated obstinately:

'It's a plot!'

'And the A B C's that were found in the cupboard?'

'I know nothing about them. I thought they were all stockings.'

'Why did you tick off the name of Mrs Ascher in that first list of people in Andover?'

'Because I decided to start with her. One must begin somewhere.'

'Yes, that is true. *One must begin somewhere.*'

'I don't mean that!' said Mr Cust. 'I don't mean what you mean!'

'*But you know what I meant?*'

Mr Cust said nothing. He was trembling.

'I didn't do it!' he said. 'I'm perfectly innocent! It's all a mistake. Why, look at that second crime—that Bexhill one. I was playing dominoes at Eastbourne. You've got to admit that!'

His voice was triumphant.

'Yes,' said Poirot. His voice was meditative—silky. 'But it's so easy, isn't it, to make a mistake of one day? And if you're an obstinate, positive man, like Mr Strange, you'll never consider the possibility of having been mistaken. What you've said you'll stick to… He's that kind of man. And the hotel register—it's very easy to put down the wrong date when you're signing it—probably no one will notice it at the time.'

'I was playing dominoes that evening!'

'You play dominoes very well, I believe.'

Mr Cust was a little flurried by this.

'I—I—well, I believe I do.'

'It is a very absorbing game, is it not, with a lot of skill in it?'

'Oh, there's a lot of play in it—a lot of play! We used to play a lot in the city, in the lunch hour. You'd be surprised the way total strangers come together over a game of dominoes.'

He chuckled.

'I remember one man—I've never forgotten him because of something he told me—we just got talking over a cup of coffee, and we started dominoes. Well, I felt after twenty minutes that I'd known that man all my life.'

'What was it that he told you?' asked Poirot.

Mr Cust's face clouded over.

'It gave me a turn—a nasty turn. Talking of your fate being written in your hand, he was. And he showed me his hand and the lines that showed he'd have two near escapes of being drowned—and he had had two near escapes. And then he looked at mine and he told me some amazing things. Said I was going to be one of the most celebrated men in England before I died. Said the whole country would be talking about me. But he said—he said…'

Mr Cust broke down—faltered…

'Yes?'

Poirot's gaze held a quiet magnetism. Mr Cust looked at him, looked away, then back again like a fascinated rabbit.

'He said—he said—that it looked as though I might die

a violent death—and he laughed and said: "Almost looks as though you might die on the scaffold," and then he laughed and said that was only his joke...'

He was silent suddenly. His eyes left Poirot's face—they ran from side to side...

'My head—I suffer very badly with my head... the headaches are something cruel sometimes. And then there are times when I don't know—when I don't know...'

He broke down.

Poirot leant forward. He spoke very quietly but with great assurance.

'*But you do know, don't you,*' he said, '*that you committed the murders?*'

Mr Cust looked up. His glance was quite simple and direct. All resistance had left him. He looked strangely at peace.

'Yes,' he said, 'I know.'

'But—I am right, am I not?—*you don't know why you did them?*'

Mr Cust shook his head.

'No,' he said. 'I don't.'

CHAPTER 34

Poirot Explains

We were sitting in a state of tense attention to listen to Poirot's final explanation of the case.

'All along,' he said, 'I have been worried over the *why* of this case. Hastings said to me the other day that the case was ended. I replied to him that the case was the *man!* The mystery was *not the mystery of the murders*, but the *mystery of A B C*. Why did he find it necessary to commit these murders? Why did he select *me* as his adversary?

'It is no answer to say that the man was mentally unhinged. To say a man does mad things because he is mad is merely unintelligent and stupid. A madman is as logical and reasoned in his actions as a sane man—*given his peculiar biased point of view*. For example, if a man insists on going out and squatting about in nothing but a loin cloth his conduct seems eccentric in the extreme. But once you know *that the man himself is firmly convinced that he is Mahatma Gandhi*, then his conduct becomes perfectly reasonable and logical.

Agatha Christie

'What was necessary in this case was to imagine a mind so constituted *that it was logical and reasonable to commit four or more murders* and to announce them beforehand by letters written to Hercule Poirot.

'My friend Hastings will tell you that from the moment I received the first letter I was upset and disturbed. It seemed to me at once that there was something very wrong about the letter.'

'You were quite right,' said Franklin Clarke dryly.

'Yes. But there, at the very start, I made a grave error. I permitted my feeling—my very strong feeling about the letter—to remain a mere impression. I treated it as though it had been an intuition. In a well-balanced, reasoning mind there is no such thing as an intuition—an inspired guess! You *can* guess, of course—and a guess is either right or wrong. If it is right you call it an intuition. If it is wrong you usually do not speak of it again. But what is often called an intuition is really *an impression based on logical deduction or experience*. When an expert feels that there is something wrong about a picture or a piece of furniture or the signature on a cheque he is really basing that feeling on a host of small signs and details. He has no need to go into them minutely—his experience obviates that—the net result is *the definite impression that something is wrong*. But it is not a *guess*, it is an impression based on *experience*.

'*Eh bien*, I admit that I did not regard that first letter in the way I should. It just made me extremely uneasy. The police regarded it as a hoax. I myself took it seriously. I was convinced that a murder would take place in Andover as stated. As you know, a murder *did* take place.

'There was no means at that point, as I well realized, of knowing who the *person* was who had done the deed. The only course open to me was to try and understand just what kind of a person had done it.

'I had certain indications. The letter—the manner of the crime—the person murdered. What I had to discover was: the motive of the crime, the motive of the letter.'

'Publicity,' suggested Clarke.

'Surely an inferiority complex covers that,' added Thora Grey.

'That was, of course, the obvious line to take. But why *me*? *Why Hercule Poirot*? Greater publicity could be ensured by sending the letters to Scotland Yard. More again by sending them to a newspaper. A newspaper might not print the first letter, but by the time the second crime took place, A B C could have been assured of all the publicity the press could give. Why, then, Hercule Poirot? Was it for some *personal* reason? There was, discernible in the letter, a slight anti-foreign bias—but not enough to explain the matter to my satisfaction.

'Then the second letter arrived—and was followed by the murder of Betty Barnard at Bexhill. It became clear now (what I had already suspected) that the murders were to proceed on an alphabetical plan, but the fact, which seemed final to most people, left the main question unaltered to my mind. Why did A B C *need* to commit these murders?'

Megan Barnard stirred in her chair.

Agatha Christie

'Isn't there such a thing as—as a blood lust?' she said.

Poirot turned to her.

'You are quite right, mademoiselle. There *is* such a thing. The lust to kill. But that did not quite fit the facts of the case. A homicidal maniac who desires to kill usually desires to kill *as many victims as possible*. It is a recurring *craving*. The great idea of such a killer is to *hide his tracks*—not to *advertise* them. When we consider the four victims selected—or at any rate three of them (for I know very little of Mr Downes or Mr Earlsfield), we realize that *if he had chosen*, the murderer could have done away with them without incurring any suspicion. Franz Ascher, Donald Fraser or Megan Barnard, possibly Mr Clarke—those are the people the police would have suspected even if they had been unable to get direct proof. An unknown homicidal murderer would not have been thought of! Why, then, did the murderer feel it necessary to call attention to himself? Was it the necessity of leaving on each body a copy of an A B C railway guide? Was *that* the compulsion? Was there some complex connected *with the railway guide*?

'I found it quite inconceivable at this point *to enter into the mind of the murderer*. Surely it could not be magnanimity? A horror of responsibility for the crime being fastened on an innocent person?

'Although I could not answer the main question, certain things I did feel I was learning about the murderer.'

'Such as?' asked Fraser.

'To begin with—that he had a tabular mind. His crimes were listed by alphabetical progression—that was obviously important to him. On the other hand, he had no particular taste in victims—Mrs Ascher, Betty Barnard, Sir Carmichael Clarke, they all differed widely from each other. There was no sex complex—no particular age complex, and that seemed to me to be a very curious fact. If a man kills indiscriminately it is usually because he removes anyone who stands in his way or annoys him. *But the alphabetical progression showed that such was not the case here.* The other type of killer usually selects *a particular type of victim*—nearly always of the opposite sex. There was something haphazard about the procedure of A B C that seemed to me to be at war with the alphabetical selection.

'One slight inference I permitted myself to make. The choice of the A B C suggested to me what I may call a *railway-minded man*. This is more common in men than women. Small boys love trains better than small girls do. It might be the sign, too, of an in some ways undeveloped mind. The "boy" motif still predominated.

'The death of Betty Barnard and the manner of it gave me certain other indications. The manner of her death was particularly suggestive. (Forgive me, Mr Fraser.) To begin with, she was strangled with her own belt—therefore she must almost certainly have been killed by someone with whom she was on friendly or affectionate terms. When I learnt something of her character a picture grew up in my mind.

'Betty Barnard was a flirt. She liked attention from a personable male. Therefore A B C, to persuade her to come out with him, must have had a certain amount of

Agatha Christie

attraction—of *le sex appeal!* He must be able, as you English say, to "get off". He must be capable of the click! I visualize the scene on the beach thus: the man admires her belt. She takes it off, he passes it playfully round her neck—says, perhaps, "I shall strangle you." It is all very playful. She giggles—and he pulls—'

Donald Fraser sprang up. He was livid.

'M. Poirot—for God's sake.'

Poirot made a gesture.

'It is finished. I say no more. It is over. We pass to the next murder, that of Sir Carmichael Clarke. Here the murderer goes back to his first method—the blow on the head. The same alphabetical complex—but one fact worries me a little. To be consistent the murderer should have chosen his towns in some definite sequence.

'If Andover is the 155th name under A, then the B crime should be the 155th also—or it should be the 156th and the C the 157th. Here again the towns seemed to be chosen in rather too *haphazard* a fashion.'

'Isn't that because you're rather biased on that subject, Poirot?' I suggested. 'You yourself are normally methodical and orderly. It's almost a disease with you.'

'No, it is *not* a disease! *Quelle idée!* But I admit that I may be over-stressing that point. *Passons!*

'The Churston crime gave me very little extra help. We were unlucky over it, since the letter announcing it went astray, hence no preparations could be made.

'But by the time the D crime was announced, a very formidable system of defence had been evolved. It must have been obvious that A B C could not much longer hope to get away with his crimes.

'Moreover, it was at this point that the clue of the stockings came into my hand. It was perfectly clear that the presence of an individual selling stockings on and near the scene of each crime could not be a coincidence. Hence the stocking-seller must be the murderer. I may say that his description, as given me by Miss Grey, did not quite correspond with my own picture of the man who strangled Betty Barnard.

'I will pass over the next stages quickly. A fourth murder was committed—the murder of a man named George Earlsfield—it was supposed in mistake for a man named Downes, who was something of the same build and who was sitting near him in the cinema.

'*And now at last comes the turn of the tide*. Events play against A B C instead of into his hands. He is marked down—hunted—and at last arrested.

'The case, as Hastings says, is ended!

'True enough as far as the public is concerned. The man is in prison and will eventually, no doubt, go to Broadmoor. There will be no more murders. Exit! Finis! R.I.P.

'*But not for me!* I know nothing—nothing at all! Neither the *why* nor the *wherefore*.

'And there is one small vexing fact. The man Cust has an alibi for the night of the Bexhill crime.'

'That's been worrying me all along,' said Franklin Clarke.

'Yes. It worried me. For the alibi, it has the air of being *genuine*. But it cannot be genuine unless—and now we come to two very interesting speculations.

Agatha Christie

'Supposing, my friends, that while Cust committed *three* of the crimes—the A, C, and D crimes—*he did not commit the B crime*.'

'M. Poirot. It isn't—'

Poirot silenced Megan Barnard with a look.

'Be quiet, mademoiselle. I am for the truth, I am! I have done with lies. Supposing, I say, *that A B C did not commit the second crime*. It took place, remember, in the early hours of the 25th—the day he had arrived for the crime. Supposing someone had forestalled him? What in those circumstances would he do? Commit a *second* murder, or lie low and *accept the first as a kind of macabre present?*'

'M. Poirot!' said Megan. 'That's a fantastic thought! All the crimes *must* have been committed by the same person!'

He took no notice of her and went steadily on:

'Such a hypothesis had the merit of explaining one fact—*the discrepancy between the personality of Alexander Bonaparte Cust* (who could never have made the click with any girl) *and the personality of Betty Barnard's murderer*. And it has been known, before now, that would-be murderers *have* taken advantage of the crimes committed by other people. Not all the crimes of Jack the Ripper were committed by Jack the Ripper, for instance. So far, so good.

'But then I came up against a definite difficulty.

'Up to the time of the Barnard murder, *no facts about the A B C murders had been made public*. The Andover murder had created little interest. The incident of the open railway guide had not even been mentioned in the press. It therefore followed that whoever killed Betty Barnard *must have had access to facts known only to certain persons*—myself, the police, and certain relations and neighbours of Mrs Ascher.

'That line of research seemed to lead me up against a blank wall.'

The faces that looked at him were blank too. Blank and puzzled.

Donald Fraser said thoughtfully:

'The police, after all, are human beings. And they're good-looking men—'

He stopped, looking at Poirot inquiringly.

Poirot shook his head gently.

'No—it is simpler than that. I told you that there was a second speculation.

'Supposing that Cust was *not* responsible for the killing of Betty Barnard? Supposing that *someone else* killed her. Could that someone else have been responsible *for the other murders too*?'

'But that doesn't make sense!' cried Clarke.

'Doesn't it? I did then *what I ought to have done at first*. I examined the letters I had received from a totally different point of view. I had felt from the beginning that there was something wrong with them—just as a picture expert knows a picture is wrong...

'I had assumed, without pausing to consider, that what was wrong with them was the fact that they were written by a madman.

'Now I examined them again—and this time I came to a totally different conclusion. What was wrong with them was *the fact that they were written by a sane man!*'

'What?' I cried.

'But yes—just that precisely! They were wrong as a picture is wrong—*because they were a fake!* They pretended to be the letters of a madman—of a homicidal lunatic, but in reality they were nothing of the kind.'

'It doesn't make sense,' Franklin Clarke repeated.

'*Mais si!* One must reason—reflect. What would be the object of writing such letters? To focus attention on the writer, to call attention to the murders! *En vérité*, it did not seem to make sense at first sight. And then I saw light. It was to focus attention on several murders—on a *group* of murders... Is it not your great Shakespeare who has said "You cannot see the trees for the wood."'

I did not correct Poirot's literary reminiscences. I was trying to see his point. A glimmer came to me. He went on:

'When do you notice a pin least? When it is in a pin-cushion! When do you notice an individual murder least? When it is one of *a series of related murders*.

'I had to deal with an intensely clever, resourceful murderer—reckless, daring and a thorough gambler. *Not* Mr Cust! He could never have committed these murders! No, I had to deal with a very different stamp of man—a man with a boyish temperament (witness the schoolboy-like letters and the railway guide), an attractive man to women, and a man with a ruthless disregard for human life, a man who was necessarily a prominent person in *one* of the crimes!

'Consider when a man or woman is killed, what are the questions that the police ask? Opportunity. Where everybody was at the time of the crime? Motive. Who benefited by the deceased's death? If the motive and the opportunity are fairly obvious, what is a would-be murderer to do? Fake an alibi—that is, manipulate *time* in some way? But that is always a hazardous proceeding. Our murderer thought of a more fantastic defence. Create a *homicidal* murderer!

'I had now only to review the various crimes and find the possible guilty person. The Andover crime? The most likely suspect for that was Franz Ascher, but I could not imagine Ascher inventing and carrying out such an elaborate scheme, nor could I see him planning a premeditated murder. The Bexhill crime? Donald Fraser was a possibility. He had brains and ability, and a methodical turn of mind. But his motive for killing his sweetheart could only be jealousy—and jealousy does not tend to premeditation. Also I learned that he had his holidays *early* in August, which rendered it unlikely he had anything to do with the Churston crime. We come to the Churston crime next—and at once we are on infinitely more promising ground.

'Sir Carmichael Clarke was an immensely wealthy man. Who inherits his money? His wife, who is dying, has a life interest in it, and it then goes to *his brother Franklin*.'

Poirot turned slowly round till his eyes met those of Franklin Clarke.

'I was quite sure then. The man I had known a long time in my secret mind *was the same as the man whom I had known as a person. A B C and Franklin Clarke were one and the same!* The daring adventurous character, the roving life, the partiality for England that had showed

Agatha Christie

itself, very faintly, in the jeer at foreigners. The attractive free and easy manner—nothing easier for him than to pick up a girl in a café. The methodical tabular mind—he made a list here one day, ticked off over the headings A B C—and finally, the boyish mind—mentioned by Lady Clarke and even shown by his taste in fiction—I have ascertained that there is a book in the library called *The Railway Children* by E. Nesbit. I had no further doubt in my own mind—A B C, the man who wrote the letters and committed the crimes, was *Franklin Clarke*.'

Clarke suddenly burst out laughing.

'Very ingenious! And what about our friend Cust, caught red-handed? What about the blood on his coat? And the knife he hid in his lodgings? He may deny he committed the crimes—'

Poirot interrupted.

'You are quite wrong. He admits the fact.'

'What?' Clarke looked really startled.

'Oh, yes,' said Poirot gently. 'I had no sooner spoken to him than I was aware that Cust *believed himself to be guilty*.'

'And even that didn't satisfy M. Poirot?' said Clarke.

'No. Because as soon as I saw him *I also knew that he could not be guilty!* He has neither the nerve nor the daring—nor, I may add, the *brains* to plan! All along I have been aware of the dual personality of the murderer. Now I see wherein it consisted. Two people were involved—the real murderer, cunning, resourceful and daring—and the *pseudo* murderer, stupid, vacillating and suggestible.

'Suggestible—it is in that word that the mystery of Mr

Cust consists! It was not enough for you, Mr Clarke, to devise this plan of a *series* to distract attention from a *single* crime. You had also to have a stalking horse.

'I think the idea first originated in your mind as the result of a chance encounter in a city coffee den with this odd personality with his bombastic Christian names. You were at that time turning over in your mind various plans for the murder of your brother.'

'Really? And why?'

'Because you were seriously alarmed for the future. I do not know whether you realize it, Mr Clarke, but you played into my hands when you showed me a certain letter written to you by your brother. In it he displayed very clearly his affection and absorption in Miss Thora Grey. His regard may have been a paternal one—or he may have preferred to think it so. Nevertheless, there was a very real danger that on the death of your sister-in-law he might, in his loneliness, turn to this beautiful girl for sympathy and comfort and it might end—as so often happens with elderly men—in his marrying her. Your fear was increased by your knowledge of Miss Grey. You are, I fancy, an excellent, if somewhat cynical judge of character. You judged, whether correctly or not, that Miss Grey was a type of young woman "on the make". You had no doubt that she would jump at the chance of becoming Lady Clarke. Your brother was an extremely healthy and vigorous man. There might be children and your chance of inheriting your brother's wealth would vanish.

'You have been, I fancy, in essence a disappointed man

Agatha Christie

all your life. You have been the rolling stone—and you have gathered very little moss. You were bitterly jealous of your brother's wealth.

'I repeat then that, turning over various schemes in your mind, your meeting with Mr Cust gave you an idea. His bombastic Christian names, his account of his epileptic seizures and of his headaches, his whole shrinking and insignificant personality, struck you as fitting him for the tool you wanted. The whole alphabetical plan sprang into your mind—Cust's initials—the fact that your brother's name began with a C and that he lived at Churston were the nucleus of the scheme. You even went so far as to hint to Cust at his possible end—though you could hardly hope that that suggestion would bear the rich fruit that it did!

'Your arrangements were excellent. In Cust's name you wrote for a large consignment of hosiery to be sent to him. You yourself sent a number of A B C's looking like a similar parcel. You wrote to him—a typed letter purporting to be from the same firm offering him a good salary and commission. Your plans were so well laid beforehand that you typed all the letters that were sent subsequently, *and then presented him with the machine on which they had been typed*.

'You had now to look about for two victims whose names began with A and B respectively and who lived at places also beginning with those same letters.

'You hit on Andover as quite a likely spot and your preliminary reconnaissance there led you to select Mrs Ascher's shop as the scene of the first crime. Her name was written clearly over the door, and you found by experiment

The A B C Murders

that she was usually alone in the shop. Her murder needed nerve, daring and reasonable luck.

'For the letter B you had to vary your tactics. Lonely women in shops might conceivably have been warned. I should imagine that you frequented a few cafés and teashops, laughing and joking with the girls there and finding out whose name began with the right letter and who would be suitable for your purpose.

'In Betty Barnard you found just the type of girl you were looking for. You took her out once or twice, explaining to her that you were a married man, and that outings must therefore take place in a somewhat hole-and-corner manner.

'Then, your preliminary plans completed, you set to work! You sent the Andover list to Cust, directing him to go there on a certain date, and you sent off the first A B C letter to me.

'On the appointed day you went to Andover—and killed Mrs Ascher—without anything occurring to damage your plans.

'Murder No. 1 was successfully accomplished.

'For the second murder, you took the precaution of committing it, in reality, *the day before*. I am fairly certain that Betty Barnard was killed well before midnight on the 24th July.

'We now come to murder No. 3—the important—in fact, the *real* murder from your point of view.

'And here a full meed of praise is due to Hastings, who made a simple and obvious remark to which no attention was paid.

'*He suggested that the third letter went astray intentionally!*

Agatha Christie

'And he was right!...

'In that one simple fact lies the answer to the question that has puzzled me so all along. Why were the letters addressed in the first place to Hercule Poirot, a private detective, and not to the police?

'Erroneously I imagined some personal reason.

'Not at all! The letters were sent to me because the essence of your plan was that one of them *should be wrongly addressed and go astray*—but you cannot arrange for a letter addressed to the Criminal Investigation Department of Scotland Yard to go astray! It is necessary to have a *private* address. You chose me as a fairly well-known person, and a person who was sure to take the letters to the police—and also, in your rather insular mind, you enjoyed scoring off a foreigner.

'You addressed your envelope very cleverly—Whitehaven—Whitehorse—quite a natural slip. Only Hastings was sufficiently perspicacious to disregard subtleties and go straight for the obvious!

'Of course the letter was *meant* to go astray! The police were to be set on the trail *only when the murder was safely over*. Your brother's nightly walk provided you with the opportunity. And so successfully had the A B C terror taken hold on the public mind that the possibility of your guilt never occurred to anyone.

'After the death of your brother, of course, your object was accomplished. You had no wish to commit any more murders. On the other hand, if the murders stopped without reason, a suspicion of the truth might come to someone.

'Your stalking horse, Mr Cust, had so successfully lived up

to his role of the invisible—because insignificant—man, that so far no one had noticed that the same person had been seen in the vicinity of the three murders! To your annoyance, even his visit to Combeside had not been mentioned. The matter had passed completely out of Miss Grey's head.

'Always daring, you decided that one more murder must take place but this time the trail must be well blazed.

'You selected Doncaster for the scene of operations.

'Your plan was very simple. You yourself would be on the scene in the nature of things. Mr Cust would be ordered to Doncaster by his firm. Your plan was to follow him round and trust to opportunity. Everything fell out well. Mr Cust went to a cinema. That was simplicity itself. You sat a few seats away from him. When he got up to go, you did the same. You pretended to stumble, leaned over and stabbed a dozing man in the row in front, slid the A B C on to his knees and managed to collide heavily with Mr Cust in the darkened doorway, wiping the knife on his sleeve and slipping it into his pocket.

'You were not in the least at pains to choose a victim whose name began with D. Anyone would do! You assumed—and quite rightly—that it would be considered to be a *mistake*. There was sure to be someone whose name began with D not far off in the audience. It would be assumed that he had been intended to be the victim.

'And now, my friends, let us consider the matter from the point of view of the false A B C—from the point of view of Mr Cust.

'The Andover crime means nothing to him. He is shocked

and surprised by the Bexhill crime—why, he himself was there about the time! Then comes the Churston crime and the headlines in the newspapers. An A B C crime at Andover when he was there, an A B C crime at Bexhill, and now another close by... Three crimes *and he has been at the scene of each of them*. Persons suffering from epilepsy often have blanks when they cannot remember what they have done... Remember that Cust was a nervous, highly neurotic subject and extremely suggestible.

'Then he receives the order to go to Doncaster.

'Doncaster! And the next A B C crime is to be in Doncaster. He must have felt as though it was fate. He loses his nerve, fancies his landlady is looking at him suspiciously, and tells her he is going to Cheltenham.

'He goes to Doncaster because it is his duty. In the afternoon he goes to a cinema. Possibly he dozes off for a minute or two.

'Imagine his feelings when on his return to his inn he discovers *that there is blood on his coat sleeve and a bloodstained knife in his pocket*. All his vague forebodings leap into certainty.

'*He—he himself—is the killer!* He remembers his headaches—his lapses of memory. He is quite sure of the truth—*he, Alexander Bonaparte Cust, is a homicidal lunatic*.

'His conduct after that is the conduct of a hunted animal. He gets back to his lodgings in London. He is safe there—known. They think he has been in Cheltenham. He has the knife with him still—a thoroughly stupid thing to do, of course. He hides it behind the hall stand.

'Then, one day, he is warned that the police are coming. It is the end! They *know*!

'The hunted animal does his last run...

'I don't know why he went to Andover—a morbid desire, I think, to go and look at the place where the crime was committed—the crime *he* committed though he can remember nothing about it...

'He has no money left—he is worn out... his feet lead him of his own accord to the police station.

'But even a cornered beast will fight. Mr Cust fully believes that he did the murders but he sticks strongly to his plea of innocence. And he holds with desperation to that alibi for the second murder. At least that cannot be laid to his door.

'As I say, when I saw him, I knew at once that he was *not* the murderer and that my name *meant* nothing to *him*. I knew, too, that he *thought* himself the murderer!

'After he had confessed his guilt to me, I knew more strongly than ever that my own theory was right.'

'Your theory,' said Franklin Clarke, 'is absurd!'

Poirot shook his head.

'No, Mr Clarke. You were safe enough *so long as no one suspected you*. Once you *were* suspected proofs were easy to obtain.'

'Proofs?'

'Yes. I found the stick that you used in the Andover and Churston murders in a cupboard at Combeside. An ordinary stick with a thick knob handle. A section of wood had been removed and melted lead poured in. Your photograph was picked out from half a dozen others by two people who saw you leaving the cinema when you were supposed to be on the race-course at Doncaster. You were identified at Bexhill the other day by Milly Higley and a girl from the Scarlet Runner Roadhouse, where you took Betty Barnard to dine on the fatal evening. And finally—most damning of all—you *overlooked a most elementary precaution*. You left a fingerprint on Cust's typewriter—the typewriter that, if you are innocent, you *could never have handled*.'

Clarke sat quite still for a minute, then he said:

'*Rouge, impair, manque!*—you win, M. Poirot! But it was worth trying!'

With an incredibly rapid motion he whipped out a small automatic from his pocket and held it to his head.

I gave a cry and involuntarily flinched as I waited for the report.

But no report came—the hammer clicked harmlessly.

Clarke stared at it in astonishment and uttered an oath.

'No, Mr Clarke,' said Poirot. 'You may have noticed I had a new manservant today—a friend of mine—an expert sneak thief. He removed your pistol from your pocket, unloaded it, and returned it, all without you being aware of the fact.'

'You unutterable little jackanapes of a foreigner!' cried Clarke, purple with rage.

'Yes, yes, that is how you feel. No, Mr Clarke, no easy death for you. You told Mr Cust that you had had near escapes from drowning. You know what that means—that you were born for another fate.'

'You—'

Words failed him. His face was livid. His fists clenched menacingly.

Two detectives from Scotland Yard emerged from the next room. One of them was Crome. He advanced and uttered his time-honoured formula: 'I warn you that anything you say may be used as evidence.'

'He has said quite enough,' said Poirot, and he added to Clarke: 'You are very full of an insular superiority, but for myself I consider your crime not an English crime at all—not above-board—not *sporting*—'

CHAPTER 35

Finale

I am sorry to relate that as the door closed behind Franklin Clarke I laughed hysterically.

Poirot looked at me in mild surprise.

'It's because you told him his crime was not sporting,' I gasped.

'It was quite true. It was abominable—not so much the murder of his brother—but the cruelty that condemned an unfortunate man to a living death. *To catch a fox and put him in a box and never let him go!* That is not *le sport*!'

Megan Barnard gave a deep sigh.

'I can't believe it—I can't. Is it true?'

'Yes, mademoiselle. The nightmare is over.'

She looked at him and her colour deepened.

Poirot turned to Fraser.

'Mademoiselle Megan, all along, was haunted by a fear that it was you who had committed the second crime.'

Donald Fraser said quietly:

'I fancied so myself at one time.'

'Because of your dream?' He drew a little nearer to the young man and dropped his voice confidentially. 'Your dream has a very natural explanation. It is that you find that already the image of one sister fades in your memory and that its place is taken by the other sister. Mademoiselle Megan replaces her sister in your heart, but since you cannot bear to think of yourself being unfaithful so soon to the dead, you strive to stifle the thought, to kill it! That is the explanation of the dream.'

Fraser's eyes went towards Megan.

'Do not be afraid to forget,' said Poirot gently. 'She was not so well worth remembering. In Mademoiselle Megan you have one in a hundred—*un coeur magnifique!*'

Donald Fraser's eyes lit up.

'I believe you are right.'

We all crowded round Poirot asking questions, elucidating this point and that.

'Those questions, Poirot? That you asked of everybody. Was there any point in them?'

'Some of them were *simplement une blague*. But I learnt one thing that I wanted to know—*that Franklin Clarke was in London when the first letter was posted*—and also I wanted to see his face when I asked my question of Mademoiselle Thora. He was off his guard. I saw all the malice and anger in his eyes.'

'You hardly spared my feelings,' said Thora Grey.

'I do not fancy you returned me a truthful answer, mademoiselle,' said Poirot dryly. 'And now your second expectation is disappointed. Franklin Clarke will not inherit his brother's money.'

She flung up her head.

'Is there any need for me to stay here and be insulted?'

'None whatever,' said Poirot and held the door open politely for her.

'That fingerprint clinched things, Poirot,' I said thoughtfully. 'He went all to pieces when you mentioned that.'

'Yes, they are useful—fingerprints.'

He added thoughtfully:

'I put that in to please you, my friend.'

'But, Poirot,' I cried, 'wasn't it *true*?'

'Not in the least, *mon ami*,' said Hercule Poirot.

I must mention a visit we had from Mr Alexander Bonaparte Cust a few days later. After wringing Poirot's hand and endeavouring very incoherently and unsuccessfully to thank him, Mr Cust drew himself up and said:

'Do you know, a newspaper has actually offered me a hundred pounds—*a hundred pounds*—for a brief account of my life and history—I—I really don't know what to do about it.'

'I should not accept a hundred,' said Poirot. 'Be firm. Say five hundred is your price. And do not confine yourself to one newspaper.'

'Do you really think—that I might—'

'You must realize,' said Poirot, smiling, 'that you are a very famous man. Practically the most famous man in England today.'

Mr Cust drew himself up still further. A beam of delight irradiated his face.

'Do you know, I believe you're right! Famous! In all the papers. I shall take your advice, M. Poirot. The money will be most agreeable—most agreeable. I shall have a little holiday... And then I want to give a nice wedding present to Lily Marbury—a dear girl—really a dear girl, M. Poirot.'

Poirot patted him encouragingly on the shoulder.

'You are quite right. Enjoy yourself. And—just a little word—what about a visit to an oculist? Those headaches, it is probably that you want new glasses.'

'You think that it may have been that all the time?'

'I do.'

Mr Cust shook him warmly by the hand.

'You're a very great man, M. Poirot.'

Poirot, as usual, did not disdain the compliment. He did not even succeed in looking modest.

When Mr Cust had strutted importantly out, my old friend smiled across at me.

'So, Hastings—we went hunting once more, did we not? *Vive le sport.*'

THE HOLLOW

ALSO BY AGATHA CHRISTIE

Mysteries
The Man in the Brown Suit
The Secret of Chimneys
The Seven Dials Mystery
The Mysterious Mr Quin
The Sittaford Mystery
The Hound of Death
The Listerdale Mystery
Why Didn't They Ask Evans?
Parker Pyne Investigates
Murder Is Easy
And Then There Were None
Towards Zero
Death Comes as the End
Sparkling Cyanide
Crooked House
They Came to Baghdad
Destination Unknown
Spider's Web *
The Unexpected Guest *
Ordeal by Innocence
The Pale Horse
Endless Night
Passenger To Frankfurt
Problem at Pollensa Bay
While the Light Lasts

Poirot
The Mysterious Affair at Styles
The Murder on the Links
Poirot Investigates
The Murder of Roger Ackroyd
The Big Four
The Mystery of the Blue Train
Black Coffee *
Peril at End House
Lord Edgware Dies
Murder on the Orient Express
Three-Act Tragedy
Death in the Clouds
The ABC Murders
Murder in Mesopotamia
Cards on the Table
Murder in the Mews
Dumb Witness
Death on the Nile
Appointment with Death
Hercule Poirot's Christmas
Sad Cypress
One, Two, Buckle My Shoe
Evil Under the Sun
Five Little Pigs
The Hollow
The Labours of Hercules
Taken at the Flood
Mrs McGinty's Dead
After the Funeral
Hickory Dickory Dock
Dead Man's Folly
Cat Among the Pigeons
The Adventure of the Christmas Pudding
The Clocks
Third Girl
Hallowe'en Party
Elephants Can Remember
Poirot's Early Cases
Curtain: Poirot's Last Case

Marple
The Murder at the Vicarage
The Thirteen Problems
The Body in the Library
The Moving Finger
A Murder Is Announced
They Do It with Mirrors
A Pocket Full of Rye
4.50 from Paddington
The Mirror Crack'd from Side to Side
A Caribbean Mystery
At Bertram's Hotel
Nemesis
Sleeping Murder
Miss Marple's Final Cases

Tommy & Tuppence
The Secret Adversary
Partners in Crime
N or M?
By the Pricking of My Thumbs
Postern of Fate

Published as Mary Westmacott
Giant's Bread
Unfinished Portrait
Absent in the Spring
The Rose and the Yew Tree
A Daughter's a Daughter
The Burden

Memoirs
An Autobiography
Come, Tell Me How You Live
The Grand Tour

Plays and Stories
Akhnaton
The Mousetrap and Other Plays
The Floating Admiral †
Star Over Bethlehem
Hercule Poirot and the Greenshore Folly

* novelized by Charles Osborne † contributor

Agatha Christie®

The Hollow

HarperCollins*Publishers*

HarperCollins*Publishers* Ltd
1 London Bridge Street
London SE1 9GF
www.harpercollins.co.uk

This paperback edition 2015

First published in Great Britain by
Collins 1946

10

Agatha Christie® Poirot® The Hollow™
Copyright © 1946 Agatha Christie Limited. All rights reserved.
www.agathachristie.com

A catalogue record for this book is
available from the British Library

ISBN 978-0-00-812958-3

Set in Sabon by Born Group using Atomik ePublisher from Easypress

Printed and bound in by
CPI Group (UK) Ltd, Croydon, CR0 4YY

All rights reserved. No part of this publication may be
reproduced, stored in a retrieval system, or transmitted,
in any form or by any means, electronic, mechanical,
photocopying, recording or otherwise, without the prior
written permission of the publishers.

This book is sold subject to the condition that it shall not,
by way of trade or otherwise, be lent, re-sold, hired out or
otherwise circulated without the publisher's prior consent
in any form of binding or cover other than that in which it
is published and without a similar condition including this
condition being imposed on the subsequent purchaser.

MIX
Paper from
responsible sources
FSC **FSC C007454**
www.fsc.org

FSC is a non-profit international organisation established to promote
the responsible management of the world's forests. Products carrying the
FSC label are independently certified to assure consumers that they come
from forests that are managed to meet the social, economic and
ecological needs of present and future generations,
and other controlled sources.

Find out more about HarperCollins and the environment at
www.harpercollins.co.uk/green

For
LARRY and DANAE
With apologies for using their swimming pool
as the scene of a murder

CHAPTER 1

At six thirteen am on a Friday morning Lucy Angkatell's big blue eyes opened upon another day and, as always, she was at once wide awake and began immediately to deal with the problems conjured up by her incredibly active mind. Feeling urgently the need of consultation and conversation, and selecting for the purpose her young cousin, Midge Hardcastle, who had arrived at The Hollow the night before, Lady Angkatell slipped quickly out of bed, threw a négligée round her still graceful shoulders, and went along the passage to Midge's room. Since she was a woman of disconcertingly rapid thought processes, Lady Angkatell, as was her invariable custom, commenced the conversation in her own mind, supplying Midge's answers out of her own fertile imagination.

The conversation was in full swing when Lady Angkatell flung open Midge's door.

'—And so, darling, you really must agree that the weekend *is* going to present difficulties!'

'Eh? Hwah!' Midge grunted inarticulately, aroused thus abruptly from a satisfying and deep sleep.

Lady Angkatell crossed to the window, opening the shutters

Agatha Christie

and jerking up the blind with a brisk movement, letting in the pale light of a September dawn.

'Birds!' she observed, peering with kindly pleasure through the pane. 'So sweet.'

'What?'

'Well, at any rate, the weather isn't going to present difficulties. It looks as though it has set in fine. That's something. Because if a lot of discordant personalities are boxed up indoors, I'm sure you will agree with me that it makes it ten times worse. Round games perhaps, and that would be like last year when I shall never forgive myself about poor Gerda. I said to Henry afterwards it was most thoughtless of me—and one *has* to have her, of course, because it would be so rude to ask John without her, but it really does make things difficult—and the worst of it is that she is so nice—really it seems odd sometimes that anyone so nice as Gerda is should be so devoid of any kind of intelligence, and if that is what they mean by the law of compensation I don't really think it is at all fair.'

'What *are* you talking about, Lucy?'

'The weekend, darling. The people who are coming tomorrow. I have been thinking about it all night and I have been dreadfully bothered about it. So it really is a relief to talk it over with you, Midge. You are always so sensible and practical.'

'Lucy,' said Midge sternly. 'Do you know what time it is?'

'Not exactly, darling. I never do, you know.'

'It's quarter-past six.'

'Yes, dear,' said Lady Angkatell, with no signs of contrition.

The Hollow

Midge gazed sternly at her. How maddening, how absolutely impossible Lucy was! Really, thought Midge, I don't know why we put up with her!

Yet even as she voiced the thought to herself, she was aware of the answer. Lucy Angkatell was smiling, and as Midge looked at her, she felt the extraordinary pervasive charm that Lucy had wielded all her life and that even now, at over sixty, had not failed her. Because of it, people all over the world, foreign potentates, ADCs, Government officials, had endured inconvenience, annoyance and bewilderment. It was the childlike pleasure and delight in her own doings that disarmed and nullified criticism. Lucy had but to open those wide blue eyes and stretch out those fragile hands, and murmur, 'Oh! but I'm so *sorry...*' and resentment immediately vanished.

'Darling,' said Lady Angkatell, 'I'm so *sorry*. You should have told me!'

'I'm telling you now—but it's too late! I'm thoroughly awake.'

'What a shame! But you *will* help me, won't you?'

'About the weekend? Why? What's wrong with it?'

Lady Angkatell sat down on the edge of the bed. It was not, Midge thought, like anyone else sitting on your bed. It was as insubstantial as though a fairy had poised itself there for a minute.

Lady Angkatell stretched out fluttering white hands in a lovely, helpless gesture.

'All the wrong people coming—the wrong people to be *together*, I mean—not in themselves. They're all charming really.'

Agatha Christie

'Who *is* coming?'

Midge pushed thick wiry black hair back from her square forehead with a sturdy brown arm. Nothing insubstantial or fairylike about her.

'Well, John and Gerda. That's all right by itself. I mean, John is delightful—*most* attractive. And as for poor Gerda—well, I mean, we must all be very kind. Very, very kind.'

Moved by an obscure instinct of defence, Midge said:

'Oh, come now, she's not as bad as that.'

'Oh, darling, she's pathetic. Those *eyes*. And she never seems to understand a single word one says.'

'She doesn't,' said Midge. 'Not what you say—but I don't know that I blame her. Your mind, Lucy, goes so fast, that to keep pace with it your conversation takes the most amazing leaps. All the connecting links are left out.'

'Just like a monkey,' said Lady Angkatell vaguely.

'But who else is coming besides the Christows? Henrietta, I suppose?'

Lady Angkatell's face brightened.

'Yes—and I really do feel that she will be a tower of strength. She always is. Henrietta, you know, is really kind—kind all through, not just on top. She will help a lot with poor Gerda. She was simply wonderful last year. That was the time we played limericks, or word-making, or quotations—or one of those things, and we had all finished and were reading them out when we suddenly discovered that poor dear Gerda hadn't even begun. She wasn't even sure what the game was. It was dreadful, wasn't it, Midge?'

The Hollow

'Why anyone ever comes to stay with the Angkatells, I don't know,' said Midge. 'What with the brainwork, and the round games, and your peculiar style of conversation, Lucy.'

'Yes, darling, we must be trying—and it must always be hateful for Gerda, and I often think that if she had any spirit she would stay away—but however, there it was, and the poor dear looked so bewildered and—well—mortified, you know. And John looked so dreadfully impatient. And I simply couldn't think of how to make things all right again—and it was then that I felt so grateful to Henrietta. She turned right round to Gerda and asked about the pullover she was wearing—really a dreadful affair in faded lettuce green—too depressing and jumble sale, darling—and Gerda brightened up at once, it seems that she had knitted it herself, and Henrietta asked her for the pattern, and Gerda looked so happy and proud. And that is what I mean about Henrietta. She can always *do* that sort of thing. It's a kind of knack.'

'She takes trouble,' said Midge slowly.

'Yes, and she knows what to say.'

'Ah,' said Midge. 'But it goes further than saying. Do you know, Lucy, that Henrietta actually knitted that pullover?'

'Oh, my dear.' Lady Angkatell looked grave. 'And wore it?'

'And wore it. Henrietta carries things through.'

'And was it very dreadful?'

'No. On Henrietta it looked very nice.'

'Well, of course it would. That's just the difference between Henrietta and Gerda. Everything Henrietta does she does well and it turns out right. She's clever about nearly everything, as well as in her own line. I must say, Midge, that if anyone carries us through this weekend, it will be Henrietta. She will be nice to Gerda and she will amuse Henry, and she'll keep John in a good temper and I'm sure she'll be most helpful with David.'

'David Angkatell?'

'Yes. He's just down from Oxford—or perhaps Cambridge. Boys of that age are so difficult—especially when they are intellectual. David is very intellectual. One wishes that they could put off being intellectual until they were rather older. As it is, they always glower at one so and bite their nails and seem to have so many spots and sometimes an Adam's apple as well. And they either won't speak at all, or else are very loud and contradictory. Still, as I say, I am trusting to Henrietta. She is very tactful and asks the right kind of questions, and being a sculptress they respect her, especially as she doesn't just carve animals or children's heads but does advanced things like that curious affair in metal and plaster that she exhibited at the New Artists last year. It looked rather like a Heath Robinson step-ladder. It was called Ascending Thought—or something like that. It is the kind of thing that would impress a boy like David... I thought myself it was just silly.'

'Dear Lucy!'

'But some of Henrietta's things I think are quite lovely. That Weeping Ash-tree figure, for instance.'

'Henrietta has a touch of real genius, I think. And she is a very lovely and satisfying person as well,' said Midge.

Lady Angkatell got up and drifted over to the window again. She played absent-mindedly with the blind cord.

'Why acorns, I wonder?' she murmured.

'Acorns?'

'On the blind cord. Like pineapples on gates. I mean, there must be a *reason*. Because it might just as easily be a fir-cone or a pear, but it's always an acorn. Mast, they call it in crosswords—you know, for pigs. So curious, I always think.'

'Don't ramble off, Lucy. You came in here to talk about the weekend and I can't see why you were so anxious about it. If you manage to keep off round games, and try to be coherent when you're talking to Gerda, and put Henrietta on to tame intellectual David, where is the difficulty?'

'Well, for one thing, darling, Edward is coming.'

'Oh, Edward.' Midge was silent for a moment after saying the name.

Then she asked quietly:

'What on earth made you ask Edward for this weekend?'

'I didn't, Midge. That's just it. He asked himself. Wired to know if we could have him. You know what Edward is. How sensitive. If I'd wired back "No," he'd probably never have asked himself again. He's like that.'

Midge nodded her head slowly.

Yes, she thought, Edward was like that. For an instant she saw his face clearly, that very dearly loved face. A face with something of Lucy's insubstantial charm; gentle, diffident, ironic...

'Dear Edward,' said Lucy, echoing the thought in Midge's mind.

She went on impatiently:

Agatha Christie

'If only Henrietta would make up her mind to marry him. She is really fond of him, I know she is. If they had been here some weekend without the Christows... As it is, John Christow has always the most unfortunate effect on Edward. John, if you know what I mean, becomes so much *more* so and Edward becomes so much *less* so. You understand?'

Again Midge nodded.

'And I can't put the Christows off because this weekend was arranged long ago, but I do feel, Midge, that it is all going to be difficult, with David glowering and biting his nails, and with trying to keep Gerda from feeling out of it, and with John being so positive and dear Edward so negative—'

'The ingredients of the pudding are not promising,' murmured Midge.

Lucy smiled at her.

'Sometimes,' she said meditatively, 'things arrange themselves quite simply. I've asked the Crime man to lunch on Sunday. It will make a distraction, don't you think so?'

'Crime man?'

'Like an egg,' said Lady Angkatell. 'He was in Baghdad, solving something, when Henry was High Commissioner. Or perhaps it was afterwards? We had him to lunch with some other Duty people. He had on a white duck suit, I remember, and a pink flower in his buttonhole, and black patent-leather shoes. I don't remember much about it because I never think it's very interesting who killed who. I mean, once they are dead it doesn't seem to matter why, and to make a fuss about it all seems so silly...'

The Hollow

'But have you any crimes down here, Lucy?'

'Oh, no, darling. He's in one of those funny new cottages—you know, beams that bump your head and a lot of very good plumbing and quite the wrong kind of garden. London people like that sort of thing. There's an actress in the other, I believe. They don't live in them all the time like we do. Still,' Lady Angkatell moved vaguely across the room, 'I dare say it pleases them. Midge, darling, it's sweet of you to have been so helpful.'

'I don't think I have been so very helpful.'

'Oh, haven't you?' Lucy Angkatell looked surprised. 'Well, have a nice sleep now and don't get up to breakfast, and when you do get up, do be as rude as ever you like.'

'Rude?' Midge looked surprised. 'Why! Oh!' she laughed. 'I see! Penetrating of you, Lucy. Perhaps I'll take you at your word.'

Lady Angkatell smiled and went out. As she passed the open bathroom door and saw the kettle and gas-ring, an idea came to her.

People were fond of tea, she knew—and Midge wouldn't be called for hours. She would make Midge some tea. She put the kettle on and then went on down the passage.

She paused at her husband's door and turned the handle, but Sir Henry Angkatell, that able administrator, knew his Lucy. He was extremely fond of her, but he liked his morning sleep undisturbed. The door was locked.

Lady Angkatell went on into her own room. She would have liked to have consulted Henry, but later would do. She stood by her open window, looked out for a moment

Agatha Christie

or two, then she yawned. She got into bed, laid her head on the pillow and in two minutes was sleeping like a child.

In the bathroom the kettle came to the boil and went on boiling...

'Another kettle gone, Mr Gudgeon,' said Simmons, the housemaid.

Gudgeon, the butler, shook his grey head.

He took the burnt-out kettle from Simmons and, going into the pantry, produced another kettle from the bottom of the plate cupboard where he had a stock of half a dozen.

'There you are, Miss Simmons. Her ladyship will never know.'

'Does her ladyship often do this sort of thing?' asked Simmons.

Gudgeon sighed.

'Her ladyship,' he said, 'is at once kind-hearted and very forgetful, if you know what I mean. But in this house,' he continued, 'I see to it that everything possible is done to spare her ladyship annoyance or worry.'

CHAPTER 2

Henrietta Savernake rolled up a little strip of clay and patted it into place. She was building up the clay head of a girl with swift practised skill.

In her ears, but penetrating only to the edge of her understanding, was the thin whine of a slightly common voice:

'And I do think, Miss Savernake, that I was quite right! "Really," I said, "if *that's* the line you're going to take!" Because I do think, Miss Savernake, that a girl owes it to herself to make a stand about these sort of things—if you know what I mean. "I'm not accustomed," I said, "to having things like that said to me, and I can only say that you must have a very nasty imagination!" One does hate unpleasantness, but I do think I was right to make a stand, don't you, Miss Savernake?'

'Oh, absolutely,' said Henrietta with a fervour in her voice which might have led someone who knew her well to suspect that she had not been listening very closely.

'"And if your wife says things of that kind," I said, "well, I'm sure *I* can't help it!" I don't know how it is, Miss Savernake, but it seems to be trouble wherever I go, and I'm sure it's not *my* fault. I mean, men are so susceptible, aren't they?' The model gave a coquettish little giggle.

Agatha Christie

'Frightfully,' said Henrietta, her eyes half-closed.

'Lovely,' she was thinking. 'Lovely that plane just below the eyelid—and the other plane coming up to meet it. That angle by the jaw's wrong... I must scrape off there and build up again. It's tricky.'

Aloud she said in her warm, sympathetic voice:

'It must have been *most* difficult for you.'

'I do think jealousy's so unfair, Miss Savernake, and so *narrow*, if you know what I mean. It's just envy, if I may say so, because someone's better-looking and younger than they are.'

Henrietta, working on the jaw, said absently, 'Yes, of course.'

She had learned the trick, years ago, of shutting her mind into watertight compartments. She could play a game of bridge, conduct an intelligent conversation, write a clearly constructed letter, all without giving more than a fraction of her essential mind to the task. She was now completely intent on seeing the head of Nausicaa build itself up under her fingers, and the thin, spiteful stream of chatter issuing from those very lovely childish lips penetrated not at all into the deeper recesses of her mind. She kept the conversation going without effort. She was used to models who wanted to talk. Not so much the professional ones—it was the amateurs who, uneasy at their forced inactivity of limb, made up for it by bursting into garrulous self-revelation. So an inconspicuous part of Henrietta listened and replied, and, very far and remote, the real Henrietta commented, 'Common mean spiteful little piece—but what eyes... Lovely lovely lovely eyes...'

The Hollow

Whilst she was busy on the eyes, let the girl talk. She would ask her to keep silent when she got to the mouth. Funny when you came to think of it, that that thin stream of spite should come out through those perfect curves.

'Oh, damn,' thought Henrietta with sudden frenzy, 'I'm ruining that eyebrow arch! What the hell's the matter with it? I've over-emphasized the bone—it's sharp, not thick...'

She stood back again frowning from the clay to the flesh and blood sitting on the platform.

Doris Saunders went on:

'"Well," I said, "I really don't see why your husband shouldn't give me a present if he likes, and I don't think," I said, "you ought to make insinuations of that kind." It was ever such a nice bracelet, Miss Savernake, reely quite lovely—and of course I dare say the poor fellow couldn't reely afford it, but I do think it was nice of him, and I certainly wasn't going to give it back!'

'No, no,' murmured Henrietta.

'And it's not as though there was anything between us—anything *nasty*, I mean—there was nothing of *that* kind.'

'No,' said Henrietta, 'I'm sure there wouldn't be...'

Her brow cleared. For the next half-hour she worked in a kind of fury. Clay smeared itself on her forehead, clung to her hair, as she pushed an impatient hand through it. Her eyes had a blind intense ferocity. It was coming... She was getting it...

Now, in a few hours, she would be out of her agony—the agony that had been growing upon her for the last ten days.

Nausicaa—she had been Nausicaa, she had got up with Nausicaa and had breakfast with Nausicaa and gone out

Agatha Christie

with Nausicaa. She had tramped the streets in a nervous excitable restlessness, unable to fix her mind on anything but a beautiful blind face somewhere just beyond her mind's eye—hovering there just not able to be clearly seen. She had interviewed models, hesitated over Greek types, felt profoundly dissatisfied...

She wanted something—something to give her the start—something that would bring her own already partially realized vision alive. She had walked long distances, getting physically tired out and welcoming the fact. And driving her, harrying her, was that urgent incessant longing—to *see*—

There was a blind look in her own eyes as she walked. She saw nothing of what was around her. She was straining—straining the whole time to make that face come nearer... She felt sick, ill, miserable...

And then, suddenly, her vision had cleared and with normal human eyes she had seen opposite her in the bus which she had boarded absent-mindedly and with no interest in its destination—she had seen—yes, *Nausicaa*! A foreshortened childish face, half-parted lips and eyes—lovely vacant, blind eyes.

The girl rang the bell and got out. Henrietta followed her.

She was now quite calm and businesslike. She had got what she wanted—the agony of baffled search was over.

'Excuse me speaking to you. I'm a professional sculptor and to put it frankly, your head is just what I have been looking for.'

She was friendly, charming and compelling as she knew how to be when she wanted something.

The Hollow

Doris Saunders had been doubtful, alarmed, flattered.

'Well, I don't know, I'm sure. If it's just the *head*. Of course, I've never *done* that sort of thing!'

Suitable hesitations, delicate financial inquiry.

'Of course I should insist on your accepting the proper professional fee.'

And so here was Nausicaa, sitting on the platform, enjoying the idea of her attractions being immortalized (though not liking very much the examples of Henrietta's work which she could see in the studio!) and enjoying also the revelation of her personality to a listener whose sympathy and attention seemed to be so complete.

On the table beside the model were her spectacles—the spectacles that she put on as seldom as possible owing to vanity, preferring to feel her way almost blindly sometimes, since she admitted to Henrietta that without them she was so short-sighted that she could hardly see a yard in front of her.

Henrietta had nodded comprehendingly. She understood now the physical reason for that blank and lovely stare.

Time went on. Henrietta suddenly laid down her modelling tools and stretched her arms widely.

'All right,' she said, 'I've finished. I hope you're not too tired?'

'Oh, no, thank you, Miss Savernake. It's been very interesting, I'm sure. Do you mean, it's really done—so soon?'

Henrietta laughed.

'Oh, no, it's not actually finished. I shall have to work on it quite a bit. But it's finished as far as you're concerned. I've got what I wanted—built up the planes.'

Agatha Christie

The girl came down slowly from the platform. She put on her spectacles and at once the blind innocence and vague confiding charm of the face vanished. There remained now an easy, cheap prettiness.

She came to stand by Henrietta and looked at the clay model.

'Oh,' she said doubtfully, disappointment in her voice. 'It's not very like me, is it?'

Henrietta smiled.

'Oh, no, it's not a portrait.'

There was, indeed, hardly a likeness at all. It was the setting of the eyes—the line of the cheekbones—that Henrietta had seen as the essential keynote of her conception of Nausicaa. This was not Doris Saunders, it was a blind girl about whom a poem could be made. The lips were parted as Doris's were parted, but they were not Doris's lips. They were lips that would speak another language and would utter thoughts that were not Doris's thoughts—

None of the features were clearly defined. It was Nausicaa remembered, not seen...

'Well,' said Miss Saunders doubtfully, 'I suppose it'll look better when you've got on with it a bit... And you reely don't want me any more?'

'No, thank you,' said Henrietta ('And thank God I don't!' said her inner mind). 'You've been simply splendid. I'm very grateful.'

She got rid of Doris expertly and returned to make herself some black coffee. She was tired—she was horribly tired. But happy—happy and at peace.

'Thank goodness,' she thought, 'now I can be a human being again.'

And at once her thoughts went to John.

'John,' she thought. Warmth crept into her cheeks, a sudden quick lifting of the heart made her spirits soar.

'Tomorrow,' she thought, 'I'm going to The Hollow... I shall see John...'

She sat quite still, sprawled back on the divan, drinking down the hot, strong liquid. She drank three cups of it. She felt vitality surging back.

It was nice, she thought, to be a human being again... and not that other thing. Nice to have stopped feeling restless and miserable and driven. Nice to be able to stop walking about the streets unhappily, looking for something, and feeling irritable and impatient because, really, you didn't know what you were looking for! Now, thank goodness, there would be only hard work—and who minded hard work?

She put down the empty cup and got up and strolled back to Nausicaa. She looked at it for some time, and slowly a little frown crept between her brows.

It wasn't—it wasn't quite—

What was it that was wrong?...

Blind eyes.

Blind eyes that were more beautiful than any eyes that could see... Blind eyes that tore at your heart because they were blind... Had she got that or hadn't she?

She'd got it, yes—but she'd got something else as well. Something that she hadn't meant or thought about... The structure was all right—yes, surely. But where did it come from—that faint, insidious suggestion?...

The suggestion, somewhere, of a common spiteful mind.

She hadn't been listening, not really listening. Yet somehow, in through her ears and out at her fingers, it had worked its way into the clay.

And she wouldn't, she knew she wouldn't, be able to get it out again...

Henrietta turned away sharply. Perhaps it was fancy. Yes, surely it was fancy. She would feel quite differently about it in the morning. She thought with dismay:

'How vulnerable one is...'

She walked, frowning, up to the end of the studio. She stopped in front of her figure of The Worshipper.

That was all right—a lovely bit of pearwood, graining just right. She'd saved it up for ages, hoarding it.

She looked at it critically. Yes, it was good. No doubt about that. The best thing she had done for a long time—it was for the International Group. Yes, quite a worthy exhibit.

She'd *got* it all right: the humility, the strength in the neck muscles, the bowed shoulders, the slightly upraised face—a featureless face, since worship drives out personality.

Yes, submission, adoration—and that final devotion that is beyond, not this side, idolatry...

Henrietta sighed. If only, she thought, John had not been so angry.

It had startled her, that anger. It had told her something about him that he did not, she thought, know himself.

He had said flatly: 'You can't exhibit that!'

The Hollow

And she had said, as flatly, 'I shall.'

She went slowly back to Nausicaa. There was nothing there, she thought, that she couldn't put right. She sprayed it and wrapped it up in the damp cloths. It would have to stand over until Monday or Tuesday. There was no hurry now. The urgency had gone—all the essential planes were there. It only needed patience.

Ahead of her were three happy days with Lucy and Henry and Midge—and John!

She yawned, stretched herself like a cat stretches itself with relish and abandon, pulling out each muscle to its fullest extent. She knew suddenly how very tired she was.

She had a hot bath and went to bed. She lay on her back staring at a star or two through the skylight. Then from there her eyes went to the one light always left on, the small bulb that illuminated the glass mask that had been one of her earliest bits of work. Rather an obvious piece, she thought now. Conventional in its suggestion.

Lucky, thought Henrietta, that one outgrew oneself...

And now, sleep! The strong black coffee that she had drunk did not bring wakefulness in its train unless she wished it to do so. Long ago she had taught herself the essential rhythm that could bring oblivion at call.

You took thoughts, choosing them out of your store, and then, not dwelling on them, you let them slip through the fingers of your mind, never clutching at them, never dwelling on them, no concentration...just letting them drift gently past.

Outside in the Mews a car was being revved up—somewhere there was hoarse shouting and laughing. She took

Agatha Christie

the sounds into the stream of her semi-consciousness.

The car, she thought, was a tiger roaring...yellow and black...striped like the striped leaves—leaves and shadows—a hot jungle...and then down the river—a wide tropical river...to the sea and the liner starting...and hoarse voices calling goodbye—and John beside her on the deck...she and John starting—blue sea and down into the dining-saloon—smiling at him across the table—like dinner at the Maison Dorée—poor John, so angry!...out into the night air—and the car, the feeling of sliding in the gears—effortless, smooth, racing out of London...up over Shovel Down...the trees...tree worship... The Hollow... Lucy... John... John... Ridgeway's Disease...dear John...

Passing into unconsciousness now, into a happy beatitude.

And then some sharp discomfort, some haunting sense of guilt pulling her back. Something she ought to have done. Something that she had shirked.

Nausicaa?

Slowly, unwillingly, Henrietta got out of bed. She switched on the lights, went across to the stand and unwrapped the cloths.

She took a deep breath.

Not Nausicaa—Doris Saunders!

A pang went through Henrietta. She was pleading with herself, 'I can get it right—I can get it right...'

'Stupid,' she said to herself. 'You know quite well what you've got to do.'

Because if she didn't do it now, at once—tomorrow she wouldn't have the courage. It was like destroying your flesh and blood. It hurt—yes, it hurt.

The Hollow

Perhaps, thought Henrietta, cats feel like this when one of their kittens has something wrong with it and they kill it.

She took a quick, sharp breath, then she seized the clay, twisting it off the armature, carrying it, a large heavy lump, to dump it in the clay bin.

She stood there breathing deeply, looking down at her clay-smeared hands, still feeling the wrench to her physical and mental self. She cleaned the clay off her hands slowly.

She went back to bed feeling a curious emptiness, yet a sense of peace.

Nausicaa, she thought sadly, would not come again. She had been born, had been contaminated and had died.

'Queer,' thought Henrietta, 'how things can seep into you without your knowing it.'

She hadn't been listening—not really listening—and yet knowledge of Doris's cheap, spiteful little mind had seeped into her mind and had, unconsciously, influenced her hands.

And now the thing that had been Nausicaa—Doris—was only clay—just the raw material that would, soon, be fashioned into something else.

Henrietta thought dreamily, 'Is that, then, what *death* is? Is what we call personality just the shaping of it—the impress of somebody's thought? Whose thought? God's?'

That was the idea, wasn't it, of Peer Gynt? Back into the Button Moulder's ladle.

> '*Where am I myself, the whole man, the true man? Where am I with God's mark upon my brow?*'

Agatha Christie

Did John feel like that? He had been so tired the other night—so disheartened. Ridgeway's Disease... Not one of those books told you who Ridgeway was! Stupid, she thought, she would like to know... Ridgeway's Disease.

CHAPTER 3

John Christow sat in his consulting-room, seeing his last patient but one for that morning. His eyes, sympathetic and encouraging, watched her as she described—explained—went into details. Now and then he nodded his head, understandingly. He asked questions, gave directions. A gentle glow pervaded the sufferer. Dr Christow was really wonderful! He was so interested—so truly concerned. Even talking to him made one feel stronger.

John Christow drew a sheet of paper towards him and began to write. Better give her a laxative, he supposed. That new American proprietary—nicely put up in cellophane and attractively coated in an unusual shade of salmon pink. Very expensive, too, and difficult to get—not every chemist stocked it. She'd probably have to go to that little place in Wardour Street. That would be all to the good—probably buck her up no end for a month or two, then he'd have to think of something else. There was nothing he could do for her. Poor physique and nothing to be done about it! Nothing to get your teeth into. Not like old mother Crabtree...

A boring morning. Profitable financially—but nothing else. God, he was tired! Tired of sickly women and their

Agatha Christie

ailments. Palliation, alleviation—nothing to it but that. Sometimes he wondered if it was worth it. But always then he remembered St Christopher's, and the long row of beds in the Margaret Russell Ward, and Mrs Crabtree grinning up at him with her toothless smile.

He and she understood each other! She was a fighter, not like that limp slug of a woman in the next bed. She was on his side, she wanted to live—though God knew why, considering the slum she lived in, with a husband who drank and a brood of unruly children, and she herself obliged to work day in day out, scrubbing endless floors of endless offices. Hard unremitting drudgery and few pleasures! But she wanted to live—she enjoyed life—just as he, John Christow, enjoyed life! It wasn't the circumstances of life they enjoyed, it was life itself—the zest of existence. Curious—a thing one couldn't explain. He thought to himself that he must talk to Henrietta about that.

He got up to accompany his patient to the door. His hand took hers in a warm clasp, friendly, encouraging. His voice was encouraging too, full of interest and sympathy. She went away revived, almost happy. Dr Christow took such an interest!

As the door closed behind her, John Christow forgot her, he had really been hardly aware of her existence even when she had been there. He had just done his stuff. It was all automatic. Yet, though it had hardly ruffled the surface of his mind, he had given out strength. His had been the automatic response of the healer and he felt the sag of depleted energy.

The Hollow

'God,' he thought again, 'I'm tired.'

Only one more patient to see and then the clear space of the weekend. His mind dwelt on it gratefully. Golden leaves tinged with red and brown, the soft moist smell of autumn—the road down through the woods—the wood fires, Lucy, *most* unique and delightful of creatures—with her curious, elusive will-o'-the-wisp mind. He'd rather have Henry and Lucy than any host and hostess in England. And The Hollow was the most delightful house he knew. On Sunday he'd walk through the woods with Henrietta—up on to the crest of the hill and along the ridge. Walking with Henrietta he'd forget that there were any sick people in the world. Thank goodness, he thought, there's never anything the matter with Henrietta.

And then with a sudden, quick twist of humour:

'She'd never let on to me if there were!'

One more patient to see. He must press the bell on his desk. Yet, unaccountably, he delayed. Already he was late. Lunch would be ready upstairs in the dining-room. Gerda and the children would be waiting. He must get on.

Yet he sat there motionless. He was so tired—so very tired.

It had been growing on him lately, this tiredness. It was at the root of the constantly increasing irritability which he was aware of but could not check. Poor Gerda, he thought, she has a lot to put up with. If only she was not so submissive—so ready to admit herself in the wrong when, half the time, it was *he* who was to blame! There were days when everything that Gerda said or did conspired to irritate him, and mainly, he thought ruefully, it was her virtues that irritated him. It was her patience, her unselfishness, her

Agatha Christie

subordination of her wishes to his, that aroused his ill-humour. And she never resented his quick bursts of temper, never stuck to her own opinion in preference to his, never attempted to strike out a line of her own.

(*Well, he thought, that's why you married her, isn't it? What are you complaining about? After that summer at San Miguel...*)

Curious, when you came to think of it, that the very qualities that irritated him in Gerda were the qualities he wanted so badly to find in Henrietta. What irritated him in Henrietta (no, that was the wrong word—it was anger, not irritation, that she inspired)—what angered him there was Henrietta's unswerving rectitude where he was concerned. It was so at variance to her attitude to the world in general. He had said to her once:

'I think you are the greatest liar I know.'

'Perhaps.'

'You are always willing to say anything to people if only it pleases them.'

'That always seems to me more important.'

'More important than speaking the truth?'

'Much more.'

'Then why in God's name can't you lie a little more to *me*?'

'Do you want me to?'

'Yes.'

'I'm sorry, John, but I can't.'

'You must know so often what I want you to say—'

Come now, he mustn't start thinking of Henrietta. He'd be seeing her this very afternoon. The thing to do now was

The Hollow

to get on with things! Ring the bell and see this last damned woman. Another sickly creature! One-tenth genuine ailment and nine-tenths hypochondria! Well, why shouldn't she enjoy ill-health if she cared to pay for it? It balanced the Mrs Crabtrees of this world.

But still he sat there motionless.

He was tired—he was so very tired. It seemed to him that he had been tired for a very long time. There was something he wanted—wanted badly.

And there shot into his mind the thought: '*I want to go home.*'

It astonished him. Where had that thought come from? And what did it mean? Home? He had never had a home. His parents had been Anglo-Indians, he had been brought up, bandied about from aunt to uncle, one set of holidays with each. The first permanent home he had had, he supposed, was this house in Harley Street.

Did he think of this house as home? He shook his head. He knew that he didn't.

But his medical curiosity was aroused. What had he meant by that phrase that had flashed out suddenly in his mind?

I want to go home.

There must be something—some image.

He half-closed his eyes—there must be some *background*.

And very clearly, before his mind's eye, he saw the deep blue of the Mediterranean Sea, the palms, the cactus and the prickly pear; he smelt the hot summer dust, and remembered the cool feeling of the water after lying on the beach in the sun. *San Miguel!*

Agatha Christie

He was startled—a little disturbed. He hadn't thought of San Miguel for years. He certainly didn't want to go back there. All that belonged to a past chapter in his life.

That was twelve—fourteen—fifteen years ago. And he'd done the right thing! His judgment had been absolutely right! He'd been madly in love with Veronica but it wouldn't have done. Veronica would have swallowed him body and soul. She was the complete egoist and she had made no bones about admitting it! Veronica had grabbed most things that she wanted, but she hadn't been able to grab him! He'd escaped. He had, he supposed, treated her badly from the conventional point of view. In plain words, he had jilted her! But the truth was that he intended to live his own life, and that was a thing that Veronica would not have allowed him to do. She intended to live *her* life and carry John along as an extra.

She had been astonished when he had refused to come with her to Hollywood.

She had said disdainfully:

'If you really want to be a doctor you can take a degree over there, I suppose, but it's quite unnecessary. You've got enough to live on, and *I* shall be making heaps of money.'

And he had replied vehemently:

'But I'm *keen* on my profession. I'm going to work with *Radley*.'

His voice—a young enthusiastic voice—was quite awed.

Veronica sniffed.

'That funny snuffy old man?'

'That funny snuffy old man,' John had said angrily, 'has done some of the most valuable research work on Pratt's Disease—'

The Hollow

She had interrupted: Who cared for Pratt's Disease? California, she said, was an enchanting climate. And it was fun to see the world. She added: 'I shall hate it without you. I want you, John—I *need* you.'

And then he had put forward the, to Veronica, amazing suggestion that she should turn down the Hollywood offer and marry him and settle down in London.

She was amused and quite firm. She was going to Hollywood, and she loved John, and John must marry her and come too. She had had no doubts of her beauty and of her power.

He had seen that there was only one thing to be done and he had done it. He had written to her breaking off the engagement.

He had suffered a good deal, but he had had no doubts as to the wisdom of the course he had taken. He'd come back to London and started work with Radley, and a year later he had married Gerda, who was as unlike Veronica in every way as it was possible to be...

The door opened and his secretary, Beryl Collins, came in.

'You've still got Mrs Forrester to see.'

He said shortly, 'I know.'

'I thought you might have forgotten.'

She crossed the room and went out at the farther door. Christow's eyes followed her calm withdrawal. A plain girl, Beryl, but damned efficient. He'd had her six years. She never made a mistake, she was never flurried or worried or hurried. She had black hair and a muddy complexion and a determined chin. Through strong glasses, her clear grey eyes surveyed him and the rest of the universe with the same dispassionate attention.

He had wanted a plain secretary with no nonsense about her, and he had got a plain secretary with no nonsense about her, but sometimes, illogically, John Christow felt aggrieved! By all the rules of stage and fiction, Beryl should have been hopelessly devoted to her employer. But he had always known that he cut no ice with Beryl. There was no devotion, no self-abnegation—Beryl regarded him as a definitely fallible human being. She remained unimpressed by his personality, uninfluenced by his charm. He doubted sometimes whether she even *liked* him.

He had heard her once speaking to a friend on the telephone.

'No,' she had been saying, 'I don't really think he is *much* more selfish than he was. Perhaps rather more thoughtless and inconsiderate.'

He had known that she was speaking of him, and for quite twenty-four hours he had been annoyed about it.

Although Gerda's indiscriminate enthusiasm irritated him, Beryl's cool appraisal irritated him too. In fact, he thought, nearly everything irritates me...

Something wrong there. Overwork? Perhaps. No, that was the excuse. This growing impatience, this irritable tiredness, it had some deeper significance. He thought: 'This won't do. I can't go on this way. What's the matter with me? If I could get *away*...'

There it was again—the blind idea rushing up to meet the formulated idea of escape.

I want to go home...

The Hollow

Damn it all, 404 Harley Street *was* his home!

And Mrs Forrester was sitting in the waiting-room. A tiresome woman, a woman with too much money and too much spare time to think about her ailments.

Someone had once said to him: 'You must get very tired of these rich patients always fancying themselves ill. It must be so satisfactory to get to the poor, who only come when there is something *really* the matter with them!' He had grinned. Funny the things people believed about the Poor with a capital P. They should have seen old Mrs Pearstock, on five different clinics, up every week, taking away bottles of medicine, liniments for her back, linctus for her cough, aperients, digestive mixtures. 'Fourteen years I've 'ad the brown medicine, Doctor, and it's the only thing does me any good. That young doctor last week writes me down a *white* medicine. No good at all! It stands to reason, doesn't it, Doctor? I mean, I've 'ad me brown medicine for fourteen years, and if I don't 'ave me liquid paraffin and them brown pills...'

He could hear the whining voice now—excellent physique, sound as a bell—even all the physic she took couldn't really do her any harm!

They were the same, sisters under the skin, Mrs Pearstock from Tottenham and Mrs Forrester of Park Lane Court. You listened and you wrote scratches with your pen on a piece of stiff expensive notepaper, or on a hospital card as the case might be...

God, he was tired of the whole business...
Blue sea, the faint sweet smell of mimosa, hot dust...

Fifteen years ago. All that was over and done with—yes, done with, thank heaven. He'd had the courage to break off the whole business.

Courage? said a little imp somewhere. Is *that* what you call it?

Well, he'd done the sensible thing, hadn't he? It had been a wrench. Damn it all, it had hurt like hell! But he'd gone through with it, cut loose, come home, and married Gerda.

He'd got a plain secretary and he'd married a plain wife. That was what he wanted, wasn't it? He'd had enough of beauty, hadn't he? He'd seen what someone like Veronica could do with her beauty—seen the effect it had on every male within range. After Veronica, he'd wanted safety. Safety and peace and devotion and the quiet, enduring things of life. He'd wanted, in fact, Gerda! He'd wanted someone who'd take her ideas of life from him, who would accept his decisions and who wouldn't have, for one moment, any ideas of her own...

Who was it who had said that the real tragedy of life was that you got what you wanted?

Angrily he pressed the buzzer on his desk.

He'd deal with Mrs Forrester.

It took him a quarter of an hour to deal with Mrs Forrester. Once again it was easy money. Once again he listened, asked questions, reassured, sympathized, infused something of his own healing energy. Once more he wrote out a prescription for an expensive proprietary.

The sickly neurotic woman who had trailed into the room left it with a firmer step, with colour in her cheeks, with a feeling that life might possibly after all be worth while.

The Hollow

John Christow leant back in his chair. He was free now—free to go upstairs to join Gerda and the children—free from the preoccupations of illness and suffering for a whole weekend.

But he felt still that strange disinclination to move, that new queer lassitude of the will.

He was tired—tired—tired...

CHAPTER 4

In the dining-room of the flat above the consulting room Gerda Christow was staring at a joint of mutton.

Should she or should she not send it back to the kitchen to be kept warm?

If John was going to be much longer it would be cold—congealed, and that would be dreadful.

But on the other hand the last patient had gone, John would be up in a moment, if she sent it back there would be delay—John was so impatient. 'But surely you knew I was just coming…' There would be that tone of suppressed exasperation in his voice that she knew and dreaded. Besides, it would get over-cooked, dried up—John hated over-cooked meat.

But on the other hand he disliked cold food very much indeed.

At any rate the dish was nice and hot.

Her mind oscillated to and fro, and her sense of misery and anxiety deepened.

The whole world had shrunk to a leg of mutton getting cold on a dish.

On the other side of the table her son Terence, aged twelve, said:

'Boracic salts burn with a green flame, sodium salts are yellow.'

The Hollow

Gerda looked distractedly across the table at his square, freckled face. She had no idea what he was talking about.

'Did you know that, Mother?'

'Know what, dear?'

'About salts.'

Gerda's eye flew distractedly to the salt-cellar. Yes, salt and pepper were on the table. That was all right. Last week Lewis had forgotten them and that had annoyed John. There was always something...

'It's one of the chemical tests,' said Terence in a dreamy voice. 'Jolly interesting. *I* think.'

Zena, aged nine, with a pretty, vacuous face, whimpered:

'I want my dinner. Can't we start, Mother?'

'In a minute, dear, we must wait for Father.'

'*We* could start,' said Terence. 'Father wouldn't mind. You know how fast he eats.'

Gerda shook her head.

Carve the mutton? But she never could remember which was the right side to plunge the knife in. Of course, perhaps Lewis had put it the right way on the dish—but sometimes she didn't—and John was always annoyed if it was done the wrong way. And, Gerda reflected desperately, it always *was* the wrong way when she did it. Oh, dear, how cold the gravy was getting—a skin was forming on the top of it—she *must* send it back—but then if John were just coming—and surely he would be coming now.

Her mind went round and round unhappily...like a trapped animal.

*

Agatha Christie

Sitting back in his consulting-room chair, tapping with one hand on the table in front of him, conscious that upstairs lunch must be ready, John Christow was nevertheless unable to force himself to get up.

San Miguel...blue sea...smell of mimosa...a scarlet tritoma upright against green leaves...the hot sun...the dust...that desperation of love and suffering...

He thought: 'Oh, God, not that. Never that again! That's over...'

He wished suddenly that he had never known Veronica, never married Gerda, never met Henrietta...

Mrs Crabtree, he thought, was worth the lot of them. That had been a bad afternoon last week. He'd been so pleased with the reactions. She could stand .005 by now. And then had come that alarming rise in toxicity and the DL reaction had been negative instead of positive.

The old bean had lain there, blue, gasping for breath—peering up at him with malicious, indomitable eyes.

'Making a bit of a guinea pig out of me, ain't you, dearie? Experimenting—that kinder thing.'

'We want to get you well,' he had said, smiling down at her.

'Up to your tricks, yer mean!' She had grinned suddenly. 'I don't mind, bless yer. You carry on, Doctor! Someone's got to be first, that's it, ain't it? 'Ad me 'air permed, I did, when I was a kid. It wasn't 'alf a difficult business then. Couldn't get a comb through it. But there—I enjoyed the fun. You can 'ave yer fun with me. *I* can stand it.'

'Feel pretty bad, don't you?' His hand was on her pulse. Vitality passed from him to the panting old woman on the bed.

The Hollow

'Orful, I feel. You're about right! 'Asn't gone according to plan—that's it, isn't it? Never you mind. Don't you lose 'eart. I can stand a lot, I can!'

John Christow said appreciatively:

'You're fine. I wish all my patients were like you.'

'I wanter get well—that's why! I wanter get well. Mum, she lived to be eighty-eight—and old Grandma was ninety when she popped off. We're long-livers in our family, we are.'

He had come away miserable, racked with doubt and uncertainty. He'd been so sure he was on the right track. Where had he gone wrong? How diminish the toxicity and keep up the hormone content and at the same time neutralize the pantratin?...

He'd been too cocksure—he'd taken it for granted that he'd circumvented all the snags.

And it was then, on the steps of St Christopher's, that a sudden desperate weariness had overcome him—a hatred of all this long, slow, wearisome clinical work, and he'd thought of Henrietta, thought of her suddenly not as herself, but of her beauty and her freshness, her health and her radiant vitality—and the faint smell of primroses that clung about her hair.

And he had gone to Henrietta straight away, sending a curt telephone message home about being called away. He had strode into the studio and taken Henrietta in his arms, holding her to him with a fierceness that was new in their relationship.

There had been a quick, startled wonder in her eyes. She had freed herself from his arms and had made him coffee. And as she moved about the studio she had thrown out desultory questions. Had he come, she asked, straight from the hospital?

Agatha Christie

He didn't want to talk about the hospital. He wanted to make love to Henrietta and forget that the hospital and Mrs Crabtree and Ridgeway's Disease and all the rest of the caboodle existed.

But, at first unwillingly, then more fluently, he answered her questions. And presently he was striding up and down, pouring out a spate of technical explanations and surmises. Once or twice he paused, trying to simplify—to explain:

'You see, you have to get a reaction—'

Henrietta said quickly:

'Yes, yes, the DL reaction has to be positive. I understand that. Go on.'

He said sharply, 'How do *you* know about the DL reaction?'

'I got a book—'

'What book? Whose?'

She motioned towards the small book table. He snorted.

'Scobell? Scobell's no good. He's fundamentally unsound. Look here, if you want to read—don't—'

She interrupted him.

'I only want to understand some of the terms you use— enough so as to understand you without making you stop to explain everything the whole time. Go on. I'm following you all right.'

'Well,' he said doubtfully, 'remember Scobell's unsound.' He went on talking. He talked for two hours and a half. Reviewing the setbacks, analysing the possibilities, outlining possible theories. He was hardly conscious of Henrietta's presence. And yet, more than once, as he hesitated, her quick intelligence took him a step on the way, seeing, almost before

The Hollow

he did, what he was hesitating to advance. He was interested now, and his belief in himself was creeping back. He had been right—the main theory was correct—and there were ways, more ways than one, of combating the toxic symptoms.

And then, suddenly, he was tired out. He'd got it all clear now. He'd get on to it tomorrow morning. He'd ring up Neill, tell him to combine the two solutions and try that. Yes, try that. By God, he wasn't going to be beaten!

'I'm tired,' he said abruptly. 'My God, I'm tired.'

And he had flung himself down and slept—slept like the dead.

He had awoken to find Henrietta smiling at him in the morning light and making tea and he had smiled back at her.

'Not at all according to plan,' he said.

'Does it matter?'

'No. No. You are rather a nice person, Henrietta.' His eye went to the bookcase. 'If you're interested in this sort of thing, I'll get you the proper stuff to read.'

'I'm not interested in this sort of thing. I'm interested in you, John.'

'You can't read Scobell.' He took up the offending volume. 'The man's a charlatan.'

And she had laughed. He could not understand why his strictures on Scobell amused her so.

But that was what, every now and then, startled him about Henrietta. The sudden revelation, disconcerting to him, that she was able to laugh at him.

He wasn't used to it. Gerda took him in deadly earnest. And Veronica had never thought about anything but herself.

Agatha Christie

But Henrietta had a trick of throwing her head back, of looking at him through half-closed eyes, with a sudden tender half-mocking little smile, as though she were saying: 'Let me have a good look at this funny person called John... Let me get a long way away and look at him...'

It was, he thought, very much the same as the way she screwed up her eyes to look at her work—or a picture. It was—damn it all—it was *detached*. He didn't want Henrietta to be detached. He wanted Henrietta to think only of him, never to let her mind stray away from him.

('Just what you object to in Gerda, in fact,' said his private imp, bobbing up again.)

The truth of it was that he was completely illogical. He didn't know what he wanted.

('*I want to go home.*' What an absurd, what a ridiculous phrase. It didn't *mean* anything.)

In an hour or so at any rate he'd be driving out of London—forgetting about sick people with their faint sour 'wrong' smell...sniffing wood smoke and pines and soft wet autumn leaves... The very motion of the car would be soothing—that smooth, effortless increase of speed.

But it wouldn't, he reflected suddenly, be at all like that because owing to a slightly strained wrist, Gerda would have to drive, and Gerda, God help her, had never been able to begin to drive a car! Every time she changed gear he would be silent, grinding his teeth together, managing not to say anything because he knew, by bitter experience, that when he did say anything Gerda became immediately worse. Curious that no one had ever been able to teach

The Hollow

Gerda to change gear—not even Henrietta. He'd turned her over to Henrietta, thinking that Henrietta's enthusiasm might do better than his own irritability.

For Henrietta loved cars. She spoke of cars with the lyrical intensity that other people gave to spring, or the first snowdrop.

'Isn't he a beauty, John? Doesn't he just purr along?' (For Henrietta's cars were always masculine.) 'He'll do Bale Hill in third—not straining at all—quite effortlessly. Listen to the even way he ticks over.'

Until he had burst out suddenly and furiously:

'Don't you think, Henrietta, you could pay *some* attention to me and forget the damned car for a minute or two!'

He was always ashamed of these outbursts.

He never knew when they would come upon him out of a blue sky.

It was the same thing over her work. He realized that her work was good. He admired it—and hated it—at the same time.

The most furious quarrel he had had with her had arisen over that.

Gerda had said to him one day:

'Henrietta has asked me to sit for her.'

'What?' His astonishment had not, if he came to think of it, been flattering. '*You?*'

'Yes, I'm going over to the studio tomorrow.'

'What on earth does she want you for?'

Yes, he hadn't been very polite about it. But luckily Gerda hadn't realized that fact. She had looked pleased about it.

Agatha Christie

He suspected Henrietta of one of those insincere kindnesses of hers—Gerda, perhaps, had hinted that she would like to be modelled. Something of that kind.

Then, about ten days later, Gerda had shown him triumphantly a small plaster statuette.

It was a pretty thing—technically skilful like all Henrietta's work. It idealized Gerda—and Gerda herself was clearly pleased about it.

'I really think it's rather charming, John.'

'Is that Henrietta's work? It means nothing—nothing at all. I don't see how she came to do a thing like that.'

'It's different, of course, from her abstract work—but I think it's good, John, I really do.'

He had said no more—after all, he didn't want to spoil Gerda's pleasure. But he tackled Henrietta about it at the first opportunity.

'What did you want to make that silly thing of Gerda for? It's unworthy of you. After all, you usually turn out decent stuff.'

Henrietta said slowly:

'I didn't think it was bad. Gerda seemed quite pleased.'

'Gerda was delighted. She would be. Gerda doesn't know art from a coloured photograph.'

'It wasn't bad art, John. It was just a portrait statuette—quite harmless and not at all pretentious.'

'You don't usually waste your time doing that kind of stuff—'

He broke off, staring at a wooden figure about five feet high.

'Hallo, what's this?'

'It's for the International Group. Pearwood. The Worshipper.'

The Hollow

She watched him. He stared and then—suddenly, his neck swelled and he turned on her furiously.

'So that's what you wanted Gerda for? How dare you?'

'I wondered if you'd see...'

'See it? Of course I see it. It's *here*.' He placed a finger on the broad heavy neck muscles.

Henrietta nodded.

'Yes, it's the neck and shoulders I wanted—and that heavy forward slant—the submission—that bowed look. It's wonderful!'

'Wonderful? Look here, Henrietta, I won't have it. You're to leave Gerda alone.'

'Gerda won't know. Nobody will know. You know Gerda would never recognize herself here—nobody else would either. And it *isn't* Gerda. It isn't *anybody*.'

'*I* recognized it, didn't I?'

'You're different, John. You—see things.'

'It's the damned cheek of it! I won't have it, Henrietta! I won't have it. Can't you see that it was an indefensible thing to do?'

'Was it?'

'Don't you know it was? Can't you *feel* it was? Where's your usual sensitiveness?'

Henrietta said slowly:

'You don't understand, John. I don't think I could ever make you understand... You don't know what it is to want something—to look at it day after day—that line of the neck—those muscles—the angle where the head goes forward—that heaviness round the jaw. I've been looking at them, wanting them—every time I saw Gerda... In the end I just had to have them!'

'Unscrupulous!'

'Yes, I suppose just that. But when you want things, in that way, you just have to take them.'

'You mean you don't care a damn about anybody else. You don't care about Gerda—'

'Don't be stupid, John. That's why I made that statuette thing. To please Gerda and make her happy. I'm not inhuman!'

'Inhuman is exactly what you are.'

'Do you think—honestly—that Gerda would ever recognize herself in this?'

John looked at it unwillingly. For the first time his anger and resentment became subordinated to his interest. A strange submissive figure, a figure offering up worship to an unseen deity—the face raised—blind, dumb, devoted—terribly strong, terribly fanatical... He said:

'That's rather a terrifying thing that you have made, Henrietta!'

Henrietta shivered slightly.

She said, 'Yes—*I* thought that...'

John said sharply:

'What's she looking at—who is it? There in front of her?'

Henrietta hesitated. She said, and her voice had a queer note in it:

'I don't know. But I *think*—she might be looking at *you*, John.'

CHAPTER 5

In the dining-room the child Terry made another scientific statement.

'Lead salts are more soluble in cold water than hot. If you add potassium iodide you get a yellow precipitate of lead iodide.'

He looked expectantly at his mother but without any real hope. Parents, in the opinion of young Terence, were sadly disappointing.

'Did you know that, Mother?'

'I don't know anything about chemistry, dear.'

'You could read about it in a book,' said Terence.

It was a simple statement of fact, but there was a certain wistfulness behind it.

Gerda did not hear the wistfulness. She was caught in the trap of her anxious misery. Round and round and round. She had been miserable ever since she woke up this morning and realized that at last this long-dreaded weekend with the Angkatells was upon her. Staying at The Hollow was always a nightmare to her. She always felt bewildered and forlorn. Lucy Angkatell with her sentences that were never finished, her swift inconsequences, and her obvious

Agatha Christie

attempts at kindliness, was the figure she dreaded most. But the others were nearly as bad. For Gerda it was two days of sheer martyrdom—to be endured for John's sake.

For John that morning as he stretched himself had remarked in tones of unmitigated pleasure:

'Splendid to think we'll be getting into the country this weekend. It will do you good, Gerda, just what you need.'

She had smiled mechanically and had said with unselfish fortitude: 'It will be delightful.'

Her unhappy eyes had wandered round the bedroom. The wallpaper, cream striped with a black mark just by the wardrobe, the mahogany dressing-table with the glass that swung too far forward, the cheerful bright blue carpet, the watercolours of the Lake District. All dear familiar things and she would not see them again until Monday.

Instead, tomorrow a housemaid who rustled would come into the strange bedroom and put down a little dainty tray of early tea by the bed and pull up the blinds, and would then rearrange and fold Gerda's clothes—a thing which made Gerda feel hot and uncomfortable all over. She would lie miserably, enduring these things, trying to comfort herself by thinking, 'Only one morning more.' Like being at school and counting the days.

Gerda had not been happy at school. At school there had been even less reassurance than elsewhere. Home had been better. But even home had not been very good. For they had all, of course, been quicker and cleverer than she was. Their comments, quick, impatient, not quite unkind, had whistled about her ears like a hailstorm. 'Oh, do be quick,

The Hollow

Gerda.' 'Butter-fingers, give it to me!' 'Oh don't let Gerda do it, she'll be *ages*.' 'Gerda never takes in anything…'

Hadn't they seen, all of them, that that was the way to make her slower and stupider still? She'd got worse and worse, more clumsy with her fingers, more slow-witted, more inclined to stare vacantly at what was said to her.

Until, suddenly, she had reached the point where she had found a way out. Almost accidentally, really, she found her weapon of defence.

She had grown slower still, her puzzled stare had become even blanker. But now, when they said impatiently: 'Oh, Gerda, how stupid you are, don't you understand *that*?' she had been able, behind her blank expression, to hug herself a little in her secret knowledge… For she wasn't as stupid as they thought. Often, when she pretended not to understand, she *did* understand. And often, deliberately, she slowed down in her task of whatever it was, smiling to herself when someone's impatient fingers snatched it away from her.

For, warm and delightful, was a secret knowledge of superiority. She began to be, quite often, a little amused. Yes, it was amusing to know more than they thought you knew. To be able to do a thing, but not let anybody know that you could do it.

And it had the advantage, suddenly discovered, that people often did things for you. That, of course, saved you a lot of trouble. And, in the end, if people got into the habit of doing things for you, you didn't have to do them at all, and then people didn't know that you did them badly.

Agatha Christie

And so, slowly, you came round again almost to where you started. To feeling that you could hold your own on equal terms with the world at large.

(But that wouldn't, Gerda feared, hold good with the Angkatells; the Angkatells were always so far ahead that you didn't feel even in the same street with them. How she hated the Angkatells! It was good for John—John liked it there. He came home less tired—and sometimes less irritable.)

Dear John, she thought. John was wonderful. Everyone thought so. Such a clever doctor, so terribly kind to his patients. Wearing himself out—and the interest he took in his hospital patients—all that side of his work that didn't pay at all. John was so *disinterested*—so truly noble.

She had always known, from the very first, that John was brilliant and was going to get to the top of the tree. And he had chosen her, when he might have married somebody far more brilliant. He had not minded her being slow and rather stupid and not very pretty. 'I'll look after you,' he had said. Nicely, rather masterfully. 'Don't worry about things, Gerda, I'll take care of you...'

Just what a man ought to be. Wonderful to think John should have chosen her.

He had said with that sudden, very attractive, half-pleading smile of his, 'I like my own way, you know, Gerda.'

Well, that was all right. She had always tried to give in to him in everything. Even lately when he had been so difficult and nervy—when nothing seemed to please him. When, somehow, nothing she did was right. One couldn't blame him. He was so busy, so unselfish—

Oh, dear, that mutton! She ought to have sent it back. Still no sign of John. Why couldn't she, sometimes, decide right? Again those dark waves of misery swept over her. The mutton! This awful weekend with the Angkatells. She felt a sharp pain through both temples. Oh, dear, now she was going to have one of her headaches. And it did so annoy John when she had headaches. He never would give her anything for them, when surely it would be so easy, being a doctor. Instead he always said: 'Don't think about it. No use poisoning yourself with drugs. Take a brisk walk.'

The mutton! Staring at it, Gerda felt the words repeating themselves in her aching head, 'The mutton, the MUTTON, THE MUTTON...'

Tears of self-pity sprang to her eyes. 'Why,' she thought, 'does nothing *ever* go right for me?'

Terence looked across at the table at his mother and then at the joint. He thought: 'Why can't *we* have our dinner? How stupid grown-up people are. They haven't any sense!'

Aloud he said in a careful voice:

'Nicholson Minor and I are going to make nitroglycerine in his father's shrubbery. They live at Streatham.'

'Are you, dear? That will be very nice,' said Gerda.

There was still time. If she rang the bell and told Lewis to take the joint down now—

Terence looked at her with faint curiosity. He had felt instinctively that the manufacture of nitroglycerine was not the kind of occupation that would be encouraged by parents. With base opportunism he had selected a moment when he felt tolerably certain that he had a good chance of getting

Agatha Christie

away with his statement. And his judgement had been justified. If, by any chance, there should be a fuss—if, that is, the properties of nitroglycerine should manifest themselves too evidently, he would be able to say in an injured voice, 'I *told* Mother.'

All the same, he felt vaguely disappointed.

'Even *Mother*,' he thought, 'ought to know about nitroglycerine.'

He sighed. There swept over him that intense sense of loneliness that only childhood can feel. His father was too impatient to listen, his mother was too inattentive. Zena was only a silly kid.

Pages of interesting chemical tests. And who cared about them? Nobody!

Bang! Gerda started. It was the door of John's consulting-room. It was John running upstairs.

John Christow burst into the room, bringing with him his own particular atmosphere of intense energy. He was good-humoured, hungry, impatient.

'God,' he exclaimed as he sat down and energetically sharpened the carving knife against the steel. 'How I hate sick people!'

'Oh, John.' Gerda was quickly reproachful. 'Don't say things like that. *They'll* think you mean it.'

She gestured slightly with her head towards the children.

'I do mean it,' said John Christow. 'Nobody ought to be ill.'

'Father's joking,' said Gerda quickly to Terence.

Terence examined his father with the dispassionate attention he gave to everything.

The Hollow

'I don't think he is,' he said.

'If you hated sick people, you wouldn't be a doctor, dear,' said Gerda, laughing gently.

'That's exactly the reason,' said John Christow. 'No doctors like sickness. Good God, this meat's stone cold. Why on earth didn't you have it sent down to keep hot?'

'Well, dear, I didn't know. You see, I thought you were just coming—'

John Christow pressed the bell, a long, irritated push. Lewis came promptly.

'Take this down and tell Cook to warm it up.'

He spoke curtly.

'Yes, sir.' Lewis, slightly impertinent, managed to convey in the two innocuous words exactly her opinion of a mistress who sat at the dining-table watching a joint of meat grow cold.

Gerda went on rather incoherently:

'I'm so sorry, dear, it's all my fault, but first, you see, I thought you were coming, and then I thought, well, if I did send it back...'

John interrupted her impatiently.

'Oh, what does it matter? It isn't important. Not worth making a song and dance about.'

Then he asked:

'Is the car here?'

'I think so. Collie ordered it.'

'Then we can get away as soon as lunch is over.'

Across Albert Bridge, he thought, and then over Clapham Common—the short-cut by the Crystal Palace—Croydon—Purley Way, then avoid the main road—take that right-hand

Agatha Christie

fork up Metherly Hill—along Haverston Ridge—get suddenly right of the suburban belt, through Cormerton, and then up Shovel Down—trees golden red—woodland below one everywhere—the soft autumn smell, and down over the crest of the hill.

Lucy and Henry... Henrietta...

He hadn't seen Henrietta for four days. When he had last seen her, he'd been angry. She'd had that look in her eyes. Not abstracted, not inattentive—he couldn't quite describe it—that look of *seeing* something—something that wasn't there—something (and that was the crux of it) something that wasn't John Christow!

He said to himself: 'I know she's a sculptor. I know her work's good. But damn it all, can't she put it aside sometimes? Can't she sometimes think of me—and nothing else?'

He was unfair. He knew he was unfair. Henrietta seldom talked of her work—was indeed less obsessed by it than most artists he knew. It was only on very rare occasions that her absorption with some inner vision spoiled the completeness of her interest in him. But it always roused his furious anger.

Once he had said, his voice sharp and hard, 'Would you give all this up if I asked you to?'

'All—what?' Her warm voice held surprise.

'All—this.' He waved a comprehensive hand round the studio.

And immediately he thought to himself, 'Fool! Why did you ask her that?' And again: 'Let her say: "Of course." Let her lie to me! If she'll only say: "Of course I will." It doesn't matter

The Hollow

if she means it or not! But let her say it. I *must* have peace.'

Instead she had said nothing for some time. Her eyes had gone dreamy and abstracted. She had frowned a little. Then she had said slowly:

'I suppose so. If it was *necessary*.'

'Necessary? What do you mean by necessary?'

'I don't really know what I mean by it, John. Necessary, as an amputation might be necessary.'

'Nothing short of a surgical operation, in fact!'

'You are angry. What did you want me to say?'

'You know well enough. One word would have done. *Yes*. Why couldn't you say it? You say enough things to people to please them, without caring whether they're true or not. Why not to me? For God's sake, why not to me?'

And still very slowly she had answered:

'I don't know...really, I don't know, John. I can't—that's all. I can't.'

He had walked up and down for a minute or two. Then he said:

'You will drive me mad, Henrietta. I never feel that I have any influence over you at all.'

'Why should you want to have?'

'I don't know. I do.'

He threw himself down on a chair.

'I want to come first.'

'You do, John.'

'No. If I were dead, the first thing you'd do, with the tears streaming down your face, would be to start modelling some damned mourning woman or some figure of grief.'

Agatha Christie

'I wonder. I believe—yes, perhaps I would. It's rather horrible.'
She had sat there looking at him with dismayed eyes.

The pudding was burnt. Christow raised his eyebrows over it and Gerda hurried into apologies.

'I'm sorry, dear. I can't think *why* that should happen. It's my fault. Give me the top and you take the underneath.'

The pudding was burnt because he, John Christow, had stayed sitting in his consulting-room for a quarter of an hour after he need, thinking about Henrietta and Mrs Crabtree and letting ridiculous nostalgic feelings about San Miguel sweep over him. The fault was his. It was idiotic of Gerda to try and take the blame, maddening of her to try and eat the burnt part herself. Why did she always have to make a martyr of herself? Why did Terence stare at him in that slow, interested way? Why, oh why, did Zena have to sniff so continually? Why were they all so damned irritating?

His wrath fell on Zena.

'Why on earth don't you blow your nose?'

'She's got a little cold, I think, dear.'

'No, she hasn't. You're always thinking they have colds! She's all right.'

Gerda sighed. She had never been able to understand why a doctor, who spent his time treating the ailments of others, could be so indifferent to the health of his own family. He always ridiculed any suggestions of illness.

'I sneezed eight times before lunch,' said Zena importantly.

'Heat sneeze!' said John.

The Hollow

'It's not hot,' said Terence. 'The thermometer in the hall is 55.'

John got up. 'Have we finished? Good, let's get on. Ready to start, Gerda?'

'In a minute, John. I've just a few things to put in.'

'Surely you could have done that *before*. What have you been doing all the morning?'

He went out of the dining-room fuming. Gerda had hurried off into her bedroom. Her anxiety to be quick would make her much slower. But why couldn't she have been ready? His own suitcase was packed and in the hall. Why on earth—

Zena was advancing on him, clasping some rather sticky cards.

'Can I tell your fortune, Daddy? I know how. I've told Mother's and Terry's and Lewis's and Jane's and Cook's.'

'All right.'

He wondered how long Gerda was going to be. He wanted to get away from this horrible house and this horrible street and this city full of ailing, sniffling, diseased people. He wanted to get to woods and wet leaves—and the graceful aloofness of Lucy Angkatell, who always gave you the impression she hadn't even got a body.

Zena was importantly dealing out cards.

'That's you in the middle, Father, the King of Hearts. The person whose fortune's told is always the King of Hearts. And then I deal the others face down. Two on the left of you and two on the right of you and one over your head—that has power over you, and one under your feet—you have power over it. And this one—covers you!

'*Now.*' Zena drew a deep breath. 'We turn them over. On the right of you is the Queen of Diamonds—quite close.'

'Henrietta,' he thought, momentarily diverted and amused by Zena's solemnity.

'And the next one is the knave of clubs—he's some quiet young man.

'On the left of you is the eight of spades—that's a secret enemy. Have you got a secret enemy, Father?'

'Not that I know of.'

'And beyond is the Queen of Spades—that's a much older lady.'

'Lady Angkatell,' he said.

'Now this is what's over your head and has power over you—the Queen of Hearts.'

'Veronica,' he thought. 'Veronica!' And then, 'What a fool I am! Veronica doesn't mean a thing to me now.'

'And this is under your feet and you have power over it—the Queen of Clubs.'

Gerda hurried into the room.

'I'm quite ready now, John.'

'Oh, wait, Mother, wait, I'm telling Daddy's fortune. Just the last card, Daddy—the most important of all. The one that covers you.'

Zena's small sticky fingers turned it over. She gave a gasp.

'Oh—it's the Ace of Spades! That's usually a *death*—but—'

'Your mother,' said John, 'is going to run over someone on the way out of London. Come on, Gerda. Goodbye, you two. Try and behave.'

CHAPTER 6

Midge Hardcastle came downstairs about eleven on Saturday morning. She had had breakfast in bed and had read a book and dozed a little and then got up.

It was nice lazing this way. About time she had a holiday! No doubt about it, Madame Alfrege's got on your nerves.

She came out of the front door into the pleasant autumn sunshine. Sir Henry Angkatell was sitting on a rustic seat reading *The Times*. He looked up and smiled. He was fond of Midge.

'Hallo, my dear.'

'Am I very late?'

'You haven't missed lunch,' said Sir Henry, smiling.

Midge sat down beside him and said with a sigh:

'It's nice being here.'

'You're looking rather peaked.'

'Oh, I'm all right. How delightful to be somewhere where no fat women are trying to get into clothes several sizes too small for them!'

'Must be dreadful!' Sir Henry paused and then said, glancing down at his wrist-watch: 'Edward's arriving by the 12.15.'

Agatha Christie

'Is he?' Midge paused, then said, 'I haven't seen Edward for a long time.'

'He's just the same,' said Sir Henry. 'Hardly ever comes up from Ainswick.'

'Ainswick,' thought Midge. 'Ainswick!' Her heart gave a sick pang. Those lovely days at Ainswick. Visits looked forward to for months! 'I'm going to Ainswick.' Lying awake for nights beforehand thinking about it. And at last—the day! The little country station at which the train—the big London express—had to stop if you gave notice to the guard! The Daimler waiting outside. The drive—the final turn in through the gate and up through the woods till you came out into the open and there the house was—big and white and welcoming. Old Uncle Geoffrey in his patchwork tweed coat.

'Now then, youngsters—enjoy yourselves.' And they had enjoyed themselves. Henrietta over from Ireland. Edward, home from Eton. She herself, from the North-country grimness of a manufacturing town. How like heaven it had been.

But always centring about Edward. Edward, tall and gentle and diffident and always kind. But never, of course, noticing her very much because Henrietta was there.

Edward, always so retiring, so very much of a visitor so that she had been startled one day when Tremlet, the head gardener, had said:

'The place will be Mr Edward's some day.'

'But why, Tremlet? He's not Uncle Geoffrey's son.'

'He's the *heir*, Miss Midge. Entailed, that's what they call it. Miss Lucy, she's Mr Geoffrey's only child, but she can't

The Hollow

inherit because she's a female, and Mr Henry, as she married, he's only a second cousin. Not so near as Mr Edward.'

And now Edward lived at Ainswick. Lived there alone and very seldom came away. Midge wondered, sometimes, if Lucy minded. Lucy always looked as though she never minded about anything.

Yet Ainswick had been her home, and Edward was only her first cousin once removed, and over twenty years younger than she was. Her father, old Geoffrey Angkatell, had been a great 'character' in the country. He had had considerable wealth as well, most of which had come to Lucy, so that Edward was a comparatively poor man, with enough to keep the place up, but not much over when that was done.

Not that Edward had expensive tastes. He had been in the diplomatic service for a time, but when he inherited Ainswick he had resigned and come to live on his property. He was of a bookish turn of mind, collected first editions, and occasionally wrote rather hesitating ironical little articles for obscure reviews. He had asked his second cousin, Henrietta Savernake, three times to marry him.

Midge sat in the autumn sunshine thinking of these things. She could not make up her mind whether she was glad she was going to see Edward or not. It was not as though she were what is called 'getting over it'. One simply did not get over any one like Edward. Edward of Ainswick was just as real to her as Edward rising to greet her from a restaurant table in London. She had loved Edward ever since she could remember...

Agatha Christie

Sir Henry's voice recalled her.

'How do you think Lucy is looking?'

'Very well. She's just the same as ever.' Midge smiled a little. 'More so.'

'Ye—es.' Sir Henry drew on his pipe. He said unexpectedly: 'Sometimes, you know, Midge, I get worried about Lucy.'

'Worried?' Midge looked at him in surprise. 'Why?'

Sir Henry shook his head.

'Lucy,' he said, 'doesn't realize that there are things that she can't do.'

Midge stared. He went on:

'She gets away with things. She always has.' He smiled. 'She's flouted the traditions of Government House—she's played merry hell with precedence at dinner parties (and that, Midge, is a black crime!). She's put deadly enemies next to each other at the dinner table, and run riot over the colour question! And instead of raising one big almighty row and setting everyone at loggerheads and bringing disgrace on the British Raj—I'm damned if she hasn't got away with it! That trick of hers—smiling at people and looking as though she couldn't help it! Servants are the same—she gives them any amount of trouble and they adore her.'

'I know what you mean,' said Midge thoughtfully. 'Things that you wouldn't stand from anyone else, you feel are all right if Lucy does them. What is it, I wonder? Charm? Magnetism?'

Sir Henry shrugged his shoulders.

'She's always been the same from a girl—only sometimes I feel it's growing on her. I mean that she doesn't realize that there *are* limits. Why, I really believe, Midge,' he said, amused, 'that Lucy would feel she could get away with murder!'

Henrietta got the Delage out from the garage in the Mews and, after a wholly technical conversation with her friend Albert, who looked after the Delage's health, she started off.

'Running a treat, miss,' said Albert.

Henrietta smiled. She shot away down the Mews, savouring the unfailing pleasure she always felt when setting off in the car alone. She much preferred to be alone when driving. In that way she could realize to the full the intimate personal enjoyment that driving a car brought to her.

She enjoyed her own skill in traffic, she enjoyed nosing out new short-cuts out of London. She had routes of her own and when driving in London itself had as intimate a knowledge of its streets as any taxi-driver.

She took now her own newly discovered way southwest, turning and twisting through intricate mazes of suburban streets.

When she came finally to the long ridge of Shovel Down it was half-past twelve. Henrietta had always loved the view from that particular place. She paused now just at the point where the road began to descend. All around and below her were trees, trees whose leaves were turning from gold to brown. It was a world incredibly golden and splendid in the strong autumn sunlight.

Henrietta thought, 'I love autumn. It's so much richer than spring.'

Agatha Christie

And suddenly one of those moments of intense happiness came to her—a sense of the loveliness of the world—of her own intense enjoyment of that world.

She thought, 'I shall never be as happy again as I am now—never.'

She stayed there a minute, gazing out over that golden world that seemed to swim and dissolve into itself, hazy and blurred with its own beauty.

Then she came down over the crest of the hill, down through the woods, down the long steep road to The Hollow.

When Henrietta drove in, Midge was sitting on the low wall of the terrace, and waved to her cheerfully. Henrietta was pleased to see Midge, whom she liked.

Lady Angkatell came out of the house and said:

'Oh, there you are, Henrietta. When you've taken your car into the stables and given it a bran mash, lunch will be ready.'

'What a penetrating remark of Lucy's,' said Henrietta as she drove round the house, Midge accompanying her on the step. 'You know, I always prided myself on having completely escaped the horsy taint of my Irish forebears. When you've been brought up amongst people who talk nothing but horse, you go all superior about not caring for them. And now Lucy has just shown me that I treat my car exactly like a horse. It's quite true. I do.'

'I know,' said Midge. 'Lucy is quite devastating. She told me this morning that I was to be as rude as I liked whilst I was here.'

The Hollow

Henrietta considered this for a moment and then nodded. 'Of course,' she said. 'The *shop*!'

'Yes. When one has to spend every day of one's life in a damnable little box being polite to rude women, calling them Madam, pulling frocks over their heads, smiling and swallowing their damned cheek whatever they like to say to one—well, one does want to cuss! You know, Henrietta, I always wonder why people think it's so humiliating to go "into service" and that it's grand and independent to be in a shop. One puts up with far more insolence in a shop than Gudgeon or Simmons or any decent domestic does.'

'It must be foul, darling. I wish you weren't so grand and proud and insistent on earning your own living.'

'Anyway, Lucy's an angel. I shall be gloriously rude to everyone this weekend.'

'Who's here?' said Henrietta as she got out of the car.

'The Christows are coming.' Midge paused and then went on, 'Edward's just arrived.'

'Edward? How nice. I haven't seen Edward for ages. Anybody else?'

'David Angkatell. That, according to Lucy, is where you are going to come in useful. You're going to stop him biting his nails.'

'It sounds very unlike me,' said Henrietta. 'I hate interfering with people, and I wouldn't dream of checking their personal habits. What did Lucy really say?'

'It amounted to that! He's got an Adam's apple, too!'

'I'm not expected to do anything about that, am I?' asked Henrietta, alarmed.

'And you're to be kind to Gerda.'

Agatha Christie

'How I should hate Lucy if I were Gerda!'

'And someone who solves crimes is coming to lunch tomorrow.'

'We're not going to play the Murder Game, are we?'

'I don't think so. I think it is just neighbourly hospitality.' Midge's voice changed a little.

'Here's Edward coming out to meet us.'

'Dear Edward,' thought Henrietta with a sudden rush of warm affection.

Edward Angkatell was very tall and thin. He was smiling now as he came towards the two young women.

'Hallo, Henrietta, I haven't seen you for over a year.'

'Hallo, Edward.'

How nice Edward was! That gentle smile of his, the little creases at the corners of his eyes. And all his nice knobbly bones. 'I believe it's his *bones* I like so much,' thought Henrietta. The warmth of her affection for Edward startled her. She had forgotten that she liked Edward so much.

After lunch Edward said: 'Come for a walk, Henrietta.'

It was Edward's kind of walk—a stroll.

They went up behind the house, taking a path that zigzagged up through the trees. Like the woods at Ainswick, thought Henrietta. Dear Ainswick, what fun they had had there! She began to talk to Edward about Ainswick. They revived old memories.

'Do you remember our squirrel? The one with the broken paw. And we kept it in a cage and it got well?'

The Hollow

'Of course. It had a ridiculous name—what was it now?'
'Cholmondeley-Marjoribanks!'
'That's it.'
They both laughed.
'And old Mrs Bondy, the housekeeper—she always *said* it would go up the chimney one day.'
'And we were so indignant.'
'And then it *did*.'
'She made it,' said Henrietta positively. 'She put the thought into the squirrel's head.'
She went on:
'Is it all the same, Edward? Or is it changed? I always imagine it just the same.'
'Why don't you come and see, Henrietta? It's a long long time since you've been there.'
'I know.'
Why, she thought, had she let so long a time go by? One got busy—interested—tangled up with people...
'You know you're always welcome there at any time.'
'How sweet you are, Edward!'
Dear Edward, she thought, with his *nice* bones.
He said presently:
'I'm glad you're fond of Ainswick, Henrietta.'
She said dreamily, 'Ainswick is the loveliest place in the world.'
A long-legged girl, with a mane of untidy brown hair...a happy girl with no idea at all of the things that life was going to do to her...a girl who loved trees...
To have been so happy and not to have known it! '*If I could go back,*' she thought.

And aloud she said suddenly:

'Is Ygdrasil still there?'

'It was struck by lightning.'

'Oh, no, not *Ygdrasil*!'

She was distressed. Ygdrasil—her own special name for the big oak tree. If the gods could strike down Ygdrasil, then nothing was safe! Better not go back.

'Do you remember your special sign, the Ygdrasil sign?'

'The funny tree like no tree that ever was I used to draw on bits of paper? I still do, Edward! On blotters, and on telephone books, and on bridge scores. I doodle it all the time. Give me a pencil.'

He handed her a pencil and notebook, and laughing, she drew the ridiculous tree.

'Yes,' he said, 'that's Ygdrasil.'

They had come almost to the top of the path. Henrietta sat on a fallen tree-trunk. Edward sat down beside her.

She looked down through the trees.

'It's a little like Ainswick here—a kind of pocket Ainswick. I've sometimes wondered—Edward, do you think that that is why Lucy and Henry came here?'

'It's possible.'

The Hollow

'One never knows,' said Henrietta slowly, 'what goes on in Lucy's head.' Then she asked, 'What have you been doing with yourself, Edward, since I saw you last?'

'Nothing, Henrietta.'

'That sounds very peaceful.'

'I've never been very good at—doing things.'

She threw him a quick glance. There had been something in his tone. But he was smiling at her quietly.

And again she felt that rush of deep affection.

'Perhaps,' she said, 'you are wise.'

'Wise?'

'Not to do things.'

Edward said slowly, 'That's an odd thing for you to say, Henrietta. You, who've been so successful.'

'Do you think of me as successful? How funny.'

'But you are, my dear. You're an artist. You must be proud of yourself; you can't help being.'

'I know,' said Henrietta. 'A lot of people say that to me. They don't understand—they don't understand the first thing about it. *You* don't, Edward. Sculpture isn't a thing you set out to do and succeed in. It's a thing that gets *at* you, that nags at you—and haunts you—so that you've got, sooner or later, to make terms with it. And then, for a bit, you get some peace—until the whole thing starts over again.'

'Do you want to be peaceful, Henrietta?'

'Sometimes I think I want to be peaceful more than anything in the world, Edward!'

'You could be peaceful at Ainswick. I think you could be happy there. Even—even if you had to put up with *me*.

Agatha Christie

What about it, Henrietta? Won't you come to Ainswick and make it your home? It's always been there, you know, waiting for you.'

Henrietta turned her head slowly. She said in a low voice:

'I wish I wasn't so dreadfully fond of you, Edward. It makes it so very much harder to go on saying No.'

'It *is* No, then?'

'I'm sorry.'

'You've said No before—but this time—well, I thought it might be different. You've been happy this afternoon, Henrietta. You can't deny that.'

'I've been very happy.'

'Your face even—it's younger than it was this morning.'

'I know.'

'We've been happy together, talking about Ainswick, thinking about Ainswick. Don't you see what that means, Henrietta?'

'It's *you* who don't see what it means, Edward! We've been living all this afternoon in the past.'

'The past is sometimes a very good place to live.'

'One can't go back. That's the one thing one can't do—go back.'

He was silent for a minute or two. Then he said in a quiet, pleasant and quite unemotional voice:

'What you really mean is that you won't marry me because of John Christow?'

Henrietta did not answer, and Edward went on:

'That's it, isn't it? If there were no John Christow in the world you would marry me.'

The Hollow

Henrietta said harshly, 'I can't imagine a world in which there was no John Christow! That's what *you've* got to understand.'

'If it's like that, why on earth doesn't the fellow get a divorce from his wife and then you could marry?'

'John doesn't want to get a divorce from his wife. And I don't know that I should want to marry John if he did. It isn't—it isn't in the least like you think.'

Edward said in a thoughtful, considering way:

'John Christow. There are too many John Christows in this world.'

'You're wrong,' said Henrietta. 'There are very few people like John.'

'If that's so—it's a good thing! At least, that's what I think!'

He got up. 'We'd better go back again.'

CHAPTER 7

As they got into the car and Lewis shut the front door of the Harley Street house, Gerda felt the pang of exile go through her. That shut door was so final. She was barred out—this awful weekend was upon her. And there were things, quite a lot of things, that she ought to have done before leaving. Had she turned off that tap in the bathroom? And that note for the laundry—she'd put it—where had she put it? Would the children be all right with Mademoiselle? Mademoiselle was so—so—Would Terence, for instance, ever do anything that Mademoiselle told him to? French governesses never seemed to have any authority.

She got into the driving-seat, still bowed down by misery, and nervously pressed the starter. She pressed it again and again. John said: 'The car will start better, Gerda, if you switch on the engine.'

'Oh, dear, how stupid of me.' She shot a quick, alarmed glance at him. If John was going to become annoyed straight away—But to her relief he was smiling.

'That's because,' thought Gerda, with one of her flashes of acumen, 'he's so pleased to be going to the Angkatells.'

Poor John, he worked so hard! His life was so unselfish, so completely devoted to others. No wonder he looked forward to this long weekend. And, her mind harking back to the conversation at lunch, she said, as she let in the clutch rather too suddenly so that the car leapt forward from the kerb:

'You know, John, you really shouldn't make jokes about hating sick people. It's wonderful of you to make light of all you do, and *I* understand. But the children don't. Terry, in particular, has such a very literal mind.'

'There are times,' said John Christow, 'when Terry seems to me almost human—not like Zena! How long do girls go on being a mass of affectation?'

Gerda gave a little quite sweet laugh. John, she knew, was teasing her. She stuck to her point. Gerda had an adhesive mind.

'I really think, John, that it's *good* for children to realize the unselfishness and devotion of a doctor's life.'

'Oh God!' said Christow.

Gerda was momentarily deflected. The traffic lights she was approaching had been green for a long time. They were almost sure, she thought, to change before she got to them. She began to slow down. Still green.

John Christow forgot his resolutions of keeping silent about Gerda's driving and said, 'What are you stopping for?'

'I thought the lights might change—'

She pressed her foot on the accelerator, the car moved forward a little, just beyond the lights, then, unable to pick up, the engine stalled. The lights changed.

Agatha Christie

The cross-traffic hooted angrily.

John said, but quite pleasantly:

'You really are the worst driver in the world, Gerda!'

'I always find traffic lights so worrying. One doesn't know just when they are going to change.'

John cast a quick sideways look at Gerda's anxious unhappy face.

'Everything worries Gerda,' he thought, and tried to imagine what it must feel like to live in that state. But since he was not a man of much imagination, he could not picture it at all.

'You see,' Gerda stuck to her point, 'I've always impressed on the children just what a doctor's life is—the self-sacrifice, the dedication of oneself to helping pain and suffering—the desire to serve others. It's such a noble life—and I'm so proud of the way you give your time and energy and never spare yourself—'

John Christow interrupted her.

'Hasn't it ever occurred to you that I *like* doctoring—that it's a pleasure, not a sacrifice!—Don't you realize that the damned thing's *interesting*!'

But no, he thought, Gerda would never realize a thing like that! If he told her about Mrs Crabtree and the Margaret Russell Ward she would only see him as a kind of angelic helper of the Poor with a capital P.

'Drowning in treacle,' he said under his breath.

'What?' Gerda leaned towards him.

He shook his head.

If he were to tell Gerda that he was trying to 'find a cure for cancer', she would respond—she could understand a

The Hollow

plain sentimental statement. But she would never understand the peculiar fascination of the intricacies of Ridgeway's Disease—he doubted if he could even make her understand what Ridgeway's Disease actually was. ('Particularly,' he thought with a grin, 'as we're not really quite sure ourselves! We don't really know *why* the cortex degenerates!')

But it occurred to him suddenly that Terence, child though he was, might be interested in Ridgeway's Disease. He had liked the way that Terence had eyed him appraisingly before stating: 'I think Father does mean it.'

Terence had been out of favour the last few days for breaking the Cona coffee machine—some nonsense about trying to make ammonia. Ammonia? Funny kid, why should he want to make ammonia? Interesting in a way.

Gerda was relieved at John's silence. She could cope with driving better if she were not distracted by conversation. Besides, if John was absorbed in thought, he was not so likely to notice that jarring noise of her occasional forced changes of gear. (She never changed down if she could help it.)

There were times, Gerda knew, when she changed gear quite well (though never with confidence), but it never happened if John were in the car. Her nervous determination to do it right this time was almost disastrous, her hand fumbled, she accelerated too much or not enough, and then she pushed the gear lever quickly and clumsily so that it shrieked in protest.

'Stroke it in, Gerda, stroke it in,' Henrietta had pleaded once, years ago. Henrietta had demonstrated. 'Can't you feel the way it wants to go—it wants to slide in—keep your

Agatha Christie

hand flat till you get the feeling of it—don't just push it anywhere—*feel* it.'

But Gerda had never been able to feel anything about a gear lever. If she was pushing it more or less in the proper direction it ought to go in! Cars ought to be made so that you didn't have that horrible grinding noise.

On the whole, thought Gerda, as she began the ascent of Mersham Hill, this drive wasn't going too badly. John was still absorbed in thought—and he hadn't noticed rather a bad crashing of gears in Croydon. Optimistically, as the car gained speed, she changed up into third, and immediately the car slackened. John, as it were, woke up.

'What on earth's the point of changing up just when you're coming to a steep bit?'

Gerda set her jaw. Not very much farther now. Not that she wanted to get there. No, indeed, she'd much rather drive on for hours and hours, even if John *did* lose his temper with her!

But now they were driving along Shovel Down—flaming autumn woods all round them.

'Wonderful to get out of London into this,' exclaimed John. 'Think of it, Gerda, most afternoons we're stuck in that dingy drawing-room having tea—sometimes with the light on.'

The image of the somewhat dark drawing-room of the flat rose up before Gerda's eyes with the tantalizing delight of a mirage. Oh, if only she could be sitting there now.

'The country looks lovely,' she said heroically.

Down the steep hill—no escape now. That vague hope that something, she didn't know what, might intervene

The Hollow

to save her from the nightmare, was unrealized. They were there.

She was a little comforted as she drove in to see Henrietta sitting on a wall with Midge and a tall thin man. She felt a certain reliance on Henrietta, who would sometimes unexpectedly come to the rescue if things were getting very bad.

John was glad to see Henrietta too. It seemed to him exactly the fitting journey's end to that lovely panorama of autumn, to drop down from the hilltop and find Henrietta waiting for him.

She had on the green tweed coat and the skirt he liked her in and which he thought suited her so much better than London clothes. Her long legs were stuck out in front of her, ending in well polished brown brogues.

They exchanged a quick smile—a brief recognition of the fact that each was glad of the other's presence. John didn't want to talk to Henrietta now. He just enjoyed feeling that she was there—knowing that without her the weekend would be barren and empty.

Lady Angkatell came out from the house and greeted them. Her conscience made her more effusive to Gerda than she would have been normally to any guest.

'But how *very* nice to see you, Gerda! It's been such a *long* time. *And* John!'

The idea was clearly that Gerda was the eagerly awaited guest, and John the mere adjunct. It failed miserably of its object, making Gerda stiff and uncomfortable.

Lucy said, 'You know Edward? Edward Angkatell?'

John nodded to Edward and said, 'No, I don't think so.'

Agatha Christie

The afternoon sun lighted up the gold of John's hair and the blue of his eyes. So might a Viking look who had just come ashore on a conquering mission. His voice, warm and resonant, charmed the ear, and the magnetism of his whole personality took charge of the scene.

That warmth and that objectiveness did no damage to Lucy. It set off, indeed, that curious elfin elusiveness of hers. It was Edward who seemed, suddenly, by contrast with the other man, bloodless—a shadowy figure, stooping a little.

Henrietta suggested to Gerda that they should go and look at the kitchen garden.

'Lucy is sure to insist on showing us the rock garden and the autumn border,' she said as she led the way. 'But I always think kitchen gardens are nice and peaceful. One can sit on the cucumber frames, or go inside a greenhouse if it's cold, and nobody bothers one and sometimes there's something to eat.'

They found, indeed, some late peas, which Henrietta ate raw, but which Gerda did not much care for. She was glad to have got away from Lucy Angkatell, whom she had found more alarming than ever.

She began to talk to Henrietta with something like animation. The questions Henrietta asked always seemed to be questions to which Gerda knew the answers. After ten minutes Gerda felt very much better and began to think that perhaps the weekend wouldn't be so bad after all.

Zena was going to dancing class now and had just had a new frock. Gerda described it at length. Also she had found a very nice new leathercraft shop. Henrietta asked

The Hollow

whether it would be difficult to make herself a handbag. Gerda must show her.

It was really very easy, she thought, to make Gerda look happy, and what an enormous difference it made to her when she did look happy!

'She only wants to be allowed to curl up and purr,' thought Henrietta.

They sat happily on the corner of the cucumber frames where the sun, now low in the sky, gave an illusion of a summer day.

Then a silence fell. Gerda's face lost its expression of placidity. Her shoulders drooped. She sat there, the picture of misery. She jumped when Henrietta spoke.

'Why do you come,' said Henrietta, 'if you hate it so much?'

Gerda hurried into speech.

'Oh, I don't! I mean, I don't know why you should think—'

She paused, then went on:

'It is really delightful to get out of London, and Lady Angkatell is so *very* kind.'

'Lucy? She's not a bit kind.'

Gerda looked faintly shocked.

'Oh, but she *is*. She's so very nice to me always.'

'Lucy has got good manners and she can be gracious. But she is rather a cruel person. I think really because she isn't quite human—she doesn't know what it's like to feel and think like ordinary people. And you *are* hating being here, Gerda! You know you are. And why should you come if you feel like that?'

'Well, you see, John likes it—'

'Oh, John likes it all right. But you could let him come by himself?'

'He wouldn't like that. He wouldn't enjoy it without me. John is so unselfish. He thinks it is good for me to get out into the country.'

'The country is all right,' said Henrietta. 'But there's no need to throw in the Angkatells.'

'I—I don't want you to feel that I'm ungrateful.'

'My dear Gerda, why should you like us? I always have thought the Angkatells were an odious family. We all like getting together and talking an extraordinary language of our own. I don't wonder outside people want to murder us.'

Then she added:

'I expect it's about teatime. Let's go back.'

She was watching Gerda's face as the latter got up and started to walk towards the house.

'It's interesting,' thought Henrietta, one portion of whose mind was always detached, 'to see exactly what a female Christian martyr's face looked like before she went into the arena.'

As they left the walled kitchen garden, they heard shots, and Henrietta remarked, 'Sounds as though the massacre of the Angkatells has begun!'

It turned out to be Sir Henry and Edward discussing firearms and illustrating their discussion by firing revolvers. Henry Angkatell's hobby was firearms and he had quite a collection of them.

He had brought out several revolvers and some target cards, and he and Edward were firing at them.

The Hollow

'Hallo, Henrietta, want to try if you could kill a burglar?'

Henrietta took the revolver from him.

'That's right—yes, so, aim like this.'

Bang!

'Missed him,' said Sir Henry.

'You try, Gerda.'

'Oh, I don't think I—'

'Come on, Mrs Christow. It's quite simple.'

Gerda fired the revolver, flinching, and shutting her eyes. The bullet went even wider than Henrietta's had done.

'Oh, I want to do it,' said Midge, strolling up.

'It's more difficult than you'd think,' she remarked after a couple of shots. 'But it's rather fun.'

Lucy came out from the house. Behind her came a tall, sulky young man with an Adam's apple.

'Here's David,' she announced.

She took the revolver from Midge, as her husband greeted David Angkatell, reloaded it, and without a word put three holes close to the centre of the target.

'Well done, Lucy,' exclaimed Midge. 'I didn't know shooting was one of your accomplishments.'

'Lucy,' said Sir Henry gravely, 'always kills her man!'

Then he added reminiscently, 'Came in useful once. Do you remember, my dear, those thugs that set upon us that day on the Asian side of the Bosphorus? I was rolling about with two of them on top of me feeling for my throat.'

'And what did Lucy do?' asked Midge.

'Fired two shots in the mêlée. I didn't even know she had the pistol with her. Got one bad man through the leg and the other in the shoulder. Nearest escape in the world *I've* ever had. I can't think how she didn't hit me.'

Lady Angkatell smiled at him.

'I think one always has to take some risk,' she said gently. 'And one should do it quickly and not think too much about it.'

'An admirable sentiment, my dear,' said Sir Henry. 'But I have always felt slightly aggrieved that *I* was the risk you took!'

CHAPTER 8

After tea John said to Henrietta, 'Come for a walk,' and Lady Angkatell said that she *must* show Gerda the rock garden though of course it was quite the wrong time of year.

Walking with John, thought Henrietta, was as unlike walking with Edward as anything could be.

With Edward one seldom did more than potter. Edward, she thought, was a born potterer. Walking with John, it was all she could do to keep up, and by the time they got up to Shovel Down she said breathlessly: 'It's not a marathon, John!'

He slowed down and laughed.

'Am I walking you off your feet?'

'I can do it—but is there any need? We haven't got a train to catch. Why do you have this ferocious energy? Are you running away from yourself?'

He stopped dead. 'Why do you say that?'

Henrietta looked at him curiously.

'I didn't mean anything particular by it.'

John went on again, but walking more slowly.

'As a matter of fact,' he said, 'I'm tired. I'm very tired.'

She heard the lassitude in his voice.

'How's the Crabtree?'

'It's early days to say, but I think, Henrietta, that I've got the hang of things. If I'm right'—his footsteps began to quicken—'a lot of our ideas will be revolutionized—we'll have to reconsider the whole question of hormone secretion—'

'You mean that there will be a cure for Ridgeway's Disease? That people won't die?'

'That, incidentally.'

What odd people doctors were, thought Henrietta. Incidentally!

'Scientifically, it opens up all sorts of possibilities!'

He drew a deep breath. 'But it's good to get down here—good to get some air into your lungs—good to see you.' He gave her one of his sudden quick smiles. 'And it will do Gerda good.'

'Gerda, of course, simply loves coming to The Hollow!'

'Of course she does. By the way, have I met Edward Angkatell before?'

'You've met him twice,' said Henrietta dryly.

'I couldn't remember. He's one of those vague, indefinite people.'

'Edward's a dear. I've always been very fond of him.'

'Well, don't let's waste time on Edward! None of these people count.'

Henrietta said in a low voice:

'Sometimes, John—I'm afraid for you!'

'Afraid for me—what do you mean?'

He turned an astonished face upon her.

'You are so oblivious—so—yes, *blind*.'

'Blind?'

The Hollow

'You don't know—you don't see—you're curiously insensitive! You don't know what other people are feeling and thinking.'

'I should have said just the opposite.'

'You see what you're looking *at*, yes. You're—you're like a searchlight. A powerful beam turned on to the one spot where your interest is, and behind it and each side of it, darkness!'

'Henrietta, my dear, what is all this?'

'It's *dangerous*, John. You assume that everyone likes you, that they mean well to you. People like Lucy, for instance.'

'Doesn't Lucy like me?' he said, surprised. 'I've always been extremely fond of her.'

'And so you assume that she likes you. But I'm not sure. And Gerda and Edward—oh, and Midge and Henry. How do you know what they feel towards you?'

'And Henrietta? Do I know how she feels?' He caught her hand for a moment. 'At least—I'm sure of you.'

She took her hand away.

'You can be sure of no one in this world, John.'

His face had grown grave.

'No, I won't believe that. I'm sure of you and I'm sure of myself. At least—' His face changed.

'What is it, John?'

'Do you know what I found myself saying today? Something quite ridiculous. "*I want to go home.*" That's what I said and I hadn't the least idea what I meant by it.'

Henrietta said slowly, 'You must have had some picture in your mind.'

He said sharply, 'Nothing. Nothing at all!'

*

83

Agatha Christie

At dinner that night, Henrietta was put next to David, and from the end of the table Lucy's delicate eyebrows telegraphed not a command—Lucy never commanded—but an appeal.

Sir Henry was doing his best with Gerda and succeeding quite well. John, his face amused, was following the leaps and bounds of Lucy's discursive mind. Midge talked in rather a stilted way to Edward, who seemed more absent-minded than usual.

David was glowering and crumbling his bread with a nervous hand.

David had come to The Hollow in a spirit of considerable unwillingness. Until now, he had never met either Sir Henry or Lady Angkatell, and disapproving of the Empire generally, he was prepared to disapprove of these relatives of his. Edward, whom he did not know, he despised as a dilettante. The remaining four guests he examined with a critical eye. Relations, he thought, were pretty awful, and one was expected to talk to people, a thing which he hated doing.

Midge and Henrietta he discounted as empty-headed. This Dr Christow was just one of these Harley Street charlatans—all manner and social success—his wife obviously did not count.

David shifted his neck in his collar and wished fervently that all these people could know how little he thought of them! They were really all quite negligible.

When he had repeated that three times to himself he felt rather better. He still glowered but he was able to leave his bread alone.

Henrietta, though responding loyally to the eyebrows, had some difficulty in making headway. David's curt rejoinders were snubbing in the extreme. In the end she had recourse to a method she had employed before with the tongue-tied young.

She made, deliberately, a dogmatic and quite unjustifiable pronouncement on a modern composer, knowing that David had much technical and musical knowledge.

To her amusement the plan worked. David drew himself up from his slouching position where he had been more or less reclining on his spine. His voice was no longer low and mumbling. He stopped crumbling his bread.

'That,' he said in loud, clear tones, fixing a cold eye on Henrietta, 'shows that you don't know the first thing about the subject!'

From then on until the end of dinner he lectured her in clear and biting accents, and Henrietta subsided into the proper meekness of one instructed.

Lucy Angkatell sent a benignant glance down the table, and Midge grinned to herself.

'So clever of you, darling,' muttered Lady Angkatell as she slipped an arm through Henrietta's on the way to the drawing-room. 'What an awful thought it is that if people had less in their heads they would know better what to do with their hands! Do you think Hearts or Bridge or Rummy or something terribly terribly simple like Animal Grab?'

'I think David would be rather insulted by Animal Grab.'

'Perhaps you are right. Bridge, then. I am sure he will feel that Bridge is rather worthless, and then he can have a nice glow of contempt for us.'

They made up two tables. Henrietta played with Gerda against John and Edward. It was not her idea of the best grouping. She had wanted to segregate Gerda from Lucy and if possible from John also—but John had shown determination. And Edward had then forestalled Midge.

The atmosphere was not, Henrietta thought, quite comfortable, but she did not quite know from whence the discomfort arose. Anyway, if the cards gave them anything like a break, she intended that Gerda should win. Gerda was not really a bad Bridge player—away from John she was quite average—but she was a nervous player with bad judgment and with no real knowledge of the value of her hand. John was a good, if slightly over-confident player. Edward was a very good player indeed.

The evening wore on, and at Henrietta's table they were still playing the same rubber. The scores rose above the line on either side. A curious tensity had come into the play of which only one person was unaware.

To Gerda this was just a rubber of Bridge which she happened for once to be quite enjoying. She felt indeed a pleasurable excitement. Difficult decisions had been unexpectedly eased by Henrietta's over-calling her own bids and playing the hand.

Those moments when John, unable to refrain from that critical attitude which did more to undermine Gerda's self-confidence than he could possibly have imagined, exclaimed: 'Why on earth did you lead that club, Gerda?' were countered almost immediately by Henrietta's swift, 'Nonsense, John, of course she had to lead the club! It was the only possible thing to do.'

Finally, with a sigh, Henrietta drew the score towards her.

The Hollow

'Game and rubber, but I don't think we shall make much out of it, Gerda.'

John said, 'A lucky finesse,' in a cheerful voice.

Henrietta looked up sharply. She knew his tone. She met his eyes and her own dropped.

She got up and went to the mantelpiece, and John followed her. He said conversationally, 'You don't *always* look deliberately into people's hands, do you?'

Henrietta said calmly, 'Perhaps I was a little obvious. How despicable it is to want to win at games!'

'You wanted Gerda to win the rubber, you mean. In your desire to give pleasure to people, you don't draw the line at cheating.'

'How horribly you put things! And you are always quite right.'

'Your wishes seemed to be shared by my partner.'

So he *had* noticed, thought Henrietta. She had wondered herself, if she had been mistaken. Edward was so skilful—there was nothing you could have taken hold of. A failure, once, to call the game. A lead that had been sound and obvious—but when a less obvious lead would have assured success.

It worried Henrietta. Edward, she knew, would never play his cards in order that she, Henrietta, might win. He was far too imbued with English sportsmanship for that. No, she thought, it was just one more success for John Christow that he was unable to endure.

She felt suddenly keyed up, alert. She didn't like this party of Lucy's.

Agatha Christie

And then dramatically, unexpectedly—with the unreality of a stage entrance, Veronica Cray came through the window.

The french windows had been pushed to, not closed, for the evening was warm. Veronica pushed them wide, came through them and stood there framed against the night, smiling, a little rueful, wholly charming, waiting just that infinitesimal moment before speaking so that she might be sure of her audience.

'You must forgive me—bursting in upon you this way. I'm your neighbour, Lady Angkatell—from that ridiculous cottage Dovecotes—and the most frightful catastrophe has occurred!'

Her smile broadened—became more humorous.

'Not a match! Not a single match in the house! And Saturday evening. So stupid of me. But what could I do? I came along here to beg help from my only neighbour within miles.'

Nobody spoke for a moment, for Veronica had rather that effect. She was lovely—not quietly lovely, not even dazzlingly lovely—but so efficiently lovely that it made you gasp! The waves of pale shimmering hair, the curving mouth—the platinum foxes that swathed her shoulders and the long sweep of white velvet underneath them.

She was looking from one to the other of them, humorous, charming!

'And I smoke,' she said, 'like a chimney! And my lighter won't work! And besides there's breakfast—gas stoves—' She thrust out her hands. 'I do feel such a complete fool.'

Lucy came forward, gracious, faintly amused.

'Why, of course—' she began, but Veronica Cray interrupted.

The Hollow

She was looking at John Christow. An expression of utter amazement, of incredulous delight, was spreading over her face. She took a step towards him, hands outstretched.

'Why, surely—*John*! It's John Christow! Now isn't that too extraordinary? I haven't seen you for years and years and years! And suddenly—to find you *here*!'

She had his hands in hers by now. She was all warmth and simple eagerness. She half-turned her head to Lady Angkatell.

'This is just the most wonderful surprise. John's an old old friend of mine. Why, John's the first man I ever loved! I was crazy about you, John.'

She was half-laughing now—a woman moved by the ridiculous remembrance of first love.

'I always thought John was just wonderful!'

Sir Henry, courteous and polished, had moved forward to her.

She must have a drink. He manoeuvred glasses. Lady Angkatell said:

'Midge, dear, ring the bell.'

When Gudgeon came, Lucy said:

'A box of matches, Gudgeon—at least, has Cook got plenty?'

'A new dozen came in today, m'lady.'

'Then bring in half a dozen, Gudgeon.'

'Oh, no, Lady Angkatell—just one!'

Veronica protested, laughing. She had her drink now and was smiling round at everyone. John Christow said:

'This is my wife, Veronica.'

'Oh, but how lovely to meet you.' Veronica beamed upon Gerda's air of bewilderment.

Gudgeon brought in the matches, stacked on a silver salver.

Lady Angkatell indicated Veronica Cray with a gesture and he brought the salver to her.

'Oh, dear Lady Angkatell, not all these!'

Lucy's gesture was negligently royal.

'It's so tiresome only having one of a thing. We can spare them quite easily.'

Sir Henry was saying pleasantly:

'And how do you like living at Dovecotes?'

'I adore it. It's wonderful here, near London, and yet one feels so beautifully isolated.'

Veronica put down her glass. She drew the platinum foxes a little closer round her. She smiled on them all.

'Thank you *so* much! You've been so kind.' The words floated between Sir Henry, Lady Angkatell, and for some reason, Edward. 'I shall now carry home the spoils. John,' she gave him an artless, friendly smile, 'you must see me safely back, because I want dreadfully to hear all you've been doing in the years and years since I've seen you. It makes me feel, of course, dreadfully *old*.'

She moved to the window, and John Christow followed her. She flung a last brilliant smile at them all.

'I'm so dreadfully sorry to have bothered you in this stupid way. Thank you *so* much, Lady Angkatell.'

She went out with John. Sir Henry stood by the window looking after them.

'Quite a fine warm night,' he said.

Lady Angkatell yawned.

The Hollow

'Oh, dear,' she murmured, 'we must go to bed. Henry, we must go and see one of her pictures. I'm sure, from tonight, she must give a lovely performance.'

They went upstairs. Midge, saying goodnight, asked Lucy:

'A lovely performance?'

'Didn't you think so, darling?'

'I gather, Lucy, that you think it's just possible she may have some matches in Dovecotes all the time.'

'Dozens of boxes, I expect, darling. But we mustn't be uncharitable. And it *was* a lovely performance!'

Doors were shutting all down the corridor, voices were murmuring goodnights. Sir Henry said: 'I'll leave the window for Christow.' His own door shut.

Henrietta said to Gerda, 'What fun actresses are. They make such marvellous entrances and exits!' She yawned and added, 'I'm frightfully sleepy.'

Veronica Cray moved swiftly along the narrow path through the chestnut woods.

She came out from the woods to the open space by the swimming pool. There was a small pavilion here where the Angkatells sat on days that were sunny but when there was a cold wind.

Veronica Cray stood still. She turned and faced John Christow.

Then she laughed. With her hand she gestured towards the leaf-strewn surface of the swimming pool.

'Not quite like the Mediterranean, is it, John?' she said.

Agatha Christie

He knew then what he had been waiting for—knew that in all those fifteen years of separation from Veronica she had still been with him. *The blue sea, the scent of mimosa, the hot dust*—pushed down, thrust out of sight, but never really forgotten. They all meant one thing—Veronica. He was a young man of twenty-four, desperately and agonizingly in love, and this time he was not going to run away.

CHAPTER 9

John Christow came out from the chestnut woods on to the green slope by the house. There was a moon and the house basked in the moonlight with a strange innocence in its curtained windows. He looked down at the wrist-watch he wore.

It was three o'clock. He drew a deep breath and his face was anxious. He was no longer, even remotely, a young man of twenty-four in love. He was a shrewd, practical man of just on forty, and his mind was clear and level-headed.

He'd been a fool, of course, a complete damned fool, but he didn't regret that! For he was, he now realized, completely master of himself. It was as though, for years, he had dragged a weight upon his leg—and now the weight was gone. He was free.

He was free and himself, John Christow—and he knew that to John Christow, successful Harley Street specialist, Veronica Cray meant nothing whatsoever. All that had been in the past—and because that conflict had never been resolved, because he had always suffered humiliatingly from the fear that he had, in plain language, 'run away', so Veronica's image had never completely left him. She had

Agatha Christie

come to him tonight out of a dream, and he had accepted the dream, and now, thank God, he was delivered from it for ever. He was back in the present—and it was 3 am, and it was just possible that he had mucked up things rather badly.

He'd been with Veronica for three hours. She had sailed in like a frigate, and cut him out of the circle and carried him off as her prize, and he wondered now what on earth everybody had thought about it.

What, for instance, would Gerda think?

And Henrietta? (But he didn't care quite so much about Henrietta. He could, he felt, at a pinch explain to Henrietta. He could never explain to Gerda.)

And he didn't, definitely he didn't want to lose anything.

All his life he had been a man who took a justifiable number of risks. Risks with patients, risks with treatment, risks with investments. Never a fantastic risk—only the kind of risk that was just beyond the margin of safety.

If Gerda guessed—if Gerda had the least suspicion...

But would she have? How much did he really know about Gerda? Normally, Gerda would believe white was black if he told her so. But over a thing like this...

What had he looked like when he followed Veronica's tall, triumphant figure out of that window? What had he shown in his face? Had they seen a boy's dazed, lovesick face? Or had they only observed a man doing a polite duty? He didn't know. He hadn't the least idea.

But he was afraid—afraid for the ease and order and safety of his life. He'd been mad—quite mad, he thought with exasperation—and then took comfort in that very thought.

The Hollow

Nobody would believe, surely, he could have been as mad as that?

Everybody was in bed and asleep, that was clear. The french window of the drawing-room stood half-open, left for his return. He looked up again at the innocent, sleeping house. It looked, somehow, too innocent.

Suddenly he started. He had heard, or he had imagined he heard, the faint closing of a door.

He turned his head sharply. If someone had come down to the pool, following him there. If someone had waited and followed him back that someone could have taken a higher path and so gained entrance to the house again by the side garden door, and the soft closing of the garden door would have made just the sound that he had heard.

He looked up sharply at the windows. Was that curtain moving, had it been pushed aside for someone to look out, and then allowed to fall? Henrietta's room.

Henrietta! Not Henrietta, his heart cried in a sudden panic. I can't lose Henrietta!

He wanted suddenly to fling up a handful of pebbles at her window, to cry out to her.

'Come out, my dear love. Come out to me now and walk with me up through the woods to Shovel Down and there listen—listen to everything that I now know about myself and that you must know, too, if you do not know it already.'

He wanted to say to Henrietta:

'I am starting again. A new life begins from today. The things that crippled and hindered me from living have fallen away. You were right this afternoon when you asked me

Agatha Christie

if I was running away from myself. That is what I have been doing for years. Because I never knew whether it was strength or weakness that took me away from Veronica. I have been afraid of myself, afraid of life, afraid of you.'

If he were to wake Henrietta and make her come out with him now—up through the woods to where they could watch, together, the sun come up over the rim of the world.

'You're mad,' he said to himself. He shivered. It was cold now, late September after all. 'What the devil is the matter with you?' he asked himself. 'You've behaved quite insanely enough for one night. If you get away with it as it is, you're damned lucky!' What on earth would Gerda think if he stayed out all night and came home with the milk?

What, for the matter of that, would the Angkatells think?

But that did not worry him for a moment. The Angkatells took Greenwich time, as it were, from Lucy Angkatell. And to Lucy Angkatell, the unusual always appeared perfectly reasonable.

But Gerda, unfortunately, was not an Angkatell.

Gerda would have to be dealt with, and he'd better go in and deal with Gerda as soon as possible.

Supposing it had been Gerda who had followed him tonight?

No good saying people didn't do such things. As a doctor, he knew only too well what people, high-minded, sensitive, fastidious, honourable people, constantly did. They listened at doors, and opened letters and spied and snooped—not because for one moment they approved of such conduct, but because before the sheer necessity of human anguish they were rendered desperate.

The Hollow

Poor devils, he thought, poor suffering human devils. John Christow knew a good deal about human suffering. He had not very much pity for weakness, but he had for suffering, for it was, he knew, the strong who suffer.

If Gerda knew—

Nonsense, he said to himself, why should she? She's gone up to bed and she's fast asleep. She's no imagination, never has had.

He went in through the french windows, switched on a lamp, closed and locked the windows. Then, switching off the light, he left the room, found the switch in the hall, went quickly and lightly up the stairs. A second switch turned off the hall light. He stood for a moment by the bedroom door, his hand on the door-knob, then he turned it and went in.

The room was dark and he could hear Gerda's even breathing. She stirred as he came in and closed the door. Her voice came to him, blurred and indistinct with sleep.

'Is that you, John?'

'Yes.'

'Aren't you very late? What time is it?'

He said easily:

'I've no idea. Sorry I woke you up. I had to go in with the woman and have a drink.'

He made his voice sound bored and sleepy.

Gerda murmured, 'Oh? Goodnight, John.'

There was a rustle as she turned over in bed.

It was all right! As usual, he'd been lucky. As *usual*—just for a moment it sobered him, the thought of how often his luck had held! Time and again there had been a moment when he'd held his breath and said, 'If *this* goes wrong.' And it hadn't gone wrong! But some day, surely, his luck would change.

He undressed quickly and got into bed. Funny that kid's fortune. '*And this one is over your head and has power over you...*' Veronica! And she *had* had power over him all right.

'But not any more, my girl,' he thought with a kind of savage satisfaction. 'All that's over. I'm quit of you now!'

CHAPTER 10

It was ten o'clock the next morning when John came down. Breakfast was on the sideboard. Gerda had had her breakfast sent up to her in bed and had been rather perturbed since perhaps she might be 'giving trouble'.

Nonsense, John had said. People like the Angkatells who still managed to have butlers and servants might just as well give them something to do.

He felt very kindly towards Gerda this morning. All that nervous irritation that had so fretted him of late seemed to have died down and disappeared.

Sir Henry and Edward had gone out shooting, Lady Angkatell told him. She herself was busy with a gardening basket and gardening gloves. He stayed talking to her for a while until Gudgeon approached him with a letter on a salver.

'This has just come by hand, sir.'

He took it with slightly raised eyebrows.

Veronica!

He strolled into the library, tearing it open.

Please come over this morning. I must see you.
  Veronica.

Imperious as ever, he thought. He'd a good mind not to go. Then he thought he might as well and get it over. He'd go at once.

He took the path opposite the library window, passed by the swimming pool which was a kind of nucleus with paths radiating from it in every direction, one up the hill to the woods proper, one from the flower walk above the house, one from the farm and the one that led on to the lane which he took now. A few yards up the lane was the cottage called Dovecotes.

Veronica was waiting for him. She spoke from the window of the pretentious half-timbered building.

'Come inside, John. It's cold this morning.'

There was a fire lit in the sitting-room, which was furnished in off-white with pale cyclamen cushions.

Looking at her this morning with an appraising eye, he saw the differences there were from the girl he remembered, as he had not been able to see them last night.

Strictly speaking, he thought, she was more beautiful now than then. She understood her beauty better, and she cared for it and enhanced it in every way. Her hair, which had been deep golden, was now a silvery platinum colour. Her eyebrows were different, giving much more poignancy to her expression.

Hers had never been a mindless beauty. Veronica, he remembered, had qualified as one of our 'intellectual actresses'. She had a university degree and had views on Strindberg and on Shakespeare.

He was struck now with what had only been dimly apparent to him in the past—that she was a woman whose

The Hollow

egoism was quite abnormal. Veronica was accustomed to getting her own way, and beneath the smooth beautiful contours of flesh he seemed to sense an ugly iron determination.

'I sent for you,' said Veronica, as she handed him a box of cigarettes, 'because we've got to talk. We've got to make arrangements. For our future, I mean.'

He took a cigarette and lighted it. Then he said quite pleasantly:

'But have we a future?'

She gave him a sharp glance.

'What do you mean, John? Of course we have got a future. We've wasted fifteen years. There's no need to waste any more time.'

He sat down.

'I'm sorry, Veronica. But I'm afraid you've got all this taped out wrong. I've—enjoyed meeting you again very much. But your life and mine don't touch anywhere. They are quite divergent.'

'Nonsense, John. I love you and you love me. We've always loved each other. You were incredibly obstinate in the past! But never mind that now. Our lives needn't clash. I don't mean to go back to the States. When I've finished this picture I'm working on now, I'm going to play a straight part on the London stage. I've got a wonderful play—Elderton's written it for me. It will be a terrific success.'

'I'm sure it will,' he said politely.

'And you can go on being a doctor.' Her voice was kind and condescending. 'You're quite well known, they tell me.'

'My dear girl, I'm married. I've got children.'

'I'm married myself at the moment,' said Veronica. 'But all these things are easily arranged. A good lawyer can fix up everything.' She smiled at him dazzlingly. 'I always did mean to marry you, darling. I can't think why I have this terrible passion for you, but there it is!'

'I'm sorry, Veronica, but no good lawyer is going to fix up anything. Your life and mine have nothing to do with each other.'

'Not after last night?'

'You're not a child, Veronica. You've had a couple of husbands, and by all accounts several lovers. What does last night mean actually? Nothing at all, and you know it.'

'Oh, my dear John.' She was still amused, indulgent. 'If you'd seen your face—there in that stuffy drawing-room! You might have been in San Miguel again.'

John sighed. He said:

'I *was* in San Miguel. Try to understand, Veronica. You came to me out of the past. Last night, I, too, was in the past, but today—today's different. I'm a man fifteen years older. A man you don't even know—and whom I dare say you wouldn't like much if you did know.'

'You prefer your wife and children to me?'

She was genuinely amazed.

'Odd as it may seem to you, I do.'

'Nonsense, John, you love me.'

'I'm sorry, Veronica.'

She said incredulously:

'You don't love me?'

The Hollow

'It's better to be quite clear about these things. You are an extraordinarily beautiful woman, Veronica, but I don't love you.'

She sat so still that she might have been a waxwork. That stillness of hers made him just a little uneasy.

When she spoke it was with such venom that he recoiled.

'Who is she?'

'She? Who do you mean?'

'That woman by the mantelpiece last night?'

Henrietta! he thought. How the devil did she get on to Henrietta? Aloud he said:

'Who are you talking about? Midge Hardcastle?'

'Midge? That's the square, dark girl, isn't it? No, I don't mean her. And I don't mean your wife. I mean that insolent devil who was leaning against the mantelpiece! It's because of *her* that you're turning me down! Oh, don't pretend to be so moral about your wife and children. It's that other woman.'

She got up and came towards him.

'Don't you understand, John, that ever since I came back to England, eighteen months ago, I've been thinking about you? Why do you imagine I took this idiotic place here? Simply because I found out that you often came down for weekends with the Angkatells!'

'So last night was all planned, Veronica?'

'You *belong* to me, John. You always have!'

'I don't belong to anyone, Veronica. Hasn't life taught you even now that you can't own other human beings body and soul? I loved you when I was a young man. I wanted you to share my life. You wouldn't do it!'

'*My* life and career were much more important than *yours*. Anyone can be a doctor!'

He lost his temper a little.

'Are you *quite* as wonderful as you think you are?'

'You mean that I haven't got to the top of the tree. I shall! *I shall*!'

John Christow looked at her with a sudden, quite dispassionate interest.

'I don't believe, you know, that you will. There's a *lack* in you, Veronica. You're all grab and snatch—no real generosity—I think that's it.'

Veronica got up. She said in a quiet voice:

'You turned me down fifteen years ago. You've turned me down again today. I'll make you sorry for this.'

John got up and went to the door.

'I'm sorry, Veronica, if I've hurt you. You're very lovely, my dear, and I once loved you very much. Can't we leave it at that?'

'Goodbye, John. We're not leaving it at that. You'll find that out all right. I think—I think I hate you more than I believed I could hate anyone.'

He shrugged his shoulders.

'I'm sorry. Goodbye.'

John walked back slowly through the wood. When he got to the swimming pool he sat down on the bench there. He had no regrets for his treatment of Veronica. Veronica, he thought dispassionately, was a nasty bit of work. She always had been a nasty bit of work, and the best thing he had ever done was to get clear of her in time. God alone knew what would have happened to him by now if he hadn't!

As it was, he had that extraordinary sensation of starting a new life, unfettered and unhampered by the past. He must have been extremely difficult to live with for the last year or two. Poor Gerda, he thought, with her unselfishness and her continual anxiety to please him. He would be kinder in future.

And perhaps now he would be able to stop trying to bully Henrietta. Not that one could really bully Henrietta—she wasn't made that way. Storms broke over her and she stood there, meditative, her eyes looking at you from very far away.

He thought: 'I shall go to Henrietta and tell her.'

He looked up sharply, disturbed by some small unexpected sound. There had been shots in the woods higher up, and there had been the usual small noises of woodlands, birds, and the faint melancholy dropping of leaves. But this was another noise—a very faint business-like click.

And suddenly, John was acutely conscious of danger. How long had he been sitting here? Half an hour? An hour? There was someone watching him. Someone—

And that click was—of course it was—

He turned sharply, a man very quick in his reactions. But he was not quick enough. His eyes widened in surprise, but there was no time for him to make a sound.

The shot rang out and he fell, awkwardly, sprawled out by the edge of the swimming pool.

A dark stain welled up slowly on his left side and trickled slowly on to the concrete of the pool edge; and from there dripped red into the blue water.

CHAPTER 11

Hercule Poirot flicked a last speck of dust from his shoes. He had dressed carefully for his luncheon party and he was satisfied with the result.

He knew well enough the kind of clothes that were worn in the country on a Sunday in England, but he did not choose to conform to English ideas. He preferred his own standards of urban smartness. He was not an English country gentleman. He was Hercule Poirot!

He did not, he confessed it to himself, really like the country. The weekend cottage—so many of his friends had extolled it—he had allowed himself to succumb, and had purchased Resthaven, though the only thing he had liked about it was its shape, which was quite square like a box. The surrounding landscape he did not care for though it was, he knew, supposed to be a beauty spot. It was, however, too wildly asymmetrical to appeal to him. He did not care much for trees at any time—they had that untidy habit of shedding their leaves. He could endure poplars and he approved of a monkey puzzle—but this riot of beech and oak left him unmoved. Such a landscape was best enjoyed from a car on a fine afternoon.

The Hollow

You exclaimed, '*Quel beau paysage!*' and drove back to a good hotel.

The best thing about Resthaven, he considered, was the small vegetable garden neatly laid out in rows by his Belgian gardener Victor. Meanwhile Françoise, Victor's wife, devoted herself with tenderness to the care of her employer's stomach.

Hercule Poirot passed through the gate, sighed, glanced down once more at his shining black shoes, adjusted his pale grey Homburg hat, and looked up and down the road.

He shivered slightly at the aspect of Dovecotes. Dovecotes and Resthaven had been erected by rival builders, both of whom had acquired a small piece of land. Further enterprise on their part had been swiftly curtailed by a National Trust for preserving the beauties of the countryside. The two houses remained representative of two schools of thought. Resthaven was a box with a roof, severely modern and a little dull. Dovecotes was a riot of half-timbering and Olde Worlde packed into as small a space as possible.

Hercule Poirot debated within himself as to how he should approach The Hollow. There was, he knew, a little higher up the lane, a small gate and a path. This, the unofficial way, would save a half-mile *détour* by the road. Nevertheless Hercule Poirot, a stickler for etiquette, decided to take the longer way round and approach the house correctly by the front entrance.

This was his first visit to Sir Henry and Lady Angkatell. One should not, he considered, take shortcuts uninvited, especially when one was the guest of people of social importance. He was, it must be admitted, pleased by their invitation.

'*Je suis un peu snob*,' he murmured to himself.

He had retained an agreeable impression of the Angkatells from the time in Baghdad, particularly of Lady Angkatell. '*Une originale!*' he thought to himself.

His estimation of the time required for walking to The Hollow by road was accurate. It was exactly one minute to one when he rang the front-door bell. He was glad to have arrived and felt slightly tired. He was not fond of walking.

The door was opened by the magnificent Gudgeon, of whom Poirot approved. His reception, however, was not quite as he had hoped. 'Her ladyship is in the pavilion by the swimming pool, sir. Will you come this way?'

The passion of the English for sitting out of doors irritated Hercule Poirot. Though one had to put up with this whimsy in the height of summer, surely, Poirot thought, one should be safe from it by the end of September! The day was mild, certainly, but it had, as autumn days always had, a certain dampness. How infinitely pleasanter to have been ushered into a comfortable drawing-room with, perhaps, a small fire in the grate. But no, here he was being led out through french windows across a slope of lawn, past a rockery and then through a small gate and along a narrow track between closely planted young chestnuts.

It was the habit of the Angkatells to invite guests for one o'clock, and on fine days they had cocktails and sherry in the small pavilion by the swimming pool. Lunch itself was scheduled for one-thirty, by which time the most unpunctual of guests should have managed to arrive, which permitted Lady Angkatell's excellent cook to embark on soufflés and such accurately timed delicacies without too much trepidation.

To Hercule Poirot, the plan did not commend itself.

'In a little minute,' he thought, 'I shall be almost back where I started.'

With an increasing awareness of his feet in his shoes, he followed Gudgeon's tall figure.

It was at that moment from just ahead of him that he heard a little cry. It increased, somehow, his dissatisfaction. It was incongruous, in some way unfitting. He did not classify it, nor indeed think about it. When he thought about it afterwards he was hard put to it to remember just what emotions it had seemed to convey. Dismay? Surprise? Horror? He could only say that it suggested, very definitely, the unexpected.

Gudgeon stepped out from the chestnuts. He was moving to one side, deferentially, to allow Poirot to pass and at the same time clearing his throat preparatory to murmuring, 'M. Poirot, my lady' in the proper subdued and respectful tones when his suppleness became suddenly rigid. He gasped. It was an unbutlerlike noise.

Hercule Poirot stepped out on to the open space surrounding the swimming pool, and immediately he, too, stiffened, but with annoyance.

It was too much—it was really too much! He had not suspected such cheapness of the Angkatells. The long walk by the road, the disappointment at the house—and now *this*! The misplaced sense of humour of the English!

Agatha Christie

He was annoyed and he was bored—oh, how he was bored. Death was not, to him, amusing. And here they had arranged for him, by way of a joke, a set-piece.

For what he was looking at was a highly artificial murder scene. By the side of the pool was the body, artistically arranged with an outflung arm and even some red paint dripping gently over the edge of the concrete into the pool. It was a spectacular body, that of a handsome fair-haired man. Standing over the body, revolver in hand, was a woman, a short, powerfully built, middle-aged woman with a curiously blank expression.

And there were three other actors. On the far side of the pool was a tall young woman whose hair matched the autumn leaves in its rich brown; she had a basket in her hand full of dahlia heads. A little farther off was a man, a tall, inconspicuous man in a shooting-coat, carrying a gun. And immediately on his left, with a basket of eggs in her hand, was his hostess, Lady Angkatell.

It was clear to Hercule Poirot that several different paths converged here at the swimming pool and that these people had each arrived by a different path.

It was all very mathematical and artificial.

He sighed. *Enfin*, what did they expect him to do? Was he to pretend to believe in this 'crime'? Was he to register dismay—alarm? Or was he to bow, to congratulate his hostess: 'Ah, but it is very charming, what you arrange for me here'?

Really, the whole thing was very stupid—not *spirituel* at all! Was it not Queen Victoria who had said: 'We are not

The Hollow

amused'? He felt very inclined to say the same. 'I, Hercule Poirot, am not amused.'

Lady Angkatell had walked towards the body. He followed, conscious of Gudgeon, still breathing hard, behind him. 'He is not in the secret, that one,' Hercule Poirot thought to himself. From the other side of the pool, the other two people joined them. They were all quite close now, looking down on that spectacular sprawling figure by the pool's edge.

And suddenly, with a terrific shock, with that feeling as of blurring on a cinematograph screen before the picture comes into focus, Hercule Poirot realized that this artificially set scene had a point of reality.

For what he was looking down at was, if not a dead, at least a dying man.

It was not red paint dripping off the edge of the concrete, it was blood. This man had been shot, and shot a very short time ago.

He darted a quick glance at the woman who stood there, revolver in hand. Her face was quite blank, without feeling of any kind. She looked dazed and rather stupid.

'Curious,' he thought.

Had she, he wondered, drained herself of all emotion, all feeling, in the firing of the shot? Was she now all passion spent, nothing but an exhausted shell? It might be so, he thought.

Then he looked down on the shot man, and he started. For the dying man's eyes were open. They were intensely blue eyes and they held an expression that Poirot could not read but which he described to himself as a kind of intense awareness.

Agatha Christie

And suddenly, or so it felt to Poirot, there seemed to be in all this group of people only one person who was really alive—the man who was at the point of death.

Poirot had never received so strong an impression of vivid and intense vitality. The others were pale shadowy figures, actors in a remote drama, but this man was *real*.

John Christow opened his mouth and spoke. His voice was strong, unsurprised and urgent.

'*Henrietta*—' he said.

Then his eyelids dropped, his head jerked sideways.

Hercule Poirot knelt down, made sure, then rose to his feet, mechanically dusting the knees of his trousers.

'Yes,' he said. 'He is dead.'

The picture broke up, wavered, refocused itself. There were individual reactions now—trivial happenings. Poirot was conscious of himself as a kind of magnified eyes and ears— recording. Just that, *recording*.

He was aware of Lady Angkatell's hand relaxing its grip on her basket and Gudgeon springing forward, quickly taking it from her.

'Allow me, my lady.'

Mechanically, quite naturally, Lady Angkatell murmured:

'Thank you, Gudgeon.'

And then, hesitantly, she said:

'Gerda—'

The woman holding the revolver stirred for the first time. She looked round at them all. When she spoke, her

The Hollow

voice held what seemed to be pure bewilderment.

'John's dead,' she said. 'John's *dead*.'

With a kind of swift authority, the tall young woman with the leaf-brown hair came swiftly to her.

'Give that to me, Gerda,' she said.

And dexterously, before Poirot could protest or intervene, she had taken the revolver out of Gerda Christow's hand.

Poirot took a quick step forward.

'You should not do that, Mademoiselle—'

The young woman started nervously at the sound of his voice. The revolver slipped through her fingers. She was standing by the edge of the pool and the revolver fell with a splash into the water.

Her mouth opened and she uttered an 'Oh' of consternation, turning her head to look at Poirot apologetically.

'What a fool I am,' she said. 'I'm sorry.'

Poirot did not speak for a moment. He was staring into a pair of clear hazel eyes. They met his quite steadily and he wondered if his momentary suspicion had been unjust.

He said quietly:

'Things should be handled as little as possible. Everything must be left exactly as it is for the police to see.'

There was a little stir then—very faint, just a ripple of uneasiness.

Lady Angkatell murmured distastefully, 'Of course. I suppose—yes, the police—'

In a quiet, pleasant voice, tinged with fastidious repulsion, the man in the shooting-coat said, 'I'm afraid, Lucy, it's inevitable.'

Into that moment of silence and realization there came the sound of footsteps and voices, assured, brisk footsteps and cheerful, incongruous voices.

Along the path from the house came Sir Henry Angkatell and Midge Hardcastle, talking and laughing together.

At the sight of the group round the pool, Sir Henry stopped short, and exclaimed in astonishment:

'What's the matter? What's happened?'

His wife answered, 'Gerda has—' She broke off sharply. 'I mean—John is—'

Gerda said in her flat, bewildered voice:

'John has been shot. He's dead.'

They all looked away from her, embarrassed.

Then Lady Angkatell said quickly:

'My dear, I think you'd better go and—and lie down. Perhaps we had better all go back to the house? Henry, you and M. Poirot can stay here and—and wait for the police.'

'That will be the best plan, I think,' said Sir Henry. He turned to Gudgeon. 'Will you ring up the police station, Gudgeon? Just state exactly what has occurred. When the police arrive, bring them straight out here.'

Gudgeon bent his head a little and said, 'Yes, Sir Henry.' He was looking a little white about the gills, but he was still the perfect servant.

The tall young woman said, 'Come, Gerda,' and putting her hand through the other woman's arm, she led her unresistingly away and along the path towards the house. Gerda walked as though in a dream. Gudgeon stood back a little to let them pass, and then followed carrying the basket of eggs.

Sir Henry turned sharply to his wife. 'Now, Lucy, what is all this? What happened exactly?'

Lady Angkatell stretched out vague hands, a lovely helpless gesture. Hercule Poirot felt the charm of it and the appeal.

'My dear, I hardly know. I was down by the hens. I heard a shot that seemed very near, but I didn't really think anything about it. After all,' she appealed to them all, 'one *doesn't*! And then I came up the path to the pool and there was John lying there and Gerda standing over him with the revolver. Henrietta and Edward arrived almost at the same moment—from over there.'

She nodded towards the farther side of the pool, where two paths ran into the woods.

Hercule Poirot cleared his throat.

'Who are they, this John and this Gerda? If I may know,' he added apologetically.

'Oh, of course.' Lady Angkatell turned to him in quick apology. 'One forgets—but then one doesn't exactly *introduce* people—not when somebody has just been killed. John is John Christow, Dr Christow. Gerda Christow is his wife.'

'And the lady who went with Mrs Christow to the house?'

'My cousin, Henrietta Savernake.'

There was a movement, a very faint movement from the man on Poirot's left.

'*Henrietta* Savernake,' thought Poirot, 'and he does not like that she should say it—but it is, after all, inevitable that I should know...'

('*Henrietta!*' the dying man had said. He had said it in a very curious way. A way that reminded Poirot of something—of some incident...now, what was it? No matter, it would come to him.)

Lady Angkatell was going on, determined now on fulfilling her social duties.

'And this is another cousin of ours, Edward Angkatell. And Miss Hardcastle.'

Poirot acknowledged the introductions with polite bows. Midge felt suddenly that she wanted to laugh hysterically; she controlled herself with an effort.

'And now, my dear,' said Sir Henry, 'I think that, as you suggested, you had better go back to the house. I will have a word or two here with M. Poirot.'

Lady Angkatell looked thoughtfully at them.

'I do hope,' she said, 'that Gerda *is* lying down. Was that the right thing to suggest? I really couldn't think what to say. I mean, one has no *precedent*. What *does* one say to a woman who has just killed her husband?'

She looked at them as though hoping that some authoritative answer might be given to her question.

Then she went along the path towards the house. Midge followed her. Edward brought up the rear.

Poirot was left with his host.

Sir Henry cleared his throat. He seemed a little uncertain what to say.

'Christow,' he observed at last, 'was a very able fellow—a *very* able fellow.'

Poirot's eyes rested once more on the dead man. He still had the curious impression that the dead man was more alive than the living.

He wondered what gave him that impression.

The Hollow

He responded politely to Sir Henry.

'Such a tragedy as this is very unfortunate,' he said.

'This sort of thing is more in your line than mine,' said Sir Henry. 'I don't think I have ever been at close quarters with a murder before. I hope I've done the right thing so far?'

'The procedure has been quite correct,' said Poirot. 'You have summoned the police, and until they arrive and take charge there is nothing for us to do—except to make sure that nobody disturbs the body or tampers with the evidence.'

As he said the last word he looked down into the pool where he could see the revolver lying on the concrete bottom, slightly distorted by the blue water.

The evidence, he thought, had perhaps already been tampered with before he, Hercule Poirot, had been able to prevent it.

But no—that had been an accident.

Sir Henry murmured distastefully:

'Think we've got to stand about? A bit chilly. It would be all right, I should think, if we went inside the pavilion?'

Poirot, who had been conscious of damp feet and a disposition to shiver, acquiesced gladly. The pavilion was at the side of the pool farthest from the house, and through its open door they commanded a view of the pool and the body and the path to the house along which the police would come.

The pavilion was luxuriously furnished with comfortable settees and gay native rugs. On a painted iron table a tray was set with glasses and a decanter of sherry.

'I'd offer you a drink,' said Sir Henry, 'but I suppose I'd better not touch anything until the police come—not, I should imagine, that there's anything to interest them

Agatha Christie

in here. Still, it is better to be on the safe side. Gudgeon hadn't brought out the cocktails yet, I see. He was waiting for you to arrive.'

The two sat down rather gingerly in two wicker chairs near the door so that they could watch the path from the house.

A constraint settled over them. It was an occasion on which it was difficult to make small talk.

Poirot glanced round the pavilion, noting anything that struck him as unusual. An expensive cape of platinum fox had been flung carelessly across the back of one of the chairs. He wondered whose it was. Its rather ostentatious magnificence did not harmonize with any of the people he had seen up to now. He could not, for instance, imagine it round Lady Angkatell's shoulders.

It worried him. It breathed a mixture of opulence and self-advertisement—and those characteristics were lacking in anyone he had seen so far.

'I suppose we can smoke,' said Sir Henry, offering his case to Poirot.

Before taking the cigarette, Poirot sniffed the air.

French perfume—an expensive French perfume.

Only a trace of it lingered, but it was there, and again the scent was not the scent that associated itself in his mind with any of the occupants of The Hollow.

As he leaned forward to light his cigarette at Sir Henry's lighter, Poirot's glance fell on a little pile of matchboxes—six of them—stacked on a small table near one of the settees.

It was a detail that struck him as definitely odd.

CHAPTER 12

'Half-past two,' said Lady Angkatell.

She was in the drawing-room, with Midge and Edward. From behind the closed door of Sir Henry's study came the murmur of voices. Hercule Poirot, Sir Henry and Inspector Grange were in there.

Lady Angkatell sighed:

'You know, Midge, I still feel one ought to do something about lunch. It seems, of course, quite heartless to sit down round the table as though nothing had happened. But after all, M. Poirot was asked to lunch—and he is probably hungry. And it can't be upsetting to *him* that poor John Christow has been killed like it is to us. And I must say that though I really do not feel like eating myself, Henry and Edward must be extremely hungry after being out shooting all the morning.'

Edward Angkatell said, 'Don't worry on my account, Lucy, dear.'

'You are always considerate, Edward. And then there is David—I noticed that he ate a great deal at dinner last night. Intellectual people always seem to need a good deal of food. Where *is* David, by the way?'

Agatha Christie

'He went up to his room,' said Midge, 'after he had heard what had happened.'

'Yes—well, that was rather tactful of him. I dare say it made him feel awkward. Of course, say what you like, a murder is an awkward thing—it upsets the servants and puts the general routine out—we were having ducks for lunch—fortunately they are quite nice eaten cold. What does one do about Gerda, do you think? Something on a tray? A little strong soup, perhaps?'

'Really,' thought Midge, 'Lucy is inhuman!' And then with a qualm she reflected that it was perhaps because Lucy was too human that it shocked one so! Wasn't it the plain unvarnished truth that all catastrophes were hedged round with these little trivial wonderings and surmises? Lucy merely gave utterance to the thoughts which most people did not acknowledge. One did remember the servants, and worry about meals. And one did, even, feel hungry. She felt hungry herself at this very moment! Hungry, she thought, and at the same time, rather sick. A curious mixture.

And there was, undoubtedly, just plain awkward embarrassment in not knowing how to react to a quiet, commonplace woman whom one had referred to, only yesterday, as 'poor Gerda' and who was now, presumably, shortly to be standing in the dock accused of murder.

'These things happen to other people,' thought Midge. 'They can't happen to *us*.'

She looked across the room at Edward. 'They oughtn't,' she thought, 'to happen to people like Edward. People who

The Hollow

are so very *un*violent.' She took comfort in looking at Edward. Edward, so quiet, so reasonable, so kind and calm.

Gudgeon entered, inclined himself confidentially and spoke in a suitably muted voice.

'I have placed sandwiches and some coffee in the dining-room, my lady.'

'Oh, *thank* you, Gudgeon!

'Really,' said Lady Angkatell as Gudgeon left the room. 'Gudgeon is wonderful: I don't know what I should do without Gudgeon. He always knows the right thing to do. Some really substantial sandwiches are as good as lunch—and nothing *heartless* about them, if you know what I mean!'

'Oh, Lucy, *don't*.'

Midge suddenly felt warm tears running down her cheek. Lady Angkatell looked surprised, murmured:

'Poor darling. It's all been too much for you.'

Edward crossed to the sofa and sat down by Midge. He put his arm round her.

'Don't worry, little Midge,' he said.

Midge buried her face on his shoulder and sobbed there comfortably. She remembered how nice Edward had been to her when her rabbit had died at Ainswick one Easter holidays.

Edward said gently, 'It's been a shock. Can I get her some brandy, Lucy?'

'On the sideboard in the dining-room. I don't think—'

She broke off as Henrietta came into the room. Midge sat up. She felt Edward stiffen and sit very still.

What, thought Midge, does Henrietta feel? She felt almost reluctant to look at her cousin—but there was nothing to see.

Agatha Christie

Henrietta looked, if anything, belligerent. She had come in with her chin up, her colour high, and with a certain swiftness.

'Oh, there you are, Henrietta,' cried Lady Angkatell. 'I have been wondering. The police are with Henry and M. Poirot. What have you given Gerda? Brandy? Or tea and aspirin?'

'I gave her some brandy—and a hot-water bottle.'

'Quite right,' said Lady Angkatell approvingly. 'That's what they tell you in First Aid classes—the hot-water bottle, I mean, for shock—*not* the brandy; there is a reaction nowadays against stimulants. But I think that is only a fashion. We always gave brandy for shock when I was a girl at Ainswick. Though, really, I suppose, it can't be exactly *shock* with Gerda. I don't know really *what* one would feel if one had killed one's husband—it's the sort of thing one just can't begin to imagine—but it wouldn't exactly give one a *shock*. I mean, there wouldn't be any element of *surprise*.'

Henrietta's voice, icy cold, cut into the placid atmosphere. She said, 'Why are you all so sure that Gerda killed John?'

There was a moment's pause—and Midge felt a curious shifting in the atmosphere. There was confusion, strain and, finally, a kind of slow watchfulness.

Then Lady Angkatell said, her voice quite devoid of any inflection:

'It seemed—self-evident. What else do you suggest?'

'Isn't it possible that Gerda came along to the pool, that she found John lying there, and that she had just picked up the revolver when—when we came upon the scene?'

Again there was that silence. Then Lady Angkatell asked:
'Is that what Gerda says?'

'Yes.'

It was not a simple assent. It had force behind it. It came out like a revolver shot.

Lady Angkatell raised her eyebrows, then she said with apparent irrelevancy:

'There are sandwiches and coffee in the dining-room.'

She broke off with a little gasp as Gerda Christow came through the open door. She said hurriedly and apologetically:

'I—I really didn't feel I could lie down any longer. One is—one is so terribly restless.'

Lady Angkatell cried:

'You must sit down—you must sit down *at once*.'

She displaced Midge from the sofa, settled Gerda there, put a cushion at her back.

'You poor dear,' said Lady Angkatell.

She spoke with emphasis, but the words seemed quite meaningless.

Edward walked to the window and stood there looking out.

Gerda pushed back the untidy hair from her forehead. She spoke in a worried, bewildered tone.

'I—I really am only just beginning to realize it. You know I haven't been able to feel—I still can't feel—that it's *real*—that John—is *dead*.' She began to shake a little. 'Who can have killed him? Who can possibly have killed him?'

Lady Angkatell drew a deep breath—then she turned her head sharply. Sir Henry's door had opened. He came in accompanied by Inspector Grange, who was a large, heavily built man with a down-drooping, pessimistic moustache.

'This is my wife—Inspector Grange.'

Grange bowed and said:

'I was wondering, Lady Angkatell, if I could have a few words with Mrs Christow—'

He broke off as Lady Angkatell indicated the figure on the sofa.

'Mrs Christow?'

Gerda said eagerly:

'Yes, I am Mrs Christow.'

'I don't want to distress you, Mrs Christow, but I would like to ask you a few questions. You can, of course, have your solicitor present if you prefer it—'

Sir Henry put in:

'It is sometimes wiser, Gerda—'

She interrupted:

'A solicitor? Why a solicitor? Why should a solicitor know anything about John's death?'

Inspector Grange coughed. Sir Henry seemed about to speak. Henrietta put in:

'The inspector only wants to know just what happened this morning.'

Gerda turned to him. She spoke in a wondering voice:

'It seems all like a bad dream—not real. I—I haven't been able to cry or anything. One just doesn't feel anything at all.'

Grange said soothingly:

'That's the shock, Mrs Christow.'

'Yes, yes—I suppose it is. But you see it was all so *sudden*. I went out from the house and along the path to the swimming pool—'

'At what time, Mrs Christow?'

The Hollow

'It was just before one o'clock—about two minutes to one. I know because I looked at that clock. And when I got there—there was John, lying there—and blood on the edge of the concrete.'

'Did you hear a shot, Mrs Christow?'

'Yes,—no—I don't know. I knew Sir Henry and Mr Angkatell were out shooting. I—I just saw John—'

'Yes, Mrs Christow?'

'John—and blood—and a revolver. I picked up the revolver—'

'Why?'

'I beg your pardon?'

'Why did you pick up the revolver, Mrs Christow?'

'I—I don't know.'

'You shouldn't have touched it, you know.'

'Shouldn't I?' Gerda was vague, her face vacant. 'But I did. I held it in my hands.'

She looked down now at her hands as though she was, in fancy, seeing the revolver lying in them.

She turned sharply to the inspector. Her voice was suddenly sharp—anguished.

'Who could have killed John? Nobody could have wanted to kill him. He was—he was the best of men. So kind, so unselfish—he did everything for other people. Everybody loved him, Inspector. He was a wonderful doctor. The best and kindest of husbands. It must have been an accident—it must—it *must*!'

She flung out a hand to the room.

'Ask anyone, Inspector. Nobody could have wanted to kill John, could they?'

She appealed to them all.

Inspector Grange closed up his notebook.

Agatha Christie

'Thank you, Mrs Christow,' he said in an unemotional voice. 'That will be all for the present.'

Hercule Poirot and Inspector Grange went together through the chestnut woods to the swimming pool. The thing that had been John Christow but which was now 'the body' had been photographed and measured and written about and examined by the police surgeon, and had now been taken away to the mortuary. The swimming pool, Poirot thought, looked curiously innocent. Everything about today, he thought, had been strangely fluid. Except John Christow—he had not been fluid. Even in death he had been purposeful and objective. The swimming pool was not now pre-eminently a swimming pool, it was the place where John Christow's body had lain and where his life-blood had welled away over concrete into artificially blue water.

Artificial—for a moment Poirot grasped at the word. Yes, there had been something artificial about it all. As though—

A man in a bathing suit came up to the inspector.

'Here's the revolver, sir,' he said.

Grange took the dripping object gingerly.

'No hope of fingerprints now,' he remarked, 'but luckily it doesn't matter in this case. Mrs Christow was actually holding the revolver when you arrived, wasn't she, M. Poirot?'

'Yes.'

'Identification of the revolver is the next thing,' said Grange. 'I should imagine Sir Henry will be able to do that for us. She got it from his study, I should say.'

The Hollow

He cast a glance round the pool.

'Now, let's have that again to be quite clear. The path below the pool comes up from the farm and that's the way Lady Angkatell came. The other two, Mr Edward Angkatell and Miss Savernake, came down from the woods—but not together. He came by the left-hand path, and she by the right-hand one which leads out of the long flower walk above the house. But they were both standing on the far side of the pool when you arrived?'

'Yes.'

'And this path here, beside the pavilion, leads on to Podder's Lane. Right—we'll go along it.'

As they walked, Grange spoke, without excitement, just with knowledge and quiet pessimism.

'Never like these cases much,' he said. 'Had one last year—down near Ashridge. Retired military man, he was—distinguished career. Wife was the nice quiet, old-fashioned kind, sixty-five, grey hair—rather pretty hair with a wave in it. Did a lot of gardening. One day she goes up to his room, gets out his service revolver, and walks out into the garden and shoots him. Just like that! A good deal behind it, of course, that one had to dig out. Sometimes they think up some fool story about a tramp! We pretend to accept it, of course, keep things quiet whilst we're making inquiries, but we know what's what.'

'You mean,' said Poirot, 'that you have decided that Mrs Christow shot her husband.'

Grange gave him a look of surprise.

'Well, don't you think so?'

Agatha Christie

Poirot said slowly, 'It could all have happened as she said.'

Inspector Grange shrugged his shoulders.

'It *could* have—yes. But it's a thin story. And *they* all think she killed him! They know something we don't.' He looked curiously at his companion. 'You thought she'd done it all right, didn't you, when you arrived on the scene?'

Poirot half-closed his eyes. Coming along the path... Gudgeon stepping... Gerda Christow standing over her husband with the revolver in her hand and that blank look on her face. Yes, as Grange had said, he *had* thought she had done it...had thought, at least, that that was the impression he was meant to have.

Yes, but that was not the same thing.

A scene staged—set to deceive.

Had Gerda Christow looked like a woman who had just shot her husband? That was what Inspector Grange wanted to know.

And with a sudden shock of surprise, Hercule Poirot realized that in all his long experience of deeds of violence he had never actually come face to face with a woman who had just killed her husband. What would a woman look like in such circumstances? Triumphant, horrified, satisfied, dazed, incredulous, empty?

Any one of these things, he thought.

Inspector Grange was talking. Poirot caught the end of his speech.

'—Once you get all the facts behind the case, and you can usually get all that from the servants.'

'Mrs Christow is going back to London?'

'Yes. There's a couple of kids there. Have to let her go. Of course, we keep a sharp eye on her, but she won't know that. She thinks she's got away with it all right. Looks rather a stupid kind of woman to me...'

Did Gerda Christow realize, Poirot wondered, what the police thought—and what the Angkatells thought? She had looked as though she did not realize anything at all. She had looked like a woman whose reactions were slow and who was completely dazed and heartbroken by her husband's death.

They had come out into the lane.

Poirot stopped by his gate. Grange said:

'This your little place? Nice and snug. Well, goodbye for the present, M. Poirot. Thanks for your cooperation. I'll drop in some time and give you the lowdown on how we're getting on.'

His eye travelled up the lane.

'Who's your neighbour? That's not where our new celebrity hangs out, is it?'

'Miss Veronica Cray, the actress, comes there for weekends, I believe.'

'Of course. Dovecotes. I liked her in *Lady Rides on Tiger*, but she's a bit high-brow for my taste. Give me Deanna Durbin or Hedy Lamarr.'

He turned away.

'Well, I must get back to the job. So long, M. Poirot.'

'You recognize this, Sir Henry?'

Inspector Grange laid the revolver on the desk in front of Sir Henry and looked at him expectantly.

'I can handle it?' Sir Henry's hand hesitated over the revolver as he asked the question.

Grange nodded.

'It's been in the pool. Destroyed whatever fingerprints there were on it. A pity, if I may say so, that Miss Savernake let it slip out of her hand.'

'Yes, yes—but of course it was a very tense moment for all of us. Women are apt to get flustered and—er—drop things.'

Again Inspector Grange nodded. He said:

'Miss Savernake seems a cool, capable young lady on the whole.'

The words were devoid of emphasis, yet something in them made Sir Henry look up sharply. Grange went on:

'Now, do you recognize it, sir?'

Sir Henry picked up the revolver and examined it. He noted the number and compared it with a list in a small leather-bound book. Then, closing the book with a sigh, he said:

'Yes, Inspector, this comes from my collection here.'

'When did you see it last?'

'Yesterday afternoon. We were doing some shooting in the garden with a target, and this was one of the firearms we were using.'

'Who actually fired this revolver on that occasion?'

'I think everybody had at least one shot with it.'

'Including Mrs Christow?'

'Including Mrs Christow.'

'And after you had finished shooting?'

'I put the revolver away in its usual place. Here.'

The Hollow

He pulled out the drawer of a big bureau. It was half-full of guns.

'You've got a big collection of firearms, Sir Henry.'

'It's been a hobby of mine for many years.'

Inspector Grange's eyes rested thoughtfully on the ex-Governor of the Hollowene Islands. A good-looking, distinguished man, the kind of man he would be quite pleased to serve under himself—in fact, a man he would much prefer to his own present Chief Constable. Inspector Grange did not think much of the Chief Constable of Wealdshire—a fussy despot and a tuft-hunter. He brought his mind back to the job in hand.

'The revolver was not, of course, loaded when you put it away, Sir Henry?'

'Certainly not.'

'And you keep your ammunition—where?'

'Here.' Sir Henry took a key from a pigeon-hole and unlocked one of the lower drawers of the desk.

'Simple enough,' thought Grange. The Christow woman had seen where it was kept. She'd only got to come along and help herself. Jealousy, he thought, plays the dickens with women. He'd lay ten to one it *was* jealousy. The thing would come clear enough when he'd finished the routine here and got on to the Harley Street end. But you'd got to do things in their proper order.

He got up and said:

'Well, thank you, Sir Henry. I'll let you know about the inquest.'

CHAPTER 13

They had the cold ducks for supper. After the ducks there was a caramel custard which, Lady Angkatell said, showed just the right feeling on the part of Mrs Medway.

Cooking, she said, really gave great scope to delicacy of feeling.

'We are only, as she knows, moderately fond of caramel custard. There would be something very gross, just after the death of a friend, in eating one's favourite pudding. But caramel custard is so easy—slippery if you know what I mean—and then one leaves a little on one's plate.'

She sighed and said that she hoped they had done right in letting Gerda go back to London.

'But quite correct of Henry to go with her.'

For Sir Henry had insisted on driving Gerda to Harley Street.

'She will come back here for the inquest, of course,' went on Lady Angkatell, meditatively eating caramel custard. 'But naturally she wanted to break it to the children—they might see it in the papers and only a Frenchwoman in the house—one knows how excitable—a *crise de nerfs*, possibly. But Henry will deal with her, and I really think Gerda will be quite all right. She will probably send for

The Hollow

some relations—sisters perhaps. Gerda is the sort of person who is sure to have sisters—three or four, I should think, probably living at Tunbridge Wells.'

'What extraordinary things you do say, Lucy,' said Midge.

'Well, darling, Torquay if you prefer it—no, not Torquay. They would be at least sixty-five if they were living at Torquay. Eastbourne, perhaps, or St Leonards.'

Lady Angkatell looked at the last spoonful of caramel custard, seemed to condole with it, and laid it down very gently uneaten.

David, who only liked savouries, looked down gloomily at his empty plate.

Lady Angkatell got up.

'I think we shall all want to go to bed early tonight,' she said. 'So much has happened, hasn't it? One has no idea from reading about these things in the paper how *tiring* they are. I feel, you know, as though I had walked about fifteen miles. Instead of actually having done nothing but sit down—but that is tiring, too, because one does not like to read a book or a newspaper, it looks so heartless. Though I think perhaps the leading article in *The Observer* would have been all right—but *not* the News of the World. Don't you agree with me, David? I like to know what the young people think, it keeps one from losing touch.'

David said in a gruff voice that he never read the *News of the World*.

'I always do,' said Lady Angkatell. 'We pretend we get it for the servants, but Gudgeon is very understanding and never takes it out until after tea. It is a most interesting paper, all about women who put their heads in gas ovens—an incredible number of them!'

'What will they do in the houses of the future which are all electric?' asked Edward Angkatell with a faint smile.

'I suppose they will just have to decide to make the best of things—so much more sensible.'

'I disagree with you, sir,' said David, 'about the houses of the future being all electric. There can be communal heating laid on from a central supply. Every working-class house should be completely labour-saving.'

Edward Angkatell said hastily that he was afraid that was a subject he was not very well up in. David's lip curled with scorn.

Gudgeon brought in coffee on a tray, moving a little slower than usual to convey a sense of mourning.

'Oh, Gudgeon,' said Lady Angkatell, 'about those eggs. I meant to write the date in pencil on them as usual. Will you ask Mrs Medway to see to it?'

'I think you will find, my lady, that everything has been attended to quite satisfactorily.' He cleared his throat. 'I have seen to things myself.'

'Oh, thank you, Gudgeon.'

As Gudgeon went out she murmured, 'Really, Gudgeon is wonderful. The servants are all being marvellous. And one does so sympathize with them having the police here—it must be dreadful for them. By the way, are there any left?'

'Police, do you mean?' asked Midge.

'Yes. Don't they usually leave one standing in the hall? Or perhaps he's watching the front door from the shrubbery outside.'

The Hollow

'Why should he watch the front door?'

'I don't know, I'm sure. They do in books. And then somebody else is murdered in the night.'

'Oh, Lucy, don't,' said Midge.

Lady Angkatell looked at her curiously.

'Darling, I am so sorry. Stupid of me. And of course nobody else could be murdered. Gerda's gone home—I mean—Oh, Henrietta dear, I am sorry. I didn't mean to say *that*.'

But Henrietta did not answer. She was standing by the round table staring down at the bridge score she had kept last night.

She said, rousing herself, 'Sorry, Lucy, what did you say?'

'I wondered if there were any police left over.'

'Like remnants in a sale? I don't think so. They've all gone back to the police station, to write out what we said in proper police language.'

'What are you looking at, Henrietta?'

'Nothing.'

Henrietta moved across to the mantelpiece.

'What do you think Veronica Cray is doing tonight?' she asked.

A look of dismay crossed Lady Angkatell's face.

'My dear! You don't think she might come over here again? She must have heard by now.'

'Yes,' said Henrietta thoughtfully. 'I suppose she's heard.'

'Which reminds me,' said Lady Angkatell. 'I really must telephone to the Careys. We can't have them coming to lunch tomorrow just as though nothing had happened.'

She left the room.

Agatha Christie

David, hating his relations, murmured that he wanted to look up something in the *Encyclopædia Britannica*. The library, he thought, would be a peaceful place.

Henrietta went to the french windows, opened them, and passed through. After a moment's hesitation Edward followed her.

He found her standing outside looking up at the sky. She said:

'Not so warm as last night, is it?'

In his pleasant voice, Edward said: 'No, distinctly chilly.'

She was standing looking up at the house. Her eyes were running along the windows. Then she turned and looked towards the woods. He had no clue to what was in her mind.

He made a movement towards the open window.

'Better come in. It's cold.'

She shook her head.

'I'm going for a stroll. To the swimming pool.'

'Oh, my dear.' He took a quick step towards her. 'I'll come with you.'

'No, thank you, Edward.' Her voice cut sharply through the chill of the air. 'I want to be alone with my dead.'

'Henrietta! My dear—I haven't said anything. But you do know how—how sorry I am.'

'Sorry? That John Christow is dead?'

There was still the brittle sharpness in her tone.

'I meant—sorry for you, Henrietta. I know it must have been a—a great shock.'

'Shock? Oh, but I'm very tough, Edward. I can stand shocks. Was it a shock to you? What did you feel when

The Hollow

you saw him lying there? Glad, I suppose. You didn't like John Christow.'

Edward murmured, 'He and I—hadn't much in common.'

'How nicely you put things! In such a restrained way. But as a matter of fact you did have one thing in common. Me! You were both fond of me, weren't you? Only that didn't make a bond between you—quite the opposite.'

The moon came fitfully through a cloud and he was startled as he suddenly saw her face looking at him. Unconsciously he always saw Henrietta as a projection of the Henrietta he had known at Ainswick. She was always to him a laughing girl, with dancing eyes full of eager expectation. The woman he saw now seemed to him a stranger, with eyes that were brilliant but cold and which seemed to look at him inimically.

He said earnestly:

'Henrietta, dearest, do believe this—that I do sympathize with you—in—in your grief, your loss.'

'*Is* it grief?'

The question startled him. She seemed to be asking it, not of him, but of herself.

She said in a low voice:

'So quick—it can happen so quickly. One moment living, breathing, and the next—dead—gone—emptiness. Oh, the emptiness! And here we are, all of us, eating caramel custard and calling ourselves alive—and John, who was more alive than any of us, is dead. I say the word, you know, over and over again to myself. Dead—dead—dead—dead—*dead*. And soon it hasn't got any meaning—not any meaning at all.

It's just a funny little word like the breaking off of a rotten branch. *Dead—dead—dead—dead.* It's like a tom-tom, isn't it, beating in the jungle. Dead—dead—dead—dead—dead—'

'Henrietta, stop! For God's sake, stop!'

She looked at him curiously.

'Didn't you know I'd feel like this? What did you think? That I'd sit gently crying into a nice little pocket handkerchief while you held my hand? That it would all be a great shock but that presently I'd begin to get over it? And that you'd comfort me very nicely? You *are* nice, Edward. You're very nice, but you're so—so inadequate.'

He drew back. His face stiffened. He said in a dry voice: 'Yes, I've always known that.'

She went on fiercely:

'What do you think it's been like all the evening, sitting round, with John dead and nobody caring but me and Gerda! With you glad, and David embarrassed and Midge distressed and Lucy delicately enjoying the *News of the World* come from print into real life! Can't you see how like a fantastic nightmare it all is?'

Edward said nothing. He stepped back a pace, into shadows.

Looking at him, Henrietta said:

'Tonight—nothing seems real to me, nobody *is* real—but John!'

Edward said quietly, 'I know... I am not very real.'

'What a brute I am, Edward. But I can't help it. I can't help resenting that John, who was so alive, is dead.'

'And that I who am half-dead, am alive.'

'I didn't mean that, Edward.'

The Hollow

'I think you did, Henrietta. I think, perhaps, you are right.'

But she was saying, thoughtfully, harking back to an earlier thought:

'But it is not grief. Perhaps I cannot feel grief. Perhaps I never shall. And yet—I would like to grieve for John.'

Her words seemed to him fantastic. Yet he was even more startled when she added suddenly, in an almost business-like voice:

'I must go to the swimming pool.'

She glided away through the trees.

Walking stiffly, Edward went through the open window.

Midge looked up as Edward came through the window with unseeing eyes. His face was grey and pinched. It looked bloodless.

He did not hear the little gasp that Midge stifled immediately.

Almost mechanically he walked to a chair and sat down. Aware of something expected of him, he said:

'It's cold.'

'Are you very cold, Edward? Shall we—shall I—light a fire?'

'What?'

Midge took a box of matches from the mantelpiece. She knelt down and set a match to the fire. She looked cautiously sideways at Edward. He was quite oblivious, she thought, of everything.

She said, 'A fire is nice. It warms one.'

'How cold he looks,' she thought. 'But it can't be as cold as that outside? It's Henrietta! What has she said to him?'

'Bring your chair nearer, Edward. Come close to the fire.'
'What?'
'Your chair. To the fire.'
She was talking to him now loudly and slowly, as though to a deaf person.
And suddenly, so suddenly that her heart turned over with relief, Edward, the real Edward, was there again. Smiling at her gently.
'Have you been talking to me, Midge? I'm sorry. I'm afraid I was thinking—thinking of something.'
'Oh, it was nothing. Just the fire.'
The sticks were crackling and some fir-cones were burning with a bright, clean flame. Edward looked at them. He said:
'It's a nice fire.'
He stretched out his long, thin hands to the blaze, aware of relief from tension.
Midge said, 'We always had fir-cones at Ainswick.'
'I still do. A basket of them is brought every day and put by the grate.'
Edward at Ainswick. Midge half-closed her eyes, picturing it. He would sit, she thought, in the library, on the west side of the house. There was a magnolia that almost covered one window and which filled the room with a golden green light in the afternoons. Through the other window you looked out on the lawn and a tall Wellingtonia stood up like a sentinel. And to the right was the big copper beech.
Oh, Ainswick—Ainswick.
She could smell the soft air that drifted in from the magnolia which would still, in September, have some great

The Hollow

white sweet-smelling waxy flowers on it. And the pinecones on the fire. And a faintly musty smell from the kind of book that Edward was sure to be reading. He would be sitting in the saddle-back chair, and occasionally, perhaps, his eyes would go from the book to the fire, and he would think, just for a minute, of Henrietta.

Midge stirred and asked:

'Where is Henrietta?'

'She went to the swimming pool.'

Midge stared. 'Why?'

Her voice, abrupt and deep, roused Edward a little.

'My dear Midge, surely you knew—oh, well—guessed. She knew Christow pretty well.'

'Oh, of course one knew *that*. But I don't see why she should go mooning off to where he was shot. That's not at all like Henrietta. She's never melodramatic.'

'Do any of us know what anyone else is like? Henrietta, for instance.'

Midge frowned. She said:

'After all, Edward, you and I have known Henrietta all our lives.'

'She has changed.'

'Not really. I don't think one changes.'

'Henrietta has changed.'

Midge looked at him curiously.

'More than we have, you and I?'

'Oh, I have stood still, I know that well enough. And you—'

His eyes, suddenly focusing, looked at her where she knelt by the fender. It was as though he was looking at her from a long way away, taking in the square chin, the dark eyes, the resolute mouth. He said:

'I wish I saw you more often, Midge, my dear.'

She smiled up at him. She said:

'I know. It isn't easy, these days, to keep in touch.'

There was a sound outside and Edward got up.

'Lucy was right,' he said. 'It has been a tiring day—one's first introduction to murder. I shall go to bed. Goodnight.'

He had left the room when Henrietta came through the window.

Midge turned on her.

'What have you done to Edward?'

'Edward?' Henrietta was vague. Her forehead was puckered. She seemed to be thinking of something a long way away.

'Yes, Edward. He came in looking dreadful—so cold and grey.'

'If you care about Edward so much, Midge, why don't you do something about him?'

'Do something? What do you mean?'

'I don't know. Stand on a chair and shout! Draw attention to yourself. Don't you know that's the only hope with a man like Edward?'

'Edward will never care about anyone but you, Henrietta. He never has.'

'Then it's very unintelligent of him.' She threw a quick glance at Midge's white face. 'I've hurt you. I'm sorry. But I hate Edward tonight.'

'Hate Edward? You *can't*.'

'Oh, yes, I can! You don't know—'

The Hollow

'What?'

Henrietta said slowly:

'He reminds me of such a lot of things I would like to forget.'

'What things?'

'Well, Ainswick, for instance.'

'Ainswick? You want to forget Ainswick?'

Midge's tone was incredulous.

'Yes, yes, *yes*! I was happy there. I can't stand, just now, being reminded of happiness. Don't you understand? A time when one didn't know what was coming. When one said confidently, everything is going to be lovely! Some people are wise—they never expect to be happy. I did.'

She said abruptly:

'I shall never go back to Ainswick.'

Midge said slowly:

'I wonder.'

CHAPTER 14

Midge woke up abruptly on Monday morning.

For a moment she lay there bemused, her eyes going confusedly towards the door, for she half-expected Lady Angkatell to appear. What was it Lucy had said when she came drifting in that first morning?

A difficult weekend? She had been worried—had thought that something unpleasant might happen.

Yes, and something unpleasant had happened—something that was lying now upon Midge's heart and spirits like a thick black cloud. Something that she didn't want to think about—didn't want to remember. Something, surely, that *frightened* her. Something to do with Edward.

Memory came with a rush. One ugly stark word—*Murder!*

'Oh, no,' thought Midge, 'it can't be true. It's a dream I've been having. John Christow, murdered, shot—lying there by the pool. Blood and blue water—like the jacket of a detective story. Fantastic, unreal. The sort of thing that doesn't happen to oneself. If we were at Ainswick now. It couldn't have happened at Ainswick.'

The black weight moved from her forehead. It settled in the pit of her stomach, making her feel slightly sick.

The Hollow

It was not a dream. It was a real happening—a *News of the World* happening—and she and Edward and Lucy and Henry and Henrietta were all mixed up with it.

Unfair—surely unfair—since it was nothing to do with them if Gerda had shot her husband.

Midge stirred uneasily.

Quiet, stupid, slightly pathetic Gerda—you couldn't associate Gerda with melodrama—with violence.

Gerda, surely, couldn't shoot *anybody*.

Again that inward uneasiness rose. No, no, one mustn't think like that. Because who else *could* have shot John? And Gerda had been standing there by his body with the revolver in her hand. The revolver she had taken from Henry's study.

Gerda had said that she had found John dead and picked up the revolver. Well, what else could she say? She'd have to say *something*, poor thing.

All very well for Henrietta to defend her—to say that Gerda's story was perfectly possible. Henrietta hadn't considered the impossible alternatives.

Henrietta had been very odd last night.

But that, of course, had been the shock of John Christow's death.

Poor Henrietta—who had cared so terribly for John.

But she would get over it in time—one got over everything. And then she would marry Edward and live at Ainswick—and Edward would be happy at last.

Henrietta had always loved Edward very dearly. It was only the aggressive, dominant personality of John Christow that had come in the way. He had made Edward look so—so *pale* by comparison.

It struck Midge when she came down to breakfast that morning that already Edward's personality, freed from John Christow's dominance, had begun to assert itself. He seemed more sure of himself, less hesitant and retiring.

He was talking pleasantly to the glowering and unresponsive David.

'You must come more often to Ainswick, David. I'd like you to feel at home there and to get to know all about the place.'

Helping himself to marmalade, David said coldly:

'These big estates are completely farcical. They should be split up.'

'That won't happen in my time, I hope,' said Edward, smiling. 'My tenants are a contented lot.'

'They shouldn't be,' said David. 'Nobody should be contented.'

'If apes had been content with tails—' murmured Lady Angkatell from where she was standing by the sideboard looking vaguely at a dish of kidneys. 'That's a poem I learnt in the nursery, but I simply can't remember how it goes on. I must have a talk with you, David, and learn all the new ideas. As far as I can see, one must hate everybody, but at the same time give them free medical attention and a lot of extra education (poor things, all those helpless little children herded into schoolhouses every day)—and cod-liver oil forced down babies' throats whether they like it or not—such nasty-smelling stuff.'

Lucy, Midge thought, was behaving very much as usual.

The Hollow

And Gudgeon, when she passed him in the hall, also looked just as usual. Life at The Hollow seemed to have resumed its normal course. With the departure of Gerda, the whole business seemed like a dream.

Then there was a scrunch of wheels on the gravel outside, and Sir Henry drew up in his car. He had stayed the night at his club and driven down early.

'Well, dear,' said Lucy, 'was everything all right?'

'Yes. The secretary was there—competent sort of girl. She took charge of things. There's a sister, it seems. The secretary telegraphed to her.'

'I knew there would be,' said Lady Angkatell. 'At Tunbridge Wells?'

'Bexhill, I think,' said Sir Henry, looking puzzled.

'I dare say'—Lucy considered Bexhill—'Yes—quite probably.'

Gudgeon approached.

'Inspector Grange telephoned, Sir Henry. The inquest will be at eleven o'clock on Wednesday.'

Sir Henry nodded. Lady Angkatell said:

'Midge, you'd better ring up your shop.'

Midge went slowly to the telephone.

Her life had always been so entirely normal and commonplace that she felt she lacked the phraseology to explain to her employers that after four days' holiday she was unable to return to work owing to the fact that she was mixed up in a murder case.

It did not sound credible. It did not even feel credible.

And Madame Alfrege was not a very easy person to explain things to at any time.

Agatha Christie

Midge set her chin resolutely and picked up the receiver.

It was all just as unpleasant as she had imagined it would be. The raucous voice of the vitriolic little Jewess came angrily over the wires.

'What ith that, Mith Hardcathle? A death? A funeral? Do you not know very well I am short-handed? Do you think I am going to stand for these excutheth? Oh, yeth, you are having a good time, I dare thay!'

Midge interrupted, speaking sharply and distinctly.

'The poleeth? The poleeth, you thay?' It was almost a scream. 'You are mixed up with the poleeth?'

Setting her teeth, Midge continued to explain. Strange how sordid that woman at the other end made the whole thing seem. A vulgar police case. What alchemy there was in human beings!

Edward opened the door and came in, then seeing that Midge was telephoning, he was about to go out. She stopped him.

'Do stay, Edward. Please. Oh, I *want* you to.'

The presence of Edward in the room gave her strength—counteracted the poison.

She took her hand from where she had laid it over the mouthpiece.

'What? Yes. I am sorry, Madame. But after all, it is hardly my fault—'

The ugly raucous voice was screaming angrily.

'Who are thethe friendth of yourth? What thort of people are they to have the poleeth there and a man shot? I've a good mind not to have you back at all! I can't have the tone of my ethtablishment lowered.'

The Hollow

Midge made a few submissive non-committal replies. She replaced the receiver at last, with a sigh of relief. She felt sick and shaken.

'It's the place I work,' she explained. 'I had to let them know that I wouldn't be back until Thursday because of the inquest and the—the police.'

'I hope they were decent about it? What is it like, this dress shop of yours? Is the woman who runs it pleasant and sympathetic to work for?'

'I should hardly describe her as that! She's a Whitechapel Jewess with dyed hair and a voice like a corncrake.'

'But my dear Midge—'

Edward's face of consternation almost made Midge laugh. He was so concerned.

'But my dear child—you can't put up with that sort of thing. If you must have a job, you must take one where the surroundings are harmonious and where you like the people you are working with.'

Midge looked at him for a moment without answering.

How explain, she thought, to a person like Edward? What did Edward know of the labour market, of jobs?

And suddenly a tide of bitterness rose in her. Lucy, Henry, Edward—yes, even Henrietta—they were all divided from her by an impassable gulf—the gulf that separates the leisured from the working.

They had no conception of the difficulties of getting a job, and once you had got it, of keeping it! One might say, perhaps, that there was no need, actually, for her to earn her living. Lucy and Henry would gladly give her a home—they would with equal gladness have made her an allowance. Edward would also willingly have done the latter.

But something in Midge rebelled against the acceptance of ease offered her by her well-to-do relations. To come on rare occasions and sink into the well-ordered luxury of Lucy's life was delightful. She could revel in that. But some sturdy independence of spirit held her back from accepting that life as a gift. The same feeling had prevented her from starting a business on her own with money borrowed from relations and friends. She had seen too much of that.

She would borrow no money—use no influence. She had found a job for herself at four pounds a week, and if she had actually been given the job because Madame Alfrege hoped that Midge would bring her 'smart' friends to buy, Madame Alfrege was disappointed. Midge discouraged any such notion sternly on the part of her friends.

She had no particular illusions about working. She disliked the shop, she disliked Madame Alfrege, she disliked the eternal subservience to ill-tempered and impolite customers, but she doubted very much whether she could obtain any other job which she would like better since she had none of the necessary qualifications.

Edward's assumption that a wide range of choice was open to her was simply unbearably irritating this morning. What right had Edward to live in a world so divorced from reality?

They were Angkatells, all of them. And she—was only half an Angkatell! And sometimes, like this morning, she did not feel like an Angkatell at all! She was all her father's daughter.

The Hollow

She thought of her father with the usual pang of love and compunction, a grey-haired, middle-aged man with a tired face. A man who had struggled for years running a small family business that was bound, for all his care and efforts, to go slowly down the hill. It was not incapacity on his part—it was the march of progress.

Strangely enough, it was not to her brilliant Angkatell mother but to her quiet, tired father that Midge's devotion had always been given. Each time, when she came back from those visits to Ainswick, which were the wild delight of her life, she would answer the faint deprecating questions in her father's tired face by flinging her arms round his neck and saying: 'I'm *glad* to be home—I'm glad to be *home*.'

Her mother had died when Midge was thirteen. Sometimes Midge realized that she knew very little about her mother. She had been vague, charming, gay. Had she regretted her marriage, the marriage that had taken her outside the circle of the Angkatell clan? Midge had no idea. Her father had grown greyer and quieter after his wife's death. His struggles against the extinction of his business had grown more unavailing. He had died quietly and inconspicuously when Midge was eighteen.

Midge had stayed with various Angkatell relations, had accepted presents from the Angkatells, had had good times with the Angkatells, but she had refused to be financially dependent on their goodwill. And much as she loved them, there were times, such as these, when she felt suddenly and violently divergent from them.

She thought with rancour, 'They don't know *anything*!'

Edward, sensitive as always, was looking at her with a puzzled face. He asked gently:

'I've upset you? Why?'

Lucy drifted into the room. She was in the middle of one of her conversations.

'—you see, one doesn't really know whether she'd *prefer* the White Hart to us or not?'

Midge looked at her blankly—then at Edward.

'It's no use looking at Edward,' said Lady Angkatell. 'Edward simply wouldn't know; you, Midge, are always so practical.'

'I don't know what you are talking about, Lucy.'

Lucy looked surprised.

'The *inquest*, darling. Gerda has to come down for it. Should she stay here? Or go to the White Hart? The associations here are painful, of course—but then at the White Hart there will be people who will stare and quantities of reporters. Wednesday, you know, at eleven, or is it eleven-thirty?' A smile lit up Lady Angkatell's face. 'I have never been to an inquest! I thought my grey—and a hat, of course, like church—but *not* gloves.

'You know,' went on Lady Angkatell, crossing the room and picking up the telephone receiver and gazing down at it earnestly, 'I don't believe I've *got* any gloves except gardening gloves nowadays! And of course lots of long evening ones put away from the Government House days. Gloves are rather stupid, don't you think so?'

'The only use is to avoid fingerprints in crimes,' said Edward, smiling.

The Hollow

'Now, it's very interesting that you should say that, Edward—very interesting. What am I doing with this thing?' Lady Angkatell looked at the telephone receiver with faint distaste.

'Were you going to ring up someone?'

'I don't think so.' Lady Angkatell shook her head vaguely and put the receiver back on its stand very gingerly.

She looked from Edward to Midge.

'I don't think, Edward, that you ought to upset Midge. Midge minds sudden deaths more than we do.'

'My dear Lucy,' exclaimed Edward. 'I was only worrying about this place where Midge works. It sounds all wrong to me.'

'Edward thinks I ought to have a delightful sympathetic employer who would appreciate me,' said Midge dryly.

'Dear Edward,' said Lucy with complete appreciation.

She smiled at Midge and went out again.

'Seriously, Midge,' said Edward, 'I am worried.'

She interrupted him:

'The damned woman pays me four pounds a week. That's all that matters.'

She brushed past him and went out into the garden.

Sir Henry was sitting in his usual place on the low wall, but Midge turned away and walked up towards the flower walk.

Her relations were charming, but she had no use for their charm this morning.

David Angkatell was sitting on the seat at the top of the path.

There was no overdone charm about David, and Midge made straight for him and sat down by him, noting with malicious pleasure his look of dismay.

How extraordinarily difficult it was, thought David, to get away from people.

He had been driven from his bedroom by the brisk incursion of housemaids, purposeful with mops and dusters.

The library (and the *Encyclopædia Britannica*) had not been the sanctuary he had hoped optimistically it might be. Twice Lady Angkatell had drifted in and out, addressing him kindly with remarks to which there seemed no possible intelligent reply.

He had come out here to brood upon his position. The mere weekend to which he had unwillingly committed himself had now lengthened out owing to the exigencies connected with sudden and violent death.

David, who preferred the contemplation of an Academic past or the earnest discussion of a Left Wing future, had no aptitude for dealing with a violent and realistic present. As he had told Lady Angkatell, he did not read the *News of the World*. But now the *News of the World* seemed to have come to The Hollow.

Murder! David shuddered distastefully. What would his friends think? How did one, so to speak, *take* murder? What was one's attitude? Bored? Disgusted? Lightly amused?

Trying to settle these problems in his mind, he was by no means pleased to be disturbed by Midge. He looked at her uneasily as she sat beside him.

He was rather startled by the defiant stare with which she returned his look. A disagreeable girl of no intellectual value.

The Hollow

She said, 'How do you like your relations?'

David shrugged his shoulders. He said:

'Does one really *think* about relations?'

Midge said:

'Does one really think about anything?'

Doubtless, David thought, *she* didn't. He said almost graciously:

'I was analysing my reactions to murder.'

'It is certainly odd,' said Midge, 'to be *in* one.'

David sighed and said:

'Wearisome.' That was quite the best attitude. 'All the clichés that one thought only existed in the pages of detective fiction!'

'You must be sorry you came,' said Midge.

David sighed.

'Yes, I might have been staying with a friend of mine in London.' He added, 'He keeps a Left Wing bookshop.'

'I expect it's more comfortable here,' said Midge.

'Does one really care about being comfortable?' David asked scornfully.

'There are times,' said Midge, 'when I feel I don't care about anything else.'

'The pampered attitude to life,' said David. 'If you were a worker—'

Midge interrupted him.

'I *am* a worker. That's just why being comfortable is so attractive. Box beds, down pillows—early-morning tea softly deposited beside the bed—a porcelain bath with lashings of hot water—and delicious bath salts. The kind of easy-chair you really sink into...'

Agatha Christie

Midge paused in her catalogue.

'The workers,' said David, 'should have all these things.'

But he was a little doubtful about the softly deposited early-morning tea, which sounded impossibly sybaritic for an earnestly organized world.

'I couldn't agree with you more,' said Midge heartily.

CHAPTER 15

Hercule Poirot, enjoying a mid-morning cup of chocolate, was interrupted by the ringing of the telephone. He got up and lifted the receiver.

"*Allo?*"

'M. Poirot?'

'Lady Angkatell?'

'How nice of you to know my voice! Am I disturbing you?'

'But not at all. You are, I hope, none the worse for the distressing events of yesterday?'

'No, indeed. Distressing, as you say, but one feels, I find, quite *detached*. I rang you up to know if you could possibly come over—an imposition, I know, but I am really in great distress.'

'But certainly, Lady Angkatell. Did you mean now?'

'Well, yes, I did mean now. As quickly as you can. That's very sweet of you.'

'Not at all. I will come by the woods, then?'

'Oh, of course—the shortest way. Thank you so much, dear M. Poirot.'

Pausing only to brush a few specks of dust off the lapels of his coat and to slip on a thin overcoat, Poirot crossed

Agatha Christie

the lane and hurried along the path through the chestnuts. The swimming pool was deserted—the police had finished their work and gone. It looked innocent and peaceful in the soft misty autumn light.

Poirot took a quick look into the pavilion. The platinum fox cape, he noted, had been removed. But the six boxes of matches still stood upon the table by the settee. He wondered more than ever about those matches.

'It is not a place to keep matches—here in the damp. One box, for convenience, perhaps—but not six.'

He frowned down on the painted iron table. The tray of glasses had been removed. Someone had scrawled with a pencil on the table—a rough design of a nightmarish tree. It pained Hercule Poirot. It offended his tidy mind.

He clicked his tongue, shook his head, and hurried on towards the house, wondering at the reason for this urgent summons.

Lady Angkatell was waiting for him at the french windows and swept him into the empty drawing-room.

'It was nice of you to come, M. Poirot.'

She clasped his hand warmly.

'Madame, I am at your service.'

Lady Angkatell's hands floated out expressively. Her wide, beautiful eyes opened.

'You see, it's all so difficult. The inspector person is interviewing—no, questioning—taking a statement—what *is* the term they use?—*Gudgeon*. And really our whole life here depends on Gudgeon, and one does so sympathize with him. Because naturally it is terrible for him to be questioned by

The Hollow

the police—even Inspector Grange, who I do feel is really nice and probably a family man—boys, I think, and he helps them with Meccano in the evenings—and a wife who has everything spotless but a little overcrowded...'

Hercule Poirot blinked as Lady Angkatell developed her imaginary sketch of Inspector Grange's home life.

'By the way his moustache droops,' went on Lady Angkatell, 'I think that a home that is too spotless might be sometimes depressing—like soap on hospital nurses' faces. Quite a *shine*! But that is more in the country where things lag behind—in London nursing homes they have lots of powder and really *vivid* lipstick. But I was saying, M. Poirot, that you really must come to lunch *properly* when all this ridiculous business is over.'

'You are very kind.'

'I do not mind the police myself,' said Lady Angkatell. 'I really find it all quite interesting. "Do let me help you in any way I can," I said to Inspector Grange. He seems rather a bewildered sort of person, but methodical.

'Motive seems so important to policemen,' she went on. 'Talking of hospital nurses just now, I believe that John Christow—a nurse with red hair and an upturned nose—quite attractive. But of course it was a long time ago and the police might not be interested. One doesn't really know how much poor Gerda had to put up with. She is the loyal type, don't you think? Or possibly she believes what is told her. I think if one has not a great deal of intelligence, it is wise to do that.'

Quite suddenly, Lady Angkatell flung open the study door and ushered Poirot in, crying brightly, 'Here is M.

Poirot.' She swept round him and out, shutting the door. Inspector Grange and Gudgeon were sitting by the desk. A young man with a notebook was in a corner. Gudgeon rose respectfully to his feet.

Poirot hastened into apologies.

'I retire immediately. I assure you I had no idea that Lady Angkatell—'

'No, no, you wouldn't have.' Grange's moustache looked more pessimistic than ever this morning. 'Perhaps,' thought Poirot, fascinated by Lady Angkatell's recent sketch of Grange, 'there has been too much cleaning or perhaps a Benares brass table has been purchased so that the good inspector he really cannot have space to move.'

Angrily he dismissed these thoughts. Inspector Grange's clean but overcrowded home, his wife, his boys and their addiction to Meccano were all figments of Lady Angkatell's busy brain.

But the vividness with which they assumed concrete reality interested him. It was quite an accomplishment.

'Sit down, M. Poirot,' said Grange. 'There's something I want to ask you about, and I've nearly finished here.'

He turned his attention back to Gudgeon, who deferentially and almost under protest resumed his seat and turned an expressionless face towards his interlocutor.

'And that's all you can remember?'

'Yes, sir. Everything, sir, was very much as usual. There was no unpleasantness of any kind.'

'There's a fur cape thing—out in that summer-house by the pool. Which of the ladies did it belong to?'

The Hollow

'Are you referring, sir, to a cape of platinum fox? I noticed it yesterday when I took out the glasses to the pavilion. But it is not the property of anyone in this house, sir.'

'Whose is it, then?'

'It might possibly belong to Miss Cray, sir. Miss Veronica Cray, the motion-picture actress. She was wearing something of the kind.'

'When?'

'When she was here the night before last, sir.'

'You didn't mention her as having been a guest here?'

'She was not a guest, sir. Miss Cray lives at Dovecotes, the—er—cottage up the lane, and she came over after dinner, having run out of matches, to borrow some.'

'Did she take away six boxes?' asked Poirot.

Gudgeon turned to him.

'That is correct, sir. Her ladyship, after having inquired if we had plenty, insisted on Miss Cray's taking half a dozen boxes.'

'Which she left in the pavilion,' said Poirot.

'Yes, sir, I observed them there yesterday morning.'

'There is not much that that man does not observe,' remarked Poirot as Gudgeon departed, closing the door softly and deferentially behind him.

Inspector Grange merely remarked that servants were the devil!

'However,' he said with a little renewed cheerfulness, 'there's always the kitchenmaid. Kitchenmaids *talk*—not like these stuck-up upper servants.

'I've put a man on to make inquiries at Harley Street,' he went on. 'And I shall be there myself later in the day.

We ought to get something there. Dare say, you know, that wife of Christow's had a good bit to put up with. Some of these fashionable doctors and their lady patients—well, you'd be surprised! And I gather from Lady Angkatell that there was some trouble over a hospital nurse. Of course, she was very vague about it.'

'Yes,' Poirot agreed. 'She would be vague.'

A skilfully built-up picture... John Christow and amorous intrigues with hospital nurses...the opportunities of a doctor's life...plenty of reasons for Gerda Christow's jealousy which had culminated at last in murder.

Yes, a skilfully suggested picture, drawing attention to a Harley Street background—away from The Hollow—away from the moment when Henrietta Savernake, stepping forward, had taken the revolver from Gerda Christow's unresisting hand... Away from that other moment when John Christow, dying, had said '*Henrietta*'.

Suddenly opening his eyes, which had been half-closed, Hercule Poirot demanded with irresistible curiosity:

'Do your boys play with Meccano?'

'Eh, what?' Inspector Grange came back from a frowning reverie to stare at Poirot. 'Why, what on earth? As a matter of fact, they're a bit young—but I was thinking of giving Teddy a Meccano set for Christmas. What made you ask?'

Poirot shook his head.

What made Lady Angkatell dangerous, he thought, was the fact that those intuitive, wild guesses of hers might be often right. With a careless (seemingly careless?) word she built up a picture—and if part of the picture was right,

The Hollow

wouldn't you, in spite of yourself, believe in the other half of the picture?...

Inspector Grange was speaking.

'There's a point I want to put to you, M. Poirot. This Miss Cray, the actress—she traipses over here borrowing matches. If she wanted to borrow matches, why didn't she come to your place, only a step or two away? Why come about half a mile?'

Hercule Poirot shrugged his shoulders.

'There might be reasons. Snob reasons, shall we say? My little cottage, it is small, unimportant. I am only a weekender, but Sir Henry and Lady Angkatell are important—they live here—they are what is called in the country. This Miss Veronica Cray, she may have wanted to get to know them—and after all, this was a way.'

Inspector Grange got up.

'Yes,' he said, 'that's perfectly possible, of course, but one doesn't want to overlook anything. Still, I've no doubt that everything's going to be plain sailing. Sir Henry has identified the gun as one of his collection. It seems they were actually practising with it the afternoon before. All Mrs Christow had to do was to go into the study and get it from where she'd seen Sir Henry put it and the ammunition away. It's all quite simple.'

'Yes,' Poirot murmured. 'It seems all quite simple.'

Just so, he thought, would a woman like Gerda Christow commit a crime. Without subterfuge or complexity—driven suddenly to violence by the bitter anguish of a narrow but deeply loving nature.

Agatha Christie

And yet surely—*surely*, she would have had *some* sense of self-preservation. Or had she acted in that blindness—that darkness of the spirit—when reason is entirely laid aside?

He recalled her blank, dazed face.

He did not know—he simply did not know.

But he felt that he ought to know.

CHAPTER 16

Gerda Christow pulled the black dress up over her head and let it fall on a chair.

Her eyes were piteous with uncertainty.

She said, 'I don't know—I really don't know. Nothing seems to matter.'

'I know, dear, I know.' Mrs Patterson was kind but firm. She knew exactly how to treat people who had had a bereavement. 'Elsie is *wonderful* in a crisis,' her family said of her.

At the present moment she was sitting in her sister Gerda's bedroom in Harley Street being wonderful. Elsie Patterson was tall and spare with an energetic manner. She was looking now at Gerda with a mixture of irritation and compassion.

Poor dear Gerda—tragic for her to lose her husband in such an awful way. And really, even now, she didn't seem to take in the—well, the *implications*, properly. Of course, Mrs Patterson reflected, Gerda always was terribly slow. And there was shock, too, to take into account.

She said in a brisk voice, 'I think I should decide on that black marocain at twelve guineas.'

One always did have to make up Gerda's mind for her.

Gerda stood motionless, her brow puckered. She said hesitantly:

'I don't really know if John liked mourning. I think I once heard him say he didn't.'

'John,' she thought. 'If only John were here to tell me what to do.'

But John would never be there again. Never—never—never... Mutton getting cold—congealing on the table...the bang of the consulting-room door, John running up two steps at a time, always in a hurry, so vital, so alive...

Alive.

Lying on his back by the swimming pool...the slow drip of blood over the edge...the feel of the revolver in her hand...

A nightmare, a bad dream, presently she would wake up and none of it would be true.

Her sister's crisp voice came cutting through her nebulous thoughts.

'You *must* have something black for the inquest. It would look most odd if you turned up in bright blue.'

Gerda said, 'That awful inquest!' and half-shut her eyes.

'Terrible for you, darling,' said Elsie Patterson quickly. 'But after it is all over you will come straight down to us and we shall take great care of you.'

The nebulous blur of Gerda Christow's thoughts hardened. She said, and her voice was frightened, almost panic-stricken:

'What am I going to do without John?'

Elsie Patterson knew the answer to that one. 'You've got your children. You've got to live for *them*.'

The Hollow

Zena, sobbing and crying, 'My Daddy's dead!' Throwing herself on her bed. Terry, pale, inquiring, shedding no tears.

An accident with a revolver, she had told them—poor Daddy has had an accident.

Beryl Collins (so thoughtful of her) had confiscated the morning papers so that the children should not see them. She had warned the servants too. Really, Beryl had been most kind and thoughtful.

Terence coming to his mother in the dim drawing-room, his lips pursed close together, his face almost greenish in its odd pallor.

'Why was Father shot?'

'An accident, dear. I—I can't talk about it.'

'It wasn't an accident. Why do you say what isn't true? Father was killed. It was murder. The paper says so.'

'Terry, how did you get hold of a paper? I told Miss Collins—'

He had nodded—queer repeated nods like a very old man.

'I went out and bought one, of course. I knew there must be something in them that you weren't telling us, or else why did Miss Collins hide them?'

It was never any good hiding truth from Terence. That queer, detached, scientific curiosity of his had always to be satisfied.

'*Why* was he killed, Mother?'

She had broken down then, becoming hysterical.

'Don't ask me about it—don't talk about it—I can't talk about it...it's all too dreadful.'

'But they'll find out, won't they? I mean, they have to find out. It's necessary.'

So reasonable, so detached. It made Gerda want to scream and laugh and cry. She thought: 'He doesn't care—he can't care—he just goes on asking questions. Why, he hasn't cried, even.'

Terence had gone away, evading his Aunt Elsie's ministrations, a lonely little boy with a stiff, pinched face. He had always felt alone. But it hadn't mattered until today.

Today, he thought, was different. If only there was someone who would answer questions reasonably and intelligently.

Tomorrow, Tuesday, he and Nicholson Minor were going to make nitroglycerine. He had been looking forward to it with a thrill. The thrill had gone. He didn't care if he never made nitroglycerine.

Terence felt almost shocked at himself. Not to care any more about scientific experiment. But when a chap's father had been murdered... He thought: 'My father—murdered.'

And something stirred—took root—grew...a slow anger.

Beryl Collins tapped on the bedroom door and came in. She was pale, composed, efficient. She said:

'Inspector Grange is here.' And as Gerda gasped and looked at her piteously, Beryl went on quickly, 'He said there was no need for him to worry you. He'll have a word with you before he goes, but it is just routine questions about Dr Christow's practice and I can tell him everything he wants to know.'

'Oh thank you, Collie.'

Beryl made a rapid exit and Gerda sighed out:

'Collie is such a help. She's so practical.'

'Yes, indeed,' said Mrs Patterson. 'An excellent secretary, I'm sure. Very plain, poor girl, isn't she? Oh, well, I always think that's just as well. Especially with an attractive man like John.'

The Hollow

Gerda flamed out at her:

'What do you mean, Elsie? John would never—he never—you talk as though John would have flirted or something horrid if he had had a pretty secretary. John wasn't like that at all.'

'Of course not, darling,' said Mrs Patterson. 'But after all, one knows what men are *like*!'

In the consulting-room Inspector Grange faced the cool, belligerent glance of Beryl Collins. It *was* belligerent, he noted that. Well, perhaps that was only natural.

'Plain bit of goods,' he thought. 'Nothing between her and the doctor, I shouldn't think. *She* may have been sweet on *him*, though. It works that way sometimes.'

But not this time, he came to the conclusion, when he leaned back in his chair a quarter of an hour later. Beryl Collins's answers to his questions had been models of clearness. She replied promptly, and obviously had every detail of the doctor's practice at her fingertips. He shifted his ground and began to probe gently into the relations existing between John Christow and his wife.

They had been, Beryl said, on excellent terms.

'I suppose they quarrelled every now and then like most married couples?' The inspector sounded easy and confidential.

'I do not remember any quarrels. Mrs Christow was quite devoted to her husband—really quite slavishly so.'

There was a faint edge of contempt in her voice. Inspector Grange heard it.

'Bit of a feminist, this girl,' he thought.

Aloud he said:

'Didn't stand up for herself at all?'

'No. Everything revolved round Dr Christow.'

'Tyrannical, eh?'

Beryl considered.

'No, I wouldn't say that. But he was what I should call a very selfish man. He took it for granted that Mrs Christow would always fall in with *his* ideas.'

'Any difficulties with patients—women, I mean? You needn't think about being frank, Miss Collins. One knows doctors have their difficulties in that line.'

'Oh, that sort of thing!' Beryl's voice was scornful. 'Dr Christow was quite equal to dealing with any difficulties in *that* line. He had an excellent manner with patients.' She added, 'He was really a wonderful doctor.'

There was an almost grudging admiration in her voice.

Grange said, 'Was he tangled up with any woman? Don't be loyal, Miss Collins, it's important that we should know.'

'Yes, I can appreciate that. Not to my knowledge.'

A little too brusque, he thought. She doesn't know, but perhaps she guesses.

He said sharply, 'What about Miss Henrietta Savernake?'

Beryl's lips closed tightly.

'She was a close friend of the family's.'

'No—trouble between Dr and Mrs Christow on her account?'

'Certainly not.'

The answer was emphatic. (Over-emphatic?)

The inspector shifted his ground.

The Hollow

'What about Miss Veronica Cray?'

'Veronica Cray?'

There was pure astonishment in Beryl's voice.

'She was a friend of Dr Christow's, was she not?'

'I never heard of her. At least, I seem to know the *name*—'

'The motion-picture actress.'

Beryl's brow cleared.

'Of course! I wondered why the name was familiar. But I didn't even know that Dr Christow knew her.'

She seemed so positive on the point that the inspector abandoned it at once. He went on to question her about Dr Christow's manner on the preceding Saturday. And here, for the first time, the confidence of Beryl's replies wavered. She said slowly:

'His manner *wasn't* quite as usual.'

'What was the difference?'

'He seemed distrait. There was quite a long gap before he rang for his last patient—and yet normally he was always in a hurry to get through when he was going away. I thought—yes, I definitely thought he had something on his mind.'

But she could not be more definite.

Inspector Grange was not very satisfied with his investigations. He'd come nowhere near establishing motive—and motive had to be established before there was a case to go to the Public Prosecutor.

He was quite certain in his own mind that Gerda Christow had shot her husband. He suspected jealousy as the motive—but so far he had found nothing to go on. Sergeant Coombes had been working on the maids but they all told the same story. Mrs Christow worshipped the ground her husband walked on.

Whatever happened, he thought, must have happened down at The Hollow. And remembering The Hollow he felt a vague disquietude. They were an odd lot down there.

The telephone on the desk rang and Miss Collins picked up the receiver.

She said, 'It's for you, Inspector,' and passed the instrument to him.

'Hallo, Grange here. What's that?' Beryl heard the alteration in his tone and looked at him curiously. The wooden-looking face was impassive as ever. He was grunting—listening.

'Yes...yes, I've got that. That's absolutely certain, is it? No margin of error. Yes...yes...yes, I'll be down. I've about finished here. Yes.'

He put the receiver back and sat for a moment motionless. Beryl looked at him curiously.

He pulled himself together and asked in a voice that was quite different from the voice of his previous questions:

'You've no ideas of your own, I suppose, Miss Collins, about this matter?'

'You mean—'

'I mean no ideas as to who it was killed Dr Christow?'

She said flatly:

'I've absolutely no idea at all, Inspector.'

Grange said slowly:

'When the body was found, Mrs Christow was standing beside it with the revolver in her hand—'

The Hollow

He left it purposely as an unfinished sentence.

Her reaction came promptly. Not heated, cool and judicial.

'If you think Mrs Christow killed her husband, I am quite sure you are wrong. Mrs Christow is not at all a violent woman. She is very meek and submissive, and she was entirely under the doctor's thumb. It seems to me quite ridiculous that anyone could imagine for a moment that she shot him, however much appearances may be against her.'

'Then if she didn't, who did?' he asked sharply.

Beryl said slowly, 'I've no idea.'

The inspector moved to the door. Beryl asked:

'Do you want to see Mrs Christow before you go?'

'No—yes, perhaps I'd better.'

Again Beryl wondered; this was not the same man who had been questioning her before the telephone rang. What news had he got that had altered him so much?

Gerda came into the room nervously. She looked unhappy and bewildered. She said in a low, shaky voice:

'Have you found out any more about who killed John?'

'Not yet, Mrs Christow.'

'It's so impossible—so absolutely impossible.'

'But it happened, Mrs Christow.'

She nodded, looking down, screwing a handkerchief into a little ball.

He said quietly:

'Had your husband any enemies, Mrs Christow?'

'John? Oh, no. He was wonderful. Everyone adored him.'

'You can't think of anyone who had a grudge against him'—he paused—'or against you?'

'Against me?' She seemed amazed. 'Oh, no, Inspector.'

Inspector Grange sighed.

'What about Miss Veronica Cray?'

'Veronica Cray? Oh, you mean the one who came that night to borrow matches?'

'Yes, that's the one. You knew her?'

Gerda shook her head.

'I'd never seen her before. John knew her years ago—or so she said.'

'I suppose she might have had a grudge against him that you didn't know about.'

Gerda said with dignity:

'I don't believe anybody could have had a grudge against John. He was the kindest and most unselfish—oh, and one of the noblest men.'

'H'm,' said the inspector. 'Yes. Quite so. Well, good morning, Mrs Christow. You understand about the inquest? Eleven o'clock Wednesday in Market Depleach. It will be very simple—nothing to upset you—probably be adjourned for a week so that we can make further inquiries.'

'Oh, I see. Thank you.'

She stood there staring after him. He wondered whether, even now, she had grasped the fact that she was the principal suspect.

He hailed a taxi—justifiable expense in view of the piece of information he had just been given over the telephone. Just where that piece of information was leading him, he did not know. On the face of it, it seemed completely irrelevant—crazy. It simply did not make sense. Yet in some way he could not yet see, it must make sense.

The only inference to be drawn from it was that the case was not quite the simple, straightforward one that he had hitherto assumed it to be.

CHAPTER 17

Sir Henry stared curiously at Inspector Grange.

He said slowly, 'I'm not quite sure that I understand you, Inspector.'

'It's quite simple, Sir Henry. I'm asking you to check over your collection of firearms. I presume they are catalogued and indexed?'

'Naturally. But I have already identified the revolver as part of my collection.'

'It isn't quite so simple as that, Sir Henry.' Grange paused a moment. His instincts were always against giving out any information, but his hand was being forced in this particular instance. Sir Henry was a person of importance. He would doubtless comply with the request that was being made to him, but he would also require a reason. The inspector decided that he had got to give him the reason.

He said quietly:

'Dr Christow was not shot with the revolver you identified this morning.'

Sir Henry's eyebrows rose.

'Remarkable!' he said.

Grange felt vaguely comforted. Remarkable was exactly

what he felt himself. He was grateful to Sir Henry for saying so, and equally grateful for his not saying any more. It was as far as they could go at the moment. The thing was remarkable—and beyond that simply did not make sense.

Sir Henry asked:

'Have you any reason to believe that the weapon from which the fatal shot was fired comes from my collection?'

'No reason at all. But I have got to make sure, shall we say, that it doesn't.'

Sir Henry nodded his head in confirmation.

'I appreciate your point. Well, we will get to work. It will take a little time.'

He opened the desk and took out a leather-bound volume. As he opened it he repeated:

'It will take a little time to check up—'

Grange's attention was held by something in his voice. He looked up sharply. Sir Henry's shoulders sagged a little—he seemed suddenly an older and more tired man.

Inspector Grange frowned.

He thought, 'Devil if I know what to make of these people down here.'

'Ah—'

Grange spun round. His eyes noted the time by the clock, thirty minutes—twenty minutes—since Sir Henry had said, 'It will take a little time.'

Grange said sharply:

'Yes, sir?'

'A .38 Smith and Wesson is missing. It was in a brown leather holster and was at the end of the rack in this drawer.'

'Ah!' The inspector kept his voice calm, but he was excited. 'And when, sir, to your certain knowledge, did you last see it in its proper place?'

Sir Henry reflected for a moment or two.

'That is not very easy to say, Inspector. I last had this drawer open about a week ago and I think—I am almost certain—that if the revolver had been missing then I should have noticed the gap. But I should not like to swear definitely that I *saw* it there.'

Inspector Grange nodded his head.

'Thank you, sir, I quite understand. Well, I must be getting on with things.'

He left the room, a busy, purposeful man.

Sir Henry stood motionless for a while after the inspector had gone, then he went out slowly through the french windows on to the terrace. His wife was busy with a gardening basket and gloves. She was pruning some rare shrubs with a pair of secateurs.

She waved to him brightly.

'What did the inspector want? I hope he is not going to worry the servants again. You know, Henry, they *don't* like it. They can't see it as amusing or as a novelty like we do.'

'Do we see it like that?'

His tone attracted her attention. She smiled up at him sweetly.

'How tired you look, Henry. Must you let all this worry you so much?'

'Murder *is* worrying, Lucy.'

Lady Angkatell considered a moment, absently clipping off some branches, then her face clouded over.

The Hollow

'Oh, dear—that is the worst of secateurs, they are so fascinating—one can't stop and one always clips off more than one means. What was it you were saying—something about murder being worrying? But really, Henry, I have never seen *why*. I mean, if one has to die, it may be cancer, or tuberculosis in one of those dreadful bright sanatoriums, or a stroke—horrid, with one's face all on one side—or else one is shot or stabbed or strangled perhaps. But the whole thing comes to the same in the end. There one is, I mean, dead! Out of it all. And all the worry over. And the relations have all the difficulties—money quarrels and whether to wear black or not—and who was to have Aunt Selina's writing-desk—things like that!'

Sir Henry sat down on the stone coping. He said:

'This is all going to be more upsetting than we thought, Lucy.'

'Well, darling, we shall have to bear it. And when it's all over we might go away somewhere. Let's not bother about present troubles but look forward to the future. I really *am* happy about that. I've been wondering whether it would be nice to go to Ainswick for Christmas—or leave it until Easter. What do you think?'

'Plenty of time to make plans for Christmas.'

'Yes, but I like to *see* things in my mind. Easter, perhaps... yes.' Lucy smiled happily. 'She will certainly have got over it by then.'

'Who?' Sir Henry was startled.

Lady Angkatell said calmly:

'Henrietta. I think if they were to have the wedding in October—October of next year, I mean, then we could go

Agatha Christie

and stop for *that* Christmas. I've been thinking, Henry—'

'I wish you wouldn't, my dear. You think too much.'

'You know the barn? It will make a perfect studio. And Henrietta will need a studio. She has real talent, you know. Edward, I am sure, will be immensely proud of her. Two boys and a girl would be nice—or two boys and two girls.'

'Lucy—Lucy! How you run on.'

'But, darling,' Lady Angkatell opened wide, beautiful eyes. 'Edward will never marry anyone but Henrietta. He is very, *very* obstinate. Rather like my father in that way. He gets an idea in his head! So of course Henrietta *must* marry him—and she *will* now that John Christow is out of the way. He was really the greatest misfortune that could possibly have happened to her.'

'Poor devil!'

'Why? Oh, you mean because he's dead? Oh, well, everyone has to die sometime. I never worry over people dying...'

He looked at her curiously.

'I always thought you liked Christow, Lucy?'

'I found him amusing. And he had charm. But I never think one ought to attach too much importance to *anybody*.'

And gently, with a smiling face, Lady Angkatell clipped remorselessly at a *Viburnum Carlesii*.

CHAPTER 18

Hercule Poirot looked out of his window and saw Henrietta Savernake walking up the path to the front door. She was wearing the same green tweeds that she had worn on the day of the tragedy. There was a spaniel with her.

He hastened to the front door and opened it. She stood smiling at him.

'Can I come in and see your house? I like looking at people's houses. I'm just taking the dog for a walk.'

'But most certainly. How English it is to take the dog for a walk!'

'I know,' said Henrietta. 'I thought of that. Do you know that nice poem: "The days passed slowly one by one. I fed the ducks, reproved my wife, played Handel's *Largo* on the fife and took the dog a run."'

Again she smiled, a brilliant, insubstantial smile.

Poirot ushered her into his sitting-room. She looked round its neat and prim arrangement and nodded her head.

'Nice,' she said, 'two of everything. How you would hate my studio.'

'Why should I hate it?'

'Oh, a lot of clay sticking to things—and here and there

just one thing that I happen to like and which would be ruined if there were two of them.'

'But I can understand that, Mademoiselle. You are an artist.'

'Aren't you an artist, too, M. Poirot?'

Poirot put his head on one side.

'It is a question, that. But on the whole I would say, no. I have known crimes that were artistic—they were, you understand, supreme exercises of imagination. But the solving of them—no, it is not the creative power that is needed. What is required is a passion for the truth.'

'A passion for the truth,' said Henrietta meditatively. 'Yes, I can see how dangerous that might make you. Would the truth satisfy you?'

He looked at her curiously.

'What do you mean, Miss Savernake?'

'I can understand that you would want to *know*. But would knowledge be enough? Would you have to go a step further and translate knowledge into action?'

He was interested in her approach.

'You are suggesting that if I knew the truth about Dr Christow's death—I might be satisfied to keep that knowledge to myself. Do *you* know the truth about his death?'

Henrietta shrugged her shoulders.

'The obvious answer seems to be Gerda. How cynical it is that a wife or a husband is always the first suspect.'

'But you do not agree?'

'I always like to keep an open mind.'

Poirot said quietly:

'Why did you come here, Miss Savernake?'

The Hollow

'I must admit that I haven't your passion for truth, M. Poirot. Taking the dog for a walk was such a nice English countryside excuse. But of course the Angkatells haven't got a dog—as you may have noticed the other day.'

'The fact had not escaped me.'

'So I borrowed the gardener's spaniel. I am not, you must understand, M. Poirot, very truthful.'

Again that brilliant brittle smile flashed out. He wondered why he should suddenly find it unendurably moving. He said quietly:

'No, but you have integrity.'

'Why on earth do you say that?'

She was startled—almost, he thought, dismayed.

'Because I believe it to be true.'

'Integrity,' Henrietta repeated thoughtfully. 'I wonder what that word really means.'

She sat very still, staring down at the carpet, then she raised her head and looked at him steadily.

'Don't you want to know why I did come?'

'You find a difficulty, perhaps, in putting it into words.'

'Yes, I think I do. The inquest, M. Poirot, is tomorrow. One has to make up one's mind just how much—'

She broke off. Getting up, she wandered across to the mantelpiece, displaced one or two of the ornaments and moved a vase of Michaelmas daisies from its position in the middle of a table to the extreme corner of the mantelpiece. She stepped back, eyeing the arrangement with her head on one side.

'How do you like that, M. Poirot?'

'Not at all, Mademoiselle.'

'I thought you wouldn't.' She laughed, moved everything quickly and deftly back to its original position. 'Well, if one wants to say a thing one has to say it! You are, somehow, the sort of person one can talk to. Here goes. Is it necessary, do you think, that the police should know that I was John Christow's mistress?'

Her voice was quite dry and unemotional. She was looking, not at him, but at the wall over his head. With one forefinger she was following the curve of the jar that held the purple flowers. He had an idea that in the touch of that finger was her emotional outlet.

Hercule Poirot said precisely and also without emotion:

'I see. You were lovers?'

'If you prefer to put it like that.'

He looked at her curiously.

'It was not how you put it, Mademoiselle.'

'No.'

'Why not?'

Henrietta shrugged her shoulders. She came and sat down by him on the sofa. She said slowly:

'One likes to describe things as—as accurately as possible.'

His interest in Henrietta Savernake grew stronger. He said:

'You had been Dr Christow's mistress—for how long?'

'About six months.'

'The police will have, I gather, no difficulty in discovering the fact?'

Henrietta considered.

'I imagine not. That is, if they are looking for something of that kind.'

The Hollow

'Oh, they will be looking, I can assure you of that.'

'Yes, I rather thought they would.' She paused, stretched out her fingers on her knee and looked at them, then gave him a swift, friendly glance. 'Well, M. Poirot, what does one do? Go to Inspector Grange and say—what does one say to a moustache like that? It's such a domestic, family moustache.'

Poirot's hand crawled upwards to his own proudly borne adornment.

'Whereas mine, Mademoiselle?'

'Your moustache, M. Poirot, is an artistic triumph. It has no associations with anything but itself. It is, I am sure, unique.'

'Absolutely.'

'And it is probably the reason why I am talking to you as I am. Granted that the police have to know the truth about John and myself, will it necessarily have to be made public?'

'That depends,' said Poirot. 'If the police think it had no bearing on the case, they will be quite discreet. You—are very anxious on this point?'

Henrietta nodded. She stared down at her fingers for a moment or two, then suddenly lifted her head and spoke. Her voice was no longer dry and light.

'Why should things be made worse than they are for poor Gerda? She adored John and he's dead. She's lost him. Why should she have to bear an added burden?'

'It is for her that you mind?'

'Do you think that is hypocritical? I suppose you're thinking that if I cared at all about Gerda's peace of mind, I would never have become John's mistress. But you don't understand—it was not like that. I did not break up his married life. I was only one—of a procession.'

'Ah, it was like that?'

She turned on him sharply.

'No, no, *no*! Not what you are thinking. That's what I mind most of all! The false idea that everybody will have of what John was like. That's why I'm here talking to you—because I've got a vague, foggy hope that I can make you understand. Understand, I mean, the sort of person John was. I can see so well what will happen—the headlines in the papers—A Doctor's Love Life—Gerda, myself, Veronica Cray. John wasn't like that—he wasn't, actually, a man who thought much about women. It wasn't women who mattered to him most, it was his *work*. It was in his work that his interest and excitement—yes, and his sense of adventure—really lay. If John had been taken unawares at any moment and asked to name the woman who was most in his mind, do you know who he would have said?—Mrs Crabtree.'

'Mrs Crabtree?' Poirot was surprised. 'Who, then, is this Mrs Crabtree?'

There was something between tears and laughter in Henrietta's voice as she went on:

'She's an old woman—ugly, dirty, wrinkled, quite indomitable. John thought the world of her. She's a patient in St Christopher's Hospital. She's got Ridgeway's Disease. That's a disease that's very rare, but if you get it you're bound to die—there just isn't any cure. But John was finding a cure—I can't explain technically—it was all very complicated—some question of hormone secretions. He'd been making

The Hollow

experiments and Mrs Crabtree was his prize patient—you see, she's got *guts*, she *wants* to live—and she was fond of John. She and he were fighting on the same side. Ridgeway's Disease and Mrs Crabtree is what has been uppermost in John's mind for months—night and day—nothing else really counted. That's what being the kind of doctor John was really means—not all the Harley Street stuff and the rich, fat women, that's only a sideline. It's the intense scientific curiosity and the achievement. I—oh, I wish I could make you understand.'

Her hands flew out in a curiously despairing gesture, and Hercule Poirot thought how very lovely and sensitive those hands were.

He said:

'*You* seem to understand very well.'

'Oh, yes, I understood. John used to come and talk, do you see? Not quite to me—partly, I think, to himself. He got things clear that way. Sometimes he was almost despairing—he couldn't see how to overcome the heightened toxicity—and then he'd get an idea for varying the treatment. I can't explain to you what it was like—it was like, yes, a *battle*. You can't imagine the—the fury of it and the concentration—and yes, sometimes the agony. And sometimes the sheer tiredness…'

She was silent for a minute or two, her eyes dark with remembrance.

Poirot said curiously:

'You must have a certain technical knowledge yourself?'

She shook her head.

Agatha Christie

'Not really. Only enough to understand what John was talking about. I got books and read about it.'

She was silent again, her face softened, her lips half-parted. She was, he thought, remembering.

With a sigh, her mind came back to the present. She looked at him wistfully.

'If I could only make you see—'

'But you have, Mademoiselle.'

'Really?'

'Yes. One recognizes authenticity when one hears it.'

'Thank you. But it won't be so easy to explain to Inspector Grange.'

'Probably not. He will concentrate on the personal angle.'

Henrietta said vehemently:

'And that was so unimportant—so completely unimportant.'

Poirot's eyebrows rose slowly. She answered his unspoken protest.

'But it was! You see—after a while—I got between John and what he was thinking of. I affected him, as a woman. He couldn't concentrate as he wanted to concentrate—because of me. He began to be afraid that he was beginning to love me—he didn't want to love anyone. He—he made love to me because he didn't want to think about me too much. He wanted it to be light, easy, just an affair like other affairs that he had had.'

'And you—' Poirot was watching her closely. 'You were content to have it—like that.'

Henrietta got up. She said, and once more it was her dry voice:

'No, I wasn't—content. After all, one is human...'

The Hollow

Poirot waited a minute then he said:

'Then why, Mademoiselle—'

'Why?' She whirled round on him. 'I wanted John to be satisfied, I wanted *John* to have what he wanted. I wanted him to be able to go on with the thing he cared about—his work. If he didn't want to be hurt—to be vulnerable again—why—why, that was all right by me.'

Poirot rubbed his nose.

'Just now, Miss Savernake, you mentioned Veronica Cray. Was she also a friend of John Christow's?'

'Until last Saturday night, he hadn't seen her for fifteen years.'

'He knew her fifteen years ago?'

'They were engaged to be married.' Henrietta came back and sat down. 'I see I've got to make it all clearer. John loved Veronica desperately. Veronica was, and is, a bitch of the first water. She's the supreme egoist. Her terms were that John was to chuck everything he cared about and become Miss Veronica Cray's little tame husband. John broke up the whole thing—quite rightly. But he suffered like hell. His one idea was to marry someone as unlike Veronica as possible. He married Gerda, whom you might describe inelegantly as a first-class chump. That was all very nice and safe, but as anyone could have told him the day came when being married to a chump irritated him. He had various affairs—none of them important. Gerda, of course, never knew about them. But I think, myself, that for fifteen years there has been something wrong with John—something connected with Veronica.

He never really got over her. And then, last Saturday, he met her again.'

After a long pause, Poirot recited dreamily:

'He went out with her that night to see her home and returned to The Hollow at 3 am.'

'How do you know?'

'A housemaid had the toothache.'

Henrietta said irrelevantly, 'Lucy has far too many servants.'

'But you yourself knew that, Mademoiselle.'

'Yes.'

'How did you know?'

Again there was an infinitesimal pause. Then Henrietta replied slowly:

'I was looking out of my window and saw him come back to the house.'

'The toothache, Mademoiselle?'

She smiled at him.

'Quite another kind of ache, M. Poirot.'

She got up and moved towards the door, and Poirot said:

'I will walk back with you, Mademoiselle.'

They crossed the lane and went through the gate into the chestnut plantation.

Henrietta said:

'We need not go past the pool. We can go up to the left and along the top path to the flower walk.'

A track led steeply uphill towards the woods. After a while they came to a broader path at right angles across the hillside above the chestnut trees. Presently they came to a bench and Henrietta sat down, Poirot beside her. The woods were above and behind them, and below were the closely planted chestnut groves. Just in front of the seat a curving path led downwards, to where just a glimmer of blue water could be seen.

Poirot watched Henrietta without speaking. Her face had relaxed, the tension had gone. It looked rounder and younger. He realized what she must have looked like as a young girl.

He said very gently at last:

'Of what are you thinking, Mademoiselle?'

'Of Ainswick.'

'What is Ainswick?'

'Ainswick? It's a place.' Almost dreamily, she described Ainswick to him. The white, graceful house, the big magnolia growing up it, the whole set in an amphitheatre of wooded hills.

'It was your home?'

'Not really. I lived in Ireland. It was where we came, all of us, for holidays. Edward and Midge and myself. It was Lucy's home actually. It belonged to her father. After his death it came to Edward.'

'Not to Sir Henry? But it is he who has the title.'

'Oh, that's a KCB,' she explained. 'Henry was only a distant cousin.'

'And after Edward Angkatell, to whom does it go, this Ainswick?'

'How odd, I've never really thought. If Edward doesn't marry—' She paused. A shadow passed over her face. Hercule Poirot wondered exactly what thought was passing through her mind.

'I suppose,' said Henrietta slowly, 'it will go to David. So that's why—'

'Why what?'

'Why Lucy asked him here... David and Ainswick?' She shook her head. 'They don't fit somehow.'

Poirot pointed to the path in front of them.

'It is by that path, Mademoiselle, that you went down to the swimming pool yesterday?'

She gave a quick shiver.

'No, by the one nearer the house. It was Edward who came this way.' She turned on him suddenly. 'Must we talk about it any more? I hate the swimming pool. I even hate The Hollow.'

Poirot murmured:

'I hate the dreadful hollow behind the little wood;
Its lips in the field above are dabbled with blood-red heath,
The red-ribb'd ledges drip with a silent horror of blood
And Echo there, whatever is ask'd her, answers "Death."'

Henrietta turned an astonished face on him.

'Tennyson,' said Hercule Poirot, nodding his head proudly. 'The poetry of your Lord Tennyson.'

Henrietta was repeating:

'*And Echo there, whatever is ask'd her...*' She went on, almost to herself, 'But of course—I see—that's what it is—Echo!'

'How do you mean, Echo?'

'This place—The Hollow itself ! I almost saw it before—on Saturday when Edward and I walked up to the ridge. An echo of Ainswick. And that's what we are, we Angkatells.

The Hollow

Echoes! We're not real—not real as John was real.' She turned to Poirot. 'I wish you had known him, M. Poirot. We're all shadows compared to John. John was really alive.'

'I knew that even when he was dying, Mademoiselle.'

'I know. One felt it... And John is dead, and we, the echoes, are alive... It's like, you know, a very bad joke.'

The youth had gone from her face again. Her lips were twisted, bitter with sudden pain.

When Poirot spoke, asking a question, she did not, for a moment, take in what he was saying.

'I am sorry. What did you say, M. Poirot?'

'I was asking whether your aunt, Lady Angkatell, liked Dr Christow?'

'Lucy? She is a cousin, by the way, not an aunt. Yes, she liked him very much.'

'And your—also a cousin?—Mr Edward Angkatell—did he like Dr Christow?'

Her voice was, he thought, a little constrained, as she replied:

'Not particularly—but then he hardly knew him.'

'And your—yet another cousin? Mr David Angkatell?'

Henrietta smiled.

'David, I think, hates all of us. He spends his time immured in the library reading the *Encyclopædia Britannica*.'

'Ah, a serious temperament.'

'I am sorry for David. He has had a difficult home life. His mother was unbalanced—an invalid. Now his only way of protecting himself is to try to feel superior to everyone. It's all right as long as it works, but now and then it breaks down and the vulnerable David peeps through.'

'Did he feel himself superior to Dr Christow?'

'He tried to—but I don't think it came off. I suspect that John Christow was just the kind of man that David would like to be. He disliked John in consequence.'

Poirot nodded his head thoughtfully.

'Yes—self-assurance, confidence, virility—all the intensive male qualities. It is interesting—very interesting.'

Henrietta did not answer.

Through the chestnuts, down by the pool, Hercule Poirot saw a man stooping, searching for something, or so it seemed.

He murmured, 'I wonder—'

'I beg your pardon?'

Poirot said, 'That is one of Inspector Grange's men. He seems to be looking for something.'

'Clues, I suppose. Don't policemen look for clues? Cigarette ash, footprints, burnt matches.'

Her voice held a kind of bitter mockery. Poirot answered seriously.

'Yes, they look for these things—and sometimes they find them. But the real clues, Miss Savernake, in a case like this, usually lie in the personal relationships of the people concerned.'

'I don't think I understand you.'

'Little things,' said Poirot, his head thrown back, his eyes half-closed. 'Not cigarette ash, or a rubber heel mark—but a gesture, a look, an unexpected action…'

Henrietta turned her head sharply to look at him. He felt her eyes, but he did not turn his head. She said:

'Are you thinking of—anything in particular?'

The Hollow

'I was thinking of how you stepped forward and took the revolver out of Mrs Christow's hand then dropped it in the pool.'

He felt the slight start she gave. But her voice was quite normal and calm.

'Gerda, M. Poirot, is rather a clumsy person. In the shock of the moment, and if the revolver had had another cartridge in it, she might have fired it and—and hurt someone.'

'But it was rather clumsy of *you*, was it not, to drop it in the pool?'

'Well, I had had a shock too.' She paused. 'What are you suggesting, M. Poirot?'

Poirot sat up, turned his head, and spoke in a brisk, matter-of-fact way.

'If there were fingerprints on that revolver, that is to say, fingerprints made *before Mrs Christow handled it*, it would be interesting to know whose they were—and that we shall never know now.'

Henrietta said quietly but steadily:

'Meaning that you think they were *mine*. You are suggesting that I shot John and then left the revolver beside him so that Gerda could come along and pick it up and be left holding the baby. That is what you are suggesting, isn't it? But surely, if I did that, you will give me credit for enough intelligence to have wiped off my own fingerprints first!'

'But surely *you* are intelligent enough to see, Mademoiselle, that if you had done so and if the revolver had had *no fingerprints on it but Mrs Christow's, that* would have been very remarkable! For you were all shooting with that revolver the day before. Gerda Christow would hardly have wiped the revolver clean of fingerprints *before* using it—why should she?'

Henrietta said slowly:

'So you think I killed John?'

'When Dr Christow was dying, he said: "*Henrietta*."'

'And you think that that was an accusation? It was not.'

'What was it then?'

Henrietta stretched out her foot and traced a pattern with the toe. She said in a low voice:

'Aren't you forgetting—what I told you not very long ago? I mean—the terms we were on?'

'Ah, yes—he was your lover—and so, as he is dying, he says: "*Henrietta*". That is very touching.'

She turned blazing eyes upon him.

'Must you sneer?'

'I am not sneering. But I do not like being lied to—and that, I think, is what you are trying to do.'

Henrietta said quietly:

'I have told you that I am not very truthful—but when John said: "*Henrietta*" he was not accusing me of having murdered him. Can't you understand that people of my kind, who *make* things, are quite incapable of taking life? I don't kill people, M. Poirot. I *couldn't* kill anyone. That's the plain stark truth. You suspect me simply because my name was murmured by a dying man who hardly knew what he was saying.'

'Dr Christow knew perfectly what he was saying. His voice was as alive and conscious as that of a doctor doing

The Hollow

a vital operation who says sharply and urgently: "Nurse, the forceps, please."'

'But—' She seemed at a loss, taken aback. Hercule Poirot went on rapidly:

'And it is not just on account of what Dr Christow said when he was dying. I do not believe for one moment that you are capable of premeditated murder—that, no. But you might have fired that shot in a sudden moment of fierce resentment—and if so—*if* so, Mademoiselle, you have the creative imagination and ability to cover your tracks.'

Henrietta got up. She stood for a moment, pale and shaken, looking at him. She said with a sudden, rueful smile:

'And I thought you liked me.'

Hercule Poirot sighed. He said sadly:

'That is what is so unfortunate for me. I do.'

CHAPTER 19

When Henrietta had left him, Poirot sat on until he saw below him Inspector Grange walk past the pool with a resolute, easy stride and take the path on past the pavilion.

The inspector was walking in a purposeful way.

He must be going, therefore, either to Resthaven or to Dovecotes. Poirot wondered which.

He got up and retraced his steps along the way he had come. If Inspector Grange was coming to see him, he was interested to hear what the inspector had to say.

But when he got back to Resthaven there was no sign of a visitor. Poirot looked thoughtfully up the lane in the direction of Dovecotes. Veronica Cray had not, he knew, gone back to London.

He found his curiosity rising about Veronica Cray. The pale, shining fox furs, the heaped boxes of matches, that sudden imperfectly explained invasion on the Saturday night, and finally Henrietta Savernake's revelations about John Christow and Veronica.

It was, he thought, an interesting pattern. Yes, that was how he saw it: a pattern.

A design of intermingled emotions and the clash of

The Hollow

personalities. A strange involved design, with dark threads of hate and desire running through it.

Had Gerda Christow shot her husband? Or was it not quite so simple as that?

He thought of his conversation with Henrietta and decided that it was not so simple.

Henrietta had jumped to the conclusion that he suspected her of the murder, but actually he had not gone nearly as far as that in his mind. No further indeed than the belief that Henrietta knew something. Knew something or was concealing something—which?

He shook his head, dissatisfied.

The scene by the pool. A set scene. A stage scene.

Staged by whom? Staged *for* whom?

The answer to the second question was, he strongly suspected, Hercule Poirot. He had thought so at the time. But he had thought then that it was an impertinence—a joke.

It was still an impertinence—but not a joke.

And the answer to the first question?

He shook his head. He did not know. He had not the least idea.

But he half-closed his eyes and conjured them up—all of them—seeing them clearly in his mind's eye. Sir Henry, upright, responsible, trusted administrator of Empire. Lady Angkatell, shadowy, elusive, unexpectedly and bewilderingly charming, with that deadly power of inconsequent suggestion. Henrietta Savernake, who had loved John Christow better than she loved herself. The gentle and negative Edward Angkatell. The dark, positive girl called Midge

Hardcastle. The dazed, bewildered face of Gerda Christow clasping a revolver in her hand. The offended adolescent personality of David Angkatell.

There they all were, caught and held in the meshes of the law. Bound together for a little while in the relentless aftermath of sudden and violent death. Each of them had their own tragedy and meaning, their own story.

And somewhere in that interplay of characters and emotions lay the truth.

To Hercule Poirot there was only one thing more fascinating than the study of human beings, and that was the pursuit of truth.

He meant to know the truth of John Christow's death.

'But of course, Inspector,' said Veronica. 'I'm only too anxious to help you.'

'Thank you, Miss Cray.'

Veronica Cray was not, somehow, at all what the inspector had imagined.

He had been prepared for glamour, for artificiality, even possibly for heroics. He would not have been at all surprised if she had put on an act of some kind.

In fact, she was, he shrewdly suspected, putting on an act. But it was not the kind of act he had expected.

There was no overdone feminine charm—glamour was not stressed.

Instead he felt that he was sitting opposite to an exceedingly good-looking and expensively dressed woman who

The Hollow

was also a good business woman. Veronica Cray, he thought, was no fool.

'We just want a clear statement, Miss Cray. You came over to The Hollow on Saturday evening?'

'Yes, I'd run out of matches. One forgets how important these things are in the country.'

'You went all the way to The Hollow? Why not to your next-door neighbour, M. Poirot?'

She smiled—a superb, confident camera smile.

'I didn't know who my next-door neighbour was—otherwise I should have. I just thought he was some little foreigner and I thought, you know, he might become a bore—living so near.'

'Yes,' thought Grange, 'quite plausible.' She'd worked that one out ready for the occasion.

'You got your matches,' he said. 'And you recognized an old friend in Dr Christow, I understand?'

She nodded.

'Poor John. Yes, I hadn't seen him for fifteen years.'

'Really?' There was polite disbelief in the inspector's tone.

'Really.' Her tone was firmly assertive.

'You were pleased to see him?'

'Very pleased. It's always delightful, don't you think, Inspector, to come across an old friend?'

'It can be on some occasions.'

Veronica Cray went on without waiting for further questioning:

'John saw me home. You'll want to know if he said anything that could have a bearing on the tragedy, and I've been thinking over our conversation very carefully—but really there wasn't a pointer of any kind.'

'What did you talk about, Miss Cray?'

'Old days. "Do you remember this, that and the other?"' She smiled pensively. 'We had known each other in the South of France. John had really changed very little—older, of course, and more assured. I gather he was quite well known in his profession. He didn't talk about his personal life at all. I just got the impression that his married life wasn't perhaps frightfully happy—but it was only the vaguest impression. I suppose his wife, poor thing, was one of those dim, jealous women—probably always making a fuss about his better-looking lady patients.'

'No,' said Grange. 'She doesn't really seem to have been that way.'

Veronica said quickly:

'You mean—it was all *underneath*? Yes—yes, I can see that that would be far more dangerous.'

'I see you think Mrs Christow shot him, Miss Cray?'

'I oughtn't to have said that. One mustn't comment—is that it—before a trial? I'm extremely sorry, Inspector. It was just that my maid told me she'd been found actually standing over the body with the revolver still in her hand. You know how in these quiet country places everything gets so exaggerated and servants do pass things on.'

'Servants can be very useful sometimes, Miss Cray.'

'Yes, I suppose you get a lot of your information that way?'

Grange went on stolidly:

'It's a question, of course, of who had a motive—'

The Hollow

He paused. Veronica said with a faint, rueful smile:

'And a wife is always the first suspect? How cynical! But there's usually what's called "the other woman". I suppose *she* might be considered to have a motive too?'

'You think there was another woman in Dr Christow's life?'

'Well—yes, I did rather imagine there might be. One just gets an impression, you know.'

'Impressions can be very helpful sometimes,' said Grange.

'I rather imagined—from what he said—that that sculptress woman was, well, a very close friend. But I expect you know all about that already?'

'We have to look into all these things, of course.'

Inspector Grange's voice was strictly non-committal, but he saw, without appearing to see, a quick, spiteful flash of satisfaction in those large blue eyes.

He said, making the question very official:

'Dr Christow saw you home, you say. What time was it when you said goodnight to him?'

'Do you know, I really can't remember! We talked for some time, I do know that. It must have been quite late.'

'He came in?'

'Yes, I gave him a drink.'

'I see. I imagined your conversation might have taken place in the—er—pavilion by the swimming pool.'

He saw her eyelids flicker. There was hardly a moment's hesitation before she said:

'You really *are* a detective, aren't you? Yes, we sat there and smoked and talked for some time. How did you know?'

Her face bore the pleased, eager expression of a child asking to be shown a clever trick.

'You left your furs behind there, Miss Cray.' He added just without emphasis, 'And the matches.'

'Yes, of course I did.'

'Dr Christow returned to The Hollow at 3 am,' announced the inspector, again without emphasis.

'Was it really as late as that?' Veronica sounded quite amazed.

'Yes, it was, Miss Cray.'

'Of course, we had so much to talk over—not having seen each other for so many years.'

'Are you sure it was quite so long since you had seen Dr Christow?'

'I've just told you I hadn't seen him for fifteen years.'

'Are you quite sure you're not making a mistake? I've got the impression you might have been seeing quite a lot of him.'

'What on earth makes you think that?'

'Well, this note for one thing.' Inspector Grange took out a letter from his pocket, glanced down at it, cleared his throat and read:

Please come over this morning. I must see you.
   Veronica.

'Ye-es.' She smiled. 'It *is* a little peremptory, perhaps. I'm afraid Hollywood makes one—well, rather arrogant.'

'Dr Christow came over to your house the following morning in answer to that summons. You had a quarrel. Would

The Hollow

you care to tell me, Miss Cray, what that quarrel was about?'

The inspector had unmasked his batteries. He was quick to seize the flash of anger, the ill-tempered tightening of the lips. She snapped out:

'We didn't quarrel.'

'Oh, yes, you did, Miss Cray. Your last words were, "I think I hate you more than I believed I could hate anyone."'

She was silent now. He could feel her thinking—thinking quickly and warily. Some women might have rushed into speech. But Veronica Cray was too clever for that.

She shrugged her shoulders and said lightly:

'I see. More servants' tales. My little maid has rather a lively imagination. There are different ways of saying things, you know. I can assure you that I wasn't being melodramatic. It was really a mildly flirtatious remark. We had been sparring together.'

'The words were not intended to be taken seriously?'

'Certainly not. And I can assure you, Inspector, that it *was* fifteen years since I had last seen John Christow. You can verify that for yourself.'

She was poised again, detached, sure of herself.

Grange did not argue or pursue the subject. He got up.

'That's all for the moment, Miss Cray,' he said pleasantly.

He went out of Dovecotes and down the lane, and turned in at the gate of Resthaven.

Hercule Poirot stared at the inspector in the utmost surprise. He repeated incredulously:

'The revolver that Gerda Christow was holding and which was subsequently dropped into the pool was not the revolver that fired the fatal shot? But that is extraordinary.'

'Exactly, M. Poirot. Put bluntly, it just doesn't make sense.'

Poirot murmured softly:

'No, it does not make sense. But all the same, Inspector, it has got to make sense, eh?'

The inspector sighed heavily: 'That's just it, M. Poirot. We've got to find some way that it does make sense—but at the moment I can't see it. The truth is that we shan't get much further until we've found the gun that *was* used. It came from Sir Henry's collection all right—at least, there's one missing—and that means that the whole thing is still tied up with The Hollow.'

'Yes,' murmured Poirot. 'It is still tied up with The Hollow.'

'It seemed a simple, straightforward business,' went on the inspector. 'Well, it isn't so simple or so straightforward.'

'No,' said Poirot, 'it is not simple.'

'We've got to admit the possibility that the thing was a frame-up—that's to say that it was all set to implicate Gerda Christow. But if that was so, why not leave the right revolver lying by the body for her to pick up?'

'She might not have picked it up.'

'That's true, but even if she didn't, so long as nobody else's fingerprints were on the gun—that's to say if it was wiped after use—she would probably have been suspected all right. And that's what the murderer wanted, wasn't it?'

'Was it?'

Grange stared.

The Hollow

'Well, if you'd done a murder, you'd want to plant it good and quick on someone else, wouldn't you? That would be a murderer's normal reaction.'

'Ye-es,' said Poirot. 'But then perhaps we have here a rather unusual type of murderer. It is possible that *that* is the solution of our problem.'

'What is the solution?'

Poirot said thoughtfully:

'An unusual type of murderer.'

Inspector Grange stared at him curiously. He said:

'But then—what *was* the murderer's idea? What was he or she getting at?'

Poirot spread out his hands with a sigh.

'I have no idea—I have no idea at all. But it seems to me—dimly—'

'Yes?'

'That the murderer is someone who wanted to kill John Christow but who did not want to implicate Gerda Christow.'

'H'm! Actually, we suspected her right away.'

'Ah, yes, but it was only a matter of time before the facts about the gun came to light, and that was bound to give a new angle. In the interval the murderer has had time—'

Poirot came to a full stop.

'Time to do what?'

'Ah, *mon ami*, there you have me. Again I have to say I do not know.'

Inspector Grange took a turn or two up and down the room. Then he stopped and came to a stand in front of Poirot.

Agatha Christie

'I've come to you this afternoon, M. Poirot, for two reasons. One is because I know—it's pretty well known in the Force—that you're a man of wide experience who's done some very tricky work on this type of problem. That's reason number one. But there's another reason. You were there. You were an eye-witness. You *saw* what happened.'

Poirot nodded.

'Yes, I *saw* what happened—but the eyes, Inspector Grange, are very unreliable witnesses.'

'What do you mean, M. Poirot?'

'The eyes see, sometimes, what they are *meant* to see.'

'You think that it was planned out beforehand?'

'I suspect it. It was exactly, you understand, like a stage scene. What I *saw* was clear enough. A man who had just been shot and the woman who had shot him holding in her hand the gun she had just used. That is what I *saw*, and already we know that in one particular the picture is wrong. That gun had *not* been used to shoot John Christow.'

'Hm!' The inspector pulled his drooping moustache firmly downwards. 'What you are getting at is that some of the other particulars of the picture may be wrong too?'

Poirot nodded. He said:

'There were three other people present—three people who had *apparently* just arrived on the scene. But that may not be true either. The pool is surrounded by a thick grove of young chestnuts. From the pool five paths lead away, one to the house, one up to the woods, one up to the flower walk, one down from the pool to the farm and one to the lane here.

The Hollow

'Of those three people, each one came along a different path, Edward Angkatell from the woods above, Lady Angkatell up from the farm, and Henrietta Savernake from the flower border above the house. Those three arrived upon the scene of the crime almost simultaneously, and a few minutes after Gerda Christow.

'But one of those three, Inspector, could have been at the pool *before* Gerda Christow arrived, could have shot John Christow, and could have retreated up or down one of the paths and then, turning round, could have arrived at the same time as the others.'

Inspector Grange said:

'Yes, it's possible.'

'And another possibility, not envisaged at the time. Someone could have come along the path from the lane, could have shot John Christow, and could have gone back the same way, unseen.'

Grange said, 'You're dead right. There are two other possible suspects besides Gerda Christow. We've got the same motive—jealousy. It's definitely a *crime passionel*. There were two other women mixed up with John Christow.'

He paused and said:

'Christow went over to see Veronica Cray that morning. They had a row. She told him that she'd make him sorry for what he'd done, and she said she hated him more than she believed she could hate anyone.'

'Interesting,' murmured Poirot.

'She's straight from Hollywood—and by what I read in the papers they do a bit of shooting each other out there

Agatha Christie

sometimes. She could have come along to get her furs, which she'd left in the pavilion the night before. They could have met—the whole thing could have flared up—she fired at him—and then, hearing someone coming, she could have dodged back the way she came.'

He paused a moment and added irritably:

'And now we come to the part where it all goes haywire. That damned gun! Unless,' his eyes brightened, 'she shot him with her own gun and dropped one that she'd pinched from Sir Henry's study so as to throw suspicion on the crowd at The Hollow. She mightn't know about our being able to identify the gun used from the marks on the rifling.'

'How many people do know that, I wonder?'

'I put the point to Sir Henry. He said he thought quite a lot of people would know—on account of all the detective stories that are written. Quoted a new one, *The Clue of the Dripping Fountain*, which he said John Christow himself had been reading on Saturday and which emphasized that particular point.'

'But Veronica Cray would have had to have got the gun somehow from Sir Henry's study.'

'Yes, it would mean premeditation.' The inspector took another tug at his moustache, then he looked at Poirot. 'But you've hinted yourself at another possibility, M. Poirot. There's Miss Savernake. And here's where your eye-witness stuff, or rather I should say, ear-witness stuff, comes in again. Dr Christow said: "*Henrietta*" when he was dying. You heard him—they all heard him, though Mr Angkatell doesn't seem to have caught what he said.'

The Hollow

'Edward Angkatell did not hear? That is interesting.'

'But the others did. Miss Savernake herself says he tried to speak to her. Lady Angkatell says he opened his eyes, saw Miss Savernake, and said: "*Henrietta.*" She doesn't, I think, attach any importance to it.'

Poirot smiled. 'No—she would not attach importance to it.'

'Now, M. Poirot, what about you? You were there—you saw—you heard. Was Dr Christow trying to tell you all that it was Henrietta who had shot him? In short, was that word an *accusation*?'

Poirot said slowly:

'I did not think so at the time.'

'But now, M. Poirot? What do you think *now*?'

Poirot sighed. Then he said slowly:

'It may have been so. I cannot say more than that. It is an impression only for which you are asking me, and when the moment is past there is a temptation to read into things a meaning which was not there at the time.'

Grange said hastily:

'Of course, this is all off the record. What M. Poirot thought isn't evidence—I know that. It's only a pointer I'm trying to get.'

'Oh, I understand you very well—and an impression from an eye-witness can be a very useful thing. But I am humiliated to have to say that my impressions are valueless. I was under the misconception, induced by the visual evidence, that Mrs Christow had just shot her husband; so that when Dr Christow opened his eyes and said "*Henrietta*"

Agatha Christie

I never thought of it as being an accusation. It is tempting now, looking back, to read into that scene something that was not there.'

'I know what you mean,' said Grange. 'But it seems to me that since "*Henrietta*" was the last word Christow spoke, it must have meant one of two things. It was either an accusation of murder or else it was—well, purely emotional. She's the woman he's in love with and he's dying. Now, bearing everything in mind, which of the two did it sound like to you?'

Poirot sighed, stirred, closed his eyes, opened them again, stretched out his hands in acute vexation. He said:

'His voice was urgent—that is all I can say—*urgent*. It seemed to me neither accusing nor emotional—but urgent, yes! And of one thing I am sure. He was in full possession of his faculties. He spoke—yes, he spoke like a doctor—a doctor who has, say, a sudden surgical emergency on his hands—a patient who is bleeding to death, perhaps.' Poirot shrugged his shoulders. 'That is the best I can do for you.'

'Medical, eh?' said the inspector. 'Well, yes, that *is* a third way of looking at it. He was shot, he suspected he was dying, he wanted something done for him quickly. And if, as Lady Angkatell says, Miss Savernake was the first person he saw when his eyes opened, then he would appeal to her. It's not very satisfactory, though.'

'Nothing about this case is satisfactory,' said Poirot with some bitterness.

A murder scene, set and staged to deceive Hercule Poirot— and which *had* deceived him! No, it was not satisfactory.

The Hollow

Inspector Grange was looking out of the window.

'Hallo,' he said, 'here's Clark, my sergeant. Looks as though he's got something. He's been working on the servants—the friendly touch. He's a nice-looking chap, got a way with women.'

Sergeant Clark came in a little breathlessly. He was clearly pleased with himself, though subduing the fact under a respectful official manner.

'Thought I'd better come and report, sir, since I knew where you'd gone.'

He hesitated, shooting a doubtful glance at Poirot, whose exotic foreign appearance did not commend itself to his sense of official reticence.

'Out with it, my lad,' said Grange. 'Never mind M. Poirot here. He's forgotten more about this game than you'll know for many years to come.'

'Yes, sir. It's this way, sir. I got something out of the kitchenmaid—'

Grange interrupted. He turned to Poirot triumphantly.

'What did I tell you? There's always hope where there's a kitchenmaid. Heaven help us when domestic staffs are so reduced that nobody keeps a kitchenmaid any more. Kitchenmaids talk, kitchenmaids babble. They're so kept down and in their place by the cook and the upper servants that it's only human nature to talk about what they know to someone who wants to hear it. Go on, Clark.'

'This is what the girl says, sir. That on Sunday afternoon she saw Gudgeon, the butler, walking across the hall with a revolver in his hand.'

Agatha Christie

'Gudgeon?'

'Yes, sir.' Clark referred to a notebook. 'These are her own words. "I don't know what to do, but I think I ought to say what I saw that day. I saw Mr Gudgeon, he was standing in the hall with a revolver in his hand. Mr Gudgeon looked very peculiar indeed."

'I don't suppose,' said Clark, breaking off, 'that the part about looking peculiar means anything. She probably put that in out of her head. But I thought you ought to know about it at once, sir.'

Inspector Grange rose, with the satisfaction of a man who sees a task ahead of him which he is well fitted to perform.

'*Gudgeon?*' he said. 'I'll have a word with Mr Gudgeon right away.'

CHAPTER 20

Sitting once more in Sir Henry's study, Inspector Grange stared at the impassive face of the man in front of him.

So far, the honours lay with Gudgeon.

'I am very sorry, sir,' he repeated. 'I suppose I ought to have mentioned the occurrence, but it had slipped my memory.'

He looked apologetically from the inspector to Sir Henry.

'It was about 5.30 if I remember rightly, sir. I was crossing the hall to see if there were any letters for the post when I noticed a revolver lying on the hall table. I presumed it was from the master's collection, so I picked it up and brought it in here. There was a gap on the shelf by the mantelpiece where it had come from, so I replaced it where it belonged.'

'Point it out to me,' said Grange.

Gudgeon rose and went to the shelf in question, the inspector close behind him.

'It was this one, sir.' Gudgeon's finger indicated a small Mauser pistol at the end of the row.

It was a .25—quite a small weapon. It was certainly not the gun that had killed John Christow.

Grange, with his eyes on Gudgeon's face, said:

'That's an automatic pistol, not a revolver.'

Gudgeon coughed.

'Indeed, sir? I'm afraid that I am not at all well up in firearms. I may have used the term revolver rather loosely, sir.'

'But you are quite sure that that is the gun you found in the hall and brought in here?'

'Oh, yes, sir, there can be no possible doubt about that.'

Grange stopped him as he was about to stretch out a hand.

'Don't touch it, please. I must examine it for fingerprints and to see if it is loaded.'

'I don't think it is loaded, sir. None of Sir Henry's collection is kept loaded. And, as for fingerprints, I polished it over with my handkerchief before replacing it, sir, so there will only be my fingerprints on it.'

'Why did you do that?' asked Grange sharply.

But Gudgeon's apologetic smile did not waver.

'I fancied it might be dusty, sir.'

The door opened and Lady Angkatell came in. She smiled at the inspector.

'How nice to see you, Inspector Grange! What is all this about a revolver and Gudgeon? That child in the kitchen is in floods of tears. Mrs Medway has been bullying her—but of course the girl was quite right to say what she saw if she thought she ought to do so. I always find right and wrong so bewildering myself—easy, you know, if right is unpleasant and wrong is agreeable, because then one knows where one is—but confusing when it is the other way about—and I think, don't you, Inspector, that everyone must do what they think right themselves. What have you been telling them about that pistol, Gudgeon?'

Gudgeon said with respectful emphasis:

'The pistol was in the hall, my lady, on the centre table. I have no idea where it came from. I brought it in here and put it away in its proper place. That is what I have just told the inspector and he quite understands.'

Lady Angkatell shook her head. She said gently:

'You really shouldn't have said that, Gudgeon. I'll talk to the inspector myself.'

Gudgeon made a slight movement, and Lady Angkatell said very charmingly:

'I do appreciate your motives, Gudgeon. I know how you always try to save us trouble and annoyance.' She added in gentle dismissal, 'That will be all now.'

Gudgeon hesitated, threw a fleeting glance towards Sir Henry and then at the inspector, then bowed and moved towards the door.

Grange made a motion as though to stop him, but for some reason he was not able to define to himself, he let his arm fall again. Gudgeon went out and closed the door.

Lady Angkatell dropped into a chair and smiled at the two men. She said conversationally:

'You know, I really do think that was very charming of Gudgeon. Quite feudal, if you know what I mean. Yes, feudal is the right word.'

Grange said stiffly:

'Am I to understand, Lady Angkatell, that you yourself have some further knowledge about the matter?'

'Of course. Gudgeon didn't find it in the hall at all. He found it when he took the eggs out.'

'The eggs?' Inspector Grange stared at her.

'Out of the basket,' said Lady Angkatell.

She seemed to think that everything was now quite clear. Sir Henry said gently:

'You must tell us a little more, my dear. Inspector Grange and I are still at sea.'

'Oh.' Lady Angkatell set herself to be explicit. 'The pistol, you see, was *in* the basket, *under* the eggs.'

'What basket and what eggs, Lady Angkatell?'

'The basket I took down to the farm. The pistol was in it, and then I put the eggs in on top of the pistol and forgot all about it. And when we found poor John Christow dead by the pool, it was such a shock I let go of the basket and Gudgeon just caught it in time (because of the eggs, I mean. If I'd dropped it they would have been broken). And he brought it back to the house. And later I asked him about writing the date on the eggs—a thing I always do—otherwise one eats the fresher eggs sometimes before the older ones—and he said all that had been attended to—and now that I remember, he was rather emphatic about it. And that is what I mean by being feudal. He found the pistol and put it back in here—I suppose really because there were police in the house. Servants are always so worried by police, I find. Very nice and loyal—but also quite stupid, because of course, Inspector, it's the truth you want to hear, isn't it?'

And Lady Angkatell finished up by giving the inspector a beaming smile.

'The truth is what I mean to get,' said Grange rather grimly.

Lady Angkatell sighed.

The Hollow

'It all seems such a fuss, doesn't it?' she said. 'I mean, all this hounding people down. I don't suppose whoever it was who shot John Christow really meant to shoot him—not seriously, I mean. If it was Gerda, I'm sure she didn't. In fact, I'm really surprised that she didn't miss—it's the sort of thing that one would expect of Gerda. And she's really a very nice kind creature. And if you go and put her in prison and hang her, what on earth is going to happen to the children? If she did shoot John, she's probably dreadfully sorry about it now. It's bad enough for children to have a father who's been murdered—but it will make it infinitely worse for them to have their mother hanged for it. Sometimes I don't think you policemen *think* of these things.'

'We are not contemplating arresting anyone at present, Lady Angkatell.'

'Well, that's sensible at any rate. But I have thought all along, Inspector Grange, that you were a very sensible sort of man.'

Again that charming, almost dazzling smile.

Inspector Grange blinked a little. He could not help it, but he came firmly to the point at issue.

'As you said just now, Lady Angkatell, it's the truth I want to get at. You took the pistol from here—which gun was it, by the way?'

Lady Angkatell nodded her head towards the shelf by the mantelpiece. 'The second from the end. The Mauser .25.' Something in the crisp, technical way she spoke jarred on Grange. He had not, somehow, expected Lady Angkatell, whom up to now he had labelled in his own mind as

219

'vague' and 'just a bit batty', to describe a firearm with such technical precision.

'You took the pistol from here and put it in your basket. Why?'

'I knew you'd ask me that,' said Lady Angkatell. Her tone, unexpectedly, was almost triumphant. 'And of course there must be some reason. Don't you think so, Henry?' She turned to her husband. 'Don't you think I must have had a reason for taking a pistol out that morning?'

'I should certainly have thought so, my dear,' said Sir Henry stiffly.

'One does things,' said Lady Angkatell, gazing thoughtfully in front of her, 'and then one doesn't remember why one has done them. But I think, you know, Inspector, that there always is a reason if one can only get at it. I must have had *some* idea in my head when I put the Mauser into my egg basket.' She appealed to him. 'What do you think it can have been?'

Grange stared at her. She displayed no embarrassment—just a childlike eagerness. It beat him. He had never yet met anyone like Lucy Angkatell, and just for the moment he didn't know what to do about it.

'My wife,' said Sir Henry, 'is extremely absent-minded, Inspector.'

'So it seems, sir,' said Grange. He did not say it very nicely.

'Why *do* you think I took that pistol?' Lady Angkatell asked him confidentially.

'I have no idea, Lady Angkatell.'

'I came in here,' mused Lady Angkatell. 'I had been talking to Simmons about the pillow-cases—and I remember

The Hollow

dimly crossing over to the fireplace—and thinking we must get a new poker—the curate, not the rector—'

Inspector Grange stared. He felt his head going round.

'And I remember picking up the Mauser—it was a nice handy little gun, I've always liked it—and dropping it into the basket—I'd just got the basket from the flower-room. But there were so many things in my head—Simmons, you know, and the bindweed in the Michaelmas daisies—and hoping Mrs Medway would make a really *rich* Mud Pie—'

'A mud pie?' Inspector Grange had to break in.

'Chocolate, you know, and eggs—and then covered with whipped cream. Just the sort of sweet a foreigner would like for lunch.'

Inspector Grange spoke fiercely and brusquely, feeling like a man who brushes away fine spiders' webs which are impairing his vision.

'Did you load the pistol?'

He had hoped to startle her—perhaps even to frighten her a little, but Lady Angkatell only considered the question with a kind of desperate thoughtfulness.

'Now did I? That's so stupid. I can't remember. But I should think I must have, don't you, Inspector? I mean, what's the good of a pistol without ammunition? I wish I could remember exactly what was in my head at the time.'

'My dear Lucy,' said Sir Henry. 'What goes on or does not go on in your head has been the despair of everyone who knows you well for years.'

She flashed him a very sweet smile.

'I *am* trying to remember, Henry dear. One does such curious things. I picked up the telephone receiver the other morning and found myself looking down at it quite bewildered. I couldn't imagine what I wanted with it.'

'Presumably you were going to ring someone up,' said the inspector coldly.

'No, funnily enough, I wasn't. I remembered afterwards—I'd been wondering why Mrs Mears, the gardener's wife, held her baby in such an odd way, and I picked up the telephone receiver to try, you know, just how one would hold a baby, and of course I realized that it had looked odd because Mrs Mears was left-handed and had its head the other way round.'

She looked triumphantly from one to the other of the two men.

'Well,' thought the inspector, 'I suppose it's possible that there are people like this.'

But he did not feel very sure about it.

The whole thing, he realized, might be a tissue of lies. The kitchenmaid, for instance, had distinctly stated that it was a revolver Gudgeon had been holding. Still, you couldn't set much store by that. The girl knew nothing of firearms. She had heard a revolver talked about in connection with the crime, and revolver or pistol would be all one to her.

Both Gudgeon and Lady Angkatell had specified the Mauser pistol—but there was nothing to prove their statement. It might actually have been the missing revolver that Gudgeon had been handling and he might have returned it, not to the study, but to Lady Angkatell herself. The

The Hollow

servants all seemed absolutely besotted about the damned woman.

Supposing it was actually she who had shot John Christow? (But why should she? He couldn't see why.) Would they still back her up and tell lies for her? He had an uncomfortable feeling that that was just what they would do.

And now this fantastic story of hers about not being able to remember—surely she could think up something better than that. And looking so natural about it—not in the least embarrassed or apprehensive. Damn it all, she gave you the impression that she was speaking the literal truth.

He got up.

'When you remember a little more, perhaps you'll tell me, Lady Angkatell,' he said dryly.

She answered, 'Of course I will, Inspector. Things come to one quite suddenly sometimes.'

Grange went out of the study. In the hall he put a finger round the inside of a collar and drew a deep breath.

He felt all tangled up in the thistledown. What he needed was his oldest and foulest pipe, a pint of ale and a good steak and chips. Something plain and objective.

CHAPTER 21

In the study Lady Angkatell flitted about touching things here and there with a vague forefinger. Sir Henry sat back in his chair watching her. He said at last:

'Why did you take the pistol, Lucy?'

Lady Angkatell came back and sank down gracefully into a chair.

'I'm not really quite sure, Henry. I suppose I had some vague ideas of an accident.'

'Accident?'

'Yes. All those roots of trees, you know,' said Lady Angkatell vaguely, 'sticking out—so easy, just to trip over one. One might have had a few shots at the target and left one shot in the magazine—careless, of course—but then people *are* careless. I've always thought, you know, that accident would be the simplest way to do a thing of that kind. One would be dreadfully sorry, of course, and blame oneself...'

Her voice died away. Her husband sat very still without taking his eyes off her face. He spoke again in the same quiet, careful voice.

'Who was to have had—the accident?'

Lucy turned her head a little, looking at him in surprise.

The Hollow

'John Christow, of course.'

'Good God, Lucy—' He broke off.

She said earnestly:

'Oh, Henry, I've been so dreadfully worried. About Ainswick.'

'I see. It's Ainswick. You've always cared too much about Ainswick, Lucy. Sometimes I think it's the only thing you do care for.'

'Edward and David are the last—the last of the Angkatells. And David won't do, Henry. He'll never marry—because of his mother and all that. He'll get the place when Edward dies, and he won't marry, and you and I will be dead long before he's even middle-aged. He'll be the last of the Angkatells and the whole thing will die out.'

'Does it matter so much, Lucy?'

'Of course it matters! *Ainswick* !'

'You should have been a boy, Lucy.'

But he smiled a little—for he could not imagine Lucy being anything but feminine.

'It all depends on Edward's marrying—and Edward's so obstinate—that long head of his, like my father's. I hoped he'd get over Henrietta and marry some nice girl—but I see now that that's hopeless. Then I thought that Henrietta's affair with John would run the usual course. John's affairs were never, I imagine, very permanent. But I saw him looking at her the other evening. He really *cared* about her. If only John were out of the way I felt that Henrietta would marry Edward. She's not the kind of person to cherish a memory and live in the past. So, you see, it all came to that—get rid of John Christow.'

'Lucy. You didn't—What did you do, Lucy?'

225

Lady Angkatell got up again. She took two dead flowers out of a vase.

'Darling,' she said. 'You don't imagine for a moment, do you, that *I* shot John Christow? I did have that silly idea about an accident. But then, you know, I remembered that we'd *asked* John Christow here—it's not as though he proposed himself. One can't ask someone to be your guest and then arrange accidents. Even Arabs are most particular about hospitality. So don't worry, will you, Henry?'

She stood looking at him with a brilliant, affectionate smile. He said heavily:

'I always worry about you, Lucy.'

'There's no need, darling. And you see, everything has actually turned out all right. John has been got rid of without our doing anything about it. It reminds me,' said Lady Angkatell reminiscently, 'of that man in Bombay who was so frightfully rude to me. He was run over by a tram three days later.'

She unbolted the french windows and went out into the garden.

Sir Henry sat still, watching her tall, slender figure wander down the path. He looked old and tired, and his face was the face of a man who lives at close quarters with fear.

In the kitchen a tearful Doris Emmott was wilting under the stern reproof of Mr Gudgeon. Mrs Medway and Miss Simmons acted as a kind of Greek chorus.

'Putting yourself forward and jumping to conclusions in a way only an inexperienced girl would do.'

The Hollow

'That's right,' said Mrs Medway.

'If you see me with a pistol in my hand, the proper thing to do is to come to me and say: "Mr Gudgeon, will you be so kind as to give me an explanation?"'

'Or you could have come to me,' put in Mrs Medway. '*I'm* always willing to tell a young girl what doesn't know the world what she ought to think.'

'What you should *not* have done,' said Gudgeon severely, 'is to go babbling off to a policeman—and only a sergeant at that! Never get mixed up with the police more than you can help. It's painful enough having them in the house at all.'

'Inexpressibly painful,' murmured Miss Simmons. 'Such a thing never happened to *me* before.'

'We all know,' went on Gudgeon, 'what her ladyship is like. Nothing her ladyship does would ever surprise me—but the police don't know her ladyship the way we do, and it's not to be thought of that her ladyship should be worried with silly questions and suspicions just because she wanders about with firearms. It's the sort of thing she would do, but the police have the kind of mind that just sees murder and nasty things like that. Her ladyship is the kind of absent-minded lady who wouldn't hurt a fly, but there's no denying that she puts things in funny places. I shall never forget,' added Gudgeon with feeling, 'when she brought back a live lobster and put it in the card tray in the hall. Thought I was seeing things!'

'That must have been before my time,' said Simmons with curiosity.

Mrs Medway checked these revelations with a glance at the erring Doris.

Agatha Christie

'Some other time,' she said. 'Now then, Doris, we've only been speaking to you for your own good. It's *common* to be mixed up with the police, and don't you forget it. You can get on with the vegetables now, and be more careful with the runner-beans than you were last night.'

Doris sniffed.

'Yes, Mrs Medway,' she said, and shuffled over to the sink.

Mrs Medway said forebodingly:

'I don't feel as I'm going to have a light hand with my pastry. That nasty inquest tomorrow. Gives me a turn every time I think of it. A thing like that—happening to *us*.'

CHAPTER 22

The latch of the gate clicked and Poirot looked out of the window in time to see the visitor who was coming up the path to the front door. He knew at once who she was. He wondered very much what brought Veronica Cray to see him.

She brought a delicious faint scent into the room with her, a scent that Poirot recognized. She wore tweeds and brogues as Henrietta had done—but she was, he decided, very different from Henrietta.

'M. Poirot.' Her tone was delightful, a little thrilled. 'I've only just discovered who my neighbour is. And I've always wanted to know you so much.'

He took her outstretched hands, bowed over them.

'Enchanted, Madame.'

She accepted the homage smilingly, refused his offer of tea, coffee or cocktail.

'No, I've just come to talk to you. To talk seriously. I'm worried.'

'You are worried? I am sorry to hear that.'

Veronica sat down and sighed.

'It's about John Christow's death. The inquest's tomorrow. You know that?'

'Yes, yes, I know.'

'And the whole thing has really been so extraordinary—' She broke off.

'Most people really wouldn't believe it. But you would, I think, because you know something about human nature.'

'I know a little about human nature,' admitted Poirot.

'Inspector Grange came to see me. He'd got it into his head that I'd quarrelled with John—which is true in a way though not in the way he meant. I told him that I hadn't seen John for fifteen years—and he simply didn't believe me. But it's true, M. Poirot.'

Poirot said, 'Since it is true, it can easily be proved, so why worry?'

She returned his smile in the friendliest fashion.

'The real truth is that I simply haven't dared to tell the inspector what actually happened on Saturday evening. It's so absolutely fantastic that he certainly wouldn't believe it. But I felt I must tell someone. That's why I have come to you.'

Poirot said quietly, 'I am flattered.'

That fact, he noted, she took for granted. She was a woman, he thought, who was very sure of the effect she was producing. So sure that she might, occasionally, make a mistake.

'John and I were engaged to be married fifteen years ago. He was very much in love with me—so much so that it rather alarmed me sometimes. He wanted me to give up acting—to give up having any mind or life of my own. He was so possessive and masterful that I felt I couldn't go through with it, and I broke off the engagement. I'm afraid he took that very hard.'

Poirot clicked a discreet and sympathetic tongue.

The Hollow

'I didn't see him again until last Saturday night. He walked home with me. I told the inspector that we talked about old times—that's true in a way. But there was far more than that.'

'Yes?'

'John went mad—quite mad. He wanted to leave his wife and children, he wanted me to get a divorce from my husband and marry him. He said he'd never forgotten me—that the moment he saw me time stood still.'

She closed her eyes, she swallowed. Under her makeup her face was very pale.

She opened her eyes again and smiled almost timidly at Poirot.

'Can you believe that a—a feeling like that is possible?' she asked.

'I think it is possible, yes,' said Poirot.

'Never to forget—to go on waiting—planning—hoping. To determine with all one's heart and mind to get what one wants in the end. There are men like that, M. Poirot.'

'Yes—and women.'

She gave him a hard stare.

'I'm talking about men—about John Christow. Well, that's how it was. I protested at first, laughed, refused to take him seriously. Then I told him he was mad. It was quite late when he went back to the house. We'd argued and argued. He was still—just as determined.'

She swallowed again.

'That's why I sent him a note the next morning. I couldn't leave things like that. I had to make him realize that what he wanted was—impossible.'

'It *was* impossible?'

'Of course it was impossible! He came over. He wouldn't listen to what I had to say. He was just as insistent. I told him that it was no good, that I didn't love him, that I hated him...' She paused, breathing hard. 'I had to be brutal about it. So we parted in anger... And now—he's dead.'

He saw her hands creep together, saw the twisted fingers and the knuckles stand out. They were large, rather cruel hands.

The strong emotion that she was feeling communicated itself to him. It was not sorrow, not grief—no, it was anger. The anger, he thought, of a baffled egoist.

'Well, M. Poirot?' Her voice was controlled and smooth again. 'What am I to do? Tell the story, or keep it to myself? It's what happened—but it takes a bit of believing.'

Poirot looked at her, a long, considering gaze.

He did not think that Veronica Cray was telling the truth, and yet there was an undeniable under-current of sincerity. It happened, he thought, but it did not happen like that.

And suddenly he got it. It was a true story, inverted. It was she who had been unable to forget John Christow. It was she who had been baffled and repulsed. And now, unable to bear in silence the furious anger of a tigress deprived of what she considered her legitimate prey, she had invented a version of the truth that should satisfy her wounded pride and feed a little the aching hunger for a man who had gone beyond the reach of her clutching hands. Impossible to admit that she, Veronica Cray, could not have what she wanted! So she had changed it all round.

Poirot drew a deep breath and spoke.

'If all this had any bearing on John Christow's death, you would have to speak out, but if it has not—and I cannot see why it should have—then I think you are quite justified in keeping it to yourself.'

He wondered if she was disappointed. He had a fancy that in her present mood she would like to hurl her story into the printed page of a newspaper. She had come to him—why? To try out her story? To test his reactions? Or to use him—to induce him to pass the story on?

If his mild response disappointed her, she did not show it. She got up and gave him one of those long, well-manicured hands.

'Thank you, M. Poirot. What you say seems eminently sensible. I'm so glad I came to you. I—I felt I wanted somebody to know.'

'I shall respect your confidence, Madame.'

When she had gone, he opened the windows a little. Scents affected him. He did not like Veronica's scent. It was expensive but cloying, overpowering like her personality.

He wondered, as he flapped the curtains, whether Veronica Cray had killed John Christow.

She would have been willing to kill him—he believed that. She would have enjoyed pressing the trigger—would have enjoyed seeing him stagger and fall.

But behind that vindictive anger was something cold and shrewd, something that appraised chances, a cool, calculating intelligence. However much Veronica Cray wished to kill John Christow, he doubted whether she would have taken the risk.

CHAPTER 23

The inquest was over. It had been the merest formality of an affair, and though warned of this beforehand, yet nearly everyone had a resentful sense of anti-climax.

Adjourned for a fortnight at the request of the police.

Gerda had driven down with Mrs Patterson from London in a hired Daimler. She had on a black dress and an unbecoming hat, and looked nervous and bewildered.

Preparatory to stepping back into the Daimler, she paused as Lady Angkatell came up to her.

'How are you, Gerda dear? Not sleeping too badly, I hope. I think it went off as well as we could hope for, don't you? So sorry we haven't got you with us at The Hollow, but I quite understand how distressing that would be.'

Mrs Patterson said in her bright voice, glancing reproachfully at her sister for not introducing her properly:

'This was Miss Collins's idea—to drive straight down and back. Expensive, of course, but we thought it was worth it.'

'Oh, I do so agree with you.'

Mrs Patterson lowered her voice.

'I am taking Gerda and the children straight down to Bexhill. What she needs is rest and quiet. The reporters!

You've no idea! Simply swarming round Harley Street.'

A young man snapped off a camera, and Elsie Patterson pushed her sister into the car and they drove off.

The others had a momentary view of Gerda's face beneath the unbecoming hat brim. It was vacant, lost—she looked for the moment like a half-witted child.

Midge Hardcastle muttered under her breath: 'Poor devil.'

Edward said irritably:

'What did everybody see in Christow? That wretched woman looks completely heartbroken.'

'She was absolutely wrapped up in him,' said Midge.

'But why? He was a selfish sort of fellow, good company in a way, but—' He broke off. Then he asked, 'What did you think of him, Midge?'

'I?' Midge reflected. She said at last, rather surprised at her own words, 'I think I respected him.'

'Respected him? For what?'

'Well, he knew his job.'

'You're thinking of him as a doctor?'

'Yes.'

There was no time for more.

Henrietta was driving Midge back to London in her car. Edward was returning to lunch at The Hollow and going up by the afternoon train with David. He said vaguely to Midge: 'You must come out and lunch one day,' and Midge said that that would be very nice but that she couldn't take more than an hour off. Edward gave her his charming smile and said:

'Oh, it's a special occasion. I'm sure they'll understand.'

Then he moved towards Henrietta. 'I'll ring you up, Henrietta.'

Agatha Christie

'Yes, do, Edward. But I may be out a good deal.'

'Out?'

She gave him a quick, mocking smile.

'Drowning my sorrow. You don't expect me to sit at home and mope, do you?'

He said slowly, 'I don't understand you nowadays, Henrietta. You are quite different.'

Her face softened. She said unexpectedly: 'Darling Edward,' and gave his arm a quick squeeze.

Then she turned to Lucy Angkatell. 'I can come back if I want to, can't I, Lucy?'

Lady Angkatell said, 'Of course, darling. And anyway there will be the inquest again in a fortnight.'

Henrietta went to where she had parked the car in the market square. Her suitcases and Midge's were already inside.

They got in and drove off.

The car climbed the long hill and came out on the road over the ridge. Below them the brown and golden leaves shivered a little in the chill of a grey autumn day.

Midge said suddenly, 'I'm glad to get away—even from Lucy. Darling as she is, she gives me the creeps sometimes.'

Henrietta was looking intently into the small driving-mirror. She said rather inattentively:

'Lucy has to give the coloratura touch—even to murder.'

'You know, I'd never thought about murder before.'

'Why should you? It isn't a thing one thinks about. It's a six-letter word in a crossword, or a pleasant entertainment between the covers of a book. But the real thing—'

She paused. Midge finished:

'*Is* real. That is what startles one.'

Henrietta said:

'It needn't be startling to you. *You* are outside it. Perhaps the only one of us who is.'

Midge said:

'We're all outside it now. We've got away.'

Henrietta murmured, 'Have we?'

She was looking in the driving-mirror again. Suddenly she put her foot down on the accelerator. The car responded. She glanced at the speedometer. They were doing over fifty. Presently the needle reached sixty.

Midge looked sideways at Henrietta's profile. It was not like Henrietta to drive recklessly. She liked speed, but the winding road hardly justified the pace they were going. There was a grim smile hovering round Henrietta's mouth.

She said, 'Look over your shoulder, Midge. See that car way back there?'

'Yes?'

'It's a Ventnor 10.'

'Is it?' Midge was not particularly interested.

'They're useful little cars, low petrol consumption, keep the road well, but they're not fast.'

'No?'

Curious, thought Midge, how fascinated Henrietta always was by cars and their performance. 'As I say, they're not fast—but that car, Midge, has managed to keep its distance although we've been going over sixty.'

Midge turned a startled face to her.

'Do you mean that—'

Henrietta nodded. 'The police, I believe, have special engines in very ordinary-looking cars.'

Midge said:

'You mean they're still keeping an eye on us all?'

'It seems rather obvious.'

Midge shivered.

'Henrietta, can you understand the meaning of this second gun business?'

'No, it lets Gerda out. But beyond that it just doesn't seem to add up to anything.'

'But, if it was one of Henry's guns—'

'We don't know that it was. It hasn't been found yet, remember.'

'No, that's true. It could be someone outside altogether. Do you know who I'd like to think killed John, Henrietta? That woman.'

'Veronica Cray?'

'Yes.'

Henrietta said nothing. She drove on with her eyes fixed sternly on the road ahead of her.

'Don't you think it's possible?' persisted Midge.

'*Possible*, yes,' said Henrietta slowly.

'Then you don't think—'

'It's no good thinking a thing because you *want* to think it. It's the perfect solution—letting all of us out!'

'Us? But—'

'We're in it—all of us. Even you, Midge darling—though they'd be hard put to it to find a motive for your shooting John. Of course I'd *like* it to be Veronica. Nothing would please me better than to see her giving a lovely performance, as Lucy would put it, in the dock!'

Midge shot a quick look at her.

'Tell me, Henrietta, does it all make you feel vindictive?'

'You mean'—Henrietta paused a moment—'because I loved John?'

'Yes.'

As she spoke, Midge realized with a slight sense of shock that this was the first time the bald fact had been put into words. It had been accepted by them all, by Lucy and Henry, by Midge, by Edward even, that Henrietta loved John Christow, but nobody had ever so much as hinted at the fact in words before.

There was a pause whilst Henrietta seemed to be thinking. Then she said in a thoughtful voice:

'I can't explain to you what I feel. Perhaps I don't know myself.'

They were driving now over Albert Bridge.

Henrietta said:

'You'd better come to the studio, Midge. We'll have tea, and I'll drive you to your digs afterwards.'

Here in London the short afternoon light was already fading. They drew up at the studio door and Henrietta put her key into the door. She went in and switched on the light.

'It's chilly,' she said. 'We'd better light the gas fire. Oh, bother—I meant to get some matches on the way.'

'Won't a lighter do?'

'Mine's no good, and anyway it's difficult to light a gas fire with one. Make yourself at home. There's an old blind man stands on the corner. I usually get my matches off him. I shan't be a minute or two.'

Left alone in the studio, Midge wandered round looking at Henrietta's work. It gave her an eerie feeling to be sharing the empty studio with these creations of wood and bronze.

There was a bronze head with high cheek-bones and a tin hat, possibly a Red Army soldier, and there was an airy structure of twisted ribbon-like aluminium which intrigued her a good deal. There was a vast static frog in pinkish granite, and at the end of the studio she came to an almost life-sized wooden figure.

She was staring at it when Henrietta's key turned in the door and Henrietta herself came in slightly breathless.

Midge turned.

'What's this, Henrietta? It's rather frightening.'

'That? That's The Worshipper. It's going to the International Group.'

Midge repeated, staring at it:

'It's frightening.'

Kneeling to light the gas fire, Henrietta said over her shoulder:

'It's interesting your saying that. Why do you find it frightening?'

'I think—because it hasn't any face.'

'How right you are, Midge.'

'It's very good, Henrietta.'

Henrietta said lightly:

'It's a nice bit of pearwood.'

She rose from her knees. She tossed her big satchel bag and her furs on to the divan, and threw down a couple of boxes of matches on the table.

The Hollow

Midge was struck by the expression on her face—it had a sudden quite inexplicable exultation.

'Now for tea,' said Henrietta, and in her voice was the same warm jubilation that Midge had already glimpsed in her face.

It struck an almost jarring note—but Midge forgot it in a train of thought aroused by the sight of the two boxes of matches.

'You remember those matches Veronica Cray took away with her?'

'When Lucy insisted on foisting a whole half-dozen on her? Yes.'

'Did anyone ever find out whether she had matches in her cottage all the time?'

'I expect the police did. They're very thorough.'

A faintly triumphant smile was curving Henrietta's lips. Midge felt puzzled and almost repelled.

She thought, 'Can Henrietta really have cared for John? Can she? Surely not.'

And a faint desolate chill struck through her as she reflected:

'Edward will not have to wait very long...'

Ungenerous of her not to let that thought bring warmth. She wanted Edward to be happy, didn't she? It wasn't as though she could have Edward herself. To Edward she would be always 'little Midge'. Never more than that. Never a woman to be loved.

Edward, unfortunately, was the faithful kind. Well, the faithful kind usually got what they wanted in the end.

Edward and Henrietta at Ainswick...that was the proper ending to the story. Edward and Henrietta living happy ever afterwards.

She could see it all very clearly.

'Cheer up, Midge,' said Henrietta. 'You mustn't let murder get you down. Shall we go out later and have a spot of dinner together?'

But Midge said quickly that she must get back to her rooms. She had things to do—letters to write. In fact, she'd better go as soon as she'd finished her cup of tea.

'All right. I'll drive you there.'

'I could get a taxi.'

'Nonsense. Let's use the car, as it's there.'

They went out into damp evening air. As they drove past the end of the Mews Henrietta pointed out a car drawn in to the side.

'A Ventnor 10. Our shadow. You'll see. He'll follow us.'

'How beastly it all is!'

'Do you think so? I don't really mind.'

Henrietta dropped Midge at her rooms and came back to the Mews and put her car away in the garage.

Then she let herself into the studio once more.

For some minutes she stood abstractedly drumming with her fingers on the mantelpiece. Then she sighed and murmured to herself:

'Well—to work. Better not waste time.'

She threw off her tweeds and got into her overall.

An hour and a half later she drew back and studied what she had done. There were dabs of clay on her cheek and her hair was dishevelled, but she nodded approval at the model on the stand.

It was the rough similitude of a horse. The clay had been slapped on in great irregular lumps. It was the kind of horse that would have given the colonel of a cavalry regiment apoplexy, so unlike was it to any flesh and blood horse that had ever been foaled. It would also have distressed Henrietta's Irish hunting forebears. Nevertheless it was a horse—a horse conceived in the abstract.

Henrietta wondered what Inspector Grange would think of it if he ever saw it, and her mouth widened a little in amusement as she pictured his face.

CHAPTER 24

Edward Angkatell stood hesitantly in the swirl of foot traffic in Shaftesbury Avenue. He was nerving himself to enter the establishment which bore the gold-lettered sign: 'Madame Alfrege'.

Some obscure instinct had prevented him from merely ringing up and asking Midge to come out and lunch. That fragment of telephone conversation at The Hollow had disturbed him—more, had shocked him. There had been in Midge's voice a submission, a subservience that had outraged all his feelings.

For Midge, the free, the cheerful, the outspoken, to have to adopt that attitude. To have to submit, as she clearly was submitting, to rudeness and insolence on the other end of the wire. It was all wrong—the whole thing was wrong! And then, when he had shown his concern, she had met him point-blank with the unpalatable truth that one had to keep one's job, that jobs weren't easy to get, and that the holding down of jobs entailed more unpleasantness than the mere performing of a stipulated task.

Up till then Edward had vaguely accepted the fact that a great many young women had 'jobs' nowadays. If he had thought about it at all, he had thought that on the whole they had jobs because they liked jobs—that it flattered their sense of independence and gave them an interest of their own in life.

The fact that a working day of nine to six, with an hour off for lunch, cut a girl off from most of the pleasures and relaxations of a leisured class had simply not occurred to Edward. That Midge, unless she sacrificed her lunch hour, could not drop into a picture gallery, that she could not go to an afternoon concert, drive out of town on a fine summer's day, lunch in a leisurely way at a distant restaurant, but had instead to relegate her excursions into the country to Saturday afternoons and Sundays, and to snatch her lunch in a crowded Lyons or a snack bar, was a new and unwelcome discovery. He was very fond of Midge. Little Midge—that was how he thought of her. Arriving shy and wide-eyed at Ainswick for the holidays, tongue-tied at first, then opening up into enthusiasm and affection.

Edward's tendency to live exclusively in the past, and to accept the present dubiously as something yet untested, had delayed his recognition of Midge as a wage-earning adult.

It was on that evening at The Hollow when he had come in cold and shivering from that strange, upsetting clash with Henrietta, and when Midge had knelt to build up the fire, that he had been first aware of a Midge who was not an affectionate child but a woman. It had been an upsetting vision—he had felt for a moment that he had lost something—something that was a precious part of Ainswick. And he had said impulsively, speaking out of that suddenly aroused feeling, 'I wish I saw more of you, little Midge…'

Agatha Christie

Standing outside in the moonlight, speaking to a Henrietta who was no longer startlingly the familiar Henrietta he had loved for so long—he had known sudden panic. And he had come in to a further disturbance of the set pattern which was his life. Little Midge was also a part of Ainswick—and this was no longer little Midge, but a courageous and sad-eyed adult whom he did not know.

Ever since then he had been troubled in his mind, and had indulged in a good deal of self-reproach for the unthinking way in which he had never bothered about Midge's happiness or comfort. The idea of her uncongenial job at Madame Alfrege's had worried him more and more, and he had determined at last to see for himself just what this dress shop of hers was like.

Edward peered suspiciously into the show window at a little black dress with a narrow gold belt, some rakish-looking, skimpy jumper suits, and an evening gown of rather tawdry coloured lace.

Edward knew nothing about women's clothes except by instinct, but had a shrewd idea that all these exhibits were somehow of a meretricious order. No, he thought, this place was not worthy of her. Someone—Lady Angkatell, perhaps—must do something about it.

Overcoming his shyness with an effort, Edward straightened his slightly stooping shoulders and walked in.

He was instantly paralysed with embarrassment. Two platinum blonde little minxes with shrill voices were examining dresses in a show-case, with a dark saleswoman in attendance. At the back of the shop a small woman with a thick nose, henna red hair and a disagreeable voice was arguing with a stout and bewildered customer over some alterations to an evening gown. From an adjacent cubicle a woman's fretful voice was raised.

'Frightful—perfectly frightful—can't you bring me anything *decent* to try?'

In response he heard the soft murmur of Midge's voice—a deferential, persuasive voice.

'This wine model is really very smart. And I think it would suit you. If you'd just slip it on—'

'I'm not going to waste my time trying on things that I can see are no good. Do take a little trouble. I've told you I don't want reds. If you'd listen to what you are told—'

The colour surged up into Edward's neck. He hoped Midge would throw the dress in the odious woman's face. Instead she murmured:

'I'll have another look. You wouldn't care for green I suppose, Madam? Or this peach?'

'Dreadful—perfectly dreadful! No, I won't see anything more. Sheer waste of time—'

But now Madame Alfrege, detaching herself from the stout customer, had come down to Edward and was looking at him inquiringly.

He pulled himself together.

'Is—could I speak—is Miss Hardcastle here?'

Madame Alfrege's eyebrows went up, but she took in the Savile Row cut of Edward's clothes, and she produced a smile whose graciousness was rather more unpleasant than her bad temper would have been.

Agatha Christie

From inside the cubicle the fretful voice rose sharply.

'Do be careful! How clumsy you are. You've torn my hairnet.'

And Midge, her voice unsteady:

'I'm very sorry, Madam.'

'Stupid clumsiness.' (The voice appeared muffled.) 'No, I'll do it myself. My belt, please.'

'Miss Hardcastle will be free in a minute,' said Madame Alfrege. Her smile was now a leer.

A sandy-haired, bad-tempered-looking woman emerged from the cubicle carrying several parcels and went out into the street. Midge, in a severe black dress, opened the door for her. She looked pale and unhappy.

'I've come to take you out to lunch,' said Edward without preamble.

Midge gave a harried glance up at the clock.

'I don't get off until quarter-past one,' she began.

It was ten past one.

Madame Alfrege said graciously:

'You can go off now if you like, Miss Hardcastle, as your *friend* has called for you.'

Midge murmured, 'Oh thank you, Madame Alfrege,' and to Edward, 'I'll be ready in a minute,' and disappeared into the back of the shop.

Edward, who had winced under the impact of Madame Alfrege's heavy emphasis on 'friend', stood helplessly waiting.

Madame Alfrege was just about to enter into arch conversation with him when the door opened and an opulent-looking woman with a Pekinese came in, and Madame Alfrege's business instincts took her forward to the newcomer.

The Hollow

Midge reappeared with her coat on, and taking her by the elbow, Edward steered her out of the shop into the street.

'My God,' he said, 'is that the sort of thing you have to put up with? I heard that damned woman talking to you behind the curtain. How can you stick it, Midge? Why didn't you throw the damned frocks at her head?'

'I'd soon lose my job if I did things like that.'

'But don't you want to fling things at a woman of that kind?'

Midge drew a deep breath.

'Of course I do. And there are times, especially at the end of a hot week during the summer sales, when I am afraid that one day I shall let go and just tell everyone exactly where they get off—instead of "Yes, Madam," "No, Madam"—"I'll see if we have anything else, Madam."'

'Midge, dear little Midge, you can't put up with all this!'

Midge laughed a little shakily.

'Don't be upset, Edward. Why on earth did you have to come here? Why not ring up?'

'I wanted to see for myself. I've been worried.' He paused and then broke out, 'Why, Lucy wouldn't talk to a scullery maid the way that woman talked to you. It's all wrong that you should have to put up with insolence and rudeness. Good God, Midge, I'd like to take you right out of it all down to Ainswick. I'd like to hail a taxi, bundle you into it, and take you down to Ainswick now by the 2.15.'

Midge stopped. Her assumed nonchalance fell from her. She had had a long tiring morning with trying customers, and Madame at her most bullying. She turned on Edward with a sudden flare of resentment.

'Well, then, why don't you? There are plenty of taxis!'

He stared at her, taken aback by her sudden fury. She went on, her anger flaming up:

'Why do you have to come along and *say* these things? You don't mean them. Do you think it makes it any easier after I've had the hell of a morning to be reminded that there are places like Ainswick? Do you think I'm grateful to you for standing there and babbling about how much you'd like to take me out of it all? All very sweet and insincere. You don't really mean a word of it. Don't you know that I'd sell my soul to catch the 2.15 to Ainswick and get away from everything? I can't bear even to *think* of Ainswick, do you understand? You mean well, Edward, but you're cruel! Saying things—just *saying* things...'

They faced each other, seriously incommoding the lunchtime crowd in Shaftesbury Avenue. Yet they were conscious of nothing but each other. Edward was staring at her like a man suddenly aroused from sleep.

He said, 'All right then, damn it. You're coming to Ainswick by the 2.15!'

He raised his stick and hailed a passing taxi. It drew into the kerb. Edward opened the door, and Midge, slightly dazed, got in. Edward said: 'Paddington Station' to the driver and followed her in.

They sat in silence. Midge's lips were set together. Her eyes were defiant and mutinous. Edward stared straight ahead of him.

As they waited for the traffic lights in Oxford Street, Midge said disagreeably:

The Hollow

'I seem to have called your bluff.'

Edward said shortly:

'It wasn't bluff.'

The taxi started forward again with a jerk.

It was not until the taxi turned left in Edgware Road into Cambridge Terrace that Edward suddenly regained his normal attitude to life.

He said, 'We can't catch the 2.15,' and tapping on the glass he said to the driver: 'Go to the Berkeley.'

Midge said coldly, 'Why can't we catch the 2.15? It's only twenty-five past one now.'

Edward smiled at her.

'You haven't got any luggage, little Midge. No nightgowns or toothbrushes or country shoes. There's a 4.15, you know. We'll have some lunch now and talk things over.'

Midge sighed.

'That's so like you, Edward. To remember the practical side. Impulse doesn't carry you very far, does it? Oh, well, it was a nice dream while it lasted.'

She slipped her hand into his and gave him her old smile.

'I'm sorry I stood on the pavement and abused you like a fishwife,' she said. 'But you know, Edward, you *were* irritating.'

'Yes,' he said. 'I must have been.'

They went into the Berkeley happily side by side. They got a table by the window and Edward ordered an excellent lunch.

As they finished their chicken, Midge sighed and said, 'I ought to hurry back to the shop. My time's up.'

Agatha Christie

'You're going to take decent time over your lunch today, even if I have to go back and buy half the clothes in the shop!'

'Dear Edward, you are really rather sweet.'

They ate Crêpes Suzette, and then the waiter brought them coffee. Edward stirred his sugar in with his spoon.

He said gently:

'You really do love Ainswick, don't you?'

'Must we talk about Ainswick? I've survived not catching the 2.15—and I quite realize that there isn't any question of the 4.15—but don't rub it in.'

Edward smiled. 'No, I'm not proposing that we catch the 4.15. But I am suggesting that you come to Ainswick, Midge. I'm suggesting that you come there for good—that is, if you can put up with me.'

She stared at him over the rim of her coffee cup—put it down with a hand that she managed to keep steady.

'What do you really mean, Edward?'

'I'm suggesting that you should marry me, Midge. I don't suppose that I'm a very romantic proposition. I'm a dull dog, I know that, and not much good at anything. I just read books and potter around. But although I'm not a very exciting person, we've known each other a long time and I think that Ainswick itself would—well, would compensate. I think you'd be happy at Ainswick, Midge. Will you come?'

Midge swallowed once or twice, then she said:

'But I thought—Henrietta—' and stopped.

Edward said, his voice level and unemotional:

'Yes, I've asked Henrietta to marry me three times. Each time she has refused. Henrietta knows what she doesn't want.'

The Hollow

There was a silence, and then Edward said:

'Well, Midge dear, what about it?'

Midge looked up at him. There was a catch in her voice. She said:

'It seems so extraordinary—to be offered heaven on a plate as it were, at the Berkeley!'

His face lighted up. He laid his hand over hers for a brief moment.

'Heaven on a plate,' he said. 'So you feel like that about Ainswick. Oh, Midge, I'm glad.'

They sat there happily. Edward paid the bill and added an enormous tip. The people in the restaurant were thinning out. Midge said with an effort:

'We'll have to go. I suppose I'd better go back to Madame Alfrege. After all, she's counting on me. I can't just walk out.'

'No, I suppose you'll have to go back and resign or hand in your notice or whatever you call it. You're not to go on working there, though. I won't have it. But first I thought we'd better go to one of those shops in Bond Street where they sell rings.'

'Rings?'

'It's usual, isn't it?'

Midge laughed.

In the dimmed lighting of the jeweller's shop, Midge and Edward bent over trays of sparkling engagement rings, whilst a discreet salesman watched them benignantly.

Edward said, pushing away a velvet-covered tray:

'Not emeralds.'

Henrietta in green tweeds—Henrietta in an evening dress like Chinese jade...

No, not emeralds.

Midge pushed away the tiny stabbing pain at her heart.

'Choose for me,' she said to Edward.

He bent over the tray before them. He picked out a ring with a single diamond. Not a very large stone, but a stone of beautiful colour and fire.

'I'd like this.'

Midge nodded. She loved this display of Edward's unerring and fastidious taste. She slipped it on her finger as Edward and the shopman drew aside.

Edward wrote out a cheque for three hundred and forty-two pounds and came back to Midge smiling.

He said, 'Let's go and be rude to Madame Alfrege.'

CHAPTER 25

'But, darling, I *am* so delighted!'

Lady Angkatell stretched out a fragile hand to Edward and touched Midge softly with the other.

'You did quite right, Edward, to make her leave that horrid shop and bring her right down here. She'll stay here, of course, and be married from here. St George's, you know, three miles by the road, though only a mile through the woods, but then one doesn't go to a wedding through woods. And I suppose it will have to be the vicar—poor man, he has such dreadful colds in the head every autumn. The curate, now, has one of those high Anglican voices, and the whole thing would be far more impressive—and more religious, too, if you know what I mean. It is so hard to keep one's mind reverent when somebody is saying things through their noses.'

It was, Midge decided, a very Lucyish reception. It made her want to both laugh and cry.

'I'd love to be married from here, Lucy,' she said.

'Then that's settled, darling. Off-white satin, I think, and an ivory prayer-book—*not* a bouquet. Bridesmaids?'

'No. I don't want a fuss. Just a very quiet wedding.'

Agatha Christie

'I know what you mean, darling, and I think perhaps you are right. With an autumn wedding it's nearly always chrysanthemums—such an uninspiring flower, I always think. And unless one takes a lot of time to choose them carefully bridesmaids never *match* properly, and there's nearly always one terribly plain one who ruins the whole effect—but one has to have her because she's usually the bridegroom's sister. But of course—' Lady Angkatell beamed, 'Edward hasn't got any sisters.'

'That seems to be one point in my favour,' said Edward, smiling.

'But children are really the worst at weddings,' went on Lady Angkatell, happily pursuing her own train of thought. 'Everyone says: "How sweet!" but, my dear, the *anxiety*! They step on the train, or else they howl for Nannie, and quite often they're sick. I always wonder how a girl can go up the aisle in a proper frame of mind, while she's so uncertain about what is happening behind her.'

'There needn't be anything behind me,' said Midge cheerfully. 'Not even a train. I can be married in a coat and skirt.'

'Oh, no, Midge, that's so like a widow. No, off-white satin and *not* from Madame Alfrege's.'

'Certainly not from Madame Alfrege's,' said Edward.

'I shall take you to Mireille,' said Lady Angkatell.

'My dear Lucy, I can't possibly afford Mireille.'

'Nonsense, Midge. Henry and I are going to give you your trousseau. And Henry, of course, will give you away. I do hope the band of his trousers won't be too tight. It's nearly two years since he last went to a wedding. And I shall wear—'

Lady Angkatell paused and closed her eyes.

The Hollow

'Yes, Lucy?'

'Hydrangea blue,' announced Lady Angkatell in a rapt voice. 'I suppose, Edward, you will have one of your own friends for best man, otherwise, of course, there is David. I cannot help feeling it would be frightfully good for David. It would give him poise, you know, and he would feel we all *liked* him. That, I am sure, is very important with David. It must be disheartening, you know, to feel you are clever and intellectual and yet nobody likes you any the better for it! But of course it would be rather a risk. He would probably lose the ring, or drop it at the last minute. I expect it would worry Edward too much. But it would be nice in a way to keep it to the same people we've had here for the murder.'

Lady Angkatell uttered the last few words in the most conversational of tones.

'Lady Angkatell has been entertaining a few friends for a murder this autumn,' Midge could not help saying.

'Yes,' said Lucy meditatively. 'I suppose it *did* sound like that. A party for the shooting. You know, when you come to think of it, that's just what it has been!'

Midge gave a faint shiver and said:

'Well, at any rate, it's over now.'

'It's not exactly over—the inquest was only adjourned. And that nice Inspector Grange has got men all over the place simply crashing through the chestnut woods and startling all the pheasants, and springing up like jacks in the box in the most unlikely places.'

'What are they looking for?' asked Edward. 'The revolver that Christow was shot with?'

'I imagine that must be it. They even came to the house with a search warrant. The inspector was most apologetic about it, quite *shy*, but of course I told him we should be delighted. It was really most interesting. They looked absolutely *everywhere*. I followed them round, you know, and I suggested one or two places which even they hadn't thought of. But they didn't find anything. It was most disappointing. Poor Inspector Grange, he is growing quite thin and he pulls and pulls at that moustache of his. His wife ought to give him specially nourishing meals with all this worry he is having— but I have a vague idea that she must be one of those women who care more about having the linoleum really well polished than in cooking a tasty little meal. Which reminds me, I must go and see Mrs Medway. Funny how servants cannot bear the police. Her cheese soufflé last night was quite uneatable. Soufflés and pastry always show if one is off balance. If it weren't for Gudgeon keeping them all together I really believe half the servants would leave. Why don't you two go and have a nice walk and help the police look for the revolver?'

Hercule Poirot sat on the bench overlooking the chestnut groves above the pool. He had no sense of trespassing since Lady Angkatell had very sweetly begged him to wander where he would at any time. It was Lady Angkatell's sweetness which Hercule Poirot was considering at this moment.

From time to time he heard the cracking of twigs in the woods above or caught sight of a figure moving through the chestnut groves below him.

The Hollow

Presently Henrietta came along the path from the direction of the lane. She stopped for a moment when she saw Poirot, then she came and sat down by him.

'Good morning, M. Poirot. I have just been to call upon you. But you were out. You look very Olympian. Are you presiding over the hunt? The inspector seems very active. What are they looking for, the revolver?'

'Yes, Miss Savernake.'

'Will they find it, do you think?'

'I think so. Quite soon now, I should say.'

She looked at him inquiringly.

'Have you an idea, then, where it is?'

'No. But I *think* it will be found soon. It is *time* for it to be found.'

'You do say odd things, M. Poirot!'

'Odd things happen here. You have come back very soon from London, Mademoiselle.'

Her face hardened. She gave a short, bitter laugh.

'The murderer returns to the scene of the crime? That is the old superstition, isn't it? So you *do* think that I—did it! You don't believe me when I tell you that I wouldn't—that I *couldn't* kill anybody?'

Poirot did not answer at once. At last he said thoughtfully:

'It has seemed to me from the beginning that either this crime was very simple—so simple that it was difficult to believe its simplicity (and simplicity, Mademoiselle, can be strangely baffling) or else it was extremely complex. That is to say, we were contending against a mind capable of intricate and ingenious inventions, so that every time we seemed to be heading for the truth, we were actually being led on a trail that twisted away from the truth and led us to a point which—ended in nothingness. This apparent futility, this continual barrenness, is not *real*—it is artificial, it is *planned*. A very subtle and ingenious mind is plotting against us the whole time—and succeeding.'

'Well?' said Henrietta. 'What has that to do with me?'

'The mind that is plotting against us is a creative mind, Mademoiselle.'

'I see—that's where I come in?'

She was silent, her lips set together bitterly. From her jacket pocket she had taken a pencil and now she was idly drawing the outline of a fantastic tree on the white painted wood of the bench, frowning as she did so.

Poirot watched her. Something stirred in his mind—standing in Lady Angkatell's drawing-room on the afternoon of the crime, looking down at a pile of bridge-markers, standing by a painted iron table in the pavilion the next morning, and a question that he had put to Gudgeon.

He said:

'That is what you drew on your bridge-marker—a tree.'

'Yes.' Henrietta seemed suddenly aware of what she was doing. 'Ygdrasil, M. Poirot.' She laughed.

'Why do you call it Ygdrasil?'

She explained the origin of Ygdrasil.

'And so, when you "doodle" (that is the word, is it not?) it is always Ygdrasil you draw?'

'Yes. Doodling is a funny thing, isn't it?'

'Here on the seat—on the bridge-marker on Saturday evening—in the pavilion on Sunday morning...'

The Hollow

The hand that held the pencil stiffened and stopped. She said in a tone of careless amusement:

'In the pavilion?'

'Yes, on the round iron table there.'

'Oh, that must have been on—on Saturday afternoon.'

'It was not on Saturday afternoon. When Gudgeon brought the glasses out to the pavilion about twelve o'clock on Sunday morning, there was nothing drawn on the table. I asked him and he is quite definite about that.'

'Then it must have been'—she hesitated for just a moment—'of course, on Sunday afternoon.'

But still smiling pleasantly, Hercule Poirot shook his head.

'I think not. Grange's men were at the pool all Sunday afternoon, photographing the body, getting the revolver out of the water. They did not leave until dusk. They would have seen anyone go into the pavilion.'

Henrietta said slowly:

'I remember now. I went along there quite late in the evening—after dinner.'

Poirot's voice came sharply:

'People do not "doodle" in the dark, Miss Savernake. Are you telling me that you went into the pavilion at night and stood by a table and drew a tree without being able to see what you were drawing?'

Henrietta said calmly, 'I am telling you the truth. Naturally you don't believe it. You have your own ideas. What is your idea, by the way?'

'I am suggesting that you were in the pavilion on *Sunday morning after twelve o'clock* when Gudgeon brought the glasses out. That you stood by that table watching someone, or waiting for someone, and unconsciously took out a pencil and drew Ygdrasil without being fully aware of what you were doing.'

'I was not in the pavilion on Sunday morning. I sat out on the terrace for a while, then I got the gardening basket and went up to the dahlia border and cut off heads and tied up some of the Michaelmas daisies that were untidy. Then just on one o'clock I went along to the pool. I've been through it all with Inspector Grange. I never came near the pool until one o'clock, just after John had been shot.'

'That,' said Hercule Poirot, 'is your story. But Ygdrasil, Mademoiselle, testifies against you.'

'I was in the pavilion and I shot John, that's what you mean?'

'You were there and you shot Dr Christow, or you were there and you saw who shot Dr Christow—or someone else was there who knew about Ygdrasil and deliberately drew it on the table to put suspicion on *you*.'

Henrietta got up. She turned on him with her chin lifted.

'You still think that I shot John Christow. You think that you can prove I shot him. Well, I will tell you this. You will never prove it. *Never*!'

'You think that you are cleverer than I am?'

'You will never prove it,' said Henrietta, and, turning, she walked away down the winding path that led to the swimming pool.

CHAPTER 26

Grange came in to Resthaven to drink a cup of tea with Hercule Poirot. The tea was exactly what he had had apprehensions it might be—extremely weak and China tea at that.

'These foreigners,' thought Grange, 'don't know how to make tea. You can't teach 'em.' But he did not mind much. He was in a condition of pessimism when one more thing that was unsatisfactory actually afforded him a kind of grim satisfaction.

He said, 'The adjourned inquest's the day after tomorrow and where have we got? Nowhere at all. What the hell, that gun must be *somewhere*! It's this damned country—miles of woods. It would take an army to search them properly. Talk of a needle in a haystack. It may be anywhere. The fact is, we've got to face up to it—we may *never* find that gun.'

'You will find it,' said Poirot confidently.

'Well, it won't be for want of trying!'

'You will find it, sooner or later. And I should say sooner. Another cup of tea?'

'I don't mind if I do—no, no hot water.'

'Is it not too strong?'

'Oh, no, it's not too strong.' The inspector was conscious of understatement.

Agatha Christie

Gloomily he sipped at the pale, straw-coloured beverage.

'This case is making a monkey of me, M. Poirot—a monkey of me! I can't get the hang of these people. They *seem* helpful—but everything they tell you seems to lead you away on a wild-goose chase.'

'Away?' said Poirot. A startled look came into his eyes. 'Yes, I see. *Away...*'

The inspector was now developing his grievance.

'Take the gun now. Christow was shot—according to the medical evidence—only a minute or two before your arrival. Lady Angkatell had that egg basket, Miss Savernake had a gardening basket full of dead flower heads, and Edward Angkatell was wearing a loose shooting-coat with large pockets stuffed with cartridges. Any one of them could have carried the revolver away with them. It wasn't hidden anywhere near the pool—my men have raked the place, so that's definitely out.'

Poirot nodded. Grange went on:

'Gerda Christow was framed—but who by? That's where every clue I follow seems to vanish into thin air.'

'Their stories of how they spent the morning are satisfactory?'

'The *stories* are all right. Miss Savernake was gardening. Lady Angkatell was collecting eggs. Edward Angkatell and Sir Henry were shooting and separated at the end of the morning—Sir Henry coming back to the house and Edward Angkatell coming down here through the woods. The young fellow was up in his bedroom reading. (Funny place to read on a nice day, but he's the indoor, bookish kind.) Miss Hardcastle took a book down to the orchard. All sounds very natural and likely, and there's no means of checking up on it. Gudgeon took a tray of glasses out to the pavilion about twelve o'clock. He can't say where any of the house party were or what they were doing. In a way, you know, there's something against almost all of them.'

'Really?'

'Of course the most obvious person is Veronica Cray. She had quarrelled with Christow, she hated his guts, she's quite *likely* to have shot him—but I can't find the least iota of proof that she *did* shoot him. No evidence as to her having had any opportunity to pinch the revolvers from Sir Henry's collection. No one who saw her going to or from the pool that day. And the missing revolver definitely isn't in her possession now.'

'Ah, you have made sure of that?'

'What do you think? The evidence would have justified a search warrant but there was no need. She was quite gracious about it. It's not anywhere in that tin-pot bungalow. After the inquest was adjourned we made a show of letting up on Miss Cray and Miss Savernake, and we've had a tail on them to see where they went and what they'd do. We've had a man on at the film studios watching Veronica—no sign of her trying to ditch the gun there.'

'And Henrietta Savernake?'

'Nothing there either. She went straight back to Chelsea and we've kept an eye on her ever since. The revolver isn't in her studio or in her possession. She was quite pleasant about the search—seemed amused. Some of her fancy stuff gave our man quite a turn. He said it beat him why people wanted to do that kind of thing—statues all lumps and swellings, bits of brass and aluminium twisted into fancy shapes, horses that you wouldn't know were horses.'

Poirot stirred a little.

'Horses, you say?'

'Well, *a* horse. If you'd call it a horse! If people want to model a horse, why don't they go and *look* at a horse!'

'A *horse*,' repeated Poirot.

Grange turned his head.

'What is there about that that interests you so, M. Poirot? I don't get it.'

'Association—a point of the psychology.'

'Word association? Horse and cart? Rocking-horse? Clothes horse. No, I don't get it. Anyway, after a day or two, Miss Savernake packs up and comes down here again. You know that?'

'Yes, I have talked with her and I have seen her walking in the woods.'

'Restless, yes. Well, she was having an affair with the doctor all right, and his saying: "*Henrietta*" as he died is pretty near to an accusation. But it's not quite near enough, M. Poirot.'

'No,' said Poirot thoughtfully, 'it is not near enough.'

Grange said heavily:

'There's something in the atmosphere here—it gets you all tangled up! It's as though they all *knew* something. Lady Angkatell now—she's never been able to put out a decent reason *why* she took out a gun with her that day. It's a crazy thing to do—sometimes I think she is crazy.'

Poirot shook his head very gently.

The Hollow

'No,' he said, 'she is not crazy.'

'Then there's Edward Angkatell. I thought I was getting something on *him*. Lady Angkatell said—no, hinted—that he'd been in love with Miss Savernake for years. Well, that gives him a motive. And now I find it's the *other* girl—Miss Hardcastle—that he's engaged to. So bang goes the case against *him*.'

Poirot gave a sympathetic murmur.

'Then there's the young fellow,' pursued the inspector. 'Lady Angkatell let slip something about him. His mother, it seems, died in an asylum—persecution mania—thought everybody was conspiring to kill her. Well, you can see what that might mean. If the boy had inherited that particular strain of insanity, he might have got ideas into his head about Dr Christow—might have fancied the doctor was planning to certify him. Not that Christow was that kind of doctor. Nervous affections of the alimentary canal and diseases of the super—super something. That was Christow's line. But if the boy was a bit touched, he *might* imagine Christow was here to keep him under observation. He's got an extraordinary manner, that young fellow, nervous as a cat.'

Grange sat unhappily for a moment or two.

'You see what I mean? All vague suspicions, leading *nowhere*.'

Poirot stirred again. He murmured softly:

'*Away*—not *towards*. *From*, not to. *Nowhere* instead of *somewhere*... Yes, of course, that *must* be it.'

Grange stared at him. He said:

'They're queer, all these Angkatells. I'd swear, sometimes, that they know all about it.'

Poirot said quietly:

'*They do.*'

'You mean, they know, all of them, who did it?' the inspector asked incredulously.

Poirot nodded.

'Yes, they know. I have thought so for some time. I am quite sure now.'

'I see.' The inspector's face was grim. 'And they're hiding it up between them? Well, I'll beat them yet. *I'm going to find that gun.*'

It was, Poirot reflected, quite the inspector's theme song.

Grange went on with rancour:

'I'd give anything to get even with them.'

'With—'

'All of them! Muddling me up! Suggesting things! Hinting! Helping my men—*helping* them! All gossamer and spiders' webs, nothing tangible. What I want is a good solid *fact*!'

Hercule Poirot had been staring out of the window for some moments. His eye had been attracted by an irregularity in the symmetry of his domain.

He said now:

'You want a solid fact? *Eh bien*, unless I am much mistaken, there is a solid fact in the hedge by my gate.'

They went down the garden path. Grange went down on his knees, coaxed the twigs apart till he disclosed more fully the thing that had been thrust between them. He drew a deep sigh as something black and steel was revealed.

He said: 'It's a revolver all right.'

Just for a moment his eye rested doubtfully on Poirot.

The Hollow

'No, no, my friend,' said Poirot. '*I* did not shoot Dr Christow and I did not put the revolver in my own hedge.'

'Of course you didn't, M. Poirot! Sorry! Well, we've got it. Looks like the one missing from Sir Henry's study. We can verify that as soon as we get the number. Then we'll see if it was the gun that shot Christow. Easy does it now.'

With infinite care and the use of a silk handkerchief he eased the gun out of the hedge.

'To give us a break, we want fingerprints. I've a feeling, you know, that our luck's changed at last.'

'Let me know.'

'Of course I will, M. Poirot. I'll ring you up.'

Poirot received two telephone calls. The first came through that same evening. The inspector was jubilant.

'That you, M. Poirot? Well, here's the dope. It's the gun all right. The gun missing from Sir Henry's collection *and* the gun that shot John Christow! That's definite. And there are a good set of prints on it. Thumb, first finger, part of middle finger. Didn't I tell you our luck had changed?'

'You have identified the fingerprints?'

'Not yet. They're certainly not Mrs Christow's. We took hers. They look more like a man's than a woman's for size. Tomorrow I'm going along to The Hollow to speak my little piece and get a sample from everyone. And then, M. Poirot, *we shall know where we are*!'

'I hope so, I am sure,' said Poirot politely.

The second telephone call came through on the following day and the voice that spoke was no longer jubilant. In tones of unmitigated gloom, Grange said:

'Want to hear the latest? Those fingerprints aren't the prints of anybody connected with the case! No, sir! They're not Edward Angkatell's, nor David's, nor Sir Henry's! They're not Gerda Christow's, nor the Savernake's, nor our Veronica's, nor her ladyship's, nor the little dark girl's! They're not even the kitchenmaid's—let alone any of the other servants'!'

Poirot made consoling noises. The sad voice of Inspector Grange went on:

'So it looks as though, after all, it *was* an outside job. Someone, that is to say, who had a down on Dr Christow and who we don't know anything about. Someone invisible and inaudible who pinched the guns from the study, and who went away after the shooting by the path to the lane. Someone who put the gun in your hedge and then vanished into thin air!'

'Would you like *my* fingerprints, my friend?'

'I don't mind if I do! It strikes me, M. Poirot, that you were on the spot, and that taking it all round you're far and away the most suspicious character in the case!'

CHAPTER 27

The coroner cleared his throat and looked expectantly at the foreman of the jury.

The latter looked down at the piece of paper he held in his hand. His Adam's apple wagged up and down excitedly. He read out in a careful voice:

'We find that the deceased came to his death by wilful murder by some person or persons unknown.'

Poirot nodded his head quietly in his corner by the wall.

There could be no other possible verdict.

Outside the Angkatells stopped a moment to talk to Gerda and her sister. Gerda was wearing the same black clothes. Her face had the same dazed, unhappy expression. This time there was no Daimler. The train service, Elsie Patterson explained, was really very good. A fast train to Waterloo and they could easily catch the 1.20 to Bexhill.

Lady Angkatell, clasping Gerda's hand, murmured:

'You must keep in touch with us, my dear. A little lunch, perhaps, one day in London? I expect you come up to do shopping occasionally.'

'I—I don't know,' said Gerda.

Elsie Patterson said:

'We must hurry, dear, our train,' and Gerda turned away with an expression of relief.

Midge said:

'Poor Gerda. The only thing John's death has done for her is to set her free from your terrifying hospitality, Lucy.'

'How unkind you are, Midge. Nobody could say I didn't try.'

'You are much worse when you try, Lucy.'

'Well, it's very nice to think it's all over, isn't it?' said Lady Angkatell, beaming at them. 'Except, of course, for poor Inspector Grange. I do feel so sorry for him. Would it cheer him up, do you think, if we asked him back to lunch? As a *friend*, I mean.'

'I should let well alone, Lucy,' said Sir Henry.

'Perhaps you are right,' said Lady Angkatell meditatively. 'And anyway it isn't the right kind of lunch today. Partridges au Choux—and that delicious Soufflé Surprise that Mrs Medway makes so well. Not at all Inspector Grange's kind of lunch. A really good steak, a little underdone, and a good old-fashioned apple tart with no nonsense about it—or perhaps apple dumplings—that's what I should order for Inspector Grange.'

'Your instincts about food are always very sound, Lucy. I think we had better get home to those partridges. They sound delicious.'

'Well, I thought we ought to have *some* celebration. It's wonderful, isn't it, how everything always seems to turn out for the best?'

'Ye-es.'

'I know what you're thinking, Henry, but don't worry. I shall attend to it this afternoon.'

The Hollow

'What are you up to now, Lucy?'

Lady Angkatell smiled at him.

'It's quite all right, darling. Just tucking in a loose end.'

Sir Henry looked at her doubtfully.

When they reached The Hollow, Gudgeon came out to open the door of the car.

'Everything went off very satisfactorily, Gudgeon,' said Lady Angkatell. 'Please tell Mrs Medway and the others. I know how unpleasant it has been for you all, and I should like to tell you now how much Sir Henry and I have appreciated the loyalty you have all shown.'

'We have been deeply concerned for you, my lady,' said Gudgeon.

'Very sweet of Gudgeon,' said Lucy as she went into the drawing-room, 'but really quite wasted. I have really almost *enjoyed* it all—so different, you know, from what one is accustomed to. Don't you feel, David, that an experience like this has broadened your mind? It must be so different from Cambridge.'

'I am at Oxford,' said David coldly.

Lady Angkatell said vaguely, 'The dear Boat Race. So English, don't you think?' and went towards the telephone.

She picked up the receiver and, holding it in her hand, she went on:

'I do hope, David, that you will come and stay with us again. It's so difficult, isn't it, to get to know people when there is a murder? And quite impossible to have any really intellectual conversation.'

'Thank you,' said David. 'But when I come down I am going to Athens—to the British School.'

Lady Angkatell turned to her husband.

'Who's got the Embassy now? Oh, of course. Hope-Remmington. No, I don't think David would like them. Those girls of theirs are so terribly hearty. They play hockey and cricket and the funny game where you catch the thing in a net.'

She broke off, looking down at the telephone receiver.

'Now, what am I doing with this thing?'

'Perhaps you were going to ring someone up,' said Edward.

'I don't think so.' She replaced it. 'Do you like telephones, David?'

It was the sort of question, David reflected irritably, that she would ask; one to which there could be no intelligent answer. He replied coldly that he supposed they were useful.

'You mean,' said Lady Angkatell, 'like mincing machines? Or elastic bands? All the same, one wouldn't—'

She broke off as Gudgeon appeared in the doorway to announce lunch.

'But you like partridges,' said Lady Angkatell to David anxiously.

David admitted that he liked partridges.

'Sometimes I think Lucy really is a bit touched,' said Midge as she and Edward strolled away from the house and up towards the woods.

The partridges and the Soufflé Surprise had been excellent, and with the inquest over a weight had lifted from the atmosphere.

The Hollow

Edward said thoughtfully:

'I always think Lucy has a brilliant mind that expresses itself like a missing word competition. To mix metaphors—the hammer jumps from nail to nail and never fails to hit each one squarely on the head.'

'All the same,' Midge said soberly, 'Lucy frightens me sometimes.' She added, with a tiny shiver: 'This place has frightened me lately.'

'The Hollow?'

Edward turned an astonished face to her.

'It always reminds me a little of Ainswick,' he said. 'It's not, of course, the real thing—'

Midge interrupted:

'That's just it, Edward. I'm frightened of things that aren't the real thing. You don't know, you see, what's *behind* them. It's like—oh, it's like a *mask*.'

'You mustn't be fanciful, little Midge.'

It was the old tone, the indulgent tone he had used years ago. She had liked it then, but now it disturbed her. She struggled to make her meaning clear—to show him that behind what he called fancy, was some shape of dimly apprehended reality.

'I got away from it in London, but now that I'm back here it all comes over me again. I feel that everyone knows who killed John Christow. That the only person who doesn't know—is *me*.'

Edward said irritably:

'Must we think and talk about John Christow? He's dead. Dead and gone.'

Agatha Christie

Midge murmured:

> *'He is dead and gone, lady,*
> *He is dead and gone.*
> *At his head a grass green turf,*
> *At his heels a stone.'*

She put her hand on Edward's arm. 'Who *did* kill him, Edward? We thought it was Gerda—but it wasn't Gerda. Then who was it? Tell me what *you* think? Was it someone we've never heard of ?'

He said irritably:

'All this speculation seems to me quite unprofitable. If the police can't find out, or can't get sufficient evidence, then the whole thing will have to be allowed to drop—and we shall be rid of it.'

'Yes—but it's the not knowing.'

'Why should we want to know? What has John Christow to do with us?'

With *us*, she thought, with Edward and me? Nothing! Comforting thought—she and Edward, linked, a dual entity. And yet—and yet—John Christow, for all that he had been laid in his grave and the words of the burial service read over him, was not buried deep enough. *He is dead and gone, lady*—But John Christow was not dead and gone—for all that Edward wished him to be. John Christow was still here at The Hollow.

Edward said: 'Where are we going?'

Something in his tone surprised her. She said:

The Hollow

'Let's walk up on to the top of the ridge? Shall we?'

'If you like.'

For some reason he was unwilling. She wondered why. It was usually his favourite walk. He and Henrietta used nearly always—Her thought snapped and broke off. *He and Henrietta!* She said: 'Have you been this way yet this autumn?'

He said stiffly:

'Henrietta and I walked up here that first afternoon.'

They went on in silence.

They came at last to the top and sat on the fallen tree. Midge thought, '*He and Henrietta sat here, perhaps.*'

She turned the ring on her finger round and round. The diamond flashed coldly at her. ('*Not emeralds,*' he had said.)

She said with a slight effort:

'It will be lovely to be at Ainswick again for Christmas.'

He did not seem to hear her. He had gone far away.

She thought, 'He is thinking of Henrietta and of John Christow.'

Sitting here he had said something to Henrietta or she had said something to him. Henrietta might know what she didn't want, but he belonged to Henrietta still. He always would, Midge thought, belong to Henrietta...

Pain swooped down upon her. The happy bubble world in which she had lived for the last week quivered and broke.

She thought, 'I can't live like that—with Henrietta always there in his mind. I can't face it. I can't bear it.'

The wind sighed through the trees—the leaves were falling fast now—there was hardly any golden left, only brown.

Agatha Christie

She said: 'Edward!'

The urgency of her voice aroused him. He turned his head. 'Yes?'

'I'm sorry, Edward.' Her lips were trembling but she forced her voice to be quiet and self-controlled. 'I've got to tell you. It's no use. I can't marry you. It wouldn't work, Edward.'

He said: 'But, Midge—surely Ainswick—'

She interrupted:

'I can't marry you just for Ainswick, Edward. You—you must see that.'

He sighed then, a long gentle sigh. It was like an echo of the dead leaves slipping gently off the branches of the trees.

'I see what you mean,' he said. 'Yes, I suppose you are right.'

'It was dear of you to ask me, dear and sweet. But it wouldn't do, Edward. It wouldn't *work*.'

She had had a faint hope, perhaps, that he would argue with her, that he would try to persuade her, but he seemed, quite simply, to feel just as she did about it. Here, with the ghost of Henrietta close beside him, he too, apparently, saw that it couldn't work.

'No,' he said, echoing her words, 'it wouldn't work.'

She slipped the ring off her finger and held it out to him.

She would always love Edward and Edward would always love Henrietta and life was just plain unadulterated hell.

She said with a little catch in her voice:

'It's a lovely ring, Edward.'

'I wish you'd keep it, Midge. I'd like you to have it.'

She shook her head.

'I couldn't do that.'

The Hollow

He said with a faint, humorous twist of the lips:

'I shan't give it to anyone else, you know.'

It was all quite friendly. He didn't know—he would never know—just what she was feeling. Heaven on a plate—and the plate was broken and heaven had slipped between her fingers or had, perhaps, never been there.

That afternoon, Poirot received his third visitor.

He had been visited by Henrietta Savernake and Veronica Cray. This time it was Lady Angkatell. She came floating up the path with her usual appearance of insubstantiality.

He opened the door and she stood smiling at him.

'I have come to see you,' she announced.

So might a fairy confer a favour on a mere mortal.

'I am enchanted, Madame.'

He led the way into the sitting-room. She sat down on the sofa and once more she smiled.

Hercule Poirot thought, 'She is old—her hair is grey—there are lines in her face. Yet she has magic—she will always have magic...'

Lady Angkatell said softly:

'I want you to do something for me.'

'Yes, Lady Angkatell?'

'To begin with, I must talk to you—about John Christow.'

'About Dr Christow?'

'Yes. It seems to me that the only thing to do is to put a full stop to the whole thing. You understand what I mean, don't you?'

Agatha Christie

'I am not sure that I do know what you mean, Lady Angkatell.'

She gave him her lovely dazzling smile again and she put one long white hand on his sleeve.

'Dear M. Poirot, you know perfectly. The police will have to hunt about for the owner of those fingerprints and they won't find him, and they'll have, in the end, to let the whole thing drop. But I'm afraid, you know, that *you* won't let it drop.'

'No, I shall not let it drop,' said Hercule Poirot.

'That is just what I thought. And that is why I came. It's the truth you want, isn't it?'

'Certainly I want the truth.'

'I see I haven't explained myself very well. I'm trying to find out just *why* you won't let things drop. It isn't because of your prestige—or because you want to hang a murderer (such an unpleasant kind of death, I've always thought—so *mediæval*). It's just, I think, that you want to *know*. You do see what I mean, don't you? If you were to know the truth—if you were to be *told* the truth, I think—I think perhaps that might satisfy you? Would it satisfy you, M. Poirot?'

'You are offering to tell me the truth, Lady Angkatell?'

She nodded.

'You yourself know the truth, then?'

Her eyes opened very wide.

'Oh, yes, I've known for a long time. I'd *like* to tell you. And then we could agree that—well, that it was all over and done with.'

She smiled at him.

The Hollow

'Is it a bargain, M. Poirot?'

It was quite an effort for Hercule Poirot to say:

'No, Madame, it is not a bargain.'

He wanted—he wanted, very badly, to let the whole thing drop, simply because Lady Angkatell asked him to do so.

Lady Angkatell sat very still for a moment. Then she raised her eyebrows.

'I wonder,' she said. 'I wonder if you really know what you are doing.'

CHAPTER 28

Midge, lying dry-eyed and awake in the darkness, turned restlessly on her pillows.

She heard a door unlatch, a footstep in the corridor outside passing her door.

It was Edward's door and Edward's step.

She switched on the lamp by her bed and looked at the clock that stood by the lamp on the table.

It was ten minutes to three.

Edward passing her door and going down the stairs at this hour in the morning. It was odd.

They had all gone to bed early, at half-past ten. She herself had not slept, had lain there with burning eyelids and with a dry, aching misery racking her feverishly.

She had heard the clock strike downstairs—had heard owls hoot outside her bedroom window. Had felt that depression that reaches its nadir at 2 am. Had thought to herself: 'I can't bear it—I can't bear it. Tomorrow coming—another day. Day after day to be got through.'

Banished by her own act from Ainswick—from all the loveliness and dearness of Ainswick which might have been her very own possession.

The Hollow

But better banishment, better loneliness, better a drab and uninteresting life, than life with Edward and Henrietta's ghost. Until that day in the wood she had not known her own capacity for bitter jealousy.

And after all, Edward had never told her that he loved her. Affection, kindliness, he had never pretended to more than that. She had accepted the limitation, and not until she had realized what it would mean to live at close quarters with an Edward whose mind and heart had Henrietta as a permanent guest, did she know that for her Edward's affection was not enough.

Edward walking past her door, down the front stairs.

It was odd—very odd. Where was he going?

Uneasiness grew upon her. It was all part and parcel of the uneasiness that The Hollow gave her nowadays. What was Edward doing downstairs in the small hours of the morning? Had he gone out?

Inactivity at last became too much for her. She got up, slipped on her dressing-gown, and, taking a torch, she opened her door and came out into the passage.

It was quite dark, no lights had been switched on. Midge turned to the left and came to the head of the staircase. Below all was dark too. She ran down the stairs and after a moment's hesitation switched on the light in the hall. Everything was silent. The front door was closed and locked. She tried the side door but that, too, was locked.

Edward, then, had not gone out. Where could he be?

And suddenly she raised her head and sniffed.

A whiff, a very faint whiff of gas.

Agatha Christie

The baize door to the kitchen quarters was just ajar. She went through it—a faint light was shining from the open kitchen door. The smell of gas was much stronger.

Midge ran along the passage and into the kitchen. Edward was lying on the floor with his head inside the gas oven, which was turned full on.

Midge was a quick, practical girl. Her first act was to swing open the shutters. She could not unlatch the window, and, winding a glass-cloth round her arm, she smashed it. Then, holding her breath, she stooped down and tugged and pulled Edward out of the gas oven and switched off the taps.

He was unconscious and breathing queerly, but she knew that he could not have been unconscious long. He could only just have gone under. The wind sweeping through from the window to the open door was fast dispelling the gas fumes. Midge dragged Edward to a spot near the window where the air would have full play. She sat down and gathered him into her strong young arms.

She said his name, first softly, then with increasing desperation.

'Edward, Edward, *Edward*...'

He stirred, groaned, opened his eyes and looked up at her. He said very faintly, 'Gas oven,' and his eyes went round to the gas stove.

'I know, darling, but why—*why*?'

He was shivering now, his hands were cold and lifeless. He said, 'Midge?' There was a kind of wondering surprise and pleasure in his voice.

She said, 'I heard you pass my door. I didn't know... I came down.'

The Hollow

He sighed, a very long sigh as though from very far away. 'Best way out,' he said. And then, inexplicably until she remembered Lucy's conversation on the night of the tragedy, '*News of the World.*'

'But, Edward, why, *why?*'

He looked up at her, and the blank, cold darkness of his stare frightened her.

'Because I know I've never been any good. Always a failure. Always ineffectual. It's men like Christow who do things. They get there and women admire them. I'm nothing—I'm not even quite alive. I inherited Ainswick and I've enough to live on—otherwise I'd have gone under. No good at a career—never much good as a writer. Henrietta didn't want me. No one wanted me. That day—at the Berkeley—I thought—but it was the same story. You couldn't care either, Midge. Even for Ainswick you couldn't put up with me. So I thought better get out altogether.'

Her words came with a rush. 'Darling, darling, you don't understand. It was because of Henrietta—because I thought you still loved Henrietta so much.'

'Henrietta?' He murmured it vaguely, as though speaking of someone infinitely remote. 'Yes, I loved her very much.'

And from even farther away she heard him murmur:

'It's so cold.'

'*Edward*—my darling.'

Her arms closed round him firmly. He smiled at her, murmuring:

'You're so warm, Midge—you're so warm.'

Yes, she thought, that was what despair was. A cold thing—a thing of infinite coldness and loneliness. She'd never understood until now that despair was a cold thing. She had thought of it as something hot and passionate, something violent, a hot-blooded desperation. But that was not so. *This* was despair—this utter outer darkness of coldness and loneliness. And the sin of despair, that priests talked of, was a cold sin, the sin of cutting oneself off from all warm and living human contacts.

Edward said again, 'You're so warm, Midge.' And suddenly with a glad, proud confidence she thought, 'But that's what he *wants*—that's what I can give him!' They were all cold, the Angkatells. Even Henrietta had something in her of the will-o'-the-wisp, of the elusive fairy coldness in the Angkatell blood. Let Edward love Henrietta as an intangible and unpossessable dream. It was warmth, permanence, stability that was his real need. It was daily companionship and love and laughter at Ainswick.

She thought, 'What Edward needs is someone to light a fire on his hearth—and *I* am the person to do that.'

Edward looked up. He saw Midge's face bending over him, the warm colouring of the skin, the generous mouth, the steady eyes and the dark hair that lay back from her forehead like two wings.

He saw Henrietta always as a projection from the past. In the grown woman he sought and wanted only to see the seventeen-year-old girl he had first loved. But now, looking up at Midge, he had a queer sense of seeing a continuous Midge. He saw the schoolgirl with her winged hair springing back into two pigtails, he saw its dark waves framing her face now, and he saw exactly how those

The Hollow

wings would look when the hair was not dark any longer but grey.

'Midge,' he thought, 'is *real*. The only real thing I have ever known...' He felt the warmth of her, and the strength—dark, positive, alive, *real* ! 'Midge,' he thought, 'is the rock on which I can build my life.'

He said, 'Darling Midge, I love you so, never leave me again.'

She bent down to him and he felt the warmth of her lips on his, felt her love enveloping him, shielding him, and happiness flowered in that cold desert where he had lived alone so long.

Suddenly Midge said with a shaky laugh:

'Look, Edward, a blackbeetle has come out to look at us. Isn't he a *nice* blackbeetle? I never thought I could like a blackbeetle so much!'

She added dreamily, 'How odd life is. Here we are sitting on the floor in a kitchen that still smells of gas all amongst the blackbeetles, and feeling that it's heaven.'

He murmured dreamily, 'I could stay here for ever.'

'We'd better go and get some sleep. It's four o'clock. How on earth are we to explain that broken window to Lucy?'

Fortunately, Midge reflected, Lucy was an extraordinarily easy person to explain things to!

Taking a leaf out of Lucy's own book, Midge went into her room at six o'clock.

She made a bald statement of fact.

'Edward went down and put his head in the gas oven in the night,' she said. 'Fortunately I heard him, and went down after him. I broke the window because I couldn't get it open quickly.'

Lucy, Midge had to admit, was wonderful.

She smiled sweetly with no sign of surprise.

'Dear Midge,' she said, 'you are always so practical. I'm sure you will always be the greatest comfort to Edward.'

After Midge had gone, Lady Angkatell lay thinking. Then she got up and went into her husband's room, which for once was unlocked.

'Henry.'

'My dear Lucy! It's not cockcrow yet.'

'No, but listen, Henry, this is really important. We must have electricity installed to cook by and get rid of that gas stove.'

'Why, it's quite satisfactory, isn't it?'

'Oh, yes, dear. But it's the sort of thing that gives people ideas, and everybody mightn't be as practical as dear Midge.'

She flitted elusively away. Sir Henry turned over with a grunt. Presently he awoke with a start just as he was dozing off. 'Did I dream it,' he murmured, 'or did Lucy come in and start talking about gas stoves?'

Outside in the passage, Lady Angkatell went into the bathroom and put a kettle on the gas ring. Sometimes, she knew, people liked an early cup of tea. Fired with self-approval, she returned to bed and lay back on her pillows, pleased with life and with herself.

Edward and Midge at Ainswick—the inquest over. She would go and talk to M. Poirot again. A nice little man...

Suddenly another idea flashed into her head. She sat upright in bed. 'I wonder now,' she speculated, 'if she has thought of *that*.'

She got out of bed and drifted along the passage to Henrietta's room, beginning her remarks as usual long before she was within earshot.

The Hollow

'—and it suddenly came to me, dear, that you *might* have overlooked that.'

Henrietta murmured sleepily, 'For heaven's sake, Lucy, the birds aren't up yet!'

'Oh, I know, dear, it *is* rather early, but it seems to have been a very disturbed night—Edward and the gas stove and Midge and the kitchen window—and thinking of what to say to M. Poirot and everything—'

'I'm sorry, Lucy, but everything you say sounds like complete gibberish. Can't it wait?'

'It was only the holster, dear. I thought, you know, that you might not have thought about the holster.'

'Holster?' Henrietta sat up in bed. She was suddenly wide awake. 'What's this about a holster?'

'That revolver of Henry's was in a holster, you know. And the holster hasn't been found. And of course nobody may think of it—but on the other hand somebody might—'

Henrietta swung herself out of bed. She said:

'One always forgets something—that's what they say! And it's true!'

Lady Angkatell went back to her room.

She got into bed and quickly went fast asleep.

The kettle on the gas ring boiled and went on boiling.

CHAPTER 29

Gerda rolled over to the side of the bed and sat up.

Her head felt a little better now but she was still glad that she hadn't gone with the others on the picnic. It was peaceful and almost comforting to be alone in the house for a bit.

Elsie, of course, had been very kind—very kind—especially at first. To begin with, Gerda had been urged to stay in bed for breakfast, trays had been brought up to her. Everybody urged her to sit in the most comfortable armchair, to put her feet up, not to do anything at all strenuous.

They were all so sorry for her about John. She had stayed cowering gratefully in that protective dim haze. She hadn't wanted to think, or to feel, or to remember.

But now, every day, she felt it coming nearer—she'd have to start living again, to decide what to do, where to live. Already Elsie was showing a shade of impatience in her manner. 'Oh, Gerda, don't be so *slow*!'

It was all the same as it had been—long ago, before John came and took her away. They all thought her slow and stupid. There was nobody to say, as John had said, 'I'll look after you.'

The Hollow

Her head ached and Gerda thought, 'I'll make myself some tea.'

She went down to the kitchen and put the kettle on. It was nearly boiling when she heard a ring at the front door.

The maids had been given the day out. Gerda went to the door and opened it. She was astonished to see Henrietta's rakish-looking car drawn up to the kerb and Henrietta herself standing on the doorstep.

'Why, Henrietta!' she exclaimed. She fell back a step or two. 'Come in. I'm afraid my sister and the children are out but—'

Henrietta cut her short. 'Good, I'm glad. I wanted to get you alone. Listen, Gerda, *what did you do with the holster?*'

Gerda stopped. Her eyes looked suddenly vacant and uncomprehending. She said, 'Holster?'

Then she opened a door on the right of the hall.

'You'd better come in here. I'm afraid it's rather dusty. You see, we haven't had much time this morning.'

Henrietta interrupted again urgently.

She said: 'Listen, Gerda, you've got to tell me. Apart from the holster everything's all right—absolutely watertight. There's nothing to connect you with the business. I found the revolver where you'd shoved it into that thicket by the pool. I hid it in a place where you couldn't possibly have put it—and there are fingerprints on it which they'll never identify. So there's only the holster. I must know what you did with that?'

She paused, praying desperately that Gerda would react quickly.

She had no idea why she had this vital sense of urgency, but it was there. Her car had not been followed—she had made sure of that. She had started on the London road, had filled up at a garage and had mentioned that she was on her way to London. Then, a little farther on, she had swung across country until she had reached a main road leading south to the coast.

Gerda was still staring at her. The trouble with Gerda, thought Henrietta, was that she was so slow.

'If you've still got it, Gerda, you must give it to me. I'll get rid of it somehow. It's the only possible thing, you see, that can connect you now with John's death. *Have* you got it?'

There was a pause and then Gerda slowly nodded her head.

'Didn't you know it was madness to keep it?' Henrietta could hardly conceal her impatience.

'I forgot about it. It was up in my room.'

She added: 'When the police came up to Harley Street I cut it in pieces and put it in the bag with my leather work.'

Henrietta said: 'That was clever of you.'

Gerda said: 'I'm not quite so stupid as everybody thinks.' She put her hand up to her throat. She said, 'John—*John*!' Her voice broke.

Henrietta said, 'I know, my dear, I know.'

Gerda said, 'But you can't know... John wasn't—he wasn't—' She stood there, dumb and strangely pathetic. She raised her eyes suddenly to Henrietta's face. 'It was all a lie—everything! All the things I thought he was. I saw his face when he followed that woman out that evening. Veronica Cray. I knew he'd cared for her, of course, years ago before he married me, but I thought it was all over.'

Henrietta said gently:

'But it *was* all over.'

Gerda shook her head.

'No. She came there and pretended that she hadn't seen John for years—but I saw John's face. He went out with her. I went up to bed. I lay there trying to read—I tried to read that detective story that John was reading. And John didn't come. And at last I went out...'

Her eyes seemed to be turning inwards, seeing the scene.

'It was moonlight. I went along the path to the swimming pool. There was a light in the pavilion. They were *there*—John and that woman.'

Henrietta made a faint sound.

Gerda's face had changed. It had none of its usual slightly vacant amiability. It was remorseless, implacable.

'I'd trusted John. I'd believed in him—as though he were God. I thought he was the noblest man in the world. I thought he was everything that was fine and noble. And it was all a *lie*! I was left with nothing at all. I—I'd *worshipped* John!'

Henrietta was gazing at her fascinated. For here, before her eyes, was what she had guessed at and brought to life, carving it out of wood. Here was The Worshipper. Blind devotion thrown back on itself, disillusioned, dangerous.

Gerda said, 'I couldn't bear it! I had to kill him! I *had* to—you do see that, Henrietta?'

She said it quite conversationally, in an almost friendly tone.

'And I knew I must be careful because the police are very clever. But then I'm not really as stupid as people think! If you're very slow and just stare, people think you don't take things in—and sometimes, underneath, you're laughing at them! I knew I could kill John and nobody would know because I'd read in that detective story about the police being able to tell which gun a bullet has been fired from. Sir Henry had shown me how to load and fire a revolver that afternoon. I'd take *two* revolvers. I'd shoot John with one and then hide it, and let people find me holding the other, and first they'd think *I'd* shot him and then they'd find he couldn't have been killed with that revolver and so they'd say I hadn't done it after all!'

She nodded her head triumphantly.

'But I forgot about the leather thing. It was in the drawer in my bedroom. What do you call it, a holster? Surely the police won't bother about that *now*!'

'They might,' said Henrietta. 'You'd better give it to me, and I'll take it away with me. Once it's out of your hands, you're quite safe.'

She sat down. She felt suddenly unutterably weary.

Gerda said, 'You don't look well. I was just making tea.'

She went out of the room. Presently she came back with a tray. On it was a teapot, milk jug and two cups. The milk jug had slopped over because it was over-full. Gerda put the tray down and poured out a cup of tea and handed it to Henrietta.

'Oh, dear,' she said, dismayed, 'I don't believe the kettle can have been boiling.'

'It's quite all right,' said Henrietta. 'Go and get that holster, Gerda.'

Gerda hesitated and then went out of the room. Henrietta leant forward and put her arms on the table and her head down on them. She was so tired, so dreadfully tired. But

The Hollow

now it was nearly done. Gerda would be safe, as John had wanted her to be safe.

She sat up, pushed the hair off her forehead and drew the teacup towards her. Then at a sound in the doorway she looked up. Gerda had been quite quick for once.

But it was Hercule Poirot who stood in the doorway.

'The front door was open,' he remarked as he advanced to the table, 'so I took the liberty of walking in.'

'You!' said Henrietta. 'How did you get here?'

'When you left The Hollow so suddenly, naturally I knew where you would go. I hired a very fast car and came straight here.'

'I see.' Henrietta sighed. 'You would.'

'You should not drink that tea,' said Poirot, taking the cup from her and replacing it on the tray. 'Tea that has not been made with boiling water is not good to drink.'

'Does a little thing like boiling water really matter?'

Poirot said gently, 'Everything matters.'

There was a sound behind him and Gerda came into the room. She had a workbag in her hands. Her eyes went from Poirot's face to Henrietta's.

Henrietta said quickly:

'I'm afraid, Gerda, I'm rather a suspicious character. M. Poirot seems to have been shadowing me. He thinks that I killed John—but he can't prove it.'

She spoke slowly and deliberately. So long as Gerda did not give herself away.

Gerda said vaguely, 'I'm so sorry. Will you have some tea, M. Poirot?'

Agatha Christie

'No, thank you, Madame.'

Gerda sat down behind the tray. She began to talk in her apologetic, conversational way.

'I'm so sorry that everybody is out. My sister and the children have all gone for a picnic. I didn't feel very well, so they left me behind.'

'I am sorry, Madame.'

Gerda lifted a teacup and drank.

'It is all so very worrying. Everything is so worrying. You see, John always arranged *everything* and now John is gone...' Her voice tailed off. 'Now John is gone.'

Her gaze, piteous, bewildered, went from one to the other.

'I don't know what to do without John. John looked after me. He took care of me. Now he is gone, everything is gone. And the children—they ask me questions and I can't answer them properly. I don't know what to say to Terry. He keeps saying, "Why was Father killed?" Some day, of course, he will find out why. Terry always has to *know*. What puzzles me is that he always asks *why*, not *who*!'

Gerda leaned back in her chair. Her lips were very blue. She said stiffly:

'I feel—not very well—if John—John—'

Poirot came round the table to her and eased her sideways down in the chair. Her head dropped forward. He bent and lifted her eyelid. Then he straightened up.

'An easy and comparatively painless death.'

Henrietta stared at him.

'Heart? No.' Her mind leaped forward. 'Something in the tea. Something she put there herself. She chose that way out?'

The Hollow

Poirot shook his head gently.

'Oh, no, it was meant for *you*. It was in *your* teacup.'

'For *me*?' Henrietta's voice was incredulous. 'But I was trying to help her.'

'That did not matter. Have you not seen a dog caught in a trap—it sets its teeth into anyone who touches it. She saw only that you knew her secret and so you, too, must die.'

Henrietta said slowly:

'And you made me put the cup back on the tray—you meant—you meant *her*—'

Poirot interrupted her quietly:

'No, no, Mademoiselle. I did not *know* that there was anything in your teacup. I only knew that there *might* be. And when the cup was on the tray it was an even chance if she drank from that or the other—if you call it chance. I say myself that an end such as this is merciful. For her—and for two innocent children.'

He said gently to Henrietta: 'You are very tired, are you not?'

She nodded. She asked him, 'When did you guess?'

'I do not know exactly. The scene was set; I felt that from the first. But I did not realize for a long time that it was set *by Gerda Christow*—that her attitude was stagey because she was, actually, acting a part. I was puzzled by the simplicity and at the same time the complexity. I recognized fairly soon that it was *your* ingenuity that I was fighting against, and that you were being aided and abetted by your relations as soon as they understood what you wanted done!' He paused and added: 'Why did *you* want it done?'

Agatha Christie

'Because John asked me to! That's what he meant when he said "*Henrietta.*" It was all there in that one word. He was asking me to protect Gerda. You see, he loved Gerda. I think he loved Gerda much better than he ever knew he did. Better than Veronica Cray. Better than me. Gerda *belonged* to him, and John liked things that belonged to him. He knew that if anyone could protect Gerda from the consequences of what she'd done, I could. And he knew that I would do anything he wanted, because I loved him.'

'And you started at once,' said Poirot grimly.

'Yes, the first thing I could think of was to get the revolver away from her and drop it in the pool. That would obscure the fingerprint business. When I discovered later that he had been shot with a different gun, I went out to look for it, and naturally found it at once because I knew just the sort of place Gerda would have put it. I was only a minute or two ahead of Inspector Grange's men.'

She paused and then went on, 'I kept it with me in that satchel bag of mine until I could take it up to London. Then I hid it in the studio until I could bring it back, and put it where the police would not find it.'

'The clay horse,' murmured Poirot.

'How did you know? Yes, I put it in a sponge bag and wired the armature round it, and then slapped up the clay model round it. After all, the police couldn't very well destroy an artist's masterpiece, could they? What made you know where it was?'

'The fact that you chose to model a horse. The horse of Troy was the unconscious association in your mind. But the fingerprints—how did you manage the fingerprints?'

The Hollow

'An old blind man who sells matches in the street. He didn't know what it was I asked him to hold for a moment while I got some money out!'

Poirot looked at her for a moment.

'*C'est formidable!*' he murmured. 'You are one of the best antagonists, Mademoiselle, that I have ever had.'

'It's been dreadfully tiring always trying to keep one move ahead of *you*!'

'I know. I began to realize the truth as soon as I saw that the pattern was always designed not to implicate any one person but to implicate *everyone*—other than Gerda Christow. Every indication always pointed *away* from her. You deliberately planted Ygdrasil to catch my attention and bring yourself under suspicion. Lady Angkatell, who knew perfectly what you were doing, amused herself by leading poor Inspector Grange in one direction after another. David, Edward, herself.

'Yes, there is only one thing to do if you want to clear a person from suspicion who is actually guilty. You must suggest guilt elsewhere but never localize it. That is why every clue *looked* promising and then petered out and ended in nothing.'

Henrietta looked at the figure huddled pathetically in the chair. She said, 'Poor Gerda.'

'Is that what you have felt all along?'

'I think so. Gerda loved John terribly, but she didn't want to love him for what he was. She built up a pedestal for him and attributed every splendid and noble and unselfish characteristic to him. And if you cast down an idol, *there's nothing left.*' She paused and then went on: 'But John was something much finer than an idol on a pedestal. He was a real, living, vital human being. He was generous and warm and alive, and he was a great doctor—yes, a *great* doctor. And he's dead, and the world has lost a very great man. And I have lost the only man I shall ever love.'

Poirot put his hand gently on her shoulder. He said:

'But you are one of those who can live with a sword in their hearts—who can go on and smile—'

Henrietta looked up at him. Her lips twisted into a bitter smile.

'That's a little melodramatic, isn't it?'

'It is because I am a foreigner and I like to use fine words.'

Henrietta said suddenly:

'You have been very kind to me.'

'That is because I have admired you always very much.'

'M. Poirot, what are we going to do? About Gerda, I mean.'

Poirot drew the raffia workbag towards him. He turned out its contents, scraps of brown suède and other coloured leathers. There were some pieces of thick shiny brown leather. Poirot fitted them together.

'The holster. I take this. And poor Madame Christow, she was overwrought, her husband's death was too much for her. It will be brought in that she took her life whilst of unsound mind—'

Henrietta said slowly:

'And no one will ever know what really happened?'

'I think one person will know. Dr Christow's son. I think that one day he will come to me and ask me for the truth.'

The Hollow

'But you won't tell him,' cried Henrietta.

'Yes. I shall tell him.'

'Oh, *no*!'

'You do not understand. To you it is unbearable that anyone should be hurt. But to some minds there is something more unbearable still—not to *know*. You heard the poor woman just a little while ago say: "Terry always has to *know*." To the scientific mind, truth comes first. Truth, however bitter, can be accepted, and woven into a design for living.'

Henrietta got up.

'Do you want me here, or had I better go?'

'It would be better if you went, I think.'

She nodded. Then she said, more to herself than to him:

'Where shall I go? What shall I do—without John?'

'You are speaking like Gerda Christow. You will know where to go and what to do.'

'Shall I? I'm so tired, M. Poirot, so tired.'

He said gently:

'Go, my child. Your place is with the living. I will stay here with the dead.'

CHAPTER 30

As she drove towards London, the two phrases echoed through Henrietta's mind. 'What shall I do? Where shall I go?'

For the last few weeks she had been strung up, excited, never relaxing for a moment. She had had a task to perform—a task laid on her by John. But now that was over—she had failed—or succeeded? One could look at it either way. But however one looked at it, the task was over. And she experienced the terrible weariness of the reaction.

Her mind went back to the words she had spoken to Edward that night on the terrace—the night of John's death—the night when she had gone along to the pool and into the pavilion and had deliberately, by the light of a match, drawn Ygdrasil upon the iron table. Purposeful, planning—not yet able to sit down and mourn—mourn for her dead. 'I should like,' she had said to Edward, 'to grieve for John.'

But she had not dared to relax then—not dared to let sorrow take command over her.

But now she could grieve. Now she had all the time there was.

She said under her breath, 'John... John.'

The Hollow

Bitterness and black rebellion broke over her.

She thought, 'I wish I'd drunk that cup of tea.'

Driving the car soothed her, gave her strength for the moment. But soon she would be in London. Soon she would put the car in the garage and go along to the empty studio. Empty since John would never sit there again bullying her, being angry with her, loving her more than he wanted to love her, telling her eagerly about Ridgeway's Disease—about his triumphs and despairs, about Mrs Crabtree and St Christopher's.

And suddenly, with a lifting of the dark pall that lay over her mind, she thought:

'Of course. That's where I will go. To St Christopher's.'

Lying in her narrow hospital bed, old Mrs Crabtree peered up at her visitor out of rheumy, twinkling eyes.

She was exactly as John had described her, and Henrietta felt a sudden warmth, a lifting of the spirit. This was real—this would last! Here, for a little space, she had found John again.

'The pore doctor. Orful, ain't it?' Mrs Crabtree was saying. There was relish in her voice as well as regret, for Mrs Crabtree loved life; and sudden deaths, particularly murders or deaths in childbed, were the richest parts of the tapestry of life. 'Getting 'imself bumped off like that! Turned my stomach right over, it did, when I 'eard. I read all about it in the papers. Sister let me 'ave all she could get 'old of. Reely nice about it, she was. There was pictures and everythink. That swimming pool and all. 'Is wife leaving the inquest, pore thing, and that Lady Angkatell what the

Agatha Christie

swimming pool belonged to. Lots of pictures. Real mystery the 'ole thing, weren't it?'

Henrietta was not repelled by her ghoulish enjoyment. She liked it because she knew that John himself would have liked it. If he had to die he would much prefer old Mrs Crabtree to get a kick out of it, than to sniff and shed tears.

'All I 'ope is that they catch 'ooever done it and 'ang 'im,' continued Mrs Crabtree vindictively. 'They don't 'ave 'angings in public like they used to once—more's the pity. I've always thought I'd like to go to an 'anging. And I'd go double quick, if you understand me, to see 'ooever killed the doctor 'anged! Real wicked, 'e must 'ave been. Why, the doctor was one in a thousand. Ever so clever, 'e was! And a nice way with 'im! Got you laughing whether you wanted to or not. The things 'e used to say sometimes! I'd 'ave done anythink for the doctor, I would!'

'Yes,' said Henrietta, 'he was a very clever man. He was a great man.'

'Think the world of 'im in the 'orspital, they do! All them nurses. *And* 'is patients! Always felt you were going to get well when 'e'd been along.'

'So you are going to get well,' said Henrietta.

The little shrewd eyes clouded for a moment.

'I'm not so sure about that, ducks. I've got that mealy-mouthed young fellow with the spectacles now. Quite different to Dr Christow. Never a laugh! 'E was a one, Dr Christow was—always up to his jokes! Given me some norful times, 'e 'as, with this treatment of 'is. "I carn't stand any more of in, Doctor," I'd say to him, and "Yes, you can,

The Hollow

Mrs Crabtree," 'e'd say to me. "You're tough, you are. You can take it. Going to make medical 'istory, you and I are." And he'd jolly you along like. Do anything for the doctor, I would 'ave! Expected a lot of you, 'e did, but you felt you couldn't let him down, if you know what I mean.'

'I know,' said Henrietta.

The little sharp eyes peered at her.

'Excuse me, dearie, you're not the doctor's wife by any chance?'

'No,' said Henrietta, 'I'm just a friend.'

'*I* see,' said Mrs Crabtree.

Henrietta thought that she did see.

'What made you come along if you don't mind me asking?'

'The doctor used to talk to me a lot about you—and about his new treatment. I wanted to see how you were.'

'I'm slipping back—that's what I'm doing.'

Henrietta cried:

'But you mustn't slip back! You've got to get well.'

Mrs Crabtree grinned.

'*I* don't want to peg out, don't you think it!'

'Well, fight then! Dr Christow said you were a fighter.'

'Did 'e now?' Mrs Crabtree lay still a minute, then she said slowly:

'Ooever shot 'im it's a wicked shame! There aren't many of 'is sort.'

We shall not see his like again. The words passed through Henrietta's mind. Mrs Crabtree was regarding her keenly.

'Keep your pecker up, dearie,' she said. She added: "E 'ad a nice funeral, I 'ope.'

305

'He had a lovely funeral,' said Henrietta obligingly.

'Ar! I wish I could of gorn to it!'

Mrs Crabtree sighed.

'Be going to me own funeral next, I expect.'

'No,' cried Henrietta. 'You mustn't let go. You said just now that Dr Christow told you that you and he were going to make medical history. Well, you've got to carry on by yourself. The treatment's just the same. You've got to have the guts for two—you've got to make medical history by yourself—for him.'

Mrs Crabtree looked at her for a moment or two.

'Sounds a bit grand! I'll do my best, ducks. Carn't say more than that.'

Henrietta got up and took her hand.

'Goodbye. I'll come and see you again if I may.'

'Yes, do. It'll do me good to talk about the doctor a bit.' The bawdy twinkle came into her eye again. 'Proper man in every kind of way, Dr Christow.'

'Yes,' said Henrietta. 'He was.'

The old woman said:

'Don't fret, ducks—what's gorn's gorn. You can't 'ave it back.'

Mrs Crabtree and Hercule Poirot, Henrietta thought, expressed the same idea in different language.

She drove back to Chelsea, put away the car in the garage and walked slowly to the studio.

'Now,' she thought, 'it has come. The moment I have been dreading—the moment when I am alone.

'Now I can put it off no longer. Now grief is here with me.'

What had she said to Edward? 'I should like to grieve for John.'

She dropped down on a chair and pushed back the hair from her face.

Alone—empty—destitute. This awful emptiness.

The tears pricked at her eyes, flowed slowly down her cheeks.

Grief, she thought, grief for John. Oh, John—John.

Remembering, remembering—his voice, sharp with pain:

'If I were dead, the first thing you'd do, with the tears streaming down your face, would be to start modelling some damn' mourning woman or some figure of grief.'

She stirred uneasily. Why had that thought come into her head?

Grief—Grief... A veiled figure—its outline barely perceptible—its head cowled.

Alabaster.

She could see the lines of it—tall, elongated, its sorrow hidden, revealed only by the long, mournful lines of the drapery.

Sorrow, emerging from clear, transparent alabaster.

'If I were dead...'

And suddenly bitterness came over her full tide!

She thought, *'That's what I am*! John was right. I cannot love—I cannot mourn—not with the whole of me.

'It's Midge, it's people like Midge who are the salt of the earth.'

Midge and Edward at Ainswick.

That was reality—strength—warmth.

'But I,' she thought, 'am not a whole person. I belong not to myself, but to something outside me. I cannot grieve

Agatha Christie

for my dead. Instead I must take my grief and make it into a figure of alabaster...'

Exhibit No. 58. 'Grief'. Alabaster. Miss Henrietta Savernake...

She said under her breath:

'John, forgive me, forgive me, for what I can't help doing.'

The Agatha Christie Collection

THE HERCULE POIROT MYSTERIES
Match your wits with the famous Belgian detective.

- *The Mysterious Affair at Styles*
- *The Murder on the Links*
- *Poirot Investigates*
- *The Murder of Roger Ackroyd*
- *The Big Four*
- *The Mystery of the Blue Train*
- *Black Coffee*
- *Peril at End House*
- *Lord Edgware Dies*
- *Murder on the Orient Express*
- *Three Act Tragedy*
- *Death in the Clouds*
- *The ABC Murders*
- *Murder in Mesopotamia*
- *Cards on the Table*
- *Murder in the Mews*
- *Dumb Witness*
- *Death on the Nile*
- *Appointment With Death*
- *Hercule Poirot's Christmas*
- *Sad Cypress*
- *One, Two, Buckle My Shoe*
- *Evil Under the Sun*
- *Five Little Pigs*
- *The Hollow*
- *The Labours of Hercules*
- *Taken at the Flood*
- *Mrs McGinty's Dead*
- *After the Funeral*
- *Hickory Dickory Dock*
- *Dead Man's Folly*
- *Cat Among the Pigeons*
- *The Adventure of the Christmas Pudding*
- *The Clocks*
- *Third Girl*
- *Hallowe'en Party*
- *Elephants Can Remember*
- *Poirot's Early Cases*
- *Curtain: Poirot's Last Case*

Find out all about the Queen of Crime
and her stories at **www.agathachristie.com**

Keep up to date with launches and news from the world of Agatha Christie and discuss all things Agatha on the forum!

Shop online for books, audiobooks, DVDs and other merchandise

/agathachristie /officialagathachristie /QueenofCrime

For a touch of Christie mystery, scan the code!

The *Agatha Christie* Collection

THE MISS MARPLE MYSTERIES
Join the legendary spinster sleuth from St Mary Mead in solving murders far and wide.

The Murder at the Vicarage
The Thirteen Problems
The Body in the Library
The Moving Finger
A Murder is Announced
They Do It With Mirrors
A Pocket Full of Rye

4.50 from Paddington
The Mirror Crack'd from Side to Side
A Caribbean Mystery
At Bertram's Hotel
Nemesis
Sleeping Murder
Miss Marple's Final Cases

THE TOMMY & TUPPENCE MYSTERIES
Jump on board with the entertaining crime-solving couple from Young Adventurers Ltd.

The Secret Adversary
Partners in Crime
N or M?
By the Pricking of My Thumbs
Postern of Fate

Find out all about the Queen of Crime
and her stories at **www.agathachristie.com**

Keep up to date with launches and news from the world
of Agatha Christie and discuss all things Agatha on the forum!

Shop online for books, audiobooks, DVDs and other merchandise

For a touch of Christie mystery, scan the code!

/agathachristie   /officialagathachristie   /QueenofCrime

The *Agatha Christie* Collection

Don't miss a single one of Agatha Christie's classic novels and short story collections.

The Man in the Brown Suit

The Secret of Chimneys

The Seven Dials Mystery

The Mysterious Mr Quin

The Sittaford Mystery

The Hound of Death

The Listerdale Mystery

Why Didn't They Ask Evans?

Parker Pyne Investigates

Murder Is Easy

And Then There Were None

Death Comes as the End

Sparkling Cyanide

Crooked House

They Came to Baghdad

Destination Unknown

Spider's Web

The Unexpected Guest

Ordeal by Innocence

The Pale Horse

Endless Night

Passenger to Frankfurt

Find out all about the Queen of Crime
and her stories at **www.agathachristie.com**

Keep up to date with launches and news from the world
of Agatha Christie and discuss all things Agatha on the forum!

Shop online for books, audiobooks, DVDs and other merchandise

/agathachristie   /officialagathachristie   /QueenofCrime

For a touch of Christie mystery, scan the code!

Agatha Christie
Short stories for your E-reader
HERCULE POIROT

The Jewel Robbery at the Grand Metropolitan

The King of Clubs

The Disappearance of Mr Davenheim

The Plymouth Express

The Adventure of the 'Western Star'

The Tragedy of Marsdon Manor

The Kidnapped Prime Minister

The Million Dollar Bond Robbery

The Adventure of the Cheap Flat

The Mystery of Hunter's Lodge

The Chocolate Box

The Adventure of the Egyptian Tomb

The Veiled Lady

The Adventure of Johnny Waverley

The Market Basing Mystery

The Adventure of the Italian Nobleman

The Case of the Missing Will

The Incredible Theft

The Adventure of the Clapham Cook

The Lost Mine

The Cornish Mystery

The Double Clue

The Adventure of the Christmas Pudding

The Lemesurier Inheritance

The Under Dog

Triangle at Rhodes

Yellow Iris

The Dream

Four-and-Twenty Blackbirds

Poirot and the Regatta Mystery

The Mystery of the Baghdad Chest

The Second Gong

Find out all about the Queen of Crime and her stories at **www.agathachristie.com**

Keep up to date with launches and news from the world of Agatha Christie and discuss all things Agatha on the forum!

Shop online for books, audiobooks, DVDs and other merchandise

/agathachristie /officialagathachristie /QueenofCrime

For a touch of Christie mystery, scan the code!

Agatha Christie

THE LIFE OF A LEGEND
Travel Memoirs

The Grand Tour

Unpublished for 90 years, Agatha Christie's extensive and evocative letters and photographs from her year-long round-the-world trip to South Africa, Australia, New Zealand, Canada and America as part of the British trade mission for the famous 1924 Empire Exhibition.

Come Tell Me How You Live

Agatha Christie's personal memoirs about her travels to Syria and Iraq in the 1930s with her archaeologist husband Max Mallowan, where she worked on the digs and wrote some of her most evocative novels.

Find out all about the Queen of Crime and her stories at **www.agathachristie.com**

Keep up to date with launches and news from the world of Agatha Christie and discuss all things Agatha on the forum!

Shop online for books, audiobooks, DVDs and other merchandise

/agathachristie /officialagathachristie /QueenofCrime

For a touch of Christie mystery, scan the code!

CAT AMONG THE PIGEONS

THE AGATHA CHRISTIE COLLECTION

Mysteries
The Man in the Brown Suit
The Secret of Chimneys
The Seven Dials Mystery
The Mysterious Mr Quin
The Sittaford Mystery
The Hound of Death
The Listerdale Mystery
Why Didn't They Ask Evans?
Parker Pyne Investigates
Murder Is Easy
And Then There Were None
Towards Zero
Death Comes as the End
Sparkling Cyanide
Crooked House
They Came to Baghdad
Destination Unknown
Spider's Web*
The Unexpected Guest*
Ordeal by Innocence
The Pale Horse
Endless Night
Passenger To Frankfurt
Problem at Pollensa Bay
While the Light Lasts

Poirot
The Mysterious Affair at Styles
The Murder on the Links
Poirot Investigates
The Murder of Roger Ackroyd
The Big Four
The Mystery of the Blue Train
Black Coffee*
Peril at End House
Lord Edgware Dies
Murder on the Orient Express
Three Act Tragedy
Death in the Clouds
The ABC Murders
Murder in Mesopotamia
Cards on the Table
Murder in the Mews
Dumb Witness
Death on the Nile
Appointment With Death
Hercule Poirot's Christmas
Sad Cypress
One, Two, Buckle My Shoe
Evil Under the Sun
Five Little Pigs
The Hollow
The Labours of Hercules
Taken at the Flood
Mrs McGinty's Dead
After the Funeral
Hickory Dickory Dock
Dead Man's Folly
Cat Among the Pigeons
The Adventure of the Christmas Pudding
The Clocks
Third Girl
Hallowe'en Party
Elephants Can Remember
Poirot's Early Cases
Curtain: Poirot's Last Case

Marple
The Murder at the Vicarage
The Thirteen Problems
The Body in the Library
The Moving Finger
A Murder Is Announced
They Do It With Mirrors
A Pocket Full of Rye
4.50 from Paddington
The Mirror Crack'd from Side to Side
A Caribbean Mystery
At Bertram's Hotel
Nemesis
Sleeping Murder
Miss Marple's Final Cases

Tommy & Tuppence
The Secret Adversary
Partners in Crime
N or M?
By the Pricking of My Thumbs
Postern of Fate

Published as Mary Westmacott
Giant's Bread
Unfinished Portrait
Absent in the Spring
The Rose and the Yew Tree
A Daughter's a Daughter
The Burden

Memoirs
An Autobiography
Come, Tell Me How You Live
The Grand Tour

Plays and Stories
Akhnaton
The Mousetrap and Other Plays
The Floating Admiral (contributor)
Star Over Bethlehem

* novelized by Charles Osborne

Agatha Christie

Cat Among the Pigeons

HarperCollinsPublishers

HarperCollins*Publishers* Ltd
1 London Bridge Street
London SE1 9GF
www.harpercollins.co.uk

This paperback edition 2014

10

First published in Great Britain by
Collins 1959

Agatha Christie® Poirot® Cat Among Pigeons™
Copyright © 1959 Agatha Christie Limited. All rights reserved.
www.agathachristie.com

A catalogue record for this book is
available from the British Library

ISBN 978-0-00-752756-4 (PB)
ISBN 978-0-00-825574-9 (POD PB)

Set in Sabon by Palimpsest Book Production Ltd., Falkirk, Stirlingshire

Printed and bound by
CPI Group (UK) Ltd, Croydon, CR0 4YY

All rights reserved. No part of this publication may be
reproduced, stored in a retrieval system, or transmitted,
in any form or by any means, electronic, mechanical,
photocopying, recording or otherwise, without the prior
permission of the publishers.

This book is sold subject to the condition that it shall not,
by way of trade or otherwise, be lent, re-sold, hired out or
otherwise circulated without the publisher's prior consent
in any form of binding or cover other than that in which it
is published and without a similar condition including this
condition being imposed on the subsequent purchaser.

MIX
Paper from
responsible sources
FSC
www.fsc.org FSC C007454

FSC™ is a non-profit international organisation established to promote
the responsible management of the world's forests. Products carrying the
FSC label are independently certified to assure consumers that they come
from forests that are managed to meet the social, economic and
ecological needs of present and future generations,
and other controlled sources.

Find out more about HarperCollins and the environment at
www.harpercollins.co.uk/green

For Stella and Larry Kirwan

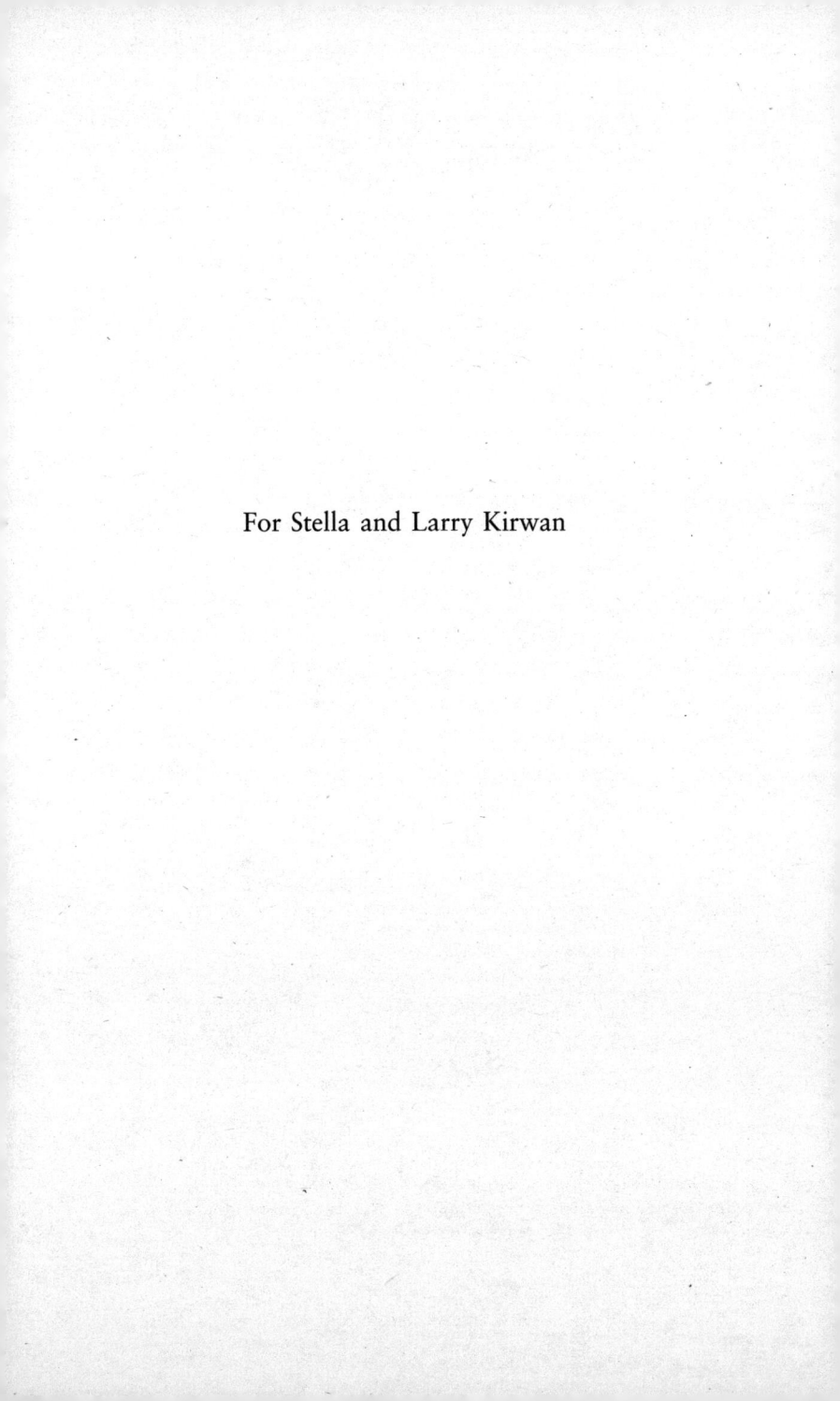

CONTENTS

Prologue Summer Term	1
1. Revolution in Ramat	19
2. The Woman on the Balcony	27
3. Introducing Mr Robinson	39
4. Return of a Traveller	54
5. Letters from Meadowbank School	69
6. Early Days	78
7. Straws in the Wind	89
8. Murder	102
9. Cat Among the Pigeons	117
10. Fantastic Story	130
11. Conference	144
12. New Lamps for Old	152
13. Catastrophe	165
14. Miss Chadwick Lies Awake	178
15. Murder Repeats Itself	188
16. The Riddle of the Sports Pavilion	196
17. Aladdin's Cave	211

18. Consultation	224
19. Consultation Continued	234
20. Conversation	243
21. Gathering Threads	252
22. Incident in Anatolia	265
23. Showdown	268
24. Poirot Explains	286
25. Legacy	298

PROLOGUE

Summer Term

It was the opening day of the summer term at Meadowbank school. The late afternoon sun shone down on the broad gravel sweep in front of the house. The front door was flung hospitably wide, and just within it, admirably suited to its Georgian proportions, stood Miss Vansittart, every hair in place, wearing an impeccably cut coat and skirt.

Some parents who knew no better had taken her for the great Miss Bulstrode herself, not knowing that it was Miss Bulstrode's custom to retire to a kind of holy of holies to which only a selected and privileged few were taken.

To one side of Miss Vansittart, operating on a slightly different plane, was Miss Chadwick, comfortable, knowledgeable, and so much a part of Meadowbank that it would have been impossible to imagine Meadowbank without her. It had never been without her. Miss Bulstrode and Miss Chadwick had started Meadowbank school together. Miss Chadwick wore pince-nez, stooped, was

Agatha Christie

dowdily dressed, amiably vague in speech, and happened to be a brilliant mathematician.

Various welcoming words and phrases, uttered graciously by Miss Vansittart, floated through the house.

'How do you do, Mrs Arnold? Well, Lydia, did you enjoy your Hellenic cruise? What a wonderful opportunity! Did you get some good photographs?

'Yes, Lady Garnett, Miss Bulstrode had your letter about the Art Classes and everything's been arranged.

'How are you, Mrs Bird?... Well? I don't think Miss Bulstrode will have time *today* to discuss the point. Miss Rowan is somewhere about if you'd like to talk to her about it?

'We've moved your bedroom, Pamela. You're in the far wing by the apple tree...

'Yes, indeed, Lady Violet, the weather has been terrible so far this spring. Is this your youngest? What is your name? Hector? What a nice aeroplane you have, Hector.

'*Très heureuse de vous voir, Madame. Ah, je regrette, ce ne serait pas possible, cette après-midi. Mademoiselle Bulstrode est tellement occupée.*

'Good afternoon, Professor. Have you been digging up some more interesting things?'

II

In a small room on the first floor, Ann Shapland, Miss Bulstrode's secretary, was typing with speed and efficiency.

Ann was a nice-looking young woman of thirty-five, with hair that fitted her like a black satin cap. She could be attractive when she wanted to be but life had taught her that efficiency and competence often paid better results and avoided painful complications. At the moment she was concentrating on being everything that a secretary to the headmistress of a famous girls' school should be.

From time to time, as she inserted a fresh sheet in her machine, she looked out of the window and registered interest in the arrivals.

'Goodness!' said Ann to herself, awed, 'I didn't know there were so many chauffeurs left in England!'

Then she smiled in spite of herself, as a majestic Rolls moved away and a very small Austin of battered age drove up. A harassed-looking father emerged from it with a daughter who looked far calmer than he did.

As he paused uncertainly, Miss Vansittart emerged from the house and took charge.

'Major Hargreaves? And this is Alison? Do come into the house. I'd like you to see Alison's room for yourself. I—'

Ann grinned and began to type again.

'Good old Vansittart, the glorified understudy,' she said to herself. 'She can copy all the Bulstrode's tricks. In fact she's word perfect!'

An enormous and almost incredibly opulent Cadillac, painted in two tones, raspberry fool and azure blue, swept (with difficulty owing to its length) into the drive and drew up behind Major the Hon. Alistair Hargreaves' ancient Austin.

Agatha Christie

The chauffeur sprang to open the door, an immense bearded, dark-skinned man, wearing a flowing aba, stepped out, a Parisian fashion plate followed and then a slim dark girl.

That's probably Princess Whatshername herself, thought Ann. Can't imagine her in school uniform, but I suppose the miracle will be apparent tomorrow...

Both Miss Vansittart and Miss Chadwick appeared on this occasion.

'They'll be taken to the Presence,' decided Ann.

Then she thought that, strangely enough, one didn't quite like making jokes about Miss Bulstrode. Miss Bulstrode was Someone.

'So you'd better mind your P.s and Q.s, my girl,' she said to herself, 'and finish these letters without making any mistakes.'

Not that Ann was in the habit of making mistakes. She could take her pick of secretarial posts. She had been P.A. to the chief executive of an oil company, private secretary to Sir Mervyn Todhunter, renowned alike for his erudition, his irritability and the illegibility of his handwriting. She numbered two Cabinet Ministers and an important Civil Servant among her employers. But on the whole, her work had always lain amongst men. She wondered how she was going to like being, as she put it herself, completely submerged in women. Well—it was all experience! And there was always Dennis! Faithful Dennis returning from Malaya, from Burma, from various parts of the world, always the same, devoted, asking her once again to marry him. Dear Dennis! But it would be very dull to be married to Dennis.

She would miss the company of men in the near future. All these schoolmistressy characters—not a man about the place, except a gardener of about eighty.

But here Ann got a surprise. Looking out of the window, she saw there was a man clipping the hedge just beyond the drive—clearly a gardener but a long way from eighty. Young, dark, good-looking. Ann wondered about him—there had been some talk of getting extra labour—but this was no yokel. Oh well, nowadays people did every kind of job. Some young man trying to get together some money for some project or other, or indeed just to keep body and soul together. But he was cutting the hedge in a very expert manner. Presumably he was a real gardener after all!

'He looks,' said Ann to herself, 'he looks as though he *might* be amusing...'

Only one more letter to do, she was pleased to note, and then she might stroll round the garden...

III

Upstairs, Miss Johnson, the matron, was busy allotting rooms, welcoming newcomers, and greeting old pupils.

She was pleased it was term time again. She never knew quite what to do with herself in the holidays. She had two married sisters with whom she stayed in turn, but they were naturally more interested in their own doings and families

Agatha Christie

than in Meadowbank. Miss Johnson, though dutifully fond of her sisters, was really only interested in Meadowbank.

Yes, it was nice that term had started—

'Miss Johnson?'

'Yes, Pamela.'

'I say, Miss Johnson. I think something's broken in my case. It's oozed all over things. I *think* it's hair oil.'

'Chut, chut!' said Miss Johnson, hurrying to help.

IV

On the grass sweep of lawn beyond the gravelled drive, Mademoiselle Blanche, the new French mistress, was walking. She looked with appreciative eyes at the powerful young man clipping the hedge.

'*Assez bien,*' thought Mademoiselle Blanche.

Mademoiselle Blanche was slender and mouselike and not very noticeable, but she herself noticed everything.

Her eyes went to the procession of cars sweeping up to the front door. She assessed them in terms of money. This Meadowbank was certainly *formidable*! She summed up mentally the profits that Miss Bulstrode must be making.

Yes, indeed! *Formidable*!

V

Miss Rich, who taught English and Geography, advanced towards the house at a rapid pace, stumbling a little now and then because, as usual, she forgot to look where she was going. Her hair, also as usual, had escaped from its bun. She had an eager ugly face.

She was saying to herself:

'To be back again! To be *here*... It seems years...' She fell over a rake, and the young gardener put out an arm and said:

'Steady, miss.'

Eileen Rich said 'Thank you,' without looking at him.

VI

Miss Rowan and Miss Blake, the two junior mistresses, were strolling towards the Sports Pavilion. Miss Rowan was thin and dark and intense, Miss Blake was plump and fair. They were discussing with animation their recent adventures in Florence: the pictures they had seen, the sculpture, the fruit blossom, and the attentions (hoped to be dishonourable) of two young Italian gentlemen.

'Of course one knows,' said Miss Blake, 'how Italians go on.'

'Uninhibited,' said Miss Rowan, who had studied Psychology as well as Economics. 'Thoroughly healthy, one feels. No repressions.'

'But Guiseppe was quite impressed when he found I taught at Meadowbank,' said Miss Blake. 'He became much more respectful at once. He has a cousin who wants to come here, but Miss Bulstrode was not sure she had a vacancy.'

'Meadowbank is a school that really counts,' said Miss

Rowan, happily. 'Really, the new Sports Pavilion looks most impressive. I never thought it would be ready in time.'

'Miss Bulstrode said it had to be,' said Miss Blake in the tone of one who has said the last word.

'Oh,' she added in a startled kind of way.

The door of the Sports Pavilion had opened abruptly, and a bony young woman with ginger-coloured hair emerged. She gave them a sharp unfriendly stare and moved rapidly away.

'That must be the new Games Mistress,' said Miss Blake. 'How uncouth!'

'*Not* a very pleasant addition to the staff,' said Miss Rowan. 'Miss Jones was always so friendly and sociable.'

'She absolutely glared at us,' said Miss Blake resentfully.

They both felt quite ruffled.

VII

Miss Bulstrode's sitting-room had windows looking out in two directions, one over the drive and lawn beyond, and another towards a bank of rhododendrons behind the house. It was quite an impressive room, and Miss Bulstrode was rather more than quite an impressive woman. She was tall, and rather noble looking, with well-dressed grey hair, grey eyes with plenty of humour in them, and a firm mouth. The success of her school (and Meadowbank was one of the most successful schools in England) was entirely due to the personality of its Headmistress. It was a very expensive school, but that was not really the point. It could be put better by saying that though you paid through the nose, you got what you paid for.

Your daughter was educated in the way you wished, and also in the way Miss Bulstrode wished, and the result of the two together seemed to give satisfaction. Owing to the high fees, Miss Bulstrode was able to employ a full staff. There was nothing mass produced about the school, but if it was individualistic, it also had discipline. Discipline without regimentation, was Miss Bulstrode's motto. Discipline, she held, was reassuring to the young, it gave them a feeling of security; regimentation gave rise to irritation. Her pupils were a varied lot. They included several foreigners of good family, often foreign royalty. There were also English girls of good family or of wealth, who wanted a training in culture and the arts, with a general knowledge of life and social facility who would be turned out agreeable, well groomed and able to take part in intelligent discussion on any subject. There were girls who wanted to work hard and pass entrance examinations, and eventually take degrees and who, to do so, needed only good teaching and special attention. There were girls who had reacted unfavourably to school life of the conventional type. But Miss Bulstrode had her rules, she did not accept morons, or juvenile delinquents, and she preferred to accept girls whose parents she liked, and girls in whom she herself saw a prospect of development. The ages of her pupils varied within wide limits. There were girls who would have been labelled in the past as 'finished', and there were girls little more than children, some of them with parents abroad,

Agatha Christie

and for whom Miss Bulstrode had a scheme of interesting holidays. The last and final court of appeal was Miss Bulstrode's own approval.

She was standing now by the chimneypiece listening to Mrs Gerald Hope's slightly whining voice. With great foresight, she had not suggested that Mrs Hope should sit down.

'Henrietta, you see, is very highly strung. Very highly strung indeed. Our doctor says—'

Miss Bulstrode nodded, with gentle reassurance, refraining from the caustic phrase she sometimes was tempted to utter.

'Don't you know, you idiot, that that is what every fool of a woman says about her child?'

She spoke with firm sympathy.

'You need have no anxiety, Mrs Hope. Miss Rowan, a member of our staff, is a fully trained psychologist. You'll be surprised, I'm sure, at the change you'll find in Henrietta' (who's a nice intelligent child, and far too good for you) 'after a term or two here.'

'Oh I know. You did wonders with the Lambeth child— absolutely wonders! So I am quite happy. And I—oh yes, I forgot. We're going to the South of France in six weeks' time. I thought I'd take Henrietta. It would make a little break for her.'

'I'm afraid that's quite impossible,' said Miss Bulstrode, briskly and with a charming smile, as though she were granting a request instead of refusing one.

'Oh! but—' Mrs Hope's weak petulant face wavered, showed temper. 'Really, I must insist. After all, she's *my* child.'

'Exactly. But it's *my* school,' said Miss Bulstrode.

'Surely I can take the child away from a school any time I like?'

'Oh yes,' said Miss Bulstrode. 'You can. Of course you can. But then, *I* wouldn't have her back.'

Mrs Hope was in a real temper now.

'Considering the size of the fees I pay here—'

'Exactly,' said Miss Bulstrode. 'You wanted my school for your daughter, didn't you? But it's take it as it is, or leave it. Like that very charming Balenciaga model you are wearing. It is Balenciaga, isn't it? It is so delightful to meet a woman with real clothes sense.'

Her hand enveloped Mrs Hope's, shook it, and imperceptibly guided her towards the door.

'Don't worry at all. Ah, here is Henrietta waiting for you.' (She looked with approval at Henrietta, a nice well-balanced intelligent child if ever there was one, and who deserved a better mother.) 'Margaret, take Henrietta Hope to Miss Johnson.'

Miss Bulstrode retired into her sitting-room and a few moments later was talking French.

'But certainly, Excellence, your niece can study modern ballroom dancing. Most important socially. And languages, also, are most necessary.'

The next arrivals were prefaced by such a gust of expensive perfume as almost to knock Miss Bulstrode backwards.

'Must pour a whole bottle of the stuff over herself every day,' Miss Bulstrode noted mentally, as she greeted the exquisitely dressed dark-skinned woman.

Agatha Christie

'*Enchantée, Madame.*'

Madame giggled very prettily.

The big bearded man in Oriental dress took Miss Bulstrode's hand, bowed over it, and said in very good English, 'I have the honour to bring to you the Princess Shaista.'

Miss Bulstrode knew all about her new pupil who had just come from a school in Switzerland, but was a little hazy as to who it was escorting her. Not the Emir himself, she decided, probably the Minister, or Chargé d'Affaires. As usual when in doubt, she used that useful title *Excellence*, and assured him that Princess Shaista would have the best of care.

Shaista was smiling politely. She was also fashionably dressed and perfumed. Her age, Miss Bulstrode knew, was fifteen, but like many Eastern and Mediterranean girls, she looked older—quite mature. Miss Bulstrode spoke to her about her projected studies and was relieved to find that she answered promptly in excellent English and without giggling. In fact, her manners compared favourably with the awkward ones of many English school girls of fifteen. Miss Bulstrode had often thought that it might be an excellent plan to send English girls abroad to the Near Eastern countries to learn courtesy and manners there. More compliments were uttered on both sides and then the room was empty again though still filled with such heavy perfume that Miss Bulstrode opened both windows to their full extent to let some of it out.

The next comers were Mrs Upjohn and her daughter Julia.

Mrs Upjohn was an agreeable young woman in the late thirties with sandy hair, freckles and an unbecoming hat which was clearly a concession to the seriousness of the occasion, since she was obviously the type of young woman who usually went hatless.

Julia was a plain freckled child, with an intelligent forehead, and an air of good humour.

The preliminaries were quickly gone through and Julia was despatched via Margaret to Miss Johnson, saying cheerfully as she went, 'So long, Mum. *Do* be careful lighting that gas heater now that I'm not there to do it.'

Miss Bulstrode turned smilingly to Mrs Upjohn, but did not ask her to sit. It was possible that, despite Julia's appearance of cheerful common-sense, her mother, too, might want to explain that her daughter was highly strung.

'Is there anything special you want to tell me about Julia?' she asked.

Mrs Upjohn replied cheerfully:

'Oh no, I don't think so. Julia's a very ordinary sort of child. Quite healthy and all that. I think she's got reasonably good brains, too, but I daresay mothers usually think that about their children, don't they?'

'Mothers,' said Miss Bulstrode grimly, 'vary!'

'It's wonderful for her to be able to come here,' said Mrs Upjohn. 'My aunt's paying for it, really, or helping. I couldn't afford it myself. But I'm awfully pleased about it. And so is Julia.' She moved to the window as she said enviously, 'How lovely your garden is. And so tidy. You must have lots of real gardeners.'

Agatha Christie

'We had three,' said Miss Bulstrode, 'but just now we're short-handed except for local labour.'

'Of course the trouble nowadays,' said Mrs Upjohn, 'is that what one calls a gardener usually isn't a gardener, just a milkman who wants to do something in his spare time, or an old man of eighty. I sometimes think—Why!' exclaimed Mrs Upjohn, still gazing out of the window— 'how extraordinary!'

Miss Bulstrode paid less attention to this sudden exclamation than she should have done. For at that moment she herself had glanced casually out of the other window which gave on to the rhododendron shrubbery, and had perceived a highly unwelcome sight, none other than Lady Veronica Carlton-Sandways, weaving her way along the path, her large black velvet hat on one side, muttering to herself and clearly in a state of advanced intoxication.

Lady Veronica was not an unknown hazard. She was a charming woman, deeply attached to her twin daughters, and very delightful when she was, as they put it, *herself*— but unfortunately at unpredictable intervals, she was not herself. Her husband, Major Carlton-Sandways, coped fairly well. A cousin lived with them, who was usually at hand to keep an eye on Lady Veronica and head her off if necessary. On Sports Day, with both Major Carlton-Sandways and the cousin in close attendance, Lady Veronica arrived completely sober and beautifully dressed and was a pattern of what a mother should be. But there were times when Lady Veronica gave her well-wishers the slip, tanked herself up and made a bee-line for her daughters to assure them of her maternal love. The twins had arrived by train early today, but no one had expected Lady Veronica.

Mrs Upjohn was still talking. But Miss Bulstrode was not listening. She was reviewing various courses of action, for she recognized that Lady Veronica was fast approaching the truculent stage. But suddenly, an answer to prayer, Miss Chadwick appeared at a brisk trot, slightly out of breath. Faithful Chaddy, thought Miss Bulstrode. Always to be relied upon, whether it was a severed artery or an intoxicated parent.

'Disgraceful,' said Lady Veronica to her loudly. 'Tried to keep me away—didn't want me to come down here—I fooled Edith all right. Went to have my rest—got out car—gave silly old Edith slip... regular old maid... no man would ever look at her twice... Had a row with police on the way... said I was unfit to drive car... nonshense... Going to tell Miss Bulstrode I'm taking the girls home—want 'em home, mother love. Wonderful thing, mother love—'

'Splendid, Lady Veronica,' said Miss Chadwick. 'We're so pleased you've come. I particularly want you to see the new Sports Pavilion. You'll love it.'

Adroitly she turned Lady Veronica's unsteady footsteps in the opposite direction, leading her away from the house.

'I expect we'll find your girls there,' she said brightly. 'Such a nice Sports Pavilion, new lockers, and a drying room for the swim suits—' their voices trailed away.

Miss Bulstrode watched. Once Lady Veronica tried to break away and return to the house, but Miss Chadwick

Agatha Christie

was a match for her. They disappeared round the corner of the rhododendrons, headed for the distant loneliness of the new Sports Pavilion.

Miss Bulstrode heaved a sigh of relief. Excellent Chaddy. So reliable! Not modern. Not brainy—apart from mathematics—but always a present help in time of trouble.

She turned with a sigh and a sense of guilt to Mrs Upjohn who had been talking happily for some time…

'… though, of course,' she was saying, 'never real cloak and dagger stuff. Not dropping by parachute, or sabotage, or being a courier. I shouldn't have been brave enough. It was mostly dull stuff. Office work. And plotting. Plotting things on a map, I mean—not the story telling kind of plotting. But of course it was exciting sometimes and it was often quite funny, as I just said—all the secret agents followed each other round and round Geneva, all knowing each other by sight, and often ending up in the same bar. I wasn't married then, of course. It was all great fun.'

She stopped abruptly with an apologetic and friendly smile.

'I'm sorry I've been talking so much. Taking up your time. When you've got such lots of people to see.'

She held out a hand, said goodbye and departed.

Miss Bulstrode stood frowning for a moment. Some instinct warned her that she had missed something that might be important.

She brushed the feeling aside. This was the opening day of summer term, and she had many more parents to see. Never had her school been more popular, more assured of success. Meadowbank was at its zenith.

There was nothing to tell her that within a few weeks Meadowbank would be plunged into a sea of trouble; that disorder, confusion and murder would reign there, that already certain events had been set in motion...

CHAPTER 1

Revolution in Ramat

About two months earlier than the first day of the summer term at Meadowbank, certain events had taken place which were to have unexpected repercussions in that celebrated girls' school.

In the Palace of Ramat, two young men sat smoking and considering the immediate future. One young man was dark, with a smooth olive face and large melancholy eyes. He was Prince Ali Yusuf, Hereditary Sheikh of Ramat, which, though small, was one of the richest states in the Middle East. The other young man was sandy haired and freckled and more or less penniless, except for the handsome salary he drew as private pilot to His Highness Prince Ali Yusuf. In spite of this difference in status, they were on terms of perfect equality. They had been at the same public school and had been friends then and ever since.

'They shot at us, Bob,' said Prince Ali almost incredulously.

Agatha Christie

'They shot at us all right,' said Bob Rawlinson.

'And they meant it. They meant to bring us down.'

'The bastards meant it all right,' said Bob grimly.

Ali considered for a moment.

'It would hardly be worth while trying again?'

'We mightn't be so lucky this time. The truth is, Ali, we've left things too late. You should have got out two weeks ago. I told you so.'

'One doesn't like to run away,' said the ruler of Ramat.

'I see your point. But remember what Shakespeare or one of these poetical fellows said about those who run away living to fight another day.'

'To think,' said the young Prince with feeling, 'of the money that has gone into making this a Welfare State. Hospitals, schools, a Health Service—'

Bob Rawlinson interrupted the catalogue.

'Couldn't the Embassy do something?'

Ali Yusuf flushed angrily.

'Take refuge in your Embassy? That, never. The extremists would probably storm the place—they wouldn't respect diplomatic immunity. Besides, if I did that, it really would be the end! Already the chief accusation against me is of being pro-Western.' He sighed. 'It is so difficult to understand.' He sounded wistful, younger than his twenty-five years. 'My grandfather was a cruel man, a real tyrant. He had hundreds of slaves and treated them ruthlessly. In his tribal wars, he killed his enemies unmercifully and executed them horribly. The mere whisper of his name made everyone turn pale. And yet—*he* is a legend still! Admired! Respected! The great

Achmed Abdullah! And I? What have I done? Built hospitals and schools, welfare, housing... all the things people are said to want. Don't they want them? Would they prefer a reign of terror like my grandfather's?'

'I expect so,' said Bob Rawlinson. 'Seems a bit unfair, but there it is.'

'But why, Bob? *Why*?'

Bob Rawlinson sighed, wriggled and endeavoured to explain what he felt. He had to struggle with his own inarticulateness.

'Well,' he said. 'He put up a show—I suppose that's it really. He was—sort of—dramatic, if you know what I mean.'

He looked at his friend who was definitely not dramatic. A nice quiet decent chap, sincere and perplexed, that was what Ali was, and Bob liked him for it. He was neither picturesque nor violent, but whilst in England people who are picturesque and violent cause embarrassment and are not much liked, in the Middle East, Bob was fairly sure, it was different.

'But democracy—' began Ali.

'Oh, democracy—' Bob waved his pipe. 'That's a word that means different things everywhere. One thing's certain. It never means what the Greeks originally meant by it. I bet you anything you like that if they boot you out of here, some spouting hot air merchant will take over, yelling his own praises, building himself up into God Almighty, and stringing up, or cutting off the heads of anyone who dares to disagree with him in any way. And, mark you, he'll *say*

Agatha Christie

it's a Democratic Government—of the people and for the people. I expect the people will like it too. Exciting for them. Lots of bloodshed.'

'But we are not savages! We are civilized nowadays.'

'There are different kinds of civilization...' said Bob vaguely. 'Besides—I rather think we've all got a bit of savage in us—if we can think up a good excuse for letting it rip.'

'Perhaps you are right,' said Ali sombrely.

'The thing people don't seem to want anywhere, nowadays,' said Bob, 'is anyone who's got a bit of common sense. I've never been a brainy chap—well, you know that well enough, Ali—but I often think that that's what the world really needs—just a bit of common sense.' He laid aside his pipe and sat in his chair. 'But never mind all that. The thing is how we're going to get you out of here. Is there anybody in the Army you can really trust?'

Slowly, Prince Ali Yusuf shook his head.

'A fortnight ago, I should have said "Yes." But now, I do not know... cannot be *sure*—'

Bob nodded. 'That's the hell of it. As for this palace of yours, it gives me the creeps.'

Ali acquiesced without emotion.

'Yes, there are spies everywhere in palaces... They hear everything—they—know everything.'

'Even down at the hangars—' Bob broke off. 'Old Achmed's all right. He's got a kind of sixth sense. Found one of the mechanics trying to tamper with the plane—one of the men we'd have sworn was absolutely trustworthy.

Look here, Ali, if we're going to have a shot at getting you away, it will have to be soon.'

'I know—I know. I think—I am quite certain now—that if I stay I shall be killed.'

He spoke without emotion, or any kind of panic: with a mild detached interest.

'We'll stand a good chance of being killed anyway,' Bob warned him. 'We'll have to fly out north, you know. They can't intercept us that way. But it means going over the mountains—and at this time of year—'

He shrugged his shoulders. 'You've got to understand. It's damned risky.'

Ali Yusuf looked distressed.

'If anything happened to you, Bob—'

'Don't worry about me, Ali. That's not what I meant. I'm not important. And anyway, I'm the sort of chap that's sure to get killed sooner or later. I'm always doing crazy things. No—it's you—I don't want to persuade you one way or the other. If a portion of the Army *is* loyal—'

'I don't like the idea of running away,' said Ali simply. 'But I do not in the least want to be a martyr, and be cut to pieces by a mob.'

He was silent for a moment or two.

'Very well then,' he said at last with a sigh. 'We will make the attempt. When?'

Bob shrugged his shoulders.

'Sooner the better. We've got to get you to the airstrip in some natural way... How about saying you're going to inspect the new road construction out at Al Jasar? Sudden

Agatha Christie

whim. Go this afternoon. Then, as your car passes the airstrip, stop there—I'll have the bus all ready and tuned up. The idea will be to go up to inspect the road construction from the air, see? We take off and *go!* We can't take any baggage, of course. It's got to be all quite impromptu.'

'There is nothing I wish to take with me—except one thing—'

He smiled, and suddenly the smile altered his face and made a different person of him. He was no longer the modern conscientious Westernized young man—the smile held all the racial guile and craft which had enabled a long line of his ancestors to survive.

'You are my friend, Bob, you shall see.'

His hand went inside his shirt and fumbled. Then he held out a little chamois leather bag.

'This?' Bob frowned and looked puzzled.

Ali took it from him, untied the neck, and poured the contents on the table.

Bob held his breath for a moment and then expelled it in a soft whistle.

'Good lord. Are they *real*?'

Ali looked amused.

'Of course they are real. Most of them belonged to my father. He acquired new ones every year. I, too. They have come from many places, bought for our family by men we can trust—from London, from Calcutta, from South Africa. It is a tradition of our family. To have these in case of need.' He added in a matter of fact voice: 'They are worth, at today's prices, about three quarters of a million.'

'Three quarters of a million pounds.' Bob let out a whistle, picked up the stones, let them run through his fingers. 'It's fantastic. Like a fairy tale. It does things to you.'

'Yes.' The dark young man nodded. Again that age-long weary look was on his face. 'Men are not the same when it comes to jewels. There is always a trail of violence to follow such things. Deaths, bloodshed, murder. And women are the worst. For with women it will not only be the value. It is something to do with the jewels themselves. Beautiful jewels drive women mad. They want to own them. To wear them round their throats, on their bosoms. I would not trust any woman with these. But I shall trust you.'

'Me?' Bob stared.

'Yes. I do not want these stones to fall into the hands of my enemies. I do not know when the rising against me will take place. It may be planned for today. I may not live to reach the airstrip this afternoon. Take the stones and do the best you can.'

'But look here—I don't understand. What am I to do with them?'

'Arrange somehow to get them out of the country.'

Ali stared placidly at his perturbed friend.

'You mean, you want *me* to carry them instead of you?'

'You can put it that way. But I think, really, you will be able to think of some better plan to get them to Europe.'

'But look here, Ali, I haven't the first idea how to set about such a thing.'

Ali leaned back in his chair. He was smiling in a quietly amused manner.

Agatha Christie

'You have common sense. And you are honest. And I remember, from the days when you were my fag, that you could always think up some ingenious idea... I will give you the name and address of a man who deals with such matters for me—that is—in case I should not survive. Do not look so worried, Bob. Do the best you can. That is all I ask. I shall not blame you if you fail. It is as Allah wills. For me, it is simple. I do not want those stones taken from my dead body. For the rest—' he shrugged his shoulders. 'It is as I have said. All will go as Allah wills.'

'You're nuts!'

'No. I am a fatalist, that is all.'

'But look here, Ali. You said just now I was honest. But three quarters of a million... Don't you think that might sap any man's honesty?'

Ali Yusuf looked at his friend with affection.

'Strangely enough,' he said, 'I have no doubt on that score.'

CHAPTER 2

The Woman on the Balcony

As Bob Rawlinson walked along the echoing marble corridors of the Palace, he had never felt so unhappy in his life. The knowledge that he was carrying three quarters of a million pounds in his trousers pocket caused him acute misery. He felt as though every Palace official he encountered must know the fact. He felt even that the knowledge of his precious burden must show in his face. He would have been relieved to learn that his freckled countenance bore exactly its usual expression of cheerful good nature.

The sentries outside presented arms with a clash. Bob walked down the main crowded street of Ramat, his mind still dazed. Where was he going? What was he planning to do? He had no idea. And time was short.

The main street was like most main streets in the Middle East. It was a mixture of squalor and magnificence. Banks reared their vast newly built magnificence. Innumerable small shops presented a collection of cheap plastic goods. Babies' bootees and cheap cigarette lighters were displayed

Agatha Christie

in unlikely juxtaposition. There were sewing machines, and spare parts for cars. Pharmacies displayed flyblown proprietary medicines, and large notices of penicillin in every form and antibiotics galore. In very few of the shops was there anything that you could normally want to buy, except possibly the latest Swiss watches, hundreds of which were displayed crowded into a tiny window. The assortment was so great that even there one would have shrunk from purchase, dazzled by sheer mass.

Bob, still walking in a kind of stupor, jostled by figures in native or European dress, pulled himself together and asked himself again where the hell he was going?

He turned into a native café and ordered lemon tea. As he sipped it, he began, slowly, to come to. The atmosphere of the café was soothing. At a table opposite him an elderly Arab was peacefully clicking through a string of amber beads. Behind him two men played tric trac. It was a good place to sit and think.

And he'd got to think. Jewels worth three quarters of a million had been handed to him, and it was up to him to devise some plan of getting them out of the country. No time to lose either. At any minute the balloon might go up...

Ali was crazy, of course. Tossing three quarters of a million light-heartedly to a friend in that way. And then sitting back quietly himself and leaving everything to Allah. Bob had not got that recourse. Bob's God expected his servants to decide on and perform their own actions to the best of the ability their God had given them.

What the hell was he going to do with those damned stones?

He thought of the Embassy. No, he couldn't involve the Embassy. The Embassy would almost certainly refuse to be involved.

What he needed was some person, some perfectly ordinary person who was leaving the country in some perfectly ordinary way. A business man, or a tourist would be best. Someone with no political connections whose baggage would, at most, be subjected to a superficial search or more probably no search at all. There was, of course, the other end to be considered... Sensation at London Airport. Attempt to smuggle in jewels worth three quarters of a million. And so on and so on. One would have to risk that—

Somebody ordinary—a *bona fide* traveller. And suddenly Bob kicked himself for a fool. Joan, of course. His sister Joan Sutcliffe. Joan had been out here for two months with her daughter Jennifer who after a bad bout of pneumonia had been ordered sunshine and a dry climate. They were going back by 'long sea' in four or five days' time.

Joan was the ideal person. What was it Ali had said about women and jewels? Bob smiled to himself. Good old Joan! *She* wouldn't lose her head over jewels. Trust her to keep her feet on the earth. Yes—he could trust Joan.

Wait a minute, though... could he trust Joan? Her honesty, yes. But her discretion? Regretfully Bob shook his head. Joan would talk, would not be able to help talking. Even worse. She would hint. 'I'm taking home something very important, I mustn't say a word to *anyone*. It's really rather exciting...'

Agatha Christie

Joan had never been able to keep a thing to herself though she was always very incensed if one told her so. Joan, then, mustn't know what she was taking. It would be safer for her that way. He'd make the stones up into a parcel, an innocent-looking parcel. Tell her some story. A present for someone? A commission? He'd think of something...

Bob glanced at his watch and rose to his feet. Time was getting on.

He strode along the street oblivious of the midday heat. Everything seemed so normal. There was nothing to show on the surface. Only in the Palace was one conscious of the banked-down fires, of the spying, the whispers. The Army—it all depended on the Army. Who was loyal? Who was disloyal? A *coup d'état* would certainly be attempted. Would it succeed or fail?

Bob frowned as he turned into Ramat's leading hotel. It was modestly called the Ritz Savoy and had a grand modernistic façade. It had opened with a flourish three years ago with a Swiss manager, a Viennese chef, and an Italian *Maître d'hôtel*. Everything had been wonderful. The Viennese chef had gone first, then the Swiss manager. Now the Italian head waiter had gone too. The food was still ambitious, but bad, the service abominable, and a good deal of the expensive plumbing had gone wrong.

The clerk behind the desk knew Bob well and beamed at him.

'Good morning, Squadron Leader. You want your sister? She has gone on a picnic with the little girl—'

'A picnic?' Bob was taken aback—of all the silly times to go for a picnic.

'With Mr and Mrs Hurst from the Oil Company,' said the clerk informatively. Everyone always knew everything. 'They have gone to the Kalat Diwa dam.'

Bob swore under his breath. Joan wouldn't be home for hours.

'I'll go up to her room,' he said and held out his hand for the key which the clerk gave him.

He unlocked the door and went in. The room, a large double-bedded one, was in its usual confusion. Joan Sutcliffe was not a tidy woman. Golf clubs lay across a chair, tennis racquets had been flung on the bed. Clothing lay about, the table was littered with rolls of film, postcards, paper-backed books and an assortment of native curios from the South, mostly made in Birmingham and Japan.

Bob looked round him, at the suitcases and the zip bags. He was faced with a problem. He wouldn't be able to see Joan before flying Ali out. There wouldn't be time to get to the dam and back. He could parcel up the stuff and leave it with a note—but almost immediately he shook his head. He knew quite well that he was nearly always followed. He'd probably been followed from the Palace to the café and from the café here. He hadn't spotted anyone—but he knew that they were good at the job. There was nothing suspicious in his coming to the hotel to see his sister—but if he left a parcel and a note, the note would be read and the parcel opened.

Time... time... He'd no *time*...

Agatha Christie

Three quarters of a million in precious stones in his trousers pocket.

He looked round the room...

Then, with a grin, he fished out from his pocket the little tool kit he always carried. His niece Jennifer had some plasticine, he noted, that would help.

He worked quickly and skilfully. Once he looked up, suspicious, his eyes going to the open window. No, there was no balcony outside this room. It was just his nerves that made him feel that someone was watching him.

He finished his task and nodded in approval. Nobody would notice what he had done—he felt sure of that. Neither Joan nor anyone else. Certainly not Jennifer, a self-centred child, who never saw or noticed anything outside herself.

He swept up all evidences of his toil and put them into his pocket... Then he hesitated, looking round.

He drew Mrs Sutcliffe's writing pad towards him and sat frowning—

He must leave a note for Joan—

But what could he say? It must be something that Joan would understand—but which would mean nothing to anyone who read the note.

And really that was impossible! In the kind of thriller that Bob liked reading to fill up his spare moments, you left a kind of cryptogram which was always successfully puzzled out by someone. But he couldn't even begin to think of a cryptogram—and in any case Joan was the sort of common-sense person who would need the i's dotted and the t's crossed before she noticed anything at all—

Then his brow cleared. There was another way of doing it—divert attention away from Joan—leave an ordinary everyday note. Then leave a message with someone else to be given to Joan in England.

He wrote rapidly—

Dear Joan—Dropped in to ask if you'd care to play a round of golf this evening but if you've been up at the dam, you'll probably be dead to the world. What about tomorrow? Five o'clock at the Club.
  Yours, Bob.

A casual sort of a message to leave for a sister that he might never see again—but in some ways the more casual the better. Joan mustn't be involved in any funny business, mustn't even know that there was any funny business. Joan could not dissimulate. Her protection would be the fact that she clearly knew nothing.

And the note would accomplish a dual purpose. It would seem that he, Bob, had no plan for departure himself.

He thought for a minute or two, then he crossed to the telephone and gave the number of the British Embassy. Presently he was connected with Edmundson, the third secretary, a friend of his.

'John? Bob Rawlinson here. Can you meet me somewhere when you get off?... Make it a bit earlier than that?... You've got to, old boy. It's important. Well, actually, it's a girl...' He gave an embarrassed cough. 'She's wonderful, quite wonderful. Out of this world. Only it's a bit tricky.'

Edmundson's voice, sounding slightly stuffed-shirt and disapproving, said, 'Really, Bob, you and your girls. All right, 2 o'clock do you?' and rang off. Bob heard the little echoing click as whoever had been listening in, replaced the receiver.

Good old Edmundson. Since all the telephones in Ramat had been tapped, Bob and John Edmundson had worked out a little code of their own. A wonderful girl who was 'out of this world' meant something urgent and important.

Edmundson would pick him up in his car outside the new Merchants Bank at 2 o'clock and he'd tell Edmundson of the hiding place. Tell him that Joan didn't know about it but that, if anything happened to him, it was important. Going by the long sea route Joan and Jennifer wouldn't be back in England for six weeks. By that time the revolution would almost certainly have happened and either been successful or have been put down. Ali Yusuf might be in Europe, or he and Bob might both be dead. He would tell Edmundson enough, but not too much.

Bob took a last look around the room. It looked exactly the same, peaceful, untidy, domestic. The only thing added was his harmless note to Joan. He propped it up on the table and went out. There was no one in the long corridor.

II

The woman in the room next to that occupied by Joan Sutcliffe stepped back from the balcony. There was a mirror in her hand.

She had gone out on the balcony originally to examine more closely a single hair that had had the audacity to spring up on her chin. She dealt with it with tweezers, then subjected her face to a minute scrutiny in the clear sunlight.

It was then, as she relaxed, that she saw something else. The angle at which she was holding her mirror was such that it reflected the mirror of the hanging wardrobe in the room next to hers and in that mirror she saw a man doing something very curious.

So curious and unexpected that she stood there motionless, watching. He could not see her from where he sat at the table, and she could only see him by means of the double reflection.

If he had turned his head behind him, he might have caught sight of her mirror in the wardrobe mirror, but he was too absorbed in what he was doing to look behind him...

Once, it was true, he did look up suddenly towards the window, but since there was nothing to see there, he lowered his head again.

The woman watched him while he finished what he was doing. After a moment's pause he wrote a note which he propped up on the table. Then he moved out of her line of vision but she could just hear enough to realize that he was making a telephone call. She couldn't catch what was said, but it sounded light-hearted—casual. Then she heard the door close.

The woman waited a few minutes. Then she opened her door. At the far end of the passage an Arab was flicking idly with a feather duster. He turned the corner out of sight.

Agatha Christie

The woman slipped quickly to the door of the next room. It was locked, but she had expected that. The hairpin she had with her and the blade of a small knife did the job quickly and expertly.

She went in, pushing the door to behind her. She picked up the note. The flap had only been stuck down lightly and opened easily. She read the note, frowning. There was no explanation there.

She sealed it up, put it back, and walked across the room.

There, with her hand outstretched, she was disturbed by voices through the window from the terrace below.

One was a voice that she knew to be the occupier of the room in which she was standing. A decided didactic voice, fully assured of itself.

She darted to the window.

Below on the terrace, Joan Sutcliffe, accompanied by her daughter Jennifer, a pale solid child of fifteen, was telling the world and a tall unhappy looking Englishman from the British Consulate just what she thought of the arrangements he had come to make.

'But it's absurd! I never *heard* such nonsense. Everything's perfectly quiet here and everyone quite pleasant. I think it's all a lot of panicky fuss.'

'We hope so, Mrs Sutcliffe, we certainly hope so. But H.E. feels that the responsibility is such—'

Mrs Sutcliffe cut him short. She did not propose to consider the responsibility of ambassadors.

'We've a lot of baggage, you know. We were going home by long sea—next Wednesday. The sea voyage will be good for Jennifer. The doctor said so. I really must absolutely decline to alter all my arrangements and be flown to England in this silly flurry.'

The unhappy looking man said encouragingly that Mrs Sutcliffe and her daughter could be flown, not to England, but to Aden and catch their boat there.

'With our baggage?'

'Yes, yes, that can be arranged. I've got a car waiting—a station wagon. We can load everything right away.'

'Oh well.' Mrs Sutcliffe capitulated. 'I suppose we'd better pack.'

'At once, if you don't mind.'

The woman in the bedroom drew back hurriedly. She took a quick glance at the address on a luggage label on one of the suitcases. Then she slipped quickly out of the room and back into her own just as Mrs Sutcliffe turned the corner of the corridor.

The clerk from the office was running after her.

'Your brother, the Squadron Leader, has been here, Mrs Sutcliffe. He went up to your room. But I think that he has left again. You must just have missed him.'

'How tiresome,' said Mrs Sutcliffe. 'Thank you,' she said to the clerk and went on to Jennifer, 'I suppose Bob's fussing too. I can't see any sign of disturbance *myself* in the streets. This door's unlocked. How careless these people are.'

'Perhaps it was Uncle Bob,' said Jennifer.

'I wish I hadn't missed him... Oh, there's a note.' She tore it open.

'At any rate *Bob* isn't fussing,' she said triumphantly. 'He

Agatha Christie

obviously doesn't know a thing about all this. Diplomatic wind up, that's all it is. How I hate trying to pack in the heat of the day. This room's like an oven. Come on, Jennifer, get your things out of the chest of drawers and the wardrobe. We must just shove everything in anyhow. We can repack later.'

'I've never been in a revolution,' said Jennifer thoughtfully.

'I don't expect you'll be in one this time,' said her mother sharply. 'It will be just as I say. Nothing will happen.'

Jennifer looked disappointed.

CHAPTER 3

Introducing Mr Robinson

It was some six weeks later that a young man tapped discreetly on the door of a room in Bloomsbury and was told to come in.

It was a small room. Behind a desk sat a fat middle-aged man slumped in a chair. He was wearing a crumpled suit, the front of which was smothered in cigar ash. The windows were closed and the atmosphere was almost unbearable.

'Well?' said the fat man testily, and speaking with half-closed eyes. 'What is it now, eh?'

It was said of Colonel Pikeaway that his eyes were always just closing in sleep, or just opening after sleep. It was also said that his name was not Pikeaway and that he was not a colonel. But some people will say anything!

'Edmundson, from the F.O., is here sir.'

'Oh,' said Colonel Pikeaway.

Agatha Christie

He blinked, appeared to be going to sleep again and muttered:

'Third secretary at our Embassy in Ramat at the time of the Revolution. Right?'

'That's right, sir.'

'I suppose, then, I'd better see him,' said Colonel Pikeaway without any marked relish. He pulled himself into a more upright position and brushed off a little of the ash from his paunch.

Mr Edmundson was a tall fair young man, very correctly dressed with manners to match, and a general air of quiet disapproval.

'Colonel Pikeaway? I'm John Edmundson. They said you—er—might want to see me.'

'Did they? Well, they should know,' said Colonel Pikeaway. 'Siddown,' he added.

His eyes began to close again, but before they did so, he spoke:

'You were in Ramat at the time of the Revolution?'

'Yes, I was. A nasty business.'

'I suppose it would be. You were a friend of Bob Rawlinson's, weren't you?'

'I know him fairly well, yes.'

'Wrong tense,' said Colonel Pikeaway. 'He's dead.'

'Yes, sir, I know. But I wasn't sure—' he paused.

'You don't have to take pains to be discreet here,' said Colonel Pikeaway. 'We know everything here. Or if we don't, we pretend we do. Rawlinson flew Ali Yusuf out of

Ramat on the day of the Revolution. Plane hasn't been heard of since. Could have landed in some inaccessible place, or could have crashed. Wreckage of a plane has been found in the Arolez mountains. Two bodies. News will be released to the Press tomorrow. Right?'

Edmundson admitted that it was quite right.

'We know all about things here,' said Colonel Pikeaway. 'That's what we're for. Plane flew into the mountain. Could have been weather conditions. Some reason to believe it was sabotage. Delayed action bomb. We haven't got the full reports yet. The plane crashed in a pretty inaccessible place. There was a reward offered for finding it, but these things take a long time to filter through. Then we had to fly out experts to make an examination. All the red tape, of course. Applications to a foreign government, permission from ministers, palm greasing—to say nothing of the local peasantry appropriating anything that might come in useful.'

He paused and looked at Edmundson.

'Very sad, the whole thing,' said Edmundson. 'Prince Ali Yusuf would have made an enlightened ruler, with democratic principles.'

'That's what probably did the poor chap in,' said Colonel Pikeaway. 'But we can't waste time in telling sad stories of the deaths of kings. We've been asked to make certain— inquiries. By interested parties. Parties, that is, to whom Her Majesty's Government is well disposed.' He looked hard at the other. 'Know what I mean?'

Agatha Christie

'Well, I have heard something.' Edmundson spoke reluctantly.

'You've heard perhaps, that nothing of value was found on the bodies, or amongst the wreckage, or as far as is known, had been pinched by the locals. Though as to that, you can never tell with peasants. They can clam up as well as the Foreign Office itself. And what else have you heard?'

'Nothing else.'

'You haven't heard that perhaps something of value *ought* to have been found? What did they send you to me for?'

'They said you might want to ask me certain questions,' said Edmundson primly.

'If I ask you questions I shall expect answers,' Colonel Pikeaway pointed out.

'Naturally.'

'Doesn't seem natural to you, son. Did Bob Rawlinson say anything to you before he flew out of Ramat? He was in Ali's confidence if anyone was. Come now, let's have it. Did he say anything?'

'As to what, sir?'

Colonel Pikeaway stared hard at him and scratched his ear.

'Oh, all right,' he grumbled. 'Hush up this and don't say that. Overdo it in my opinion! If you don't know what I'm talking about, you don't know, and there it is.'

'I think there was something—' Edmundson spoke cautiously and with reluctance. 'Something important that Bob might have wanted to tell me.'

'Ah,' said Colonel Pikeaway, with the air of a man who has at last pulled the cork out of a bottle. 'Interesting. Let's have what you know.'

'It's very little, sir. Bob and I had a kind of simple code. We'd cottoned on to the fact that all the telephones in Ramat were being tapped. Bob was in the way of hearing things at the Palace, and I sometimes had a bit of useful information to pass on to him. So if one of us rang the other up and mentioned a girl or girls, in a certain way, using the term "out of this world" for her, it meant something was up!'

'Important information of some kind or other?'

'Yes. Bob rang me up using those terms the day the whole show started. I was to meet him at our usual rendezvous—outside one of the banks. But rioting broke out in that particular quarter and the police closed the road. I couldn't make contact with Bob or he with me. He flew Ali out the same afternoon.'

'I see,' said Pikeaway. 'No idea where he was telephoning from?'

'No. It might have been anywhere.'

'Pity.' He paused and then threw out casually:

'Do you know Mrs Sutcliffe?'

'You mean Bob Rawlinson's sister? I met her out there, of course. She was there with a schoolgirl daughter. I don't know her well.'

'Were she and Bob Rawlinson very close?'

Edmundson considered.

'No, I shouldn't say so. She was a good deal older than

he was, and rather much of the elder sister. And he didn't much like his brother-in-law—always referred to him as a pompous ass.'

'So he is! One of our prominent industrialists—and how pompous can they get! So you don't think it likely that Bob Rawlinson would have confided an important secret to his sister?'

'It's difficult to say—but no, I shouldn't think so.'

'I shouldn't either,' said Colonel Pikeaway.

He sighed. 'Well, there we are, Mrs Sutcliffe and her daughter are on their way home by the long sea route. Dock at Tilbury on the *Eastern Queen* tomorrow.'

He was silent for a moment or two, whilst his eyes made a thoughtful survey of the young man opposite him. Then, as though having come to a decision, he held out his hand and spoke briskly.

'Very good of you to come.'

'I'm only sorry I've been of such little use. You're sure there's nothing I can do?'

'No. No. I'm afraid not.'

John Edmundson went out.

The discreet young man came back.

'Thought I might have sent him to Tilbury to break the news to the sister,' said Pikeaway. 'Friend of her brother's—all that. But I decided against it. Inelastic type. That's the F.O. training. Not an opportunist. I'll send round what's his name.'

'Derek?'

'That's right,' Colonel Pikeaway nodded approval. 'Getting to know what I mean quite well, ain't you?'

'I try my best, sir.'

'Trying's not enough. You have to succeed. Send me along Ronnie first. I've got an assignment for him.'

II

Colonel Pikeaway was apparently just going off to sleep again when the young man called Ronnie entered the room. He was tall, dark, muscular, and had a gay and rather impertinent manner.

Colonel Pikeaway looked at him for a moment or two and then grinned.

'How'd you like to penetrate into a girls' school?' he asked.

'A girls' school?' The young man lifted his eyebrows. 'That will be something new! What are they up to? Making bombs in the chemistry class?'

'Nothing of that kind. Very superior high-class school. Meadowbank.'

'Meadowbank!' the young man whistled. 'I can't believe it!'

'Hold your impertinent tongue and listen to me. Princess Shaista, first cousin and only near relative of the late Prince Ali Yusuf of Ramat, goes there this next term. She's been at school in Switzerland up to now.'

'What do I do? Abduct her?'

'Certainly not. I think it possible she may become a focus of interest in the near future. I want you to keep an eye on developments. I'll have to leave it vague. I don't know

Agatha Christie

what or who may turn up, but if any of our more unlikeable friends seem to be interested, report it... A watching brief, that's what you've got.'

The young man nodded.

'And how do I get in to watch? Shall I be the drawing master?'

'The visiting staff is all female.' Colonel Pikeaway looked at him in a considering manner. 'I think I'll have to make you a gardener.'

'A gardener?'

'Yes. I'm right in thinking you know something about gardening?'

'Yes, indeed. I ran a column on *Your Garden* in the *Sunday Mail* for a year in my younger days.'

'Tush!' said Colonel Pikeaway. 'That's nothing! I could do a column on gardening myself without knowing a thing about it—just crib from a few luridly illustrated Nurseryman's catalogues and a Gardening Encyclopedia. I know all the patter. "*Why not break away from tradition and sound a really tropical note in your border this year? Lovely Amabellis Gossiporia, and some of the wonderful new Chinese hybrids of Sinensis Maka foolia. Try the rich blushing beauty of a clump of Sinistra Hopaless, not very hardy but they should be all right against a west wall.*"' He broke off and grinned. 'Nothing to it! The fools buy the things and early frost sets in and kills them and they wish they'd stuck to wallflowers and forget-me-nots! No, my boy, I mean the real stuff. Spit on your hands and use the spade, be well acquainted with the compost heap, mulch diligently, use the Dutch hoe and every other kind of hoe, trench really deep for your sweet peas—and all the rest of the beastly business. Can you do it?'

'All these things I have done from my youth upwards!'

'Of course you have. I know your mother. Well, that's settled.'

'Is there a job going as a gardener at Meadowbank?'

'Sure to be,' said Colonel Pikeaway. 'Every garden in England is short staffed. I'll write you some nice testimonials. You'll see, they'll simply jump at you. No time to waste, summer term begins on the 29th.'

'I garden and I keep my eyes open, is that right?'

'That's it, and if any oversexed teenagers make passes at you, Heaven help you if you respond. I don't want you thrown out on your ear too soon.'

He drew a sheet of paper towards him. 'What do you fancy as a name?'

'Adam would seem appropriate.'

'Last name?'

'How about Eden?'

'I'm not sure I like the way your mind is running. Adam Goodman will do very nicely. Go and work out your past history with Jenson and then get cracking.' He looked at his watch. 'I've no more time for you. I don't want to keep Mr Robinson waiting. He ought to be here by now.'

Agatha Christie (signature)

Adam (to give him his new name) stopped as he was moving to the door.

'Mr Robinson?' he asked curiously. 'Is *he* coming?'

'I said so.' A buzzer went on the desk. 'There he is now. Always punctual, Mr Robinson.'

'Tell me,' said Adam curiously. 'Who is he really? What's his real name?'

'His name,' said Colonel Pikeaway, 'is Mr Robinson. That's all I know, and that's all anybody knows.'

III

The man who came into the room did not look as though his name was, or could ever have been, Robinson. It might have been Demetrius, or Isaacstein, or Perenna—though not one or the other in particular. He was not definitely Jewish, nor definitely Greek nor Portuguese nor Spanish, nor South American. What did seem highly unlikely was that he was an Englishman called Robinson. He was fat and well dressed, with a yellow face, melancholy dark eyes, a broad forehead, and a generous mouth that displayed rather over-large very white teeth. His hands were well shaped and beautifully kept. His voice was English with no trace of accent.

He and Colonel Pikeaway greeted each other rather in the manner of two reigning monarchs. Politenesses were exchanged.

Then, as Mr Robinson accepted a cigar, Colonel Pikeaway said:

Cat Among the Pigeons

'It is very good of you to offer to help us.'

Mr Robinson lit his cigar, savoured it appreciatively, and finally spoke.

'My dear fellow. I just thought—I hear things, you know. I know a lot of people, and they tell me things. I don't know why.'

Colonel Pikeaway did not comment on the reason why. He said:

'I gather you've heard that Prince Ali Yusuf's plane has been found?'

'Wednesday of last week,' said Mr Robinson. 'Young Rawlinson was the pilot. A tricky flight. But the crash wasn't due to an error on Rawlinson's part. The plane had been tampered with—by a certain Achmed—senior mechanic. Completely trustworthy—or so Rawlinson thought. But he wasn't. He's got a very lucrative job with the new *régime* now.'

'So it was sabotage! We didn't know that for sure. It's a sad story.'

'Yes. That poor young man—Ali Yusuf, I mean—was ill equipped to cope with corruption and treachery. His public school education was unwise—or at least that is my view. But we do not concern ourselves with him now, do we? He is yesterday's news. Nothing is so dead as a dead king. We are concerned, you in your way, I in mine, with what dead kings leave behind them.'

'Which is?'

Mr Robinson shrugged his shoulders.

'A substantial bank balance in Geneva, a modest balance

in London, considerable assets in his own country now taken over by the glorious new *régime* (and a little bad feeling as to how the spoils have been divided, or so I hear!), and finally a small personal item.'

'Small?'

'These things are relative. Anyway, small in bulk. Handy to carry upon the person.'

'They weren't on Ali Yusuf's person, as far as we know.'

'No. Because he had handed them over to young Rawlinson.'

'Are you sure of that?' asked Pikeaway sharply.

'Well, one is never sure,' said Mr Robinson apologetically. 'In a palace there is so much gossip. It cannot *all* be true. But there was a very strong rumour to that effect.'

'They weren't on young Rawlinson's person, either—'

'In that case,' said Mr Robinson, 'it seems as though they must have been got out of the country by some other means.'

'What other means? Have you any idea?'

'Rawlinson went to a café in the town after he had received the jewels. He was not seen to speak to anyone or approach anyone whilst he was there. Then he went to the Ritz Savoy Hotel where his sister was staying. He went up to her room and was there for about 20 minutes. She herself was out. He then left the hotel and went to the Merchants Bank in Victory Square where he cashed a cheque. When he came out of the bank a disturbance was beginning. Students rioting about something. It was some time before the square was cleared. Rawlinson then went straight to the airstrip where, in company with Sergeant Achmed, he went over the plane.

'Ali Yusuf drove out to see the new road construction, stopped his car at the airstrip, joined Rawlinson and expressed a desire to take a short flight and see the dam and the new highway construction from the air. They took off and did not return.'

'And your deductions from that?'

'My dear fellow, the same as yours. Why did Bob Rawlinson spend twenty minutes in his sister's room when she was out and he had been told that she was not likely to return until evening? He left her a note that would have taken him at most three minutes to scribble. What did he do for the rest of the time?'

'You are suggesting that he concealed the jewels in some appropriate place amongst his sister's belongings?'

'It seems indicated, does it not? Mrs Sutcliffe was evacuated that same day with other British subjects. She was flown to Aden with her daughter. She arrives at Tilbury, I believe, tomorrow.'

Pikeaway nodded.

'Look after her,' said Mr Robinson.

'We're going to look after her,' said Pikeaway. 'That's all arranged.'

'If she has the jewels, she will be in danger.' He closed his eyes. 'I so much dislike violence.'

'You think there is likely to be violence?'

'There are people interested. Various undesirable people—if you understand me.'

Agatha Christie

'I understand you,' said Pikeaway grimly.

'And they will, of course, double cross each other.'

Mr Robinson shook his head. 'So confusing.'

Colonel Pikeaway asked delicately: 'Have you yourself any—er—special interest in the matter?'

'I represent a certain group of interests,' said Mr Robinson. His voice was faintly reproachful. 'Some of the stones in question were supplied by my syndicate to his late highness—at a very fair and reasonable price. The group of people I represent who were interested in the recovery of the stones, would, I may venture to say, have had the approval of the late owner. I shouldn't like to say more. These matters are so delicate.'

'But you are definitely on the side of the angels,' Colonel Pikeaway smiled.

'Ah, angels! Angels—yes.' He paused. 'Do you happen to know who occupied the rooms in the hotel on either side of the room occupied by Mrs Sutcliffe and her daughter?'

Colonel Pikeaway looked vague.

'Let me see now—I believe I do. On the left hand side was Señora Angelica de Toredo—a Spanish—er—dancer appearing at the local cabaret. Perhaps not strictly Spanish and perhaps not a very good dancer. But popular with the clientèle. On the other side was one of a group of schoolteachers, I understand—'

Mr Robinson beamed approvingly.

'You are always the same. I come to tell you things, but nearly always you know them already.'

'No no.' Colonel Pikeaway made a polite disclaimer.
'Between us,' said Mr Robinson, 'we know a good deal.'
Their eyes met.
'I hope,' Mr Robinson said, rising, 'that we know enough—'

CHAPTER 4

Return of a Traveller

'Really!' said Mrs Sutcliffe, in an annoyed voice, as she looked out of her hotel window, 'I don't see why it always has to rain when one comes back to England. It makes it all seem so depressing.'

'I think it's lovely to be back,' said Jennifer. 'Hearing everyone talk English in the streets! And we'll be able to have a really good tea presently. Bread and butter and jam and proper cakes.'

'I wish you weren't so insular, darling,' said Mrs Sutcliffe. 'What's the good of my taking you abroad all the way to the Persian Gulf if you're going to say you'd rather have stayed at home?'

'I don't mind going abroad for a month or two,' said Jennifer. 'All I said was I'm glad to be back.'

'Now do get out of the way, dear, and let me make sure that they've brought up all the luggage. Really, I do feel—I've felt ever since the war that people have got very dishonest nowadays. I'm sure if I hadn't kept an eye on

Cat Among the Pigeons

things that man would have gone off with my green zip bag at Tilbury. And there was another man hanging about near the luggage. I saw him afterwards on the train. I believe, you know, that these sneak thieves meet the boats and if the people are flustered or seasick they go off with some of the suitcases.'

'Oh, you're always thinking things like that, Mother,' said Jennifer. 'You think everybody you meet is dishonest.'

'Most of them are,' said Mrs Sutcliffe grimly.

'Not English people,' said the loyal Jennifer.

'That's worse,' said her mother. 'One doesn't expect anything else from Arabs and foreigners, but in England one's off guard and that makes it easier for dishonest people. Now do let me count. That's the big green suitcase and the black one, and the two small brown and the zip bag and the golf clubs and the racquets and the hold-all and the canvas suitcase—and where's the green bag? Oh, there it is. And that local tin we bought to put the extra things in—yes, one, two, three, four, five, six—yes, that's all right. All fourteen things are here.'

'Can't we have some tea now?' said Jennifer.

'Tea? It's only three o'clock.'

'I'm awfully hungry.'

'All right, all right. Can you go down by yourself and order it? I really feel I must have a rest, and then I'll just unpack the things we'll need for tonight. It's too bad your father couldn't have met us. Why he had to have an important directors' meeting in Newcastle-on-Tyne today I simply cannot imagine. You'd think his wife and

Agatha Christie

daughter would come first. Especially as he hasn't seen us for three months. Are you sure you can manage by yourself?'

'Good gracious, Mummy,' said Jennifer, 'what age do you think I am? Can I have some money, please? I haven't got any English money.'

She accepted the ten shilling note her mother handed to her, and went out scornfully.

The telephone rang by the bed. Mrs Sutcliffe went to it and picked up the receiver.

'Hallo... Yes... Yes, Mrs Sutcliffe speaking...'

There was a knock at the door. Mrs Sutcliffe said, 'Just one moment' to the receiver, laid it down and went over to the door. A young man in dark blue overalls was standing there with a small kit of tools.

'Electrician,' he said briskly. 'The lights in this suite aren't satisfactory. I've been sent up to see to them.'

'Oh—all right...'

She drew back. The electrician entered.

'Bathroom?'

'Through there—beyond the other bedroom.'

She went back to the telephone.

'I'm so sorry... What were you saying?'

'My name is Derek O'Connor. Perhaps I might come up to your suite, Mrs Sutcliffe. It's about your brother.'

'Bob? Is there—news of him?'

'I'm afraid so—yes.'

'Oh... Oh, I see... Yes, come up. It's on the third floor, 310.'

She sat down on the bed. She already knew what the news must be.

Presently there was a knock on the door and she opened it to admit a young man who shook hands in a suitably subdued manner.

'Are you from the Foreign Office?'

'My name's Derek O'Connor. My chief sent me round as there didn't seem to be anybody else who could break it to you.'

'Please tell me,' said Mrs Sutcliffe. 'He's been killed. Is that it?'

'Yes, that's it, Mrs Sutcliffe. He was flying Prince Ali Yusuf out from Ramat and they crashed in the mountains.'

'Why haven't I heard—why didn't someone wireless it to the boat?'

'There was no definite news until a few days ago. It was known that the plane was missing, that was all. But under the circumstances there might still have been hope. But now the wreck of the plane has been found... I am sure you will be glad to know that death was instantaneous.'

'The Prince was killed as well?'

'Yes.'

'I'm not at all surprised,' said Mrs Sutcliffe. Her voice shook a little but she was in full command of herself. 'I knew Bob would die young. He was always reckless, you know—always flying new planes, trying new stunts. I've hardly seen anything of him for the last four years. Oh well, one can't change people, can one?'

'No,' said her visitor, 'I'm afraid not.'

'Henry always said he'd smash himself up sooner or later,' said Mrs Sutcliffe. She seemed to derive a kind of melancholy satisfaction from the accuracy of her husband's prophecy. A tear rolled down her cheek and she looked for her handkerchief. 'It's been a shock,' she said.

'I know—I'm awfully sorry.'

'Bob couldn't run away, of course,' said Mrs Sutcliffe. 'I mean, he'd taken on the job of being the Prince's pilot. I wouldn't have wanted him to throw in his hand. And he was a good flier too. I'm sure if he ran into a mountain it wasn't his fault.'

'No,' said O'Connor, 'it certainly wasn't his fault. The only hope of getting the Prince out was to fly in no matter what conditions. It was a dangerous flight to undertake and it went wrong.'

Mrs Sutcliffe nodded.

'I quite understand,' she said. 'Thank you for coming to tell me.'

'There's something more,' said O'Connor, 'something I've got to ask you. Did your brother entrust anything to you to take back to England?'

'Entrust something to me?' said Mrs Sutcliffe. 'What do you mean?'

'Did he give you any—package—any small parcel to bring back and deliver to anyone in England?'

She shook her head wonderingly. 'No. Why should you think he did?'

'There was a rather important package which we think

Cat Among the Pigeons

your brother may have given to someone to bring home. He called on you at your hotel that day—the day of the Revolution, I mean.'

'I know. He left a note. But there was nothing in that—just some silly thing about playing tennis or golf the next day. I suppose when he wrote that note, he couldn't have known that he'd have to fly the Prince out that very afternoon.'

'That was all it said?'

'The note? Yes.'

'Have you kept it, Mrs Sutcliffe?'

'Kept the note he left? No, of course I haven't. It was quite trivial. I tore it up and threw it away. Why should I keep it?'

'No reason,' said O'Connor. 'I just wondered.'

'Wondered what?' said Mrs Sutcliffe crossly.

'Whether there might have been some—other message concealed in it. After all—' he smiled, '—there is such a thing as invisible ink, you know.'

'Invisible ink!' said Mrs Sutcliffe, with a great deal of distaste, 'do you mean the sort of thing they use in spy stories?'

'Well, I'm afraid I do mean just that,' said O'Connor, rather apologetically.

'How idiotic,' said Mrs Sutcliffe. 'I'm sure Bob would never use anything like invisible ink. Why should he? He was a dear matter-of-fact sensible person.' A tear dripped down her cheek again. 'Oh dear, where *is* my bag? I must have a handkerchief. Perhaps I left it in the other room.'

Agatha Christie

'I'll get it for you,' said O'Connor.

He went through the communicating door and stopped as a young man in overalls who was bending over a suitcase straightened up to face him, looking rather startled.

'Electrician,' said the young man hurriedly. 'Something wrong with the lights here.'

O'Connor flicked a switch.

'They seem all right to me,' he said pleasantly.

'Must have given me the wrong room number,' said the electrician.

He gathered up his tool bag and slipped out quickly through the door to the corridor.

O'Connor frowned, picked up Mrs Sutcliffe's bag from the dressing-table and took it back to her.

'Excuse me,' he said, and picked up the telephone receiver.

'Room 310 here. Have you just sent up an electrician to see to the light in this suite? Yes... Yes, I'll hang on.'

He waited.

'No? No, I thought you hadn't. No, there's nothing wrong.'

He replaced the receiver and turned to Mrs Sutcliffe.

'There's nothing wrong with any of the lights here,' he said. 'And the office didn't send up an electrician.'

'Then what was that man doing? Was he a thief?'

'He may have been.'

Mrs Sutcliffe looked hurriedly in her bag. 'He hasn't taken anything out of my bag. The money is all right.'

'Are you sure, Mrs Sutcliffe, absolutely *sure* that your brother didn't give you anything to take home, to pack among your belongings?'

'I'm absolutely sure,' said Mrs Sutcliffe.
'Or your daughter—you have a daughter, haven't you?'
'Yes. She's downstairs having tea.'
'Could your brother have given anything to her?'
'No, I'm sure he couldn't.'
'There's another possibility,' said O'Connor. 'He might have hidden something in your baggage among your belongings that day when he was waiting for you in your room.'
'But why should Bob do such a thing? It sounds absolutely absurd.'
'It's not quite so absurd as it sounds. It seems possible that Prince Ali Yusuf gave your brother something to keep for him and that your brother thought it would be safer among your possessions than if he kept it himself.'
'Sounds very unlikely to me,' said Mrs Sutcliffe.
'I wonder now, would you mind if we searched?'
'Searched through my luggage, do you mean? Unpack?' Mrs Sutcliffe's voice rose with a wail on that word.
'I know,' said O'Connor. 'It's a terrible thing to ask you. But it might be very important. I could help you, you know,' he said persuasively. 'I often used to pack for my mother. She said I was quite a good packer.'
He exerted all the charm which was one of his assets to Colonel Pikeaway.
'Oh well,' said Mrs Sutcliffe, yielding, 'I suppose—If you say so—if, I mean, it's really important—'
'It might be very important,' said Derek O'Connor. 'Well, now,' he smiled at her. 'Suppose we begin.'

II

Three quarters of an hour later Jennifer returned from her tea. She looked round the room and gave a gasp of surprise.

'Mummy, what *have* you been doing?'

'We've been unpacking,' said Mrs Sutcliffe crossly. 'Now we're packing things up again. This is Mr O'Connor. My daughter Jennifer.'

'But why are you packing and unpacking?'

'Don't ask me why,' snapped her mother. 'There seems to be some idea that your Uncle Bob put something in my luggage to bring home. He didn't give you anything, I suppose, Jennifer?'

'Uncle Bob give me anything to bring back? No. Have you been unpacking my things too?'

'We've unpacked everything,' said Derek O'Connor cheerfully, 'and we haven't found a thing and now we're packing them up again. I think you ought to have a drink of tea or something, Mrs Sutcliffe. Can I order you something? A brandy and soda perhaps?' He went to the telephone.

'I wouldn't mind a good cup of tea,' said Mrs Sutcliffe.

'I had a smashing tea,' said Jennifer. 'Bread and butter and sandwiches and cake and then the waiter brought me more sandwiches because I asked him if he'd mind and he said he didn't. It was lovely.'

O'Connor ordered the tea, then he finished packing up Mrs Sutcliffe's belongings again with a neatness and a dexterity which forced her unwilling admiration.

Cat Among the Pigeons

'Your mother seems to have trained you to pack very well,' she said.

'Oh, I've all sorts of handy accomplishments,' said O'Connor smiling.

His mother was long since dead, and his skill in packing and unpacking had been acquired solely in the service of Colonel Pikeaway.

'There's just one thing more, Mrs Sutcliffe. I'd like you to be very careful of yourself.'

'Careful of myself? In what way?'

'Well,' O'Connor left it vague. 'Revolutions are tricky things. There are a lot of ramifications. Are you staying in London long?'

'We're going down to the country tomorrow. My husband will be driving us down.'

'That's all right then. But—don't take any chances. If anything in the least out of the ordinary happens, ring 999 straight away.'

'Ooh!' said Jennifer, in high delight. 'Dial 999. I've always wanted to.'

'Don't be silly, Jennifer,' said her mother.

III

Extract from account in a local paper.

A man appeared before the Magistrate's court yesterday charged with breaking into the residence of Mr Henry Sutcliffe with intent to steal. Mrs Sutcliffe's bedroom was

Agatha Christie

ransacked and left in wild confusion whilst the members of the family were at Church on Sunday morning. The kitchen staff who were preparing the mid-day meal, heard nothing. Police arrested the man as he was making his escape from the house. Something had evidently alarmed him and he had fled without taking anything.

Giving his name as Andrew Ball of no fixed abode, he pleaded guilty. He said he had been out of work and was looking for money. Mrs Sutcliffe's jewellery, apart from a few pieces which she was wearing, is kept at her bank.

'I told you to have the lock of that drawing-room french window seen to,' had been the comment of Mr Sutcliffe in the family circle.

'My dear Henry,' said Mrs Sutcliffe, 'you don't seem to realize that I have been abroad for the last three months. And anyway, I'm sure I've read somewhere that if burglars *want* to get in they always can.'

She added wistfully, as she glanced again at the local paper:

'How beautifully grand "kitchen staff" sounds. So different from what it really is, old Mrs Ellis who is quite deaf and can hardly stand up and that half-witted daughter of the Bardwells who comes in to help on Sunday mornings.'

'What I don't see,' said Jennifer, 'is how the police found out the house was being burgled and got here in time to catch him?'

Cat Among the Pigeons

'It seems extraordinary that he didn't take anything,' commented her mother.

'Are you quite sure about that, Joan?' demanded her husband. 'You were a little doubtful at first.'

Mrs Sutcliffe gave an exasperated sigh.

'It's impossible to tell about a thing like that straight away. The mess in my bedroom—things thrown about everywhere, drawers pulled out and overturned. I had to look through *everything* before I could be sure—though now I come to think of it, I don't remember seeing my best Jacqmar scarf.'

'I'm sorry, Mummy. That was me. It blew overboard in the Mediterranean. I'd borrowed it. I meant to tell you but I forgot.'

'Really, Jennifer, how often have I asked you not to borrow things without telling me first?'

'Can I have some more pudding?' said Jennifer, creating a diversion.

'I suppose so. Really, Mrs Ellis has a wonderfully light hand. It makes it worth while having to shout at her so much. I do hope, though, that they won't think you too greedy at school. Meadowbank isn't quite an ordinary school, remember.'

'I don't know that I really want to go to Meadowbank,' said Jennifer. 'I knew a girl whose cousin had been there, and she said it was awful. They spent all their time telling you how to get in and out of Rolls-Royces, and how to behave if you went to lunch with the Queen.'

'That will do, Jennifer,' said Mrs Sutcliffe. 'You don't

Agatha Christie

appreciate how extremely fortunate you are in being admitted to Meadowbank. Miss Bulstrode doesn't take every girl, I can tell you. It's entirely owing to your father's important position and the influence of your Aunt Rosamond. You are exceedingly lucky. And if,' added Mrs Sutcliffe, 'you are ever asked to lunch with the Queen, it will be a good thing for you to know how to behave.'

'Oh well,' said Jennifer. 'I expect the Queen often has to have people to lunch who don't know how to behave—African chiefs and jockeys and sheikhs.'

'African chiefs have the most polished manners,' said her father, who had recently returned from a short business trip to Ghana.

'So do Arab sheikhs,' said Mrs Sutcliffe. 'Really courtly.'

'D'you remember that sheikh's feast we went to,' said Jennifer. 'And how he picked out the sheep's eye and gave it to you, and Uncle Bob nudged you not to make a fuss and to eat it? I mean, if a sheikh did that with roast lamb at Buckingham Palace, it would give the Queen a bit of a jolt, wouldn't it?'

'That will do, Jennifer,' said her mother and closed the subject.

IV

When Andrew Ball of no fixed abode had been sentenced to three months for breaking and entering, Derek O'Connor, who had been occupying a modest position at the back of the Magistrate's Court, put through a call to a Museum number.

'Not a thing on the fellow when we picked him up,' he said. 'We gave him plenty of time too.'

'Who was he? Anyone we know?'

'One of the Gecko lot, I think. Small time. They hire him out for this sort of thing. Not much brain but he's said to be thorough.'

'And he took his sentence like a lamb?' At the other end of the line Colonel Pikeaway grinned as he spoke.

'Yes. Perfect picture of a stupid fellow lapsed from the straight and narrow path. You'd never connect him with any big time stuff. That's his value, of course.'

'And he didn't find anything,' mused Colonel Pikeaway. 'And *you* didn't find anything. It rather looks, doesn't it, as though there isn't anything to find? Our idea that Rawlinson planted these things on his sister seems to have been wrong.'

'Other people appear to have the same idea.'

'It's a bit obvious really... Maybe we are meant to take the bait.'

'Could be. Any other possibilities?'

'Plenty of them. The stuff may still be in Ramat. Hidden somewhere in the Ritz Savoy Hotel, maybe. Or Rawlinson passed it to someone on his way to the airstrip. Or there may be something in that hint of Mr Robinson's. A woman may have got hold of it. Or it could be that Mrs Sutcliffe had it all the time unbeknownst to herself, and flung it overboard in the Red Sea with something she had no further use for.

Agatha Christie

'And that,' he added thoughtfully, 'might be all for the best.'

'Oh, come now, it's worth a lot of money, sir.'

'Human life is worth a lot, too,' said Colonel Pikeaway.

CHAPTER 5

Letters from Meadowbank School

Letter from Julia Upjohn to her mother:

Dear Mummy,
I've settled in now and am liking it very much. There's a girl who is new this term too called Jennifer and she and I rather do things together. We're both awfully keen on tennis. She's rather good. She has a really smashing serve when it comes off, but it doesn't usually. She says her racquet's got warped from being out in the Persian Gulf. It's very hot out there. She was in all that Revolution that happened. I said wasn't it very exciting, but she said no, they didn't see anything at all. They were taken away to the Embassy or something and missed it.

Miss Bulstrode is rather a lamb, but she's pretty frightening too—or can be. She goes easy on you when you're new. Behind her back everyone calls her The Bull

Agatha Christie

or Bully. We're taught English literature by Miss Rich, who's terrific. When she gets in a real state her hair comes down. She's got a queer but rather exciting face and when she reads bits of Shakespeare it all seems different and real. She went on at us the other day about Iago, and what he felt—and a lot about jealousy and how it ate into you and you suffered until you went quite mad wanting to hurt the person you loved. It gave us all the shivers—except Jennifer, because nothing upsets her. Miss Rich teaches us Geography, too. I always thought it was such a dull subject, but it isn't with Miss Rich. This morning she told us all about the spice trade and why they had to have spices because of things going bad so easily.

I'm starting Art with Miss Laurie. She comes twice a week and takes us up to London to see picture galleries as well. We do French with Mademoiselle Blanche. She doesn't keep order very well. Jennifer says French people can't. She doesn't get cross, though, only bored. She says 'Enfin, vous m'ennuiez, mes enfants!' Miss Springer is awful. She does gym and P.T. She's got ginger hair and smells when she's hot. Then there's Miss Chadwick (Chaddy)—she's been here since the school started. She teaches mathematics and is rather fussy, but quite nice. And there's Miss Vansittart who teaches History and German. She's a sort of Second Miss Bulstrode with the pep left out.

There are a lot of foreign girls here, two Italians and some Germans, and a rather jolly Swede (she's a Princess or something) and a girl who's half Turkish and half

Persian and who says she would have been married to Prince Ali Yusuf who got killed in that aeroplane crash, but Jennifer says that isn't true, that Shaista only says so because she was a kind of cousin, and you're supposed to marry a cousin. But Jennifer says he wasn't going to. He liked someone else. Jennifer knows a lot of things but she won't usually tell them.

I suppose you'll be starting on your trip soon. Don't leave your passport behind you like you did last time!!! And take your first aid kit in case you have an accident.

Love from Julia

Letter from Jennifer Sutcliffe to her mother:

Dear Mummy,

It really isn't bad here. I'm enjoying it more than I expected to do. The weather has been very fine. We had to write a composition yesterday on 'Can a good quality be carried to excess?' I couldn't think of anything to say. Next week it will be 'Contrast the characters of Juliet and Desdemona.' That seems silly too. Do you think I could have a new tennis racquet? I know you had mine restrung last Autumn—but it feels all wrong. Perhaps it's got warped. I'd rather like to learn Greek. Can I? I love languages. Some of us are going to London to see the ballet next week. It's Swan Lake. The food here is jolly good. Yesterday we had chicken for lunch, and we had lovely home made cakes for tea.

I can't think of any more news—have you had any more burglaries?

Your loving daughter,
Jennifer

Letter from Margaret Gore-West, Senior Prefect, to her mother:

Dear Mummy,

There is very little news. I am doing German with Miss Vansittart this term. There is a rumour that Miss Bulstrode is going to retire and that Miss Vansittart will succeed her but they've been saying that for over a year now, and I'm sure it isn't true. I asked Miss Chadwick (of course I wouldn't dare ask Miss Bulstrode!) and she was quite sharp about it. Said certainly not and don't listen to gossip. We went to the ballet on Tuesday. Swan Lake. Too dreamy for words!

Princess Ingrid is rather fun. Very blue eyes, but she wears braces on her teeth. There are two new German girls. They speak English quite well.

Miss Rich is back and looking quite well. We did miss her last term. The new Games Mistress is called Miss Springer. She's terribly bossy and nobody likes her much. She coaches you in tennis very well, though. One of the new girls, Jennifer Sutcliffe, is going to be really good, I think. Her backhand's a bit weak. Her great friend is a girl called Julia. We call them the Jays!

You won't forget about taking me out on the 20th, will you? Sports Day is June 19th.
Your loving
Margaret

Letter from Ann Shapland to Dennis Rathbone:

Dear Dennis,
I shan't get any time off until the third week of term. I should like to dine with you then very much. It would have to be Saturday or Sunday. I'll let you know.
I find it rather fun working in a school. But thank God I'm not a schoolmistress! I'd go raving mad.
Yours ever,
Ann

Letter from Miss Johnson to her sister:

Dear Edith,
Everything much the same as usual here. The summer term is always nice. The garden is looking beautiful and we've got a new gardener to help old Briggs—young and strong! Rather good looking, too, which is a pity. Girls are so silly.
Miss Bulstrode hasn't said anything more about retiring, so I hope she's got over the idea. Miss Vansittart wouldn't be at all the same thing. I really don't believe I would stay on.

Agatha Christie

*Give my love to Dick and to the children, and
remember me to Oliver and Kate when you see them.
Elspeth*

Letter from Mademoiselle Angèle Blanche to René Dupont,
Post Restante, Bordeaux.

*Dear René,
All is well here, though I cannot say that I amuse
myself. The girls are neither respectful nor well behaved.
I think it better, however, not to complain to Miss
Bulstrode. One has to be on one's guard when dealing
with that one!
There is nothing interesting at present to tell you.
Mouche*

Letter from Miss Vansittart to a friend:

*Dear Gloria,
The summer term has started smoothly. A very
satisfactory set of new girls. The foreigners are settling
down well. Our little Princess (the Middle East one, not
the Scandinavian) is inclined to lack application, but I
suppose one has to expect that. She has very charming
manners.
The new Games Mistress, Miss Springer, is not a success.
The girls dislike her and she is far too high-handed with
them. After all, this is not an ordinary school. We don't
stand or fall by P.T.! She is also very inquisitive, and asks*

far too many personal questions. That sort of thing can be very trying, and is so ill bred. Mademoiselle Blanche, the new French Mistress, is quite amiable but not up to the standard of Mademoiselle Depuy.

We had a near escape on the first day of term. Lady Veronica Carlton-Sandways turned up completely intoxicated!! But for Miss Chadwick spotting it and heading her off, we might have had a most unpleasant incident. The twins are such nice girls, too.

Miss Bulstrode has not said anything definite yet about the future—but from her manner, I think her mind is definitely made up. Meadowbank is a really fine achievement, and I shall be proud to carry on its traditions.

Give my love to Marjorie when you see her.
Yours ever,
Eleanor

Letter to Colonel Pikeaway, sent through the usual channels:

Talk about sending a man into danger! I'm the only able-bodied male in an establishment of, roughly, some hundred and ninety females.

Her Highness arrived in style. Cadillac of squashed strawberry and pastel blue, with Wog Notable in native dress, fashion-plate-from-Paris wife, and junior edition of same (H.R.H.).

Hardly recognized her the next day in her school

Agatha Christie

uniform. There will be no difficulty in establishing friendly relations with her. She has already seen to that. Was asking me the names of various flowers in a sweet innocent way, when a female Gorgon with freckles, red hair, and a voice like a corncrake bore down upon her and removed her from my vicinity. She didn't want to go. I'd always understood these Oriental girls were brought up modestly behind the veil. This one must have had a little worldly experience during her schooldays in Switzerland, I think.

The Gorgon, alias Miss Springer, the Games Mistress, came back to give me a raspberry. Garden staff were not to talk to the pupils, etc. My turn to express innocent surprise. 'Sorry, Miss. The young lady was asking what these here delphiniums was. Suppose they don't have them in the parts she comes from.' The Gorgon was easily pacified, in the end she almost simpered. Less success with Miss Bulstrode's secretary. One of these coat and skirt country girls. French mistress is more cooperative. Demure and mousy to look at, but not such a mouse really. Also have made friends with three pleasant gigglers, Christian names, Pamela, Lois and Mary, surnames unknown, but of aristocratic lineage. A sharp old war-horse called Miss Chadwick keeps a wary eye on me, so I'm careful not to blot my copybook.

My boss, old Briggs, is a crusty kind of character whose chief subject of conversation is what things used to be in the good old days, when he was, I suspect, the fourth of a staff of five. He grumbles about most things and people, but has a wholesome respect for Miss Bulstrode herself. So have I. She had a few words, very pleasant, with me, but I had a horrid feeling she was seeing right through me and knowing all about me.

No sign, so far, of anything sinister—but I live in hope.

CHAPTER 6

Early Days

In the Mistresses' Common Room news was being exchanged. Foreign travel, plays seen, Art Exhibitions visited. Snapshots were handed round. The menace of coloured transparencies was in the offing. All the enthusiasts wanted to show their own pictures, but to get out of being forced to see other people's.

Presently conversation became less personal. The new Sports Pavilion was both criticized and admired. It was admitted to be a fine building, but naturally everybody would have liked to improve its design in one way or another.

The new girls were then briefly passed in review, and, on the whole, the verdict was favourable.

A little pleasant conversation was made to the two new members of the staff. Had Mademoiselle Blanche been in England before? What part of France did she come from?

Mademoiselle Blanche replied politely but with reserve.

Miss Springer was more forthcoming.

She spoke with emphasis and decision. It might almost

have been said that she was giving a lecture. Subject: The excellence of Miss Springer. How much she had been appreciated as a colleague. How headmistresses had accepted her advice with gratitude and had re-organized their schedules accordingly.

Miss Springer was not sensitive. A restlessness in her audience was not noticed by her. It remained for Miss Johnson to ask in her mild tones:

'All the same, I expect your ideas haven't always been accepted in the way they—er—should have been.'

'One must be prepared for ingratitude,' said Miss Springer. Her voice, already loud, became louder. 'The trouble is, people are so cowardly—won't face facts. They often prefer not to see what's under their noses all the time. I'm not like that. I go straight to the point. More than once I've unearthed a nasty scandal—brought it into the open. I've a good nose—once I'm on the trail, I don't leave it—not till I've pinned down my quarry.' She gave a loud jolly laugh. 'In my opinion, no one should teach in a school whose life isn't an open book. If anyone's got anything to hide, one can soon tell. Oh! you'd be surprised if I told you some of the things I've found out about people. Things that nobody else had dreamed of.'

'You enjoyed that experience, yes?' said Mademoiselle Blanche.

'Of course not. Just doing my duty. But I wasn't backed up. Shameful laxness. So I resigned—as a protest.'

She looked round and gave her jolly sporting laugh again.

'Hope nobody here has anything to hide,' she said gaily.

Agatha Christie

Nobody was amused. But Miss Springer was not the kind of woman to notice that.

II

'Can I speak to you, Miss Bulstrode?'

Miss Bulstrode laid her pen aside and looked up into the flushed face of the matron, Miss Johnson.

'Yes, Miss Johnson.'

'It's that girl Shaista—the Egyptian girl or whatever she is.'

'Yes?'

'It's her—er—underclothing.'

Miss Bulstrode's eyebrows rose in patient surprise.

'Her—well—her bust bodice.'

'What is wrong with her brassière?'

'Well—it isn't an ordinary kind—I mean it doesn't hold her in, exactly. It—er—well it pushes her up—really quite unnecessarily.'

Miss Bulstrode bit her lip to keep back a smile, as so often when in colloquy with Miss Johnson.

'Perhaps I'd better come and look at it,' she said gravely.

A kind of inquest was then held with the offending contraption held up to display by Miss Johnson, whilst Shaista looked on with lively interest.

'It's this sort of wire and—er—boning arrangement,' said Miss Johnson with disapprobation.

Shaista burst into animated explanation.

'But you see my breasts they are not very big—not nearly

big enough. I do not look enough like a woman. And it is very important for a girl—to show she is a woman and not a boy.'

'Plenty of time for that. You're only fifteen,' said Miss Johnson.

'Fifteen—that *is* a woman! And I look like a woman, do I not?'

She appealed to Miss Bulstrode who nodded gravely.

'Only my breasts, they are poor. So I want to make them look not so poor. You understand?'

'I understand perfectly,' said Miss Bulstrode. 'And I quite see your point of view. But in this school, you see, you are amongst girls who are, for the most part, English, and English girls are not very often women at the age of fifteen. I like my girls to use make-up discreetly and to wear clothes suitable to their stage of growth. I suggest that you wear your brassière when you are dressed for a party or for going to London, but not every day here. We do a good deal of sports and games here and for that your body needs to be free to move easily.'

'It is too much—all this running and jumping,' said Shaista sulkily, '*and* the P.T. I do not like Miss Springer—she always says, "Faster, faster, do not slack." I get tired.'

'That will do, Shaista,' said Miss Bulstrode, her voice becoming authoritative. 'Your family has sent you here to learn English ways. All this exercise will be very good for your complexion, *and* for developing your bust.'

Dismissing Shaista, she smiled at the agitated Miss Johnson.

'It's quite true,' she said. 'The girl is fully mature. She might easily be over twenty by the look of her. And that is what she feels like. You can't expect her to feel the same age as Julia Upjohn, for instance. Intellectually Julia is far ahead of Shaista. Physically, she could quite well wear a liberty bodice still.'

'I wish they were all like Julia Upjohn,' said Miss Johnson.

'I don't,' said Miss Bulstrode briskly. 'A schoolful of girls all alike would be very dull.'

Dull, she thought, as she went back to her marking of Scripture essays. That word had been repeating itself in her brain for some time now. *Dull...*

If there was one thing her school was not, it was dull. During her career as its headmistress, she herself had never felt dull. There had been difficulties to combat, unforeseen crises, irritations with parents, with children: domestic upheavals. She had met and dealt with incipient disasters and turned them into triumphs. It had all been stimulating, exciting, supremely worth while. And even now, though she had made up her mind to it, she did not want to go.

She was physically in excellent health, almost as tough as when she and Chaddy (faithful Chaddy!) had started the great enterprise with a mere handful of children and backing from a banker of unusual foresight. Chaddy's academic distinctions had been better than hers, but it was she who had had the vision to plan and make of the school a place of such distinction that it was known all over Europe. She had never been afraid to experiment, whereas Chaddy had been content to teach soundly but unexcitingly what she knew. Chaddy's supreme achievement had always been to be *there*, at hand, the faithful buffer, quick to render assistance when assistance was needed. As on the opening day of term with Lady Veronica. It was on her solidity, Miss Bulstrode reflected, that an exciting edifice had been built.

Well, from the material point of view, both women had done very well out of it. If they retired now, they would both have a good assured income for the rest of their lives. Miss Bulstrode wondered if Chaddy would want to retire when she herself did? Probably not. Probably, to her, the school was home. She would continue, faithful and reliable, to buttress up Miss Bulstrode's successor.

Because Miss Bulstrode had made up her mind—a successor there must be. Firstly associated with herself in joint rule and then to rule alone. To know when to go—that was one of the great necessities of life. To go before one's powers began to fail, one's sure grip to loosen, before one felt the faint staleness, the unwillingness to envisage continuing effort.

Miss Bulstrode finished marking the essays and noted that the Upjohn child had an original mind. Jennifer Sutcliffe had a complete lack of imagination, but showed an unusually sound grasp of facts. Mary Vyse, of course, was scholarship class—a wonderful retentive memory. But what a dull girl! Dull—that word again. Miss Bulstrode dismissed it from her mind and rang for her secretary.

She began to dictate letters.

Dear Lady Valence. Jane has had some trouble with her ears. I enclose the doctor's report—etc.

Agatha Christie

Dear Baron Von Eisenger. We can certainly arrange for Hedwig to go to the Opera on the occasion of Hellstern's taking the role of Isolda—

An hour passed swiftly. Miss Bulstrode seldom paused for a word. Ann Shapland's pencil raced over the pad.

A very good secretary, Miss Bulstrode thought to herself. Better than Vera Lorrimer. Tiresome girl, Vera. Throwing up her post so suddenly. A nervous breakdown, she had said. Something to do with a man, Miss Bulstrode thought resignedly. It was usually a man.

'That's the lot,' said Miss Bulstrode, as she dictated the last word. She heaved a sigh of relief.

'So many dull things to be done,' she remarked. 'Writing letters to parents is like feeding dogs. Pop some soothing platitude into every waiting mouth.'

Ann laughed. Miss Bulstrode looked at her appraisingly.

'What made you take up secretarial work?'

'I don't quite know. I had no special bent for anything in particular, and it's the sort of thing almost everybody drifts into.'

'You don't find it monotonous?'

'I suppose I've been lucky. I've had a lot of different jobs. I was with Sir Mervyn Todhunter, the archaeologist, for a year, then I was with Sir Andrew Peters in Shell. I was secretary to Monica Lord, the actress, for a while—that really was hectic!' She smiled in remembrance.

'There's a lot of that nowadays amongst you girls,' said Miss Bulstrode. 'All this chopping and changing.' She sounded disapproving.

'Actually, I can't do anything for very long. I've got an invalid mother. She's rather—well—difficult from time to time. And then I have to go back home and take charge.'

'I see.'

'But all the same, I'm afraid I should chop and change anyway. I haven't got the gift for continuity. I find chopping and changing far less dull.'

'Dull…' murmured Miss Bulstrode, struck again by the fatal word.

Ann looked at her in surprise.

'Don't mind me,' said Miss Bulstrode. 'It's just that sometimes one particular word seems to crop up all the time. How would you have liked to be a schoolmistress?' she asked, with some curiosity.

'I'm afraid I should hate it,' said Ann frankly.

'Why?'

'I'd find it terribly dull—Oh, I am sorry.'

She stopped in dismay.

'Teaching isn't in the least dull,' said Miss Bulstrode with spirit. 'It can be the most exciting thing in the world. I shall miss it terribly when I retire.'

'But surely—' Ann stared at her. 'Are you thinking of retiring?'

'It's decided—yes. Oh, I shan't go for another year—or even two years.'

'But—why?'

'Because I've given my best to the school—and had the best from it. I don't want second best.'

'The school will carry on?'

'Oh yes. I have a good successor.'

'Miss Vansittart, I suppose?'

'So you fix on her automatically?' Miss Bulstrode looked at her sharply. 'That's interesting—'

'I'm afraid I hadn't really thought about it. I've just overheard the staff talking. I should think she'll carry on very well—exactly in your tradition. And she's very striking looking, handsome and with quite a presence. I imagine that's important, isn't it?'

'Yes, it is. Yes, I'm sure Eleanor Vansittart is the right person.'

'She'll carry on where you leave off,' said Ann gathering up her things.

But do I want that? thought Miss Bulstrode to herself as Ann went out. Carry on where I leave off? That's just what Eleanor *will* do! No new experiments, nothing revolutionary. That wasn't the way I made Meadowbank what it is. I took chances. I upset lots of people. I bullied and cajoled, and refused to follow the pattern of other schools. Isn't that what I want to follow on here now? Someone to pour new life into the school. Some dynamic personality… like—yes—Eileen Rich.

But Eileen wasn't old enough, hadn't enough experience. She was stimulating, though, she could teach. She had ideas. She would never be dull—Nonsense, she must get that word out of her mind. Eleanor Vansittart was not dull…

She looked up as Miss Chadwick came in.

'Oh, Chaddy,' she said. 'I *am* pleased to see you!'

Miss Chadwick looked a little surprised.

'Why? Is anything the matter?'

'I'm the matter. I don't know my own mind.'

'That's very unlike you, Honoria.'

'Yes, isn't it? How's the term going, Chaddy?'

'Quite all right, I think.' Miss Chadwick sounded a little unsure.

Miss Bulstrode pounced.

'Now then. Don't hedge. What's wrong?'

'Nothing. Really, Honoria, nothing at all. It's just—' Miss Chadwick wrinkled up her forehead and looked rather like a perplexed Boxer dog—'Oh, a feeling. But really it's nothing that I can put a finger on. The new girls seem a pleasant lot. I don't care for Mademoiselle Blanche very much. But then I didn't like Geneviève Depuy, either. *Sly.*'

Miss Bulstrode did not pay very much attention to this criticism. Chaddy always accused the French mistresses of being sly.

'She's not a good teacher,' said Miss Bulstrode. 'Surprising really. Her testimonials were so good.'

'The French never can teach. No discipline,' said Miss Chadwick. 'And really Miss Springer is a little too much of a good thing! Leaps about so. Springer by nature as well as by name...'

'She's good at her job.'

'Oh yes, first class.'

'New staff is always upsetting,' said Miss Bulstrode.

'Yes,' agreed Miss Chadwick eagerly. 'I'm sure it's nothing more than that. By the way, that new gardener is quite young. So unusual nowadays. No gardeners seem to be young. A pity he's so good-looking. We shall have to keep a sharp eye open.'

The two ladies nodded their heads in agreement. They knew, none better, the havoc caused by a good-looking young man to the hearts of adolescent girls.

CHAPTER 7

Straws in the Wind

'Not too bad, boy,' said old Briggs grudgingly, 'not too bad.'

He was expressing approval of his new assistant's performance in digging a strip of ground. It wouldn't do, thought Briggs, to let the young fellow get above himself.

'Mind you,' he went on, 'you don't want to rush at things. Take it steady, that's what I say. Steady is what does it.'

The young man understood that his performance had compared rather too favourably with Briggs's own tempo of work.

'Now, along this here,' continued Briggs, 'we'll put some nice asters out. *She* don't like asters—but I pay no attention. Females has their whims, but if you don't pay no attention, ten to one they never notice. Though I will say *She* is the noticing kind on the whole. You'd think she 'ad enough to bother her head about, running a place like this.'

Adam understood that '*She*' who figured so largely in Briggs's conversation referred to Miss Bulstrode.

'And who was it I saw you talking to just now?' went

Agatha Christie

on Briggs suspiciously, 'when you went along to the potting shed for them bamboos?'

'Oh, that was just one of the young ladies,' said Adam.

'Ah. One of them two Eye-ties, wasn't it? Now you be careful, my boy. Don't you get mixed up with no Eye-ties, I know what I'm talkin' about. I knew Eye-ties, I did, in the first war and if I'd known then what I know now I'd have been more careful. See?'

'Wasn't no harm in it,' said Adam, putting on a sulky manner. 'Just passed the time of day with me, she did, and asked the names of one or two things.'

'Ah,' said Briggs, 'but you be careful. It's not your place to talk to any of the young ladies. *She* wouldn't like it.'

'I wasn't doing no harm and I didn't say anything I shouldn't.'

'I don't say you did, boy. But I say a lot o' young females penned up together here with not so much as a drawing master to take their minds off things—well, you'd better be careful. That's all. Ah, here comes the Old Bitch now. Wanting something difficult, I'll be bound.'

Miss Bulstrode was approaching with a rapid step. 'Good morning, Briggs,' she said. 'Good morning—er—'

'Adam, miss.'

'Ah yes, Adam. Well, you seem to have got that piece dug very satisfactorily. The wire netting's coming down by the far tennis court, Briggs. You'd better attend to that.'

'All right, ma'am, all right. It'll be seen to.'

'What are you putting in front here?'

'Well ma'am, I had thought—'

'*Not* asters,' said Miss Bulstrode, without giving him time to finish. 'Pom Pom dahlias,' and she departed briskly.

'Coming along—giving orders,' said Briggs. 'Not that she isn't a sharp one. She soon notices if you haven't done work properly. And remember what I've said and be careful, boy. About Eye-ties and the others.'

'If she's any fault to find with me, I'll soon know what I can do,' said Adam sulkily. 'Plenty o' jobs going.'

'Ah. That's like you young men all over nowadays. Won't take a word from anybody. All I say is, mind your step.'

Adam continued to look sulky, but bent to his work once more.

Miss Bulstrode walked back along the path towards the school. She was frowning a little.

Miss Vansittart was coming in the opposite direction.

'What a hot afternoon,' said Miss Vansittart.

'Yes, it's very sultry and oppressive.' Again Miss Bulstrode frowned. 'Have you noticed that young man—the young gardener?'

'No, not particularly.'

'He seems to me—well—an odd type,' said Miss Bulstrode thoughtfully. 'Not the usual kind around here.'

'Perhaps he's just come down from Oxford and wants to make a little money.'

'He's good-looking. The girls notice him.'

'The usual problem.'

Miss Bulstrode smiled. 'To combine freedom for the girls *and* strict supervision—is that what you mean, Eleanor?'

'Yes.'

Agatha Christie

'We manage,' said Miss Bulstrode.

'Yes, indeed. You've never had a scandal at Meadowbank, have you?'

'We've come near it once or twice,' said Miss Bulstrode. She laughed. 'Never a dull moment in running a school.' She went on, 'Do you ever find life dull here, Eleanor?'

'No, indeed,' said Miss Vansittart. 'I find the work here most stimulating and satisfying. You must feel very proud and happy, Honoria, at the great success you have achieved.'

'I think I made a good job of things,' said Miss Bulstrode thoughtfully. 'Nothing, of course, is ever quite as one first imagined it...

'Tell me, Eleanor,' she said suddenly, 'if you were running this place instead of me, what changes would you make? Don't mind saying. I shall be interested to hear.'

'I don't think I should want to make any changes,' said Eleanor Vansittart. 'It seems to me the spirit of the place and the whole organization is well-nigh perfect.'

'You'd carry on on the same lines, you mean?'

'Yes, indeed. I don't think they could be bettered.'

Miss Bulstrode was silent for a moment. She was thinking to herself: I wonder if she said that in order to please me. One never knows with people. However close to them you may have been for years. Surely, she can't really mean that. Anybody with any creative feeling at all *must* want to make changes. It's true, though, that it mightn't have seemed tactful to say so... And tact *is* very important. It's important with parents, it's important with the girls, it's important with the staff. Eleanor certainly has tact.

Aloud, she said, 'There must always be adjustments, though, mustn't there? I mean with changing ideas and conditions of life generally.'

'Oh, that, yes,' said Miss Vansittart. 'One has, as they say, to go with the times. But it's *your* school, Honoria, you've made it what it is and your traditions are the essence of it. I think tradition is very important, don't you?'

Miss Bulstrode did not answer. She was hovering on the brink of irrevocable words. The offer of a partnership hung in the air. Miss Vansittart, though seeming unaware in her well-bred way, must be conscious of the fact that it was there. Miss Bulstrode did not know really what was holding her back. Why did she so dislike to commit herself? Probably, she admitted ruefully, because she hated the idea of giving up control. Secretly, of course, she wanted to stay, she wanted to go on running her school. But surely nobody could be a worthier successor than Eleanor? So dependable, so reliable. Of course, as far as that went, so was dear Chaddy—reliable as they came. And yet you could never envisage Chaddy as headmistress of an outstanding school.

'What *do* I want?' said Miss Bulstrode to herself. 'How tiresome I am being! Really, indecision has never been one of my faults up to now.'

A bell sounded in the distance.

'My German class,' said Miss Vansittart. 'I must go in.' She moved at a rapid but dignified step towards the school buildings. Following her more slowly, Miss Bulstrode almost collided with Eileen Rich, hurrying from a side path.

'Oh, I'm so sorry, Miss Bulstrode. I didn't see you.' Her

hair, as usual, was escaping from its untidy bun. Miss Bulstrode noted anew the ugly but interesting bones of her face, a strange, eager, compelling young woman.

'You've got a class?'

'Yes. English—'

'You enjoy teaching, don't you?' said Miss Bulstrode.

'I love it. It's the most fascinating thing in the world.'

'Why?'

Eileen Rich stopped dead. She ran a hand through her hair. She frowned with the effort of thought.

'How interesting. I don't know that I've really *thought* about it. Why *does* one like teaching? Is it because it makes one feel grand and important? No, no... it's not as bad as that. No, it's more like fishing, I think. You don't know what catch you're going to get, what you're going to drag up from the sea. It's the quality of the *response*. It's so exciting when it comes. It doesn't very often, of course.'

Miss Bulstrode nodded in agreement. She had been right! This girl had something!

'I expect you'll run a school of your own some day,' she said.

'Oh, I hope so,' said Eileen Rich. 'I do hope so. That's what I'd like above anything.'

'You've got ideas already, haven't you, as to how a school should be run?'

'Everyone has ideas, I suppose,' said Eileen Rich. 'I daresay a great many of them are fantastic and they'd go utterly wrong. That would be a risk, of course. But one would have to try them out. I would have to learn by experience... The awful thing is that one can't go by other people's experience, can one?'

'Not really,' said Miss Bulstrode. 'In life one has to make one's own mistakes.'

'That's all right in life,' said Eileen Rich. 'In life you can pick yourself up and start again.' Her hands, hanging at her sides, clenched themselves into fists. Her expression was grim. Then suddenly it relaxed into humour. 'But if a school's gone to pieces, you can't very well pick that up and start again, can you?'

'If *you* ran a school like Meadowbank,' said Miss Bulstrode, 'would you make changes—experiment?'

Eileen Rich looked embarrassed. 'That's—that's an awfully hard thing to say,' she said.

'You mean you would,' said Miss Bulstrode. 'Don't mind speaking your mind, child.'

'One would always want, I suppose, to use one's own ideas,' said Eileen Rich. 'I don't say they'd work. They mightn't.'

'But it would be worth taking a risk?'

'It's always worth taking a risk, isn't it?' said Eileen Rich. 'I mean if you feel strongly enough about anything.'

'You don't object to leading a dangerous life. I see...' said Miss Bulstrode.

'I think I've always led a dangerous life.' A shadow passed over the girl's face. 'I must go. They'll be waiting.' She hurried off.

Miss Bulstrode stood looking after her. She was still

Agatha Christie

standing there lost in thought when Miss Chadwick came hurrying to find her.

'Oh! there you are. We've been looking everywhere for you. Professor Anderson has just rung up. He wants to know if he can take Meroe this next weekend. He knows it's against the rules so soon but he's going off quite suddenly to—somewhere that sounds like Azure Basin.'

'Azerbaijan,' said Miss Bulstrode automatically, her mind still on her own thoughts.

'Not enough experience,' she murmured to herself. 'That's the risk. What did you say, Chaddy?'

Miss Chadwick repeated her message.

'I told Miss Shapland to say that we'd ring him back, and sent her to find you.'

'Say it will be quite all right,' said Miss Bulstrode. 'I recognize that this is an exceptional occasion.'

Miss Chadwick looked at her keenly.

'You're worrying, Honoria.'

'Yes, I am. I don't really know my own mind. That's unusual for me—and it upsets me... I know what I'd like to do—but I feel that to hand over to someone without the necessary experience wouldn't be fair to the school.'

'I wish you'd give up this idea of retirement. You belong here. Meadowbank needs you.'

'Meadowbank means a lot to you, Chaddy, doesn't it?'

'There's no school like it anywhere in England,' said Miss Chadwick. 'We can be proud of ourselves, you and I, for having started it.'

Miss Bulstrode put an affectionate arm round her shoulders. 'We can indeed, Chaddy. As for you, you're the comfort of my life. There's nothing about Meadowbank you don't know. You care for it as much as I do. And that's saying a lot, my dear.'

Miss Chadwick flushed with pleasure. It was so seldom that Honoria Bulstrode broke through her reserve.

II

'I simply can't play with the beastly thing. It's no good.'

Jennifer flung her racquet down in despair.

'Oh, Jennifer, what a fuss you make.'

'It's the balance,' Jennifer picked it up again and waggled it experimentally. 'It doesn't balance right.'

'It's much better than my old thing,' Julia compared her racquet. 'Mine's like a sponge. Listen to the sound of it.' She twanged. 'We meant to have it restrung, but Mummy forgot.'

'I'd rather have it than mine, all the same.' Jennifer took it and tried a swish or two with it.

'Well, I'd rather have *yours*. I could really hit something then. I'll swap, if you will.'

'All right then, swap.'

The two girls peeled off the small pieces of adhesive plaster on which their names were written, and re-affixed them, each to the other's racquet.

'I'm not going to swap back again,' said Julia warningly. 'So it's no use saying you don't like my old sponge.'

III

Adam whistled cheerfully as he tacked up the wire netting round the tennis court. The door of the Sports Pavilion opened and Mademoiselle Blanche, the little mousy French Mistress, looked out. She seemed startled at the sight of Adam. She hesitated for a moment and then went back inside.

'Wonder what she's been up to,' said Adam to himself. It would not have occurred to him that Mademoiselle Blanche had been up to anything, if it had not been for her manner. She had a guilty look which immediately roused surmise in his mind. Presently she came out again, closing the door behind her, and paused to speak as she passed him.

'Ah, you repair the netting, I see.'

'Yes, miss.'

'They are very fine courts here, and the swimming pool and the pavilion too. Oh! *le sport*! You think a lot in England of *le sport*, do you not?'

'Well, I suppose we do, miss.'

'Do you play tennis yourself?' Her eyes appraised him in a definitely feminine way and with a faint invitation in her glance. Adam wondered once more about her. It struck him that Mademoiselle Blanche was a somewhat unsuitable French Mistress for Meadowbank.

'No,' he said untruthfully, 'I don't play tennis. Haven't got the time.'

'You play cricket, then?'

'Oh well, I played cricket as a boy. Most chaps do.'

'I have not had much time to look around,' said Angèle Blanche. 'Not until today and it was so fine I thought I would like to examine the Sports Pavilion. I wish to write home to my friends in France who keep a school.'

Again Adam wondered a little. It seemed a lot of unnecessary explanation. It was almost as though Mademoiselle Blanche wished to excuse her presence out here at the Sports Pavilion. But why should she? She had a perfect right to go anywhere in the school grounds that she pleased. There was certainly no need to apologize for it to a gardener's assistant. It raised queries again in his mind. What had this young woman been doing in the Sports Pavilion?

He looked thoughtfully at Mademoiselle Blanche. It would be a good thing perhaps to know a little more about her. Subtly, deliberately, his manner changed. It was still respectful but not quite so respectful. He permitted his eyes to tell her that she was an attractive-looking young woman.

'You must find it a bit dull sometimes working in a girls' school, miss,' he said.

'It does not amuse me very much, no.'

'Still,' said Adam, 'I suppose you get your times off, don't you?'

There was a slight pause. It was as though she were debating with herself. Then, he felt it was with slight regret, the distance between them was deliberately widened.

'Oh yes,' she said, 'I have adequate time off. The

conditions of employment here are excellent.' She gave him a little nod of the head. 'Good morning.' She walked off towards the house.

'You've been up to something,' said Adam to himself, 'in the Sports Pavilion.'

He waited till she was out of sight, then he left his work, went across to the Sports Pavilion and looked inside. But nothing that he could see was out of place. 'All the same,' he said to himself, 'she was up to something.'

As he came out again, he was confronted unexpectedly by Ann Shapland.

'Do you know where Miss Bulstrode is?' she asked.

'I think she's gone back to the house, miss. She was talking to Briggs just now.'

Ann was frowning.

'What are you doing in the Sports Pavilion?'

Adam was slightly taken aback. Nasty suspicious mind *she's* got, he thought. He said, with a faint insolence in his voice:

'Thought I'd like to take a look at it. No harm in looking, is there?'

'Oughtn't you to be getting on with your work?'

'I've just about finished nailing the wire round the tennis court.' He turned, looking up at the building behind him. 'This is new, isn't it? Must have cost a packet. The best of everything the young ladies here get, don't they?'

'They pay for it,' said Ann dryly.

'Pay through the nose, so I've heard,' agreed Adam.

He felt a desire he hardly understood himself, to wound

or annoy this girl. She was so cool always, so self-sufficient. He would really enjoy seeing her angry.

But Ann did not give him that satisfaction. She merely said:

'You'd better finish tacking up the netting,' and went back towards the house. Half-way there, she slackened speed and looked back. Adam was busy at the tennis wire. She looked from him to the Sports Pavilion in a puzzled manner.

CHAPTER 8

Murder

On night duty in Hurst St Cyprian Police Station, Sergeant Green yawned. The telephone rang and he picked up the receiver. A moment later his manner had changed completely. He began scribbling rapidly on a pad.

'Yes? Meadowbank? Yes—and the name? Spell it, please. S-P-R-I-N-G-for greengage?-E-R. Springer. Yes. Yes, please see that nothing is disturbed. Someone'll be with you very shortly.'

Rapidly and methodically he then proceeded to put into motion the various procedures indicated.

'Meadowbank?' said Detective Inspector Kelsey when his turn came. 'That's the girls' school, isn't it? Who is it who's been murdered?

'Death of a Games Mistress,' said Kelsey, thoughtfully. 'Sounds like the title of a thriller on a railway bookstall.'

'Who's likely to have done her in, d'you think?' said the Sergeant. 'Seems unnatural.'

'Even Games Mistresses may have their love lives,' said Detective Inspector Kelsey. 'Where did they say the body was found?'

'In the Sports Pavilion. I suppose that's a fancy name for the gymnasium.'

'Could be,' said Kelsey. 'Death of a Games Mistress in the Gymnasium. Sounds a highly athletic crime, doesn't it? Did you say she was shot?'

'Yes.'

'They find the pistol?'

'No.'

'Interesting,' said Detective Inspector Kelsey, and having assembled his retinue, he departed to carry out his duties.

II

The front door at Meadowbank was open, with light streaming from it, and here Inspector Kelsey was received by Miss Bulstrode herself. He knew her by sight, as indeed most people in the neighbourhood did. Even in this moment of confusion and uncertainty, Miss Bulstrode remained eminently herself, in command of the situation and in command of her subordinates.

'Detective Inspector Kelsey, madam,' said the Inspector.

'What would you like to do first, Inspector Kelsey? Do you wish to go out to the Sports Pavilion or do you want to hear full details?'

'The doctor is with me,' said Kelsey. 'If you will show

Agatha Christie

him and two of my men to where the body is, I should like a few words with you.'

'Certainly. Come into my sitting-room. Miss Rowan, will you show the doctor and the others the way?' She added, 'One of my staff is out there seeing that nothing is disturbed.'

'Thank you, madam.'

Kelsey followed Miss Bulstrode into her sitting-room. 'Who found the body?'

'The matron, Miss Johnson. One of the girls had earache and Miss Johnson was up attending to her. As she did so, she noticed the curtains were not pulled properly and going to pull them she observed that there was a light on in the Sports Pavilion which there should not have been at 1 a.m.,' finished Miss Bulstrode dryly.

'Quite so,' said Kelsey. 'Where is Miss Johnson now?'

'She is here if you want to see her?'

'Presently. Will you go on, madam.'

'Miss Johnson went and woke up another member of my staff, Miss Chadwick. They decided to go out and investigate. As they were leaving by the side door they heard the sound of a shot, whereupon they ran as quickly as they could towards the Sports Pavilion. On arrival there—'

The Inspector broke in. 'Thank you, Miss Bulstrode. If, as you say, Miss Johnson is available, I will hear the next part from her. But first, perhaps, you will tell me something about the murdered woman.'

'Her name is Grace Springer.'

'She has been with you long?'

'No. She came to me this term. My former Games Mistress left to take up a post in Australia.'

'And what did you know about this Miss Springer?'

'Her testimonials were excellent,' said Miss Bulstrode.

'You didn't know her personally before that?'

'No.'

'Have you any idea at all, even the vaguest, of what might have precipitated this tragedy? Was she unhappy? Any unfortunate entanglements?'

Miss Bulstrode shook her head. 'Nothing that I know of. I may say,' she went on, 'that it seems to me most unlikely. She was not that kind of a woman.'

'You'd be surprised,' said Inspector Kelsey darkly.

'Would you like me to fetch Miss Johnson now?'

'If you please. When I've heard her story I'll go out to the gym—or the—what d'you call it—Sports Pavilion?'

'It is a newly built addition to the school this year,' said Miss Bulstrode. 'It is built adjacent to the swimming pool and it comprises a squash court and other features. The racquets, lacrosse and hockey sticks are kept there, and there is a drying room for swim suits.'

'Was there any reason why Miss Springer should be in the Sports Pavilion at night?'

'None whatever,' said Miss Bulstrode unequivocally.

'Very well, Miss Bulstrode. I'll talk to Miss Johnson now.'

Miss Bulstrode left the room and returned bringing the matron with her. Miss Johnson had had a sizeable dollop of brandy administered to her to pull her together after her discovery of the body. The result was a slightly added loquacity.

'This is Detective Inspector Kelsey,' said Miss Bulstrode. 'Pull yourself together, Elspeth, and tell him exactly what happened.'

'It's dreadful,' said Miss Johnson, 'it's really dreadful. Such a thing has never happened before in all my experience. Never! I couldn't have believed it, I really couldn't've believed it. Miss Springer too!'

Inspector Kelsey was a perceptive man. He was always willing to deviate from the course of routine if a remark struck him as unusual or worth following up.

'It seems to you, does it,' he said, 'very strange that it was Miss Springer who was murdered?'

'Well yes, it does, Inspector. She was so—well, so tough, you know. So hearty. Like the sort of woman one could imagine taking on a burglar single-handed—or two burglars.'

'Burglars? H'm,' said Inspector Kelsey. 'Was there anything to steal in the Sports Pavilion?'

'Well, no, really I can't see what there can have been. Swim suits of course, sports paraphernalia.'

'The sort of thing a sneak-thief might have taken,' agreed Kelsey. 'Hardly worth breaking in for, I should have thought. Was it broken into, by the way?'

'Well, really, I never thought to look,' said Miss Johnson. 'I mean, the door was open when we got there and—'

'It had not been broken into,' said Miss Bulstrode.

'I see,' said Kelsey. 'A key was used.' He looked at Miss Johnson. 'Was Miss Springer well liked?' he asked.

'Well, really, I couldn't say. I mean, after all, she's dead.'

'So, you didn't like her,' said Kelsey perceptively, ignoring Miss Johnson's finer feelings.

'I don't think anyone could have liked her very much,' said Miss Johnson. 'She had a very positive manner, you know. Never minded contradicting people flatly. She was very efficient and took her work very seriously I should say, wouldn't you, Miss Bulstrode?'

'Certainly,' said Miss Bulstrode.

Kelsey returned from the by-path he had been pursuing. 'Now, Miss Johnson, let's hear just what happened.'

'Jane, one of our pupils, had earache. She woke up with a rather bad attack of it and came to me. I got some remedies and when I'd got her back to bed, I saw the window curtains were flapping and thought perhaps it would be better for once if her window was not opened at night as it was blowing rather in that direction. Of course the girls always sleep with their windows open. We have difficulties sometimes with the foreigners, but I always insist that—'

'That really doesn't matter now,' said Miss Bulstrode. 'Our general rules of hygiene would not interest Inspector Kelsey.'

'No, no, of course not,' said Miss Johnson. 'Well, as I say I went to shut the window and what was my surprise to see a light in the Sports Pavilion. It was quite distinct, I couldn't mistake it. It seemed to be moving about.'

'You mean it was not the electric light turned on but the light of a torch or flashlight?'

'Yes, yes, that's what it must have been. I thought at once "Dear me, what's anyone doing out there at this time of night?" Of course I didn't think of burglars. That would have been a very fanciful idea, as you said just now.'

'What did you think of?' asked Kelsey.

Miss Johnson shot a glance at Miss Bulstrode and back again.

'Well, really, I don't know that I had any ideas in particular. I mean, well—well really, I mean I couldn't think—'

Miss Bulstrode broke in. 'I should imagine that Miss Johnson had the idea that one of our pupils might have gone out there to keep an assignation with someone,' she said. 'Is that right, Elspeth?'

Miss Johnson gasped. 'Well, yes, the idea did come into my head just for the moment. One of our Italian girls, perhaps. Foreigners are so much more precocious than English girls.'

'Don't be so insular,' said Miss Bulstrode. 'We've had plenty of English girls trying to make unsuitable assignations. It was a very natural thought to have occurred to you and probably the one that would have occurred to me.'

'Go on,' said Inspector Kelsey.

'So I thought the best thing,' went on Miss Johnson, 'was to go to Miss Chadwick and ask her to come out with me and see what was going on.'

Cat Among the Pigeons

'Why Miss Chadwick?' asked Kelsey. 'Any particular reason for selecting that particular mistress?'

'Well, I didn't want to disturb Miss Bulstrode,' said Miss Johnson, 'and I'm afraid it's rather a habit of ours always to go to Miss Chadwick if we don't want to disturb Miss Bulstrode. You see, Miss Chadwick's been here a very long time and has had so much experience.'

'Anyway,' said Kelsey, 'you went to Miss Chadwick and woke her up. Is that right?'

'Yes. She agreed with me that we must go out there immediately. We didn't wait to dress or anything, just put on pullovers and coats and went out by the side door. And it was then, just as we were standing on the path, that we heard a shot from the Sports Pavilion. So we ran along the path as fast as we could. Rather stupidly we hadn't taken a torch with us and it was hard to see where we were going. We stumbled once or twice but we got there quite quickly. The door was open. We switched on the light and—'

Kelsey interrupted. 'There was no light then when you got there. Not a torch or any other light?'

'No. The place was in darkness. We switched on the light and there she was. She—'

'That's all right,' said Inspector Kelsey kindly, 'you needn't describe anything. I shall be going out there now and I shall see for myself. You didn't meet anyone on your way there?'

'No.'

'Or hear anybody running away?'

Agatha Christie

'No. We didn't hear anything.'

'Did anybody else hear the shot in the school building?' asked Kelsey looking at Miss Bulstrode.

She shook her head. 'No. Not that I know of. Nobody has said that they heard it. The Sports Pavilion is some distance away and I rather doubt if the shot would be noticeable.'

'Perhaps from one of the rooms on the side of the house giving on the Sports Pavilion?'

'Hardly, I think, unless one were listening for such a thing. I'm sure it wouldn't be loud enough to wake anybody up.'

'Well, thank you,' said Inspector Kelsey. 'I'll be going out to the Sports Pavilion now.'

'I will come with you,' said Miss Bulstrode.

'Do you want me to come too?' asked Miss Johnson. 'I will if you like. I mean it's no good shirking things, is it? I always feel that one must face whatever comes and—'

'Thank you,' said Inspector Kelsey, 'there's no need, Miss Johnson. I wouldn't think of putting you to any further strain.'

'So awful,' said Miss Johnson, 'it makes it worse to feel I didn't like her very much. In fact, we had a disagreement only last night in the Common Room. I stuck to it that too much P.T. was bad for some girls—the more delicate girls. Miss Springer said nonsense, that they were just the ones who needed it. Toned them up and made new women of them, she said. I said to her that really she didn't know everything though she might think she did. After all I have been professionally trained and I know a great deal more about delicacy and illness than Miss Springer does—did, though I've no doubt that Miss Springer knows everything about parallel bars and vaulting horses and coaching tennis. But, oh dear, now I think of what's happened, I wish I hadn't said quite what I did. I suppose one always feels like that afterwards when something dreadful has occurred. I really do blame myself.'

'Now sit down there, dear,' said Miss Bulstrode, settling her on the sofa. 'You just sit down and rest and pay no attention to any little disputes you may have had. Life would be very dull if we agreed with each other on every subject.'

Miss Johnson sat down shaking her head, then yawned. Miss Bulstrode followed Kelsey into the hall.

'I gave her rather a lot of brandy,' she said, apologetically. 'It's made her a little voluble. But not confused, do you think?'

'No,' said Kelsey. 'She gave quite a clear account of what happened.'

Miss Bulstrode led the way to the side door.

'Is this the way Miss Johnson and Miss Chadwick went out?'

'Yes. You see it leads straight on to the path through the rhododendrons there which comes out at the Sports Pavilion.'

The Inspector had a powerful torch and he and Miss

Agatha Christie

Bulstrode soon reached the building where the lights were now glaring.

'Fine bit of building,' said Kelsey, looking at it.

'It cost us a pretty penny,' said Miss Bulstrode, 'but we can afford it,' she added serenely.

The open door led into a fair-sized room. There were lockers there with the names of the various girls on them. At the end of the room there was a stand for tennis racquets and one for lacrosse sticks. The door at the side led off to showers and changing cubicles. Kelsey paused before going in. Two of his men had been busy. A photographer had just finished his job and another man who was busy testing for fingerprints looked up and said,

'You can walk straight across the floor, sir. You'll be all right. We haven't finished down this end yet.'

Kelsey walked forward to where the police surgeon was kneeling by the body. The latter looked up as Kelsey approached.

'She was shot from about four feet away,' he said. 'Bullet penetrated the heart. Death must have been pretty well instantaneous.'

'Yes. How long ago?'

'Say an hour or thereabouts.'

Kelsey nodded. He strolled round to look at the tall figure of Miss Chadwick where she stood grimly, like a watchdog, against one wall. About fifty-five, he judged, good forehead, obstinate mouth, untidy grey hair, no trace of hysteria. The kind of woman, he thought, who could be depended upon in a crisis though she might be overlooked in ordinary everyday life.

'Miss Chadwick?' he said.

'Yes.'

'You came out with Miss Johnson and discovered the body?'

'Yes. She was just as she is now. She was dead.'

'And the time?'

'I looked at my watch when Miss Johnson roused me. It was ten minutes to one.'

Kelsey nodded. That agreed with the time that Miss Johnson had given him. He looked down thoughtfully at the dead woman. Her bright red hair was cut short. She had a freckled face, with a chin which jutted out strongly, and a spare, athletic figure. She was wearing a tweed skirt and a heavy, dark pullover. She had brogues on her feet with no stockings.

'Any sign of the weapon?' asked Kelsey.

One of his men shook his head. 'No sign at all, sir.'

'What about the torch?'

'There's a torch there in the corner.'

'Any prints on it?'

'Yes. The dead woman's.'

'So she's the one who had the torch,' said Kelsey thoughtfully. 'She came out here with a torch—why?' He asked it partly of himself, partly of his men, partly of Miss Bulstrode and Miss Chadwick. Finally he seemed to concentrate on the latter. 'Any ideas?'

Agatha Christie

Miss Chadwick shook her head. 'No idea at all. I suppose she might have left something here—forgotten it this afternoon or evening—and come out to fetch it. But it seems rather unlikely in the middle of the night.'

'It must have been something very important if she did,' said Kelsey.

He looked round him. Nothing seemed disturbed except the stand of racquets at the end. That seemed to have been pulled violently forward. Several of the racquets were lying about on the floor.

'Of course,' said Miss Chadwick, 'she could have seen a light here, like Miss Johnson did later, and have come out to investigate. That seems the most likely thing to me.'

'I think you're right,' said Kelsey. 'There's just one small matter. Would she have come out here alone?'

'Yes.' Miss Chadwick answered without hesitation.

'Miss Johnson,' Kelsey reminded her, 'came and woke you up.'

'I know,' said Miss Chadwick, 'and that's what I should have done if I'd seen the light. I would have woken up Miss Bulstrode or Miss Vansittart or somebody. But Miss Springer wouldn't. She would have been quite confident—indeed would have preferred to tackle an intruder on her own.'

'Another point,' said the Inspector. 'You came out through the side door with Miss Johnson. Was the side door unlocked?'

'Yes, it was.'

'Presumably left unlocked by Miss Springer?'

'That seems the natural conclusion,' said Miss Chadwick.

'So we assume,' said Kelsey, 'that Miss Springer saw a light out here in the gymnasium—Sports Pavilion—whatever you call it—that she came out to investigate and that whoever was here shot her.' He wheeled round on Miss Bulstrode as she stood motionless in the doorway. 'Does that seem right to you?' he asked.

'It doesn't seem right at all,' said Miss Bulstrode. 'I grant you the first part. We'll say Miss Springer saw a light out here and that she went out to investigate by herself. That's perfectly probable. But that the person she disturbed here should shoot her—that seems to me all wrong. If anyone was here who had no business to be here they would be more likely to run away, or to try to run away. Why should someone come to this place at this hour of night with a pistol? It's ridiculous, that's what it is. Ridiculous! There's nothing here worth stealing, certainly nothing for which it would be worth while doing murder.'

'You think it more likely that Miss Springer disturbed a rendezvous of some kind?'

'That's the natural and most probable explanation,' said Miss Bulstrode. 'But it doesn't explain the fact of murder, does it? Girls in my school don't carry pistols about with them and any young man they might be meeting seems very unlikely to have a pistol either.'

Kelsey agreed. 'He'd have had a flick knife at most,' he said. 'There's an alternative,' he went on. 'Say Miss Springer came out here to meet a man—'

Miss Chadwick giggled suddenly. 'Oh no,' she said, 'not Miss Springer.'

Agatha Christie

'I do not mean necessarily an amorous assignment,' said the Inspector dryly. 'I'm suggesting that the murder was deliberate, that someone intended to murder Miss Springer, that they arranged to meet her here and shot her.'

CHAPTER 9

Cat Among the Pigeons

Letter from Jennifer Sutcliffe to her mother:

Dear Mummy,

We had a murder last night. Miss Springer, the gym mistress. It happened in the middle of the night and the police came and this morning they're asking everybody questions.

Miss Chadwick told us not to talk to anybody about it but I thought you'd like to know.

With love,
Jennifer

II

Meadowbank was an establishment of sufficient importance to merit the personal attention of the Chief Constable. While routine investigation was going on Miss Bulstrode had not been inactive. She rang up a Press magnate and

Agatha Christie

the Home Secretary, both personal friends of hers. As a result of those manoeuvres, very little had appeared about the event in the papers. A games mistress had been found dead in the school gymnasium. She had been shot, whether by accident or not was as yet not determined. Most of the notices of the event had an almost apologetic note in them, as though it were thoroughly tactless of any games mistress to get herself shot in such circumstances.

Ann Shapland had a busy day taking down letters to parents. Miss Bulstrode did not waste time in telling her pupils to keep quiet about the event. She knew that it would be a waste of time. More or less lurid reports would be sure to be penned to anxious parents and guardians. She intended her own balanced and reasonable account of the tragedy to reach them at the same time.

Later that afternoon she sat in conclave with Mr Stone, the Chief Constable, and Inspector Kelsey. The police were perfectly amenable to having the Press play the thing down as much as possible. It enabled them to pursue their inquiries quietly and without interference.

'I'm very sorry about this, Miss Bulstrode, very sorry indeed,' said the Chief Constable. 'I suppose it's—well—a bad thing for you.'

'Murder's a bad thing for any school, yes,' said Miss Bulstrode. 'It's no good dwelling on that now, though. We shall weather it, no doubt, as we have weathered other storms. All I do hope is that the matter will be cleared up *quickly*.'

'Don't see why it shouldn't, eh?' said Stone. He looked at Kelsey.

Kelsey said, 'It may help when we get her background.'

'D'you really think so?' asked Miss Bulstrode dryly.

'Somebody may have had it in for her,' Kelsey suggested.

Miss Bulstrode did not reply.

'You think it's tied up with this place?' asked the Chief Constable.

'Inspector Kelsey does really,' said Miss Bulstrode. 'He's only trying to save my feelings, I think.'

'I think it does tie up with Meadowbank,' said the Inspector slowly. 'After all, Miss Springer had her times off like all the other members of the staff. She could have arranged a meeting with anyone if she had wanted to do so at any spot she chose. Why choose the gymnasium here in the middle of the night?'

'You have no objection to a search being made of the school premises, Miss Bulstrode?' asked the Chief Constable.

'None at all. You're looking for the pistol or revolver or whatever it is, I suppose?'

'Yes. It was a small pistol of foreign make.'

'Foreign,' said Miss Bulstrode thoughtfully.

'To your knowledge, do any of your staff or any of the pupils have such a thing as a pistol in their possession?'

'Certainly not to my knowledge,' said Miss Bulstrode. 'I am fairly certain that none of the pupils have. Their possessions are unpacked for them when they arrive and such a thing would have been seen and noted, and would, I may say, have aroused considerable comment. But please, Inspector Kelsey, do exactly as you like in that respect. I see your men have been searching the grounds today.'

Agatha Christie

The Inspector nodded. 'Yes.'

He went on: 'I should also like interviews with the other members of your staff. One or other of them may have heard some remark made by Miss Springer that will give us a clue. Or may have observed some oddity of behaviour on her part.'

He paused, then went on, 'The same thing might apply to the pupils.'

Miss Bulstrode said: 'I had formed the plan of making a short address to the girls this evening after prayers. I would ask that if any of them has any knowledge that might possibly bear upon Miss Springer's death that they should come and tell me of it.'

'Very sound idea,' said the Chief Constable.

'But you must remember this,' said Miss Bulstrode, 'one or other of the girls may wish to make herself important by exaggerating some incident or even by inventing one. Girls do very odd things: but I expect you are used to dealing with that form of exhibitionism.'

'I've come across it,' said Inspector Kelsey. 'Now,' he added, 'please give me a list of your staff, also the servants.'

III

'I've looked through all the lockers in the Pavilion, sir.'

'And you didn't find anything?' said Kelsey.

'No, sir, nothing of importance. Funny things in some of them, but nothing in our line.'

120

'None of them were locked, were they?'

'No, sir, they can lock. There were keys in them, but none of them were locked.'

Kelsey looked round the bare floor thoughtfully. The tennis and lacrosse sticks had been replaced tidily on their stands.

'Oh well,' he said, 'I'm going up to the house now to have a talk with the staff.'

'You don't think it was an inside job, sir?'

'It could have been,' said Kelsey. 'Nobody's got an alibi except those two mistresses, Chadwick and Johnson and the child Jane that had the earache. Theoretically, everyone else was in bed and asleep, but there's no one to vouch for that. The girls all have separate rooms and naturally the staff do. Any one of them, including Miss Bulstrode herself, could have come out and met Springer here, or could have followed her here. Then, after she'd been shot, whoever it was could dodge back quietly through the bushes to the side door, and be nicely back in bed again when the alarm was given. It's motive that's difficult. Yes,' said Kelsey, 'it's motive. Unless there's something going on here that we don't know anything about, there doesn't seem to *be* any motive.'

He stepped out of the Pavilion and made his way slowly back to the house. Although it was past working hours, old Briggs, the gardener, was putting in a little work on a flower bed and he straightened up as the Inspector passed.

'You work late hours,' said Kelsey, smiling.

'Ah,' said Briggs. 'Young 'uns don't know what gardening

Agatha Christie

is. Come on at eight and knock off at five—that's what they think it is. You've got to study your weather, some days you might as well not be out in the garden at all, and there's other days as you can work from seven in the morning until eight at night. That is if you love the place and have pride in the look of it.'

'You ought to be proud of this one,' said Kelsey. 'I've never seen any place better kept these days.'

'These days is right,' said Briggs. 'But I'm lucky I am. I've got a strong young fellow to work for me. A couple of boys, too, but they're not much good. Most of these boys and young men won't come and do this sort of work. All for going into factories, they are, or white collars and working in an office. Don't like to get their hands soiled with a bit of honest earth. But I'm lucky, as I say. I've got a good man working for me as come and offered himself.'

'Recently?' said Inspector Kelsey.

'Beginning of the term,' said Briggs. 'Adam, his name is. Adam Goodman.'

'I don't think I've seen him about,' said Kelsey.

'Asked for the day off today, he did,' said Briggs. 'I give it him. Didn't seem to be much doing today with you people tramping all over the place.'

'Somebody should have told me about him,' said Kelsey sharply.

'What do you mean, told you about him?'

'He's not on my list,' said the Inspector. 'Of people employed here, I mean.'

'Oh, well, you can see him tomorrow, mister,' said Briggs. 'Not that he can tell you anything, I don't suppose.'

'You never know,' said the Inspector.

A strong young man who had offered himself at the beginning of the term? It seemed to Kelsey that here was the first thing that he had come across which might be a little out of the ordinary.

IV

The girls filed into the hall for prayers that evening as usual, and afterwards Miss Bulstrode arrested their departure by raising her hand.

'I have something to say to you all. Miss Springer, as you know, was shot last night in the Sports Pavilion. If any of you has heard or seen anything in the past week—anything that has puzzled you relating to Miss Springer, anything Miss Springer may have said or someone else may have said of her that strikes you as at all significant, I should like to know it. You can come to me in my sitting-room any time this evening.'

'Oh,' Julia Upjohn sighed, as the girls filed out, 'how I wish we *did* know something! But we don't, do we, Jennifer?'

'No,' said Jennifer, 'of course we don't.'

'Miss Springer always seemed so very ordinary,' said Julia sadly, 'much too ordinary to get killed in a mysterious way.'

'I don't suppose it was so mysterious,' said Jennifer. 'Just a burglar.'

Agatha Christie

'Stealing our tennis racquets, I suppose,' said Julia with sarcasm.

'Perhaps someone was blackmailing her,' suggested one of the other girls hopefully.

'What about?' said Jennifer.

But nobody could think of any reason for blackmailing Miss Springer.

V

Inspector Kelsey started his interviewing of the staff with Miss Vansittart. A handsome woman, he thought, summing her up. Possibly forty or a little over; tall, well-built, grey hair tastefully arranged. She had dignity and composure, with a certain sense, he thought, of her own importance. She reminded him a little of Miss Bulstrode herself: she was the schoolmistress type all right. All the same, he reflected, Miss Bulstrode had something that Miss Vansittart had not. Miss Bulstrode had a quality of unexpectedness. He did not feel that Miss Vansittart would ever be unexpected.

Question and answer followed routine. In effect, Miss Vansittart had seen nothing, had noticed nothing, had heard nothing. Miss Springer had been excellent at her job. Yes, her manner had perhaps been a trifle brusque, but not, she thought, unduly so. She had not perhaps had a very attractive personality but that was really not a necessity in a Games Mistress. It was better, in fact, *not* to have mistresses who had attractive personalities. It did not do to let the girls get emotional about the mistresses. Miss Vansittart, having contributed nothing of value, made her exit.

'See no evil, hear no evil, think no evil. Same like the monkeys,' observed Sergeant Percy Bond, who was assisting Inspector Kelsey in his task.

Kelsey grinned. 'That's about right, Percy,' he said.

'There's something about schoolmistresses that gives me the hump,' said Sergeant Bond. 'Had a terror of them ever since I was a kid. Knew one that was a holy terror. So upstage and la-di-da you never knew what she was trying to teach you.'

The next mistress to appear was Eileen Rich. Ugly as sin was Inspector Kelsey's first reaction. Then he qualified it; she had a certain attraction. He started his routine questions, but the answers were not quite so routine as he had expected. After saying No, she had not heard or noticed anything special that anyone else had said about Miss Springer or that Miss Springer herself had said, Eileen Rich's next answer was not what he anticipated. He had asked:

'There was no one as far as you know who had a personal grudge against her?'

'Oh no,' said Eileen Rich quickly. 'One couldn't have. I think that was her tragedy, you know. That she wasn't a person one could ever hate.'

'Now just what do you mean by that, Miss Rich?'

'I mean she wasn't a person one could ever have wanted to destroy. Everything she did and was, was on the surface. She annoyed people. They often had sharp words with her,

Agatha Christie

but it didn't mean anything. Not anything deep. I'm sure she wasn't killed for *herself*, if you know what I mean.'

'I'm not quite sure that I do, Miss Rich.'

'I mean if you had something like a bank robbery, she might quite easily be the cashier that gets shot, but it would be as a cashier, not as Grace Springer. Nobody would love her or hate her enough to want to do away with her. I think she probably felt that without thinking about it, and that's what made her so officious. About finding fault, you know, and enforcing rules and finding out what people were doing that they shouldn't be doing, and showing them up.'

'Snooping?' asked Kelsey.

'No, not exactly snooping.' Eileen Rich considered. 'She wouldn't tiptoe round on sneakers or anything of that kind. But if she found something going on that she didn't understand she'd be quite determined to get to the bottom of it. And she *would* get to the bottom of it.'

'I see.' He paused a moment. 'You didn't like her yourself much, did you, Miss Rich?'

'I don't think I ever thought about her. She was just the Games Mistress. Oh! What a horrible thing that is to say about anybody! Just this—just that! But that's how *she* felt about her job. It was a job that she took pride in doing well. She didn't find it fun. She wasn't keen when she found a girl who might be really good at tennis, or really fine at some form of athletics. She didn't rejoice in it or triumph.'

Kelsey looked at her curiously. An odd young woman, this, he thought.

'You seem to have your ideas on most things, Miss Rich,' he said.

'Yes. Yes, I suppose I do.'

'How long have you been at Meadowbank?'

'Just over a year and a half.'

'There's never been any trouble before?'

'At Meadowbank?' She sounded startled.

'Yes.'

'Oh no. Everything's been quite all right until this term.'

Kelsey pounced.

'What's been wrong this term? You don't mean the murder, do you? You mean something else—'

'I don't—' she stopped—'Yes, perhaps I do—but it's all very nebulous.'

'Go on.'

'Miss Bulstrode's not been happy lately,' said Eileen slowly. 'That's one thing. You wouldn't know it. I don't think anybody else has even noticed it. But I have. And she's not the only one who's unhappy. But that isn't what you mean, is it? That's just people's feelings. The kind of things you get when you're cooped up together and think about one thing too much. You meant, was there anything that didn't seem right just this term. That's it, isn't it?'

'Yes,' said Kelsey, looking at her curiously, 'yes, that's it. Well, what about it?'

'I think there *is* something wrong here,' said Eileen Rich slowly. 'It's as though there were someone among us who didn't belong.' She looked at him, smiled, almost laughed and said, 'Cat among the pigeons, that's the sort of feeling.

Agatha Christie

We're the pigeons, all of us, and the cat's amongst us. But we can't *see* the cat.'

'That's very vague, Miss Rich.'

'Yes, isn't it? It sounds quite idiotic. I can hear that myself. What I really mean, I suppose, is that there has been something, some little thing that I've noticed but I don't know what I've noticed.'

'About anyone in particular?'

'No, I told you, that's just it. I don't know who it is. The only way I can sum it up is to say that there's *someone* here, who's—somehow—wrong! There's someone here—I don't know who—who makes me uncomfortable. Not when I'm looking at her but when she's looking at me because it's when she's looking at me that it shows, whatever it is. Oh, I'm getting more incoherent than ever. And anyway, it's only a feeling. It's not what you want. It isn't evidence.'

'No,' said Kelsey, 'it isn't evidence. Not yet. But it's interesting, and if your feeling gets any more definite, Miss Rich, I'd be glad to hear about it.'

She nodded. 'Yes,' she said, 'because it's serious, isn't it? I mean, someone's been killed—we don't know why—and the killer may be miles away, or, on the other hand, the killer may be here in the school. And if so that pistol or revolver or whatever it is, must be here too. That's not a very nice thought, is it?'

She went out with a slight nod. Sergeant Bond said,

'Crackers—or don't you think so?'

'No,' said Kelsey, 'I don't think she's crackers. I think she's what's called a sensitive. You know, like the people who know when there's a cat in the room long before they see it. If she'd been born in an African tribe she might have been a witch doctor.'

'They go round smelling out evil, don't they?' said Sergeant Bond.

'That's right, Percy,' said Kelsey. 'And that's exactly what I'm trying to do myself. Nobody's come across with any concrete facts so I've got to go about smelling out things. We'll have the French woman next.'

CHAPTER 10

Fantastic Story

Mademoiselle Angèle Blanche was thirty-five at a guess. No make-up, dark brown hair arranged neatly but unbecomingly. A severe coat and skirt.

It was Mademoiselle Blanche's first term at Meadowbank, she explained. She was not sure that she wished to remain for a further term.

'It is not nice to be in a school where murders take place,' she said disapprovingly.

Also, there did not seem to be burglar alarms anywhere in the house—that was dangerous.

'There's nothing of any great value, Mademoiselle Blanche, to attract burglars.'

Mademoiselle Blanche shrugged her shoulders.

'How does one know? These girls who come here, some of them have very rich fathers. They may have something with them of great value. A burglar knows about that, perhaps, and he comes here because he thinks this is an easy place to steal it.'

'If a girl had something of value with her it wouldn't be in the gymnasium.'

'How do you know?' said Mademoiselle. 'They have lockers there, do they not, the girls?'

'Only to keep their sports kit in, and things of that kind.'

'Ah yes, that is what is supposed. But a girl could hide anything in the toe of a gym shoe, or wrapped up in an old pullover or in a scarf.'

'What sort of thing, Mademoiselle Blanche?'

But Mademoiselle Blanche had no idea what sort of thing.

'Even the most indulgent fathers don't give their daughters diamond necklaces to take to school,' the Inspector said.

Again Mademoiselle Blanche shrugged her shoulders.

'Perhaps it is something of a different kind of value—a scarab, say, or something that a collector would give a lot of money for. One of the girls has a father who is an archaeologist.'

Kelsey smiled. 'I don't really think that's likely, you know, Mademoiselle Blanche.'

She shrugged her shoulders. 'Oh well, I only make the suggestion.'

'Have you taught in any other English schools, Mademoiselle Blanche?'

'One in the north of England some time ago. Mostly I have taught in Switzerland and in France. Also in Germany. I think I will come to England to improve my English. I have a friend here. She went sick and she told me I could take her position here as Miss Bulstrode would be glad to find somebody quickly. So I came. But I do not like it very much. As I tell you, I do not think I shall stay.'

'Why don't you like it?' Kelsey persisted.

'I do not like places where there are shootings,' said Mademoiselle Blanche. 'And the children, they are not respectful.'

'They are not quite children, are they?'

'Some of them behave like babies, some of them might be twenty-five. There are all kinds here. They have much freedom. I prefer an establishment with more routine.'

'Did you know Miss Springer well?'

'I knew her practically not at all. She had bad manners and I conversed with her as little as possible. She was all bones and freckles and a loud ugly voice. She was like caricatures of Englishwomen. She was rude to me often and I did not like it.'

'What was she rude to you about?'

'She did not like me coming to her Sports Pavilion. That seems to be how she feels about it—or felt about it, I mean—that it was *her* Sports Pavilion! I go there one day because I am interested. I have not been in it before and it is a new building. It is very well arranged and planned and I am just looking round. Then Miss Springer she comes and says "What are you doing here? This is no business of yours to be in here." She says that to me—*me*, a mistress in the school! What does she think I am, a pupil?'

'Yes, yes, very irritating, I'm sure,' said Kelsey, soothingly.

'The manners of a pig, that is what she had. And then she calls out "Do not go away with the key in your hand." She upset me. When I pull the door open the key fell out and I pick it up. I forget to put it back, because she has offended me. And then she shouts after me as though she thinks I was meaning to steal it. *Her* key, I suppose, as well as *her* Sports Pavilion.'

'That seems a little odd, doesn't it?' said Kelsey. 'That she should feel like that about the gymnasium, I mean. As though it were her private property, as though she were afraid of people finding something she had hidden there.' He made the faint feeler tentatively, but Angèle Blanche merely laughed.

'Hide something there—what could you hide in a place like that? Do you think she hides her love letters there? I am sure she has never had a love letter written to her! The other mistresses, they are at least polite. Miss Chadwick, she is old-fashioned and she fusses. Miss Vansittart, she is very nice, *grande dame*, sympathetic. Miss Rich, she is a little crazy I think, but friendly. And the younger mistresses are quite pleasant.'

Angèle Blanche was dismissed after a few more unimportant questions.

'Touchy,' said Bond. 'All the French are touchy.'

'All the same, it's interesting,' said Kelsey. 'Miss Springer didn't like people prowling about *her* gymnasium—Sports Pavilion—I don't know what to call the thing. Now *why*?'

'Perhaps she thought the Frenchwoman was spying on her,' suggested Bond.

Agatha Christie

'Well, but *why* should she think so? I mean, ought it to have mattered to her that Angèle Blanche should spy on her unless there was something she was afraid of Angèle Blanche finding out?

'Who have we got left?' he added.

'The two junior mistresses, Miss Blake and Miss Rowan, and Miss Bulstrode's secretary.'

Miss Blake was young and earnest with a round good-natured face. She taught Botany and Physics. She had nothing much to say that could help. She had seen very little of Miss Springer and had no idea of what could have led to her death.

Miss Rowan, as befitted one who held a degree in psychology, had views to express. It was highly probable, she said, that Miss Springer had committed suicide.

Inspector Kelsey raised his eyebrows.

'Why should she? Was she unhappy in any way?'

'She was aggressive,' said Miss Rowan, leaning forward and peering eagerly through her thick lenses. 'Very aggressive. I consider that significant. It was a defence mechanism, to conceal a feeling of inferiority.'

'Everything I've heard so far,' said Inspector Kelsey, 'points to her being very sure of herself.'

'*Too* sure of herself,' said Miss Rowan darkly. 'And several of the things she said bear out my assumption.'

'Such as?'

'She hinted at people being "not what they seemed". She mentioned that at the last school where she was employed, she had "unmasked" someone. The Headmistress, however, had been prejudiced, and refused to listen to what she had found out. Several of the other mistresses, too, had been what she called "against her".

'You see what that means, Inspector?' Miss Rowan nearly fell off her chair as she leaned forward excitedly. Strands of lank dark hair fell forward across her face. 'The beginnings of a persecution complex.'

Inspector Kelsey said politely that Miss Rowan might be correct in her assumptions, but that he couldn't accept the theory of suicide, unless Miss Rowan could explain how Miss Springer had managed to shoot herself from a distance of at least four feet away, and had also been able to make the pistol disappear into thin air afterwards.

Miss Rowan retorted acidly that the police were well known to be prejudiced against psychology.

She then gave place to Ann Shapland.

'Well, Miss Shapland,' said Inspector Kelsey, eyeing her neat and businesslike appearance with favour, 'what light can you throw upon this matter?'

'Absolutely none, I'm afraid. I've got my own sitting-room, and I don't see much of the staff. The whole thing's unbelievable.'

'In what way unbelievable?'

'Well, first that Miss Springer should get shot at all. Say somebody broke into the gymnasium and she went out to see who it was. That's all right, I suppose, but who'd want to break into the gymnasium?'

'Boys, perhaps, some young locals who wanted to help themselves to equipment of some kind or another, or who did it for a lark.'

'If that's so, I can't help feeling that what Miss Springer would have said was: "Now then, what are you doing here? Be off with you," and they'd have gone off.'

'Did it ever seem to you that Miss Springer adopted any particular attitude about the Sports Pavilion?'

Ann Shapland looked puzzled. 'Attitude?'

'I mean did she regard it as her special province and dislike other people going there?'

'Not that I know of. Why should she? It was just part of the school buildings.'

'You didn't notice anything yourself? You didn't find that if you went there she resented your presence—anything of that kind?'

Ann Shapland shook her head. 'I haven't been out there myself more than a couple of times. I haven't the time. I've gone out there once or twice with a message for one of the girls from Miss Bulstrode. That's all.'

'You didn't know that Miss Springer had objected to Mademoiselle Blanche being out there?'

'No, I didn't hear anything about that. Oh yes, I believe I did. Mademoiselle Blanche was rather cross about something one day, but then she is a little bit touchy, you know. There was something about her going into the drawing class one day and resenting something the drawing mistress said to her. Of course she hasn't really very much to do—Mademoiselle Blanche, I mean. She only teaches one subject—French, and she has a lot of time on her hands. I think—' she hesitated, 'I think she is perhaps rather an inquisitive person.'

'Do you think it likely that when she went into the Sports Pavilion she was poking about in any of the lockers?'

'The girls' lockers? Well, I wouldn't put it past her. She might amuse herself that way.'

'Does Miss Springer herself have a locker out there?'

'Yes, of course.'

'If Mademoiselle Blanche was caught poking about in Miss Springer's locker, then I can imagine that Miss Springer *would* be annoyed?'

'She certainly would!'

'You don't know anything about Miss Springer's private life?'

'I don't think anyone did,' said Ann. 'Did she have one, I wonder?'

'And there's nothing else—nothing connected with the Sports Pavilion, for instance, that you haven't told me?'

'Well—' Ann hesitated.

'Yes, Miss Shapland, let's have it.'

'It's nothing really,' said Ann slowly. 'But one of the gardeners—not Briggs, the young one. I saw him come out of the Sports Pavilion one day, and he had no business to be in there at all. Of course it was probably just curiosity on his part—or perhaps an excuse to slack off a bit from work—he was supposed to be nailing down the wire on the tennis court. I don't suppose really there's anything in it.'

'Still, you remembered it,' Kelsey pointed out. 'Now why?'

'I think—' she frowned. 'Yes, because his manner was a little odd. Defiant. And—he sneered at all the money that was spent here on the girls.'

'That sort of attitude... I see.'

'I don't suppose there's really anything in it.'

'Probably not—but I'll make a note of it, all the same.'

'Round and round the mulberry bush,' said Bond when Ann Shapland had gone. 'Same thing over and over again! For goodness' sake let's hope we get something out of the servants.'

But they got very little out of the servants.

'It's no use asking me anything, young man,' said Mrs Gibbons, the cook. 'For one thing I can't hear what you say, and for another I don't know a thing. I went to sleep last night and I slept unusually heavy. Never heard anything of all the excitement there was. Nobody woke me up and told me anything about it.' She sounded injured. 'It wasn't until this morning I heard.'

Kelsey shouted a few questions and got a few answers that told him nothing.

Miss Springer had come new this term, and she wasn't as much liked as Miss Jones who'd held the post before her. Miss Shapland was new, too, but she was a nice young lady. Mademoiselle Blanche was like all the Frenchies—thought the other mistresses were against her and let the young ladies treat her something shocking in class. 'Not a one for crying, though,' Mrs Gibbons admitted. 'Some schools I've been in the French mistresses used to cry something awful!'

Most of the domestic staff were dailies. There was only one other maid who slept in the house, and she proved equally uninformative, though able to hear what was said to her. She couldn't say, she was sure. She didn't know nothing. Miss Springer was a bit sharp in her manner. She didn't know nothing about the Sports Pavilion nor what was kept there, and she'd never seen nothing like a pistol nowhere.

This negative spate of information was interrupted by Miss Bulstrode. 'One of the girls would like to speak to you, Inspector Kelsey,' she said.

Kelsey looked up sharply. 'Indeed? She knows something?'

'As to that I'm rather doubtful,' said Miss Bulstrode, 'but you had better talk to her yourself. She is one of our foreign girls. Princess Shaista—niece of the Emir Ibrahim. She is inclined to think, perhaps, that she is of rather more importance than she is. You understand?'

Kelsey nodded comprehendingly. Then Miss Bulstrode went out and a slight dark girl of middle height came in.

She looked at them, almond eyed and demure.

'You are the police?'

'Yes,' said Kelsey smiling, 'we are the police. Will you sit down and tell me what you know about Miss Springer?'

'Yes, I will tell you.'

She sat down, leaned forward, and lowered her voice dramatically.

'There have been people watching this place. Oh, they do not show themselves clearly, but they are there!'

She nodded her head significantly.

Inspector Kelsey thought that he understood what Miss Bulstrode had meant. This girl was dramatizing herself—and enjoying it.

Agatha Christie

'And why should they be watching the school?'

'Because of *me*! They want to kidnap me.'

Whatever Kelsey had expected, it was not this. His eyebrows rose.

'Why should they want to kidnap you?'

'To hold me to ransom, of course. Then they would make my relations pay much money.'

'Er—well—perhaps,' said Kelsey dubiously. 'But—er—supposing this is so, what has it got to do with the death of Miss Springer?'

'She must have found out about them,' said Shaista. 'Perhaps she told them she had found out something. Perhaps she threatened them. Then perhaps they promised to pay her money if she would say nothing. And she believed them. So she goes out to the Sports Pavilion where they say they will pay her the money, and then they shoot her.'

'But surely Miss Springer would never have accepted blackmail money?'

'Do you think it is such fun to be a school teacher—to be a teacher of gymnastics?' Shaista was scornful. 'Do you not think it would be nice instead to have money, to travel, to do what you want? Especially someone like Miss Springer who is not beautiful, at whom men do not even look! Do you not think that money would attract her more than it would attract other people?'

'Well—er—' said Inspector Kelsey, 'I don't know quite what to say.' He had not had this point of view presented to him before.

'This is just—er—your own idea?' he said. 'Miss Springer never said anything to you?'

'Miss Springer never said anything except "Stretch and bend", and "Faster", and "Don't slack",' said Shaista with resentment.

'Yes—quite so. Well, don't you think you may have imagined all this about kidnapping?'

Shaista was immediately much annoyed.

'You do not understand *at all*! My cousin was Prince Ali Yusuf of Ramat. He was killed in a revolution, or at least in fleeing from a revolution. It was understood that when I grew up I should marry him. So you see I am an important person. It may be perhaps the Communists who come here. Perhaps it is not to kidnap. Perhaps they intend to assassinate me.'

Inspector Kelsey looked still more incredulous.

'That's rather far fetched, isn't it?'

'You think such things could not happen? I say they can. They are very very wicked, the Communists! Everybody knows that.'

As he still looked dubious, she went on:

'Perhaps they think I know where the jewels are!'

'What jewels?'

'My cousin had jewels. So had his father. My family always has a hoard of jewels. For emergencies, you comprehend.'

She made it sound very matter of fact.

Kelsey stared at her.

'But what has all this got to do with you—or with Miss Springer?'

Agatha Christie

'But I already tell you! They think, perhaps, I know where the jewels are. So they will take me prisoner and force me to speak.'

'*Do* you know where the jewels are?'

'No, of course I do not know. They disappeared in the Revolution. Perhaps the wicked Communists take them. But again, perhaps not.'

'Who do they belong to?'

'Now my cousin is dead, they belong to me. No men in his family any more. His aunt, my mother, is dead. He would want them to belong to me. If he were not dead, I marry him.'

'That was the arrangement?'

'I have to marry him. He is my cousin, you see.'

'And you would have got the jewels when you married him?'

'No, I would have had new jewels. From Cartier in Paris. These others would still be kept for emergencies.'

Inspector Kelsey blinked, letting this Oriental insurance scheme for emergencies sink into his consciousness.

Shaista was racing on with great animation.

'I think that is what happens. Somebody gets the jewels out of Ramat. Perhaps good person, perhaps bad. Good person would bring them to me, would say: "These are yours," and I should reward him.'

She nodded her head regally, playing the part.

Quite a little actress, thought the Inspector.

'But if it was a bad person, he would keep the jewels and sell them. Or he would come to me and say: "What will you give me as a reward if I bring them to you?" And if it worth while, he brings—but if not, then not!'

'But in actual fact, nobody has said anything at all to you?'

'No,' admitted Shaista.

Inspector Kelsey made up his mind.

'I think, you know,' he said pleasantly, 'that you're really talking a lot of nonsense.'

Shaista flashed a furious glance at him.

'I tell you what I know, that is all,' she said sulkily.

'Yes—well, it's very kind of you, and I'll bear it in mind.'

He got up and opened the door for her to go out.

'The Arabian Nights aren't in it,' he said, as he returned to the table. 'Kidnapping and fabulous jewels! What next?'

CHAPTER 11

Conference

When Inspector Kelsey returned to the station, the sergeant on duty said:

'We've got Adam Goodman here, waiting, sir.'

'Adam Goodman? Oh yes. The gardener.'

A young man had risen respectfully to his feet. He was tall, dark and good-looking. He wore stained corduroy trousers loosely held up by an aged belt, and an open-necked shirt of very bright blue.

'You wanted to see me, I hear.'

His voice was rough, and as that of so many young men of today, slightly truculent.

Kelsey said merely:

'Yes, come into my room.'

'I don't know anything about the murder,' said Adam Goodman sulkily. 'It's nothing to do with me. I was at home and in bed last night.'

Kelsey merely nodded noncommittally.

He sat down at his desk, and motioned to the young

man to take the chair opposite. A young policeman in plain clothes had followed the two men in unobtrusively and sat down a little distance away.

'Now then,' said Kelsey. 'You're Goodman—' he looked at a note on his desk—'Adam Goodman.'

'That's right, sir. But first, I'd like to show you this.'

Adam's manner had changed. There was no truculence or sulkiness in it now. It was quiet and deferential. He took something from his pocket and passed it across the desk. Inspector Kelsey's eyebrows rose very slightly as he studied it. Then he raised his head.

'I shan't need you, Barber,' he said.

The discreet young policeman got up and went out. He managed not to look surprised, but he was.

'Ah,' said Kelsey. He looked across at Adam with speculative interest. 'So that's who you are? And what the hell, I'd like to know, are you—'

'Doing in a girls' school?' the young man finished for him. His voice was still deferential, but he grinned in spite of himself. 'It's certainly the first time I've had an assignment of that kind. Don't I look like a gardener?'

'Not around these parts. Gardeners are usually rather ancient. Do you know anything about gardening?'

'Quite a lot. I've got one of these gardening mothers. England's speciality. She's seen to it that I'm a worthy assistant to her.'

'And what exactly is going on at Meadowbank—to bring you on the scene?'

'We don't know, actually, that there's anything going on

at Meadowbank. My assignment is in the nature of a watching brief. Or was—until last night. Murder of a Games Mistress. Not quite in the school's curriculum.'

'It could happen,' said Inspector Kelsey. He sighed. 'Anything could happen—anywhere. I've learnt that. But I'll admit that it's a little off the beaten track. What's behind all this?'

Adam told him. Kelsey listened with interest.

'I did that girl an injustice,' he remarked—'But you'll admit it sounds too fantastic to be true. Jewels worth between half a million and a million pounds? Who do you say they belong to?'

'That's a very pretty question. To answer it, you'd have to have a gaggle of international lawyers on the job—and they'd probably disagree. You could argue the case a lot of ways. They belonged, three months ago, to His Highness Prince Ali Yusuf of Ramat. But now? If they'd turned up in Ramat they'd have been the property of the present Government, they'd have made sure of that. Ali Yusuf may have willed them to someone. A lot would then depend on where the will was executed and whether it could be proved. They may belong to his family. But the real essence of the matter is, that if you or I happened to pick them up in the street and put them in our pockets, they would for all practical purposes belong to us. That is, I doubt if any legal machine exists that could get them away from us. They could try, of course, but the intricacies of international law are quite incredible…'

'You mean that, practically speaking, it's findings are

keepings?' asked Inspector Kelsey. He shook his head disapprovingly. 'That's not very nice,' he said primly.

'No,' said Adam firmly. 'It's not very nice. There's more than one lot after them, too. None of them scrupulous. Word's got around, you see. It may be a rumour, it may be true, but the story is that they were got out of Ramat just before the bust up. There are a dozen different tales of *how*.'

'But why Meadowbank? Because of little Princess Butter-won't-melt-in-my-mouth?'

'Princess Shaista, first cousin of Ali Yusuf. Yes. Someone may try and deliver the goods to her or communicate with her. There are some questionable characters from our point of view hanging about the neighbourhood. A Mrs Kolinsky, for instance, staying at the Grand Hotel. Quite a prominent member of what one might describe as International Riff Raff Ltd. Nothing in *your* line, always strictly within the law, all perfectly respectable, but a grand picker-up of useful information. Then there's a woman who was out in Ramat dancing in cabaret there. She's reported to have been working for a certain foreign government. Where she is now we don't know, we don't even know what she looks like, but there's a rumour that she *might* be in this part of the world. Looks, doesn't it, as though it were all centring round Meadowbank? And last night, Miss Springer gets herself killed.'

Kelsey nodded thoughtfully.

'Proper mix up,' he observed. He struggled a moment with his feelings. 'You see this sort of thing on the telly...

Agatha Christie

far fetched—that's what you think... can't really happen. And it doesn't—not in the normal course of events.'

'Secret agents, robbery, violence, murder, double crossing,' agreed Adam. 'All preposterous—but that side of life exists.'

'But not at Meadowbank!'

The words were wrung from Inspector Kelsey.

'I perceive your point,' said Adam. 'Lese-majesty.'

There was a silence, and then Inspector Kelsey asked:

'What do *you* think happened last night?'

Adam took his time, then he said slowly:

'Springer was in the Sports Pavilion—in the middle of the night. Why? We've got to start there. It's no good asking ourselves who killed her until we've made up our minds why she was there, in the Sports Pavilion at that time of night. We can say that in spite of her blameless and athletic life she wasn't sleeping well, and got up and looked out of her window and saw a light in the Sports Pavilion—her window does look out that way?'

Kelsey nodded.

'Being a tough and fearless young woman, she went out to investigate. She disturbed someone there who was—doing what? We don't know. But it was someone desperate enough to shoot her dead.'

Again Kelsey nodded.

'That's the way we've been looking at it,' he said. 'But your last point had me worried all along. You don't shoot to kill—and come prepared to do so, unless—'

'Unless you're after something big? Agreed! Well, that's the case of what we might call Innocent Springer—shot down in the performance of duty. But there's another possibility. Springer, as a result of private information, gets a job at Meadowbank or is detailed for it by her bosses—because of her qualification—She waits until a suitable night, then slips out to the Sports Pavilion (again our stumbling-block of a question—*why?*)—Somebody is following her—or waiting for her—someone who carries a pistol and is prepared to use it... But again—why? What for? In fact, what the devil is there about the Sports Pavilion? It's not the sort of place that one can imagine hiding anything.'

'There wasn't anything hidden there, I can tell you that. We went through it with a tooth comb—the girls' lockers, Miss Springer's ditto. Sports equipment of various kinds, all normal and accounted for. *And* a brand new building! There wasn't anything there in the nature of jewellery.'

'Whatever it was it could have been removed, of course. By the murderer,' said Adam. 'The other possibility is that the Sports Pavilion was simply used as a rendezvous—by Miss Springer or by someone else. It's quite a handy place for that. A reasonable distance from the house. Not too far. And if anyone was noticed going out there, a simple answer would be that whoever it was thought they had seen a light, etc., etc. Let's say that Miss Springer went out to meet someone—there was a disagreement and she got shot. Or, a variation, Miss Springer noticed someone leaving the house, followed that someone, intruded upon something she wasn't meant to see or hear.'

'I never met her alive,' said Kelsey, 'but from the way

Agatha Christie

everyone speaks of her, I get the impression that she might have been a nosey woman.'

'I think that's really the most probable explanation,' agreed Adam. 'Curiosity killed the cat. Yes, I think that's the way the Sports Pavilion comes into it.'

'But if it was a rendezvous, then—' Kelsey paused.

Adam nodded vigorously.

'Yes. It looks as though there is someone in the school who merits our very close attention. Cat among the pigeons, in fact.'

'Cat among the pigeons,' said Kelsey, struck by the phrase. 'Miss Rich, one of the mistresses, said something like that today.'

He reflected a moment or two.

'There were three newcomers to the staff this term,' he said. 'Shapland, the secretary. Blanche, the French Mistress, and, of course, Miss Springer herself. She's dead and out of it. If there is a cat among the pigeons, it would seem that one of the other two would be the most likely bet.' He looked towards Adam. 'Any ideas, as between the two of them?'

Adam considered.

'I caught Mademoiselle Blanche coming out of the Sports Pavilion one day. She had a guilty look. As though she'd been doing something she ought not to have done. All the same, on the whole—I think I'd plump for the other. For Shapland. She's a cool customer and she's got brains. I'd go into her antecedents rather carefully if I were you. What the devil are you laughing for?'

Kelsey was grinning.

'*She* was suspicious of *you*,' he said. 'Caught *you* coming out of the Sports Pavilion—and thought there was something odd about your manner!'

'Well, I'm damned!' Adam was indignant. 'The cheek of her!'

Inspector Kelsey resumed his authoritative manner.

'The point is,' he said, 'that we think a lot of Meadowbank round these parts. It's a fine school. And Miss Bulstrode's a fine woman. The sooner we can get to the bottom of all this, the better for the school. We want to clear things up and give Meadowbank a clean bill of health.'

He paused, looking thoughtfully at Adam.

'I think,' he said, 'we'll have to tell Miss Bulstrode who you are. She'll keep her mouth shut—don't fear for that.'

Adam considered for a moment. Then he nodded his head.

'Yes,' he said. 'Under the circumstances, I think it's more or less inevitable.'

CHAPTER 12

New Lamps for Old

Miss Bulstrode had another faculty which demonstrated her superiority over most other women. She could listen.

She listened in silence to both Inspector Kelsey and Adam. She did not so much as raise an eyebrow. Then she uttered one word.

'Remarkable.'

It's you who are remarkable, thought Adam, but he did not say so aloud.

'Well,' said Miss Bulstrode, coming as was habitual to her straight to the point. 'What do you want me to do?'

Inspector Kelsey cleared his throat.

'It's like this,' he said. 'We felt that you ought to be fully informed—for the sake of the school.'

Miss Bulstrode nodded.

'Naturally,' she said, 'the school is my first concern. It has to be. I am responsible for the care and safety of my pupils—and in a lesser degree for that of my staff. And I would like to add now that if there can be as little publicity as possible about Miss Springer's death—the better it will be for me. This is a purely selfish point of view—though I think my school is important in itself—not only to me. And I quite realize that if full publicity is necessary for you, then you will have to go ahead. But is it?'

'No,' said Inspector Kelsey. 'In this case I should say the less publicity the better. The inquest will be adjourned and we'll let it get about that we think it was a local affair. Young thugs—or juvenile delinquents, as we have to call them nowadays—out with guns amongst them, trigger happy. It's usually flick knives, but some of these boys do get hold of guns. Miss Springer surprised them. They shot her. That's what I should like to let it go at—then we can get to work quiet-like. Not more than can be helped in the Press. But of course, Meadowbank's famous. It's news. And murder at Meadowbank will be hot news.'

'I think I can help you there,' said Miss Bulstrode crisply, 'I am not without influence in high places.' She smiled and reeled off a few names. These included the Home Secretary, two Press barons, a bishop and the Minister of Education. 'I'll do what I can.' She looked at Adam. 'You agree?'

Adam spoke quickly.

'Yes, indeed. We always like things nice and quiet.'

'Are you continuing to be my gardener?' inquired Miss Bulstrode.

'If you don't object. It puts me right where I want to be. And I can keep an eye on things.'

This time Miss Bulstrode's eyebrows did rise.

'I hope you're not expecting any more murders?'

'No, no.'

'I'm glad of that. I doubt if any school could survive two murders in one term.'

She turned to Kelsey.

'Have you people finished with the Sports Pavilion? It's awkward if we can't use it.'

'We've finished with it. Clean as a whistle—from our point of view, I mean. For whatever reason the murder was committed—there's nothing there now to help us. It's just a Sports Pavilion with the usual equipment.'

'Nothing in the girls' lockers?'

Inspector Kelsey smiled.

'Well—this and that—copy of a book—French—called *Candide*—with—er—illustrations. Expensive book.'

'Ah,' said Miss Bulstrode. 'So that's where she keeps it! Giselle d'Aubray, I suppose?'

Kelsey's respect for Miss Bulstrode rose.

'You don't miss much, M'am,' he said.

'She won't come to harm with *Candide*,' said Miss Bulstrode. 'It's a classic. Some forms of pornography I do confiscate. Now I come back to my first question. You have relieved my mind about the publicity connected with the school. Can the school help you in anyway? Can *I* help you?'

'I don't think so, at the moment. The only thing I can ask is, has anything caused you uneasiness this term? Any incident? Or any person?'

Miss Bulstrode was silent for a moment or two. Then she said slowly:

'The answer, literally, is: I don't know.'

Adam said quickly:

'You've got a feeling that something's wrong?'

'Yes—just that. It's not definite. I can't put my finger on any person, or any incident—unless—'

She was silent for a moment, then she said:

'I feel—I felt at the time—that I'd missed something that I ought not to have missed. Let me explain.'

She recited briefly the little incident of Mrs Upjohn and the distressing and unexpected arrival of Lady Veronica.

Adam was interested.

'Let me get this clear, Miss Bulstrode. Mrs Upjohn, looking out of the window, this front window that gives on the drive, recognized someone. There's nothing in that. You have over a hundred pupils and nothing is more likely than for Mrs Upjohn to see some parent or relation that she knew. But you are definitely of the opinion that she was *astonished* to recognize that person—in fact, that it was someone whom she would *not* have expected to see at Meadowbank?'

'Yes, that was exactly the impression I got.'

'And then through the window looking in the opposite direction you saw one of the pupils' mothers, in a state of intoxication, and that completely distracted your mind from what Mrs Upjohn was saying?'

Miss Bulstrode nodded.

'She was talking for some minutes?'

'Yes.'

'And when your attention did return to her, she was

speaking of espionage, of Intelligence work she had done in the war before she married?'

'Yes.'

'It might tie up,' said Adam thoughtfully. 'Someone she had known in her war days. A parent or relation of one of your pupils, or it could have been a member of your teaching staff.'

'Hardly a member of my staff,' objected Miss Bulstrode.

'It's possible.'

'We'd better get in touch with Mrs Upjohn,' said Kelsey. 'As soon as possible. You have her address, Miss Bulstrode?'

'Of course. But I believe she is abroad at the moment. Wait—I will find out.'

She pressed her desk buzzer twice, then went impatiently to the door and called to a girl who was passing.

'Find Julia Upjohn for me, will you, Paula?'

'Yes, Miss Bulstrode.'

'I'd better go before the girl comes,' Adam said. 'It wouldn't be natural for me to assist in the inquiries the Inspector is making. Ostensibly he's called me in here to get the low down on me. Having satisfied himself that he's got nothing on me for the moment, he now tells me to take myself off.'

'Take yourself off and remember I've got my eye on you!' growled Kelsey with a grin.

'By the way,' said Adam, addressing Miss Bulstrode as he paused by the door, 'will it be all right with you if I slightly abuse my position here? If I get, shall we say, a little too friendly with some members of your staff?'

'With which members of my staff?'

'Well—Mademoiselle Blanche, for instance.'

'Mademoiselle Blanche? You think that she—?'

'I think she's rather bored here.'

'Ah!' Miss Bulstrode looked rather grim. 'Perhaps you're right. Anyone else?'

'I shall have a good try all round,' said Adam cheerfully. 'If you should find that some of your girls are being rather silly, and slipping off to assignations in the garden, please believe that my intentions are strictly sleuthial—if there is such a word.'

'You think the girls are likely to know something?'

'Everybody always knows something,' said Adam, 'even if it's something they don't know they know.'

'You may be right.'

There was a knock on the door, and Miss Bulstrode called—'Come in.'

Julia Upjohn appeared, very much out of breath.

'Come in, Julia.'

Inspector Kelsey growled.

'You can go now, Goodman. Take yourself off and get on with your work.'

'I've told you I don't know a thing about anything,' said Adam sulkily. He went out, muttering 'Blooming Gestapo.'

'I'm sorry I'm so out of breath, Miss Bulstrode,' apologized Julia. 'I've run all the way from the tennis courts.'

'That's quite all right. I just wanted to ask you your mother's address—that is, where can I get in touch with her?'

Agatha Christie

'Oh! You'll have to write to Aunt Isabel. Mother's abroad.'

'I have your aunt's address. But I need to get in touch with your mother personally.'

'I don't see how you can,' said Julia, frowning. 'Mother's gone to Anatolia on a bus.'

'On a *bus*?' said Miss Bulstrode, taken aback.

Julia nodded vigorously.

'She likes that sort of thing,' she explained. 'And of course it's frightfully cheap. A bit uncomfortable, but Mummy doesn't mind that. Roughly, I should think she'd fetch up in Van in about three weeks or so.'

'I see—yes. Tell me, Julia, did your mother ever mention to you seeing someone here whom she'd known in her war service days?'

'No, Miss Bulstrode, I don't think so. No, I'm sure she didn't.'

'Your mother did Intelligence work, didn't she?'

'Oh, yes. Mummy seems to have loved it. Not that it sounds really exciting to me. She never blew up anything. Or got caught by the Gestapo. Or had her toe nails pulled out. Or anything like that. She worked in Switzerland, I think—or was it Portugal?'

Julia added apologetically: 'One gets rather bored with all that old war stuff; and I'm afraid I don't always listen properly.'

'Well, thank you, Julia. That's all.'

'Really!' said Miss Bulstrode, when Julia had departed. 'Gone to Anatolia on a bus! The child said it exactly as though she were saying her mother had taken a 73 bus to Marshall and Snelgrove's.'

II

Jennifer walked away from the tennis courts rather moodily, swishing her racquet. The amount of double faults she had served this morning depressed her. Not, of course, that you could get a hard serve with this racquet, anyway. But she seemed to have lost control of her service lately. Her backhand, however, had definitely improved. Springer's coaching had been helpful. In many ways it was a pity that Springer was dead.

Jennifer took tennis very seriously. It was one of the things she thought about.

'Excuse me—'

Jennifer looked up, startled. A well-dressed woman with golden hair, carrying a long flat parcel, was standing a few feet away from her on the path. Jennifer wondered why on earth she hadn't seen the woman coming along towards her before. It did not occur to her that the woman might have been hidden behind a tree or in the rhododendron bushes and just stepped out of them. Such an idea would not have occurred to Jennifer, since why should a woman hide behind rhododendron bushes and suddenly step out of them?

Speaking with a slightly American accent the woman said, 'I wonder if you could tell me where I could find a girl called'—she consulted a piece of paper—'Jennifer Sutcliffe.'

Agatha Christie

Jennifer was surprised.

'I'm Jennifer Sutcliffe.'

'Why! How ridiculous! That *is* a coincidence. That in a big school like this I should be looking for one girl and I should happen upon the girl herself to ask. And they say things like that don't happen.'

'I suppose they do happen sometimes,' said Jennifer, uninterested.

'I was coming down to lunch today with some friends down here,' went on the woman, 'and at a cocktail party yesterday I happened to mention I was coming, and your aunt—or was it your godmother?—I've got such a terrible memory. She told me her name and I've forgotten that too. But anyway, she said could I possibly call here and leave a new tennis racquet for you. She said you had been asking for one.'

Jennifer's face lit up. It seemed like a miracle, nothing less.

'It must have been my godmother, Mrs Campbell. I call her Aunt Gina. It wouldn't have been Aunt Rosamond. She never gives me anything but a mingy ten shillings at Christmas.'

'Yes, I remember now. That *was* the name. Campbell.'

The parcel was held out. Jennifer took it eagerly. It was quite loosely wrapped. Jennifer uttered an exclamation of pleasure as the racquet emerged from its coverings.

'Oh, it's smashing!' she exclaimed. 'A really *good* one. I've been longing for a new racquet—you can't play decently if you haven't got a decent racquet.'

'Why I guess that's so.'

'Thank you very much for bringing it,' said Jennifer gratefully.

'It was really no trouble. Only I confess I felt a little shy. Schools always make me feel shy. So many girls. Oh, by the way, I was asked to bring back your old racquet with me.'

She picked up the racquet Jennifer had dropped.

'Your aunt—no—godmother—said she would have it restrung. It needs it badly, doesn't it?'

'I don't think that it's really worth while,' said Jennifer, but without paying much attention.

She was still experimenting with the swing and balance of her new treasure.

'But an extra racquet is always useful,' said her new friend. 'Oh dear,' she glanced at her watch. 'It is much later than I thought. I must run.'

'Have you—do you want a taxi? I could telephone—'

'No, thank you, dear. My car is right by the gate. I left it there so that I shouldn't have to turn in a narrow space. Goodbye. So pleased to have met you. I hope you enjoy the racquet.'

She literally ran along the path towards the gate. Jennifer called after her once more. 'Thank you *very* much.'

Then, gloating, she went in search of Julia.

'Look,' she flourished the racquet dramatically.

'I say! Where did you get that?'

'My godmother sent it to me. Aunt Gina. She's not my aunt, but I call her that. She's frightfully rich. I expect

Agatha Christie

Mummy told her about me grumbling about my racquet. It *is* smashing, isn't it? I *must* remember to write and thank her.'

'I should hope so!' said Julia virtuously.

'Well, you know how one does forget things sometimes. Even things you really mean to do. Look, Shaista,' she added as the latter girl came towards them. 'I've got a new racquet. Isn't it a beauty?'

'It must have been very expensive,' said Shaista, scanning it respectfully. 'I wish I could play tennis well.'

'You always run into the ball.'

'I never seem to know where the ball is going to come,' said Shaista vaguely. 'Before I go home, I must have some really good shorts made in London. Or a tennis dress like the American champion Ruth Allen wears. I think that is very smart. Perhaps I will have both,' she smiled in pleasurable anticipation.

'Shaista never thinks of anything except things to wear,' said Julia scornfully as the two friends passed on. 'Do you think *we* shall ever be like that?'

'I suppose so,' said Jennifer gloomily. 'It will be an awful bore.'

They entered the Sports Pavilion, now officially vacated by the police, and Jennifer put her racquet carefully into her press.

'Isn't it lovely?' she said, stroking it affectionately.

'What have you done with the old one?'

'Oh, she took it.'

'Who?'

'The woman who brought this. She'd met Aunt Gina at a cocktail party, and Aunt Gina asked her to bring me this as she was coming down here today, and Aunt Gina said to bring up my old one and she'd have it restrung.'

'Oh, I see...' But Julia was frowning.

'What did Bully want with you?' asked Jennifer.

'Bully? Oh, nothing really. Just Mummy's address. But she hasn't got one because she's on a bus. In Turkey somewhere. Jennifer—look here. Your racquet didn't *need* restringing.'

'Oh, it did, Julia. It was like a sponge.'

'I know. But it's *my* racquet really. I mean, we exchanged. It was *my* racquet that needed restringing. Yours, the one I've got now, *was* restrung. You said yourself your mother had had it restrung before you went abroad.'

'Yes, that's true.' Jennifer looked a little startled. 'Oh well, I suppose this woman—whoever she was—I ought to have asked her name, but I was so entranced—just saw that it needed restringing.'

'But you said that *she* said that it was your *Aunt Gina* who had said it needed restringing. And your Aunt Gina couldn't have thought it needed restringing if it didn't.'

'Oh, well—' Jennifer looked impatient. 'I suppose—I suppose—'

'You suppose what?'

'Perhaps Aunt Gina just thought that *if* I wanted a new racquet, it was because the old one wanted restringing. Anyway what does it matter?'

'I suppose it doesn't matter,' said Julia slowly. 'But I do

Agatha Christie

think it's odd, Jennifer. It's like—like new lamps for old. Aladdin, you know.'

Jennifer giggled.

'Fancy rubbing my old racquet—your old racquet, I mean, and having a genie appear! If you rubbed a lamp and a genie did appear, what would you ask him for, Julia?'

'Lots of things,' breathed Julia ecstatically. 'A tape recorder, and an Alsatian—or perhaps a Great Dane, and a hundred thousand pounds, and a black satin party frock, and oh! lots of other things... What would you?'

'I don't really know,' said Jennifer. 'Now I've got this smashing new racquet, I don't really want anything else.'

CHAPTER 13

Catastrophe

The third weekend after the opening of term followed the usual plan. It was the first weekend on which parents were allowed to take pupils out. As a result Meadowbank was left almost deserted.

On this particular Sunday there would only be twenty girls left at the school itself for the midday meal. Some of the staff had weekend leave, returning late Sunday night or early Monday morning. On this particular occasion Miss Bulstrode herself was proposing to be absent for the weekend. This was unusual since it was not her habit to leave the school during term time. But she had her reasons. She was going to stay with the Duchess of Welsham at Welsington Abbey. The duchess had made a special point of it and had added that Henry Banks would be there. Henry Banks was the Chairman of the Governors. He was an important industrialist and he had been one of the original backers of the school. The invitation was therefore almost in the nature of a command. Not that Miss Bulstrode would have allowed herself to be commanded if she had not wished to do so. But as it happened, she welcomed the invitation gladly. She was by no means indifferent to duchesses and the Duchess of Welsham was an influential duchess, whose own daughters had been sent to Meadowbank. She was also particularly glad to have the opportunity of talking to Henry Banks on the subject of the school's future and also to put forward her own account of the recent tragic occurrence.

Owing to the influential connections at Meadowbank the murder of Miss Springer had been played down very tactfully in the Press. It had become a sad fatality rather than a mysterious murder. The impression was given, though not said, that possibly some young thugs had broken into the Sports Pavilion and that Miss Springer's death had been more accident than design. It was reported vaguely that several young men had been asked to come to the police station and 'assist the police'. Miss Bulstrode herself was anxious to mitigate any unpleasant impression that might have been given to these two influential patrons of the school. She knew that they wanted to discuss the veiled hint that she had thrown out of her coming retirement. Both the duchess and Henry Banks were anxious to persuade her to remain on. Now was the time, Miss Bulstrode felt, to push the claims of Eleanor Vansittart, to point out what a splendid person she was, and how well fitted to carry on the traditions of Meadowbank.

On Saturday morning Miss Bulstrode was just finishing off her correspondence with Ann Shapland when the telephone rang. Ann answered it.

'It's the Emir Ibrahim, Miss Bulstrode. He's arrived at Claridge's and would like to take Shaista out tomorrow.'

Miss Bulstrode took the receiver from her and had a brief conversation with the Emir's equerry. Shaista would be ready any time from eleven-thirty onwards on Sunday morning, she said. The girl must be back at the school by eight p.m.

She rang off and said:

'I wish Orientals sometimes gave you a little more warning. It has been arranged for Shaista to go out with Giselle d'Aubray tomorrow. Now that will have to be cancelled. Have we finished all the letters?'

'Yes, Miss Bulstrode.'

'Good, then I can go off with a clear conscience. Type them and send them off, and then you, too, are free for the weekend. I shan't want you until lunch time on Monday.'

'Thank you, Miss Bulstrode.'

'Enjoy yourself, my dear.'

'I'm going to,' said Ann.

'Young man?'

'Well—yes.' Ann coloured a little. 'Nothing serious, though.'

'Then there ought to be. If you're going to marry, don't leave it too late.'

'Oh this is only an old friend. Nothing exciting.'

'Excitement,' said Miss Bulstrode warningly, 'isn't always a good foundation for married life. Send Miss Chadwick to me, will you?'

Agatha Christie

Miss Chadwick bustled in.

'The Emir Ibrahim, Shaista's uncle, is taking her out tomorrow Chaddy. If he comes himself, tell him she is making good progress.'

'She's not very bright,' said Miss Chadwick.

'She's immature intellectually,' agreed Miss Bulstrode. 'But she has a remarkably mature mind in other ways. Sometimes, when you talk to her, she might be a woman of twenty-five. I suppose it's because of the sophisticated life she's led. Paris, Teheran, Cairo, Istanbul and all the rest of it. In this country we're inclined to keep our children too young. We account it a merit when we say: "She's still quite a child." It isn't a merit. It's a grave handicap in life.'

'I don't know that I quite agree with you there, dear,' said Miss Chadwick. 'I'll go now and tell Shaista about her uncle. You go away for your weekend and don't worry about anything.'

'Oh! I shan't,' said Miss Bulstrode. 'It's a good opportunity, really, for leaving Eleanor Vansittart in charge and seeing how she shapes. With you and her in charge nothing's likely to go wrong.'

'I hope not, indeed. I'll go and find Shaista.'

Shaista looked surprised and not at all pleased to hear that her uncle had arrived in London.

'He wants to take me out tomorrow?' she grumbled. 'But Miss Chadwick, it is all arranged that I go out with Giselle d'Aubray and her mother.'

'I'm afraid you'll have to do that another time.'

'But I would much rather go out with Giselle,' said Shaista crossly. 'My uncle is not at all amusing. He eats and then he grunts and it is all very dull.'

'You mustn't talk like that. It is impolite,' said Miss Chadwick. 'Your uncle is only in England for a week, I understand, and naturally he wants to see you.'

'Perhaps he has arranged a new marriage for me,' said Shaista, her face brightening. 'If so, that would be fun.'

'If that is so, he will no doubt tell you so. But you are too young to get married yet awhile. You must first finish your education.'

'Education is very boring,' said Shaista.

II

Sunday morning dawned bright and serene—Miss Shapland had departed soon after Miss Bulstrode on Saturday. Miss Johnson, Miss Rich and Miss Blake left on Sunday morning.

Miss Vansittart, Miss Chadwick, Miss Rowan and Mademoiselle Blanche were left in charge.

'I hope all the girls won't talk too much,' said Miss Chadwick dubiously. 'About poor Miss Springer I mean.'

'Let us hope,' said Eleanor Vansittart, 'that the whole affair will soon be forgotten.' She added: 'If any parents talk to *me* about it, I shall discourage them. It will be best, I think, to take quite a firm line.'

The girls went to church at 10 o'clock accompanied by Miss Vansittart and Miss Chadwick. Four girls who were Roman Catholics were escorted by Angèle Blanche to a rival religious establishment. Then, about half past eleven, the cars began to roll into the drive. Miss Vansittart, graceful, poised and dignified, stood in the hall. She greeted mothers smilingly, produced their offspring and adroitly turned aside any unwanted references to the recent tragedy.

'Terrible,' she said, 'yes, quite terrible, but, you do understand, *we don't talk about it here*. All these young minds—such a pity for them to dwell on it.'

Chaddy was also on the spot greeting old friends among the parents, discussing plans for the holidays and speaking affectionately of the various daughters.

'I do think Aunt Isabel might have come and taken *me* out,' said Julia who with Jennifer was standing with her nose pressed against the window of one of the classrooms, watching the comings and goings on the drive outside.

'Mummy's going to take me out next weekend,' said Jennifer. 'Daddy's got some important people coming down this weekend so she couldn't come today.'

'There goes Shaista,' said Julia, 'all togged up for London. Oo-ee! Just look at the heels on her shoes. I bet old Johnson doesn't like those shoes.'

A liveried chauffeur was opening the door of a large Cadillac. Shaista climbed in and was driven away.

'You can come out with me next weekend, if you like,' said Jennifer. 'I told Mummy I'd got a friend I wanted to bring.'

'I'd love to,' said Julia. 'Look at Vansittart doing her stuff.'

'Terribly gracious, isn't she?' said Jennifer.

'I don't know why,' said Julia, 'but somehow it makes me want to laugh. It's a sort of copy of Miss Bulstrode, isn't it? Quite a good copy, but it's rather like Joyce Grenfell or someone doing an imitation.'

'There's Pam's mother,' said Jennifer. 'She's brought the little boys. How they can all get into that tiny Morris Minor I don't know.'

'They're going to have a picnic,' said Julia. 'Look at all the baskets.'

'What are you going to do this afternoon?' asked Jennifer. 'I don't think I need write to Mummy this week, do you, if I'm going to see her next week?'

'You are slack about writing letters, Jennifer.'

'I never can think of anything to say,' said Jennifer.

'I can,' said Julia, 'I can think of lots to say.' She added mournfully, 'But there isn't really anyone much to write to at present.'

'What about your mother?'

'I told you she's gone to Anatolia in a bus. You can't write letters to people who go to Anatolia in buses. At least you can't write to them all the time.'

'Where do you write to when you do write?'

'Oh, consulates here and there. She left me a list. Stamboul is the first and then Ankara and then some funny name.' She added, 'I wonder why Bully wanted to get in touch with Mummy so badly? She seemed quite upset when I said where she'd gone.'

'It can't be about you,' said Jennifer. 'You haven't done anything awful, have you?'

'Not that I know of,' said Julia. 'Perhaps she wanted to tell her about Springer.'

'Why should she?' said Jennifer. 'I should think she'd be jolly glad that there's at least one mother who *doesn't* know about Springer.'

'You mean mothers might think that their daughters were going to get murdered too?'

'I don't think my mother's quite as bad as that,' said Jennifer. 'But she did get in quite a flap about it.'

'If you ask me,' said Julia, in a meditative manner, 'I think there's a lot that they haven't told us about Springer.'

'What sort of things?'

'Well, funny things seem to be happening. Like your new tennis racquet.'

'Oh, I meant to tell you,' said Jennifer, 'I wrote and thanked Aunt Gina and this morning I got a letter from her saying she was very glad I'd got a new racquet but that she never sent it to me.'

'I told you that racquet business was peculiar,' said Julia triumphantly, 'and you had a burglary, too, at your home, didn't you?'

'Yes, but they didn't take anything.'

'That makes it even more interesting,' said Julia. 'I think,' she added thoughtfully, 'that we shall probably have a second murder soon.'

'Oh really, Julia, why should we have a second murder?'

'Well, there's usually a second murder in books,' said

Julia. 'What I think is, Jennifer, that you'll have to be frightfully careful that it isn't *you* who gets murdered.'

'Me?' said Jennifer, surprised. 'Why should anyone murder me?'

'Because somehow you're mixed up in it all,' said Julia. She added thoughtfully, 'We must try and get a bit more out of your mother next week, Jennifer. Perhaps somebody gave her some secret papers out in Ramat.'

'What sort of secret papers?'

'Oh, how should I know,' said Julia. 'Plans or formulas for a new atomic bomb. That sort of thing.'

Jennifer looked unconvinced.

III

Miss Vansittart and Miss Chadwick were in the Common Room when Miss Rowan entered and said:

'Where is Shaista? I can't find her anywhere. The Emir's car has just arrived to call for her.'

'What?' Chaddy looked up surprised. 'There must be some mistake. The Emir's car came for her about three quarters of an hour ago. I saw her get into it and drive off myself. She was one of the first to go.'

Eleanor Vansittart shrugged her shoulders. 'I suppose a car must have been ordered twice over, or something,' she said.

She went out herself and spoke to the chauffeur. 'There must be some mistake,' she said. 'The young lady has already left for London three quarters of an hour ago.'

Agatha Christie

The chauffeur seemed surprised. 'I suppose there must be some mistake, if you say so, madam,' he said. 'I was definitely given instructions to call at Meadowbank for the young lady.'

'I suppose there's bound to be a muddle sometimes,' said Miss Vansittart.

The chauffeur seemed unperturbed and unsurprised. 'Happens all the time,' he said. 'Telephone messages taken, written down, forgotten. All that sort of thing. But we pride ourselves in our firm that we *don't* make mistakes. Of course, if I may say so, you never know with these Oriental gentlemen. They've sometimes got quite a big entourage with them, and orders get given twice and even three times over. I expect that's what must have happened in this instance.' He turned his large car with some adroitness and drove away.

Miss Vansittart looked a little doubtful for a moment or two, but she decided there was nothing to worry about and began to look forward with satisfaction to a peaceful afternoon.

After luncheon the few girls who remained wrote letters or wandered about the grounds. A certain amount of tennis was played and the swimming pool was well patronized. Miss Vansittart took her fountain pen and her writing pad to the shade of the cedar tree. When the telephone rang at half past four it was Miss Chadwick who answered it.

'Meadowbank School?' The voice of a well-bred young Englishman spoke. 'Oh, is Miss Bulstrode there?'

'Miss Bulstrode's not here today. This is Miss Chadwick speaking.'

'Oh, it's about one of your pupils. I am speaking from Claridge's, the Emir Ibrahim's suite.'

'Oh yes? You mean about Shaista?'

'Yes. The Emir is rather annoyed at not having got a message of any kind.'

'A message? Why should he get a message?'

'Well, to say that Shaista couldn't come, or wasn't coming.'

'Wasn't coming! Do you mean to say she hasn't arrived?'

'No, no, she's certainly not arrived. Did she leave Meadowbank then?'

'Yes. A car came for her this morning—oh, about half past eleven I should think, and she drove off.'

'That's extraordinary because there's no sign of her here... I'd better ring up the firm that supplies the Emir's cars.'

'Oh dear,' said Miss Chadwick, 'I do hope there hasn't been an accident.'

'Oh, don't let's assume the worst,' said the young man cheerfully. 'I think you'd have heard, you know, if there'd been an accident. Or we would. I shouldn't worry if I were you.'

But Miss Chadwick did worry.

'It seems to me very odd,' she said.

'I suppose—' the young man hesitated.

'Yes?' said Miss Chadwick.

'Well, it's not quite the sort of thing I want to suggest

Agatha Christie

to the Emir, but just between you and me there's no—er—well, no boy friend hanging about, is there?'

'Certainly not,' said Miss Chadwick with dignity.

'No, no, well I didn't think there would be, but, well one never knows with girls, does one? You'd be surprised at some of the things I've run into.'

'I can assure you,' said Miss Chadwick with dignity, 'that anything of that kind is quite impossible.'

But was it impossible? Did one ever know with girls?

She replaced the receiver and rather unwillingly went in search of Miss Vansittart. There was no reason to believe that Miss Vansittart would be any better able to deal with the situation than she herself but she felt the need of consulting with someone. Miss Vansittart said at once,

'The second car?'

They looked at each other.

'Do you think,' said Chaddy slowly, 'that we ought to report this to the police?'

'Not to the *police*,' said Eleanor Vansittart in a shocked voice.

'She did say, you know,' said Chaddy, 'that somebody might try to kidnap her.'

'Kidnap her? Nonsense!' said Miss Vansittart sharply.

'You don't think—' Miss Chadwick was persistent.

'Miss Bulstrode left me in charge here,' said Eleanor Vansittart, 'and I shall certainly not sanction anything of the kind. We don't want any more trouble here with the police.'

Miss Chadwick looked at her without affection. She

thought Miss Vansittart was being short-sighted and foolish. She went back into the house and put through a call to the Duchess of Welsham's house. Unfortunately everyone was out.

CHAPTER 14

Miss Chadwick Lies Awake

Miss Chadwick was restless. She turned to and fro in her bed counting sheep, and employing other time-honoured methods of invoking sleep. In vain.

At eight o'clock, when Shaista had not returned, and there had been no news of her, Miss Chadwick had taken matters into her own hands and rung up Inspector Kelsey. She was relieved to find that he did not take the matter too seriously. She could leave it all to him, he assured her. It would be an easy matter to check up on a possible accident. After that, he would get in touch with London. Everything would be done that was necessary. Perhaps the girl herself was playing truant. He advised Miss Chadwick to say as little as possible at the school. Let it be thought that Shaista was staying the night with her uncle at Claridge's.

'The last thing you want, or that Miss Bulstrode would want, is any more publicity,' said Kelsey. 'It's most unlikely that the girl has been kidnapped. So don't worry, Miss Chadwick. Leave it all to us.'

But Miss Chadwick did worry.

Lying in bed, sleepless, her mind went from possible kidnapping back to murder.

Murder at Meadowbank. It was terrible! Unbelievable! *Meadowbank*. Miss Chadwick loved Meadowbank. She loved it, perhaps, even more than Miss Bulstrode did, though in a somewhat different way. It had been such a risky, gallant enterprise. Following Miss Bulstrode faithfully into the hazardous undertaking, she had endured panic more than once. Supposing the whole thing should fail. They hadn't really had much capital. If they did not succeed—if their backing was withdrawn—Miss Chadwick had an anxious mind and could always tabulate innumerable ifs. Miss Bulstrode had enjoyed the adventure, the hazard of it all, but Chaddy had not. Sometimes, in an agony of apprehension, she had pleaded for Meadowbank to be run on more conventional lines. It would be *safer*, she urged. But Miss Bulstrode had been uninterested in safety. She had her vision of what a school should be and she had pursued it unafraid. And she had been justified in her audacity. But oh, the relief to Chaddy when success was a *fait accompli*. When Meadowbank was established, safely established, as a great English institution. It was then that her love for Meadowbank had flowed most fully. Doubts, fears, anxieties, all slipped from her. Peace and

Agatha Christie

prosperity had come. She basked in the prosperity of Meadowbank like a purring tabby cat.

She had been quite upset when Miss Bulstrode had first begun to talk of retirement. Retire *now*—when everything was set fair? What madness! Miss Bulstrode talked of travel, of all the things in the world to see. Chaddy was unimpressed. Nothing, anywhere, could be half as good as Meadowbank! It had seemed to her that nothing could affect the well-being of Meadowbank— But now—Murder!

Such an ugly violent word—coming in from the outside world like an ill-mannered storm wind. Murder—a word associated by Miss Chadwick only with delinquent boys with flick knives, or evil-minded doctors poisoning their wives. But murder here—at a school—and not any school— at Meadowbank. Incredible.

Really, Miss Springer—poor Miss Springer, naturally it wasn't her *fault*—but, illogically, Chaddy felt that it must have been her fault in some way. She didn't know the traditions of Meadowbank. A tactless woman. She must in some way have invited murder. Miss Chadwick rolled over, turned her pillow, said 'I mustn't go on thinking of it all. Perhaps I had better get up and take some aspirin. I'll just try counting to fifty...'

Before she had got to fifty, her mind was off again on the same track. Worrying. Would all this—and perhaps kidnapping too—get into the papers? Would parents, reading, hasten to take their daughters away...

Oh dear, she *must* calm down and go to sleep. What

time was it? She switched on her light and looked at her watch—Just after a quarter to one. Just about the time that poor Miss Springer... No, she would *not* think of it any more. And, how stupid of Miss Springer to have gone off by herself like that without waking up somebody else.

'Oh dear,' said Miss Chadwick. 'I'll have to take some aspirin.'

She got out of bed and went over to the washstand. She took two aspirins with a drink of water. On her way back, she pulled aside the curtain of the window and peered out. She did so to reassure herself more than for any other reason. She wanted to feel that of course there would never again be a light in the Sports Pavilion in the middle of the night.

But there was.

In a minute Chaddy had leapt to action. She thrust her feet into stout shoes, pulled on a thick coat, picked up her electric torch and rushed out of her room and down the stairs. She had blamed Miss Springer for not obtaining support before going out to investigate, but it never occurred to her to do so. She was only eager to get out to the Pavilion and find out who the intruder was. She did pause to pick up a weapon—not perhaps a very good one, but a weapon of kinds, and then she was out of the side door and following quickly along the path through the shrubbery. She was out of breath, but completely resolute. Only when she got at last to the door, did she slacken up and take care to move softly.

Agatha Christie

The door was slightly ajar. She pushed it further open and looked in...

II

At about the time when Miss Chadwick was rising from bed in search of aspirin, Ann Shapland, looking very attractive in a black dance frock, was sitting at a table in Le Nid Sauvage eating Supreme of Chicken and smiling at the young man opposite her. Dear Dennis, thought Ann to herself, always so exactly the same. It is what I simply couldn't bear if I married him. He *is* rather a pet, all the same. Aloud she remarked:

'What fun this is, Dennis. Such a glorious *change*.'

'How is the new job?' said Dennis.

'Well, actually, I'm rather enjoying it.'

'Doesn't seem to me quite your sort of thing.'

Ann laughed. 'I'd be hard put to it to say what is my sort of thing. I like variety, Dennis.'

'I never can see why you gave up your job with old Sir Mervyn Todhunter.'

'Well, chiefly because of Sir Mervyn Todhunter. The attention he bestowed on me was beginning to annoy his wife. And it's part of my policy never to annoy wives. They can do you a lot of harm, you know.'

'Jealous cats,' said Dennis.

'Oh no, not really,' said Ann. 'I'm rather on the wives' side. Anyway I liked Lady Todhunter much better than old Mervyn. Why are you surprised at my present job?'

'Oh, a school. You're not scholastically minded at all, I should have said.'

'I'd hate to *teach* in a school. I'd hate to be penned up. Herded with a lot of women. But the work as the secretary of a school like Meadowbank is rather fun. It really is a unique place, you know. And Miss Bulstrode's unique. She's really something, I can tell you. Her steel-grey eye goes through you and sees your innermost secrets. And she keeps you on your toes. I'd hate to make a mistake in any letters I'd taken down for her. Oh yes, she's certainly something.'

'I wish you'd get tired of all these jobs,' said Dennis. 'It's quite time, you know, Ann, that you stopped all this racketing about with jobs here and jobs there and—and settled down.'

'You are sweet, Dennis,' said Ann in a noncommittal manner.

'We could have quite fun, you know,' said Dennis.

'I daresay,' said Ann, 'but I'm not ready yet. And anyway, you know, there's my mamma.'

'Yes, I was—going to talk to you about that.'

'About my mamma? What were you going to say?'

'Well, Ann, you know I think you're wonderful. The way you get an interesting job and then you chuck it all up and go home to her.'

'Well, I have to now and again when she gets a really bad attack.'

'I know. As I say, I think it's wonderful of you. But all the same there are places, you know, very good places nowadays where—where people like your mother are well looked after and all that sort of thing. Not really loony bins.'

'And which cost the earth,' said Ann.

'No, no, not necessarily. Why, even under the Health Scheme—'

A bitter note crept into Ann's voice. 'Yes, I daresay it will come to that one day. But in the meantime I've got a nice old pussy who lives with Mother and who can cope normally. Mother is quite reasonable most of the time—And when she—isn't, I come back and lend a hand.'

'She's—she isn't—she's never—?'

'Are you going to say violent, Dennis? You've got an extraordinarily lurid imagination. No. My dear mamma is *never* violent. She just gets fuddled. She forgets where she is and who she is and wants to go for long walks, and then as like as not she'll jump into a train or a bus and take off somewhere and—well, it's all very difficult, you see. Sometimes it's too much for one person to cope with. But she's quite happy, even when she *is* fuddled. And sometimes quite funny about it. I remember her saying: "Ann, darling, it really is very embarrassing. I knew I was going to Tibet and there I was sitting in that hotel in Dover with no idea how to get there. Then I thought why was I going to Tibet? And I thought I'd better come home. Then I couldn't remember how long ago it was when I left home. It makes it very embarrassing, dear, when you can't quite remember things." Mummy was really very funny over it all, you know. I mean she quite sees the humorous side herself.'

'I've never actually met her,' Dennis began.

'I don't encourage people to meet her,' said Ann. 'That's the one thing I think you *can* do for your people. Protect them from—well, curiosity and pity.'

'It's not curiosity, Ann.'

'No, I don't think it would be that with you. But it would be pity. I don't want that.'

'I can see what you mean.'

'But if you think I mind giving up jobs from time to time and going home for an indefinite period, I don't,' said Ann. 'I never meant to get embroiled in anything too deeply. Not even when I took my first post after my secretarial training. I thought the thing was to get really good at the job. Then if you're really good you can pick and choose your posts. You see different places and you see different kinds of life. At the moment I'm seeing school life. The best school in England seen from within! I shall stay there, I expect, about a year and a half.'

'You never really get caught up in things, do you, Ann?'

'No,' said Ann thoughtfully, 'I don't think I do. I think I'm one of those people who is a born observer. More like a commentator on the radio.'

'You're so detached,' said Dennis gloomily. 'You don't really care about anything or anyone.'

'I expect I shall some day,' said Ann encouragingly.

Agatha Christie

'I do understand more or less how you're thinking and feeling.'

'I doubt it,' said Ann.

'Anyway, I don't think you'll last a year. You'll get fed up with all those women,' said Dennis.

'There's a very good-looking gardener,' said Ann. She laughed when she saw Dennis's expression. 'Cheer up, I'm only trying to make you jealous.'

'What's this about one of the mistresses having been killed?'

'Oh, that.' Ann's face became serious and thoughtful.

'That's odd, Dennis. Very odd indeed. It was the Games Mistress. You know the type. I-am-a-plain-Games Mistress. I think there's a lot more behind it than has come out yet.'

'Well, don't you get mixed up in anything unpleasant.'

'That's easy to say. I've never had any chance at displaying my talents as a sleuth. I think I *might* be rather good at it.'

'Now, Ann.'

'Darling, I'm not going to trail dangerous criminals. I'm just going to—well, make a few logical deductions. Why and who. And what for? That sort of thing. I've come across one piece of information that's rather interesting.'

'Ann!'

'Don't look so agonized. Only it doesn't seem to link up with anything,' said Ann thoughtfully. 'Up to a point it all fits in very well. And then, suddenly, it doesn't.' She added cheerfully, 'Perhaps there'll be a second murder, and that will clarify things a little.'

It was at exactly that moment that Miss Chadwick pushed open the Sports Pavilion door.

CHAPTER 15

Murder Repeats Itself

'Come along,' said Inspector Kelsey, entering the room with a grim face. 'There's been another.'

'Another what?' Adam looked up sharply.

'Another murder,' said Inspector Kelsey. He led the way out of the room and Adam followed him. They had been sitting in the latter's room drinking beer and discussing various probabilities when Kelsey had been summoned to the telephone.

'Who is it?' demanded Adam, as he followed Inspector Kelsey down the stairs.

'Another mistress—Miss Vansittart.'

'Where?'

'In the Sports Pavilion.'

'The Sports Pavilion again,' said Adam. 'What is there about this Sports Pavilion?'

'*You'd* better give it the once-over this time,' said Inspector Kelsey. 'Perhaps your technique of searching may be more successful than ours has been. There must be *something* about that Sports Pavilion or why should everyone get killed there?'

He and Adam got into his car. 'I expect the doctor will be there ahead of us. He hasn't so far to go.'

It was, Kelsey thought, like a bad dream repeating itself as he entered the brilliantly lighted Sports Pavilion. There, once again, was a body with the doctor kneeling beside it. Once again the doctor rose from his knees and got up.

'Killed about half an hour ago,' he said. 'Forty minutes at most.'

'Who found her?' said Kelsey.

One of his men spoke up. 'Miss Chadwick.'

'That's the old one, isn't it?'

'Yes. She saw a light, came out here, and found her dead. She stumbled back to the house and more or less went into hysterics. It was the matron who telephoned, Miss Johnson.'

'Right,' said Kelsey. 'How was she killed? Shot again?'

The doctor shook his head. 'No. Slugged on the back of the head, this time. Might have been a cosh or a sandbag. Something of that kind.'

A golf club with a steel head was lying near the door. It was the only thing that looked remotely disorderly in the place.

'What about that?' said Kelsey, pointing. 'Could she have been hit with that?'

The doctor shook his head. 'Impossible. There's no mark on her. No, it was definitely a heavy rubber cosh or a sandbag, something of that sort.'

'Something—professional?'

Agatha Christie

'Probably, yes. Whoever it was, didn't mean to make any noise this time. Came up behind her and slugged her on the back of the head. She fell forward and probably never knew what hit her.'

'What was she doing?'

'She was probably kneeling down,' said the doctor. 'Kneeling in front of this locker.'

The Inspector went up to the locker and looked at it. 'That's the girl's name on it, I presume,' he said. 'Shaista—let me see, that's the—that's the Egyptian girl, isn't it? Her Highness Princess Shaista.' He turned to Adam. 'It seems to tie in, doesn't it? Wait a minute—that's the girl they reported this evening as missing?'

'That's right, sir,' said the Sergeant. 'A car called for her here, supposed to have been sent by her uncle who's staying at Claridge's in London. She got into it and drove off.'

'No reports come in?'

'Not as yet, sir. Got a network out. And the Yard is on it.'

'A nice simple way of kidnapping anyone,' said Adam. 'No struggle, no cries. All you've got to know is that the girl's expecting a car to fetch her and all you've got to do is to look like a high-class chauffeur and arrive there before the other car does. The girl will step in without a second thought and you can drive off without her suspecting in the least what's happening to her.'

'No abandoned car found anywhere?' asked Kelsey.

'We've had no news of one,' said the Sergeant. 'The Yard's on it now as I said,' he added, 'and the Special Branch.'

'May mean a bit of a political schemozzle,' said the

Inspector. 'I don't suppose for a minute they'll be able to take her out of the country.'

'What do they want to kidnap her for anyway?' asked the doctor.

'Goodness knows,' said Kelsey gloomily. 'She told me she was afraid of being kidnapped and I'm ashamed to say I thought she was just showing off.'

'I thought so, too, when you told me about it,' said Adam.

'The trouble is we don't know enough,' said Kelsey. 'There are far too many loose ends.' He looked around. 'Well, there doesn't seem to be anything more that I can do here. Get on with the usual stuff—photographs, fingerprints, etc. I'd better go along to the house.'

At the house he was received by Miss Johnson. She was shaken but preserved her self-control.

'It's terrible, Inspector,' she said. 'Two of our mistresses killed. Poor Miss Chadwick's in a dreadful state.'

'I'd like to see her as soon as I can.'

'The doctor gave her something and she's much calmer now. Shall I take you to her?'

'Yes, in a minute or two. First of all, just tell me what you can about the last time you saw Miss Vansittart.'

'I haven't seen her at all today,' said Miss Johnson. 'I've been away all day. I arrived back here just before eleven and went straight up to my room. I went to bed.'

'You didn't happen to look out of your window towards the Sports Pavilion?'

'No. No, I never thought of it. I'd spent the day with my sister whom I hadn't seen for some time and my mind was full of home news. I took a bath and went to bed and read a book, and I turned off the light and went to sleep. The next thing I knew was when Miss Chadwick burst in, looking as white as a sheet and shaking all over.'

'Was Miss Vansittart absent today?'

'No, she was here. She was in charge. Miss Bulstrode's away.'

'Who else was here, of the mistresses, I mean?'

Miss Johnson considered a moment. 'Miss Vansittart, Miss Chadwick, the French mistress, Mademoiselle Blanche, Miss Rowan.'

'I see. Well, I think you'd better take me to Miss Chadwick now.'

Miss Chadwick was sitting in a chair in her room. Although the night was a warm one the electric fire had been turned on and a rug was wrapped round her knees. She turned a ghastly face towards Inspector Kelsey.

'She's dead—she *is* dead? There's no chance that—that she might come round?'

Kelsey shook his head slowly.

'It's so awful,' said Miss Chadwick, 'with Miss Bulstrode away.' She burst into tears. 'This will ruin the school,' she said. 'This will ruin Meadowbank. I can't bear it—I really can't bear it.'

Kelsey sat down beside her. 'I know,' he said sympathetically, 'I know. It's been a terrible shock to you, but I want you to be brave, Miss Chadwick, and tell me all you know. The sooner we can find out who did it, the less trouble and publicity there will be.'

'Yes, yes, I can see that. You see, I—I went to bed early because I thought it would be nice for once to have a nice long night. But I couldn't go to sleep. I was worrying.'

'Worrying about the school?'

'Yes. And about Shaista being missing. And then I began thinking of Miss Springer and whether—whether her murder would affect the parents, and whether perhaps they wouldn't send their girls back here next term. I was so terribly upset for Miss Bulstrode. I mean, she's *made* this place. It's been such a fine achievement.'

'I know. Now go on telling me—you were worried, and you couldn't sleep?'

'No, I counted sheep and everything. And then I got up and took some aspirin and when I'd taken it I just happened to draw back the curtains from the window. I don't quite know why. I suppose because I'd been thinking about Miss Springer. Then you see, I saw... I saw a light there.'

'What kind of a light?'

'Well, a sort of dancing light. I mean—I think it must have been a torch. It was just like the light that Miss Johnson and I saw before.'

'It was just the same, was it?'

'Yes. Yes, I think so. Perhaps a little feebler, but I don't know.'

'Yes. And then?'

'And then,' said Miss Chadwick, her voice suddenly becoming more resonant, 'I was determined that *this* time I would see who it was out there and what they were doing.

Agatha Christie

So I got up and pulled on my coat and my shoes, and I rushed out of the house.'

'You didn't think of calling anyone else?'

'No. No, I didn't. You see I was in such a hurry to get there, I was so afraid the person—whoever it was—would go away.'

'Yes. Go on, Miss Chadwick.'

'So I went as fast as I could. I went up to the door and just before I got there I went on tiptoe so that—so that I should be able to look in and nobody would hear me coming. I got there. The door was not shut—just ajar and I pushed it very slightly open. I looked round it and—and there she was. Fallen forward on her face, *dead*...'

She began to shake all over.

'Yes, yes, Miss Chadwick, it's all right. By the way, there was a golf club out there. Did you take it out? Or did Miss Vansittart?'

'A golf club?' said Miss Chadwick vaguely. 'I can't remember—Oh, yes, I think I picked it up in the hall. I took it out with me in case—well, in case I should have to use it. When I saw Eleanor I suppose I just dropped it. Then I got back to the house somehow and I found Miss Johnson—Oh! I can't bear it. I can't bear it—this will be the end of Meadowbank—'

Miss Chadwick's voice rose hysterically. Miss Johnson came forward.

'To discover two murders is too much of a strain for anyone,' said Miss Johnson. 'Certainly for anyone her age. You don't want to ask her any more, do you?'

Inspector Kelsey shook his head.

As he was going downstairs, he noticed a pile of old-fashioned sandbags with buckets in an alcove. Dating from the war, perhaps, but the uneasy thought occurred to him that it needn't have been a professional with a cosh who had slugged Miss Vansittart. Someone in the building, someone who hadn't wished to risk the sound of a shot a second time, and who, very likely, had disposed of the incriminating pistol after the last murder, could have helped themselves to an innocent-looking but lethal weapon—and possibly even replaced it tidily afterwards!

CHAPTER 16

The Riddle of the Sports Pavilion

'*My head is bloody but unbowed,*' said Adam to himself.

He was looking at Miss Bulstrode. He had never, he thought, admired a woman more. She sat, cool and unmoved, with her lifework falling in ruins about her.

From time to time telephone calls came through announcing that yet another pupil was being removed.

Finally Miss Bulstrode had taken her decision. Excusing herself to the police officers, she summoned Ann Shapland, and dictated a brief statement. The school would be closed until the end of term. Parents who found it inconvenient to have their children home, were welcome to leave them in her care and their education would be continued.

'You've got the list of parents' names and addresses? And their telephone numbers?'

'Yes, Miss Bulstrode.'

'Then start on the telephone. After that see a typed notice goes to everyone.'

'Yes, Miss Bulstrode.'

On her way out, Ann Shapland paused near the door. She flushed and her words came with a rush.

'Excuse me, Miss Bulstrode. It's not my business—but isn't it a pity to—to be premature? I mean—after the first panic, when people have had time to think—surely they won't want to take the girls away. They'll be sensible and think better of it.'

Miss Bulstrode looked at her keenly.

'You think I'm accepting defeat too easily?'

Ann flushed.

'I know—you think it's cheek. But—but, well then, yes, I do.'

'You're a fighter, child, I'm glad to see. But you're quite wrong. I'm not accepting defeat. I'm going on my knowledge of human nature. Urge people to take their children away, force it on them—and they won't want to nearly so much. They'll think up reasons for letting them remain. Or at the worst they'll decide to let them come back next term—if there is a next term,' she added grimly.

She looked at Inspector Kelsey.

'That's up to you,' she said. 'Clear these murders up—catch whoever is responsible for them—and we'll be all right.'

Inspector Kelsey looked unhappy. He said: 'We're doing our best.'

Ann Shapland went out.

'Competent girl,' said Miss Bulstrode. 'And loyal.'

Agatha Christie

This was in the nature of a parenthesis. She pressed her attack.

'Have you absolutely *no* idea of who killed two of my mistresses in the Sports Pavilion? You ought to, by this time. And this kidnapping on top of everything else. I blame myself there. The girl talked about someone wanting to kidnap her. I thought, God forgive me, she was making herself important. I see now that there must have been something behind it. Someone must have hinted, or warned—one doesn't know which—' She broke off, resuming: 'You've no news of any kind?'

'Not yet. But I don't think you need worry too much about that. It's been passed to the C.I.D. The Special Branch is on to it, too. They ought to find her within twenty-four hours, thirty-six at most. There are advantages in this being an island. All the ports, airports, etc., are alerted. And the police in every district are keeping a lookout. It's actually easy enough to kidnap anyone—it's keeping them hidden that's the problem. Oh, we'll find her.'

'I hope you'll find her alive,' said Miss Bulstrode grimly. 'We seem to be up against someone who isn't too scrupulous about human life.'

'They wouldn't have troubled to kidnap her if they'd meant to do away with her,' said Adam. 'They could have done that here easily enough.'

He felt that the last words were unfortunate. Miss Bulstrode gave him a look.

'So it seems,' she said dryly.

The telephone rang. Miss Bulstrode took up the receiver.

'Yes?'

She motioned to Inspector Kelsey.

'It's for you.'

Adam and Miss Bulstrode watched him as he took the call. He grunted, jotted down a note or two, said finally: 'I see. Alderton Priors. That's Wallshire. Yes, we'll cooperate. Yes, Super. I'll carry on here, then.'

He put down the receiver and stayed a moment lost in thought. Then he looked up.

'His Excellency got a ransom note this morning. Typed on a new Corona. Postmark Portsmouth. Bet that's a blind.'

'Where and how?' asked Adam.

'Crossroads two miles north of Alderton Priors. That's a bit of bare moorland. Envelope containing money to be put under stone behind A.A. box there at 2 a.m. tomorrow morning.'

'How much?'

'Twenty thousand.' He shook his head. 'Sounds amateurish to me.'

'What are you going to do?' asked Miss Bulstrode.

Inspector Kelsey looked at her. He was a different man. Official reticence hung about him like a cloak.

'The responsibility isn't mine, madam,' he said. 'We have our methods.'

'I hope they're successful,' said Miss Bulstrode.

'Ought to be easy,' said Adam.

'Amateurish?' said Miss Bulstrode, catching at a word they had used. 'I wonder...'

Agatha Christie

Then she said sharply:

'What about my staff? What remains of it, that is to say? Do I trust them, or don't I?'

As Inspector Kelsey hesitated, she said,

'You're afraid that if you tell me who is *not* cleared, I should show it in my manner to them. You're wrong. I shouldn't.'

'I don't think you would,' said Kelsey. 'But I can't afford to take any chances. It doesn't look, on the face of it, as though any of your staff *can* be the person we're looking for. That is, not so far as we've been able to check up on them. We've paid special attention to those who are new this term—that is Mademoiselle Blanche, Miss Springer and your secretary, Miss Shapland. Miss Shapland's past is completely corroborated. She's the daughter of a retired general, she has held the posts she says she did and her former employers vouch for her. In addition she has an alibi for last night. When Miss Vansittart was killed, Miss Shapland was with a Mr Dennis Rathbone at a night club. They're both well known there, and Mr Rathbone has an excellent character. Mademoiselle Blanche's antecedents have also been checked. She has taught at a school in the north of England and at two schools in Germany, and has been given an excellent character. She is said to be a first-class teacher.'

'Not by our standards,' sniffed Miss Bulstrode.

'Her French background has also been checked. As regards Miss Springer, things are not quite so conclusive. She did her training where she says, but there have been gaps since in her periods of employment which are not fully accounted for.

'Since, however, she was killed,' added the Inspector, 'that seems to exonerate her.'

'I agree,' said Miss Bulstrode dryly, 'that both Miss Springer and Miss Vansittart are *hors de combat* as suspects. Let us talk sense. Is Mademoiselle Blanche, in spite of her blameless background, still a suspect merely because she is still alive?'

'She *could* have done both murders. She was here, in the building, last night,' said Kelsey. 'She *says* she went to bed early and slept and heard nothing until the alarm was given. There's no evidence to the contrary. We've got nothing against her. But Miss Chadwick says definitely that she's sly.'

Miss Bulstrode waved that aside impatiently.

'Miss Chadwick always finds the French Mistresses sly. She's got a thing about them.' She looked at Adam. 'What do *you* think?'

'I think she pries,' said Adam slowly. 'It may be just natural inquisitiveness. It may be something more. I can't make up my mind. She doesn't *look* to me like a killer, but how does one know?'

'That's just it,' said Kelsey. 'There *is* a killer here, a ruthless killer who has killed twice—but it's very hard to believe that it's one of the staff. Miss Johnson was with her sister last night at Limeston on Sea, and anyway she's been with you seven years. Miss Chadwick's been with you since you started. Both of them, anyway, are clear of Miss Springer's death. Miss Rich has been with you over a year and was staying last night at the Alton Grange Hotel, twenty miles away, Miss Blake was with friends at Littleport, Miss Rowan has been with you for a year and has a good background. As for your servants, frankly I can't see any of them as murderers. They're all local, too...'

Miss Bulstrode nodded pleasantly.

'I quite agree with your reasoning. It doesn't leave much, does it? So—' She paused and fixed an accusing eye on Adam. 'It looks really—as though it must be *you*.'

His mouth opened in astonishment.

'On the spot,' she mused. 'Free to come and go... Good story to account for your presence here. Background OK but you *could* be a double crosser, you know.'

Adam recovered himself.

'Really, Miss Bulstrode,' he said admiringly, 'I take off my hat to you. You think of *everything*!'

II

'Good gracious!' cried Mrs Sutcliffe at the breakfast table. 'Henry!'

She had just unfolded her newspaper.

The width of the table was between her and her husband since her weekend guests had not yet put in an appearance for the meal.

Mr Sutcliffe, who had opened his paper to the financial page, and was absorbed in the unforeseen movements of certain shares, did not reply.

Cat Among the Pigeons

'*Henry!*'

The clarion call reached him. He raised a startled face.

'What's the matter, Joan?'

'The matter? Another murder! At Meadowbank! At Jennifer's school.'

'What? Here, let *me* see!'

Disregarding his wife's remark that it would be in his paper, too, Mr Sutcliffe leant across the table and snatched the sheet from his wife's grasp.

'Miss Eleanor Vansittart... Sports Pavilion... same spot where Miss Springer, the Games Mistress... hm... hm...'

'I can't believe it!' Mrs Sutcliffe was wailing. 'Meadowbank. Such an exclusive school. Royalty there and everything...'

Mr Sutcliffe crumpled up the paper and threw it down on the table.

'Only one thing to be done,' he said. 'You get over there right away and take Jennifer out of it.'

'You mean take her away—altogether?'

'That's what I mean.'

'You don't think that would be a little too drastic? After Rosamond being so good about it and managing to get her in?'

'You won't be the only one taking your daughter away! Plenty of vacancies soon at your precious Meadowbank.'

'Oh, Henry, do you think so?'

'Yes, I do. Something badly wrong there. Take Jennifer away today.'

'Yes—of course—I suppose you're right. What shall we do with her?'

Agatha Christie

'Send her to a secondary modern somewhere handy. They don't have murders there.'

'Oh, Henry, but they *do*. Don't you remember? There was a boy who shot the science master at one. It was in last week's *News of the World*.'

'I don't know what England's coming to,' said Mr Sutcliffe.

Disgusted, he threw his napkin on the table and strode from the room.

III

Adam was alone in the Sports Pavilion... His deft fingers were turning over the contents of the lockers. It was unlikely that he would find anything where the police had failed but after all, one could never be sure. As Kelsey had said every department's technique varied a little.

What was there that linked this expensive modern building with sudden and violent death? The idea of a rendezvous was out. No one would choose to keep a rendezvous a second time in the same place where murder had occurred. It came back to it, then, that there was something here that someone was looking for. Hardly a *cache* of jewels. That seemed ruled out. There could be no secret hiding place, false drawers, spring catches, etc. And the contents of the lockers were pitifully simple. They had their secrets, but they were the secrets of school life. Photographs of pin up heroes, packets of cigarettes, an occasional unsuitable cheap paperback. Especially he returned to Shaista's locker. It was while bending over that that Miss Vansittart had been killed. What had Miss Vansittart expected to find there? Had she found it? Had her killer taken it from her dead hand and then slipped out of the building in the nick of time to miss being discovered by Miss Chadwick?

In that case it was no good looking. Whatever it was, was gone.

The sound of footsteps outside aroused him from his thoughts. He was on his feet and lighting a cigarette in the middle of the floor when Julia Upjohn appeared in the doorway, hesitating a little.

'Anything you want, miss?' asked Adam.

'I wondered if I could have my tennis racquet.'

'Don't see why not,' said Adam. 'Police constable left me here,' he explained mendaciously. 'Had to drop back to the station for something. Told me to stop here while he was away.'

'To see if he came back, I suppose,' said Julia.

'The police constable?'

'No. I mean, the murderer. They do, don't they? Come back to the scene of the crime. They have to! It's a compulsion.'

'You may be right,' said Adam. He looked up at the serried rows of racquets in their presses. 'Whereabouts is yours?'

'Under U,' said Julia. 'Right at the far end. We have our names on them,' she explained, pointing out the adhesive tape as he handed the racquet to her.

'Seen some service,' said Adam. 'But been a good racquet once.'

'Can I have Jennifer Sutcliffe's too?' asked Julia.

'New,' said Adam appreciatively, as he handed it to her.

'Brand new,' said Julia. 'Her aunt sent it to her only the other day.'

'Lucky girl.'

'She ought to have a good racquet. She's very good at tennis. Her backhand's come on like anything this term.' She looked round. 'Don't you think he *will* come back?'

Adam was a moment or two getting it.

'Oh. The murderer? No, I don't think it's really likely. Bit risky, wouldn't it be?'

'You don't think murderers feel they *have* to?'

'Not unless they've left something behind.'

'You mean a clue? I'd like to find a clue. Have the police found one?'

'They wouldn't tell me.'

'No. I suppose they wouldn't... Are you interested in crime?'

She looked at him inquiringly. He returned her glance. There was, as yet, nothing of the woman in her. She must be of much the same age as Shaista, but her eyes held nothing but interested inquiry.

'Well—I suppose—up to a point—we all are.'

Julia nodded in agreement.

'Yes. I think so, too... I can think of all sorts of

solutions—but most of them are very far fetched. It's rather fun, though.'

'You weren't fond of Miss Vansittart?'

'I never really thought about her. She was all right. A bit like the Bull—Miss Bulstrode—but not really like her. More like an understudy in a theatre. I didn't mean it was fun she was dead. I'm sorry about that.'

She walked out holding the two racquets.

Adam remained looking round the Pavilion.

'What the hell could there ever have been here?' he muttered to himself.

IV

'Good lord,' said Jennifer, allowing Julia's forehand drive to pass her. 'There's Mummy.'

The two girls turned to stare at the agitated figure of Mrs Sutcliffe, shepherded by Miss Rich, rapidly arriving and gesticulating as she did so.

'More fuss, I suppose,' said Jennifer resignedly. 'It's the murder. You *are* lucky, Julia, that your mother's safely on a bus in the Caucasus.'

'There's still Aunt Isabel.'

'Aunts don't mind in the same way.'

'Hallo, Mummy,' she added, as Mrs Sutcliffe arrived.

'You must come and pack your things, Jennifer. I'm taking you back with me.'

'Back home?'

'Yes.'

Agatha Christie

'But—you don't mean altogether? Not for good?'

'Yes. I do.'

'But you can't—really. My tennis has come on like anything. I've got a very good chance of winning the singles and Julia and I *might* win the doubles, though I don't think it's very likely.'

'You're coming home with me today.'

'Why?'

'Don't ask questions.'

'I suppose it's because of Miss Springer and Miss Vansittart being murdered. But no one's murdered any of the girls. I'm sure they wouldn't want to. And Sports Day is in three weeks' time. I *think* I shall win the Long Jump and I've a good chance for the Hurdling.'

'Don't argue with me, Jennifer. You're coming back with me today. Your father insists.'

'But, Mummy—'

Arguing persistently Jennifer moved towards the house by her mother's side.

Suddenly she broke away and ran back to the tennis court.

'Goodbye, Julia. Mummy seems to have got the wind up thoroughly. Daddy, too, apparently. Sickening, isn't it? Goodbye, I'll write to you.'

'I'll write to you, too, and tell you all that happens.'

'I hope they don't kill Chaddy next. I'd rather it was Mademoiselle Blanche, wouldn't you?'

'Yes. She's the one we could spare best. I say, did you notice how black Miss Rich was looking?'

'She hasn't said a word. She's furious at Mummy coming and taking me away.'

'Perhaps she'll stop her. She's very forceful, isn't she? Not like anyone else.'

'She reminds me of someone,' said Jennifer.

'I don't think she's a bit like anybody. She always seems to be quite different.'

'Oh yes. She is different. I meant in appearance. But the person I knew was quite fat.'

'I can't imagine Miss Rich being fat.'

'Jennifer...' called Mrs Sutcliffe.

'I do think parents are trying,' said Jennifer crossly. 'Fuss, fuss, fuss. They never stop. I do think you're lucky to—'

'I know. You said that before. But just at the moment, let me tell you, I wish Mummy were a good deal nearer, and *not* on a bus in Anatolia.'

'*Jennifer...*'

'Coming...'

Julia walked slowly in the direction of the Sports Pavilion. Her steps grew slower and slower and finally she stopped altogether. She stood, frowning, lost in thought.

The luncheon bell sounded, but she hardly heard it. She stared down at the racquet she was holding, moved a step or two along the path, then wheeled round and marched determinedly towards the house. She went in by the front door, which was not allowed, and thereby avoided meeting any of the other girls. The hall was empty. She ran up the stairs to her small bedroom, looked

Agatha Christie

round her hurriedly, then lifting the mattress on her bed, shoved the racquet flat beneath it. Then, rapidly smoothing her hair, she walked demurely downstairs to the dining-room.

CHAPTER 17

Aladdin's Cave

The girls went up to bed that night more quietly than usual. For one thing their numbers were much depleted. At least thirty of them had gone home. The others reacted according to their several dispositions. Excitement, trepidation, a certain amount of giggling that was purely nervous in origin and there were some again who were merely quiet and thoughtful.

Julia Upjohn went up quietly amongst the first wave. She went into her room and closed the door. She stood there listening to the whispers, giggles, footsteps and goodnights. Then silence closed down—or a near silence. Faint voices echoed in the distance, and footsteps went to and fro to the bathroom.

There was no lock on the door. Julia pulled a chair against it, with the top of the chair wedged under the handle. That would give her warning if anyone should come in. But no one was likely to come in. It was strictly forbidden for the girls to go into each other's rooms, and the only mistress who did so was Miss Johnson, if one of the girls was ill or out of sorts.

Julia went to her bed, lifted up the mattress and groped under it. She brought out the tennis racquet and stood a moment holding it. She had decided to examine it now, and not later. A light in her room showing under the door might attract attention when all lights were supposed to be off. Now was the time when a light was normal for undressing and for reading in bed until half past ten if you wanted to do so.

She stood staring down at the racquet. How could there be anything hidden in a tennis racquet?

'But there must be,' said Julia to herself. 'There *must*. The burglary at Jennifer's home, the woman who came with that silly story about a new racquet...'

Only Jennifer would have believed that, thought Julia scornfully.

No, it was 'new lamps for old' and that meant, like in Aladdin, that there was *something* about this particular tennis racquet. Jennifer and Julia had never mentioned to anyone that they had swopped racquets—or at least, she herself never had.

So really then, *this* was the racquet that everyone was looking for in the Sports Pavilion. And it was up to her to find out *why*! She examined it carefully. There was nothing unusual about it to look at. It was a good quality racquet, somewhat the worse for wear, but restrung and eminently usable. Jennifer had complained of the balance.

The only place you could possibly conceal anything in

Cat Among the Pigeons

a tennis racquet was in the handle. You could, she supposed, hollow out the handle to make a hiding place. It sounded a little far fetched but it was possible. And if the handle had been tampered with, that probably *would* upset the balance.

There was a round of leather with lettering on it, the lettering almost worn away. That of course was only stuck on. If one removed that? Julia sat down at her dressing table and attacked it with a penknife and presently managed to pull the leather off. Inside was a round of thin wood. It didn't look quite right. There was a join all round it. Julia dug in her penknife. The blade snapped. Nail scissors were more effective. She succeeded at last in prising it out. A mottled red and blue substance now showed. Julia poked it and enlightenment came to her. *Plasticine!* But surely handles of tennis racquets didn't normally contain plasticine? She grasped the nail scissors firmly and began to dig out lumps of plasticine. The stuff was encasing something. Something that felt like buttons or pebbles.

She attacked the plasticine vigorously.

Something rolled out on the table—then another something. Presently there was quite a heap.

Julia leaned back and gasped.

She stared and stared and stared...

Liquid fire, red and green and deep blue and dazzling white...

In that moment, Julia grew up. She was no longer a child. She became a woman. A woman looking at jewels...

All sorts of fantastic snatches of thought raced through

her brain. Aladdin's cave... Marguerite and her casket of jewels... (They had been taken to Covent Garden to hear Faust last week)... Fatal stones... the Hope diamond... Romance... herself in a black velvet gown with a flashing necklace round her throat...

She sat and gloated and dreamed... She held the stones in her fingers and let them fall through in a rivulet of fire, a flashing stream of wonder and delight.

And then something, some slight sound perhaps, recalled her to herself.

She sat thinking, trying to use her common sense, deciding what she ought to do. That faint sound had alarmed her. She swept up the stones, took them to the washstand and thrust them into her sponge bag and rammed her sponge and nail brush down on top of them. Then she went back to the tennis racquet, forced the plasticine back inside it, replaced the wooden top and tried to gum down the leather on top again. It curled upwards, but she managed to deal with that by applying adhesive plaster the wrong way up in thin strips and then pressing the leather on to it.

It was done. The racquet looked and felt just as before, its weight hardly altered in feel. She looked at it and then cast it down carelessly on a chair.

She looked at her bed, neatly turned down and waiting. But she did not undress. Instead she sat listening. Was that a footstep outside?

Suddenly and unexpectedly she knew fear. Two people had been killed. If anyone knew what she had found, *she* would be killed....

Cat Among the Pigeons

There was a fairly heavy oak chest of drawers in the room. She managed to drag it in front of the door, wishing that it was the custom at Meadowbank to have keys in the locks. She went to the window, pulled up the top sash and bolted it. There was no tree growing near the window and no creepers. She doubted if it was possible for anyone to come in that way but she was not going to take any chances.

She looked at her small clock. Half past ten. She drew a deep breath and turned out the light. No one must notice anything unusual. She pulled back the curtain a little from the window. There was a full moon and she could see the door clearly. Then she sat down on the edge of the bed. In her hand she held the stoutest shoe she possessed.

'If anyone tries to come in,' Julia said to herself, 'I'll rap on the wall here as hard as I can. Mary King is next door and that will wake her up. *And* I'll scream—at the top of my voice. And then, if lots of people come, I'll say I had a nightmare. Anyone might have a nightmare after all the things that have been going on here.'

She sat there and time passed. Then she heard it—a soft step along the passage. She heard it stop outside her door. A long pause and then she saw the handle slowly turning.

Should she scream? Not yet.

The door was pushed—just a crack, but the chest of drawers held it. That must have puzzled the person outside.

Another pause, and then there was a knock, a very gentle little knock, on the door.

Julia held her breath. A pause, and then the knock came again—but still soft and muted.

'I'm asleep,' said Julia to herself. 'I don't hear *anything*.'

Who would come and knock on her door in the middle of the night? If it was someone who had a right to knock, they'd call out, rattle the handle, make a noise. But this person couldn't afford to make a noise...

For a long time Julia sat there. The knock was not repeated, the handle stayed immovable. But Julia sat tense and alert.

She sat like that for a long time. She never knew herself how long it was before sleep overcame her. The school bell finally awoke her, lying in a cramped and uncomfortable heap on the edge of the bed.

II

After breakfast, the girls went upstairs and made their beds, then went down to prayers in the big hall and finally dispersed to various classrooms.

It was during that last exercise, when girls were hurrying in different directions, that Julia went into one classroom, out by a further door, joined a group hurrying round the house, dived behind a rhododendron, made a series of further strategic dives and arrived finally near the wall of the grounds where a lime tree had thick growth almost down to the ground. Julia climbed the tree with ease, she had climbed trees all her life. Completely hidden in the leafy branches, she sat, glancing from time to time at her watch. She was fairly sure she would not be missed for some time. Things were disorganized, two teachers were missing, and more than half the girls had gone home. That meant that all classes would have been reorganized, so nobody would be likely to observe the absence of Julia Upjohn until lunch time and by then—

Julia looked at her watch again, scrambled easily down the tree to the level of the wall, straddled it and dropped neatly on the other side. A hundred yards away was a bus stop where a bus ought to arrive in a few minutes. It duly did so, and Julia hailed and boarded it, having by now abstracted a felt hat from inside her cotton frock and clapped it on her slightly dishevelled hair. She got out at the station and took a train to London.

In her room, propped up on the washstand, she had left a note addressed to Miss Bulstrode.

Dear Miss Bulstrode,
 I have not been kidnapped or run away, so don't worry. I will come back as soon as I can.
 Yours very sincerely,
 Julia Upjohn

III

At 228 Whitehouse Mansions, George, Hercule Poirot's immaculate valet and manservant, opened the door and contemplated with some surprise a schoolgirl with a rather dirty face.

'Can I see M. Hercule Poirot, please?'

George took just a shade longer than usual to reply. He found the caller unexpected.

'Mr Poirot does not see anyone without an appointment,' he said.

'I'm afraid I haven't time to wait for that. I really must see him now. It is very urgent. It's about some murders and a robbery and things like that.'

'I will ascertain,' said George, 'if Mr Poirot will see you.'

He left her in the hall and withdrew to consult his master.

'A young lady, sir, who wishes to see you urgently.'

'I daresay,' said Hercule Poirot. 'But things do not arrange themselves as easily as that.'

'That is what I told her, sir.'

'What kind of a young lady?'

'Well, sir, she's more of a little girl.'

'A little girl? A young lady? Which do you mean, Georges? They are really not the same.'

'I'm afraid you did not quite get my meaning sir. She is, I should say, a little girl—of school age, that is to say. But though her frock is dirty and indeed torn, she is essentially a young lady.'

'A social term. I see.'

'And she wishes to see you about some murders and a robbery.'

Poirot's eyebrows went up.

'*Some* murders, and *a robbery*. Original. Show the little girl—the young lady—in.'

Julia came into the room with only the slightest trace of diffidence. She spoke politely and quite naturally.

'How do you do, M. Poirot. I am Julia Upjohn. I think you know a great friend of Mummy's. Mrs Summerhayes.

We stayed with her last summer and she talked about you a lot.'

'Mrs Summerhayes...' Poirot's mind went back to a village that climbed a hill and to a house on top of that hill. He recalled a charming freckled face, a sofa with broken springs, a large quantity of dogs, and other things both agreeable and disagreeable.

'Maureen Summerhayes,' he said. 'Ah yes.'

'I call her Aunt Maureen, but she isn't really an aunt at all. She told us how wonderful you'd been and saved a man who was in prison for murder, and when I couldn't think of what to do and who to go to, I thought of you.'

'I am honoured,' said Poirot gravely.

He brought forward a chair for her.

'Now tell me,' he said. 'Georges, my servant, told me you wanted to consult me about a robbery and some murders—more than one murder, then?'

'Yes,' said Julia. 'Miss Springer and Miss Vansittart. And of course there's the kidnapping, too—but I don't think that's really my business.'

'You bewilder me,' said Poirot. 'Where have all these exciting happenings taken place?'

'At my school—Meadowbank.'

'Meadowbank,' exclaimed Poirot. 'Ah.' He stretched out his hand to where the newspapers lay neatly folded beside him. He unfolded one and glanced over the front page, nodding his head.

'I begin to comprehend,' he said. 'Now tell me, Julia, tell me everything from the beginning.'

Agatha Christie

Julia told him. It was quite a long story and a comprehensive one—but she told it clearly—with an occasional break as she went back over something she had forgotten.

She brought her story up to the moment when she had examined the tennis racquet in her bedroom last night.

'You see, I thought it was just like Aladdin—new lamps for old—and there must be something about that tennis racquet.'

'And there was?'

'Yes.'

Without any false modesty, Julia pulled up her skirt, rolled up her knicker leg nearly to her thigh and exposed what looked like a grey poultice attached by adhesive plaster to the upper part of her leg.

She tore off the strips of plaster, uttering an anguished 'Ouch' as she did so, and freed the poultice which Poirot now perceived to be a packet enclosed in a portion of grey plastic sponge bag. Julia unwrapped it and without warning poured a heap of glittering stones on the table.

'*Nom d'un nom d'un nom!*' ejaculated Poirot in an awe-inspired whisper.

He picked them up, letting them run through his fingers.

'*Nom d'un nom d'un nom!* But they are *real*. Genuine.'

Julia nodded.

'I think they must be. People wouldn't kill other people for them otherwise, would they? But I can understand people killing for *these*!'

And suddenly, as had happened last night, a woman looked out of the child's eyes.

Poirot looked keenly at her and nodded.

'Yes—you understand—you feel the spell. They cannot be to you just pretty coloured playthings—more is the pity.'

'They're *jewels*!' said Julia, in tones of ecstasy.

'And you found them, you say, in this tennis racquet?'

Julia finished her recital.

'And you have now told me everything?'

'I think so. I may, perhaps, have exaggerated a little here and there. I do exaggerate sometimes. Now Jennifer, my great friend, she's the other way round. She can make the most exciting things sound dull.' She looked again at the shining heap. 'M. Poirot, who do they really belong to?'

'It is probably very difficult to say. But they do not belong to either you or to me. We have to decide now what to do next.'

Julia looked at him in an expectant fashion.

'You leave yourself in my hands? Good.'

Hercule Poirot closed his eyes.

Suddenly he opened them and became brisk.

'It seems that this is an occasion when I cannot, as I prefer, remain in my chair. There must be order and method, but in what you tell me, there is no order and method. That is because we have here many threads. But they all converge and meet at one place, Meadowbank. Different people, with different aims, and representing different interests—all converge at Meadowbank. So, I, too, go to Meadowbank. And as for you—where is your mother?'

'Mummy's gone in a bus to Anatolia.'

'Ah, your mother has gone in a bus to Anatolia. *Il ne*

manquait que ça! I perceive well that she might be a friend of Mrs Summerhayes! Tell me, did you enjoy your visit with Mrs Summerhayes?'

'Oh yes, it was great fun. She's got some lovely dogs.'

'The dogs, yes, I well remember.'

'They come in and out through all the windows—like in a pantomime.'

'You are so right! And the food? Did you enjoy the food?'

'Well, it was a bit peculiar sometimes,' Julia admitted.

'Peculiar, yes, indeed.'

'But Aunt Maureen makes smashing omelettes.'

'She makes smashing omelettes.' Poirot's voice was happy. He sighed.

'Then Hercule Poirot has not lived in vain,' he said. 'It was *I* who taught your Aunt Maureen to make an omelette.' He picked up the telephone receiver.

'We will now reassure your good schoolmistress as to your safety and announce my arrival with you at Meadowbank.'

'She knows I'm all right. I left a note saying I hadn't been kidnapped.'

'Nevertheless, she will welcome further reassurance.'

In due course he was connected, and was informed that Miss Bulstrode was on the line.

'Ah, Miss Bulstrode? My name is Hercule Poirot. I have with me here your pupil Julia Upjohn. I propose to motor down with her immediately, and for the information of the police officer in charge of the case, a certain packet of some value has been safely deposited in the bank.'

He rang off and looked at Julia.

'You would like a *sirop*?' he suggested.

'Golden syrup?' Julia looked doubtful.

'No, a syrup of fruit juice. Blackcurrant, raspberry, *groseille*—that is, red currant?'

Julia settled for red currant.

'But the jewels aren't in the bank,' she pointed out.

'They will be in a very short time,' said Poirot. 'But for the benefit of anyone who listens in at Meadowbank, or who overhears, or who is told, it is as well to think they are already there and no longer in your possession. To obtain jewels from a bank requires time and organization. And I should very much dislike anything to happen to you, my child. I will admit that I have formed a high opinion of your courage and your resource.'

Julia looked pleased but embarrassed.

CHAPTER 18

Consultation

Hercule Poirot had prepared himself to beat down an insular prejudice that a headmistress might have against aged foreigners with pointed patent leather shoes and large moustaches. But he was agreeably surprised. Miss Bulstrode greeted him with cosmopolitan aplomb. She also, to his gratification, knew all about him.

'It was kind of you, M. Poirot,' she said, 'to ring up so promptly and allay our anxiety. All the more so because that anxiety had hardly begun. You weren't missed at lunch, Julia, you know,' she added, turning to the girl. 'So many girls were fetched away this morning, and there were so many gaps at table, that half the school could have been missing, I think, without any apprehension being aroused. These are unusual circumstances,' she said, turning back to Poirot. 'I assure you we would not be so slack normally. When I received your telephone call,' she went on, 'I went to Julia's room and found the note she had left.'

'I didn't want you to think I'd been kidnapped, Miss Bulstrode,' said Julia.

'I appreciate that, but I think, Julia, that you might have told me what you were planning to do.'

'I thought I'd better not,' said Julia, and added unexpectedly, '*Les oreilles ennemies nous écoutent.*'

'Mademoiselle Blanche doesn't seem to have done much to improve your accent yet,' said Miss Bulstrode, briskly. 'But I'm not scolding you, Julia.' She looked from Julia to Poirot. 'Now, if you please, I want to hear exactly what has happened.'

'You permit?' said Hercule Poirot. He stepped across the room, opened the door and looked out. He made an exaggerated gesture of shutting it. He returned beaming.

'We are alone,' he said mysteriously. 'We can proceed.'

Miss Bulstrode looked at him, then she looked at the door, then she looked at Poirot again. Her eyebrows rose. He returned her gaze steadily. Very slowly Miss Bulstrode inclined her head. Then, resuming her brisk manner, she said, 'Now then, Julia, let's hear all about this.'

Julia plunged into her recital. The exchange of tennis racquets, the mysterious woman. And finally her discovery of what the racquet contained. Miss Bulstrode turned to Poirot. He nodded his head gently.

'Mademoiselle Julia has stated everything correctly,' he said. 'I took charge of what she brought me. It is safely lodged in a bank. I think therefore that you need anticipate no further developments of an unpleasant nature here.'

'I see,' said Miss Bulstrode. 'Yes, I see…' She was quiet

Agatha Christie

for a moment or two and then she said, 'You think it wise for Julia to remain here? Or would it be better for her to go to her aunt in London?'

'Oh please,' said Julia, 'do let me stay here.'

'You're happy here then?' said Miss Bulstrode.

'I love it,' said Julia. 'And besides, there have been such exciting things going on.'

'That is *not* a normal feature of Meadowbank,' said Miss Bulstrode, dryly.

'I think that Julia will be in no danger here now,' said Hercule Poirot. He looked again towards the door.

'I think I understand,' said Miss Bulstrode.

'But for all that,' said Poirot, 'there should be discretion. Do you understand discretion, I wonder?' he added, looking at Julia.

'M. Poirot means,' said Miss Bulstrode, 'that he would like you to hold your tongue about what you found. Not talk about it to the other girls. Can you hold your tongue?'

'Yes,' said Julia.

'It is a very good story to tell to your friends,' said Poirot. 'Of what you found in a tennis racquet in the dead of night. But there are important reasons why it would be advisable that that story should not be told.'

'I understand,' said Julia.

'Can I trust you, Julia?' said Miss Bulstrode.

'You can trust me,' said Julia. 'Cross my heart.'

Miss Bulstrode smiled. 'I hope your mother will be home before long,' she said.

'Mummy? Oh, I do hope so.'

'I understand from Inspector Kelsey,' said Miss Bulstrode, 'that every effort is being made to get in touch with her. Unfortunately,' she added, 'Anatolian buses are liable to unexpected delays and do not always run to schedule.'

'I can tell Mummy, can't I?' said Julia.

'Of course. Well, Julia, that's all settled. You'd better run along now.'

Julia departed. She closed the door after her. Miss Bulstrode looked very hard at Poirot.

'I have understood you correctly, I think,' she said. 'Just now, you made a great parade of closing that door. Actually—you deliberately left it slightly open.'

Poirot nodded.

'So that what we said could be overheard?'

'Yes—if there was anyone who wanted to overhear. It was a precaution of safety for the child—the news must get round that what she found is safely in a bank, and not in her possession.'

Miss Bulstrode looked at him for a moment—then she pursed her lips grimly together.

'There's got to be an end to all this,' she said.

II

'The idea is,' said the Chief Constable, 'that we try to pool our ideas and information. We are very glad to have you with us, M. Poirot,' he added. 'Inspector Kelsey remembers you well.'

'It's a great many years ago,' said Inspector Kelsey. 'Chief

Agatha Christie

Inspector Warrender was in charge of the case. I was a fairly raw sergeant, knowing my place.'

'The gentleman called, for convenience's sake by us—Mr Adam Goodman, is not known to you, M. Poirot, but I believe you do know his—his—er—chief. Special Branch,' he added.

'Colonel Pikeaway?' said Hercule Poirot thoughtfully.

'Ah, yes, it is some time since I have seen him. Is he still as sleepy as ever?' he asked Adam.

Adam laughed. 'I see you know him all right, M. Poirot. I've never seen him wide awake. When I do, I'll know that for once he isn't paying attention to what goes on.'

'You have something there, my friend. It is well observed.'

'Now,' said the Chief Constable, 'let's get down to things. I shan't push myself forward or urge my own opinions. I'm here to listen to what the men who are actually working on the case know and think. There are a great many sides to all this, and one thing perhaps I ought to mention first of all. I'm saying this as a result of representations that have been made to me from—er—various quarters high up.' He looked at Poirot. 'Let's say,' he said, 'that a little girl—a schoolgirl—came to you with a pretty tale of something she'd found in the hollowed-out handle of a tennis racquet. Very exciting for her. A collection, shall we say, of coloured stones, paste, good imitation—something of that kind—or even semi-precious stones which often look as attractive as the other kind. Anyway let's say something that a child would be excited to find. She might even have exaggerated ideas of its value. That's quite possible, don't you think?' He looked very hard at Hercule Poirot.

'It seems to me eminently possible,' said Hercule Poirot.

'Good,' said the Chief Constable. 'Since the person who brought these—er—coloured stones into the country did so quite unknowingly and innocently, we don't want any question of illicit smuggling to arise.

'Then there is the question of our foreign policy,' he went on. 'Things, I am led to understand, are rather—delicate just at present. When it comes to large interests in oil, mineral deposits, all that sort of thing, we have to deal with whatever government's in power. We don't want any awkward questions to arise. You can't keep murder out of the Press, and murder hasn't been kept out of the Press. But there's been no mention of anything like jewels in connection with it. For the present, at any rate, there needn't be.'

'I agree,' said Poirot. 'One must always consider international complications.'

'Exactly,' said the Chief Constable. 'I think I'm right in saying that the late ruler of Ramat was regarded as a friend of this country, and that the powers that be would like his wishes in respect of any property of his that *might* be in this country to be carried out. What that amounts to, I gather, nobody knows at present. If the new Government of Ramat is claiming certain property which they allege belongs to them, it will be much better if we know nothing about such property being in this country. A plain refusal would be tactless.'

'One does not give plain refusals in diplomacy,' said Hercule Poirot. 'One says instead that such a matter shall receive the utmost attention but that at the moment nothing definite is known about any little—nest egg, say—that the late ruler of Ramat may have possessed. It may be still in Ramat, it may be in the keeping of a faithful friend of the late Prince Ali Yusuf, it may have been taken out of the country by half a dozen people, it may be hidden somewhere in the city of Ramat itself.' He shrugged his shoulders. 'One simply does not know.'

The Chief Constable heaved a sigh. 'Thank you,' he said. 'That's just what I mean.' He went on, 'M. Poirot, you have friends in very high quarters in this country. They put much trust in you. Unofficially they would like to leave a certain article in your hands if you do not object.'

'I do not object,' said Poirot. 'Let us leave it at that. We have more serious things to consider, have we not?' He looked round at them. 'Or perhaps you do not think so? But after all, what is three quarters of a million or some such sum in comparison with human life?'

'You're right, M. Poirot,' said the Chief Constable.

'You're right every time,' said Inspector Kelsey. 'What we want is a murderer. We shall be glad to have your opinion, M. Poirot,' he added, 'because it's largely a question of guess and guess again and your guess is as good as the next man's and sometimes better. The whole thing's like a snarl of tangled wool.'

'That is excellently put,' said Poirot, 'one has to take up

that snarl of wool and pull out the one colour that we seek, the colour of a murderer. Is that right?'

'That's right.'

'Then tell me, if it is not too tedious for you to indulge in repetition, all that is known so far.'

He settled down to listen.

He listened to Inspector Kelsey, and he listened to Adam Goodman. He listened to the brief summing up of the Chief Constable. Then he leaned back, closed his eyes, and slowly nodded his head.

'Two murders,' he said, 'committed in the same place and roughly under the same conditions. One kidnapping. The kidnapping of a girl who might be the central figure of the plot. Let us ascertain first *why* she was kidnapped.'

'I can tell you what she said herself,' said Kelsey.

He did so, and Poirot listened.

'It does not make sense,' he complained.

'That's what I thought at the time. As a matter of fact I thought she was just making herself important…'

'But the fact remains that she *was* kidnapped. Why?'

'There have been ransom demands,' said Kelsey slowly, 'but—' he paused.

'But they have been, you think, phoney? They have been sent merely to bolster up the kidnapping theory?'

'That's right. The appointments made weren't kept.'

'Shaista, then, was kidnapped for some other reason. What reason?'

'So that she could be made to tell where the—er—valuables were hidden?' suggested Adam doubtfully.

Poirot shook his head.

'She did not know where they were hidden,' he pointed out. 'That at least, is clear. No, there must be something...'

His voice tailed off. He was silent, frowning, for a moment or two. Then he sat up, and asked a question.

'Her knees,' he said. 'Did you ever notice her knees?'

Adam stared at him in astonishment.

'No,' he said. 'Why should I?'

'There are many reasons why a man notices a girl's knees,' said Poirot severely. 'Unfortunately, you did not.'

'Was there something odd about her knees? A scar? Something of that kind? I wouldn't know. They all wear stockings most of the time, and their skirts are just below knee length.'

'In the swimming pool, perhaps?' suggested Poirot hopefully.

'Never saw her go in,' said Adam. 'Too chilly for her, I expect. She was used to a warm climate. What are you getting at? A scar? Something of that kind?'

'No, no, that is not it at all. Ah well, a pity.'

He turned to the Chief Constable.

'With your permission, I will communicate with my old friend, the Préfet, at Geneva. I think he may be able to help us.'

'About something that happened when she was at school there?'

'It is possible, yes. You do permit? Good. It is just a little idea of mine.' He paused and went on: 'By the way, there has been nothing in the papers about the kidnapping?'

'The Emir Ibrahim was most insistent.'

'But I did notice a little remark in a gossip column. About a certain foreign young lady who had departed from school very suddenly. A budding romance, the columnist suggested? To be nipped in the bud if possible!'

'That was my idea,' said Adam. 'It seemed a good line to take.'

'Admirable. So now we pass from kidnapping to something more serious. Murder. Two murders at Meadowbank.'

CHAPTER 19

Consultation Continued

'Two murders at Meadowbank,' repeated Poirot thoughtfully.

'We've given you the facts,' said Kelsey. 'If you've any ideas—'

'Why the Sports Pavilion?' said Poirot. 'That was your question, wasn't it?' he said to Adam. 'Well, now we have the answer. Because in the Sports Pavilion there was a tennis racquet containing a fortune in jewels. Someone knew about that racquet. Who was it? It could have been Miss Springer herself. She was, so you all say, rather peculiar about that Sports Pavilion. Disliked people coming there—unauthorized people, that is to say. She seemed to be suspicious of their motives. Particularly was that so in the case of Mademoiselle Blanche.'

'Mademoiselle Blanche,' said Kelsey thoughtfully.

Hercule Poirot again spoke to Adam.

'You yourself considered Mademoiselle Blanche's manner odd where it concerned the Sports Pavilion?'

'She explained,' said Adam. 'She explained too much. I should never have questioned her right to be there if she had not taken so much trouble to explain it away.'

Poirot nodded.

'Exactly. That certainly gives one to think. But all we *know* is that Miss Springer was killed in the Sports Pavilion at one o'clock in the morning when she had no business to be there.'

He turned to Kelsey.

'Where was Miss Springer before she came to Meadowbank?'

'We don't know,' said the Inspector. 'She left her last place of employment,' he mentioned a famous school, 'last summer. Where she has been since we do not know.' He added dryly: 'There was no occasion to ask the question until she was dead. She has no near relatives, nor, apparently, any close friends.'

'She *could* have been in Ramat, then,' said Poirot thoughtfully.

'I believe there was a party of school teachers out there at the time of the trouble,' said Adam.

'Let us say, then, that she was there, that in some way she learned about the tennis racquet. Let us assume that after waiting a short time to familiarize herself with the routine at Meadowbank she went out one night to the Sports Pavilion. She got hold of the racquet and was about to remove the jewels from their hiding place when—' he paused—'when *someone* interrupted her. Someone who had been watching her? Following her that evening? Whoever it was had a pistol—and shot her—but had no time to prise out the jewels, or to take the racquet away, because people were approaching the Sports Pavilion who had heard the shot.'

He stopped.

'You think that's what happened?' asked the Chief Constable.

'I do not know,' said Poirot. 'It is one possibility. The other is that that person with the pistol was there *first*, and was surprised by Miss Springer. Someone whom Miss Springer was already suspicious of. She was, you have told me, that kind of woman. A noser out of secrets.'

'And the other woman?' asked Adam.

Poirot looked at him. Then, slowly, he shifted his gaze to the other two men.

'*You* do not know,' he said. 'And *I* do not know. It could have been someone from outside—?'

His voice half asked a question.

Kelsey shook his head.

'I think not. We have sifted the neighbourhood very carefully. Especially, of course, in the case of strangers. There was a Madam Kolinsky staying nearby—known to Adam here. But she could not have been concerned in either murder.'

'Then it comes back to Meadowbank. And there is only one method to arrive at the truth—elimination.'

Kelsey sighed.

'Yes,' he said. 'That's what it amounts to. For the first murder, it's a fairly open field. Almost anybody could have killed Miss Springer. The exceptions are Miss Johnson and Miss Chadwick—and a child who had the earache. But the second murder narrows things down. Miss Rich, Miss Blake and Miss Shapland are out of it. Miss Rich was staying at the Alton Grange Hotel, twenty miles away, Miss Blake was at Littleport on Sea, Miss Shapland was in London at a night club, the Nid Sauvage, with Mr Dennis Rathbone.'

'And Miss Bulstrode was also away, I understand?'

Adam grinned. The Inspector and the Chief Constable looked shocked.

'Miss Bulstrode,' said the Inspector severely, 'was staying with the Duchess of Welsham.'

'That eliminates Miss Bulstrode then,' said Poirot gravely. 'And leaves us—what?'

'Two members of the domestic staff who sleep in, Mrs Gibbons and a girl called Doris Hogg. I can't consider either of them seriously. That leaves Miss Rowan and Mademoiselle Blanche.'

'And the pupils, of course.'

Kelsey looked startled.

'Surely you don't suspect them?'

'Frankly, no. But one must be exact.'

Kelsey paid no attention to exactitude. He plodded on.

'Miss Rowan has been here over a year. She has a good record. We know nothing against her.'

'So we come, then, to Mademoiselle Blanche. It is there that the journey ends.'

There was a silence.

Agatha Christie

'There's no evidence,' said Kelsey. 'Her credentials seem genuine enough.'

'They would have to be,' said Poirot.

'She snooped,' said Adam. 'But snooping isn't evidence of murder.'

'Wait a minute,' said Kelsey, 'there was something about a key. In our first interview with her—I'll look it up—something about the key of the Pavilion falling out of the door and she picked it up and forgot to replace it—walked out with it and Springer bawled her out.'

'Whoever wanted to go out there at night and look for the racquet would have had to have a key to get in with,' said Poirot. 'For that, it would have been necessary to take an impression of the key.'

'Surely,' said Adam, 'in that case she would never have mentioned the key incident to you.'

'That doesn't follow,' said Kelsey. 'Springer might have talked about the key incident. If so, she might think it better to mention it in a casual fashion.'

'It is a point to be remembered,' said Poirot.

'It doesn't take us very far,' said Kelsey.

He looked gloomily at Poirot.

'There would seem,' said Poirot, '(that is, if I have been informed correctly), one possibility. Julia Upjohn's mother, I understand, recognized someone here on the first day of term. Someone whom she was surprised to see. From the context, it would seem likely that that someone was connected with foreign espionage. If Mrs Upjohn definitely points out Mademoiselle as the person she recognized, then I think we could proceed with some assurance.'

'Easier said than done,' said Kelsey. 'We've been trying to get in contact with Mrs Upjohn, but the whole thing's a headache! When the child said a bus, I thought she meant a proper coach tour, running to schedule, and a party all booked together. But that's not it at all. Seems she's just taking local buses to any place she happens to fancy! She's not done it through Cook's or a recognized travel agency. She's all on her own, wandering about. What can you do with a woman like that? She might be anywhere. There's a lot of Anatolia!'

'It makes it difficult, yes,' said Poirot.

'Plenty of nice coach tours,' said the Inspector in an injured voice. 'All made easy for you—where you stop and what you see, and all-in fares so that you know exactly where you are.'

'But clearly, that kind of travel does not appeal to Mrs Upjohn.'

'And in the meantime, here *we* are,' went on Kelsey. 'Stuck! That Frenchwoman can walk out any moment she chooses. We've nothing on which we could hold her.'

Poirot shook his head.

'She will not do that.'

'You can't be sure.'

'I am sure. If you have committed murder, you do not want to do anything out of character, that may draw attention to you. Mademoiselle Blanche will remain here quietly until the end of the term.'

'I hope you're right.'

'I am sure I am right. And remember, the person whom Mrs Upjohn saw, *does not know that Mrs Upjohn saw her*. The surprise when it comes will be complete.'

Kelsey sighed.

'If that's all we've got to go on—'

'There are other things. Conversation, for instance.'

'Conversation?'

'It is very valuable, conversation. Sooner or later, if one has something to hide, one says too much.'

'Gives oneself away?' The Chief Constable sounded sceptical.

'It is not quite so simple as that. One is guarded about the thing one is trying to hide. But often one says too much about other things. And there are other uses for conversation. There are the innocent people who know things, but are unaware of the importance of what they know. And that reminds me—'

He rose to his feet.

'Excuse me, I pray. I must go and demand of Miss Bulstrode if there is someone here who can draw.'

'Draw?'

'Draw.'

'Well,' said Adam, as Poirot went out. 'First girls' knees, and now draughtsmanship! What next, I wonder?'

II

Miss Bulstrode answered Poirot's questions without evincing any surprise.

'Miss Laurie is our visiting Drawing Mistress,' she said briskly. 'But she isn't here today. What do you want her to draw for you?' she added in a kindly manner as though to a child.

'Faces,' said Poirot.

'Miss Rich is good at sketching people. She's clever at getting a likeness.'

'That is exactly what I need.'

Miss Bulstrode, he noted with approval, asked him no questions as to his reasons. She merely left the room and returned with Miss Rich.

After introductions, Poirot said: 'You can sketch people? Quickly? With a pencil?'

Eileen Rich nodded.

'I often do. For amusement.'

'Good. Please, then, sketch for me the late Miss Springer.'

'That's difficult. I knew her for such a short time. I'll try.' She screwed up her eyes, then began to draw rapidly.

'*Bien*,' said Poirot, taking it from her. 'And now, if you please, Miss Bulstrode, Miss Rowan, Mademoiselle Blanche and—yes—the gardener Adam.'

Eileen Rich looked at him doubtfully, then set to work. He looked at the result, and nodded appreciatively.

'You are good—you are very good. So few strokes—and yet the likeness is there. Now I will ask you to do something more difficult. Give, for example, to Miss Bulstrode a different hair arrangement. Change the shape of her eyebrows.'

Eileen stared at him as though she thought he was mad.

Agatha Christie

'No,' said Poirot. 'I am not mad. I make an experiment, that is all. Please do as I ask.'

In a moment or two she said: 'Here you are.'

'Excellent. Now do the same for Mademoiselle Blanche and Miss Rowan.'

When she had finished he lined up the three sketches.

'Now I will show you something,' he said. 'Miss Bulstrode, in spite of the changes you have made is still unmistakably Miss Bulstrode. But look at the other two. Because their features are negative, and since they have not Miss Bulstrode's personality, they appear almost different people, do they not?'

'I see what you mean,' said Eileen Rich.

She looked at him as he carefully folded the sketches away.

'What are you going to do with them?' she asked.

'Use them,' said Poirot.

CHAPTER 20

Conversation

'Well—I don't know what to say,' said Mrs Sutcliffe. 'Really I don't know what to say—'

She looked with definite distaste at Hercule Poirot.

'Henry, of course,' she said, 'is not at home.'

The meaning of this pronouncement was slightly obscure, but Hercule Poirot thought that he knew what was in her mind. Henry, she was feeling, would be able to deal with this sort of thing. Henry had so many international dealings. He was always flying to the Middle East and to Ghana and to South America and to Geneva, and even occasionally, but not so often, to Paris.

'The whole thing,' said Mrs Sutcliffe, 'has been *most* distressing. I was so glad to have Jennifer safely at home with me. Though, I must say,' she added, with a trace of vexation, 'Jennifer has really been most tiresome. After having made a great fuss about going to Meadowbank and being quite sure she wouldn't like it there, and saying it was a snobby kind of school and not the kind she wanted

Agatha Christie

to go to, *now* she sulks all day long because I've taken her away. It's really too bad.'

'It is undeniably a very good school,' said Hercule Poirot. 'Many people say the best school in England.'

'It *was*, I daresay,' said Mrs Sutcliffe.

'And will be again,' said Hercule Poirot.

'You think so?' Mrs Sutcliffe looked at him doubtfully. His sympathetic manner was gradually piercing her defences. There is nothing that eases the burden of a mother's life more than to be permitted to unburden herself of the difficulties, rebuffs and frustrations which she has in dealing with her offspring. Loyalty so often compels silent endurance. But to a foreigner like Hercule Poirot Mrs Sutcliffe felt that this loyalty was not applicable. It was not like talking to the mother of another daughter.

'Meadowbank,' said Hercule Poirot, 'is just passing through an unfortunate phase.'

It was the best thing he could think of to say at the moment. He felt its inadequacy and Mrs Sutcliffe pounced upon the inadequacy immediately.

'Rather more than unfortunate!' she said. 'Two murders! And a girl kidnapped. You can't send your daughter to a school where the mistresses are being murdered all the time.'

It seemed a highly reasonable point of view.

'If the murders,' said Poirot, 'turn out to be the work of one person and that person is apprehended, that makes a difference, does it not?'

'Well—I suppose so. Yes,' said Mrs Sutcliffe doubtfully. 'I

244

mean—you mean—oh, I see, you mean like Jack the Ripper or that other man—who was it? Something to do with Devonshire. Cream? Neil Cream. Who went about killing an unfortunate type of woman. I suppose this murderer just goes about killing schoolmistresses! If once you've got him safely in prison, and hanged too, I hope, because you're only allowed one murder, aren't you?—like a dog with a bite—what was I saying? Oh yes, if he's safely caught, well, then I suppose it *would* be different. Of course there can't be many people like that, can there?'

'One certainly hopes not,' said Hercule Poirot.

'But then there's this kidnapping too,' pointed out Mrs Sutcliffe. 'You don't want to send your daughter to a school where she may be kidnapped, either, do you?'

'Assuredly not, madame. I see how clearly you have thought out the whole thing. You are so right in all you say.'

Mrs Sutcliffe looked faintly pleased. Nobody had said anything like that to her for some time. Henry had merely said things like 'What did you want to send her to Meadowbank for anyway?' and Jennifer had sulked and refused to answer.

'I *have* thought about it,' she said. 'A great deal.'

'Then I should not let kidnapping worry you, madame. *Entre nous*, if I may speak in confidence, about Princess Shaista—It is not exactly a kidnapping—one suspects a romance—'

'You mean the naughty girl just ran away to marry somebody?'

Agatha Christie

'My lips are sealed,' said Hercule Poirot. 'You comprehend it is not desired that there should be any scandal. This is in confidence *entre nous*. I know you will say nothing.'

'Of course not,' said Mrs Sutcliffe virtuously. She looked down at the letter that Poirot had brought with him from the Chief Constable. 'I don't quite understand who you are, M.—er—Poirot. Are you what they call in books—a private eye?'

'I am a consultant,' said Hercule Poirot loftily.

This flavour of Harley Street encouraged Mrs Sutcliffe a great deal.

'What do you want to talk to Jennifer about?' she demanded.

'Just to get her impressions of things,' said Poirot. 'She is observant—yes?'

'I'm afraid I wouldn't say that,' said Mrs Sutcliffe. 'She's not what I call a noticing kind of child at all. I mean, she is always so matter of fact.'

'It is better than making up things that have never happened at all,' said Poirot.

'Oh, Jennifer wouldn't do *that* sort of thing,' said Mrs Sutcliffe, with certainty. She got up, went to the window and called 'Jennifer.'

'I wish,' she said, to Poirot, as she came back again, 'that you'd try and get it into Jennifer's head that her father and I are only doing our best for her.'

Jennifer came into the room with a sulky face and looked with deep suspicion at Hercule Poirot.

'How do you do?' said Poirot. 'I am a very old friend of Julia Upjohn. She came to London to find me.'

'Julia went to London?' said Jennifer, slightly surprised. 'Why?'

'To ask my advice,' said Hercule Poirot.

Jennifer looked unbelieving.

'I was able to give it to her,' said Poirot. 'She is now back at Meadowbank,' he added.

'So her Aunt Isabel didn't *take* her away,' said Jennifer, shooting an irritated look at her mother.

Poirot looked at Mrs Sutcliffe and for some reason, perhaps because she had been in the middle of counting the laundry when Poirot arrived and perhaps because of some unexplained compulsion, she got up and left the room.

'It's a bit hard,' said Jennifer, 'to be out of all that's going on there. All this fuss! I told Mummy it was silly. After all, none of the *pupils* have been killed.'

'Have you any ideas of your own about the murders?' asked Poirot.

Jennifer shook her head. 'Someone who's batty?' she offered. She added thoughtfully, 'I suppose Miss Bulstrode will have to get some new mistresses now.'

'It seems possible, yes,' said Poirot. He went on, 'I am interested, Mademoiselle Jennifer, in the woman who came and offered you a new racquet for your old one. Do you remember?'

'I should think I do remember,' said Jennifer. 'I've never found out to this day who really sent it. It wasn't Aunt Gina at all.'

Agatha Christie

'What did this woman look like?' said Poirot.

'The one who brought the racquet?' Jennifer half closed her eyes as though thinking. 'Well, I don't know. She had on a sort of fussy dress with a little cape, I think. Blue, and a floppy sort of hat.'

'Yes?' said Poirot. 'I meant perhaps not so much her clothes as her face.'

'A good deal of make-up, I think,' said Jennifer vaguely. 'A bit too much for the country, I mean, and fair hair. I think she was an American.'

'Had you ever seen her before?' asked Poirot.

'Oh no,' said Jennifer. 'I don't think she lived down there. She said she'd come down for a luncheon party or a cocktail party or something.'

Poirot looked at her thoughtfully. He was interested in Jennifer's complete acceptance of everything that was said to her. He said gently,

'But she might not have been speaking the truth?'

'Oh,' said Jennifer. 'No, I suppose not.'

'You're quite sure you hadn't seen her before? She could not have been, for instance, one of the girls dressed up? Or one of the mistresses?'

'Dressed up?' Jennifer looked puzzled.

Poirot laid before her the sketch Eileen Rich had done for him of Mademoiselle Blanche.

'This was not the woman, was it?'

Jennifer looked at it doubtfully.

'It's a little like her—but I don't think it's her.'

Poirot nodded thoughtfully.

There was no sign that Jennifer recognized that this was actually a sketch of Mademoiselle Blanche.

'You see,' said Jennifer, 'I didn't really look at her much. She was an American and a stranger, and then she told me about the racquet—'

After that, it was clear, Jennifer would have had eyes for nothing but her new possession.

'I see,' said Poirot. He went on, 'Did you ever see at Meadowbank anyone that you'd seen out in Ramat?'

'In Ramat?' Jennifer thought. 'Oh no—at least—I don't think so.'

Poirot pounced on the slight expression of doubt. 'But you are not *sure*, Mademoiselle Jennifer.'

'Well,' Jennifer scratched her forehead with a worried expression, 'I mean, you're always seeing people who look like somebody else. You can't quite remember who it is they look like. Sometimes you see people that you *have* met but you don't remember who they are. And they say to you "You don't remember me," and then that's awfully awkward because really you don't. I mean, you sort of know their face but you can't remember their names or where you saw them.'

'That is very true,' said Poirot. 'Yes, that is very true. One often has that experience.' He paused a moment then he went on, prodding gently, 'Princess Shaista, for instance, you probably recognized *her* when you saw her because you must have seen her in Ramat.'

'Oh, was she in Ramat?'

'Very likely,' said Poirot. 'After all she is a relation of the ruling house. You might have seen her there?'

Agatha Christie

'I don't think I did,' said Jennifer frowning. 'Anyway, she wouldn't go about with her face showing there, would she? I mean, they all wear veils and things like that. Though they take them off in Paris and Cairo, I believe. And in London, of course,' she added.

'Anyway, you had no feeling of having seen anyone at Meadowbank whom you had seen before?'

'No, I'm sure I hadn't. Of course most people do look rather alike and you might have seen them anywhere. It's only when somebody's got an odd sort of face like Miss Rich, that you notice it.'

'Did you think you'd seen Miss Rich somewhere before?'

'I hadn't really. It must have been someone like her. But it was someone much fatter than she was.'

'Someone much fatter,' said Poirot thoughtfully.

'You couldn't imagine Miss Rich being fat,' said Jennifer with a giggle. 'She's so frightfully thin and nobbly. And anyway Miss Rich couldn't have been in Ramat because she was away ill last term.'

'And the other girls?' said Poirot, 'had you seen any of the girls before?'

'Only the ones I knew already,' said Jennifer. 'I did know one or two of them. After all, you know, I was only there three weeks and I really don't know half of the people there even by sight. I wouldn't know most of them if I met them tomorrow.'

'You should notice things more,' said Poirot severely.

'One can't notice everything,' protested Jennifer. She went on: 'If Meadowbank is carrying on I would like to go back.

See if you can do anything with Mummy. Though really,' she added, 'I think it's Daddy who's the stumbling-block. It's awful here in the country. I get *no* opportunity to improve my tennis.'

'I assure you I will do what I can,' said Poirot.

CHAPTER 21

Gathering Threads

'I want to talk to you, Eileen,' said Miss Bulstrode.

Eileen Rich followed Miss Bulstrode into the latter's sitting-room. Meadowbank was strangely quiet. About twenty-five pupils were still there. Pupils whose parents had found it either difficult or unwelcome to fetch them. The panic-stricken rush had, as Miss Bulstrode had hoped, been checked by her own tactics. There was a general feeling that by next term everything would have been cleared up. It was much wiser of Miss Bulstrode, they felt, to close the school.

None of the staff had left. Miss Johnson fretted with too much time on her hands. A day in which there was too little to do did not in the least suit her. Miss Chadwick, looking old and miserable, wandered round in a kind of coma of misery. She was far harder hit to all appearance than Miss Bulstrode. Miss Bulstrode, indeed, managed apparently without difficulty to be completely herself, unperturbed, and with no sign of strain or collapse. The two younger mistresses were not averse to the extra leisure. They bathed in the swimming pool, wrote long letters to friends and relations and sent for cruise literature to study and compare. Ann Shapland had a good deal of time on her hands and did not appear to resent the fact. She spent a good deal of that time in the garden and devoted herself to gardening with quite unexpected efficiency. That she preferred to be instructed in the work by Adam rather than by old Briggs was perhaps a not unnatural phenomenon.

'Yes, Miss Bulstrode?' said Eileen Rich.

'I've been wanting to talk to you,' said Miss Bulstrode. 'Whether this school can continue or not I do not know. What people will feel is always fairly incalculable because they will all feel differently. But the result will be that whoever feels most strongly will end by converting all the rest. So either Meadowbank is finished—'

'No,' said Eileen Rich, interrupting, 'not finished.' She almost stamped her foot and her hair immediately began coming down. 'You mustn't let it be stopped,' she said. 'It would be a sin—a crime.'

'You speak very strongly,' said Miss Bulstrode.

'I feel strongly. There are so many things that really don't seem worth while a bit, but Meadowbank does seem worth while. It seemed worth while to me the first moment I came here.'

'You're a fighter,' said Miss Bulstrode. 'I like fighters, and I assure you that I don't intend to give in tamely. In a way I'm going to enjoy the fight. You know, when everything's too easy and things go too well one gets—I don't know the exact word I mean—complacent? Bored? A kind of hybrid of the two. But I'm not bored now and I'm not complacent and I'm going to fight with every ounce of strength I've got, and with every penny I've got, too. Now what I want to say to you is this: If Meadowbank continues, will you come in on a partnership basis?'

'Me?' Eileen Rich stared at her. 'Me?'

'Yes, my dear,' said Miss Bulstrode. 'You.'

'I couldn't,' said Eileen Rich. 'I don't know enough. I'm too young. Why, I haven't got the experience, the knowledge that you'd want.'

'You must leave it to me to know what I want,' said Miss Bulstrode. 'Mind you, this isn't, at the present moment of talking, a good offer. You'd probably do better for yourself elsewhere. But I want to tell you this, and you've got to believe me. I had already decided before Miss Vansittart's unfortunate death, that you were the person I wanted to carry on this school.'

'You thought so then?' Eileen Rich stared at her. 'But I thought—we all thought—that Miss Vansittart...'

'There was no arrangement made with Miss Vansittart,' said Miss Bulstrode. 'I had her in mind, I will confess. I've had her in mind for the last two years. But something's always held me back from saying anything definite to her about it. I daresay everyone assumed that she'd be my successor. She may have thought so herself. I myself thought so until very recently. And then I decided that she was not what I wanted.'

'But she was so suitable in every way,' said Eileen Rich. 'She would have carried out things in exactly your ways, in exactly your ideas.'

'Yes,' said Miss Bulstrode, 'and that's just what would have been wrong. You can't hold on to the past. A certain amount of tradition is good but never too much. A school is for the children of *today*. It's not for the children of fifty years ago or even of thirty years ago. There are some schools in which tradition is more important than others, but Meadowbank is not one of those. It's not a school with a long tradition behind it. It's a creation, if I may say it, of one woman. Myself. I've tried certain ideas and carried them out to the best of my ability, though occasionally I've had to modify them when they haven't produced the results I'd expected. It's not been a conventional school, but it has not prided itself on being an unconventional school either. It's a school that tries to make the best of both worlds: the past and the future, but the real stress is on the present. That's how it's going to go on, how it ought to go on. Run by someone with ideas—ideas of the present day. Keeping what is wise from the past, looking forward towards the future. You're very much the age I was when I started here but you've got what I no longer can have. You'll find it written in the Bible. *Their old men dream dreams and their young men have visions.* We don't need dreams here, we need vision. I believe you to have vision and that's why I decided that you were the person and not Eleanor Vansittart.'

'It would have been wonderful,' said Eileen Rich. 'Wonderful. The thing I should have liked above all.'

Miss Bulstrode was faintly surprised by the tense, although she did not show it. Instead she agreed promptly.

'Yes,' she said, 'it would have been wonderful. But it isn't wonderful now? Well, I suppose I understand that.'

'No, no, I don't mean that at all,' said Eileen Rich. 'Not at all. I—I can't go into details very well, but if you had—if you had asked me, spoken to me like this a week or a fortnight ago, I should have said at once that I couldn't, that it would have been quite impossible. The only reason why it—why it might be possible now is because—well, because it *is* a case of fighting—of taking on things. May I—may I think it over, Miss Bulstrode? I don't know what to say now.'

'Of course,' said Miss Bulstrode. She was still surprised. One never really knew, she thought, about anybody.

II

'There goes Rich with her hair coming down again,' said Ann Shapland as she straightened herself up from a flower bed. 'If she can't control it I can't think why she doesn't get it cut off. She's got a good-shaped head and she would look better.'

'You ought to tell her so,' said Adam.

'We're not on those terms,' said Ann Shapland. She went on, 'D'you think this place will be able to carry on?'

Cat Among the Pigeons

'That's a very doubtful question,' said Adam, 'and who am I to judge?'

'You could tell as well as another I should think,' said Ann Shapland. 'It might, you know. The old Bull, as the girls call her, has got what it takes. A hypnotizing effect on parents to begin with. How long is it since the beginning of term—only a month? It seems like a year. I shall be glad when it comes to an end.'

'Will you come back if the school goes on?'

'No,' said Ann with emphasis, 'no indeed. I've had enough of schools to last me for a lifetime. I'm not cut out for being cooped up with a lot of women anyway. And, frankly, I don't like murder. It's the sort of thing that's fun to read about in the paper or to read yourself to sleep with in the way of a nice book. But the real thing isn't so good. I think,' added Ann thoughtfully, 'that when I leave here at the end of the term I shall marry Dennis and settle down.'

'Dennis?' said Adam. 'That's the one you mentioned to me, wasn't it? As far as I remember his work takes him to Burma and Malaya and Singapore and Japan and places like that. It won't be exactly settling down, will it, if you marry him?'

Ann laughed suddenly. 'No, no, I suppose it won't. Not in the physical, geographical sense.'

'I think you can do better than Dennis,' said Adam.

'Are you making me an offer?' said Ann.

'Certainly not,' said Adam. 'You're an ambitious girl, you wouldn't like to marry a humble jobbing gardener.'

Agatha Christie

'I was wondering about marrying into the C.I.D.,' said Ann.

'I'm not in the C.I.D.,' said Adam.

'No, no, of course not,' said Ann. 'Let's preserve the niceties of speech. You're not in the C.I.D. Shaista wasn't kidnapped, everything in the garden's lovely. It is rather,' she added, looking round. 'All the same,' she said after a moment or two, 'I don't understand in the least about Shaista turning up in Geneva or whatever the story is. How did she get there? All you people must be very slack to allow her to be taken out of this country.'

'My lips are sealed,' said Adam.

'I don't think you know the first thing about it,' said Ann.

'I will admit,' said Adam, 'that we have to thank Monsieur Hercule Poirot for having had a bright idea.'

'What, the funny little man who brought Julia back and came to see Miss Bulstrode?'

'Yes. He calls himself,' said Adam, 'a consultant detective.'

'I think he's pretty much of a has-been,' said Ann.

'I don't understand what he's up to at all,' said Adam. 'He even went to see my mother—or some friend of his did.'

'Your mother?' said Ann. 'Why?'

'I've no idea. He seems to have a kind of morbid interest in mothers. He went to see Jennifer's mother too.'

'Did he go and see Miss Rich's mother, and Chaddy's?'

'I gather Miss Rich hasn't got a mother,' said Adam. 'Otherwise, no doubt, he would have gone to see her.'

'Miss Chadwick's got a mother in Cheltenham, she told me,' said Ann, 'but she's about eighty-odd, I believe. Poor Miss Chadwick, she looks about eighty herself. She's coming to talk to us now.'

Adam looked up. 'Yes,' he said, 'she's aged a lot in the last week.'

'Because she really loves the school,' said Ann. 'It's her whole life. She can't bear to see it go downhill.'

Miss Chadwick indeed looked ten years older than she had done on the day of the opening term. Her step had lost its brisk efficiency. She no longer trotted about, happy and bustling. She came up to them now, her steps dragging a little.

'Will you please come to Miss Bulstrode,' she said to Adam. 'She has some instruction about the garden.'

'I'll have to clean up a bit first,' said Adam. He laid down his tools and moved off in the direction of the potting shed.

Ann and Miss Chadwick walked together towards the house.

'It does seem quiet, doesn't it,' said Ann, looking round. 'Like an empty house at the theatre,' she added thoughtfully, 'with people spaced out by the box office as tactfully as possible to make them look like an audience.'

'It's dreadful,' said Miss Chadwick, 'dreadful! Dreadful to think that Meadowbank has come to *this*. I can't get over it. I can't sleep at night. Everything in ruins. All the years of work, of building up something really fine.'

'It may get all right again,' said Ann cheerfully. 'People have got very short memories, you know.'

'Not as short as all that,' said Miss Chadwick grimly.

Ann did not answer. In her heart she rather agreed with Miss Chadwick.

III

Mademoiselle Blanche came out of the classroom where she had been teaching French literature.

She glanced at her watch. Yes, there would be plenty of time for what she intended to do. With so few pupils there was always plenty of time these days.

She went upstairs to her room and put on her hat. She was not one of those who went about hatless. She studied her appearance in the mirror with satisfaction. Not a personality to be noticed! Well, there could be advantages in that! She smiled to herself. It had made it easy for her to use her sister's testimonials. Even the passport photograph had gone unchallenged. It would have been a thousand pities to waste those excellent credentials when Angèle had died. Angèle had really enjoyed teaching. For herself, it was unutterable boredom. But the pay was excellent. Far above what she herself had ever been able to earn. And besides, things had turned out unbelievably well. The future was going to be very different. Oh yes, very different. The drab Mademoiselle Blanche would be transformed. She saw it all in her mind's eye. The Riviera. Herself smartly dressed, suitably made up. All one needed in this world was money. Oh yes, things were going to be very pleasant indeed. It was worth having come to this detestable English school.

She picked up her handbag, went out of her room and along the corridor. Her eyes dropped to the kneeling woman who was busy there. A new daily help. A police spy, of course. How simple they were—to think that one would not know!

A contemptuous smile on her lips, she went out of the house and down the drive to the front gate. The bus stop was almost opposite. She stood at it, waiting. The bus should be here in a moment or two.

There were very few people about in this quiet country road. A car, with a man bending over the open bonnet. A bicycle leaning against a hedge. A man also waiting for the bus.

One or other of the three would, no doubt, follow her. It would be skilfully done, not obviously. She was quite alive to the fact, and it did not worry her. Her 'shadow' was welcome to see where she went and what she did.

The bus came. She got in. A quarter of an hour later, she got out in the main square of the town. She did not trouble to look behind her. She crossed to where the shop windows of a fairly large departmental store showed their display of new model gowns. Poor stuff, for provincial tastes, she thought, with a curling lip. But she stood looking at them as though much attracted.

Presently she went inside, made one or two trivial purchases, then went up to the first floor and entered the Ladies Rest Room. There was a writing table there, some easy chairs, and a telephone box. She went into the box, put the necessary coins in, dialled the number she wanted, waiting to hear if the right voice answered.

She nodded in approval, pressed button A and spoke.

'This is the Maison Blanche. You understand me, the Maison *Blanche*? I have to speak of an account that is owed. You have until tomorrow evening. Tomorrow evening. To pay into the account of the Maison Blanche at the Credit Nationale in London, Ledbury St branch the sum that I tell you.'

She named the sum.

'If that money is not paid in, then it will be necessary for me to report in the proper quarters what I observed on the night of the 12th. The reference—pay—attention—is to Miss Springer. You have a little over twenty-four hours.'

She hung up and emerged into the rest room. A woman had just come in from outside. Another customer of the shop, perhaps, or again perhaps not. But if the latter, it was too late for anything to be overheard.

Mademoiselle Blanche freshened herself up in the adjoining cloak room, then she went and tried on a couple of blouses, but did not buy them; she went out into the street again, smiling to herself. She looked into a bookshop, and then caught a bus back to Meadowbank.

She was still smiling to herself as she walked up the drive. She had arranged matters very well. The sum she had demanded had not been too large—not impossible to raise at short notice. And it would do very well to go on with. Because, of course, in the future, there would be further demands...

Yes, a very pretty little source of income this was going to be. She had no qualms of conscience. She did not consider it in any way her duty to report what she knew and had seen to the police. That Springer had been a detestable woman, rude, *mal élevée*. Prying into what was no business of hers. Ah, well, she had got her deserts.

Mademoiselle Blanche stayed for a while by the swimming pool. She watched Eileen Rich diving. Then Ann Shapland, too, climbed up and dived—very well, too. There was laughing and squeals from the girls.

A bell rang, and Mademoiselle Blanche went in to take her junior class. They were inattentive and tiresome, but Mademoiselle Blanche hardly noticed. She would soon have done with teaching for ever.

She went up to her room to tidy herself for supper. Vaguely, without really noticing, she saw that, contrary to her usual practice, she had thrown her garden coat across a chair in the corner instead of hanging it up as usual.

She leaned forward, studying her face in the glass. She applied powder, lipstick—

The movement was so quick that it took her completely by surprise. Noiseless! Professional. The coat on the chair seemed to gather itself together, drop to the ground and in an instant behind Mademoiselle Blanche a hand with a sandbag rose and, as she opened her lips to scream, fell, dully, on the back of her neck.

CHAPTER 22

Incident in Anatolia

Mrs Upjohn was sitting by the side of the road overlooking a deep ravine. She was talking partly in French and partly with gestures to a large and solid-looking Turkish woman who was telling her with as much detail as possible under these difficulties of communications all about her last miscarriage. Nine children she had had, she explained. Eight of them boys, and five miscarriages. She seemed as pleased at the miscarriages as she did at the births.

'And you?' she poked Mrs Upjohn amiably in the ribs. '*Combien?—garçons?—filles?—combien?*' She held up her hands ready to indicate on the fingers.

'*Une fille,*' said Mrs Upjohn.

'*Et garçons?*'

Seeing that she was about to fall in the Turkish woman's estimation, Mrs Upjohn in a surge of nationalism proceeded to perjure herself. She held up five fingers of her right hand.

'*Cinq,*' she said.

'*Cinq garçons? Très bien!*'

Agatha Christie

The Turkish woman nodded with approbation and respect. She added that if only her cousin who spoke French really fluently was here they could understand each other a great deal better. She then resumed the story of her last miscarriage.

The other passengers were sprawled about near them, eating odd bits of food from the baskets they carried with them. The bus, looking slightly the worse for wear, was drawn up against an overhanging rock, and the driver and another man were busy inside the bonnet. Mrs Upjohn had lost complete count of time. Floods had blocked two of the roads, *detours* had been necessary and they had once been stuck for seven hours until the river they were fording subsided. Ankara lay in the not impossible future and that was all she knew. She listened to her friend's eager and incoherent conversation, trying to gauge when to nod admiringly, when to shake her head in sympathy.

A voice cut into her thoughts, a voice highly incongruous with her present surroundings.

'Mrs Upjohn, I believe,' said the voice.

Mrs Upjohn looked up. A little way away a car had driven up. The man standing opposite her had undoubtedly alighted from it. His face was unmistakably British, as was his voice. He was impeccably dressed in a grey flannel suit.

'Good heavens,' said Mrs Upjohn. 'Dr Livingstone?'

'It must seem rather like that,' said the stranger pleasantly. 'My name's Atkinson. I'm from the Consulate in Ankara. We've been trying to get in touch with you for two or three days, but the roads have been cut.'

'You wanted to get in touch with me? Why?' Suddenly Mrs Upjohn rose to her feet. All traces of the gay traveller had disappeared. She was all mother, every inch of her. 'Julia?' she said sharply. 'Has something happened to Julia?'

'No, no,' Mr Atkinson reassured her. 'Julia's quite all right. It's not that at all. There's been a spot of trouble at Meadowbank and we want to get you home there as soon as possible. I'll drive you back to Ankara, and you can get on a plane in about an hour's time.'

Mrs Upjohn opened her mouth and then shut it again. Then she rose and said, 'You'll have to get my bag off the top of that bus. It's the dark one.' She turned, shook hands with her Turkish companion, said: 'I'm sorry, I have to go home now,' waved to the rest of the bus load with the utmost friendliness, called out a Turkish farewell greeting which was part of her small stock of Turkish, and prepared to follow Mr Atkinson immediately without asking any further questions. It occurred to him as it had occurred to many other people that Mrs Upjohn was a very sensible woman.

CHAPTER 23

Showdown

In one of the smaller classrooms Miss Bulstrode looked at the assembled people. All the members of her staff were there: Miss Chadwick, Miss Johnson, Miss Rich and the two younger mistresses. Ann Shapland sat with her pad and pencil in case Miss Bulstrode wanted her to take notes. Beside Miss Bulstrode sat Inspector Kelsey and beyond him, Hercule Poirot. Adam Goodman sat in a no-man's-land of his own halfway between the staff and what he called to himself the executive body. Miss Bulstrode rose and spoke in her practised, decisive voice.

'I feel it is due to you all,' she said, 'as members of my staff, and interested in the fortunes of the school, to know exactly to what point this inquiry has progressed. I have been informed by Inspector Kelsey of several facts. M. Hercule Poirot who has international connections, has obtained valuable assistance from Switzerland and will report himself on that particular matter. We have not yet come to the end of the inquiry, I am sorry to say, but certain minor matters have been cleared up and I thought it would be a relief to you all to know how matters stand at the present moment.' Miss Bulstrode looked towards Inspector Kelsey, and he rose.

'Officially,' he said, 'I am not in a position to disclose all that I know. I can only reassure you to the extent of saying that we are making progress and we are beginning to have a good idea who is responsible for the three crimes that have been committed on the premises. Beyond that I will not go. My friend, M. Hercule Poirot, who is not bound by official secrecy and is at perfect liberty to give you his own ideas, will disclose to you certain information which he himself has been influential in procuring. I am sure you are all loyal to Meadowbank and to Miss Bulstrode and will keep to yourselves various matters upon which M. Poirot is going to touch and which are not of any public interest. The less gossip or speculation about them the better, so I will ask you to keep the facts that you will learn here today to yourselves. Is that understood?'

'Of course,' said Miss Chadwick, speaking first and with emphasis. 'Of course we're all loyal to Meadowbank, I should hope.'

'Naturally,' said Miss Johnson.

'Oh yes,' said the two younger mistresses.

'I agree,' said Eileen Rich.

'Then perhaps, M. Poirot?'

Hercule Poirot rose to his feet, beamed on his audience and carefully twisted his moustaches. The two younger mistresses had a sudden desire to giggle, and looked away from each other pursing their lips together.

'It has been a difficult and anxious time for you all,' he said. 'I want you to know first that I do appreciate that. It has naturally been worst of all for Miss Bulstrode herself, but you have all suffered. You have suffered first the loss of three of your colleagues, one of whom has been here for a considerable period of time. I refer to Miss Vansittart. Miss Springer and Mademoiselle Blanche were, of course, newcomers, but I do not doubt that their deaths were a great shock to you and a distressing happening. You must also have suffered a good deal of apprehension yourselves, for it must have seemed as though there were a kind of vendetta aimed against the mistresses of Meadowbank school. That I can assure you, and Inspector Kelsey will assure you also, is not so. Meadowbank by a fortuitous series of chances became the centre for the attentions of various undesirable interests. There has been, shall we say, a cat among the pigeons. There have been three murders here and also a kidnapping. I will deal first with the kidnapping, for all through this business the difficulty has been to clear out of the way extraneous matters which, though criminal in themselves, obscure the most important thread— the thread of a ruthless and determined killer in your midst.'

He took from his pocket a photograph.

'First, I will pass round this photograph.'

Kelsey took it, handed it to Miss Bulstrode and she in turn handed it to the staff. It was returned to Poirot. He looked at their faces, which were quite blank.

'I ask you, all of you, do you recognize the girl in that photograph?'

One and all they shook their heads.

'You should do so,' said Poirot. 'Since that is a photograph obtained by me from Geneva of Princess Shaista.'

'But it's not Shaista at all,' cried Miss Chadwick.

'Exactly,' said Poirot. 'The threads of all this business start in Ramat where, as you know, a revolutionary *coup d'état* took place about three months ago. The ruler, Prince Ali Yusuf, managed to escape, flown out by his own private pilot. Their plane, however, crashed in the mountains north of Ramat and was not discovered until later in the year. A certain article of great value, which was always carried on Prince Ali's person, was missing. It was not found in the wreck and there were rumours that it had been brought to this country. Several groups of people were anxious to get hold of this very valuable article. One of their leads to it was Prince Ali Yusuf's only remaining relation, his first cousin, a girl who was then at a school in Switzerland. It seemed likely that if the precious article had been safely got out of Ramat it would be brought to Princess Shaista or to her relatives and guardians. Certain agents were detailed to keep an eye on her uncle, the Emir Ibrahim, and others to keep an eye on the Princess herself. It was known that she was due to come to this school, Meadowbank, this term. Therefore it would have been only natural that someone should be detailed to obtain employment here and to keep a close watch on anyone who approached the

Agatha Christie

Princess, her letters, and any telephone messages. But an even simpler and more efficacious idea was evolved, that of kidnapping Shaista and sending one of their own number to the school as Princess Shaista herself. This could be done successfully since the Emir Ibrahim was in Egypt and did not propose to visit England until late summer. Miss Bulstrode herself had not seen the girl and all arrangements that she had made concerning her reception had been made with the Embassy in London.

'The plan was simple in the extreme. The real Shaista left Switzerland accompanied by a representative from the Embassy in London. Or so it was supposed. Actually, the Embassy in London was informed that a representative from the Swiss school would accompany the girl to London. The real Shaista was taken to a very pleasant chalet in Switzerland where she has been ever since, and an entirely different girl arrived in London, was met there by a representative of the Embassy and subsequently brought to this school. This substitute, of course, was necessarily much older than the real Shaista. But that would hardly attract attention since Eastern girls noticeably look much more mature than their age. A young French actress who specializes in playing schoolgirl parts was the agent chosen.

'I did ask,' said Hercule Poirot, in a thoughtful voice, 'as to whether anyone had noticed Shaista's knees. Knees are a very good indication of age. The knees of a woman of twenty-three or twenty-four can never really be mistaken for the knees of a girl of fourteen or fifteen. Nobody, alas, had noticed her knees.

'The plan was hardly as successful as had been hoped. Nobody attempted to get in touch with Shaista, no letters or telephone calls of significance arrived for her and as time went on an added anxiety arose. The Emir Ibrahim might arrive in England ahead of schedule. He was not a man who announced his plans ahead. He was in the habit, I understand, of saying one evening, "Tomorrow I go to London" and thereupon to go.

'The false Shaista, then, was aware that at any moment someone who knew the real Shaista might arrive. Especially was this so after the murder and therefore she began to prepare the way for a kidnapping by talking about it to Inspector Kelsey. Of course, the actual kidnapping was nothing of the kind. As soon as she learned that her uncle was coming to take her out the following morning, she sent a brief message by telephone, and half an hour earlier than the genuine car, a showy car with false C.D. plates on it arrived and Shaista was officially "kidnapped". Actually, of course, she was set down by the car in the first large town where she at once resumed her own personality. An amateurish ransom note was sent just to keep up the fiction.'

Hercule Poirot paused, then said, 'It was, as you can see, merely the trick of the conjurer. Misdirection. You focus the eyes on the kidnapping *here* and it does not occur to anyone that the kidnapping *really* occurred three weeks earlier in Switzerland.'

What Poirot really meant, but was too polite to say, was that it had not occurred to anyone but himself!

Agatha Christie

'We pass now,' he said, 'to something far more serious than kidnapping—murder.

'The false Shaista could, of course, have killed Miss Springer but she could not have killed Miss Vansittart or Mademoiselle Blanche, and would have had no motive to kill anybody, nor was such a thing required of her. Her role was simply to receive a valuable packet if, as seemed likely, it should be brought to her: or, alternatively, to receive news of it.

'Let us go back now to Ramat where all this started. It was widely rumoured in Ramat that Prince Ali Yusuf had given this valuable packet to Bob Rawlinson, his private pilot, and that Bob Rawlinson had arranged for its despatch to England. On the day in question Rawlinson went to Ramat's principal hotel where his sister, Mrs Sutcliffe, and her daughter Jennifer were staying. Mrs Sutcliffe and Jennifer were out, but Bob Rawlinson went up to their room where he remained for at least twenty minutes. That is rather a long time under the circumstances. He might of course have been writing a long letter to his sister. But that was not so. He merely left a short note which he could have scribbled in a couple of minutes.

'It was a very fair inference then, inferred by several separate parties, that during his time in her room he had placed this object amongst his sister's effects and that she had brought it back to England. Now we come to what I may call the dividing of two separate threads. One set of interests—(or possibly more than one set)—assumed that Mrs Sutcliffe had brought this article back to England and in consequence her house in the country was ransacked and a thorough search made. This showed that whoever was searching *did not know where exactly the article was hidden.* Only that it was probably *somewhere* in Mrs Sutcliffe's possession.

'But somebody else knew very definitely exactly where that article was, and I think that by now it will do no harm for me to tell you where, in fact, Bob Rawlinson did conceal it. He concealed it in the handle of a tennis racquet, hollowing out the handle and afterwards piecing it together again so skilfully that it was difficult to see what had been done.

'The tennis racquet belonged, not to his sister, but to her daughter Jennifer. Someone who knew exactly where the cache was, went out to the Sports Pavilion one night, having previously taken an impression of the key and got a key cut. At that time of night everyone should have been in bed and asleep. But that was not so. Miss Springer saw the light of a torch in the Sports Pavilion from the house, and went out to investigate. She was a tough hefty young woman and had no doubts of her own ability to cope with anything she might find. The person in question was probably sorting through the tennis racquets to find the right one. Discovered and recognized by Miss Springer, there was no hesitation... The searcher was a killer, and shot Miss Springer dead. Afterwards, however, the killer had to act fast. The shot had been heard, people were approaching. At all costs the killer must get out of the Sports Pavilion unseen. The racquet must be left where it was for the moment...

Agatha Christie

'Within a few days another method was tried. A strange woman with a faked American accent waylaid Jennifer Sutcliffe as she was coming from the tennis courts, and told her a plausible story about a relative of hers having sent her down a new tennis racquet. Jennifer unsuspiciously accepted this story and gladly exchanged the racquet she was carrying for the new, expensive one the stranger had brought. But a circumstance had arisen which the woman with the American accent knew nothing about. That was that a few days previously Jennifer Sutcliffe and Julia Upjohn had exchanged racquets so that what the strange woman took away with her was in actual fact Julia Upjohn's old racquet, though the identifying tape on it bore Jennifer's name.

'We come now to the second tragedy. Miss Vansittart for some unknown reason, but possibly connected with the kidnapping of Shaista which had taken place that afternoon, took a torch and went out to the Sports Pavilion after everybody had gone to bed. Somebody who had followed her there struck her down with a cosh or a sandbag, as she was stooping down by Shaista's locker. Again the crime was discovered almost immediately. Miss Chadwick saw a light in the Sports Pavilion and hurried out there.

'The police once more took charge at the Sports Pavilion, and again the killer was debarred from searching and examining the tennis racquets there. But by now, Julia Upjohn, an intelligent child, had thought things over and had come to the logical conclusion that the racquet she possessed and which had originally belonged to Jennifer, was in some way important. She investigated on her own behalf, found that she was correct in her surmise, and brought the contents of the racquet to me.

'These are now,' said Hercule Poirot, 'in safe custody and need concern us here no longer.' He paused and then went on, 'It remains to consider the third tragedy.

'What Mademoiselle Blanche knew or suspected we shall never know. She may have seen someone leaving the house on the night of Miss Springer's murder. Whatever it was that she knew or suspected, she knew the identity of the murderer. And she kept that knowledge to herself. She planned to obtain money in return for her silence.

'There is nothing,' said Hercule Poirot, with feeling, 'more dangerous than levying blackmail on a person who has killed perhaps twice already. Mademoiselle Blanche may have taken her own precautions but whatever they were, they were inadequate. She made an appointment with the murderer and she was killed.'

He paused again.

'So there,' he said, looking round at them, 'you have the account of this whole affair.'

They were all staring at him. Their faces, which at first had reflected interest, surprise, excitement, seemed now frozen into a uniform calm. It was as though they were terrified to display any emotion. Hercule Poirot nodded at them.

'Yes,' he said, 'I know how you feel. It has come, has it not, very near home? That is why, you see, I and Inspector

Kelsey and Mr Adam Goodman have been making the inquiries. We have to know, you see, if there is still a cat among the pigeons! You understand what I mean? Is there still someone here who is masquerading under false colours?'

There was a slight ripple passing through those who listened to him, a brief almost furtive sidelong glance as though they wished to look at each other, but did not dare do so.

'I am happy to reassure you,' said Poirot. 'All of you here at this moment *are exactly who you say you are*. Miss Chadwick, for instance, is Miss Chadwick—that is certainly not open to doubt, she has been here as long as Meadowbank itself! Miss Johnson, too, is unmistakably Miss Johnson. Miss Rich is Miss Rich. Miss Shapland is Miss Shapland. Miss Rowan and Miss Blake are Miss Rowan and Miss Blake. To go further,' said Poirot, turning his head, 'Adam Goodman who works here in the garden, is, if not precisely Adam Goodman, at any rate the person whose name is on his credentials. So then, where are we? We must seek not for someone masquerading as someone else, but for someone who is, in his or her proper identity, a murderer.'

The room was very still now. There was menace in the air.

Poirot went on.

'We want, primarily, *someone who was in Ramat three months ago*. Knowledge that the prize was concealed in the tennis racquet could only have been acquired in one way. Someone must have *seen* it put there by Bob Rawlinson. It is as simple as that. Who then, of all of you present here, was in Ramat three months ago? Miss Chadwick was here, Miss Johnson was here.' His eyes went on to the two junior Mistresses. 'Miss Rowan and Miss Blake were here.'

His finger went out pointing.

'But Miss Rich—Miss Rich was not here last term, was she?'

'I—no. I was ill.' She spoke hurriedly. 'I was away for a term.'

'That is the thing we did not know,' said Hercule Poirot, 'until a few days ago somebody mentioned it casually. When questioned by the police originally, you merely said that you had been at Meadowbank for a year and a half. That in itself is true enough. But you were absent last term. You could have been in Ramat—I think you were in Ramat. Be careful. It can be verified, you know, from your passport.'

There was a moment's silence, then Eileen Rich looked up.

'Yes,' she said quietly. 'I was in Ramat. Why not?'

'Why did you go to Ramat, Miss Rich?'

'You already know. I had been ill. I was advised to take a rest—to go abroad. I wrote to Miss Bulstrode and explained that I must take a term off. She quite understood.'

'That is so,' said Miss Bulstrode. 'A doctor's certificate was enclosed which said that it would be unwise for Miss Rich to resume her duties until the following term.'

'So—you went to Ramat?' said Hercule Poirot.

'Why shouldn't I go to Ramat?' said Eileen Rich. Her voice trembled slightly. 'There are cheap fares offered to schoolteachers. I wanted a rest. I wanted sunshine. I went out to Ramat. I spent two months there. *Why not? Why not, I say?*'

'You have never mentioned that you were at Ramat at the time of the Revolution.'

'Why should I? What has it got to do with anyone here? I haven't killed anyone, I tell you. I haven't killed anyone.'

'You were recognized, you know,' said Hercule Poirot. 'Not recognized definitely, but indefinitely. The child Jennifer was very vague. She said she thought she'd seen you in Ramat but concluded it couldn't be you because, she said, the person she had seen was *fat*, not thin.' He leaned forward, his eyes boring into Eileen Rich's face.

'What have you to say, Miss Rich?'

She wheeled round. 'I know what you're trying to make out!' she cried. 'You're trying to make out that it wasn't a secret agent or anything of that kind who did these murders. That it was someone who just *happened* to be there, someone who *happened* to see this treasure hidden in a tennis racquet. Someone who realized that the child was coming to Meadowbank and that she'd have an opportunity to take for herself this hidden thing. But I tell you it isn't *true*!'

'I think that is what happened. Yes,' said Poirot. 'Someone saw the jewels being hidden and forgot all other duties or interests in the determination to possess them!'

'It isn't true, I tell you. I saw nothing—'

'Inspector Kelsey.' Poirot turned his head.

Inspector Kelsey nodded—went to the door, opened it, and Mrs Upjohn walked into the room.

II

'How do you do, Miss Bulstrode,' said Mrs Upjohn, looking rather embarrassed. 'I'm sorry I'm looking rather untidy, but I was somewhere near Ankara yesterday and I've just flown home. I'm in a terrible mess and I really haven't had time to clean myself up or do *anything*.'

'That does not matter,' said Hercule Poirot. 'We want to ask you something.'

'Mrs Upjohn,' said Kelsey, 'when you came here to bring your daughter to the school and you were in Miss Bulstrode's sitting-room, you looked out of the window—the window which gives on the front drive—and you uttered an exclamation as though you recognized someone you saw there. That is so, is it not?'

Mrs Upjohn stared at him. 'When I was in Miss Bulstrode's sitting-room? I looked—oh, yes, of *course*! Yes, I did see someone.'

'Someone you were surprised to see?'

'Well, I was rather... You see, it had all been such years ago.'

Agatha Christie

'You mean the days when you were working in Intelligence towards the end of the war?'

'Yes. It was about fifteen years ago. Of course, she looked much older, but I recognized her at once. And I wondered what on earth she could be doing *here*.'

'Mrs Upjohn, will you look round this room and tell me if you see that person here now?'

'Yes, of course,' said Mrs Upjohn. 'I saw her as soon as I came in. That's her.'

She stretched out a pointing finger. Inspector Kelsey was quick and so was Adam, but they were not quick enough. Ann Shapland had sprung to her feet. In her hand was a small wicked-looking automatic and it pointed straight at Mrs Upjohn. Miss Bulstrode, quicker than the two men, moved sharply forward, but swifter still was Miss Chadwick. It was not Mrs Upjohn that she was trying to shield, it was the woman who was standing between Ann Shapland and Mrs Upjohn.

'No, you shan't,' cried Chaddy, and flung herself on Miss Bulstrode just as the small automatic went off.

Miss Chadwick staggered, then slowly crumpled down. Miss Johnson ran to her. Adam and Kelsey had got hold of Ann Shapland now. She was struggling like a wild cat, but they wrested the small automatic from her.

Mrs Upjohn said breathlessly:

'They said then that she was a killer. Although she was so young. One of the most dangerous agents they had. Angelica was her code name.'

'You lying bitch!' Ann Shapland fairly spat out the words.

Hercule Poirot said:

'She does not lie. You are dangerous. You have always led a dangerous life. Up to now, you have never been suspected in your own identity. All the jobs you have taken in your own name have been perfectly genuine jobs, efficiently performed—but they have all been jobs with a purpose, and that purpose has been the gaining of information. You have worked with an Oil Company, with an archaeologist whose work took him to a certain part of the globe, with an actress whose protector was an eminent politician. Ever since you were seventeen you have worked as an agent—though for many different masters. Your services have been for hire and have been highly paid. You have played a dual role. Most of your assignments have been carried out in your own name, but there were certain jobs for which you assumed different identities. Those were the times when ostensibly you had to go home and be with your mother.

'But I strongly suspect, Miss Shapland, that the elderly woman I visited who lives in a small village with a nurse-companion to look after her, an elderly woman who is genuinely a mental patient with a confused mind, is not your mother at all. She has been your excuse for retiring from employment and from the circle of your friends. The three months this winter that you spent with your "mother" who had one of her "bad turns" covers the time when you went out to Ramat. Not as Ann Shapland but as Angelica de Toredo, a Spanish, or near-Spanish cabaret dancer. You occupied the room in the hotel next to that of Mrs Sutcliffe and somehow you managed to see Bob Rawlinson conceal the jewels in the racquet. You had no opportunity of taking the racquet then for there was the sudden evacuation of all British people, but you had read the labels on their luggage and it was easy to find out something about them. To obtain a secretarial post here was not difficult. I have made some inquiries. You paid a substantial sum to Miss Bulstrode's former secretary to vacate her post on the plea of a "breakdown". And you had quite a plausible story. You had been commissioned to write a series of articles on a famous girls' school "from within".

'It all seemed quite easy, did it not? If a child's racquet was missing, what of it? Simpler still, you would go out at night to the Sports Pavilion, and abstract the jewels. But you had not reckoned with Miss Springer. Perhaps she had already seen you examining the racquets. Perhaps she just happened to wake that night. She followed you out there and you shot her. Later, Mademoiselle Blanche tried to blackmail you, and you killed her. It comes natural to you, does it not, to kill?'

He stopped. In a monotonous official voice, Inspector Kelsey cautioned his prisoner.

She did not listen. Turning towards Hercule Poirot, she burst out in a low-pitched flood of invective that startled everyone in the room.

'Whew!' said Adam, as Kelsey took her away. 'And I thought she was a nice girl!'

Miss Johnson had been kneeling by Miss Chadwick.

'I'm afraid she's badly hurt,' she said. 'She'd better not be moved until the doctor comes.'

CHAPTER 24

Poirot Explains

Mrs Upjohn, wandering through the corridors of Meadowbank School, forgot the exciting scene she had just been through. She was for the moment merely a mother seeking her young. She found her in a deserted classroom. Julia was bending over a desk, her tongue protruding slightly, absorbed in the agonies of composition.

She looked up and stared. Then flung herself across the room and hugged her mother.

'Mummy!'

Then, with the self-consciousness of her age, ashamed of her unrestrained emotion, she detached herself and spoke in a carefully casual tone—indeed almost accusingly.

'Aren't you back rather *soon*, Mummy?'

'I flew back,' said Mrs Upjohn, almost apologetically, 'from Ankara.'

'Oh,' said Julia. 'Well—I'm glad you're back.'

'Yes,' said Mrs Upjohn, 'I am very glad too.'

They looked at each other, embarrassed. 'What are you doing?' said Mrs Upjohn, advancing a little closer.

'I'm writing a composition for Miss Rich,' said Julia. 'She really does set the most exciting subjects.'

'What's this one?' said Mrs Upjohn. She bent over.

The subject was written at the top of the page. Some nine or ten lines of writing in Julia's uneven and sprawling hand-writing came below. 'Contrast the Attitudes of Macbeth and Lady Macbeth to Murder' read Mrs Upjohn.

'Well,' she said doubtfully, 'you can't say that the subject isn't topical!'

She read the start of her daughter's essay. 'Macbeth,' Julia had written, 'liked the idea of murder and had been thinking of it a lot, but he needed a push to get him started. Once he'd got started he enjoyed murdering people and had no more qualms or fears. Lady Macbeth was just greedy and ambitious. She thought she didn't mind what she did to get what she wanted. But once she'd done it she found she didn't like it after all.'

'Your language isn't very elegant,' said Mrs Upjohn. 'I think you'll have to polish it up a bit, but you've certainly got something there.'

II

Inspector Kelsey was speaking in a slightly complaining tone.

'It's all very well for you, Poirot,' he said. 'You can say and do a lot of things we can't: and I'll admit the whole thing was well stage managed. Got her off her guard, made her think we were after Rich, and then, Mrs Upjohn's sudden appearance made her lose her head. Thank the lord she kept that automatic after shooting Springer. If the bullet corresponds—'

'It will, *mon ami*, it will,' said Poirot.

'Then we've got her cold for the murder of Springer. And I gather Miss Chadwick's in a bad way. But look here, Poirot, I still can't see how she can possibly have killed Miss Vansittart. It's physically impossible. She's got a cast iron alibi—unless young Rathbone and the whole staff of the Nid Sauvage are in it with her.'

Poirot shook his head. 'Oh, no,' he said. 'Her alibi is perfectly good. She killed Miss Springer and Mademoiselle Blanche. But Miss Vansittart—' he hesitated for a moment, his eyes going to where Miss Bulstrode sat listening to them. 'Miss Vansittart was killed by Miss Chadwick.'

'Miss Chadwick?' exclaimed Miss Bulstrode and Kelsey together.

Poirot nodded. 'I am sure of it.'

'But—why?'

'I think,' said Poirot, 'Miss Chadwick loved Meadowbank too much…' His eyes went across to Miss Bulstrode.

'I see…' said Miss Bulstrode. 'Yes, yes, I see… I ought to have known.' She paused. 'You mean that she—?'

'I mean,' said Poirot, 'that she started here with you, that all along she has regarded Meadowbank as a joint venture between you both.'

'Which in one sense it was,' said Miss Bulstrode.

'Quite so,' said Poirot. 'But that was merely the financial aspect. When you began to talk of retiring she regarded herself as the person who would take over.'

'But she's far too old,' objected Miss Bulstrode.

'Yes,' said Poirot, 'she is too old and she is not suited to be a headmistress. But she herself did not think so. She thought that when you went she would be headmistress of Meadowbank as a matter of course. And then she found that was not so. That you were considering someone else, that you had fastened upon Eleanor Vansittart. And she loved Meadowbank. She loved the school and she did not like Eleanor Vansittart. I think in the end she hated her.'

'She might have done,' said Miss Bulstrode. 'Yes, Eleanor Vansittart was—how shall I put it?—she was always very complacent, very superior about everything. That would be hard to bear if you were jealous. That's what you mean, isn't it? Chaddy was jealous.'

'Yes,' said Poirot. 'She was jealous of Meadowbank and jealous of Eleanor Vansittart. She couldn't bear the thought of the school and Miss Vansittart together. And then perhaps something in your manner led her to think that you were weakening?'

'I did weaken,' said Miss Bulstrode. 'But I didn't weaken in the way that perhaps Chaddy thought I would weaken. Actually I thought of someone younger still than Miss Vansittart—I thought it over and then I said No, she's too young… Chaddy was with me then, I remember.'

'And she thought,' said Poirot, 'that you were referring to Miss Vansittart. That you were saying Miss Vansittart was

Agatha Christie

too young. She thoroughly agreed. She thought that experience and wisdom such as she had got were far more important things. But then, after all, you returned to your original decision. You chose Eleanor Vansittart as the right person and left her in charge of the school that weekend. This is what I think happened. On that Sunday night Miss Chadwick was restless, she got up and she saw the light in the squash court. She went out there exactly as she says she went. There is only one thing different in her story from what she said. It wasn't a golf club she took with her. She picked up one of the sandbags from the pile in the hall. She went out there all ready to deal with a burglar, with someone who for a second time had broken into the Sports Pavilion. She had the sandbag ready in her hand to defend herself if attacked. And what did she find? She found Eleanor Vansittart kneeling down looking in a locker, and she thought, it may be—(for I am good,' said Hercule Poirot in a parenthesis, '—at putting myself into other people's minds—) she thought *if* I were a marauder, a burglar, I would come up behind her and strike her down. And as the thought came into her mind, only half conscious of what she was doing, she raised the sandbag and struck. And there was Eleanor Vansittart dead, out of her way. She was appalled then, I think, at what she had done. It has preyed on her ever since—for she is not a natural killer, Miss Chadwick. She was driven, as some are driven, by jealousy and by obsession. The obsession of love for Meadowbank. Now that Eleanor Vansittart was dead she was quite sure that she would succeed you at Meadowbank. So she didn't confess. She told her story to the police exactly as it had occurred but for the one vital fact, that it was *she* who had struck the blow. But when she was asked about the golf club which presumably Miss Vansittart took with her being nervous after all that had occurred, Miss Chadwick said quickly that she had taken it out there. She didn't want you to think even for a moment that she had handled the sandbag.'

'Why did Ann Shapland also choose a sandbag to kill Mademoiselle Blanche?' asked Miss Bulstrode.

'For one thing, she could not risk a pistol shot in the school building, and for another she is a very clever young woman. She wanted to tie up this third murder with the second one, for which she had an alibi.'

'I don't really understand what Eleanor Vansittart was doing herself in the Sports Pavilion,' said Miss Bulstrode.

'I think one could make a guess. She was probably far more concerned over the disappearance of Shaista than she allowed to appear on the surface. She was as upset as Miss Chadwick was. In a way it was worse for her, because she had been left by you in charge—and the kidnapping had happened whilst she was responsible. Moreover she had pooh-poohed it as long as possible through an unwillingness to face unpleasant facts squarely.'

'So there was weakness behind the *façade*,' mused Miss Bulstrode. 'I sometimes suspected it.'

'She, too, I think, was unable to sleep. And I think she went out quietly to the Sports Pavilion to make an examination of Shaista's locker in case there might be some clue there to the girl's disappearance.'

Agatha Christie

'You seem to have explanations for everything, Mr Poirot.'

'That's his speciality,' said Inspector Kelsey with slight malice.

'And what was the point of getting Eileen Rich to sketch various members of my staff?'

'I wanted to test the child Jennifer's ability to recognize a face. I soon satisfied myself that Jennifer was so entirely preoccupied by her own affairs, that she gave outsiders at most a cursory glance, taking in only the external details of their appearance. She did not recognize a sketch of Mademoiselle Blanche with a different hairdo. Still less, then, would she have recognized Ann Shapland who, as your secretary, she seldom saw at close quarters.'

'You think that the woman with the racquet was Ann Shapland herself.'

'Yes. It has been a one woman job all through. You remember that day, you rang for her to take a message to Julia but in the end, as the buzzer went unanswered, sent a girl to find Julia. Ann was accustomed to quick disguise. A fair wig, differently pencilled eyebrows, a "fussy" dress and hat. She need only be absent from her typewriter for about twenty minutes. I saw from Miss Rich's clever sketches how easy it is for a woman to alter her appearance by purely external matters.'

'Miss Rich—I wonder—' Miss Bulstrode looked thoughtful.

Poirot gave Inspector Kelsey a look and the Inspector said he must be getting along.

'Miss Rich?' said Miss Bulstrode again.

'Send for her,' said Poirot. 'It is the best way.'

Eileen Rich appeared. She was white faced and slightly defiant.

'You want to know,' she said to Miss Bulstrode, 'what I was doing in Ramat?'

'I think I have an idea,' said Miss Bulstrode.

'Just so,' said Poirot. 'Children nowadays know all the facts of life—but their eyes often retain innocence.'

He added that he, too, must be getting along, and slipped out.

'That was it, wasn't it?' said Miss Bulstrode. Her voice was brisk and businesslike. 'Jennifer merely described it as fat. She didn't realize it was a pregnant woman she had seen.'

'Yes,' said Eileen Rich. 'That was it. I was going to have a child. I didn't want to give up my job here. I carried on all right through the autumn, but after that, it was beginning to show. I got a doctor's certificate that I wasn't fit to carry on, and I pleaded illness. I went abroad to a remote spot where I thought I wasn't likely to meet anyone who knew me. I came back to this country and the child was born—dead. I came back this term and I hoped that no one would ever know... But you understand now, don't you, why I said I should have had to refuse your offer of a partnership if you'd made it? Only now, with the school in such a disaster, I thought that, after all, I might be able to accept.'

She paused and said in a matter of fact voice,

Agatha Christie

'Would you like me to leave now? Or wait until the end of term?'

'You'll stay till the end of the term,' said Miss Bulstrode, 'and if there is a new term here, which I still hope, you'll come back.'

'Come back?' said Eileen Rich. 'Do you mean you still want me?'

'Of course I want you,' said Miss Bulstrode. 'You haven't murdered anyone, have you?—not gone mad over jewels and planned to kill to get them? I'll tell you what you've done. You've probably denied your instincts too long. There was a man, you fell in love with him, you had a child. I suppose you couldn't marry.'

'There was never any question of marriage,' said Eileen Rich. 'I knew that. He isn't to blame.'

'Very well, then,' said Miss Bulstrode. 'You had a love affair and a child. You wanted to have that child?'

'Yes,' said Eileen Rich. 'Yes, I wanted to have it.'

'So that's that,' said Miss Bulstrode. 'Now I'm going to tell you something. I believe that in spite of this love affair, your real vocation in life is teaching. I think your profession means more to you than any normal woman's life with a husband and children would mean.'

'Oh yes,' said Eileen Rich. 'I'm sure of that. I've known that all along. That's what I really want to do—that's the real passion of my life.'

'Then don't be a fool,' said Miss Bulstrode. 'I'm making you a very good offer. If, that is, things come right. We'll spend two or three years together putting Meadowbank back on the map. You'll have different ideas as to how that should be done from the ideas that I have. I'll listen to your ideas. Maybe I'll even give in to some of them. You want things to be different, I suppose, at Meadowbank?'

'I do in some ways, yes,' said Eileen Rich. 'I won't pretend. I want more emphasis on getting girls that really matter.'

'Ah,' said Miss Bulstrode, 'I see. It's the snob element that you don't like, is that it?'

'Yes,' said Eileen, 'it seems to me to spoil things.'

'What you don't realize,' said Miss Bulstrode, 'is that to get the kind of girl you want you've *got* to have that snob element. It's quite a small element really, you know. A few foreign royalties, a few great names and everybody, all the silly parents all over this country and other countries want their girls to come to Meadowbank. Fall over themselves to get their girl admitted to Meadowbank. What's the result? An enormous waiting list, and I look at the girls and I see the girls and I choose! You get your pick, do you see? I choose my girls. I choose them very carefully, some for character, some for brains, some for pure academic intellect. Some because I think they haven't had a chance but are capable of being made something of that's worth while. You're young, Eileen. You're full of ideals—it's the teaching that matters to you and the ethical side of it. Your vision's quite right. It's the girls that matter, but if you want to make a success of anything, you know, you've got to be a good tradesman as well. Ideas are like everything else. They've got to be marketed. We'll have to do some pretty slick work in future to get Meadowbank going again. I'll have to get

Agatha Christie

my hooks into a few people, former pupils, bully them, plead with them, get them to send their daughters here. And then the others will come. You let me be up to my tricks, and then you shall have your way. Meadowbank will go on and it'll be a fine school.'

'It'll be the finest school in England,' said Eileen Rich enthusiastically.

'Good,' said Miss Bulstrode, '—and Eileen, I should go and get your hair properly cut and shaped. You don't seem able to manage that bun. And now,' she said, her voice changing, 'I must go to Chaddy.'

She went in and came up to the bed. Miss Chadwick was lying very still and white. The blood had all gone from her face and she looked drained of life. A policeman with a notebook sat nearby and Miss Johnson sat on the other side of the bed. She looked at Miss Bulstrode and shook her head gently.

'Hallo, Chaddy,' said Miss Bulstrode. She took up the limp hand in hers. Miss Chadwick's eyes opened.

'I want to tell you,' she said, 'Eleanor—it was—it was me.'

'Yes, dear, I know,' said Miss Bulstrode.

'Jealous,' said Chaddy. 'I wanted—'

'I know,' said Miss Bulstrode.

Tears rolled very slowly down Miss Chadwick's cheeks. 'It's so awful... I didn't mean—I don't know how I came to do such a thing!'

'Don't think about it any more,' said Miss Bulstrode.

'But I can't—you'll never—I'll never forgive myself—'

'Listen, dear,' she said. 'You saved my life, you know.

My life and the life of that nice woman, Mrs Upjohn. That counts for something, doesn't it?'

'I only wish,' said Miss Chadwick, 'I could have given *my* life for you both. That would have made it all right...'

Miss Bulstrode looked at her with great pity. Miss Chadwick took a great breath, smiled, then, moving her head very slightly to one side, she died...

'You *did* give your life, my dear,' said Miss Bulstrode softly. 'I hope you realize that—now.'

CHAPTER 25

Legacy

'A Mr Robinson has called to see you, sir.'

'Ah!' said Hercule Poirot. He stretched out his hand and picked up a letter from the desk in front of him. He looked down on it thoughtfully.

He said: 'Show him in, Georges.'

The letter was only a few lines,

Dear Poirot,

A Mr Robinson may call upon you in the near future. You may already know something about him. Quite a prominent figure in certain circles. There is a demand for such men in our modern world... I believe, if I may so put it, that he is, in this particular matter, on the side of the angels. This is just a recommendation, if you should be in doubt. Of course, and I underline this, we have no *idea as to the matter on which he wishes to consult you...*

Ha ha! and likewise ho ho!

Yours ever,
Ephraim Pikeaway

Poirot laid down the letter and rose as Mr Robinson came into the room. He bowed, shook hands, indicated a chair.

Mr Robinson sat, pulled out a handkerchief and wiped his large yellow face. He observed that it was a warm day.

'You have not, I hope, walked here in this heat?'

Poirot looked horrified at the idea. By a natural association of ideas, his fingers went to his moustache. He was reassured. There was no limpness.

Mr Robinson looked equally horrified.

'No, no, indeed. I came in my Rolls. But these traffic blocks... One sits for half an hour sometimes.'

Poirot nodded sympathetically.

There was a pause—the pause that ensues on part one of conversation before entering upon part two.

'I was interested to hear—of course one hears so many things—most of them quite untrue—that you had been concerning yourself with the affairs of a girls' school.'

'Ah,' said Poirot. 'That!'

He leaned back in his chair.

'Meadowbank,' said Mr Robinson thoughtfully. 'Quite one of the premier schools of England.'

'It is a fine school.'

'Is? Or was?'

'I hope the former.'

'I hope so, too,' said Mr Robinson. 'I fear it may be touch and go. Ah well, one must do what one can. A little financial backing to tide over a certain inevitable period of depression. A few carefully chosen new pupils. I am not without influence in European circles.'

'I, too, have applied persuasion in certain quarters. If, as you say, we can tide things over. Mercifully, memories are short.'

'That is what one hopes. But one must admit that events have taken place there that might well shake the nerves of fond mammas—and papas also. The Games Mistress, the French Mistress, and yet another mistress—all murdered.'

'As you say.'

'I hear,' said Mr Robinson, '(one hears so many things), that the unfortunate young woman responsible has suffered from a phobia about schoolmistresses since her youth. An unhappy childhood at school. Psychiatrists will make a good deal of this. They will try at least for a verdict of diminished responsibility, as they call it nowadays.'

'That line would seem to be the best choice,' said Poirot. 'You will pardon me for saying that I hope it will not succeed.'

'I agree with you entirely. A most cold-blooded killer. But they will make much of her excellent character, her work as secretary to various well-known people, her war record—quite distinguished, I believe—counter espionage—'

He let the last words out with a certain significance—a hint of a question in his voice.

'She was very good, I believe,' he said more briskly. 'So young—but quite brilliant, of great use—to both sides. That was her métier—she should have stuck to it. But I can understand the temptation—to play a lone hand, and gain a big prize.' He added softly, 'A very big prize.'

Poirot nodded.

Mr Robinson leaned forward.

'Where are they, M. Poirot?'

'I think you know where they are.'

'Well, frankly, yes. Banks are such useful institutions are they not?'

Poirot smiled.

'We needn't beat about the bush really, need we, my dear fellow? What are you going to do about them?'

'I have been waiting.'

'Waiting for what?'

'Shall we say—for suggestions?'

'Yes—I see.'

'You understand they do not belong to me. I would like to hand them over to the person they do belong to. But that, if I appraise the position correctly, is not so simple.'

'Governments are in such a difficult position,' said Mr Robinson. 'Vulnerable, so to speak. What with oil, and steel, and uranium, and cobalt and all the rest of it, foreign relations are a matter of the utmost delicacy. The great thing is to be able to say that Her Majesty's Government, etc., etc., has absolutely *no* information on the subject.'

'But I cannot keep this important deposit at my bank indefinitely.'

'Exactly. That is why I have come to propose that you should hand it over to me.'

'Ah,' said Poirot. 'Why?'

Agatha Christie

'I can give you some excellent reasons. These jewels—mercifully we are not official, we can call things by their right names—were unquestionably the personal property of the late Prince Ali Yusuf.'

'I understand that is so.'

'His Highness handed them over to Squadron Leader Robert Rawlinson with certain instructions. They were to be got out of Ramat, and they were to be delivered to *me*.'

'Have you proof of that?'

'Certainly.'

Mr Robinson drew a long envelope from his pocket. Out of it he took several papers. He laid them before Poirot on the desk.

Poirot bent over them and studied them carefully.

'It seems to be as you say.'

'Well, then?'

'Do you mind if I ask a question?'

'Not at all.'

'What do you, personally, get out of this?'

Mr Robinson looked surprised.

'My dear fellow. Money, of course. Quite a lot of money.'

Poirot looked at him thoughtfully.

'It is a very old trade,' said Mr Robinson. 'And a lucrative one. There are quite a lot of us, a network all over the globe. We are, how shall I put it, the Arrangers behind the scenes. For kings, for presidents, for politicians, for all those, in fact, upon whom the fierce light beats, as a poet has put it. We work in with one another and remember this: we keep faith. Our profits are large but we are honest. Our services are costly—but we do render service.'

'I see,' said Poirot. '*Eh bien!* I agree to what you ask.'

'I can assure you that that decision will please everyone.' Mr Robinson's eyes just rested for a moment on Colonel Pikeaway's letter where it lay at Poirot's right hand.

'But just one little moment. I am human. I have curiosity. What are you going to do with these jewels?'

Mr Robinson looked at him. Then his large yellow face creased into a smile. He leaned forward.

'I shall tell you.'

He told him.

II

Children were playing up and down the street. Their raucous cries filled the air. Mr Robinson, alighting ponderously from his Rolls, was cannoned into by one of them.

Mr Robinson put the child aside with a not unkindly hand and peered up at the number on the house.

No. 15. This was right. He pushed open the gate and went up the three steps to the front door. Neat white curtains at the windows, he noted, and a well-polished brass knocker. An insignificant little house in an insignificant street in an insignificant part of London, but it was well kept. It had self-respect.

The door opened. A girl of about twenty-five, pleasant looking, with a kind of fair, chocolate box prettiness, welcomed him with a smile.

Agatha Christie

'Mr Robinson? Come in.'

She took him into the small sitting-room. A television set, cretonnes of a Jacobean pattern, a cottage piano against the wall. She had on a dark skirt and a grey pullover.

'You'll have some tea? I've got the kettle on.'

'Thank you, but no. I never drink tea. And I can only stay a short time. I have only come to bring you what I wrote to you about.'

'From Ali?'

'Yes.'

'There isn't—there couldn't be—any hope? I mean—it's really true—that he was killed? There couldn't be any mistake?'

'I'm afraid there was no mistake,' said Mr Robinson gently.

'No—no, I suppose not. Anyway, I never expected— When he went back there I didn't think really I'd ever see him again. I don't mean I thought he was going to be killed or that there would be a Revolution. I just mean—well, you know—he'd have to carry on, do his stuff—what was expected of him. Marry one of his own people—all that.'

Mr Robinson drew out a package and laid it down on the table.

'Open it, please.'

Her fingers fumbled a little as she tore the wrappings off and then unfolded the final covering...

She drew her breath in sharply.

Red, blue, green, white, all sparkling with fire, with life, turning the dim little room into Aladdin's cave...

Cat Among the Pigeons

Mr Robinson watched her. He had seen so many women look at jewels...

She said at last in a breathless voice,

'Are they—they can't be—*real*?'

'They are real.'

'But they must be worth—they must be worth—'

Her imagination failed.

Mr Robinson nodded.

'If you wish to dispose of them, you can probably get at least half a million pounds for them.'

'No—no, it's not possible.'

Suddenly she scooped them up in her hands and re-wrapped them with shaking fingers.

'I'm scared,' she said. 'They frighten me. What am I to do with them?'

The door burst open. A small boy rushed in.

'Mum, I got a smashing tank off Billy. He—'

He stopped, staring at Mr Robinson.

An olive skinned, dark boy.

His mother said,

'Go in the kitchen, Allen, your tea's all ready. Milk and biscuits and there's a bit of gingerbread.'

'Oh good.' He departed noisily.

'You call him Allen?' said Mr Robinson.

She flushed.

'It was the nearest name to Ali. I couldn't call him Ali—too difficult for him and the neighbours and all.'

She went on, her face clouding over again.

'What am I to do?'

Agatha Christie

'First, have you got your marriage certificate? I have to be sure you're the person you say you are.'

She stared a moment, then went over to a small desk. From one of the drawers she brought out an envelope, extracted a paper from it and brought it to him.

'Hm... yes... Register of Edmonstow... Ali Yusuf, student... Alice Calder, spinster... Yes, all in order.'

'Oh it's legal all right—as far as it goes. And no one ever tumbled to who he was. There's so many of these foreign Moslem students, you see. We knew it didn't mean anything really. He was a Moslem and he could have more than one wife, and he knew he'd have to go back and do just that. We talked about it. But Allen was on the way, you see, and he said this would make it all right for him—we were married all right in this country and Allen would be legitimate. It was the best he could do for me. He really did love me, you know. He really did.'

'Yes,' said Mr Robinson. 'I am sure he did.'

He went on briskly.

'Now, supposing that you put yourself in my hands. I will see to the selling of these stones. And I will give you the address of a lawyer, a really good and reliable solicitor. He will advise you, I expect, to put most of the money in a trust fund. And there will be other things, education for your son, and a new way of life for you. You'll want social education and guidance. You're going to be a very rich woman and all the sharks and the confidence tricksters and the rest of them will be after you. Your life's not going to be easy except in the purely material sense. Rich people don't have an easy time in life, I can tell you—I've seen too many of them to have that illusion. But you've got character. I think you'll come through. And that boy of yours may be a happier man than his father ever was.'

He paused. 'You agree?'

'Yes. Take them.' She pushed them towards him, then said suddenly: 'That schoolgirl—the one who found them—I'd like her to have one of them—which—what colour do you think she'd like?'

Mr Robinson reflected. 'An emerald, I think—green for mystery. A good idea of yours. She will find that very thrilling.'

He rose to his feet.

'I shall charge you for my services, you know,' said Mr Robinson. 'And my charges are pretty high. But I shan't cheat you.'

She gave him a level glance.

'No, I don't think you will. And I need someone who knows about business, because I don't.'

'You seem a very sensible woman if I may say so. Now then, I'm to take these? You don't want to keep—just one—say?'

He watched her with curiosity, the sudden flicker of excitement, the hungry covetous eyes—and then the flicker died.

'No,' said Alice. 'I won't keep—even one.' She flushed. 'Oh I daresay that seems daft to you—not to keep just one big ruby or an emerald—just as a keepsake. But you see, he and I—he was a Moslem but he let me read bits now and again out of the Bible. And we read that bit—about a woman whose price was above rubies. And so—I won't have any jewels. I'd rather not...'

'A most unusual woman,' said Mr Robinson to himself as he walked down the path and into his waiting Rolls.

He repeated to himself,

'A most unusual woman...'

The Agatha Christie Collection

THE HERCULE POIROT MYSTERIES
Match your wits with the famous Belgian detective.

The Mysterious Affair at Styles
The Murder on the Links
Poirot Investigates
The Murder of Roger Ackroyd
The Big Four
The Mystery of the Blue Train
Black Coffee
Peril at End House
Lord Edgware Dies
Murder on the Orient Express
Three Act Tragedy
Death in the Clouds
The ABC Murders
Murder in Mesopotamia
Cards on the Table
Murder in the Mews
Dumb Witness
Death on the Nile
Appointment With Death
Hercule Poirot's Christmas
Sad Cypress
One, Two, Buckle My Shoe
Evil Under the Sun
Five Little Pigs
The Hollow
The Labours of Hercules
Taken at the Flood
Mrs McGinty's Dead
After the Funeral
Hickory Dickory Dock
Dead Man's Folly
Cat Among the Pigeons
The Adventure of the Christmas Pudding
The Clocks
Third Girl
Hallowe'en Party
Elephants Can Remember
Poirot's Early Cases
Curtain: Poirot's Last Case

Find out all about the Queen of Crime
and her stories at **www.agathachristie.com**
Keep up to date with launches and news from the world
of Agatha Christie and discuss all things Agatha on the forum!
Shop online for books, audiobooks, DVDs and other merchandise

/agathachristie   /officialagathachristie   /QueenofCrime

For a touch of Christie mystery, scan the code!

The
Agatha Christie
Collection

**Don't miss a single one of Agatha Christie's
classic novels and short story collections.**

The Man in the Brown Suit	*Death Comes as the End*
The Secret of Chimneys	*Sparkling Cyanide*
The Seven Dials Mystery	*Crooked House*
The Mysterious Mr Quin	*They Came to Baghdad*
The Sittaford Mystery	*Destination Unknown*
The Hound of Death	*Spider's Web*
The Listerdale Mystery	*The Unexpected Guest*
Why Didn't They Ask Evans?	*Ordeal by Innocence*
Parker Pyne Investigates	*The Pale Horse*
Murder Is Easy	*Endless Night*
And Then There Were None	*Passenger to Frankfurt*

Find out all about the Queen of Crime
and her stories at **www.agathachristie.com**

Keep up to date with launches and news from the world
of Agatha Christie and discuss all things Agatha on the forum!

Shop online for books, audiobooks, DVDs and other merchandise

/agathachristie   /officialagathachristie   /QueenofCrime

For a touch of
Christie mystery,
scan the code!

COMING SEPTEMBER 2014

THE NEW *Agatha Christie*

HERCULE POIROT MYSTERY

BY SOPHIE HANNAH

DEATH ON THE NILE

THE AGATHA CHRISTIE COLLECTION

Mysteries
The Man in the Brown Suit
The Secret of Chimneys
The Seven Dials Mystery
The Mysterious Mr Quin
The Sittaford Mystery
The Hound of Death
The Listerdale Mystery
Why Didn't They Ask Evans?
Parker Pyne Investigates
Murder Is Easy
And Then There Were None
Towards Zero
Death Comes as the End
Sparkling Cyanide
Crooked House
They Came to Baghdad
Destination Unknown
Spider's Web*
The Unexpected Guest*
Ordeal by Innocence
The Pale Horse
Endless Night
Passenger To Frankfurt
Problem at Pollensa Bay
While the Light Lasts

Poirot
The Mysterious Affair at Styles
The Murder on the Links
Poirot Investigates
The Murder of Roger Ackroyd
The Big Four
The Mystery of the Blue Train
Black Coffee*
Peril at End House
Lord Edgware Dies
Murder on the Orient Express
Three Act Tragedy
Death in the Clouds
The ABC Murders
Murder in Mesopotamia
Cards on the Table
Murder in the Mews
Dumb Witness
Death on the Nile
Appointment With Death
Hercule Poirot's Christmas
Sad Cypress
One, Two, Buckle My Shoe
Evil Under the Sun
Five Little Pigs
The Hollow
The Labours of Hercules
Taken at the Flood
Mrs McGinty's Dead
After the Funeral
Hickory Dickory Dock
Dead Man's Folly
Cat Among the Pigeons
The Adventure of the Christmas Pudding
The Clocks
Third Girl
Hallowe'en Party
Elephants Can Remember
Poirot's Early Cases
Curtain: Poirot's Last Case

Marple
The Murder at the Vicarage
The Thirteen Problems
The Body in the Library
The Moving Finger
A Murder Is Announced
They Do It With Mirrors
A Pocket Full of Rye
4.50 from Paddington
The Mirror Crack'd from Side to Side
A Caribbean Mystery
At Bertram's Hotel
Nemesis
Sleeping Murder
Miss Marple's Final Cases

Tommy & Tuppence
The Secret Adversary
Partners in Crime
N or M?
By the Pricking of My Thumbs
Postern of Fate

Published as Mary Westmacott
Giant's Bread
Unfinished Portrait
Absent in the Spring
The Rose and the Yew Tree
A Daughter's a Daughter
The Burden

Memoirs
An Autobiography
Come, Tell Me How You Live
The Grand Tour

Plays and Stories
Akhnaton
The Mousetrap and Other Plays
The Floating Admiral (contributor)
Star Over Bethlehem

* novelized by Charles Osborne

Agatha Christie

Death on the Nile

HarperCollins*Publishers*

HarperCollins*Publishers* Ltd
1 London Bridge Street
London SE1 9GF
www.harpercollins.co.uk

This paperback edition 2014

7

First published in Great Britain by
Collins 1937

Agatha Christie® Poirot® Death on the Nile™
Copyright © Agatha Christie Limited 1937. All rights reserved.
www.agathachristie.com

A catalogue record for this book is
available from the British Library

ISBN 978-0-00-752755-7 (PB)
ISBN 978-0-00-825607-4 (POD PB)

Set in Sabon by Palimpsest Book Production Ltd., Falkirk, Stirlingshire

Printed and bound in Great Britain by
CPI Group (UK) Ltd, Croydon CR0 4YY

All rights reserved. No part of this publication may be
reproduced, stored in a retrieval system, or transmitted,
in any form or by any means, electronic, mechanical,
photocopying, recording or otherwise, without the prior
written permission of the publishers.

This book is sold subject to the condition that it shall not,
by way of trade or otherwise, be lent, re-sold, hired out or
otherwise circulated without the publisher's prior consent
in any form of binding or cover other than that in which it
is published and without a similar condition including this
condition being imposed on the subsequent purchaser.

MIX
Paper from
responsible sources
FSC
www.fsc.org FSC® C007454

FSC™ is a non-profit international organisation established to promote
the responsible management of the world's forests. Products carrying
the FSC label are independently certified to assure consumers that they come
from forests that are managed to meet the social, economic and
ecological needs of present and future generations,
and other controlled sources.

Find out more about HarperCollins and the environment at
www.harpercollins.co.uk/green

TO
SYBIL BURNETT
WHO ALSO LOVES WANDERING ABOUT
THE WORLD

AUTHOR'S FOREWORD

Death on the Nile was written after coming back from a winter in Egypt. When I read it now I feel myself back again on the steamer from Aswan to Wadi Halfa. There were quite a number of passengers on board, but the ones in this book travelled in my mind and became increasingly real to me—in the setting of a Nile steamer. The book has a lot of characters and a very elaborately worked out plot. I think the central situation is intriguing and has dramatic possibilities, and the three characters, Simon, Linnet, and Jacqueline, seem to me to be real and alive.

My friend, Francis L. Sullivan, liked the book so much that he kept urging me to adapt it for the stage, which in the end I did.

I think, myself, that the book is one of the best of my 'foreign travel' ones, and if detective stories are 'escape

Agatha Christie

literature' (and why shouldn't they be!) the reader can escape to sunny skies and blue water as well as to crime in the confines of an armchair.

AGATHA CHRISTIE

PART ONE

Characters in Order
of their Appearance

I

'Linnet Ridgeway!'

'That's *Her!*' said Mr Burnaby, the landlord of the Three Crowns.

He nudged his companion.

The two men stared with round bucolic eyes and slightly open mouths.

A big scarlet Rolls-Royce had just stopped in front of the local post office.

A girl jumped out, a girl without a hat and wearing a frock that looked (but only *looked*) simple. A girl with golden hair and straight autocratic features—a girl with a lovely shape—a girl such as was seldom seen in Malton-under-Wode.

With a quick imperative step she passed into the post office.

'That's her!' said Mr Burnaby again. And he went on in

Agatha Christie

a low awed voice: 'Millions she's got.... Going to spend thousands on the place. Swimming-pools there's going to be, and Italian gardens and a ballroom and half of the house pulled down and rebuilt....'

'She'll bring money into the town,' said his friend.

He was a lean, seedy-looking man. His tone was envious and grudging.

Mr Burnaby agreed.

'Yes, it's a great thing for Malton-under-Wode. A great thing it is.'

Mr Burnaby was complacent about it.

'Wake us all up proper,' he added.

'Bit of difference from Sir George,' said the other.

'Ah, it was the 'orses did for him,' said Mr Burnaby indulgently. 'Never 'ad no luck.'

'What did he get for the place?'

'A cool sixty thousand, so I've heard.'

The lean man whistled.

Mr Burnaby went on triumphantly:

'And they say she'll have spent another sixty thousand before she's finished!'

'Wicked!' said the lean man. 'Where'd she *get* all that money from?'

'America, so I've heard. Her mother was the only daughter of one of those millionaire blokes. Quite like the pictures, isn't it?'

The girl came out of the post office and climbed into the car.

As she drove off, the lean man followed her with his eyes.

He muttered:

'It seems all wrong to me—her looking like that. Money *and* looks—it's too much! If a girl's as rich as that she's no right to be a good-looker as well. And she *is* a good-looker.... Got everything, that girl has. Doesn't seem fair....'

II

Extract from the social column of the *Daily Blague*.

Among those supping at Chez Ma Tante I noticed beautiful Linnet Ridgeway. She was with the Hon. Joanna Southwood, Lord Windlesham and Mr Toby Bryce. Miss Ridgeway, as everyone knows, is the daughter of Melhuish Ridgeway who married Anna Hartz. She inherits from her grandfather, Leopold Hartz, an immense fortune. The lovely Linnet is the sensation of the moment and it is rumoured that an engagement may be announced shortly. Certainly Lord Windlesham seemed very épris!

III

The Hon. Joanna Southwood said:

'Darling, I think it's going to be all perfectly *marvellous!*'

She was sitting in Linnet Ridgeway's bedroom at Wode Hall.

From the window the eye passed over the gardens to open country with blue shadows of woodlands.

'It's rather perfect, isn't it?' said Linnet.

Agatha Christie

She leaned her arms on the window sill. Her face was eager, alive, dynamic. Beside her, Joanna Southwood seemed, somehow, a little dim—a tall thin young woman of twenty-seven, with a long clever face and freakishly plucked eyebrows.

'And you've done so much in the time! Did you have lots of architects and things?'

'Three.'

'What are architects like? I don't think I've ever seen any.'

'They were all right. I found them rather unpractical sometimes.'

'Darling, you soon put *that* right! You are the *most* practical creature!'

Joanna picked up a string of pearls from the dressing table.

'I suppose these are real, aren't they, Linnet?'

'Of course.'

'I know it's "of course" to you, my sweet, but it wouldn't be to most people. Heavily cultured or even Woolworth! Darling, they really are *incredible*, so exquisitely matched. They must be worth the *most* fabulous sums!'

'Rather vulgar, you think?'

'No, not at all—just pure beauty. What *are* they worth?'

'About fifty thousand.'

'What a lovely lot of money! Aren't you afraid of having them stolen?'

'No, I always wear them—and anyway they're insured.'

'Let me wear them till dinnertime, will you, darling? It would give me such a thrill.'

Linnet laughed.

'Of course, if you like.'

'You know, Linnet, I really do envy you. You've simply got *everything*. Here you are at twenty, your own mistress, with any amount of money, looks, superb health. You've even got *brains!* When are you twenty-one?'

'Next June. I shall have a grand coming-of-age party in London.'

'And then are you going to marry Charles Windlesham? All the dreadful little gossip writers are getting so excited about it. And he really is frightfully devoted.'

Linnet shrugged her shoulders.

'I don't know. I don't really want to marry anyone yet.'

'Darling, how right you are! It's never quite the same afterwards, is it?'

The telephone shrilled and Linnet went to it.

'Yes? Yes?'

The butler's voice answered her.

'Miss de Bellefort is on the line. Shall I put her through?'

'Bellefort? Oh, of course, yes, put her through.'

A click and a voice, an eager, soft, slightly breathless voice. 'Hullo, is that Miss Ridgeway? *Linnet!*'

'*Jackie darling!* I haven't heard anything of you for ages and *ages!*'

'I know. It's awful. Linnet, I want to see you terribly.'

'Darling, can't you come down here? My new toy. I'd love to show it to you.'

'That's just what I want to do.'

'Well, jump into a train or a car.'

'Right, I will. A frightfully dilapidated two-seater. I

Agatha Christie

bought it for fifteen pounds, and some days it goes beautifully. But it has moods. If I haven't arrived by teatime you'll know it's had a mood. So long, my sweet.'

Linnet replaced the receiver. She crossed back to Joanna.

'That's my oldest friend, Jacqueline de Bellefort. We were together at a convent in Paris. She's had the most terribly bad luck. Her father was a French Count, her mother was American—a Southerner. The father went off with some woman, and her mother lost all her money in the Wall Street crash. Jackie was left absolutely broke. I don't know how she's managed to get along the last two years.'

Joanna was polishing her deep blood-coloured nails with her friend's nail pad. She leant back with her head on one side scrutinizing the effect.

'Darling,' she drawled, 'won't that be rather *tiresome*? If any misfortunes happen to my friends I always drop them *at once!* It sounds heartless, but it saves such a lot of trouble later! They always want to borrow money off you, or else they start a dressmaking business and you have to get the most terrible clothes from them. Or they paint lampshades, or do batik scarves.'

'So, if I lost all my money, you'd drop me tomorrow?'

'Yes, darling, I would. You can't say I'm not honest about it! I only like successful people. And you'll find that's true of nearly everybody—only most people won't admit it. They just say that really they "can't put up with Mary or Emily or Pamela any more! Her troubles have made her so *bitter* and peculiar, poor dear!"'

'How beastly you are, Joanna!'

'I'm only on the make, like everyone else.'

'*I'm* not on the make!'

'For obvious reasons! You don't have to be sordid when good-looking, middle-aged American trustees pay you over a vast allowance every quarter.'

'And you're wrong about Jacqueline,' said Linnet. 'She's not a sponge. I've wanted to help her, but she won't let me. She's as proud as the devil.'

'What's she in such a hurry to see you for? I'll bet she wants something! You just wait and see.'

'She sounded excited about something,' admitted Linnet. 'Jackie always did get frightfully worked up over things. She once stuck a penknife into someone!'

'Darling, how thrilling!'

'A boy who was teasing a dog. Jackie tried to get him to stop. He wouldn't. She pulled him and shook him but he was much stronger than she was, and at last she whipped out a penknife and plunged it right into him. There was the *most* awful row!'

'I should think so. It sounds most uncomfortable!'

Linnet's maid entered the room. With a murmured word of apology, she took down a dress from the wardrobe and went out of the room with it.

'What's the matter with Marie?' asked Joanna. 'She's been crying.'

'Poor thing! You know I told you she wanted to marry a man who has a job in Egypt. She didn't know much about him, so I thought I'd better make sure he was all right. It turned out that he had a wife already—and three children.'

'What a lot of enemies you must make, Linnet.'

'Enemies?' Linnet looked surprised.

Joanna nodded and helped herself to a cigarette.

'Enemies, my sweet. You're so devastatingly efficient. And you're so frightfully good at doing the right thing.'

Linnet laughed.

'Why, I haven't got an enemy in the world.'

IV

Lord Windlesham sat under the cedar tree. His eyes rested on the graceful proportions of Wode Hall. There was nothing to mar its old-world beauty; the new buildings and additions were out of sight round the corner. It was a fair and peaceful sight bathed in the autumn sunshine. Nevertheless, as he gazed, it was no longer Wode Hall that Charles Windlesham saw. Instead, he seemed to see a more imposing Elizabethan mansion, a long sweep of park, a bleaker background... It was his own family seat, Charltonbury, and in the foreground stood a figure—a girl's figure, with bright golden hair and an eager confident face... Linnet as mistress of Charltonbury!

He felt very hopeful. That refusal of hers had not been at all a definite refusal. It had been little more than a plea for time. Well, he could afford to wait a little...

How amazingly suitable the whole thing was. It was certainly advisable that he should marry money, but not such a matter of necessity that he could regard himself as forced to put his own feelings on one side. And he loved Linnet. He would have wanted to marry her even if she had been practically penniless, instead of one of the richest girls in England. Only, fortunately, she *was* one of the richest girls in England…

His mind played with attractive plans for the future. The Mastership of the Roxdale perhaps, the restoration of the west wing, no need to let the Scotch shooting…

Charles Windlesham dreamed in the sun.

V

It was four o'clock when the dilapidated little two-seater stopped with a sound of crunching gravel. A girl got out of it—a small slender creature with a mop of dark hair. She ran up the steps and tugged at the bell.

A few minutes later she was being ushered into the long stately drawing room, and an ecclesiastical butler was saying with the proper mournful intonation: 'Miss de Bellefort.'

'Linnet!'

'Jackie!'

Windlesham stood a little aside, watching sympathetically as this fiery little creature flung herself open-armed upon Linnet.

'Lord Windlesham—Miss de Bellefort—my best friend.'

A pretty child, he thought—not really pretty but decidedly attractive with her dark curly hair and her enormous eyes. He murmured a few tactful nothings and then managed unobtrusively to leave the two friends together.

Jacqueline pounced—in a fashion that Linnet remembered as being characteristic of her.

'Windlesham? Windlesham? *That's* the man the papers always say you're going to marry! Are you, Linnet? *Are you?*'

Linnet murmured:

'Perhaps.'

'Darling—I'm so glad! He looks nice.'

'Oh, don't make up your mind about it—I haven't made up my own mind yet.'

'Of course not! Queens always proceed with due deliberation to the choosing of a consort!'

'Don't be ridiculous, Jackie.'

'But you *are* a queen, Linnet! You always were. *Sa Majesté, la reine Linette. Linette la blonde!* And I—I'm the Queen's confidante! The trusted Maid of Honour.'

'What nonsense you talk, Jackie darling! Where have you been all this time? You just disappear. And you never write.'

'I hate writing letters. Where have I been? Oh, about three parts submerged, darling. In JOBS, you know. Grim jobs with grim women!'

'Darling, I wish you'd—'

'Take the Queen's bounty? Well, frankly, darling, that's what I'm here for. No, not to borrow money. It's not got to that yet! But I've come to ask a great big important favour!'

'Go on.'

'If you're going to marry the Windlesham man, you'll understand, perhaps.'

Linnet looked puzzled for a minute, then her face cleared.

'Jackie, do you mean—?'

'Yes, darling, *I'm engaged!*'

'So that's it! I thought you were looking particularly alive somehow. You always do, of course, but even more than usual.'

'That's just what I feel like.'

'Tell me all about him.'

'His name's Simon Doyle. He's big and square and incredibly simple and boyish and utterly adorable! He's poor—got no money. He's what you call "county" all right—but very impoverished county—a younger son and all that. His people come from Devonshire. He loves the country and country things. And for the last five years he's been in the City in a stuffy office. And now they're cutting down and he's out of a job. Linnet, I shall *die* if I can't marry him! I shall die! I shall die! I shall *die*…!'

'Don't be ridiculous, Jackie.'

'I shall die, I tell you! I'm crazy about him. He's crazy about me. We can't live without each other.'

'Darling, you *have* got it badly!'

'I know. It's awful, isn't it? This love business gets hold of you and you can't do anything about it.'

She paused for a minute. Her dark eyes dilated, looked suddenly tragic. She gave a little shiver.

'It's—even frightening sometimes! Simon and I were made

Agatha Christie

for each other. I shall never care for anyone else. And *you've* got to help us, Linnet. I heard you'd bought this place and it put an idea into my head. Listen, you'll have to have a land agent—perhaps two. I want you to give the job to Simon.'

'Oh!' Linnet was startled.

Jacqueline rushed on.

'He's got all that sort of thing at his fingertips. He knows all about estates—was brought up on one. And he's got his business training too. Oh, Linnet, you will give him a job, won't you, for love of me? If he doesn't make good, sack him. But he will. And we can live in a little house and I shall see lots of you and everything in the garden will be too, too divine.'

She got up.

'Say you will, Linnet. Say you will. Beautiful Linnet! Tall golden Linnet! My own very special Linnet! Say you will!'

'Jackie—'

'You will?'

Linnet burst out laughing.

'Ridiculous Jackie! Bring along your young man and let me have a look at him and we'll talk it over.'

Jackie darted at her, kissing her exuberantly.

'*Darling Linnet*—you're a real friend! I knew you were. You wouldn't let me down—ever. You're just the loveliest thing in the world. Goodbye.'

'But, Jackie, you're *staying*.'

'Me? No, I'm not. I'm going back to London and tomorrow I'll come back and bring Simon and we'll settle it all up. You'll adore him. He really is a *pet*.'

'But can't you wait and just have tea?'

'No, I can't wait, Linnet. I'm too excited. I must get back and tell Simon. I know I'm mad, darling, but I can't help it. Marriage will cure me, I expect. It always seems to have a very sobering effect on people.'

She turned at the door, stood a moment, then rushed back for a last quick birdlike embrace.

'Dear Linnet—there's no one like you.'

VI

M. Gaston Blondin, the proprietor of that modish little restaurant Chez Ma Tante, was not a man who delighted to honour many of his clientele. The rich, the beautiful, the notorious and the well-born might wait in vain to be singled out and paid special attention. Only in the rarest cases did M. Blondin, with gracious condescension, greet a guest, accompany him to a privileged table, and exchange with him suitable and apposite remarks.

On this particular night, M. Blondin had exercised his royal prerogative three times—once for a Duchess, once for a famous racing peer, and once for a little man of comical appearance with immense black moustaches and who, a casual onlooker would have thought, could bestow no favour on Chez Ma Tante by his presence there.

M. Blondin, however, was positively fulsome in his attentions.

Though clients had been told for the last half hour that a table was not to be had, one now mysteriously appeared, placed in a most favourable position. M. Blondin conducted the client to it with every appearance of *empressement*.

'But naturally, for *you* there is *always* a table, Monsieur Poirot! How I wish that you would honour us oftener!'

Hercule Poirot smiled, remembering that past incident wherein a dead body, a waiter, M. Blondin, and a very lovely lady had played a part.

'You are too amiable, Monsieur Blondin,' he said.

'And you are alone, Monsieur Poirot?'

'Yes, I am alone.'

'Oh, well, Jules here will compose for you a little meal that will be a poem—positively a poem! Women, however charming, have this disadvantage: they distract the mind from food! You will enjoy your dinner, Monsieur Poirot, I promise you that. Now as to wine—'

A technical conversation ensued, Jules, the *maître d'hotel*, assisting.

Before departing, M. Blondin lingered a moment, lowering his voice confidentially.

'You have grave affairs on hand?'

Poirot shook his head.

'I am, alas, a man of leisure,' he said softly. 'I have made the economies in my time and I have now the means to enjoy the life of idleness.'

'I envy you.'

'No, no, you would be unwise to do so. I can assure you, it is not so gay as it sounds.' He sighed. 'How true is the saying that man was forced to invent work in order to escape the strain of having to think.'

M. Blondin threw up his hands.

'But there is so much! There is travel!'

'Yes, there is travel. Already I have done not so badly. This winter I shall visit Egypt, I think. The climate, they say, is superb! One will escape from the fogs, the greyness, the monotony of the constantly falling rain.'

'Ah! Egypt,' breathed M. Blondin.

'One can even voyage there now, I believe, by train, escaping all sea travel except the Channel.'

'Ah, the sea, it does not agree with you?'

Hercule Poirot shook his head and shuddered slightly.

'I, too,' said M. Blondin with sympathy. 'Curious the effect it has upon the stomach.'

'But only upon certain stomachs! There are people on whom the motion makes no impression whatever. They actually *enjoy* it!'

'An unfairness of the good God,' said M. Blondin.

He shook his head sadly, and, brooding on the impious thought, withdrew.

Smooth-footed, deft-handed waiters ministered to the table. Toast Melba, butter, an ice pail, all the adjuncts to a meal of quality.

The Negro orchestra broke into an ecstasy of strange discordant noises. London danced.

Hercule Poirot looked on, registered impressions in his neat orderly mind.

How bored and weary most of the faces were! Some of those stout men, however, were enjoying themselves... whereas a patient endurance seemed to be the sentiment exhibited on their partners' faces. The fat woman in purple was looking radiant... Undoubtedly the fat had certain compensations in life... a zest—a gusto—denied to those of more fashionable contours.

A good sprinkling of young people—some vacant-looking—some bored—some definitely unhappy. How absurd to call youth the time of happiness—youth, the time of greatest vulnerability!

His glance softened as it rested on one particular couple. A well-matched pair—tall broad-shouldered man, slender delicate girl. Two bodies that moved in a perfect rhythm of happiness. Happiness in the place, the hour, and in each other.

The dance stopped abruptly. Hands clapped and it started again. After a second encore the couple returned to their table close by Poirot.

The girl was flushed, laughing. As she sat, he could study her face as it was lifted laughing to her companion.

There was something else beside laughter in her eyes.

Hercule Poirot shook his head doubtfully.

'She cares too much, that little one,' he said to himself. 'It is not safe. No, it is not safe.'

And then a word caught his ear. Egypt.

Their voices came to him clearly—the girl's young, fresh, arrogant, with just a trace of soft-sounding foreign Rs, and the man's pleasant, low-toned, well-bred English.

'I'm *not* counting my chickens before they're hatched, Simon. I tell you Linnet won't let us down!'

'*I* might let *her* down.'

'Nonsense—it's just the right job for you.'

'As a matter of fact I think it is... I haven't really any doubts as to my capability. And I mean to make good—for *your* sake!'

The girl laughed softly, a laugh of pure happiness.

'We'll wait three months—to make sure you don't get the sack—and then—'

'And then I'll endow thee with my worldly goods—that's the hang of it, isn't it?'

'And, as I say, we'll go to Egypt for our honeymoon. Damn the expense! I've always wanted to go to Egypt all my life. The Nile and the Pyramids and the sand...'

He said, his voice slightly indistinct:

'We'll see it together, Jackie... together. Won't it be marvellous?'

'I wonder. Will it be as marvellous to you as it is to me? Do you really care—as much as I do?'

Her voice was suddenly sharp—her eyes dilated—almost with fear.

The man's answer came with an equal sharpness: 'Don't be absurd, Jackie.'

But the girl repeated: 'I wonder...'

Then she shrugged her shoulders: 'Let's dance.'

Hercule Poirot murmured to himself:

'*Une qui aime et un qui se laisse aimer.* Yes, I wonder too.'

VII

Joanna Southwood said:
'And suppose he's a terrible tough?'

Linnet shook her head. 'Oh, he won't be. I can trust Jacqueline's taste.'

Joanna murmured:

'Ah, but people don't run true to form in love affairs.'

Linnet shook her head impatiently. Then she changed the subject.

'I must go and see Mr Pierce about those plans.'

'Plans?'

'Yes, some dreadful insanitary old cottages. I'm having them pulled down and the people moved.'

'How sanitary and public-spirited of you, darling!'

'They'd have had to go anyway. Those cottages would have overlooked my new swimming pool.'

'Do the people who live in them like going?'

'Most of them are delighted. One or two are being rather stupid about it—really tiresome in fact. They don't seem to realize how vastly improved their living conditions will be!'

'But you're being quite high-handed about it, I presume.'

'My dear Joanna, it's to their advantage really.'

'Yes, dear. I'm sure it is. Compulsory benefit.'

Linnet frowned. Joanna laughed.

'Come now, you *are* a tyrant, admit it. A beneficent tyrant if you like!'

'I'm not the least bit of a tyrant.'

'But you like your own way!'

'Not especially.'

'Linnet Ridgeway, can you look me in the face and tell me of *any one occasion* on which you've failed to do exactly as you wanted?'

'Heaps of times.'

'Oh, yes, "heaps of times"—just like that—but no concrete example. And you simply can't think up one, darling, however hard you try! The triumphal progress of Linnet Ridgeway in her golden car.'

Linnet said sharply:

'You think I'm selfish?'

'No—just irresistible. The combined effect of money and charm. Everything goes down before you. What you can't buy with cash you buy with a smile. Result: Linnet Ridgeway, the Girl Who Has Everything.'

'Don't be ridiculous, Joanna!'

'Well, haven't you got everything?'

'I suppose I have… It sounds rather disgusting, somehow!'

'Of course it's disgusting, darling! You'll probably get terribly bored and blasé by and by. In the meantime, enjoy the triumphal progress in the golden car. Only I wonder, I really do wonder, what will happen when you want to go down a street which has a board saying No Thoroughfare.'

'Don't be idiotic, Joanna.' As Lord Windlesham joined them, Linnet said, turning to him: 'Joanna is saying the nastiest things to me.'

'All spite, darling, all spite,' said Joanna vaguely as she got up from her seat.

She made no apology for leaving them. She had caught the glint in Windlesham's eye.

He was silent for a minute or two. Then he went straight to the point.

'Have you come to a decision, Linnet?'

Linnet said slowly:

'Am I being a brute? I suppose, if I'm not sure, I ought to say No—'

He interrupted her:

'Don't say it: You shall have time—as much time as you want. But I think, you know, we should be happy together.'

'You see,' Linnet's tone was apologetic, almost childish, 'I'm enjoying myself so much—especially with all this.' She waved a hand. 'I wanted to make Wode Hall into my real ideal of a country house, and I do think I've got it nice, don't you?'

'It's beautiful. Beautifully planned. Everything perfect. You're very clever, Linnet.'

He paused a minute and went on:

'And you like Charltonbury, don't you? Of course it wants modernizing and all that—but you're so clever at that sort of thing. You enjoy it.'

'Why, of course, Charltonbury's divine.'

She spoke with ready enthusiasm, but inwardly she was conscious of a sudden chill. An alien note had sounded, disturbing her complete satisfaction with life.

She did not analyse the feeling at the moment, but later, when Windlesham had left her, she tried to probe the recesses of her mind.

Charltonbury—yes, that was it—she had resented the mention of Charltonbury. But why? Charltonbury was modestly famous. Windlesham's ancestors had held it since the time of Elizabeth. To be mistress of Charltonbury was a position unsurpassed in society. Windlesham was one of the most desirable *partis* in England.

Naturally he couldn't take Wode seriously... It was not in any way to be compared with Charltonbury.

Ah, but Wode was *hers*! She had seen it, acquired it, rebuilt and re-dressed it, lavished money on it. It was her own possession, her kingdom.

But in a sense it wouldn't count if she married Windlesham. What would they want with two country places? And of the two, naturally Wode Hall would be the one to be given up.

She, Linnet Ridgeway, wouldn't exist any longer. She would be Countess of Windlesham, bringing a fine dowry to Charltonbury and its master. She would be queen consort, not queen any longer.

'I'm being ridiculous,' said Linnet to herself.

But it was curious how she did hate the idea of abandoning Wode...

And wasn't there something else nagging at her?

Jackie's voice with that queer blurred note in it saying: 'I shall *die* if I can't marry him! I shall die. I shall die...'

So positive, so earnest. Did she, Linnet, feel like that about Windlesham? Assuredly she didn't. Perhaps she could never feel like that about anyone. It must be—rather wonderful—to feel like that...

The sound of a car came through the open window.

Linnet shook herself impatiently. That must be Jackie and her young man. She'd go out and meet them.

She was standing in the open doorway as Jacqueline and Simon Doyle got out of the car.

'Linnet!' Jackie ran to her. 'This is Simon. Simon, here's Linnet. She's just the most wonderful person in the world.'

Agatha Christie

Linnet saw a tall, broad-shouldered young man, with very dark blue eyes, crisply curling brown hair, a square chin, and a boyish, appealing, simple smile...

She stretched out a hand. The hand that clasped hers was firm and warm... She liked the way he looked at her, the naïve genuine admiration.

Jackie had told him she was wonderful, and he clearly thought that she was wonderful...

A warm sweet feeling of intoxication ran through her veins.

'Isn't this all lovely?' she said. 'Come in, Simon, and let me welcome my new land agent properly.'

And as she turned to lead the way she thought: 'I'm frightfully—frightfully happy. I like Jackie's young man... I like him enormously...'

And then a sudden pang: 'Lucky Jackie...'

VIII

Tim Allerton leant back in his wicker chair and yawned as he looked out over the sea. He shot a quick sidelong glance at his mother.

Mrs Allerton was a good-looking, white-haired woman of fifty. By imparting an expression of pinched severity to her mouth every time she looked at her son, she sought to disguise the fact of her intense affection for him. Even total strangers were seldom deceived by this device and Tim himself saw through it perfectly.

He said:

'Do you really like Majorca, Mother?'

'Well—,' Mrs Allerton considered, 'it's cheap.'

'And cold,' said Tim with a slight shiver.

He was a tall, thin young man, with dark hair and a rather narrow chest. His mouth had a very sweet expression, his eyes were sad and his chin was indecisive. He had long delicate hands.

Threatened by consumption some years ago, he had never displayed a really robust physique. He was popularly supposed 'to write', but it was understood among his friends that enquiries as to literary output were not encouraged.

'What are you thinking of, Tim?'

Mrs Allerton was alert. Her bright dark-brown eyes looked suspicious.

Tim Allerton grinned at her:

'I was thinking of Egypt.'

'Egypt?' Mrs Allerton sounded doubtful.

'Real warmth, darling. Lazy golden sands. The Nile. I'd like to go up the Nile, wouldn't you?'

'Oh, I'd *like* it.' Her tone was dry. 'But Egypt's expensive, my dear. Not for those who have to count the pennies.'

Tim laughed. He rose, stretched himself. Suddenly he looked alive and eager. There was an excited note in his voice.

'The expense will be my affair. Yes, darling. A little flutter on the Stock Exchange. With thoroughly satisfactory results. I heard this morning.'

'This morning?' said Mrs Allerton sharply. 'You only had one letter and that—'

Agatha Christie

She stopped and bit her lip.

Tim looked momentarily undecided whether to be amused or annoyed. Amusement gained the day.

'And that was from Joanna,' he finished coolly. 'Quite right, Mother. What a queen of detectives you'd make! The famous Hercule Poirot would have to look to his laurels if you were about.'

Mrs Allerton looked rather cross.

'I just happened to see the handwriting—'

'And knew it wasn't that of a stockbroker? Quite right. As a matter of fact it was yesterday I heard from them. Poor Joanna's handwriting *is* rather noticeable—sprawls about all over the envelope like an inebriated spider.'

'What does Joanna say? Any news?'

Mrs Allerton strove to make her voice sound casual and ordinary. The friendship between her son and his second cousin, Joanna Southwood, always irritated her. Not, as she put it to herself, that there was 'anything in it'. She was quite sure there wasn't. Tim had never manifested a sentimental interest in Joanna, nor she in him. Their mutual attraction seemed to be founded on gossip and the possession of a large number of friends and acquaintances in common. They both liked people and discussing people. Joanna had an amusing if caustic tongue.

It was not because Mrs Allerton feared that Tim might fall in love with Joanna that she found herself always becoming a little stiff in manner if Joanna were present or when letters from her arrived.

It was some other feeling hard to define—perhaps an

unacknowledged jealousy in the unfeigned pleasure Tim always seemed to take in Joanna's society. He and his mother were such perfect companions that the sight of him absorbed and interested in another woman always startled Mrs Allerton slightly. She fancied, too, that her own presence on these occasions set some barrier between the two members of the younger generation. Often she had come upon them eagerly absorbed in some conversation and, at sight of her, their talk had wavered, had seemed to include her rather too purposefully and as in duty bound. Quite definitely, Mrs Allerton did not like Joanna Southwood. She thought her insincere, affected, and essentially superficial. She found it very hard to prevent herself saying so in unmeasured tones.

In answer to her question, Tim pulled the letter out of his pocket and glanced through it. It was quite a long letter, his mother noted.

'Nothing much,' he said. 'The Devenishes are getting a divorce. Old Monty's been had up for being drunk in charge of a car. Windlesham's gone to Canada. Seems he was pretty badly hit when Linnet Ridgeway turned him down. She's definitely going to marry this land agent person.'

'How extraordinary! Is he very dreadful?'

'No, no, not at all. He's one of the Devonshire Doyles. No money, of course—and he was actually engaged to one of Linnet's best friends. Pretty thick, that.'

'I don't think it's at all nice,' said Mrs Allerton, flushing.

Tim flashed her a quick affectionate glance.

'I know, darling. You don't approve of snaffling other people's husbands and all that sort of thing.'

Agatha Christie

'In my day we had our standards,' said Mrs Allerton. 'And a very good thing too! Nowadays young people seem to think they can just go about doing anything they choose.'

Tim smiled. 'They don't only think it. They do it. *Vide* Linnet Ridgeway!'

'Well, I think it's horrid!'

Tim twinkled at her.

'Cheer up, you old die-hard! Perhaps I agree with you. Anyway, *I* haven't helped myself to anyone's wife or fiancée yet.'

'I'm sure you'd never do such a thing,' said Mrs Allerton. She added with spirit, 'I've brought you up properly.'

'So the credit is yours, not mine.'

He smiled teasingly at her as he folded the letter and put it away again. Mrs Allerton let the thought just flash across her mind: 'Most letters he shows to me. He only reads me snippets from Joanna's.'

But she put the unworthy thought away from her, and decided, as ever, to behave like a gentlewoman.

'Is Joanna enjoying life?' she asked.

'So so. Says she thinks of opening a delicatessen shop in Mayfair.'

'She always talks about being hard up,' said Mrs Allerton with a tinge of spite, 'but she goes about everywhere and her clothes must cost her a lot. She's always beautifully dressed.'

'Ah, well,' said Tim, 'she probably doesn't pay for them. No, mother, I don't mean what your Edwardian mind suggests to you. I just mean quite literally that she leaves her bills unpaid.'

Mrs Allerton sighed.

'I never know how people manage to do that.'

'It's a kind of special gift,' said Tim. 'If only you have sufficiently extravagant tastes, and absolutely no sense of money values, people will give you any amount of credit.'

'Yes, but you come to the Bankruptcy Court in the end like poor Sir George Wode.'

'You have a soft spot for that old horse coper—probably because he called you a rosebud in 1879 at a dance.'

'I wasn't born in 1879,' Mrs Allerton retorted with spirit. 'Sir George has charming manners, and I won't have you calling him a horse coper.'

'I've heard funny stories about him from people that know.'

'You and Joanna don't mind what you say about people; anything will do so long as it's sufficiently ill-natured.'

Tim raised his eyebrows.

'My dear, you're quite heated. I didn't know old Wode was such a favourite of yours.'

'You don't realize how hard it was for him, having to sell Wode Hall. He cared terribly about that place.'

Tim suppressed the easy retort. After all, who was he to judge? Instead he said thoughtfully:

'You know, I think you're not far wrong there. Linnet asked him to come down and see what she'd done to the place, and he refused quite rudely.'

'Of course. She ought to have known better than to ask him.'

'And I believe he's quite venomous about her—mutters things under his breath whenever he sees her. Can't forgive her for having given him an absolutely top price for the worm-eaten family estate.'

'And you can't understand that?' Mrs Allerton spoke sharply.

'Frankly,' said Tim calmly, 'I can't. Why live in the past? Why cling on to things that have been?'

'What are you going to put in their place?'

He shrugged his shoulders. 'Excitement, perhaps. Novelty. The joy of never knowing what may turn up from day to day. Instead of inheriting a useless tract of land, the pleasure of making money for yourself—by your own brains and skill.'

'A successful deal on the Stock Exchange, in fact!'

He laughed: 'Why not?'

'And what about an equal *loss* on the Stock Exchange?'

'That, dear, is rather tactless. And quite inappropriate today... What about this Egypt plan?'

'Well—'

He cut in smiling at her: 'That's settled. We've both always wanted to see Egypt.'

'When do you suggest?'

'Oh, next month. January's about the best time there. We'll enjoy the delightful society in this hotel a few weeks longer.'

'Tim,' said Mrs Allerton reproachfully. Then she added

guiltily: 'I'm afraid I promised Mrs Leech that you'd go with her to the police station. She doesn't understand any Spanish.'

Tim made a grimace.

'About her ring? The blood-red ruby of the horseleech's daughter? Does she still persist in thinking it's been stolen? I'll go if you like, but it's a waste of time. She'll only get some wretched chambermaid into trouble. I distinctly saw it on her finger when she went into the sea that day. It came off in the water and she never noticed.'

'She says she is quite sure she took it off and left it on her dressing table.'

'Well, she didn't. I saw it with my own eyes. The woman's a fool. Any woman's a fool who goes prancing into the sea in December, pretending the water's quite warm just because the sun happens to be shining rather brightly at the moment. Stout women oughtn't to be allowed to bathe anyway; they look so revolting in bathing dresses.'

Mrs Allerton murmured:

'I really feel I ought to give up bathing.'

Tim gave a shout of laughter.

'You? You can give most of the young things points and to spare.'

Mrs Allerton sighed and said, 'I wish there were a few more young people for you here.'

Tim Allerton shook his head decidedly.

'I don't. You and I get along rather comfortably without outside distractions.'

'You'd like it if Joanna were here.'

Agatha Christie

'I wouldn't.' His tone was unexpectedly resolute. 'You're all wrong there. Joanna amuses me, but I don't really like her, and to have her around much gets on my nerves. I'm thankful she isn't here. I should be quite resigned if I were never to see Joanna again.'

He added, almost below his breath:

'There's only one woman in the world I've got a real respect and admiration for, and I think, Mrs Allerton, you know very well who that woman is.'

His mother blushed and looked quite confused.

Tim said gravely:

'There aren't very many really nice women in the world. You happen to be one of them.'

IX

In an apartment overlooking Central Park in New York Mrs Robson exclaimed:

'If that isn't just too lovely! You really are the luckiest girl, Cornelia.'

Cornelia Robson flushed responsively.

She was a big clumsy-looking girl with brown doglike eyes.

'Oh, it will be wonderful!' she gasped.

Old Miss Van Schuyler inclined her head in a satisfied fashion at this correct attitude on the part of poor relations.

'I've always dreamed of a trip to Europe,' sighed Cornelia, 'but I just didn't feel I'd ever get there.'

'Miss Bowers will come with me as usual, of course,'

said Miss Van Schuyler, 'but as a social companion I find her limited—very limited. There are many little things that Cornelia can do for me.'

'I'd just love to, Cousin Marie,' said Cornelia eagerly.

'Well, well, then that's settled,' said Miss Van Schuyler. 'Just run and find Miss Bowers, my dear. It's time for my eggnog.'

Cornelia departed.

Her mother said:

'My dear Marie, I'm really *most* grateful to you! You know I think Cornelia suffers a lot from not being a social success. It makes her feel kind of mortified. If I could afford to take her to places—but you know how it's been since Ned died.'

'I'm very glad to take her,' said Miss Van Schuyler. 'Cornelia has always been a nice handy girl, willing to run errands, and not so selfish as some of these young people nowadays.'

Mrs Robson rose and kissed her rich relative's wrinkled and slightly yellow face.

'I'm just ever so grateful,' she declared.

On the stairs she met a tall capable-looking woman who was carrying a glass containing a yellow foamy liquid.

'Well, Miss Bowers, so you're off to Europe?'

'Why, yes, Mrs Robson.'

'What a lovely trip!'

'Why, yes, I should think it would be very enjoyable.'

'But you've been abroad before?'

'Oh, yes, Mrs Robson. I went over to Paris with Miss Van Schuyler last fall. But I've never been to Egypt before.'

Agatha Christie

Mrs Robson hesitated.

'I do hope—there won't be any—trouble.'

She had lowered her voice.

Miss Bowers, however, replied in her usual tone:

'Oh, *no*, Mrs Robson; I shall take good care of *that*. I keep a very sharp look-out always.'

But there was still a faint shadow on Mrs Robson's face as she slowly continued down the stairs.

X

In his office downtown Mr Andrew Pennington was opening his personal mail. Suddenly his fist clenched itself and came down on his desk with a bang; his face crimsoned and two big veins stood out on his forehead. He pressed a buzzer on his desk and a smart-looking stenographer appeared with commendable promptitude.

'Tell Mr Rockford to step in here.'

'Yes, Mr Pennington.'

A few minutes later, Sterndale Rockford, Pennington's partner, entered the office. The two men were not unlike—both tall, spare, with greying hair and clean-shaven clever faces.

'What's up, Pennington?'

Pennington looked up from the letter he was rereading. He said:

'Linnet's married…'

'*What?*'

'You heard what I said! Linnet Ridgeway's *married*!'

'How? When? Why didn't we hear about it?'

Death on the Nile

Pennington glanced at the calendar on his desk.

'She wasn't married when she wrote this letter, but she's married now. Morning of the fourth. That's today.'

Rockford dropped into a chair.

'Whew! No warning! Nothing? Who's the man?'

Pennington referred again to the letter.

'Doyle. Simon Doyle.'

'What sort of a fellow is he? Ever heard of him?'

'No. She doesn't say much…' He scanned the lines of clear, upright hand writing. 'Got an idea there's something hole-and-corner about this business… That doesn't matter. The whole point is, she's married.'

The eyes of the two men met. Rockford nodded.

'This needs a bit of thinking out,' he said quietly.

'What are we going to do about it?'

'I'm asking you.'

The two men sat silent.

Then Rockford said:

'Got any plan?'

Pennington said slowly:

'The *Normandie* sails today. One of us could just make it.'

'You're crazy! What's the big idea?'

Pennington began:

'Those Britisher lawyers—' and stopped.

'What about 'em. Surely you're not going over to tackle 'em? You're mad!'

'I'm not suggesting that you—or I—should go to England.'

'What's the big idea, then?'

Pennington smoothed out the letter on the table.

'Linnet's going to Egypt for her honeymoon. Expects to be there a month or more...'

'Egypt—eh?'

Rockford considered. Then he looked up and met the other's glance.

'Egypt,' he said; '*that's* your idea!'

'Yes—a chance meeting. Over on a trip. Linnet and her husband—honeymoon atmosphere. It might be done.'

Rockford said doubtfully:

'She's sharp, Linnet is... but—'

Pennington said softly: 'I think there might be ways of—managing it.'

Again their eyes met. Rockford nodded.

'All right, big boy.'

Pennington looked at the clock.

'We'll have to hustle—whichever of us is going.'

'You go,' said Rockford promptly. 'You always made a hit with Linnet. "Uncle Andrew." That's the ticket!'

Pennington's face had hardened.

He said: 'I hope I can pull it off.'

His partner said:

'You've got to pull it off. 'The situation's critical...'

XI

William Carmichael said to the thin, weedy youth who opened the door inquiringly:

'Send Mr Jim to me, please.'

Jim Fanthorp entered the room and looked inquiringly at his uncle. The older man looked up with a nod and a grunt.

'Humph, there you are.'

'You asked for me?'

'Just cast an eye over this.'

The young man sat down and drew the sheaf of papers towards him. The elder man watched him.

'Well?'

The answer came promptly.

'Looks fishy to me, sir.'

Again the senior partner of Carmichael, Grant & Carmichael uttered his characteristic grunt.

Jim Fanthorp reread the letter which had just arrived by air mail from Egypt:

...It seems wicked to be writing business letters on such a day. We have spent a week at Mena House and made an expedition to the Fayum. The day after tomorrow we are going up the Nile to Luxor and Aswan by steamer, and perhaps on to Khartoum. When we went into Cook's this morning to see about our tickets who do you think was the first person I saw?—my American trustee, Andrew Pennington. I think you met him two years ago when he was over. I had no idea he was in Egypt and he had no idea that I was! Nor that I was married! My letter, telling him of my marriage, must just have missed him. He is actually going up the Nile on the same trip that we are.

Isn't it a coincidence? Thank you so much for all you have done in this busy time. I—

As the young man was about to turn the page, Mr Carmichael took the letter from him.

'That's all,' he said. 'The rest doesn't matter. Well, what do you think?'

His nephew considered for a moment—then he said:

'Well—I think—not a coincidence…'

The other nodded approval.

'Like a trip to Egypt?' he barked out.

'You think that's advisable?'

'I think there's no time to lose.'

'But, why me?'

'Use your brains, boy; use your brains. Linnet Ridgeway has never met you; no more has Pennington. If you go by air you may get there in time.'

'I—I don't like it, sir. What am I to do?'

'Use your eyes. Use your ears. Use your brains—if you've got any. And if necessary—act.'

'I—I don't like it.'

'Perhaps not—but you've got to do it.'

'It's—necessary?'

'In my opinion,' said Mr Carmichael, 'it's absolutely vital.'

XII

Mrs Otterbourne, readjusting the turban of native material that she wore draped round her head, said fretfully:

'I really don't see why we shouldn't go on to Egypt. I'm sick and tired of Jerusalem.'

As her daughter made no reply, she said:

'You might at least answer when you're spoken to.'

Rosalie Otterbourne was looking at a newspaper reproduction of a face. Below it was printed:

> Mrs Simon Doyle, who before her marriage was the well-known society beauty, Miss Linnet Ridgeway. Mr and Mrs Doyle are spending their honeymoon in Egypt.

Rosalie said, 'You'd like to move on to Egypt, Mother?'

'Yes, I would,' Mrs Otterbourne snapped. 'I consider they've treated us in a most cavalier fashion here. My being here is an advertisement—I ought to get a special reduction in terms. When I hinted as much, I consider they were most impertinent—*most* impertinent. I told them exactly what I thought of them.'

The girl sighed. She said:

'One place is very like another. I wish we could get right away.'

'And this morning,' went on Mrs Otterbourne, 'the manager actually had the impertinence to tell me that all the rooms had been booked in advance and that he would require ours in two days' time.'

'So we've got to go somewhere.'

'Not at all. I'm quite prepared to fight for my rights.'

Rosalie murmured: 'I suppose we might as well go on to Egypt. It doesn't make any difference.'

Agatha Christie

'It's certainly not a matter of life or death,' said Mrs Otterbourne.

But there she was quite wrong—for a matter of life and death was exactly what it was.

PART TWO

Egypt

CHAPTER 1

'That's Hercule Poirot, the detective,' said Mrs Allerton.

She and her son were sitting in brightly painted scarlet basket chairs outside the Cataract Hotel in Aswan. They were watching the retreating figures of two people—a short man dressed in a white silk suit and a tall slim girl.

Tim Allerton sat up in an unusually alert fashion.

'That funny little man?' he asked incredulously.

'That funny little man!'

'What on earth's he doing out here?' Tim asked.

His mother laughed. 'Darling, you sound quite excited. Why do men enjoy crime so much? I hate detective stories and never read them. But I don't think Monsieur Poirot is here with any ulterior motive. He's made a good deal of money and he's seeing life, I fancy.'

'Seems to have an eye for the best-looking girl in the place.'

Mrs Allerton tilted her head a little on one side as

she considered the retreating backs of M. Poirot and his companion.

The girl by his side overtopped him by some three inches. She walked well, neither stiffly nor slouchingly.

'I suppose she *is* quite good-looking,' said Mrs Allerton.

She shot a little glance sideways at Tim. Somewhat to her amusement the fish rose at once.

'She's more than quite. Pity she looks so bad-tempered and sulky.'

'Perhaps that's just expression, dear.'

'Unpleasant young devil, I think. But she's pretty enough.'

The subject of these remarks was walking slowly by Poirot's side. Rosalie Otterbourne was twirling an unopened parasol, and her expression certainly bore out what Tim had just said. She looked both sulky and bad-tempered. Her eyebrows were drawn together in a frown, and the scarlet line of her mouth was drawn downwards.

They turned to the left out of the hotel gate and entered the cool shade of the public gardens.

Hercule Poirot was prattling gently, his expression that of beatific good humour. He wore a white silk suit, carefully pressed, and a panama hat, and carried a highly ornamental fly whisk with a sham amber handle.

'—it enchants me,' he was saying. 'The black rocks of Elephantine, and the sun, the little boats on the river. Yes, it is good to be alive.'

He paused and then added:

'You do not find it so, Mademoiselle?'

Rosalie Otterbourne said shortly:

Death on the Nile

'It's all right, I suppose. I think Aswan's a gloomy sort of place. The hotel's half empty, and everyone's about a hundred—'

She stopped—biting her lip.

Hercule Poirot's eyes twinkled.

'It is true, yes, I have one leg in the grave.'

'I—I wasn't thinking of you,' said the girl. 'I'm sorry. That sounded rude.'

'Not at all. It is natural you should wish for young companions of your own age. Ah, well, there is *one* young man, at least.'

'The one who sits with his mother all the time? I like *her*—but I think he looks dreadful—so conceited!'

Poirot smiled.

'And I—am I conceited?'

'Oh, I don't think so.'

She was obviously uninterested—but the fact did not seem to annoy Poirot. He merely remarked with placid satisfaction:

'My best friend says that I am very conceited.'

'Oh, well,' said Rosalie vaguely, 'I suppose you have something to be conceited about. Unfortunately crime doesn't interest me in the least.'

Poirot said solemnly:

'I am delighted to learn that you have no guilty secret to hide.'

Just for a moment the sulky mask of her face was transformed as she shot him a swift questioning glance. Poirot did not seem to notice it as he went on.

Agatha Christie

'Madame, your mother, was not at lunch today. She is not indisposed, I trust?'

'This place doesn't suit her,' said Rosalie briefly. 'I shall be glad when we leave.'

'We are fellow passengers, are we not? We both make the excursion up to Wadi Halfa and the Second Cataract?'

'Yes.'

They came out from the shade of the gardens on to a dusty stretch of road bordered by the river. Five watchful bead sellers, two vendors of postcards, three sellers of plaster scarabs, a couple of donkey boys and some detached but hopeful infantile riff-raff closed in upon them. 'You want beads, sir? Very good, sir. Very cheap...'

'Lady, you want scarab? Look—great queen—very lucky...'

'You look, sir—real lapis. Very good, very cheap...'

'You want ride donkey, sir? This very good donkey. This donkey Whiskey and Soda, sir...'

'You want to go granite quarries, sir? This very good donkey. Other donkey very bad, sir, that donkey fall down...'

'You want postcard—very cheap—very nice...'

'Look, lady... Only ten piastres—very cheap—lapis—this ivory...'

'This very good fly whisk—this all amber...'

'You go out in boat, sir? I got very good boat, sir...'

'You ride back to hotel, lady? This first-class donkey...'

Hercule Poirot made vague gestures to rid himself of this human cluster of flies. Rosalie stalked through them like a sleep walker.

'It's best to pretend to be deaf and blind,' she remarked.

The infantile riff-raff ran alongside murmuring plaintively: 'Bakshish? Bakshish? Hip hip hurrah—very good, very nice...'

Their gaily coloured rags trailed picturesquely, and the flies lay in clusters on their eyelids.

They were the most persistent. The others fell back and launched a fresh attack on the next corner. Now Poirot and Rosalie only ran the gauntlet of the shops—suave, persuasive accents here...

'You visit my shop today, sir?' 'You want that ivory crocodile, sir?' 'You not been in my shop yet, sir? I show you very beautiful things.'

They turned into the fifth shop and Rosalie handed over several rolls of film—the object of the walk.

Then they came out again and walked towards the river's edge.

One of the Nile steamers was just mooring. Poirot and Rosalie looked interestedly at the passengers.

'Quite a lot, aren't there?' commented Rosalie.

She turned her head as Tim Allerton came up and joined them. He was a little out of breath as though he had been walking fast.

They stood there for a moment or two, and then Tim spoke.

'An awful crowd as usual, I suppose,' he remarked disparagingly, indicating the disembarking passengers.

'They're usually quite terrible,' agreed Rosalie.

All three wore the air of superiority assumed by people who are already in a place when studying new arrivals.

'Hallo!' exclaimed Tim, his voice suddenly excited. 'I'm damned if that isn't Linnet Ridgeway.'

If the information left Poirot unmoved, it stirred Rosalie's interest. She leaned forward and her sulkiness quite dropped from her as she asked:

'Where? That one in white?'

'Yes, there with the tall man. They're coming ashore now. He's the new husband, I suppose. Can't remember her name now.'

'Doyle,' said Rosalie. 'Simon Doyle. It was in all the newspapers. She's simply rolling, isn't she?'

'Only about the richest girl in England,' said Tim cheerfully.

The three lookers-on were silent watching the passengers come ashore. Poirot gazed with interest at the subject of the remarks of his companions. He murmured:

'She is beautiful.'

'Some people have got everything,' said Rosalie bitterly.

There was a queer grudging expression on her face as she watched the other girl come up the gangplank.

Linnet Doyle was looking as perfectly turned out as if she were stepping on to the centre of the stage in a revue. She had something too of the assurance of a famous actress. She was used to being looked at, to being admired, to being the centre of the stage wherever she went.

She was aware of the keen glances bent upon her—and at the same time almost unaware of them; such tributes were part of her life.

She came ashore playing a role, even though she played

Death on the Nile

it unconsciously. The rich, beautiful society bride on her honeymoon. She turned, with a little smile and a light remark, to the tall man by her side. He answered, and the sound of his voice seemed to interest Hercule Poirot. His eyes lit up and he drew his brows together.

The couple passed close to him. He heard Simon Doyle say:

'We'll try and make time for it, darling. We can easily stay a week or two if you like it here.'

His face was turned towards her, eager, adoring, a little humble.

Poirot's eyes ran over him thoughtfully—the square shoulders, the bronzed face, the dark blue eyes, the rather childlike simplicity of the smile.

'Lucky devil,' said Tim after they had passed. 'Fancy finding an heiress who hasn't got adenoids and flat feet!'

'They look frightfully happy,' said Rosalie with a note of envy in her voice. She said suddenly, but so low that Tim did not catch the words: 'It isn't fair.'

Poirot heard, however. He had been frowning somewhat perplexedly, but now he flashed a quick glance towards her.

Tim said:

'I must collect some stuff for my mother now.'

He raised his hat and moved off. Poirot and Rosalie retraced their steps slowly in the direction of the hotel, waving aside fresh proffers of donkeys.

'So it is not fair, Mademoiselle?' asked Poirot gently.

The girl flushed angrily.

'I don't know what you mean.'

'I am repeating what you said just now under your breath. Oh, yes, you did.'

Rosalie Otterbourne shrugged her shoulders.

'It really seems a little too much for one person. Money, good looks, marvellous figure and—'

She paused and Poirot said:

'And love? Eh? And love? But you do not know—she may have been married for her money!'

'Didn't you see the way he looked at her?'

'Oh, yes, Mademoiselle. I saw all there was to see—indeed I saw something that you did not.'

'What was that?'

Poirot said slowly: 'I saw, Mademoiselle, dark lines below a woman's eyes. I saw a hand that clutched a sunshade so tight that the knuckles were white…'

Rosalie was staring at him.

'What do you mean?'

'I mean that all is not the gold that glitters—I mean that though this lady is rich and beautiful and beloved, there is all the same *something* that is not right. And I know something else.'

'Yes?'

'I know,' said Poirot, frowning, 'that somewhere, at some time, *I have heard that voice before*—the voice of Monsieur Doyle—and I wish I could remember where.'

But Rosalie was not listening. She had stopped dead. With the point of her sunshade she was tracing patterns in the loose sand. Suddenly she broke out fiercely:

'I'm odious. I'm quite odious. I'm just a beast through

and through. I'd like to tear the clothes off her back and stamp on her lovely, arrogant, self-confident face. I'm just a jealous cat—but that's what I feel like. She's so horribly successful and poised and assured.'

Hercule Poirot looked a little astonished by the outburst. He took her by the arm and gave her a friendly little shake.

'*Tenez*—you will feel better for having said that!'

'I just hate her! I've never hated anyone so much at first sight.'

'Magnificent!'

Rosalie looked at him doubtfully. Then her mouth twitched and she laughed.

'*Bien*,' said Poirot, and laughed too.

They proceeded amicably back to the hotel.

'I must find Mother,' said Rosalie, as they came into the cool dim hall.

Poirot passed out on the other side on to the terrace overlooking the Nile. Here were little tables set for tea, but it was early still. He stood for a few moments looking down on to the river, then strolled down through the gardens.

Some people were playing tennis in the hot sun. He paused to watch them for a while, then went on down the steep path. It was there, sitting on a bench overlooking the Nile, that he came upon the girl of Chez Ma Tante. He recognized her at once. Her face, as he had seen it that night, was securely etched upon his memory. The expression on it now was very different. She was paler, thinner, and there were lines that told of a great weariness and misery of spirit.

He drew back a little. She had not seen him, and he watched her for a while without her suspecting his presence. Her small foot tapped impatiently on the ground. Her eyes, dark with a kind of smouldering fire, had a queer kind of suffering dark triumph in them. She was looking out across the Nile where the white-sailed boats glided up and down the river.

A face—and a voice. He remembered them both. This girl's face and the voice he had heard just now, the voice of a newly made bridegroom...

And even as he stood there considering the unconscious girl, the next scene in the drama was played.

Voices sounded above. The girl on the seat started to her feet. Linnet Doyle and her husband came down the path. Linnet's voice was happy and confident. The look of strain and tenseness of muscle had quite disappeared, Linnet was happy.

The girl who was standing there took a step or two forward.

The other two stopped dead.

'Hallo, Linnet,' said Jacqueline de Bellefort. 'So here you are! We never seem to stop running into each other. Hallo, Simon, how are you?'

Linnet Doyle had shrunk back against the rock with a little cry. Simon Doyle's good-looking face was suddenly convulsed with rage. He moved forward as though he would have liked to strike the slim girlish figure.

With a quick birdlike turn of her head she signalled her realization of a stranger's presence. Simon turned his head and noticed Poirot.

He said awkwardly:
'Hullo, Jacqueline; we didn't expect to see you here.'
The words were unconvincing in the extreme.
The girl flashed white teeth at them.
'Quite a surprise?' she asked.
Then, with a little nod, she walked up the path.
Poirot moved delicately in the opposite direction.
As he went, he heard Linnet Doyle say:
'Simon—for God's sake—Simon—what can we do?'

CHAPTER 2

Dinner was over.

The terrace outside the Cataract Hotel was softly lit. Most of the guests staying at the hotel were there sitting at little tables.

Simon and Linnet Doyle came out, a tall distinguished looking grey-haired man with a keen clean-shaven American face beside them. As the little group hesitated for a moment in the doorway, Tim Allerton rose from his chair nearby and came forward.

'You don't remember me, I'm sure,' he said pleasantly to Linnet, 'but I'm Joanna Southwood's cousin.'

'Of course—how stupid of me. You're Tim Allerton. This is my husband'—a faint tremor in the voice, pride, shyness?—'and this is my American trustee, Mr Pennington.'

Tim said:

'You must meet my mother.'

A few minutes later they were sitting together in a party— Linnet in the corner, Tim and Pennington each side of her, both talking to her, vying for her attention. Mrs Allerton talked to Simon Doyle.

The swing doors revolved. A sudden tension came into the beautiful upright figure sitting in the corner between the two men. Then it relaxed as a small man came out and walked across the terrace.

Mrs Allerton said:

'You're not the only celebrity here, my dear. That funny little man is Hercule Poirot.'

She had spoken lightly, just out of instinctive social tact to bridge an awkward pause, but Linnet seemed struck by the information.

'Hercule Poirot? Of course—I've heard of him…'

She seemed to sink into a fit of abstraction. The two men on either side of her were momentarily at a loss.

Poirot had strolled across to the edge of the terrace, but his attention was immediately solicited.

'Sit down, Monsieur Poirot. What a lovely night!'

He obeyed.

'*Mais oui, Madame*, it is indeed beautiful.'

He smiled politely at Mrs Otterbourne. What draperies of black ninon and that ridiculous turban effect!

Mrs Otterbourne went on in her high complaining voice:

'Quite a lot of notabilities here now, aren't there? I expect we shall see a paragraph about it in the papers soon. Society beauties, famous novelists—'

She paused with a slight mock-modest laugh.

Poirot felt, rather than saw, the sulky frowning girl

opposite him flinch and set her mouth in a sulkier line than before.

'You have a novel on the way at present, Madame?' he inquired.

Mrs Otterbourne gave her little self-conscious laugh again.

'I'm being dreadfully lazy. I really must set to. My public is getting terribly impatient—and my publisher, poor man! Appeals by every post! Even cables!'

Again he felt the girl shift in the darkness.

'I don't mind telling you, Monsieur Poirot, I am partly here for local colour. *Snow on the Desert's Face*—that is the title of my new book. Powerful—suggestive. Snow—on the desert—melted in the first flaming breath of passion.'

Rosalie got up, muttering something, and moved away down into the dark garden.

'One must be strong,' went on Mrs Otterbourne, wagging the turban emphatically. 'Strong meat—that is what my books are. Libraries may ban them—no matter! I speak the truth. Sex—ah! Monsieur Poirot—why is everyone so afraid of sex? The pivot of the universe! You have read my books?'

'Alas, Madame! You comprehend, I do not read many novels. My work—'

Mrs Otterbourne said firmly:

'I must give you a copy of *Under the Fig Tree*. I think you will find it significant. It is outspoken—but it is *real*!'

'That is most kind of you, Madame. I will read it with pleasure.'

Mrs Otterbourne was silent a minute or two. She fidgeted

with a long chain of beads that was wound twice round her neck. She looked swiftly from side to side.

'Perhaps—I'll just slip up and get it for you now.'

'Oh, Madame, pray do not trouble yourself. Later—'

'No, no. It's no trouble.' She rose. 'I'd like to show you—'

'What is it, Mother?'

Rosalie was suddenly at her side.

'Nothing, dear. I was just going up to get a book for Monsieur Poirot.'

'The *Fig Tree*? I'll get it.'

'You don't know where it is, dear. I'll go.'

'Yes, I do.'

The girl went swiftly across the terrace and into the hotel.

'Let me congratulate you, Madame, on a very lovely daughter,' said Poirot, with a bow.

'Rosalie? Yes, yes—she is good looking. But she's very *hard*, Monsieur Poirot. And no sympathy with illness. She always thinks she knows best. She imagines she knows more about my health than I do myself—'

Poirot signalled to a passing waiter.

'A liqueur, Madame? A chartreuse? A créme de menthe?'

Mrs Otterbourne shook her head vigorously.

'No, no. I am practically a teetotaller. You may have noticed I never drink anything but water—or perhaps lemonade. I cannot bear the taste of spirits.'

'Then may I order you a lemon squash, Madame?'

He gave the order—one lemon squash and one benedictine.

Agatha Christie

The swing door revolved. Rosalie passed through and came towards them, a book in her hand.

'Here you are,' she said. Her voice was quite expressionless—almost remarkably so.

'Monsieur Poirot has just ordered me a lemon squash,' said her mother.

'And you, Mademoiselle, what will you take?'

'Nothing.' She added, suddenly conscious of the curtness: 'Nothing, thank you.'

Poirot took the volume which Mrs Otterbourne held out to him. It still bore its original jacket, a gaily coloured affair representing a lady with smartly shingled hair and scarlet fingernails sitting on a tiger skin in the traditional costume of Eve. Above her was a tree with the leaves of an oak, bearing large and improbably coloured apples.

It was entitled *Under the Fig Tree*, by Salome Otterbourne. On the inside was a publisher's blurb. It spoke enthusiastically of the superb courage and realism of this study of a modern woman's love life. Fearless, unconventional, realistic were the adjectives used.

Poirot bowed and murmured:

'I am honoured, Madame.'

As he raised his head, his eyes met those of the authoress's daughter. Almost involuntarily he made a little movement. He was astonished and grieved at the eloquent pain they revealed.

It was at that moment that the drinks arrived and created a welcome diversion.

Poirot lifted his glass gallantly.

'*A votre santé, Madame—Mademoiselle.*'

Mrs Otterbourne, sipping her lemonade, murmured: 'So refreshing—delicious.'

Silence fell on the three of them. They looked down to the shining black rocks in the Nile. There was something fantastic about them in the moonlight. They were like vast prehistoric monsters lying half out of the water. A little breeze came up suddenly and as suddenly died away.

There was a feeling in the air of hush—of expectancy.

Hercule Poirot brought his gaze to the terrace and its occupants. Was he wrong, or was there the same hush of expectancy there? It was like a moment on the stage when one is waiting for the entrance of the leading lady.

And just at that moment the swing doors began to revolve once more. This time it seemed as though they did so with a special air of importance. Everyone had stopped talking and was looking towards them.

A dark slender girl in a wine-coloured evening frock came through. She paused for a minute, then walked deliberately across the terrace and sat down at an empty table. There was nothing flaunting, nothing out of the way about her demeanour, and yet it had somehow the studied effect of a stage entrance.

'Well,' said Mrs Otterbourne. She tossed her turbaned head. 'She seems to think she is somebody, that girl!'

Poirot did not answer. He was watching. The girl had sat down in a place where she could look deliberately across at Linnet Doyle. Presently, Poirot noticed, Linnet Doyle leant forward and said something and a moment later got up and changed her seat. She was now sitting facing in the opposite direction.

Poirot nodded thoughtfully to himself.

It was about five minutes later that the other girl changed her seat to the opposite side of the terrace. She sat smoking and smiling quietly, the picture of contented ease. But always, as though unconsciously, her meditative gaze was on Simon Doyle's wife.

After a quarter of an hour Linnet Doyle got up abruptly and went into the hotel. Her husband followed her almost immediately.

Jacqueline de Bellefort smiled and twisted her chair round. She lit a cigarette and stared out over the Nile. She went on smiling to herself.

CHAPTER 3

'Monsieur Poirot.'

Poirot got hastily to his feet. He had remained sitting out on the terrace alone after everyone else had left. Lost in meditation, he had been staring at the smooth shiny black rocks when the sound of his name recalled him to himself.

It was a well-bred, assured voice, a charming voice, although perhaps a trifle arrogant.

Hercule Poirot, rising quickly, looked into the commanding eyes of Linnet Doyle.

She wore a wrap of rich purple velvet over her white satin gown and she looked more lovely and more regal than Poirot had imagined possible.

'You are Monsieur Hercule Poirot?' said Linnet.

It was hardly a question.

'At your service, Madame.'

'You know who I am, perhaps?'

'Yes, Madame. I have heard your name. I know exactly who you are.'

Agatha Christie

Linnet nodded. That was only what she had expected. She went on, in her charming autocratic manner: 'Will you come with me into the card room, Monsieur Poirot? I am very anxious to speak to you.'

'Certainly, Madame.'

She led the way into the hotel. He followed. She led him into the deserted card room and motioned him to close the door. Then she sank down on a chair at one of the tables and he sat down opposite her.

She plunged straightaway into what she wanted to say. There were no hesitations. Her speech came flowingly.

'I have heard a great deal about you, Monsieur Poirot, and I know that you are a very clever man. It happens that I am urgently in need of someone to help me—and I think very possibly that you are the man who could do it.'

Poirot inclined his head.

'You are very amiable, Madame. But you see, I am on holiday, and when I am on holiday I do not take cases.'

'That could be arranged.'

It was not offensively said—only with the quiet confidence of a young woman who had always been able to arrange matters to her satisfaction.

Linnet Doyle went on:

'I am the subject, Monsieur Poirot, of an intolerable persecution. That persecution has got to stop! My own idea was to go to the police about it, but my—my husband seems to think that the police would be powerless to do anything.'

Death on the Nile

'Perhaps—if you would explain a little further?' murmured Poirot politely.

'Oh, yes, I will do so. The matter is perfectly simple.'

There was still no hesitation—no faltering. Linnet Doyle had a clear-cut businesslike mind. She only paused a minute so as to present the facts as concisely as possible.

'Before I met my husband, he was engaged to a Miss de Bellefort. She was also a friend of mine. My husband broke off his engagement to her—they were not suited in any way. She, I am sorry to say, took it rather hard... I—am very sorry about that—but these things cannot be helped. She made certain—well, threats—to which I paid very little attention, and which, I may say, she has not attempted to carry out. But instead she has adopted the extraordinary course of—of following us about wherever we go.'

Poirot raised his eyebrows.

'Ah—rather an unusual—er—revenge.'

'Very unusual—and very ridiculous! But also—annoying.'

She bit her lip.

Poirot nodded.

'Yes, I can imagine that. You are, I understand, on your honeymoon?'

'Yes. It happened—the first time—at Venice. She was there—at Danielli's. I thought it was just coincidence. Rather embarrassing, but that was all. Then we found her on board the boat at Brindisi. We—we understood that she was going on to Palestine. We left her, as we thought, on the boat.

Agatha Christie

But—but when we got to Mena House she was there—waiting for us.'

Poirot nodded.

'And now?'

'We came up the Nile by boat. I—I was half expecting to find her on board. When she wasn't there I thought she had stopped being so—so childish. But when we got here—she—she was here—waiting.'

Poirot eyed her keenly for a moment. She was still perfectly composed, but the knuckles of the hand that was gripping the table were white with the force of her grip.

He said:

'And you are afraid this state of things may continue?'

'Yes.' She paused. 'Of course the whole thing is idiotic! Jacqueline is making herself utterly ridiculous. I am surprised she hasn't got more pride—more dignity.'

Poirot made a slight gesture.

'There are times, Madame, when pride and dignity—they go by the board! There are other—stronger emotions.'

'Yes, possibly.' Linnet spoke impatiently. 'But what on earth can she hope to *gain* by all this?'

'It is not always a question of gain, Madame.'

Something in his tone struck Linnet disagreeably. She flushed and said quickly:

'You are right. A discussion of motives is beside the point. The crux of the matter is that this has got to be stopped.'

'And how do you propose that that should be accomplished, Madame?' Poirot asked.

'Well—naturally—my husband and I cannot continue being subjected to this annoyance. There must be some kind of legal redress against such a thing.'

She spoke impatiently. Poirot looked at her thoughtfully as he asked:

'Has she threatened you in actual words in public? Used insulting language? Attempted any bodily harm?'

'No.'

'Then, frankly, Madame, *I do not see what you can do.* If it is a young lady's pleasure to travel in certain places, and those places are the same where you and your husband find yourselves—*eh bien*—what of it? The air is free to all! There is no question of her forcing herself upon your privacy? It is always in public that these encounters take place?'

'You mean there is nothing that I can do about it?'

Linnet sounded incredulous.

Poirot said placidly:

'Nothing at all, as far as I can see. Mademoiselle de Bellefort is within her rights.'

'But—but it is maddening! It is *intolerable* that I should have to put up with this!'

Poirot said dryly:

'I must sympathize with you, Madame—especially as I imagine that you have not often had to put up with things.'

Linnet was frowning.

'There *must* be some way of stopping it,' she murmured.

Poirot shrugged his shoulders.

'You can always leave—move on somewhere else,' he suggested.

Agatha Christie

'Then she will follow!'

'Very possibly—yes.'

'It's absurd!'

'Precisely.'

'Anyway, why should I—we—run away? As though—as though—'

She stopped.

'Exactly, Madame. As though—! It is all there, is it not?'

Linnet lifted her head and stared at him.

'What do you mean?'

Poirot altered his tone. He leant forward; his voice was confidential, appealing. He said very gently:

'*Why do you mind so much, Madame?*'

'Why? But it's maddening! Irritating to the last degree! I've told you why!'

Poirot shook his head.

'Not altogether.'

Linnet said again: 'What do you mean?'

Poirot leant back, folded his arms and spoke in a detached impersonal manner.

'*Ecoutez*, Madame. I will recount to you a little history. It is that one day, a month or two ago, I am dining in a restaurant in London. At the table next to me are two people, a man and a girl. They are very happy, so it seems, very much in love. They talk with confidence of the future. It is not that I listen to what is not meant for me—they are quite oblivious of who hears them and who does not. The man's back is to me, but I can watch the girl's face. It is very intense. She is in love—heart, soul, and body—and she is not of those who love lightly and often. With her it is clearly the life and the death. They are engaged to be married, these two; that is what I gather; and they talk of where they shall pass the days of their honeymoon. They plan to go to Egypt.'

He paused. Linnet said sharply:

'Well?'

Poirot went on.

'That is a month or two ago, but the girl's face—I do not forget it. I know that I shall remember if I see it again. And I remember too the man's voice. And I think you can guess, Madame, when it is I see the one and hear the other again. It is here in Egypt. The man is on his honeymoon, yes—but he is on his honeymoon *with another woman.*'

Linnet said sharply:

'What of it? I had already mentioned the facts.'

'The facts—yes.'

'Well then?'

Poirot said slowly:

'The girl in the restaurant mentioned a friend—a friend who she was very positive would not let her down. That friend, I think, was you, Madame.'

'Yes. I told you we had been friends.'

Linnet flushed.

'And she trusted you?'

'Yes.'

She hesitated for a moment, biting her lip impatiently;

then, as Poirot did not seem disposed to speak, she broke out:

'Of course the whole thing was very unfortunate. But these things happen, Monsieur Poirot.'

'Ah! yes, they happen, Madame.' He paused. 'You are of the Church of England, I presume?'

'Yes.' Linnet looked slightly bewildered.

'Then you have heard portions of the Bible read aloud in church. You have heard of King David and of the rich man who had many flocks and herds and the poor man who had one ewe lamb—and of how the rich man took the poor man's one ewe lamb. That was something that happened, Madame.'

Linnet sat up. Her eyes flashed angrily.

'I see perfectly what you are driving at, Monsieur Poirot! You think, to put it vulgarly, that I stole my friend's young man. Looking at the matter sentimentally—which is, I suppose, the way people of your generation cannot help looking at things—that is possibly true. But the real hard truth is different. I don't deny that Jackie was passionately in love with Simon, but I don't think you take into account that he may not have been equally devoted to her. He was very fond of her, but I think that even before he met me he was beginning to feel that he had made a mistake. Look at it clearly, Monsieur Poirot. Simon discovers that it is I he loves, not Jackie. What is he to do? Be heroically noble and marry a woman he does not care for—and thereby probably ruin three lives—for it is doubtful whether he could make Jackie happy under those circumstances? If he were actually married to her when he met me I agree that it *might* be his duty to stick to her—though I'm not really sure of that. If one person is unhappy the other suffers too. But an engagement is not really binding. If a mistake has been made, then surely it is better to face the fact before it is too late. I admit that it was very hard on Jackie, and I'm very sorry about it—but there it is. It was inevitable.'

'I wonder.'

She stared at him.

'What do you mean?'

'It is very sensible, very logical—all that you say! But it does not explain one thing.'

'What is that?'

'Your own attitude, Madame. See you, this pursuit of you, you might take it in two ways. It might cause you annoyance—yes, or it might stir your pity—that your friend should have been so deeply hurt as to throw all regard for the conventions aside. But that is not the way you react. No, to you this persecution is *intolerable*—and why? It can be for one reason only—*that you feel a sense of guilt.*'

Linnet sprang to her feet.

'How dare you? Really, Monsieur Poirot, this is going too far.'

'But I do dare, Madame! I am going to speak to you quite frankly. I suggest to you that, although you may have endeavoured to gloss over the fact to yourself, *you did deliberately set about taking your husband from your friend.*

Agatha Christie

I suggest that you felt strongly attracted to him at once. But I suggest that there was a moment when you hesitated, when you realized that there was a *choice*—that you could refrain or go on. I suggest that the initiative rested with *you*—not with Monsieur Doyle. You are beautiful, Madame, you are rich, you are clever, intelligent—and you have charm. You could have exercised that charm or you could have restrained it. You had everything, Madame, that life can offer. Your friend's life was bound up in one person. You knew that—but though you hesitated, you did not hold your hand. You stretched it out and, like King David, you took the poor man's one ewe lamb.'

There was a silence. Linnet controlled herself with an effort and said in a cold voice:

'All this is quite beside the point!'

'No, it is not beside the point. I am explaining to you just why the unexpected appearances of Mademoiselle de Bellefort have upset you so much. It is because though she may be unwomanly and undignified in what she is doing, you have the inner conviction that she has right on her side.'

'That's not true.'

Poirot shrugged his shoulders.

'You refuse to be honest with yourself.'

'Not at all.'

Poirot said gently:

'I should say, Madame, that you have had a happy life, that you have been generous and kindly in your attitude towards others.'

'I have tried to be,' said Linnet.

The impatient anger died out of her face. She spoke simply—almost forlornly.

'And that is why the feeling that you have deliberately caused injury to someone upsets you so much, and why you are so reluctant to admit the fact. Pardon me if I have been impertinent, but the psychology, it is the most important factor in a case.'

Linnet said slowly: 'Even supposing what you say were true—and I don't admit it, mind—what can be done about it now? One can't alter the past; one must deal with things as they are.'

Poirot nodded.

'You have the clear brain. Yes, one cannot go back over the past. One must accept things as they are. And sometimes, Madame, that is all one can do—accept the consequences of one's past deeds.'

'You mean,' said Linnet incredulously, 'that I can do nothing—*nothing*?'

'You must have courage, Madame; that is what it seems like to me.'

Linnet said slowly:

'Couldn't you—talk to Jackie—to Miss de Bellefort? Reason with her?'

'Yes, I could do that. I will do that if you would like me to do so. But do not expect much result. I fancy that Mademoiselle de Bellefort is so much in the grip of a fixed idea that nothing will turn her from it.'

'But surely we can do *something* to extricate ourselves?'

Agatha Christie

'You could, of course, return to England and establish yourselves in your own house.'

'Even then, I suppose, Jacqueline is capable of planting herself in the village, so that I should see her every time I went out of the grounds.'

'True.'

'Besides,' said Linnet slowly, 'I don't think that Simon would agree to run away.'

'What is his attitude in this?'

'He's furious—simply furious.'

Poirot nodded thoughtfully.

Linnet said appealingly:

'You will—talk to her?'

'Yes, I will do that. But it is my opinion that I shall not be able to accomplish anything.'

Linnet said violently: 'Jackie is extraordinary! One can't tell what she will do!'

'You spoke just now of certain threats she had made. Would you tell me what those threats were?'

Linnet shrugged her shoulders.

'She threatened to—well—kill us both. Jackie can be rather—Latin sometimes.'

'I see.' Poirot's tone was grave.

Linnet turned to him appealingly.

'You will act for me?'

'No, Madame.' His tone was firm. 'I will not accept a commission from you. I will do what I can in the interests of humanity. That, yes. There is here a situation that is full of difficulty and danger. I will do what I can to clear it up—but I am not very sanguine as to my chance of success.'

Linnet Doyle said slowly:

'But you will not act for *me*?'

'No, Madame,' said Hercule Poirot.

CHAPTER 4

Hercule Poirot found Jacqueline de Bellefort sitting on the rocks directly overlooking the Nile. He had felt fairly certain that she had not retired for the night and that he would find her somewhere about the grounds of the hotel.

She was sitting with her chin cupped in the palms of her hands, and she did not turn her head or look around at the sound of his approach.

'Mademoiselle de Bellefort?' asked Poirot. 'You permit that I speak to you for a little moment?'

Jacqueline turned her head slightly. A faint smile played round her lips.

'Certainly,' she said. 'You are Monsieur Hercule Poirot, I think? Shall I make a guess? You are acting for Mrs Doyle, who has promised you a large fee if you succeed in your mission.'

Poirot sat down on the bench near her.

'Your assumption is partially correct,' he said, smiling. 'I have just come from Madame Doyle, but I am not accepting any fee from her and, strictly speaking, I am not acting for her.'

'Oh!'

Jacqueline studied him attentively.

'Then why have you come?' she asked abruptly.

Hercule Poirot's reply was in the form of another question.

'Have you ever seen me before, Mademoiselle?'

She shook her head.

'No, I do not think so.'

'Yet I have seen you. I sat next to you once at Chez Ma Tante. You were there with Monsieur Simon Doyle.'

A strange masklike expression came over the girl's face. She said, 'I remember that evening...'

'Since then,' said Poirot, 'many things have occurred.'

'As you say, many things have occurred.'

Her voice was hard with an undertone of desperate bitterness.

'Mademoiselle, I speak as a friend. *Bury your dead!*'

She looked startled.

'What do you mean?'

'Give up the past! Turn to the future! What is done is done. Bitterness will not undo it.'

'I'm sure that that would suit dear Linnet admirably.'

Poirot made a gesture.

'I am not thinking of her at this moment! I am thinking of *you*. You have suffered—yes—but what you are doing now will only prolong that suffering.'

She shook her head.

Agatha Christie

'You're wrong. There are times when I almost enjoy myself.'

'And that, Mademoiselle, is the worst of all.'

She looked up swiftly.

'You're not stupid,' she said. She added slowly, 'I believe you mean to be kind.'

'Go home, Mademoiselle. You are young, you have brains—the world is before you.'

Jacqueline shook her head slowly.

'You don't understand—or you won't. Simon is my world.'

'Love is not everything, Mademoiselle,' Poirot said gently. 'It is only when we are young that we think it is.'

But the girl still shook her head.

'You don't understand.' She shot him a quick look. 'You know all about it, of course? You've talked to Linnet? And you were in the restaurant that night... Simon and I loved each other.'

'I know that you loved him.'

She was quick to perceive the inflection of his words. She repeated with emphasis:

'*We loved each other*. And I loved Linnet... I trusted her. She was my best friend. All her life Linnet has been able to buy everything she wanted. She's never denied herself anything. When she saw Simon she wanted him—and she just took him.'

'And he allowed himself to be—bought?'

Jacqueline shook her dark head slowly.

'No, it's not quite like that. If it were, I shouldn't be here now… You're suggesting that Simon isn't worth caring for… If he'd married Linnet for her money, that would be true. But he didn't marry her for her money. It's more complicated than that. There's such a thing as *glamour*, Monsieur Poirot. And money helps that. Linnet had an "atmosphere", you see. She was the queen of a kingdom—the young princess—luxurious to her fingertips. It was like a stage setting. She had the world at her feet, one of the richest and most sought-after peers in England wanting to marry her. And she stoops instead to the obscure Simon Doyle… Do you wonder it went to his head?' She made a sudden gesture. 'Look at the moon up there. You see her very plainly, don't you? She's very real. *But if the sun were to shine you wouldn't be able to see her at all.* It was rather like that. I was the moon… When the sun came out, Simon couldn't see me any more… He was dazzled. He couldn't see anything but the sun—Linnet.'

She paused and then she went on:

'So you see it was—glamour. She went to his head. And then there's her complete assurance—her habit of command. She's so sure of herself that she makes other people sure. Simon was—weak, perhaps, but then he's a very simple person. He would have loved me and me only if Linnet hadn't come along and snatched him up in her golden chariot. And I know—I know perfectly—that he wouldn't ever have fallen in love with her if she hadn't made him.'

'That is what you think—yes.'

'I *know* it. He loved me—he will always love me.'

Poirot said:

Agatha Christie

'Even now?'

A quick answer seemed to rise to her lips, then be stifled. She looked at Poirot and a deep burning colour spread over her face. She looked away, her head dropped down. She said in a low stifled voice:

'Yes, I know. He hates me now. Yes, hates me… He'd better be careful.'

With a quick gesture she fumbled in a little silk bag that lay on the seat. Then she held out her hand. On the palm of it was a small pearl-handled pistol—a dainty toy it looked.

'Nice little thing, isn't it? she said. 'Looks too foolish to be real, but it is real! One of those bullets would kill a man or a woman. And I'm a good shot.' She smiled a faraway, reminiscent smile. 'When I went home as a child with my mother to South Carolina, my grandfather taught me to shoot. He was the old-fashioned kind that believes in shooting—especially where honour is concerned. My father, too, he fought several duels as a young man. He was a good swordsman. He killed a man once. That was over a woman. So you see, Monsieur Poirot'—she met his eyes squarely—'I've hot blood in me! I bought this when it first happened. I meant to kill one or other of them—the trouble was I couldn't decide which. Both of them would have been unsatisfactory. If I'd thought Linnet would have looked afraid—but she's got plenty of physical courage. She can stand up to physical action. And then I thought I'd—wait! That appealed to me more and more. After all, I could do it any time; it would be more fun to wait and—think about it! And then this idea came to my mind—to follow them! Whenever they arrived at some faraway spot and were together and happy, they should see—*me*! And it worked! It got Linnet badly—in a way nothing else could have done! It got right under her skin... That was when I began to enjoy myself... And there's nothing she can do about it! I'm always perfectly pleasant and polite! There's not a word they can take hold of! It's poisoning everything—everything—for them.'

Her laugh rang out, clear and silvery.

Poirot grasped her arm.

'Be quiet. Quiet, I tell you.'

Jacqueline looked at him.

'Well?' she said.

Her smile was definitely challenging.

'Mademoiselle, I beseech you, do not do what you are doing.'

'Leave dear Linnet alone, you mean!'

'It is deeper than that. Do not open your heart to evil.'

Her lips fell apart; a look of bewilderment came into her eyes.

Poirot went on gravely:

'Because—if you do—*evil will come*... Yes, very surely evil will come... It will enter in and make its home within you, and after a little while it will no longer be possible to drive it out.'

Jacqueline stared at him. Her glance seemed to waver, to flicker uncertainly.

She said: 'I—don't know—'

Then she cried out definitely:

'You can't stop me.'

AgathaChristie

'No,' said Hercule Poirot. 'I cannot stop you.'

His voice was sad.

'Even if I were to—kill her, you couldn't stop me.'

'No—not if you were willing—to pay the price.'

Jacqueline de Bellefort laughed.

'Oh, I'm not afraid of death! What have I got to live for, after all? I suppose you believe it's very wrong to kill a person who has injured you—even if they've taken away everything you had in the world?'

Poirot said steadily:

'Yes, Mademoiselle. I believe it is the unforgivable offence—to kill.'

Jacqueline laughed again.

'Then you ought to approve of my present scheme of revenge. Because, you see, *as long as it works*, I shan't use that pistol... But I'm afraid—yes, afraid sometimes—it all goes red—I want to hurt her—to stick a knife into her, to put my dear little pistol close against her head and then—just press with my finger—*Oh!*'

The exclamation startled him.

'What is it, Mademoiselle!'

She turned her head and was staring into the shadows.

'Someone—standing over there. He's gone now.'

Hercule Poirot looked round sharply.

The place seemed quite deserted.

'There seems no one here but ourselves, Mademoiselle.'

He got up.

'In any case I have said all I came to say. I wish you good night.'

Death on the Nile

Jacqueline got up too. She said almost pleadingly:

'You do understand—that I can't do what you ask me to do?'

Poirot shook his head.

'No—for *you could do it*! There is always a moment! Your friend Linnet—there was a moment, too, in which she could have held her hand... She let it pass by. And if one does that, then one is committed to the enterprise and there comes no second chance.'

'No second chance...' said Jacqueline de Bellefort.

She stood brooding for a moment, then she lifted her head defiantly.

'Good night, Monsieur Poirot.'

He shook his head sadly and followed her up the path to the hotel.

CHAPTER 5

On the following morning Simon Doyle joined Hercule Poirot as the latter was leaving the hotel to walk down to the town.

'Good morning, Monsieur Poirot.'

'Good morning, Monsieur Doyle.'

'You going to the town? Mind if I stroll along with you?'

'But certainly. I shall be delighted.'

The two men walked side by side, passed out through the gateway and turned into the cool shade of the gardens. Then Simon removed his pipe from his mouth and said, 'I understand, Monsieur Poirot, that my wife had a talk with you last night?'

'That is so.'

Simon Doyle was frowning a little. He belonged to that type of men of action who find it difficult to put thoughts into words and who have trouble in expressing themselves clearly.

'I'm glad of one thing,' he said. 'You've made her realize that we're more or less powerless in the matter.'

'There is clearly no legal redress,' agreed Poirot.

'Exactly. Linnet didn't seem to understand that.' He gave a faint smile. 'Linnet's been brought up to believe that every annoyance can automatically be referred to the police.'

'It would be pleasant if such were the case,' said Poirot.

There was a pause. Then Simon said suddenly, his face going very red as he spoke:

'It's—it's infamous that she should be victimized like this! She's done nothing! If anyone likes to say I behaved like a cad, they're welcome to say so! I suppose I did. But I won't have the whole thing visited on Linnet. She had nothing whatever to do with it.'

Poirot bowed his head gravely but said nothing.

'Did you—er—have you—talked to Jackie—Miss de Bellefort?'

'Yes, I have spoken with her.'

'Did you get her to see sense?'

'I'm afraid not.'

Simon broke out irritably.

'Can't she see what an ass she's making of herself? Doesn't she realize that no decent woman would behave as she is doing? Hasn't she got any pride or self-respect?'

Poirot shrugged his shoulders.

'She has only a sense of—injury, shall we say?' he replied.

'Yes, but damn it all, man, decent girls don't behave like this! I admit I was entirely to blame. I treated her damned badly and all that. I should quite understand her being thoroughly fed up with me and never wishing to see me again. But this following me round—it's—it's *indecent*! Making a show of herself! What the devil does she hope to get out of it?'

'Perhaps—revenge!'

'Idiotic! I'd really understand better if she'd tried to do something melodramatic—like taking a pot shot at me.'

'You think that would be more like her—yes?'

'Frankly I do. She's hot-blooded—and she's got an ungovernable temper. I shouldn't be surprised at her doing anything while she was in a white-hot rage. But this spying business—' He shook his head.

'It is more subtle—yes! It is intelligent!'

Doyle stared at him.

'You don't understand. It's playing hell with Linnet's nerves.'

'And yours?'

Simon looked at him with momentary surprise.

'Me? I'd like to wring the little devil's neck.'

'There is nothing, then, of the old feeling left?'

'My dear Monsieur Poirot—how can I put it? It's like the moon when the sun comes out. You don't know it's there any more. When once I'd met Linnet—Jackie didn't exist.'

'*Tiens, c'est drôle, ça!*' muttered Poirot.

'I beg your pardon?'

'Your simile interested me, that is all.'

Again flushing, Simon said: 'I suppose Jackie told you

that I'd only married Linnet for her money? Well, that's a damned lie! I wouldn't marry any woman for money! What Jackie doesn't understand is that it's difficult for a fellow when—when—a woman cares for him as she cared for me.'

'Ah?'

Poirot looked up sharply.

Simon blundered on.

'It—it—sounds a caddish thing to say, but Jackie was *too* fond of me!'

'*Une qui aime et un qui se laisse aimer*,' murmured Poirot.

'Eh? What's that you say? You see, a man doesn't want to feel that a woman cares more for him than he does for her.' His voice grew warm as he went on. 'He doesn't want to feel *owned*, body and soul. It's that damned *possessive* attitude! This man is *mine*—he *belongs* to me! That's the sort of thing I can't stick—no man could stick! He wants to get away—to get free. He wants to own his woman—he doesn't want *her* to own *him*.'

He broke off, and with fingers that trembled slightly he lit a cigarette.

Poirot said:

'And it is like that that you felt with Mademoiselle Jacqueline?'

'Eh?' Simon stared and then admitted:

'Er—yes—well, yes, as a matter of fact I did. She doesn't realize that, of course. And it's not the sort of thing I could ever tell her. But I *was* feeling restless—and then I met

Linnet, and she just swept me off my feet! I'd never seen anything so lovely. It was all so amazing. Everyone kowtowing to her—and then her singling out a poor chump like me.'

His tone held boyish awe and astonishment.

'I see,' said Poirot. He nodded thoughtfully. 'Yes—I see.'

'Why can't Jackie take it like a man?' demanded Simon resentfully.

A very faint smile twitched Poirot's upper lip.

'Well, you see, Monsieur Doyle, to begin with she is *not* a man.'

'No, no—but I meant take it like a good sport! After all, you've got to take your medicine when it comes to you. The fault's mine, I admit. But there it is! If you no longer care for a girl, it's simply madness to marry her. And now that I see what Jackie's really like and the lengths she is likely to go to, I feel I've had rather a lucky escape.'

'The lengths she is likely to go to,' Poirot repeated thoughtfully. 'Have you an idea, Monsieur Doyle, what those lengths are?'

Simon looked at him rather startled.

'No—at least, what do you mean?'

'You know she carries a pistol about with her?'

Simon frowned, then shook his head.

'I don't believe she'll use that—now. She might have done so earlier. But I believe it's got past that. She's just spiteful now—trying to take it out of us both.'

Poirot shrugged his shoulders.

'It may be so,' he said doubtfully.

Death on the Nile

'It's Linnet I'm worrying about,' said Simon somewhat unnecessarily.

'I quite realize that,' said Poirot.

'I'm not really afraid of Jackie doing any melodramatic shooting stuff, but this spying and following business has absolutely got Linnet on the raw. I'll tell you the plan I've made, and perhaps you can suggest improvements on it. To begin with, I've announced fairly openly that we're going to stay here ten days. But tomorrow—the steamer *Karnak* starts from Shellal to Wadi Halfa. I propose to book passages on that under an assumed name. Tomorrow we'll go on an excursion to Philae. Linnet's maid can take the luggage. We'll join the *Karnak* at Shellal. When Jackie finds we don't come back, it will be too late—we shall be well on our way. She'll assume we have given her the slip and gone back to Cairo. In fact I might even bribe the porter to say so. Enquiry at the tourist offices won't help her, because our names won't appear. How does that strike you?'

'It is well imagined, yes. And suppose she waits here till you return?'

'We may not return. We would go on to Khartoum and then perhaps by air to Kenya. She can't follow us all over the globe.'

'No, there must come a time when financial reasons forbid. She has very little money, I understand.'

Simon looked at him with admiration.

'That's clever of you. Do you know, I hadn't thought of that. Jackie's as poor as they make them.'

'And yet she has managed to follow you so far?'

Simon said doubtfully:

'She's got a small income, of course. Something under two hundred a year, I imagine. I suppose—yes, I suppose she must have sold out the capital to do what she's doing.'

'So that the time will come when she has exhausted her resources and is quite penniless?'

'Yes...'

Simon wriggled uneasily. The thought seemed to make him uncomfortable. Poirot watched him attentively.

'No,' he remarked. 'No, it is not a pretty thought...'

Simon said rather angrily:

'Well, *I* can't help it!' Then he added, 'What do you think of my plan?'

'I think it may work, yes. But it is, of course, a *retreat.*'

Simon flushed.

'You mean, we're running away? Yes, that's true... But Linnet—'

Poirot watched him, then gave a short nod.

'As you say, it may be the best way. But remember, Mademoiselle de Bellefort has brains.'

Simon said sombrely:

'Some day, I feel, we've got to make a stand and fight it out. Her attitude isn't reasonable.'

'Reasonable, *mon Dieu*!' cried Poirot.

'There's no reason why women shouldn't behave like rational beings,' said Simon stolidly.

Poirot said dryly:

'Quite frequently they do. That is even more upsetting!'

Death on the Nile

He added, 'I, too, shall be on the *Karnak*. It is part of my itinerary.'

'Oh!' Simon hesitated, then said, choosing his words with some embarrassment: 'That isn't—isn't—er—on our account in any way? I mean I wouldn't like to think—'

Poirot disabused him quickly.

'Not at all. It was all arranged before I left London. I always make my plans well in advance.'

'You don't just move on from place to place as the fancy takes you? Isn't the latter really pleasanter?'

'Perhaps. But to succeed in life every detail should be arranged well beforehand.'

Simon laughed and said:

'That is how the more skilful murderer behaves, I suppose.'

'Yes—though I must admit that the most brilliant crime I remember and one of the most difficult to solve was committed on the spur of the moment.'

Simon said boyishly:

'You must tell us something about your cases on board the *Karnak*.'

'No, no; that would be to talk—what do you call it?—the shop.'

'Yes, but your kind of shop is rather thrilling. Mrs Allerton thinks so. She's longing to get a chance to cross-question you.'

'Mrs Allerton? That is the charming grey-haired woman who has such a devoted son?'

'Yes. She'll be on the *Karnak* too.'

'Does she know that you—?'

'Certainly not,' said Simon with emphasis. 'Nobody knows. I've gone on the principle that it's better not to trust anybody.'

'An admirable sentiment—and one which I always adopt. By the way, the third member of your party, the tall grey-haired man—'

'Pennington?'

'Yes. He is travelling with you?'

Simon said grimly: 'Not very usual on a honeymoon, you were thinking? Pennington is Linnet's American trustee. We ran across him by chance in Cairo.'

'*Ah, vraiment*! You permit a question? She is of age, Madame your wife?'

Simon looked amused.

'She isn't actually twenty-one yet—but she hadn't got to ask anyone's consent before marrying me. It was the greatest surprise to Pennington. He left New York on the *Carmanic* two days before Linnet's letter got there telling him of our marriage. So he knew nothing about it.'

'The *Carmanic*—' murmured Poirot.

'It was the greatest surprise to him when we ran into him at Shepheard's in Cairo.'

'That was indeed the coincidence!'

'Yes, and we found that he was coming on this Nile trip—so naturally we foregathered—couldn't have done anything else decently. Besides that, it's been—well, a relief in some ways.' He looked embarrassed again. 'You see, Linnet's been all strung up—expecting Jackie to turn up anywhere and everywhere. While we were alone together, the subject kept coming up. Andrew Pennington's a help that way—we have to talk of outside matters.'

'Your wife has not confided in Mr Pennington?'

'No.' Simon's jaw looked aggressive. 'It's nothing to do with anyone else. Besides, when we started on this Nile trip we thought we'd seen the end of the business.'

Poirot shook his head.

'You have not seen the end of it yet. No—the end is not yet at hand. I am very sure of that.'

'I must say, Monsieur Poirot, you're not very encouraging.'

Poirot looked at him with a slight feeling of irritation. He thought to himself: 'The Anglo-Saxon, he takes nothing seriously but playing games! He does not grow up.'

Linnet Doyle—Jacqueline de Bellefort—both of them took the business seriously enough. But in Simon's attitude he could find nothing but male impatience and annoyance.

He said:

'You will permit me an impertinent question? Was it *your* idea to come to Egypt for your honeymoon?'

Simon flushed.

'No, of course not. As a matter of fact I'd rather have gone anywhere else. But Linnet was absolutely set upon it. And so—and so—'

He stopped rather lamely.

'Naturally,' said Poirot gravely.

He appreciated the fact that if Linnet Doyle was set upon anything, that thing had to happen.

Agatha Christie

He thought to himself: 'I have now heard three separate accounts of the affair—Linnet Doyle's, Jacqueline de Bellefort's, Simon Doyle's. Which of them is nearest to the truth?'

CHAPTER 6

Simon and Linnet Doyle set off on their expedition to Philae about eleven o'clock the following morning. Jacqueline de Bellefort, sitting on the hotel balcony, watched them set off in the picturesque sailing boat. What she did not see was the departure of a car—laden with luggage, and in which sat a demure-looking maid—from the front door of the hotel. It turned to the right in the direction of Shellal.

Hercule Poirot decided to pass the remaining two hours before lunch on the island of Elephantine, immediately opposite the hotel.

He went down to the landing-stage. There were two men just stepping into one of the hotel boats, and Poirot joined them. The men were obviously strangers to each other. The younger of them had arrived by train the day before. He was a tall, dark-haired young man, with a thin face and a pugnacious chin. He was wearing an extremely dirty pair of grey flannel trousers and a high-necked polo jumper singularly unsuited to the climate. The other was a slightly podgy middle-aged man who lost no time in entering into conversation with Poirot in idiomatic but slightly broken English. Far from taking part in the conversation, the younger man merely scowled at them both and then deliberately turned his back on them and proceeded to admire the agility with which the Nubian boatman steered the boat with his toes as he manipulated the sail with his hands.

It was very peaceful on the water, the great smooth slippery black rocks gliding by and the soft breeze fanning their faces. Elephantine was reached very quickly and on going ashore Poirot and his loquacious acquaintance made straight for the museum. By this time the latter had produced a card which he handed to Poirot with a little bow. It bore the inscription:

'Signor Guido Richetti, Archeologo.'

Not to be outdone, Poirot returned the bow and extracted his own card. These formalities completed, the two men stepped into the Museum together, the Italian pouring forth a stream of erudite information. They were by now conversing in French.

The young man in the flannel trousers strolled listlessly round the Museum, yawning from time to time, and then escaped to the outer air.

Poirot and Signor Richetti at last found him. The Italian was energetic in examining the ruins, but presently Poirot, espying a green-lined sunshade which he recognized on the rocks down by the river, escaped in that direction.

Mrs Allerton was sitting on a large rock, a sketchbook by her side and a book on her lap.

Poirot removed his hat politely and Mrs Allerton at once entered into conversation.

'Good morning,' she said. 'I suppose it would be quite impossible to get rid of some of these awful children.'

A group of small black figures surrounded her, all grinning and posturing and holding out imploring hands as they lisped 'Bakshish' at intervals hopefully.

'I thought they'd get tired of me,' said Mrs Allerton sadly. 'They've been watching me for over two hours now—and they close in on me little by little; and then I yell "Imshi" and brandish my sunshade at them and they scatter for a minute or two. And then they come back and stare and stare, and their eyes are simply disgusting, and so are their noses, and I don't believe I really like children—not unless they're more or less washed and have the rudiments of manners.'

She laughed ruefully.

Poirot gallantly attempted to disperse the mob for her, but without avail. They scattered and then reappeared, closing in once more.

'If there were only any peace in Egypt, I should like it better,' said Mrs Allerton. 'But you can never be alone anywhere—someone is always pestering you for money, or offering you donkeys, or beads, or expeditions to native villages, or duck shooting.'

'It is the great disadvantage, that is true,' said Poirot.

He spread his handkerchief cautiously on the rock and sat somewhat gingerly upon it.

'Your son is not with you this morning?' he went on.

'No, Tim had some letters to get off before we leave. We're doing the trip to the Second Cataract, you know.'

'I, too.'

'I'm so glad. I want to tell you that I'm quite thrilled to meet you. When we were in Majorca, there was a Mrs Leech there, and she was telling us the most wonderful things about you. She'd lost a ruby ring bathing, and she was just lamenting that you weren't there to find it for her.

'Ah, *parbleu*, but I am not the diving seal!'

They both laughed.

Mrs Allerton went on.

'I saw you from my window walking down the drive with Simon Doyle this morning. Do tell me what you make of him! We're so excited about him.'

'Ah? Truly?'

'Yes. You know his marriage to Linnet Ridgeway was the greatest surprise. She was supposed to be going to marry Lord Windlesham and then suddenly she gets engaged to this man no one had ever heard of!'

'You know her well, Madame?'

'No, but a cousin of mine, Joanna Southwood, is one of her best friends.'

'Ah, yes, I have read that name in the papers.' He was silent a moment and then went on, 'She is a young lady very much in the news, Mademoiselle Joanna Southwood.'

'Oh, she knows how to advertise herself all right,' snapped Mrs Allerton.

'You do not like her, Madame?'

'That was a nasty remark of mine.' Mrs Allerton looked

penitent. 'You see, I'm old-fashioned. I don't like her much. Tim and she are the greatest of friends, though.'

'I see,' said Poirot.

His companion shot a quick look at him. She changed the subject.

'How very few young people there are out here! That pretty girl with the chestnut hair and the appalling mother in the turban is almost the only young creature in the place. You have talked to her a good deal, I notice. She interests me, that child.'

'Why is that, Madame?'

'I feel sorry for her. You can suffer so much when you are young and sensitive. I think she is suffering.'

'Yes, she is not happy, poor little one.'

'Tim and I call her the "sulky girl". I've tried to talk to her once or twice, but she's snubbed me on each occasion. However, I believe she's going on this Nile trip too, and I expect we'll have to be more or less all matey together, shan't we?'

'It is a possible contingency, Madame.'

'I'm very matey really—people interest me enormously. All the different types.' She paused, then said: 'Tim tells me that that dark girl—her name is de Bellefort—is the girl who was engaged to Simon Doyle. It's rather awkward for them—meeting like this.'

'It is awkward—yes,' agreed Poirot.

Mrs Allerton shot a quick glance at him.

'You know, it may sound foolish, but she almost frightened me. She looked so—intense.'

Poirot nodded his head slowly.

'You were not far wrong, Madame. A great force of emotion is always frightening.'

'Do people interest you too, Monsieur Poirot? Or do you reserve your interest for potential criminals?'

'Madame—that category would not leave many people outside it.'

Mrs Allerton looked a trifle startled.

'Do you really mean that?'

'Given the particular incentive, that is to say,' Poirot added.

'Which would differ?'

'Naturally.'

Mrs Allerton hesitated—a little smile on her lips.

'Even I perhaps?'

'Mothers, Madame, are particularly ruthless when their children are in danger.'

She said gravely:

'I think that's true—yes, you're quite right.'

She was silent a minute or two, then she said, smiling:

'I'm trying to imagine motives for crime suitable for everyone in the hotel. It's quite entertaining. Simon Doyle, for instance?'

Poirot said, smiling:

'A very simple crime—a direct short cut to his objective. No subtlety about it.'

'And therefore very easily detected?'

'Yes; he would not be ingenious.'

'And Linnet?'

Death on the Nile

'That would be like the Queen in your *Alice in Wonderland*, "Off with her head."'

'Of course. The divine right of monarchy! Just a little bit of the Naboth's vineyard touch. And the dangerous girl—Jacqueline de Bellefort—could *she* do a murder?'

Poirot hesitated for a minute or two, then he said doubtfully:

'Yes, I think she could.'

'But you're not sure?'

'No. She puzzles me, that little one.'

'I don't think Mr Pennington could do one, do you? He looks so desiccated and dyspeptic—with no red blood in him.'

'But possibly a strong sense of self-preservation.'

'Yes, I suppose so. And poor Mrs Otterbourne in her turban?'

'There is always vanity.'

'As a motive for murder?' Mrs Allerton asked doubtfully.

'Motives for murder are sometimes very trivial, Madame.'

'What are the most usual motives, Monsieur Poirot?'

'Most frequent—money. That is to say, gain in its various ramifications. Then there is revenge, and love, and fear—and pure hate, and beneficence—'

'Monsieur Poirot!'

'Oh, yes, Madame. I have known of—shall we say A?—being removed by B solely in order to benefit C. Political murders often come under that heading. Someone is considered to be harmful to civilization and is removed on that account. Such people forget that life and death are the affair of the good God.'

He spoke gravely.

Mrs Allerton said quietly:

'I am glad to hear you say that. All the same, God chooses his instruments.'

'There is a danger in thinking like that, Madame.'

She adopted a lighter tone:

'After this conversation, Monsieur Poirot, I shall wonder that there is anyone left alive!'

She got up.

'We must be getting back. We have to start immediately after lunch.'

When they reached the landing stage they found the young man in the polo jumper just taking his place in the boat. The Italian was already waiting. As the Nubian boatman cast the sail loose and they started, Poirot addressed a polite remark to the stranger:

'There are very wonderful things to be seen in Egypt, are there not?'

The young man was now smoking a somewhat noisome pipe. He removed it from his mouth and remarked briefly and emphatically in astonishingly well-bred accents:

'They make me sick.'

Mrs Allerton put on her pince-nez and surveyed him with pleasurable interest. Poirot said:

'Indeed? And why is that?'

'Take the Pyramids. Great blocks of useless masonry Put up to minister to the egoism of a despotic bloated king.

Think of the sweated masses who toiled to build them and died doing it. It makes me sick to think of the suffering and torture they represent.'

Mrs Allerton said cheerfully:

'You'd rather have no Pyramids, no Parthenon, no beautiful tombs or temples—just the solid satisfaction of knowing that people got three meals a day and died in their beds.'

The young man directed his scowl in her direction.

'I think human beings matter more than stones.'

'But they do not endure as well,' remarked Hercule Poirot.

'I'd rather see a well fed worker than any so-called work of art. What matters is the future—not the past.'

This was too much for Signor Richetti, who burst into a torrent of impassioned speech not too easy to follow.

The young man retorted by telling everybody exactly what he thought of the capitalist system. He spoke with the utmost venom.

When the tirade was over they had arrived at the hotel landing-stage.

Mrs Allerton murmured cheerfully: 'Well, well,' and stepped ashore. The young man directed a baleful glance after her.

In the hall of the hotel Poirot encountered Jacqueline de Bellefort. She was dressed in riding clothes. She gave him an ironical little bow.

'I'm going donkey-riding. Do you recommend the native villages, Monsieur Poirot?'

'Is that your excursion today, Mademoiselle? *Eh bien*, they

Agatha Christie

are picturesque—but do not spend large sums on native curios.'

'Which are shipped here from Europe? No, I am not so easy to deceive as that.'

With a little nod she passed out into the brilliant sunshine.

Poirot completed his packing—a very simple affair, since his possessions were always in the most meticulous order. Then he repaired to the dining room and ate an early lunch.

After lunch the hotel bus took the passengers for the Second Cataract to the station where they were to catch the daily express from Cairo to Shellal—a ten-minute run.

The Allertons, Poirot, the young man in the dirty flannel trousers and the Italian were the passengers. Mrs Otterbourne and her daughter had made the expedition to the Dam and to Philae and would join the steamer at Shellal.

The train from Cairo and Luxor was about twenty minutes late. However, it arrived at last, and the usual scenes of wild activity occurred. Native porters taking suitcases out of the train collided with other porters putting them in.

Finally, somewhat breathless, Poirot found himself with an assortment of his own, the Allertons', and some totally unknown luggage in one compartment, while Tim and his mother were elsewhere with the remains of the assorted baggage.

The compartment in which Poirot found himself was occupied by an elderly lady with a very wrinkled face, a stiff white stock, a good many diamonds and an expression of reptilian contempt for the majority of mankind.

She treated Poirot to an aristocratic glare and retired

behind the pages of an American magazine. A big, rather clumsy young woman of under thirty was sitting opposite her. She had eager brown eyes rather like a dog's, untidy hair, and a terrific air of willingness to please. At intervals the old lady looked over the top of her magazine and snapped an order at her.

'Cornelia, collect the rugs. When we arrive look after my dressing-case. On no account let anyone else handle it. Don't forget my paper-cutter.'

The train run was brief. In ten minutes' time they came to rest on the jetty where the S.S. *Karnak* was awaiting them. The Otterbournes were already on board.

The *Karnak* was a smaller steamer than the *Papyrus* and the *Lotus*, the First Cataract steamers, which are too large to pass through the locks of the Aswan dam. The passengers went on board and were shown their accommodation. Since the boat was not full, most of the passengers had accommodation on the promenade deck. The entire forward part of this deck was occupied by an observation saloon, all glass-enclosed, where the passengers could sit and watch the river unfold before them. On the deck below were a smoking room and a small drawing room and on the deck below that, the dining saloon.

Having seen his possessions disposed in his cabin, Poirot came out on the deck again to watch the process of departure. He joined Rosalie Otterbourne, who was leaning over the side.

'So now we journey into Nubia. You are pleased, Mademoiselle?'

Agatha Christie

The girl drew a deep breath.

'Yes. I feel that one's really getting away from things at last.'

She made a gesture with her hand. There was a savage aspect about the sheet of water in front of them, the masses of rock without vegetation that came down to the water's edge—here and there a trace of houses abandoned and ruined as a result of the damming up of the waters. The whole scene had a melancholy, almost sinister charm.

'Away from *people*,' said Rosalie Otterbourne.

'Except those of our own number, Mademoiselle?'

She shrugged her shoulders. Then she said: 'There's something about this country that makes me feel—wicked. It brings to the surface all the things that are boiling inside one. Everything's so unfair—so unjust.'

'I wonder. You cannot judge by material evidence.'

Rosalie muttered:

'Look at—at some people's mothers—and look at mine. There is no God but Sex, and Salome Otterbourne is its Prophet.' She stopped. 'I shouldn't have said that, I suppose.'

Poirot made a gesture with his hands.

'Why not say it—to me? I am one of those who hear many things. If, as you say, you boil inside—like the jam—*Eh bien*, let the scum come to the surface, and then one can take it off with a spoon, so.'

He made a gesture of dropping something into the Nile.

'Then, it has gone.'

Rosalie said:

'What an extraordinary man you are!' Her sulky mouth

twisted into a smile. Then she suddenly stiffened as she exclaimed: 'Well, here are Mrs Doyle and her husband! I'd no idea *they* were coming on this trip!'

Linnet had just emerged from a cabin halfway down the deck. Simon was behind her. Poirot was almost startled by the look of her—so radiant, so assured. She looked positively arrogant with happiness. Simon Doyle, too, was a transformed being. He was grinning from ear to ear and looking like a happy schoolboy.

'This is grand,' he said as he too leaned on the rail. 'I'm really looking forward to this trip, aren't you, Linnet? It feels somehow so much less touristy—as though we were really going into the heart of Egypt.'

His wife responded quickly:

'I know. It's so much—wilder, somehow.'

Her hand slipped through his arm. He pressed it close to his side.

'We're off, Lin,' he murmured.

The steamer was drawing away from the jetty. They had started on their seven-day journey to the Second Cataract and back.

Behind them a light silvery laugh rang out. Linnet whipped round.

Jacqueline de Bellefort was standing there. She seemed amused.

'Hullo, Linnet! I didn't expect to find you here. I thought you said you were staying in Aswan another ten days. This is a surprise!'

'You—you didn't—'Linnet's tongue stammered. She

Agatha Christie

forced a ghastly conventional smile. 'I didn't expect to see you either.'

'No?'

Jacqueline moved away to the other side of the boat. Linnet's grasp on her husband's arm tightened.

'Simon—Simon—'

All Doyle's good-natured pleasure had gone. He looked furious. His hands clenched themselves in spite of his effort at self-control.

The two of them moved a little away. Without turning his head Poirot caught scraps of disjointed words.

'...turn back... impossible... we could...' and then, slightly louder, Doyle's voice, despairing but grim.

'We can't run away for ever, Lin. *We've got to go through with it now...*'

It was some hours later. Daylight was just fading. Poirot stood in the glass-enclosed saloon looking straight ahead. The *Karnak* was going through a narrow gorge. The rocks came down with a kind of sheer ferocity to the river flowing deep and swift between them. They were in Nubia now.

He heard a movement and Linnet Doyle stood by his side.

Her fingers twisted and untwisted themselves; she looked as he had never yet seen her look. There was about her the air of a bewildered child. She said:

'Monsieur Poirot, I'm afraid—I'm afraid of everything. I've never felt like this before. All these wild rocks and the awful grimness and starkness. Where are we going? What's going to happen? I'm afraid, I tell you. Everyone hates me. I've never felt like that before. I've always been nice to people—I've done things for them—and they hate me—lots of people hate me. Except for Simon, I'm surrounded by enemies... It's terrible to feel—that there are people who hate you...'

'But what is all this, Madame?'

She shook her head.

'I suppose—it's nerves... I just feel that—everything's unsafe all round me.'

She cast a quick nervous glance over his shoulder. Then she said abruptly: 'How will all this end? We're caught here. Trapped. There's no way out. We've got to go on. I—I don't know where I am.'

She slipped down on to a seat. Poirot looked down on her gravely; his glance was not untinged with compassion.

She said:

'How did she know we were coming on this boat? How could she have known?'

Poirot shook his head as he answered:

'She has brains, you know.'

'I feel as though I shall never escape from her.'

Poirot said: 'There is one plan you might have adopted. In fact I am surprised that it did not occur to you. After all, with you, Madame, money is no object. Why did you not engage in your own private dahabeeyah?'

Linnet shook her head rather helplessly.

'If we'd known about all this—but you see we didn't—then. And it was difficult...' She flashed out with sudden

Agatha Christie

impatience: 'Oh! you don't understand half my difficulties. I've got to be careful with Simon... He's—he's absurdly sensitive—about money. About my having so much! He wanted me to go to some little place in Spain with him—he—he wanted to pay all our honeymoon expenses himself. As if it *mattered*! Men are stupid! He's got to get used to—to—living comfortably. The mere idea of a dahabeeyah upset him—the—the needless expense. I've got to educate him—gradually.'

She looked up, bit her lip vexedly, as though feeling that she had been led into discussing her difficulties rather too unguardedly.

She got up.

'I must change. I'm sorry, Monsieur Poirot. I'm afraid I've been talking a lot of foolish nonsense.'

CHAPTER 7

Mrs Allerton, looking quiet and distinguished in her simple black lace evening gown, descended two decks to the dining room. At the door of it her son caught her up.

'Sorry, darling. I thought I was going to be late.'

'I wonder where we sit.' The saloon was dotted with little tables. Mrs Allerton paused till the steward, who was busy seating a party of people, could attend to them.

'By the way,' she added, 'I asked little Hercule Poirot to sit at our table.'

'Mother, you didn't!' Tim sounded really taken aback and annoyed.

His mother stared at him in surprise. Tim was usually so easy going.

'My dear, do you mind?'

'Yes, I do. He's an unmitigated little bounder!'

'Oh, no, Tim! I don't agree with you.'

'Anyway, what do we want to get mixed up with an

Agatha Christie

outsider for? Cooped up like this on a small boat, that sort of thing is always a bore. He'll be with us morning, noon and night.'

'I'm sorry, dear.' Mrs Allerton looked distressed. 'I thought really it would amuse you. After all, he must have had a varied experience. And you love detective stories.'

Tim grunted:

'I wish you wouldn't have these bright ideas, Mother. We can't get out of it now, I suppose?'

'Really, Tim, I don't see how we can.'

'Oh, well, we shall have to put up with it, I suppose.'

The steward came to them at this minute and led them to a table. Mrs Allerton's face wore rather a puzzled expression as she followed him. Tim was usually so easy-going and good-tempered. This outburst was quite unlike him. It wasn't as though he had the ordinary Britisher's dislike— and mistrust—of foreigners. Tim was very cosmopolitan. Oh, well—she sighed. Men were incomprehensible! Even one's nearest and dearest had unsuspected reactions and feelings.

As they took their places, Hercule Poirot came quickly and silently into the dining-saloon. He paused with his hand on the back of the third chair.

'You really permit, Madame, that I avail myself of your kind suggestion?'

'Of course. Sit down, Monsieur Poirot.'

'You are most amiable.'

She was uneasily conscious that as he seated himself he

shot a swift glance at Tim, and that Tim had not quite succeeded in masking a somewhat sullen expression.

Mrs Allerton set herself to produce a pleasant atmosphere. As they drank their soup, she picked up the passenger list which had been placed beside her plate.

'Let's try and identify everybody,' she suggested cheerfully. 'I always think that's rather fun.'

She began reading.

'Mrs Allerton, Mr T. Allerton. That's easy enough! Miss de Bellefort. They've put her at the same table as the Otterbournes, I see. I wonder what she and Rosalie will make of each other. Who comes next? Dr Bessner. Dr Bessner? Who can identify Dr Bessner?'

She bent her glance on a table at which four men sat together.

'I think he must be the fat one with the closely shaved head and the moustache. A German, I should imagine. He seems to be enjoying his soup very much.'

Certain succulent noises floated across to them.

Mrs Allerton continued:

'Miss Bowers? Can we make a guess at Miss Bowers? There are three or four women—no, we'll leave her for the present. Mr and Mrs Doyle. Yes, indeed, the lions of this trip. She really is very beautiful, and what a perfectly lovely frock she is wearing.'

Tim turned round in his chair. Linnet and her husband and Andrew Pennington had been given a table in the corner. Linnet was wearing a white dress and pearls.

Agatha Christie

'It looks frightfully simple to me,' said Tim. 'Just a length of stuff with a kind of cord round the middle.'

'Yes, darling,' said his mother. 'A very nice manly description of an eighty-guinea model.'

'I can't think why women pay so much for their clothes,' Tim said. 'It seems absurd to me.'

Mrs Allerton proceeded with her study of her fellow passengers.

'Mr Fanthorp must be the intensely quiet young man who never speaks, at the same table as the German. Rather a nice face, cautious but intelligent.'

Poirot agreed.

'He is intelligent—yes. He does not talk, but he listens very attentively and he also watches. Yes, he makes good use of his eyes Not quite the type you would expect to find travelling for pleasure in this part of the world. I wonder what he is doing here.'

'Mr Ferguson,' read Mrs Allerton. 'I feel that Ferguson must be our anti-capitalist friend. Mrs Otterbourne, Miss Otterbourne. We know all about them. Mr Pennington? Alias Uncle Andrew. He's a good-looking man, I think—'

'Now, Mother,' said Tim.

'I think he's very good-looking in a dry sort of way,' said Mrs Allerton. 'Rather a ruthless jaw. Probably the kind of man one reads about in the paper, who operates on Wall Street—or is it *in* Wall Street? I'm sure he must be extremely rich. Next—Monsieur Hercule Poirot—whose talents are really being wasted. Can't you get up a crime for Monsieur Poirot, Tim?'

But her well-meant banter only seemed to annoy her son anew.

He scowled and Mrs Allerton hurried on. 'Mr Richetti. Our Italian archaeological friend. Then Miss Robson and last of all Miss Van Schuyler. The last's easy. The very ugly old American lady who obviously feels herself the queen of the boat and who is clearly going to be very exclusive and speak to nobody who doesn't come up to the most exacting standards! She's rather marvellous, isn't she, really? A kind of period piece. The two women with her must be Miss Bowers and Miss Robson—perhaps a secretary, the thin one with pince-nez, and a poor relation, the rather pathetic young woman who is obviously enjoying herself in spite of being treated like a black slave. I think Robson's the secretary woman and Bowers is the poor relation.'

'Wrong, Mother,' said Tim, grinning. He had suddenly recovered his good humour.

'How do you know?'

'Because I was in the lounge before dinner and the old bean said to the companion woman: "Where's Miss Bowers? Fetch her at once, Cornelia." And away trotted Cornelia like an obedient dog.'

'I shall have to talk to Miss Van Schuyler,' mused Mrs Allerton.

Tim grinned again.

'She'll snub you, Mother.'

'Not at all. I shall pave the way by sitting near her and conversing in low (but penetrating) well-bred tones about any titled relations and friends I can remember. I think a casual mention of your second cousin once removed, the Duke of Glasgow, would probably do the trick.'

'How unscrupulous you are, Mother!'

Events after dinner were not without their amusing side to a student of human nature.

The socialistic young man (who turned out to be Mr Ferguson as deduced) retired to the smoking room, scorning the assemblage of passengers in the observation saloon on the top deck.

Miss Van Schuyler duly secured the best and most undraughty position there by advancing firmly on a table at which Mrs Otterbourne was sitting and saying:

'You'll excuse me, I am sure, but I *think* my knitting was left here!'

Fixed by a hypnotic eye, the turban rose and gave ground. Miss Van Schuyler established herself and her suite. Mrs Otterbourne sat down nearby and hazarded various remarks, which were met with such chilling politeness that she soon gave up. Miss Van Schuyler then sat in glorious isolation. The Doyles sat with the Allertons. Dr Bessner retained the quiet Mr Fanthorp as a companion. Jacqueline de Bellefort sat by herself with a book. Rosalie Otterbourne was restless. Mrs Allerton spoke to her once or twice and tried to draw her into their group, but the girl responded ungraciously.

M. Hercule Poirot spent his evening listening to an account of Mrs Otterbourne's mission as a writer.

On his way to his cabin that night he encountered Jacqueline de Bellefort. She was leaning over the rail and as she turned her head he was struck by the look of acute misery on her face. There was now no insouciance, no malicious defiance, no dark flaming triumph.

'Good night, Mademoiselle.'

'Good night, Monsieur Poirot.' She hesitated, then said: 'You were surprised to find me here?'

'I was not so much surprised as sorry—very sorry...'

He spoke gravely.

'You mean sorry—for *me*?'

'That is what I meant. You have chosen, Mademoiselle, the dangerous course... As we here in this boat have embarked on a journey, so you too have embarked on your own private journey—a journey on a swift-moving river, between dangerous rocks, and heading for who knows what currents of disaster...'

'Why do you say this?'

'Because it is true... You have cut the bonds that moored you to safety. I doubt now if you could turn back if you would.'

She said very slowly:

'That is true...'

Then she flung her head back.

'Ah, well—one must follow one's star—wherever it leads.'

'Beware, Mademoiselle, that it is not a false star...'

She laughed and mimicked the parrot cry of the donkey boys:

'That very bad star, sir! That star fall down...'

He was just dropping off to sleep when the murmur of voices awoke him.

Agatha Christie

It was Simon Doyle's voice he heard, repeating the same words he had used when the steamer left Shellal.

'We've got to go through with it now...'

'Yes,' thought Hercule Poirot to himself, 'we have got to go through with it now...'

He was not happy.

CHAPTER 8

The steamer arrived early next morning at Ez-Zebua. Cornelia Robson, her face beaming, a large flapping hat on her head, was one of the first to hurry on shore. Cornelia was not good at snubbing people. She was of an amiable disposition and disposed to like all her fellow creatures. The sight of Hercule Poirot, in a white suit, pink shirt, large black bow tie and a white topee, did not make her wince as the aristocratic Miss Van Schuyler would assuredly have winced.

As they walked together up an avenue of sphinxes, she responded readily to his conventional opening, 'Your companions are not coming ashore to view the temple?'

'Well, you see, Cousin Marie—that's Miss Van Schuyler—never gets up very early. She has to be very, very careful of her health. And of course she wanted Miss Bowers, that's her hospital nurse, to do things for her. And she said, too, that this isn't one of the best temples—but she was frightfully kind and said it would be quite all right for me to come.'

Agatha Christie

'That was very gracious of her,' said Poirot dryly.

The ingenuous Cornelia agreed unsuspectingly.

'Oh, she's very kind. It's simply wonderful of her to bring me on this trip. I do feel I'm a lucky girl. I just could hardly believe it when she suggested to Mother that I should come too.'

'And you have enjoyed it—yes?'

'Oh, it's been wonderful. I've seen Italy—Venice and Padua and Pisa—and then Cairo—only Cousin Marie wasn't very well in Cairo, so I couldn't get around much, and now this wonderful trip up to Wadi Halfa and back.'

Poirot said, smiling:

'You have the happy nature, Mademoiselle.'

He looked thoughtfully from her to the silent, frowning Rosalie, who was walking ahead by herself.

'She's very nice looking, isn't she?' said Cornelia, following his glance. 'Only kind of scornful looking. She's very English, of course. She's not as lovely as Mrs Doyle. I think Mrs Doyle's the loveliest, the most elegant woman I've ever seen! And her husband just worships the ground she walks on, doesn't he? I think that grey-haired lady is kind of distinguished looking, don't you? She's a cousin of a duke, I believe. She was talking about him right near us last night. But she isn't actually titled herself, is she?'

She prattled on until the dragoman in charge called a halt and began to intone: 'This temple was dedicated to Egyptian God Amon and the Sun God Re-Harakhte—whose symbol was hawk's head...'

It droned on. Dr Bessner, Baedeker in hand, mumbled to himself in German. He preferred the written word.

Tim Allerton had not joined the party. His mother was breaking the ice with the reserved Mr Fanthorp. Andrew Pennington, his arm through Linnet Doyle's, was listening attentively, seemingly most interested in the measurements as recited by the guide.

'Sixty-five feet high, is that so? Looks a little less to me. Great fellow, this Rameses. An Egyptian live wire.'

'A big business man, Uncle Andrew.'

Andrew Pennington looked at her appreciatively.

'You look fine this morning, Linnet. I've been a mite worried about you lately. You've looked kind of peaky.'

Chatting together, the party returned to the boat. Once more the *Karnak* glided up the river. The scenery was less stern now. There were palms, cultivation.

It was as though the change in the scenery had relieved some secret oppression that had brooded over the passengers. Tim Allerton had got over his fit of moodiness. Rosalie looked less sulky. Linnet seemed almost light hearted.

Pennington said to her: 'It's tactless to talk business to a bride on her honeymoon, but there are just one or two things—'

'Why, of course, Uncle Andrew.' Linnet at once became businesslike. 'My marriage has made a difference, of course.'

'That's just it. Some time or other I want your signature to several documents.'

'Why not now?'

Andrew Pennington glanced round. Their corner of the observation saloon was quite untenanted. Most of the people were outside on the deck space between the observation saloon and the cabin. The only occupants of the saloon were Mr Ferguson—who was drinking beer at a small table in the middle, his legs encased in their dirty flannel trousers stuck out in front of him, whilst he whistled to himself in the intervals of drinking—M. Hercule Poirot, who was sitting before him, and Miss Van Schuyler, who was sitting in a corner reading a book on Egypt.

'That's fine,' said Andrew Pennington.

He left the saloon.

Linnet and Simon smiled at each other—a slow smile that took a few minutes to come to full fruition.

He said:

'All right, sweet?'

'Yes, still all right… Funny how I'm not rattled any more.'

Simon said with deep conviction in his tone:

'You're marvellous.'

Pennington came back. He brought with him a sheaf of closely written documents.

'Mercy!' cried Linnet. 'Have I got to sign all these?'

Andrew Pennington was apologetic.

'It's tough on you, I know. But I'd just like to get your affairs put in proper shape. First of all there's the lease of the Fifth Avenue property… then there are the Western Land Concessions…'

He talked on, rustling and sorting the papers. Simon yawned.

The door to the deck swung open and Mr Fanthorp came in. He gazed aimlessly round, then strolled forward and

Death on the Nile

stood by Poirot looking out at the pale blue water and the yellow enveloping sands...

'—you sign just there,' concluded Pennington, spreading a paper before Linnet and indicating a space.

Linnet picked up the document and glanced through it. She turned back once to the first page, then, taking up the fountain pen Pennington had laid beside her, she signed her name *Linnet Doyle*...

Pennington took away the paper and spread out another.

Fanthorp wandered over in their direction. He peered out through the side window at something that seemed to interest him on the bank they were passing.

'That's just the transfer,' said Pennington. 'You needn't read it.'

But Linnet took a brief glance through it. Pennington laid down a third paper. Again Linnet perused it carefully.

'They're all quite straightforward,' said Andrew. 'Nothing of interest. Only legal phraseology.'

Simon yawned again.

'My dear girl, you're not going to read the whole lot through, are you? You'll be at it till lunch time and longer.'

'I always read everything through,' said Linnet. 'Father taught me to do that. He said there might be some clerical error.'

Pennington laughed rather harshly.

'You're a grand woman of business, Linnet.'

'She's much more conscientious than I'd be,' said Simon, laughing. 'I've never read a legal document in my life. I sign where they tell me to sign on the dotted line—and that's that.'

'That's frightfully slipshod,' said Linnet disapprovingly.

'I've no business head,' said Simon cheerfully. 'Never had. A fellow tells me to sign—I sign. It's much the simplest way.'

Andrew Pennington was looking at him thoughtfully. He said dryly, stroking his upper lip,

'A little risky sometimes, Doyle?'

'Nonsense,' replied Simon. 'I'm not one of those people who believe the whole world is out to do one down. I'm a trusting kind of fellow—and it pays, you know. I've hardly ever been let down.'

Suddenly, to everyone's surprise, the silent Mr Fanthorp swung around and addressed Linnet.

'I hope I'm not butting in, but you must let me say how much I admire your businesslike capacity. In my profession—er—I am a lawyer—I find ladies sadly unbusinesslike. Never to sign a document unless you read it through is admirable—altogether admirable.'

He gave a little bow. Then, rather red in the face, he turned once more to contemplate the banks of the Nile.

Linnet said rather uncertainly, 'Er—thank you…' She bit her lip to repress a giggle. The young man had looked so preternaturally solemn.

Andrew Pennington looked seriously annoyed.

Simon Doyle looked uncertain whether to be annoyed or amused.

The backs of Mr Fanthorp's ears were bright crimson.

'Next, please,' said Linnet, smiling up at Pennington.

But Pennington looked decidedly ruffled.

'I think perhaps some other time would be better,' he said stiffly. 'As—er—Doyle says, if you have to read through all these we shall be here till lunch time. We mustn't miss enjoying the scenery. Anyway those first two papers were the only urgent ones. We'll settle down to business later.'

Linnet said:

'It's frightfully hot in here. Let's go outside.'

The three of them passed through the swing door. Hercule Poirot turned his head. His gaze rested thoughtfully on Mr Fanthorp's back; then it shifted to the lounging figure of Mr Ferguson, who had his head thrown back and was still whistling softly to himself.

Finally Poirot looked over at the upright figure of Miss Van Schuyler in her corner. Miss Van Schuyler was glaring at Mr Ferguson.

The swing door on the port side opened and Cornelia Robson hurried in.

'You've been a long time,' snapped the old lady. 'Where've you been?'

'I'm so sorry, Cousin Marie. The wool wasn't where you said it was. It was in another case altogther—'

'My dear child, you are perfectly hopeless at finding anything! You are willing, I know, my dear, but you must try to be a little cleverer and quicker. It only needs *concentration*.'

'I'm so sorry, Cousin Marie. I'm afraid I am very stupid.'

Agatha Christie

'Nobody need be stupid if they *try*, my dear. I have brought you on this trip, and I expect a little attention in return.'

Cornelia flushed.

'I'm very sorry, Cousin Marie.'

'And where is Miss Bowers? It was time for my drops ten minutes ago. Please go and find her at once. The doctor said it was most important—'

But at this stage Miss Bowers entered, carrying a small medicine glass.

'Your drops, Miss Van Schuyler.'

'I should have had them at eleven,' snapped the old lady. 'If there's one thing I detest it's unpunctuality.'

'Quite,' said Miss Bowers. She glanced at her wristwatch. 'It's exactly half a minute to eleven.'

'By my watch it's ten past.'

'I think you'll find my watch is right. It's a perfect timekeeper. It never loses or gains.'

Miss Bowers was quite imperturbable.

Miss Van Schuyler swallowed the contents of the medicine glass.

'I feel definitely worse,' she snapped.

'I'm sorry to hear that, Miss Van Schuyler.'

Miss Bowers did not sound sorry. She sounded completely uninterested. She was obviously making the correct reply mechanically.

'It's too hot in here,' snapped Miss Van Schuyler. 'Find me a chair on the deck, Miss Bowers. Cornelia, bring my knitting. Don't be clumsy or drop it. And then I shall want you to wind some wool.'

Death on the Nile

The procession passed out.

Mr Ferguson sighed, stirred his legs and remarked to the world at large:

'Gosh, I'd like to scrag that dame.'

Poirot asked interestedly:

'She is a type you dislike, eh?'

'Dislike? I should say so. What good has that woman ever been to anyone or anything? She's never worked or lifted a finger. She's just battened on other people. She's a parasite—and a damned unpleasant parasite. There are a lot of people on this boat I'd say the world could do without.'

'Really?'

'Yes. That girl in here just now, signing share transfers and throwing her weight about. Hundreds and thousands of wretched workers slaving for a mere pittance to keep her in silk stockings and useless luxuries. One of the richest women in England, so someone told me—and never done a hand's turn in her life.'

'Who told you she was one of the richest women in England?'

Mr Ferguson cast a belligerent eye at him.

'A man you wouldn't be seen speaking to! A man who works with his hands and isn't ashamed of it! Not one of your dressed-up, foppish good-for-nothings.'

His eye rested unfavourably on the bow tie and pink shirt.

'Me, I work with my brains and am not ashamed of it,' said Poirot, answering the glance.

Mr Ferguson merely snorted.

125

'Ought to be shot—the lot of them!' he asserted.

'My dear young man,' said Poirot, 'what a passion you have for violence!'

'Can you tell me of any good that can be done without it? You've got to break down and destroy before you can build up.'

'It is certainly much easier and much noisier and much more spectacular.'

'What do *you* do for a living? Nothing at all, I bet. Probably call yourself a middle man.'

'I am not a middle man. I am a top man,' said Hercule Poirot with a slight arrogance.

'What *are* you?'

'I am a detective,' said Hercule Poirot with the modest air of one who says "I am a king."

'Good God!' The young man seemed seriously taken aback. 'Do you mean that girl actually totes about a dumb dick? Is she as careful of her precious skin as *that*?'

'I have no connection whatever with Monsieur and Madame Doyle,' said Poirot stiffly. 'I am on a holiday.'

'Enjoying a vacation—eh?'

'And you? Is it not that you are on holiday also?'

'Holiday!' Mr Ferguson snorted. Then he added cryptically: 'I'm studying conditions.'

'Very interesting,' murmured Poirot and moved gently out on to the deck.

Miss Van Schuyler was established in the best corner. Cornelia knelt in front of her, her arms outstretched with a skein of grey wool upon them. Miss Bowers was sitting very upright reading the *Saturday Evening Post*.

Poirot wandered gently onward down the starboard deck. As he passed round the stern of the boat he almost ran into a woman who turned a startled face towards him—a dark, piquant, Latin face. She was neatly dressed in black and had been standing talking to a big burly man in uniform—one of the engineers, by the look of him. There was a queer expression on both their faces—guilt and alarm. Poirot wondered what they had been talking about.

He rounded the stern and continued his walk along the port side. A cabin door opened and Mrs Otterbourne emerged and nearly fell into his arms. She was wearing a scarlet satin dressing gown.

'So sorry,' she apologized. 'Dear Mr Poirot—so very sorry. The motion—just the motion, you know. Never did have any sea legs. If the boat would only keep still...' She clutched at his arm. 'It's the pitching I can't stand... Never really happy at sea... And left all alone here hour after hour. That girl of mine—no sympathy—no understanding of her poor old mother who's done everything for her...' Mrs Otterbourne began to weep. 'Slaved for her I have—worn myself to the bone—to the bone. A *grande amoureuse*—that's what I might have been—a *grande amoureuse*—sacrificed everything—everything... And nobody cares! But I'll tell everyone—I'll tell them now—how she neglects me—how hard she is—making me come on this journey—bored to death... I'll go and tell them now—'

She surged forward. Poirot gently repressed the action.

Agatha Christie

'I will send her to you, Madame. Re-enter your cabin. It is best that way—'

'No. I want to tell everyone—everyone on the boat—'

'It is too dangerous, Madame. The sea is too rough. You might be swept overboard.'

Mrs Otterbourne looked at him doubtfully.

'You think so. You really think so?'

'I do.'

He was successful. Mrs Otterbourne wavered, faltered and re-entered her cabin.

Poirot's nostrils twitched once or twice. Then he nodded and walked on to where Rosalie Otterbourne was sitting between Mrs Allerton and Tim.

'Your mother wants you, Mademoiselle.'

She had been laughing quite happily. Now her face clouded over. She shot a quick suspicious look at him and hurried along the deck.

'I can't make that child out,' said Mrs Allerton. 'She varies so. One day she's friendly—the next day, she's positively rude.'

'Thoroughly spoilt and bad-tempered,' said Tim.

Mrs Allerton shook her head.

'No. I don't think it's that. I think she's unhappy.'

Tim shrugged his shoulders.

'Oh, well, I suppose we've all got our private troubles.' His voice sounded hard and curt.

A booming noise was heard.

'Lunch,' cried Mrs Allerton delightedly. 'I'm starving.'

That evening, Poirot noticed that Mrs Allerton was sitting

talking to Miss Van Schuyler. As he passed, Mrs Allerton closed one eye and opened it again.

She was saying, 'Of course at Calfries Castle—the dear Duke—'

Cornelia, released from attendance, was out on the deck. She was listening to Dr Bessner, who was instructing her somewhat ponderously in Egyptology as culled from the pages of Baedeker. Cornelia listened with rapt attention.

Leaning over the rail Tim Allerton was saying:

'Anyhow, it's a rotten world...'

Rosalie Otterbourne answered:

'It's unfair... some people have everything.'

Poirot sighed.

He was glad that he was no longer young.

CHAPTER 9

On the Monday morning various expressions of delight and appreciation were heard on the deck of the *Karnak*. The steamer was moored to the bank and a few hundred yards away, the morning sun just striking it, was a great temple carved out of the face of the rock. Four colossal figures, hewn out of the cliff, look out eternally over the Nile and face the rising sun.

Cornelia Robson said incoherently:

'Oh, Monsieur Poirot, isn't it wonderful? I mean they're so big and peaceful—and looking at them makes one feel that one's so small—and rather like an insect—and that nothing matters very much really, does it?'

Mr Fanthorp, who was standing near by, murmured, 'Very—er—impressive.'

'Grand, isn't it?' said Simon Doyle, strolling up. He went on confidentially to Poirot: 'You know, I'm not much of a fellow for temples and sightseeing and all that, but a place like this sort of gets you, if you know what

Death on the Nile

I mean. Those old Pharaohs must have been wonderful fellows.'

The other had drifted away. Simon lowered his voice.

'I'm no end glad we came on this trip. It's—well, it's cleared things up. Amazing why it should—but there it is. Linnet's got her nerve back. She says it's because she's actually *faced* the business at last.'

'I think that is very probable,' said Poirot.

'She says that when she actually saw Jackie on the boat she felt terrible—and then, suddenly, it didn't matter any more. We're both agreed that we won't try to dodge her any more. We'll just meet her on her own ground and show her that this ridiculous stunt of hers doesn't worry us a bit. It's just damned bad form—that's all. She thought she'd got us badly rattled—but now, well, we just aren't rattled any more. That ought to show her.'

'Yes,' said Poirot thoughtfully.

'So that's splendid, isn't it?'

'Oh, yes, yes.'

Linnet came along the deck. She was dressed in a soft shade of apricot linen. She was smiling.

She greeted Poirot with no particular enthusiasm, just gave him a cool nod and then drew her husband away.

Poirot realized with a momentary flicker of amusement that he had not made himself popular by his critical attitude. Linnet was used to unqualified admiration of all she was or did. Hercule Poirot had sinned noticeably against this creed.

Mrs Allerton, joining him, murmured: 'What a difference

in that girl! She looked worried and not very happy at Aswan. Today she looks so happy that one might almost be afraid she was fey.'

Before Poirot could respond as he meant, the party was called to order. The official dragoman took charge and the party was led ashore to visit Abu Simbel.

Poirot himself fell into step with Andrew Pennington.

'It is your first visit to Egypt—yes?' he asked.

'Why, no, I was here in 1923. That is to say, I was in Cairo. I've never been this trip up the Nile before.'

'You came over on the *Carmanic*, I believe—at least so Madame Doyle was telling me.'

Pennington shot a shrewd glance in his direction.

'Why, yes, that is so,' he admitted.

'I wondered if you had happened to come across some friends of mine who were aboard—the Rushington Smiths.'

'I can't recall anyone of that name. The boat was full and we had bad weather. A lot of passengers hardly appeared, and in any case the voyage is so short one doesn't get to know who is on board and who isn't.'

'Yes, that is very true. What a pleasant surprise your running into Madame Doyle and her husband. You had no idea they were married?'

'No. Mrs Doyle had written me, but the letter was forwarded on and I only received it some days after our unexpected meeting in Cairo.'

'You have known her for many years, I understand?'

'Why, I should say I have, Monsieur Poirot. I've known Linnet Ridgeway since she was just a cute little thing so high—' He made an illustrating gesture. 'Her father and I were lifelong friends. A very remarkable man, Melhuish Ridgeway—and a very successful one.'

'His daughter comes into a considerable fortune, I understand... Ah, *pardon*—perhaps it is not delicate what I say there.'

Andrew Pennington seemed slightly amused.

'Oh, that's pretty common knowledge. Yes, Linnet's a wealthy woman.'

'I suppose, though, that the recent slump is bound to affect any stocks, however sound they may be?'

Pennington took a moment or two to answer. He said at last:

'That, of course, is true to a certain extent. The position is very difficult in these days.'

Poirot murmured:

'I should imagine, however, that Madame Doyle has a keen business head.'

'That is so. Yes, that is so. Linnet is a clever practical girl.'

They came to a halt. The guide proceeded to instruct them on the subject of the temple built by the great Rameses. The four colossi of Rameses himself, one pair on each side of the entrance, hewn out of the living rock, looked down on the straggling little party of tourists.

Signor Richetti, disdaining the remarks of the dragoman, was busy examining the reliefs of Negro and Syrian captives on the bases of the colossi on either side of the entrance.

When the party entered the temple, a sense of dimness

Agatha Christie

and peace came over them. The still vividly coloured reliefs on some of the inner walls were pointed out, but the party tended to break up into groups.

Dr Bessner read sonorously in German from a Baedeker, pausing every now and then to translate for the benefit of Cornelia, who walked in a docile manner beside him. This was not to continue, however. Miss Van Schuyler, entering on the arm of the phlegmatic Miss Bowers, uttered a commanding, 'Cornelia, come here,' and the instruction had perforce to cease. Dr Bessner beamed after her vaguely through his thick lenses.

'A very nice maiden, that,' he announced to Poirot. 'She does not look so starved as some of these young women—no, she has the nice curves. She listens too very intelligently; it is a pleasure to instruct her.'

It fleeted across Poirot's mind that it seemed to be Cornelia's fate either to be bullied or instructed. In any case she was always the listener, never the talker.

Miss Bowers, momentarily released by the peremptory summons of Cornelia, was standing in the middle of the temple, looking about her with her cool, incurious gaze. Her reaction to the wonders of the past was succinct.

'The guide says the name of one of these gods or goddesses was Mut. Can you beat it?'

There was an inner sanctuary where sat four figures eternally presiding, stangely dignified in their dim aloofness.

Before them stood Linnet and her husband. Her arm was in his, her face lifted—a typical face of the new civilization, intelligent, curious, untouched by the past.

Death on the Nile

Simon said suddenly:

'Let's get out of here. I don't like these four fellows—especially the one in the high hat.'

'That's Amon, I suppose. And that one is Rameses. Why don't you like them? I think they're very impressive.'

'They're a damned sight too impressive—there's something uncanny about them. Come out into the sunlight.'

Linnet laughed, but yielded.

They came out of the temple into the sunshine with the sand yellow and warm about their feet. Linnet began to laugh. At their feet in a row, presenting a momentarily gruesome appearance as though sawn from their bodies, were the heads of half a dozen Nubian boys. The eyes rolled, the heads moved rhythmically from side to side, the lips chanted a new invocation:

'Hip, hip *hurray*! Hip, hip *hurray*! Very good, very nice. Thank you very much.'

'How absurd! How do they do it? Are they really buried very deep?'

Simon produced some small change.

'Very good, very nice, very expensive,' he mimicked.

Two small boys in charge of the 'show' picked up the coins neatly.

Linnet and Simon passed on.

They had no wish to return to the boat, and they were weary of sightseeing. They settled themselves with their backs to the cliff and let the warm sun bake them through.

'How lovely the sun is,' thought Linnet. 'How

warm—how safe... How lovely it is to be happy... How lovely to be me—me—me—Linnet—'

Her eyes closed. She was half asleep, half awake, drifting in the midst of thought that was like the sand drifting and blowing.

Simon's eyes were open. They too held contentment. What a fool he'd been to be rattled that first night... There was nothing to be rattled about... Everything was all right... After all, one could trust Jackie—

There was a shout—people running towards him waving their arms—shouting...

Simon stared stupidly for a moment. Then he sprang to his feet and dragged Linnet with him.

Not a minute too soon. A big boulder hurtling down the cliff crashed past them. If Linnet had remained where she was she would have been crushed to atoms.

White-faced they clung together. Hercule Poirot and Tim Allerton ran up to them.

'*Ma foi*, Madame, that was a near thing.'

All four instinctively looked up at the cliff. There was nothing to be seen. But there was a path along the top. Poirot remembered seeing some natives walking along there when they had first come ashore.

He looked at the husband and wife. Linnet looked dazed still—bewildered. Simon, however, was inarticulate with rage.

'God damn her!' he ejaculated.

He checked himself with a quick glance at Tim Allerton. The latter said:

Death on the Nile

'Phew, that was near! Did some fool bowl that thing over, or did it get detached on its own?'

Linnet was very pale. She said with difficulty:

'I think—some fool must have done it.'

'Might have crushed you like an eggshell. Sure you haven't got an enemy, Linnet?'

Linnet swallowed twice and found difficulty in answering the light-hearted raillery.

Poirot said quickly:

'Come back to the boat, Madame. You must have a restorative.'

They walked quickly, Simon still full of pent-up rage, Tim trying to talk cheerfully and distract Linnet's mind from the danger she had run, Poirot with a grave face.

And then, just as they reached the gangplank, Simon stopped dead. A look of amazement spread over his face.

Jacqueline de Bellefort was just coming ashore. Dressed in blue gingham, she looked childish this morning.

'Good God!' said Simon under his breath. 'So it *was* an accident, after all.'

The anger went out of his face. An overwhelming relief showed so plainly that Jacqueline noticed something amiss.

'Good morning,' she said. 'I'm afraid I'm a little on the late side.'

She gave them all a nod and stepped ashore and proceeded in the direction of the temple.

Simon clutched Poirot's arm. The other two had gone on.

'My God, that's a relief. I thought—I thought—'

Poirot nodded.

'Yes, yes, I know what you thought.'

But he himself still looked grave and preoccupied.

He turned his head and noted carefully what had become of the rest of the party from the ship.

Miss Van Schuyler was slowly returning on the arm of Miss Bowers.

A little farther away Mrs Allerton was standing laughing at the little Nubian row of heads. Mrs Otterbourne was with her.

The others were nowhere in sight.

Poirot shook his head as he followed Simon slowly onto the boat.

CHAPTER 10

'Will you explain to me, Madame, the meaning of the word "fey"?'

Mrs Allerton looked slightly surprised.

She and Poirot were toiling slowly up to the rock overlooking the Second Cataract. Most of the others had gone up on camels, but Poirot had felt that the motion of the camel was slightly reminiscent of that of a ship. Mrs Allerton had put it on the grounds of personal indignity.

They had arrived at Wadi Halfa the night before. This morning two launches had conveyed all the party to the Second Cataract, with the exception of Signor Richetti, who had insisted on making an excursion of his own to a remote spot called Semna, which he explained was of paramount interest as being the gateway of Nubia in the time of Amenemhet III, and where there was a stele recording the fact that on entering Egypt Negroes must pay customs duties. Everything had been done to discourage this example of individuality, but with no avail. Signor Richetti was determined and had waved aside each objection: (1) that the expedition was not worth making, (2) that the expedition could not be made, owing to the impossibility of getting a car there, (3) that no car could be obtained to do the trip, (4) that a car would be a prohibitive price. Having scoffed at (1), expressed incredulity at (2), offered to find a car himself to (3), and bargained fluently in Arabic for (4), Signor Richetti had at last departed—his departure being arranged in a secret and furtive manner in case some of the other tourists should take it into their heads to stray from the appointed paths of sightseeing.

'Fey?' Mrs Allerton put her head on one side as she considered her reply. 'Well, it's a Scotch word, really. It means the kind of exalted happiness that comes before disaster. You know—it's too good to be true.'

She enlarged on the theme. Poirot listened attentively.

'I thank you, Madame. I understand now. It is odd that you should have said that yesterday—when Madame Doyle was to escape death so shortly afterwards.'

Mrs Allerton gave a little shiver.

'It must have been a very near escape. Do you think some of these little black wretches rolled it over for fun? It's the sort of thing boys might do all over the world—not perhaps really meaning any harm.'

Poirot shrugged his shoulders.

'It may be, Madame.'

He changed the subject, talking of Majorca and asking various practical questions from the point of view of a possible visit.

Mrs Allerton had grown to like the little man very much—partly perhaps out of a contradictory spirit. Tim, she felt, was always trying to make her less friendly to Hercule Poirot, whom he had summarized firmly as 'the worst kind of bounder'. But she herself did not call him a bounder; she supposed it was his somewhat foreign exotic clothing which roused her son's prejudices. She herself found him an intelligent and stimulating companion. He was also extremely sympathetic. She found herself suddenly confiding in him her dislike of Joanna Southwood. It eased her to talk of the matter. And after all, why not? He did not know Joanna—would probably never meet her. Why should she not ease herself of that constantly borne burden of jealous thought?

At the same moment Tim and Rosalie Otterbourne were talking of her.

Tim had just been half-jestingly abusing his luck. His rotten health, never bad enough to be really interesting, yet not good enough for him to have led the life he would have chosen. Very little money, no congenial occupation.

'A thoroughly lukewarm, tame existence,' he finished discontentedly.

Rosalie said abruptly:

'You've got something heaps of people would envy you.'

'What's that?'

'Your mother.'

Tim was surprised and pleased.

'Mother? Yes, of course she is quite unique. It's nice of you to see it.'

Agatha Christie

'I think she's marvellous. She looks so lovely—so composed and calm—as though nothing could ever touch her, and yet—and yet somehow she's always ready to be funny about things too...'

Rosalie was stammering slightly in her earnestness.

Tim felt a rising warmth towards the girl. He wished he could return the compliment, but lamentably Mrs Otterbourne was his idea of the world's greatest menace. The inability to respond in kind made him embarrassed.

Miss Van Schuyler had stayed in the launch. She could not risk the ascent either on a camel or on her legs. She had said snappily:

'I'm sorry to have to ask you to stay with me, Miss Bowers. I intended you to go and Cornelia to stay, but girls are so selfish. She rushed off without a word to me. And I actually saw her talking to that very unpleasant and ill-bred young man, Ferguson. Cornelia has disappointed me sadly. She has absolutely no social sense.'

Miss Bowers replied in her usual matter-of-fact fashion:

'That's quite all right, Miss Van Schuyler. It would have been a hot walk up there, and I don't fancy the look of those saddles on the camels. Fleas, as likely as not.'

She adjusted her glasses, screwed up her eyes to look at the party descending the hill and remarked:

'Miss Robson isn't with that young man any more. She's with Dr Bessner.'

Miss Van Schuyler grunted.

Since she had discovered that Dr Bessner had a large clinic in Czechoslovakia and a European reputation as a fashionable physician, she was disposed to be gracious to him. Besides, she might need his professional services before the journey was over.

When the party returned to the *Karnak,* Linnet gave a cry of surprise.

'A telegram for me.'

She snatched it off the board and tore it open.

'Why—I don't understand—potatoes, beetroots—what does it mean, Simon?'

Simon was just coming to look over her shoulder when a furious voice said:

'Excuse me, that telegram is for me.

And Signor Richetti snatched it rudely from her hand, fixing her with a furious glare as he did so.

Linnet stared in surprise for a moment, then turned over the envelope.

'Oh, Simon, what a fool I am! It's Richetti—not Ridgeway—and anyway of course my name isn't Ridgeway now. I must apologize.'

She followed the little archaeologist up to the stern of the boat.

'I am so sorry, Signor Richetti. You see my name was Ridgeway before I married, and I haven't been married very long, and so...'

She paused, her face dimpled with smiles, inviting him to smile upon a young bride's *faux pas.*

But Richetti was obviously 'not amused'. Queen Victoria at her most disapproving could not have looked more grim.

Agatha Christie

'Names should be read carefully. It is inexcusable to be careless in these matters.'

Linnet bit her lip and her colour rose. She was not accustomed to have her apologies received in this fashion. She turned away and, rejoining Simon, said angrily, 'These Italians are really insupportable.'

'Never mind, darling; let's go and look at that big ivory crocodile you liked.'

They went ashore together.

Poirot, watching them walk up the landing stage, heard a sharp indrawn breath. He turned to see Jacqueline de Bellefort at his side. Her hands were clenched on the rail. The expression on her face as she turned it towards him quite startled him. It was no longer gay or malicious. She looked devoured by some inner consuming fire.

'They don't care any more.' The words came low and fast. 'They've got beyond me. I can't reach them... They don't mind if I'm here or not... I can't—I can't hurt them any more...'

Her hands on the rail trembled.

'Mademoiselle—'

She broke in: 'Oh, it's too late now—too late for warnings... You were right. I ought not to have come. Not on this journey. What did you call it? A journey of the soul? I can't go back—I've got to go on. And I'm going on. They shan't be happy together—they shan't. I'd kill him sooner...'

She turned abruptly away. Poirot, staring after her, felt a hand on his shoulder.

'Your girl friend seems a trifle upset, Monsieur Poirot.'

Poirot turned. He stared in surprise, seeing an old acquaintance.

'Colonel Race.'

The tall bronzed man smiled.

'Bit of a surprise, eh?'

Hercule Poirot had come across Colonel Race a year previously in London. They had been fellow guests at a very strange dinner party—a dinner party that had ended in death for that strange man, their host.

Poirot knew that Race was a man of unadvertised goings and comings. He was usually to be found in one of the outposts of Empire where trouble was brewing.

'So you are here at Wadi Halfa,' Poirot marked thoughtfully.

'I am here on this boat.'

'You mean?'

'That I am making the return journey with you to Shellal.'

Hercule Poirot's eyebrows rose.

'That is very interesting. Shall we, perhaps, have a little drink?'

They went into the observation saloon, now quite empty. Poirot ordered a whisky for the Colonel and a double orangeade full of sugar for himself.

'So you make the return journey with us,' said Poirot as he sipped. 'You would go faster, would you not, on the Government steamer, which travels by night as well as day?'

Colonel Race's face creased appreciatively.

'You're right on the spot as usual, Monsieur Poirot,' he said pleasantly.

'It is, then, the passengers?'

'One of the passengers.'

'Now which one, I wonder?' Hercule Poirot asked of the ornate ceiling.

'Unfortunately I don't know myself,' said Race ruefully.

Poirot looked interested.

Race said:

'There's no need to be mysterious to you. We've had a good deal of trouble out here—one way and another. It isn't the people who ostensibly lead the rioters that we're after. It's the men who very cleverly put the match to the gunpowder. There were three of them. One's dead. One's in prison. I want the third man—a man with five or six cold-blooded murders to his credit. He's one of the cleverest paid agitators that ever existed… He's on this boat. I know that from a passage in a letter that passed through our hands. Decoded it said: "X will be on the *Karnak* trip February seventh to thirteenth." It didn't say under what name X would be passing.'

'Have you any description of him?'

'No. American, Irish, and French descent. Bit of a mongrel. That doesn't help us much. Have you got any ideas?'

'An idea—it is all very well,' said Poirot meditatively.

Such was the understanding between them that Race pressed him no further. He knew Hercule Poirot did not ever speak unless he was sure.

Poirot rubbed his nose and said unhappily:

'There passes itself something on this boat that causes me much inquietude.'

Race looked at him inquiringly.

'Figure to yourself,' said Poirot, 'a person A who has grievously wronged a person B. The person B desires the revenge. The person B makes the threats.'

'A and B being both on this boat?'

Poirot nodded.

'Precisely.'

'And B, I gather, being a woman?'

'Exactly.'

Race lit a cigarette.

'I shouldn't worry. People who go about talking of what they are going to do don't usually do it.'

'And particularly is that the case with *les femmes*, you would say! Yes, that is true.'

But he still did not look happy.

'Anything else?' asked Race.

'Yes, there is something. Yesterday the person A had a very near escape from death. The kind of death that might very conveniently be called an accident.'

'Engineered by B?'

'No, that is just the point. B could have had nothing to do with it.'

'Then it *was* an accident.'

'I suppose so—but I do not like such accidents.'

'You're quite sure B could have had no hand in it?'

'Absolutely.'

'Oh, well, coincidences do happen. Who is A, by the way? A particularly disagreeable person?'

'On the contrary. A is a charming, rich, and beautiful young lady.'

Race grinned.

'Sounds quite like a novelette.'

'*Peut-être*. But I tell you, I am not happy, my friend. If I am right, and after all I am constantly in the habit of being right'—Race smiled into his moustache at this typical utterance—'then there is matter for grave inquietude. And now, *you* come to add yet another complication. You tell me that there is a man on the *Karnak* who kills.'

'He doesn't usually kill charming young ladies.'

Poirot shook his head in a dissatisfied manner.

'I am afraid, my friend,' he said. 'I am afraid... Today, I advised this lady, Madame Doyle, to go with her husband to Khartoum, not to return on this boat. But they would not agree. I pray to Heaven that we may arrive at Shellal without catastrophe.'

'Aren't you taking rather a gloomy view?'

Poirot shook his head.

'I am afraid,' he said simply. 'Yes, I, Hercule Poirot, am afraid...'

CHAPTER 11

Cornelia Robson stood inside the temple of Abu Simbel. It was the evening of the following day—a hot still evening. The *Karnak* was anchored once more at Abu Simbel to permit a second visit to be made to the temple, this time by artificial light. The difference this made was considerable, and Cornelia commented wonderingly on the fact to Mr Ferguson, who was standing by her side.

'Why, you see it ever so much better now!' she exclaimed. 'All those enemies having their heads cut off by the King—they just stand right out. That's a cute kind of castle there that I never noticed before. I wish Dr Bessner was here, he'd tell me what it was.'

'How you can stand that old fool beats me,' said Ferguson gloomily.

'Why, he's just one of the kindest men I've ever met.'

'Pompous old bore.'

'I don't think you ought to speak that way.'

The young man gripped her suddenly by the arm. They were just emerging from the temple into the moonlight.

'Why do you stick being bored by fat old men—and bullied and snubbed by a vicious old harridan?'

'Why, Mr Ferguson!'

'Haven't you got any spirit? Don't you know you're just as good as she is?'

'But I'm not!' Cornelia spoke with honest conviction.

'You're not as rich; that's all you mean.'

'No, it isn't. Cousin Marie's very cultured, and—'

'Cultured!' The young man let go of her arm as suddenly as he had taken it. 'That word makes me sick.'

Cornelia looked at him in alarm.

'She doesn't like you talking to me, does she?' said the young man.

Cornelia blushed and looked embarrassed.

'Why? Because she thinks I'm not her social equal! Pah! Doesn't that make you see red?'

Cornelia faltered out:

'I wish you wouldn't get so mad about things.'

'Don't you realize—and you an American—that everyone is born free and equal?'

'They're not,' said Cornelia with calm certainty.

'My good girl, it's part of your constitution!'

'Cousin Marie says politicians aren't gentlemen,' said Cornelia. 'And of course people aren't equal. It doesn't make sense. I know I'm kind of homely looking, and I used to feel mortified about it sometimes, but I've got over that. I'd like to have been born elegant and beautiful like Mrs Doyle, but I wasn't, so I guess it's no use worrying.'

'Mrs Doyle!' exclaimed Ferguson with deep contempt. 'She's the sort of woman who ought to be shot as an example.'

Cornelia looked at him anxiously.

'I believe it's your digestion,' she said kindly. 'I've got a special kind of pepsin that Cousin Marie tried once. Would you like to try it?'

Mr Ferguson said:

'You're impossible!'

He turned and strode away. Cornelia went on towards the boat. Just as she was crossing onto the gangway he caught her up once more.

'You're the nicest person on the boat,' he said. 'And mind you remember it.'

Blushing with pleasure Cornelia repaired to the observation saloon.

Miss Van Schuyler was conversing with Dr Bessner—an agreeable conversation dealing with certain royal patients of his.

Cornelia said guiltily:

'I do hope I haven't been a long time, Cousin Marie.'

Glancing at her watch, the old lady snapped:

'You haven't exactly hurried, my dear. And what have you done with my velvet stole?'

Cornelia looked round.

'Shall I see if it's in the cabin, Cousin Marie?'

'Of course it isn't! I had it just after dinner in here, and I haven't moved out of the place. It was on that chair.'

Agatha Christie

Cornelia made a desultory search.

'I can't see it anywhere, Cousin Marie.'

'Nonsense,' said Miss Van Schuyler. 'Look about.' It was an order such as one might give to a dog, and in her doglike fashion Cornelia obeyed. The quiet Mr Fanthorp, who was sitting at a table near by, rose and assisted her. But the stole could not be found.

The day had been such an unusually hot and sultry one that most people had retired early after going ashore to view the temple. The Doyles were playing bridge with Pennington and Race at a table in a corner. The only other occupant of the saloon was Hercule Poirot, who was yawning his head off at a small table near the door.

Miss Van Schuyler, making a Royal Progress bedward, with Cornelia and Miss Bowers in attendance, paused by his chair. He sprang politely to his feet, stifling a yawn of gargantuan dimensions.

Miss Van Schuyler said:

'I have only just realized who you are, Monsieur Poirot. I may tell you that I have heard of you from my old friend Rufus Van Aldin. You must tell me about your cases sometime.'

Poirot, his eyes twinkling a little through their sleepiness, bowed in an exaggerated manner. With a kindly but condescending nod, Miss Van Schuyler passed on.

Then he yawned once more. He felt heavy and stupid with sleep and could hardly keep his eyes open. He glanced over at the bridge players, absorbed in their game, then at

Death on the Nile

young Fanthorp, who was deep in a book. Apart from them the saloon was empty.

He passed through the swinging door out on to the deck. Jacqueline de Bellefort, coming precipitately along the deck, almost collided with him.

'Pardon, Mademoiselle.'

She said: 'You look sleepy, Monsieur Poirot.'

He admitted it frankly.

'*Mais oui*—I am consumed with sleep. I can hardly keep my eyes open. It has been a day very close and oppressive.'

'Yes.' She seemed to brood over it. 'It's been the sort of day when things—snap! Break! When one can't go on...'

Her voice was low and charged with passion.

She looked not at him, but towards the sandy shore. Her hands were clenched, rigid...

Suddenly the tension relaxed. She said: 'Good night, Monsieur Poirot.'

'Good night, Mademoiselle.'

Her eyes met his, just for a swift moment. Thinking it over the next day, he came to the conclusion that there had been appeal in that glance. He was to remember it afterwards.

Then he passed on to his cabin and she went towards the saloon.

Cornelia, having dealt with Miss Van Schuyler's many needs and fantasies, took some needlework with her back to the saloon. She herself did not feel in the least sleepy. On the contrary she felt wide awake and slightly excited.

The bridge four were still at it. In another chair the

quiet Fanthorp read a book. Cornelia sat down to her needlework.

Suddenly the door opened and Jacqueline de Bellefort came in. She stood in the doorway, her head thrown back. Then she pressed a bell and sauntered across to Cornelia and sat down.

'Been ashore?' she asked.

'Yes. I thought it was just fascinating in the moonlight.'

Jacqueline nodded.

'Yes, lovely night... A real honeymoon night.'

Her eyes went to the bridge table—rested a moment on Linnet Doyle.

The boy came in answer to the bell.

Jacqueline ordered a double gin. As she gave the order Simon Doyle shot a quick glance at her. A faint line of anxiety showed between his eyebrows.

His wife said:

'Simon, we're waiting for you to call.'

Jacqueline hummed a little tune to herself.

When the drink came, she picked it up, said: 'Well, here's to crime,' drank it off and ordered another.

Again Simon looked across from the bridge table. His calls became slightly absent-minded. His partner, Pennington, took him to task.

Jacqueline began to hum again, at first under her breath, then louder:

'He was her man and he did her wrong...'

'Sorry,' said Simon to Pennington. 'Stupid of me not to return your lead. That gives 'em rubber.'

Linnet rose to her feet.

'I'm sleepy. I think I'll go to bed.'

'About time to turn in,' said Colonel Race.

'I'm with you,' agreed Pennington.

'Coming, Simon?'

Doyle said slowly:

'Not just yet. I think I'll have a drink first.'

Linnet nodded and went out. Race followed her. Pennington finished his drink and then followed suit.

Cornelia began to gather up her embroidery.

'Don't go to bed, Miss Robson,' said Jacqueline. 'Please don't. I feel like making a night of it. Don't desert me.'

Cornelia sat down again.

'We girls must stick together,' said Jacqueline.

She threw back her head and laughed—a shrill laugh without merriment.

The second drink came.

'Have something,' said Jacqueline.

'No, thank you very much,' replied Cornelia.

Jacqueline tilted back her chair. She hummed now loudly: *'He was her man and he did her wrong...'*

Mr Fanthorp turned a page of *Europe from Within*.

Simon Doyle picked up a magazine.

'Really, I think I'll go to bed,' said Cornelia. 'It's getting very late.'

'You can't go to bed yet,' Jacqueline declared. 'I forbid you to. Tell me about yourself.'

'Well—I don't know—there isn't much to tell,' Cornelia faltered. 'I've just lived at home and I haven't been around much. This is my first trip to Europe. I'm just loving every minute of it.'

Jacqueline laughed.

'You're a happy sort of person, aren't you? God, I'd like to be you.'

'Oh, would you? But I mean—I'm sure—'

Cornelia felt flustered.

Undoubtedly Miss de Bellefort was drinking too much. That wasn't exactly a novelty to Cornelia. She had seen plenty of drunkenness during Prohibition years. But there was something else... Jacqueline de Bellefort was talking to her—was looking at her—and yet, Cornelia felt, it was as though, somehow, she was talking to someone else...

But there were only two other people in the room, Mr Fanthorp and Mr Doyle. Mr Fanthorp seemed quite absorbed in his book. Mr Doyle was looking rather odd—a queer sort of watchful look on his face.

Jacqueline said again:

'Tell me all about yourself.'

Always obedient, Cornelia tried to comply. She talked, rather heavily, going into unnecessary small details about her daily life. She was so unused to being the talker. Her role was so constantly that of the listener.

And yet Miss de Bellefort seemed to want to know. When Cornelia faltered to a standstill, the other girl was quick to prompt her.

'Go on—tell me more.'

And so Cornelia went on ('Of course, Mother's very delicate—some days she touches nothing but cereals—')

unhappily conscious that all she said was supremely uninteresting, yet flattered by the other girl's seeming interest. But was she interested? Wasn't she, somehow, listening to something else—or, perhaps, *for* something else? She was looking at Cornelia, yes, but wasn't there *someone else*, sitting in the room...?

'And of course we get very good art classes, and last winter I had a course of—'

(How late was it? Surely very late. She had been talking and talking. If only something definite would happen...)

And immediately, as though in answer to the wish, something did happen. Only, at that moment, it seemed very natural.

Jacqueline turned her head and spoke to Simon Doyle.

'Ring the bell, Simon. I want another drink.'

Simon Doyle looked up from his magazine and said quietly:

'The stewards have gone to bed. It's after midnight.'

'I tell you I want another drink.'

Simon said:

'You've had quite enough to drink, Jackie.'

She swung round at him.

'What damned business is it of yours?'

He shrugged his shoulders.

'None.'

She watched him for a minute or two. Then she said:

'What's the matter, Simon? Are you afraid?'

Simon did not answer. Rather elaborately he picked up his magazine again.

Cornelia murmured:

Agatha Christie

'Oh, dear—as late as that—I—must—'

She began to fumble, dropped a thimble...

Jacqueline said:

'Don't go to bed. I'd like another woman here—to support me.' She began to laugh again. 'Do you know what Simon over there is afraid of? He's afraid *I'm* going to tell you the story of *my* life.'

'Oh—er—' Cornelia spluttered a little.

Jacqueline said clearly:

'You see, he and I were once engaged.'

'Oh, really?'

Cornelia was the prey of conflicting emotions. She was deeply embarrassed but at the same time pleasurably thrilled. How—how *black* Simon Doyle was looking.

'Yes, it's a very sad story,' said Jacqueline; her soft voice was low and mocking. 'He treated me rather badly, didn't you, Simon?'

Simon Doyle said brutally:

'Go to bed, Jackie. You're drunk.'

'If you're embarrassed, Simon dear, you'd better leave the room.'

Simon Doyle looked at her. The hand that held the magazine shook a little, but he spoke bluntly.

'I'm staying,' he said.

Cornelia murmured for the third time, 'I really must—it's so late—'

'You're not to go,' said Jacqueline. Her hand shot out and held the other girl in her chair. 'You're to stay and hear what I've go to say.'

Death on the Nile

'Jackie,' said Simon sharply, 'you're making a fool of yourself! For God's sake, go to bed.'

Jacqueline sat up suddenly in her chair. Words poured from her rapidly in a soft hissing stream.

'You're afraid of a scene, aren't you? That's because you're so English—so reticent! You want me to behave "decently", don't you? But I don't care whether I behave decently or not! You'd better get out of here quickly—because I'm going to talk—a lot.'

Jim Fanthorp carefully shut his book, yawned, glanced at his watch, got up and strolled out. It was a very British and utterly unconvincing performance.

Jacqueline swung round in her chair and glared at Simon.

'You damned fool,' she said thickly, 'do you think you can treat me as you have done and get away with it?'

Simon Doyle opened his lips, then shut them again. He sat quite still as though he were hoping that her outburst would exhaust itself if he said nothing to provoke her further.

Jacqueline's voice came thick and blurred. It fascinated Cornelia, totally unused to naked emotions of any kind.

'I told you,' said Jacqueline, 'that I'd kill you sooner than see you go to another woman... You don't think I meant that? *You're wrong.* I've only been—waiting! You're *my* man! Do you hear? You belong to me...'

Still half did not speak. Jacqueline's hand fumbled a moment or two on her lap. She leant forward.

'I told you I'd kill you and I meant it...' Her hand came

Agatha Christie

up suddenly with something in it that flashed and gleamed. 'I'll shoot you like a dog—like the dirty dog you are...'

Now at last Simon acted. He sprang to his feet, but at the same moment she pulled the trigger...

Simon half twisted—fell across a chair... Cornelia screamed and rushed to the door. Jim Fanthorp was on the deck leaning over the rail. She called to him.

'Mr Fanthorp... Mr Fanthorp...'

He ran to her; she clutched at him incoherently...

'She's shot him—Oh! She's shot him...'

Simon Doyle still lay as he had fallen half into and across a chair... Jacqueline stood as though paralysed. She was trembling violently, and her eyes, dilated and frightened, were staring at the crimson stain slowly soaking through Simon's trouser leg just below the knee where he held a handkerchief close against the wound.

She stammered out:

'I didn't mean... Oh, my God, I didn't really mean...'

The pistol dropped from her nervous fingers with a clatter on the floor. She kicked it away with her foot. It slid under one of the settees.

Simon, his voice faint, murmured:

'Fanthorp, for heaven's sake—there's someone coming... Say it's all right—an accident—something. There mustn't be a scandal over this.'

Fanthorp nodded in quick comprehension. He wheeled round to the door where a startled Nubian face showed. He said:

'All right—all right—just fun!'

The black face looked doubtful, puzzled, then reassured. The teeth showed in a wide grin. The boy nodded and went off.

Fanthorp turned back.

'That's all right. Don't think anybody else heard. Only sounded like a cork, you know. Now the next thing—'

He was startled. Jacqueline suddenly began to weep hysterically.

'Oh, God, I wish I were dead... I'll kill myself. I'll be better dead... Oh, what have I done—what have I done?'

Cornelia hurried to her.

'Hush, dear, hush.'

Simon, his brow wet, his face twisted with pain, said urgently:

'Get her away. For God's sake, get her out of here! Get her to her cabin, Fanthorp. Look here, Miss Robson, get that hospital nurse of yours.' He looked appealingly from one to the other of them.

'Don't leave her. Make quite sure she's safe with the nurse looking after her. Then get hold of old Bessner and bring him here. For God's sake, don't let any news of this get to my wife.'

Jim Fanthorp nodded comprehendingly. The quiet young man was cool and competent in an emergency.

Between them he and Cornelia got the weeping, struggling girl out of the saloon and along the deck to her cabin. There they had more trouble with her. She fought to free herself; her sobs redoubled.

'I'll drown myself... I'll drown myself... I'm not fit to live... Oh, Simon—Simon!'

Fanthorp said to Cornelia:

'Better get hold of Miss Bowers. I'll stay while you get her.'

Cornelia nodded and hurried out.

As soon as she left, Jacqueline clutched Fanthorp.

'His leg—it's bleeding—broken... He may bleed to death. I must go to him... Oh, Simon—Simon—how could I?'

Her voice rose. Fanthorp said urgently:

'Quietly—quietly... He'll be all right.'

She began to struggle again.

'Let me go! Let me throw myself overboard... Let me kill myself!'

Fanthorp, holding her by the shoulders, forced her back on to the bed.

'You must stay here. Don't make a fuss. Pull yourself together. It's all right, I tell you.'

To his relief, the distraught girl did manage to control herself a little, but he was thankful when the curtains were pushed aside and the efficient Miss Bowers, neatly dressed in a hideous kimono, entered accompanied by Cornelia.

'Now then,' said Miss Bowers briskly, 'what's all this?'

She took charge without any sign of surprise and alarm.

Fanthorp thankfully left the overwrought girl in her capable hands and hurried along to the cabin occupied by Dr Bessner.

He knocked and entered on top of the knock.

Death on the Nile

'Dr Bessner?'

A terrific snore resolved itself, and a startled voice said:

'So? What is it?'

By this time Fanthorp had switched the light on. The doctor blinked up at him, looking rather like a large owl.

'It's Doyle. He's been shot. Miss de Bellefort shot him. He's in the saloon. Can you come?'

The stout doctor reacted promptly. He asked a few curt questions, pulled on his bedroom slippers and a dressinggown, picked up a little case of necessaries and accompanied Fanthorp to the lounge.

Simon had managed to get the window beside him open. He was leaning his head against it, inhaling the air. His face was a ghastly colour.

Dr Bessner came over to him.

'Ha? So? What have we here?'

A handkerchief sodden with blood lay on the carpet, and on the carpet itself was a dark stain.

The doctor's examination was punctuated with Teutonic grunts and exclamations.

'Yes, it is bad this... The bone is fractured. And a big loss of blood. Herr Fanthorp, you and I must get him to my cabin. So—like this. He cannot walk. We must carry him, thus.'

As they lifted him Cornelia appeared in the doorway. Catching sight of her, the doctor uttered a grunt of satisfaction.

'Ach, it is you? Goot. Come with us. I have need of

assistance. You will be better than my friend here. He looks a little pale already.'

Fanthorp emitted a rather sickly smile.

'Shall I get Miss Bowers?' he asked.

Dr Bessner threw a considering glance over Cornelia.

'You will do very well, young lady,' he announced. 'You will not faint or be foolish, hein?'

'I can do what you tell me,' said Cornelia eagerly.

Bessner nodded in a satisfied fashion.

The procession passed along the deck.

The next ten minutes were purely surgical and Mr Jim Fanthorp did not enjoy it at all. He felt secretly ashamed of the superior fortitude exhibited by Cornelia.

'So, that is the best I can do,' announced Dr Bessner at last. 'You have been a hero, my friend.' He patted Simon approvingly on the shoulder.

Then he rolled up his sleeve and produced a hypodermic needle.

'And now I will give you something to make you sleep. Your wife, what about her?'

Simon said weakly:

'She needn't know till the morning…' He went on: 'I—you mustn't blame Jackie… It's been all my fault. I treated her disgracefully… poor kid—she didn't know what she was doing…'

Dr Bessner nodded comprehendingly.

'Yes, yes—I understand…'

'My fault—' Simon urged. His eyes went to Cornelia. 'Someone—ought to stay with her. She might—hurt herself—'

Death on the Nile

Dr Bessner injected the needle. Cornelia said, with quiet competence:

'It's all right, Mr Doyle. Miss Bowers is going to stay with her all night...'

A grateful look flashed over Simon's face. His body relaxed. His eyes closed. Suddenly he jerked them open. 'Fanthorp?'

'Yes, Doyle.'

'The pistol... Ought not to leave it... lying about... The boys will find it in the morning...'

Fanthorp nodded.

'Quite right. I'll go and get hold of it now.'

He went out of the cabin and along the deck. Miss Bowers appeared at the door of Jacqueline's cabin.

'She'll be all right now,' she announced. 'I've given her a morphine injection.'

'But you'll stay with her?'

'Oh, yes. Morphia excites some people. I shall stay all night.'

Fanthorp went on to the lounge.

Some three minutes later there was a tap on Bessner's cabin door.

'Dr Bessner?'

'Yes?' The stout man appeared.

Fanthorp beckoned him out on the deck.

'Look here—I can't find that pistol...'

'What is that?'

'The pistol. It dropped out of the girl's hand. She kicked it away and it went under a settee. *It isn't under that settee now.*'

Agatha Christie

They stared at each other.

'But who can have taken it?'

Fanthorp shrugged his shoulders.

Bessner said:

'It is curious, that. But I do not see what we can do about it.'

Puzzled and vaguely alarmed, the two men separated.

CHAPTER 12

Hercule Poirot was just wiping the lather from his freshly shaved face when there was a quick tap on the door and hard on top of it Colonel Race entered unceremoniously.

He closed the door behind him.

He said:

'Your instinct was quite correct. It's happened.'

Poirot straightened up and asked sharply:

'What has happened?'

'Linnet Doyle's dead—shot through the head last night.'

Poirot was silent for a minute, two memories vividly before him—a girl in a garden at Aswan saying in a hard breathless voice, 'I'd like to put my dear little pistol against her head and just press the trigger,' and another more recent memory, the same voice saying: 'One feels one can't go on—the kind of day when something breaks'—and that strange momentary flash of appeal in her eyes. What had been the matter with him not to respond to that appeal? He had been blind, deaf, stupid with his need for sleep...

S.S. KARNAK
PROMENADE DECK

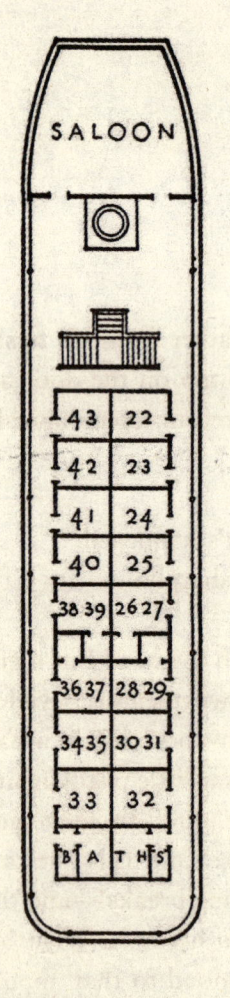

43	22 JAMES FANTHORP
42	23 TIM ALLERTON
41 CORNELIA ROBSON.	24 MRS ALLERTON
40 JACQUELINE DE BELLEFORT	25 SIMON DOYLE
38 39 ANDREW PENNINGTON	26 27 LINNET DOYLE
36 37 DR BESSNER	28 29 MISS VAN SCHUYLER
34 35 MRS AND MISS OTTERBOURNE	30 31 HERCULE POIROT
33 MISS BOWERS	32 COLONEL RACE

PLAN   CABINS

Race went on:

'I've got some slight official standing—they sent for me, put it in my hands. The boat's due to start in half an hour, but it will be delayed till I give the word. There's a possibility, of course, that the murderer came from the shore.'

Poirot shook his head.

Race acquiesced in the gesture.

'I agree. One can pretty well rule that out. Well, man, it's up to you. This is your show.'

Poirot had been attiring himself with a neat-fingered celerity. He said now:

'I am at your disposal.'

The two men stepped out on the deck.

Race said:

'Bessner should be there by now. I sent the steward for him.'

There were four cabins de luxe, with bathrooms, on the boat. Of the two on the port side one was occupied by Dr Bessner, the other by Andrew Pennington. On the starboard side the first was occupied by Miss Van Schuyler, and the one next to it by Linnet Doyle. Her husband's dressing cabin was next door.

A white-faced steward was standing outside the door of Linnet Doyle's cabin. He opened the door for them and they passed inside. Dr Bessner was bending over the bed. He looked up and grunted as the other two entered.

'What can you tell us, Doctor, about this business?' asked Race.

Bessner rubbed his unshaven jaw meditatively.

'Ach! She was shot—shot at close quarters. See—here just above the ear—that is where the bullet entered. A very little bullet—I should say a .22. The pistol, it was held close against her head—see, there is blackening here, the skin is scorched.'

Again in a sick wave of memory Poirot thought of those words uttered in Aswan.

Bessner went on.

'She was asleep—there was no struggle—the murderer crept up in the dark and shot her as she lay there.'

'Ah! non!' Poirot cried out. His sense of psychology was outraged. Jacqueline de Bellefort creeping into a darkened cabin, pistol in hand—no, it did not 'fit', that picture.

Bessner stared at him with his thick lenses.

'But that is what happened, I tell you.'

'Yes, yes. I did not mean what you thought. I was not contradicting you.'

Bessner gave a satisfied grunt.

Poirot came up and stood beside him. Linnet Doyle was lying on her side. Her attitude was natural and peaceful. But above the ear was a tiny hole with an incrustation of dried blood round it.

Poirot shook his head sadly.

Then his gaze fell on the white painted wall just in front of him and he drew in his breath sharply. Its white neatness was marred by a big wavering letter J scrawled in some brownish-red medium.

Poirot stared at it, then he leaned over the dead girl and

very gently picked up her right hand. One finger of it was stained a brownish-red.

'*Non d'un nom d'un nom!*' ejaculated Hercule Poirot.

'Eh? What is that?'

Dr Bessner looked up.

'Ach! *That.*'

Race said:

'Well, I'm damned. What do you make of that, Poirot?'

Poirot swayed a little on his toes.

'You ask me what I make of it. *Eh bien*, it is very simple, is it not? Madame Doyle is dying; she wishes to indicate her murderer, and so she writes with her finger, dipped in her own blood, the initial letter of her murderer's name. Oh, yes, it is astonishingly simple.'

'Ach, but—'

Dr Bessner was about to break out, but a peremptory gesture from Race silenced him.

'So it strikes you that?' he asked slowly.

Poirot turned round on him, nodding his head.

'Yes, yes. It is, as I say, of an astonishing simplicity! It is so familiar, is it not? *It has been done so often*, in the pages of the romance of crime! It is now, indeed, a little *vieux jeu*! It leads one to suspect that our murderer is—old-fashioned!'

Race drew a long breath.

'I see,' he said. 'I thought at first—'

He Stopped.

Poirot said with a very faint smile:

'That I believed in all the old cliche's of melodrama? But pardon, Dr Bessner, you were about to say—?'

Agatha Christie

Bessner broke out gutturally:

'What do I say? Pah! I say it is absurd—it is the nonsense! The poor lady she died instantaneously. To dip her finger in the blood (and as you see, there is hardly any blood) and write the latter J upon the wall. Bah—it is the nonsense—the melodramatic nonsense!'

'*C'est l'enfantillage*,' agreed Poirot.

'But it was done with a purpose,' suggested Race.

'That—naturally,' agreed Poirot, and his face was grave. Race said.

'What does J stand for?'

Poirot replied promptly: 'J stands for Jacqueline de Bellefort, a young lady who declared to me less than a week ago that she would like nothing better than to—' he paused and then deliberately quoted, '"to put my dear little pistol close against her head and then just press with my finger..."'

'*Gott im Himmel!* exclaimed Dr Bessner.

There was a momentary silence. Then Race drew a deep breath and said:

'*Which is just what was done here?*'

Bessner nodded.

'That is so, yes. It was a pistol of very small calibre—as I say, probably a .22. The bullet has got to be extracted, of course, before we can say definitely.'

Race nodded in swift comprehension. Then he said:

'What about time of death?'

Bessner stroked his jaw again. His finger made a rasping sound.

'I would not care to be too precise. It is now eight o'clock. I will say, with due regard to the temperature last night, that she has been dead certainly six hours and probably not longer than eight.'

'That puts it between midnight and two a.m.'

'That is so.'

There was a pause. Race looked around.

'What about her husband? I suppose he sleeps in the cabin next door.'

'At the moment,' said Dr Bessner, 'he is asleep in my cabin.'

Both men looked very surprised.

Bessner nodded his head several times.

'Ach, so. I see you have not been told about that. Mr Doyle was shot last night in the saloon.'

'Shot? By whom?'

'By the young lady, Jacqueline de Bellefort.'

Race asked sharply:

'Is he badly hurt?'

'Yes, the bone was splintered. I have done all that is possible at the moment, but it is necessary, you understand, that the fracture should be X-rayed as soon as possible and proper treatment given, such as is impossible on this boat.'

Poirot murmured:

'Jacqueline de Bellefort.'

His eyes went again to the J on the wall.

Race said abruptly:

'If there is nothing more we can do here for the moment,

Agatha Christie

let's go below. The management has put the smoking room at our disposal. We must get the details of what happened last night.'

They left the cabin. Race locked the door and took the key with him.

'We can come back later,' he said. 'The first thing to do is to get all the facts clear.'

They went down to the deck below, where they found the manager of the *Karnak* waiting uneasily in the doorway of the smoking room.

The poor man was terribly upset and worried over the whole business, and was eager to leave everything in Colonel Race's hands.

'I feel I can't do better than leave it to you, sir, seeing your official position. I'd had orders to put myself at your disposal in the—er—other matter. If you will take charge, I'll see that everything is done as you wish.'

'Good man! To begin with I'd like this room kept clear for me and Monsieur Poirot during this inquiry.'

'Certainly, sir.'

'That's all at present. Go on with your own work. I know where to find you.'

Looking slightly relieved, the manager left the room.

Race said:

'Sit down, Bessner, and let's have the whole story of what happened last night.'

They listened in silence to the doctor's rumbling voice.

'Clear enough,' said Race, when he had finished. 'The girl worked herself up, helped by a drink or two, and finally

Death on the Nile

took a pot shot at the man with a .22 pistol. Then she went along to Linnet Doyle's cabin and shot her as well.'

But Dr Bessner was shaking his head.

'No, no, I do not think so. I do not think that was *possible*. For one thing she would not write her own initial on the wall—it would be ridiculous, *nicht wahr?*'

'She might,' Race declared, 'if she were as blindly mad and jealous as she sounds; she might want to—well—sign her name to the crime, so to speak.'

Poirot shook his head.

'No, no, I do not think she would be as—as *crude* as that.'

'Then there's only one reason for that J. It was put there by someone else deliberately to throw suspicion on her.'

The doctor said:

'Yes, and the criminal was unlucky, because, you see, it is not only *unlikely* that the young Fräulein did the murder—it is also I think *impossible*.'

'How's that?'

Bessner explained Jacqueline's hysterics and the circumstances which had led Miss Bowers to take charge of her.

'And I think—I am sure—that Miss Bowers stayed with her all night.'

Race said:

'If that's so, it's going to simplify matters very much.'

Poirot asked:

'Who discovered the crime?'

'Mrs Doyle's maid, Louise Bourget. She went to call her mistress as usual, found her dead, and came out and flopped into the steward's arms in a dead faint. He went to the manager, who came to me. I got hold of Bessner and then came for you.'

Poirot nodded.

Race said:

'Doyle's got to know. You say he's asleep still?'

The doctor said:

'Yes, he's still asleep in my cabin. I gave him a strong opiate last night.'

Race turned to Poirot.

'Well,' he said, 'I don't think we need detain the doctor any longer, eh? Thank you, Doctor.'

Bessner rose.

'I will have my breakfast, yes. And then I will go back to my cabin and see if Mr Doyle is ready to wake.'

'Thanks.'

Bessner went out. The two men looked at each other.

'Well, what about it, Poirot?' Race asked. 'You're the man in charge. I'll take my orders from you. You say what's to be done.'

Poirot bowed.

'*Eh bien!*' he said, 'we must hold the court of inquiry. First of all, I think we must verify the story of the affair last night. That is to say, we must question Fanthorp and Miss Robson, who were the actual witnesses of what occurred. The disappearance of the pistol is very significant.'

Race rang a bell and sent a message by the steward.

Poirot sighed and shook his head.

'It is bad, this,' he murmured. 'It is bad.'

Death on the Nile

'Have you any ideas?' asked Race curiously.

'My ideas conflict. They are not well arranged—they are not orderly. There is, you see, the big fact that this girl hated Linnet Doyle and wanted to kill her.'

'You think she's capable of it?'

'I think so—yes.' Poirot sounded doubtful.

'But not in this way? That's what's worrying you, isn't it? Not to creep into her cabin in the dark and shoot her while she was sleeping. It's the cold-bloodedness that strikes you as not ringing true.'

'In a sense, yes.'

'You think that this girl, Jacqueline de Bellefort, is incapable of a premeditated cold-blooded murder.'

Poirot said slowly:

'I am not sure, you see. She would have the brains—yes. But I doubt if, physically, she could bring herself to do the *act*...'

Race nodded.

'Yes, I see... Well, according to Bessner's story, it would also have been physically impossible.'

'If that is true it clears the ground considerably. Let us hope it is true.' Poirot paused and then added simply: 'I shall be glad if it is so, for I have for that little one much sympathy.'

The door opened and Fanthorp and Cornelia came in. Bessner followed them.

Cornelia gasped out:

'Isn't this just awful? Poor, poor Mrs Doyle! And she was so lovely too. It must have been a real *fiend* who could hurt her! And poor Mr Doyle, he'll go half crazy when he knows! Why, even last night he was so frightfully worried lest she should hear about his accident.'

'That is just what we want you to tell us about, Miss Robson,' said Race. 'We want to know exactly what happened last night.'

Cornelia began a little confusedly, but a question or two from Poirot helped matters.

'Ah, yes, I understand. After the bridge, Madame Doyle went to her cabin. Did she really go to her cabin, I wonder?'

'She did,' said Race. 'I actually saw her. I said good night to her at the door.'

'And the time?'

'Mercy, I couldn't say,' replied Cornelia.

'It was twenty past eleven,' said Race.

'*Bien*. Then at twenty past eleven, Madame Doyle was alive and well. At that moment there was in the saloon—who?

Fanthorp answered.

'Doyle was there. And Miss de Bellefort. Myself and Miss Robson.'

'That's so,' agreed Cornelia. 'Mr Pennington had a drink and then went off to bed.'

'That was how much later?'

'Oh, about three or four minutes.'

'Before half-past eleven, then?'

'Oh, yes.'

'So that there were left in the saloon you, Mademoiselle Robson, Mademoiselle de Bellefort, Monsieur Doyle and Monsieur Fanthorp. What were you all doing?'

Death on the Nile

'Mr Fanthorp was reading a book. I'd got some embroidery. Miss de Bellefort was—she was—'

Fanthorp came to the rescue.

'She was drinking pretty heavily.'

'Yes,' agreed Cornelia. 'She was talking to me mostly and asking me about things at home. And she kept saying things—to me mostly, but I think they were kind of meant for Mr Doyle. He was getting kind of mad at her, but he didn't say anything. I think he thought if he kept quiet she might simmer down.

'But she didn't?'

Cornelia shook her head.

'I tried to go once or twice, but she made me stop, and I was getting very, very uncomfortable. And then Mr Fanthorp got up and went out—'

'It was a little embarrassing,' said Fanthorp. 'I thought I'd make an unobtrusive exit. Miss de Bellefort was clearly working up for a scene.'

'And then she pulled out the pistol,' went on Cornelia, 'and Mr Doyle jumped up to try and get it away from her, and it went off and shot him through the leg, and then she began to sob and cry—and I was scared to death and ran out after Mr Fanthorp and he came back with me, and Mr Doyle said not to make a fuss, and one of the Nubian boys heard the noise of the shot and came along, but Mr Fanthorp told him it was all right, and then we got Jacqueline away to her cabin and Mr Fanthorp stayed with her while I got Miss Bowers.'

Cornelia paused breathless.

'What time was this?' asked Race.

Cornelia said again, 'Mercy, I don't know,' but Fanthorp answered promptly:

'It must have been about twenty minutes past twelve. I know that it was actually half past twelve when I finally got to my cabin.'

'Now let me be quite sure on one or two points,' said Poirot. 'After Madame Doyle left the saloon, did any of you four leave it?'

'No.'

'You are quite certain Mademoiselle de Bellefort did not leave the saloon at all?'

Fanthorp answered promptly:

'Positive. Neither Doyle, Miss de Bellefort, Miss Robson, nor myself left the saloon.'

'Good. That establishes the fact that Mademoiselle de Bellefort could not possibly have shot Madame Doyle before—let us say—twenty past twelve. Now, Mademoiselle Robson, you went to fetch Mademoiselle Bowers. Was Mademoiselle de Bellefort alone in her cabin during that period?'

'No. Mr Fanthorp stayed with her.'

'Good! So far, Mademoiselle de Bellefort has a perfect alibi. Mademoiselle Bowers is the next person to interview, but, before I send for her I should like to have your opinion on one or two points. Monsieur Doyle, you say, was very anxious that Mademoiselle de Bellefort should not be left alone. Was he afraid, do you think, that she was contemplating some further rash act?'

'That is my opinion,' said Fanthorp.

'He was definitely afraid she might attack Madame Doyle?'

'No.' Fanthorp shook his head. 'I don't think that was his idea at all. I think he was afraid she might—er—do something rash to herself.'

'Suicide?'

'Yes. You see, she seemed completely sobered and heartbroken at what she had done. She was full of self-reproach. She kept saying she would be better dead.'

Cornelia said timidly:

'I think he was rather upset about her. He spoke—quite nicely. He said it was all his fault—that he'd treated her badly. He—he was really very nice.'

Hercule Poirot nodded thoughtfully.

'Now about that pistol,' he went on. 'What happened to that?'

'She dropped it,' said Cornelia.

'And afterwards?'

Fanthorp explained how he had gone back to search for it, but had not been able to find it.

'Aha!' said Poirot. 'Now we begin to arrive. Let us, I pray you, be very precise. Describe to me exactly what happened.'

'Miss de Bellefort let it fall. Then she kicked it away from her with her foot.'

'She sort of hated it,' explained Cornelia. 'I know just what she felt.'

'And it went under a settee, you say. Now be very careful.

Agatha Christie

Mademoiselle de Bellefort did not recover that pistol before she left the saloon?'

Both Fanthorp and Cornelia were positive on that point.

'*Précisément*. I seek only to be very exact, you comprehend. Then we arrive at this point. When Mademoiselle de Bellefort leaves the saloon the pistol is under the settee. And since Mademoiselle de Bellefort is not left alone—Monsieur Fanthorp, Mademoiselle Robson or Mademoiselle Bowers being with her—she has no opportunity to get back the pistol after she left the saloon. What time was it, Monsieur Fanthorp, when you went back to look for it?'

'It must have been just before half past twelve.'

'And how long would have elapsed between the time you and Dr Bessner carried Monsieur Doyle out of the saloon until you returned to look for the pistol?'

'Perhaps five minutes—perhaps a little more.'

'Then in that five minutes *someone removes that pistol from where it lay out of sight under the settee.* That someone was *not* Mademoiselle de Bellefort. Who was it? It seems highly probable that the person who removed it was the murderer of Madame Doyle. We may assume, too, that that person had overheard or seen something of the events immediately preceding.'

'I don't see how you make that out,' objected Fanthorp.

'Because,' said Hercule Poirot, 'you have just told us that *the pistol was out of sight under the settee*. Therefore it is hardly credible that it was discovered by *accident*. It was taken by *someone who knew it was there*. Therefore that someone must have assisted at the scene.'

Fanthorp shook his head.

'I saw no one when I went out on the deck just before the shot was fired.'

'Ah, but you went out by the door on the starboard side.'

'Yes. The same side as my cabin.'

'Then if there had been anybody at the port door looking through the glass you would not have seen him?'

'No,' admitted Fanthorp.

'Did anyone hear the shot except the Nubian boy?'

'Not as far as I know.'

Fanthorp went on:

'You see, the windows in here were all closed. Miss Van Schuyler felt a draught earlier in the evening. The swing doors were shut. I doubt if the shot would be clearly heard. It would only sound like the pop of a cork.'

Race said:

'As far as I know, no one seems to have heard the other shot—the shot that killed Mrs Doyle.'

'That we will inquire into presently,' said Poirot. 'For the moment we still concern ourselves with Mademoiselle de Bellefort. We must speak to Mademoiselle Bowers. But first, before you go'—he arrested Fanthorp and Cornelia with a gesture—'you will give me a little information about yourselves. Then it will not be necessary to call you again later. You first, Monsieur—your full name.'

'James Lechdale Fanthorp.'

'Address?'

'Glasmore House, Market Donnington, Northamptonshire.'

'Your profession?'

Agatha Christie

'I am a lawyer.'

'And your reasons for visiting this country?'

There was a pause. For the first time the impassive Mr Fanthorp seemed taken a back. He said at last—almost mumbling the words:

'Er—pleasure.'

'Aha!' said Poirot. 'You take the holiday; that is it, yes?'

'Er—yes.'

'Very well, Monsieur Fanthorp. Will you give me a brief account of your own movements last night after the events we have just been narrating?'

'I went straight to bed.'

'That was at—?'

'Just after half past twelve.'

'Your cabin is number twenty-two on the starboard side—the one nearest the saloon.'

'Yes.'

'I will ask you one more question. Did you hear anything—anything at all—after you went to your cabin?'

Fanthorp considered.

'I turned in very quickly. I *think* I heard a kind of splash just as I was dropping off to sleep. Nothing else.'

'You heard a kind of splash? Near at hand?'

Fanthorp shook his head.

'Really, I couldn't say. I was half asleep.'

'And what time would that be?'

'It might have been about one o'clock. I can't really say.'

'Thank you, Monsieur Fanthorp. That is all.'

Poirot turned his attention to Cornelia.

Death on the Nile

'And now, Mademoiselle Robson. Your full name?'

'Cornelia Ruth. And my address is The Red House, Bellfield, Connecticut.'

'What brought you to Egypt?'

'Cousin Marie, Miss Van Schuyler, brought me along on a trip.'

'Had you ever met Madame Doyle previous to this journey?'

'No, never.'

'And what did you do last night?'

'I went right to bed after helping Dr Bessner with Mr Doyle's leg.'

'Your cabin is—?'

'Forty-one on the port side—right next door to Miss de Bellefort.'

'And did you hear anything?'

Cornelia shook her head. 'I didn't hear a thing.'

'No splash?'

'No, but then I wouldn't, because the boat's against the bank on my side.'

Poirot nodded.

'Thank you, Mademoiselle Robson. Now perhaps you will be so kind as to ask Mademoiselle Bowers to come here.'

Fanthorp and Cornelia went out.

'That seems clear enough,' said Race. 'Unless three independent witnesses are lying, Jacqueline de Bellefort couldn't have got hold of the pistol. But somebody did. And somebody overheard the scene. And somebody was B.F. enough to write a big J on the wall.'

Agatha Christie

There was a tap on the door and Miss Bowers entered. The hospital nurse sat down in her usual composed efficient manner. In answer to Poirot she gave her name, address, and qualifications, adding:

'I've been looking after Miss Van Schuyler for over two years now.'

'Is Mademoiselle Van Schuyler's health very bad?'

'Why, no, I wouldn't say that,' replied Miss Bowers. 'She's not very young, and she's nervous about herself, and she likes to have a nurse around handy. There's nothing serious the matter with her. She just likes plenty of attention, and she's willing to pay for it.'

Poirot nodded comprehendingly. Then he said:

'I understand that Mademoiselle Robson fetched you last night?'

'Why, yes, that's so.'

'Will you tell me exactly what happened?'

'Well, Miss Robson just gave me a brief outline of what had occurred, and I came along with her. I found Miss de Bellefort in a very excited, hysterical condition.'

'Did she utter any threats against Madame Doyle?'

'No, nothing of that kind. She was in a condition of morbid self-reproach. She'd taken a good deal of alcohol, I should say, and she was suffering from reaction. I didn't think she ought to be left. I gave her a shot of morphia and sat up with her.'

'Now, Mademoiselle Bowers, I want you to answer this. Did Mademoiselle de Bellefort leave her cabin at all?'

'No, she did not.'

'And you yourself?'

'I stayed with her until early this morning.'

'You are quite sure of that?'

'Absolutely sure.'

'Thank you, Mademoiselle Bowers.'

The nurse went out. The two men looked at each other.

Jacqueline de Bellefort was definitely cleared of the crime. Who then had shot Linnet Doyle?

CHAPTER 13

Race said:

'Someone pinched the pistol. *It wasn't Jacqueline de Bellefort*. Someone knew enough to feel that his crime would be attributed to her. But that someone did *not* know that a hospital nurse was going to give her morphia and sit up with her all night. Add one thing more. Someone had already attempted to kill Linnet Doyle by rolling a boulder over the cliff; that someone was *not* Jacqueline de Bellefort. *Who was it*?'

Poirot said:

'It will be simpler to say who it could not have been. Neither Monsieur Doyle, Madame Allerton, Monsieur Tim Allerton, Mademoiselle Van Schuyler nor Mademoiselle Bowers could have had anything to do with it. They were all within my sight.'

'H'm,' said Race, 'that leaves rather a large field. What about motive?

Death on the Nile

'That is where I hope Monsieur Doyle may be able to help us. There have been several incidents—'

The door opened and Jacqueline de Bellefort entered.

She was very pale and she stumbled a little as she walked.

'I didn't do it,' she said. Her voice was that of a frightened child. 'I didn't do it. Oh, please believe me. Everyone will think I did it—but I didn't—I didn't. It's—it's awful. I wish it hadn't happened. I might have killed Simon last night—I was mad, I think. But I didn't do the other...'

She sat down and burst into tears.

Poirot patted her on the shoulder.

'There, there. We know that you did not kill Madame Doyle. It is proved—yes, proved, *mon enfant*. It was not you.'

Jackie sat up suddenly, her wet handkerchief clasped in her hand.

'But who did?'

'That,' said Poirot, 'is just the question we are asking ourselves. You cannot help us there, my child?'

Jacqueline shook her head.

'I don't know... I can't imagine... No, I haven't the faintest idea.'

She frowned deeply. 'No,' she said at last. 'I can't think of anyone who wanted her dead'—her voice faltered a little—'except me.'

Race said:

'Excuse me a minute—just thought of something.'

Agatha Christie

He hurried out of the room.

Jacqueline de Bellefort sat with her head downcast, nervously twisting her fingers.

She broke out suddenly: 'Death's horrible—horrible! I—hate the thought of it.'

Poirot said:

'Yes. It is not pleasant to think, is it, that now, at this very moment, someone is rejoicing at the successful carrying out of his or her plan.'

'Don't—don't!' cried Jackie. 'It sounds horrible, the way you put it.'

Poirot shrugged his shoulders.

'It is true.'

Jackie said in a low voice:

'I—I wanted her dead—and she *is* dead... And, what is worse... she died—just like I said.'

'Yes, Mademoiselle. She was shot through the head.'

She cried out:

'Then I was right, that night at the Cataract Hotel. There *was* someone listening!'

'Ah!' Poirot nodded his head. 'I wondered if you would remember that. Yes, it is altogether too much of a coincidence—that Madame Doyle should be killed in just the way you described.'

Jackie shuddered.

'That man that night—who can he have been?'

Poirot was silent for a minute or two, then he said in quite a different tone of voice:

'You are sure it was a man, Mademoiselle?'

Jackie looked at him in surprise.

'Yes, of course. At least—'

'Well, Mademoiselle?'

She frowned, half closing her eyes in an effort to remember. She said slowly:

'I *thought* it was a man...'

'But now you are not so sure?'

Jackie said slowly:

'No, I can't be certain. I just assumed it was a man—but it was really just a—a figure—a shadow...'

She paused and then, as Poirot did not speak, she added: 'You think it must have been a woman? But surely none of the women on this boat can have wanted to kill Linnet?'

Poirot merely moved his head from side to side.

The door opened and Bessner appeared.

'Will you come and speak with Mr Doyle, please, Monsieur Poirot? He would like to see you.'

Jackie sprang up. She caught Bessner by the arm.

'How is he? Is he—all right?'

'Naturally he is not all right,' replied Dr Bessner reproachfully. 'The bone is fractured, you understand.'

'But he's not going to die?' cried Jackie.

'Ach, who said anything about dying? We will get him to civilization and there we will have an X-ray and proper treatment.'

'Oh!' The girl's hands came together in a convulsive pressure. She sank down again on a chair.

Poirot stepped out on to the deck with the doctor and

at that moment Race joined them. They went up to the promenade deck and along to Bessner's cabin.

Simon Doyle was lying propped with cushions and pillows, an improvised cage over his leg. His face was ghastly in colour, the ravages of pain with shock on top of it. But the predominant expression on his face was bewilderment—the sick bewilderment of a child.

He muttered:

'Please come in. The doctor's told me—told me—about Linnet... I can't believe it. I simply can't believe it's true.'

'I know. It's a bad knock,' said Race.

Simon stammered:

'You know—Jackie didn't do it. I'm certain Jackie didn't do it! It looks black against her, I dare say, but *she didn't do it*. She—she was a bit tight last night, and all worked up, and that's why she went for me. But she wouldn't—she wouldn't do *murder*... not cold-blooded murder...'

Poirot said gently:

'Do not distress yourself, Monsieur Doyle. Whoever shot your wife, it was not Mademoiselle de Bellefort.'

Simon looked at him doubtfully.

'Is that on the level?'

'But since it was not Mademoiselle de Bellefort,' continued Poirot, 'can you give us any idea of who it might have been?'

Simon shook his head. The look of bewilderment increased.

'It's crazy—impossible. Apart from Jackie nobody could have wanted to do her in.'

'Reflect, Monsieur Doyle. Had she no enemies? Is there no one who had a grudge against her?'

Again Simon shook his head with the same hopeless gesture.

'It sounds absolutely fantastic. There's Windlesham, of course. She more or less chucked him to marry me—but I can't see a polite stick like Windlesham committing murder, and anyway he's miles away. Same thing with old Sir George Wode. He'd got a down on Linnet over the house—disliked the way she was pulling it about; but he's miles away in London, and anyway to think of murder in such a connection would be fantastic.'

'Listen, Monsieur Doyle.' Poirot spoke very earnestly. 'On the first day we came on board the *Karnak* I was impressed by a little conversation which I had with Madame your wife. She was very upset—very distraught. She said—mark this well—that *everybody* hated her. She said she felt afraid—unsafe—as though *everyone* round her were an enemy.'

'She was pretty upset at finding Jackie aboard. So was I,' said Simon.

'That is true, but it does not quite explain those words. When she said she was surrounded by enemies, she was almost certainly exaggerating, but all the same she did mean *more than one person*.'

'You might be right there,' admitted Simon. 'I think I can explain that. It was a name in the passenger list that upset her.'

'A name in the passenger list? What name?'

Agatha Christie

'Well, you see, she didn't actually tell me. As a matter of fact I wasn't even listening very carefully. I was going over the Jacqueline business in my mind. As far as I remember, Linnet said something about doing people down in business, and that it made her uncomfortable to meet anyone who had a grudge against her family. You see, although I don't really know the family history very well, I gather that Linnet's mother was a millionaire's daughter. Her father was only just ordinary plain wealthy, but after his marriage he naturally began playing the markets or whatever you call it. And as a result of that, of course, several people got it in the neck. You know, affluence one day, the gutter the next. Well, I gather there was someone on board whose father had got up against Linnet's father and taken a pretty hard knock. I remember Linnet saying: "It's pretty awful when people hate you without even knowing you."'

'Yes,' said Poirot thoughtfully. 'That would explain what she said to me. For the first time she was feeling the burden of her inheritance and not its advantages. You are quite sure, Monsieur Doyle, that she did not mention this man's name?'

Simon shook his head ruefully.

'I didn't really pay much attention. Just said: "Oh, nobody minds what happened to their fathers nowadays. Life goes too fast for that." Something of that kind.'

Bessner said dryly:

'Ach, but I can have a guess. There is certainly a young man with a grievance on board.'

'You mean Ferguson?' said Poirot.

'Yes. He spoke against Mrs Doyle once or twice. I myself have heard him.'

'What can we do to find out?' asked Simon.

Poirot replied: 'Colonel Race and I must interview all the passengers. Until we have got their stories it would be unwise to form theories. Then there is the maid. We ought to interview her first of all. It would, perhaps, be as well if we did that here. Monsieur Doyle's presence might be helpful.'

'Yes, that's a good idea,' said Simon.

'Had she been with Mrs Doyle long?'

'Just a couple of months, that's all.'

'Only a couple of months!' exclaimed Poirot.

'Why, you don't think—'

'Had Madame any valuable jewellery?'

'There were her pearls,' said Simon. 'She once told me they were worth forty or fifty thousand.'

He shivered.

'My God, do you think those damned pearls—?'

'Robbery is a possible motive,' said Poirot. 'All the same it seems hardly credible... Well, we shall see. Let us have the maid here.'

Louise Bourget was that same vivacious Latin brunette who Poirot had seen one day and noticed.

She was anything but vivacious now. She had been crying and looked frightened. Yet there was a kind of sharp cunning apparent in her face which did not prepossess the two men favourably towards her.

'You are Louise Bourget?'

'Yes, Monsieur.'

'When did you last see Madame Doyle alive?'

'Last night, Monsieur. I was in her cabin to undress her.'

'What time was that?'

'It was some time after eleven, Monsieur. I cannot say exactly when. I undress Madame and put her to bed, and then I leave.'

'How long did all that take?'

'Ten minutes, Monsieur. Madame was tired. She told me to put the lights out when I went.'

'And when you had left her, what did you do?'

'I went to my own cabin, Monsieur, on the deck below.'

'And you heard or saw nothing more that can help us?'

'How could I, Monsieur?'

'That, Mademoiselle, is for you to say, not for us,' Hercule Poirot retorted.

She stole a sideways glance at him.

'But, Monsieur, I was nowhere near... What could I have seen or heard? I was on the deck below. My cabin, it was on the other side of the boat, even. It is impossible that I should have heard anything. Naturally if I had been unable to sleep, if I had mounted the stairs, *then* perhaps I might have seen the assassin, this monster, enter or leave Madame's cabin, but as it is—'

She threw out her hands appealingly to Simon.

'Monsieur, I implore you—you see how it is? What can I say?'

'My good girl,' said Simon harshly, 'don't be a fool. Nobody thinks you saw or heard anything. You'll be quite all right. I'll look after you. Nobody's accusing you of anything.'

Louise murmured, 'Monsieur is very good,' and dropped her eyelids modestly.

'We take it, then, that you saw and heard nothing?' asked Race impatiently.

'That is what I said, Monsieur.'

'And you know of no one who had a grudge against your mistress?'

To the surprise of the listeners Louise nodded her head vigorously.

'Oh, yes. That I do know. To that question I can answer Yes most emphatically.'

Poirot said:

'You mean Mademoiselle de Bellefort?'

'She, certainly. But it is not of her I speak. There was someone else on this boat who disliked Madame, who was very angry because of the way Madame had injured him.'

'Good lord!' Simon exclaimed. 'What's all this?'

Louise went on, still emphatically nodding her head with the utmost vigour.

'Yes, yes, yes, it is as I say! It concerns the former maid of Madame—my predecessor. There was a man, one of the engineers on this boat, who wanted her to marry him. And my predecessor, Marie her name was, she would have done so. But Madame Doyle, she made enquiries and she discovered that this Fleetwood already he had a wife—a wife of colour, you understand, a wife of this country. She had gone back to her own people, but he was still married to her, you understand. And so Madame she told all this to Marie, and Marie she was very unhappy and she would not see Fleetwood any more. And this Fleetwood, he was infuriated, and when he found out that this Madame Doyle had formerly been Mademoiselle Linnet Ridgeway he tells me that he would like to kill her! Her interference ruined his life, he said.'

Louise paused triumphantly.

'This is interesting,' said Race.

Poirot turned to Simon.

'Had you any idea of this?'

'None whatever,' Simon replied with patent sincerity. 'I doubt if Linnet even knew the man was on the boat. She had probably forgotten all about the incident.'

He turned sharply to the maid.

'Did you say anything to Mrs Doyle about this?'

'No, Monsieur, of course not.'

Poirot said:

'Do you know anything about your mistress's pearls?'

'Her pearls? Louise's eyes opened very wide. 'She was wearing them last night.'

'You saw them when she came to bed?'

'Yes, Monsieur.'

'Where did she put them?'

'On the table by the side as always.'

'That is where you last saw them?'

'Yes, Monsieur.'

'Did you see them there this morning?'

A startled look came into the girl's face.

'*Mon Dieu*! I did not even look. I come up to the bed, I see—I see Madame, and then I cry out and rush out of the door and I faint.'

Hercule Poirot nodded his head.

'You did not look. But I, I have the eyes which notice, and there were *no pearls on the table beside the bed this morning.*'

CHAPTER 14

Hercule Poirot's observation had not been at fault. There were no pearls on the table by Linnet Doyle's bed.

Louise Bourget was bidden to make a search among Linnet's belongings.

According to her, all was in order. Only the pearls had disappeared.

As they emerged from the cabin a steward was waiting to tell them that breakfast had been served in the smoking room.

As they passed along the deck, Race paused to look over the rail.

'Aha! I see you have had an idea, my friend.'

'Yes. It suddenly came to me, when Fanthorp mentioned thinking he had heard a splash that I too had been awakened some time last night by a splash. It's perfectly possible that after the murder, the murderer threw the pistol overboard.'

Poirot said slowly:

'You really think that is possible, my friend?'

Race shrugged his shoulders.

'It's a suggestion. After all, the pistol wasn't any where in the cabin. First thing I looked for.'

'All the same,' said Poirot, 'it is incredible that it should have been thrown overboard.'

Race said:

'Where is it then?'

Poirot said thoughtfully:

'If it is not in Madame Doyle's cabin, there is, logically, only one other place where it could be.'

'Where's that?'

'In Mademoiselle de Bellefort's cabin.'

Race said thoughtfully: 'Yes. I see—'

He stopped suddenly.

'She's out of her cabin. Shall we go and have a look now?'

Poirot shook his head. 'No, my friend, that would be precipitate. *It may not yet have been put there.*'

'What about an immediate search of the whole boat.'

'That way we should show our hand. We must work with great care. It is very delicate, our position at the moment. Let us discuss the situation as we eat.'

Race agreed. They went into the smoking room.

'Well?' said Race as he poured himself out a cup of coffee. 'We've got two definite leads. There's the disappearance of the pearls. And there's the man Fleetwood. As regards the pearls, robbery seems indicated, but—I don't know whether you'll agree with me—'

Agatha Christie

Poirot said quickly:

'But it was an odd moment to choose?'

'Exactly. To steal the pearls at such a moment invites *a close search of everybody on board*. How then could the thief hope to get away with his booty?'

'He might have gone ashore and dumped it.'

'The company always has a watchman on the bank.'

'Then that is not feasible. Was the murder committed to divert attention from the robbery? No, that does not make sense—it is profoundly unsatisfactory. But supposing that Madame Doyle woke up and caught the thief in the act?'

'And therefore the thief shot her? But she was shot whilst she slept.'

'So that too does not make sense... You know, I have a little idea about those pearls—and yet—no—it is impossible. Because if my idea was right the pearls would not have disappeared. Tell me, what did you think of the maid?'

'I wondered,' said Race slowly, 'if she knew more than she said.'

'Ah, you too had that impression?'

'Definitely not a nice girl,' said Race.

Hercule Poirot nodded.

'Yes, I would not trust her, that one.'

'You think she had something to do with the murder?'

'No, I would not say that.'

'With the theft of the pearls, then?'

'That is more probable. She had only been with Madame Doyle a very short time. She may be a member of a gang that specializes in jewel robberies. In such a case there is often a maid with excellent references. Unfortunately we are not in a position to seek information on these points. And yet that explanation does not quite satisfy me... Those pearls—ah, *sacré,* my little idea *ought* to be right. And yet nobody would be so imbecile—' He broke off.

'What about the man Fleetwood?'

'We must question him. It may be that we have there the solution. If Louise Bourget's story is true, he had a definite motive for revenge. He could have overheard the scene between Jacqueline and Monsieur Doyle, and when they had left the saloon he could have darted in and secured the gun. Yes, it is all quite possible. And that letter J scrawled in blood. That, too, would accord with a simple, rather crude nature.'

'In fact, he's just the person we are looking for?'

'Yes—only—'

Poirot rubbed his nose. He said with a slight grimace:

'See you, I recognize my own weaknesses. It has been said of me that I like to make a case difficult. This solution that you put to me—it is too simple, too easy. I cannot feel that it really happened. And yet, that may be sheer prejudice on my part.'

'Well, we'd better have the fellow here.'

Race rang the bell and gave the order. Then he said:

'Any other—possibilities?'

'Plenty, my friend. There is, for example, the American trustee.'

'Pennington?'

'Yes, Pennington. There was a curious little scene in here the other day.'

He narrated the happenings to Race.

'You see—it is significant. Madame, she wanted to read all the papers before signing. So he makes the excuse of another day. And then, the husband, he makes a very significant remark.'

'What was that?'

'He says—"*I never read anything. I sign where I am told to sign.*" You perceive the significance of that. *Pennington did.* I saw it in his eye. He looked at Doyle as though an entirely new idea had come into his head. Just imagine, my friend, that you have been left trustee to the daughter of an intensely wealthy man. You use, perhaps, that money to speculate with. I know it is so in all detective novels—but you read of it too in the newspapers. It happens, my friend, it *happens*.'

'I don't dispute it,' said Race.

'There is, perhaps, still time to make good by speculating wildly. Your ward is not yet of age. And then—she marries! The control passes from your hands into hers at a moment's notice! A disaster! But there is still a chance. She is on a honeymoon. She will perhaps be careless about business. A casual paper slipped in among others, signed without reading. But Linnet Doyle was not like that. Honeymoon or no honeymoon, she was a business woman. And then her husband makes a remark, and a new idea comes to that desperate man who is seeking a way out from ruin. If Linnet Doyle were to die, her fortune would pass to her

Death on the Nile

husband—and he would be easy to deal with; he would be a child in the hands of an astute man like Andrew Pennington. *Mon cher* Colonel, I tell you I *saw* the thought pass through Andrew Pennington's head. "If only it were *Doyle* I had got to deal with…" That is what he was thinking.'

'Quite possible, I daresay,' said Race dryly, 'but you've no evidence.'

'Alas, no.'

'Then there's young Ferguson,' said Race. 'He talks bitterly enough. Not that I go by talk. Still, he *might* be the fellow whose father was ruined by old Ridgeway. It's a little far-fetched but it's *possible*. People do brood over bygone wrongs sometimes.'

He paused a minute and then said:

'And there's my fellow.'

'Yes, there is "your fellow" as you call him.'

'He's a killer,' said Race. 'We know that. On the other hand, I can't see any way in which he could have come up against Linnet Doyle. Their orbits don't touch.'

Poirot said slowly:

'Unless, accidentally, she had become possessed of evidence showing his identity.'

'That's possible, but it seems highly unlikely.' There was a knock at the door. 'Ah, here's our would-be bigamist.'

Fleetwood was a big, truculent-looking man. He looked suspiciously from one to the other of them as he entered the room. Poirot recognized him as the man he had seen talking to Louise Bourget.

Agatha Christie

Fleetwood said suspiciously:

'You wanted to see me?'

'We did,' said Race. 'You probably know that a murder was committed on this boat last night?'

Fleetwood nodded.

'And I believe it is true that you had reason to feel anger against the woman who was killed.'

A look of alarm sprang up in Fleetwood's eyes.

'Who told you that?'

'You considered that Mrs Doyle had interfered between you and a young woman.'

'I know who told you that—that lying French hussy. She's a liar through and through, that girl.'

'But this particular story happens to be true.'

'It's a dirty lie!'

'You say that although you don't know what it is yet.'

The shot told. The man flushed and gulped.

'It is true, is it not, that you were going to marry the girl Marie, and that she broke it off when she discovered that you were a married man already?'

'What business was it of hers?'

'You mean, what business was it of Mrs Doyle's? Well, you know, bigamy is bigamy.'

'It wasn't like that. I married one of the locals out here. It didn't answer. She went back to her people. I've not seen her for a half a dozen years.'

'Still you were married to her.'

The man was silent. Race went on.

'Mrs Doyle, or Miss Ridgeway as she then was, found out all this?'

'Yes, she did, curse her! Nosing about where no one ever asked her to. I'd have treated Marie right. I'd have done anything for her. And she'd never have known about the other, if it hadn't been for that meddlesome young lady of hers. Yes, I'll say it, I *did* have a grudge against the lady, and I felt bitter about it when I saw her on this boat, all dressed up in pearls and diamonds and lording it all over the place with never a thought that she'd broken up a man's life for him! I felt bitter all right. But if you think I'm a dirty murderer—if you think I went and shot her with a gun, well, that's a damned lie! I never touched her. And that's God's truth.'

He stopped. The sweat was rolling down his face.

'Where were you last night between the hours of twelve and two?'

'In my bunk asleep—and my mate will tell you so.'

'We shall see,' said Race. He dismissed him with a curt nod. 'That'll do.'

'*Eh bien?*' inquired Poirot as the door closed behind Fleetwood.

Race shrugged his shoulders.

'He tells quite a straight story. He's nervous, of course, but not unduly so. We'll have to investigate his alibi—though I don't suppose it will be decisive. His mate was probably asleep, and this fellow could have slipped in and out if he wanted to. It depends whether anyone else saw him.'

Agatha Christie

'Yes, one must enquire as to that.'

'The next thing, I think,' said Race, 'is whether anyone heard anything which might give a clue to the time of the crime. Bessner places it as having occurred between twelve and two. It seems reasonable to hope that someone among the passengers may have heard the shot—even if they did not recognize it for what it was. I didn't hear anything of the kind myself. What about you?'

Poirot shook his head.

'Me, I slept absolutely like the log. I heard nothing—but nothing at all. I might have been drugged, I slept so soundly.'

'A pity,' said Race. 'Well, let's hope we have a bit of luck with the people who have cabins on the starboard side. Fanthorp we've done. The Allertons come next. I'll send the steward to fetch them.'

Mrs Allerton came in briskly. She was wearing a soft grey striped silk dress. Her face looked distressed.

'It's too horrible,' she said as she accepted the chair that Poirot placed for her. 'I can hardly believe it. That lovely creature with everything to live for—dead. I almost feel I can't believe it.'

'I know how you feel, Madame,' said Poirot sympathetically.

'I'm glad *you* are on board,' said Mrs Allerton simply. 'You'll be able to find out who did it. I'm so glad it isn't that poor tragic girl.'

'You mean Mademoiselle de Bellefort. Who told you she did not do it?'

'Cornelia Robson,' said Mrs Allerton, with a faint smile. 'You know, she's simply thrilled by it all. It's probably the only exciting thing that has ever happened to her, and probably the only exciting thing that ever will happen to her. But she's so nice that she's terribly ashamed of enjoying it. She thinks it's awful of her.'

Mrs Allerton gave a look at Poirot and then added:

'But I mustn't chatter. You want to ask me questions.'

'If you please. You went to bed at what time, Madame?'

'Just after half past ten.'

'And you went to sleep at once?'

'Yes. I was sleepy.'

'And did you hear anything—anything at all—during the night?'

Mrs Allerton wrinkled her brows.

'Yes, I think I heard a splash and someone running—or was it the other way about? I'm rather hazy. I just had a vague idea that someone had fallen overboard at sea—a dream, you know—and then I woke up and listened, but it was all quite quiet.'

'Do you know what time that was?'

'No, I'm afraid I don't. But I don't think it was very long after I went to sleep. I mean it was within the first hour or so.'

'Alas, Madame, that is not very definite.'

'No, I know it isn't. But it's no good trying to guess, is it, when I haven't really the vaguest idea?'

'And that is all you can tell us, Madame?'

'I'm afraid so.'

'Had you ever actually met Madame Doyle before?'

'No, Tim had met her. And I'd heard a good deal about her—through a cousin of ours, Joanna Southwood, but I'd never spoken to her till we met at Aswan.'

'I have one other question, Madame, if you will pardon me for asking.'

Mrs Allerton murmured with a faint smile, 'I should love to be asked an indiscreet question.'

'It is this. *Did you, or your family, ever suffer any financial loss through the operations of Madame Doyle's father, Melhuish Ridgeway?*'

Mrs Allerton looked throughly astonished.

'Oh, no! The family finances have never suffered except by dwindling... you know, everything paying less interest than it used to. There's never been anything melodramatic about our poverty. My husband left very little money, but what he left I still have, though it doesn't yield as much as it used to yield.'

'I thank you, Madame. Perhaps you will ask your son to come to us.'

Tim said lightly, when his mother came to him:

'Ordeal over? My turn now! What sort of things did they ask you?'

'Only whether I heard anything last night,' said Mrs Allerton. 'And unluckily I didn't hear anything at all. I can't think why not. After all, Linnet's cabin is only one away from mine. I should think I'd have been bound to hear the shot. Go along, Tim; they're waiting for you.'

To Tim Allerton Poirot repeated his previous questions.

Death on the Nile

Tim answered:

'I went to bed early, half past ten or so. I read for a bit. Put out my light just after eleven.'

'Did you hear anything after that?'

'Heard a man's voice saying good night, I think, not far away.'

'That was me saying good night to Mrs Doyle,' said Race.

'Yes. After that I went to sleep. Then, later, I heard a kind of hullabaloo going on, somebody calling Fanthorp, I remember.'

'Mademoiselle Robson when she ran out from the observation saloon.'

'Yes, I suppose that was it. And then a lot of different voices. And then somebody running along the deck. And then a splash. And then I heard old Bessner booming out something about "Careful now" and "Not too quick."'

'You heard a splash.'

'Well, something of that kind.'

'You are sure it was not a *shot* you heard?'

'Yes, I suppose it might have been... I did hear a cork pop. Perhaps that was the shot. I may have imagined the splash from connecting the idea of the cork with liquid pouring into a glass... I know my foggy idea was that there was some kind of party on. And I wished they'd all go to bed and shut up.'

'Anything more after that?'

Tim thought.

'Only Fanthorp barging around in his cabin next door. I thought he'd never go to bed.'

Agatha Christie

'And after that?'
Tim shrugged his shoulders.
'After that—oblivion.'
'You heard nothing more?'
'Nothing whatever.'
'Thank you, Monsieur Allerton.'
Tim got up and left the cabin.

CHAPTER 15

Race pored thoughtfully over a plan of the promenade deck of the *Karnak*.

'Fanthorp, young Allerton, Mrs Allerton. Then an empty cabin—Simon Doyle's. Now who's on the other side of Mrs Doyle's? The old American dame. If anyone heard anything she would have done. If she's up we'd better have her along.'

Miss Van Schuyler entered the room. She looked even older and yellower than usual this morning. Her small dark eyes had an air of venomous displeasure in them.

Race rose and bowed.

'We're very sorry to trouble you, Miss Van Schuyler. It's very good of you. Please sit down.'

Miss Van Schuyler said sharply:

'I dislike being mixed up in this. I resent it very much. I do not wish to be associated in any way with this—er—very unpleasant affair.'

'Quite—quite. I was just saying to Monsieur Poirot that

the sooner we took your statement the better, as then you need have no further trouble.'

Miss Van Schuyler looked at Poirot with something approaching favour.

'I'm glad you both realize my feelings. I am not accustomed to anything of this kind.'

Poirot said soothingly:

'Precisely, Mademoiselle. That is why we wish to free you from unpleasantness as quickly as possible. Now you went to bed last night—at what time?'

'Ten o'clock is my usual time. Last night I was rather later, as Cornelia Robson, very inconsiderately, kept me waiting.'

'*Très bien*, Mademoiselle. Now what did you hear after you had retired?'

Miss Van Schuyler said:

'I sleep very lightly.'

'A *merveille*! That is very fortunate for us.'

'I was awakened by that rather flashy young woman, Mrs Doyle's maid, who said, "*Bonne nuit, Madame*" in what I cannot but think an unnecessarily loud voice.'

'And after that?'

'I went to sleep again. I woke up thinking someone was in my cabin, but I realized that it was someone in the cabin next door.'

'In Madame Doyle's cabin?'

'Yes. Then I heard someone outside on the deck and then a splash.'

'You have no idea what time this was?'

'I can tell you the time exactly. It was ten minutes past one.'

'You are sure of that?'

'Yes. I looked at my little clock that stands by my bed.'

'You did not hear a shot?'

'No, nothing of the kind.'

'But it might possibly have been a shot that awakened you?'

Miss Van Schuyler considered the question, her toad-like head on one side.

'It might,' she admitted rather grudgingly.

'And you have no idea what caused the splash you heard?'

'Not at all—I know perfectly.'

Colonel Race sat up alertly.

'You know?'

'Certainly. I did not like this sound of prowling around. I got up and went to the door of my cabin. Miss Otterbourne was leaning over the side. She had just dropped something into the water.'

'Miss Otterbourne?'

Race sounded really surprised.

'Yes.'

'You are quite sure it was Miss Otterbourne?'

'I saw her face distinctly.'

'She did not see you?'

'I do not think so.'

Poirot leant forward.

'And what did her face look like, Mademoiselle?'

'She was in a condition of considerable emotion.'

Race and Poirot exchanged a quick glance.

'And then?' Race prompted.

'Miss Otterbourne went away round the stern of the boat and I returned to bed.'

There was a knock at the door and the manager entered. He carried in his hand a dripping bundle.

'We've got it, Colonel.'

Race took the package. He unwrapped fold after fold of sodden velvet. Out of it fell a coarse handkerchief faintly stained with pink, wrapped round a small pearl-handled pistol.

Race gave Poirot a glance of slightly malicious triumph.

'You see,' he said, 'my idea was right. It *was* thrown overboard.'

He held the pistol out on the palm of his hand.

'What do you say, Monsieur Poirot? Is this the pistol you saw at the Cataract Hotel that night?'

Poirot examined it carefully, then he said quietly: 'Yes— that is it. There is the ornamental work on it—and the initials J.B. It is an *article de luxe*—a very feminine production—but it is none the less a lethal weapon.'

'.22,' murmured Race. He took out the clip. 'Two bullets fired. Yes, there doesn't seem much doubt about it.'

Miss Van Schuyler coughed significantly.

'And what about my stole?' she demanded.

'Your stole, Mademoiselle?'

'Yes, that is my velvet stole you have there.'

Race picked up the dripping folds of material.

'This is yours, Miss Van Schuyler?'

'Certainly it's mine!' the old lady snapped. 'I missed it last night. I was asking everyone if they'd seen it.'

Poirot questioned Race with a glance, and the latter gave a slight nod of assent.

'Where did you see it last, Miss Van Schuyler?'

'I had it in the saloon yesterday evening. When I came to go to bed I could not find it anywhere.'

Race said quickly:

'You realize what it's been used for?'

He spread it out, indicating with a finger the scorching and several small holes.

'The murderer wrapped it round the pistol to deaden the noise of the shot.'

'Impertinence!' snapped Miss Van Schuyler.

The colour rose in her wizened cheeks.

Race said:

'I shall be glad, Miss Van Schuyler, if you will tell me the extent of your previous acquaintance with Mrs Doyle.'

'There was no previous acquaintance.'

'But you knew of her?'

'I knew who she was, of course.'

'But your families were not acquainted?'

'As a family we have always prided ourselves on being exclusive, Colonel Race. My dear mother would never have dreamed of calling upon any of the Hartz family, who, outside their wealth, were nobodies.'

'That is all you have to say, Miss Van Schuyler?'

'I have nothing to add to what I have told you. Linnet Ridgeway was brought up in England and I never saw her till I came aboard this boat.'

She rose.

Poirot opened the door and she marched out.

The eyes of the two men met.

'That's her story,' said Race, 'and she's going to stick to it! It may be true. I don't know. But—Rosalie Otterbourne? I hadn't expected that.'

Poirot shook his head in a perplexed manner. Then he brought down his hand on the table with a sudden bang.

'But it does not make sense,' he cried. '*Nom d'un nom d'un nom!* It does not make sense.'

Race looked at him.

'What do you mean exactly?'

'I mean that up to a point it is all the clear sailing. Someone wished to kill Linnet Doyle. Someone overheard the scene in the saloon last night. Someone sneaked in there and retrieved the pistol—Jacqueline de Bellefort's pistol, remember. Somebody shot Linnet Doyle with that pistol and wrote the letter J on the wall... All so clear, is it not? All pointing to Jacqueline de Bellefort as the murderess. And then what does the murderer do? Leave the pistol—the damning pistol—Jacqueline de Bellefort's pistol, for everyone to find? No, he—or she—throws the pistol, *that particular damning bit of evidence*, overboard. Why, my friend, why?'

Race shook his head.

'It's odd.'

'It is more than odd—it is *impossible!*'

'Not impossible, since it happened!'

'I do not mean that. I mean *the sequence of events is impossible*. Something is wrong.'

CHAPTER 16

Colonel Race glanced curiously at his colleague. He respected—he had reason to respect—the brain of Hercule Poirot. Yet for the moment he did not follow the other's process of thought. He asked no question, however. He seldom did ask questions. He proceeded straightforwardly with the matter in hand.

'What's the next thing to be done? Question the Otterbourne girl?'

'Yes, that may advance us a little.'

Rosalie Otterbourne entered ungraciously. She did not look nervous or frightened in any way—merely unwilling and sulky.

'Well?' she said. 'What is it?'

Race was the spokesman.

'We're investigating Mrs Doyle's death,' he explained.

Rosalie nodded.

'Will you tell me what you did last night?'

Rosalie reflected a minute.

Agatha Christie

'Mother and I went to bed early—before eleven. We didn't hear anything in particular, except a bit of fuss outside Dr Bessner's cabin. I heard the old man's German voice booming away. Of course I didn't know what it was all about till this morning.'

'You didn't hear a shot?'

'No.'

'Did you leave your cabin at all last night?'

'No.'

'You are quite sure of that?'

Rosalie stared at him.

'What do you mean? Of course I'm sure of it.'

'You did not, for instance, go round to the starboard side of the boat and throw something overboard?'

The colour rose in her face.

'Is there any rule against throwing things overboard?'

'No, of course not. Then you did?'

'No, I didn't. I never left my cabin, I tell you.'

'Then if anyone says that they saw you—?'

She interrupted him.

'Who says they saw me?'

'Miss Van Schuyler.'

'Miss Van Schuyler?' She sounded genuinely astonished.

'Yes. Miss Van Schuyler says she looked out of her cabin and saw you throw something over the side.'

Rosalie said clearly:

'That's a damned lie.'

Then, as though struck by a sudden thought, she asked:

'What time was this?'

Death on the Nile

It was Poirot who answered.

'It was ten minutes past one, Mademoiselle.'

She nodded her head thoughtfully.

'Did she see anything else?'

Poirot looked at her curiously. He stroked his chin.

'See—no,' he replied, 'but she heard something.'

'What did she hear?'

'Someone moving about in Madame Doyle's cabin.'

'I see,' muttered Rosalie.

She was pale now—deadly pale.

'And you persist in saying that you threw nothing overboard, Mademoiselle?'

'What on earth should I run about throwing things overboard for in the middle of the night?'

'There might be a reason—an innocent reason.'

'Innocent?' repeated the girl sharply.

'That's what I said. You see, Mademoiselle, something *was* thrown overboard last night—something that was not innocent.'

Race silently held out the bundle of stained velvet, opening it to display its contents.

Rosalie Otterbourne shrank back.

'Was that—what—she was killed with?'

'Yes, Mademoiselle.'

'And you think that I—I did it? What utter nonsense! Why on earth should I want to kill Linnet Doyle? I don't even know her!'

She laughed and stood up scornfully.

'The whole thing is too ridiculous.'

'Remember, Miss Otterbourne,' said Race, 'that Miss Van Schuyler is prepared to swear she saw your face quite clearly in the moonlight.'

Rosalie laughed again. 'That old cat? She's probably half blind anyway. It wasn't me she saw.'

She paused.

'Can I go now?'

Race nodded and Rosalie Otterbourne left the room.

The eyes of the two men met. Race lighted a cigarette.

'Well, that's that. Flat contradiction. Which of 'em do we believe?'

Poirot shook his head.

'I have a little idea that neither of them was being quite frank.'

'That's the worst of our job,' said Race despondently. 'So many people keep back the truth for positively futile reasons. What's our next move? Get on with the questioning of the passengers?'

'I think so. It is always well to proceed with order and method.'

Race nodded.

Mrs Otterbourne, dressed in floating batik material, succeeded her daughter.

She corroborated Rosalie's statement that they had both gone to bed before eleven o'clock. She herself had heard nothing of interest during the night. She could not say whether Rosalie had left their cabin or not. On the subject of the crime she was inclined to hold forth.

'The *crime passionel*!' she exclaimed. 'The primitive

instinct—to kill! So closely allied to the sex instinct. That girl, Jacqueline, half Latin, hot blooded, obeying the deepest instincts of her being, stealing forth, revolver in hand—'

'But Jacqueline de Bellefort did not shoot Madame Doyle. That we know for certain. It is proved,' explained Poirot.

'Her husband, then,' said Mrs Otterbourne, rallying from the blow. 'The blood lust and the sex instinct—a sexual crime. There are many well-known instances.'

'Mr Doyle was shot through the leg and he was quite unable to move—the bone was fractured,' explained Colonel Race. 'He spent the night with Dr Bessner.'

Mrs Otterbourne was even more disappointed. She searched her mind hopefully.

'Of course!' she said. 'How foolish of me! Miss Bowers!'

'Miss Bowers?'

'Yes. Naturally. It's so *clear* psychologically. Repression! The repressed virgin! Maddened by the sight of these two—a young husband and wife passionately in love with each other. Of course it was her! She's just the type—sexually unattractive, innately respectable. In my book, *The Barren Vine*—'

Colonel Race interposed tactfully:

'Your suggestions have been most helpful, Mrs Otterbourne. We must get on with our job now. Thank you so much.'

He escorted her gallantly to the door and came back wiping his brow.

'What a poisonous woman! Whew! Why didn't somebody murder *her*!'

'It may yet happen,' Poirot consoled him.

Agatha Christie

'There might be some sense in that. Whom have we got left? Pennington—we'll keep him for the end, I think. Richetti—Ferguson.'

Signor Richetti was very voluble, very agitated.

'But what a horror, what an infamy—a woman so young and so beautiful—indeed an inhuman crime—'

Signor Richetti's hands flew expressively up in the air.

His answers were prompt. He had gone to bed early—very early. In fact immediately after dinner. He had read for a while—a very interesting pamphlet lately published—*Prähistorische Forschung in Kleinasien*—throwing an entirely new light on the painted pottery of the Anatolian foothills.

He had put out his light some time before eleven. No, he had not heard any shot. Not any sound like the pop of a cork. The only thing he had heard—but that was later, in the middle of the night—was a splash, a big splash, just near his porthole.

'Your cabin is on the lower deck, on the starboard side, is it not?'

'Yes, yes, that is so. And I heard the big splash.' His arms flew up once more to describe the bigness of the splash.

'Can you tell me at all what time that was?'

Signor Richetti reflected.

'It was one, two, three hours after I go to sleep. Perhaps two hours.'

'About ten minutes past one, for instance?'

'It might very well be, yes. Ah! but what a terrible crime—how inhuman... So charming a woman...'

Death on the Nile

Exit Signor Richetti, still gesticulating freely.

Race looked at Poirot. Poirot raised his eyebrows expressively. Then shrugged his shoulders. They passed on to Mr Ferguson.

Ferguson was difficult. He sprawled insolently in a chair.

'Grand to-do about this business!' he sneered. 'What's it really matter? Lot of superfluous women in the world!'

Race said coldly:

'Can we have an account of your movements last night, Mr Ferguson?'

'Don't see why you should, but I don't mind. I mooched around a good bit. Went ashore with Miss Robson. When she went back to the boat I mooched around by myself for a while. Came back and turned in round about midnight.'

'Your cabin is on the lower deck, starboard side?'

'Yes. I'm up among the nobs.'

'Did you hear a shot? It might only have sounded like the popping of a cork.'

Ferguson considered.

'Yes, I think I did hear something like a cork... Can't remember when—before I went to sleep. But there were still a lot of people about then—commotion, running about on the deck above.'

'That was probably the shot fired by Miss de Bellefort. You didn't hear another?'

Ferguson shook his head.

'Nor a splash?'

'A splash? Yes, I believe I did hear a splash. But there was so much row going on I can't be sure about it.'

'Did you leave your cabin during the night?'

Ferguson grinned.

'No, I didn't. And I didn't participate in the good work, worse luck.'

'Come, come, Mr Ferguson, don't behave childishly.'

The young man reacted angrily.

'Why shouldn't I say what I think? I believe in violence.'

'But you don't practice what you preach?' murmured Poirot. 'I wonder.'

He leaned forward.

'It was the man, Fleetwood, was it not, who told you that Linnet Doyle was one of the richest women in England?'

'What's Fleetwood got to do with this?'

'Fleetwood, my friend, had an excellent motive for killing Linnet Doyle. He had a special grudge against her.'

Mr Ferguson came up out of his seat like a jack-in-the-box.

'So that's your dirty game, is it?' he demanded wrathfully. 'Put it on to a poor devil like Fleetwood who can't defend himself—who's got no money to hire lawyers. But I tell you this—if you try and saddle Fleetwood with this business you'll have me to deal with.'

'And who exactly are you?' asked Poirot sweetly.

Mr Ferguson got rather red.

'I can stick by my friends anyway,' he said gruffly.

'Well, Mr Ferguson, I think that's all we need for the present,' said Race.

As the door closed behind Ferguson he remarked unexpectedly:

'Rather a likeable young cub, really.'

'You don't think he is the man *you* are after?' asked Poirot.

'I hardly think so. I suppose he *is* on board. The information was very precise. Oh, well, one job at a time. Let's have a go at Pennington.'

CHAPTER 17

Andrew Pennington displayed all the conventional reactions of grief and shock. He was, as usual, carefully dressed. He had changed into a black tie. His long clean-shaven face bore a bewildered expression.

'Gentlemen,' he said sadly, 'this business has got me right down! Little Linnet—why, I remember her as the cutest little thing you can imagine. How proud of her Melhuish Ridgeway used to be, too! Well, there's no point in going into that. Just tell me what I can do—that's all I ask.'

Race said:

'To begin with, Mr Pennington, did you hear anything last night?'

'No, sir, I can't say I did. I have the cabin right next to Dr Bessner's—number thirty-eight thrity-nine—and I heard a certain commotion going on in there round about midnight or so. Of course I didn't know what it was at the time.'

'You heard nothing else? No shots?'

Andrew Pennington shook his head.

'Nothing whatever of that kind.'

'And you went to bed?'

'Must have been some time after eleven.'

He leaned forward.

'I don't suppose it's news to you to know that there's plenty of rumours going about the boat. That half-French girl—Jacqueline de Bellefort—there was something fishy there, you know. Linnet didn't tell me anything, but naturally I wasn't born blind and deaf. There'd been some affair between her and Simon, some time, hadn't there? *Cherchez la femme*—that's a pretty good sound rule, and I should say you wouldn't have to *cherchez* far.'

Poirot said:

'You mean that in your belief Jacqueline de Bellefort shot Madame Doyle?'

'That's what it looks like to me. Of course I don't *know* anything...'

'Unfortunately we *do* know something!'

'Eh?' Mr Pennington looked startled.

'We know that it is quite impossible for Mademoiselle de Bellefort to have shot Madame Doyle.'

He explained carefully the circumstances. Pennington seemed reluctant to accept them.

'I agree it looks all right on the face of it—but this hospital nurse woman, I'll bet she didn't stay awake all night. She dozed off and the girl slipped out and in again.'

'Hardly likely, Monsieur Pennington. She had administered

Agatha Christie

a strong opiate, remember. And anyway a nurse is in the habit of sleeping lightly and waking when her patient wakes.'

'It all sounds rather fishy to me,' declared Pennington.

Race said in a gently authoritative manner:

'I think you must take it from me, Mr Pennington, that we have examined all the possibilities very carefully. The result is quite definite—Jacqueline de Bellefort did not shoot Mrs Doyle. So we are forced to look elsewhere. That is where we hope you may be able to help us.'

'I?'

Pennington gave a nervous start.

'Yes. You were an intimate friend of the dead woman. You know the circumstances of her life, in all probability, much better than her husband does, since he only made her acquaintance a few months ago. You would know, for instance, of anyone who had a grudge against her. You would know, perhaps, whether there was anyone who had a motive for desiring her death.'

Andrew Pennington passed his tongue over rather dry-looking lips.

'I assure you, I have no idea... You see Linnet was brought up in England. I know very little of her surroundings and associations.'

'And yet,' mused Poirot, 'there was someone on board who was interested in Madame Doyle's removal. She had a near escape before, you remember, at this very place, when that boulder crashed down—ah! but you were not there, perhaps?'

'No. I was inside the temple at the time. I heard about it afterwards, of course. A very near escape. But possibly an accident, don't you think?'

Poirot shrugged his shoulders.

'One thought so at the time. Now—one wonders.'

'Yes—yes, of course.' Pennington wiped his face with a fine silk handkerchief.

Colonel Race went on:

'Mr Doyle happened to mention someone being on board who bore a grudge—not against her personally, but against her family. Do you know who that could be?'

Pennington looked genuinely astonished.

'No, I've no idea.'

'She didn't mention the matter to you?'

'No.'

'You were an intimate friend of her father's—you cannot remember any business operations of his that might have resulted in ruin for some business opponent?'

Pennington shook his head helplessly.

'No outstanding case. Such operations were frequent, of course, but I can't recall anyone who uttered threats—nothing of that kind.'

In short, Mr Pennington, you cannot help us?'

'It seems so. I deplore my inadequacy, gentlemen.'

Race interchanged a glance with Poirot, then he said:

'I'm sorry too. We'd had hopes.'

He got up as a sign the interview was at an end.

Andrew Pennington said:

'As Doyle's laid up, I expect he'd like me to see to things. Pardon me, Colonel, but what exactly are the arrangements?'

'When we leave here we shall make a non-stop run to Shellal, arriving there tomorrow morning.'

'And the body?'

'Will be removed to one of the cold storage chambers.'

Andrew Pennington bowed his head. Then he left the room.

Poirot and Race again interchanged a glance.

'Mr Pennington,' said Race, lighting a cigarette, 'was not at all comfortable.'

Poirot nodded.

'And,' he said, 'Mr Pennington was sufficiently perturbed to tell a rather stupid lie. He was *not* in the temple of Abu Simbel when that boulder fell. I—*moi qui vous parle*—can swear to that. I had just come from there.'

'A very stupid lie,' said Race, 'and a very revealing one.'

Again Poirot nodded.

'But for the moment,' he said, and smiled, 'we handle him with the gloves of kid, is it not so?'

'That was the idea,' agreed Race.

'My friend, you and I understand each other to a marvel.'

There was a faint grinding noise, a stir beneath their feet. The *Karnak* had started on her homeward journey to Shellal.

Death on the Nile

'The pearls,' said Race. 'That is the next thing to be cleared up.'

'You have a plan?'

'Yes.' He glanced at his watch. 'It will be lunch time in half an hour. At the end of the meal I propose to make an announcement—just state the fact that the pearls have been stolen, and that I must request everyone to stay in the dining-saloon while a search is conducted.'

Poirot nodded approvingly.

'It is well imagined. *Whoever took the pearls still has them.* By giving no warning beforehand, there will be no chance of their being thrown overboard in a panic.'

Race drew some sheets of paper towards him. He murmured apologetically:

'I'd like to make a brief précis of the facts as I go along. It keeps one's mind free of confusion.'

'You do well. Method and order, they are everything,' replied Poirot.

Race wrote for some minutes in his small neat script. Finally he pushed the result of his labours towards Poirot.

'Anything you don't agree with there?'

Poirot took up the sheets. They were headed:

MURDER OF MRS LINNET DOYLE

Mrs Doyle was last seen alive by her maid, Louise Bourget. Time: 11.30 (approx.).

From 11.30—12.20 following have alibis: Cornelia Robson, James Fanthorp, Simon Doyle, Jacqueline de

Bellefort—*nobody else*—but crime almost certainly committed *after* that time, since it is practically certain that pistol used was Jacqueline de Bellefort's, which was then in her handbag. That her pistol was used is not *absolutely* certain until after post-mortem and expert evidence re bullet—but it may be taken as overwhelmingly probable.

Probable course of events: X (murderer) was witness of scene between Jacqueline and Simon Doyle in observation saloon and noted where pistol went under settee. After the saloon was vacant, X procured pistol—his or her idea being that Jacqueline de Bellefort would be thought guilty of crime. On this theory certain people are automatically cleared of suspicion:

Cornelia Robson, since she had no opportunity to take pistol before James Fanthorp returned to search for it.

Miss Bowers—same.

Dr Bessner—same.

N.B.—Fanthorp is not definitely excluded from suspicion, since he could actually have pocketed pistol while declaring himself unable to find it.

Any other person could have taken the pistol during that ten minutes' interval.

Possible motives for the murder:

Andrew Pennington. This is on the assumption that he has been guilty of fraudulent practices. There is a certain amount of evidence in favour of that assumption, but not enough to justify making out a case against him. If it was he who rolled down the boulder, he is a man who can seize

Death on the Nile

a chance when it presents itself. The crime, clearly, was not premeditated except in a *general* way. Last night's shooting scene was an ideal opportunity.

Objections to the theory of Pennington's guilt: *why did he throw the pistol overboard, since it constituted a valuable clue against J.B.?*

Fleetwood. Motive, revenge. Fleetwood considered himself injured by Linnet Doyle. Might have overheard scene and noted position of pistol. He may have taken pistol because it was a handy weapon, rather than with the idea of throwing guilt on Jacqueline. This would fit in with throwing it overboard. *But if that were the case, why did he write J in blood on the wall?*

N.B.—Cheap handkerchief found with pistol more likely to have belonged to a man like Fleetwood than to one of the well-to-do passengers.

Rosalie Otterbourne. Are we to accept Miss Van Schuyler's evidence or Rosalie's denial? Something *was* thrown overboard at the time, and that something was presumably the pistol wrapped up in the velvet stole.

Points to be noted. Had Rosalie any motive? She may have disliked Linnet Doyle and even been envious of her—but as a motive for murder that seems grossly inadequate. The evidence against her can be convincing only if we discover an adequate *motive*. As far as we know, there is no previous knowledge or link between Rosalie Otterbourne and Linnet Doyle.

Miss Van Schuyler. The velvet stole in which pistol was wrapped belonged to Miss Van Schuyler. According to her own statement she last saw it in the observation saloon. She drew attention to its loss during the evening, and a search was made for it without success.

How did the stole come into the possession of X? Did X purloin it some time early in the evening? But if so, why? Nobody could tell *in advance* that there was going to be a scene between Jacqueline and Simon. Did X find the stole in the saloon when he went to get the pistol from under the settee? But if so, why was it not found when the search for it was made? *Did it never leave Miss Van Schuyler's possession?*

That is to say:

Did Miss Van Schuyler murder Linnet Doyle? Is her accusation of Rosalie Otterbourne a deliberate lie? If she did murder her, what was her *motive*?

Other possibilities:

Robbery as a motive. Possible, since the pearls have disappeared, and Linnet Doyle was certainly wearing them last night.

Someone with a grudge against the Ridgeway family. Possible—again no evidence.

We know that there is a dangerous man on board—a killer. Here we have a killer and a death. May not the two be connected? But we should have to show that Linnet Doyle possessed dangerous knowledge concerning this man.

Conclusions: We can group the persons on board into two classes—those who had a possible motive or against whom there is definite evidence, and those who, as far as we know, are free of suspicion.

Group I	*Group II*
Andrew Pennington	Mrs Allerton
Fleetwood	Tim Allerton
Rosalie Otterbourne	Cornelia Robson
Miss Van Schuyler	Miss Bowers
Louise Bourget (Robbery?)	Dr Bessner
Ferguson (Political?)	Signor Richetti
	Mrs Otterbourne
	James Fanthorp

Poirot pushed the paper back.

'It is very just, very exact, what you have written there.'

'You agree with it?'

'Yes.'

'And now what is your contribution?'

Poirot drew himself up in an important manner.

'Me, I pose myself one question:

"*Why was the pistol thrown overboard?*"'

'That's all?'

'At the moment, yes. Until I can arrive at a satisfactory answer to that question, there is not sense anywhere. That is—that *must* be—the starting point. You will notice, my friend, that in your summary of where we stand, you have not attempted to answer that point.'

Race shrugged his shoulders.

'Panic.'

Poirot shook his head perplexedly.

He picked up the sodden velvet wrap and smoothed it

out, wet and limp, on the table. His fingers traced the scorched marks and the burnt holes.

'Tell me, my friend,' he said suddenly. 'You are more conversant with firearms than I am. Would such a thing as this, wrapped round a pistol, make much difference in muffling the sound?'

'No, it wouldn't. Not like a silencer, for instance.'

Poirot nodded. He went on:

'A man—certainly a man who had had much handling of firearms—would know that. But a woman—a woman would *not* know.'

Race looked at him curiously.

'Probably not.'

'No. She would have read the detective stories where they are not always very exact as to details.'

Race flicked the little pearl-handled pistol with his finger.

'This little fellow wouldn't make much noise anyway,' he said. 'Just a pop, that's all. With any other noise around, ten to one you wouldn't notice it.'

'Yes, I have reflected as to that.'

Poirot picked up the handkerchief and examined it.

'A man's handkerchief—but not a gentleman's handkerchief. *Ce cher* Woolworth, I imagine. Three pence at most.'

'The sort of handkerchief a man like Fleetwood would own.'

'Yes. Andrew Pennington, I notice, carries a very fine silk handkerchief.'

'Ferguson?' suggested Race.

'Possibly. As a gesture. But then it ought to be a bandana.'

'Used it instead of a glove, I suppose, to hold the pistol and obviate fingerprints.' Race added, with slight facetiousness, '"The Clue of the Blushing Handkerchief."'

'Ah, yes. Quite a *jeune fille* colour, is it not?' He laid it down and returned to the stole, once more examining the powder marks.

'All the same,' he murmured, 'it is odd...'

'What's that?'

Poirot said gently:

'*Cette pauvre* Madame Doyle. Lying there so peacefully... with the little hole in her head. You remember how she looked?'

Race looked at him curiously.

'You know,' he said, 'I've got an idea you're trying to tell me something—but I haven't the faintest idea what it is.'

CHAPTER 18

There was a tap on the door.

'Come in,' Race called.

A steward entered.

'Excuse me, sir,' he said to Poirot, 'but Mr Doyle is asking for you.'

'I will come.'

Poirot rose. He went out of the room and up the companionway to the promenade deck and along it to Dr Bessner's cabin.

Simon, his face flushed and feverish, was propped up with pillows.

He looked embarrassed.

'Awfully good of you to come along, Monsieur Poirot. Look here, there's something I want to ask you.'

'Yes?'

Simon got still redder in the face.

'It's—it's about Jackie. I want to see her. Do you think—would you mind—would she mind, d'you think—if you asked her to come along here? You know I've been lying here thinking... That wretched kid—she is only a kid after all—and I treated her damn' badly—and—'

He stammered to silence.

Poirot looked at him with interest.

'You desire to see Mademoiselle Jacqueline? I will fetch her.'

'Thanks. Awfully good of you.'

Poirot went on his quest. He found Jacqueline de Bellefort sitting huddled up in a corner of the observation saloon. There was an open book on her lap but she was not reading.

Poirot said gently:

'Will you come with me, Mademoiselle? Monsieur Doyle wants to see you.'

She started up. Her face flushed—then paled. She looked bewildered.

'Simon? He wants to see me—to see *me*?'

He found her incredulity moving.

'Will you come, Mademoiselle?'

She went with him in a docile fashion, like a child, but like a puzzled child.

'I—yes, of course I will.'

Poirot passed into the cabin.

'Here is Mademoiselle.'

She stepped in after him, wavered, stood still... standing there mute and dumb, her eyes fixed on Simon's face.

'Hallo, Jackie.'

He, too, was embarrassed. He went on:

Agatha Christie

'Awfully good of you to come. I wanted to say—I mean—what I mean is—'

She interrupted him then. Her words came out in a rush—breathless, desperate...

'Simon—I didn't kill Linnet. You know I didn't do that... I—I—was mad last night. Oh, can you ever forgive me?'

Words came more easily to him now.

'Of course. That's all right! Absolutely all right! That's what I wanted to say. Thought you might be worrying a bit, you know...'

'*Worrying? A bit? Oh! Simon!*'

'That's what I wanted to see you about. It's quite all right, see, old girl? You just got a bit rattled last night—a shade tight. All perfectly natural.'

'Oh, Simon! I might have killed you...'

'Not you. Not with a rotten little peashooter like that...'

'And your leg! Perhaps you'll never walk again...'

'Now, look here, Jackie, don't be maudlin. As soon as we get to Aswan they're going to put the X-rays to work, and dig out that tinpot bullet, and everything will be as right as rain.'

Jacqueline gulped twice, then she rushed forward and knelt down by Simon's bed, burying her face and sobbing. Simon patted her awkwardly on the head. His eyes met Poirot's and, with a reluctant sigh, the latter left the cabin.

He heard broken murmurs as he went:

'How could I be such a devil? Oh, Simon!... I'm so dreadfully sorry...'

Outside Cornelia Robson was leaning over the rail.

She turned her head.

Death on the Nile

'Oh, it's you, Monsieur Poirot. It seems so awful somehow that it should be such a lovely day.'

Poirot looked up at the sky.

'When the sun shines you cannot see the moon,' he said. 'But when the sun is gone—ah, when the sun is gone.'

Cornelia's mouth fell open.

'I beg your pardon?'

'I was saying, Mademoiselle, that when the sun has gone down, we shall see the moon. That is so, is it not?'

'Why—why, yes—certainly.'

She looked at him doubtfully.

Poirot laughed gently.

'I utter the imbecilities,' he said. 'Take no notice.'

He strolled gently towards the stern of the boat. As he passed the next cabin he paused for a minute. He caught fragments of speech from within.

'Utterly ungrateful—after all I've done for you—no consideration for your wretched mother... no idea of what I suffer...'

Poirot's lips stiffened as he pressed them together. He raised a hand and knocked.

There was a startled silence and Mrs Otterbourne's voice called out:

'Who's that?'

'Is Mademoiselle Rosalie there?'

Rosalie appeared in the doorway. Poirot was shocked at her appearance. There were dark circles under her eyes and drawn lines round her mouth.

'What's the matter?' she said ungraciously. 'What do you want?'

Agatha Christie

'The pleasure of a few minutes' conversation with you, Mademoiselle. Will you come?'

Her mouth went sulky at once. She shot him a suspicious look.

'Why should I?'

'I entreat you, Mademoiselle.'

'Oh, I suppose—'

She stepped out on the deck, closing the door behind her. 'Well?'

Poirot took her gently by the arm and drew her along the deck, still in the direction of the stern. They passed the bathrooms and round the corner. They had the stern part of the deck to themselves. The Nile flowed away behind them.

Poirot rested his elbows on the rail. Rosalie stood up straight and stiff.

'Well?' she asked again, and her voice held the same ungracious tone.

Poirot spoke slowly, choosing his words.

'I could ask you certain questions, Mademoiselle, but I do not think for one moment that you would consent to answer them.'

'Seems rather a waste to bring me along here then.'

Poirot drew a finger slowly along the wooden rail.

'You are accustomed, Mademoiselle, to carrying your own burdens... But you can do that too long. The strain becomes too great. For you, Mademoiselle, the strain is becoming too great.'

'I don't know what you are talking about,' said Rosalie.

'I am talking about facts, Mademoiselle—plain ugly facts.

Death on the Nile

Let us call the spade the spade and say it in one little short sentence. Your mother drinks, Mademoiselle.'

Rosalie did not answer. Her mouth opened, then she closed it again. For once she seemed at a loss.

'There is no need for you to talk, Mademoiselle. I will do all the talking. I was interested at Aswan in the relations existing between you. I saw at once that, in spite of your carefully studied unfilial remarks, you were in reality passionately protecting her from something. I very soon knew what that something was. I knew it long before I encountered your mother one morning in an unmistakable state of intoxication. Moreover, her case, I could see, was one of secret bouts of drinking—by far the most difficult kind of case with which to deal. You were coping with it manfully. Nevertheless, she had all the secret drunkard's cunning. She managed to get hold of a secret supply of spirits and to keep it successfully hidden from you. I should not be surprised if you discovered its hiding place only yesterday. Accordingly, last night, as soon as your mother was really soundly asleep, you stole out with the contents of the cache, went round to the other side of the boat (since your own side was up against the bank) and cast it overboard into the Nile.'

He paused.

'I am right, am I not?'

'Yes—you're quite right.' Rosalie spoke with sudden passion. 'I was a fool not to say so, I suppose! But I didn't want everyone to know. It would go all over the boat. And it seemed so—so silly—I mean—that I—'

Poirot finished the sentence for her.

'So silly that you should be suspected of committing a murder?'

Rosalie nodded.

Then she burst out again.

'I've tried so hard to—keep everyone from knowing... It isn't really her fault. She got discouraged. Her books didn't sell any more. People are tired of all that cheap sex stuff... It hurt her—it hurt her dreadfully. And so she began to—to drink. For a long time I didn't know why she was so queer. Then, when I found out, I tried to—to stop it. She'd be all right for a bit, and then, suddenly, she'd start, and there would be dreadful quarrels and rows with people. It was awful.' She shuddered. 'I had always to be on the watch—to get her away...'

'And then—she began to dislike me for it. She—she's turned right against me. I think she almost hates me sometimes.'

'*Pauvre petite*,' said Poirot.

She turned on him vehemently.

'Don't be sorry for me. Don't be kind. It's easier if you're not.' She sighed—a long heart-rending sigh. 'I'm so tired... I'm so deadly, deadly tired.'

'I know,' said Poirot.

'People think I'm awful. Stuck-up and cross and bad-tempered. I can't help it. I've forgotten how to be—to be nice.'

'That is what I said to you—you have carried your burden by yourself too long.'

Rosalie said slowly:

'It's a relief—to talk about it. You—you've always been kind to me, Monsieur Poirot. I'm afraid I've been rude to you often.'

'*La politesse*, it is not necessary between friends.'

The suspicion came back to her face suddenly.

'Are you—are you going to tell everyone? I suppose you must, because of those damned bottles I threw overboard.'

'No, no, it is not necessary. Just tell me what I want to know. At what time was this? Ten minutes past one?'

'About that, I should think. I don't remember exactly.'

'Now tell me, Mademoiselle. Mademoiselle Van Schuyler saw *you*, did you see *her*?'

Rosalie shook her head.

'No, I didn't.'

'She says that she looked out of the door of her cabin.'

'I don't think I should have seen her. I just looked along the deck and then out to the river.'

Poirot nodded.

'And did you see anyone at all when you looked down the deck?'

There was a pause—quite a long pause. Rosalie was frowning. She seemed to be thinking earnestly.

At last she shook her head quite decisively.

'No,' she said. 'I saw nobody.'

Hercule Poirot slowly nodded his head. But his eyes were grave.

CHAPTER 19

People crept into the dining saloon by ones and twos in a very subdued manner. There seemed a general feeling that to sit down eagerly to food displayed an unfortunate heartlessness. It was with an almost apologetic air that one passenger after another came and sat down at their tables.

Tim Allerton arrived some few minutes after his mother had taken her seat. He was looking in a thoroughly bad temper.

'I wish we'd never come on this blasted trip,' he growled.

Mrs Allerton shook her head sadly.

'Oh, my dear, so do I. That beautiful girl! It all seems such a *waste*. To think that anyone could shoot her in cold blood. It seems awful to me that anyone could do such a thing. And that other poor child.'

'Jacqueline?'

'Yes; my heart aches for her. She looks so dreadfully unhappy.'

'Teach her not to go round loosing off toy firearms,' said Tim unfeelingly as he helped himself to butter.

'I expect she was badly brought up.'

'Oh, for God's sake, Mother, don't go all maternal about it.'

'You're in a shocking bad temper, Tim.'

'Yes I am. Who wouldn't be?'

'I don't see what there is to be cross about. It's just frightfully sad.'

Tim said crossly:

'You're taking the romantic point of view! What you don't seem to realize is that it's no joke being mixed up in a murder case.'

Mrs Allerton looked a little startled.

'But surely—'

'That's just it. There's no "But surely" about it. Everyone on this damned boat is under suspicion—you and I as well as the rest of them.'

Mrs Allerton demurred.

'Technically we are, I suppose—but actually it's ridiculous!'

'There's nothing ridiculous where murder's concerned! You may sit there, darling, just exuding virtue and conscious rectitude, but a lot of unpleasant policeman at Shellal or Aswan won't take you at your face value.'

'Perhaps the truth will be known before then.'

'Why should it be?'

'Monsieur Poirot may find out.'

'That old mountebank? He won't find out anything. He's all talk and moustaches.'

'Well, Tim,' said Mrs Allerton. 'I daresay everything you

Agatha Christie

say is true, but even if it is, we've got to go through with it, so we might as well make up our minds to it and go through with it as cheerfully as we can.'

But her son showed no abatement of gloom.

'There's this blasted business of the pearls being missing, too.'

'Linnet's pearls?'

'Yes. It seems somebody must have pinched 'em.'

'I suppose that was the motive for the crime,' said Mrs Allerton.

'Why should it be? You're mixing up two perfectly different things.'

'Who told you that they were missing?'

'Ferguson. He got it from his tough friend in the engine room, who got it from the maid.'

'They were lovely pearls,' said Mrs Allerton.

Poirot sat down at the table, bowing to Mrs Allerton.

'I am a little late,' he said.

'I expect you have been busy,' said Mrs Allerton.

'Yes, I have been much occupied.'

He ordered a fresh bottle of wine from the waiter.

'We're very catholic in our tastes,' said Mrs Allerton. 'You drink wine always, Tim drinks whisky and soda, and I try all the different brands of mineral water in turn.'

'*Tiens*!' said Poirot. He stared at her for a moment. He murmured to himself: 'It is an idea, that...'

Then, with an impatient shrug of his shoulders, he dismissed the sudden preoccupation that had distracted him and began to chat lightly of other matters.

'Is Mr Doyle badly hurt?' asked Mrs Allerton.

'Yes, it is a fairly serious injury. Dr Bessner is anxious to reach Aswan so that his leg can be X-rayed and the bullet removed. But he hopes that there will be no permanent lameness.'

'Poor Simon,' said Mrs Allerton. 'Only yesterday he looked such a happy boy, with everything in the world he wanted. And now his beautiful wife killed and he himself laid up and helpless. I do hope, though—'

'What do you hope, Madame?' asked Poirot as Mrs Allerton paused.

'I hope he's not too angry with that poor child.'

'With Mademoiselle Jacqueline? Quite the contrary. He was full of anxiety on her behalf.'

He turned to Tim.

'You know, it is a pretty little problem of psychology, that. All the time that Mademoiselle Jacqueline was following them from place to place he was absolutely furious—but now, when she has actually shot him, and wounded him dangerously—perhaps made him lame for life—all his anger seems to have evaporated. Can you understand that?'

'Yes,' said Tim thoughtfully, 'I think I can. The first thing made him feel a fool—'

Poirot nodded.

'You are right. It offended his male dignity.'

'But now—if you look at it a certain way, it's *she* who's made a fool of herself. Everyone's down on her, and so—'

'He can be generously forgiving,' finished Mrs Allerton. 'What children men are!'

'A profoundly untrue statement that women always make,' murmured Tim.

Poirot smiled. Then he said to Tim:

'Tell me, Madame Doyle's cousin, Miss Joanna Southwood, did she resemble Madame Doyle?'

'You've got it a little wrong, Monsieur Poirot. She was our cousin and Linnet's friend.'

'Ah, pardon—I was confused. She is a young lady much in the news, that. I have been interested in her for some time.'

'Why?' asked Tim sharply.

Poirot half rose to bow to Jacqueline de Bellefort, who had just come in and passed their table on the way to her own. Her cheeks were flushed and her eyes bright, and her breath came a little unevenly. As he resumed his seat Poirot seemed to have forgotten Tim's question. He murmured vaguely:

'I wonder if all young ladies with valuable jewels are as careless as Madame Doyle was?'

'It is true, then, that they were stolen?' asked Mrs Allerton.

'Who told you so, Madame?'

'Ferguson said so,' said Tim.

Poirot nodded gravely.

'It is quite true.'

'I suppose,' said Mrs Allerton nervously, 'that this will mean a lot of unpleasantness for all of us. Tim says it will.'

Her son scowled. But Poirot had turned to him.

'Ah! You have had previous experience, perhaps? You have been in a house where there was a robbery?'

'Never,' said Tim.

'Oh, yes, darling, you were at the Portarlingtons' that time—when that awful woman's diamonds were stolen.'

'You always get things hopelessly wrong, Mother. I was there when it was discovered that the diamonds she was wearing round her fat neck were only paste! The actual substitution was probably done months earlier. As a matter of fact, a lot a people said she'd had it done herself!'

'Joanna said so, I expect.'

'Joanna wasn't there.'

'But she knew them quite well. And it's very like her to make that kind of suggestion.'

'You're always down on Joanna, Mother.'

Poirot hastily changed the subject. He had it in mind to make a really big purchase at one of the Aswan shops. Some very attractive purple and gold material at one of the Indian merchants. There would, of course, be the duty to pay, but—

'They tell me that they can—how do you say—expedite it for me. And that the charges will not be too high. How think you, will it arrive all right?'

Mrs Allerton said that many people, so she had heard, had had things sent straight to England from the shops in question and that everything had arrived safely.

'*Bien*. Then I will do that. But the trouble one has, when one is abroad, if a parcel comes out from England! Have you had experience of that? Have you had any parcels arrive since you have been on your travels?'

Agatha Christie

'I don't think we have, have we, Tim? You get books sometimes, but of course there is never any trouble about them.'

'Ah, no, books are different.'

Dessert had been served. Now, without any previous warning, Colonel Race stood up and made his speech.

He touched on the circumstances of the crime and announced the theft of the pearls. A search of the boat was about to be instituted, and he would be obliged if all the passengers would remain in the saloon until this was completed. Then, after that, if the passengers agreed, as he was sure they would, they themselves would be kind enough to submit to a search.

Poirot slipped nimbly along to his side. There was a little buzz and hum all round them. Voices doubtful, indignant, excited...

Poirot reached Race's side and murmured something in his ear just as the latter was about to leave the dining saloon.

Race listened, nodded assent, and beckoned a steward. He said a few brief words to him; then, together with Poirot, he passed out on to the deck, closing the door behind him.

They stood for a minute or two by the rail. Race lit a cigarette.

'Not a bad idea of yours,' he said. 'We'll soon see if there's anything in it. I'll give 'em three minutes.'

The door of the dining saloon opened and the same steward to whom they had spoken came out. He saluted Race and said: 'Quite right, sir. There's a lady who says it's urgent she should speak to you at once without delay.'

'Ah!' Race's face showed satisfaction. 'Who is it?'

'Miss Bowers, sir, the hospital nurse lady.'

A slight shade of surprise showed on Race's face. He said:

'Bring her to the smoking-room. Don't let anyone else leave.'

'No, sir—the other steward will attend to that.'

He went back into the dining room. Poirot and Race went to the smoking room.

'Bowers, eh?' muttered Race.

They had hardly got inside the smoking room before the steward reappeared with Miss Bowers. He ushered her in and left, shutting the door behind him.

'Well, Miss Bowers?' Colonel Race looked at her inquiringly. 'What's all this?'

Miss Bowers looked her usual composed, unhurried self. She displayed no particular emotion.

'You'll excuse me, Colonel Race,' she said, 'but under the circumstances I thought the best thing to do would be to speak to you at once'—she opened her neat black handbag—'and to return you these.'

She took out a string of pearls and laid them on the table.

CHAPTER 20

If Miss Bowers had been the kind of woman who enjoyed creating a sensation, she would have been richly repaid by the result of her action.

A look of utter astonishment passed over Colonel Race's face as he picked up the pearls from the table.

'This is most extraordinary,' he said. 'Will you kindly explain, Miss Bowers?'

'Of course. That's what I've come to do.' Miss Bowers settled herself comfortably in a chair. 'Naturally it was a little difficult for me to decide what it was best for me to do. The family would naturally be averse to scandal of any kind, and they trusted my discretion, but the circumstances are so very unusual that it really leaves me no choice. Of course, when you didn't find anything in the cabins, your next move would be a search of the passengers, and, if the pearls were then found in my possession, it would be rather an awkward situation and the truth would come out just the same.'

'And just what is the truth? Did you take these pearls from Mrs Doyle's cabin?'

'Oh, no, Colonel Race, of course not. Miss Van Schuyler did.'

'Miss Van Schuyler?'

'Yes. She can't help it, you know, but she does—er—take things. Especially jewellery. That's really why I'm always with her. It's not her health at all—it's this little idiosyncrasy. I keep on the alert, and fortunately there's never been any trouble since I've been with her. It just means being watchful, you know. And she always hides the things she takes in the same place—rolled up in a pair of stockings—so that it makes it very simple. I look each morning. Of course I'm a light sleeper, and I always sleep next door to her, and with the communicating door open if it's in a hotel, so that I usually hear. Then I go after her and persuade her to go back to bed. Of course it's been rather more difficult on a boat. But she doesn't usually do it at night. It's more just picking up things that she sees left about. Of course, pearls have a great attraction for her always.'

Miss Bowers ceased speaking.

Race asked:

'How did you discover they had been taken?'

'They were in her stockings this morning. I knew whose they were, of course. I've often noticed them. I went along to put them back, hoping that Mrs Doyle wasn't up yet and hadn't discovered her loss. But there was a steward standing there, and he told me about the murder and that no one could go in. So then, you see, I was in a regular

Agatha Christie

quandary. But I still hoped to slip them back in the cabin later, before their absence had been noticed. I can assure you I've passed a very unpleasant morning wondering what was the best thing to do. You see, the Van Schuyler family is so *very* particular and exclusive. It would never do if this got into the newspapers. But that won't be necessary, will it?'

Miss Bowers really looked worried.

'That depends on circumstances,' said Colonel Race cautiously. 'But we shall do our best for you, of course. What does Miss Van Schuyler say to this?'

'Oh, she'll deny it, of course. She always does. Says some wicked person has put it there. She never admits taking anything. That's why if you catch her in time she goes back to bed like a lamb. Says she just went out to look at the moon. Something like that.'

'Does Miss Robson know about this—er—failing?'

'No, she doesn't. Her mother knows, but she's a very simple kind of girl and her mother thought it best she should know nothing about it. I was quite equal to dealing with Miss Van Schuyler,' added the competent Miss Bowers.

'We have to thank you, Mademoiselle, for coming to us so promptly,' said Poirot.

Miss Bowers stood up.

'I'm sure I hope I acted for the best.'

'Be assured that you have.'

'You see, what with there being a murder as well—'

Colonel Race interrupted her. His voice was grave.

'Miss Bowers, I am going to ask you a question, and I want to impress upon you that it has got to be answered truthfully. Miss Van Schuyler is unhinged mentally to the extent of being a kleptomaniac. Has she also a tendency to homicidal mania?'

Miss Bowers' answer came immediately.

'Oh, dear me, no! Nothing of that kind. You can take my word for it absolutely. The old lady wouldn't hurt a fly.'

The reply came with such positive assurance that there seemed nothing more to be said. Nevertheless Poirot did interpolate one mild inquiry.

'Does Miss Van Schuyler suffer at all from deafness?'

'As a matter of fact she does, Monsieur Poirot. Not so that you'd notice in any way, not if you were speaking to her, I mean. But quite often she doesn't hear you when you come into a room. Things like that.'

'Do you think she would have heard anyone moving about in Mrs Doyle's cabin, which is next door to her own?'

'Oh, I shouldn't think so—not for a minute. You see, the bunk is the other side of the cabin, not even against the partition wall. No, I don't think she would have heard anything.'

'Thank you, Miss Bowers.'

Race said: 'Perhaps you will now go back to the dining saloon and wait with the others?'

He opened the door for her and watched her go down the staircase and enter the saloon. Then he shut the door

Agatha Christie

and came back to the table. Poirot had picked up the pearls.

'Well,' said Race grimly, 'that reaction came pretty quickly. That's a very cool-headed and astute young woman—perfectly capable of holding out on us still further if she thinks it suits her book. What about Miss Marie Van Schuyler now? I don't think we can eliminate her from the possible suspects. You know, she *might* have committed murder to get hold of those jewels. We can't take the nurse's word for it. She's all out to do the best for the family.'

Poirot nodded in agreement. He was very busy with the pearls, running them through his fingers, holding them up to his eyes.

He said:

'We may take it, I think, that part of the old lady's story to us is true. She *did* look out of her cabin and she *did* see Rosalie Otterbourne. But I don't think she *heard* anything or anyone in Linnet Doyle's cabin. I think she was just peering out from *her* cabin preparatory to slipping along and purloining the pearls.'

'The Otterbourne girl was there, then?'

'Yes. Throwing her mother's secret cache of drink overboard.'

Colonel Race shook his head sympathetically.

'So that's it! Tough on a young 'un.'

'Yes, her life has not been very gay, *cette pauvre petite Rosalie*.'

'Well, I'm glad that's been cleared up. *She* didn't see or hear anything?'

260

'I asked her that. She responded—after a lapse of quite twenty seconds—that she saw nobody.'

'Oh?' Race looked alert.

'Yes, it is suggestive, that.'

Race said slowly: 'If Linnet Doyle was shot round about ten minutes past one, or indeed any time after the boat had quieted down, it has seemed amazing to me that no one heard the shot. I grant you that a little pistol like that wouldn't make much noise, but all the same the boat would be deadly quiet, and any noise, even a little pop, should have been heard. But I begin to understand better now. The cabin on the forward side of hers was unoccupied—since her husband was in Dr Bessner's cabin. The one aft was occupied by the Van Schuyler woman, who was deaf. That leaves only—'

He paused and looked expectantly at Poirot, who nodded.

'The cabin next to her on the other side of the boat. In other words—Pennington. We always seem to come back to Pennington.'

'We will come back to him presently with the kid gloves removed! Ah, yes, I am promising myself that pleasure.'

'In the meantime we'd better get on with our search of the boat. The pearls still make a convenient excuse, even though they have been returned—but Miss Bowers is not likely to advertise the fact.'

'Ah, these pearls!' Poirot held them up against the light once more. He stuck out his tongue and licked them—he even gingerly tried one of them between his teeth. Then, with a sigh, he threw them down on the table.

Agatha Christie

'Here are more complications, my friend,' he said. 'I am not an expert on precious stones, but I have had a good deal to do with them in my time and I am fairly certain of what I say. *These pearls are only a clever imitation.*'

CHAPTER 21

Colonel Race swore hastily.

'This damned case gets more and more involved.' He picked up the pearls. 'I suppose you've not made a mistake? They look all right to me.'

'They are a very good imitation—yes.'

'Now where does that lead us? I suppose Linnet Doyle didn't deliberately have an imitation made and bring it abroad with her for safety. Many women do.'

'I think, if that were so, her husband would know about it.'

'She may not have told him.'

Poirot shook his head in a dissatisfied manner.

'No, I do not think that is so. I was admiring Madame Doyle's pearls the first evening on the boat—their wonderful sheen and lustre. I am sure that she was wearing the genuine ones then.'

'That brings us up against two possibilities. First, that Miss Van Schuyler only stole the imitation string after the real ones had been stolen by someone else. Second, that the whole kleptomaniac story is a fabrication. Either Miss Bowers is a thief, and quickly invented the story and allayed suspicion by handing over the false pearls, or else that whole party is in it together. That is to say, they are a gang of clever jewel thieves masquerading as an exclusive American family.'

'Yes,' Poirot murmured. 'It is difficult to say. But I will point out to you one thing—to make a perfect and exact copy of the pearls, clasp and all, good enough to stand a chance of deceiving Madame Doyle, is a highly skilled technical performance. It could not be done in a hurry. Whoever copied those pearls must have had a good opportunity of studying the original.'

Race rose to his feet.

'Useless to speculate about it any further now. Let's get on with the job. We've got to find the real pearls. And at the same time we'll keep our eyes open.'

They disposed of the cabins occupied on the lower deck.

That of Signor Richetti contained various archaeological works in different languages, a varied assortment of clothing, hair lotions of a highly scented kind and two personal letters—one from an archaeological expedition in Syria, and one from, apparently, a sister in Rome. His handkerchiefs were all of coloured silk.

They passed on to Ferguson's cabin.

There was a sprinkling of communistic literature, a good many snapshots, Samuel Butler's *Erewhon* and a cheap edition of Pepys' *Diary*. His personal possessions were not many. Most of what outer clothing there was was torn and dirty; the underclothing, on the other hand, was of really good quality. The handkerchiefs were expensive linen ones.

'Some interesting discrepancies,' murmured Poirot.

Race nodded. 'Rather odd that there are absolutely no personal papers, letters, etc.'

'Yes; that gives one to think. An odd young man, Monsieur Ferguson.' He looked thoughtfully at a signet ring he held in his hand, before replacing it in the drawer where he had found it.

They went along to the cabin occupied by Louise Bourget. The maid had her meals after the other passengers, but Race had sent word that she was to be taken to join the others. A cabin steward met them.

'I'm sorry, sir,' he apologized, 'but I've not been able to find the young woman anywhere. I can't think where she can have got to.'

Race glanced inside the cabin. It was empty.

They went up to the promenade deck and started on the starboard side. The first cabin was that occupied by James Fanthorp. Here all was in meticulous order. Mr Fanthorp travelled light, but all that he had was of good quality.

'No letters,' said Poirot thoughtfully. 'He is careful, our Mr Fanthorp, to destroy his correspondence.'

They passed on to Tim Allerton's cabin, next door.

There were evidences here of an Anglo-Catholic turn of mind—an exquisite little triptych, and a big rosary of intricately carved wood. Besides personal clothing, there was a half-completed manuscript, a good deal annotated and scribbled over, and a good collection of books, most of them recently published. There were also a quantity of letters thrown carelessly into a drawer. Poirot, never in the least scrupulous about reading other people's correspondence, glanced through them. He noted that amongst them there were no letters from Joanna Southwood. He picked up a tube of Seccotine, fingered it absently for a minute or two, then said:

'Let us pass on.'

'No Woolworth handkerchiefs,' reported Race, rapidly replacing the contents of a drawer.

Mrs Allerton's cabin was the next. It was exquisitely neat, and a faint old-fashioned smell of lavender hung about it.

The two men's search was soon over. Race remarked as they left it:

'Nice woman, that.'

The next cabin was that which had been used as a dressing-room by Simon Doyle. His immediate necessities—pyjamas, toilet things, etc.—had been moved to Bessner's cabin, but the remainder of his possessions were still there—two good-sized leather suitcases and a kitbag. There were also some clothes in the wardrobe.

'We will look carefully here, my friend,' said Poirot, 'for it is possible that the thief hid the pearls here.'

'You think it is likely?'

'But yes, indeed. Consider! The thief, whoever he or she may be, must know that sooner or later a search will be made, and therefore a hiding place in his or her own cabin would be injudicious in the extreme. The public rooms present other difficulties. But here is a cabin belonging to a man *who cannot possibly visit it himself*. So that if the pearls are found here it tells us nothing at all.'

But the most meticulous search failed to reveal any trace of the missing necklace.

Poirot murmured '*Zut!*' to himself and they emerged once more on the deck.

Linnet Doyle's cabin had been locked after the body was removed, but Race had the key with him. He unlocked the door and the two men stepped inside.

Except for the removal of the girl's body, the cabin was exactly as it had been that morning.

'Poirot,' said Race, 'if there's anything to be found here, for God's sake go ahead and find it. You can if anyone can—I know that.'

'This time you do not mean the pearls, *mon ami*?'

'No. The murder's the main thing. There may be something I overlooked this morning.'

Quietly, deftly, Poirot went about his search. He went down on his knees and scrutinized the floor inch by inch. He examined the bed. He went rapidly through the wardrobe and chest of drawers. He went through the wardrobe trunk and the two costly suitcases. He looked through the expensive gold-fitted dressing-case. Finally he turned his attention to the washstand. There were various creams, powders, face lotions. But the only thing that seemed to interest Poirot were two little bottles labelled Nailex. He picked them up at last and brought them to the dressing table. One, which bore the inscription Nailex Rose, was empty but for a drop or two of dark red fluid at the bottom. The other, the same size, but labelled Nailex Cardinal, was nearly full. Poirot uncorked first the empty, then the full one, and sniffed them both delicately.

An odour of pear drops billowed into the room. With a slight grimace he recorked them.

'Get anything?' asked Race.

Poirot replied by a French proverb: '*On no prend pas les mouches avec le vinaigre.*'

Then he said with a sigh:

'My friend, we have not been fortunate. The murderer has not been obliging. He has not dropped for us the cuff link, the cigarette end, the cigar ash—or, in the case of the woman, the handkerchief, the lipstick, or the hair slide.'

'Only the bottle of nail polish?'

Poirot shrugged his shoulders. 'I must ask the maid. There is something—yes—a little curious there.'

'I wonder where the devil the girl's got to?' said Race.

They left the cabin, locking the door behind them, and passed on to that of Miss Van Schuyler.

Here again were all the appurtenances of wealth, expensive toilet fittings, good luggage, a certain number of private letters and papers all perfectly in order.

The next cabin was the double one occupied by Poirot, and beyond it that of Race.

'Hardly like to hide 'em in either of these,' said the Colonel.

Poirot demurred. 'It might be. Once, on the Orient

Express, I investigated a murder. There was a little matter of a scarlet kimono. It had disappeared, and yet it must be on the train. I found it—where do you think? *In my own locked suitcase!* Ah! It was an impertinence, that!'

'Well, let's see if anybody has been impertinent with you or me this time.'

But the thief of the pearls had not been impertinent with Hercule Poirot or with Colonel Race.

Rounding the stern they made a very careful search of Miss Bowers' cabin but could find nothing of a suspicious nature. Her handkerchiefs were of plain linen with an initial.

The Otterbournes' cabin came next. Here, again, Poirot made a very meticulous search—but with no result.

The next cabin was Bessner's. Simon Doyle lay with an untasted tray of food beside him.

'Off my feed,' he said apologetically.

He was looking feverish and very much worse than earlier in the day. Poirot appreciated Bessner's anxiety to get him as swiftly as possible to hospital and skilled appliances.

The little Belgian explained what the two of them were doing, and Simon nodded approval. On learning that the pearls had been restored by Miss Bowers but proved to be merely imitation, he expressed the most complete astonishment.

'You are quite sure, Monsieur Doyle, that your wife did not have an imitation string which she brought abroad with her instead of the real ones?'

Simon shook his head decisively.

'Oh, no. I'm quite sure of that. Linnet loved those

pearls and she wore 'em everywhere. They were insured against every possible risk, so I think that made her a bit careless.'

'Then we must continue our search.'

He started opening drawers. Race attacked a suitcase.

Simon stared. 'Look here, you surely don't suspect old Bessner pinched them?'

Poirot shrugged his shoulders.

'It might be so. After all, what do we know of Dr Bessner? Only what he himself gives out.'

'But he couldn't have hidden them in here without my seeing him.'

'He could not have hidden anything *today* without your having seen him. But we do not know when the substitution took place. He may have effected the exchange some days ago.'

'I never thought of that.'

But the search was unavailing.

The next cabin was Pennington's. The two men spent some time in their search. In particular, Poirot and Race examined carefully a case full of legal and business documents, most of them requiring Linnet's signature.

Poirot shook his head gloomily. 'These seem all square and above board. You agree?'

'Absolutely. Still, the man isn't a born fool. If there *had* been a compromising document there—a power of attorney or something of that kind—he'd be pretty sure to have destroyed it first thing.'

'That is so, yes.'

Poirot lifted a heavy Colt revolver out of the top drawer of the chest of drawers, looked at it and put it back.

'So it seems there are still some people who travel with revolvers,' he murmured.

'Yes, a little suggestive, perhaps. Still, Linnet Doyle wasn't shot with a thing that size.' Race paused and then said, 'You know, I've thought of a possible answer to your point about the pistol being thrown overboard. Supposing that the actual murderer *did* leave it in Linnet Doyle's cabin, and that someone else—some second person—took it away and threw it into the river?'

'Yes, that is possible. I have thought of it. But it opens up a whole string of questions. Who was that second person? What interest had they in endeavouring to shield Jacqueline de Bellefort by taking away the pistol? What was the second person doing there? The only other person we know of who went into the cabin was Mademoiselle Van Schuyler. Was it conceivably Mademoiselle Van Schuyler who removed it? Why should *she* wish to shield Jacqueline de Bellefort? And yet—what other reason can there be for the removal of the pistol?'

Race suggested:

'She may have recognized the stole as hers, got the wind up, and thrown the whole bag of tricks over on that account.'

'The stole, perhaps, but would she have got rid of the pistol, too? Still, I agree that it is a possible solution. But it is always—*bon Dieu*, it is clumsy. And you still have not appreciated one point about the stole—'

Agatha Christie

As they emerged from Pennington's cabin Poirot suggested that Race should search the remaining cabins, those occupied by Jacqueline, Cornelia and two empty ones at the end, while he himself had a few words with Simon Doyle.

Accordingly he retraced his steps along the deck and re-entered Bessner's cabin.

Simon said:

'Look here, I've been thinking. I'm perfectly sure that these pearls were all right yesterday.'

'Why is that, Monsieur Doyle?'

'Because Linnet'—he winced as he uttered his wife's name—'was passing them through her hands just before dinner and talking about them. She knew something about pearls. I feel certain she'd have known if they were a fake.'

'They were a very good imitation, though. Tell me, was Madame Doyle in the habit of letting those pearls out of her hands? Did she ever lend them to a friend for instance?'

Simon flushed with slight embarrassment.

'You see, Monsieur Poirot, it's difficult for me to say... I—I—well, you see, I hadn't known Linnet very long.'

'Ah, no, it was a quick romance—yours.'

Simon went on:

'And so—really—I shouldn't know a thing like that. But Linnet was awfully generous with her things. I should think she might have done.'

'She never, for instance'—Poirot's voice was very smooth—' she never, for instance, lent them to Mademoiselle de Bellefort?'

'What d' you mean?' Simon flushed brick-red, tried to

sit up and, wincing, fell back. 'What are you getting at? That Jackie stole the pearls? She didn't. I'll swear she didn't. Jackie's as straight as a die. The mere idea of her being a thief is ridiculous—absolutely ridiculous.'

Poirot looked at him with gently twinkling eyes.

'Oh, la! la! la!' he said unexpectedly. 'That suggestion of mine, it has indeed stirred up the nest of hornets.'

Simon repeated doggedly, unmoved by Poirot's lighter note, 'Jackie's straight!'

Poirot remembered a girl's voice by the Nile in Aswan saying, 'I love Simon—and he loves me...'

He had wondered which of the three statements he had heard that night was the true one. It seemed to him that it had turned out to be Jacqueline who had come closest to the truth.

The door opened and Race came in.

'Nothing,' he said brusquely. 'Well, we didn't expect it. I see the stewards coming along with their report as to the searching of the passengers.'

A steward and stewardess appeared in the doorway. The former spoke first. 'Nothing, sir.'

'Any of the gentlemen make any fuss?'

'Only the Italian gentleman, sir. He carried on a good deal. Said it was a dishonour—something of that kind. He'd got a gun on him, too.'

'What kind of a gun?'

'Mauser automatic .25, sir.'

'Italians are pretty hot tempered,' said Simon. 'Richetti got in no end of a stew at Wadi Halfa just because of a

Agatha Christie

mistake over a telegram. He was darned rude to Linnet over it.'

Race turned to the stewardess. She was a big handsome-looking woman.

'Nothing on any of the ladies, sir. They made a good deal of fuss—except for Mrs Allerton, who was as nice as nice could be. Not a sign of the pearls. By the way, the young lady, Miss Rosalie Otterbourne, had a little pistol in her handbag.'

'What kind?'

'It was a very small one, sir, with a pearl handle. A kind of toy.'

Race stared. 'Devil take this case,' he muttered. 'I thought we'd got *her* cleared of suspicion, and now—Does every girl on this blinking boat carry around pearl-handled toy pistols?'

He shot a question at the stewardess. 'Did she show any feeling over your finding it?'

The woman shook her head. 'I don't think she noticed. I had my back turned whilst I was going through the handbag.'

'Still, she must have known you'd come across it. Oh, well, it beats me. What about the maid?'

'We've looked all over the boat, sir. We can't find her anywhere.'

'What's this?' asked Simon.

'Mrs Doyle's maid—Louise Bourget. She's disappeared.'

'*Disappeared?*'

Race said thoughtfully:

'She might have stolen the pearls. She is the one person who had ample opportunity to get a replica made.'

'And then, when she found a search was being instituted, she threw herself overboard?' suggested Simon.

'Nonsense,' replied Race, irritably. 'A woman can't throw herself overboard in broad daylight, from a boat like this, without somebody realizing the fact. She's bound to be somewhere on board.'

He addressed the stewardess once more. 'When was she last seen?'

'About half an hour before the bell went for lunch, sir.'

'We'll have a look at her cabin anyway,' said Race. 'That may tell us something.'

He led the way to the deck below. Poirot followed him. They unlocked the door of the cabin and passed inside.

Louise Bourget, whose trade it was to keep other people's belongings in order, had taken a holiday where her own were concerned. Odds and ends littered the top of the chest of drawers; a suitcase gaped open, with clothes hanging out of the side of it and preventing it shutting; under-clothing hung limply over the sides of the chairs.

As Poirot, with swift neat fingers, opened the drawers of the dressing chest, Race examined the suitcase.

Louise's shoes were lined along by the bed. One of them, a black patent leather, seemed to be resting at an extraordinary angle, almost unsupported. The appearance of it was so odd that it attracted Race's attention.

He closed the suitcase and bent over the line of shoes. Then he uttered a sharp exclamation.

Agatha Christie

Poirot whirled round.
'*Qu'est-ce qu'ily a?*'
Race said grimly:
'She hasn't disappeared. *She's here—under the bed...*'

CHAPTER 22

The body of a dead woman who in life had been Louise Bourget lay on the floor of her cabin. The two men bent over it.

Race straightened himself first.

'Been dead close on an hour, I should say. We'll get Bessner on to it. Stabbed to the heart. Death pretty well instantaneous, I should imagine. She doesn't look pretty, does she?'

'No.'

Poirot shook his head with a slight shudder.

The dark feline face was convulsed as though with surprise and fury, the lips drawn back from the teeth.

Poirot bent again gently and picked up the right hand. Something just showed within the fingers. He detached it and held it out to Race—a little sliver of flimsy paper coloured a pale mauvish pink.

'You see what it is?'

'Money,' said Race.

Agatha Christie

'The corner of a thousand-franc note, I fancy.'

'Well, it's clear what happened,' said Race. 'She knew something—and she was blackmailing the murderer with her knowledge. We thought she wasn't being quite straight this morning.'

Poirot cried out:

'We have been idiots—fools! We should have known—then. What did she say? "What could I have seen or heard? I was on the deck below. Naturally, if I had been unable to sleep, if I had mounted the stairs, *then* perhaps I might have seen this assassin, this monster, enter or leave Madame's cabin, but as it is—" Of course, that is what did happen! She did come up. She *did* see someone gliding into Linnet Doyle's cabin—or coming out of it. And, because of her greed, her insensate greed, she lies here—'

'And we are no nearer to knowing who killed her,' finished Race disgustedly.

Poirot shook his head. 'No, no. We know much more now. We know—we know almost everything. Only what we know seems incredible... Yet it must be so. Only I do not see... Pah! what a fool I was this morning! We felt—both of us felt—that she was keeping something back, and yet we never realized that logical reason—blackmail.'

'She must have demanded hush money straight away,' said Race. 'Demanded it with threats. The murderer was forced to accede to that request and paid her in French notes. Anything there?'

Poirot shook his head thoughtfully. 'I hardly think so. Many people take a reserve of money with them when travelling—sometimes five-pound notes, sometimes dollars, but very often French notes as well. Possibly the murderer paid her all he had in a mixture of currencies. Let us continue our reconstruction.'

'The murderer comes to her cabin, gives her the money, and then—'

'And then,' said Poirot, 'she counts it. Oh, yes, I know that class. She would count the money, and while she counted it she was completely off her guard. The murderer struck. Having done so successfully, he gathered up the money and fled—not noticing that the corner of one of the notes was torn.'

'We may get him that way,' suggested Race doubtfully.

'I doubt it,' said Poirot. 'He will examine those notes, and will probably notice the tear. Of course if he were of a parsimonious disposition he would not be able to bring himself to destroy a *mille* note—but I fear—I very much fear that his temperament is just the opposite.'

'How do you make that out?'

'Both this crime and the murder of Madame Doyle demanded certain qualities—courage, audacity, bold execution, lightning action; those qualities do not accord with a saving, prudent disposition.'

Race shook his head sadly.

'I'd better get Bessner down,' he said.

The stout doctor's examination did not take long. Accompanied by a good many *Ach*s and *So*s, he went to work.

'She has been dead not more than an hour,' he announced. 'Death it was very quick—at once.'

Agatha Christie

'And what weapon do you think was used?'

'Ach, it is interesting that. It was something very sharp, very thin, very delicate. I could show you the kind of thing.'

Back again in his cabin he opened a case and extracted a long, delicate, surgical knife.

'It was something like that, my friend—it was not a common table knife.'

'I suppose,' suggested Race smoothly, 'that none of your own knives are—er—missing, Doctor?'

Bessner stared at him, then his face grew red with indignation.

'What is that you say? Do you think I—I, Carl Bessner—who so well-known is all over Austria—I with my clients, my highly born patients—I have killed a miserable little *femme de chambre*? Ah, but it is ridiculous—absurd, what you say! None of my knives are missing—not one, I tell you. They are all here, correct, in their places. You can see for yourself. And this insult to my profession I will not forget.'

Dr Bessner closed his case with a snap, flung it down and stamped out on to the deck.

'Whew!' said Simon. 'You've put the old boy's back up.'

Poirot shrugged his shoulders. 'It is regrettable.'

'You're on the wrong tack. Old Bessner's one of the best, even though he is a kind of Boche.'

Dr Bessner reappeared suddenly.

'Will you be so kind as to leave me now my cabin? I have to do the dressing of my patient's leg.'

Miss Bowers had entered with him and stood, brisk and professional, waiting for the others to go.

Race and Poirot crept out meekly. Race muttered something and went off. Poirot turned to his left.

He heard scraps of girlish conversation, a little laugh. Jacqueline and Rosalie were together in the latter's cabin.

The door was open and the two girls were standing near it. As his shadow fell on them they looked up. He saw Rosalie Otterbourne smile at him for the first time—a shy welcoming smile—a little uncertain in its lines, as of one who does a new and unfamiliar thing.

'You talk the scandal, Mesdemoiselles?' he accused them.

'No, indeed,' said Rosalie. 'As a matter of fact we were just comparing lipsticks.'

Poirot smiled. '*Les chiffons d'aujourd'hui*,' he murmured.

But there was something a little mechanical about his smile, and Jacqueline de Bellefort, quicker and more observant than Rosalie, saw it. She dropped the lipstick she was holding and came out upon the deck.

'Has something—what has happened now?'

'It is as you guess, Mademoiselle; something has happened.'

'What?' Rosalie came out too.

'Another death,' said Poirot.

Rosalie caught her breath sharply. Poirot was watching her narrowly. He saw alarm and something more—consternation—show for a minute or two in her eyes.

'Madame Doyle's maid has been killed,' he said bluntly.

'Killed?' cried Jacqueline. '*Killed*, do you say?'

'Yes, that is what I said.' Though his answer was nominally to her, it was Rosalie whom he watched. It was Rosalie

Agatha Christie

to whom he spoke as he went on. 'You see, this maid she saw something she was not intended to see. And so—she was silenced in case she should not hold her tongue.'

'What was it she saw?'

Again it was Jacqueline who asked, and again Poirot's answer was to Rosalie. It was an odd little three-cornered scene.

'There is, I think, very little doubt what it was she saw,' said Poirot. 'She saw someone enter and leave Linnet Doyle's cabin on that fatal night.'

His ears were quick. He heard the sharp intake of breath and saw the eyelids flicker. Rosalie Otterbourne had reacted just as he intended she should.

'Did she say who it was she saw?' Rosalie asked.

Gently—regretfully—Poirot shook his head.

Footsteps pattered up the deck. It was Cornelia Robson, her eyes wide and startled.

'Oh, Jacqueline,' she cried, 'something awful has happened. Another dreadful thing!'

Jacqueline turned to her. The two moved a few steps forward. Almost unconsciously Poirot and Rosalie Otterbourne moved in the other direction.

Rosalie said sharply:

'Why do you look at me? What have you got in your mind?'

'That is two questions you ask me. I will ask you only one in return. *Why do you not tell me all the truth, Mademoiselle?*'

'I don't know what you mean. I told you—everything—this morning.'

Death on the Nile

'No, there were things you did not tell me. You did not tell me that you carry about in your handbag a small-calibre pistol with a pearl handle. You did not tell me all that you saw last night.'

She flushed. Then she said sharply:

'It's quite untrue. I haven't got a revolver.'

'I did not say a revolver. I said a small pistol that you carry about in your handbag.'

She wheeled round, darted into her cabin and out again and thrust her grey leather handbag into his hands.

'You're talking nonsense. Look for yourself if you like.'

Poirot opened the bag. There was no pistol inside.

He handed the bag back to her, meeting her scornful triumphant glance.

'No,' he said pleasantly. 'It is not there.'

'You see. You're not always right, Monsieur Poirot. And you're wrong about that other ridiculous thing you said.'

'No, I do not think so.'

'You're infuriating!' She stamped an angry foot. 'You get an idea into your head and you go on and on and on about it.'

'Because I want you to tell me the truth.'

'What is the truth? You seem to know it better than I do.'

Poirot said:

'You want me to tell what it was you saw? If I am right, will you admit that I am right? I will tell you my little idea. I think that when you came round the stern of the boat you stopped involuntarily because you saw a man come

Agatha Christie

out of a cabin about halfway down the deck—Linnet Doyle's cabin, as you realized next day. You saw him come out, close the door behind him, and walk away from you down the deck and—perhaps—enter *one of the two end cabins*. Now, then, am I right, Mademoiselle?'

She did not answer.

Poirot said:

'Perhaps you think it is wiser not to speak. Perhaps you are afraid that if you do, you too will be killed.'

For a moment he thought she had risen to the easy bait—that the accusation against her courage would succeed where more subtle arguments would have failed.

Her lips opened—trembled—then:

'I saw no one,' said Rosalie Otterbourne.

CHAPTER 23

Miss Bowers came out of Dr Bessner's cabin, smoothing her cuffs over her wrists.

Jacqueline left Cornelia abruptly and accosted the hospital nurse.

'How is he?' she demanded.

Poirot came up in time to hear the answer. Miss Bowers was looking rather worried.

'Things aren't going too badly,' she said.

Jacqueline cried:

'You mean, he's worse?'

'Well, I must say I shall be relieved when we get in and can get a proper X-ray done and the whole thing cleaned up under an anaesthetic. When do you think we shall get to Shellal, Monsieur Poirot?'

'Tomorrow morning.'

Miss Bowers pursed her lips and shook her head.

'It's very unfortunate. We are doing all we can, but there's always such a danger of septicæmia.'

Agatha Christie

Jacqueline caught Miss Bowers' arm and shook it.

'Is he going to die? Is he going to die?'

'Dear me, no, Miss de Bellefort. That is, I hope not, I'm sure. The wound in itself isn't dangerous, but there's no doubt it ought to be X-rayed as soon as possible. And then, of course, poor Mr Doyle ought to have been kept absolutely quiet today. He's had far too much worry and excitement. No wonder his temperature is rising. What with the shock of his wife's death, and one thing and another—'

Jacqueline relinquished her grasp of the nurse's arm and turned away. She stood leaning over the side, her back to the other two.

'What I say is, we've got to hope for the best always,' said Miss Bowers. 'Of course Mr Doyle has a very strong constitution—one can see that—probably never had a day's illness in his life. So that's in his favour. But there's no denying that this rise in temperature is a nasty sign and—'

She shook her head, adjusted her cuffs once more, and moved briskly away.

Jacqueline turned and walked gropingly, blinded by tears, towards her cabin. A hand below her elbow steadied and guided her. She looked up through the tears to find Poirot by her side. She leaned on him a little and he guided her through the cabin door.

She sank down on the bed and the tears came more freely, punctuated by great shuddering sobs.

'He'll die! He'll die! I know he'll die… And I shall have killed him. Yes, I shall have killed him…'

Death on the Nile

Poirot shrugged his shoulders. He shook his head a little, sadly.

'Mademoiselle, what is done is done. One cannot take back the accomplished action. It is too late to regret.'

She cried out more vehemently:

'I shall have killed him! And I love him so... I love him so.'

Poirot sighed. 'Too much...'

It had been his thought long ago in the restaurant of M. Blondin. It was his thought again now.

He said, hesitating a little:

'Do not, at all events, go by what Miss Bowers says. Hospital nurses—me, I find them always gloomy! The night nurse, always, she is astonished to find her patient alive in the evening; the day nurse, always, she is surprised to find him alive in the morning! They know too much, you see, of the possibilities that may arise. When one is motoring one might easily say to oneself: "If a car came out from that cross-road—or if that lorry backed suddenly—or if the wheel came off the car that is approaching—or if a dog jumped off the hedge on to my driving arm—*eh bien*, I should probably be killed!" But one assumes—and usually rightly—that none of these things *will* happen, and that one will get to one's journey's end. But if, of course, one has been in an accident, or seen one or more accidents, then one is inclined to take the opposite point of view.'

Jacqueline asked, half smiling through her tears:

'Are you trying to console me, Monsieur Poirot?'

Agatha Christie

'The *bon Dieu* knows what I am trying to do! You should not have come on this journey.'

'No—I wish I hadn't. It's been—so awful. But—it will be soon over now.'

'*Mais oui—mais oui.*'

'And Simon will go to the hospital and they'll give the proper treatment and everything will be all right.'

'You speak like the child! *And they lived happily ever afterwards*. That is it, is it not?'

She flushed suddenly scarlet.

'Monsieur Poirot, I never meant—never—'

'It is too soon to think of such a thing! That is the proper hypocritical thing to say, is it not? But you are partly a Latin, Mademoiselle Jacqueline. You should be able to admit facts even if they do not sound very decorous. *Le roi est mort— vive le roi!* The sun has gone and the moon rises. That is so, is it not?'

'You don't understand. He's just sorry for me—awfully sorry for me, because he knows how terrible it is for me to know I've hurt him so badly.'

'Ah, well,' said Poirot. 'The pure pity, it is a very lofty sentiment.'

He looked at her half mockingly, half with some other emotion. He murmured softly under his breath words in French:

> '*La vie est vaine.*
> *Un peu d'amour,*
> *Un peu de haine,*
> *Et puis bonjour.*

*La vie est brève.
Un peu d'espoir,
Un peu de rêve,
Et puis bonsoir.'*

He went out again onto the deck. Colonel Race was striding along the deck and hailed him at once.

'Poirot. Good man! I want you. I've got an idea.'

Thrusting his arm through Poirot's he walked him up the deck.

'Just a chance remark of Doyle's. I hardly noticed it at the time. Something about a telegram.'

'*Tiens—c'est vrai.*'

'Nothing in it, perhaps, but one can't leave any avenue unexplored. Damn it all, man, two murders and we're still in the dark.'

Poirot shook his head. 'No, not in the dark. In the light.'

Race looked at him curiously. 'You have an idea?'

'It is more than an idea now. *I am sure.*'

'Since—when?'

'Since the death of the maid, Louise Bourget.'

'Damned if I see it!'

'My friend, it is so clear—so clear. Only—there are difficulties! Embarrassments—impediments! See you, around a person like Linnet Doyle there is so much—so many conflicting hates and jealousies and envies and meannesses. It is like a cloud of flies—buzzing, buzzing...'

'But you think you know?' The other looked at him curiously. 'You wouldn't say so unless you were sure.

Can't say I've any real light, myself. I've suspicions, of course...'

Poirot stopped. He laid an impressive hand on Race's arm. 'You are a great man, *mon Colonel*... You do not say: "Tell me. What is it that you think?" You know that if I could speak now I would. But there is much to be cleared away first. But think, think for a moment along the lines that I shall indicate. There are certain points... There is the statement of Mademoiselle de Bellefort that someone overheard our conversation that night in the garden at Aswan. There is the statement of Monsieur Tim Allerton as to what he heard and did on the night of the crime. There are Louise Bourget's significant answers to our questions this morning. There is the fact that Madame Allerton drinks water, that her son drinks whisky and soda and that I drink wine. Add to that the fact of two bottles of nail polish and the proverb I quoted. And finally we come to the crux of the whole business, the fact that the pistol was wrapped up in a cheap handkerchief and a velvet stole and thrown overboard...'

Race was silent a minute or two, then he shook his head.

'No,' he said. 'I don't see it. Mind, I've got a faint idea what you're driving at. But as far as I can see it doesn't work.'

'But yes—but yes—you are seeing only half the truth. And remember this—we must start again from the beginning, since our first conception was entirely wrong.'

Race made a slight grimace.

'I'm used to that. It often seems to me that's all detective work is, wiping out your false starts and beginning again.'

'Yes, it is very true, that. And it is just what some people will not do. They conceive a certain theory, and everything has to fit into that theory. If one little fact will not fit it, they throw it aside. But it is always the facts *that will not fit in* that are significant. All along I have realized *the significance of that pistol being removed from the scene of the crime.* I knew that it meant something—but what that something was I only realized one little half hour ago.'

'And I still don't see it!'

'But you will! Only reflect along the lines I indicated. And now let us clear up this matter of a telegram. That is, if the Herr Doktor will admit us.'

Dr Bessner was still in a very bad humour. In answer to their knock he disclosed a scowling face.

'What is it? Once more you wish to see my patient? But I tell you it is not wise. He has fever. He has had more than enough excitement today.'

'Just one question,' said Race. 'Nothing more, I assure you.'

With an unwilling grunt the doctor moved aside and the two men entered the cabin.

Dr Bessner, growling to himself, pushed past them.

'I return in three minutes,' he said. 'And then—positively—you go!'

They heard him stumping down the deck.

Simon Doyle looked from one to the other of them inquiringly.

'Yes,' he said, 'what is it?'

'A very little thing,' Race replied. 'Just now, when the

Agatha Christie

stewards were reporting to me, they mentioned that Signor Richetti had been particularly troublesome. You said that that didn't surprise you, as you knew he had a bad temper, and that he had been rude to your wife over some matter of a telegram. Now can you tell me about the incident?'

'Easily. It was at Wadi Halfa. We'd just come back from the Second Cataract. Linnet thought she saw a telegram for her sticking up on the board. She'd forgotten, you see, that she wasn't called Ridgeway any longer, and Richetti and Ridgeway do look rather alike when written in an atrocious handwriting. So she tore it open, couldn't make head or tail of it, and was puzzling over it when this fellow Richetti came along, fairly tore it out of her hand and gibbered with rage. She went after him to apologize and he was frightfully rude to her about it.'

Race drew a deep breath. 'And do you know at all, Mr Doyle, what was in that telegram?'

'Yes. Linnet read part of it out aloud. It said—'

He paused. There was a commotion outside. A high-pitched voice was rapidly approaching.

'Where are Monsieur Poirot and Colonel Race? I must see them *immediately*! It is most important. I have vital information. I—Are they with Mr Doyle?'

Bessner had not closed the door. Only the curtain hung across the open doorway. Mrs Otterbourne swept it to one side and entered like a tornado. Her face was suffused with colour, her gait slightly unsteady, her command of words not quite under her control.

Death on the Nile

'Mr Doyle,' she said dramatically, 'I know who killed your wife!'

'What?'

Simon stared at her. So did the other two.

Mrs Otterbourne swept all three of them with a triumphant glance. She was happy—superbly happy.

'Yes,' she said. 'My theories are completely vindicated. The deep, primeval, primordial urges—it may appear impossible—fantastic—but it is the truth!'

Race said sharply:

'Do I understand that you have evidence in your possession to show who killed Mrs Doyle?'

Mrs Otterbourne sat down in a chair and leaned forward, nodding her head vigorously.

'Certainly I have. You will agree, will you not, that *whoever killed Louise Bourget also killed Linnet Doyle*—that the two crimes were committed by one and the same hand?'

'Yes, yes,' said Simon impatiently. 'Of course. That stands to reason. Go on.'

'Then my assertion holds. I know who killed Louise Bourget—therefore I know who killed Linnet Doyle.'

'You mean, you have a theory as to who killed Louise Bourget,' suggested Race sceptically.

Mrs Otterbourne turned on him like a tiger.

'No, I have exact knowledge. I *saw* the person with my own eyes.'

Simon, fevered, shouted out:

'For God's sake, start at the beginning. You know the person who killed Louise Bourget, you say.'

Agatha Christie

Mrs Otterbourne nodded.

'I will tell you exactly what occurred.'

Yes, she was very happy—no doubt of it! This was her moment—her triumph! What of it if her books were failing to sell, if the stupid public that once had bought them and devoured them voraciously now turned to newer favourites? Salome Otterbourne would once again be notorious. Her name would be in all the papers. She would be principal witness for the prosecution at the trial.

She took a deep breath and opened her mouth.

'It was when I went down to lunch. I hardly felt like eating—all the horror of the recent tragedy—Well, I needn't go into that.

'Halfway down I remembered that I had—er—left something in my cabin. I told Rosalie to go on without me. She did.'

Mrs Otterbourne paused a minute.

The curtain across the door moved slightly as though lifted by the wind, but none of the three men noticed it.

'I—er—' Mrs Otterbourne paused. Thin ice to skate over here, but it must be done somehow. 'I—er—had an arrangement with one of the—er—personnel of the ship. He was to—er—get me something I needed, but I did not wish my daughter to know of it. She is inclined to be tiresome in certain ways—'

Not too good, this, but she could think of something that sounded better before it came to telling the story in court.

Race's eyebrows lifted as his eyes asked a question of Poirot.

Death on the Nile

Poirot gave an infinitesimal nod. His lips formed the word: 'Drink.'

The curtain across the door moved again. Between it and the door itself something showed with a faint steel-blue gleam.

Mrs Otterbourne continued.

'The arrangement was that I should go round to the stern on the deck below this, and there I should find the man waiting for me. As I went along the deck a cabin door opened and somebody looked out. It was this girl—Louise Bourget or whatever her name is. She seemed to be expecting someone. When she saw it was me, she looked disappointed and went abruptly inside again. I didn't think anything of it, of course. I went along just as I had said I would and got the—the stuff from the man. I paid him and—er—just had a word with him. Then I started back. Just as I came around the corner I saw someone knock on the maid's door and go into the cabin.'

Race said:

'And that person was—?'

Bang!

The noise of the explosion filled the cabin. There was an acrid sour smell of smoke. Mrs Otterbourne turned slowly sideways, as though in supreme inquiry, then her body slumped forward and she fell to the ground with a crash. From just behind her ear the blood flowed from a round neat hole.

There was a moment's stupefied silence.

Then both the able-bodied men jumped to their feet. The

woman's body hindered their movements a little. Race bent over her while Poirot made a catlike jump for the door and the deck.

The deck was empty. On the ground just in front of the sill lay a big Colt revolver.

Poirot glanced in both directions. The deck was empty. He then sprinted towards the stern. As he rounded the corner he ran into Tim Allerton, who was coming full tilt from the opposite direction.

'What the devil was that?' cried Tim breathlessly.

Poirot said sharply: 'Did you meet anyone on your way here?'

'Meet anyone? No.'

'Then come with me.' He took the young man by the arm and retraced his steps. A little crowd had assembled by now. Rosalie, Jacqueline, and Cornelia had rushed out of their cabins. More people were coming along the deck from the saloon—Ferguson, Jim Fanthorp and Mrs Allerton.

Race stood by the revolver. Poirot turned his head and said sharply to Tim Allerton:

'Got any gloves in your pocket?'

Tim fumbled.

'Yes, I have.'

Poirot seized them from him, put them on, and bent to examine the revolver. Race did the same. The others watched breathlessly.

Race said:

'He didn't go the other way. Fanthorp and Ferguson were sitting on this deck lounge; they'd have seen him.'

Poirot responded, 'And Mr Allerton would have met him if he'd gone aft.'

Race said, pointing to the revolver:

'Rather fancy we've seen this not so very long ago. Must make sure, though.'

He knocked on the door of Pennington's cabin. There was no answer. The cabin was empty. Race strode to the right-hand drawer of the chest and jerked it open. The revolver was gone.

'Settles that,' said Race. 'Now then, where's Pennington himself?'

They went out again on deck. Mrs Allerton had joined the group. Poirot moved swiftly over to her.

'Madame, take Miss Otterbourne with you and look after her. Her mother has been'—he consulted Race with an eye and Race nodded—'killed.'

Dr Bessner came bustling along.

'*Gott im Himmel!* What is there now?'

They made way for him. Race indicated the cabin. Bessner went inside.

'*Find Pennington*,' said Race. 'Any fingerprints on that revolver?'

'None,' said Poirot.

They found Pennington on the deck below. He was sitting in the little drawing-room writing letters. He lifted a handsome, clean-shaven face.

'Anything new?' he asked.

'Didn't you hear a shot?'

'Why—now you mention it—I believe I did hear a kind of a bang. But I never dreamed—Who's been shot?'

Agatha Christie

'Mrs Otterbourne.'

'*Mrs Otterbourne?*' Pennington sounded quite astounded. 'Well, you do surprise me. Mrs Otterbourne.' He shook his head. 'I can't see that at all.' He lowered his voice. 'Strikes me, gentlemen, we've got a homicidal maniac aboard. We ought to organize a defence system.'

'Mr Pennington,' said Race, 'how long have you been in this room?'

'Why, let me see.' Mr Pennington gently rubbed his chin. 'I should say a matter of twenty minutes or so.'

'And you haven't left it?'

'Why no—certainly not.'

He looked inquiringly at the two men.

'You see, Mr Pennington,' said Race, 'Mrs Otterbourne was shot with your revolver.'

CHAPTER 24

Mr Pennington was shocked. Mr Pennington could hardly believe it.

'Why, gentlemen,' he said, 'this is a very serious matter. Very serious indeed.'

'Extremely serious for you, Mr Pennington.'

'For me?' Pennington's eyebrows rose in startled surprise. 'But, my dear sir, I was sitting quietly writing in here when that shot was fired.'

'You have, perhaps, a witness to prove that?'

Pennington shook his head.

'Why, no—I wouldn't say that. But it's clearly impossible that I should have gone to the deck above, shot this poor woman (and why should I shoot her anyway?) and come down again with no one seeing me. There are always plenty of people on the deck lounge this time of day.'

'How do you account for your pistol being used?'

'Well—I'm afraid I may be to blame there. Quite soon after getting aboard there was a conversation in the saloon one evening, I remember, about firearms, and I mentioned then that I always carried a revolver with me when I travel.'

'Who was there?'

'Well, I can't remember exactly. Most people, I think. Quite a crowd, anyway.'

He shook his head gently.

'Why, yes,' he said. 'I am certainly to blame there.'

He went on: 'First Linnet, then Linnet's maid, and now Mrs Otterbourne. There seems no reason in it all!'

'There *was* reason,' said Race.

'There was?'

'Yes. Mrs Otterbourne was on the point of telling us that she had seen a certain person go into Louise's cabin. Before she could name that person she was shot dead.'

Andrew Pennington passed a fine silk handkerchief over his brow.

'All this is terrible,' he murmured.

Poirot said:

'Monsieur Pennington, I would like to discuss certain aspects of the case with you. Will you come to my cabin in half an hour's time?'

'I should be delighted.'

Pennington did not sound delighted. He did not look delighted either. Race and Poirot exchanged glances and then abruptly left the room.

'Cunning old devil,' said Race, 'but he's afraid. Eh?'

Poirot nodded. 'Yes, he is not happy, our Monsieur Pennington.'

Death on the Nile

As they reached the promenade deck again, Mrs Allerton came out of her cabin and, seeing Poirot, beckoned him imperiously.

'Madame?'

'That poor child! Tell me, Monsieur Poirot, is there a double cabin somewhere that I could share with her? She oughtn't to go back to the one she shared with her mother, and mine is only a single one.'

'That can be arranged, Madame. It is very good of you.'

'It's mere decency. Besides, I'm very fond of the girl. I've always liked her.'

'Is she very—upset?'

'Terribly. She seems to have been absolutely devoted to that odious woman. That is what is so pathetic about it all. Tim says he believes she drank. Is that true?'

Poirot nodded.

'Oh, well, poor woman—one must not judge her, I suppose, but that girl must have had a terrible life.'

'She did, Madame. She is very proud and she was very loyal.'

'Yes, I like that—loyalty, I mean. It's out of fashion nowadays. She's an odd character, that girl—proud, reserved, stubborn, and terribly warm-hearted underneath, I fancy.'

'I see that I have given her into good hands, Madame.'

'Yes, don't worry. I'll look after her. She's inclined to cling to me in the most pathetic fashion.'

Mrs Allerton went back into the cabin. Poirot returned to the scene of the tragedy.

Agatha Christie

Cornelia was still standing on the deck, her eyes wide. She said: 'I don't understand, Monsieur Poirot. How did the person who shot her get away without our seeing him?'

'Yes, how?' echoed Jacqueline.

'Ah,' said Poirot, 'it was not quite such a disappearing trick as you think, Mademoiselle. There were three distinct ways the murderer might have gone.'

Jacqueline looked puzzled. She said, '*Three?*'

'He might have gone to the right, or he might have gone to the left, but I don't see any other way,' puzzled Cornelia.

Jacqueline too frowned. Then her brow cleared. She said:

'Of course. He could move in two directions on one plane—*but he could go at right angles to that plane too.* That is, he couldn't go *up* very well, but he could go *down*.'

Poirot smiled. 'You have brains, Mademoiselle.'

Cornelia said:

'I know I'm just a plain mutt, but I still don't see.'

Jacqueline said:

'Monsieur Poirot means, darling, that he could swing himself over the rail and down on to the deck below.'

'My!' gasped Cornelia. 'I never thought of that. He'd have to be mighty quick about it, though. I suppose he could just do it?'

'He could do it easily enough,' said Tim Allerton. 'Remember, there's always a minute of shock after a thing like this. One hears a shot and one's too paralysed to move for a second or two.'

'That was your experience, Monsieur Allerton?'

'Yes, it was. I just stood like a dummy for quite five seconds. Then I fairly sprinted round the deck.'

Race came out of Bessner's cabin and said authoritatively:

'Would you mind all clearing off? We want to bring out the body.'

Everyone moved away obediently. Poirot went with them. Cornelia said to him with sad earnestness:

'I'll never forget this trip as long as I live. Three deaths... It's just like living in a nightmare.'

Ferguson overheard her. He said aggressively:

'That's because you're over-civilized. You should look on death as the Oriental does. It's a mere incident—hardly noticeable.'

Cornelia said:

'That's all very well—they're not educated, poor creatures.'

'No, and a good thing too. Education has devitalized the white races. Look at America—goes in for an orgy of culture. Simply disgusting.'

'I think you're talking nonsense,' said Cornelia, flushing. 'I attend lectures every winter on Greek Art and the Renaissance, and I went to some on famous Women of History.'

Mr Ferguson groaned in agony. 'Greek Art! Renaissance! Famous Women of History! It makes me quite sick to hear you. It's the *future* that matters, woman, not the past.

Three women are dead on this boat—well, what of it? They're no loss! Linnet Doyle and her money! The French maid—a domestic parasite. Mrs Otterbourne—a useless fool of a woman. Do you think anyone really cares whether they're dead or not? *I* don't. I think it's a damned good thing!'

'Then you're wrong!' Cornelia blazed out at him. 'And it makes me sick to hear you talk and talk, as though nobody mattered but *you*. I didn't like Mrs Otterbourne much, but her daughter was ever so fond of her and she's all broken up over her mother's death. I don't know much about the French maid, but I expect somebody was fond of her somewhere; and as for Linnet Doyle—well, apart from everything else, she was just lovely! She was so beautiful when she came into a room that it made a lump come in your throat. I'm homely myself, and that makes me appreciate beauty a lot more. She was as beautiful—just as a woman—as anything in Greek Art. And when anything beautiful's dead, it's a loss to the world. So there!'

Mr Ferguson stepped back a pace. He caught hold of his hair with both hands and tugged at it vehemently.

'I give it up,' he said. 'You're unbelievable. Just haven't got a bit of natural female spite in you anywhere.' He turned to Poirot. 'Do you know, sir, that Cornelia's father was practically ruined by Linnet Ridgeway's old man? But does the girl gnash her teeth when she sees the heiress sailing about in pearls and Paris models? No, she just bleats out, "Isn't she beautiful?" like a blessed baa lamb. I don't believe she even felt sore at her.'

Cornelia flushed. 'I did—just for a minute. Poppa kind of died of discouragement, you know, because he hadn't made good.'

'Felt sore for a minute! I ask you.'

Cornelia flashed round on him.

'Well, didn't you say just now it was the future that mattered, not the past? All that was in the past, wasn't it? It's over.'

'Got me there,' said Ferguson. 'Cornelia Robson, you're the only nice woman I've ever come across. Will you marry me?'

'Don't be absurd.'

'It's a genuine proposal—even if it is made in the presence of Old Man Sleuth. Anyway, you're a witness, Monsieur Poirot. I've deliberately offered marriage to this female—against all my principles, because I don't believe in legal contracts between the sexes; but I don't think she'd stand for anything else, so marriage it shall be. Come on, Cornelia, say yes.'

'I think you're utterly ridiculous,' said Cornelia, flushing.

'Why won't you marry me?'

'You're not serious,' said Cornelia.

'Do you mean not serious in proposing or do you mean not serious in character?'

'Both, but I really meant character. You laugh at all sorts of serious things. Education and Culture—and—and Death. You wouldn't be *reliable*.'

She broke off, flushed again, and hurried along into her cabin.

Ferguson stared after her. 'Damn the girl! I believe she really means it. She wants a man to be reliable. *Reliable*—ye gods!' He paused and then said curiously, 'What's the matter with you, Monsieur Poirot? You seem very deep in thought.'

Poirot roused himself with a start.

'I reflect, that is all. I reflect.'

'Meditation on Death. Death, the Recurring Decimal, by Hercule Poirot. One of his well-known monographs.'

'Monsieur Ferguson,' said Poirot, 'you are a very impertinent young man.'

'You must excuse me. I like attacking established institutions.'

'And I—am an established institution?'

'Precisely. What do you think of that girl?'

'Of Miss Robson?'

'Yes.'

'I think that she has a great deal of character.'

'You're right. She's got spirit. She looks meek, but she isn't. She's got guts. She's—oh, damn it, I want that girl. It mightn't be a bad move if I tackled the old lady. If I could once get her thoroughly against me, it might cut some ice with Cornelia.'

He wheeled and went into the observation saloon.

Miss Van Schuyler was seated in her usual corner. She looked even more arrogant than usual. She was knitting. Ferguson strode up to her. Hercule Poirot, entering unobtrusively, took a seat a discreet distance away and appeared to be absorbed in a magazine.

'Good afternoon, Miss Van Schuyler.'

Miss Van Schuyler raised her eyes for a bare second, dropped them again and murmured frigidly, 'Er—good afternoon.'

'Look here, Miss Van Schuyler, I want to talk to you about something pretty important. It's just this. I want to marry your cousin.'

Miss Van Schuyler's ball of wool dropped on to the ground and ran wildly across the saloon.

She said in a venomous tone:

'You must be out of your senses, young man.'

'Not at all. I'm determined to marry her. I've asked her to marry me!'

Miss Van Schuyler surveyed him coldly, with the kind of speculative interest she might have accorded to an odd sort of beetle.

'Indeed? And I presume she sent you about your business.'

'She refused me.'

'Naturally.'

'Not "naturally" at all. I'm going to go on asking her till she agrees.'

'I can assure you, sir, that I shall take steps to see that my young cousin is not subjected to any such persecution,' said Miss Van Schuyler in a biting tone.

'What have you got against me?'

Miss Van Schuyler merely raised her eyebrows and gave a vehement tug to her wool, preparatory to regaining it and closing the interview.

'Come now,' persisted Mr Ferguson, 'what have you got against me?'

'I should think that was quite obvious, Mr—er—I don't know your name.'

'Ferguson.'

'Mr Ferguson.' Miss Van Schuyler uttered the name with definite distaste. 'Any such idea is quite out of the question.'

'You mean,' said Ferguson, 'that I'm not good enough for her?'

'I should think that would have been obvious to you.'

'In what way am I not good enough?'

Miss Van Schuyler again did not answer.

'I've got two legs, two arms, good health, and quite reasonable brains. What's wrong with that?'

'There is such a thing as social position, Mr Ferguson.'

'Social position is bunk!'

The door swung open and Cornelia came in. She stopped dead on seeing her redoubtable Cousin Marie in conversation with her would-be suitor.

The outrageous Mr Ferguson turned his head, grinned broadly and called out:

'Come along, Cornelia. I'm asking for your hand in marriage in the best conventional manner.'

'Cornelia,' said Miss Van Schuyler, and her voice was truly awful in quality, *have you encouraged this young man?*'

'I—no, of course not—at least—not exactly—I mean—'

'What do you mean?'

'She hasn't encouraged me,' said Mr Ferguson helpfully. 'I've done it all. She hasn't actually pushed me in the face, because she's got too kind a heart. Cornelia, your cousin says I'm not good enough for you. That, of course, is true, but not in the way she means it. My moral nature certainly doesn't equal yours, but her point is that I'm hopelessly below you socially.'

'That I think, is equally obvious to Cornelia,' said Miss Van Schuyler.

'Is it?' Mr Ferguson looked at her searchingly. 'Is that why you won't marry me?'

'No, it isn't.' Cornelia flushed. 'If—if I liked you, I'd marry you no matter who you were.'

'But you don't like me?'

'I—I think you're just outrageous. The way you say things... The *things* you say... I—I've never met anyone the least like you. I—'

Tears threatened to overcome her. She rushed from the room.

'On the whole,' said Mr Ferguson, 'that's not too bad for a start.' He leaned back in his chair, gazed at the ceiling, whistled, crossed his disreputable knees and remarked, 'I'll be calling you Cousin yet.'

Miss Van Schuyler trembled with rage.

'Leave this room at once, sir, or I'll ring for the steward.'

'I've paid for my ticket,' said Mr Ferguson. 'They can't possibly turn me out of the public lounge. But I'll humour you.' He sang softly, 'Yo ho ho, and a bottle of rum.' Rising, he sauntered nonchalantly to the door and passed out.

Agatha Christie

Choking with anger Miss Van Schuyler struggled to her feet. Poirot, discreetly emerging from retirement behind his magazine, sprang up and retrieved the ball of wool.

'Thank you, Monsieur Poirot. If you would send Miss Bowers to me—I feel quite upset—that insolent young man.'

'Rather eccentric, I'm afraid,' said Poirot. 'Most of that family are. Spoilt, of course. Always inclined to tilt at windmills.' He added carelessly, 'You recognized him, I suppose?'

'Recognized him?'

'Calls himself Ferguson and won't use his title because of his advanced ideas.'

'His *title*?' Miss Van Schuyler's tone was sharp.

'Yes, that's young Lord Dawlish. Rolling in money, of course, but he became a communist when he was at Oxford.'

Miss Van Schuyler, her face a battleground of contradictory emotions, said:

'How long have you known this, Monsieur Poirot?'

Poirot shrugged his shoulders.

'There was a picture in one of these papers—I noticed the resemblance. Then I found a signet ring with a coat of arms on it. Oh, there's no doubt about it, I assure you.'

He quite enjoyed reading the conflicting expressions that succeeded each other on Miss Van Schuyler's face. Finally, with a gracious inclination of the head, she said, 'I am very much obliged to you, Monsieur Poirot.'

Poirot looked after her and smiled as she went out of

the saloon. Then he sat down and his face grew grave once more. He was following out a train of thought in his mind. From time to time he nodded his head.

'*Mais oui*,' he said at last. 'It all fits in.'

CHAPTER 25

Race found him still sitting there.

'Well, Poirot, what about it? Pennington's due in ten minutes. I'm leaving this in your hands.'

Poirot rose quickly to his feet. 'First, get hold of young Fanthorp.'

'Fanthorp?' Race looked surprised.

'Yes. Bring him to my cabin.'

Race nodded and went off. Poirot went along to his cabin. Race arrived with young Fanthorp a minute or two afterward.

Poirot indicated chairs and offered cigarettes.

'Now, Monsieur Fanthorp,' he said, 'to our business! I perceive that you wear the same tie that my friend Hastings wears.'

Jim Fanthorp looked down at his neckwear with some bewilderment.

'It's an O.E. tie,' he said.

'Exactly. You must understand that, though I am a

foreigner, I know something of the English point of view. I know, for instance, that there are "things which are done" and "things which are not done".'

Jim Fanthorp grinned.

'We don't say that sort of thing much nowadays, sir.'

'Perhaps not, but the custom, it still remains. The Old School Tie is the Old School Tie, and there are certain things (I know this from experience) that the Old School Tie does not do! One of those things, Monsieur Fanthorp, is to butt into a private conversation unasked when one does not know the people who are conducting it.'

Fanthorp stared.

Poirot went on:

'But the other day, Monsieur Fanthorp, *that is exactly what you did do*. Certain persons were quietly transacting some private business in the observation saloon. You strolled near them, obviously in order to overhear what it was that was in progress, and presently you actually turned round and congratulated a lady—Madame Simon Doyle—on the soundness of her business methods.'

Jim Fanthorp's face got very red. Poirot swept on, not waiting for a comment.

'Now that, Monsieur Fanthorp, was not at all the behaviour of one who wears a tie similar to that worn by my friend Hastings! Hastings is all delicacy, would die of shame before he did such a thing! Therefore, taking that action of yours in conjunction with the fact that you are a very young man to be able to afford an expensive holiday, that you are a member of a country solicitor's firm and therefore probably not extravagantly well off, and that you show no signs of recent illness such as might necessitate a prolonged visit abroad, I ask myself—and am now asking you—*what is the reason for your presence on this boat?*'

Jim Fanthorp jerked his head back.

'I decline to give you any information whatever, Monsieur Poirot. I really think you must be mad.'

'I am not mad. I am very, very sane. Where is your firm? In Northampton; that is not very far from Wode Hall. What conversation did you try to overhear? One concerning legal documents. What was the object of your remark—a remark which you uttered with obvious embarrassment and malaise? Your object was *to prevent Madame Doyle from signing any document unread.*'

He paused.

'On this boat we have had a murder, and following that murder two other murders in rapid succession. If I further give you the information that the weapon which killed Madame Otterbourne was *a revolver owned by Monsieur Andrew Pennington*, then perhaps you will realize that it is actually your duty to tell us all you can.'

Jim Fanthorp was silent for some minutes. At last he said:

'You have rather an odd way of going about things, Monsieur Poirot, but I appreciate the points you have made. The trouble is that I have no exact information to lay before you.'

'You mean that it is a case, merely, of suspicion.'

'Yes.'

'And therefore you think it injudicious to speak? That may be true, legally speaking. But this is not a court of law. Colonel Race and myself are endeavouring to track down a murderer. Anything that can help us to do so may be valuable.'

Again Jim Fanthorp reflected. Then he said:

'Very well. What is it you want to know?'

'Why did you come on this trip?'

'My uncle, Mr Carmichael, Mrs Doyle's English solicitor, sent me. He handled a good many of her affairs. In this way, he was often in correspondence with Mr Andrew Pennington, who was Mrs Doyle's American trustee. Several small incidents (I cannot enumerate them all) made my uncle suspicious that all was not quite as it should be.'

'In plain language,' said Race, 'your uncle suspected that Pennington was a crook?'

Jim Fanthorp nodded, a faint smile on his face.

'You put it rather more bluntly than I should, but the main idea is correct. Various excuses made by Pennington, certain plausible explanations of the disposal of funds, aroused my uncle's distrust.

'While these suspicions of his were still nebulous, Miss Ridgeway married unexpectedly and went off on her honeymoon to Egypt. Her marriage relieved my uncle's mind, as he knew that on her return to England the estate would have to be formally settled and handed over.

'However, in a letter she wrote him from Cairo, she mentioned casually that she had unexpectedly run across Andrew Pennington. My uncle's suspicions became acute.

Agatha Christie

He felt sure that Pennington, perhaps by now in a desperate position, was going to try and obtain signatures from her which would cover his own defalcations. Since my uncle had no definite evidence to lay before her, he was in a most difficult position. The only thing he could think of was to send me out here, travelling by air, with instruction to discover what was in the wind. I was to keep my eyes open and act summarily if necessary—a most unpleasant mission, I can assure you. As a matter of fact, on the occasion you mention I had to behave more or less as a cad! It was awkward, but on the whole I was satisfied with the result.'

'You mean you put Madame Doyle on her guard?' asked Race.

'Not so much that, but I think I put the wind up Pennington. I felt convinced he wouldn't try any more funny business for some time, and by then I hoped to have got intimate enough with Mr and Mrs Doyle to convey some kind of a warning. As a matter of fact I hoped to do so through Doyle. Mrs Doyle was so attached to Mr Pennington that it would have been a bit awkward to suggest things to her about him. It would have been easier for me to approach the husband.'

Race nodded.

Poirot asked, 'Will you give me a candid opinion on one point, Monsieur Fanthorp? If you were engaged in putting a swindle over, would you choose Madame Doyle or Monsieur Doyle as a victim?'

Fanthorp smiled faintly.

'Mr Doyle, every time. Linnet Doyle was very shrewd in

business matters. Her husband, I should fancy, is one of those trustful fellows who know nothing of business and are always ready to "sign on the dotted line" as he himself put it.'

'I agree,' said Poirot. He looked at Race. '*And there's your motive.*'

Jim Fanthorp said:

'But this is all pure conjecture. It isn't *evidence.*'

Poirot said easily:

'Ah, bah! we will get evidence!'

'How?'

'Possibly from Mr Pennington himself.'

Fanthorp looked doubtful.

'I wonder. I very much wonder.'

Race glanced at his watch. 'He's about due now.'

Jim Fanthorp was quick to take the hint. He left them.

Two minutes later Andrew Pennington made his appearance. His manner was all smiling urbanity. Only the taut line of his jaw and the wariness of his eyes betrayed the fact that a thoroughly experienced fighter was on his guard.

'Well, gentlemen,' he said, 'here I am.'

He sat down and looked at them inquiringly.

'We asked you to come here, Monsieur Pennington,' began Poirot, 'because it is fairly obvious that you have a very special and immediate interest in the case.'

Pennington raised his eyebrows slightly.

'Is that so?'

Poirot said gently: 'Surely. You have known Linnet Ridgeway, I understand, since she was quite a child.'

'Oh! that—' His face altered, became less alert. 'I beg pardon, I didn't quite get you. Yes, as I told you this morning, I've known Linnet since she was a cute little thing in pinafores.'

'You were on terms of close intimacy with her father?'

'That's so. Melhuish Ridgeway and I were very close—very close.'

'You were so intimately associated that on his death he appointed you business guardian to his daughter and trustee to the vast fortune she inherited?'

'Why, roughly, that is so.' The wariness was back again. The note was more cautious. 'I was not the only trustee, naturally—others were associated with me.'

'Who have since died?'

'Two of them are dead. The other, Mr Sterndale Rockford, is alive.'

'Your partner?'

'Yes.'

'Mademoiselle Ridgeway, I understand, was not yet of age when she married?'

'She would have been twenty-one next July.'

'And in the normal course of events she would have come into control of her fortune then?'

'Yes.'

'But her marriage precipitated matters?'

Pennington's jaw hardened. He shot out his chin at them aggressively.

'You'll pardon me, gentlemen, but what exact business is all this of yours?'

'If you dislike answering the question—'

'There's no dislike about it. I don't mind what you ask me. But I don't see the relevance of all this.'

'Oh, but surely, Monsieur Pennington'—Poirot leaned forward, his eyes green and catlike—'there is the question of motive. In considering that, financial considerations must always be taken into account.'

Pennington said sullenly:

'By Ridgeway's will, Linnet got control of her dough when she was twenty-one or when she married.'

'No conditions of any kind?'

'No conditions.'

'And it is a matter, I am credibly assured, of millions.'

'Millions it is.'

Poirot said softly:

'Your responsibility, Mr Pennington, and that of your partner, has been a very grave one.'

Pennington said curtly:

'We're used to responsibility. Doesn't worry us any.'

'I wonder.'

Something in his tone flicked the other man on the raw. He asked angrily: 'What the devil do you mean?'

Poirot replied with an air of engaging frankness.

'I was wondering, Mr Pennington, whether Linnet Ridgeway's sudden marriage caused any—consternation in your office?'

'Consternation?'

'That was the word I used.'

'What the hell are you driving at?'

'Something quite simple. Are Linnet Doyle's affairs in the perfect order they should be?'

Pennington rose to his feet.

'That's enough. I'm through.' He made for the door.

'But you will answer my question first?'

Pennington snapped:

'They're in perfect order.'

'You were not so alarmed when the news of Linnet Ridgeway's marriage reached you that you rushed over to Europe by the first boat and staged an apparently fortuitous meeting in Egypt?'

Pennington came back towards them. He had himself under control once more.

'What you are saying is absolute balderdash! I didn't even know that Linnet was married till I met her in Cairo. I was utterly astonished. Her letter must have missed me by a day in New York. It was forwarded and I got it about a week later.'

'You came over by the *Carmanic*, I think you said.'

'That's right.'

'And the letter reached New York after the *Carmanic* sailed?'

'How many times have I got to repeat it?'

'It is strange,' said Poirot.

'What's strange?'

'That on your luggage there are no labels of the *Carmanic*. The only recent labels of transatlantic sailing are the *Normandie*. The *Normandie*, I remember, sailed two days after the *Carmanic*.'

For a moment the other was at a loss. His eyes wavered. Colonel Race weighed in with telling effect.

'Come now, Mr Pennington,' he said. 'We've several reasons for believing that you came over on the *Normandie* and not by the *Carmanic*, as you said. In that case, *you received Mrs Doyle's letter before you left New York*. It's no good denying it, for it's the easiest thing in the world to check up the steamship companies.'

Andrew Pennington felt absent-mindedly for a chair and sat down. His face was impassive—a poker face. Behind that mask his agile brain looked ahead to the next move.

'I'll have to hand it to you, gentlemen. You've been too smart for me. But I had my reasons for acting as I did.'

'No doubt.' Race's tone was curt.

'If I give them to you, it must be understood I do so in confidence.'

'I think you can trust us to behave fittingly. Naturally I cannot give assurances blindly.'

'Well—' Pennington sighed. 'I'll come clean. There was some monkey business going on in England. It worried me. I couldn't do much about it by letter. The only thing was to come over and see for myself.'

'What do you mean by monkey business?'

'I'd good reason to believe that Linnet was being swindled.'

'By whom?'

'Her Britisher lawyer. Now that's not the kind of accusation you can fling around anyhow. I made up my mind to come over right away and see into matters myself.'

Agatha Christie

'That does great credit to your vigilance, I am sure. But why the little deception about not having received the letter?'

'Well, I ask you—' Pennington spread out his hands. 'You can't butt in on a honeymoon couple without more or less coming down to brass tacks and giving your reasons. I thought it best to make the meeting accidental. Besides, I didn't know anything about the husband. He might have been mixed up in the racket for all I knew.'

'In fact all your actions were actuated by pure disinterestedness,' said Colonel Race dryly.

'You've said it, Colonel.'

There was a pause.

Race glanced at Poirot. The little man leant forward.

'Monsieur Pennington, we do not believe a word of your story.'

'The hell you don't! And what the hell do you believe?'

'We believe that Linnet Ridgeway's unexpected marriage put you in a financial quandary. That you came over posthaste to try and find some way out of the mess you were in—that is to say, some way of gaining time. That, with that end in view, you endeavoured to obtain Madame Doyle's signature to certain documents and failed. That on the journey up the Nile, when walking along the cliff top at Abu Simbel, you dislodged a boulder which fell and only very narrowly missed its object—'

'You're crazy.'

'We believe that the same kind of circumstances occurred on the return journey. That is to say, an opportunity presented itself of putting Madame Doyle out of the way *at the moment when her death would be almost certainly ascribed to the action of another person*. We not only believe, but *know*, that it was your revolver which killed a woman who was about to reveal to us the name of the person who she had reason to believe killed both Linnet Doyle and the maid Louise—'

'Hell!' The forcible ejaculation broke forth and interrupted Poirot's stream of eloquence. 'What are you getting at? Are you crazy? What motive had I to kill Linnet? I wouldn't get her money—that goes to her husband. Why don't you pick on him? *He's* the one to benefit—not me.'

Race said coldly:

'Doyle never left the lounge on the night of the tragedy till he was shot at and wounded in the leg. The impossibility of his walking a step after that is attested to by a doctor and a nurse—both independent and reliable witnesses. Simon Doyle could not have killed his wife. He could not have killed Louise Bourget. He most definitely did not kill Mrs Otterbourne! You know that as well as we do.'

'I know he didn't kill her.' Pennington sounded a little calmer. 'All I say is, why pick on me when I don't benefit by her death?'

'But, my dear sir,' Poirot's voice came soft as a purring cat, 'that is rather a matter of opinion. Madame Doyle was a keen woman of business, fully conversant with her own affairs and very quick to spot any irregularity. As soon as she took up the control of her property, which she would have done on her return to England, her suspicions were bound to be aroused. But now that she is dead and that her husband, as you have just pointed out, inherits, *the whole thing is different*. Simon Doyle knows nothing whatever of his wife's affairs except that she was a rich woman. He is of a simple, trusting disposition. You will find it easy to place complicated statements before him, to involve the real issue in a net of figures, and to delay settlement with pleas of legal formalities and the recent depression. *I think that it makes a very considerable difference to you whether you deal with the husband or the wife.*'

Pennington shrugged his shoulders.

'Your ideas are—fantastic.'

'Time will show.'

'What did you say?'

'I said, "Time will show!" This is a matter of three deaths—three murders. The law will demand the most searching investigation into the condition of Madame Doyle's estate.'

He saw the sudden sag in the other's shoulders and knew that he had won. Jim Fanthorp's suspicions were well founded.

Poirot went on:

'You've played—and lost. Useless to go on bluffing.'

Pennington muttered:

'You don't understand—it's all square enough really. It's been this damned slump—Wall Street's been crazy. But I'd staged a comeback. With luck everything will be O.K. by the middle of June.'

With shaking hands he took a cigarette, tried to light it—failed.

'I suppose,' mused Poirot, 'that the boulder was a sudden temptation. You thought nobody saw you.'

'That was an accident—I swear it was an accident.' The man leaned forward, his face working, his eyes terrified. 'I stumbled and fell against it. I swear it was an accident…'

The two men said nothing.

Pennington suddenly pulled himself together. He was still a wreck of a man but his fighting spirit had returned in a certain measure. He moved towards the door.

'You can't pin that on me, gentlemen. It was an accident. And it wasn't I who shot her! D'you hear? You can't pin that on me either—and you never will.'

He went out.

CHAPTER 26

As the door closed behind him, Race gave a deep sigh.

'We got more than I thought we should. Admission of fraud. Admission of attempted murder. Further than that it's impossible to go. A man will confess, more or less, to attempted murder, but you won't get him to confess to the real thing.'

'Sometimes it can be done,' said Poirot. His eyes were dreamy—catlike.

Race looked at him curiously.

'Got a plan?'

Poirot nodded. Then he said, ticking off the items on his fingers:

'The garden at Aswan. Mr Allerton's statement. The two bottles of nail polish. My bottle of wine. The velvet stole. The stained handkerchief. The pistol that was left on the scene of the crime. The death of Louise. The death of Madame Otterbourne... Yes, it's all there. *Pennington didn't do it, Race!*'

'What?' Race was startled.

'*Pennington didn't do it.* He had the motive, yes. He had the *will* to do it, yes. He got as far as *attempting* to do it. *Mais c'est tout.* Something was wanted for this crime *that Pennington hasn't got!* This is a crime that needed audacity, swift and faultless execution, courage, indifference to danger, and a resourceful, calculating brain. *Pennington hasn't got those attributes*. He couldn't do a crime unless he knew it to be safe. This crime wasn't safe! It hung on a razor edge. It needed boldness. Pennington isn't bold. He's only astute.'

Race looked at him with the respect one able man gives to another.

'You've got it all well taped,' he said.

'I think so, yes. There are one or two things— that telegram for instance, that Linnet Doyle read. I should like to get that cleared up.'

'By Jove, we forgot to ask Doyle. He was telling us when poor old Ma Otterbourne came along. We'll ask him again.'

'Presently. First, I have someone else to whom I wish to speak.'

'Who's that?'

'Tim Allerton.'

Race raised his eyebrows.

'Allerton? Well, we'll get him here.'

He pressed a bell and sent the steward with a message. Tim Allerton entered with a questioning look.

'Steward said you wanted to see me?'

'That is right, Monsieur Allerton. Sit down.'

Agatha Christie

Tim sat. His face was attentive but very slightly bored.

'Anything I can do?' His tone was polite but not enthusiastic.

Poirot said:

'In a sense, perhaps. What I really require is for you to listen.'

Tim's eyebrows rose in polite surprise.

'Certainly. I'm the world's best listener. Can be relied on to say "Oo-er!" at the right moments.'

'That is very satisfactory. "Oo-er!" will be very expressive. *Eh bien*, let us commence. When I met you and your mother at Aswan, Monsieur Allerton, I was attracted to your company very strongly. To begin with, I thought your mother was one of the most charming people I had ever met—'

The weary face flickered for a moment—a shade of expression came into it.

'She is—unique,' he said.

'But the second thing that interested me was your mention of a certain lady.'

'Really?'

'Yes, a Mademoiselle Joanna Southwood. You see, I had recently been hearing that name.'

He paused and went on.

'For the last three years there have been certain jewel robberies that have been worrying Scotland Yard a good deal. They are what may be described as society robberies. The method is usually the same—the substitution of an imitation piece of jewellery for an original. My friend, Chief

Inspector Japp, came to the conclusion that the robberies were not the work of one person, but of two people working in with each other very cleverly. He was convinced, from the considerable inside knowledge displayed, that the robberies were the work of people in a good social position. And finally his attention became riveted on Mademoiselle Joanna Southwood.

'Every one of the victims had been either a friend or acquaintance of hers, and in each case she had either handled or been lent the piece of jewellery in question. Also, her style of living was far in excess of her income. On the other hand it was quite clear that the actual robbery—that is to say the substitution—had *not* been accomplished by her. In some cases she had been out of England during the period when the jewellery must have been replaced.

'So gradually a little picture grew up in Chief Inspector Japp's mind. Mademoiselle Southwood was at one time associated with a Guild of Modern Jewellery. He suspected that she handled the jewels in question, made accurate drawings of them, got them copied by some humble but dishonest working jeweller and that the third part of the operation was the successful substitution by another person—somebody who could have been proved never to have handled the jewels and never to have had anything to do with copies or imitations of precious stones. Of the identity of this other person Japp was ignorant.

'Certain things that fell from you in conversation interested me. A ring that disappeared when you were in

Majorca, the fact that you had been in a house party where one of these fake substitutions had occurred, your close association with Mademoiselle Southwood. There was also the fact that you obviously resented my presence and tried to get your mother to be less friendly towards me. That might, of course, have been just personal dislike, but I thought not. You were too anxious to try and hide your distaste under a genial manner.

'*Eh bien*—after the murder of Linnet Doyle it is discovered that her pearls are missing. You comprehend, at once I think of you! But I am not quite satisfied. For if you are working, as I suspect, with Mademoiselle Southwood (who was an intimate friend of Madame Doyle's), then substitution would be the method employed—not barefaced theft. But then, the pearls quite unexpectedly are returned, and what do I discover? That they are not genuine, but *imitation*.

'I know then who the real thief is. It was the imitation string which was stolen and returned—an imitation which you had previously substituted for the real necklace.'

He looked at the young man in front of him. Tim was white under his tan. He was not so good a fighter as Pennington—his stamina was bad. He said, with an effort to sustain his mocking manner:

'Indeed? And if so, what did I do with them?'

'That I know also.'

The young man's face changed—broke up.

Poirot went on slowly.

'There is only one place where they can be. I have

reflected, and my reason tells me that that is so. Those pearls, Monsieur Allerton, are concealed in a rosary that hangs in your cabin. The beads of it are very elaborately carved. I think you had it made specially. Those beads unscrew, though you would never think so to look at them. Inside each is a pearl, stuck with Seccotine. Most police searchers respect religious symbols unless there is something obviously queer about them. You counted on that. I endeavoured to find out how Mademoiselle Southwood sent the imitation necklace out to you. She must have done so, since you came here from Majorca on hearing that Madame Doyle would be here for her honeymoon. My theory is that it was sent in a book—a square hole being cut out of the pages in the middle. A book goes with the ends open and is practically never opened in the post.'

There was a pause—a long pause. Then Tim said quietly:

'You win! It's been a good game, but it's over at last. There's nothing for it now, I suppose, but to take my medicine.'

Poirot nodded gently.

'Do you realize that you were seen that night?'

'Seen?' Tim started.

'Yes, on the night that Linnet Doyle died, someone saw you leave her cabin just after one in the morning.'

Tim said: 'Look here—you aren't thinking... it wasn't I who killed her! I'll swear that! I've been in the most awful stew. To have chosen that night of all others... God, it's been awful!'

Poirot said:

'Yes, you must have had uneasy moments. But, now that the truth has come out, you may be able to help us. Was Madame Doyle alive or dead when you stole the pearls?'

Tim said hoarsely:

'I don't know—Honest to God, Monsieur Poirot, I don't know! I'd found out where she put them at night—on the little table by the bed. I crept in, felt very softly on the table and grabbed 'em, put down the others and crept out again. I assumed, of course, that she was asleep.'

'Did you hear her breathing? Surely you would have listened for that?'

Tim thought earnestly.

'It was very still—very still indeed. No, I can't remember actually hearing her breathe...'

'Was there any smell of smoke lingering in the air, as there would have been if a firearm had been discharged recently?'

'I don't think so. I don't remember it.'

Poirot sighed.

'Then we are no further.'

Tim asked curiously, 'Who was it saw me?'

'Rosalie Otterbourne. She came round from the other side of the boat and saw you leave Linnet Doyle's cabin and go to your own.'

'So it was she who told you.'

Poirot said gently, 'Excuse me—she did not tell me.'

'But then, how do you know?'

'Because I am Hercule Poirot! *I do not need to be told.*

When I taxed her with it, do you know what she said? She said, "*I saw nobody.*" And she lied.'

'But why?'

Poirot said in a detached voice:

'Perhaps because she thought the man she saw was the murderer. It looked like that, you know.'

'That seems to me all the more reason for telling you.'

Poirot shrugged his shoulders.

'She did not think so, it seems.'

Tim said, a queer note in his voice:

'She's an extraordinary sort of a girl. She must have been through a pretty rough time with that mother of hers.'

'Yes, life has not been easy for her.'

'Poor kid,' Tim muttered. Then he looked towards Race.

'Well, sir, where do we go from here? I admit taking the pearls from Linnet's cabin, and you'll find them just where you say they are. I'm guilty all right. But as far as Miss Southwood is concerned, I'm not admitting anything. You've no evidence whatever against her. How I got hold of the fake necklace is my own business.'

Poirot murmured:

'A very correct attitude.'

Tim said with a flash of humour:

'Always the gentleman!'

He added: 'Perhaps you can imagine how annoying it was to me to find my mother cottoning on to you! I'm not a sufficiently hardened criminal to enjoy sitting cheek by jowl with a successful detective just before bringing off a

Agatha Christie

rather risky coup! Some people might get a kick out of it. I didn't. Frankly, it gave me cold feet.'

'But it did not deter you from making your attempt?'

Tim shrugged his shoulders.

'I couldn't funk it to that extent. The exchange had to be made sometime and I'd got a unique opportunity on this boat—a cabin only two doors off, and Linnet herself so preoccupied with her own troubles that she wasn't likely to detect the change.'

'I wonder if that was so—'

Tim looked up sharply. 'What do you mean?'

Poirot pressed the bell. 'I am going to ask Miss Otterbourne if she will come here for a minute.'

Tim frowned but said nothing. A steward came, received the order and went away with the message.

Rosalie came after a few minutes. Her eyes, reddened with recent weeping, widened a little at seeing Tim, but her old attitude of suspicion and defiance seemed entirely absent. She sat down and with a new docility looked from Race to Poirot.

'We're very sorry to bother you, Miss Otterbourne,' said Race gently. He was slightly annoyed with Poirot.

The girl said in a low voice:

'It doesn't matter.'

Poirot said:

'It is necessary to clear up one or two points. When I asked you whether you saw anyone on the starboard deck at 1.10 this morning, your answer was that you saw nobody. Fortunately I have been able to arrive at the truth without

Death on the Nile

your help. Monsieur Allerton has admitted that he was in Linnet Doyle's cabin last night.'

She flashed a swift glance at Tim. Tim, his face grim and set, gave a curt nod.

'The time is correct, Monsieur Allerton?'

Allerton replied, 'Quite correct.'

Rosalie was staring at him. Her lips trembled—fell apart...

'But you didn't—you didn't—'

He said quickly:

'No, I didn't kill her. I'm a thief, not a murderer. It's all going to come out, so you might as well know. I was after her pearls.'

Poirot said, 'Mr Allerton's story is that he went to her cabin last night and exchanged a string of fake pearls for the real ones.'

'Did you?' asked Rosalie. Her eyes, grave, sad, childlike, questioned his.

'Yes,' said Tim.

There was a pause. Colonel Race shifted restlessly.

Poirot said in a curious voice:

'That, as I say, is Monsieur Allerton's story, partially confirmed by your evidence. That is to say, there is evidence that he did visit Linnet Doyle's cabin last night, *but there is no evidence to show why he did so.*'

Tim stared at him. 'But you know!'

'What do I know?'

'Well—you know I've got the pearls.'

'*Mais oui—mais oui!* I know you have the pearls, *but*

Agatha Christie

I do not know when you got them. It may have been *before* last night... You said just now that Linnet Doyle would not have noticed the substitution. I am not so sure of that. Supposing she *did* notice it... Supposing, even, she knew who did it... Supposing that last night she threatened to expose the whole business, and that you knew she meant to do so... and supposing that you overheard the scene in the saloon between Jacqueline de Bellefort and Simon Doyle and, as soon as the saloon was empty, you slipped in and secured the pistol, and then, an hour later, when the boat had quieted down, you crept along to Linnet Doyle's cabin and made quite sure that no exposure would come...'

'My God!' said Tim. Out of his ashen face, two tortured, agonized eyes gazed dumbly at Hercule Poirot.

The latter went on:

'But somebody else saw you—the girl Louise. The next day she came to you and blackmailed you. You must pay her handsomely or she would tell what she knew. You realized that to submit to blackmail would be the beginning of the end. You pretended to agree, made an appointment to come to her cabin just before lunch with the money. Then, when she was counting the notes, you stabbed her.

'But again luck was against you. Somebody saw you go to her cabin—'he half turned to Rosalie. 'Your mother. Once again you had to act—dangerously, foolhardily—but it was the only chance. You had heard Pennington talk about his revolver. You rushed into his cabin, got hold of it, listened outside Dr Bessner's cabin door and shot Madame Otterbourne before she could reveal your name—'

'No-o!' cried Rosalie. 'He didn't! He didn't!'

'After that, you did *the only thing you could do*—rushed round the stern. And when I rushed after you, you had turned and pretended to be coming in the *opposite* direction. You had handled the revolver in gloves; those gloves *were in your pocket when I asked for them...*'

Tim said, 'Before God, I swear it isn't true—not a word of it.' But his voice, ill assured and trembling, failed to convince.

It was then that Rosalie Otterbourne surprised them.

'Of course it isn't true! And Monsieur Poirot knows it isn't! He's saying it for some reason of his own.'

Poirot looked at her. A faint smile came to his lips. He spread out his hands in token surrender.

'Mademoiselle is too clever... But you agree—it was a good case?'

'What the devil—' Tim began with rising anger, but Poirot held up a hand.

'There is a very good case against you, Monsieur Allerton. I wanted you to realize that. Now I will tell you something more pleasant. I have not yet examined that rosary in your cabin. It may be that, when I do, *I shall find nothing there*. And then, since Mademoiselle Otterbourne sticks to it that she saw no one on the deck last night—*eh bien*, there is no case against you at all. The pearls were taken by a kleptomaniac who has since returned them. They are in a little box on the table by the door, if you would like to examine them with Mademoiselle.'

Tim got up. He stood for a moment unable to speak. When he did, his words seemed inadequate, but it is possible that they satisfied his listeners.

'Thanks!' he said. 'You won't have to give me another chance!'

He held the door open for the girl; she passed out and, picking up the little cardboard box, he followed her.

Side by side they went. Tim opened the box, took out the sham string of pearls and hurled it far from him into the Nile.

'There!' he said. 'That's gone. When I return the box to Poirot the real string will be in it. What a damned fool I've been!'

Rosalie said in a low voice:

'Why did you come to do it in the first place?'

'How did I come to start, do you mean? Oh, I don't know. Boredom—laziness—the fun of the thing. Such a much more attractive way of earning a living than just pegging away at a job. Sounds pretty sordid to you, I expect, but you know there was an attraction about it—mainly the risk, I suppose.'

'I think I understand.'

'Yes, but you wouldn't ever do it.'

Rosalie considered for a moment or two, her grave young head bent.

'No,' she said simply. 'I wouldn't.'

He said: 'Oh, my dear—you're so lovely... so utterly lovely. Why wouldn't you say you'd seen me last night?'

Rosalie said:

'I thought—they might suspect you.'

'Did you suspect me?'

'No. I couldn't believe that you'd kill anyone.'

'No. I'm not the strong stuff murderers are made of. I'm only a miserable sneak-thief.'

She put out a timid hand and touched his arm.

'Don't say that...'

He caught her hand in his.

'Rosalie, would you—you know what I mean? Or would you always despise me and throw it in my teeth?'

She smiled faintly. 'There are things you could throw in my teeth, too...'

'Rosalie—darling...'

But she held back a minute longer. 'This—Joanna—'

Tim gave a sudden shout.

'Joanna? You're as bad as Mother. I don't care a damn about Joanna. She's got a face like a horse and a predatory eye. A most unattractive female.'

Presently Rosalie said:

'Your mother need never know about you.'

Tim said thoughtfully:

'I'm not sure.' 'I think I shall tell her. Mother's got plenty of stuffing, you know. She can stand up to things. Yes, I think I shall shatter her maternal illusions about me. She'll be so relieved to know that my relations with Joanna were purely of a business nature that she'll forgive me everything else.'

They had come to Mrs Allerton's cabin and Tim knocked

Agatha Christie

firmly on the door. It opened and Mrs Allerton stood on the threshold.

'Rosalie and I—' began Tim.

He paused.

'Oh, my dears,' said Mrs Allerton. She folded Rosalie in her arms. 'My dear, dear child... I always hoped—but Tim was so tiresome, and pretended he didn't like you. But of course I saw through *that!*'

Rosalie said in a broken voice:

'You've been so sweet to me—always. I used to wish—to wish—'

She broke off and sobbed happily on Mrs Allerton's shoulder.

CHAPTER 27

As the door closed behind Tim and Rosalie, Poirot looked somewhat apologetically at Colonel Race. The Colonel was looking rather grim.

'You will consent to my little arrangement, yes?' Poirot pleaded. 'It is irregular—I know it is irregular, yes—but I have a high regard for human happiness.'

'You've none for mine,' said Race.

'That *jeune fille*. I have a tenderness towards her, and she loves that young man. It will be an excellent match—she has the stiffening he needs, the mother likes her—everything is thoroughly suitable.'

'In fact the marriage has been arranged by heaven and Hercule Poirot. All I have to do is to compound a felony.'

'But, *mon ami*, I told you, it was all conjecture on my part.'

Race grinned suddenly.

'It's all right by me,' he said. 'I'm not a damned policeman, thank God! I dare say the young fool will go straight enough

Agatha Christie

now. The girl's straight all right. No, what I'm complaining of is your treatment of *me*! I'm a patient man—but there are limits to patience! *Do* you know who committed the three murders on this boat or *don't* you?'

'I do.'

'Then why all this beating about the bush?'

'You think that I am just amusing myself with side issues? And it annoys you? But it is not that. Once I went professionally to an archæological expedition—and I learnt something there. In the course of an excavation, when something comes up out of the ground, everything is cleared away very carefully all around it. You take away the loose earth, and you scrape here and there with a knife until finally your object is there, all alone, ready to be drawn and photographed with no extraneous matter confusing it. That is what I have been seeking to do—clear away the extraneous matter so that we can see the truth— the naked shining truth.'

'Good,' said Race. 'Let's have this naked shining truth. It wasn't Pennington. It wasn't young Allerton. I presume it wasn't Fleetwood. Let's hear who it was for a change.'

'My friend, I am just about to tell you.'

There was a knock on the door. Race uttered a muffled curse.

It was Dr Bessner and Cornelia. The latter was looking upset.

'Oh, Colonel Race,' she exclaimed, 'Miss Bowers has just told me about Cousin Marie. It's been the most dreadful shock. She said she couldn't bear the responsibility all by herself any longer, and that I'd better know as I was one of the family. I just couldn't believe it at first, but Dr Bessner here has been just wonderful.'

'No, no,' protested the doctor modestly.

'He's been so kind, explaining it all, and how people really can't help it. He's had kleptomaniacs in his clinic. And he's explained to me how it's very often due to a deep-seated neurosis.'

Cornelia repeated the words with awe.

'It's planted very deeply in the subconscious—sometimes it's just some little thing that happened when you were a child. And he's cured people by getting them to think back and remember what that little thing was.'

Cornelia paused, drew a deep breath, and started off again.

'But it's worrying me dreadfully in case it all gets out. It would be too, too terrible in New York. Why, all the tabloids would have it. Cousin Marie and Mother and everybody—they'd never hold up their heads again.'

Race sighed. 'That's all right,' he said. 'This is Hush Hush House.'

'I beg your pardon, Colonel Race?'

'What I was endeavouring to say was that anything short of murder is being hushed up.'

'Oh!' Cornelia clasped her hands. 'I'm *so* relieved. I've just been worrying and worrying.'

'You have the heart too tender,' said Dr Bessner, and patted her benevolently on the shoulder. He said to the others: 'She has a very sensitive and beautiful nature.'

'Oh, I haven't really. You're too kind.'

Poirot murmured, 'Have you seen any more of Mr Ferguson?'

Cornelia blushed.

'No—but Cousin Marie's been talking about him.'

'It seems the young man is highly born,' said Dr Bessner. 'I must confess he does not look it. His clothes are terrible. Not for a moment does he appear a well-bred man.'

'And what do you think, Mademoiselle?'

'I think he must be just plain crazy,' said Cornelia.

Poirot turned to the doctor. 'How is your patient?'

'Ach, he is going on splendidly. I have just reassured the Fräulein de Bellefort. Would you believe it, I found her in despair. Just because the fellow had a bit of a temperature this afternoon! But what could be more natural? It is amazing that he is not in a high fever now. But no, he is like some of our peasants; he has a magnificent constitution, the constitution of an ox. I have seen them with deep wounds that they hardly notice. It is the same with Mr Doyle. His pulse is steady, his temperature only slightly above normal. I was able to pooh-pooh the little lady's fears. All the same, it is ridiculous, *nicht wahr*? One minute you shoot a man, the next you are in hysterics in case he may not be doing well.'

Cornelia said:

'She loves him terribly, you see.'

'Ach! but it is not sensible, that. If *you* loved a man, would you try and shoot him? No, you are sensible.'

'I don't like things that go off with bangs anyway,' said Cornelia.

'Naturally you do not. You are very feminine.'

Race interrupted this scene of heavy approval. 'Since Doyle is all right there's no reason I shouldn't come along and resume our talk of this afternoon. He was just telling me about a telegram.'

Dr Bessner's bulk moved up and down appreciatively.

'Ho, ho, ho, it was very funny that! Doyle, he tells me about it. It was a telegram all about vegetables—potatoes, artichokes, leeks—Ach! pardon?'

With a stifled exclamation, Race had sat up in his chair.

'My God,' he said. 'So that's it! Richetti!'

He looked round on three uncomprehending faces.

'A new code—it was used in the South African rebellion. Potatoes mean machine guns, artichokes are high explosives—and so on. Richetti is no more an archæologist than I am! He's a very dangerous agitator, a man who's killed more than once. And I'll swear that he's killed once again. Mrs Doyle opened that telegram by mistake, you see. *If she were ever to repeat what was in it before me*, he knew his goose would be cooked!'

He turned to Poirot. 'Am I right?' he asked. 'Is Richetti the man?'

'He is *your* man,' said Poirot. 'I always thought there was something wrong about him! He was almost too word-perfect in his role—he was all archæologist, not enough human being.'

He paused and then said:

Agatha Christie

'But it was not Richetti who killed Linnet Doyle. For some time now I have known what I may express as the "first half" of the murderer. Now I know the "second half" also. The picture is complete. But you understand that, although I know what must have happened, *I have no proof that it happened*. Intellectually the case is satisfying. Actually it is profoundly unsatisfactory. There is only one hope—a confession from the murderer.'

Dr Bessner raised his shoulders sceptically. 'Ah! but that—it would be a miracle.'

'I think not. Not under the circumstances.'

Cornelia cried out: 'But who is it? Aren't you going to tell us?'

Poirot's eyes ranged quietly over the three of them. Race, smiling sardonically, Bessner, still looking sceptical, Cornelia, her mouth hanging a little open, gazing at him with eager eyes.

'*Mais oui*,' he said. 'I like an audience, I must confess. I am vain, you see. I am puffed up with conceit. I like to say, "See how clever is Hercule Poirot!"'

Race shifted a little in his chair.

'Well,' he asked gently, 'just how clever *is* Hercule Poirot?'

Shaking his head sadly from side to side Poirot said:

'To begin with I was stupid—incredibly stupid. To me the stumbling block was the pistol—Jacqueline de Bellefort's pistol. Why had that pistol not been left on the scene of the crime? The idea of the murderer was quite plainly to incriminate her. Why then did the murderer take it away?

I was so stupid that I thought of all sorts of fantastic reasons. The real one was very simple. The murderer took it away because he *had* to take it away—because *he had no choice in the matter*.'

CHAPTER 28

'You and I, my friend,' Poirot leaned towards Race, 'started our investigation with a preconceived idea. That idea was that the crime was committed on the spur of the moment, without any preliminary planning. Somebody wished to remove Linnet Doyle and had seized their opportunity to do so at a moment when the crime would almost certainly be attributed to Jacqueline de Bellefort. It therefore followed that the person in question had overheard the scene between Jacqueline and Simon Doyle and had obtained possession of the pistol after the others had left the saloon.

'But, my friends, *if that preconceived idea was wrong,* the whole aspect of the case altered. And it *was* wrong! This was no spontaneous crime committed on the spur of the moment. It was, on the contrary, very carefully planned and accurately timed, with all the details meticulously worked out beforehand, even to the drugging of Hercule Poirot's bottle of wine on the night in question!

'But yes, that is so! I was put to sleep so that there should be no possibility of my participating in the events of the night. It did just occur to me as a possibility. I drink wine; my two companions at table drink whisky and mineral water respectively. Nothing easier than to slip a dose of harmless narcotic into my bottle of wine—the bottles stand on the tables all day. But I dismissed the thought. It had been a hot day, I had been unusually tired—it was not really extraordinary that I should for once have slept heavily instead of lightly as I usually do.

'You see, I was still in the grip of the preconceived idea. If I had been drugged, that would have implied premeditation, it would mean that before 7.30, when dinner is served, *the crime had already been decided upon*; and that (always from the point of view of the preconceived idea) was absurd.

'The first blow to the preconceived idea was when the pistol was recovered from the Nile. To begin with, if we were right in our assumptions, *the pistol ought never to have been thrown overboard at all*... And there was more to follow.'

Poirot turned to Dr Bessner.

'You, Dr Bessner, examined Linnet Doyle's body. You will remember that the wound showed signs of scorching—that is to say, that the pistol had been placed close against the head before being fired.'

Bessner nodded. 'So. That is exact.'

'But when the pistol was found it was wrapped in a velvet stole, and that velvet showed definite signs that a pistol had been fired through its folds, presumably under the impression that that would deaden the sound of the shot. *But if the pistol had been fired through the velvet, there would have been no signs of burning on the victim's skin.* Therefore, the shot fired through the stole *could not have been the shot that killed Linnet Doyle.* Could it have been the other shot—the one fired by Jacqueline de Bellefort at Simon Doyle? Again no, for there had been two witnesses of that shooting, and we knew all about it. It appeared, therefore, as though a *third* shot had been fired—one we knew nothing about. But only two shots had been fired from the pistol, and there was no hint or suggestion of another shot.

'Here we were face to face with a very curious unexplained circumstance. The next interesting point was the fact that in Linnet Doyle's cabin I found two bottles of coloured nail polish. Now ladies very often vary the colour of their nails, but so far Linnet Doyle's nails had always been the shade called Cardinal—a deep dark red. The other bottle was labelled Rose, which is a shade of pale pink, but the few drops remaining in the bottle were not pale pink but a bright red. I was sufficiently curious to take out the stopper and sniff. Instead of the usual strong odour of pear drops, the bottle smelt of vinegar! That is to say, it suggested that the drop or two of fluid in it was *red ink*. Now there is no reason why Madame Doyle should not have had a bottle of red ink, but it would have been more natural if she had had red ink in a red ink bottle and not in a nail polish bottle. It suggested a link with the faintly stained handkerchief which had been wrapped round the pistol. Red ink washes out quickly but always leaves a pale pink stain.

'I should perhaps have arrived at the truth with these slender indications, but an event occurred which rendered all doubt superfluous. Louise Bourget was killed in circumstances which pointed unmistakably to the fact that she had been blackmailing the murderer. Not only was a fragment of a *mille* franc note still clasped in her hand, but I remembered some very significant words she had used this morning.

'Listen carefully, for here is the crux of the whole matter. When I asked her if she had seen anything the previous night she gave this very curious answer: "Naturally, if I had been unable to sleep, if I had mounted the stairs, *then* perhaps I might have seen this assassin, this monster enter or leave Madame's cabin..." Now what exactly did that tell us?'

Bessner, his nose wrinkling with intellectual interest, replied promptly:

'It told you that she *had* mounted the stairs.'

'No, no—you fail to see the point. Why should she have said that, to *us*?'

'To convey a hint.'

'But why *hint* to us? If she knows who the murderer is, there are two courses open to her—to tell us the truth, or to hold her tongue and demand money for her silence from the person concerned! But she does neither. She neither says promptly: "I saw nobody. I was asleep." Nor does she say: "Yes, I saw someone, and it was so and so." Why use that significant indeterminate rigmarole of words? *Parbleu*, there can be only one reason! *She is hinting to the murderer*;

Agatha Christie

therefore the murderer *must have been present at the time*. But, besides myself and Colonel Race, only two people were present—Simon Doyle and Dr Bessner.'

The doctor sprang up with a roar.

'Ach! what is that you say? You accuse me? Again? But it is ridiculous—beneath contempt.'

Poirot said sharply:

'Be quiet. I am telling you what I thought at the time. Let us remain impersonal.'

'He doesn't mean he thinks it's you now,' said Cornelia soothingly.

Poirot went on quickly.

'So it lay there—between Simon Doyle and Dr Bessner. But what reason has Bessner to kill Linnet Doyle? None, *so far as I know*. Simon Doyle, then? But that was impossible! There were plenty of witnesses who could swear that Doyle never left the saloon that evening until the quarrel broke out. After that he was wounded and it would then have been physically impossible for him to have done so. Had I good evidence on both those points? Yes, I had the evidence of Mademoiselle Robson, of Jim Fanthorp and of Jacqueline de Bellefort as to the first, and I had the skilled testimony of Dr Bessner and of Mademoiselle Bowers as to the other. No doubt was possible.

'So Dr Bessner *must* be the guilty one. In favour of this theory there was the fact that the maid had been stabbed *with a surgical knife*. On the other hand Bessner had deliberately called attention to this fact.

'And then, my friends, a second perfectly indisputable

Death on the Nile

fact became apparent to me. Louise Bourget's hint could not have been intended for Dr Bessner, *because she could perfectly well have spoken to him in private at any time she liked*. There was one person, *and one person only*, who corresponded to her necessity—*Simon Doyle!* Simon Doyle was wounded, was constantly attended by a doctor, was in that doctor's cabin. It was to him therefore that she risked saying those ambiguous words in case she might not get another chance. And I remember how she had gone on, turning to him: "Monsieur, I implore you—you see how it is? What can I say?" And this answer: "My good girl, don't be a fool. Nobody thinks you saw or heard anything. You'll be quite all right. I'll look after you. Nobody's accusing you of anything." That was the assurance she wanted, and she got it!'

Bessner uttered a colossal snort.

'Ach! it is foolish, that! Do you think a man with a fractured bone and a splint on his leg could go walking about the boat and stabbing people? I tell you, it was *impossible* for Simon Doyle to leave his cabin.'

Poirot said gently:

'I know. That is quite true. The thing was impossible. It was impossible—but it was also true! There could be *only one logical meaning* behind Louise Bourget's words.

'So I returned to the beginning and reviewed the crime in the light of this new knowledge. Was it possible that in the period preceding the quarrel Simon Doyle had left the saloon and the others had forgotten or not noticed it? I could not see that that was possible. Could the skilled testimony of Dr

Agatha Christie

Bessner and Mademoiselle Bowers be disregarded? Again I felt sure it could not. But, I remembered, *there was a gap between the two*. Simon Doyle had been alone in the saloon for a period of five minutes, and the skilled testimony of Dr Bessner only applied to the time *after that period*. For that period we had only the evidence of *visual appearance*, and, though apparently that was perfectly sound, it was no longer *certain*. What had actually been *seen*—leaving assumption out of the question?

'Mademoiselle Robson had seen Mademoiselle de Bellefort fire her pistol, had seen Simon Doyle collapse on to a chair, had seen him clasp a handkerchief to his leg and seen that handkerchief gradually soak through red. What had Monsieur Fanthorp heard and seen? He heard a shot, he found Doyle with a red-stained handkerchief clasped to his leg. What had happened then? Doyle had been very insistent that Mademoiselle de Bellefort should be got away, that she should not be left alone. After that, he suggested that Fanthorp should get hold of the doctor.

'Accordingly Mademoiselle Robson and Monsieur Fanthorp got out with Mademoiselle de Bellefort and for the next five minutes they are busy, *on the port side of the deck*. Mademoiselle Bowers', Dr Bessner's and Mademoiselle de Bellefort's cabins are all on the port side. Two minutes are all that Simon Doyle needs. He picks up the pistol from under the sofa, slips out of his shoes, runs like a hare silently along the starboard deck, enters his wife's cabin, creeps up to her as she lies asleep, shoots her through the head, puts the bottle that has contained the red ink on her washstand (it mustn't be found on him), runs back, gets hold of Mademoiselle Van Schuyler's velvet stole, which he has quietly stuffed down the side of a chair in readiness, muffles it round the pistol and fires a bullet into his leg. His chair into which he falls (in genuine agony this time) is by a window. He lifts the window and throws the pistol (wrapped up with the tell-tale handkerchief in the velvet stole) into the Nile.'

'Impossible!' said Race.

'No, my friend, not *impossible*. Remember the evidence of Tim Allerton. He heard a pop—*followed* by a splash. And he heard something else—the footsteps of a man running—a man running past his door. *But nobody could have been running along the starboard side of the deck.* What he heard was the stockinged feet of Simon Doyle running past his cabin.'

Race said: 'I still say it's impossible. No man could work out the whole caboodle like that in a flash—especially a chap like Doyle who is slow in his mental processes.'

'But very quick and deft in his physical actions!'

'That, yes. But he wouldn't be capable of thinking the whole thing out.'

'But he did not think it out himself, my friend. That is where we were all wrong. It looked like a crime committed on the spur of the moment, but it was *not* a crime committed on the spur of the moment. As I say, it was a very cleverly planned and well thought out piece of work. It could not be *chance* that Simon Doyle had a bottle of red ink in his pocket. No, it must be *design*. It was not *chance* that he had a plain unmarked handkerchief with him. It was not *chance* that Jacqueline de Bellefort's foot kicked the pistol under the settee, where it would be out of sight and unremembered until later.'

'Jacqueline?'

'Certainly. The two halves of the murderer. What gave *Simon* his alibi? The shot fired by *Jacqueline*. What gave Jacqueline *her* alibi? The insistence of *Simon* which resulted in a hospital nurse remaining with her all night. There, between the two of them, you get all the qualities you require—the cool, resourceful, planning brain, Jacqueline de Bellefort's brain, and the man of action to carry it out with incredible swiftness and timing.'

'Look at it the right way, and it answers every question. Simon Doyle and Jacqueline had been lovers. Realize that they are still lovers, and it is all clear. Simon does away with his rich wife, inherits her money, *and in due course will marry his old love*. It was all very ingenious. The persecution of Madame Doyle by Jacqueline, all part of the plan. Simon's pretended rage. And yet—there were lapses. He held forth to me once about possessive women—held forth with real bitterness. It ought to have been clear to me *that it was his wife he was thinking about*—not Jacqueline. Then his manner to his wife in public. An ordinary, inarticulate Englishman, such as Simon Doyle, is very embarrassed at showing any affection. Simon was not a really good actor. He overdid the devoted manner. That conversation I had with Mademoiselle Jacqueline, too, when she pretended that somebody had overheard, *I* saw no one.

And there *was* no one! But it was to be a useful red herring later. Then one night on this boat I thought I heard Simon and Linnet outside my cabin. He was saying, "We've got to go through with it now." It was Doyle all right, but it was to Jacqueline he was speaking.

'The final drama was perfectly planned and timed. There was a sleeping draught for me, in case I might put an inconvenient finger in the pie. There was the selection of Mademoiselle Robson as a witness—the working up of the scene, Mademoiselle de Bellefort's exaggerated remorse and hysterics. She made a good deal of noise, in case the shot should be heard. *En vérité*, it was an extraordinarily clever idea. Jacqueline says she has shot Doyle, Mademoiselle Robson says so, Fanthorp says so—and when Simon's leg is examined he *has* been shot. It looks unanswerable! For both of them there is a perfect alibi—at the cost, it is true, of a certain amount of pain and risk to Simon Doyle, but it is necessary that his wound should definitely disable him.

'And then the plan goes wrong. Louise Bourget has been wakeful. She has come up the stairway and she has seen Simon Doyle run along to his wife's cabin and come back. Easy enough to piece together what has happened the following day. And so she makes her greedy bid for hush money, and in so doing signs her death warrant.'

'But Mr Doyle couldn't have killed *her*?' Cornelia objected.

'No, the other partner did that murder. As soon as he can, Simon Doyle asks to see Jacqueline. He even asks me to leave them alone together. He tells her then of the new danger. They must act at once. He knows where Bessner's scalpels are kept. After the crime the scalpel is wiped and returned, and then, very late and rather out of breath, Jacqueline de Bellefort hurries in to lunch.

'And still all is not well. *For Madame Otterbourne has seen Jacqueline go into Louise Bourget's cabin.* And she comes hot-foot to tell Simon about it. Jacqueline is the murderess. Do you remember how Simon shouted at the poor woman? Nerves, we thought. But the door was open and he was trying to convey the danger to his accomplice. She heard and she acted—acted like lightning. She remembered Pennington had talked about a revolver. She got hold of it, crept up outside the door, listened and, at the critical moment, fired. She boasted once that she was a good shot, and her boast was not an idle one.

'I remarked after that third crime that there were three ways the murderer could have gone. I meant that he could have gone aft (in which case Tim Allerton was the criminal), he could have gone over the side (very improbable) or he could have gone into a cabin. Jacqueline's cabin was just two away from Dr Bessner's. She had only to throw down the revolver, bolt into the cabin, ruffle her hair and fling herself down on the bunk. It was risky, but it was the only possible chance.'

There was a silence, then Race asked:

'What happened to the first bullet fired at Doyle by the girl?'

'I think it went into the table. There is a recently made hole there. I think Doyle had time to dig it out with a penknife and fling it through the window. He had, of course, a spare cartridge, so that it would appear that only two shots had been fired.'

Cornelia sighed. 'They thought of everything,' she said. 'It's—horrible!'

Poirot was silent. But it was not a modest silence. His eyes seemed to be saying: 'You are wrong. They didn't allow for Hercule Poirot.'

Aloud he said, 'And now, Doctor, we will go and have a word with your patient...'

CHAPTER 29

It was very much later that evening that Hercule Poirot came and knocked on the door of a cabin.

A voice said 'Come in' and he entered.

Jacqueline de Bellefort was sitting in a chair. In another chair, close against the wall, sat the big stewardess.

Jacqueline's eyes surveyed Poirot thoughtfully. She made a gesture towards the stewardess.

'Can she go?'

Poirot nodded to the woman and she went out. Poirot drew up her chair and sat down near Jacqueline. Neither of them spoke. Poirot's face was unhappy.

In the end it was the girl who spoke first.

'Well,' she said, 'it is all over! You were too clever for us, Monsieur Poirot.'

Poirot sighed. He spread out his hands. He seemed strangely dumb.

'All the same,' said Jacqueline reflectively, 'I can't really see that you had much proof. You were quite right, of course, but if we'd bluffed you out—'

'In no other way, Mademoiselle, could the thing have happened.'

'That's proof enough for a logical mind, but I don't believe it would have convinced a jury. Oh, well—it can't be helped. You sprang it all on Simon, and he went down like a ninepin. He just lost his head utterly, poor lamb, and admitted everything.'

She shook her head. 'He's a bad loser.'

'But you, Mademoiselle, are a good loser.'

She laughed suddenly—a queer, gay, defiant little laugh.

'Oh, yes, I'm a good loser all right.' She looked at him.

She said suddenly and impulsively:

'Don't mind so much, Monsieur Poirot! About me, I mean. You do mind, don't you?'

'Yes, Mademoiselle.'

'But it wouldn't have occurred to you to let me off?'

Hercule Poirot said quietly, 'No.'

She nodded her head in quiet agreement.

'No, it's no use being sentimental. I might do it again... I'm not a safe person any longer. I can feel that myself...' She went on broodingly: 'It's so dreadfully easy—killing people. And you begin to feel that it doesn't matter... that it's only *you* that matters! It's dangerous—that.'

She paused, then said with a little smile:

'You did your best for me, you know. That night at Aswan—you told me not to open my heart to evil... Did you realize then what was in my mind?'

He shook his head.

'I only knew that what I said was true.'

'It was true... I could have stopped, then, you know. I nearly did... I could have told Simon that I wouldn't go on with it... But then perhaps—'

She broke off. She said:

'Would you like to hear about it? From the beginning?'

'If you care to tell me, Mademoiselle.'

'I think I want to tell you. It was all very simple really. You see, Simon and I loved each other...'

It was a matter-of-fact statement, yet, underneath the lightness of her tone, there were echoes...

Poirot said simply:

'And for you love would have been enough, but not for him.'

'You might put it that way, perhaps. But you don't quite understand Simon. You see, he's always wanted money so dreadfully. He liked all the things you get with money—horses and yachts and sport—nice things all of them, things a man ought to be keen about. And he'd never been able to have any of them. He's awfully simple, Simon is. He wants things just as a child wants them—you know—terribly.

'All the same he never tried to marry anybody rich and horrid. He wasn't that sort. And then we met—and—and that sort of settled things. Only we didn't see when we'd be able to marry. He'd had rather a decent job, but he'd lost it. In a way it was his own fault. He tried to do something smart over money and got found out at once. I don't believe he really meant to be dishonest. He just thought it was the sort of thing people did in the City.'

A flicker passed over her listener's face, but he guarded his tongue.

'There we were, up against it; and then I thought of Linnet and her new country house, and I rushed off to her. You know, Monsieur Poirot, I loved Linnet, really I did. She was my best friend, and I never dreamed that anything would ever come between us. I just thought how lucky it was she was rich. It might make all the difference to me and Simon if she'd give him a job. And she was awfully sweet about it and told me to bring Simon down to see her. It was about then you saw us that night at Chez Ma Tante. We were making whoopee, although we couldn't really afford it.'

She paused, sighed, then went on.

'What I'm going to say now is quite true, Monsieur Poirot. Even though Linnet is dead, it doesn't alter the truth. That's why I'm not really sorry about her, even now. She went all out to get Simon away from me. That's the absolute truth! I don't think she even hesitated for more than about a minute. I was her friend, but she didn't care. She just went bald-headed for Simon...

'And Simon didn't care a damn about her! I talked a lot to you about glamour, but of course that wasn't true. He didn't want Linnet. He thought her good-looking but terribly bossy, and he hated bossy women! The whole thing embarrassed him frightfully. But he did like the thought of her money.

'Of course I saw that... And at last I suggested to him that it might be a good thing if he—got rid of me and married Linnet. But he scouted the idea. He said, money or no money, it would be hell to be married to her. He said his idea of having money was to have it himself—not to have a rich wife holding the purse strings. "I'd be a kind of damned Prince Consort," he said to me. He said, too, that he didn't want anyone but me...

'I think I know when the idea came into his head. He said one day: "If I'd any luck, I'd marry her and she'd die in about a year and leave me all the boodle." And then a queer startled look came into his eyes. That was when he first thought of it...

'He talked about it a good deal, one way and another—about how convenient it would be if Linnet died. I said it was an awful idea, and then he shut up about it. Then, one day, I found him reading up all about arsenic. I taxed him with it then, and he laughed and said: "Nothing venture, nothing have! It's about the only time in my life I shall be near to touching a far lot of money."

'After a bit I saw that he'd made up his mind. And I was terrified—simply terrified. Because, you see, *I realized that he'd never pull it off*. He's so childishly simple. He'd have no kind of subtlety about it—and he's got no imagination. He would probably have just bunged arsenic into her and assumed the doctor would say she'd died of gastritis. He always thought things would go right.

'So I had to come into it, too, to look after him...'

She said it very simply but in complete good faith. Poirot had no doubt whatever that her motive had been exactly what she said it was. She herself had not coveted Linnet Ridgeway's money, but she had loved Simon Doyle, had loved him beyond reason and beyond rectitude and beyond pity.

'I thought and I thought—trying to work out a plan. It seemed to me that the basis of the idea ought to be a kind of two-handed alibi. You know—if Simon and I could somehow or other give evidence against each other, but actually that evidence would clear us of everything. It would be easy enough for me to pretend to hate Simon. It was quite a likely thing to happen under the circumstances. Then, if Linnet was killed, I should probably be suspected, so it would be better if I was suspected right away. We worked out details little by little. I wanted it to be so that if anything went wrong, they'd get me and not Simon. But Simon was worried about me.

'The only thing I was glad about was that I hadn't got to do it. I simply couldn't have! Not go along in cold blood and kill her when she was asleep! You see, I hadn't forgiven her—I think I could have killed her face to face, but not the other way...

'We worked everything out carefully. Even then, Simon went and wrote a J in blood which was a silly melodramatic thing to do. It's just the sort of thing he *would* think of! But it went off all right.'

Poirot nodded.

Agatha Christie

'Yes. It was not your fault that Louise Bourget could not sleep that night... And afterwards, Mademoiselle?'

She met his eyes squarely.

'Yes,' she said 'it's rather horrible isn't it? I can't believe that I—did that! I know now what you meant by opening your heart to evil... You know pretty well how it happened. Louise made it clear to Simon that she knew. Simon got you to bring me to him. As soon as we were alone together he told me what had happened. He told me what I'd got to do. I wasn't even horrified. I was so afraid—so deadly afraid... That's what murder does to you... Simon and I were safe—quite safe—except for this miserable blackmailing French girl. I took her all the money we could get hold of. I pretended to grovel. And then, when she was counting the money, I—did it! It was quite easy. That's what's so horribly, horribly frightening about it... It's so terribly easy...

'And even then we weren't safe. Mrs Otterbourne had seen me. She came triumphantly along the deck looking for you and Colonel Race. I'd no time to think. I just acted like a flash. It was almost exciting. I knew it was touch or go that time. That seemed to make it better...'

She stopped again.

'Do you remember when you came into my cabin afterwards? You said you were not sure why you had come. I was so miserable—so terrified. I thought Simon was going to die...'

'And I—was hoping it,' said Poirot.

Jacqueline nodded.

'Yes, it would have been better for him that way.'
'That was not my thought.'
Jacqueline looked at the sternness of his face.
She said gently:
'Don't mind so much for me, Monsieur Poirot. After all, I've lived hard always, you know. If we'd won out, I'd have been very happy and enjoyed things and probably should never have regretted anything. As it is—well, one goes through with it.'
She added:
'I suppose the stewardess is in attendance to see I don't hang myself or swallow a miraculous capsule of prussic acid as people always do in books. You needn't be afraid! I shan't do that. It will be easier for Simon if I'm standing by.'
Poirot got up. Jacqueline rose also. She said with a sudden smile:
'Do you remember when I said I must follow my star? You said it might be a false star. And I said: "That very bad star, that star fall down."'
He went out to the deck with her laughter ringing in his ears.

CHAPTER 30

It was early dawn when they came into Shellal. The rocks came down grimly to the water's edge.

Poirot murmured: '*Quel pays sauvage!*'

Race stood beside him. 'Well,' he said, 'we've done our job. I've arranged for Richetti to be taken ashore first. Glad we've got him. He's been a slippery customer, I can tell you. Given us the slip dozens of times.'

He went on: 'We must get hold of a stretcher for Doyle. Remarkable how he went to pieces.'

'Not really,' said Poirot. 'That boyish type of criminal is usually intensely vain. Once prick the bubble of their self-esteem and it is finished! They go to pieces like children.'

'Deserves to be hanged,' said Race. 'He's a cold-blooded scoundrel. I'm sorry for the girl—but there's nothing to be done about it.'

Poirot shook his head.

'People say love justifies everything, but that is not true... Women who care for men as Jacqueline cares for Simon

Doyle are very dangerous. It is what I said when I saw her first. "She cares too much, that little one!" It is true.'

Cornelia Robson came up beside him.

'Oh,' she said, 'we're nearly in.'

She paused a minute or two, then added, 'I've been with her.'

'With Mademoiselle de Bellefort?'

'Yes. I felt it was kind of awful for her boxed up with that stewardess. Cousin Marie's very angry, though, I'm afraid.'

Miss Van Schuyler was progressing slowly down the deck towards them. Her eyes were venomous.

'Cornelia,' she snapped, 'you've behaved outrageously. I shall send you straight home.'

Cornelia took a deep breath.

'I'm sorry, Cousin Marie, but I'm not going home. I'm going to get married.'

'So you've seen sense at last,' snapped the old lady.

Ferguson came striding round the corner of the deck. He said: 'Cornelia, what's this I hear? It's not true!'

'It's quite true,' said Cornelia. 'I'm going to marry Dr Bessner. He asked me last night.'

'And why are you going to marry him?' said Ferguson furiously. 'Simply because he's rich?'

'No, I'm not,' said Cornelia indignantly. 'I like him. He's kind, and he knows a lot. And I've always been interested in sick folks and clinics, and I shall have just a wonderful life with him.'

'Do you mean to say,' said Mr Ferguson incredulously, 'that you'd rather marry that disgusting old man than me?'

'Yes, I would. You're not reliable! You wouldn't be at

all a comfortable sort of person to live with. And he's *not* old. He's not fifty yet.'

'He's got a stomach,' said Mr Ferguson venomously.

'Well, I've got round shoulders,' retorted Cornelia. 'What one looks like doesn't matter. He says I really could help him in his work, and he's going to teach me all about neuroses.'

She moved away.

Ferguson said to Poirot: 'Do you think she really means that?'

'Certainly.'

'She prefers that pompous old bore to me?'

'Undoubtedly.'

'The girl's mad,' declared Ferguson.

Poirot's eyes twinkled.

'She is a woman of an original mind,' he said. 'It is probably the first time you have met one.'

The boat drew in to the landing stage. A cordon had been drawn round the passengers. They had been asked to wait before disembarking.

Richetti, dark-faced and sullen, was marched ashore by two engineers.

Then, after a certain amount of delay, a stretcher was brought. Simon Doyle was carried along the deck to the gangway.

He looked a different man—cringing, frightened, all his boyish insouciance vanished.

Jacqueline de Bellefort followed. A stewardess walked beside her. She was pale but otherwise looked much as usual. She came up to the stretcher.

Death on the Nile

'Hallo, Simon!' she said.

He looked up at her quickly. The old boyish look came back to his face for a moment.

'I messed it up,' he said. 'Lost my head and admitted everything! Sorry, Jackie. I've let you down.'

She smiled at him then.

'It's all right, Simon,' she said. 'A fool's game, and we've lost. That's all.'

She stood aside. The bearers picked up the handles of the stretcher.

Jacqueline bent down and tied the lace of her shoe. Then her hand went to her stocking top and she straightened up with something in her hand.

There was a sharp explosive *pop*.

Simon Doyle gave one convulsed shudder and then lay still.

Jacqueline de Bellefort nodded. She stood for a minute, pistol in hand. She gave a fleeting smile at Poirot.

Then, as Race jumped forward, she turned the little glittering toy against her heart and pressed the trigger.

She sank down in a soft huddled heap.

Race shouted:

'Where the devil did she get that pistol?'

Poirot felt a hand on his arm. Mrs Allerton said softly, 'You—knew?'

He nodded. 'She had a pair of these pistols. I realized that when I heard that one had been found in Rosalie Otterbourne's handbag the day of the search. Jacqueline sat at the same table as they did. When she realized that there was going to be a search, she slipped it into the other girl's handbag. Later she went to Rosalie's cabin and got it back, after having distracted her attention with a comparison of lipsticks. As both she and her cabin had been searched yesterday, it wasn't thought necessary to do it again.'

Mrs Allerton said:

'You wanted her to take that way out?'

'Yes. But she would not take it alone. That is why Simon Doyle has died an easier death than he deserved.'

Mrs Allerton shivered. 'Love can be a very frightening thing.'

'That is why most great love stories are tragedies.'

Mrs Allerton's eyes rested upon Tim and Rosalie, standing side by side in the sunlight, and she said suddenly and passionately:

'But thank God, there is happiness in the world.'

'As you say, Madame, thank God for it.'

Presently the passengers went ashore.

Later the bodies of Louise Bourget and Mrs Otterbourne were carried off the *Karnak*.

Lastly the body of Linnet Doyle was brought ashore, and all over the world wires began to hum, telling the public that Linnet Doyle, who had been Linnet Ridgeway, the famous, the beautiful, the wealthy Linnet Doyle was dead.

Sir George Wode read about it in his London club, and Sterndale Rockford in New York, and Joanna Southwood in Switzerland, and it was discussed in the bar of the Three Crowns in Malton-under-Wode.

And Mr Burnaby's lean friend said:

'Well, it didn't seem fair, her having everything.'

And Mr Burnaby said acutely:

'Well, it doesn't seem to have done her much good, poor lass.'

But after a while they stopped talking about her and discussed instead who was going to win the Grand National. For, as Mr Ferguson was saying at that minute in Luxor, it is not the past that matters but the future.

The *Agatha Christie* Collection

THE HERCULE POIROT MYSTERIES
Match your wits with the famous Belgian detective.

The Mysterious Affair at Styles
The Murder on the Links
Poirot Investigates
The Murder of Roger Ackroyd
The Big Four
The Mystery of the Blue Train
Black Coffee
Peril at End House
Lord Edgware Dies
Murder on the Orient Express
Three Act Tragedy
Death in the Clouds
The ABC Murders
Murder in Mesopotamia
Cards on the Table
Murder in the Mews
Dumb Witness
Death on the Nile
Appointment With Death
Hercule Poirot's Christmas

Sad Cypress
One, Two, Buckle My Shoe
Evil Under the Sun
Five Little Pigs
The Hollow
The Labours of Hercules
Taken at the Flood
Mrs McGinty's Dead
After the Funeral
Hickory Dickory Dock
Dead Man's Folly
Cat Among the Pigeons
The Adventure of the Christmas Pudding
The Clocks
Third Girl
Hallowe'en Party
Elephants Can Remember
Poirot's Early Cases
Curtain: Poirot's Last Case

Find out all about the Queen of Crime
and her stories at **www.agathachristie.com**

Keep up to date with launches and news from the world
of Agatha Christie and discuss all things Agatha on the forum!

Shop online for books, audiobooks, DVDs and other merchandise

/agathachristie   /officialagathachristie   /QueenofCrime

For a touch of Christie mystery, scan the code!

itv
STUDIOS
GLOBAL ENTERTAINMENT
Agatha Christie
POIROT
Watch every case
Available on
iTunes

COMING SEPTEMBER 2014

THE NEW *Agatha Christie*

HERCULE POIROT MYSTERY

BY SOPHIE HANNAH

EVIL UNDER THE SUN

THE AGATHA CHRISTIE COLLECTION

Mysteries
The Man in the Brown Suit
The Secret of Chimneys
The Seven Dials Mystery
The Mysterious Mr Quin
The Sittaford Mystery
The Hound of Death
The Listerdale Mystery
Why Didn't They Ask Evans?
Parker Pyne Investigates
Murder Is Easy
And Then There Were None
Towards Zero
Death Comes as the End
Sparkling Cyanide
Crooked House
They Came to Baghdad
Destination Unknown
Spider's Web*
The Unexpected Guest*
Ordeal by Innocence
The Pale Horse
Endless Night
Passenger To Frankfurt
Problem at Pollensa Bay
While the Light Lasts

Poirot
The Mysterious Affair at Styles
The Murder on the Links
Poirot Investigates
The Murder of Roger Ackroyd
The Big Four
The Mystery of the Blue Train
Black Coffee*
Peril at End House
Lord Edgware Dies
Murder on the Orient Express
Three Act Tragedy
Death in the Clouds
The ABC Murders
Murder in Mesopotamia
Cards on the Table
Murder in the Mews
Dumb Witness
Death on the Nile
Appointment With Death
Hercule Poirot's Christmas
Sad Cypress
One, Two, Buckle My Shoe
Evil Under the Sun
Five Little Pigs
The Hollow
The Labours of Hercules
Taken at the Flood
Mrs McGinty's Dead
After the Funeral
Hickory Dickory Dock
Dead Man's Folly
Cat Among the Pigeons
The Adventure of the Christmas Pudding
The Clocks
Third Girl
Hallowe'en Party
Elephants Can Remember
Poirot's Early Cases
Curtain: Poirot's Last Case

Marple
The Murder at the Vicarage
The Thirteen Problems
The Body in the Library
The Moving Finger
A Murder Is Announced
They Do It With Mirrors
A Pocket Full of Rye
4.50 from Paddington
The Mirror Crack'd from Side to Side
A Caribbean Mystery
At Bertram's Hotel
Nemesis
Sleeping Murder
Miss Marple's Final Cases

Tommy & Tuppence
The Secret Adversary
Partners in Crime
N or M?
By the Pricking of My Thumbs
Postern of Fate

Published as Mary Westmacott
Giant's Bread
Unfinished Portrait
Absent in the Spring
The Rose and the Yew Tree
A Daughter's a Daughter
The Burden

Memoirs
An Autobiography
Come, Tell Me How You Live
The Grand Tour

Plays and Stories
Akhnaton
The Mousetrap and Other Plays
The Floating Admiral (contributor)
Star Over Bethlehem

* novelized by Charles Osborne

Agatha Christie

Evil Under the Sun

HarperCollins*Publishers*

HarperCollins*Publishers* Ltd
1 London Bridge Street
London SE1 9GF
www.harpercollins.co.uk

This paperback edition 2014
13

First published in Great Britain by
Collins 1941

Agatha Christie® Poirot® Evil Under the Sun™
Copyright © 1941 Agatha Christie Limited. All rights reserved.
www.agathachristie.com

A catalogue record for this book is
available from the British Library

ISBN 978-0-00-752757-1 (PB)
ISBN 978-0-00-825587-9 (POD PB)

Set in Sabon by Palimpsest Book Production Ltd., Falkirk, Stirlingshire

Printed and bound by
CPI Group (UK) Ltd, Croydon, CR0 4YY

All rights reserved. No part of this publication may be
reproduced, stored in a retrieval system, or transmitted,
in any form or by any means, electronic, mechanical,
photocopying, recording or otherwise, without the prior
permission of the publishers.

This book is sold subject to the condition that it shall not,
by way of trade or otherwise, be lent, re-sold, hired out or
otherwise circulated without the publisher's prior consent
in any form of binding or cover other than that in which it
is published and without a similar condition including this
condition being imposed on the subsequent purchaser.

MIX
Paper from
responsible sources
FSC
www.fsc.org
FSC® C007454

FSC™ is a non-profit international organisation established to promote
the responsible management of the world's forests. Products carrying the
FSC label are independently certified to assure consumers that they come
from forests that are managed to meet the social, economic and
ecological needs of present and future generations,
and other controlled sources.

Find out more about HarperCollins and the environment at
www.harpercollins.co.uk/green

TO JOHN
In memory of our last season in Syria

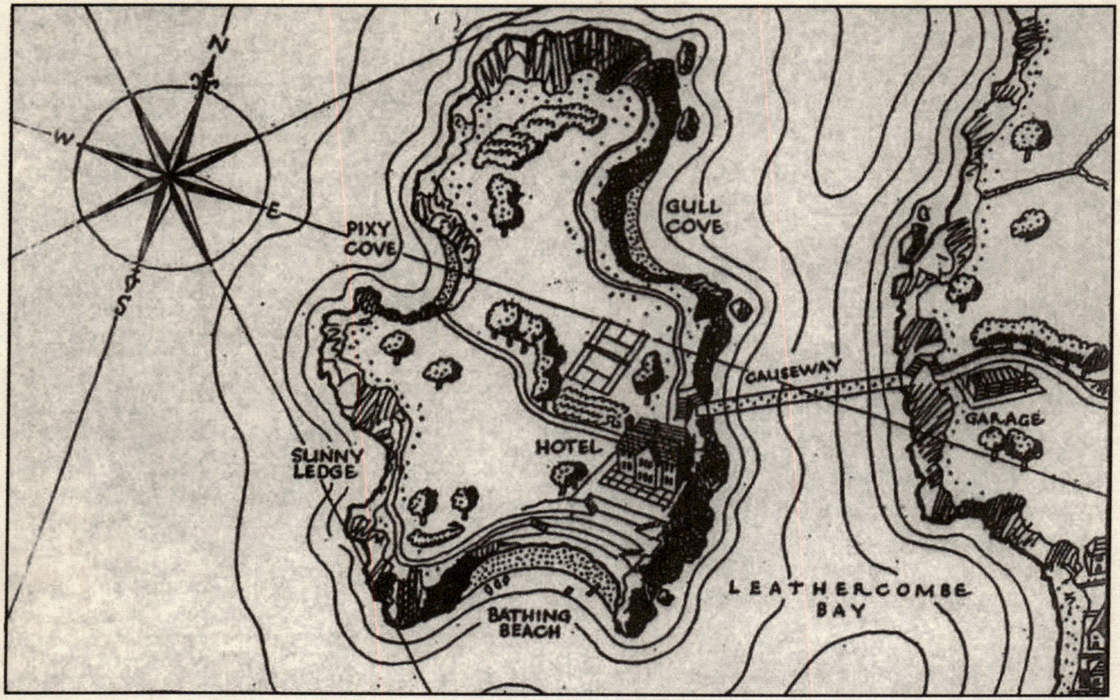
N
W
E
S
PIXY COVE
GULL COVE
CAUSEWAY
GARAGE
HOTEL
SUNNY LEDGE
BATHING BEACH
LEATHERCOMBE BAY

CHAPTER 1

When Captain Roger Angmering built himself a house in the year 1782 on the island off Leathercombe Bay, it was thought the height of eccentricity on his part. A man of good family such as he was should have had a decorous mansion set in wide meadows with, perhaps, a running stream and good pasture.

But Captain Roger Angmering had only one great love, the sea. So he built his house—a sturdy house too, as it needed to be, on the little windswept gull-haunted promontory—cut off from land at each high tide.

He did not marry, the sea was his first and last spouse, and at his death the house and island went to a distant cousin. That cousin and his descendants thought little of the bequest. Their own acres dwindled, and their heirs grew steadily poorer.

In 1922 when the great cult of the Seaside for Holidays was finally established and the coast of Devon and Cornwall was no longer thought too hot in the summer,

Agatha Christie

Arthur Angmering found his vast inconvenient late Georgian house unsaleable, but he got a good price for the odd bit of property acquired by the seafaring Captain Roger.

The sturdy house was added to and embellished. A concrete causeway was laid down from the mainland to the island. 'Walks' and 'Nooks' were cut and devised all round the island. There were two tennis courts, sun-terraces leading down to a little bay embellished with rafts and diving boards. The Jolly Roger Hotel, Smugglers' Island, Leathercombe Bay, came triumphantly into being. And from June till September (with a short season at Easter) the Jolly Roger Hotel was usually packed to the attics. It was enlarged and improved in 1934 by the addition of a cocktail bar, a bigger dining-room and some extra bathrooms. The prices went up.

People said:

'Ever been to Leathercombe Bay? Awfully jolly hotel there, on a sort of island. Very comfortable and no trippers or charabancs. Good cooking and all that. You ought to go.'

And people did go.

II

There was one very important person (in his own estimation at least) staying at the Jolly Roger. Hercule Poirot, resplendent in a white duck suit, with a panama hat tilted over his eyes, his moustaches magnificently befurled, lay back in an improved type of deck chair and surveyed the bathing beach. A series of terraces led down to it from the hotel. On the beach itself were floats, lilos, rubber and canvas boats, balls and rubber toys. There was a long springboard and three rafts at varying distances from the shore.

Of the bathers, some were in the sea, some were lying stretched out in the sun, and some were anointing themselves carefully with oil.

On the terrace immediately above, the non-bathers sat and commented on the weather, the scene in front of them, the news in the morning papers and any other subject that appealed to them.

On Poirot's left a ceaseless flow of conversation poured in a gentle monotone from the lips of Mrs Gardener while at the same time her needles clacked as she knitted vigorously. Beyond her, her husband, Odell C. Gardener, lay in a hammock chair, his hat tilted forward over his nose, and occasionally uttered a brief statement when called upon to do so.

On Poirot's right, Miss Brewster, a tough athletic woman with grizzled hair and a pleasant weather-beaten face, made gruff comments. The result sounded rather like a sheepdog whose short stentorian barks interrupted the ceaseless yapping of a Pomeranian.

Mrs Gardener was saying:

'And so I said to Mr Gardener, why, I said, sightseeing is all very well, and I do like to do a place thoroughly. But, after all, I said, we've done England pretty well and all I

Agatha Christie

want now is to get to some quiet spot by the seaside and just relax. That's what I said, wasn't it, Odell? Just *relax*. I feel I must relax, I said. That's so, isn't it, Odell?'

Mr Gardener, from behind his hat, murmured:

'Yes, darling.'

Mrs Gardener pursued the theme.

'And so, when I mentioned it to Mr Kelso, at Cook's—He's arranged all our itinerary for us and been *most* helpful in every way. I don't really know what we'd have done without him!—well, as I say, when I mentioned it to him, Mr Kelso said that we couldn't do better than come here. A most picturesque spot, he said, quite out of the world, and at the same time very comfortable and most exclusive in every way. And, of course, Mr Gardener, he chipped in there and said what about the sanitary arrangements? Because, if you'll believe me M. Poirot, a sister of Mr Gardener's went to stay at a guesthouse once, very exclusive they said it was, and in the heart of the moors, but would you believe me, *nothing but an earth closet!* So naturally that made Mr Gardener suspicious of these out-of-the-world places, didn't it, Odell?'

'Why, yes, darling,' said Gardener.

'But Mr Kelso reassured us at once. The sanitation, he said, was absolutely the latest word, and the cooking was excellent. And I'm sure that's so. And what I like about it is, it's *intime*, if you know what I mean. Being a small place we all talk to each other and everybody knows everybody. If there is a fault about the British it is that they're inclined to be a bit standoffish until they've known you a couple

Evil Under the Sun

of years. After that nobody could be nicer. Mr Kelso said that interesting people came here, and I see he was right. There's you M. Poirot, and Miss Darnley. Oh! I was just tickled to death when I found out who you were, wasn't I, Odell?'

'You were, darling.'

'Ha!' said Miss Brewster, breaking in explosively. 'What a thrill, eh, M. Poirot?'

Hercule Poirot raised his hands in deprecation. But it was no more than a polite gesture. Mrs Gardener flowed smoothly on.

'You see, M. Poirot, I'd heard a lot about you from Cornelia Robson who was. Mr Gardener and I were at Badenhof in May. And of course Cornelia told us all about that business in Egypt when Linnet Ridgeway was killed. She said you were wonderful and I've always been simply crazy to meet you, haven't I, Odell?'

'Yes, darling.'

'And then Miss Darnley, too. I get a lot of my things at Rose Mond's and of course she *is* Rose Mond, isn't she? I think her clothes are ever so clever. Such a marvellous line. That dress I had on last night was one of hers. She's just a lovely woman in every way, I think.'

From beyond Miss Brewster, Major Barry, who had been sitting with protuberant eyes glued to the bathers, grunted out:

'Distinguished lookin' gal!'

Mrs Gardener clacked her needles.

'I've just got to confess one thing, M. Poirot. It gave me

Agatha Christie

a kind of a *turn* meeting you here—not that I wasn't just thrilled to meet you, because I was. Mr Gardener knows that. But it just came to me that you might be here—well, *professionally*. You know what I mean? Well, I'm just terribly sensitive, as Mr Gardener will tell you, and I just couldn't bear it if I was to be mixed up in crime of any kind. You see—'

Mr Gardener cleared his throat. He said:

'You see, M. Poirot, Mrs Gardener is very sensitive.'

The hands of Hercule Poirot shot into the air.

'But let me assure you, Madame, that I am here simply in the same way that you are here yourselves—to enjoy myself—to spend the holiday. I do not think of crime even.'

Miss Brewster said again, giving her short gruff bark:

'No bodies on Smugglers' Island.'

Hercule Poirot said:

'Ah! but that, it is not strictly true.' He pointed downward. 'Regard them there, lying out in rows. What are they? They are not men and women. There is nothing personal about them. They are just—bodies!'

Major Barry said appreciatively:

'Good-looking fillies, some of 'em. Bit on the thin side, perhaps.'

Poirot cried:

'Yes, but what appeal is there? What mystery? I, I am old, of the old school, When I was young, one saw barely the ankle. The glimpse of a foamy petticoat, how alluring!

6

The gentle swelling of the calf—a knee—a beribboned garter—'

'Naughty, naughty!' said Major Barry hoarsely.

'Much more sensible—the things we wear nowadays,' said Miss Brewster.

'Why, yes, M. Poirot,' said Mrs Gardener. 'I do think, you know, that our girls and boys nowadays lead a much more natural healthy life. They just romp about together and they—well, they—' Mrs Gardener blushed slightly, for she had a nice mind—'they think nothing *of* it, if you know what I mean?'

'I do know,' said Hercule Poirot. 'It is deplorable!'

'Deplorable?' squeaked Mrs Gardener.

'To remove all the romance—all the mystery! Today everything is *standardized!*' He waved a hand towards the recumbent figures. 'That reminds me very much of the Morgue in Paris.'

'M. Poirot!' Mrs Gardener was scandalized.

'Bodies—arranged on slabs—like butcher's meat!'

'But M. Poirot, isn't that too far-fetched for words?'

Hercule Poirot admitted:

'It may be, yes.'

'All the same,' Mrs Gardener knitted with energy, 'I'm inclined to agree with you on one point. These girls that lie out like that in the sun will grow hair on their legs and arms. I've said so to Irene—that's my daughter, M. Poirot. Irene, I said to her, if you lie out like that in the sun, you'll have hair all over you, hair on your arms and hair on your legs and hair on your bosom, and what will you look like then? I said to her. Didn't I, Odell?'

'Yes, darling,' said Mr Gardener.

Everyone was silent, perhaps making a mental picture of Irene when the worst had happened.

Mrs Gardener rolled up her knitting and said:

'I wonder now—'

Mr Gardener said:

'Yes, darling?'

He struggled out of the hammock chair and took Mrs Gardener's knitting and her book. He asked:

'What about joining us for a drink, Miss Brewster?'

'Not just now, thanks.'

The Gardeners went up to the hotel.

Miss Brewster said:

'American husbands are wonderful!'

III

Mrs Gardener's place was taken by the Reverend Stephen Lane.

Mr Lane was a tall vigorous clergyman of fifty-odd. His face was tanned and his dark grey flannel trousers were holidayfied and disreputable.

He said with enthusiasm:

'Marvellous country! I've been from Leathercombe Bay to Harford and back over the cliffs.'

'Warm work walking today,' said Major Barry, who never walked.

'Good exercise,' said Miss Brewster. 'I haven't been for my row yet. Nothing like rowing for your stomach muscles.'

The eyes of Hercule Poirot dropped somewhat ruefully to a certain protuberance in his middle.

Miss Brewster, noting the glance, said kindly:

'You'd soon get that off, M. Poirot, if you took a rowing boat out every day.'

'*Merci, Mademoiselle.* I detest boats!'

'You mean small boats?'

'Boats of all sizes!' He closed his eyes and shuddered. 'The movement of the sea, it is not pleasant.'

'Bless the man, the sea is as calm as a mill pond today.'

Poirot replied with conviction:

'There is no such thing as a really calm sea. Always, always, there is motion.'

'If you ask me,' said Major Barry, 'seasickness is nine-tenths nerves.'

'There,' said the clergyman, smiling a little, 'speaks the good sailor—eh, Major?'

'Only been ill once—and that was crossing the Channel! Don't think about it, that's my motto.'

'Seasickness is really a very odd thing,' mused Miss Brewster. 'Why should some people be subject to it and not others? It seems so unfair. And nothing to do with one's ordinary health. Quite sickly people are good sailors. Someone told me once it was something to do with one's spine. Then there's the way some people can't stand heights. I'm not very good myself, but Mrs Redfern is far worse. The other day, on the cliff path to Harford, she turned

Agatha Christie

quite giddy and simply clung to me. She told me she once got stuck halfway down that outside staircase on Milan Cathedral. She'd gone up without thinking but coming down did for her.'

'She'd better not go down the ladder to Pixy Cove, then,' observed Lane.

Miss Brewster made a face.

'I funk that myself. It's all right for the young. The Cowan boys and the young Mastermans, they run up and down and enjoy it.'

Lane said:

'Here comes Mrs Redfern now, coming up from her bathe.'

Miss Brewster remarked:

'M. Poirot ought to approve of her. She's no sun-bather.'

Young Mrs Redfern had taken off her rubber cap and was shaking out her hair. She was an ash blonde and her skin was of that dead fairness that goes with that colouring. Her legs and arms were very white.

With a hoarse chuckle, Major Barry said:

'Looks a bit uncooked among the others, doesn't she?'

Wrapping herself in a long bathrobe Christine Redfern came up the beach and mounted the steps towards them.

She had a fair serious face, pretty in a negative way, and small dainty hands and feet.

She smiled at them and dropped down beside them, tucking her bath-wrap round her.

Miss Brewster said:

'You have earned M. Poirot's good opinion. He doesn't like the sun-tanning crowd. Says they're like joints of butcher's meat, or words to that effect.'

Christine Redfern smiled ruefully. She said:

'I wish I *could* sunbathe! But I don't go brown. I only blister and get the most frightful freckles all over my arms.'

'Better than getting hair all over them like Mrs Gardener's Irene,' said Miss Brewster. In answer to Christine's enquiring glance she went on: 'Mrs Gardener's been in grand form this morning. Absolutely non-stop. "Isn't that so, Odell?" "Yes, darling."' She paused and then said: 'I wish, though, M. Poirot, that you'd played up to her a bit. Why didn't you? Why didn't you tell her that you were down here investigating a particularly gruesome murder, and that the murderer, a homicidal maniac, was certainly to be found among the guests of the hotel?'

Hercule Poirot sighed. He said:

'I very much fear she would have believed me.'

Major Barry gave a wheezy chuckle. He said:

'She certainly would.'

Emily Brewster said:

'No, I don't believe even Mrs Gardener would have believed in a crime staged here. This isn't the sort of place you'd get a body!'

Hercule Poirot stirred a little in his chair. He protested. He said:

'But why not, Mademoiselle? Why should there not be what you call a "body" here on Smugglers' Island?'

Emily Brewster said:

Agatha Christie

'I don't know. I suppose some places *are* more unlikely than others. This isn't the kind of spot—' She broke off, finding it difficult to explain her meaning.

'It is romantic, yes,' agreed Hercule Poirot. 'It is peaceful. The sun shines. The sea is blue. But you forget, Miss Brewster, there is evil everywhere under the sun.'

The clergyman stirred in his chair. He leaned forward. His intensely blue eyes lighted up.

Miss Brewster shrugged her shoulders.

'Oh! of course I realize that, but all the same—'

'But all the same this still seems to you an unlikely setting for crime? You forget one thing, Mademoiselle.'

'Human nature, I suppose?'

'That, yes. That, always. But that was not what I was going to say. I was going to point out to you that here everyone is on holiday.'

Emily Brewster turned a puzzled face to him.

'I don't understand.'

Hercule Poirot beamed kindly at her. He made dabs in the air with an emphatic forefinger.

'Let us say, you have an enemy. If you seek him out in his flat, in his office, in the street—*eh bien*, you must have a *reason*—you must account for yourself. But here at the seaside it is necessary for no one to account for himself. You are at Leathercombe Bay, why? *Parbleu!* it is August—one goes to the seaside in August—one is on one's holiday. It is quite natural, you see, for you to be here and for Mr Lane to be here and for Major Barry to be here and for Mrs Redfern and her husband to be here.

Because it is the custom in England to go to the seaside in August.'

'Well,' admitted Miss Brewster, 'that's certainly a very ingenious idea. But what about the Gardeners? They're American.'

Poirot smiled.

'Even Mrs Gardener, as she told us, feels the need to *relax*. Also, since she is "doing" England, she must certainly spend a fortnight at the seaside—as a good tourist, if nothing else. She enjoys watching people.'

Mrs Redfern murmured:

'You like watching the people too, I think?'

'Madame, I will confess it. I do.'

She said thoughtfully: 'You see—a good deal.'

IV

There was a pause. Stephen Lane cleared his throat and said with a trace of self-consciousness.

'I was interested, M. Poirot, in something you said just now. You said that there was evil done everywhere under the sun. It was almost a quotation from Ecclesiastes.' He paused and then quoted himself: '*Yea, also the heart of the sons of men is full of evil, and madness is in their heart while they live.*' His face lit up with an almost fanatical light. 'I was glad to hear you say that. Nowadays, no one believes in evil. It is considered, at most, a mere negation of good. Evil, people say, is done by those who know no better—who are undeveloped—who are to be pitied rather

Agatha Christie

than blamed. But M. Poirot, evil is *real!* It is a *fact!* I believe in Evil like I believe in Good. It exists! It is powerful! It walks the earth!'

He stopped. His breath was coming fast. He wiped his forehead with his handkerchief and looked suddenly apologetic.

'I'm sorry. I got carried away.'

Poirot said calmly:

'I understand your meaning. Up to a point I agree with you. Evil does walk the earth and can be recognized as such.'

Major Barry cleared his throat.

'Talking of that sort of thing, some of these fakir fellers in India—'

Major Barry had been long enough at the Jolly Roger for everyone to be on their guard against his fatal tendency to embark on long Indian stories. Both Miss Brewster and Mrs Redfern burst into speech.

'That's your husband swimming in now, isn't it, Mrs Redfern? How magnificent his crawl stroke is. He's an awfully good swimmer.'

At the same moment Mrs Redfern said:

'Oh look! What a lovely little boat that is out there with the red sails. It's Mr Blatt's, isn't it?'

The sailing boat with the red sails was just crossing the end of the bay.

Major Barry grunted:

'Fanciful idea, red sails,' but the menace of the story about the fakir was avoided.

Hercule Poirot looked with appreciation at the young man who had just swum to shore. Patrick Redfern was a good specimen of humanity. Lean, bronzed, with broad shoulders and narrow thighs, there was about him a kind of infectious enjoyment and gaiety—a native simplicity that endeared him to all women and most men.

He stood there shaking the water from him and raising a hand in gay salutation to his wife.

She waved back calling out:

'Come up here, Pat.'

'I'm coming.'

He went a little way along the beach to retrieve the towel he had left there.

It was then that a woman came down past them from the hotel to the beach.

Her arrival had all the importance of a stage entrance.

Moreover, she walked as though she knew it. There was no self-consciousness apparent. It would seem that she was too used to the invariable effect her presence produced.

She was tall and slender. She wore a simple backless white bathing dress and every inch of her exposed body was tanned a beautiful even shade of bronze. She was as perfect as a statue. Her hair was a rich flaming auburn curling richly and intimately into her neck. Her face had that slight hardness which is seen when thirty years have come and gone, but the whole effect of her was one of youth—of superb and triumphant vitality. There was a Chinese immobility about her face, and an upward slant

Agatha Christie

of the dark blue eyes. On her head she wore a fantastic Chinese hat of jade green cardboard.

There was that about her which made every other woman on the beach seem faded and insignificant. And with equal inevitability, the eye of every male present was drawn and riveted on her.

The eyes of Hercule Poirot opened, his moustache quivered appreciatively, Major Barry sat up and his protuberant eyes bulged even farther with excitement; on Poirot's left the Reverend Stephen Lane drew in his breath with a little hiss and his figure stiffened.

Major Barry said in a hoarse whisper:

'Arlena Stuart (that's who she was before she married Marshall)—I saw her in *Come and Go* before she left the stage. Something worth looking at, eh?'

Christine Redfern said slowly and her voice was cold: 'She's handsome—yes. I think—she looks rather a beast!'

Emily Brewster said abruptly:

'You talked about evil just now, M. Poirot. Now to my mind that woman's a personification of evil! She's a bad lot through and through. I happen to know a good deal about her.'

Major Barry said reminiscently:

'I remember a gal out in Simla. *She* had red hair too. Wife of a subaltern. Did she set the place by the ears? I'll say she did! Men went mad about her! All the women, of course, would have liked to gouge her eyes out! She upset the apple cart in more homes than one.'

He chuckled reminiscently.

'Husband was a nice quiet fellow. Worshipped the ground she walked on. Never saw a thing—or made out he didn't.'

Stephen Lane said in a low voice full of intense feeling: 'Such women are a menace—a menace to—'

He stopped.

Arlena Stuart had come to the water's edge. Two young men, little more than boys, had sprung up and come eagerly towards her. She stood smiling at them.

Her eyes slid past them to where Patrick Redfern was coming along the beach.

It was, Hercule Poirot thought, like watching the needle of a compass. Patrick Redfern was deflected, his feet changed their direction. The needle, do what it will, must obey the law of magnetism and turn to the north. Patrick Redfern's feet brought him to Arlena Stuart.

She stood smiling at him. Then she moved slowly along the beach by the side of the waves. Patrick Redfern went with her. She stretched herself out by a rock. Redfern dropped to the shingle beside her.

Abruptly, Christine Redfern got up and went into the hotel.

V

There was an uncomfortable little silence after she had left.

Then Emily Brewster said:

'It's rather too bad. She's a nice little thing. They've only been married a year or two.'

'Gal I was speaking of,' said Major Barry, 'the one in

Simla. She upset a couple of really happy marriages. Seemed a pity, what?'

'There's a type of woman,' said Miss Brewster, 'who *likes* smashing up homes.' She added after a minute or two, 'Patrick Redfern's a fool!'

Hercule Poirot said nothing. He was gazing down the beach, but he was not looking at Patrick Redfern and Arlena Stuart.

Miss Brewster said:

'Well, I'd better go and get hold of my boat.'

She left them.

Major Barry turned his boiled gooseberry eyes with mild curiosity on Poirot.

'Well, Poirot,' he said. 'What are you thinking about? You've not opened your mouth. What do you think of the siren? Pretty hot?'

Poirot said:

'*C'est possible.*'

'Now then, you old dog. I know you Frenchmen!'

Poirot said coldly:

'I am *not* a Frenchman!'

'Well, don't tell me you haven't got an eye for a pretty girl! What do you think of her, eh?'

Hercule Poirot said:

'She is not young.'

'What does that matter? A woman's as old as she looks! *Her* looks are all right.'

Hercule Poirot nodded. He said:

'Yes, she is beautiful. But it is not beauty that counts in

the end. It is not beauty that makes every head (except one) turn on the beach to look at her.'

'It's IT, my boy,' said the Major. 'That's what it is—IT.' Then he said with sudden curiosity.

'What are you looking at so steadily?'

Hercule Poirot replied: 'I am looking at the exception. At the one man who did not look up when she passed.'

Major Barry followed his gaze to where it rested on a man of about forty, fair-haired and suntanned. He had a quiet pleasant face and was sitting on the beach smoking a pipe and reading *The Times*.

'Oh, *that*!' said Major Barry. 'That's the husband, my boy. That's Marshall.'

Hercule Poirot said:

'Yes, I know.'

Major Barry chuckled. He himself was a bachelor. He was accustomed to think of The Husband in three lights only—as 'the Obstacle', 'the Inconvenience' or 'the Safeguard'.

He said:

'Seems a nice fellow. Quiet. Wonder if my *Times* has come?'

He got up and went up towards the hotel.

Poirot's glance shifted slowly to the face of Stephen Lane.

Stephen Lane was watching Arlena Marshall and Patrick Redfern. He turned suddenly to Poirot. There was a stern fanatical light in his eyes.

He said:

'That woman is evil through and through. Do you doubt it?'

Agatha Christie

Poirot said slowly:

'It is difficult to be sure.'

Stephen Lane said:

'But, man alive, don't you feel it in the air? All round you? The presence of Evil.'

Slowly, Hercule Poirot nodded his head.

CHAPTER 2

When Rosamund Darnley came and sat down by him, Hercule Poirot made no attempt to disguise his pleasure.

As he has since admitted, he admired Rosamund Darnley as much as any woman he had ever met. He liked her distinction, the graceful lines of her figure, the alert proud carriage of her head. He liked the neat sleek waves of her dark hair and the ironic quality of her smile.

She was wearing a dress of some navy blue material with touches of white. It looked very simple owing to the expensive severity of its line. Rosamund Darnley as Rose Mond Ltd was one of London's best-known dressmakers.

She said:

'I don't think I like this place. I'm wondering why I came here!'

'You have been here before, have you not?'

'Yes, two years ago, at Easter. There weren't so many people then.'

Hercule Poirot looked at her. He said gently:

Agatha Christie

'Something has occurred to worry you. That is right, is it not?'

She nodded. Her foot swung to and fro. She stared down at it. She said:

'I've met a ghost. That's what it is.'

'A ghost, Mademoiselle?'

'Yes.'

'The ghost of what? Or of whom?'

'Oh, the ghost of myself.'

Poirot asked gently:

'Was it a painful ghost?'

'Unexpectedly painful. It took me back, you know...'

She paused, musing. Then she said.

'Imagine my childhood. No, you can't! You're not English!'

Poirot asked:

'Was it a very English childhood?'

'Oh, incredibly so! The country—a big shabby house—horses, dogs—walks in the rain—wood fires—apples in the orchard—lack of money—old tweeds—evening dresses that went on from year to year—a neglected garden—with Michaelmas daisies coming out like great banners in the autumn...'

Poirot asked gently:

'And you want to go back?'

Rosamund Darnley shook her head. She said:

'One can't go back, can one? That—never. But I'd like to have gone on—a different way.'

Poirot said:

'I wonder.'

Rosamund Darnley laughed.

'So do I, really!'

Poirot said:

'When I was young (and that, Mademoiselle, is indeed a long time ago) there was a game entitled, "*If not yourself, who would you be?*" One wrote the answer in young ladies' albums. They had gold edges and were bound in blue leather. The answer, Mademoiselle, is not really very easy to find.'

Rosamund said:

'No—I suppose not. It would be a big risk. One wouldn't like to take on being Mussolini or Princess Elizabeth. As for one's friends, one knows too much about them. I remember once meeting a charming husband and wife. They were so courteous and delightful to one another and seemed on such good terms after years of marriage that I envied the woman. I'd have changed places with her willingly. Somebody told me afterwards that in private they'd never spoken to each other for eleven years!'

She laughed.

'That shows, doesn't it, that you never know?'

After a moment or two Poirot said:

'Many people, Mademoiselle, must envy you.'

Rosamund Darnley said coolly:

'Oh, yes. Naturally.'

She thought about it, her lips curved upward in their ironic smile.

'Yes, I'm really the perfect type of the successful woman! I enjoy the artistic satisfaction of the successful creative artist (I really do like designing clothes) and the financial satisfaction of the successful business woman. I'm very well off, I've a good figure, a passable face, and a not too malicious tongue.'

She paused. Her smiled widened.

'Of course—I haven't got a husband! I've failed there, haven't I, M. Poirot?'

Poirot said gallantly:

'Mademoiselle, if you are not married, it is because none of my sex have been sufficiently eloquent. It is from choice, not necessity, that you remain single.'

Rosamund Darnley said:

'And yet, like all men, I'm sure you believe in your heart that no woman is content unless she is married and has children.'

Poirot shrugged his shoulders.

'To marry and have children, that is the common lot of women. Only one woman in a hundred—more, in a thousand, can make for herself a name and a position as you have done.'

Rosamund grinned at him.

'And yet, all the same, I'm nothing but a wretched old maid! That's what I feel today, at any rate. I'd be happier with twopence a year and a big silent brute of a husband and a brood of brats running after me. That's true, isn't it?'

Poirot shrugged his shoulders.

'Since you say so, then, yes, Mademoiselle.'

Rosamund laughed, her equilibrium suddenly restored. She took out a cigarette and lit it.

She said:

'You certainly know how to deal with women, M. Poirot. I now feel like taking the opposite point of view and arguing with you in favour of careers for women. Of course I'm damned well off as I am—and I know it!'

'Then everything in the garden—or shall we say at the seaside? is lovely, Mademoiselle.'

'Quite right.'

Poirot, in his turn, extracted his cigarette case and lit one of those tiny cigarettes which it was his affection to smoke.

Regarding the ascending haze with a quizzical eye, he murmured:

'So Mr—no, Captain Marshall is an old friend of yours, Mademoiselle?'

Rosamund sat up. She said:

'Now how do you know that? Oh, I suppose Ken told you.'

Poirot shook his head.

'Nobody has told me anything. After all, Mademoiselle, I am a detective. It was the obvious conclusion to draw.'

Rosamund Darnley said: 'I don't see it.'

'But consider!' The little man's hands were eloquent. 'You have been here a week. You are lively, gay, without a care. Today, suddenly, you speak of ghosts, of old times. What has happened? For several days there have been no new arrivals until last night when Captain Marshall and his wife and daughter arrive. Today the change! It is obvious!'

Rosamund Darnley said:

'Well, it's true enough. Kenneth Marshall and I were more or less children together. The Marshalls lived next door to us. Ken was always nice to me—although condescending, of course, since he was four years older. I've not seen anything of him for a long time. It must be—fifteen years at least.'

Poirot said thoughtfully:

'A long time.'

Rosamund nodded.

There was a pause and then Hercule Poirot said:

'He is sympathetic, yes?'

Rosamund said warmly:

'Ken's a dear. One of the best. Frightfully quiet and reserved. I'd say his only fault is a *penchant* for making unfortunate marriages.'

Poirot said in a tone of great understanding: 'Ah—'

Rosamund Darnley went on.

'Kenneth's a fool—an utter fool where women are concerned! Do you remember the Martingdale case?'

Poirot frowned.

'Martingdale? Martingdale? Arsenic, was it not?'

'Yes. Seventeen or eighteen years ago. The woman was tried for the murder of her husband.'

'And he was proved to have been an arsenic eater and she was acquitted?'

'That's right. Well, after her acquittal, Ken married her. That's the sort of damn silly thing he does.'

Hercule Poirot murmured:

'But if she was innocent?'

26

Rosamund Darnley said impatiently:

'Oh, I dare say she *was* innocent. Nobody really knows! But there are plenty of women to marry in the world without going out of your way to marry one who's stood her trial for murder.'

Poirot said nothing. Perhaps he knew that if he kept silence Rosamund Darnley would go on. She did so.

'He was very young, of course, only just twenty-one. He was crazy about her. She died when Linda was born—a year after their marriage. I believe Ken was terribly cut up by her death. Afterwards he racketed around a lot—trying to forget, I suppose.'

She paused.

'And then came this business of Arlena Stuart. She was in Revue at the time. There was the Codrington divorce case. Lady Codrington divorced Codrington, citing Arlena Stuart. They say Lord Codrington was absolutely infatuated with her. It was understood they were to be married as soon as the decree was made absolute. Actually, when it came to it, he didn't marry her. Turned her down flat. I believe she actually sued him for breach of promise. Anyway, the thing made a big stir at the time. The next thing that happens is that Ken goes and marries her. The fool—the complete fool!'

Hercule Poirot murmured:

'A man might be excused such a folly—she is beautiful, Mademoiselle.'

'Yes, there's no doubt of that. There was another scandal about three years ago. Old Sir Roger Erskine left her every penny of his money. I should have thought that would have opened Ken's eyes if anything would.'

'And did it not?'

Rosamund Darnley shrugged her shoulders.

'I tell you I've seen nothing of him for years. People say, though, that he took it with absolute equanimity. Why, I should like to know? Has he got an absolutely blind belief in her?'

'There might be other reasons.'

'Yes. Pride! Keeping a stiff upper lip! I don't know what he really feels about her. Nobody does.'

'And she? What does she feel about him?'

Rosamund stared at him.

She said:

'She? She's the world's first gold-digger. And a man-eater as well! If anything personable in trousers comes within a hundred yards of her, it's fresh sport for Arlena! She's that kind.'

Poirot nodded his head slowly in complete agreement.

'Yes,' he said. 'That is true what you say... Her eyes look for one thing only—men.'

Rosamund said:

'She's got her eye on Patrick Redfern now. He's a good-looking man—and rather the simple kind—you know, fond of his wife, and not a philanderer. That's the kind that's meat and drink to Arlena. I like little Mrs Redfern—she's nice-looking in her fair washed-out way—but I don't think she'll stand a dog's chance against that man-eating tiger, Arlena.'

Poirot said:

'No, it is as you say.'

He looked distressed.

Rosamund said:

'Christine Redfern was a school teacher, I believe. She's the kind that thinks that mind has a pull over matter. She's got a rude shock coming to her.'

Poirot shook his head vexedly.

Rosamund got up. She said:

'It's a shame, you know.' She added vaguely: 'Somebody ought to do something about it.'

II

Linda Marshall was examining her face dispassionately in her bedroom mirror. She disliked her face very much. At this minute it seemed to her to be mostly bones and freckles. She noted with distaste her heavy bush of soft brown hair (mouse, she called it in her own mind), her greenish-grey eyes, her high cheekbones and the long aggressive line of the chin. Her mouth and teeth weren't perhaps quite so bad—but what were teeth after all? And was that a spot coming on the side of her nose?

She decided with relief that it wasn't a spot. She thought to herself:

'It's awful to be sixteen—simply *awful*.'

One didn't, somehow, know where one was. Linda was as awkward as a young colt and as prickly as a hedgehog. She was conscious the whole time of her ungainliness and

Agatha Christie

of the fact that she was neither one thing nor the other. It hadn't been so bad at school. But now she had left school. Nobody seemed to know quite what she was going to do next. Her father talked vaguely of sending her to Paris next winter. Linda didn't want to go to Paris—but then she didn't want to be at home either. She'd never realized properly, somehow, until now, how very much she disliked Arlena.

Linda's young face grew tense, her green eyes hardened. Arlena...

She thought to herself:

'She's a beast—a *beast*...'

Stepmothers! It was rotten to have a stepmother, everybody said so. And it was true! Not that Arlena was unkind to her. Most of the time she hardly noticed the girl. But when she did, there was a contemptuous amusement in her glance, in her words. The finished grace and poise of Arlena's movements emphasized Linda's own adolescent clumsiness. With Arlena about, one felt, shamingly, just how immature and crude one was.

But it wasn't that only. No, it wasn't only that.

Linda groped haltingly in the recesses of her mind. She wasn't very good at sorting out her emotions and labelling them. It was something that Arlena *did* to people—to the house—

'She's bad,' thought Linda with decision. 'She's quite, quite bad.'

But you couldn't even leave it at that. You couldn't just elevate your nose with a sniff of moral superiority and dismiss her from your mind.

Evil Under the Sun

It was something she did to people. Father, now, Father was quite different...

She puzzled over it. Father coming down to take her out from school. Father taking her once for a cruise. And Father at home—with Arlena there. All—all sort of bottled up and not—and not *there*.

Linda thought:

'And it'll go on like this. Day after day—month after month. I can't bear it.'

Life stretched before her—endless—in a series of days darkened and poisoned by Arlena's presence. She was childish enough still to have little sense of proportion. A year, to Linda, seemed like an eternity.

A big dark burning wave of hatred against Arlena surged up in her mind. She thought:

'I'd like to kill her. Oh! I wish she'd die...'

She looked out above the mirror onto the sea below.

This place was really rather fun. Or it could be fun. All those beaches and coves and queer little paths. Lots to explore. And places where one could go off by oneself and muck about. There were caves, too, so the Cowan boys had told her.

Linda thought:

'If only Arlena would go away, I could enjoy myself.'

Her mind went back to the evening of their arrival. It had been exciting coming from the mainland. The tide had been up over the causeway. They had come in a boat. The hotel had looked exciting, unusual. And then on the terrace a tall dark woman had jumped up and said:

Agatha Christie

'Why, Kenneth!'

And her father, looking frightfully surprised, had exclaimed:

'Rosamund!'

Linda considered Rosamund Darnley severely and critically in the manner of youth.

She decided that she approved of Rosamund. Rosamund, she thought, was sensible. And her hair grew nicely—as though it fitted her—most people's hair didn't fit them. And her clothes were nice. And she had a kind of funny amused face—as though it were amused at herself, not at you. Rosamund had been nice to her, Linda. She hadn't been gushing or *said* things. (Under the term of 'saying things' Linda grouped a mass of miscellaneous dislikes.) And Rosamund hadn't looked as though she thought Linda a fool. In fact she'd treated Linda as though she was a real human being. Linda so seldom felt like a real human being that she was deeply grateful when anyone appeared to consider her one.

Father, too, had seemed pleased to see Miss Darnley.

Funny—he'd looked quite different, all of a sudden. He'd looked—he'd looked—Linda puzzled it out—why, *young*, that was it! He'd laughed—a queer boyish laugh. Now Linda came to think of it, she'd very seldom heard him laugh.

She felt puzzled. It was as though she'd got a glimpse of quite a different person. She thought:

'I wonder what Father was like when he was my age...'

But that was too difficult. She gave it up.

Evil Under the Sun

An idea flashed across her mind.

What fun it would have been if they'd come here and found Miss Darnley here—just she and Father.

A vista opened out just for a minute. Father, boyish and laughing, Miss Darnley, herself—and all the fun one could have on the island—bathing—caves—

The blackness shut down again.

Arlena. One couldn't enjoy oneself with Arlena about. Why not? Well, she, Linda, couldn't anyway. You couldn't be happy when there was a person there you—hated. Yes, hated. She hated Arlena.

Very slowly that black burning wave of hatred rose up again.

Linda's face went very white. Her lips parted a little. The pupils of her eyes contracted. And her fingers stiffened and clenched themselves...

III

Kenneth Marshall tapped on his wife's door. When her voice answered, he opened the door and went in.

Arlena was just putting the finishing touches to her toilet. She was dressed in glittering green and looked a little like a mermaid. She was standing in front of the glass applying mascara to her eyelashes. She said:

'Oh, it's you, Ken.'

'Yes. I wondered if you were ready.'

'Just a minute.'

Kenneth Marshall strolled to the window. He looked out

on the sea. His face, as usual, displayed no emotion of any kind. It was pleasant and ordinary.

Turning round, he said:

'Arlena?'

'Yes?'

'You've met Redfern before, I gather?'

Arlena said easily:

'Oh yes, darling. At a cocktail party somewhere. I thought he was rather a pet.'

'So I gather. Did you know that he and his wife were coming down here?'

Arlena opened her eyes very wide.

'Oh no, darling. It was the *greatest* surprise!'

Kenneth Marshall said quietly:

'I thought, perhaps, that that was what put the idea of this place into your head. You were very keen we should come here.'

Arlena put down the mascara. She turned towards him. She smiled—a soft seductive smile. She said:

'Somebody told me about this place. I think it was the Rylands. They said it was simply too marvellous—so unspoilt! Don't you like it?'

Kenneth Marshall said:

'I'm not sure.'

'Oh, darling, but you adore bathing and lazing about. I'm sure you'll simply adore it here.'

'I can see that you mean to enjoy yourself.'

Her eyes widened a little. She looked at him uncertainly.

Kenneth Marshall said:

'I suppose the truth of it is that you told young Redfern that you were coming here?'

Arlena said:

'Kenneth darling, you're not going to be horrid, are you?'

Kenneth Marshall said:

'Look here, Arlena. I know what you're like. They're rather a nice young couple. That boy's fond of his wife, really. Must you upset the whole blinking show?'

Arlena said:

'It's so unfair blaming *me*. *I* haven't done anything—anything at all. I can't help it if—'

He prompted her.

'If what?'

Her eyelids fluttered.

'Well, of course. I know people do go crazy about me. But it's not my doing. They just get like that.'

'So you do admit that young Redfern is crazy about you?'

Arlena murmured:

'It's really rather stupid of him.'

She moved a step towards her husband.

'But you know, don't you, Ken, that I don't really care for anyone but you?'

She looked up at him through her darkened lashes.

It was a marvellous look—a look that few men could have resisted.

Agatha Christie

Kenneth Marshall looked down at her gravely. His face was composed. His voice quiet. He said:

'I think I know you pretty well, Arlena...'

IV

When you came out of the hotel on the south side the terraces and the bathing beach were immediately below you. There was also a path that led off round the cliff on the south-west side of the island. A little way along it, a few steps led down to a series of recesses cut into the cliff and labelled on the hotel map of the island as Sunny Ledge. Here cut out of the cliff were niches with seats in them.

To one of these, immediately after dinner, came Patrick Redfern and his wife. It was a lovely clear night with a bright moon.

The Redferns sat down. For a while they were silent.

At last Patrick Redfern said:

'It's a glorious evening, isn't it, Christine?'

'Yes.'

Something in her voice may have made him uneasy. He sat without looking at her.

Christine Redfern asked in her quiet voice:

'Did you know that woman was going to be here?'

He turned sharply. He said:

'I don't know what you mean.'

'I think you do.'

'Look here, Christine. I don't know what has come over you—'

She interrupted. Her voice held feeling now. It trembled.
'Over *me*? It's what has come over *you*!'
'Nothing's come over me.'
'Oh! Patrick! it *has!* You insisted so on coming here. You were quite vehement. I wanted to go to Tintagel again where—where we had our honeymoon. You were bent on coming here.'

'Well, why not? It's a fascinating spot.'

'Perhaps. But you wanted to come here because *she* was going to be here.'

'She? Who is she?'

'Mrs Marshall. You—you're infatuated with her.'

'For God's sake, Christine, don't make a fool of yourself. It's not like you to be jealous.'

His bluster was a little uncertain. He exaggerated it.

She said:

'We've been so happy.'

'Happy? Of course we've been happy! We *are* happy. But we shan't go on being happy if I can't even speak to another woman without you kicking up a row.'

'It's not like that.'

'Yes, it is. In marriage one has got to have—well—friendships with other people. This suspicious attitude is all wrong. I—I can't speak to a pretty woman without your jumping to the conclusion that I'm in love with her—'

He stopped. He shrugged his shoulders.

Christine Redfern said:

'You *are* in love with her…'

Agatha Christie

'Oh, don't be a fool, Christine! I've—I've barely spoken to her.'

'That's not true.'

'Don't for goodness' sake get into the habit of being jealous of every pretty woman we come across.'

Christine Redfern said:

'She's not just any pretty woman! She's—she's *different*! She's a bad lot! Yes, she is. She'll do you harm. Patrick, please, *give it up*. Let's go away from here.'

Patrick Redfern stuck out his chin mutinously. He looked, somehow, very young as he said defiantly:

'Don't be ridiculous, Christine. And—and don't let's quarrel about it.'

'I don't want to quarrel.'

'Then behave like a reasonable human being. Come on, let's go back to the hotel.'

He got up. There was a pause, then Christine Redfern got up too.

She said:

'Very well...'

In the recess adjoining, on the seat there, Hercule Poirot sat and shook his head sorrowfully.

Some people might have scrupulously removed themselves from earshot of a private conversation. But not Hercule Poirot. He had no scruples of that kind.

'Besides,' as he explained to his friend Hastings at a later date, 'it was a question of murder.'

Hastings said, staring:

'But the murder hadn't happened, then.'

Hercule Poirot sighed. He said:

'But already, *mon cher*, it was very clearly indicated.'

'Then why didn't you stop it?'

And Hercule Poirot, with a sigh, said as he had said once before in Egypt, that if a person is determined to commit murder it is not easy to prevent them. He does not blame himself for what happened. It was, according to him, inevitable.

CHAPTER 3

Rosamund Darnley and Kenneth Marshall sat on the short springy turf of the cliff overlooking Gull Cove. This was on the east side of the island. People came here in the morning sometimes to bathe when they wanted to be peaceful.

Rosamund said:

'It's nice to get away from people.'

Marshall murmured inaudibly:

'M—m, yes.'

He rolled over, sniffing at the short turf.

'Smells good. Remember the downs at Shipley?'

'Rather.'

'Pretty good, those days.'

'Yes.'

'You've not changed much, Rosamund.'

'Yes, I have. I've changed enormously.'

'You've been very successful and you're rich and all that, but you're the same old Rosamund.'

Rosamund murmured:

'I wish I were.'

'What's that?'

'Nothing. It's a pity, isn't it, Kenneth, that we can't keep the nice natures and high ideals that we had when we were young?'

'I don't know that your nature was ever particularly nice, my child. You used to get into the most frightful rages. You half-choked me once when you flew at me in a temper.'

Rosamund laughed. She said:

'Do you remember the day that we took Toby down to get water rats?'

They spent some minutes in recalling old adventures.

Then there came a pause.

Rosamund's fingers played with the clasp of her bag. She said at last:

'Kenneth?'

'Um.' His reply was indistinct. He was still lying on his face on the turf.

'If I say something to you that is probably outrageously impertinent will you never speak to me again?'

He rolled over and sat up.

'I don't think,' he said seriously, 'that I would ever regard anything you said as impertinent. You see, you *belong*.'

She nodded in acceptance of all that last phrase meant. She concealed only the pleasure it gave her.

'Kenneth, why don't you get a divorce from your wife?'

His face altered. It hardened—the happy expression

died out of it. He took a pipe from his pocket and began filling it.

Rosamund said:

'I'm sorry if I've offended you.'

He said quietly:

'You haven't offended me.'

'Well then, why don't you?'

'You don't understand, my dear girl.'

'Are you—so frightfully fond of her?'

'It's not just a question of that. You see, I married her.'

'I know. But she's—pretty notorious.'

He considered that for a moment, ramming in the tobacco carefully.

'Is she? I suppose she is.'

'You *could* divorce her, Ken.'

'My dear girl, you've got no business to say a thing like that. Just because men lose their heads about her a bit isn't to say that she loses hers.'

Rosamund bit off a rejoinder. Then she said:

'You could fix it so that she divorced you—if you prefer it that way.'

'I dare say I could.'

'You ought to, Ken. Really, I mean it. There's the child.'

'Linda?'

'Yes, Linda.'

'What's Linda to do with it?'

'Arlena's not good for Linda. She isn't really. Linda, I think, *feels* things a good deal.'

Kenneth Marshall applied a match to his pipe. Between puffs he said:

'Yes—there's something in that. I suppose Arlena and Linda aren't very good for each other. Not the right thing for a girl perhaps. It's a bit worrying.'

Rosamund said:

'I like Linda—very much. There's something—fine about her.'

Kenneth said:

'She's like her mother. She takes things hard like Ruth did.'

Rosamund said:

'Then don't you think—really—that you ought to get rid of Arlena?'

'Fix up a divorce?'

'Yes. People are doing that all the time.'

Kenneth Marshall said with sudden vehemence:

'Yes, and that's just what I hate.'

'Hate?' She was startled.

'Yes. Sort of attitude to life there is nowadays. If you take on a thing and don't like it, then you get yourself out of it as quick as possible! Dash it all, there's got to be such a thing as good faith. If you marry a woman and engage yourself to look after her, well, it's up to you to do it. It's your show. You've taken it on. I'm sick of quick marriage and easy divorce. Arlena's my wife, that's all there is to it.'

Rosamund leaned forward. She said in a low voice:

'So it's like that with you? "Till death do us part"?'

Kenneth Marshall nodded his head.

Agatha Christie

He said:
'That's just it.'
Rosamund said:
'I see.'

II

Mr Horace Blatt, returning to Leathercombe Bay down a narrow twisting lane, nearly ran down Mrs Redfern at a corner.

As she flattened herself into the hedge, Mr Blatt brought his Sunbeam to a halt by applying the brakes vigorously.

'Hullo-ullo-ullo,' said Mr Blatt cheerfully.

He was a large man with a red face and a fringe of reddish hair round a shining bald spot.

It was Mr Blatt's apparent ambition to be the life and soul of any place he happened to be in. The Jolly Roger Hotel, in his opinion, given somewhat loudly, needed brightening up. He was puzzled at the way people seemed to melt and disappear when he himself arrived on the scene.

'Nearly made you into strawberry jam, didn't I?' said Mr Blatt gaily.

Christine Redfern said:
'Yes, you did.'
'Jump in,' said Mr Blatt.
'Oh, thanks—I think I'll walk.'
'Nonsense,' said Mr Blatt. 'What's a car for?'
Yielding to necessity Christine Redfern got in.

Mr Blatt restarted the engine, which had stopped owing to the suddenness with which he had previously pulled up.

Mr Blatt inquired:

'And what are you doing walking about all alone? That's all wrong, a nice-looking girl like you.'

Christine said hurriedly:

'Oh! I like being alone.'

Mr Blatt gave her a terrific dig with his elbow, nearly sending the car into the hedge at the same time.

'Girls always say that,' he said. 'They don't mean it. You know, that place, the Jolly Roger, wants a bit of livening up. Nothing jolly about it. No *life* in it. Of course there's a good amount of duds staying there. A lot of kids, to begin with, and a lot of old fogeys too. There's that old Anglo-Indian bore and that athletic parson and those yapping Americans and that foreigner with the moustache—makes me laugh that moustache of his! I should say he's a hairdresser, something of that sort.'

Christine shook her head.

'Oh no, he's a detective.'

Mr Blatt nearly let the car go into the hedge again.

'A detective? D'you mean he's in *disguise?*'

Christine smiled faintly.

She said:

'Oh no, he really *is* like that. He's Hercule Poirot. You must have heard of him.'

Mr Blatt said:

'Didn't catch his name properly. Oh yes, I've *heard* of

him. But I thought he was dead... Dash it, he *ought* to be dead. What's he after down here?'

'He's not after anything—he's just on a holiday.'

'Well, I suppose that might be so.' Mr Blatt seemed doubtful about it. 'Looks a bit of a bounder, doesn't he?'

'Well,' said Christine and hesitated. 'Perhaps a little peculiar.'

'What I say is,' said Mr Blatt, 'what's wrong with Scotland Yard? Buy British every time for me.'

He reached the bottom of the hill and with a triumphant fanfare of the horn ran the car into the Jolly Roger's garage, which was situated, for tidal reasons, on the mainland opposite the hotel.

III

Linda Marshall was in the small shop which catered for the wants of visitors to Leathercombe Bay. One side of it was devoted to shelves on which were books which could be borrowed for the sum of twopence. The newest of them was ten years old, some were twenty years old and others older still.

Linda took first one and then another doubtfully from the shelf and glanced into it. She decided that she couldn't possibly read *The Four Feathers* or *Vice Versa*. She took out a small squat volume in brown calf.

The time passed...

With a start Linda shoved the book back in the shelf as Christine Redfern's voice said:

'What are you reading, Linda?'

Linda said hurriedly:

'Nothing. I'm looking for a book.'

She pulled out *The Marriage of William Ashe* at random and advanced to the counter fumbling for twopence.

Christine said:

'Mr Blatt just drove me home—after nearly running over me first. I really felt I couldn't walk all across the causeway with him, so I said I had to buy some things.'

Linda said:

'He's awful, isn't he? Always saying how rich he is and making the most terrible jokes.'

Christine said:

'Poor man. One really feels rather sorry for him.'

Linda didn't agree. She didn't see anything to be sorry for in Mr Blatt. She was young and ruthless.

She walked with Christine Redfern out of the shop and down towards the causeway.

She was busy with her own thoughts. She liked Christine Redfern. She and Rosamund Darnley were the only bearable people on the island in Linda's opinion. Neither of them talked much to her for one thing. Now, as they walked, Christine didn't say anything. That, Linda thought, was sensible. If you hadn't anything worth saying why go chattering all the time?

She lost herself in her own perplexities.

She said suddenly:

'Mrs Redfern, have you ever felt that everything's so awful—so terrible—that you'll—oh, *burst*...?'

The words were almost comic, but Linda's face, drawn and anxious, was not. Christine Redfern, looking at her at first vaguely, with scarcely comprehending eyes, certainly saw nothing to laugh at...

She caught her breath sharply.

She said:

'Yes—yes—I have felt—just that...'

IV

Mr Blatt said:

'So you're the famous sleuth, eh?'

They were in the cocktail bar, a favourite haunt of Mr Blatt's.

Hercule Poirot acknowledged the remark with his usual lack of modesty.

Mr Blatt went on.

'And what are you doing down here—on a job?'

'No, no. I repose myself. I take the holiday.'

Mr Blatt winked.

'You'd say that anyway, wouldn't you?'

Poirot replied:

'Not necessarily.'

Horace Blatt said:

'Oh! Come now. As a matter of fact you'd be safe enough with *me*. *I* don't repeat all I hear! Learnt to keep my mouth shut years ago. Shouldn't have got on the way I have if I hadn't known how to do that. But you know what most people are—yap, yap, yap about everything they hear! Now you can't afford that in your trade! That's why you've got to keep it up that you're here holiday-making and nothing else.'

Poirot asked:

'And why should you suppose the contrary?'

Mr Blatt closed one eye.

He said:

'I'm a man of the world. I know the cut of a fellow's jib. A man like you would be at Deauville or Le Touquet or down at Juan les Pins. That's your—what's the phrase?—spiritual home.'

Poirot sighed. He looked out of the window. Rain was falling and mist encircled the island. He said:

'It is possible that you are right! There, at least, in wet weather there are the distractions.'

'Good old Casino!' said Mr Blatt. 'You know, I've had to work pretty hard most of my life. No time for holidays or kickshaws. I meant to make good and I have made good. Now I can do what I please. My money's as good as any man's. I've seen a bit of life in the last few years, I can tell you.'

Poirot murmured:

'Ah, yes?'

'Don't know why I came to this place,' Mr Blatt continued.

Poirot observed:

'I, too, wondered?'

'Eh, what's that?'

Poirot waved an eloquent hand.

Agatha Christie

'I, too, am not without observation. I should have expected *you* most certainly to choose Deauville or Biarritz.'

'Instead of which, we're both here, eh?'

Mr Blatt gave a hoarse chuckle.

'Don't really know why I came here,' he mused. 'I think, you know, it sounded *romantic*. Jolly Roger Hotel, Smugglers' Island. That kind of address tickles you up, you know. Makes you think of when you were a boy. Pirates, smuggling, all that.'

He laughed rather self-consciously.

'I used to sail quite a bit as a boy. Not this part of the world. Off the East coast. Funny how a taste for that sort of thing never quite leaves you. I could have a tip-top yacht if I liked, but somehow I don't really fancy it. I like mucking about in that little yawl of mine. Redfern's keen on sailing, too. He's been out with me once or twice. Can't get hold of him now—always hanging round that red-haired wife of Marshall's.'

He paused, then lowering his voice, he went on:

'Mostly a dried up lot of sticks in this hotel! Mrs Marshall's about the only lively spot! I should think Marshall's got his hands full looking after her. All sorts of stories about her in her stage days—*and* after! Men go crazy about her. You'll see, there'll be a spot of trouble one of these days.'

Poirot asked: 'What kind of trouble?'

Horace Blatt replied:

'That depends. I'd say, looking at Marshall, that he's a man with a funny kind of temper. As a matter of fact, I know he is. Heard something about him. I've met that quiet sort. Never know where you are with that kind. Redfern had better look out—'

He broke off, as the subject of his words came into the bar. He went on speaking loudly and self-consciously.

'And, as I say, sailing round this coast is good fun. Hullo, Redfern, have one with me? What'll you have? Dry Martini? Right. What about you, M. Poirot?'

Poirot shook his head.

Patrick Redfern sat down and said:

'Sailing? It's the best fun in the world. Wish I could do more of it. Used to spend most of my time as a boy in a sailing dinghy round this coast.'

Poirot said:

'Then you know this part of the world well?'

'Rather! I knew this place before there was a hotel on it. There were just a few fishermen's cottages at Leathercombe Bay and a tumbledown old house, all shut up, on the island.'

'There was a house here?'

'Oh, yes, but it hadn't been lived in for years. Was practically falling down. There used to be all sorts of stories of secret passages from the house to Pixy's Cave. We were always looking for that secret passage, I remember.'

Horace Blatt spilt his drink. He cursed, mopped himself and asked:

'What is this Pixy's Cave?'

Patrick said:

'Oh, don't you know it? It's on Pixy Cove. You can't find the entrance to it easily. It's among a lot of piled up boulders at one end. Just a long thin crack. You can just squeeze through it. Inside it widens out into quite a big cave. You can imagine what fun it was to a boy! An old fisherman showed it to me. Nowadays, even the fishermen don't know about it. I asked one the other day why the place was called Pixy Cove and he couldn't tell me.'

Hercule Poirot said:

'But I still do not understand. What is this pixy?'

Patrick Redfern said:

'Oh! that's typically Devonshire. There's the pixy's cave at Sheepstor on the Moor. You're supposed to leave a pin, you know, as a present for the pixy. A pixy is a kind of moor spirit.'

Hercule Poirot said:

'Ah! but it is interesting, that.'

Patrick Redfern went on.

'There's a lot of pixy lore on Dartmoor still. There are tors that are said to be pixy ridden, and I expect that farmers coming home after a thick night still complain of being pixy led.'

Horace Blatt said:

'You mean when they've had a couple?'

Patrick Redfern said with a smile:

'That's certainly the commonsense explanation!'

Blatt looked at his watch. He said:

'I'm going in to dinner. On the whole, Redfern, pirates are my favourites, not pixies.'

Patrick Redfern said with a laugh as the other went out:

'Faith, I'd like to see the old boy pixy led himself!'

Poirot observed meditatively:

'For a hard-bitten business man, M. Blatt seems to have a very romantic imagination.'

Patrick Redfern said:

'That's because he's only half educated. Or so my wife says. Look at what he reads! Nothing but thrillers or Wild West stories.'

Poirot said:

'You mean that he has still the mentality of a boy?'

'Well, don't you think so, sir?'

'Me, I have not seen very much of him.'

'I haven't either. I've been out sailing with him once or twice—but he doesn't really like having anyone with him. He prefers to be on his own.'

Hercule Poirot said:

'That is indeed curious. It is singularly unlike his practice on land.'

Redfern laughed. He said:

'I know. We all have a bit of trouble keeping out of his way. He'd like to turn this place into a cross between Margate and Le Touquet.'

Poirot said nothing for a minute or two. He was studying the laughing face of his companion very attentively. He said suddenly and unexpectedly:

'I think, M. Redfern, that you enjoy living.'

Patrick stared at him, surprised.

'Indeed I do. Why not?'

'Why not indeed,' agreed Poirot. 'I make you my felicitation on the fact.'

Agatha Christie

Smiling a little, Patrick Redfern said:

'Thank you, sir.'

'That is why, as an older man, a very much older man, I venture to offer you a piece of advice.'

'Yes, sir?'

'A very wise friend of mine in the Police Force said to me years ago: "Hercule, my friend, if you would know tranquillity, avoid women."'

Patrick Redfern said:

'I'm afraid it's a bit late for that, sir. I'm married, you know.'

'I do know. Your wife is a very charming, a very accomplished woman. She is, I think, very fond of you.'

Patrick Redfern said sharply:

'I'm very fond of her.'

'Ah,' said Hercule Poirot, 'I am delighted to hear it.'

Patrick's brow was suddenly like thunder.

'Look here, M. Poirot, what are you getting at?'

'*Les femmes*.' Poirot leaned back and closed his eyes. 'I know something of them. They are capable of complicating life unbearably. And the English, they conduct their affairs indescribably. If it was necessary for you to come here, M. Redfern, why, in the name of heaven, did you bring your wife?'

Patrick Redfern said angrily:

'I don't know what you mean.'

Hercule Poirot said calmly:

'You know perfectly. I am not so foolish as to argue with an infatuated man. I utter only the word of caution.'

'You've been listening to these damned scandalmongers. Mrs Gardener, the Brewster woman—nothing to do but to clack their tongues all day. Just because a woman's good-looking—they're down on her like a sack of coals.'

Hercule Poirot got up. He murmured:

'Are you really as young as all that?'

Shaking his head, he left the bar. Patrick Redfern stared angrily after him.

V

Hercule Poirot paused in the hall on his way from the dining room. The doors were open—a breath of soft night air came in.

The rain had stopped and the mist had dispersed. It was a fine night again.

Hercule Poirot found Mrs Redfern in her favourite seat on the cliff ledge. He stopped by her and said:

'This seat is damp. You should not sit here. You will catch the chill.'

'No, I shan't. And what does it matter anyway.'

'Tscha, tscha, you are not a child! You are an educated woman. You must look at things sensibly.'

She said coldly:

'I can assure you I never take cold.'

Poirot said:

'It has been a wet day. The wind blew, the rain came down, and the mist was everywhere so that one could not see through it. *Eh bien*, what is it like now? The mists have rolled away, the sky is clear and up above the stars shine. That is like life, Madame.'

Christine said in a low fierce voice:

'Do you know what I am most sick of in this place?'

'What, Madame?'

'Pity.'

She brought the word out like the flick of a whip.

She went on:

'Do you think I don't know? That I can't see? All the time people are saying: "Poor Mrs Redfern—that poor little woman." And anyway I'm not little, I'm tall. They say little because they are sorry for me. And I can't bear it!'

Cautiously, Hercule Poirot spread his handkerchief on the seat and sat down. He said thoughtfully:

'There is something in that.'

'That woman—' said Christine and stopped.

Poirot said gravely:

'Will you allow me to tell you something, Madame? Something that is as true as the stars above us? The Arlena Stuarts—or Arlena Marshalls—of this world—do not count.'

Christine Redfern said:

'Nonsense.'

'I assure you, it is true. Their Empire is of the moment and for the moment. To count—really and truly to count—a woman must have goodness or brains.'

Christine said scornfully:

'Do you think men care for goodness or brains?'

Poirot said gravely:

'Fundamentally, yes.'

Christine laughed shortly.

She said:

'I don't agree with you.'

Poirot said:

'Your husband loves you, Madame. I know it.'

'You can't know it.'

'Yes, yes. I know it. I have seen him looking at you.'

Suddenly she broke down. She wept stormily and bitterly against Poirot's accommodating shoulder.

She said:

'I can't bear it... I can't bear it...'

Poirot patted her arm. He said soothingly:

'Patience—only patience.'

She sat up and pressed her handkerchief to her eyes. She said in a stifled voice:

'It's all right. I'm better now. Leave me. I'd—I'd rather be alone.'

He obeyed and left her sitting there while he himself followed the winding path down to the hotel.

He was nearly there when he heard the murmur of voices.

He turned a little aside from the path. There was a gap in the bushes.

He saw Arlena Marshall and Patrick Redfern beside her. He heard the man's voice, with the throb in it of emotion.

'I'm crazy about you—crazy—you've driven me mad... You do care a little—you do care?'

He saw Arlena Marshall's face—it was, he thought, like a sleek happy cat—it was animal, not human. She said softly:

Agatha Christie

'Of course, Patrick darling, I adore you. You know that…'

For once Hercule Poirot cut his eavesdropping short. He went back to the path and on down to the hotel.

A figure joined him suddenly. It was Captain Marshall. Marshall said:

'Remarkable night, what? After that foul day.' He looked up at the sky. 'Looks as though we should have fine weather tomorrow.'

CHAPTER 4

The morning of the 25th of August dawned bright and cloudless. It was a morning to tempt even an inveterate sluggard to rise early.

Several people rose early that morning at the Jolly Roger.

It was eight o'clock when Linda, sitting at her dressing table, turned a little thick calf-bound volume face downwards, sprawling it open, and looked at her own face in the mirror.

Her lips were set tight together and the pupils of her eyes contracted.

She said below her breath:

'I'll do it...'

She slipped out of her pyjamas and into her bathing dress. Over it she flung on a bathrobe and laced espadrilles on her feet.

She went out of her room and along the passage. At the end of it a door onto the balcony led to an outside staircase leading directly down to the rocks below the hotel. There was a small iron ladder clamped onto the rocks leading

Agatha Christie

down into the water which was used by many of the hotel guests for a before-breakfast dip as taking up less time than going down to the main bathing beach.

As Linda started down from the balcony she met her father coming up. He said:

'You're up early. Going to have a dip?'

Linda nodded.

They passed each other.

Instead of going on down the rocks, however, Linda skirted round the hotel to the left until she came to the path down to the causeway connecting the hotel with the mainland. The tide was high and the causeway under water, but the boat that took hotel guests across was tied to a little jetty. The man in charge of it was absent at the moment. Linda got in, untied it and rowed herself across.

She tied up the boat on the other side, walked up the slope, past the hotel garage and along until she reached the general shop.

The woman had just taken down the shutters and was engaged in sweeping out the floor. She looked amazed at the sight of Linda.

'Well, Miss, you *are* up early.'

Linda put her hand in the pocket of her bath-wrap and brought out some money. She proceeded to make her purchases.

II

Christine Redfern was standing in Linda's room when the girl returned.

'Oh, there you are,' Christine exclaimed. 'I thought you couldn't be really up yet.'

Linda said:

'No, I've been bathing.'

Noticing the parcel in her hand, Christine said with surprise:

'The post has come early today.'

Linda flushed. With her habitual nervous clumsiness the parcel slipped from her hand. The flimsy string broke and some of the contents rolled over the floor.

Christine exclaimed:

'What have you been buying *candles* for?'

But to Linda's relief she did not wait for an answer, but went on, as she helped to pick the things up from the floor.

'I came in to ask whether you would like to come with me to Gull Cove this morning. I want to sketch there.'

Linda accepted with alacrity.

In the last few days she had accompanied Christine Redfern more than once on sketching expeditions. Christine was a most indifferent artist, but it is possible that she found the excuse of painting a help to her pride since her husband now spent most of his time with Arlena Marshall.

Linda Marshall had been increasingly morose and bad tempered. She liked being with Christine who, intent on her work, spoke very little. It was, Linda felt, nearly as good as being by oneself, and in a curious way she craved for company of some kind. There was a subtle kind of sympathy between her and the elder woman, probably based on the fact of their mutual dislike of the same person.

Christine said:

'I'm playing tennis at twelve, so we'd better start fairly early. Half past ten?'

'Right. I'll be ready. Meet you in the hall.'

III

Rosamund Darnley, strolling out of the dining room after a very late breakfast, was cannoned into by Linda as the latter came tearing down the stairs.

'Oh! sorry, Miss Darnley.'

Rosamund said: 'Lovely morning, isn't it? One can hardly believe it after yesterday.'

'I know. I'm going with Mrs Redfern to Gull Cove. I said I'd meet her at half past ten. I thought I was late.'

'No, it's only twenty-five past.'

'Oh! good.'

She was panting a little and Rosamund looked at her curiously.

'You're not feverish, are you, Linda?'

The girls' eyes were very bright and she had a vivid patch of colour in each cheek.

'Oh! *no*. I'm never feverish.'

Rosamund smiled and said:

'It's such a lovely day I got up for breakfast. Usually I have it in bed. But today I came down and faced eggs and bacon like a man.'

'I know—it's heavenly after yesterday. Gull Cove is nice in the morning. I shall put a lot of oil on and get really brown.'

Rosamund said:

'Yes, Gull Cove is nice in the morning. And it's more peaceful than the beach here.'

Linda said, rather shyly:

'Come too.'

Rosamund shook her head.

She said:

'Not this morning. I've other fish to fry.'

Christine Redfern came down the stairs.

She was wearing beach pyjamas of a loose floppy pattern with long sleeves and wide legs. They were made of some green material with a yellow design. Rosamund's tongue itched to tell her that yellow and green were the most unbecoming colours possible for her fair, slightly anaemic complexion. It always annoyed Rosamund when people had no clothes sense.

She thought: 'If I dressed that girl, *I'd* soon make her husband sit up and take notice. However much of a fool Arlena is, she does know how to dress. This wretched girl looks just like a wilting lettuce.'

Aloud she said:

'Have a nice time. I'm going to Sunny Ledge with a book.'

IV

Hercule Poirot breakfasted in his room as usual off coffee and rolls.

The beauty of the morning, however, tempted him to

Agatha Christie

leave the hotel earlier than usual. It was ten o'clock, at least half an hour before his usual appearance, when he descended to the bathing beach. The beach itself was empty save for one person.

That person was Arlena Marshall.

Clad in her white bathing dress, the green Chinese hat on her head, she was trying to launch a white wooden float. Poirot came gallantly to the rescue, completely immersing a pair of white suede shoes in doing so.

She thanked him with one of those sideways glances of hers.

Just as she was pushing off, she called him.

'M. Poirot?'

Poirot leaped to the water's edge.

'Madame.'

Arlena Marshall said:

'Do something for me, will you?'

'Anything.'

She smiled at him. She murmured:

'Don't tell anyone where I am.' She made her glance appealing. 'Everyone *will* follow me about so. I just want for once to be *alone*.'

She paddled off vigorously.

Poirot walked up the beach. He murmured to himself:

'*Ah ça, jamais!* That, *par exemple*, I do not believe.'

He doubted if Arlena Stuart, to give her her stage name, had ever wanted to be alone in her life.

Hercule Poirot, that man of the world, knew better.

Evil Under the Sun

Arlena Marshall was doubtless keeping a rendezvous, and Poirot had a very good idea with whom.

Or thought he had, but there he found himself proved wrong.

For just as she floated rounded the point of the bay and disappeared out of sight, Patrick Redfern, closely followed by Kenneth Marshall, came striding down the beach from the hotel.

Marshall nodded to Poirot, ' 'Morning, Poirot. Seen my wife anywhere about?'

Poirot's answer was diplomatic.

'Has Madame then risen so early?'

Marshall said:

'She's not in her room.' He looked up at the sky. 'Lovely day. I shall have a bathe right away. Got a lot of typing to do this morning.'

Patrick Redfern, less openly, was looking up and down the beach. He sat down near Poirot and prepared to wait for the arrival of his lady.

Poirot said:

'And Madame Redfern? Has she too risen early?'

Patrick Redfern said:

'Christine? Oh, she's going off sketching. She's rather keen on art just now.'

He spoke impatiently, his mind clearly elsewhere. As time passed he displayed his impatience for Arlena's arrival only too crudely. At every footstep he turned an eager head to see who it was coming down from the hotel.

Agatha Christie

Disappointment followed disappointment.

First Mr and Mrs Gardener complete with knitting and book and then Miss Brewster arrived.

Mrs Gardener, industrious as ever, settled herself in her chair, and began to knit vigorously and talk at the same time.

'Well. M. Poirot. The beach seems very deserted this morning. Where *is* everybody?'

Poirot replied that the Mastermans and the Cowans, two families with young people in them, had gone off on an all-day sailing excursion.

'Why, that certainly does make all the difference, not having them about laughing and calling out. And only one person bathing, Captain Marshall.'

Marshall had just finished his swim. He came up the beach swinging his towel.

'Pretty good in the sea this morning,' he said. 'Unfortunately I've got a lot of work to do. Must go and get on with it.'

'Why, if that isn't too bad, Captain Marshall. On a beautiful day like this, too. My, wasn't yesterday too terrible? I said to Mr Gardener that if the weather was going to continue like that we'd just have to leave. It's the melancholy, you know, with the mist right up around the island. Gives you a kind of ghosty feeling, but then I've always been very susceptible to atmosphere ever since I was a child. Sometimes, you know, I'd feel I just had to scream and scream. And that, of course, was very trying to my parents. But my mother was a lovely woman and she said to my father, "Sinclair, if the child feels like that, we must let her do it. Screaming is her way of expressing herself." And, of course, my father agreed. He was devoted to my mother and just did everything she said. They were a perfectly lovely couple, as I'm sure Mr Gardener will agree. They were a very remarkable couple, weren't they, Odell?'

'Yes, darling,' said Mr Gardener.

'And where's your girl this morning, Captain Marshall?'

'Linda? I don't know. I expect she's mooning round the island somewhere.'

'You know, Captain Marshall, that girl looks kind of peaky to me. She needs feeding up and very very sympathetic treatment.'

Kenneth Marshall said curtly:

'Linda's all right.'

He went up to the hotel.

Patrick Redfern did not go into the water. He sat about, frankly looking up towards the hotel. He was beginning to look a shade sulky.

Miss Brewster was brisk and cheerful when she arrived.

The conversation was much as it had been on a previous morning. Gentle yapping from Mrs Gardener and short staccato barks from Miss Brewster.

She remarked at last: 'Beach seems a bit empty. Everyone off on excursions?'

Mrs Gardener said:

'I was saying to Mr Gardener only this morning that we simply must make an excursion to Dartmoor. It's quite near and the associations are all so romantic. And I'd like to see that convict prison—Princetown, isn't it? I think we'd better fix up right away and go there tomorrow, Odell.'

Mr Gardener said:

'Yes, darling.'

Hercule Poirot said to Miss Brewster.

'You are going to bathe, Mademoiselle?'

'Oh, I've had my morning dip before breakfast. Somebody nearly brained me with a bottle, too. Chucked it out of one of the hotel windows.'

'Now that's a very dangerous thing to do,' said Mrs Gardener. 'I had a very dear friend who got concussion by a toothpaste tin falling on him in the street—thrown out of a thirty-fifth storey window it was. A most dangerous thing to do. He got very substantial damages.' She began to hunt among her skeins of wool. 'Why, Odell, I don't believe I've got that second shade of purple wool. It's in the second drawer of the bureau in our bedroom or it might be the third.'

'Yes, darling.'

Mr Gardener rose obediently and departed on his search.

Mrs Gardener went on:

'Sometimes, you know, I do think that maybe we're going a little too far nowadays. What with all our great discoveries and all the electrical waves there must be in the atmosphere, I do think it leads to a great deal of mental unrest, and I just feel that maybe the time has come for a new message to humanity. I don't know, M. Poirot, if you've ever interested yourself in the prophecies from the Pyramids.'

'I have not,' said Poirot.

'Well, I do assure you that they're very, very interesting. What with Moscow being exactly a thousand miles due north of—now what was it?—would it be Nineveh?—but anyway you take a circle and it just shows the most surprising things—and one can just see that there must have been special guidance, and that those ancient Egyptians couldn't have thought of what they did all by themselves. And when you've gone into the theory of the numbers and their repetition, why it's all just so clear that I can't see how anyone can doubt the truth of it for a moment.'

Mrs Gardener paused triumphantly but neither Poirot nor Miss Emily Brewster felt moved to argue the point.

Poirot studied his white suede shoes ruefully.

Emily Brewster said:

'You been paddling with your shoes on, M. Poirot?'

Poirot murmured:

'Alas! I was precipitate.'

Emily Brewster lowered her voice. She said:

'Where's our vamp this morning? She's late.'

Mrs Gardener, raising her eyes from her knitting to study Patrick Redfern, murmured:

'He looks just like a thundercloud. Oh dear, I do feel the whole thing is such a pity. I wonder what Captain Marshall thinks about it all. He's such a nice quiet man—very British and unassuming. You just never know what he's thinking about things.'

Patrick Redfern rose and began to pace up and down the beach.

Mrs Gardener murmured:

'Just like a tiger.'

Three pairs of eyes watched his pacing. Their scrutiny seemed to make Patrick Redfern uncomfortable. He looked more than sulky now. He looked in a flaming temper.

In the stillness a faint chime from the mainland came to their ears.

Emily Brewster murmured:

'Wind's from the east again. That's a good sign when you can hear the church clock strike.'

Nobody said any more until Mr Gardener returned with a skein of brilliant magenta wool.

'Why, Odell, what a long time you have been!'

'Sorry darling, but you see it wasn't in your bureau at all. I found it on your wardrobe shelf.'

'Why, isn't that too extraordinary? I could have declared I put it in that bureau drawer. I do think it's fortunate that I've never had to give evidence in a court case. I'd just worry myself to death in case I wasn't remembering a thing just right.'

Mr Gardener said:

'Mrs Gardener is very conscientious.'

V

It was some five minutes later that Patrick Redfern said:

'Going for your row this morning, Miss Brewster? Mind if I come with you?'

Miss Brewster said heartily:

'Delighted.'

'Let's row right round the island,' proposed Redfern.

Miss Brewster consulted her watch.

'Shall we have time? Oh yes, it's not half past eleven yet. Come on, then, let's start.'

They went down the beach together.

Patrick Redfern took first turn at the oars. He rowed with a powerful stroke. The boat leapt forward.

Emily Brewster said approvingly:

'Good. We'll see if you can keep that up.'

He laughed into her eyes. His spirits had improved.

'I shall probably have a fine crop of blisters by the time we get back.' He threw up his head, tossing back his black hair. 'God, it's a marvellous day! If you do get a real summer's day in England there's nothing to beat it.'

Emily Brewster said gruffly:

'Can't beat England anyway in my opinion. Only place in the world to live in.'

'I'm with you.'

They rounded the point of the bay to the west and rowed under the cliffs. Patrick Redfern looked up.

'Anyone on Sunny Ledge this morning? Yes, there's a sunshade. Who is it, I wonder?'

Emily Brewster said:

'It's Miss Darnley, I think. She's got one of those Japanese affairs.'

They rowed up the coast. On their left was the open sea.

Emily Brewster said:

'We ought to have gone the other way round. This way we've got the current against us.'

Agatha Christie

'There's very little current. I've swum out here and not noticed it. Anyway we couldn't go the other way, the causeway wouldn't be covered.'

'Depends on the tide, of course. But they always say that bathing from Pixy Cove is dangerous if you swim out too far.'

Patrick was rowing vigorously still. At the same time he was scanning the cliffs attentively.

Emily Brewster thought suddenly:

'He's looking for the Marshall woman. That's why he wanted to come with me. She hasn't shown up this morning and he's wondering what she's up to. Probably she's done it on purpose. Just a move in the game—to make him keener.'

They rounded the jutting point of rock to the south of the little bay named Pixy Cove. It was quite a small cove, with rocks dotted fantastically about the beach. It faced nearly north-west and the cliff overhung it a good deal. It was a favourite place for picnic teas. In the morning, when the sun was off it, it was not popular and there was seldom anyone there.

On this occasion, however, there was a figure on the beach.

Patrick Redfern's stroke checked and recovered.

He said in a would-be casual tone:

'Hullo, who's that?'

Miss Brewster said dryly:

'It looks like Mrs Marshall.'

Patrick Redfern said, as though struck by the idea:

72

'So it does.'

He altered his course, rowing inshore.

Emily Brewster protested.

'We don't want to land here, do we?'

Patrick Redfern said quickly:

'Oh, plenty of time.'

His eyes looked into hers—something in them, a naïve pleading look rather like that of an importunate dog, silenced Emily Brewster. She thought to herself:

'Poor boy, he's got it badly. Oh well, it can't be helped. He'll get over it in time.'

The boat was fast approaching the beach.

Arlena Marshall was lying face downwards on the shingle, her arms outstretched. The white float was drawn up nearby.

Something was puzzling Emily Brewster. It was as though she was looking at something she knew quite well but which was in one respect quite wrong.

It was a minute or two before it came to her.

Arlena Marshall's attitude was the attitude of a sunbather. So had she lain many a time on the beach by the hotel, her bronzed body outstretched and the green cardboard hat protecting her head and neck.

But there was no sun on Pixy's Beach and there would be none for some hours yet. The overhanging cliff protected the beach from the sun in the morning. A vague feeling of apprehension came over Emily Brewster.

The boat grounded on the shingle. Patrick Redfern called:

'Hullo, Arlena.'

Agatha Christie

And then Emily Brewster's foreboding took definite shape. For the recumbent figure did not move or answer.

Emily saw Patrick Redfern's face change. He jumped out of the boat and she followed him. They dragged the boat ashore then set off up the beach to where that white figure lay so still and unresponsive near the bottom of the cliff.

Patrick Redfern got there first but Emily Brewster was close behind him.

She saw, as one sees in a dream, the bronzed limbs, the white backless bathing dress—the red curl of hair escaping under the jade-green hat; saw something else too—the curious unnatural angle of the outspread arms. Felt, in that minute, that this body had not *lain* down but had been thrown...

She heard Patrick's voice—a mere frightened whisper. He knelt down beside that still form—touched the hand—the arm...

He said in a low shuddering whisper:

'My God, she's dead...'

And then, as he lifted the hat a little, peered at the neck:

'*Oh, God, she's been strangled... murdered.*'

VI

It was one of those moments when time stands still.

With an odd feeling of unreality Emily Brewster heard herself saying:

'We mustn't touch anything... Not until the police come.'

Redfern's answer came mechanically.

'No—no—of course not.' And then in a deep agonized whisper. 'Who? *Who?* Who could have done that to Arlena. She can't have—have been murdered. It can't be true!'

Emily Brewster shook her head, not knowing quite what to answer.

She heard him draw in his breath—heard the low controlled rage in his voice as he said:

'My God, if I get my hands on the foul fiend who did this.'

Emily Brewster shivered. Her imagination pictured a lurking murderer behind one of the boulders. Then she heard her voice saying:

'Whoever did it wouldn't be hanging about. We must get the police. Perhaps—' she hesitated—'one of us ought to stay with—with the body.'

Patrick Redfern said:

'I'll stay.'

Emily Brewster drew a little sigh of relief. She was not the kind of woman who would ever admit to feeling fear, but she was secretly thankful not to have to remain on that beach alone with the faint possibility of a homicidal maniac lingering close at hand.

She said:

'Good. I'll be as quick as I can. I'll go in the boat. Can't face that ladder. There's a constable at Leathercombe Bay.'

Patrick Redfern murmured mechanically:

'Yes—yes, whatever you think best.'

As she rowed vigorously away from the shore, Emily Brewster saw Patrick drop down beside the dead woman and bury his head in his hands. There was something so forlorn about his attitude that she felt an unwilling sympathy. He looked like a dog watching by its dead master. Nevertheless her robust common sense was saying to her:

'Best thing that could have happened for him and his wife—and for Marshall and the child—but I don't suppose *he* can see it that way, poor devil.'

Emily Brewster was a woman who could always rise to an emergency.

CHAPTER 5

Inspector Colgate stood back by the cliff waiting for the police surgeon to finish with Arlena's body. Patrick Redfern and Emily Brewster stood a little to one side.

Dr Neasdon rose from his knees with a quick deft movement.

He said:

'Strangled—and by a pretty powerful pair of hands. She doesn't seem to have put up much of a struggle. Taken by surprise. Hm—well—nasty business.'

Emily Brewster had taken one look and then quickly averted her eyes from the dead woman's face. That horrible purple convulsed countenance.

Inspector Colgate asked:

'What about time of death?'

Neasden said irritably:

'Can't say definitely without knowing more about her. Lots of factors to take into account. Let's see, it's quarter to one now. What time was it when you found her?'

Patrick Redfern, to whom the question was addressed, said vaguely:

'Some time before twelve. I don't know exactly.'

Emily Brewster said:

'It was exactly a quarter to twelve when we found she was dead.'

'Ah, and you came here in the boat. What time was it when you caught sight of her lying here?'

Emily Brewster considered.

'I should say we rounded the point about five or six minutes earlier.' She turned to Redfern. 'Do you agree?'

He said vaguely:

'Yes—yes—about that, I should think.'

Neasdon asked the Inspector in a low voice:

'This the husband? Oh! I see, my mistake. Thought it might be. He seems rather done in over it.'

He raised his voice officially.

'Let's put it at twenty minutes to twelve. She cannot have been killed very long before that. Say between then and eleven—quarter to eleven at the earliest outside limit.'

The Inspector shut his notebook with a snap.

'Thanks,' he said. 'That ought to help us considerably. Puts it within very narrow limits—less than an hour all told.'

He turned to Miss Brewster.

'Now then, I think it's all clear so far. You're Miss Emily Brewster and this is Mr Patrick Redfern, both staying at the Jolly Roger Hotel. You identify this lady as a fellow guest of yours at the hotel—the wife of a Captain Marshall?'

Emily Brewster nodded.

'Then, I think,' said Inspector Colgate, 'that we'll adjourn to the hotel.'

He beckoned to a constable.

'Hawkes, you stay here and don't allow anyone onto this cove. I'll be sending Phillips along later.'

II

'Upon my soul!' said Colonel Weston. 'This is a surprise finding you here!'

Hercule Poirot replied to the Chief Constable's greeting in a suitable manner. He murmured:

'Ah, yes, many years have passed since that affair at St Loo.'

'I haven't forgotten it, though,' said Weston. 'Biggest surprise of my life. The thing I've never got over, though, is the way you got round me about that funeral business. Absolutely unorthodox, the whole thing. Fantastic!'

'*Tout de même, mon Colonel*,' said Poirot. 'It produced the goods, did it not?'

'Er—well, possibly. I dare say we should have got there by more orthodox methods.'

'It is possible,' agreed Poirot diplomatically.

'And here you are in the thick of another murder,' said the Chief Constable. 'Any ideas about this one?'

Poirot said slowly:

'Nothing definite—but it is interesting.'

'Going to give us a hand?'

Agatha Christie

'You would permit it, yes?'

'My dear fellow, delighted to have you. Don't know enough yet to decide whether it's a case for Scotland Yard or not. Offhand it looks as though our murderer must be pretty well within a limited radius. On the other hand, all these people are strangers down here. To find out about them and their motives you've got to go to London.'

Poirot said:

'Yes, that is true.'

'First of all,' said Weston, 'we've got to find out who last saw the dead woman alive. Chambermaid took her her breakfast at nine. Girl in the bureau downstairs saw her pass through the lounge and go out about ten.'

'My friend,' said Poirot, 'I suspect that I am the man you want.'

'You saw her this morning? What time?'

'At five minutes past ten. I assisted her to launch her float from the bathing beach.'

'And she went off on it?'

'Yes.'

'Alone?'

'Yes.'

'Did you see which direction she took?'

'She paddled round that point there to the right.'

'In the direction of Pixy Cove, that is?'

'Yes.'

'And the time then was—?'

'I should say she actually left the beach at a quarter past ten.'

Weston considered.

'That fits in well enough. How long should you say that it would take her to paddle round to the Cove?'

'Ah me, I am not an expert. I do not go in boats or expose myself on floats. Perhaps half an hour?'

'That's about what I think,' said the Colonel. 'She wouldn't be hurrying, I presume. Well, if she arrived there at a quarter to eleven, that fits in well enough.'

'At what time does your doctor suggest she died?'

'Oh, Neasdon doesn't commit himself. He's a cautious chap. A quarter to eleven is his earliest outside limit.'

Poirot nodded. He said:

'There is one other point that I must mention. As she left, Mrs Marshall asked me not to say I had seen her.'

Weston stared.

He said:

'Hm, that's rather suggestive, isn't it?'

Poirot murmured.

'Yes. I thought so myself.'

Weston tugged at his moustache. He said:

'Look here, Poirot. You're a man of the world. What sort of a woman was Mrs Marshall?'

A faint smile came to Poirot's lips.

He asked:

'Have you not already heard?'

The Chief Constable said dryly:

'I know what the women say of her. They would. How much truth is there in it? *Was* she having an affair with this fellow Redfern?'

'I should say undoubtedly *yes*.'

'He followed her down here, eh?'

'There is reason to suppose so.'

'And the husband? Did he know about it? What did he feel?'

Poirot said slowly:

'It is not easy to know what Captain Marshall feels or thinks. He is a man who does not display his emotions.'

Weston said sharply:

'But he might have 'em, all the same.'

Poirot nodded. He said:

'Oh yes, he might have them.'

III

The Chief Constable was being as tactful as it was in his nature to be with Mrs Castle.

Mrs Castle was the owner and proprietress of the Jolly Roger Hotel. She was a woman of forty-odd with a large bust, rather violent henna red hair, and an almost offensively refined manner of speech.

She was saying:

'That such a thing should happen in my hotel! Ay am sure it has always been the quayettest place imaginable! The people who come here are such naice people. No *rowdiness*—if you know what ay mean. Not like the big hotels in St Loo.'

'Quite so, Mrs Castle,' said Colonel Weston. 'But accidents happen in the best regulated—er households.'

'Ay'm sure Inspector Colgate will bear me out,' said Mrs Castle, sending an appealing glance towards the Inspector, who was sitting looking very official. 'As to the laycensing laws, ay am *most* particular. There has never been *any* irregularity!'

'Quite, quite,' said Weston. 'We're not blaming you in any way, Mrs Castle.'

'But it does so reflect upon an establishment,' said Mrs Castle, her large bust heaving. 'When ay think of the noisy gaping crowds. Of course no one but hotel guests are allowed upon the island—but all the same they will no doubt come and *point* from the shore.'

She shuddered.

Inspector Colgate saw his chance to turn the conversation to good account.

He said:

'In regard to that point you've just raised. Access to the island. How do you keep people off?'

'Ay am *most* particular about it.'

'Yes, but what measures do you take? *What* keeps 'em off? Holiday crowds in summer time swarm everywhere like flies.'

Mrs Castle shuddered slightly again.

She said:

'That is the fault of the charabancs. Ay have seen eighteen at one time parked by the quay at Leathercombe Bay. Eighteen!'

Agatha Christie

'Just so. How do you stop them coming here?'

'There are notices. And then, of course, at high tide, we are cut off.'

'Yes, but at low tide?'

Mrs Castle explained. At the island end of the causeway there was a gate. This said 'Jolly Roger Hotel. Private. No entry except to Hotel.' The rocks rose sheer out of the sea on either side there and could not be climbed.

'Anyone could take a boat, though, I suppose, and row round and land on one of the coves? You couldn't stop them doing that. There's a right of access to the foreshore. You can't stop people being on the beach between low and high watermark.'

But this, it seemed, very seldom happened. Boats could be obtained at Leathercombe Bay harbour, but from there it was a long row to the island, and there was also a strong current just outside Leathercombe Bay harbour.

There were notices, too, on both Gull Cove and Pixy Cove by the ladder. She added that George or William were always on the look out at the bathing beach proper, which was the nearest to the mainland.

'Who are George and William?'

'George attends to the bathing beach. He sees to the costumes and the floats. William is the gardener. He keeps the paths and marks the tennis courts and all that.'

Colonel Weston said impatiently:

'Well, that seems clear enough. That's not to say that

nobody could have come from outside, but anyone who did so took a risk—the risk of being noticed. We'll have a word with George and William presently.'

Mrs Castle said:

'Ay do not care for trippers—a very noisy crowd, and they frequently leave orange peel and cigarette boxes on the causeway and down by the rocks, but all the same ay never thought one of them would turn out to be a murderer. Oh dear! it really is too terrible for words. A lady like Mrs Marshall murdered and what's so horrible, actually—er—strangled...'

Mrs Castle could hardly bring herself to say the word. She brought it out with the utmost reluctance.

Inspector Colgate said soothingly:

'Yes, it's a nasty business.'

'And the newspapers. *My* hotel in the newspapers!'

Colgate said, with a faint grin.

'Oh well, it's advertisement, in a way.'

Mrs Castle drew herself up. Her bust heaved and whalebone creaked. She said icily:

'That is not the kind of advertisement ay care about, Mr Colgate.'

Colonel Weston broke in. He said:

'Now then, Mrs Castle, you've got a list of the guests staying here, as I asked you?'

'Yes, sir.'

Colonel Weston pored over the hotel register. He looked over to Poirot, who made the fourth member of the group assembled in the manageress's office.

Agatha Christie

'This is where you'll probably be able to help us presently.'

He read down the names.

'What about servants?'

Mrs Castle produced a second list.

'There are four chambermaids, the head waiter and three under him and Henry in the bar. William does the boots and shoes. Then there's the cook and two under her.'

'What about the waiters?'

'Well, sir, Albert, the Mater Dotel, came to me from the Vincent at Plymouth. He was there for some years. The three under him have been here for three years—one of them four. They are very naice lads and most respectable. Henry has been here since the hotel opened. He is quite an institution.'

Weston nodded. He said to Colgate:

'Seems all right. You'll check up on them, of course. Thank you, Mrs Castle.'

'That will be all you require?'

'For the moment, yes.'

Mrs Castle creaked out of the room.

Weston said:

'First thing to do is to talk with Captain Marshall.'

IV

Kenneth Marshall sat quietly answering the questions put to him. Apart from a slight hardening of his features he was quite calm. Seen here, with the sunlight falling on him from the window, you realized that he was a handsome man. Those straight features, the steady blue eyes, the firm mouth. His voice was low and pleasant.

Colonel Weston was saying:

'I quite understand, Captain Marshall, what a terrible shock this must be to you. But you realize that I am anxious to get the fullest information as soon as possible.'

Marshall nodded.

He said:

'I quite understand. Carry on.'

'Mrs Marshall was your second wife?'

'Yes.'

'And you have been married how long?'

'Just over four years.'

'And her name before she was married?'

'Helen Stuart. Her acting name was Arlena Stuart.'

'She was an actress?'

'She appeared in revue and musical shows.'

'Did she give up the stage on her marriage?'

'No. She continued to appear. She actually retired only about a year and a half ago.'

'Was there any special reason for her retirement?'

Kenneth Marshall appeared to consider.

'No,' he said. 'She simply said that she was tired of it all.'

'It was not—er—in obedience to your special wish?'

Marshall raised his eyebrows.

'Oh, no.'

Agatha Christie

'You were quite content for her to continue acting after your marriage?'

Marshall smiled very faintly.

'I should have preferred her to give it up—that, yes. But I made no fuss about it.'

'It caused no point of dissension between you?'

'Certainly not. My wife was free to please herself.'

'And—the marriage was a happy one?'

Kenneth Marshall said coldly:

'Certainly.'

Colonel Weston paused a minute. Then he said:

'Captain Marshall, have you any idea who could possibly have killed your wife?'

The answer came without the least hesitation.

'None whatever.'

'Had she any enemies?'

'Possibly.'

'Ah?'

The other went on quickly. He said:

'Don't misunderstand me, sir. My wife was an actress. She was also a very good-looking woman. In both capacities she aroused a certain amount of envy and jealousy. There were fusses over parts—there was rivalry from other women—there was a good deal, shall we say, of general envy, hatred, malice, and all uncharitableness! But that is not to say that there was anyone who was capable of deliberately murdering her.'

Hercule Poirot spoke for the first time. He said:

Evil Under the Sun

'What you really mean, Monsieur, is that her enemies were mostly or entirely, *women*?'

Kenneth Marshall looked across at him.

'Yes,' he said. 'That is so.'

The Chief Constable said:

'You know of no man who had a grudge against her?'

'No.'

'Was she previously acquainted with anyone in this hotel?'

'I believe she had met Mr Redfern before—at some cocktail party. Nobody else to my knowledge.'

Weston paused. He seemed to deliberate as to whether to pursue the subject. Then he decided against that course. He said:

'We now come to this morning. When was the last time you saw your wife?'

Marshall paused a minute, then he said:

'I looked in on my way down to breakfast—'

'Excuse me, you occupied separate rooms?'

'Yes.'

'And what time was that?'

'It must have been about nine o'clock.'

'What was she doing?'

'She was opening her letters.'

'Did she say anything?'

'Nothing of any particular interest. Just good morning—and that it was a nice day—that sort of thing.'

'What was her manner? Unusual at all?'

Agatha Christie

'No, perfectly normal.'

'She did not seem excited, or depressed, or upset in any way?'

'I certainly didn't notice it.'

Hercule Poirot said:

'Did she mention at all what were the contents of her letters?'

Again a faint smile appeared on Marshall's lips. He said:

'As far as I can remember, she said they were all bills.'

'Your wife breakfasted in bed?'

'Yes.'

'Did she always do that?'

'Invariably.'

Hercule Poirot said:

'What time did she usually come downstairs?'

'Oh! between ten and eleven—usually nearer eleven.'

Poirot went on:

'If she was to descend at ten o'clock exactly, that would be rather surprising?'

'Yes. She wasn't often down as early as that.'

'But she was this morning. Why do you think that was, Captain Marshall?'

Marshall said unemotionally:

'Haven't the least idea. Might have been the weather—extra fine day and all that.'

'You missed her?'

Kenneth Marshall shifted a little in his chair. He said:

'Looked in on her again after breakfast. Room was empty. I was a bit surprised.'

'And then you came down on the beach and asked me if I had seen her?'

'Er—yes.' He added with a faint emphasis in his voice. 'And you said you hadn't...'

The innocent eyes of Hercule Poirot did not falter. Gently he caressed his large and flamboyant moustache.

Weston asked:

'Had you any special reason for wanting to find your wife this morning?'

Marshall shifted his glance amiably to the Chief Constable.

He said:

'No, just wondered where she was, that's all.'

Weston paused. He moved his chair slightly. His voice fell into a different key. He said:

'Just now, Captain Marshall, you mentioned that your wife had a previous acquaintance with Mr Patrick Redfern. How well did your wife know Mr Redfern?'

Kenneth Marshall said:

'Mind if I smoke?' He felt through his pockets. 'Dash! I've mislaid my pipe somewhere.'

Poirot offered him a cigarette which he accepted. Lighting it, he said:

'You were asking about Redfern. My wife told me she had come across him at some cocktail party or other.'

'He was, then, just a casual acquaintance?'

'I believe so.'

'Since then—' the Chief Constable paused. 'I understand that that acquaintanceship has ripened into something rather closer.'

Marshall said sharply:

'You understand that, do you? Who told you so?'

'It is the common gossip of the hotel.'

For a moment Marshall's eyes went to Hercule Poirot. They dwelt on him with a kind of cold anger. He said:

'Hotel gossip is usually a tissue of lies!'

'Possibly. But I gather that Mr Redfern and your wife gave some grounds for the gossip.'

'What grounds?'

'They were constantly in each other's company.'

'Is that all?'

'You do not deny that that was so?'

'May have been. I really didn't notice.'

'You did not—excuse me, Captain Marshall—object to your wife's friendship with Mr Redfern?'

'I wasn't in the habit of criticizing my wife's conduct.'

'You did not protest or object in any way?'

'Certainly not.'

'Not even though it was becoming a subject of scandal and an estrangement was growing up between Mr Redfern and his wife?'

Kenneth Marshall said coldly:

'I mind my own business and I expect other people to mind theirs. I don't listen to gossip and tittle tattle.'

'You won't deny that Mr Redfern admired your wife?'

'He probably did. Most men did. She was a very beautiful woman.'

'But you yourself were persuaded that there was nothing serious in the affair?'

'I never thought about it, I tell you.'

'And suppose we have a witness who can testify that they were on terms of the greatest intimacy?'

Again those blue eyes went to Hercule Poirot. Again an expression of dislike showed on that usually impassive face.

Marshall said:

'If you want to listen to these tales, listen to 'em. My wife's dead and can't defend herself.'

'You mean that you, personally, don't believe them?'

For the first time a faint dew of sweat was observable on Marshall's brow. He said:

'I don't propose to believe anything of the kind.'

He went on:

'Aren't you getting a good way from the essentials of this business? What I believe or don't believe is surely not relevant to the plain fact of murder?'

Hercule Poirot answered before either of the others could speak. He said:

'You do not comprehend, Captain Marshall. There is no such thing as a plain fact of murder. Murder springs, nine times out of ten, out of the character and circumstances of the murdered person. *Because* the victim was the kind of person he or she was, *therefore* was he or she murdered! Until we can understand fully and completely *exactly what kind of a person Arlena Marshall was*, we shall not be able to see clearly exactly *the kind of person who murdered her*. From that springs the necessity of our questions.'

Marshall turned to the Chief Constable. He said:

'That your view, too?'

Weston boggled a little. He said:

'Well, up to a point—that is to say—'

Marshall gave a short laugh. He said:

'Thought you wouldn't agree. This character stuff is M. Poirot's speciality, I believe.'

Poirot said, smiling:

'You can at least congratulate yourself on having done nothing to assist me!'

'What do you mean?'

'What have you told us about your wife? Exactly nothing at all. You have told us only what everyone could see for themselves. That she was beautiful and admired. Nothing more.'

Kenneth Marshall shrugged his shoulders. He said simply:

'You're crazy.'

He looked towards the Chief Constable and said with emphasis:

'Anything else, sir, that *you'd* like me to tell you?'

'Yes, Captain Marshall, your own movements this morning, please.'

Kenneth Marshall nodded. He had clearly expected this. He said:

'I breakfasted downstairs about nine o'clock as usual and read the paper. As I told you I went up to my wife's room afterwards and found she had gone out. I came down to the beach, saw M. Poirot and asked if he had seen her. Then I had a quick bathe and went up to the hotel again. It was then, let me see, about twenty to eleven—yes, just about that. I saw the clock in the lounge. It was just after twenty minutes to. I went up to my room, but the chambermaid hadn't quite finished it. I asked her to finish as quickly as she could. I had some letters to type which I wanted to get off by the post. I went downstairs again and had a word or two with Henry in the bar. I went up again to my room at ten minutes to eleven. There I typed my letters. I typed until ten minutes to twelve. I then changed into tennis kit as I had a date to play tennis at twelve. We'd booked the court the day before.'

'Who was we?'

'Mrs Redfern, Miss Darnley, Mr Gardener and myself. I came down at twelve o'clock and went up to the court. Miss Darnley was there and Mr Gardener. Mrs Redfern arrived a few minutes later. We played tennis for an hour. Just as we came into the hotel afterwards I—I—got the news.'

'Thank you, Captain Marshall. Just as a matter of form, is there anyone who can corroborate the fact that you were typing in your room between—er—ten minutes to eleven and ten minutes to twelve?'

Kenneth Marshall said with a faint smile:

'Have you got some idea that I killed my own wife? Let me see now. The chambermaid was about doing the rooms. She must have heard the typewriter going. And then there are the letters themselves. With all this upset I haven't posted them. I should imagine they are as good evidence as anything.'

He took three letters from his pocket. They were addressed, but not stamped. He said:

'Their contents, by the way, are strictly confidential. But when it's a case of murder, one is forced to trust in the discretion of the police. They contain lists of figures and various financial statements. I think you will find that if you put one of your men on to type them out, he won't do it in much under an hour.'

He paused.

'Satisfied, I hope?'

Weston said smoothly.

'It is no question of suspicion. Everyone on the island will be asked to account for his or her movements between a quarter to eleven and twenty minutes to twelve this morning.'

Kenneth Marshall said:

'Quite.'

Weston said:

'One more thing, Captain Marshall. Do you know anything about the way your wife was likely to have disposed of any property she had?'

'You mean a will? I don't think she ever made a will.'

'But you are not sure?'

'Her solicitors are Barkett, Markett & Applegood, Bedford Square. They saw to all her contracts, et cetera. But I'm fairly certain she never made a will. She said once that doing a thing like that would give her the shivers.'

'In that case, if she has died intestate, you, as her husband, succeed to her property.'

'Yes, I suppose I do.'

'Had she any near relatives?'

'I don't think so. If she had, she never mentioned them. I know that her father and mother died when she was a child and she had no brothers or sisters.'

'In any case, I suppose, she had nothing very much to leave?'

Kenneth Marshall said coldly:

'On the contrary. Only two years ago, Sir Robert Erskine, who was an old friend of hers, died and left her most of his fortune. It amounted, I think, to about fifty thousand pounds.'

Inspector Colgate looked up. An alertness came into his glance. Up to now he had been silent. Now he asked:

'Then actually, Captain Marshall, your wife was a rich woman?'

Kenneth Marshall shrugged his shoulders.

'I suppose she was really.'

'And you still say she did not make a will?'

'You can ask the solicitors. But I'm pretty certain she didn't. As I tell you, she thought it unlucky.'

There was a pause then Marshall added:

'Is there anything further?'

Weston shook his head.

'Don't think so—eh Colgate? No. Once more, Captain Marshall, let me offer you all my sympathy in your loss.'

Marshall blinked. He said jerkily:

'Oh—thanks.'
He went out.

V

The three men looked at each other.

Weston said:

'Cool customer. Not giving anything away, is he? What do you make of him, Colgate?'

The Inspector shook his head.

'It's difficult to tell. He's not the kind that shows anything. That sort makes a bad impression in the witness box, and yet it's a bit unfair on them really. Sometimes they're as cut up as anything and yet can't show it. That kind of manner made the jury bring in a verdict of Guilty against Wallace. It wasn't the evidence. They just couldn't believe that a man could lose his wife and talk and act so coolly about it.'

Weston turned to Poirot.

'What do you think, Poirot?'

Hercule Poirot raised his hands.

He said:

'What can one say? He is the closed box—the fastened oyster. He has chosen his role. He has heard nothing, he has seen nothing, he knows nothing!'

'We've got a choice of motives,' said Colgate. 'There's jealousy and there's the money motive. Of course, in a way, a husband's the obvious suspect. One naturally thinks of him first. If he knew his missus was carrying on with the other chap—'

Poirot interrupted.

He said:

'I think he knew that.'

'Why do you say so?'

'Listen, my friend. Last night I had been talking with Mrs Redfern on Sunny Ledge. I came down from there to the hotel and on my way I saw those two together—Mrs Marshall and Patrick Redfern. And a moment or two after I met Captain Marshall. His face was very stiff. It says nothing—but nothing at all! It is almost *too* blank, if you understand me. Oh! he knew all right.'

Colgate grunted doubtfully.

He said:

'Oh well, if you think so—'

'I am sure of it! But even then, what does that tell us? What did Kenneth Marshall *feel* about his wife?'

Colonel Weston said:

'Takes her death coolly enough.'

Poirot shook his head in a dissatisfied manner.

Inspector Colgate said:

'Sometimes these quiet ones are the most violent underneath, so to speak. It's all bottled up. He may have been madly fond of her—and madly jealous. But he's not the kind to show it.'

Poirot said slowly:

'That is possible—yes. He is a very interesting character

this Captain Marshall. I interest myself in him greatly. And in his alibi.'

'Alibi by typewriter,' said Weston with a short bark of a laugh. 'What have you got to say about that, Colgate?'

Inspector Colgate screwed up his eyes. He said:

'Well, you know, sir, I rather fancy that alibi. It's not too good, if you know what I mean. It's—well, it's *natural*. And if we find the chambermaid was about, and did hear the typewriter going, well then, it seems to me that it's all right and that we'll have to look elsewhere.'

'Hm,' said Colonel Weston. 'Where are you going to look?'

VI

For a minute or two the three men pondered the question.

Inspector Colgate spoke first. He said:

'It boils down to this—was it an outsider, or a guest at the hotel? I'm not eliminating the servants entirely, mind, but I don't expect for a minute that we'll find any of them had a hand in it. No, it's a hotel guest, or it's someone from right outside. We've got to look at it this way. First of all—motive. There's gain. The only person to gain by her death was the lady's husband, it seems. What other motives are there? First and foremost—jealousy. It seems to me—just looking at it—that if ever you've got a *crime passionnel*—'he bowed to Poirot—'this is one.'

Poirot murmured as he looked up at the ceiling:

'There are so many passions.'

Inspector Colgate went on:

'Her husband wouldn't allow that she had any enemies—real enemies, that is, but I don't believe for a minute that that's so! I should say that a lady like her would—well, would make some pretty bad enemies—eh, sir, what do you say?'

Poirot responded. He said:

'*Mais oui*, that is so. Arlena Marshall would make enemies. But in my opinion, the enemy theory is not tenable, for you see, Inspector, Arlena Marshall's enemies would, I think, as I said just now, always be *women*.'

Colonel Weston grunted and said:

'Something in that. It's the women who've got their knife into her here all right.'

Poirot went on.

'It seems to be hardly possible that this crime was committed by a woman. What does the medical evidence say?'

Weston grunted again. He said:

'Neasdon's pretty confident that she was strangled by a man. Big hands—powerful grip. It's just possible, of course, that an unusually athletic woman might have done it—but it's damned unlikely.'

Poirot nodded.

'Exactly. Arsenic in a cup of tea—a box of poisoned chocolates—a knife—even a pistol—but strangulation—no! It is a man we have to look for.'

'And immediately,' he went on, 'it becomes more difficult. There are two people here in this hotel who have a motive for wishing Arlena Marshall out of the way—but both of them are women.'

Colonel Weston asked:

'Redfern's wife is one of them, I suppose?'

'Yes. Mrs Redfern might have made up her mind to kill Arlena Stuart. She had, let us say, ample cause. I think, too, that it would be possible for Mrs Redfern to commit a murder. But not this kind of murder. For all her unhappiness and jealousy, she is not, I should say, a woman of strong passions. In love, she would be devoted and loyal—not passionate. As I said just now—arsenic in the teacup, possibly—strangulation, no. I am sure, also, that she is physically incapable of committing this crime—her hands and feet are small, below the average.'

Weston nodded. He said:

'This isn't a woman's crime. No, a man did this.'

Inspector Colgate coughed.

'Let me put forward a solution, sir. Say that prior to meeting this Mr Redfern the lady had had another affair with someone—call him X. She turns X down for Mr Redfern. X is mad with rage and jealousy. He follows her down here, stays somewhere in the neighbourhood, comes over to the island and does her in. It's a possibility!'

Weston said:

'It's *possible*, all right. And if it's true, it ought to be easy to prove. Did he come on foot or in a boat? The latter seems more likely. If so, he must have hired a boat somewhere. You'd better make enquiries.'

He looked across at Poirot.

'What do you think of Colgate's suggestion?'
Poirot said slowly:
'It leaves, somehow, too much to chance. And besides—somewhere the picture is not true. I cannot, you see, imagine this man... the man who is mad with rage and jealousy.'
Colgate said:
'People *did* go potty about her, though, sir. Look at Redfern.'
'Yes, yes... But all the same—'
Colgate looked at him questioningly.
Poirot shook his head.
He said, frowning:
'Somewhere, there is something that we have missed...'

CHAPTER 6

Colonel Weston was poring over the hotel register.
He read aloud:

'Major and Mrs Cowan,
Miss Pamela Cowan,
Master Robert Cowan,
Master Evan Cowan,
   Rydal's Mount, Leatherhead.
Mr and Mrs Masterman,
Mr Edward Masterman,
Miss Jennifer Masterman,
Mr Roy Masterman,
Master Frederick Masterman,
   5 Marlborough Avenue, London, NW.
Mr and Mrs Gardener,
   New York.
Mr and Mrs Redfern,
   Crossgates, Seldon, Princes Risborough.

Major Barry,
   18 Cardon St., St James, London, SW1.
Mr Horace Blatt,
   5 Pickersgill Street, London, EC2.
M. Hercule Poirot,
   Whitehaven Mansions, London, W1.
Miss Rosamund Darnley,
   8 Cardigan Court, W1.
Miss Emily Brewster,
   Southgates, Sunbury-on-Thames.
Rev. Stephen Lane,
   London.
Captain and Mrs Marshall,
Miss Linda Marshall,
   73 Upcott Mansions, London, SW7.'

He stopped.
Inspector Colgate said:
'I think, sir, that we can wash out the first two entries. Mrs Castle tells me that the Mastermans and the Cowans come here regularly every summer with their children. This morning they went off on an all-day excursion sailing, taking lunch with them. They left just after nine o'clock. A man called Andrew Baston took them. We can check up from him, but I think we can put them right out of it.'
Weston nodded.
'I agree. Let's eliminate everyone we can. Can you give us a pointer on any of the rest of them, Poirot?'
Poirot said:

'Superficially, that is easy. The Gardeners are a middle-aged married couple, pleasant, travelled. All the talking is done by the lady. The husband is acquiescent. He plays tennis and golf and has a form of dry humour that is attractive when one gets him to oneself.'

'Sounds quite OK.'

'Next—the Redferns. Mr Redfern is young, attractive to women, a magnificent swimmer, a good tennis player and accomplished dancer. His wife I have already spoken of to you. She is quiet, pretty in a washed-out way. She is, I think, devoted to her husband. She has something that Arlena Marshall did not have.'

'What is that?'

'Brains.'

Inspector Colgate sighed. He said:

'Brains don't count for much when it comes to an infatuation, sir.'

'Perhaps not. And yet I do truly believe that in spite of his infatuation for Mrs Marshall, Patrick Redfern really cares for his wife.'

'That may be, sir. It wouldn't be the first time that's happened.'

Poirot murmured.

'That is the pity of it! It is always the thing women find hardest to believe.'

He went on:

'Major Barry. Retired Indian Army. An admirer of women. A teller of long and boring stories.'

Inspector Colgate sighed.

'You needn't go on. I've met a few, sir.'

'Mr Horace Blatt. He is, apparently, a rich man. He talks a good deal—about Mr Blatt. He wants to be everybody's friend. It is sad. For nobody likes him very much. And there is something else. Mr Blatt last night asked me a good many questions. Mr Blatt was uneasy. Yes, there is something not quite right about Mr Blatt.'

He paused and went on with a change of voice:

'Next comes Miss Rosamund Darnley. Her business name is Rose Mond Ltd. She is a celebrated dressmaker. What can I say of her? She has brains and charm and chic. She is very pleasing to look at.' He paused and added. 'And she is a very old friend of Captain Marshall's.'

Weston sat up in his chair.

'Oh, she is, is she?'

'Yes. They had not met for some years.'

Weston asked:

'Did she know he was going to be down here?'

'She says not.'

Poirot paused and then went on.

'Who comes next? Miss Brewster. I find her just a little alarming.' He shook his head. 'She has a voice like a man's. She is gruff and what you call hearty. She rows boats and has a handicap of four at golf.' He paused. 'I think, though, that she has a good heart.'

Weston said:

'That leaves only the Reverend Stephen Lane. Who's the Reverend Stephen Lane?'

'I can only tell you one thing. He is a man who is in a

Agatha Christie

condition of great nervous tension. Also he is, I think, a fanatic.'

Inspector Colgate said:

'Oh, that kind of person.'

Weston said:

'And that's the lot!' He looked at Poirot. 'You seem very lost in thought, my friend?'

Poirot said:

'Yes. Because, you see, when Mrs Marshall went off this morning and asked me not to tell anyone I had seen her, I jumped at once in my own mind to a certain conclusion. I thought that her friendship with Patrick Redfern had made trouble between her and her husband. I thought that she was going to meet Patrick Redfern somewhere, and that she did not want her husband to know where she was.'

He paused.

'But that, you see, was where I was wrong. Because, although her husband appeared almost immediately on the beach and asked if I had seen her, Patrick Redfern arrived also—and was most patently and obviously looking for her! And therefore, my friends, I am asking myself, *who was it that Arlena Marshall went off to meet?*'

Inspector Colgate said:

'That fits in with *my* idea. A man from London or somewhere.'

Hercule Poirot shook his head. He said:

'But, my friend, according to your theory, Arlena Marshall had broken with this mythical man. Why, then, should she take such trouble and pains to meet him?'

Inspector Colgate shook his head. He said:

'Who do *you* think it was?'

'That is just what I cannot imagine. We have just read through the list of hotel guests. They are all middle-aged—dull. Which of them would Arlena Marshall prefer to Patrick Redfern? No, that is impossible. And yet, all the same, she *did* go to meet someone—and that someone was not Patrick Redfern.'

Weston murmured:

'You don't think she just went off by herself?'

Poirot shook his head.

'*Mon cher*,' he said. 'It is very evident that you never met the dead woman. Somebody once wrote a learned treatise on the difference that solitary confinement would mean to Beau Brummel or to a man like Newton. Arlena Marshall, my dear friend, would practically not exist in solitude. She only lived in the light of a man's admiration. No, Arlena Marshall went to meet *someone* this morning. *Who was it?*'

II

Colonel Weston sighed, shook his head and said:

'Well, we can go into theories later. Got to get through these interviews now. Got to get it down in black and white where everyone was. I suppose we'd better see the Marshall girl now. She might be able to tell us something useful.'

Linda Marshall came into the room clumsily, knocking against the doorpost. She was breathing quickly and the pupils of her eyes were dilated. She looked like a startled young colt. Colonel Weston felt a kindly impulse towards her.

He thought:

'Poor kid—she's nothing but a kid after all. This must have been a pretty bad shock to her.'

He drew up a chair and said in a reassuring voice.

'Sorry to put you through this, Miss—Linda, isn't it?'

'Yes, Linda.'

Her voice had that indrawn breathy quality that is often characteristic of schoolgirls. Her hands rested helplessly on the table in front of him—pathetic hands, big and red, with large bones and long wrists. Weston thought:

'A kid oughtn't to be mixed up in this sort of thing.'

He said reassuringly:

'There's nothing very alarming about all this. We just want you to tell us anything you know that might be useful, that's all.'

Linda said:

'You mean—about Arlena?'

'Yes. Did you see her this morning at all?'

The girl shook her head.

'No. Arlena always gets down rather late. She has breakfast in bed.'

Hercule Poirot said:

'And you, Mademoiselle?'

'Oh, I get up. Breakfast in bed's so *stuffy*.'

Weston said:

'Will you tell us what you did this morning?'

'Well, I had a bathe first and then breakfast, and then I went with Mrs Redfern to Gull Cove.'

Weston said:

'What time did you and Mrs Redfern start?'

'She said she'd be waiting for me in the hall at half past ten. I was afraid I was going to be late, but it was all right. We started off at about three minutes to the half-hour.'

Poirot said:

'And what did you do at Gull Cove?'

'Oh, I oiled myself and sunbathed and Mrs Redfern sketched. Then, later, I went into the sea and Christine went back to the hotel to get changed for tennis.'

Weston said, keeping his voice quite casual:

'Do you remember what time that was?'

'When Mrs Redfern went back to the hotel? Quarter to twelve.'

'Sure of that time—quarter to twelve?'

Linda, opening her eyes wide, said:

'Oh *yes*. I looked at my watch.'

'The watch you have on now?'

Linda glanced down at her wrist.

'Yes.'

Weston said:

'Mind if I see?'

She held out her wrist. He compared the watch with his own and with the hotel clock on the wall.

He said, smiling:

'Correct to a second. And after that you had a bathe?'

'Yes.'

Agatha Christie

'And you got back to the hotel—when?'

'Just about one o'clock. And—and then—I heard—about Arlena...'

Her voice changed.

Colonel Weston said:

'Did you—er—get on with your stepmother all right?'

She looked at him for a minute without replying. Then she said:

'Oh yes.'

Poirot asked:

'Did you like her, Mademoiselle?'

Linda said again:

'Oh yes.' She added: 'Arlena was quite kind to me.'

Weston said with rather uneasy facetiousness.

'Not the cruel stepmother, eh?'

Linda shook her head without smiling.

Weston said:

'That's good. That's good. Sometimes, you know, there's a bit of difficulty in families—jealousy—all that. Girl and her father great pals and then she resents it a bit when he's all wrapped up in the new wife. You didn't feel like that, eh?'

Linda stared at him. She said with obvious sincerity:

'Oh no.'

Weston said:

'I suppose your father was—er—very wrapped up in her?'

Linda said simply:

'I don't know.'

Weston went on:

'All sorts of difficulties, as I say, arise in families. Quarrels—rows—that sort of thing. If husband and wife get ratty with each other, that's a bit awkward for a daughter too. Anything of that sort?'

Linda said clearly:

'Do you mean, did Father and Arlena quarrel?'

'Well—yes.'

Weston thought to himself:

'Rotten business—questioning a child about her father. Why is one a policeman? Damn it all, it's got to be done, though.'

Linda said positively:

'Oh no.' She added: 'Father doesn't quarrel with people. He's not like that at all.'

Weston said:

'Now, Miss Linda, I want you to think very carefully. Have you any idea at all who might have killed your stepmother? Is there anything you've ever heard or anything you know that could help us on that point?'

Linda was silent a minute. She seemed to be giving the question a serious unhurried consideration. She said at last:

'No, I don't know who could have wanted to kill Arlena.' She added: 'Except, of course, Mrs Redfern.'

Weston said:

'You think Mrs Redfern wanted to kill her? Why?'

Linda said:

'Because her husband was in love with Arlena. But I don't think she would really want to *kill* her. I mean she'd just feel that she wished she was dead—and that isn't the same thing at all, is it?'

Poirot said gently:

'No, it is not at all the same.'

Linda nodded. A queer sort of spasm passed across her face. She said:

'And anyway, Mrs Redfern could never do a thing like that—kill anybody. She isn't—she isn't *violent*, if you know what I mean.'

Weston and Poirot nodded. The latter said:

'I know exactly what you mean, my child, and I agree with you. Mrs Redfern is not of those who, as your saying goes, "sees red". She would not be'—he leaned back half-closing his eyes, picking his words with care—'shaken by a storm of feeling—seeing life narrowing in front of her—seeing a hated face—a hated white neck—feeling her hands clench—longing to feel them press into flesh—'

He stopped.

Linda moved jerkily back from the table. She said in a trembling voice:

'Can I go now? Is that all?'

Colonel Weston said:

'Yes, yes, that's all. Thank you, Miss Linda.'

He got up to open the door for her, then came back to the table and lit a cigarette.

'Phew,' he said. 'Not a nice job, ours. I can tell you I felt a bit of a cad questioning that child about the relations between her father and her stepmother. More or less inviting a daughter to put a rope round her father's neck. All the same, it had to be done. Murder is murder. And she's the person most likely to know the truth of things. I'm rather thankful, though, that she'd nothing to tell us in that line.'

Poirot said:

'Yes, I thought you were.'

Weston said with an embarrassed cough:

'By the way, Poirot, you went a bit far, I thought at the end. All that hands sinking into flesh business! Not quite the sort of idea to put into a kid's head.'

Hercule Poirot looked at him with thoughtful eyes. He said:

'So you thought I put ideas into her head?'

'Well, didn't you? Come now.'

Poirot shook his head.

Weston sheered away from the point. He said:

'On the whole we got very little useful stuff out of her. Except a more or less complete alibi for the Redfern woman. If they were together from half past ten to a quarter to twelve that lets Christine Redfern out of it. Exit the jealous wife suspect.'

Poirot said:

'There are better reasons than that for leaving Mrs Redfern out of it. It would, I am convinced, be physically impossible and mentally impossible for her to strangle anyone. She is cold rather than warm blooded, capable of deep devotion and unswerving constancy, but not of hot-blooded passion or rage. Moreover, her hands are far too small and delicate.'

Colgate said:

Agatha Christie

'I agree with M. Poirot. She's out of it. Dr Neasdon says it was a full-sized pair of hands that throttled that dame.'

Weston said:

'Well, I suppose we'd better see the Redferns next. I expect he's recovered a bit from the shock now.'

III

Patrick Redfern had recovered full composure by now. He looked pale and haggard and suddenly very young, but his manner was quite composed.

'You are Mr Patrick Redfern of Crossgates, Seldon, Princes Risborough?'

'Yes.'

'How long had you known Mrs Marshall?'

Patrick Redfern hesitated, then said:

'Three months.'

Weston went on:

'Captain Marshall has told us that you and she met casually at a cocktail party. Is that right?'

'Yes, that's how it came about.'

Weston said:

'Captain Marshall has implied that until you both met down here you did not know each other well. Is that the truth, Mr Redfern?'

Again Patrick Redfern hesitated a minute. Then he said:

'Well—not exactly. As a matter of fact I saw a fair amount of her one way and another.'

'Without Captain Marshall's knowledge?'

Redfern flushed slightly. He said:

'I don't know whether he knew about it or not.'

Hercule Poirot spoke. He murmured:

'And was it also without your wife's knowledge, Mr Redfern?'

'I believe I mentioned to my wife that I had met the famous Arlena Stuart.'

Poirot persisted.

'But she did not know how often you were seeing her?'

'Well, perhaps not.'

Weston said:

'Did you and Mrs Marshall arrange to meet down here?'

Redfern was silent a minute or two. Then he shrugged his shoulders.

'Oh well,' he said, 'I suppose it's bound to come out now. It's no good my fencing with you. I was crazy about the woman—mad—infatuated—anything you like. She wanted me to come down here. I demurred a bit and then I agreed. I—I—well, I would have agreed to do any mortal thing she liked. She had that kind of effect on people.'

Hercule Poirot murmured:

'You paint a very clear picture of her. She was the eternal Circe. Just that!'

Patrick Redfern said bitterly:

'She turned men into swine all right!' He went on: 'I'm being frank with you, gentlemen. I'm not going to hide anything. What's the use? As I say, I was infatuated with her. Whether she cared for me or not, I don't know. She pretended to, but I think she was one of those women who lose interest in a man once they've got him body and soul. She knew she'd got me all right. This morning, when I found her there on the beach, dead, it was as though'—he paused—'as though something had hit me straight between the eyes. I was dazed—knocked out!'

Poirot leaned forward. 'And now?'

Patrick Redfern met his eyes squarely.

He said:

'I've told you the truth. What I want to ask is this—*how much of it has got to be made public*? It's not as though it could have any bearing on her death. And if it all comes out, it's going to be pretty rough on my wife.

'Oh, I know,' he went on quickly. 'You think I haven't thought much about her up to now? Perhaps that's true. But, though I may sound the worst kind of hypocrite, the real truth is that I care for my wife—care for her very deeply. The other'—he twitched his shoulders—'it was a madness—the kind of idiotic fool thing men do— but Christine is different. She's *real*. Badly as I've treated her, I've known all along, deep down, that she was the person who really counted.' He paused—sighed—and said rather pathetically: 'I wish I could make you believe that.'

Hercule Poirot leant forward. He said:

'But I do believe it. Yes, yes, I do believe it!'

Patrick Redfern looked at him gratefully. He said:

'Thank you.'

Colonel Weston cleared his throat. He said:

'You may take it, Mr Redfern, that we shall not go into

irrelevancies. If your infatuation for Mrs Marshall played no part in the murder then there will be no point in dragging it into the case. But what you don't seem to realize is that that—er—intimacy—may have a very direct bearing on the murder. It might establish, you understand, a *motive* for the crime.'

Patrick Redfern said:

'Motive?'

Weston said:

'Yes, Mr Redfern, *motive!* Captain Marshall, perhaps, was unaware of the affair. Suppose that he suddenly found out?'

Redfern said:

'Oh God! You mean he got wise and—and killed her?'

The Chief Constable said rather dryly:

'That solution had not occurred to you?'

Redfern shook his head. He said:

'No—funny. I never thought of it. You see, Marshall's such a quiet chap. I—oh, it doesn't seem likely.'

Weston asked:

'What was Mrs Marshall's attitude to her husband in all this? Was she—well, uneasy—in case it should come to his ears? Or was she indifferent?'

Redfern said slowly:

'She was—a bit nervous. She didn't want him to suspect anything.'

'Did she seem afraid of him?'

'Afraid. No, I wouldn't say that.'

Poirot murmured:

'Excuse me, M. Redfern, there was not, at any time, the question of a divorce?'

Patrick Redfern shook his head decisively.

'Oh no, there was no question of anything like that. There was Christine, you see. And Arlena, I am sure, never thought of such a thing. She was perfectly satisfied married to Marshall. He's—well, rather a big bug in his way—' He smiled suddenly. 'County—all that sort of thing, and quite well off. She never thought of me as a possible *husband*. No, I was just one of a succession of poor mutts—just something to pass the time with. I knew that all along, and yet, queerly enough, it didn't alter my feeling towards her...'

His voice trailed off. He sat there thinking.

Weston recalled him to the needs of the moment.

'Now, Mr Redfern, had you any particular appointment with Mrs Marshall this morning?'

Patrick Redfern looked slightly puzzled.

He said:

'Not a particular appointment, no. We usually met every morning on the beach. We used to paddle about on floats.'

'Were you surprised not to find Mrs Marshall there this morning?'

'Yes, I was. Very surprised. I couldn't understand it at all.'

'What did you think?'

'Well, I didn't know what to think. I mean, all the time I thought she would be coming.'

'If she were keeping an appointment elsewhere you had no idea with whom that appointment might be?'

Patrick Redfern merely stared and shook his head.

'When you had a rendezvous with Mrs Marshall, where did you meet?'

'Well, sometimes I'd meet her in the afternoon down at Gull Cove. You see the sun is off Gull Cove in the afternoon and so there aren't usually many people there. We met there once or twice.'

'Never on the other cove?' Pixy Cove?'

'No. You see Pixy Cove faces west and people go round there in boats or on floats in the afternoon. We never tried to meet in the morning. It would have been too noticeable. In the afternoon people go and have a sleep or mooch around and nobody knows much where anyone else is.'

Weston nodded:

Patrick Redfern went on:

'After dinner, of course, on the fine nights, we used to go off for a stroll together to different parts of the island.'

Hercule Poirot murmured:

'Ah, yes!' and Patrick Redfern shot him an inquiring glance.

Weston said:

'Then you can give us no help whatsoever as to the cause that took Mrs Marshall to Pixy Cove this morning?'

Redfern shook his head. He said, and his voice sounded honestly bewildered:

'I haven't the faintest idea! It wasn't like Arlena.'

Weston said:

'Had she any friends down here staying in the neighbourhood?'

'Not that I know of. Oh, I'm sure she hadn't.'

'Now, Mr Redfern, I want you to think very carefully. You knew Mrs Marshall in London. You must be acquainted with various members of her circle. Is there anyone you know of who could have had a grudge against her? Someone, for instance, whom you may have supplanted in her fancy?'

Patrick Redfern thought for some minutes. Then he shook his head.

'Honestly,' he said. 'I can't think of anyone.'

Colonel Weston drummed with his fingers on the table. He said at last:

'Well, that's that. We seem to be left with three possibilities. That of an unknown killer—some monomaniac—who happened to be in the neighbourhood—and that's a pretty tall order—'

Redfern said, interrupting:

'And yet surely, it's by far the most likely explanation.'

Weston shook his head. He said:

'This isn't one of the "lonely copse" murders. This cove place was pretty inaccessible. Either the man would have to come up from the causeway past the hotel, over the top of the island and down by that ladder contraption, or else he came there by boat. Either way is unlikely for a casual killing.'

Patrick Redfern said:

'You said there were three possibilities.'

'Um—yes,' said the Chief Constable. 'That's to say, there were two people on this island who had a motive for killing her. Her husband, for one, and your wife for another.'

Redfern stared at him. He looked dumbfounded. He said:

'My wife? Christine? D'you mean that *Christine* had anything to do with this?'

He got up and stood there stammering slightly in his incoherent haste to get the words out.

'You're mad—quite mad—Christine? Why, it's *impossible*. It's laughable!'

Weston said:

'All the same, Mr Redfern, jealousy is a very powerful motive. Women who are jealous lose control of themselves completely.'

Redfern said earnestly.

'Not Christine. She's—oh she's not like that. She was unhappy, yes. But she's not the kind of person to—Oh, there's no violence in her.'

Hercule Poirot nodded thoughtfully. Violence. The same word that Linda Marshall had used. As before, he agreed with the sentiment.

'Besides,' went on Redfern confidently. 'It would be absurd. Arlena was twice as strong physically as Christine. I doubt if Christine could strangle a kitten—certainly not a strong wiry creature like Arlena. And then Christine could never have got down that ladder to the beach. She has no head for that sort of thing. And—oh, the whole thing is fantastic!'

Colonel Weston scratched his ear tentatively.

'Well,' he said. 'Put like that it doesn't seem likely. I grant you that. But motive's the first thing we've got to look for.' He added: 'Motive and opportunity.'

IV

When Redfern had left the room, the Chief Constable observed with a slight smile:

'Didn't think it necessary to tell the fellow his wife had got an alibi. Wanted to hear what he'd have to say to the idea. Shook him up a bit, didn't it?'

Hercule Poirot murmured:

'The arguments he advanced were quite as strong as any alibi.'

'Yes. Oh! she didn't do it! She couldn't have done it—physically impossible as you said. Marshall *could* have done it—but apparently he didn't.'

Inspector Colgate coughed. He said:

'Excuse me, sir, I've been thinking about that alibi. It's possible, you know, if he'd thought this thing out, that those letters were got ready *beforehand*.'

Weston said:

'That's a good idea. We must look into—'

He broke off as Christine Redfern entered the room.

She was, as always, calm and a little precise in manner. She was wearing a white tennis frock and a pale blue pullover. It accentuated her fair, rather anaemic prettiness. Yet, Hercule Poirot thought to himself, it was neither a silly face nor a weak one. It had plenty of resolution, courage and good sense. He nodded appreciatively.

Colonel Weston thought:

'Nice little woman. Bit wishy-washy, perhaps. A lot too good for that philandering young ass of a husband of hers.

Oh well, the boy's young. Women usually make a fool of you once!'

He said:

'Sit down, Mrs Redfern. We've got to go through a certain amount of routine, you see. Asking everybody for an account of their movements this morning. Just for our records.'

Christine Redfern nodded.

She said in her quiet precise voice.

'Oh yes, I quite understand. Where do you want me to begin?'

Hercule Poirot said:

'As early as possible, Madame. What did you do when you first got up this morning?'

Christine said:

'Let me see. On my way down to breakfast I went into Linda Marshall's room and fixed up with her to go to Gull Cove this morning. We agreed to meet in the lounge at half past ten.'

Poirot asked:

'You did not bathe before breakfast, Madame?'

'No. I very seldom do.' She smiled. 'I like the sea well warmed before I get into it. I'm rather a chilly person.'

'But your husband bathes then?'

'Oh, yes. Nearly always.'

'And Mrs Marshall, she also?'

A change came over Christine's voice. It became cold and almost acrid.

She said:

'Oh no, Mrs Marshall was the sort of person who never made an appearance before the middle of the morning.'

With an air of confusion, Hercule Poirot said:

'Pardon, Madame, I interrupted you. You were saying that you went to Miss Linda Marshall's room. What time was that?'

'Let me see—half past eight—no, a little later.'

'And was Miss Marshall up then?'

'Oh yes, she had been out.'

'Out?'

'Yes, she said she'd been bathing.'

There was a faint—a very faint note of embarrassment in Christine's voice. It puzzled Hercule Poirot.

Weston said:

'And then?'

'Then I went down to breakfast.'

'And after breakfast?'

'I went upstairs, collected my sketching box and sketching book and we started out.'

'You and Miss Linda Marshall?'

'Yes.'

'What time was that?'

'I think it was just on half past ten.'

'And what did you do?'

'We went to Gull Cove. You know, the cove on the east side of the island. We settled ourselves there. I did a sketch and Linda sunbathed.'

'What time did you leave the cove?'

'At a quarter to twelve. I was playing tennis at twelve and had to change.'

'You had your watch with you?'

'No, as a matter of fact I hadn't. I asked Linda the time.'

'I see. And then?'

'I packed up my sketching things and went back to the hotel.'

Poirot said:

'And Mademoiselle Linda?'

'Linda?' Oh, Linda went into the sea.'

Poirot said:

'Were you far from the sea where you were sitting?'

'Well, we were well above high-water mark. Just under the cliff—so that I could be a little in the shade and Linda in the sun.'

Poirot said:

'Did Linda Marshall actually enter the sea before you left the beach?'

Christine frowned a little in the effort to remember. She said:

'Let me see. She ran down the beach—I fastened my box—Yes, I heard her splashing in the waves as I was on the path up the cliff.'

'You are sure of that, Madame? That she really entered the sea?'

'Oh yes.'

She stared at him in surprise.

Colonel Weston also stared at him.

Then he said:

'Go on, Mrs Redfern.'

'I went back to the hotel, changed, and went to the tennis courts where I met the others.'

'Who were?'

'Captain Marshall, Mr Gardener and Miss Darnley. We played two sets. We were just going in again when the news came about—about Mrs Marshall.'

Hercule Poirot leant forward. He said:

'And what did you think, Madame, when you heard that news?'

'What did I think?'

Her face showed a faint distaste for the question.

'Yes.'

Christine Redfern said slowly:

'It was—a horrible thing to happen.'

'Ah, yes, your fastidiousness was revolted. I understand that. But what did it mean to *you*—personally?'

She gave him a quick look—a look of appeal. He responded to it. He said in a matter-of-fact voice.

'I am appealing to you, Madame, as a woman of intelligence with plenty of good sense and judgment. You had doubtless during your stay here formed an opinion of Mrs Marshall, of the kind of woman she was?'

Christine said cautiously:

'I suppose one always does that more or less when one is staying in hotels.'

'Certainly, it is the natural thing to do. So I ask you, Madame, were you really very surprised at the manner of her death?'

Christine said slowly:

'I think I see what you mean. No, I was not, perhaps, surprised. Shocked, yes. But she was the kind of woman—'

Poirot finished the sentence for her.

'She was the kind of woman to whom such a thing might happen... Yes, Madame, that is the truest and most significant thing that has been said in this room this morning. Laying all—er'—he stressed it carefully—'*personal* feeling aside, what did you really think of the late Mrs Marshall?'

Christine Redfern said calmly:

'Is it really worth while going into all that now?'

'I think it might be, yes.'

'Well, what shall I say?' Her fair skin was suddenly suffused with colour. The careful poise of her manner was relaxed. For a short space the natural raw woman looked out. 'She's the kind of woman that to my mind is absolutely worthless! She did nothing to justify her existence. She had no mind—no brains. She thought of nothing but men and clothes and admiration. Useless, a parasite! She was attractive to men, I suppose—Oh, of course, she was. And she lived for that kind of life. And so, I suppose, I wasn't really surprised at her coming to a sticky end. She was the sort of woman who would be mixed up with everything sordid—blackmail—jealousy—violence—every kind of crude emotion. She—she appealed to the worst in people.'

She stopped, panting a little. Her rather short top lip lifted itself in a kind of fastidious disgust. It occurred to Colonel Weston that you could not have found a more complete contrast to Arlena Stuart than Christine Redfern.

Agatha Christie

It also occurred to him that if you were married to Christine Redfern, the atmosphere might be so rarefied that the Arlena Stuarts of this world would hold a particular attraction for you.

And then, immediately following on these thoughts, a single word out of the words she had spoken fastened on his attention with particular intensity.

He leaned forward and said:

'Mrs Redfern, why, in speaking of her, did you mention the word *blackmail*?'

CHAPTER 7

Christine stared at him, not seeming at once to take in what he meant. She answered almost mechanically.

'I suppose—because she *was* being blackmailed. She was the sort of person who would be.'

Colonel Weston said earnestly:

'But—do you know she was being blackmailed?'

A faint colour rose in the girl's cheeks. She said rather awkwardly:

'As a matter of fact I do happen to know it. I—I overheard something.'

'Will you explain, Mrs Redfern?'

Flushing still more, Christine Redfern said:

'I—I didn't mean to overhear. It was an accident. It was two—no, three nights ago. We were playing bridge.' She turned towards Poirot. 'You remember? My husband and I, M. Poirot and Miss Darnley. I was dummy. It was very stuffy in the card room, and I slipped out of the window for a breath of fresh air. I went down towards the beach and I suddenly heard voices. One—it was Arlena Marshall's—I knew it at once—said: "It's no good pressing me. I can't get any more money now. My husband will suspect something." And then a man's voice said: "I'm not taking any excuses. You've got to cough up." And then Arlena Marshall said: "You blackmailing brute!" And the man said: "Brute or not, you'll pay up, my lady."'

Christine paused.

'I'd turned back and a minute after Arlena Marshall rushed past me. She looked—well, frightfully upset.'

Weston said:

'And the man? Do you know who he was?'

Christine Redfern shook her head.

She said:

'He was keeping his voice low. I barely heard what he said.'

'It didn't suggest the voice to you of anyone you knew?'

She thought again, but once more shook her head. She said:

'No, I don't know. It was gruff and low. It—oh, it might have been anybody's.'

Colonel Weston said:

'Thank you, Mrs Redfern.'

II

When the door had closed behind Christine Redfern Inspector Colgate said:

'Now we are getting somewhere!'

Weston said:

'You think so, eh?'

'Well, it's suggestive, sir, you can't get away from it. Somebody in this hotel was blackmailing the lady.'

Poirot murmured:

'But it is not the wicked blackmailer who lies dead. It is the victim.'

'That's a bit of a setback, I agree,' said the Inspector. 'Blackmailers aren't in the habit of bumping off their victims. But what it does give us is this, it suggests a reason for Mrs Marshall's curious behaviour this morning. She'd got a rendezvous with this fellow who was blackmailing her, and she didn't want either her husband or Redfern to know about it.'

'It certainly explains that point,' agreed Poirot.

Inspector Colgate went on:

'And think of the place chosen. The very spot for the purpose. The lady goes off on her float. That's natural enough. It's what she does every day. She goes round to Pixy Cove where no one ever goes in the morning and which will be a nice quiet place for an interview.'

Poirot said:

'But yes, I too was struck by that point. It is as you say, an ideal spot for a rendezvous. It is deserted, it is only accessible from the land side by descending a vertical steel ladder which is not everybody's money, *bien entendu*. Moreover most of the beach is invisible from above because of the overhanging cliff. And it has another advantage. Mr Redfern told me of that one day. There is a cave on it, the entrance to which is not easy to find but where anyone could wait unseen.'

Weston said:

'Of course, the Pixy's Cave—remember hearing about it.'

Inspector Colgate said:

'Haven't heard it spoken of for years, though. We'd better have a look inside it. Never know, we might find a pointer of some kind.'

Weston said:

'Yes, you're right, Colgate, we've got the solution to part one of the puzzle. *Why did Mrs Marshall go to Pixy Cove?* We want the other half of that solution, though. *Who did she go there to meet?* Presumably someone staying in this hotel. None of them fitted as a lover—but a blackmailer's a different proposition.'

He drew the register towards him.

'Excluding the waiters, boots, et cetera, whom I don't think likely, we've got the following. The American—Gardener, Major Barry, Mr Horace Blatt, and the Reverend Stephen Lane.'

Inspector Colgate said:

'We can narrow it down a bit, sir. We might almost rule out the American, I think. He was on the beach all the morning. That's so, isn't it, M. Poirot?'

Poirot replied:

'He was absent for a short time when he fetched a skein of wool for his wife.'

Colgate said:

'Oh well, we needn't count that.'

Weston said:

'And what about the other three?'

'Major Barry went out at ten o'clock this morning. He returned at 1.30. Mr Lane was earlier still. He breakfasted at eight. Said he was going for a tramp. Mr Blatt went off for a sail at 9.30 same as he does most days. Neither of them are back yet.'

'A sail, eh?' Colonel Weston's voice was thoughtful.

Inspector Colgate's voice was responsive. He said:

'Might fit in rather well, sir.'

Weston said:

'Well, we'll have a word with this Major bloke—and let me see, who else is there? Rosamund Darnley. And there's the Brewster woman who found the body with Redfern. What's she like, Colgate?'

'Oh, a sensible party, sir. No nonsense about her.'

'She didn't express any opinions on the death?'

The Inspector shook his head.

'I don't think she'll have anything more to tell us, sir, but we'll have to make sure. Then there are the Americans.'

Colonel Weston nodded. He said: 'Let's have 'em all in and get it over as soon as possible. Never know, might learn something. About the blackmailing stunt if about nothing else.'

III

Mr and Mrs Gardener came into the presence of authority together.

Agatha Christie

Mrs Gardener explained immediately.

'I hope you'll understand how it is, Colonel Weston (that is the name, I think?)' Reassured on this point she went on: 'But this has been a very bad shock to me and Mr Gardener is always very, very careful of my health—'

Mr Gardener here interpolated:

'Mrs Gardener,' he said, 'is very sensitive.'

'—and he said to me, "Why, Carrie," he said, "naturally I'm coming right along with you." It's not that we haven't the highest admiration for British police methods because we have. I've been told that British police procedure is most refined and delicate, and I've never doubted it, and certainly when I once had a bracelet missing at the Savoy Hotel nothing could have been more lovely and sympathetic than the young man who came to see me about it, and, of course, I hadn't really lost the bracelet at all, but just mislaid it; that's the worst of rushing about so much, it makes you kind of forgetful where you put things—' Mrs Gardener paused, inhaled gently and started off again. 'And what I say is, and I know Mr Gardener agrees with me, that we're only too anxious to do anything to help the British police in every way. So go right ahead and ask me anything at all you want to know—'

Colonel Weston opened his mouth to comply with this invitation, but had momentarily to postpone speech while Mrs Gardener went on.

'That's what I said, Odell, isn't it? And that's so, isn't it?'

'Yes, darling,' said Mr Gardener.

Colonel Weston spoke hastily.

'I understand, Mrs Gardener, that you and your husband were on the beach all the morning?'

For once Mr Gardener was able to get in first.

'That's so,' he said.

'Why, certainly we were,' said Mrs Gardener. 'And a lovely peaceful morning it was, just like any other morning if you get me, perhaps even more so, and not the slightest idea in our minds of what was happening round the corner on that lonely beach.'

'Did you see Mrs Marshall at all today?'

'We did not. And I said to Odell, why wherever can Mrs Marshall have got to this morning? I said. And first her husband coming looking for her and then that good-looking young man, Mr Redfern, and so impatient he was, just sitting there on the beach scowling at everyone and everything. And I said to myself why, when he has that nice pretty little wife of his own, must he go running after that dreadful woman? Because that's just what I felt she was. I always felt that about her, didn't I, Odell?'

'Yes, darling.'

'However that nice Captain Marshall came to marry such a woman I just cannot imagine—and with that nice young daughter growing up, and it's so important for girls to have the right influence. Mrs Marshall was not at all the right person—no breeding at all—and I should say a very animal nature. Now if Captain Marshall had had any sense he'd have married Miss Darnley, who's a very very charming woman and a very distinguished one. I must say

Agatha Christie

I admire the way she's gone straight ahead and built up a first-class business as she has. It takes brains to do a thing like that—and you've only got to look at Rosamund Darnley to see she's just frantic with brains. She could plan and carry out any mortal thing she liked. I just admire that woman more than I can say. And I said to Mr Gardener the other day that anyone could see she was very much in love with Captain Marshall—crazy about him was what I said, didn't I, Odell?'

'Yes, darling.'

'It seems they knew each other as children, and why now, who knows, it may all come right after all with that woman out of the way. I'm not a narrow-minded woman, Colonel Weston, and it isn't that I disapprove of the stage as such—why, quite a lot of my best friends are actresses—but I've said to Mr Gardener all along that there was something evil about that woman. And you see, I've been proved right.'

She paused triumphantly.

The lips of Hercule Poirot quivered in a little smile. His eyes met for a minute the shrewd grey eyes of Mr Gardener.

Colonel Weston said rather desperately:

'Well, thank you, Mrs Gardener. I suppose there's nothing that either of you has noticed since you've been here that might have a bearing upon the case?'

'Why no, I don't think so.' Mr Gardener spoke with a slow drawl. 'Mrs Marshall was around with young Redfern most of the time—but everybody can tell you that.'

'What about her husband? Did he mind, do you think?'

Mr Gardener said cautiously:

'Captain Marshall is a very reserved man.'

Mrs Gardener confirmed this by saying:

'Why, yes, he is a real Britisher!'

IV

On the slightly apoplectic countenance of Major Barry various emotions seemed contending for mastery. He was endeavouring to look properly horrified but could not subdue a kind of shamefaced gusto.

He was saying in his hoarse, slightly wheezy voice:

'Glad to help you any way I can. 'Course I don't know anythin' about it—nothin' at all. Not acquainted with the parties. But I've knocked about a bit in my time. Lived a lot in the East, you know. And I can tell you that after being in an Indian hill station what you don't know about human nature isn't worth knowin'.'

He paused, took a breath and was off again.

'Matter of fact this business reminds me of a case in Simla. Fellow called Robinson, or was it Falconer? Anyway he was in the East Wilts, or was it the North Surreys? Can't remember now, and anyway it doesn't matter. Quiet chap, you know, great reader—mild as milk you'd have said. Went for his wife one evening in their bungalow. Got her by the throat. She'd been carryin' on with some feller or other and he'd got wise to it. By Jove, he nearly did for her! It was touch and go. Surprised us all! Didn't think he had it in him.'

Agatha Christie

Hercule Poirot murmured:

'And you see there an analogy to the death of Mrs Marshall?'

'Well, what I mean to say—strangled, you know. Same idea. Feller suddenly sees red!'

Poirot said:

'You think that Captain Marshall felt like that?'

'Oh, look here, I never said that.' Major Barry's face went even redder. 'Never said anything about Marshall. Thoroughly nice chap. Wouldn't say a word against him for the world.'

Poirot murmured:

'Ah, *pardon*, but you *did* refer to the natural reactions of a husband.'

Major Barry said:

'Well, I mean to say, I should think she'd been pretty hot stuff. Eh? Got young Redfern on a string all right. And there were probably others before him. But the funny thing is, you know, that husbands are a dense lot. Amazin'. I've been surprised by it again and again. They see a feller sweet on their wife but they don't see that *she's* sweet on *him*! Remember a case like that in Poona. Very pretty woman, Jove, she led her husband a dance—'

Colonel Weston stirred a little restively. He said:

'Yes, yes, Major Barry. For the moment we've just got to establish the facts. You don't know of anything personally—that you've seen or noticed that might help us in this case?'

'Well, really, Weston, I can't say I do. Saw her and young

Redfern one afternoon on Gull Cove'—here he winked knowingly and gave a deep hoarse chuckle—'very pretty it was, too. But it's not evidence of that kind you're wanting. Ha, ha!'

'You did not see Mrs Marshall at all this morning?'

'Didn't see anybody this morning. Went over to St Loo. Just my luck. Sort of place here where nothin' happens for months and when it does you miss it!'

The Major's voice held a ghoulish regret.

Colonel Weston prompted him.

'You went to St Loo, you say?'

'Yes, wanted to do some telephonin'. No telephone here and that post office place at Leathercombe Bay isn't very private.'

'Were your telephone calls of a very private nature?'

The Major winked again cheerfully.

'Well, they were and they weren't. Wanted to get through to a pal of mine and get him to put somethin' on a horse. Couldn't get through to him, worse luck.'

'Where did you telephone from?'

'Call box in the GPO at St Loo. Then on the way back I got lost—these confounded lanes—twistin' and turnin' all over the place. Must have wasted an hour over that at least. Damned confusing part of the world. I only got back half an hour ago.'

Colonel Weston said:

'Speak to anyone or meet anyone in St Loo?'

Major Barry said with a chuckle:

'Wantin' me to prove an alibi? Can't think of anythin'

useful. Saw about fifty thousand people in St Loo—but that's not to say they'll remember seein' me.'

The Chief Constable said:

'We have to ask these things, you know.'

'Right you are. Call on me at any time. Glad to help you. Very fetchin' woman, the deceased. Like to help you catch the feller who did it. The Lonely Beach Murder—bet you that's what the papers will call it. Reminds me of the time—'

It was Inspector Colgate who firmly nipped this latest reminiscence in the bud and manoeuvred the garrulous Major out of the door.

Coming back he said:

'Difficult to check up on anything in St Loo. It's the middle of the holiday season.'

The Chief Constable said:

'Yes, we can't take him off the list. Not that I seriously believe he's implicated. Dozens of old bores like him going about. Remember one or two of them in my army days. Still—he's a possibility. I leave all that to you, Colgate. Check what time he took the car out—petrol—all that. It's humanly possible that he parked the car somewhere in a lonely spot, walked back here and went to the cove. But it doesn't seem feasible to me. He'd have run too much risk of being seen.'

Colgate nodded.

He said:

'Of course there are a good many charabancs here today. Fine day. They start arriving round about half past eleven.

High tide was at seven. Low tide would be about one o'clock. People would be spread out over the sands and the causeway.'

Weston said:

'Yes. But he'd have to come up from the causeway past the hotel.'

'Not right past it. He could branch off on the path that leads up over the top of the island.'

Weston said doubtfully:

'I'm not saying that he mightn't have done it without being seen. Practically all the hotel guests were on the bathing beach except for Mrs Redfern and the Marshall girl, who were down in Gull Cove, and the beginning of that path would only be overlooked by a few rooms of the hotel and there are plenty of chances against anyone looking out of those windows just at that moment. For the matter of that, I dare say it's possible for a man to walk up to the hotel, through the lounge and out again without anyone happening to see him. But what I say is, he couldn't *count* on no one seeing him.'

Colgate said:

'He could have gone round to the cove by boat.'

Weston nodded. He said:

'That's much sounder. If he'd had a boat handy in one of the coves nearby, he could have left the car, rowed or sailed to Pixy Cove, done the murder, rowed back, picked up the car and arrived back with this tale about having been to St Loo and lost his way—a story that he'd know would be pretty hard to disprove.'

'You're right, sir.'

The Chief Constable said:

'Well, I leave it to you, Colgate. Comb the neighbourhood thoroughly. You know what to do. We'd better see Miss Brewster now.'

V

Emily Brewster was not able to add anything of material value to what they already knew.

Weston said after she had repeated her story:

'And there's nothing you know of that could help us in any way?'

Emily Brewster said shortly:

'Afraid not. It's a distressing business. However, I expect you'll soon get to the bottom of it.'

Weston said:

'I hope so, I'm sure.'

Emily Brewster said dryly:

'Ought not to be difficult.'

'Now what do you mean by that, Miss Brewster?'

'Sorry. Wasn't attempting to teach you your business. All I meant was that with a woman of that kind it ought to be easy enough.'

Hercule Poirot murmured:

'That is your opinion?'

Emily Brewster snapped out:

'Of course. *De mortuis nil nisi bonum* and all that, but you can't get away from *facts*. That woman was a bad lot through and through. You've only got to hunt round a bit in her unsavoury past.'

Hercule Poirot said gently:

'You did not like her?'

'I know a bit too much about her.' In answer to the enquiring looks she went on: 'My first cousin married one of the Erskines. You've probably heard that that woman induced old Sir Robert when he was in his dotage to leave most of his fortune to her away from his own family.'

Colonel Weston said:

'And the family—er—resented that?'

'Naturally. His association with her was a scandal anyway, and on top of that, to leave her a sum like fifty thousand pounds shows just the kind of woman she was. I dare say I sound hard, but in my opinion the Arlena Stuarts of this world deserve very little sympathy. I know of something else too—a young fellow who lost his head about her completely—he'd always been a bit wild, naturally his association with her pushed him over the edge. He did something rather fishy with some shares—solely to get money to spend on her—and only just managed to escape prosecution. That woman contaminated everyone she met. Look at the way she was ruining young Redfern. No, I'm afraid I can't have any regret for her death—though of course it would have been better if she'd drowned herself, or fallen over a cliff. Strangling is rather unpleasant.'

'And you think the murderer was someone out of her past?'

'Yes, I do.'

Agatha Christie

'Someone who came from the mainland with no one seeing him?'

'Why should any one see him? We were all on the beach. I gather the Marshall child and Christine Redfern were down on Gull Cove out of the way. Captain Marshall was in his room in the hotel. Then who on earth was there to see him except possibly Miss Darnley.'

'Where was Miss Darnley?'

'Sitting up on the cutting at the top of the cliff. Sunny Ledge it's called. We saw her there, Mr Redfern and I, when we were rowing round the island.'

Colonel Weston said:

'You may be right, Miss Brewster.'

Emily Brewster said positively:

'I'm sure I'm right. When a woman's neither more nor less than a nasty mess, then she herself will provide the best possible clue. Don't you agree with me, M. Poirot?'

Hercule Poirot looked up. His eyes met her confident grey ones. He said:

'Oh, yes—I agree with that which you have just this minute said. Arlena Marshall herself is the best, the only clue, to her own death.'

Miss Brewster said sharply:

'Well, then!'

She stood there, an erect sturdy figure, her cool self-confident glance going from one man to the other.

Colonel Weston said:

'You may be sure, Miss Brewster, that any clue there may be in Mrs Marshall's past life will not be overlooked.'

Emily Brewster went out.

VI

Inspector Colgate shifted his position at the table. He said in a thoughtful voice:

'She's a determined one, she is. And she'd got her knife into the dead lady, proper, she had.'

He stopped a minute and said reflectively:

'It's a pity in a way that she's got a cast-iron alibi for the whole morning. Did you notice her hands, sir? As big as a man's. And she's a hefty woman—as strong and stronger than many a man, I'd say...'

He paused again. His glance at Poirot was almost pleading.

'And you say she never left the beach this morning, M. Poirot?'

Slowly Poirot shook his head. He said:

'My dear Inspector, she came down to the beach before Mrs Marshall could have reached Pixy Cove and she was within my sight until she set off with Mr Redfern in the boat.'

Inspector Colgate said gloomily:

'Then that washes her out.'

He seemed upset about it.

VII

As always, Hercule Poirot felt a keen sense of pleasure at the sight of Rosamund Darnley.

Even to a bare police inquiry into the ugly facts of murder she brought a distinction of her own.

She sat down opposite Colonel Weston and turned a grave and intelligent face to him.

She said:

'You want my name and address? Rosamund Anne Darnley. I carry on a dressmaking business under the name of Rose Mond Ltd at 622 Brook Street.'

'Thank you, Miss Darnley. Now can you tell us anything that may help us?'

'I don't really think I can.'

'Your own movements—'

'I had breakfast about 9.30. Then I went up to my room and collected some books and my sunshade and went out to Sunny Ledge. That must have been about twenty-five past ten. I came back to the hotel about ten minutes to twelve, went up and got my tennis racquet and went out to the tennis courts, where I played tennis until lunchtime.'

'You were in the cliff recess, called by the hotel Sunny Ledge, from about half past ten until ten minutes to twelve?'

'Yes.'

'Did you see Mrs Marshall at all this morning?'

'No.'

'Did you see her from the cliff as she paddled her float round to Pixy Cove?'

'No, she must have gone by before I got there.'

'Did you notice anyone on a float or in a boat at all this morning?'

'No, I don't think I did. You see, I was reading. Of course I looked up from my book from time to time, but as it happened the sea was quite bare each time I did so.'

'You didn't even notice Mr Redfern and Miss Brewster when they went round?'

'No.'

'You were, I think, acquainted with Mr Marshall?'

'Captain Marshall is an old family friend. His family and mine lived next door to each other. I had not seen him, however, for a good many years—it must be something like twelve years.'

'And Mrs Marshall?'

'I'd never exchanged half a dozen words with her until I met her here.'

'Were Captain and Mrs Marshall, as far as you knew, on good terms with each other?'

'On perfectly good terms, I should say.'

'Was Captain Marshall very devoted to his wife?'

Rosamund said:

'He may have been. I can't really tell you anything about that. Captain Marshall is rather old-fashioned—he hasn't got the modern habit of shouting matrimonial woes upon the housetop.'

'Did you like Mrs Marshall, Miss Darnley?'

Agatha Christie

'No.'

The monosyllable came quietly and evenly. It sounded what it was—a simple statement of fact.

'Why was that?'

A half-smile came to Rosamund's lips. She said:

'Surely you've discovered that Arlena Marshall was not popular with her own sex? She was bored to death with women and showed it. Nevertheless I should like to have had the dressing of her. She had a great gift for clothes. Her clothes were always just right and she wore them well. I should like to have had her as a client.'

'She spent a good deal on clothes?'

'She must have done. But then she had money of her own and of course Captain Marshall is quite well off.'

'Did you ever hear or did it ever occur to you that Mrs Marshall was being blackmailed, Miss Darnley?'

A look of intense astonishment came over Rosamund Darnley's expressive face.

She said:

'Blackmailed? Arlena?'

'The idea seems to surprise you.'

'Well, yes, it does rather. It seems so incongruous.'

'But surely it is possible?'

'Everything's possible, isn't it? The world soon teaches one that. But I wondered what anyone could blackmail Arlena about?'

'There are certain things, I suppose, that Mrs Marshall might be anxious should not come to her husband's ears?'

'We-ll, yes.'

She explained the doubt in her voice by saying with a half-smile:

'I sound sceptical, but then, you see, Arlena was rather notorious in her conduct. She never made much of a pose of respectability.'

'You think, then, that her husband was aware of her—intimacies with other people?'

There was a pause. Rosamund was frowning. She spoke at last in a slow, reluctant voice. She said:

'You know, I don't really know what to think. I've always assumed that Kenneth Marshall accepted his wife, quite frankly, for what she was. That he had no illusions about her. But it may not be so.'

'He may have believed in her absolutely?'

Rosamund said with semi-exasperation:

'Men are such fools. And Kenneth Marshall is unworldly under his sophisticated manner. He *may* have believed in her blindly. He may have thought she was just—admired.'

'And you know of no one—that is, you have heard of no one who was likely to have had a grudge against Mrs Marshall?'

Rosamund Darnley smiled. She said:

'Only resentful wives. And I presume, since she was strangled, that it was a man who killed her.'

'Yes.'

Rosamund said thoughtfully:

'No, I can't think of anyone. But then I probably shouldn't know. You'll have to ask someone in her own intimate set.'

Agatha Christie

'Thank you, Miss Darnley.'
Rosamund turned a little in her chair. She said:
'Hasn't M. Poirot any questions to ask?'
Her faintly ironic smile flashed out at him.
Hercule Poirot smiled and shook his head.
He said:
'I can think of nothing.'
Rosamund Darnley got up and went out.

CHAPTER 8

They were standing in the bedroom that had been Arlena Marshall's.

Two big bay windows gave onto a balcony that overlooked the bathing beach and the sea beyond. Sunshine poured into the room, flashing over the bewildering array of bottles and jars on Arlena's dressing table.

Here there was every kind of cosmetic and unguent known to beauty parlours. Amongst this panoply of woman's affairs three men moved purposefully. Inspector Colgate went about shutting and opening drawers.

Presently he gave a grunt. He had come upon a packet of folded letters. He and Weston ran through them together.

Hercule Poirot had moved to the wardrobe. He opened the door of the hanging cupboard and looked at the multiplicity of gowns and sports suits that hung there. He opened the other side. Foamy lingerie lay in piles.

Agatha Christie

On a wide shelf were hats. Two more beach cardboard hats in lacquer red and pale yellow; a Big Hawaiian straw hat; another of drooping dark-blue linen and three or four little absurdities for which, no doubt, several guineas had been paid apiece; a kind of beret in dark blue; a tuft, no more, of black velvet; a pale grey turban.

Hercule Poirot stood scanning them—a faintly indulgent smile came to his lips. He murmured:

'*Les femmes!*'

Colonel Weston was refolding the letters.

'Three from young Redfern,' he said. 'Damned young ass. He'll learn not to write letters to women in a few more years. Women always keep letters and then swear they've burnt them. There's one other letter here. Same line of country.'

He held it out and Poirot took it.

Darling Arlena,—God, I feel blue. To be going out to China—and perhaps not seeing you again for years and years. I didn't know any man could go on feeling crazy about a woman like I feel about you. Thanks for the cheque. They won't prosecute now. It was a near shave, though, and all because I wanted to make big money for you. Can you forgive me? I wanted to set diamonds in your ears—your lovely lovely ears—and clasp great milk-white pearls round your throat, only they say pearls are no good nowadays. A fabulous emerald, then? Yes, that's the thing. A great emerald, cool and green and full of hidden fire. Don't forget me—but you won't, I know. You're mine—always.

Goodbye—goodbye—goodbye.

J.N.

Inspector Colgate said:

'Might be worthwhile to find out if J.N. really did go to China. Otherwise—well, he might be the person we're looking for. Crazy about the woman, idealizing her, suddenly finding out he'd been played for a sucker. It sounds to me as though this is the boy Miss Brewster mentioned. Yes, I think this might be useful.'

Hercule Poirot nodded. He said: 'Yes, that letter is important. I find it very important.'

He turned round and stared at the room—at the bottles on the dressing table—at the open wardrobe and at a big Pierrot doll that lolled insolently on the bed.

They went into Kenneth Marshall's room.

It was next door to his wife's but with no communicating door and no balcony. It faced the same way and had two windows, but it was much smaller. Between the two windows a gilt mirror hung on the wall. In the corner beyond the right-hand window was the dressing table. On it were two ivory brushes, a clothes brush and a bottle of hair lotion. In the corner by the left-hand window was a writing table. An open typewriter stood on it and papers were ranged in a stack beside it.

Colgate went through them rapidly.

He said:

Agatha Christie

'All seems straightforward enough. Ah, here's the letter he mentioned this morning. Dated the 24th—that's yesterday. And here's the envelope postmarked Leathercombe Bay this morning. Seems all square. Now we'll have an idea if he could have prepared that answer of his beforehand.

He sat down.

Colonel Weston said:

'We'll leave you to it, for a moment. We'll just glance through the rest of the rooms. Everyone's been kept out of this corridor until now, and they're getting a bit restive about it.'

They went next into Linda Marshall's room. It faced east, looking out over the rocks down to the sea below.

Weston gave a glance round. He murmured:

'Don't suppose there's anything to see here. But it's possible Marshall might have put something in his daughter's room that he didn't want us to find. Not likely, though. It isn't as though there had been a weapon or anything to get rid of.'

He went out again.

Hercule Poirot stayed behind. He found something that interested him in the grate. Something had been burnt there recently. He knelt down, working patiently. He laid out his finds on a sheet of paper. A large irregular blob of candle grease; some fragments of green paper or cardboard, possibly a pull-off calendar, for with it was an unburnt fragment bearing a large figure 5 and a scrap of printing... *noble deeds*... There was also an ordinary pin and some burnt animal matter which might have been hair.

Poirot arranged them neatly in a row and stared at them. He murmured:

'*Do noble deeds, not dream them all day long. C'est possible.* But what is one to make of this collection? *C'est fantastique!*'

And then he picked up the pin and his eyes grew sharp and green.

He murmured:

'*Pour l'amour de Dieu!* Is it possible?'

Hercule Poirot got up from where he had been kneeling by the grate.

Slowly he looked round the room and this time there was an entirely new expression on his face. It was grave and almost stern.

To the left of the mantelpiece there were some shelves with a row of books. Hercule Poirot looked thoughtfully along the titles.

A Bible, a battered copy of Shakespeare's plays. *The Marriage of William Ashe*, by Mrs Humphry Ward. *The Young Stepmother*, by Charlotte Yonge. *The Shropshire Lad*. Eliot's *Murder in the Cathedral*. Bernard Shaw's *St Joan*. *Gone With the Wind*, by Margaret Mitchell. *The Burning Court*, by Dickson Carr.

Poirot took out two books. *The Young Stepmother* and *William Ashe*, and glanced inside at the blurred stamp affixed to the title page. As he was about to replace them, his eye caught sight of a book that had been shoved behind the other books. It was a small dumpy volume bound in brown calf.

He took it out and opened it. Very slowly he nodded his head.

He murmured:

'*So I was right*... Yes, I was right. But for the other—is that possible too? No, it is not possible, unless...'

He stayed there, motionless, stroking his moustaches whilst his mind ranged busily over the problem.

He said again, softly:

'*Unless—*'

II

Colonel Weston looked in at the door.

'Hullo, Poirot, still there?'

'I arrive. I arrive,' cried Poirot.

He hurried out into the corridor.

The room next to Linda's was that of the Redferns.

Poirot looked into it, noting automatically the traces of two different individualities—a neatness and tidiness which he associated with Christine, and a picturesque disorder which was characteristic of Patrick. Apart from these sidelights on personality the room did not interest him.

Next to it again was Rosamund Darnley's room, and here he lingered for a moment in the sheer pleasure of the owner's personality.

He noted the few books that lay on the table next to the bed, the expensive simplicity of the toilet set on the dressing table. And there came gently to his nostrils the elusive expensive perfume that Rosamund Darnley used.

Next to Rosamund Darnley's room at the northern end of the corridor was an open window leading to a balcony from which an outside stair led down to the rocks below.

Weston said:

'That's the way people go down to bathe before breakfast—that is, if they bathe off the rocks as most of them do.'

Interest came into Hercule Poirot's eyes. He stepped outside and looked down.

Below, a path led to steps cut zigzag leading down the rocks to the sea. There was also a path that led round the hotel to the left. He said:

'One could go down these stairs, go to the left round the hotel and join the main path up from the causeway.'

Weston nodded. He amplified Poirot's statement.

'One could go right across the island without going through the hotel at all.' He added: 'But one might still be seen from a window.'

'What window?'

'Two of the public bathrooms look out that way—north—and the staff bathroom, and the cloakrooms on the ground floor. Also the billiard room.'

Poirot nodded. He said:

'And all the former have frosted glass windows, and one does not play billiards on a fine morning.'

'Exactly.'

Weston paused and said:

'If he did it, that's the way he went.'

'You mean Captain Marshall?'

Agatha Christie

'Yes. Blackmail, or no blackmail. I still feel it points to him. And his manner—well, his manner is unfortunate.'

Hercule Poirot said dryly:

'Perhaps—but a manner does not make a murderer!'

Weston said:

'Then you think he's out of it?'

Poirot shook his head. He said:

'No, I would not say that.'

Weston said:

'We'll see what Colgate can make out of the typewriting alibi. In the meantime I've got the chambermaid of this floor waiting to be interviewed. A good deal may depend on her evidence.'

The chambermaid was a woman of thirty, brisk, efficient and intelligent. Her answers came readily.

Captain Marshall had come up to his room not long after 10.30. She was then finishing the room. He had asked her to be as quick as possible. She had not seen him come back but she had heard the sound of the typewriter a little later. She put it at about five minutes to eleven. She was then in Mr and Mrs Redfern's room. After she had done that she moved on to Miss Darnley's room at the end of the corridor. She could not hear the typewriter from there. She went to Miss Darnley's room, as near as she could say, at just after eleven o'clock. She remembered hearing Leathercombe Church strike the hour as she went in. At a quarter past eleven she had gone downstairs for her eleven o'clock cup of tea and 'snack'. Afterwards she had gone to do the rooms in the other wing of the hotel. In answer

Evil Under the Sun

to the Chief Constable's question she explained that she had done the rooms in this corridor in the following order:

Miss Linda Marshall's, the two public bathrooms, Mrs Marshall's room and private bath, Captain Marshall's room, Mr and Mrs Redfern's room and private bath, Miss Darnley's room and private bath. Captain Marshall's and Miss Marshall's rooms had no adjoining bathrooms.

During the time she was in Miss Darnley's room and bathroom she had not heard anyone pass the door or go out by the staircase to the rocks, but it was quite likely she wouldn't have heard if anyone went quietly.

Weston then directed his questions to the subject of Mrs Marshall.

No, Mrs Marshall wasn't one for rising early as a rule. She, Gladys Narracott, had been surprised to find the door open and Mrs Marshall gone down at just after ten. Something quite unusual, that was.

'Did Mrs Marshall always have her breakfast in bed?'

'Oh yes, sir, always. Not very much of it either. Just tea and orange juice and one piece of toast. Slimming like so many ladies.'

No, she hadn't noticed anything unusual in Mrs Marshall's manner that morning. She'd seemed quite as usual.

Hercule Poirot murmured:

'What did you think of Mrs Marshall, Mademoiselle?'

Gladys Narracott stared at him. She said:

'Well, that's hardly for me to say, is it, sir?'

'But yes, it is for you to say. We are anxious—very anxious—to hear your impression.'

Agatha Christie

Gladys gave a slightly uneasy glance towards the Chief Constable, who endeavoured to make his face sympathetic and approving, though actually he felt slightly embarrassed by his foreign colleague's methods of approach. He said:

'Er—yes, certainly. Go ahead.'

For the first time Gladys Narracott's brisk efficiency deserted her. Her fingers fumbled with her print dress. She said:

'Well, Mrs Marshall—she wasn't exactly a lady, as you might say. What I mean is she was more like an actress.'

Colonel Weston said:

'She was an actress.'

'Yes, sir, that's what I'm saying. She just went on exactly as she felt like it. She didn't—well, she didn't trouble to be polite if she wasn't feeling polite. And she'd be all smiles one minute and then, if she couldn't find something or the bell wasn't answered at once or her laundry wasn't back, well, be downright rude and nasty about it. None of us you might say *liked* her. But her clothes were beautiful, and, of course, she was a very handsome lady, so it was only natural she should be admired.'

Colonel Weston said:

'I am sorry to have to ask you what I am going to ask you, but it is a very vital matter. Can you tell me how things were between her and her husband?'

Gladys Narracott hesitated a minute.

She said:

'You don't—it wasn't—you don't think as *he* did it?'

Hercule Poirot said quickly:

'Do you?'

'Oh! I wouldn't like to think so. He's such a nice gentleman, Captain Marshall. He couldn't do a thing like that—I'm sure he couldn't.'

'But you are *not* very sure—I hear it in your voice.'

Gladys Narracott said reluctantly:

'You do read such things in the papers! When there's jealousy. If there's been goings on—and, of course, everyone's been talking about it—about her and Mr Redfern, I mean. And Mrs Redfern such a nice quiet lady! It does seem a shame! And Mr Redfern's a nice gentleman too, but it seems men can't help themselves when it's a lady like Mrs Marshall—one who's used to having her own way. Wives have to put up with a lot, I'm sure.' She sighed and paused. 'But if Captain Marshall found out about it—'

Colonel Weston said sharply:

'Well?'

Gladys Narracott said slowly:

'I did think sometimes that Mrs Marshall was frightened of her husband knowing.'

'What makes you say that?'

'It wasn't anything definite, sir. It was only I felt—that sometimes she was—afraid of him. He was a very quiet gentleman but he wasn't—he wasn't *easy*.'

Weston said:

'But you've nothing definite to go on? Nothing either of them ever said to each other.'

Slowly Gladys Narracott shook her head.

Weston sighed. He went on.

'Now, as to letters received by Mrs Marshall this morning. Can you tell us anything about those?'

'There were about six or seven, sir. I couldn't say exactly.'

'Did you take them up to her?'

'Yes, sir. I got them from the office as usual and put them on her breakfast tray.'

'Do you remember anything about the look of them?'

The girl shook her head.

'They were just ordinary-looking letters. Some of them were bills and circulars, I think, because they were torn up on the tray.'

'What happened to them?'

'They went into the dustbin, sir. One of the police gentlemen is going through that now.'

Weston nodded.

'And the contents of the wastepaper baskets, where are they?'

'They'll be in the dustbin too.'

Weston said: 'Hm—well, I think that is all at present.' He looked inquiringly at Poirot.

Poirot leaned forward.

'When you did Miss Linda Marshall's room this morning, did you do the fireplace?'

'There wasn't anything to do, sir. There had been no fire lit.'

'And there was nothing in the fireplace itself?'

'No sir, it was perfectly all right.'

'What time did you do her room?'

Evil Under the Sun

'About a quarter past nine, sir, when she'd gone down to breakfast.'

'Did she come up to her room after breakfast, do you know?'

'Yes, sir. She came up about a quarter to ten.'

'Did she stay in her room?'

'I think so, sir. She came out, hurrying rather, just before half past ten.'

'You didn't go into her room again?'

'No, sir. I had finished with it.'

Poirot nodded. He said:

'There is another thing I want to know. What people bathed before breakfast this morning?'

'I couldn't say about the other wing and the floor above. Only about this one.'

'That is all I want to know.'

'Well, sir, Captain Marshall and Mr Redfern were the only ones this morning, I think. They always go down for an early dip.'

'Did you see them?'

'No, sir, but their wet bathing things were hanging over the balcony rail as usual.'

'Miss Linda Marshall did not bathe this morning?'

'No, sir. All her bathing dresses were quite dry.'

'Ah,' said Poirot. 'That is what I wanted to know.'

Gladys Narracott volunteered:

'She does most mornings, sir.'

'And the other three, Miss Darnley, Mrs Redfern and Mrs Marshall?'

'Mrs Marshall never, sir. Miss Darnley has once or twice, I think. Mrs Redfern doesn't often bathe before breakfast—only when it's very hot, but she didn't this morning.'

Again Poirot nodded. Then he asked:

'I wonder if you have noticed whether a bottle is missing from any of the rooms you look after in this wing?'

'A bottle, sir? What kind of a bottle?'

'Unfortunately I do not know. But have you noticed—or would you be likely to notice—if one had gone?'

Gladys said frankly:

'I shouldn't from Mrs Marshall's room, sir, and that's a fact. She has ever so many.'

'And the other rooms?'

'Well, I'm not sure about Miss Darnley. She has a good many creams and lotions. But from the other rooms, yes, I would, sir. I mean if I were to look special. If I were noticing, so to speak.'

'But you haven't actually noticed?'

'No, because I wasn't looking special, as I say.'

'Perhaps you would go and look now, then.'

'Certainly, sir.'

She left the room, her print dress rustling. Weston looked at Poirot. He said: 'What's all this?'

Poirot murmured:

'My orderly mind, that is vexed by trifles! Miss Brewster, this morning, was bathing off the rocks before breakfast, and she says that a bottle was thrown from above and nearly hit her. *Eh bien*, I want to know who threw that bottle and why.'

'My dear man, anyone may have chucked a bottle away.'

'Not at all. To begin with, it could only have been thrown from a window on the east side of the hotel—that is, one of the windows of the rooms we have just examined. Now I ask you, if you have an empty bottle on your dressing table or in your bathroom what do you do with it? I will tell you, you drop it into the wastepaper basket. You do not take the trouble to go out on your balcony and hurl it into the sea! For one thing you might hit someone, for another it would be too much trouble. No, you would only do that *if you did not want anyone to see that particular bottle.*'

Weston stared at him.

Weston said:

'I know that Chief Inspector Japp, whom I met over a case not long ago, always says you have a damned tortuous mind. You're not going to tell me now that Arlena Marshall wasn't strangled at all, but poisoned out of some mysterious bottle with a mysterious drug?'

'No, no, I do not think there was poison in that bottle.'

'Then what was there?'

'I do not know at all. That's why I am interested.'

Gladys Narracott came back. She was a little breathless. She said:

'I'm sorry, sir, but I can't find anything missing. I'm sure there's nothing gone from Captain Marshall's room, or Miss Linda Marshall's room, or Mr and Mrs Redfern's room, and I'm pretty sure there's nothing gone from Miss Darnley's either. But I couldn't say about Mrs Marshall's. As I say, she's got such a lot.'

Poirot shrugged his shoulders.

He said:

'No matter. We will leave it.'

Gladys Narracott said:

'Is there anything more, sir?'

She looked from one to the other of them.

Weston said:

'Don't think so. Thank you.'

Poirot said:

'I thank you, no. You are sure, are you not, that there is nothing—nothing at all, that you have forgotten to tell us?'

'About Mrs Marshall, sir?'

'About anything at all. Anything unusual, out of the way, unexplained, slightly peculiar, rather curious—*enfin*, something that has made you say to yourself or to one of your colleagues: "That's funny!"?'

Gladys said doubtfully:

'Well, not the sort of thing that you would mean, sir.'

Hercule Poirot said:

'Never mind what I mean. You do not know what I mean. It is true, then, that you have said to yourself or to a colleague today, "That is funny!"?'

He brought out the three words with ironic detachment.

Gladys said:

'It was nothing really. Just a bath being run. And I did pass the remark to Elsie, downstairs, that it was funny somebody having a bath round about twelve o'clock.'

'Whose bath, who had a bath?'

'That I couldn't say, sir. We heard it going down the waste from this wing, that's all, and that's when I said what I did to Elsie.'

'You're sure it was a bath? Not one of the hand basins?'

'Oh! quite sure, sir. You can't mistake bath water running away.'

Poirot displaying no further desire to keep her, Gladys Narracott was permitted to depart.

Weston said:

'You don't think this bath question is important, do you, Poirot? I mean, there's no point to it. No bloodstains or anything like that to wash off. That's the—' He hesitated.

Poirot cut in:

'That, you would say, is the advantage of strangulation! No bloodstains, no weapon—nothing to get rid of or conceal! Nothing is needed but physical strength—*and the soul of a killer!*'

His voice was so fierce, so charged with feeling, that Weston recoiled a little.

Hercule Poirot smiled at him apologetically.

'No, no,' he said, 'the bath is probably of no importance. Anyone may have had a bath. Mrs Redfern before she went to play tennis, Captain Marshall, Miss Darnley. As I say, anyone. There is nothing in that.'

A police constable knocked at the door, and put in his head.

'It's Miss Darnley, sir. She says she'd like to see you again for a minute. There's something she forgot to tell you, she says.'

Weston said:

'We're coming down—now.'

III

The first person they saw was Colgate. His face was gloomy.

'Just a minute, sir.'

Weston and Poirot followed him into Mrs Castle's office. Colgate said:

'I've been checking-up with Heald on this typewriting business. Not a doubt of it, it couldn't be done under an hour. Longer, if you had to stop and think here and there. That seems to me pretty well to settle it. And look at this letter.'

He held it out.

'*My dear Marshall—Sorry to worry you on your holiday but an entirely unforseen situation has arisen over the Burley and Tender contracts...*'

'Etcetera, etcetera,' said Colgate. 'Dated the 24th—that's yesterday. Envelope postmarked yesterday evening EC1 and Leathercombe Bay this morning. Same typewriter used on envelope and in letter. And by the contents it was clearly impossible for Marshall to prepare his answer beforehand. The figures arise out of the ones in the letter—the whole thing is quite intricate.'

'Hm,' said Weston gloomily. 'That seems to let Marshall

Evil Under the Sun

out. We'll have to look elsewhere.' He added: 'I've got to see Miss Darnley again. She's waiting now.'

Rosamund came in crisply. Her smile held an apologetic *nuance*.

She said:

'I'm frightfully sorry. Probably it isn't worth bothering about. But one does forget things so.'

'Yes, Miss Darnley?'

The Chief Constable indicated a chair.

She shook her shapely black head.

'Oh, it isn't worth sitting down. It's simply this. I told you that I spent the morning lying out on Sunny Ledge. That isn't quite accurate. I forgot that once during the morning I went back to the hotel and out again.'

'What time was that, Miss Darnley?'

'It must have been about a quarter past eleven.'

'You went back to the hotel, you said?'

'Yes, I'd forgotten my glare glasses. At first I thought I wouldn't bother and then my eyes got tired and I decided to go in and get them.'

'You went straight to your room and out again?'

'Yes. At least, as a matter of fact, I just looked in on Ken—Captain Marshall. I heard his machine going and I thought it was so stupid of him to stay indoors typing on such a lovely day. I thought I'd tell him to come out.'

'And what did Captain Marshall say?'

Rosamund smiled rather shamefacedly.

'Well, when I opened the door he was typing so vigorously, and frowning and looking so concentrated, that I just went away quietly. I don't think he even saw me come in.'

'And that was—at what time, Miss Darnley?'

'Just about twenty past eleven. I noticed the clock in the hall as I went out again.'

IV

'And that puts the lid on it finally,' said Inspector Colgate. 'The chambermaid heard him typing up till five minutes to eleven. Miss Darnley saw him at twenty minutes past, and the woman was dead at a quarter to twelve. He says he spent that hour typing in his room, and it seems quite clear that he *was* typing in his room. That washes Captain Marshall right out.'

He stopped, then looking at Poirot with some curiosity, he asked:

'M. Poirot's looking very serious over something.'

Poirot said thoughtfully:

'I was wondering why Miss Darnley suddenly volunteered this extra evidence.'

Inspector Colgate cocked his head alertly.

'Think there's something fishy about it? That it isn't just a question of "forgetting"?'

He considered for a minute or two, then he said slowly:

'Look here, sir, let's look at it this way. Supposing Miss Darnley wasn't on Sunny Ledge this morning as she says. That story's a lie. Now suppose that *after* telling us her story, she finds that somebody saw her somewhere else or alternatively that someone went to the Ledge and didn't find her there. Then she thinks up this story quick and comes and tells it to us to account for her absence. You'll notice that she was careful to say Captain Marshall didn't *see* her when she looked into his room.'

Poirot murmured:

'Yes, I noticed that.'

Weston said incredulously:

'Are you suggesting that Miss Darnley's mixed up in this? Nonsense, seems absurd to me. Why should she be?'

Inspector Colgate coughed.

He said:

'You'll remember what the American lady, Mrs Gardener, said. She sort of hinted that Miss Darnley was sweet on Captain Marshall. There'd be a motive there, sir.'

Weston said impatiently:

'Arlena Marshall wasn't killed by a woman. It's a man we've got to look for. We've got to stick to the men in the case.'

Inspector Colgate sighed. He said:

'Yes, that's true, sir. We always come back to that, don't we?'

Weston went on:

'Better put a constable onto timing one or two things. From the hotel across the island to the top of the ladder. Let him do it running and walking. Same thing with the ladder itself. And somebody had better check the time it takes to go on a float from the bathing beach to the cove.'

Inspector Colgate nodded.

Agatha Christie

'I'll attend to all that, sir,' he said confidently.

The Chief Constable said:

'Think I'll go along to the cove now. See if Phillips has found anything. Then there's that Pixy's Cave we've been hearing about. Ought to see if there are any traces of a man waiting in there. Eh, Poirot? What do you think?'

'By all means. It is a possibility.'

Weston said:

'If somebody from outside had nipped over to the island that would be a good hiding place—if he knew about it. I suppose the locals know?'

Colgate said:

'Don't believe the younger generation would. You see, ever since this hotel was started the coves have been private property. Fishermen don't go there, or picnic parties. And the hotel people aren't local. Mrs Castle's a Londoner.'

Weston said:

'We might take Redfern with us. He told us about it. What about you, M. Poirot?'

Hercule Poirot hesitated. He said, his foreign intonation very pronounced:

'Me, I am like Miss Brewster and Mrs Redfern, I do not like to descend perpendicular ladders.'

Weston said: 'You can go round by boat.'

Again Hercule Poirot sighed.

'My stomach, it is not happy on the sea.'

'Nonsense, man, it's a beautiful day. Calm as a mill pond. You can't let us down, you know.'

Hercule Poirot hardly looked like responding to this British adjuration. But at that moment, Mrs Castle poked her ladylike face and elaborate coiffure round the door.

'Ay'm sure ay hope ay am not intruding,' she said. 'But Mr Lane, the clergyman, you know, has just returned. Ay thought you might like to know.'

'Ah yes, thanks, Mrs Castle. We'll see him right away.'

Mrs Castle came a little farther into the room. She said:

'Ay don't know if it is worth mentioning, but ay *have* heard that the smallest incident should not be ignored—'

'Yes, yes?' said Weston impatiently.

'It is only that there was a lady and gentleman here about one o'clock. Came over from the mainland. For luncheon. They were informed that there had been an accident and that under the circumstances no luncheons could be served.'

'Any idea who they were?'

'Ay couldn't say at all. Naturally no name was given. They expressed disappointment and a certain amount of curiosity as to the nature of the accident. Ay couldn't tell them anything, of course. Ay should say, myself, they were summer visitors of the better class.'

Weston said brusquely:

'Ah well, thank you for telling us. Probably not important but quite right—er—to remember everything.'

'Naturally,' said Mrs Castle, 'ay wish to do my Duty!'

'Quite, quite. Ask Mr Lane to come here.'

V

Stephen Lane strode into the room with his usual vigour.

Weston said:

'I'm the Chief Constable of the County, Mr Lane. I suppose you've been told what has occurred here?'

'Yes—oh yes—I heard as soon as I got here. Terrible... Terrible...' His thin frame quivered. He said in a low voice: 'All along—ever since I arrived here—I have been conscious—very conscious—of the forces of evil close at hand.'

His eyes, burning eager eyes, went to Hercule Poirot.

He said:

'You remember, M. Poirot? Our conversation some days ago? About the reality of evil?'

Weston was studying the tall, gaunt figure in some perplexity. He found it difficult to make this man out. Lane's eyes came back to him. The clergyman said with a slight smile:

'I dare say that seems fantastic to you, sir. We have left off believing in evil in these days. We have abolished Hell fire! We no longer believe in the Devil! But Satan and Satan's emissaries were never more powerful than they are today!'

Weston said:

'Er—er—yes, perhaps. That, Mr Lane, is your province. Mine is more prosaic—to clear up a case of murder.'

Stephen Lane said:

'An awful word. Murder! One of the earliest sins known

on earth—the ruthless shedding of an innocent brother's blood...' He paused, his eyes half closed. Then, in a more ordinary voice he said:

'In what way can I help you?'

'First of all, Mr Lane, will you tell me your own movements today?'

'Willingly. I started off early on one of my usual tramps. I am fond of walking. I have roamed over a good deal of the countryside round here. Today I went to St Petrock-in-the-Combe. That is about seven miles from here—a very pleasant walk along winding lanes, up and down the Devon hills and valleys. I took some lunch with me and ate it in a spinney. I visited the church—it has some fragments—only fragments alas, of early glass—also a very interesting painted screen.'

'Thank you, Mr Lane. Did you meet anyone on your walk?'

'Not to speak to. A cart passed me once and a couple of boys on bicycles and some cows. However,' he smiled, 'if you want proof of my statement, I wrote my name in the book at the church. You will find it there.'

'You did not see anyone at the church itself—the Vicar, or the verger?'

Stephen Lane shook his head. He said:

'No, there was no one about and I was the only visitor. St Petrock is a very remote spot. The village itself lies on the far side of it about half a mile farther on.'

Colonel Weston said pleasantly:

'You mustn't think we're—er—doubting what you say.

Agatha Christie

Just a matter of checking up on everybody. Just routine, you know, routine. Have to stick to routine in cases of this kind.'

Stephen Lane said gently:

'Oh yes, I quite understand.'

Weston went on:

'Now the next point. Is there anything you know that would assist us at all? Anything about the dead woman? Anything that could give us a pointer as to who murdered her? Anything you heard or saw?'

Stephen Lane said:

'I heard nothing. All I can tell you is this: that I knew instinctively as soon as I saw her that Arlena Marshall was a focus of evil. She *was* Evil! Evil personified! Woman can be man's help and inspiration in life—she can also be man's downfall. She can drag a man down to the level of the beast. The dead woman was just such a woman. She appealed to everything base in a man's nature. She was a woman such as Jezebel and Aholibah. Now—she has been struck down in the middle of her wickedness!'

Hercule Poirot stirred. He said:

'Not struck down—*strangled!* Strangled, Mr Lane, by a pair of human hands.'

The clergyman's own hands trembled. The fingers writhed and twitched. He said, and his voice came low and choked:

'That's horrible—horrible—Must you put it like that?'

Hercule Poirot said:

'It is the simple truth. Have you any idea, Mr Lane, whose hands those were?'

The other shook his head. He said: 'I know nothing—nothing...'

Weston got up. He said, after a glance at Colgate to which the latter replied by an almost imperceptible nod, 'Well, we must get on to the cove.'

Lane said:

'Is that where—it happened?'

Weston nodded.

Lane said:

'Can—can I come with you?'

About to return a curt negative, Weston was forestalled by Poirot.

'But certainly,' said Poirot. 'Accompany me there in a boat, Mr Lane. We start immediately.'

CHAPTER 9

For the second time that morning Patrick Redfern was rowing a boat into Pixy Cove. The other occupants of the boat were Hercule Poirot, very pale with a hand to his stomach, and Stephen Lane. Colonel Weston had taken the land route. Having been delayed on the way he arrived on the beach at the same time as the boat grounded. A police constable and a plainclothes sergeant were on the beach already. Weston was questioning the latter as the three from the boat walked up and joined him.

Sergeant Phillips said:

'I think I've been over every inch of the beach, sir.'

'Good, what did you find?'

'It's all together here, sir, if you'd like to come and see.'

A small collection of objects was laid out neatly on a rock. There was a pair of scissors, an empty Gold Flake packet, five patent bottle tops, a number of used matches, three pieces of string, one or two fragments of newspaper, a fragment of a smashed pipe, four buttons, the drumstick bone of a chicken and an empty bottle of sunbathing oil.

Weston looked down appraisingly on the objects.

'Hm,' he said. 'Rather moderate for a beach nowadays! Most people seem to confuse a beach with a public rubbish dump! Empty bottle's been here some time by the way the label's blurred—so have most of the other things, I should say. The scissors are new, though. Bright and shining. *They* weren't out in yesterday's rain! Where were they?'

'Close by the bottom of the ladder, sir. Also this bit of pipe.'

'Hm, probably dropped by someone going up or down. Nothing to say who they belong to?'

'No, sir. Quite an ordinary pair of nail scissors. Pipe's a good-quality brier—expensive.'

Poirot murmured thoughtfully:

'Captain Marshall told us, I think, that he had mislaid his pipe.'

Weston said:

'Marshall's out of the picture. Anyway, he's not the only person who smokes a pipe.'

Hercule Poirot was watching Stephen Lane as the latter's hand went to his pocket and away again. He said pleasantly:

'You also smoke a pipe, do you not, Mr Lane?'

The clergyman started. He looked at Poirot.

He said:

'Yes. Oh yes. My pipe is an old friend and companion.' Putting his hand into his pocket again he drew out a pipe, filled it with tobacco and lighted it.

Hercule Poirot moved away to where Redfern was standing, his eyes blank.

Redfern said in a low voice:

'I'm glad—they've taken *her* away...'

Stephen Lane asked:

'Where was she found?'

The Sergeant said cheerfully:

'Just about where you're standing, sir.'

Lane moved swiftly aside. He stared at the spot he had just vacated.

The Sergeant went on:

'Place where the float was drawn up agrees with putting the time she arrived here at 10.45. That's going by the tide. It's turned now.'

'Photography all done?' asked Weston.

'Yes, sir.'

Weston turned to Redfern.

'Now then, man, where's the entrance to this cave of yours?'

Patrick Redfern was still staring down at the beach where Lane had been standing. It was as though he was seeing that sprawling body that was no longer there.

Weston's words recalled him to himself.

He said: 'It's over here.'

He led the way to where a great mass of tumbled-down

rocks were massed picturesquely against the cliff side. He went straight to where two big rocks, side by side, showed a straight narrow cleft between them. He said:

'The entrance is here.'

Weston said:

'Here? Doesn't look as though a man could squeeze through.'

'It's deceptive, you'll find, sir. It can just be done.'

Weston inserted himself gingerly into the cleft. It was not as narrow as it looked. Inside, the space widened and proved to be a fairly roomy recess with room to stand upright and to move about.

Hercule Poirot and Stephen Lane joined the Chief Constable. The others stayed outside. Light filtered in through the opening, but Weston had also got a powerful torch which he played freely over the interior.

He observed:

'Handy place. You'd never suspect it from the outside.'

He played the torch carefully over the floor.

Hercule Poirot was delicately sniffing the air.

Noticing this, Weston said:

'Air quite fresh, not fishy or seaweedy, but of course this place is well above high-water mark.'

But to Poirot's sensitive nose, the air was more than fresh. It was delicately scented. He knew two people who used that elusive perfume...

'Weston's torch came to rest. He said:

'Don't see anything out of the way in here.'

Poirot's eyes rose to a ledge a little way above his head. He murmured:

'One might perhaps see that there is nothing up there?'

Weston said: 'If there's anything up there it would have to be deliberately put there. Still, we'd better have a look.'

Poirot said to Lane:

'You are, I think, the tallest of us, Monsieur. Could we venture to ask you to make sure there is nothing resting on that ledge?'

Lane stretched up, but he could not quite reach to the back of the shelf. Then, seeing a crevice in the rock, he inserted a toe in it and pulled himself up by one hand.

He said:

'Hullo, there's a box up here.'

In a minute or two they were out in the sunshine examining the clergyman's find.

Weston said:

'Careful, don't handle it more than you can help. May be fingerprints.'

It was a dark-green tin box and bore the word Sandwiches on it.

Sergeant Phillips said:

'Left from some picnic or other, I suppose.'

He opened the lid with his handkerchief.

Inside were small tin containers marked salt, pepper, mustard, and two larger square tins evidently for sandwiches. Sergeant Phillips lifted the lid of the salt container. It was full to the brim. He raised the next one, commenting:

'Hm, got salt in the pepper one too.'

The mustard compartment also contained salt.

His face suddenly alert, the police sergeant opened one of the bigger square tins. That, too, contained the same white crystalline powder.

Very gingerly, Sergeant Phillips dipped a finger in and applied it to his tongue.

His face changed. He said—and his voice was excited:

'This isn't *salt*, sir. Not by a long way! Bitter taste! Seems to me it's some kind of *drug*.'

II

'The third angle,' said Colonel Weston with a groan.

They were back at the hotel again.

The Chief Constable went on:

'If by any chance there's a dope gang mixed up in this, it opens up several possibilities. First of all, the dead woman may have been in with the gang herself. Think that's likely?'

Hercule Poirot said cautiously:

'It is possible.'

'She may have been a drug addict?'

Poirot shook his head.

He said:

'I should doubt that. She had steady nerves, radiant health, there were no marks of hypodermic injections (not that that proves anything—some people sniff the stuff). No, I do not think she took drugs.'

'In that case,' said Weston, 'she may have run into the

business accidentally, and she was deliberately silenced by the people running the show. We'll know presently just what the stuff is. I've sent it to Neasdon. If we're onto some dope ring, they're not the people to stick at trifles—'

He broke off as the door opened and Mr Horace Blatt came briskly into the room.

Mr Blatt was looking hot. He was wiping the perspiration from his forehead. His big hearty voice billowed out and filled the small room.

'Just this minute got back and heard the news! You the Chief Constable? They told me you were in here. My name's Blatt—Horace Blatt. Any way I can help you? Don't suppose so. I've been out in my boat since early this morning. Missed the whole blinking show. The one day that something *does* happen in this out-of-the-way spot, I'm not there. Just like life, that, isn't it? Hullo, Poirot, didn't see you at first. So you're in on this? Oh well, I suppose you would be. Sherlock Holmes *v.* the local police, is that it? Ha, ha! Lestrade—all that stuff. I'll enjoy seeing you do a bit of fancy sleuthing.'

Mr Blatt came to anchor in a chair, pulled out a cigarette case and offered it to Colonel Weston, who shook his head.

He said, with a slight smile:

'I'm an inveterate pipe smoker.'

'Same here. I smoke cigarettes as well—but nothing beats a pipe.'

Colonel Weston said with suddenly geniality:

Evil Under the Sun

'Then light up, man.'

Blatt shook his head.

'Not got my pipe on me at the moment. But put me wise about all this. All I've heard so far is that Mrs Marshall was found murdered on one of the beaches here.'

'On Pixy Cove,' said Colonel Weston, watching him.

But Mr Blatt merely asked excitedly:

'And she was strangled?'

'Yes, Mr Blatt.'

'Nasty—very nasty. Mind you, she asked for it! Hot stuff—*trés moutarde*—eh, M. Poirot? Any idea who did it, or mustn't I ask that?'

With a faint smile Colonel Weston said:

'Well, you know, it's we who are supposed to ask the questions.'

Mr Blatt waved his cigarette.

'Sorry—sorry—my mistake. Go ahead.'

'You went out sailing this morning. At what time?'

'Left here at a quarter to ten.'

'Was anyone with you?'

'Not a soul. All on my little lonesome.'

'And where did you go?'

'Along the coast in the direction of Plymouth. Took lunch with me. Not much wind so I didn't actually get very far.'

After another question or two, Weston asked:

'Now, about the Marshalls? Do you know anything that might help us?'

Agatha Christie

'Well, I've given you my opinion. *Crime passionnel!* All I can tell you is, it wasn't *me!* The fair Arlena had no use for me. Nothing doing in that quarter. She had her own blue-eyed boy! And if you ask me, Marshall was getting wise to it.'

'Have you any evidence for that?'

'Saw him give young Redfern a dirty look once or twice. Dark horse, Marshall. Looks very meek and mild and as though he were half asleep all the time—but that's not his reputation in the City. I've heard a thing or two about him. Nearly had up for assault once. Mind you, the fellow in question had put up a pretty dirty deal. Marshall had trusted him and the fellow had let him down cold. Particularly dirty business, I believe. Marshall went for him and half killed him. Fellow didn't prosecute—too afraid of what might come out. I give you that for what it's worth.'

'So you think it possible,' said Poirot, 'that Captain Marshall strangled his wife?'

'Not at all. Never said anything of the sort. Just letting you know that he's the sort of fellow who could go berserk on occasions.'

Poirot said:

'Mr Blatt, there is reason to believe that Mrs Marshall went this morning to Pixy Cove to meet someone. Have you any idea who that someone might be?'

Mr Blatt winked.

'It's not a guess. It's a certainty. Redfern!'

'It was not Mr Redfern.'

Mr Blatt seemed taken aback. He said hesitatingly:

'Then I don't know... No, I can't imagine...'

He went on, regaining a little of his aplomb:

'As I said before, it wasn't *me!* No such luck! Let me see, couldn't have been Gardener—his wife keeps far too sharp an eye on him! That old ass Barry? Rot! And it would hardly be the parson. Although, mind you, I've seen his Reverence watching her a good bit. All holy disapproval, but perhaps an eye for the contours all the same! Eh? Lot of hypocrites, most parsons. Did you read that case last month? Parson and the churchwarden's daughter! Bit of an eye-opener.'

Mr Blatt chuckled.

Colonel Weston said coldly:

'There is nothing you can think of that might help us?'

The other shook his head.

'No. Can't think of a thing.' He added: 'This will make a bit of a stir, I imagine. The Press will be onto it like hot cakes. There won't be quite so much of this high-toned exclusiveness about the Jolly Roger in future. Jolly Roger indeed. Precious little jollity about it.'

Hercule Poirot murmured:

'You have not enjoyed your stay here?'

Mr Blatt's red face got slightly redder. He said:

'Well, no, I haven't. The sailing's all right and the scenery and the service and the food—but there's no *matiness* in the place, you know what I mean! What I say is, my money's as good as another man's. We're all here to enjoy ourselves. Then why not get together and *do* it? All these cliques and people sitting by themselves and giving you frosty good-mornings—and good-evenings—and yes, very pleasant weather. No joy de viver. Lot of stuck-up dummies!'

Mr Blatt paused—by now very red indeed.

He wiped his forehead once more and said apologetically: 'Don't pay any attention to me. I get all worked up.'

III

Hercule Poirot murmured:

'And what do we think of Mr Blatt?'

Colonel Weston grinned and said:

'What do *you* think of him? You've seen more of him than I have.'

Poirot said softly:

'There are many of your English idioms that describe him. The rough diamond! The self-made man! The social climber! He is, as you choose to look at it, pathetic, ludicrous, blatant! It is a matter of opinion. But I think, too, that he is something else.'

'And what is that?'

Hercule Poirot, his eyes raised to the ceiling, murmured:

'I think that he is—*nervous!*'

IV

Inspector Colgate said:

'I've got those times worked out. From the hotel to the

ladder down to Pixy Cove three minutes. That's walking till you are out of sight of the hotel and then running like hell.'

Weston raised his eyebrows. He said:

'That's quicker than I thought.'

'Down ladder to beach one minute and three-quarters. Up same two minutes. That's PC Flint. He's a bit of an athlete. Walking and taking the ladder in the normal way, the whole business takes close on a quarter of an hour.'

Weston nodded. He said:

'There's another thing we must go into, the pipe question.'

Colgate said:

'Blatt smokes a pipe, so does Marshall, so does the parson. Redfern smokes cigarettes, the American prefers a cigar. Major Barry doesn't smoke at all. There's one pipe in Marshall's room, two in Blatt's, and one in the parson's. Chambermaid says Marshall has two pipes. The other chambermaid isn't a very bright girl. Doesn't know how many pipes the other two have. Says vaguely she's noticed two or three about in their rooms.'

Weston nodded.

'Anything else?'

'I've checked up on the staff. They all seem quite OK. Henry, in the bar, checks Marshall's statement about seeing him at ten to eleven. William, the beach attendant, was down repairing the ladder on the rocks by the hotel most of the morning. He seems all right. George marked the tennis court and then bedded out some plants round by the dining room. Neither of them would have seen anyone who came across the causeway to the island.'

'When was the causeway uncovered?'

'Round about 9.30, sir.'

Weston pulled at his moustache.

'It's possible somebody did come that way. We've got a new angle, Colgate.'

He told of the discovery of the sandwich box in the cave.

V

There was a tap on the door.

'Come in,' said Weston.

It was Captain Marshall.

He said:

'Can you tell me what arrangements I can make about the funeral?'

'I think we shall manage the inquest for the day after tomorrow, Captain Marshall.'

'Thank you.'

Inspector Colgate said:

'Excuse me, sir, allow me to return you these.'

He handed over the three letters.

Kenneth Marshall smiled rather sardonically.

He said:

'Has the police department been testing the speed of my typing? I hope my character is cleared.'

Colonel Weston said pleasantly.

Evil Under the Sun

'Yes, Captain Marshall, I think we can give you a clean bill of health. Those sheets take fully an hour to type. Moreover you were heard typing them by the chambermaid up till five minutes to eleven and you were seen by another witness at twenty minutes past.'

Captain Marshall murmured:

'Really? That all seems very satisfactory!'

'Yes. Miss Darnley came to your room at twenty minutes past eleven. You were so busy typing that you did not observe her entry.'

Kenneth Marshall's face took on an impassive expression. He said:

'Does Miss Darnley say that?' He paused. 'As a matter of fact she is wrong. I *did* see her, though she may not be aware of the fact. I saw her in the mirror.'

Poirot murmured:

'But you did not interrupt your typing?'

Marshall said shortly:

'No. I wanted to get finished.'

He paused a minute, then, in an abrupt voice, he said:

'Nothing more I can do for you?'

'No, thank you, Captain Marshall.'

Kenneth Marshall nodded and went out.

Weston said with a sigh:

'There goes our most hopeful suspect—cleared! Hullo, here's Neasdon.'

The doctor came in with a trace of excitement in his manner. He said:

'That's a nice little death lot you sent me along.'

'What is it?'

'What is it? Diamorphine hydrochloride. Stuff that's usually called heroin.'

Inspector Colgate whistled. He said:

'Now we're getting places, all right! Depend upon it, this dope stunt is at the bottom of the whole business.'

CHAPTER 10

The little crowd of people flocked out of the Red Bull. The brief inquest was over—adjourned for a fortnight.

Rosamund Darnley joined Captain Marshall. She said in a low voice:

'That wasn't so bad, was it, Ken?'

He did not answer at once. Perhaps he was conscious of the staring eyes of the villagers, the fingers that nearly pointed to him and only just did not quite do so!

'That's 'im, my dear.' 'See, that's 'er 'usband.' 'That be the 'usband.' 'Look, there 'e goes...'

The murmurs were not loud enough to reach his ears, but he was none the less sensitive to them. This was the modern-day pillory. The Press he had already encountered—self-confident, persuasive young men, adept at battering down his wall of silence of 'Nothing to say' that he had endeavoured to erect. Even the curt monosyllables that he had uttered, thinking that they at least could not lead to misapprehension, had reappeared in this morning's papers in a totally different guise. 'Asked whether he agreed that the mystery of his wife's death could only be explained on the assumption that a homicidal murderer had found his way onto the island, Captain Marshall declared that—' and so on and so forth.

Cameras had clicked ceaselessly. Now, at this minute, the well-known sound caught his ear. He half turned—a smiling young man was nodding cheerfully, his purpose accomplished.

Rosamund murmured:

'*Captain Marshall and a friend leaving the Red Bull after the inquest.*'

Marshall winced.

Rosamund said:

'It's no use, Ken! You've got to face it! I don't mean just the fact of Arlena's death—I mean all the attendant beastliness. The staring eyes and gossiping tongues, the fatuous interviews in the papers—and the best way to meet it is to find it funny! Come out with all the old inane clichés and curl a sardonic lip at them.'

He said:

'Is that your way?'

'Yes.' She paused. 'It isn't yours, I know. Protective colouring is your line. Remain rigidly non-active and fade into the background! But you can't do that here—you've no background to fade into. You stand out clear for all to see—like a striped tiger against a white backcloth. *The husband of the murdered woman!*'

'For God's sake, Rosamund—'
She said gently:
'My dear, I'm trying to be good for you!'
They walked for a few steps in silence. Then Marshall said in a different voice:
'I know you are. I'm not really ungrateful, Rosamund.'
They had progressed beyond the limits of the village. Eyes followed them but there was no one very near. Rosamund Darnley's voice dropped as she repeated a variant of her first remark.
'It didn't really go so badly, did it?'
He was silent for a moment, then he said:
'I don't know.'
'What do the police think?'
'They're non-committal.'
After a minute Rosamund said:
'That little man—Poirot—is he really taking an active interest!'
Kenneth Marshall said:
'Seemed to be sitting in the Chief Constable's pocket all right the other day.'
'I know—but is he *doing* anything?'
'How the hell should I know, Rosamund?'
She said thoughtfully:
'He's pretty old. Probably more or less ga ga.'
'Perhaps.'
They came to the causeway. Opposite them, serene in the sun, lay the island.
Rosamund said suddenly:

'Sometimes—things seem unreal. I can't believe, this minute, that it ever happened...'

Marshall said slowly:

'I think I know what you mean. Nature is so regardless! One ant the less—that's all it is in Nature!'

Rosamund said:

'Yes—and that's the proper way to look at it really.'

He gave her one very quick glance. Then he said in a low voice:

'Don't worry, my dear. It's all right. *It's all right.*'

II

Linda came down to the causeway to meet them. She moved with the spasmodic jerkiness of a nervous colt. Her young face was marred by deep black shadows under her eyes. Her lips were dry and rough.

She said breathlessly:

'What happened—what—what did they say?'

Her father said abruptly:

'Inquest adjourned for a fortnight.'

'That means they—they haven't decided?'

'Yes. More evidence is needed.'

'But—but what do they think?'

Marshall smiled a little in spite of himself.

'Oh, my dear child—who knows? And whom do you mean by they? The coroner, the jury, the police, the newspaper reporters, the fishing folk of Leathercombe Bay?'

Linda said slowly:

'I suppose I mean—the police.'

Marshall said dryly:

'Whatever the police think, they're not giving it away at present.'

His lips closed tightly after the sentence. He went into the hotel.

As Rosamund Darnley was about to follow suit, Linda said:

'Rosamund!'

Rosamund turned. The mute appeal in the girl's unhappy face touched her. She linked her arm through Linda's and together they walked away from the hotel, taking the path that led to the extreme end of the island.

Rosamund said gently:

'Try not to mind so much, Linda. I know it's all very terrible and a shock and all that, but it's no use brooding over these things. And it can be only the—horror of it that is worrying you. You weren't in the least *fond* of Arlena, you know.'

She felt the tremor that ran through the girl's body as Linda answered:

'No, I wasn't fond of her...'

Rosamund went on:

'Sorrow for a person is different—one can't put *that* behind one. But one *can* get over shock and horror by just not letting your mind *dwell* on it all the time.'

Linda said sharply:

'You don't understand.'

'I think I do, my dear.'

Linda shook her head.

Agatha Christie

'No, you don't. You don't understand in the least—and Christine doesn't understand either! Both of you have been nice to me, but you can't understand what I'm feeling. You just think it's morbid—that I'm dwelling on it all when I needn't.'

She paused.

'But it isn't that at all. If you knew what I know—'

Rosamund stopped dead. Her body did not tremble—on the contrary it stiffened. She stood for a minute or two, then she disengaged her arm from Linda's.

She said:

'What is it that you know, Linda?'

The girl gazed at her. Then she shook her head.

She muttered:

'Nothing.'

Rosamund caught her by the arm. The grip hurt and Linda winced slightly.

Rosamund said:

'Be careful, Linda. Be damned careful.'

Linda had gone dead white.

She said:

'I *am* very careful—all the time.'

Rosamund said urgently:

'Listen, Linda, what I said a minute or two ago applies just the same—only a hundred times more so. *Put the whole business out of your mind*. Never think about it. Forget— forget... You can if you try! Arlena is dead and nothing can bring her back to life... Forget everything and live in the future. And above all, *hold your tongue*.'

Evil Under the Sun

Linda shrank a little. She said:

'You—you seem to know all about it?'

Rosamund said energetically:

'I don't know *anything*! In my opinion a wandering maniac got onto the island and killed Arlena. That's much the most probable solution. I'm fairly sure that the police will have to accept that in the end. That's what *must* have happened! That's what *did* happen!'

Linda said:

'If Father—'

Rosamund interrupted her.

'Don't talk about it.'

Linda said:

'I've got to say one thing. My mother—'

'Well, what about her?'

'She—she was tried for murder, wasn't she?'

'Yes.'

Linda said slowly:

'And then Father married her. That looks, doesn't it, as though Father didn't really think murder was very wrong—not always, that is.'

Rosamund said sharply:

'Don't say things like that—even to me! The police haven't got anything against your father. He's got an alibi—an alibi that they can't break. He's perfectly safe.'

Linda whispered:

'Did they think at first that Father—?'

Rosamund cried:

'I don't know what they thought! But they know now

that he couldn't have done it. Do you understand? *He couldn't have done it.*'

She spoke with authority, her eyes commanded Linda's acquiescence. The girl uttered a long fluttering sigh.

Rosamund said:

'You'll be able to leave here soon. You'll forget everything—everything!'

Linda said with sudden unexpected violence.

'*I shall never forget.*'

She turned abruptly and ran back to the hotel. Rosamund stared after her.

III

'There is something I want to know, Madame.'

Christine Redfern glanced up at Poirot in a slightly abstracted manner. She said:

'Yes?'

Hercule Poirot took very little notice of her abstraction. He had noted the way her eyes followed her husband's figure where he was pacing up and down on the terrace outside the bar, but for the moment he had no interest in purely conjugal problems. He wanted information.

He said:

'Yes, Madame. It was a phrase—a chance phrase of yours the other day which roused my attention.'

Christine, her eyes still on Patrick, said:

'Yes? What did I say?'

'It was in answer to a question from the Chief Constable.

Evil Under the Sun

You described how you went into Miss Linda Marshall's room on the morning of the crime and how you found her absent from it and how she returned there, and it was then that the Chief Constable asked you where she had been.'

Christine said rather impatiently:

'And I said she had been bathing? Is that it?'

'Ah, but you did not say quite that. You did not say "she had been bathing". Your words were, "she said she had been bathing."'

Christine said:

'It's the same thing, surely.'

'No, it is not the same! The form of your answer suggests a certain attitude of mind on your part. Linda Marshall came into the room—she was wearing a bathing-wrap and yet—for some reason—you did not at once assume she had been bathing. That is shown by your words, "she *said* she had been bathing." What was there about her appearance—was it her manner, or something that she was wearing or something she said—that led you to feel surprised when she said she had been bathing?'

Christine's attention left Patrick and focused itself entirely on Poirot. She was interested. She said:

'That's clever of you. It's quite true, now I remember... I *was*, just faintly, surprised when Linda said she had been bathing.'

'But why, Madame, why?'

'Yes, why? That's just what I'm trying to remember. Oh yes, I think it was the parcel in her hand.'

Agatha Christie

'She had a parcel?'

'Yes.'

'You do not know what was in it?'

'Oh yes, I do. The string broke. It was loosely done up in the way they do in the village. It was *candles*—they were scattered on the floor. I helped her to pick them up.'

'Ah,' said Poirot. 'Candles.'

Christine stared at him. She said:

'You seem excited, M. Poirot.'

Poirot asked:

'Did Linda say why she had bought candles?'

Christine reflected.

'No, I don't think she did. I suppose it was to read by at night—perhaps the electric light wasn't good.'

'On the contrary, Madame, there was a bedside electric lamp in perfect order.'

Christine said:

'Then I don't know what she wanted them for.'

Poirot said:

'What was her manner—when the string broke and the candles fell out of the parcel?'

Christine said slowly:

'She was—upset—embarrassed.'

Poirot nodded his head. Then he asked:

'Did you notice a calendar in her room?'

'A calendar? What kind of a calendar?'

Poirot said:

'Possibly a green calendar—with tear-off leaves.'

Christine screwed up her eyes in an effort of memory.

'A green calendar—rather a bright green. Yes, I have seen a calendar like that—but I can't remember where. It may have been in Linda's room, but I can't be sure.'

'But you have definitely seen such a thing.'

'Yes.'

Again Poirot nodded.

Christine said rather sharply:

'What are you hinting at, M. Poirot? What is the meaning of all this?'

For answer Poirot produced a small volume bound in faded brown calf. He said:

'Have you ever seen this before?'

'Why—I think—I'm not sure—yes, Linda was looking into it in the village lending library the other day. But she shut it up and thrust it back quickly when I came up to her. It made me wonder what it was.'

Silently Poirot displayed the title.

A History of Witchcraft, Sorcery and of the Compounding of Untraceable Poisons.

Christine said:

'I don't understand. What does all this mean?'

Poirot said gravely.

'It may mean, Madame, a good deal.'

She looked at him enquiringly, but he did not go on. Instead he asked:

'One more question, Madame. Did you take a bath that morning before you went out to play tennis?'

Christine stared again.

'A bath? No. I would have had no time and, anyway, I didn't want a bath—not before tennis. I might have had one after.'

'Did you use your bathroom at all when you came in?'

'I sponged my face and hands, that's all.'

'You did not turn on the bath at all?'

'No, I'm sure I didn't.'

Poirot nodded. He said:

'It is of no importance.'

IV

Hercule Poirot stood by the table where Mrs Gardener was wrestling with a jigsaw. She looked up and jumped.

'Why, M. Poirot, how very quietly you came up beside me! I never heard you. Have you just come back from the inquest? You know, the very thought of that inquest makes me so nervous, I don't know what to do. That's why I'm doing this puzzle. I just felt I couldn't sit outside on the beach as usual. As Mr Gardener knows, when my nerves are all upset, there's nothing like one of these puzzles for calming me. There now, where *does* this white piece fit in? It must be part of the fur rug, but I don't seem to see...'

Gently Poirot's hand took the piece from her. He said:

'It fits, Madame, *here*. It is part of the cat.'

'It can't be. It's a black cat.'

Evil Under the Sun

'A black cat, yes, but you see the tip of the black cat's tail happens to be white.'

'Why, so it does! How clever of you! But I do think the people who make puzzles are kind of mean. They just go out of their way to deceive you.'

She fitted in another piece and then resumed.

'You know, M. Poirot, I've been watching you this last day or two. I just wanted to watch you detecting, if you know what I mean—not that it doesn't sound rather heartless put like that, as though it were all a game—and a poor creature killed. Oh dear, every time *I* think of it I get the shivers! I told Mr Gardener this morning I'd just *got* to get away from here, and now the inquest's over he thinks we'll be able to leave tomorrow, and that's a blessing, I'm sure. But about detecting, I would so like to know your methods—you know, I'd feel privileged if you'd just *explain* it to me.'

Hercule Poirot said:

'It is a little like your puzzle, Madame. One assembles the pieces. It is like a mosaic—many colours and patterns—and every strange-shaped little piece must be fitted into its own place.'

'Now isn't that interesting? Why, I'm sure you explain it just too beautifully.'

Poirot went on:

'And sometimes it is like that piece of your puzzle just now. One arranges very methodically the pieces of the puzzle—one sorts the colours—and then perhaps a piece

Agatha Christie

of one colour that should fit in with—say, the fur rug, fits in instead in a black cat's tail.'

'Why, if that doesn't sound too fascinating! And are there a great many pieces, M. Poirot?'

'Yes, Madame. Almost everyone here in this hotel has given me a piece for my puzzle. You amongst them.'

'Me?' Mrs Gardener's tone was shrill.

'Yes, a remark of yours, Madame, was exceedingly helpful. I might say it was illuminating.'

'Well, if that isn't too lovely! Can't you tell me some more, M. Poirot?'

'Ah! Madame, I reserve the explanations for the last chapter.'

Mrs Gardener murmured:

'If that isn't just too bad!'

V

Hercule Poirot tapped gently on the door of Captain Marshall's room. Inside there was the sound of a typewriter.

A curt 'Come in' came from the room and Poirot entered.

Captain Marshall's back was turned to him. He was sitting typing at the table between the windows. He did not turn his head but his eyes met Poirot's in the mirror that hung on the wall directly in front of him. He said irritably:

'Well, M. Poirot, what is it?'

Poirot said quickly:

'A thousand apologies for intruding. You are busy?'

Marshall said shortly: 'I am rather.'

Poirot said:

'It is one little question that I would like to ask you.'

Marshall said:

'My God, I'm sick of answering questions. I've answered the police questions. I don't feel called upon to answer yours.'

Poirot said:

'Mine is a very simple one. Only this. On the morning of your wife's death, did you have a bath after you finished typing and before you went out to play tennis?'

'A bath? No, of course I didn't! I'd had a bathe only an hour earlier!'

Hercule Poirot said:

'Thank you. That is all.'

'But look here. Oh—' the other paused irresolutely.

Poirot withdrew, gently closing the door.

Kenneth Marshall said:

'The fellow's crazy!'

VI

Just outside the bar Poirot encountered Mr Gardener. He was carrying two cocktails and was clearly on his way to where Mrs Gardener was ensconced with her jigsaw.

He smiled at Poirot in genial fashion.

'Care to join us, M. Poirot?'

Poirot shook his head. He said:

'What did you think of the inquest, Mr Gardener?'

Mr Gardener lowered his voice. He said:

'Seemed kind of indeterminate to me. Your police, I gather, have got something up their sleeves.'

'It is possible,' said Hercule Poirot.

Mr Gardener lowered his voice still further.

'I shall be glad to get Mrs Gardener away. She's a very, very sensitive woman, and this affair has got on her nerves. She's very highly strung.'

Hercule Poirot said:

'Will you permit me, Mr Gardener, to ask you one question?'

'Why, certainly, M. Poirot. Delighted to assist in any way I can.'

Hercule Poirot said:

'You are a man of the world—a man, I think, of considerable acumen. What, frankly, was your opinion of the late Mrs Marshall?'

Mr Gardener's eyebrows rose in surprise. He glanced cautiously round and lowered his voice.

'Well, M. Poirot, I've heard a few things that have been kind of going around, if you get me, especially among the women.' Poirot nodded. 'But if you ask me I'll tell you my candid opinion and that is that that woman was pretty much of a darned fool!'

Hercule Poirot said thoughtfully:

'Now that is very interesting.'

VII

Rosamund Darnley said: 'So it's my turn, is it?'

'Pardon?'

She laughed.

'The other day the Chief Constable held his inquisition. You sat by. Today, I think, you are conducting your own unofficial inquiry. I've been watching you. First Mrs Redfern, then I caught a glimpse of you through the lounge window where Mrs Gardener is doing her hateful jigsaw puzzle. Now it's my turn.'

Hercule Poirot sat down beside her. They were on Sunny Ledge. Below them the sea showed a deep-glowing green. Farther out it was a pale dazzling blue.

Poirot said:

'You are very intelligent, Mademoiselle. I have thought so ever since I arrived here. It would be a pleasure to discuss this business with you.'

Rosamund Darnley said softly:

'You want to know what I think about the whole thing?'

'It would be most interesting.'

Rosamund said:

'I think it's really very simple. The clue is in the woman's past.'

'The past? Not the present?'

'Oh! not necessarily the very remote past. I look at it like this. Arlena Marshall was attractive, fatally attractive, to men. It's possible, I think, that she also tired of them rather quickly. Amongst her—followers, shall we say—was one who resented that. Oh, don't misunderstand me, it won't be someone who sticks out a mile. Probably some tepid little man, vain and sensitive—the kind of man who broods. I think he followed her down here, waited his opportunity and killed her.'

'You mean that he was an outsider, that he came from the mainland?'

'Yes. He probably hid in that cave until he got his chance.'

Poirot shook his head. He said:

'Would she go there to meet such a man as you describe? No, she would laugh and not go.'

Rosamund said:

'She mayn't have known she was going to meet him. He may have sent her a message in some other person's name.'

Poirot murmured:

'That is possible.'

Then he said:

'But you forget one thing, Mademoiselle. A man bent on murder could not risk coming in broad daylight across the causeway and past the hotel. Someone might have seen him.'

'They might have—but I don't think that it's certain. I think it's quite possible that he could have come without anyone noticing him at all.'

'It would be *possible*, yes, that I grant you. But the point is that he could not *count* on that possibility.'

Evil Under the Sun

Rosamund said:

'Aren't you forgetting something? The weather.'

'The weather?'

'Yes. The day of the murder was a glorious day, but the day before, remember, there was rain and thick mist. Anyone could come onto the island then without being seen. He had only to go down to the beach and spend the night in the cave. That mist, M. Poirot, is important.'

Poirot looked at her thoughtfully for a minute or two. He said:

'You know, there is a good deal in what you have just said.'

Rosamund flushed. She said:

'That's my theory, for what it is worth. Now tell me yours.'

'Ah,' said Hercule Poirot. He stared down at the sea.

'*Eh bien*, Mademoiselle. I am a very simple person. I always incline to the belief that the most likely person committed the crime. At the very beginning it seemed to me that one person was very clearly indicated.'

Rosamund's voice hardened a little. She said:

'Go on.'

Hercule Poirot went on.

'But you see, there is what you call a snag in the way! It seems that it was *impossible* for that person to have committed the crime.'

He heard the quick expulsion of her breath. She said rather breathlessly:

'Well?'

Agatha Christie

Hercule Poirot shrugged his shoulders.

'Well, what do we do about it? That is my problem.' He paused and then went on. 'May I ask you a question?'

'Certainly.'

She faced him, alert and vigilant. But the question that came was an unexpected one.

'When you came in to change for tennis that morning, did you have a bath?'

Rosamund stared at him.

'A bath? What do you mean?'

'That is what I mean. A bath! The receptacle of porcelain, one turns the taps and fills it, one gets in, one gets out and ghoosh—ghoosh—ghoosh, the water goes down the waste pipe!'

'M. Poirot, are you quite mad?'

'No, I am extremely sane.'

'Well, anyway, I *didn't* take a bath.'

'Ha!' said Poirot. 'So nobody took a bath. That is extremely interesting.'

'But why should anyone take a bath?'

Hercule Poirot said: 'Why, indeed?'

Rosamund said with some exasperation:

'I suppose this is the Sherlock Holmes touch!'

Hercule Poirot smiled.

Then he sniffed the air delicately.

'Will you permit me to be impertinent, Mademoiselle?'

'I'm sure you couldn't be impertinent, M. Poirot.'

'That is very kind of you. Then may I venture to say that the scent you use is delicious—it has a *nuance*—a delicate elusive charm.' He waved his hands, and then added in a practical voice, 'Gabrielle, No 8, I think?'

'How clever you are. Yes, I always use it.'

'So did the late Mrs Marshall. It is chic, eh? And very expensive?'

Rosamund shrugged her shoulders with a faint smile.

Poirot said:

'You sat here where we are now, Mademoiselle, on the morning of the crime. You were seen here, or at least your sunshade was seen by Miss Brewster and Mr Redfern as they passed on the sea. During the morning, Mademoiselle, are you sure you did not happen to go down to Pixy Cove and enter the cave there—the famous Pixy's Cave?'

Rosamund turned her head and stared at him.

She said in a quiet level voice:

'Are you asking me if I killed Arlena Marshall?'

'No, I am asking you if you went into the Pixy's Cave.'

'I don't even know where it is. Why should I go into it? For what reason?'

'On the day of the crime, Mademoiselle, somebody had been in that cave who used Gabrielle No 8.'

Rosamund said sharply:

'You've just said yourself, M. Poirot, that Arlena Marshall used Gabrielle No 8. She was on the beach there that day. Presumably she went into the cave.'

'Why should she go into the cave? It is dark there and narrow and very uncomfortable.'

Rosamund said impatiently:

Agatha Christie

'Don't ask me for reasons. Since she was actually at the cove she was by far the most likely person. I've told you already I never left this place the whole morning.'

'Except for the time when you went into the hotel to Captain Marshall's room.' Poirot reminded her.

'Yes, of course. I'd forgotten that.'

Poirot said:

'And you were wrong, Mademoiselle, when you thought that Captain Marshall did not see you.'

Rosamund said incredulously:

'Kenneth did see me? Did—did he say so?'

Poirot nodded.

'He saw you, Mademoiselle, in the mirror that hangs over the table.'

Rosamund caught her breath. She said:

'Oh! I see.'

Poirot was no longer looking out to sea. He was looking at Rosamund Darnley's hands as they lay folded in her lap. They were well-shaped hands, beautifully moulded with very long fingers.

Rosamund, shooting a quick look at him, followed the direction of his eyes. She said sharply:

'What are you looking at my hands for? Do you think— do you think—?'

Poirot said:

'Do I think—what, Mademoiselle?'

Rosamund Darnley said:

'Nothing.'

VIII

It was perhaps an hour later that Hercule Poirot came to the top of the path leading to Gull Cove. There was someone sitting on the beach. A slight figure in a red shirt and dark blue shorts.

Poirot descended the path, stepping carefully in his tight smart shoes.

Linda Marshall turned her head sharply. He thought that she shrank a little.

Her eyes, as he came and lowered himself gingerly to the shingle beside her, rested on him with the suspicion and alertness of a trapped animal. He realized, with a pang, how young and vulnerable she was.

She said:

'What is it? What do you want?'

Hercule Poirot did not answer for a minute or two. Then he said:

'The other day you told the Chief Constable that you were fond of your stepmother and that she was kind to you.'

'Well?'

'That was not true, was it, Mademoiselle?'

'Yes, it was.'

Poirot said:

'She may not have been actively unkind—that I will grant. But you were not fond of her—Oh no—I think you disliked her very much. That was very plain to see.'

Linda said:

Agatha Christie

'Perhaps I didn't like her very much. But one can't say that when a person is dead. It wouldn't be decent.'

Poirot sighed. He said:

'They taught you that at your school?'

'More or less, I suppose.'

Hercule Poirot said:

'When a person has been murdered, it is more important to be truthful than to be decent.'

Linda said:

'I suppose you *would* say a thing like that.'

'I would say it and I do say it. It is my business, you see, to find out who killed Arlena Marshall.'

Linda muttered:

'I want to forget it all. It's so horrible.'

Poirot said gently:

'*But you can't forget, can you?*'

Linda said:

'I suppose some beastly madman killed her.'

Hercule Poirot murmured:

'No, I do not think it was quite like that.'

Linda caught her breath. She said:

'You sound—as though you *knew*?'

Poirot said:

'Perhaps I do know.' He paused and went on: 'Will you trust me, my child, to do the best I can for you in your bitter trouble?'

Linda sprang up. She said:

'I haven't any trouble. There is nothing you can do for me. I don't know what you are talking about.'

Poirot said, watching her:

'I am talking about *candles*...'

He saw the terror leap into her eyes. She cried:

'I won't listen to you. I won't listen.'

She ran across the beach, swift as a young gazelle, and went flying up the zigzag path.

Poirot shook his head. He looked grave and troubled.

CHAPTER 11

Inspector Colgate was reporting to the Chief Constable.

'I've got on to one thing, sir, and something pretty sensational. It's about Mrs Marshall's money. I've been into it with her lawyers. I'd say it's a bit of a shock to them. I've got proof of the blackmail story. You remember she was left fifty thousand pounds by old Erskine? Well, all that's left of that is about fifteen thousand.'

The Chief Constable whistled.

'Whew, what's become of the rest?'

'That's the interesting point, sir. She's sold out stuff from time to time, and each time she's handled it in cash or negotiable securities—that's to say she's handed out money to someone that she didn't want traced. Blackmail all right.'

The Chief Constable nodded.

'Certainly looks like it. And the blackmailer is here in this hotel. That means it must be one of those three men. Got anything fresh on any of them?'

'Can't say I've got anything definite, sir. Major Barry's

a retired Army man, as he says. Lives in a small flat, has a pension and a small income from stocks. *But* he's paid pretty considerable sums into his account in the last year.'

'That sounds promising. What's his explanation?'

'Says they're betting gains. It's perfectly true that he goes to all the large race meetings. Places his bets on the course too, doesn't run an account.'

The Chief Constable nodded.

'Hard to disprove that,' he said. 'But it's suggestive.'

Colgate went on.

'Next, the Reverend Stephen Lane. He's *bona fide* all right—had a living at St Helen's, Whiteridge, Surrey—resigned his living just over a year ago owing to ill-health. His ill-health amounted to his going into a nursing home for mental patients. He was there for over a year.'

'Interesting,' said Weston.

'Yes, sir. I tried to get as much as I could out of the doctor in charge but you know what these medicos are—it's difficult to pin them down to anything you can get hold of. But as far as I can make out, his reverence's trouble was an obsession about the devil—especially the devil in the guise of a woman—scarlet woman—whore of Babylon.'

'Hm,' said Weston. 'There have been precedents for murder there.'

'Yes, sir. It seems to me that Stephen Lane is at least a possibility. The late Mrs Marshall was a pretty good example of what a clergyman would call a scarlet woman—hair and going-on and all. Seems to me it's not impossible

Agatha Christie

he may have felt it his appointed task to dispose of her. That is if he is really batty.'

'Nothing to fit in with the blackmail theory?'

'No, sir, I think we can wash him out as far as that's concerned. Has some private means of his own, but not very much, and no sudden increase lately.'

'What about his story of his movements on the day of the crime?'

'Can't get any confirmation of them. Nobody remembers meeting a parson in the lanes. As to the book at the church, the last entry was three days before and nobody had looked at it for about a fortnight. He could have quite easily gone over the day before, say, or even a couple of days before, and dated his entry the 25th.'

Weston nodded. He said:

'And the third man?'

'Horace Blatt? It's my opinion, sir, that there's definitely something fishy there. Pays income tax on a sum far exceeding what he makes out of his hardware business. And mind you, he's a slippery customer. He could probably cook up a reasonable statement—he gambles a bit on the Stock Exchange, and he's in with one or two shady deals. Oh, yes, there may be plausible explanations, but there's no getting away from it that he's been making pretty big sums from unexplained sources for some years now.'

'In fact,' said Weston, 'the idea is that Mr Horace Blatt is a successful blackmailer by profession?'

'Either that, sir, or it's dope. I saw Chief Inspector Ridgeway who's in charge of the dope business, and he was no end keen. Seems there's been a good bit of heroin coming in lately. They're on to the small distributors, and they know more or less who's running it the other end, but it's the way it's coming into the country that's baffled them so far.'

Weston said:

'If the Marshall woman's death is the result of her getting mixed up, innocently or otherwise, with the dope-running stunt, then we'd better hand the whole thing over to Scotland Yard. It's their pigeon. Eh? What do you say?'

Inspector Colgate said rather regretfully:

'I'm afraid you're right, sir. If it's dope, then it's a case for the Yard.'

Weston said after a moment or two's thought:

'It really seems the most likely explanation.'

Colgate nodded gloomily.

'Yes, it does. Marshall's right out of it—though I did get some information that might have been useful if his alibi hadn't been so good. Seems his firm is very near the rocks. Not his fault or his partner's, just the general result of the crisis last year and the general state of trade and finance. And as far as he knew, he'd come into fifty thousand pounds if his wife died. And fifty thousand would have been a very useful sum.'

He sighed.

'Seems a pity when a man's got two perfectly good motives for murder, that he can be proved to have had nothing to do with it!'

Weston smiled.

'Cheer up, Colgate. There's still a chance we may distinguish ourselves. There's the blackmail angle still and there's the batty parson, but, personally, I think the dope solution is far the most likely.' He added: 'And if it was one of the dope gang who put her out we'll have been instrumental in helping Scotland Yard to solve the dope problem. In fact, take it all round, one way or another, we've done pretty well.'

An unwilling smile showed on Colgate's face.

He said:

'Well, that's the lot, sir. By the way, I checked up on the writer of that letter we found in her room. The one signed J.N. Nothing doing. He's in China safe enough. Same chap as Miss Brewster was telling us about. Bit of a young scallywag. I've checked up on the rest of Mrs Marshall's friends. No leads there. Everything there is to get, we've got, sir.'

Weston said:

'So now it's up to us.' He paused and then added: 'Seen anything of our Belgian colleague? Does he know all you've told me?'

Colgate said with a grin:

'He's a queer little cuss, isn't he? D'you know what he asked me day before yesterday? He wanted particulars of any cases of strangulation in the last three years.'

Colonel Weston sat up.

'He did, did he? Now I wonder—' he paused a minute. 'When did you say the Reverend Stephen Lane went into that mental home?'

'A year ago last Easter, sir.'

Colonel Weston was thinking deeply. He said:

'There was a case—body of a young woman found somewhere near Bagshot. Going to meet her husband somewhere and never turned up. And there was what the papers called the Lonely Copse Mystery. Both in Surrey if I remember rightly.'

His eyes met those of his Inspector. Colgate said:

'Surrey? My word, sir, it fits, doesn't it? I wonder...'

II

Hercule Poirot sat on the turf on the summit of the island.

A little to his left was the beginning of the steel ladder that led down to Pixy Cove. There were several rough boulders near the head of the ladder, he noted, forming easy concealment for anyone who proposed to descend to the beach below. Of the beach itself little could be seen from the top owing to the overhang of the cliff.

Hercule Poirot nodded his head gravely.

The pieces of his jigsaw were fitting into position.

Mentally he went over those pieces, considering each as a detached item.

A morning on the bathing beach some few days before Arlena Marshall's death.

One, two, three, four, five separate remarks uttered on that morning.

The evening of a bridge game. He, Patrick Redfern and Rosamund Darnley had been at the table. Christine had wandered out while dummy and had overheard a certain conversation. Who else had been in the lounge at that time? Who had been absent?

The evening before the crime. The conversation he had had with Christine on the cliff and the scene he had witnessed on his way back to the hotel.

Gabrielle No 8.

A pair of scissors.

A broken pipe stem.

A bottle thrown from a window.

A green calendar.

A packet of candles.

A mirror and a typewriter.

A skein of magenta wool.

A girl's wristwatch.

Bathwater rushing down the waste pipe.

Each of these unrelated facts must fit into its appointed place. There must be no loose ends.

And then, with each concrete fact fitted into position, on to the next stop: his own belief in the presence of evil on the island.

Evil...

He looked down at a typewritten paper in his hands.

Nellie Parsons—found strangled in a lonely copse near Chobham. No clue to her murderer ever discovered.

Nellie Parsons?

Alice Corrigan.

He read very carefully the details of Alice Corrigan's death.

III

To Hercule Poirot, sitting on the ledge overlooking the sea, came Inspector Colgate.

Poirot liked Inspector Colgate. He liked his rugged face, his shrewd eyes, and his slow unhurried manner.

Inspector Colgate sat down. He said, glancing down at the typewritten sheets in Poirot's hand:

'Done anything with those cases, sir?'

'I have studied them—yes.'

Colgate got up, he walked along and peered into the next niche. He came back, saying:

'One can't be too careful. Don't want to be overheard.'

Poirot said:

'You are wise.'

Colgate said:

'I don't mind telling you, M. Poirot, that I've been interested in those cases myself—though perhaps I shouldn't have thought about them if you hadn't asked for them.' He paused: 'I've been interested in one case in particular.'

'Alice Corrigan?'

'Alice Corrigan.' He paused. 'I've been on to the Surrey police about that case—wanted to get all the ins and outs of it.'

'Tell me, my friend. I am interested—very interested.'

'I thought you might be. Alice Corrigan was found strangled in Caesar's Grove on Blackridge Heath—not ten miles from Marley Copse where Nellie Parsons was found—and both those places are within twelve miles of Whiteridge where Mr Lane was vicar.'

Poirot said:

'Tell me more about the death of Alice Corrigan.'

Colgate said:

'The Surrey police didn't at first connect her death with that of Nellie Parsons. That's because they'd pitched on the husband as the guilty party. Don't quite know why except that he was a bit of what the Press calls a "mystery man"—not much known about him—who he was or where he came from. She'd married him against her people's wishes, she'd a bit of money of her own—and she'd insured her life in his favour—all that was enough to raise suspicion, as I think you'll agree, sir?'

Poirot nodded.

'But when it came down to brass tacks the husband was washed right out of the picture. The body was discovered by one of these women hikers—hefty young women in shorts. She was an absolutely competent and reliable witness—games mistress at a school in Lancashire. She noted the time when she found the body—it was exactly 4.15—and gave it as her opinion that the woman had been dead quite a short time—not more than ten minutes. That fitted in well enough with the police surgeon's view when he examined the body at 5.45. She left everything as it was and tramped across country to Bagshot police station where she reported the death. Now from three o'clock to 4.10, Edward Corrigan was in the train coming down from London, where he'd gone up for the day on business. Four other people were in the carriage with him. From the station he took the local bus, two of his fellow passengers travelling by it also. He got off at the Pine Ridge Café where he'd arranged to meet his wife for tea. Time then was 4.25. He ordered tea for them both, but said not to bring it till she came. Then he walked about outside waiting for her. When by five o'clock she hadn't turned up, he was getting alarmed—thought she might have sprained her ankle. The arrangement was that she was to walk across the moors from the village where they were staying to the Pine Ridge Café and go home by bus. Caesar's Grove is not far from the café, and it's thought that as she was ahead of time she sat down there to admire the view for a bit before going on, and that some tramp or madman came upon her there and caught her unawares. Once the husband was proved to be out of it, naturally they connected up her death with that of Nellie Parsons—that rather flighty servant girl who was found strangled in Marley Copse. They decided that the same man was responsible for both crimes, but they never caught him—and what's more they never came near to catching him! Drew a blank everywhere.'

He paused and then he said slowly:

'And now—here's a third woman strangled—and a certain gentleman we won't name right on the spot.'

He stopped.

His small shrewd eyes came round to Poirot. He waited hopefully.

Agatha Christie

Poirot's lips moved. Inspector Colgate leaned forward. Poirot was murmuring:

'—so difficult to know which pieces are part of the fur rug and which are the cat's tail.'

'I *beg* pardon, sir?' said Inspector Colgate, startled.

Poirot said quickly:

'I apologize. I was following a train of thought of my own.'

'What's this about a fur rug and a cat?'

'Nothing—nothing at all.' He paused. 'Tell me, Inspector Colgate, if you suspected someone of telling lies—many, many lies—but you had no proof, what would you do?'

Inspector Colgate considered.

'It's difficult, that is. But it's my opinion that if anyone tells enough lies, they're bound to trip up in the end.'

Poirot nodded.

'Yes, that is very true. You see, it is only in my mind that certain statements are lies. I *think* that they are lies, but I cannot *know* that they are lies. But one might perhaps make a test—a test of one little not very noticeable lie. And if that were proved to be a lie—why then, one would know that all the rest were lies, too!'

Inspector Colgate looked at him curiously.

'Your mind works a funny way, doesn't it, sir? But I dare say it comes out all right in the end. If you'll excuse me asking, what put you onto asking about strangulation cases in general?'

Poirot said slowly:

'You have a word in your language—*slick*. This crime

seemed to me a very slick crime! It made me wonder if, perhaps, it was not a first attempt.'

Inspector Colgate said:

'I see.'

Poirot went on:

'I said to myself, let us examine past crimes of a similar kind and if there is a crime that closely resembles this one—*eh bien*, we shall have there a very valuable clue.'

'You mean using the same method of death, sir?'

'No, no, I mean more than that. The death of Nellie Parsons for instance tells me nothing. But the death of Alice Corrigan—tell me, Inspector Colgate, do you not notice one striking form of similarity in this crime?'

Inspector Colgate turned the problem over in his mind. He said at last.

'No, sir, I can't say that I do really. Unless it's that in each case the husband has got a cast-iron alibi.'

Poirot said softly:

'Ah, so you *have* noticed that?'

IV

'Ha, Poirot. Glad to see you. Come in. Just the man I want.'

Hercule Poirot responded to the invitation.

The Chief Constable pushed over a box of cigarettes, took one himself and lighted it. Between puffs he said:

'I've decided, more or less, on a course of action. But I'd like your opinion on it before I act decisively.'

Hercule Poirot said:

Agatha Christie

'Tell me, my friend.'

Weston said:

'I've decided to call in Scotland Yard and hand the case over to them. In my opinion, although there have been grounds for suspicion against one or two people, the whole case hinges on dope smuggling. It seems clear to me that that place, Pixy's Cave, was a definite rendezvous for the stuff.'

Poirot nodded.

'I agree.'

'Good man. And I'm pretty certain who our dope smuggler is. Horace Blatt.'

Again Poirot assented. He said:

'That, too, is indicated.'

'I see our minds have both worked the same way. Blatt used to go sailing in that boat of his. Sometimes he'd invite people to go with him, but most of the time he went out alone. He had some rather conspicuous red sails on that boat, but we've found that he had some white sails as well stowed away. I think he sailed out on a good day to an appointed spot, and was met by another boat—sailing boat or motor yacht—something of the kind, and the stuff was handed over. Then Blatt would run ashore into Pixy Cove at a suitable time of day—'

Hercule Poirot smiled:

'Yes, yes, at half past one. The hour of the British lunch when everyone is quite sure to be in the dining room. The island is private. It is not a place where outsiders come for picnics. People take their tea sometimes from the hotel to

Pixy Cove in the afternoon when the sun is on it, or if they want a picnic they would go somewhere far afield, many miles away.'

The Chief Constable nodded.

'Quite,' he said. 'Therefore, Blatt ran ashore there and stowed the stuff on that ledge in the cave. Somebody else was to pick it up there in due course.'

Poirot murmured:

'There was a couple, you remember, who came to the island for lunch on the day of the murder? That would be a way of getting the stuff. Some summer visitors from a hotel on the Moor or at St Loo come over to Smugglers' Island. They announce that they will have lunch. They walk round the island first. How easy to descend to the beach, pick up the sandwich box, place it, no doubt, in Madame's bathing-bag which she carries—and return for lunch to the hotel—a little late, perhaps, say at ten minutes to two, having enjoyed their walk whilst everyone else was in the dining room.'

Weston said:

'Yes, it all sounds practicable enough. Now these dope organizations are pretty ruthless. If anyone blundered in and got wise to things, they wouldn't make any bones about silencing that person. It seems to me that that is the right explanation of Arlena Marshall's death. It's possible that on that morning Blatt was actually at the cove stowing the stuff away. His accomplices were to come for it that very day. Arlena arrives on her float and sees him going into the cave with the box. She asks him about it and he kills her then and there and sheers off in his boat as quick as possible.'

Poirot said:

'You think definitely that Blatt is the murderer?'

'It seems the most probable solution. Of course it's possible that Arlena might have got onto the truth earlier, said something to Blatt about it, and some other member of the gang fixed a fake appointment with her and did her in. As I say, I think the best course is to hand the case over to Scotland Yard. They've a far better chance than we have of proving Blatt's connection with the gang.'

Hercule Poirot nodded thoughtfully.

Weston said:

'You think that's the wise thing to do—eh?'

Poirot was thoughtful. He said at last: 'It may be.'

'Dash it all, Poirot, have you got something up your sleeve, or haven't you?'

Poirot said gravely:

'If I have, I am not sure that I can prove it.'

Weston said:

'Of course, I know that you and Colgate have other ideas. Seems a bit fantastic to me, but I'm bound to admit there may be something in it. But even if you're right, I still think it's a case for the Yard. We'll give them the facts and they can work in with the Surrey police. What I feel is that it isn't really a case for us. It's not sufficiently localized.'

He paused.

'What do you think, Poirot? What do you feel ought to be done about it?'

Poirot seemed lost in thought. At last he said:
'I know what I should like to do.'
'Yes, man.'
Poirot murmured:
'I should like to go for a picnic.'
Colonel Weston stared at him.

CHAPTER 12

'A picnic, M. Poirot?'

Emily Brewster stared at him as though he were out of his senses.

Poirot said engagingly:

'It sounds to you, does it not, very outrageous? But indeed it seems to me a most admirable idea. We need something of the everyday, the usual, to restore life to the normal. I am most anxious to see something of Dartmoor, the weather is good. It will—how shall I say, it will cheer everybody up! So aid me in this matter. Persuade everyone.'

The idea met with unexpected success. Everyone was at first dubious and then grudgingly admitted it might not be such a bad idea after all.

It was not suggested that Captain Marshall should be asked. He had himself announced that he had to go to Plymouth that day. Mr Blatt was of the party, enthusiastically so. He was determined to be the life and soul of it. Besides him there was Emily Brewster, the Redferns, Stephen

Lane, the Gardeners—who were persuaded to delay their departure by one day—Rosamund Darnley and Linda.

Poirot had been eloquent to Rosamund and had dwelt on the advantage it would be to Linda to have something to take her out of herself. To this Rosamund agreed. She said:

'You're quite right. The shock has been very bad for a child of that age. It has made her terribly jumpy.'

'That is only natural, Mademoiselle. But at that age one soon forgets. Persuade her to come. You can, I know.'

Major Barry had refused firmly. He said he didn't like picnics. 'Lots of baskets to carry,' he said. 'And darned uncomfortable. Eating my food at a table's good enough for me.'

The party assembled at ten o'clock. Three cars had been ordered. Mr Blatt was loud and cheerful, imitating a tourist guide.

'This way, ladies and gentlemen—this way for Dartmoor. Heather and bilberries, Devonshire cream and convicts. Bring your wives, gentlemen, or bring the other thing! Everyone welcome! Scenery guaranteed. Walk up. Walk up.'

At the last minute Rosamund Darnley came down looking concerned. She said:

'Linda's not coming. She says she's got a frightful headache.'

Poirot cried:

'But it will do her good to come. Persuade her, Mademoiselle.'

Rosamund said firmly:

'It's no good. She's absolutely determined. I've given her some aspirin and she's gone to bed.'

She hesitated and said:

'I think, perhaps, I won't go, either.

'Can't allow that, dear lady, can't allow that,' cried Mr Blatt, seizing her facetiously by the arm. '*La haute Mode* must grace the occasion. No refusals! I've taken you into custody, ha, ha. Sentenced to Dartmoor.'

He led her firmly to the first car. Rosamund threw a black look at Hercule Poirot.

'I'll stay with Linda,' said Christine Redfern. 'I don't mind a bit.'

Patrick said: 'Oh, come on, Christine.'

And Poirot said:

'No, no, you must come, Madame. With a headache one is better alone. Come, let us start.'

The three cars drove off. They went first to the real Pixy's Cave on Sheepstor, and had a good deal of fun looking for the entrance and at last finding it, aided by a picture postcard.

It was precarious going on the big boulders and Hercule Poirot did not attempt it. He watched indulgently while Christine Redfern sprang lightly from stone to stone, and observed that her husband was never far from her. Rosamund Darnley and Emily Brewster had joined in the search though the latter slipped once and gave a slight twist to her ankle. Stephen Lane was indefatigable, his long lean figure turning and twisting among the boulders. Mr Blatt contented himself with going a little way and shouting encouragement, also taking photographs of the searchers.

The Gardeners and Poirot remained staidly sitting by the wayside whilst Mrs Gardener's voice upraised itself in a pleasant even-toned monologue, punctuated now and then by the obedient 'Yes, darlings' of her spouse.

'—and what I always have felt, M. Poirot, and Mr Gardener agrees with me, is that snapshots can be very annoying. Unless, that is to say, they are taken among friends. That Mr Blatt has just no sensitiveness of any kind. He just comes right up to everyone and talks away and takes pictures of you and, as I said to Mr Gardener, that really is very ill-bred. That's what I said, Odell, wasn't it?'

'Yes, darling.'

'That group he took of us all sitting on the beach. Well, that's all very well, but he should have asked first. As it was, Miss Brewster was just getting up from the beach, and it certainly makes her look a very peculiar shape.'

'I'll say it does,' said Mr Gardener with a grin.

'And there's Mr Blatt giving round copies to everybody without so much as asking first. He gave one to you, M. Poirot, I noticed.'

Poirot nodded. He said:

'I value that group very much.'

Mrs Gardener went on:

'And look at his behaviour today—so loud and noisy and common. Why, it just makes me shudder. You ought to have arranged to leave that man at home, M. Poirot.'

Hercule Poirot murmured:

Agatha Christie

'Alas, Madame, that would have been difficult.'

'I should say it would. That man just pushes his way in anywhere. He's just not sensitive at all.'

At this moment the discovery of the Pixy's Cave was hailed from below with loud cries.

The party now drove on, under Hercule Poirot's directions, to a spot where a short walk from the car down a hillside of heather led to a delightful spot by a small river.

A narrow plank bridge crossed the river and Poirot and her husband induced Mrs Gardener to cross it to where a delightful heathery spot free from prickly furze looked an ideal spot for a picnic lunch.

Talking volubly about her sensations when crossing on a plank bridge Mrs Gardener sank down. Suddenly there was a slight outcry.

The others had run across the bridge lightly enough, but Emily Brewster was standing in the middle of the plank, her eyes shut, swaying to and fro.

Poirot and Patrick Redfern rushed to the rescue.

Emily Brewster was gruff and ashamed.

'Thanks, thanks. Sorry. Never was good at crossing running water. Get giddy. Stupid, very.'

Lunch was spread out and the picnic began.

All the people concerned were secretly surprised to find how much they enjoyed this interlude. It was, perhaps, because it afforded an escape from an atmosphere of suspicion and dread. Here, with the trickling of the water, the soft peaty smell in the air and the warm colouring of bracken and heather, a world of murder and police

Evil Under the Sun

inquiries and suspicion seemed blotted out as though it had never existed. Even Mr Blatt forgot to be the life and soul of the party. After lunch he went to sleep a little distance away and subdued snores testified to his blissful unconsciousness.

It was quite a grateful party of people who packed up the picnic baskets and congratulated Hercule Poirot on his good idea.

The sun was sinking as they returned along the narrow winding lanes. From the top of the hill above Leathercombe Bay they had a brief glimpse of the island with the white hotel on it.

It looked peaceful and innocent in the setting sun.

Mrs Gardener, not loquacious for once, sighed and said:

'I really do thank you, M. Poirot. I feel so calm. It's just wonderful.'

II

Major Barry came out to greet them on arrival.

'Hullo,' he said. 'Had a good day?'

Mrs Gardener said:

'Indeed we did. The moors were just too lovely for anything. So English and old world. And the air delicious and invigorating. You ought to be ashamed of yourself for being so lazy as to stay behind.'

The Major chuckled.

'I'm too old for that kind of thing—sitting on a patch of bog and eating sandwiches.'

Agatha Christie

A chambermaid had come out of the hotel. She was a little out of breath. She hesitated for a moment then came swiftly up to Christine Redfern.

Hercule Poirot recognized her as Gladys Narracott. Her voice came quick and uneven.

'Excuse me, Madam, but I'm worried about the young lady. About Miss Marshall. I took her up some tea just now and I couldn't get her to wake, and she looks so—so queer somehow.'

Christine looked round helplessly. Poirot was at her side in a moment. His hand under her elbow he said quietly:

'We will go up and see.'

They hurried up the stairs and along the passage to Linda's room.

One glance at her was enough to tell them both that something was very wrong. She was an odd colour and her breathing was hardly perceptible.

Poirot's hand went to her pulse. At the same time he noticed an envelope stuck up against the lamp on the bedside table. It was addressed to himself.

Captain Marshall came quickly into the room. He said: 'What's this about Linda? What's the matter with her?'

A small frightened sob came from Christine Redfern.

Hercule Poirot turned from the bed. He said to Marshall:

'Get a doctor—as quick as you possibly can. But I'm afraid—very much afraid—it may be too late.'

He took the letter with his name on it and ripped open the envelope. Inside were a few lines of writing in Linda's prim schoolgirl hand.

I think this is the best way out. Ask Father to try and forgive me. I killed Arlena. I thought I should be glad—but I'm not. I am very sorry for everything.

III

They were assembled in the lounge—Marshall, the Redferns, Rosamund Darnley and Hercule Poirot.

They sat there silent—waiting...

The door opened and Dr Neasdon came in. He said curtly:

'I've done all I can. She may pull through—but I'm bound to tell you that there's not much hope.'

He paused. Marshall, his face stiff, his eyes a cold frosty blue, asked:

'How did she get hold of the stuff?'

Neasdon opened the door again and beckoned.

The chambermaid came into the room. She had been crying.

Neasdon said:

'Just tell us again what you saw.'

Sniffing, the girl said:

'I never thought—I never thought for a minute there was anything wrong—though the young lady did seem rather strange about it.' A slight gesture of impatience from the doctor started her off again. 'She was in the other lady's room. Mrs Redfern's. Your room, Madam. Over at the washstand, and she took up a little bottle. She did give a bit of a jump when I came in, and I

Agatha Christie

thought it was queer her taking things from your room, but then, of course, it might be something she'd lent you. She just said: "Oh, this is what I'm looking for—" and went out.'

Christine said almost in a whisper.

'My sleeping tablets.'

The doctor said brusquely:

'How did she know about them?'

Christine said:

'I gave her one. The night after it happened. She told me she couldn't sleep. She—I remember her saying—"Will one be enough?"—and I said, Oh yes, they were very strong—that I'd been cautioned never to take more than two at most.'

Neasdon nodded: 'She made pretty sure,' he said. 'Took six of them.'

Christine sobbed again.

'Oh dear, I feel it's my fault. I should have kept them locked up.'

The doctor shrugged his shoulders.

'It might have been wiser, Mrs Redfern.'

Christine said despairingly:

'She's dying—and it's my fault...'

Kenneth Marshall stirred in his chair. He said:

'No, you can't blame yourself. Linda knew what she was doing. She took them deliberately. Perhaps—perhaps it was best.'

He looked down at the crumpled note in his hand—the note that Poirot had silently handed to him.

Rosamund Darnley cried out.

Evil Under the Sun

'I don't believe it. I don't believe Linda killed her. Surely it's impossible—on the evidence!'

Christine said eagerly:

'Yes, she *can't* have done it! She must have got overwrought and imagined it all.'

The door opened and Colonel Weston came in. He said:

'What's all this I hear?'

Dr Neasdon took the note from Marshall's hand and handed it to the Chief Constable. The latter read it. He exclaimed incredulously:

'What? But this is nonsense—absolute nonsense! It's impossible.' He repeated with assurance. 'Impossible! Isn't it, Poirot?'

Hercule Poirot moved for the first time. He said in a slow sad voice:

'No, I'm afraid it is not impossible.'

Christine Redfern said:

'But I was with her, M. Poirot. I was with her up to a quarter to twelve. I told the police so.'

Poirot said:

'Your evidence gave her an alibi—yes. But what was your evidence based on? It was based on *Linda Marshall's own wristwatch*. You do not know *of your own knowledge* that it was a quarter to twelve when you left her—you only know that she told you so. You said yourself the time seemed to have gone very fast.'

She stared at him, stricken.

He said:

Agatha Christie

'Now, think, Madame, when you left the beach, did you walk back to the hotel fast or slow?'

'I—well, fairly slowly, I think.'

'Do you remember much about that walk back?'

'Not very much, I'm afraid. I—I was thinking.'

Poirot said:

'I am sorry to ask you this, but will you tell just what you were thinking about during that walk?'

Christine flushed.

'I suppose—if it is necessary... I was considering the question of—of leaving here. Just going away without telling my husband. I—I was very unhappy just then, you see.'

Patrick Redfern cried:

'Oh, Christine! I know... I know...'

Poirot's precise voice cut in.

'Exactly. You were concerned over taking a step of some importance. You were, I should say, deaf and blind to your surroundings. You probably walked very slowly and occasionally stopped for some minutes whilst you puzzled things out.'

Christine nodded.

'How clever you are. It was just like that. I woke up from a kind of dream just outside the hotel and hurried in thinking I should be very late, but when I saw the clock in the lounge I realized I had plenty of time.'

Hercule Poirot said again:

'Exactly.'

He turned to Marshall.

'I must now describe to you certain things I found in

your daughter's room after the murder. In the grate was a large blob of melted wax, some burnt hair, fragments of cardboard and paper and an ordinary household pin. The paper and the cardboard might not be relevant, but the other three things were suggestive—particularly when I found tucked away in the bookshelf a volume from the local library here dealing with witchcraft and magic. It opened very easily at a certain page. On that page were described various methods of causing death by moulding in wax a figure supposed to represent the victim. This was then slowly roasted till it melted away—or alternatively you would pierce the wax figure to the heart with a pin. Death of the victim would ensue. I later heard from Mrs Redfern that Linda Marshall had been out early that morning and had bought a packet of candles, and had seemed embarrassed when her purchase was revealed. I had no doubt what had happened after that. Linda had made a crude figure of the candle wax—possibly adorning it with a snip of Arlena's red hair to give the magic force—had then stabbed it to the heart with a pin and finally melted the figure away by lighting strips of cardboard under it.

'It was crude, childish, superstitious, but it revealed one thing: the desire to kill.

'Was there any possibility that there had been more than a desire? Could Linda Marshall have *actually* killed her stepmother?

'At first sight it seemed as though she had a perfect alibi—but in actuality, as I have just pointed out, the time evidence was supplied *by Linda herself*. She could easily

Agatha Christie

have declared the time to be a quarter of an hour later than it really was.

'It was quite possible, once Mrs Redfern had left the beach, for Linda to follow her up and then strike across the narrow neck of land to the ladder, hurry down it, meet her stepmother there, strangle her and return up the ladder before the boat containing Miss Brewster and Patrick Redfern came in sight. She could then return to Gull Cove, take her bathe and return to the hotel at her leisure.

'But that entailed two things. She must have definite knowledge that Arlena Marshall would be at Pixy Cove and she must be physically capable of the deed.

'Well, the first was quite possible—if Linda Marshall had written a note to Arlena herself in someone else's name. As to the second, Linda has very large strong hands. They are as large as a man's. As to the strength, she is at the age when one is prone to be mentally unbalanced. Mental derangement often is accompanied by unusual strength. There was one other small point. Linda Marshall's mother had actually been accused and tried for murder.'

Kenneth Marshall lifted his head. He said fiercely: 'She was also acquitted.'

'She was acquitted,' Poirot agreed.

Marshall said:

'And I'll tell you this, M. Poirot. Ruth—my wife—was innocent. That I know with complete and absolute certainty. In the intimacy of our life I could not have been deceived. She was an innocent victim of circumstances.'

He paused.

'And I don't believe that Linda killed Arlena. It's ridiculous—absurd!'

Poirot said:

'Do you believe that letter, then, to be a forgery?'

Marshall held out his hand for it and Weston gave it to him. Marshall studied it attentively. Then he shook his head.

'No,' he said unwillingly. 'I believe Linda did write this.'

Poirot said:

'Then if she wrote it, there are only two explanations. Either she wrote it in all good faith, knowing herself to be the murderess or—or, I say—*she wrote it deliberately to shield someone else*, someone whom she feared was suspected.'

Kenneth Marshall said:

'You mean me?'

'It is possible, is it not?'

Marshall considered for a moment or two, then he said quietly:

'No, I think that idea is absurd. Linda may have realized that I was regarded with suspicion at first. But she knew definitely by now that that was over and done with—that the police had accepted my alibi and turned their attention elsewhere.'

Poirot said:

'And supposing that it was not so much that she thought that you were suspected as that she *knew* you were guilty.'

Marshall stared at him. He gave a short laugh.

'That's absurd.'

Poirot said:

'I wonder. There are, you know, several possibilities about Mrs Marshall's death. There is the theory that she was being blackmailed, that she went that morning to meet the blackmailer and that the blackmailer killed her. There is the theory that Pixy Cove and Cave were being used for drug-running, and that she was killed because she accidentally learned something about that. There is a third possibility—that she was killed by a religious maniac. And there is a fourth possibility—you stood to gain a lot of money by your wife's death, Captain Marshall?'

'I've just told you—'

'Yes, yes—I agree that it is impossible that you could have killed your wife—*if you were acting alone*. But supposing someone helped you?'

'What the devil do you mean?'

The quiet man was roused at last. He half-rose from his chair. His voice was menacing. There was a hard angry light in his eyes.

Poirot said:

'I mean that this is not a crime that was committed single-handed. Two people were in it. It is quite true that you could not have typed that letter and at the same time gone to the cove—but there would have been time for you to have jotted down that letter in shorthand—and for *someone else* to have typed it in your room while you yourself were absent on your murderous errand.'

Hercule Poirot looked towards Rosamund Darnley. He said:

'Miss Darnley states that she left Sunny Ledge at ten

minutes past eleven and saw you typing in your room. But just about that time Mr Gardener went up to the hotel to fetch a skein of wool for his wife. He did not meet Miss Darnley or see her. That is rather remarkable. It looks as though either Miss Darnley never left Sunny Ledge, or else she had left it much earlier and was in your room typing industriously. Another point, you stated that when Miss Darnley looked into your room at a quarter past eleven *you saw her in the mirror*. But on the day of the murder your typewriter and papers were all on the writing desk across the corner of the room, whereas the mirror was between the windows. So that that statement was a deliberate lie. Later, you moved your typewriter to the table under the mirror so as to substantiate your story—but it was too late. I was aware that both you and Miss Darnley had lied.'

Rosamund Darnley spoke. Her voice was low and clear. She said:

'How devilishly ingenious you are!'

Hercule Poirot said, raising his voice:

'But not so devilish and so ingenious as the man who killed Arlena Marshall! Think back for a moment. Who did I think—who did everybody think—that Arlena Marshall had gone to meet that morning? We all jumped to the same conclusion. *Patrick Redfern*. It was not to meet a blackmailer that she went. Her face alone would have told me that. Oh no, it was a lover she was going to meet—or thought she was going to meet.

'Yes, I was quite sure of that. Arlena Marshall was going to meet Patrick Redfern. But a minute later Patrick Redfern appeared on the beach and was obviously looking for her. So what then?'

Patrick Redfern said with subdued anger:

'Some devil used my name.'

Poirot said:

'You were very obviously upset and surprised by her non-appearance. Almost too obviously, perhaps. It is *my* theory, Mr Redfern, that she went to Pixy Cove to meet *you*, and that she *did* meet you, and that *you killed her there as you had planned to do.*'

Patrick Redfern stared. He said in his high good-humoured Irish voice:

'Is it daft you are? I was with you on the beach until I went round in the boat with Miss Brewster and found her dead.'

Hercule Poirot said:

'You killed her after Miss Brewster had gone off in the boat to fetch the police. Arlena Marshall was not dead when you got to the beach. She was waiting hidden in the cave until the coast could be clear.'

'But the body! Miss Brewster and I both saw the body.'

'A body—yes. But not a *dead* body. The *live* body of the woman who helped you, her arms and legs stained with tan, her face hidden by a green cardboard hat. Christine, your wife (or possibly not your wife—but still your partner), helping you to commit this crime as she helped you to commit that crime in the past when she 'discovered' the body of Alice Corrigan at least twenty

Evil Under the Sun

minutes before Alice Corrigan died—killed by her husband Edward Corrigan—you!'

Christine spoke. Her voice was sharp—cold. She said:

'Be careful, Patrick, don't lose your temper.'

Poirot said:

'You will be interested to hear that both you and your wife Christine were easily recognized and picked out by the Surrey police from a group of people photographed here. They identified you both at once as Edward Corrigan and Christine Deverill, the young woman who found the body.'

Patrick Redfern had risen. His handsome face was transformed, suffused with blood, blind with rage. It was the face of a killer—of a tiger. He yelled:

'You damned interfering murdering lousy little worm!'

He hurled himself forward, his fingers stretching and curling, his voice raving curses, as he fastened his fingers round Hercule Poirot's throat...

CHAPTER 13

Poirot said reflectively:

'It was on a morning when we were sitting out here that we talked of suntanned bodies lying like meat upon a slab, and it was then that I reflected how little difference there was between one body and another. If one looked closely and appraisingly—yes—but to the casual glance? One moderately well-made young woman is very like another. Two brown legs, two brown arms, a little piece of bathing suit in between—just a body lying out in the sun. When a woman walks, when she speaks, laughs, turns her head, moves a hand—then, yes then, there is personality—individuality. But in the sun ritual—no.

'It was that day that we spoke of evil—*evil under the sun* as Mr Lane put it. Mr Lane is a very sensitive person—evil affects him—he perceives its presence—but though he is a good recording instrument, he did not really know exactly where the evil was. To him, evil was focused in the

Evil Under the Sun

person of Arlena Marshall, and practically everyone present agreed with him.

'But to my mind, though evil was present, it was not centralized in Arlena Marshall at all. It was connected with her, yes—but in a totally different way. I saw her, first, last and all the time, as an eternal and predestined *victim*. Because she was beautiful, because she had glamour, because men turned their heads to look at her, it was assumed that she was the type of woman who wrecked lives and destroyed souls. But I saw her very differently. It was not she who fatally attracted men—it was men who fatally attracted her. She was the type of woman whom men care for easily and of whom they as easily tire. And everything that I was told or found out about her strengthened my conviction on this point. The first thing that was mentioned about her was how the man in whose divorce case she had been cited refused to marry her. It was then that Captain Marshall, one of those incurably chivalrous men, stepped in and asked her to marry him. To a shy retiring man of Captain Marshall's type, a public ordeal of any kind would be the worst torture—hence his love and pity for his first wife who was publicly accused and tried for a murder she had not committed. He married her and found himself amply justified in his estimate of her character. After her death another beautiful woman, perhaps something of the same type (since Linda has red hair which she probably inherited from her mother), is held up to public ignominy. Again Marshall performs a rescue act. But this time he finds little to sustain his infatuation. Arlena is stupid, unworthy of his sympathy and protection, mindless. Nevertheless, I think he always had a fairly true vision of her. Long after he ceased to love her and was irked by her presence, he remained sorry for her. She was to him like a child who cannot get farther than a certain page in the book of life.

'I saw in Arlena Marshall, with her passion for men, a predestined prey for an unscrupulous man of a certain type. In Patrick Redfern, with his good looks, his easy assurance, his undeniable charm for women, I recognized at once that type. The adventurer who makes his living, one way or another, out of women. Looking on from my place on the beach I was quite certain that Arlena was Patrick's victim, not the other way about. And I associated that focus of evil with Patrick Redfern, not with Arlena Marshall.

'Arlena had recently come into a large sum of money, left her by an elderly admirer who had not had time to grow tired of her. She was the type of woman who is invariably defrauded of money by some man or other. Miss Brewster mentioned a young man who had been "ruined" by Arlena, but a letter from him which was found in her room, though it expressed a wish (which cost nothing) to cover her with jewels, in actual *fact* acknowledged a cheque from *her* by means of which he hoped to escape prosecution. A clear case of a young waster sponging on her. I have no doubt that Patrick Redfern found it easy to induce her to hand him large sums from time to time "for investment". He probably dazzled her with stories of great opportunities—how he would make her fortune and his own. Unprotected women, living alone, are easy prey to that type of man—and he usually escapes scot free with the booty. If, however, there is a husband, or a brother, or a father about, things are apt to take an unpleasant turn for the swindler. Once Captain Marshall was to find out what had happened to his wife's fortune, Patrick Redfern might expect short shrift.

'That did not worry him, however, because he contemplated quite calmly doing away with her when he judged it necessary—encouraged by having already got away with one murder—that of a young woman whom he had married in the name of Corrigan and whom he had persuaded to insure her life for a large sum.

'In his plans he was aided and abetted by the woman who down here passed as his wife and to whom he was genuinely attached. A young woman as unlike the type of his victims as could well be imagined—cool, calm, passionless, but steadfastly loyal to him and an actress of no mean ability. From the time of her arrival here Christine Redfern played a part, the part of the "poor little wife"—frail, helpless, intellectual rather than athletic. Think of the points she made one after another. Her tendency to blister in the sun and her consequent white skin, her giddiness at heights—stories of getting stuck on Milan Cathedral, et cetera. An emphasis on her frailty and delicacy—nearly every one spoke of her as a "little woman". She was actually as tall as Arlena Marshall, but with very small hands and feet. She spoke of herself as a former schoolteacher, and thereby emphasized an impression of book learning and lack of athletic prowess. Actually, it is quite true that she had

Agatha Christie

worked in a school, but the position she held there was that of *games mistress*, and she was an extremely active young woman who could climb like a cat and run like an athlete.

'The crime itself was perfectly planned and timed. It was, as I mentioned before, a very slick crime. The timing was a work of genius.

'First of all there were certain preliminary scenes—one played on the cliff ledge when they knew me to be occupying the next recess—a conventional jealous wife dialogue between her and her husband. Later she played the same part in a scene with me. At the time I remember a vague feeling of having read all this in a book. It did not seem *real*. Because, of course, it was *not* real. Then came the day of the crime. It was a fine day—an essential. Redfern's first act was to slip out very early—by the balcony door which he unlocked from the inside (if found open it would only be thought someone had gone for an early bathe). Under his bathing-wrap he concealed a green Chinese hat, the duplicate of the one Arlena was in the habit of wearing. He slipped across the island, down the ladder, and stowed it away in an appointed place behind some rocks. Part I.

'On the previous evening he had arranged a rendezvous with Arlena. They were exercising a good deal of caution about meeting as Arlena was slightly afraid of her husband. She agreed to go round to Pixy Cove early. Nobody went there in the morning. Redfern was to join her there, taking a chance to slip away unobtrusively. If she heard anyone descending the ladder or a boat came in sight she was to

258

slip inside the Pixy's Cave, the secret of which he had told her, and wait there until the coast was clear. Part II.

'In the meantime Christine went to Linda's room at a time when she judged Linda would have gone for her early morning dip. She would then alter Linda's watch, putting it on twenty minutes. There was, of course, a risk that Linda might notice her watch was wrong, but it did not much matter if she did. Christine's real alibi was the size of her hands, which made it a physical impossibility for her to have committed the crime. Nevertheless, an additional alibi would be desirable. Then in Linda's room she noticed the book on witchcraft and magic, open at a certain page. She read it, and when Linda came in and dropped a parcel of candles she realized what was in Linda's mind. It opened up some new ideas to her. The original idea of the guilty pair had been to cast a reasonable amount of suspicion on Kenneth Marshall, hence the abstracted pipe, a fragment of which was to be planted on the cove underneath the ladder.

'On Linda's return Christine easily arranged an outing together to Gull Cove. She then returned to her own room, took out from a locked suitcase a bottle of artificial suntan, applied it carefully and threw the empty bottle out of the window where it narrowly escaped hitting Emily Brewster who was bathing. Part III successfully accomplished.

'Christine then dressed herself in a white bathing suit, and over it a pair of beach trousers and coat with long floppy sleeves which effectually concealed her newly-browned arms and legs.

Agatha Christie

'At 10.15 Arlena departed for her rendezvous, a minute or two later Patrick Redfern came down and registered surprise, annoyance, et cetera. Christine's task was easy enough. Keeping her own watch concealed she asked Linda at twenty-five past eleven what time it was. Linda looked at her watch and replied that it was a quarter to twelve. She then starts down to the sea and Christine packs up her sketching things. As soon as Linda's back is turned Christine picks up the girl's watch which she has necessarily discarded before going into the sea and alters it back to the correct time. Then she hurries up the cliff path, runs across the narrow neck of land to the top of the ladder, strips off her pyjamas and shoves them and her sketching box behind a rock and swarms rapidly down the ladder in her best gymnastic fashion.

'Arlena is on the beach below wondering why Patrick is so long in coming. She sees or hears someone on the ladder, takes a cautious observation, and to her annoyance sees that inconvenient person—the wife! She hurries along the beach and into the Pixy's Cave.

'Christine takes the hat from its hiding place, a false red curl pinned underneath the brim at the back, and disposes herself in a sprawling attitude with the hat and curl shielding her face and neck. The timing is perfect. A minute or two later the boat containing Patrick and Emily Brewster comes round the point. Remember it is *Patrick* who bends down and examines the body, *Patrick* who is stunned—shocked—broken down by the death of his lady love! His witness has been carefully chosen. Miss Brewster has not got a good head, she will not attempt to go up the ladder. She will leave the cove by boat, Patrick naturally being the one to remain with the body—"in case the murderer may still be about". Miss Brewster rows off to fetch the police. Christine, as soon as the boat has disappeared, springs up, cuts the hat into pieces with the scissors Patrick has carefully brought, stuffs them into her bathing suit and swarms up the ladder in double-quick time, slips into her beach pyjamas and runs back to the hotel. Just time to have a quick bath, washing off the brown suntan application, and into her tennis dress. One other thing she does. She burns the pieces of the green cardboard hat and the hair in Linda's grate, adding a leaf of a calendar so that it may be associated with the cardboard. Not a *hat* but a *calendar* has been burnt. As she suspected, Linda has been experimenting in magic—the blob of wax and the pin shows that.

'Then, down to the tennis court, arriving the last, but showing no signs of flurry or haste.

'And, meanwhile, Patrick has gone to the cave. Arlena has seen nothing and heard very little—a boat—voices—she has prudently remained hidden. But now it is Patrick calling.

'"All clear, darling," and she comes out, and his hands fasten round her neck—and that is the end of poor foolish beautiful Arlena Marshall...'

His voice died away.

For a moment there was silence, then Rosamund Darnley said with a little shiver:

'Yes, you make one see it all. But that's the story from

Agatha Christie

the other side. You haven't told us how *you* came to get at the truth?'

Hercule Poirot said:

'I told you once that I had a very simple mind. Always, from the beginning, it seemed to me that *the most likely person* had killed Arlena Marshall. And the most likely person was Patrick Redfern. He was the type, *par excellence*—the type of man who exploits women like her—and the type of the killer—the kind of man who will take a woman's savings and cut her throat into the bargain. Who was Arlena going to meet that morning? By the evidence of her face, her smile, her manner, her words to me—*Patrick Redfern*. And therefore, in the very nature of things, it should be Patrick who killed her.

'But at once I came up, as I told you, against impossibility. Patrick Redfern could not have killed her since he was on the beach and in Miss Brewster's company until the actual discovery of the body. So I looked about for other solutions—and there were several. She could have been killed by her husband—with Miss Darnley's connivance. (They too had both lied as to one point which looked suspicious.) She could have been killed as a result of her having stumbled on the secret of the dope smuggling. She could have been killed, as I said, by a religious maniac, and she could have been killed by her stepdaughter. The latter seemed to me at one time to be the real solution. Linda's manner in her very first interview with the police was significant. An interview that I had with her later assured me of one point. Linda considered herself guilty.'

'You mean she imagined that she had actually killed Arlena?'

Rosamund's voice was incredulous.

Hercule Poirot nodded.

'Yes. Remember—she is really little more than a child. She read that book on witchcraft and she half-believed it. She hated Arlena. She deliberately made the wax doll, cast her spell, pierced it to the heart, melted it away—*and that very day Arlena dies*. Older and wiser people than Linda have believed fervently in magic. Naturally, she believed that it was all true—that by using magic she had killed her stepmother.'

Rosamund cried:

'Oh, poor child, poor child. And I thought—I imagined—something quite different—that she knew something which would—'

Rosamund stopped. Poirot said:

'I know what it was you thought. Actually your manner frightened Linda still further. She believed that her action had really brought about Arlena's death and that you knew it. Christine Redfern worked on her too, introducing the idea of the sleeping tablets to her mind, showing her the way to a speedy and painless expiation of her crime. You see, once Captain Marshall was proved to have an alibi, it was vital for a new suspect to be found. Neither she nor her husband knew about the dope smuggling. They fixed on Linda to be the scapegoat.'

Rosamund said:

'What a devil!'

Agatha Christie

Poirot nodded.

'Yes, you are right. A cold-blooded and cruel woman. For me, I was in great difficulty. Was Linda guilty only of the childish attempt at witchcraft, or had her hate carried her still further—to the actual act? I tried to get her to confess to me. But it was no good. At that moment I was in grave uncertainty. The Chief Constable was inclined to accept the dope smuggling explanation. I couldn't let it go at that. I went over the facts again very carefully. I had, you see, a collection of jigsaw puzzle pieces, isolated happenings—plain facts. The whole must fit into a complete and harmonious pattern. There were the scissors found on the beach—a bottle thrown from a window—a bath that no one would admit to having taken—all perfectly harmless occurrences in themselves, but rendered significant by the fact that no one would admit to them. Therefore, they *must* be of significance. Nothing about them fitted in with the theories of either Captain Marshall's or Linda's, or of a dope gang's, being responsible. And yet they *must* have meaning. I went back again to my first solution—that Patrick Redfern had committed the murder. Was there anything in support of that? Yes, the fact that a very large sum of money was missing from Arlena's account. Who had got that money? Patrick Redfern, of course. She was the type of woman easily swindled by a handsome young man—but she was not at all the type of woman to be blackmailed. She was far too transparent, not good enough at keeping a secret. The blackmailer story had never rung true to my mind. And yet there *had* been that conversation

Evil Under the Sun

overheard—ah, but overheard by whom? *Patrick Redfern's wife*. It was her story—unsupported by any outside evidence. Why was it invented? The answer came to me like lightning. To account for the absence of Arlena's money!

'Patrick and Christine Redfern. The two of them were in it together. Christine hadn't got the physical strength to strangle her, or the mental make-up. No, it was Patrick who had done it—but that was impossible! Every minute of his time was accounted for until the body was found.

'Body—the word stirred something in my mind—bodies lying on the beach—*all alike*. Patrick Redfern and Emily Brewster had got to the cove and seen *a body* lying there. A body—suppose it was not Arlena's body but somebody else's? The face was hidden by the great Chinese hat.

'But there *was* only one dead body—Arlena's. Then, could it be—a *live* body—someone pretending to be dead? Could it be Arlena herself, inspired by Patrick to play some kind of a joke. I shook my head—no, too risky. A live body—whose? Was there any woman who would help Redfern? Of course—his wife. But she was a white-skinned delicate creature. Ah yes, but suntan can be applied out of bottles—bottles—a bottle—I had one of my jigsaw pieces. Yes, and afterwards, of course, a bath—to wash that telltale stain off before she went out to play tennis. And the scissors? Why, to cut up that duplicate cardboard hat—an unwieldy thing that must be got out of the way, and in the haste the scissors were left behind—the one thing that the pair of murderers forgot.

'But where was Arlena all the time? That again was

Agatha Christie

perfectly clear. Either Rosamund Darnley or Arlena Marshall had been in the Pixy's Cave, the scent they both used told me that. It was certainly not Rosamund Darnley. Then it was Arlena, hiding till the coast should clear.

'When Emily Brewster went off in the boat, Patrick had the beach to himself and full opportunity to commit the crime. Arlena Marshall was killed after a quarter to twelve, but the medical evidence was only concerned with the earliest possible time the crime could have been committed. That Arlena was dead at a quarter to twelve was what was told to the doctor, not what he told the police.

'Two more points had to be settled. Linda Marshall's evidence gave Christine Redfern an alibi. Yes, but that evidence depended on Linda Marshall's wristwatch. All that was needed was to prove that Christine had had two opportunities of tampering with the watch. I found those easily enough. She had been alone in Linda's room that morning—and there was an indirect proof. Linda was heard to say that she was "afraid she was going to be late", but when she got down it was only twenty-five past ten by the lounge clock. The second opportunity was easy—she could alter the watch back again as soon as Linda turned her back and went down to bathe.

'Then there was the question of the ladder. Christine had always declared she had no head for heights. Another carefully prepared lie.

'I had my mosaic now—each piece beautifully fitted into its place. But, unfortunately, I had no definite proof. It was all in my mind.

'It was then that an idea came to me. There was an assurance—a slickness about the crime. I had no doubt that in the future Patrick Redfern would repeat his crime. What about the past? It was remotely possible that this was not his first killing. The method employed, strangulation, was in harmony with his nature—a killer for pleasure as well as for profit. If he was already a murderer I was sure that he would have used the same means. I asked Inspector Colgate for a list of women victims of strangulation. The result filled me with joy. The death of Nellie Parsons found strangled in a lonely copse might or might not be Patrick Redfern's work—it might merely have suggested choice of locality to him—but in Alice Corrigan's death I found exactly what I was looking for. In essence the same method. Juggling with time—a murder committed not, as is the usual way, *before* it is supposed to have happened, but *afterwards*. A body supposedly discovered at a quarter past four. A husband with an alibi up to twenty-five past four.

'What really happened? It was said that Edward Corrigan arrived at the Pine Ridge, found his wife not there, *and went out and walked up and down*. Actually, of course, he ran full speed to the rendezvous, Caesar's Grove (which you will remember was quite nearby), killed her and returned to the café. The girl hiker who reported the crime was a most respectable young lady, games mistress in a well-known girls' school. Apparently she had no connection with Edward Corrigan. She had to walk some way to report the death. The police surgeon only examined the body at

Agatha Christie

a quarter to six. As in this case the time of death was accepted without question.

'I made one final test. I must know definitely if Mrs Redfern was a liar. I arranged our little excursion to Dartmoor. If anyone has a bad head for heights, they are never comfortable crossing a narrow bridge over running water. Miss Brewster, a genuine sufferer, showed giddiness. But Christine Redfern, unconcerned, ran across without a qualm. It was a small point, but it was a definite test. If she had told one unnecessary lie—then all the other lies were possible. In the meantime Colgate had got the photograph identified by the Surrey Police. I played my hand in the only way I thought likely to succeed. Having lulled Patrick Redfern into security, I turned on him and did my utmost to make him lose his self-control. The knowledge that he had been identified with Corrigan caused him to lose his head completely.'

Hercule Poirot stroked his throat reminiscently.

'What I did,' he said with importance, 'was exceedingly dangerous—but I do not regret it. I succeeded! I did not suffer in vain.'

There was a moment's silence. Then Mrs Gardener gave a deep sigh.

'Why, M. Poirot,' she said. 'It's just been too wonderful—hearing just exactly how you got your results. It's every bit as fascinating as a lecture on criminology—in fact it *is* a lecture on criminology. And to think my magenta wool and that sunbathing conversation actually had something to do with it? That really makes me too excited for words, and I'm sure Mr Gardener feels the same, don't you, Odell?'

'Yes, darling,' said Mr Gardener.

Hercule Poirot said:

'Mr Gardener too was of assistance to me. I wanted the opinion of a sensible man about Mrs Marshall. I asked Mr Gardener what he thought of her.'

'Is that so,' said Mrs Gardener. 'And what did you say about her, Odell?'

Mr Gardener coughed. He said:

'Well, darling, I never did think very much of her, you know.'

'That's the kind of thing men always say to their wives,' said Mrs Gardener. 'And if you ask me, even M. Poirot here is what I should call a shade on the indulgent side about her, calling her a natural victim and all that. Of course it's true that she wasn't a cultured woman at all, and as Captain Marshall isn't here I don't mind saying that she always did seem to me kind of dumb. I said so to Mr Gardener, didn't I, Odell?'

'Yes, darling,' said Mr Gardener.

II

Linda Marshall sat with Hercule Poirot on Gull Cove.

She said:

'Of course I'm glad I didn't die after all. But you know, M. Poirot, it's just the same as if I'd killed her, isn't it? I meant to.'

Hercule Poirot said energetically:

'It is not at all the same thing. The wish to kill and the action of killing are two different things. If in your bedroom instead of a little wax figure you had had your stepmother bound and helpless and a dagger in your hand instead of a pin, you would not have pushed it into her heart! Something within you would have said "no". It is the same with me. I enrage myself at an imbecile. I say, "I would like to kick him." Instead, I kick the table. I say, "This table, it is the imbecile, I kick him so." And then, if I have not hurt my toe too much, I feel much better and the table it is not usually damaged. But if the imbecile himself was there I should not kick him. To make the wax figures and stick in the pins, it is silly, yes, it is childish, yes—but it does something useful too. You took the hate out of yourself and put it into that little figure. And with the pin and the fire you destroyed—not your stepmother—but the hate you bore her. Afterwards, even before you heard of her death, you felt cleansed, did you not—you felt lighter—happier?'

Linda nodded. She said:

'How did you know? That's just how I did feel.'

Poirot said:

'Then do not repeat to yourself the imbecilities. Just make up your mind not to hate your next stepmother.'

Linda said startled:

'Do you think I'm going to have another? Oh, I see, you mean Rosamund. I don't mind her.' She hesitated a minute. 'She's *sensible*.'

It was not the adjective that Poirot himself would have selected for Rosamund Darnley, but he realized that it was Linda's idea of high praise.

III

Kenneth Marshall said:

'Rosamund, did you get some extraordinary idea into your head that I'd killed Arlena.'

Rosamund looked rather shamefaced. She said:

'I suppose I was a damned fool.'

'Of course you were.'

'Yes, but Ken, you are such an oyster. I never knew what you really felt about Arlena. I didn't know if you accepted her as she was and were just frightfully decent about her, or whether you—well, just believed in her blindly. And I thought if it was that, and you suddenly found out that she was letting you down, you might go mad with rage. I've heard stories about you. You're always very quiet but you're rather frightening sometimes.'

'So you thought I just took her by the throat and throttled the life out of her?'

'Well—yes—that's just exactly what I did think. And your alibi seemed a bit on the light side. That's when I suddenly decided to take a hand, and made up that silly story about seeing you typing in your room. And when I heard that you said you'd seen me look in—well, that made me quite sure you'd done it. That, and Linda's queerness.'

Kenneth Marshall said with a sigh:

'Don't you realize that I said I'd seen you in the mirror in order to back up *your* story. I—I thought you needed it corroborated.'

Rosamund stared at him.

'You don't mean you thought that I killed your wife?'

Kenneth Marshall shifted uneasily. He mumbled:

'Dash it all, Rosamund, don't you remember how you nearly killed that boy about that dog once? How you hung on to his throat and wouldn't let go.'

'But that was years ago.'

'Yes, I know—'

Rosamund said sharply:

'What earthly motive do you think I had to kill Arlena?'

His glance shifted. He mumbled something again.

Rosamund cried:

'Ken, you mass of conceit! You thought I killed her out of altruism on your behalf, did you? Or—did you think I killed her because I wanted you myself?'

'Not at all,' said Kenneth Marshall indignantly. 'But you know what you said that day—about Linda and everything—and—and you seemed to care what happened to me.'

Rosamund said:

'I've always cared about that.'

'I believe you have. You know, Rosamund—I can't usually talk about things—I'm not good at talking—but I'd like to get this clear. I didn't care for Arlena—only just a little at first—and living with her day after day was a pretty nerve-racking business. In fact it was absolute hell, but I *was* awfully sorry for her. She was such a damned fool—crazy about men—she just couldn't help it—and they always let her down and treated her rottenly. I simply felt I couldn't be the one to give her the final push. I'd married her and it was up to me to look after her as best I could. I think she knew that and was grateful to me really. She was—she was a pathetic sort of creature really.'

Rosamund said gently:

'It's all right, Ken. I understand now.'

Without looking at her Kenneth Marshall carefully filled a pipe. He mumbled:

'You're—pretty good at understanding, Rosamund.'

A faint smile curved Rosamund's ironic mouth. She said:

'Are you going to ask me to marry you now, Ken, or are you determined to wait six months?'

Kenneth Marshall's pipe dropped from his lips and crashed on the rocks below.

He said:

'Damn, that's the second pipe I've lost down here. And I haven't got another with me. How the devil did you know I'd fixed six months as the proper time?'

'I suppose because it *is* the proper time. But I'd rather have something definite now, please. Because in the intervening months you may come across some other persecuted female and rush to the rescue in chivalrous fashion again.'

He laughed.

'You're going to be the persecuted female this time,

Rosamund. You're going to give up that damned dressmaking business of yours and we're going to live in the country.'

'Don't you know that I make a very handsome income out of my business? Don't you realize that it's *my* business—that I created it and worked it up, and that I'm proud of it! And you've got the damned nerve to come along and say, "Give it all up, dear."'

'I've got the damned nerve to say it, yes.'

'And you think I care enough for you to do it?'

'If you don't,' said Kenneth Marshall, 'you'd be no good to me.'

Rosamund said softly:

'Oh, my dear, I've wanted to live in the country with you all my life. Now—it's going to come true...'

The Agatha Christie Collection

THE HERCULE POIROT MYSTERIES
Match your wits with the famous Belgian detective.

The Mysterious Affair at Styles
The Murder on the Links
Poirot Investigates
The Murder of Roger Ackroyd
The Big Four
The Mystery of the Blue Train
Black Coffee
Peril at End House
Lord Edgware Dies
Murder on the Orient Express
Three Act Tragedy
Death in the Clouds
The ABC Murders
Murder in Mesopotamia
Cards on the Table
Murder in the Mews
Dumb Witness
Death on the Nile
Appointment With Death
Hercule Poirot's Christmas
Sad Cypress
One, Two, Buckle My Shoe
Evil Under the Sun
Five Little Pigs
The Hollow
The Labours of Hercules
Taken at the Flood
Mrs McGinty's Dead
After the Funeral
Hickory Dickory Dock
Dead Man's Folly
Cat Among the Pigeons
The Adventure of the Christmas Pudding
The Clocks
Third Girl
Hallowe'en Party
Elephants Can Remember
Poirot's Early Cases
Curtain: Poirot's Last Case

Find out all about the Queen of Crime
and her stories at **www.agathachristie.com**

Keep up to date with launches and news from the world
of Agatha Christie and discuss all things Agatha on the forum!

Shop online for books, audiobooks, DVDs and other merchandise

/agathachristie /officialagathachristie /QueenofCrime

For a touch of Christie mystery, scan the code!

The *Agatha Christie* Collection

THE MISS MARPLE MYSTERIES
Join the legendary spinster sleuth from St Mary Mead in solving murders far and wide.

The Murder at the Vicarage
The Thirteen Problems
The Body in the Library
The Moving Finger
A Murder is Announced
They Do It With Mirrors
A Pocket Full of Rye
4.50 from Paddington
The Mirror Crack'd from Side to Side
A Caribbean Mystery
At Bertram's Hotel
Nemesis
Sleeping Murder
Miss Marple's Final Cases

THE TOMMY & TUPPENCE MYSTERIES
Jump on board with the entertaining crime-solving couple from Young Adventurers Ltd.

The Secret Adversary
Partners in Crime
N or M?
By the Pricking of My Thumbs
Postern of Fate

Find out all about the Queen of Crime
and her stories at **www.agathachristie.com**

Keep up to date with launches and news from the world
of Agatha Christie and discuss all things Agatha on the forum!

Shop online for books, audiobooks, DVDs and other merchandise

/agathachristie   /officialagathachristie   /QueenofCrime

For a touch of Christie mystery, scan the code!

The *Agatha Christie* Collection

Don't miss a single one of Agatha Christie's classic novels and short story collections.

The Man in the Brown Suit	*Death Comes as the End*
The Secret of Chimneys	*Sparkling Cyanide*
The Seven Dials Mystery	*Crooked House*
The Mysterious Mr Quin	*They Came to Baghdad*
The Sittaford Mystery	*Destination Unknown*
The Hound of Death	*Spider's Web*
The Listerdale Mystery	*The Unexpected Guest*
Why Didn't They Ask Evans?	*Ordeal by Innocence*
Parker Pyne Investigates	*The Pale Horse*
Murder Is Easy	*Endless Night*
And Then There Were None	*Passenger to Frankfurt*

Find out all about the Queen of Crime and her stories at **www.agathachristie.com**

Keep up to date with launches and news from the world of Agatha Christie and discuss all things Agatha on the forum!

Shop online for books, audiobooks, DVDs and other merchandise

/agathachristie   /officialagathachristie   /QueenofCrime

For a touch of Christie mystery, scan the code!

Agatha Christie
Short stories for your E-reader
HERCULE POIROT

The Jewel Robbery at the Grand Metropolitan

The King of Clubs

The Disappearance of Mr Davenheim

The Plymouth Express

The Adventure of the 'Western Star'

The Tragedy of Marsdon Manor

The Kidnapped Prime Minister

The Million Dollar Bond Robbery

The Adventure of the Cheap Flat

The Mystery of Hunter's Lodge

The Chocolate Box

The Adventure of the Egyptian Tomb

The Veiled Lady

The Adventure of Johnny Waverley

The Market Basing Mystery

The Adventure of the Italian Nobleman

The Case of the Missing Will

The Incredible Theft

The Adventure of the Clapham Cook

The Lost Mine

The Cornish Mystery

The Double Clue

The Adventure of the Christmas Pudding

The Lemesurier Inheritance

The Under Dog

Triangle at Rhodes

Yellow Iris

The Dream

Four-and-Twenty Blackbirds

Poirot and the Regatta Mystery

The Mystery of the Baghdad Chest

The Second Gong

Find out all about the Queen of Crime
and her stories at **www.agathachristie.com**

Keep up to date with launches and news from the world
of Agatha Christie and discuss all things Agatha on the forum!

Shop online for books, audiobooks, DVDs and other merchandise

/agathachristie   /officialagathachristie   /QueenofCrime

For a touch of Christie mystery, scan the code!

itv
STUDIOS
GLOBAL ENTERTAINMENT
Agatha Christie
POIROT
Watch every case
Available on
iTunes

COMING SEPTEMBER 2014

THE NEW *Agatha Christie*

HERCULE POIROT MYSTERY

BY SOPHIE HANNAH

MURDER IN MESOPOTAMIA

ALSO BY AGATHA CHRISTIE

Mysteries
The Man in the Brown Suit
The Secret of Chimneys
The Seven Dials Mystery
The Mysterious Mr Quin
The Sittaford Mystery
The Hound of Death
The Listerdale Mystery
Why Didn't They Ask Evans?
Parker Pyne Investigates
Murder Is Easy
And Then There Were None
Towards Zero
Death Comes as the End
Sparkling Cyanide
Crooked House
They Came to Baghdad
Destination Unknown
Spider's Web *
The Unexpected Guest *
Ordeal by Innocence
The Pale Horse
Endless Night
Passenger To Frankfurt
Problem at Pollensa Bay
While the Light Lasts

Poirot
The Mysterious Affair at Styles
The Murder on the Links
Poirot Investigates
The Murder of Roger Ackroyd
The Big Four
The Mystery of the Blue Train
Black Coffee *
Peril at End House
Lord Edgware Dies
Murder on the Orient Express
Three-Act Tragedy
Death in the Clouds
The ABC Murders
Murder in Mesopotamia
Cards on the Table
Murder in the Mews
Dumb Witness
Death on the Nile
Appointment with Death
Hercule Poirot's Christmas
Sad Cypress
One, Two, Buckle My Shoe
Evil Under the Sun
Five Little Pigs
The Hollow
The Labours of Hercules
Taken at the Flood
Mrs McGinty's Dead
After the Funeral
Hickory Dickory Dock
Dead Man's Folly
Cat Among the Pigeons
The Adventure of the Christmas Pudding
The Clocks
Third Girl
Hallowe'en Party
Elephants Can Remember
Poirot's Early Cases
Curtain: Poirot's Last Case

Marple
The Murder at the Vicarage
The Thirteen Problems
The Body in the Library
The Moving Finger
A Murder Is Announced
They Do It with Mirrors
A Pocket Full of Rye
4.50 from Paddington
The Mirror Crack'd from Side to Side
A Caribbean Mystery
At Bertram's Hotel
Nemesis
Sleeping Murder
Miss Marple's Final Cases

Tommy & Tuppence
The Secret Adversary
Partners in Crime
N or M?
By the Pricking of My Thumbs
Postern of Fate

Published as Mary Westmacott
Giant's Bread
Unfinished Portrait
Absent in the Spring
The Rose and the Yew Tree
A Daughter's a Daughter
The Burden

Memoirs
An Autobiography
Come, Tell Me How You Live
The Grand Tour

Play Collections
Akhnaton
The Mousetrap and Other Plays
The Floating Admiral †
Star Over Bethlehem

* novelized by Charles Osborne   † contributor

Agatha Christie

Murder in Mesopotamia

HarperCollins*Publishers*

HarperCollins*Publishers* Ltd
1 London Bridge Street
London SE1 9GF
www.harpercollins.co.uk

This paperback edition 2016

First published in Great Britain by
Collins, The Crime Club 1936

11

Agatha Christie® Poirot® Murder in Mesopotamia™
Copyright © 1936 Agatha Christie Limited. All rights reserved.
www.agathachristie.com

A catalogue record for this book is
available from the British Library

ISBN 978-0-00-816487-4 (PB)
ISBN 978-0-00-825584-8 (POD PB)

Set in Sabon by Born Group using Atomik ePublisher from Easypress

Printed and bound by
CPI Group (UK) Ltd, Croydon, CR0 4YY

All rights reserved. No part of this publication may be
reproduced, stored in a retrieval system, or transmitted,
in any form or by any means, electronic, mechanical,
photocopying, recording or otherwise, without the prior
written permission of the publishers.

This book is sold subject to the condition that it shall not,
by way of trade or otherwise, be lent, re-sold, hired out or
otherwise circulated without the publisher's prior consent
in any form of binding or cover other than that in which it
is published and without a similar condition including this
condition being imposed on the subsequent purchaser.

MIX
Paper from
responsible sources
FSC
www.fsc.org **FSC C007454**

FSC is a non-profit international organisation established to promote
the responsible management of the world's forests. Products carrying the
FSC label are independently certified to assure consumers that they come
from forests that are managed to meet the social, economic and
ecological needs of present and future generations,
and other controlled sources.

Find out more about HarperCollins and the environment at
www.harpercollins.co.uk/green

*Dedicated to
My Many Archaeological Friends in
Iraq and Syria*

Contents

	Foreword	1
1.	Frontispiece	3
2.	Introducing Amy Leatheran	5
3.	Gossip	12
4.	I Arrive in Hassanieh	17
5.	Tell Yarimjah	28
6.	First Evening	34
7.	The Man at the Window	48
8.	Night Alarm	59
9.	Mrs Leidner's Story	68
10.	Saturday Afternoon	78
11.	An Odd Business	84
12.	'I Didn't Believe…'	91
13.	Hercule Poirot Arrives	97
14.	One of Us?	109
15.	Poirot Makes a Suggestion	117
16.	The Suspects	127
17.	The Stain by the Washstand	134
18.	Tea at Dr Reilly's	143
19.	A New Suspicion	156

20.	Miss Johnson, Mrs Mercado, Mr Reiter	166
21.	Mr Mercado, Richard Carey	180
22.	David Emmott, Father Lavigny and a Discovery	190
23.	I Go Psychic	203
24.	Murder is a Habit	215
25.	Suicide or Murder?	220
26.	Next It Will Be Me!	230
27.	Beginning of a Journey	238
28.	Journey's End	268
29.	L'Envoi	278

Foreword

by Giles Reilly, MD

The events chronicled in this narrative took place some four years ago. Circumstances have rendered it necessary, in my opinion, that a straightforward account of them should be given to the public. There have been the wildest and most ridiculous rumours suggesting that important evidence was suppressed and other nonsense of that kind. Those misconstructions have appeared more especially in the American Press.

For obvious reasons it was desirable that the account should not come from the pen of one of the expedition staff, who might reasonably be supposed to be prejudiced.

I therefore suggested to Miss Amy Leatheran that she should undertake the task. She is obviously the person to do it. She had a professional character of the highest, she is not biased by having any previous connection with the University of Pittstown Expedition to Iraq and she was an observant and intelligent eye-witness.

It was not very easy to persuade Miss Leatheran to undertake this task—in fact, persuading her was one of

Agatha Christie

the hardest jobs of my professional career—and even after it was completed she displayed a curious reluctance to let me see the manuscript. I discovered that this was partly due to some critical remarks she had made concerning my daughter Sheila. I soon disposed of that, assuring her that as children criticize their parents freely in print nowadays, parents are only too delighted when their offspring come in for their share of abuse! Her other objection was extreme modesty about her literary style. She hoped I would 'put the grammar right and all that.' I have, on the contrary, refused to alter so much as a single word. Miss Leatheran's style in my opinion is vigorous, individual and entirely apposite. If she calls Hercule Poirot 'Poirot' in one paragraph and 'Mr Poirot' in the next, such a variation is both interesting and suggestive. At one moment she is, so to speak, 'remembering her manners' (and hospital nurses are great sticklers for etiquette) and at the next her interest in what she is telling is that of a pure human being—cap and cuffs forgotten!

The only thing I have done is to take the liberty of writing a first chapter—aided by a letter kindly supplied by one of Miss Leatheran's friends. It is intended to be in the nature of a frontispiece—that is, it gives a rough sketch of the narrator.

CHAPTER 1

Frontispiece

In the hall of the Tigris Palace Hotel in Baghdad a hospital nurse was finishing a letter. Her fountain-pen drove briskly over the paper.

> *... Well, dear, I think that's really all my news. I must say it's been nice to see a bit of the world—though England for me every time, thank you. The dirt and the mess in Baghdad you wouldn't believe—and not romantic at all like you'd think from the Arabian Nights! Of course, it's pretty just on the river, but the town itself is just awful—and no proper shops at all. Major Kelsey took me through the bazaars, and of course there's no denying they're quaint—but just a lot of rubbish and hammering away at copper pans till they make your head ache—and not what I'd like to use myself unless I was sure about the cleaning. You've got to be so careful of verdigris with copper pans.*
>
> *I'll write and let you know if anything comes of the job that Dr Reilly spoke about. He said this American gentleman*

Agatha Christie

was in Baghdad now and might come and see me this afternoon. It's for his wife—she has 'fancies', so Dr Reilly said. He didn't say any more than that, and of course, dear, one knows what that usually means (but I hope not actually D.T.s!). Of course, Dr Reilly didn't say anything—but he had a look—if you know what I mean. This Dr Leidner is an archaeologist and is digging up a mound out in the desert somewhere for some American museum.

Well, dear, I will close now. I thought what you told me about little Stubbins was simply killing! *Whatever did Matron say?*

No more now.

    Yours ever,
        Amy Leatheran

Enclosing the letter in an envelope, she addressed it to Sister Curshaw, St Christopher's Hospital, London.

As she put the cap on her fountain-pen, one of the native boys approached her.

'A gentleman come to see you. Dr Leidner.'

Nurse Leatheran turned. She saw a man of middle height with slightly stooping shoulders, a brown beard and gentle, tired eyes.

Dr Leidner saw a woman of thirty-five, of erect, confident bearing. He saw a good-humoured face with slightly prominent blue eyes and glossy brown hair. She looked, he thought, just what a hospital nurse for a nervous case ought to look. Cheerful, robust, shrewd and matter-of-fact.

Nurse Leatheran, he thought, would do.

CHAPTER 2

Introducing Amy Leatheran

I don't pretend to be an author or to know anything about writing. I'm doing this simply because Dr Reilly asked me to, and somehow when Dr Reilly asks you to do a thing you don't like to refuse.

'Oh, but, doctor,' I said, 'I'm not literary—not literary at all.'

'Nonsense!' he said. 'Treat it as case notes, if you like.'

Well, of course, you *can* look at it that way.

Dr Reilly went on. He said that an unvarnished plain account of the Tell Yarimjah business was badly needed.

'If one of the interested parties writes it, it won't carry conviction. They'll say it's biased one way or another.'

And of course that was true, too. I was in it all and yet an outsider, so to speak.

'Why don't you write it yourself, doctor?' I asked.

'I wasn't on the spot—you were. Besides,' he added with a sigh, 'my daughter won't let me.'

The way he knuckles under to that chit of a girl of his is downright disgraceful. I had half a mind to say so, when I

Agatha Christie

saw that his eyes were twinkling. That was the worst of Dr Reilly. You never knew whether he was joking or not. He always said things in the same slow melancholy way—but half the time there was a twinkle underneath it.

'Well,' I said doubtfully, 'I suppose I *could*.'

'Of course you could.'

'Only I don't quite know how to set about it.'

'There's a good precedent for that. Begin at the beginning, go on to the end and then leave off.'

'I don't even know quite where and what the beginning was,' I said doubtfully.

'Believe me, nurse, the difficulty of beginning will be nothing to the difficulty of knowing how to stop. At least that's the way it is with me when I have to make a spech. Someone's got to catch hold of my coat-tails and pull me down by main force.'

'Oh, you're joking, doctor.'

'It's profoundly serious I am. Now what about it?'

Another thing was worrying me. After hesitating a moment or two I said: 'You know, doctor, I'm afraid I might tend to be—well, a little *personal* sometimes.'

'God bless my soul, woman, the more personal you are the better! This is a story of human beings—not dummies! Be personal—be prejudiced—be catty—be anything you please! Write the thing your own way. We can always prune out the bits that are libellous afterwards! You go ahead. You're a sensible woman, and you'll give a sensible common-sense account of the business.'

So that was that, and I promised to do my best.

And here I am beginning, but as I said to the doctor, it's difficult to know just where to start.

I suppose I ought to say a word or two about myself. I'm thirty-two and my name is Amy Leatheran. I took my training at St Christopher's and after that did two years maternity. I did a certain amount of private work and I was for four years at Miss Bendix's Nursing Home in Devonshire Place. I came out to Iraq with a Mrs Kelsey. I'd attended her when her baby was born. She was coming out to Baghdad with her husband and had already got a children's nurse booked who had been for some years with friends of hers out there. Their children were coming home and going to school, and the nurse had agreed to go to Mrs Kelsey when they left. Mrs Kelsey was delicate and nervous about the journey out with so young a child, so Major Kelsey arranged that I should come out with her and look after her and the baby. They would pay my passage home unless we found someone needing a nurse for the return journey.

Well, there is no need to describe the Kelseys—the baby was a little love and Mrs Kelsey quite nice, though rather the fretting kind. I enjoyed the voyage very much. I'd never been a long trip on the sea before.

Dr Reilly was on board the boat. He was a black-haired, long-faced man who said all sorts of funny things in a low, sad voice. I think he enjoyed pulling my leg and used to make the most extraordinary statements to see if I would swallow them. He was the civil surgeon at a place called Hassanieh—a day and a half's journey from Baghdad.

Agatha Christie

I had been about a week in Baghdad when I ran across him and he asked when I was leaving the Kelseys. I said that it was funny his asking that because as a matter of fact the Wrights (the other people I mentioned) were going home earlier than they had meant to and their nurse was free to come straightaway.

He said that he had heard about the Wrights and that that was why he had asked me.

'As a matter of fact, nurse, I've got a possible job for you.'

'A case?'

He screwed his face up as though considering.

'You could hardly call it a case. It's just a lady who has—shall we say—fancies?'

'Oh!' I said.

(One usually knows what *that* means—drink or drugs!)

Dr Reilly didn't explain further. He was very discreet. 'Yes,' he said. 'A Mrs Leidner. Husband's an American—an American Swede to be exact. He's the head of a large American dig.'

And he explained how this expedition was excavating the site of a big Assyrian city something like Nineveh. The expedition house was not actually very far from Hassanieh, but it was a lonely spot and Dr Leidner had been worried for some time about his wife's health.

'He's not been very explicit about it, but it seems she has these fits of recurring nervous terrors.'

'Is she left alone all day amongst natives?' I asked.

'Oh, no, there's quite a crowd—seven or eight. I don't fancy she's ever been alone in the house. But there seems to be no doubt that she's worked herself up into a queer state. Leidner has any amount of work on his shoulders, but he's crazy about his wife and it worries him to know she's in this state. He felt he'd be happier if he knew that some responsible person with expert knowledge was keeping an eye on her.'

'And what does Mrs Leidner herself think about it?'

Dr Reilly answered gravely:

'Mrs Leidner is a very lovely lady. She's seldom of the same mind about anything two days on end. But on the whole she favours the idea.' He added, 'She's an odd woman. A mass of affectation and, I should fancy, a champion liar—but Leidner seems honestly to believe that she is scared out of her life by something or other.'

'What did she herself say to you, doctor?'

'Oh, she hasn't consulted me! She doesn't like me anyway—for several reasons. It was Leidner who came to me and propounded this plan. Well, nurse, what do you think of the idea? You'd see something of the country before you go home—they'll be digging for another two months. And excavation is quite interesting work.'

After a moment's hesitation while I turned the matter over in my mind: 'Well,' I said, 'I really think I might try it.'

'Splendid,' said Dr Reilly, rising. 'Leidner's in Baghdad now. I'll tell him to come round and see if he can fix things up with you.'

Dr Leidner came to the hotel that afternoon. He was a middle-aged man with a rather nervous, hesitating manner. There was something gentle and kindly and rather helpless about him.

Agatha Christie

He sounded very devoted to his wife, but he was very vague about what was the matter with her.

'You see,' he said, tugging at his beard in a rather perplexed manner that I later came to know to be characteristic of him, 'my wife is really in a very nervous state. I—I'm quite worried about her.'

'She is in good physical health?' I asked.

'Yes—oh, yes, I think so. No, I should not think there was anything the matter with her physically. But she—well—imagines things, you know.'

'What kind of things?' I asked.

But he shied off from the point, merely murmuring perplexedly: 'She works herself up over nothing at all... I really can see no foundations for these fears.'

'Fears of what, Dr Leidner?'

He said vaguely, 'Oh, just—nervous terrors, you know.'

Ten to one, I thought to myself, it's drugs. And he doesn't realize it! Lots of men don't. Just wonder why their wives are so jumpy and have such extraordinary changes of mood.

I asked whether Mrs Leidner herself approved of the idea of my coming.

His face lighted up.

'Yes. I was surprised. Most pleasurably surprised. She said it was a very good idea. She said she would feel very much safer.'

The word struck me oddly. *Safer*. A very queer word to use. I began to surmise that Mrs Leidner might be a mental case.

He went on with a kind of boyish eagerness.

'I'm sure you'll get on very well with her. She's really a very charming woman.' He smiled disarmingly. 'She feels you'll be the greatest comfort to her. I felt the same as soon as I saw you. You look, if you will allow me to say so, so splendidly healthy and full of common sense. I'm sure you're just the person for Louise.'

'Well, we can but try, Dr Leidner,' I said cheerfully. 'I'm sure I hope I can be of use to your wife. Perhaps she's nervous of natives?'

'Oh, dear me no.' He shook his head, amused at the idea. 'My wife likes Arabs very much—she appreciates their simplicity and their sense of humour. This is only her second season—we have been married less than two years—but she already speaks quite a fair amount of Arabic.'

I was silent for a moment or two, then I had one more try.

'Can't you tell me at all what it is your wife is afraid of, Dr Leidner?' I asked.

He hesitated. Then he said slowly, 'I hope—I believe—that she will tell you that herself.'

And that's all I could get out of him.

CHAPTER 3

Gossip

It was arranged that I should go to Tell Yarimjah the following week.

Mrs Kelsey was settling into her house at Alwiyah, and I was glad to be able to take a few things off her shoulders.

During that time I heard one or two allusions to the Leidner expedition. A friend of Mrs Kelsey's, a young squadron-leader, pursed his lips in surprise as he exclaimed: 'Lovely Louise. So that's her latest!' He turned to me. 'That's our nickname for her, nurse. She's always known as Lovely Louise.'

'Is she so very handsome then?' I asked.

'It's taking her at her own valuation. *She* thinks she is!'

'Now don't be spiteful, John,' said Mrs Kelsey. 'You know it's not only she who thinks so! Lots of people have been very smitten by her.'

'Perhaps you're right. She's a bit long in the tooth, but she has a certain attraction.'

'You were completely bowled over yourself,' said Mrs Kelsey, laughing.

Murder in Mesopotamia

The squadron-leader blushed and admitted rather shamefacedly: 'Well, she has a way with her. As for Leidner himself, he worships the ground she walks on—and all the rest of the expedition has to worship too! It's expected of them!'

'How many are there altogether?' I asked.

'All sorts and nationalities, nurse,' said the squadron-leader cheerfully. 'An English architect, a French Father from Carthage—he does the inscriptions—tablets and things, you know. And then there's Miss Johnson. She's English too—sort of general bottle-washer. And a little plump man who does the photography—he's an American. And the Mercados. Heaven knows what nationality they are—Dagos of some kind! She's quite young—a snaky-looking creature—and oh! doesn't she hate Lovely Louise! And there are a couple of youngsters and that's the lot. A few odd fish, but nice on the whole—don't you agree, Pennyman?'

He was appealing to an elderly man who was sitting thoughtfully twirling a pair of pince-nez.

The latter started and looked up.

'Yes—yes—very nice indeed. Taken individually, that is. Of course, Mercado is rather a queer fish—'

'He has such a very *odd* beard,' put in Mrs Kelsey. 'A queer limp kind.'

Major Pennyman went on without noticing her interruption.

'The young 'uns are both nice. The American's rather silent, and the English boy talks a bit too much. Funny, it's usually the other way round. Leidner himself is a delightful fellow—so modest and unassuming. Yes, individually they

Agatha Christie

are all pleasant people. But somehow or other, I may have been fanciful, but the last time I went to see them I got a queer impression of something being wrong. I don't know what it was exactly... Nobody seemed quite natural. There was a queer atmosphere of tension. I can explain best what I mean by saying that they all passed the butter to each other too politely.'

Blushing a little, because I don't like airing my own opinions too much, I said: 'If people are too much cooped up together it's got a way of getting on their nerves. I know that myself from experience in hospital.'

'That's true,' said Major Kelsey, 'but it's early in the season, hardly time for that particular irritation to have set in.'

'An expedition is probably like our life here in miniature,' said Major Pennyman. 'It has its cliques and rivalries and jealousies.'

'It sounds as though they'd got a good many newcomers this year,' said Major Kelsey.

'Let me see.' The squadron-leader counted them off on his fingers. 'Young Coleman is new, so is Reiter. Emmott was out last year and so were the Mercados. Father Lavigny is a newcomer. He's come in place of Dr Byrd, who was ill this year and couldn't come out. Carey, of course, is an old hand. He's been out ever since the beginning, five years ago. Miss Johnson's been out nearly as many years as Carey.'

'I always thought they got on so well together at Tell Yarimjah,' remarked Major Kelsey. 'They seemed like a happy family—which is really surprising when one considers

14

Murder in Mesopotamia

what human nature is! I'm sure Nurse Leatheran agrees with me.'

'Well,' I said, 'I don't know that you're not right! The rows I've known in hospital and starting often from nothing more than a dispute about a pot of tea.'

'Yes, one tends to get petty in close communities,' said Major Pennyman. 'All the same I feel there must be something more to it in this case. Leidner is such a gentle, unassuming man, with really a remarkable amount of tact. He's always managed to keep his expedition happy and on good terms with each other. And yet I *did* notice that feeling of tension the other day.'

Mrs Kelsey laughed.

'And you don't see the explanation? Why, it leaps to the eye!'

'What do you mean?'

'*Mrs* Leidner, of course.'

'Oh come, Mary,' said her husband, 'she's a charming woman—not at all the quarrelsome kind.'

'I didn't say she was quarrelsome. She *causes* quarrels!'

'In what way? And why should she?'

'Why? Why? Because she's bored. She's not an archaeologist, only the wife of one. She's bored shut away from any excitements and so she provides her own drama. She amuses herself by setting other people by the ears.'

'Mary, you don't know in the least. You're merely imagining.'

'Of course I'm imagining! But you'll find I'm right. Lovely Louise doesn't look like the Mona Lisa for nothing! She

Agatha Christie

mayn't mean any harm, but she likes to see what will happen.'

'She's devoted to Leidner.'

'Oh! I dare say, I'm not suggesting vulgar intrigues. But she's an *allumeuse*, that woman.'

'Women are so sweet to each other,' said Major Kelsey.

'I know. Cat, cat, cat, that's what you men say. But we're usually right about our own sex.'

'All the same,' said Major Pennyman thoughtfully, 'assuming all Mrs Kelsey's uncharitable surmises to be true, I don't think it would quite account for that curious sense of tension—rather like the feeling there is before a thunderstorm. I had the impression very strongly that the storm might break any minute.'

'Now don't frighten nurse,' said Mrs Kelsey. 'She's going there in three days' time and you'll put her right off.'

'Oh, you won't frighten me,' I said, laughing.

All the same I thought a good deal about what had been said. Dr Leidner's curious use of the word 'safer' recurred to me. Was it his wife's secret fear, unacknowledged or expressed perhaps, that was reacting on the rest of the party? Or was it the actual tension (or perhaps the unknown cause of it) that was reacting on *her* nerves?

I looked up the word *allumeuse* that Mrs Kelsey had used in a dictionary, but couldn't get any sense out of it.

'Well,' I thought to myself, 'I must wait and see.'

CHAPTER 4

I Arrive in Hassanieh

Three days later I left Baghdad.

I was sorry to leave Mrs Kelsey and the baby, who was a little love and was thriving splendidly, gaining her proper number of ounces every week. Major Kelsey took me to the station and saw me off. I should arrive at Kirkuk the following morning, and there someone was to meet me.

I slept badly, I never sleep very well in a train and I was troubled by dreams.

The next morning, however, when I looked out of the window it was a lovely day and I felt interested and curious about the people I was going to see.

As I stood on the platform hesitating and looking about me I saw a young man coming towards me. He had a round pink face, and really, in all my life, I have never seen anyone who seemed so exactly like a young man out of one of Mr P. G. Wodehouse's books.

'Hallo, 'allo, 'allo,' he said. 'Are you Nurse Leatheran? Well, I mean you must be—I can see that. Ha ha! My

Agatha Christie

name's Coleman. Dr Leidner sent me along. How are you feeling? Beastly journey and all that? Don't I know these trains! Well, here we are—had any breakfast? This your kit? I say, awfully modest, aren't you? Mrs Leidner has four suitcases and a trunk—to say nothing of a hat-box and a patent pillow, and this, that and the other. Am I talking too much? Come along to the old bus.'

There was what I heard called later a station wagon waiting outside. It was a little like a wagonette, a little like a lorry and a little like a car. Mr Coleman helped me in, explaining that I had better sit next to the driver so as to get less jolting.

Jolting! I wonder the whole contraption didn't fall to pieces! And nothing like a road—just a sort of track all ruts and holes. Glorious East indeed! When I thought of our splendid arterial roads in England it made me quite homesick.

Mr Coleman leaned forward from his seat behind me and yelled in my ear a good deal.

'Track's in pretty good condition,' he shouted just after we had been thrown up in our seats till we nearly touched the roof.

And apparently he was speaking quite seriously.

'Very good for you—jogs the liver,' he said. 'You ought to know that, nurse.'

'A stimulated liver won't be much good to me if my head's split open,' I observed tartly.

'You should come along here after it's rained! The skids are glorious. Most of the time one's going sideways.'

To this I did not respond.

Murder in Mesopotamia

Presently we had to cross the river, which we did on the craziest ferry-boat you can imagine. To my mind it was a mercy we ever got across, but everyone seemed to think it was quite usual.

It took us about four hours to get to Hassanieh, which, to my surprise, was quite a big place. Very pretty it looked, too, before we got there from the other side of the river—standing up quite white and fairy-like with minarets. It was a bit different, though, when one had crossed the bridge and come right into it. Such a smell and everything ramshackle and tumble-down, and mud and mess everywhere.

Mr Coleman took me to Dr Reilly's house, where, he said, the doctor was expecting me to lunch.

Dr Reilly was just as nice as ever, and his house was nice too, with a bathroom and everything spick and span. I had a nice bath, and by the time I got back into my uniform and came down I was feeling fine.

Lunch was just ready and we went in, the doctor apologizing for his daughter, who he said was always late.

We'd just had a very good dish of eggs in sauce when she came in and Dr Reilly said, 'Nurse, this is my daughter Sheila.'

She shook hands, hoped I'd had a good journey, tossed off her hat, gave a cool nod to Mr Coleman and sat down.

'Well, Bill,' she said. 'How's everything?'

He began to talk to her about some party or other that was to come off at the club, and I took stock of her.

I can't say I took to her much. A thought too cool for my liking. An off-hand sort of girl, though good-looking. Black hair and blue eyes—a pale sort of face and the usual

Agatha Christie

lipsticked mouth. She'd a cool, sarcastic way of talking that rather annoyed me. I had a probationer like her under me once—a girl who worked well, I'll admit, but whose manner always riled me.

It looked to me rather as though Mr Coleman was gone on her. He stammered a bit, and his conversation became slightly more idiotic than it was before, if that was possible! He reminded me of a large stupid dog wagging its tail and trying to please.

After lunch Dr Reilly went off to the hospital, and Mr Coleman had some things to get in the town, and Miss Reilly asked me whether I'd like to see round the town a bit or whether I'd rather stop in the house. Mr Coleman, she said, would be back to fetch me in about an hour.

'Is there anything to see?' I asked.

'There are some picturesque corners,' said Miss Reilly. 'But I don't know that you'd care for them. They're extremely dirty.'

The way she said it rather nettled me. I've never been able to see that picturesqueness excuses dirt.

In the end she took me to the club, which was pleasant enough, overlooking the river, and there were English papers and magazines there.

When we got back to the house Mr Coleman wasn't there yet, so we sat down and talked a bit. It wasn't easy somehow.

She asked me if I'd met Mrs Leidner yet.

'No,' I said. 'Only her husband.'

'Oh,' she said. 'I wonder what you'll think of her?'

I didn't say anything to that. And she went on: 'I like Dr Leidner very much. Everybody likes him.'

That's as good as saying, I thought, that you don't like his wife.

I still didn't say anything and presently she asked abruptly: 'What's the matter with her? Did Dr Leidner tell you?'

I wasn't going to start gossiping about a patient before I got there even, so I said evasively: 'I understand she's a bit rundown and wants looking after.'

She laughed—a nasty sort of laugh—hard and abrupt.

'Good God,' she said. 'Aren't nine people looking after her already enough?'

'I suppose they've all got their work to do,' I said.

'Work to do? Of course they've got work to do. But Louise comes first—she sees to that all right.'

'No,' I said to myself. 'You *don't* like her.'

'All the same,' went on Miss Reilly, 'I don't see what she wants with a professional hospital nurse. I should have thought amateur assistance was more in her line; not someone who'll jam a thermometer in her mouth, and count her pulse and bring everything down to hard facts.'

Well, I must admit it, I was curious.

'You think there's nothing the matter with her?' I asked.

'Of course there's nothing the matter with her! The woman's as strong as an ox. "Dear Louise hasn't slept." "She's got black circles under her eyes." Yes—put there with a blue pencil! Anything to get attention, to have everybody hovering round her, making a fuss of her!'

Agatha Christie

There was something in that, of course. I had (what nurse hasn't?) come across many cases of hypochondriacs whose delight it is to keep a whole household dancing attendance. And if a doctor or a nurse were to say to them: 'There's nothing on earth the matter with you!' Well, to begin with they wouldn't believe it, and their indignation would be as genuine as indignation can be.

Of course it was quite possible that Mrs Leidner might be a case of this kind. The husband, naturally, would be the first to be deceived. Husbands, I've found, are a credulous lot where illness is concerned. But all the same, it didn't quite square with what I'd heard. It didn't, for instance, fit in with that word 'safer'.

Funny how that word had got kind of stuck in my mind. Reflecting on it, I asked: 'Is Mrs Leidner a nervous woman? Is she nervous, for instance, of living out far from anywhere?'

'What is there to be nervous of? Good heavens, there are ten of them! And they've got guards too—because of the antiquities. Oh, no, she's not nervous—at least—'

She seemed struck by some thought and stopped—going on slowly after a minute or two.

'It's odd your saying that.'

'Why?'

'Flight-Lieutenant Jervis and I rode over the other day. It was in the morning. Most of them were up on the dig. She was sitting writing a letter and I suppose she didn't hear us coming. The boy who brings you in wasn't about for once, and we came straight up on to the verandah. Apparently she saw Flight-Lieutenant Jervis's shadow thrown on the wall—and she fairly screamed! Apologized, of course. Said she thought it was a strange man. A bit odd, that. I mean, even if it was a strange man, why get the wind up?'

I nodded thoughtfully.

Miss Reilly was silent, then burst out suddenly, 'I don't know what's the matter with them this year. They've all got the jumps. Johnson goes about so glum she can't open her mouth. David never speaks if he can help it. Bill, of course, never stops, and somehow his chatter seems to make the others worse. Carey goes about looking as though something would snap any minute. And they all watch each other as though—as though—Oh, I don't know, but it's *queer*.'

It was odd, I thought, that two such dissimilar people as Miss Reilly and Major Pennyman should have been struck in the same manner.

Just then Mr Coleman came bustling in. Bustling was just the word for it. If his tongue had hung out and he had suddenly produced a tail to wag you wouldn't have been surprised.

'Hallo-allo,' he said. 'Absolutely the world's best shopper—that's me. Have you shown nurse all the beauties of the town?'

'She wasn't impressed,' said Miss Reilly dryly.

'I don't blame her,' said Mr Coleman heartily. 'Of all the one-horse tumble-down places!'

'Not a lover of the picturesque or the antique, are you, Bill? I can't think why you are an archaeologist.'

Agatha Christie

'Don't blame me for that. Blame my guardian. He's a learned bird—fellow of his college—browses among books in bedroom slippers—that kind of man. Bit of a shock for him to have a ward like me.'

'I think it's frightfully stupid of you to be forced into a profession you don't care for,' said the girl sharply.

'Not forced, Sheila, old girl, not forced. The old man asked if I had any special profession in mind, and I said I hadn't, and so he wangled a season out here for me.'

'But haven't you any idea really what you'd *like* to do? You *must* have!'

'Of course I have. My idea would be to give work a miss altogether. What I'd like to do is to have plenty of money and go in for motor-racing.'

'You're absurd!' said Miss Reilly.

She sounded quite angry.

'Oh, I realize that it's quite out of the question,' said Mr Coleman cheerfully. 'So, if I've got to do something, I don't much care what it is so long as it isn't mugging in an office all day long. I was quite agreeable to seeing a bit of the world. Here goes, I said, and along I came.'

'And a fat lot of use you must be, I expect!'

'There you're wrong. I can stand up on the dig and shout "*Y'Allah*" with anybody! And as a matter of fact I'm not so dusty at drawing. Imitating handwriting used to be my speciality at school. I'd have made a first-class forger. Oh, well, I may come to that yet. If my Rolls-Royce splashes you with mud as you're waiting for a bus, you'll know that I've taken to crime.'

Miss Reilly said coldly: 'Don't you think it's about time you started instead of talking so much?'

'Hospitable, aren't we, nurse?'

'I'm sure Nurse Leatheran is anxious to get settled in.'

'You're always sure of everything,' retorted Mr Coleman with a grin.

That was true enough, I thought. Cocksure little minx.

I said dryly: 'Perhaps we'd better start, Mr Coleman.'

'Right you are, nurse.'

I shook hands with Miss Reilly and thanked her, and we set off.

'Damned attractive girl, Sheila,' said Mr Coleman. 'But always ticking a fellow off.'

We drove out of the town and presently took a kind of track between green crops. It was very bumpy and full of ruts.

After about half an hour Mr Coleman pointed to a big mound by the river bank ahead of us and said: 'Tell Yarimjah.'

I could see little black figures moving about it like ants.

As I was looking they suddenly began to run all together down the side of the mound.

'Fidos,' said Mr Coleman. 'Knocking-off time. We knock off an hour before sunset.'

The expedition house lay a little way back from the river.

The driver rounded a corner, bumped through an extremely narrow arch and there we were.

The house was built round a courtyard. Originally it had occupied only the south side of the courtyard with a few unimportant out-buildings on the east. The expedition had continued the building on the other two sides. As the plan of the house was to prove of special interest later, I append a rough sketch of it here.

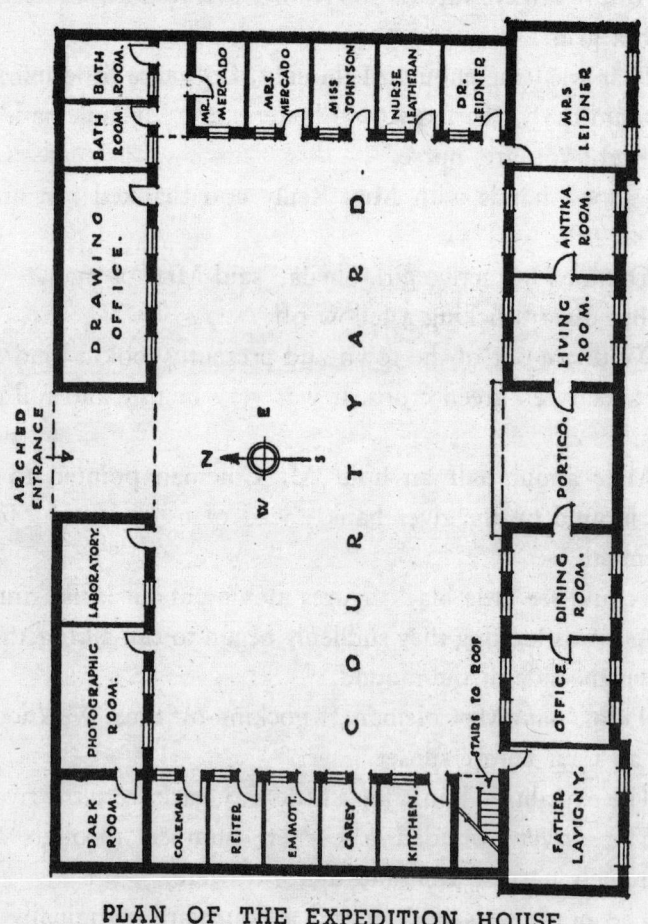

PLAN OF THE EXPEDITION HOUSE
AT TELL YARIMJAH

All the rooms opened on to the courtyard, and most of the windows—the exception being in the original south building where there were windows giving on the outside country as well. These windows, however, were barred on the outside. In the south-west corner a staircase ran up to a long flat roof with a parapet running the length of the south side of the building which was higher than the other three sides.

Mr Coleman led me along the east side of the courtyard and round to where a big open verandah occupied the centre of the south side. He pushed open a door at one side of it and we entered a room where several people were sitting round a tea-table.

'Toodle-oodle-oo!' said Mr Coleman. 'Here's Sairey Gamp.'

The lady who was sitting at the head of the table rose and came to greet me.

I had my first glimpse of Louise Leidner.

CHAPTER 5

Tell Yarimjah

I don't mind admitting that my first impression on seeing Mrs Leidner was one of downright surprise. One gets into the way of imagining a person when one hears them talked about. I'd got it firmly into my head that Mrs Leidner was a dark, discontented kind of woman. The nervy kind, all on edge. And then, too, I'd expected her to be—well, to put it frankly—a bit vulgar.

She wasn't a bit like what I'd imagined her! To begin with, she was very fair. She wasn't a Swede, like her husband, but she might have been as far as looks went. She had that blonde Scandinavian fairness that you don't very often see. She wasn't a young woman. Midway between thirty and forty, I should say. Her face was rather haggard, and there was some grey hair mingled with the fairness. Her eyes, though, were lovely. They were the only eyes I've ever come across that you might truly describe as violet. They were very large, and there were faint shadows underneath them. She was very thin and fragile-looking, and if I say that she had an air of intense weariness and was at the same time very much alive, it sounds like nonsense—but that's the feeling I got. I felt, too, that she was a lady through and through. And that means something—even nowadays.

She put out her hand and smiled. Her voice was low and soft with an American drawl in it.

'I'm so glad you've come, nurse. Will you have some tea? Or would you like to go to your room first?'

I said I'd have tea, and she introduced me to the people sitting round the table.

'This is Miss Johnson—and Mr Reiter. Mrs Mercado. Mr Emmott. Father Lavigny. My husband will be in presently. Sit down here between Father Lavigny and Miss Johnson.'

I did as I was bid and Miss Johnson began talking to me, asking about my journey and so on.

I liked her. She reminded me of a matron I'd had in my probationer days whom we had all admired and worked hard for.

She was getting on for fifty, I should judge, and rather mannish in appearance, with iron-grey hair cropped short. She had an abrupt, pleasant voice, rather deep in tone. She had an ugly rugged face with an almost laughably turned-up nose which she was in the habit of rubbing irritably when anything troubled or perplexed her. She wore a tweed coat and skirt made rather like a man's. She told me presently that she was a native of Yorkshire.

Father Lavigny I found just a bit alarming. He was a tall man with a great black beard and pince-nez. I had heard Mrs Kelsey say that there was a French monk there, and I

Agatha Christie

now saw that Father Lavigny was wearing a monk's robe of some white woollen material. It surprised me rather, because I always understood that monks went into monasteries and didn't come out again.

Mrs Leidner talked to him mostly in French, but he spoke to me in quite fair English. I noticed that he had shrewd, observant eyes which darted about from face to face.

Opposite me were the other three. Mr Reiter was a stout, fair young man with glasses. His hair was rather long and curly, and he had very round blue eyes. I should think he must have been a lovely baby, but he wasn't much to look at now! In fact he was just a little like a pig. The other young man had very short hair cropped close to his head. He had a long, rather humorous face and very good teeth, and he looked very attractive when he smiled. He said very little, though, just nodded if spoken to or answered in monosyllables. He, like Mr Reiter, was an American. The last person was Mrs Mercado, and I couldn't have a good look at her because whenever I glanced in her direction I always found her staring at me with a kind of hungry stare that was a bit disconcerting to say the least of it. You might have thought a hospital nurse was a strange animal the way she was looking at me. No manners at all!

She was quite young—not more than about twenty-five—and sort of dark and slinky-looking, if you know what I mean. Quite nice-looking in a kind of way, but rather as though she might have what my mother used to call 'a touch of the tar-brush'. She had on a very vivid pullover and her nails matched it in colour. She had a thin bird-like eager face with big eyes and rather a tight, suspicious mouth.

The tea was very good—a nice strong blend—not like the weak China stuff that Mrs Kelsey always had and that had been a sore trial to me.

There was toast and jam and a plate of rock buns and a cutting cake. Mr Emmott was very polite passing me things. Quiet as he was he always seemed to notice when my plate was empty.

Presently Mr Coleman bustled in and took the place beyond Miss Johnson. There didn't seem to be anything the matter with *his* nerves. He talked away nineteen to the dozen.

Mrs Leidner sighed once and cast a wearied look in his direction but it didn't have any effect. Nor did the fact that Mrs Mercado, to whom he was addressing most of his conversation, was far too busy watching me to do more than make perfunctory replies.

Just as we were finishing, Dr Leidner and Mr Mercado came in from the dig.

Dr Leidner greeted me in his nice kind manner. I saw his eyes go quickly and anxiously to his wife's face and he seemed to be relieved by what he saw there. Then he sat down at the other end of the table, and Mr Mercado sat down in the vacant place by Mrs Leidner. He was a tall, thin, melancholy man, a good deal older than his wife, with a sallow complexion and a queer, soft, shapeless-looking beard. I was glad when he came in, for his wife stopped staring at me and transferred her attention to him, watching

Agatha Christie

him with a kind of anxious impatience that I found rather odd. He himself stirred his tea dreamily and said nothing at all. A piece of cake lay untasted on his plate.

There was still one vacant place, and presently the door opened and a man came in.

The moment I saw Richard Carey I felt he was one of the handsomest men I'd seen for a long time—and yet I doubt if that were really so. To say a man is handsome and at the same time to say he looks like a death's head sounds a rank contradiction, and yet it was true. His head gave the effect of having the skin stretched unusually tight over the bones—but they were beautiful bones. The lean line of jaw and temple and forehead was so sharply outlined that he reminded me of a bronze statue. Out of this lean brown face looked two of the brightest and most intensely blue eyes I have ever seen. He stood about six foot and was, I should imagine, a little under forty years of age.

Dr Leidner said: 'This is Mr Carey, our architect, nurse.'

He murmured something in a pleasant, inaudible English voice and sat down by Mrs Mercado.

Mrs Leidner said: 'I'm afraid the tea is a little cold, Mr Carey.'

He said: 'Oh, that's quite all right, Mrs Leidner. My fault for being late. I wanted to finish plotting those walls.'

Mrs Mercado said, 'Jam, Mr Carey?'

Mr Reiter pushed forward the toast.

And I remembered Major Pennyman saying: '*I can explain best what I mean by saying that they all passed the butter to each other a shade too politely.*'

Yes, there was something a little odd about it...

A shade formal...

You'd have said it was a party of strangers—not people who had known each other—some of them—for quite a number of years.

CHAPTER 6

First Evening

After tea Mrs Leidner took me to show me my room.

Perhaps here I had better give a short description of the arrangement of the rooms. This was very simple and can easily be understood by a reference to the plan.

On either side of the big open porch were doors leading into the two principal rooms. That on the right led into the dining-room, where we had tea. The one on the other side led into an exactly similar room (I have called it the living-room) which was used as a sitting-room and kind of informal workroom—that is, a certain amount of drawing (other than the strictly architectural) was done there, and the more delicate pieces of pottery were brought there to be pieced together. Through the living-room one passed into the antiquities-room where all the finds from the dig were brought in and stored on shelves and in pigeon-holes, and also laid out on big benches and tables. From the antika-room there was no exit save through the living-room.

Beyond the antika-room, but reached through a door which gave on the courtyard, was Mrs Leidner's bedroom. This, like the other rooms on that side of the house, had a couple of barred windows looking out over the ploughed countryside. Round the corner next to Mrs Leidner's room, but with no actual communicating door, was Dr Leidner's room. This was the first of the rooms on the east side of the building. Next to it was the room that was to be mine. Next to me was Miss Johnson's, with Mr and Mrs Mercado's beyond. After that came two so-called bathrooms.

(When I once used that last term in the hearing of Dr Reilly he laughed at me and said a bathroom was either a bathroom or not a bathroom! All the same, when you've got used to taps and proper plumbing, it seems strange to call a couple of mud-rooms with a tin hip-bath in each of them, and muddy water brought in kerosene tins, *bathrooms*!)

All this side of the building had been added by Dr Leidner to the original Arab house. The bedrooms were all the same, each with a window and a door giving on to the courtyard. Along the north side were the drawing-office, the laboratory and the photographic rooms.

To return to the verandah, the arrangement of rooms was much the same on the other side. There was the dining-room leading into the office where the files were kept and the cataloguing and typing was done. Corresponding to Mrs Leidner's room was that of Father Lavigny, who was given the largest bedroom; he used it also for the decoding—or whatever you call it—of tablets.

Agatha Christie

In the south-west corner was the staircase running up to the roof. On the west side were first the kitchen quarters and then four small bedrooms used by the young men—Carey, Emmott, Reiter and Coleman.

At the north-west corner was the photographic-room with the dark-room leading out of it. Next to that the laboratory. Then came the only entrance—the big arched doorway through which we had entered. Outside were sleeping quarters for the native servants, the guard-house for the soldiers, and stables, etc., for the water horses. The drawing-office was to the right of the archway occupying the rest of the north side.

I have gone into the arrangements of the house rather fully here because I don't want to have to go over them again later.

As I say, Mrs Leidner herself took me round the building and finally established me in my bedroom, hoping that I should be comfortable and have everything I wanted.

The room was nicely though plainly furnished—a bed, a chest of drawers, a wash-stand and a chair.

'The boys will bring you hot water before lunch and dinner—and in the morning, of course. If you want it any other time, go outside and clap your hands, and when the boy comes say, *jib mai' har*. Do you think you can remember that?'

I said I thought so and repeated it a little haltingly.

'That's right. And be sure and shout it. Arabs don't understand anything said in an ordinary "English" voice.'

'Languages are funny things,' I said. 'It seems odd there should be such a lot of different ones.'

Mrs Leidner smiled.

'There is a church in Palestine in which the Lord's Prayer is written up in—ninety, I think it is—different languages.'

'Well!' I said. 'I must write and tell my old aunt that. She *will* be interested.'

Mrs Leidner fingered the jug and basin absently and shifted the soap-dish an inch or two.'

'I do hope you'll be happy here,' she said, 'and not get too bored.'

'I'm not often bored,' I assured her. 'Life's not long enough for that.'

She did not answer. She continued to toy with the washstand as though abstractedly.

Suddenly she fixed her dark violet eyes on my face.

'What exactly did my husband tell you, nurse?'

Well, one usually says the same thing to a question of that kind.

'I gathered you were a bit run-down and all that, Mrs Leidner,' I said glibly. 'And that you just wanted someone to look after you and take any worries off your hands.'

She bent her head slowly and thoughtfully.

'Yes,' she said. 'Yes—that will do very well.'

That was just a little bit enigmatic, but I wasn't going to question it. Instead I said: 'I hope you'll let me help you with anything there is to do in the house. You mustn't let me be idle.'

She smiled a little.

'Thank you, nurse.'

Then she sat down on the bed and, rather to my surprise, began to cross-question me rather closely. I say rather to my surprise because, from the moment I set eyes on her, I felt sure

Agatha Christie

that Mrs Leidner was a lady. And a lady, in my experience, very seldom displays curiosity about one's private affairs.

But Mrs Leidner seemed anxious to know everything there was to know about me. Where I'd trained and how long ago. What had brought me out to the East. How it had come about that Dr Reilly had recommended me. She even asked me if I had ever been in America or had any relations in America. One or two other questions she asked me that seemed quite purposeless at the time, but of which I saw the significance later.

Then, suddenly, her manner changed. She smiled—a warm sunny smile—and she said, very sweetly, that she was very glad I had come and that she was sure I was going to be a comfort to her.

She got up from the bed and said: 'Would you like to come up to the roof and see the sunset? It's usually very lovely about this time.'

I agreed willingly.

As we went out of the room she asked: 'Were there many other people on the train from Baghdad? Any men?'

I said that I hadn't noticed anybody in particular. There had been two Frenchmen in the restaurant-car the night before. And a party of three men whom I gathered from their conversation had to do with the Pipe line.

She nodded and a faint sound escaped her. It sounded like a small sigh of relief.

We went up to the roof together.

Mrs Mercado was there, sitting on the parapet, and Dr Leidner was bending over looking at a lot of stones and broken pottery that were laid out in rows. There were big things he called querns, and pestles and celts and stone axes, and more broken bits of pottery with queer patterns on them than I've ever seen all at once.

'Come over here,' called out Mrs Mercado. 'Isn't it *too* too beautiful?'

It certainly was a beautiful sunset. Hassanieh in the distance looked quite fairy-like with the setting sun behind it, and the River Tigris flowing between its wide banks looked like a dream river rather than a real one.

'Isn't it lovely, Eric?' said Mrs Leidner.

The doctor looked up with abstracted eyes, murmured, 'Lovely, lovely,' perfunctorily and went on sorting potsherds.

Mrs Leidner smiled and said: 'Archaeologists only look at what lies beneath their feet. The sky and the heavens don't exist for them.'

Mrs Mercado giggled.

'Oh, they're very queer people—you'll soon find *that* out, nurse,' she said.

She paused and then added: 'We are all *so* glad you've come. We've been so very worried about dear Mrs Leidner, haven't we, Louise?'

'Have you?'

Her voice was not encouraging.

'Oh, yes. She really has been *very* bad, nurse. All sorts of alarms and excursions. You know when anybody says to me of someone, "It's just nerves," I always say: but what could be *worse*? Nerves are the core and centre of one's being, aren't they?'

Agatha Christie

'Puss, puss,' I thought to myself.

Mrs Leidner said dryly: 'Well, you needn't be worried about me any more, Marie. Nurse is going to look after me.'

'Certainly I am,' I said cheerfully.

'I'm sure that will make all the difference,' said Mrs Mercado. 'We've all felt that she ought to see a doctor or do *something*. Her nerves have really been all to pieces, haven't they, Louise dear?'

'So much so that I seem to have got on *your* nerves with them,' said Mrs Leidner. 'Shall we talk about something more interesting than my wretched ailments?'

I understood then that Mrs Leidner was the sort of woman who could easily make enemies. There was a cool rudeness in her tone (not that I blamed her for it) which brought a flush to Mrs Mercado's rather sallow cheeks. She stammered out something, but Mrs Leidner had risen and had joined her husband at the other end of the roof. I doubt if he heard her coming till she laid her hand on his shoulder, then he looked up quickly. There was affection and a kind of eager questioning in his face.

Mrs Leidner nodded her head gently. Presently, her arm through his, they wandered to the far parapet and finally down the steps together.

'He's devoted to her, isn't he?' said Mrs Mercado.

'Yes,' I said. 'It's very nice to see.'

She was looking at me with a queer, rather eager sidelong glance.

'What do you think is really the matter with her, nurse?' she asked, lowering her voice a little.

'Oh, I don't suppose it's much,' I said cheerfully. 'Just a bit run-down, I expect.'

Her eyes still bored into me as they had done at tea. She said abruptly: 'Are you a mental nurse?'

'Oh, dear, no!' I said. 'What made you think that?'

She was silent for a moment, then she said: 'Do you know how queer she's been? Did Dr Leidner tell you?'

I don't hold with gossiping about my cases. On the other hand, it's my experience that it's often very hard to get the truth out of relatives, and until you know the truth you're often working in the dark and doing no good. Of course, when there's a doctor in charge, it's different. He tells you what it's necessary for you to know. But in this case there wasn't a doctor in charge. Dr Reilly had never been called in professionally. And in my own mind I wasn't at all sure that Dr Leidner had told me all he could have done. It's often the husband's instinct to be reticent—and more honour to him, I must say. But all the same, the more I knew the better I could tell which line to take. Mrs Mercado (whom I put down in my own mind as a thoroughly spiteful little cat) was clearly dying to talk. And frankly, on the human side as well as the professional, I wanted to hear what she had to say. You can put it that I was just everyday curious if you like.

I said, 'I gather Mrs Leidner's not been quite her normal self lately?'

Mrs Mercado laughed disagreeably.

'Normal? I should say not. Frightening us to death. One night it was fingers tapping on her window. And then it

Agatha Christie

was a hand without an arm attached. But when it came to a yellow face pressed against the window—and when she rushed to the window there was nothing there—well, I ask you, it *is* a bit creepy for all of us.'

'Perhaps somebody was playing a trick on her,' I suggested.

'Oh, no, she fancied it all. And only three days ago at dinner they were firing shots in the village—nearly a mile away—and she jumped up and screamed out—it scared us all to death. As for Dr Leidner, he rushed to her and behaved in the most ridiculous way. "It's nothing, darling, it's nothing at all," he kept saying. I think, you know, nurse, men sometimes *encourage* women in these hysterical fancies. It's a pity because it's a bad thing. Delusions shouldn't be encouraged.'

'Not if they *are* delusions,' I said dryly.

'What else could they be?'

I didn't answer because I didn't know what to say. It was a funny business. The shots and the screaming were natural enough—for anyone in a nervous condition, that is. But this queer story of a spectral face and hand was different. It looked to me like one of two things—either Mrs Leidner had made the story up (exactly as a child shows off by telling lies about something that never happened in order to make herself the centre of attraction) or else it was, as I had suggested, a deliberate practical joke. It was the sort of thing, I reflected, that an unimaginative hearty sort of young fellow like Mr Coleman might think very funny. I decided to keep a close watch on him. Nervous patients can be scared nearly out of their minds by a silly joke.

Mrs Mercado said with a sideways glance at me:

'She's very romantic-looking, nurse, don't you think so? The sort of woman things *happen* to.'

'Have many things happened to her?' I asked.

'Well, her first husband was killed in the war when she was only twenty. I think that's very pathetic and romantic, don't you?'

'It's one way of calling a goose a swan,' I said dryly.

'Oh, nurse! What an extraordinary remark!'

It was really a very true one. The amount of women you hear say, 'If Donald—or Arthur—or whatever his name was—had *only* lived.' And I sometimes think but if he had, he'd have been a stout, unromantic, short-tempered, middle-aged husband as likely as not.

It was getting dark and I suggested that we should go down. Mrs Mercado agreed and asked if I would like to see the laboratory. 'My husband will be there—working.'

I said I would like to very much and we made our way there. The place was lighted by a lamp, but it was empty. Mrs Mercado showed me some of the apparatus and some copper ornaments that were being treated, and also some bones coated with wax.

'Where can Joseph be?' said Mrs Mercado.

She looked into the drawing-office, where Carey was at work. He hardly looked up as we entered, and I was struck by the extraordinary look of strain on his face. It came to me suddenly: 'This man is at the end of his tether. Very soon, something will snap.' And I remembered somebody else had noticed that same tenseness about him.

Agatha Christie

As we went out again I turned my head for one last look at him. He was bent over his paper, his lips pressed very closely together, and that 'death's head' suggestion of his bones very strongly marked. Perhaps it was fanciful, but I thought that he looked like a knight of old who was going into battle and knew he was going to be killed.

And again I felt what an extraordinary and quite unconscious power of attraction he had.

We found Mr Mercado in the living-room. He was explaining the idea of some new process to Mrs Leidner. She was sitting on a straight wooden chair, embroidering flowers in fine silks, and I was struck anew by her strange, fragile, unearthly appearance. She looked a fairy creature more than flesh and blood.

Mrs Mercado said, her voice high and shrill: 'Oh, *there* you are, Joseph. We thought we'd find you in the lab.'

He jumped up looking startled and confused, as though her entrance had broken a spell. He said stammeringly: 'I—I must go now. I'm in the middle of—the middle of—'

He didn't complete the sentence but turned towards the door.

Mrs Leidner said in her soft, drawling voice: 'You must finish telling me some other time. It was very interesting.'

She looked up at us, smiled rather sweetly but in a far-away manner, and bent over her embroidery again.

In a minute or two she said: 'There are some books over there, nurse. We've got quite a good selection. Choose one and sit down.'

Murder in Mesopotamia

I went over to the bookshelf. Mrs Mercado stayed for a minute or two, then, turning abruptly, she went out. As she passed me I saw her face and I didn't like the look of it. She looked wild with fury.

In spite of myself I remembered some of the things Mrs Kelsey had said and hinted about Mrs Leidner. I didn't like to think they were true because I liked Mrs Leidner, but I wondered, nevertheless, if there mightn't perhaps be a grain of truth behind them.

I didn't think it was all her fault, but the fact remained that dear ugly Miss Johnson, and that common little spitfire Mrs Mercado, couldn't hold a candle to her in looks or in attraction. And after all, men are men all over the world. You soon see a lot of that in my profession.

Mercado was a poor fish, and I don't suppose Mrs Leidner really cared two hoots for his admiration—but his wife cared. If I wasn't mistaken, she minded badly and would be quite willing to do Mrs Leidner a bad turn if she could.

I looked at Mrs Leidner sitting there and sewing at her pretty flowers, so remote and far away and aloof. I felt somehow I ought to warn her. I felt that perhaps she didn't know how stupid and unreasoning and violent jealousy and hate can be—and how little it takes to set them smouldering.

And then I said to myself, 'Amy Leatheran, you're a fool. Mrs Leidner's no chicken. She's close on forty if she's a day, and she must know all about life there is to know.'

But I felt that all the same perhaps she didn't.

She had such a queer untouched look.

I began to wonder what her life had been. I knew she'd only married Dr Leidner two years ago. And according to Mrs Mercado her first husband had died about fifteen years ago.

I came and sat down near her with a book, and presently I went and washed my hands for supper. It was a good meal—some really excellent curry. They all went to bed early and I was glad, for I was tired.

Dr Leidner came with me to my room to see I had all I wanted.

He gave me a warm handclasp and said eagerly:

'She likes you, nurse. She's taken to you at once. I'm so glad. I feel everything's going to be all right now.'

His eagerness was almost boyish.

I felt, too, that Mrs Leidner had taken a liking to me, and I was pleased it should be so.

But I didn't quite share his confidence. I felt, somehow, that there was more to it all than he himself might know.

There was *something*—something I couldn't get at. But I felt it in the air.

My bed was comfortable, but I didn't sleep well for all that. I dreamt too much.

The words of a poem by Keats, that I'd had to learn as a child, kept running through my head. I kept getting them wrong and it worried me. It was a poem I'd always hated—I suppose because I'd had to learn it whether I wanted to or not. But somehow when I woke up in the dark I saw a sort of beauty in it for the first time.

'*Oh say what ails thee, knight at arms, alone—and*(what was it?)—*palely loitering*...? I saw the knight's face in my mind for the first time—it was Mr Carey's face—a grim, tense, bronzed face like some of those poor young men I remembered as a girl during the war...and I felt sorry for him—and then I fell off to sleep again and I saw that the Belle Dame sans Merci was Mrs Leidner and she was leaning sideways on a horse with an embroidery of flowers in her hands—and then the horse stumbled and everywhere there were bones coated in wax, and I woke up all goose-flesh and shivering, and told myself that curry never *had* agreed with me at night.

CHAPTER 7

The Man at the Window

I think I'd better make it clear right away that there isn't going to be any local colour in this story. I don't know anything about archaeology and I don't know that I very much want to. Messing about with people and places that are buried and done with doesn't make sense to me. Mr Carey used to tell me that I hadn't got the archaeological temperament and I've no doubt he was quite right.

The very first morning after my arrival Mr Carey asked if I'd like to come and see the palace he was—*planning* I think he called it. Though how you can plan for a thing that's happened long ago I'm sure I don't know! Well, I said I'd like to, and to tell the truth, I was a bit excited about it. Nearly three thousand years old that palace was, it appeared. I wondered what sort of palaces they had in those days, and if it would be like the pictures I'd seen of Tutankahmen's tomb furniture. But would you believe it, there was nothing to see but *mud*! Dirty mud walls about two feet high—and that's all there was to it. Mr Carey took me here and there telling me things—how this was the great court, and there were some chambers here and an upper storey and various other rooms that opened off the central court. And all I thought was, 'But how does he *know*?' though, of course, I was too polite to say so. I can tell you it *was* a disappointment! The whole excavation looked like nothing but mud to me—no marble or gold or anything handsome—my aunt's house in Cricklewood would have made a much more imposing ruin! And those old Assyrians, or whatever they were, called themselves *kings*. When Mr Carey had shown me his old 'palace', he handed me over to Father Lavigny, who showed me the rest of the mound. I was a little afraid of Father Lavigny, being a monk and a foreigner and having such a deep voice and all that, but he was very kind—though rather vague. Sometimes I felt it wasn't much more real to him than it was to me.

Mrs Leidner explained that later. She said that Father Lavigny was only interested in 'written documents'—as she called them. They wrote everything on clay, these people, queer, heathenish-looking marks too, but quite sensible. There were even school tablets—the teacher's lesson on one side and the pupil's effort on the back of it. I confess that that did interest me rather—it seemed so human, if you know what I mean.

Father Lavigny walked round the work with me and showed me what were temples or palaces and what were private houses, and also a place which he said was an early Akkadian cemetery. He spoke in a funny jerky way, just

Agatha Christie

throwing in a scrap of information and then reverting to other subjects.

He said: 'It is strange that you have come here. Is Mrs Leidner really ill, then?'

'Not exactly ill,' I said cautiously.

He said: 'She is an odd woman. A dangerous woman, I think.'

'Now what do you mean by that?' I said. 'Dangerous? How dangerous?'

He shook his head thoughtfully.

'I think she is ruthless,' he said. 'Yes, I think she could be absolutely ruthless.'

'If you'll excuse me,' I said, 'I think you're talking nonsense.'

He shook his head.

'You do not know women as I do,' he said.

And that was a funny thing, I thought, for a monk to say. But of course I suppose he might have heard a lot of things in confession. But that rather puzzled me, because I wasn't sure if monks heard confessions or if it was only priests. I supposed he *was* a monk with that long woollen robe—all sweeping up the dirt—and the rosary and all!

'Yes, she could be ruthless,' he said musingly. 'I am quite sure of that. And yet—though she is so hard—like stone, like marble—yet she is afraid. What is she afraid of?'

That, I thought, is what we should all like to know!

At least it was possible that her husband did know, but I didn't think anyone else did.

He fixed me with a sudden bright, dark eye.

'It is odd here? You find it odd? Or quite natural?'

'Not quite natural,' I said, considering. 'It's comfortable enough as far as the arrangements go—but there isn't quite a comfortable feeling.'

'It makes *me* uncomfortable. I have the idea'—he became suddenly a little more foreign—'that something prepares itself. Dr Leidner, too, he is not quite himself. Something is worrying him also.'

'His wife's health?'

'That perhaps. But there is more. There is—how shall I say it—an uneasiness.'

And that was just it, there was an uneasiness.

We didn't say any more just then, for Dr Leidner came towards us. He showed me a child's grave that had just been uncovered. Rather pathetic it was—the little bones—and a pot or two and some little specks that Dr Leidner told me were a bead necklace.

It was the workmen that made me laugh. You never saw such a lot of scarecrows—all in long petticoats and rags, and their heads tied up as though they had toothache. And every now and then, as they went to and fro carrying away baskets of earth, they began to sing—at least I suppose it was meant to be singing—a queer sort of monotonous chant that went on and on over and over again. I noticed that most of their eyes were terrible—all covered with discharge, and one or two looked half blind. I was just thinking what a miserable lot they were when Dr Leidner said, 'Rather a fine-looking lot of men, aren't they?' and I thought what a queer world it was and how two different people could see the same thing each of them

Agatha Christie

the other way round. I haven't put that very well, but you can guess what I mean.

After a bit Dr Leidner said he was going back to the house for a mid-morning cup of tea. So he and I walked back together and he told me things. When *he* explained, it was all quite different. I sort of *saw* it all—how it used to be—the streets and the houses, and he showed me ovens where they baked bread and said the Arabs used much the same kind of ovens nowadays.

We got back to the house and found Mrs Leidner had got up. She was looking better today, not so thin and worn. Tea came in almost at once and Dr Leidner told her what had turned up during the morning on the dig. Then he went back to work and Mrs Leidner asked me if I would like to see some of the finds they had made up to date. Of course I said 'Yes,' so she took me through into the antika-room. There was a lot of stuff lying about—mostly broken pots it seemed to me—or else ones that were all mended and stuck together. The whole lot might have been thrown away, I thought.

'Dear, dear,' I said, 'it's a pity they're all so broken, isn't it? Are they really worth keeping?'

Mrs Leidner smiled a little and she said: 'You mustn't let Eric hear you. Pots interest him more than anything else, and some of these are the oldest things we have—perhaps as much as seven thousand years old.' And she explained how some of them came from a very deep cut on the mound down towards the bottom, and how, thousands of years ago, they had been broken and mended with bitumen, showing people prized their things just as much then as they do nowadays.

'And now,' she said, 'we'll show you something more exciting.'

And she took down a box from the shelf and showed me a beautiful gold dagger with dark-blue stones in the handle.

I exclaimed with pleasure.

Mrs Leidner laughed.

'Yes, everybody likes gold! Except my husband.'

'Why doesn't Dr Leidner like it?'

'Well, for one thing it comes expensive. You have to pay the workmen who find it the weight of the object in gold.'

'Good gracious!' I exclaimed. 'But why?'

'Oh, it's a custom. For one thing it prevents them from stealing. You see, if they *did* steal, it wouldn't be for the archaeological value but for the intrinsic value. They could melt it down. So we make it easy for them to be honest.'

She took down another tray and showed me a really beautiful gold drinking-cup with a design of rams' heads on it.

Again I exclaimed.

'Yes, it is beautiful, isn't it? These came from a prince's grave. We found other royal graves but most of them had been plundered. This cup is our best find. It is one of the most lovely ever found anywhere. Early Akkadian. Unique.'

Suddenly, with a frown, Mrs Leidner brought the cup up close to her eyes and scratched at it delicately with her nail.

Agatha Christie

'How extraordinary! There's actually wax on it. Someone must have been in here with a candle.' She detached the little flake and replaced the cup in its place.

After that she showed me some queer little terra-cotta figurines—but most of them were just rude. Nasty minds those old people had, I say.

When we went back to the porch Mrs Mercado was sitting polishing her nails. She was holding them out in front of her admiring the effect. I thought myself that anything more hideous than that orange red could hardly have been imagined.

Mrs Leidner had brought with her from the antika-room a very delicate little saucer broken in several pieces, and this she now proceeded to join together. I watched her for a minute or two and then asked if I could help.

'Oh, yes, there are plenty more.' She fetched quite a supply of broken pottery and we set to work. I soon got into the hang of it and she praised my ability. I suppose most nurses are handy with their fingers.

'How busy everybody is!' said Mrs Mercado. 'It makes me feel dreadfully idle. Of course I *am* idle.'

'Why shouldn't you be if you like?' said Mrs Leidner.

Her voice was quite uninterested.

At twelve we had lunch. Afterwards Dr Leidner and Mr Mercado cleaned some pottery, pouring a solution of hydrochloric acid over it. One pot went a lovely plum colour and a pattern of bulls' horns came out on another one. It was really quite magical. All the dried mud that no washing would remove sort of foamed and boiled away.

Mr Carey and Mr Coleman went out on the dig and Mr Reiter went off to the photographic-room.

'What will you do, Louise?' Dr Leidner asked his wife. 'I suppose you'll rest for a bit?'

I gathered that Mrs Leidner usually lay down every afternoon.

'I'll rest for about an hour. Then perhaps I'll go out for a short stroll.'

'Good. Nurse will go with you, won't you?'

'Of course,' I said.

'No, no,' said Mrs Leidner, 'I like going alone. Nurse isn't to feel so much on duty that I'm not allowed out of her sight.'

'Oh, but I'd like to come,' I said.

'No, really, I'd rather you didn't.' She was quite firm—almost peremptory. 'I must be by myself every now and then. It's necessary to me.'

I didn't insist, of course. But as I went off for a short sleep myself it struck me as odd that Mrs Leidner, with her nervous terrors, should be quite content to walk by herself without any kind of protection.

When I came out of my room at half-past three the courtyard was deserted save for a little boy with a large copper bath who was washing pottery, and Mr Emmott, who was sorting and arranging it. As I went towards them Mrs Leidner came in through the archway. She looked more alive than I had seen her yet. Her eyes shone and she looked uplifted and almost gay.

Dr Leidner came out from the laboratory and joined her. He was showing her a big dish with bulls' horns on it.

'The prehistoric levels are being extraordinarily productive,' he said. 'It's been a good season so far. Finding that tomb right at the beginning was a real piece of luck. The only person who might complain is Father Lavigny. We've had hardly any tablets so far.'

'He doesn't seem to have done very much with the few we have had,' said Mrs Leidner dryly. 'He may be a very fine epigraphist but he's a remarkably lazy one. He spends all his afternoons sleeping.'

'We miss Byrd,' said Dr Leidner. 'This man strikes me as slightly unorthodox—though, of course, I'm not competent to judge. But one or two of his translations have been surprising, to say the least of it. I can hardly believe, for instance, that he's right about that inscribed brick, and yet he must know.'

After tea Mrs Leidner asked me if I would like to stroll down to the river. I thought that perhaps she feared that her refusal to let me accompany her earlier in the afternoon might have hurt my feelings.

I wanted her to know that I wasn't the touchy kind, so I accepted at once.

It was a lovely evening. A path led between barley fields and then through some flowering fruit trees. Finally we came to the edge of the Tigris. Immediately on our left was the Tell with the workmen singing in their queer monotonous chant. A little to our right was a big water-wheel which made a queer groaning noise. It used to set my teeth on edge at first. But in the end I got fond of it and it had a queer soothing effect on me. Beyond the water-wheel was the village from which most of the workmen came.

'It's rather beautiful, isn't it?' said Mrs Leidner.

'It's very peaceful,' I said. 'It seems funny to me to be so far away from everywhere.'

'Far from everywhere,' repeated Mrs Leidner. 'Yes. Here at least one might expect to be safe.'

I glanced at her sharply, but I think she was speaking more to herself than to me, and I don't think she realized that her words had been revealing.

We began to walk back to the house.

Suddenly Mrs Leidner clutched my arm so violently that I nearly cried out.

'Who's that, nurse? What's he doing?'

Some distance ahead of us, just where the path ran near the expedition house, a man was standing. He wore European clothes and he seemed to be standing on tiptoe and trying to look in at one of the windows.

As we watched he glanced round, caught sight of us, and immediately continued on the path towards us. I felt Mrs Leidner's clutch tighten.

'Nurse,' she whispered. 'Nurse...'

'It's all right, my dear, it's all right,' I said reassuringly.

The man came along and passed us. He was an Iraqi, and as soon as she saw him near to, Mrs Leidner relaxed with a sigh.

'He's only an Iraqi after all,' she said.

We went on our way. I glanced up at the windows as I passed. Not only were they barred, but they were too high from the ground to permit of anyone seeing in, for the level of the ground was lower here than on the inside of the courtyard.

Agatha Christie

'It must have been just curiosity,' I said.

Mrs Leidner nodded.

'That's all. But just for a minute I thought—'

She broke off.

I thought to myself. 'You thought *what*? That's what I'd like to know. *What* did you think?'

But I knew one thing now—that Mrs Leidner was afraid of a definite flesh-and-blood person.

CHAPTER 8

Night Alarm

It's a little difficult to know exactly what to note in the week that followed my arrival at Tell Yarimjah.

Looking back as I do from my present standpoint of knowledge I can see a good many little signs and indications that I was quite blind to at the time.

To tell the story properly, however, I think I ought to try to recapture the point of view that I actually held—puzzled, uneasy and increasingly conscious of *something* wrong.

For one thing *was* certain, that curious sense of strain and constraint was *not* imagined. It was genuine. Even Bill Coleman the insensitive commented upon it.

'This place gets under my skin,' I heard him say. 'Are they always such a glum lot?'

It was David Emmott to whom he spoke, the other assistant. I had taken rather a fancy to Mr Emmott, his taciturnity was not, I felt sure, unfriendly. There was something about him that seemed very steadfast and reassuring in an atmosphere where one was uncertain what anyone was feeling or thinking.

'No,' he said in answer to Mr Coleman. 'It wasn't like this last year.'

But he didn't enlarge on the theme, or say any more.

'What I can't make out is what it's all about,' said Mr Coleman in an aggrieved voice.

Emmott shrugged his shoulders but didn't answer.

I had a rather enlightening conversation with Miss Johnson. I liked her very much. She was capable, practical and intelligent. She had, it was quite obvious, a distinct hero worship for Dr Leidner.

On this occasion she told me the story of his life since his young days. She knew every site he had dug, and the results of the dig. I would almost dare swear she could quote from every lecture he had ever delivered. She considered him, she told me, quite the finest field archaeologist living.

'And he's so simple. So completely unworldly. He doesn't know the meaning of the word conceit. Only a really great man could be so simple.'

'That's true enough,' I said. 'Big people don't need to throw their weight about.'

'And he's so light-hearted too, I can't tell you what fun we used to have—he and Richard Carey and I—the first years we were out here. We were such a happy party. Richard Carey worked with him in Palestine, of course. Theirs is a friendship of ten years or so. Oh, well, I've known him for seven.'

'What a handsome man Mr Carey is,' I said.

'Yes—I suppose he is.'

She said it rather curtly.

'But he's just a little bit quiet, don't you think?'

'He usedn't to be like that,' said Miss Johnson quickly. 'It's only since—'

She stopped abruptly.

'Only since—?' I prompted.

'Oh, well.' Miss Johnson gave a characteristic motion of her shoulders. 'A good many things are changed nowadays.'

I didn't answer. I hoped she would go on—and she did—prefacing her remarks with a little laugh as though to detract from their importance.

'I'm afraid I'm rather a conservative old fogy. I sometimes think that if an archaeologist's wife isn't really interested, it would be wiser for her not to accompany the expedition. It often leads to friction.'

'Mrs Mercado—' I suggested.

'Oh, her!' Miss Johnson brushed the suggestion aside. 'I was really thinking of Mrs Leidner. She's a very charming woman—and one can quite understand why Dr Leidner "fell for her"—to use a slang term. But I can't help feeling she's out of place here. She—it unsettles things.'

So Miss Johnson agreed with Mrs Kelsey that it was Mrs Leidner who was responsible for the strained atmosphere. But then where did Mrs Leidner's own nervous fears come in?

'It unsettles *him*,' said Miss Johnson earnestly. 'Of course I'm—well, I'm like a faithful but jealous old dog. I don't like to see him so worn out and worried. His whole mind ought to be on the work—not taken up with his wife and her silly fears! If she's nervous of coming to out-of-the-way

Agatha Christie

places, she ought to have stayed in America. I've no patience with people who come to a place and then do nothing but grouse about it!'

And then, a little fearful of having said more than she meant to say, she went on: 'Of course I admire her very much. She's a lovely woman and she's got great charm of manner when she chooses.'

And there the subject dropped.

I thought to myself that it was always the same way—wherever women are cooped up together, there's bound to be jealousy. Miss Johnson clearly didn't like her chief's wife (that was perhaps natural) and unless I was much mistaken Mrs Mercado fairly hated her.

Another person who didn't like Mrs Leidner was Sheila Reilly. She came out once or twice to the dig, once in a car and twice with some young man on a horse—on two horses I mean, of course. It was at the back of my mind that she had a weakness for the silent young American, Emmott. When he was on duty at the dig she used to stay talking to him, and I thought, too, that *he* admired *her*.

One day, rather injudiciously, I thought, Mrs Leidner commented upon it at lunch.

'The Reilly girl is still hunting David down,' she said with a little laugh. 'Poor David, she chases you up on the dig even! How foolish girls are!'

Mr Emmott didn't answer, but under his tan his face got rather red. He raised his eyes and looked right into hers with a very curious expression—a straight, steady glance with something of a challenge in it.

She smiled very faintly and looked away.

I heard Father Lavigny murmur something, but when I said 'Pardon?' he merely shook his head and did not repeat his remark.

That afternoon Mr Coleman said to me: 'Matter of fact I didn't like Mrs L. any too much at first. She used to jump down my throat every time I opened my mouth. But I've begun to understand her better now. She's one of the kindest women I've ever met. You find yourself telling her all the foolish scrapes you ever got into before you know where you are. She's got her knife into Sheila Reilly, I know, but then Sheila's been damned rude to her once or twice. That's the worst of Sheila—she's got no manners. And a temper like the devil!'

That I could well believe. Dr Reilly spoilt her.

'Of course she's bound to get a bit full of herself, being the only young woman in the place. But that doesn't excuse her talking to Mrs Leidner as though Mrs Leidner were her great-aunt. Mrs L.'s not exactly a chicken, but she's a damned good-looking woman. Rather like those fairy women who come out of marshes with lights and lure you away.' He added bitterly, 'You wouldn't find Sheila luring anyone. All she does is to tick a fellow off.'

I only remember two other incidents of any kind of significance.

One was when I went to the laboratory to fetch some acetone to get the stickiness off my fingers from mending the pottery. Mr Mercado was sitting in a corner, his head was laid down on his arms and I fancied he was asleep. I took the bottle I wanted and went off with it.

Agatha Christie

That evening, to my great surprise, Mrs Mercado tackled me.

'Did you take a bottle of acetone from the lab?'

'Yes,' I said. 'I did.'

'You know perfectly well that there's a small bottle always kept in the antika-room.'

She spoke quite angrily.

'Is there? I didn't know.'

'I think you did! You just wanted to come spying round. I know what hospital nurses are.'

I stared at her.

'I don't know what you're talking about, Mrs Mercado,' I said with dignity. 'I'm sure I don't want to spy on anyone.'

'Oh, no! Of course not. Do you think I don't know what you're here for?'

Really, for a minute or two I thought she must have been drinking. I went away without saying any more. But I thought it was very odd.

The other thing was nothing very much. I was trying to entice a pi dog pup with a piece of bread. It was very timid, however, like all Arab dogs—and was convinced I meant no good. It slunk away and I followed it—out through the archway and round the corner of the house. I came round so sharply that before I knew I had cannoned into Father Lavigny and another man who were standing together—and in a minute I realized that the second man was the same one Mrs Leidner and I had noticed that day trying to peer through the window.

I apologized and Father Lavigny smiled, and with a word of farewell greeting to the other man he returned to the house with me.

'You know,' he said. 'I am very ashamed. I am a student of Oriental languages and none of the men on the work can understand me! It is humiliating, do you not think? I was trying my Arabic on that man, who is a townsman, to see if I got on better—but it still wasn't very successful. Leidner says my Arabic is too pure.'

That was all. But it just passed through my head that it was odd the same man should still be hanging round the house.

That night we had a scare.

It must have been about two in the morning. I'm a light sleeper, as most nurses have to be. I was awake and sitting up in bed by the time that my door opened.

'Nurse, nurse!'

It was Mrs Leidner's voice, low and urgent.

I struck a match and lighted the candle.

She was standing by the door in a long blue dressing-gown. She was looking petrified with terror.

'There's someone—someone—in the room next to mine... I heard him—scratching on the wall.'

I jumped out of bed and came to her.

'It's all right,' I said. 'I'm here. Don't be afraid, my dear.'

She whispered: 'Get Eric.'

I nodded and ran out and knocked on his door. In a minute he was with us. Mrs Leidner was sitting on my bed, her breath coming in great gasps.

Agatha Christie

'I heard him,' she said. 'I heard him—scratching on the wall.'

'Someone in the antika-room?' cried Dr Leidner.

He ran out quickly—and it just flashed across my mind how differently these two had reacted. Mrs Leidner's fear was entirely personal, but Dr Leidner's mind leaped at once to his precious treasures.

'The antika-room!' breathed Mrs Leidner. 'Of course! How stupid of me!'

And rising and pulling her gown round her, she bade me come with her. All traces of her panic-stricken fear had vanished.

We arrived in the antika-room to find Dr Leidner and Father Lavigny. The latter had also heard a noise, had risen to investigate, and had fancied he saw a light in the antika-room. He had delayed to put on slippers and snatch up a torch and had found no one by the time he got there. The door, moreover, was duly locked, as it was supposed to be at night.

Whilst he was assuring himself that nothing had been taken, Dr Leidner had joined him.

Nothing more was to be learned. The outside archway door was locked. The guard swore nobody could have got in from outside, but as they had probably been fast asleep this was not conclusive. There were no marks or traces of an intruder and nothing had been taken.

It was possible that what had alarmed Mrs Leidner was the noise made by Father Lavigny taking down boxes from the shelves to assure himself that all was in order.

On the other hand, Father Lavigny himself was positive that he had (*a*) heard footsteps passing his window and (*b*) seen the flicker of a light, possibly a torch, in the antika-room.

Nobody else had heard or seen anything.

The incident is of value in my narrative because it led to Mrs Leidner's unburdening herself to me on the following day.

CHAPTER 9

Mrs Leidner's Story

We had just finished lunch. Mrs Leidner went to her room to rest as usual. I settled her on her bed with plenty of pillows and her book, and was leaving the room when she called me back.

'Don't go, nurse, there's something I want to say to you.'

I came back into the room.

'Shut the door.'

I obeyed.

She got up from the bed and began to walk up and down the room. I could see that she was making up her mind to something and I didn't like to interrupt her. She was clearly in great indecision of mind.

At last she seemed to have nerved herself to the required point. She turned to me and said abruptly: 'Sit down.'

I sat down by the table very quietly. She began nervously: 'You must have wondered what all this is about?'

I just nodded without saying anything.

'I've made up my mind to tell you—everything! I must tell someone or I shall go mad.'

'Well,' I said, 'I think really it would be just as well. It's not easy to know the best thing to do when one's kept in the dark.'

She stopped in her uneasy walk and faced me.

'Do you know what I'm frightened of?'

'Some man,' I said.

'Yes—but I didn't say whom—I said what.'

I waited.

She said: *'I'm afraid of being killed!'*

Well, it was out now. I wasn't going to show any particular concern. She was near enough to hysterics as it was.

'Dear me,' I said. 'So that's it, is it?'

Then she began to laugh. She laughed and she laughed—and the tears ran down her face.

'The way you said that!' she gasped. 'The way you said it...'

'Now, now,' I said. 'This won't do.' I spoke sharply. I pushed her into a chair, went over to the washstand and got a cold sponge and bathed her forehead and wrists.

'No more nonsense,' I said. 'Tell me calmly and sensibly all about it.'

That stopped her. She sat up and spoke in her natural voice.

'You're a treasure, nurse,' she said. 'You make me feel as though I'm six. I'm going to tell you.'

'That's right,' I said. 'Take your time and don't hurry.'

She began to speak, slowly and deliberately.

'When I was a girl of twenty I married. A young man in one of our State departments. It was in 1918.'

'I know,' I said. 'Mrs Mercado told me. He was killed in the war.'

But Mrs Leidner shook her head.

'That's what she thinks. That's what everybody thinks. The truth is something different. I was a queer patriotic, enthusiastic girl, nurse, full of idealism. When I'd been married a few months I discovered—by a quite unforeseeable accident—that my husband was a spy in German pay. I learned that the information supplied by him had led directly to the sinking of an American transport and the loss of hundreds of lives. I don't know what most people would have done... But I'll tell you what I did. I went straight to my father, who was in the War Department, and told him the truth. Frederick *was* killed in the war—but he was killed in America—shot as a spy.'

'Oh dear, dear!' I ejaculated. 'How terrible!'

'Yes,' she said. 'It was terrible. He was so kind, too—so gentle... And all the time... But I never hesitated. Perhaps I was wrong.'

'It's difficult to say,' I said. 'I'm sure I don't know what one would do.'

'What I'm telling you was never generally known outside the State department. Ostensibly my husband had gone to the Front and had been killed. I had a lot of sympathy and kindness shown me as a war widow.'

Her voice was bitter and I nodded comprehendingly.

'Lots of people wanted to marry me, but I always refused. I'd had too bad a shock. I didn't feel I could ever *trust* anyone again.'

Murder in Mesopotamia

'Yes, I can imagine feeling like that.'

'And then I became very fond of a certain young man. I wavered. An amazing thing happened! I got an anonymous letter—from Frederick—saying that if I ever married another man, he'd kill me!'

'From Frederick? From your dead husband?'

'Yes. Of course, I thought at first I was mad or dreaming... At last I went to my father. He told me the truth. My husband hadn't been shot after all. He'd escaped—but his escape did him no good. He was involved in a train wreck a few weeks later and his dead body was found amongst others. My father had kept the fact of his escape from me, and since the man had died anyway he had seen no reason to tell me anything until now.

'But the letter I received opened up entirely new possibilities. Was it perhaps a fact that my husband was still alive?

'My father went into the matter as carefully as possible. And he declared that as far as one could humanly be sure the body that was buried as Frederick's *was* Frederick's. There had been a certain amount of disfiguration, so that he could not speak with absolute cast-iron certainty, but he reiterated his solemn belief that Frederick was dead and that this letter was a cruel and malicious hoax.

'The same thing happened more than once. If I seemed to be on intimate terms with any man, I would receive a threatening letter.'

'In your husband's handwriting?'

She said slowly: 'That is difficult to say. I had no letters of his. I had only my memory to go by.'

Agatha Christie

'There was no allusion or special form of words used that could make you sure?'

'No. There *were* certain terms—nicknames, for instance—private between us—if one of those had been used or quoted, then I should have been quite sure.'

'Yes,' I said thoughtfully. 'That is odd. It looks as though it *wasn't* your husband. But is there anyone else it could be?'

'There is a possibility. Frederick had a younger brother—a boy of ten or twelve at the time of our marriage. He worshipped Frederick and Frederick was devoted to him. What happened to this boy, William his name was, I don't know. It seems to me possible that, adoring his brother as fanatically as he did, he may have grown up regarding me as directly responsible for his death. He had always been jealous of me and may have invented this scheme by way of punishment.'

'It's possible,' I said. 'It's amazing the way children do remember if they've had a shock.'

'I know. This boy may have dedicated his life to revenge.'

'Please go on.'

'There isn't very much more to tell. I met Eric three years ago. I meant never to marry. Eric made me change my mind. Right up to our wedding day I waited for another threatening letter. None came. I decided that whoever the writer might be, he was either dead, or tired of his cruel sport. *Two days after our marriage I got this.*'

Drawing a small attaché-case which was on the table towards her, she unlocked it, took out a letter and handed it to me.

The ink was slightly faded. It was written in a rather womanish hand with a forward slant.

You have disobeyed. Now you cannot escape. You must be Frederick Bosner's wife only! You have got to die.

'I was frightened—but not so much as I might have been to begin with. Being with Eric made me feel safe. Then, a month later, I got a second letter.'

I have not forgotten. I am making my plans. You have got to die. Why did you disobey?

'Does your husband know about this?'

Mrs Leidner answered slowly.

'He knows that I am threatened. I showed him both letters when the second one came. He was inclined to think the whole thing a hoax. He thought also that it might be someone who wanted to blackmail me by pretending my first husband was alive.'

She paused and then went on.

'A few days after I received the second letter we had a narrow escape from death by gas poisoning. Somebody entered our apartment after we were asleep and turned on the gas. Luckily I woke and smelled the gas in time. Then I lost my nerve. I told Eric how I had been persecuted for years, and I told him that I was sure this madman, whoever he might be, did really mean to kill me. I think that for the first time I really did think it *was* Frederick. There was always something a little ruthless behind his gentleness.

'Eric was still, I think, less alarmed than I was. He wanted to go to the police. Naturally I wouldn't hear of that. In the end we agreed that I should accompany him here, and that it might be wise if I didn't return to America in the summer but stayed in London and Paris.

Agatha Christie

'We carried out our plan and all went well. I felt sure that now everything would be all right. After all, we had put half the globe between ourselves and my enemy.

'And then—a little over three weeks ago—I received a letter—with an Iraq stamp on it.'

She handed me a third letter.

You thought you could escape. You were wrong. You shall not be false to me and live. I have always told you so. Death is coming very soon.

'And a week ago—*this*! Just lying on the table here. It had not even gone through the post.'

I took the sheet of paper from her. There was just one phrase scrawled across it.

I have arrived.

She stared at me.

'You see? You understand? He's going to kill me. It may be Frederick—it may be little William—*but he's going to kill me.*'

Her voice rose shudderingly. I caught her wrist.

'Now—now,' I said warningly. 'Don't give way. We'll look after you. Have you got any sal volatile?'

She nodded towards the washstand and I gave her a good dose.

'That's better,' I said, as the colour returned to her cheeks.

'Yes, I'm better now. But oh, nurse, do you see why I'm in this state? When I saw that man looking in through my window, I thought: *he's come...* Even when *you* arrived I was suspicious. I thought you might be a man in disguise—'

'The idea!'

'Oh, I know it sounds absurd. But you might have been in league with him perhaps—not a hospital nurse at all.'

'But that's nonsense!'

'Yes, perhaps. But I've got beyond sense.'

Struck by a sudden idea, I said: 'You'd *recognize* your husband, I suppose?'

She answered slowly.

'I don't even know that. It's over fifteen years ago. I mightn't recognize his face.'

Then she shivered.

'I saw it one night—but it was a *dead* face. There was a tap, tap, tap on the window. And then I saw a face, a dead face, ghastly and grinning against the pane. I screamed and screamed... And they said there wasn't anything there!'

I remembered Mrs Mercado's story.

'You don't think,' I said hesitatingly, 'that you *dreamt* that?'

'I'm sure I didn't!'

I wasn't so sure. It was the kind of nightmare that was quite likely under the circumstances and that easily might be taken for a waking occurrence. However, I never contradict a patient. I soothed Mrs Leidner as best I could and pointed out that if any stranger arrived in the neighbourhood it was pretty sure to be known.

I left her, I think, a little comforted, and I went in search of Dr Leidner and told him of our conversation.

Agatha Christie

'I'm glad she told you,' he said simply. 'It has worried me dreadfully. I feel sure that all those faces and tappings on the window-pane have been sheer imagination on her part. I haven't known what to do for the best. What do you think of the whole thing?'

I didn't quite understand the tone in his voice, but I answered promptly enough.

'It's possible,' I said, 'that these letters may be just a cruel and malicious hoax.'

'Yes, that is quite likely. But what are we to *do*? They are driving her mad. I don't know what to think.'

I didn't either. It had occurred to me that possibly a woman might be concerned. Those letters had a feminine note about them. Mrs Mercado was at the back of my mind.

Supposing that by some chance she had learnt the facts of Mrs Leidner's first marriage? She might be indulging her spite by terrorizing the other woman.

I didn't quite like to suggest such a thing to Dr Leidner. It's so difficult to know how people are going to take things.

'Oh, well,' I said cheerfully, 'we must hope for the best. I think Mrs Leidner seems happier already from just talking about it. That's always a help, you know. It's bottling things up that makes them get on your nerves.'

'I'm very glad she has told you,' he repeated. 'It's a good sign. It shows she likes and trusts you. I've been at my wits' end to know what to do for the best.'

It was on the tip of my tongue to ask him whether he'd thought of giving a discreet hint to the local police, but afterwards I was glad I hadn't done so.

Murder in Mesopotamia

What happened was this. On the following day Mr Coleman was going in to Hassanieh to get the workmen's pay. He was also taking in all our letters to catch the air mail.

The letters, as written, were dropped into a wooden box on the dining-room window-sill. Last thing that night Mr Coleman took them out and was sorting them out into bundles and putting rubber bands round them.

Suddenly he gave a shout.

'What is it?' I asked.

He held out a letter with a grin.

'It's our Lovely Louise—she really *is* going balmy. She's addressed a letter to someone at 42nd Street, Paris, France. I don't think that can be right, do you? Do you mind taking it to her and asking what she *does* mean? She's just gone off to bed.'

I took it from him and ran off to Mrs Leidner with it and she amended the address.

It was the first time I had seen Mrs Leidner's handwriting, and I wondered idly where I had seen it before, for it was certainly quite familiar to me.

It wasn't till the middle of the night that it suddenly came to me.

Except that it was bigger and rather more straggling, *it was extraordinarily like the writing on the anonymous letters.*

New ideas flashed through my head.

Had Mrs Leidner conceivably written those letters *herself*?

And did Dr Leidner half-suspect the fact?

CHAPTER 10

Saturday Afternoon

Mrs Leidner told me her story on a Friday.

On the Saturday morning there was a feeling of slight anticlimax in the air.

Mrs Leidner, in particular, was inclined to be very offhand with me and rather pointedly avoided any possibility of a *tête-à-tête*. Well, *that* didn't surprise me! I've had the same thing happen to me again and again. Ladies tell their nurses things in a sudden burst of confidence, and then, afterwards, they feel uncomfortable about it and wish they hadn't! It's only human nature.

I was very careful not to hint or remind her in any way of what she had told me. I purposely kept my conversation as matter-of-fact as possible.

Mr Coleman had started in to Hassanieh in the morning, driving himself in the lorry with the letters in a knapsack. He also had one or two commissions to do for the members of the expedition. It was pay-day for the men, and he would have to go to the bank and bring out the money in coins of small denominations. All this was a long business and he did not expect to be back until the afternoon. I rather suspected he might be lunching with Sheila Reilly.

Work on the dig was usually not very busy on the afternoon of pay-day as at three-thirty the paying-out began.

The little boy, Abdullah, whose business it was to wash pots, was established as usual in the centre of the courtyard, and again, as usual, kept up his queer nasal chant. Dr Leidner and Mr Emmott were going to put in some work on the pottery until Mr Coleman returned, and Mr Carey went up to the dig.

Mrs Leidner went to her room to rest. I settled her as usual and then went to my own room, taking a book with me as I did not feel sleepy. It was then about a quarter to one, and a couple of hours passed quite pleasantly. I was reading *Death in a Nursing Home*—really a most exciting story—though I don't think the author knew much about the way nursing homes are run! At any rate I've never known a nursing home like that! I really felt inclined to write to the author and put him right about a few points.

When I put the book down at last (it was the red-haired parlourmaid and I'd never suspected her once!) and looked at my watch I was quite surprised to find it was twenty minutes to three!

I got up, straightened my uniform, and came out into the courtyard.

Abdullah was still scrubbing and still singing his depressing chant, and David Emmott was standing by him sorting the scrubbed pots, and putting the ones that were broken into

Agatha Christie

boxes to await mending. I strolled over towards them just as Dr Leidner came down the staircase from the roof.

'Not a bad afternoon,' he said cheerfully. 'I've made a bit of a clearance up there. Louise will be pleased. She's complained lately that there's not room to walk about. I'll go and tell her the good news.'

He went over to his wife's door, tapped on it and went in.

It must, I suppose, have been about a minute and a half later that he came out again. I happened to be looking at the door when he did so. It was like a nightmare. He had gone in a brisk, cheerful man. He came out like a drunken one—reeling a little on his feet, and with a queer dazed expression on his face.

'Nurse—' he called in a queer, hoarse voice. 'Nurse—'

I saw at once something was wrong and I ran across to him. He looked awful—his face was all grey and twitching, and I saw he might collapse any minute.

'My wife...' he said. 'My wife... Oh, my God...'

I pushed past him into the room. Then I caught my breath.

Mrs Leidner was lying in a dreadful huddled heap by the bed.

I bent over her. She was quite dead—must have been dead an hour at least. The cause of death was perfectly plain—a terrific blow on the front of the head just over the right temple. She must have got up from the bed and been struck down where she stood.

I didn't handle her more than I could help.

I glanced round the room to see if there was anything that might give a clue, but nothing seemed out of place or disturbed. The windows were closed and fastened, and there was no place where the murderer could have hidden. Obviously he had been and gone long ago.

I went out, closing the door behind me.

Dr Leidner had collapsed completely now. David Emmott was with him and turned a white, inquiring face to me.

In a few low words I told him what had happened.

As I had always suspected, he was a first-class person to rely on in trouble. He was perfectly calm and self-possessed. Those blue eyes of his opened very wide, but otherwise he gave no sign at all.

He considered for a moment and then said: 'I suppose we must notify the police as soon as possible. Bill ought to be back any minute. What shall we do with Leidner?'

'Help me to get him into his room.'

He nodded.

'Better lock this door first, I suppose,' he said.

He turned the key in the lock of Mrs Leidner's door, then drew it out and handed it to me.

'I guess you'd better keep this, nurse. Now then.'

Together we lifted Dr Leidner and carried him into his own room and laid him on his bed. Mr Emmott went off in search of brandy. He returned, accompanied by Miss Johnson.

Her face was drawn and anxious, but she was calm and capable, and I felt satisfied to leave Dr Leidner in her charge.

I hurried out into the courtyard. The station wagon was just coming in through the archway. I think it gave us all a shock to see Bill's pink, cheerful face as he jumped out

Agatha Christie

with his familiar 'Hallo, 'allo, 'allo! Here's the oof!' He went on gaily, 'No highway robberies—'

He came to a halt suddenly. 'I say, is anything up? What's the matter with you all? You look as though the cat had killed your canary.'

Mr Emmott said shortly: 'Mrs Leidner's dead—killed.'

'*What?*' Bill's jolly face changed ludicrously. He stared, his eyes goggling. 'Mother Leidner dead! You're pulling my leg.'

'Dead?' It was a sharp cry. I turned to see Mrs Mercado behind me. 'Did you say Mrs Leidner had been *killed*?'

'Yes,' I said. 'Murdered.'

'No!' she gasped. 'Oh, no! I won't believe it. Perhaps she's committed suicide.'

'Suicides don't hit themselves on the head,' I said dryly. 'It's murder all right, Mrs Mercado.'

She sat down suddenly on an upturned packing-case.

She said, 'Oh, but this is horrible—*horrible*…'

Naturally it was horrible. We didn't need *her* to tell us so! I wondered if perhaps she was feeling a bit remorseful for the harsh feelings she had harboured against the dead woman, and all the spiteful things she had said.

After a minute or two she asked rather breathlessly: 'What are you going to do?'

Mr Emmott took charge in his quiet way.

'Bill, you'd better get in again to Hassanieh as quick as you can. I don't know much about the proper procedure. Better get hold of Captain Maitland, he's in charge of the police here, I think. Get Dr Reilly first. He'll know what to do.'

Mr Coleman nodded. All the facetiousness was knocked out of him. He just looked young and frightened. Without a word he jumped into the station wagon and drove off.

Mr Emmott said rather uncertainly, 'I suppose we ought to have a hunt round.' He raised his voice and called: 'Ibrahim!'

'*Na'am.*'

The house-boy came running. Mr Emmott spoke to him in Arabic. A vigorous colloquy passed between them. The boy seemed to be emphatically denying something.

At last Mr Emmott said in a perplexed voice, 'He says there's not been a soul here this afternoon. No stranger of any kind. I suppose the fellow must have slipped in without their seeing him.'

'Of course he did,' said Mrs Mercado. 'He slunk in when the boys weren't looking.'

'Yes,' said Mr Emmott.

The slight uncertainty in his voice made me look at him inquiringly.

He turned and spoke to the little pot-boy, Abdullah, asking him a question.

The boy replied vehemently at length.

The puzzled frown on Mr Emmott's brow increased.

'I don't understand it,' he murmured under his breath. 'I don't understand it at all.'

But he didn't tell me what he didn't understand.

CHAPTER 11

An Odd Business

I'm adhering as far as possible to telling only my personal part in the business. I pass over the events of the next two hours, the arrival of Captain Maitland and the police and Dr Reilly. There was a good deal of general confusion, questioning, all the routine business, I suppose.

In my opinion we began to get down to brass tacks about five o'clock when Dr Reilly asked me to come with him into the office.

He shut the door, sat down in Dr Leidner's chair, motioned me to sit down opposite him, and said briskly: 'Now, then, nurse, let's get down to it. There's something damned odd here.'

I settled my cuffs and looked at him inquiringly.

He drew out a notebook.

'This is for my own satisfaction. Now, what time was it exactly when Dr Leidner found his wife's body?'

'I should say it was almost exactly a quarter to three,' I said.

'And how do you know that?'

'Well, I looked at my watch when I got up. It was twenty to three then.'

'Let's have a look at this watch of yours.'

I slipped it off my wrist and held it out to him.

'Right to the minute. Excellent woman. Good, that's *that* fixed. Now, did you form any opinion as to how long she'd been dead?'

'Oh, really, doctor,' I said, 'I shouldn't like to say.'

'Don't be so professional. I want to see if your estimate agrees with mine.'

'Well, I should say she'd been dead at least an hour.'

'Quite so. I examined the body at half-past four and I'm inclined to put the time of death between 1.15 and 1.45. We'll say half-past one at a guess. That's near enough.'

He stopped and drummed thoughtfully with his fingers on the table.

'Damned odd, this business,' he said. 'Can you tell me about it—you were resting, you say? Did you hear anything?'

'At half-past one? No, doctor. I didn't hear anything at half-past one or at any other time. I lay on my bed from a quarter to one until twenty to three and I didn't hear anything except that droning noise the Arab boy makes, and occasionally Mr Emmott shouting up to Dr Leidner on the roof.'

'The Arab boy—yes.'

He frowned.

At that moment the door opened and Dr Leidner and Captain Maitland came in. Captain Maitland was a fussy little man with a pair of shrewd grey eyes.

Agatha Christie

Dr Reilly rose and pushed Dr Leidner into his chair.

'Sit down, man. I'm glad you've come. We shall want you. There's something very queer about this business.'

Dr Leidner bowed his head.

'I know.' He looked at me. 'My wife confided the truth to Nurse Leatheran. We mustn't keep anything back at this juncture, nurse, so please tell Captain Maitland and Dr Reilly just what passed between you and my wife yesterday.'

As nearly as possible I gave our conversation verbatim.

Captain Maitland uttered an occasional ejaculation. When I had finished he turned to Dr Leidner.

'And this is all true, Leidner—eh?'

'Every word Nurse Leatheran has told you is correct.'

'What an extraordinary story!' said Dr Reilly. 'You can produce these letters?'

'I have no doubt they will be found amongst my wife's belongings.'

'She took them out of the attaché-case on her table,' I said.

'Then they are probably still there.'

He turned to Captain Maitland and his usually gentle face grew hard and stern.

'There must be no question of hushing this story up, Captain Maitland. The one thing necessary is for this man to be caught and punished.'

'You believe it actually is Mrs Leidner's former husband?' I asked.

'Don't you think so, nurse?' asked Captain Maitland.

'Well, I think it is open to doubt,' I said hesitatingly.

'In any case,' said Dr Leidner, 'the man is a murderer—and I should say a dangerous lunatic also. He *must* be found, Captain Maitland. He must. It should not be difficult.'

Dr Reilly said slowly: 'It may be more difficult than you think...eh, Maitland?'

Captain Maitland tugged at his moustache without replying.

Suddenly I gave a start.

'Excuse me,' I said, 'but there's something perhaps I ought to mention.'

I told my story of the Iraqi we had seen trying to peer through the window, and of how I had seen him hanging about the place two days ago trying to pump Father Lavigny.

'Good,' said Captain Maitland, 'we'll make a note of that. It will be something for the police to go on. The man may have some connection with the case.'

'Probably paid to act as a spy,' I suggested. 'To find out when the coast was clear.'

Dr Reilly rubbed his nose with a harassed gesture.

'That's the devil of it,' he said. 'Supposing the coast wasn't clear—eh?'

I stared at him in a puzzled fashion.

Captain Maitland turned to Dr Leidner.

'I want you to listen to me very carefully, Leidner. This is a review of the evidence we've got up to date. After lunch, which was served at twelve o'clock and was over by five and twenty to one, your wife went to her room accompanied by Nurse Leatheran, who settled her comfortably. You yourself went up to the roof, where you spent the next two hours, is that right?'

'Yes.'

'Did you come down from the roof at all during that time?'

'No.'

'Did anyone come up to you?'

'Yes, Emmott did pretty frequently. He went to and fro between me and the boy, who was washing pottery down below.'

'Did you yourself look over into the courtyard at all?'

'Once or twice—usually to call to Emmott about something.'

'On each occasion the boy was sitting in the middle of the courtyard washing pots?'

'Yes.'

'What was the longest period of time when Emmott was with you and absent from the courtyard?'

Dr Leidner considered.

'It's difficult to say—perhaps ten minutes. Personally I should say two or three minutes, but I know by experience that my sense of time is not very good when I am absorbed and interested in what I am doing.'

Captain Maitland looked at Dr Reilly. The latter nodded. 'We'd better get down to it,' he said.

Captain Maitland took out a small notebook and opened it.

'Look here, Leidner, I'm going to read to you exactly what every member of your expedition was doing between one and two this afternoon.'

'But surely—'

'Wait. You'll see what I'm driving at in a minute. First Mr and Mrs Mercado. Mr Mercado says he was working in his laboratory. Mrs Mercado says she was in her bedroom shampooing her hair. Miss Johnson says she was in the living-room taking impressions of cylinder seals. Mr Reiter says he was in the dark-room developing plates. Father Lavigny says he was working in his bedroom. As to the two remaining members of the expedition, Carey and Coleman, the former was up on the dig and Coleman was in Hassanieh. So much for the members of the expedition. Now for the servants. The cook—your Indian chap—was sitting immediately outside the archway chatting to the guard and plucking a couple of fowls. Ibrahim and Mansur, the house-boys, joined him there at about 1.15. They both remained there laughing and talking until 2.30—*by which time your wife was already dead.*'

Dr Leidner leaned forward.

'I don't understand—you puzzle me. What are you hinting at?'

'Is there any means of access to your wife's room except by the door into the courtyard?'

'No. There are two windows, but they are heavily barred—and besides, I think they were shut.'

He looked at me questioningly.

'They were closed and latched on the inside,' I said promptly.

'In any case,' said Captain Maitland, 'even if they had been open, no one could have entered or left the room that way. My fellows and I have assured ourselves of that. It is the same with all the other windows giving on the open country. They all have iron bars and all the bars are in good condition. To have got into your wife's room, a stranger *must* have come through the arched doorway into the courtyard. But we have the united assurance of the guard, the cook and the house-boy that *nobody did so*.'

Dr Leidner sprang up.

'What do you mean? What do you mean?'

'Pull yourself together, man,' said Dr Reilly quietly. 'I know it's a shock, but it's got to be faced. The *murderer didn't come from outside*—so he must have come from *inside*. It looks as though Mrs Leidner must have been murdered *by a member of your own expedition*.'

CHAPTER 12

'I Didn't Believe...'

'No. No!'

Dr Leidner sprang up and walked up and down in an agitated manner.

'It's impossible what you say, Reilly. Absolutely impossible. One of *us*? Why, every single member of the expedition was devoted to Louise!'

A queer little expression pulled down the corners of Dr Reilly's mouth. Under the circumstances it was difficult for him to say anything, but if ever a man's silence was eloquent his was at that minute.

'Quite impossible,' reiterated Dr Leidner. 'They were all devoted to her, Louise had such wonderful charm. Everyone felt it.'

Dr Reilly coughed.

'Excuse me, Leidner, but after all that's only your opinion. If any member of the expedition had disliked your wife they would naturally not advertise the fact to you.'

Dr Leidner looked distressed.

'True—quite true. But all the same, Reilly, I think you are wrong. I'm sure everyone was fond of Louise.'

He was silent for a moment or two and then burst out:

'This idea of yours is infamous. It's—it's frankly incredible.'

'You can't get away from—er—the facts,' said Captain Maitland.

'Facts? Facts? Lies told by an Indian cook and a couple of Arab house-boys. You know these fellows as well as I do, Reilly, so do you, Maitland. Truth as truth means nothing to them. They say what you want them to say as a mere matter of politeness.'

'In this case,' said Dr Reilly dryly, 'they are saying what we *don't* want them to say. Besides, I know the habits of your household fairly well. Just outside the gate is a kind of social club. Whenever I've been over here in the afternoon I've always found most of your staff there. It's the natural place for them to be.'

'All the same I think you are assuming too much. Why shouldn't this man—this devil—have got in earlier and concealed himself somewhere?'

'I agree that that is not actually impossible,' said Dr Reilly coolly. 'Let us assume that a stranger *did* somehow gain admission unseen. He would have to remain concealed until the right moment (and he certainly couldn't have done so in Mrs Leidner's room, there is no cover there) and take the risk of being seen entering the room and leaving it—with Emmott and the boy in the courtyard most of the time.'

'The boy. I'd forgotten the boy,' said Dr Leidner. 'A sharp little chap. But surely, Maitland, the boy *must* have seen the murderer go into my wife's room?'

'We've elucidated that. The boy was washing pots the whole afternoon with one exception. Somewhere around half-past one—Emmott can't put it closer than that—he went up to the roof and was with you for ten minutes—that's right, isn't it?'

'Yes. I couldn't have told you the exact time but it must have been about that.'

'Very good. Well, during that ten minutes, the boy, seizing his chance to be idle, strolled out and joined the others outside the gate for a chat. When Emmott came down he found the boy absent and called him angrily, asking him what he meant leaving his work. As far as I can see, *your wife must have been murdered during that ten minutes*.'

With a groan Dr Leidner sat down and hid his face in his hands.

Dr Reilly took up the tale, his voice quiet and matter-of-fact.

'The time fits in with my evidence,' he said. 'She'd been dead about three hours when I examined her. The only question is—who did it?'

There was a silence. Dr Leidner sat up in his chair and passed a hand over his forehead.

'I admit the force of your reasoning, Reilly,' he said quietly. 'It certainly *seems* as though it were what people call "an inside job". But I feel convinced that somewhere or other there is a mistake. It's plausible but there must be a flaw in

Agatha Christie

it. To begin with, you are assuming that an amazing coincidence has occurred.'

'Odd that you should use that word,' said Dr Reilly.

Without paying any attention Dr Leidner went on: 'My wife receives threatening letters. She has reason to fear a certain person. Then she is—killed. And you ask me to believe that she is killed—not by that person—but by someone entirely different! I say that that is ridiculous.'

'It seems so—yes,' said Reilly meditatively.

He looked at Captain Maitland. 'Coincidence—eh? What do you say, Maitland? Are you in favour of the idea? Shall we put it up to Leidner?'

Captain Maitland gave a nod.

'Go ahead,' he said shortly.

'Have you ever heard of a man called Hercule Poirot Leidner?'

Dr Leidner stared at him, puzzled.

'I think I have heard the name, yes,' he said vaguely. 'I once heard a Mr Van Aldin speak of him in very high terms. He is a private detective, is he not?'

'That's the man.'

'But surely he lives in London, so how will that help us?'

'He lives in London, true,' said Dr Reilly, 'but this is where the coincidence comes in. He is now, not in London, but in Syria, and *he will actually pass through Hassanieh on his way to Baghdad tomorrow!*'

'Who told you this?'

'Jean Berat, the French consul. He dined with us last night and was talking about him. It seems he has been disentangling some military scandal in Syria. He's coming through here to visit Baghdad, and afterwards returning through Syria to London. How's that for a coincidence?'

Dr Leidner hesitated a moment and looked apologetically at Captain Maitland.

'What do you think, Captain Maitland?'

'Should welcome co-operation,' said Captain Maitland promptly. 'My fellows are good scouts at scouring the countryside and investigating Arab blood feuds, but frankly, Leidner, this business of your wife's seems to me rather out of my class. The whole thing looks confoundedly fishy. I'm more than willing to have the fellow take a look at the case.'

'You suggest that I should appeal to this man Poirot to help us?' said Dr Leidner. 'And suppose he refuses?'

'He won't refuse,' said Dr Reilly.

'How do you know?'

'Because I'm a professional man myself. If a really intricate case of, say, cerebro-spinal meningitis comes my way and I'm invited to take a hand, I shouldn't be able to refuse. This isn't an ordinary crime, Leidner.'

'No,' said Dr Leidner. His lips twitched with sudden pain. 'Will you then, Reilly, approach this Hercule Poirot on my behalf?'

'I will.'

Dr Leidner made a gesture of thanks.

'Even now,' he said slowly, 'I can't realize it—that Louise is really dead.'

I could bear it no longer.

Agatha Christie

'Oh! Doctor Leidner,' I burst out, 'I—I can't tell you how badly I feel about this. I've failed so badly in my duty. It was my job to watch over Mrs Leidner—to keep her from harm.'

Dr Leidner shook his head gravely.

'No, no, nurse, you've nothing to reproach yourself with,' he said slowly. 'It's *I*, God forgive me, who am to blame... *I didn't believe*—all along I didn't believe... I didn't dream for one moment that there was any *real* danger...'

He got up. His face twitched.

'*I let her go to her death*... Yes, I let her go to her death—*not believing*—'

He staggered out of the room.

Dr Reilly looked at me.

'I feel pretty culpable too,' he said. 'I thought the good lady was playing on his nerves.'

'I didn't take it really seriously either,' I confessed.

'We were all three wrong,' said Dr Reilly gravely.

'So it seems,' said Captain Maitland.

CHAPTER 13

Hercule Poirot Arrives

I don't think I shall ever forget my first sight of Hercule Poirot. Of course, I got used to him later on, but to begin with it was a shock, and I think everyone else must have felt the same!

I don't know what I'd imagined—something rather like Sherlock Holmes—long and lean with a keen, clever face. Of course, I knew he was a foreigner, but I hadn't expected him to be *quite* as foreign as he was, if you know what I mean.

When you saw him you just wanted to laugh! He was like something on the stage or at the pictures. To begin with, he wasn't above five-foot five, I should think—an odd, plump little man, quite old, with an enormous moustache, and a head like an egg. He looked like a hairdresser in a comic play!

And this was the man who was going to find out who killed Mrs Leidner!

I suppose something of my disgust must have shown in my face, for almost straightaway he said to me with a queer kind of twinkle:

Agatha Christie

'You disapprove of me, *ma soeur*? Remember, the pudding proves itself only when you eat it.'

The proof of the pudding's in the eating, I *suppose* he meant.

Well, that's a true enough saying, but I couldn't say I felt much confidence myself!

Dr Reilly brought him out in his car soon after lunch on Sunday, and his first procedure was to ask us all to assemble together.

We did so in the dining-room, all sitting round the table. Mr Poirot sat at the head of it with Dr Leidner one side and Dr Reilly the other.

When we were all assembled, Dr Leidner cleared his throat and spoke in his gentle, hesitating voice.

'I dare say you have all heard of M. Hercule Poirot. He was passing through Hassanieh today, and has very kindly agreed to break his journey to help us. The Iraqi police and Captain Maitland are, I am sure, doing their very best, but—but there are circumstances in the case'—he floundered and shot an appealing glance at Dr Reilly—'there may, it seems, be difficulties...'

'It is not all the square and overboard—no?' said the little man at the top of the table. Why, he couldn't even speak English properly!

'Oho, he *must* be caught!' cried Mrs Mercado. 'It would be unbearable if he got away!'

I noticed the little foreigner's eyes rest on her appraisingly.

'He? Who is *he*, madame?' he asked.

'Why, the murderer, of course.'

'Ah! the murderer,' said Hercule Poirot.

Murder in Mesopotamia

He spoke as though the murderer was of no consequence at all!

We all stared at him. He looked from one face to another.

'It is likely, I think,' he said, 'that you have none of you been brought in contact with a case of murder before?'

There was a general murmur of assent.

Hercule Poirot smiled.

'It is clear, therefore, that you do not understand the A B C of the position. There are unpleasantnesses! Yes, there are a lot of unpleasantnesses. To begin with, there is *suspicion*.'

'Suspicion?'

It was Miss Johnson who spoke. Mr Poirot looked at her thoughtfully. I had an idea that he regarded her with approval. He looked as though he were thinking: 'Here is a sensible, intelligent person!'

'Yes, mademoiselle,' he said. 'Suspicion! Let us not make the bones about it. *You are all under suspicion here in this house.* The cook, the house-boy, the scullion, the pot-boy—yes, and all the members of the expedition too.'

Mrs Mercado started up, her face working.

'How *dare* you? How dare you say such a thing! This is odious—unbearable! Dr Leidner—you can't sit here and let this man—let this man—'

Dr Leidner said wearily: 'Please try and be calm, Marie.'

Mr Mercado stood up too. His hands were shaking and his eyes were bloodshot.

'I agree. It is an outrage—an insult—'

'No, no,' said Mr Poirot. 'I do not insult you. I merely ask you all to face facts. *In a house where murder has been*

Agatha Christie

committed, every inmate comes in for a certain share of suspicion. I ask you what evidence is there that the murderer came from outside at all?'

Mrs Mercado cried: 'But of course he did! It stands to reason! Why—' She stopped and said more slowly, 'Anything else would be incredible!'

'You are doubtless correct, madame,' said Poirot with a bow. 'I explain to you only how the matter must be approached. First I assure myself of the fact that everyone in this room is innocent. After that I seek the murderer elsewhere.'

'Is it not possible that that may be a little late in the day?' asked Father Lavigny suavely.

'The tortoise, *mon père*, overtook the hare.'

Father Lavigny shrugged his shoulders.

'We are in your hands,' he said resignedly. 'Convince yourself as soon as may be of our innocence in this terrible business.'

'As rapidly as possible. It was my duty to make the position clear to you, so that you may not resent the impertinence of any questions I may have to ask. Perhaps, *mon père*, the Church will set an example?'

'Ask any questions you please of me,' said Father Lavigny gravely.

'This is your first season out here?'

'Yes.'

'And you arrived—when?'

'Three weeks ago almost to a day. That is, on the 27th of February.'

'Coming from?'

'The Order of the *Pères Blancs* at Carthage.'

'Thank you, *mon père*. Were you at any time acquainted with Mrs Leidner before coming here?'

'No, I had never seen the lady until I met her here.'

'Will you tell me what you were doing at the time of the tragedy?'

'I was working on some cuneiform tablets in my own room.'

I noticed that Poirot had at his elbow a rough plan of the building.

'That is the room at the south-west corner corresponding to that of Mrs Leidner on the opposite side?'

'Yes.'

'At what time did you go to your room?'

'Immediately after lunch. I should say at about twenty minutes to one.'

'And you remained there until—when?'

'Just before three o'clock. I had heard the station wagon come back—and then I heard it drive off again. I wondered why, and came out to see.'

'During the time that you were there did you leave the room at all?'

'No, not once.'

'And you heard or saw nothing that might have any bearing on the tragedy?'

'No.'

'You have no window giving on the courtyard in your room?'

'No, both the windows give on the countryside.'

'Could you hear at all what was happening in the courtyard?'

'Not very much. I heard Mr Emmott passing my room and going up to the roof. He did so once or twice.'

'Can you remember at what time?'

'No, I'm afraid I can't. I was engrossed in my work, you see.'

There was a pause and then Poirot said:

'Can you say or suggest anything at all that might throw light on this business? Did you, for instance, notice anything in the days preceding the murder?'

Father Lavigny looked slightly uncomfortable.

He shot a half-questioning look at Dr Leidner.

'That is rather a difficult question, monsieur,' he said gravely. 'If you ask me I must reply frankly that in my opinion Mrs Leidner was clearly in dread of someone or something. She was definitely nervous about strangers. I imagine she had a reason for this nervousness of hers—but I *know* nothing. She did not confide in me.'

Poirot cleared his throat and consulted some notes that he held in his hand. 'Two nights ago I understand there was a scare of burglary.'

Father Lavigny replied in the affirmative and retailed his story of the light seen in the antika-room and the subsequent futile search.

'You believe, do you not, that some unauthorized person was on the premises at that time?'

'I don't know what to think,' said Father Lavigny frankly. 'Nothing was taken or disturbed in any way. It might have been one of the house-boys—'

'Or a member of the expedition?'

'Or a member of the expedition. But in that case there would be no reason for the person not admitting the fact.'

'But it *might* equally have been a stranger from outside?'

'I suppose so.'

'Supposing a stranger *had* been on the premises, could he have concealed himself successfully during the following day and until the afternoon of the day following that?'

He asked the question half of Father Lavigny and half of Dr Leidner. Both men considered the question carefully.

'I hardly think it would be possible,' said Dr Leidner at last with some reluctance. 'I don't see where he could possibly conceal himself, do you, Father Lavigny?'

'No—no—I don't.'

Both men seemed reluctant to put the suggestion aside.

Poirot turned to Miss Johnson.

'And you, mademoiselle? Do you consider such a hypothesis feasible?'

After a moment's thought Miss Johnson shook her head.

'No,' she said. 'I don't. Where could anyone hide? The bedrooms are all in use and, in any case, are sparsely furnished. The dark-room, the drawing-office and the laboratory were all in use the next day—so were all these rooms. There are no cupboards or corners. Perhaps, if the servants were in collusion—'

'That is possible, but unlikely,' said Poirot.

He turned once more to Father Lavigny.

'There is another point. The other day Nurse Leatheran here noticed you talking to a man outside. She had previously noticed that same man trying to peer in at one of the

Agatha Christie

windows on the outside. It rather looks as though the man were hanging round the place deliberately.'

'That is possible, of course,' said Father Lavigny thoughtfully.

'Did you speak to this man first, or did he speak to you?'

Father Lavigny considered for a moment or two.

'I believe—yes, I am sure, that he spoke to me.'

'What did he say?'

Father Lavigny made an effort of memory.

'He said, I think, something to the effect was this the American expedition house? And then something else about the Americans employing a lot of men on the work. I did not really understand him very well, but I endeavoured to keep up a conversation so as to improve my Arabic. I thought, perhaps, that being a townee he would understand me better than the men on the dig do.'

'Did you converse about anything else?'

'As far as I remember, I said Hassanieh was a big town— and we then agreed that Baghdad was bigger —and I think he asked whether I was an Armenian or a Syrian Catholic— something of that kind.'

Poirot nodded.

'Can you describe him?'

Again Father Lavigny frowned in thought.

'He was rather a short man,' he said at last, 'and squarely built. He had a very noticeable squint and was of fair complexion.'

Mr Poirot turned to me.

'Does that agree with the way you would describe him?' he asked.

'Not exactly,' I said hesitatingly. 'I should have said he was tall rather than short, and very dark-complexioned. He seemed to me of a rather slender build. I didn't notice any squint.'

Mr Poirot gave a despairing shrug of the shoulders.

'It is always so! If you were of the police how well you would know it! The description of the same man by two different people—never does it agree. Every detail is contradicted.'

'I'm fairly sure about the squint,' said Father Lavigny. 'Nurse Leatheran may be right about the other points. By the way, when I said *fair*, I only meant fair for an *Iraqi*. I expect nurse would call that dark.'

'Very dark,' I said obstinately. 'A dirty dark-yellow colour.'

I saw Dr Reilly bite his lips and smile.

Poirot threw up his hands.

'*Passons!*' he said. 'This stranger hanging about, he may be important—he may not. At any rate he must be found. Let us continue our inquiry.'

He hesitated for a minute, studying the faces turned towards him round the table, then, with a quick nod, he singled out Mr Reiter.

'Come, my friend,' he said. 'Let us have your account of yesterday afternoon.'

Mr Reiter's pink, plump face flushed scarlet.

'Me?' he said.

'Yes, you. To begin with, your name and your age?'

'Carl Reiter, twenty-eight.'

Agatha Christie

'American—yes?'

'Yes, I come from Chicago.'

'This is your first season?'

'Yes. I'm in charge of the photography.'

'Ah, yes. And yesterday afternoon, how did you employ yourself?'

'Well—I was in the dark-room most of the time.'

'*Most* of the time—eh?'

'Yes. I developed some plates first. Afterwards I was fixing up some objects to photograph.'

'Outside?'

'Oh no, in the photographic-room.'

'The dark-room opens out of the photographic-room?'

'Yes.'

'And so you never came outside the photographic-room?'

'No.'

'Did you notice anything that went on in the courtyard?'

The young man shook his head.

'I wasn't noticing anything,' he explained. 'I was busy. I heard the car come back, and as soon as I could leave what I was doing I came out to see if there was any mail. It was then that I—heard.'

'And you began to work in the photographic-room—when?'

'At ten minutes to one.'

'Were you acquainted with Mrs Leidner before you joined this expedition?'

The young man shook his head.

'No, sir. I never saw her till I actually got here.'

'Can you think of *anything*—any incident—however small—that might help us?'

Carl Reiter shook his head.

He said helplessly: 'I guess I don't know anything at all, sir.'

'Mr Emmott?'

David Emmott spoke clearly and concisely in his pleasant soft American voice.

'I was working with the pottery from a quarter to one till a quarter to three—overseeing the boy Abdullah, sorting it, and occasionally going up to the roof to help Dr Leidner.'

'How often did you go up to the roof?'

'Four times, I think.'

'For how long?'

'Usually a couple of minutes—not more. But on one occasion after I'd been working a little over half an hour I stayed as long as ten minutes—discussing what to keep and what to fling away.'

'And I understand that when you came down you found the boy had left his place?'

'Yes. I called him angrily and he reappeared from outside the archway. He had gone out to gossip with the others.'

'That was the only time he left his work?'

'Well, I sent him up once or twice to the roof with pottery.'

Poirot said gravely: 'It is hardly necessary to ask you, Mr Emmott, whether you saw anyone enter or leave Mrs Leidner's room during that time?'

Mr Emmott replied promptly.

'I saw no one at all. Nobody even came out into the courtyard during the two hours I was working.'

Agatha Christie

'And to the best of your belief it was half-past one when both you and the boy were absent and the courtyard was empty?'

'It couldn't have been far off that time. Of course, I can't say *exactly*.'

Poirot turned to Dr Reilly.

'That agrees with your estimate of the time of death, doctor?'

'It does,' said Dr Reilly.

Mr Poirot stroked his great curled moustaches.

'I think we can take it,' he said gravely, 'that Mrs Leidner met her death during that ten minutes.'

CHAPTER 14

One of Us?

There was a little pause—and in it a wave of horror seemed to float round the room.

I think it was at that moment that I first believed Dr Reilly's theory to be right.

I *felt* that the murderer was in the room. Sitting with us—listening. *One of us...*

Perhaps Mrs Mercado felt it too. For she suddenly gave a short sharp cry.

'I can't help it,' she sobbed. 'I—it's so *terrible*!'

'Courage, Marie,' said her husband.

He looked at us apologetically.

'She is so sensitive. She feels things so much.'

'I—I was so fond of Louise,' sobbed Mrs Mercado.

I don't know whether something of what I felt showed in my face, but I suddenly found that Mr Poirot was looking at me, and that a slight smile hovered on his lips.

I gave him a cold glance, and at once he resumed his inquiry.

'Tell me, madame,' he said, 'of the way you spent yesterday afternoon?'

'I was washing my hair,' sobbed Mrs Mercado. 'It seems awful not to have known anything about it. I was quite happy and busy.'

'You were in your room?'

'Yes.'

'And you did not leave it?'

'No. Not till I heard the car. Then I came out and I heard what had happened. Oh, it was *awful*!'

'Did it surprise you?'

Mrs Mercado stopped crying. Her eyes opened resentfully.

'What do you mean, M. Poirot? Are you suggesting—?'

'What should I mean, madame? You have just told us how fond you were of Mrs Leidner. She might, perhaps, have confided in you.'

'Oh, I see... No—no, dear Louise never told me anything—anything *definite*, that is. Of course, I could see she was terribly worried and nervous. And there were those strange occurrences—hands tapping on the windows and all that.'

'Fancies, I remember you said,' I put in, unable to keep silent.

I was glad to see that she looked momentarily disconcerted.

Once again I was conscious of Mr Poirot's amused eye glancing in my direction.

He summed up in a business-like way.

'It comes to this, madame, you were washing your hair—you heard nothing and you saw nothing. Is there anything at all you can think of that would be a help to us in any way?'

Murder in Mesopotamia

Mrs Mercado took no time to think.

'No, indeed there isn't. It's the deepest mystery! But I should say there is no doubt—no doubt *at all* that the murderer came from outside. Why, it stands to reason.'

Poirot turned to her husband.

'And you, monsieur, what have you to say?'

Mr Mercado started nervously. He pulled at his beard in an aimless fashion.

'Must have been. Must have been,' he said. 'Yet how could anyone wish to harm her? She was so gentle—so kind—' He shook his head. 'Whoever killed her must have been a fiend—yes, a fiend!'

'And you yourself, monsieur, how did you pass yesterday afternoon?'

'I?' he stared vaguely.

'You were in the laboratory, Joseph,' his wife prompted him.

'Ah, yes, so I was—so I was. My usual tasks.'

'At what time did you go there?'

Again he looked helplessly and inquiringly at Mrs Mercado.

'At ten minutes to one, Joseph.'

'Ah, yes, at ten minutes to one.'

'Did you come out in the courtyard at all?'

'No—I don't think so.' He considered. 'No, I am sure I didn't.'

'When did you hear of the tragedy?'

'My wife came and told me. It was terrible—shocking. I could hardly believe it. Even now, I can hardly believe it is true.'

Suddenly he began to tremble.

Agatha Christie

'It is horrible—horrible...'

Mrs Mercado came quickly to his side.

'Yes, yes, Joseph, we feel that. But we mustn't give way. It makes it so much more difficult for poor Dr Leidner.'

I saw a spasm of pain pass across Dr Leidner's face, and I guessed that this emotional atmosphere was not easy for him. He gave a half-glance at Poirot as though in appeal. Poirot responded quickly.

'Miss Johnson?' he said.

'I'm afraid I can tell you very little,' said Miss Johnson. Her cultured well-bred voice was soothing after Mrs Mercado's shrill treble. She went on: 'I was working in the living-room—taking impressions of some cylinder seals on plasticine.'

'And you saw or noticed nothing?'

'No.'

Poirot gave her a quick glance. His ear had caught what mine had—a faint note of indecision.

'Are you quite sure, mademoiselle? Is there something that comes back to you vaguely?'

'No—not really—'

'Something you saw, shall we say, out of the corner of your eye hardly knowing you saw it.'

'No, certainly not,' she replied positively.

'Something you *heard* then. Ah, yes, something you are not quite sure whether you heard or not?'

Miss Johnson gave a short, vexed laugh.

'You press me very closely, M. Poirot. I'm afraid you are encouraging me to tell you what I am, perhaps, only imagining.'

'Then there was something you—shall we say—imagined?'

Miss Johnson said slowly, weighing her words in a detached way: 'I have imagined—since—that at some time during the afternoon I heard a very faint cry... What I mean is that I daresay I *did* hear a cry. All the windows in the living-room were open and one hears all sorts of sounds from people working in the barley fields. But you see—since—I've got the idea into my head that it was—that it was Mrs Leidner I heard. And that's made me rather unhappy. Because if I'd jumped up and run along to her room—well, who knows? I might have been in time...'

Dr Reilly interposed authoritatively.

'Now, don't start getting that into your head,' he said. 'I've no doubt but that Mrs Leidner (forgive me, Leidner) was struck down almost as soon as the man entered the room, and it was that blow that killed her. No second blow was struck. Otherwise she would have had time to call for help and make a real outcry.'

'Still, I might have caught the murderer,' said Miss Johnson.

'What time was this, mademoiselle?' asked Poirot. 'In the neighbourhood of half-past one?'

'It must have been about that time—yes.' She reflected a minute.

'That would fit in,' said Poirot thoughtfully. 'You heard nothing else—the opening or shutting of a door, for instance?'

Miss Johnson shook her head.

'No, I do not remember anything of that kind.'

'You were sitting at a table, I presume. Which way were you facing? The courtyard? The antika-room? The verandah? Or the open countryside?'

'I was facing the courtyard.'

'Could you see the boy Abdullah washing pots from where you were?'

'Oh, yes, if I looked up, but of course I was very intent on what I was doing. All my attention was on that.'

'If anyone had passed the courtyard window, though, you would have noticed it?'

'Oh, yes, I am almost sure of that.'

'And nobody did so?'

'No.'

'But if anyone had walked, say, across the middle of the courtyard, would you have noticed that?'

'I think—probably not—unless, as I said before, I had happened to look up and out of the window.'

'You did not notice the boy Abdullah leave his work and go out to join the other servants?'

'No.'

'Ten minutes,' mused Poirot. 'That fatal ten minutes.'

There was a momentary silence.

Miss Johnson lifted her head suddenly and said: 'You know, M. Poirot, I think I have unintentionally misled you. On thinking it over, I do not believe that I could possibly have heard any cry uttered in Mrs Leidner's room from where I was. The antika-room lay between me and her—and I understand her windows were found closed.'

'In any case, do not distress yourself, mademoiselle,' said Poirot kindly. 'It is not really of much importance.'

'No, of course not. I understand that. But you see, it *is* of importance to me, because I feel I might have done something.'

'Don't distress yourself, dear Anne,' said Dr Leidner with affection. 'You must be sensible. What you heard was probably one Arab bawling to another some distance away in the fields.'

Miss Johnson flushed a little at the kindliness of his tone. I even saw tears spring to her eyes. She turned her head away and spoke even more gruffly than usual.

'Probably was. Usual thing after a tragedy—start imagining things that aren't so at all.'

Poirot was once more consulting his notebook.

'I do not suppose there is much more to be said. Mr Carey?'

Richard Carey spoke slowly—in a wooden mechanical manner.

'I'm afraid I can add nothing helpful. I was on duty at the dig. The news was brought to me there.'

'And you know or can think of nothing helpful that occurred in the days immediately preceding the murder?'

'Nothing at all.'

'Mr Coleman?'

'I was right out of the whole thing,' said Mr Coleman with—was it just a shade of regret—in his tone. 'I went into Hassanieh yesterday morning to get the money for the men's wages. When I came back Emmott told me what had happened and I went back in the bus to get the police and Dr Reilly.'

'And beforehand?'

'Well, sir, things were a bit jumpy—but you know that already. There was the antika-room scare and one or two before that—hands and faces at the window—you remember, sir,' he appealed to Dr Leidner, who bent his head in assent.

Agatha Christie

'I think, you know, that you'll find some Johnny *did* get in from outside. Must have been an artful sort of beggar.'

Poirot considered him for a minute or two in silence.

'You are an Englishman, Mr Coleman?' he asked at last.

'That's right, sir. All British. See the trademark. Guaranteed genuine.'

'This is your first season?'

'Quite right.'

'And you are passionately keen on archaeology?'

This description of himself seemed to cause Mr Coleman some embarrassment. He got rather pink and shot the side look of a guilty schoolboy at Dr Leidner.

'Of course—it's all very interesting,' he stammered. 'I mean—I'm not exactly a brainy chap...'

He broke off rather lamely. Poirot did not insist.

He tapped thoughtfully on the table with the end of his pencil and carefully straightened an inkpot that stood in front of him.

'It seems then,' he said, 'that that is as near as we can get for the moment. If any one of you thinks of something that has for the time being slipped his or her memory, do not hesitate to come to me with it. It will be well now, I think, for me to have a few words alone with Dr Leidner and Dr Reilly.'

It was the signal for a breaking up of the party. We all rose and filed out of the door. When I was half-way out, however, a voice recalled me.

'Perhaps,' said M. Poirot, 'Nurse Leatheran will be so kind as to remain. I think her assistance will be valuable to us.'

I came back and resumed my seat at the table.

CHAPTER 15

Poirot Makes a Suggestion

Dr Reilly had risen from his seat. When everyone had gone out he carefully closed the door. Then, with an inquiring glance at Poirot, he proceeded to shut the window giving on the courtyard. The others were already shut. Then he, too, resumed his seat at the table.

'*Bien!*' said Poirot. 'We are now private and undisturbed. We can speak freely. We have heard what the members of the expedition have to tell us and—But yes, *ma soeur*, what is it that you think?'

I got rather red. There was no denying that the queer little man had sharp eyes. He'd seen the thought passing through my mind—I suppose my face *had* shown a bit too clearly what I was thinking!

'Oh, it's nothing—' I said hesitating.

'Come on, nurse,' said Dr Reilly. 'Don't keep the specialist waiting.'

'It's nothing really,' I said hurriedly. 'It only just passed through my mind, so to speak, that perhaps even if anyone did know or suspect something it wouldn't be easy to bring it out in front of everybody else—or even, perhaps, in front of Dr Leidner.'

Rather to my astonishment, M. Poirot nodded his head in vigorous agreement.

'Precisely. Precisely. It is very just what you say there. But I will explain. That little reunion we have just had—it served a purpose. In England before the races you have a parade of the horses, do you not? They go in front of the grandstand so that everyone may have an opportunity of seeing and judging them. That is the purpose of my little assembly. In the sporting phrase, I run my eye over the possible starters.'

Dr Leidner cried out violently, 'I do not believe for one minute that *any* member of my expedition is implicated in this crime!'

Then, turning to me, he said authoritatively: 'Nurse, I should be much obliged if you would tell M. Poirot here and now exactly what passed between my wife and you two days ago.'

Thus urged, I plunged straightaway into my own story, trying as far as possible to recall the exact words and phrases Mrs Leidner had used.

When I had finished, M. Poirot said: 'Very good. Very good. You have the mind neat and orderly. You will be of great service to me here.'

He turned to Dr Leidner.

'You have these letters?'

'I have them here. I thought that you would want to see them first thing.'

Poirot took them from him, read them, and scrutinized them carefully as he did so. I was rather disappointed that he didn't dust powder over them or examine them with a microscope or anything like that—but I realized that he wasn't a very young man and that his methods were probably not very up to date. He just read them in the way that anyone might read a letter.

Having read them he put them down and cleared his throat.

'Now,' he said, 'let us proceed to get our facts clear and in order. The first of these letters was received by your wife shortly after her marriage to you in America. There had been others but these she destroyed. The first letter was followed by a second. A very short time after the second arrived you both had a near escape from coal-gas poisoning. You then came abroad and for nearly two years no further letters were received. They started again at the beginning of your season this year—that is to say within the last three weeks. That is correct?'

'Absolutely.'

'Your wife displayed every sign of panic and, after consulting Dr Reilly, you engaged Nurse Leatheran here to keep your wife company and allay her fears?'

'Yes.'

'Certain incidents occurred—hands tapping at the window—a spectral face—noises in the antika-room. You did not witness any of these phenomena yourself?'

'No.'

'In fact nobody did except Mrs Leidner?'

Agatha Christie

'Father Lavigny saw a light in the antika-room.'

'Yes, I have not forgotten that.'

He was silent for a minute or two, then he said: 'Had your wife made a will?'

'I do not think so.'

'Why was that?'

'It did not seem worth it from her point of view.'

'Is she not a wealthy woman?'

'Yes, during her lifetime. Her father left her a considerable sum of money in trust. She could not touch the principal. At her death it was to pass to any children she might have—and failing children to the Pittstown Museum.'

Poirot drummed thoughtfully on the table.

'Then we can, I think,' he said, 'eliminate one motive from the case. It is, you comprehend, what I look for first. *Who benefits by the deceased's death?* In this case it is a museum. Had it been otherwise, had Mrs Leidner died intestate but possessed of a considerable fortune, I should imagine that it would prove an interesting question as to who inherited the money—you—or a former husband. But there would have been this difficulty, the former husband would have had to resurrect himself in order to claim it, and I should imagine that he would then be in danger of arrest, though I hardly fancy that the death penalty would be exacted so long after the war. However, these speculations need not arise. As I say, I settle first the question of money. For the next step I proceed always to suspect the husband or wife of the deceased! In this case, in the first place, you are proved never to have gone near your wife's room yesterday afternoon, in the second place you lose instead of gain by your wife's death, and in the third place—'

He paused.

'Yes?' said Dr Leidner.

'In the third place,' said Poirot slowly, 'I can, I think, appreciate devotion when I see it. I believe, Dr Leidner, that your love for your wife was the ruling passion of your life. It is so, is it not?'

Dr Leidner answered quite simply: 'Yes.'

Poirot nodded.

'Therefore,' he said, 'we can proceed.'

'Hear, hear, let's get down to it,' said Dr Reilly with some impatience.

Poirot gave him a reproving glance.

'My friend, do not be impatient. In a case like this everything must be approached with order and method. In fact, that is my rule in every case. Having disposed of certain possibilities, we now approach a very important point. It is vital that, as you say—all the cards should be on the table—there must be nothing kept back.'

'Quite so,' said Dr Reilly.

'That is why I demand the whole truth,' went on Poirot.

Dr Leidner looked at him in surprise.

'I assure you, M. Poirot, that I have kept nothing back. I have told you everything that I know. There have been no reserves.'

'*Tout de même*, you have not told me *everything*.'

'Yes, indeed. I cannot think of any detail that has escaped me.'

Agatha Christie

He looked quite distressed.

Poirot shook his head gently.

'No,' he said. '*You have not told me, for instance, why you installed Nurse Leatheran in the house.*'

Dr Leidner looked completely bewildered.

'But I have explained that. It is obvious. My wife's nervousness—her fears…'

Poirot leaned forward. Slowly and emphatically he wagged a finger up and down.

'No, no, no. There is something there that is not clear. Your wife is in danger, yes—she is threatened with death, yes. You send—*not for the police*—not for a private detective even—but for a *nurse*! It does not make the sense, that!'

'I—I—' Dr Leidner stopped. The colour rose in his cheeks. 'I thought—' He came to a dead stop.

'Now we are coming to it,' Poirot encouraged him. 'You thought—what?'

Dr Leidner remained silent. He looked harassed and unwilling.

'See you,' Poirot's tone became winning and appealing, 'it all rings true what you have told me, *except for that*. Why a *nurse*? There is an answer—yes. In fact, there can be only one answer. *You did not believe yourself in your wife's danger.*'

And then with a cry Dr Leidner broke down.

'God help me,' he groaned. 'I didn't. I didn't.'

Poirot watched him with the kind of attention a cat gives a mouse-hole—ready to pounce when the mouse shows itself.

'What *did* you think then?' he asked.

'I don't know. I don't know…'

'But you do know. You know perfectly. Perhaps I can help you—with a guess. *Did you, Dr Leidner, suspect that these letters were all written by your wife herself?*'

There wasn't any need for him to answer. The truth of Poirot's guess was only too apparent. The horrified hand he held up, as though begging for mercy, told its own tale.

I drew a deep breath. So I *had* been right in my half-formed guess! I recalled the curious tone in which Dr Leidner had asked me what I thought of it all. I nodded my head slowly and thoughtfully, and suddenly awoke to the fact that M. Poirot's eyes were on me.

'Did you think the same, nurse?'

'The idea did cross my mind,' I said truthfully.

'For what reason?'

I explained the similarity of the handwriting on the letter that Mr Coleman had shown me.

Poirot turned to Dr Leidner.

'Had you, too, noticed that similarity?'

Dr Leidner bowed his head.

'Yes, I did. The writing was small and cramped—not big and generous like Louise's, but several of the letters were formed the same way. I will show you.'

From an inner breast pocket he took out some letters and finally selected a sheet from one, which he handed to Poirot. It was part of a letter written to him by his wife. Poirot compared it carefully with the anonymous letters.

'Yes,' he murmured. 'Yes. There are several similarities—a curious way of forming the letter *s*, a distinctive *e*. I am not a handwriting expert—I cannot pronounce definitely (and

Agatha Christie

for that matter, I have never found two handwriting experts who agree on any point whatsoever)—but one can at least say this—the similarity between the two handwritings is very marked. It seems highly probable that they were all written by the same person. But it is not *certain*. We must take all contingencies into mind.'

He leaned back in his chair and said thoughtfully: 'There are three possibilities. First, the similarity of the handwriting is pure coincidence. Second, that these threatening letters were written by Mrs Leidner herself for some obscure reason. Third, that they were written by someone *who deliberately copied her handwriting*. Why? There seems no sense in it. One of these three possibilities must be the correct one.'

He reflected for a minute or two and then, turning to Dr Leidner, he asked, with a resumal of his brisk manner: 'When the possibility that Mrs Leidner herself was the author of these letters first struck you, what theory did you form?'

Dr Leidner shook his head.

'I put the idea out of my head as quickly as possible. I felt it was monstrous.'

'Did you search for no explanation?'

'Well,' he hesitated. 'I wondered if worrying and brooding over the past had perhaps affected my wife's brain slightly. I thought she might possibly have written those letters to herself without being conscious of having done so. That is possible, isn't it?' he added, turning to Dr Reilly.

Dr Reilly pursed up his lips.

'The human brain is capable of almost anything,' he replied vaguely.

Murder in Mesopotamia

But he shot a lightning glance at Poirot, and as if in obedience to it, the latter abandoned the subject.

'The letters are an interesting point,' he said. 'But we must concentrate on the case as a whole. There are, as I see it, three possible solutions.'

'Three?'

'Yes. Solution one: the simplest. Your wife's first husband is still alive. He first threatens her and then proceeds to carry out his threats. If we accept this solution, our problem is to discover how he got in or out without being seen.

'Solution two: Mrs Leidner, for reasons of her own (reasons probably more easily understood by a medical man than a layman), writes herself threatening letters. The gas business is staged by her (remember, it was she who roused you by telling you she smelt gas). But, *if Mrs Leidner wrote herself the letters, she cannot be in danger from the supposed writer*. We must, therefore, look elsewhere for the murderer. We must look, in fact, amongst the members of your staff. Yes,' in answer to a murmur of protest from Dr Leidner, 'that is the only logical conclusion. To satisfy a private grudge one of them killed her. That person, I may say, was probably aware of the letters—or was at any rate aware that Mrs Leidner feared or was pretending to fear someone. That fact, in the murderer's opinion, rendered the murder quite safe for him. He felt sure it would be put down to a mysterious outsider—the writer of the threatening letters.

'A variant of this solution is that the murderer actually wrote the letters himself, being aware of Mrs Leidner's past history. But in that case it is not quite clear *why* the criminal

Agatha Christie

should have copied Mrs Leidner's own handwriting since, as far as we can see, it would be more to his or her advantage that they should appear to be written by an outsider.

'The third solution is the most interesting to my mind. I suggest that the letters are genuine. They are written by Mrs Leidner's first husband (or his younger brother), *who is actually one of the expedition staff.*'

CHAPTER 16

The Suspects

Dr Leidner sprang to his feet.

'Impossible! Absolutely impossible! The idea is absurd!'

Mr Poirot looked at him quite calmly but said nothing.

'You mean to suggest that my wife's former husband is one of the expedition *and that she didn't recognize him?*'

'Exactly. Reflect a little on the facts. Some fifteen years ago your wife lived with this man for a few months. Would she know him if she came across him after that lapse of time? I think not. His face will have changed, his build will have changed—his voice may not have changed so much, but that is a detail he can attend to himself. And remember, *she is not looking for him amongst her own household*. She visualizes him as somewhere *outside*—a stranger. No, I do not think she would recognize him. And there is a second possibility. The young brother—the child of those days who was so passionately devoted to his elder brother. He is now a man. Will she recognize a child of ten or twelve years old in a man nearing thirty? Yes, there is young William

127

Agatha Christie

Bosner to be reckoned with. Remember, his brother in his eyes may not loom as a traitor but as a patriot, a martyr for his own country—Germany. In his eyes *Mrs Leidner* is the traitor—the monster who sent his beloved brother to death! A susceptible child is capable of great hero worship, and a young mind can easily be obsessed by an idea which persists into adult life.'

'Quite true,' said Dr Reilly. 'The popular view that a child forgets easily is not an accurate one. Many people go right through life in the grip of an idea which has been impressed on them in very tender years.'

'*Bien*. You have these two possibilities. Frederick Bosner, a man by now of fifty odd, and William Bosner, whose age would be something short of thirty. Let us examine the members of your staff from these two points of view.'

'This is fantastic,' murmured Dr Leidner. '*My* staff! The members of my own expedition.'

'And consequently considered above suspicion,' said Poirot dryly. 'A very useful point of view. *Commençons!* Who could emphatically *not* be Frederick or William?'

'The women.'

'Naturally. Miss Johnson and Mrs Mercado are crossed off. Who else?'

'Carey. He and I have worked together for years before I even met Louise—'

'And also he is the wrong age. He is, I should judge, thirty-eight or nine, too young for Frederick, too old for William. Now for the rest. There is Father Lavigny and Mr Mercado. Either of them might be Frederick Bosner.'

'But, my dear sir,' cried Dr Leidner in a voice of mingled irritation and amusement, 'Father Lavigny is known all over the world as an epigraphist and Mercado has worked for years in a well-known museum in New York. It is *impossible* that either of them should be the man you think!'

Poirot waved an airy hand.

'Impossible—impossible—I take no account of the word! The impossible, always I examine it very closely! But we will pass on for the moment. Who else have you? Carl Reiter, a young man with a German name, David Emmott—'

'He has been with me two seasons, remember.'

'He is a young man with the gift of patience. *If* he committed a crime, it would not be in a hurry. All would be very well prepared.'

Dr Leidner made a gesture of despair.

'And lastly, William Coleman,' continued Poirot.

'He is an Englishman.'

'*Pourquoi pas?* Did not Mrs Leidner say that the boy left America and could not be traced? He might easily have been brought up in England.'

'You have an answer to everything,' said Dr Leidner.

I was thinking hard. Right from the beginning I had thought Mr Coleman's manner rather more like a P.G. Wodehouse book than like a real live young man. Had he really been playing a part all the time?

Poirot was writing in a little book.

'Let us proceed with order and method,' he said. 'On the first count we have two names. Father Lavigny and Mr Mercado. On the second we have Coleman, Emmott and Reiter.

'Now let us pass to the opposite aspect of the matter—means and opportunity. *Who amongst the expedition had the means and the opportunity of committing the crime?* Carey was on the dig, Coleman was in Hassanieh, you yourself were on the roof. That leaves us Father Lavigny, Mr Mercado, Mrs Mercado, David Emmott, Carl Reiter, Miss Johnson and Nurse Leatheran.'

'Oh!' I exclaimed, and I bounded in my chair.

Mr Poirot looked at me with twinkling eyes.

'Yes, I'm afraid, *ma soeur*, that you have got to be included. It would have been quite easy for you to have gone along and killed Mrs Leidner while the courtyard was empty. You have plenty of muscle and strength, and she would have been quite unsuspicious until the moment the blow was struck.'

I was so upset that I couldn't get a word out. Dr Reilly, I noticed, was looking highly amused.

'Interesting case of a nurse who murdered her patients one by one,' he murmured.

Such a look as I gave him!

Dr Leidner's mind had been running on a different tack.

'Not Emmott, M. Poirot,' he objected. 'You can't include him. He was on the roof with me, remember, during that ten minutes.'

'Nevertheless we cannot exclude him. He could have come down, gone straight to Mrs Leidner's room, killed her, and *then* called the boy back. Or he might have killed her on one of the occasions when he had *sent the boy up to you.*'

Dr Leidner shook his head, murmuring: 'What a nightmare! It's all so—fantastic.'

Murder in Mesopotamia

To my surprise Poirot agreed.

'Yes, that's true. *This is a fantastic crime.* One does not often come across them. Usually murder is very sordid—very simple. But this is unusual murder… I suspect, Dr Leidner, that your wife was an unusual woman.'

He had hit the nail on the head with such accuracy that I jumped.

'Is that true, nurse?' he asked.

Dr Leidner said quietly: 'Tell him what Louise was like, nurse. You are unprejudiced.'

I spoke quite frankly.

'She was very lovely,' I said. 'You couldn't help admiring her and wanting to do things for her. I've never met anyone like her before.'

'Thank you,' said Dr Leidner and smiled at me.

'That is valuable testimony coming from an outsider,' said Poirot politely. 'Well, let us proceed. Under the heading of *means and opportunity* we have seven names. Nurse Leatheran, Miss Johnson, Mrs Mercado, Mr Mercado, Mr Reiter, Mr Emmott and Father Lavigny.'

Once more he cleared his throat. I've always noticed that foreigners can make the oddest noises.

'Let us for the moment assume that our third theory is correct. That is that the murderer is Frederick or William Bosner, and that Frederick or William Bosner is a member of the expedition staff. By comparing both lists we can narrow down our suspects on this count to four. Father Lavigny, Mr Mercado, Carl Reiter and David Emmott.'

'Father Lavigny is out of the question,' said Dr Leidner with decision. 'He is one of the *Pères Blancs* in Carthage.'

'And his beard's quite real,' I put in.

'*Ma soeur*,' said Poirot, 'a murderer of the first class *never* wears a false beard!'

'How do you know the murderer is of the first class?' I asked rebelliously.

'Because if he were not, the whole truth would be plain to me at this instant—and it is not.'

That's pure conceit, I thought to myself.

'Anyway,' I said, reverting to the beard, 'it must have taken quite a time to grow.'

'That is a practical observation,' said Poirot.

Dr Leidner said irritably: 'But it's ridiculous—quite ridiculous. Both he and Mercado are well-known men. They've been known for years.'

Poirot turned to him.

'You have not the true vision. You do not appreciate an important point. *If Frederick Bosner is not dead—what has he been doing all these years?* He must have taken a different name. He must have built himself up a career.'

'As a *Père Blanc*?' asked Dr Reilly sceptically.

'It is a little fantastic that, yes,' confessed Poirot. 'But we cannot put it right out of court. Besides, these other possibilities.'

'The young 'uns?' said Reilly. 'If you want my opinion, on the face of it there's only one of your suspects that's even plausible.'

'And that is?'

'Young Carl Reiter. There's nothing actually against him, but come down to it and you've got to admit a few things—he's the right age, he's got a German name, he's new this year and he had the opportunity all right. He'd only got to pop out of his photographic place, cross the courtyard to do his dirty work and hare back again while the coast was clear. If anyone were to have dropped into the photographic-room while he was out of it, he can always say later that he was in the dark-room. I don't say he's your man but if you are going to suspect someone I say he's by far and away the most likely.'

M. Poirot didn't seem very receptive. He nodded gravely but doubtfully.

'Yes,' he said. 'He is the most plausible, but it may not be so simple as all that.'

Then he said: 'Let us say no more at present. I would like now, if I may, to examine the room where the crime took place.'

'Certainly.' Dr Leidner fumbled in his pockets, then looked at Dr Reilly.

'Captain Maitland took it,' he said.

'Maitland gave it to me,' said Reilly. 'He had to go off on that Kurdish business.'

He produced the key.

Dr Leidner said hesitatingly: 'Do you mind—if I don't— Perhaps, nurse—'

'Of course. Of course,' said Poirot. 'I quite understand. Never do I wish to cause you unnecessary pain. If you will be good enough to accompany me, *ma soeur*.'

'Certainly,' I said.

CHAPTER 17

The Stain by the Washstand

Mrs Leidner's body had been taken to Hassanieh for the postmortem, but otherwise her room had been left exactly as it was. There was so little in it that it had not taken the police long to go over it.

To the right of the door as you entered was the bed. Opposite the door were the two barred windows giving on the countryside. Between them was a plain oak table with two drawers that served Mrs Leidner as a dressing-table. On the east wall there was a line of hooks with dresses hung up protected by cotton bags and a deal chest of drawers. Immediately to the left of the door was the washstand. In the middle of the room was a good-sized plain oak table with a blotter and inkstand and a small attaché-case. It was in the latter that Mrs Leidner had kept the anonymous letters. The curtains were short strips of native material—white striped with orange. The floor was of stone with some goatskin rugs on it, three narrow ones of brown striped with white in front of the two windows and the washstand, and a larger better quality one of white with brown stripes lying between the bed and the writing-table.

There were no cupboards or alcoves or long curtains—nowhere, in fact, where anyone could have hidden. The bed was a plain iron one with a printed cotton quilt. The only trace of luxury in the room were three pillows all made of the best soft and billowy down. Nobody but Mrs Leidner had pillows like these.

In a few brief words Dr Reilly explained where Mrs Leidner's body had been found—in a heap on the rug beside the bed.

To illustrate his account, he beckoned me to come forward.

'If you don't mind, nurse?' he said.

I'm not squeamish. I got down on the floor and arranged myself as far as possible in the attitude in which Mrs Leidner's body had been found.

'Leidner lifted her head when he found her,' said the doctor. 'But I questioned him closely and it's obvious that he didn't actually change her position.'

'It seems quite straightforward,' said Poirot. 'She was lying on the bed, asleep or resting—someone opens the door, she looks up, rises to her feet—'

'And he struck her down,' finished the doctor. 'The blow would produce unconsciousness and death would follow very shortly. You see—'

He explained the injury in technical language.

'Not much blood, then?' said Poirot.

'No, the blood escaped internally into the brain.'

Agatha Christie

'*Eh bien*,' said Poirot, 'that seems straightforward enough—except for one thing. *If* the man who entered was a stranger, why did not Mrs Leidner cry out at once for help? If she had screamed she would have been heard. Nurse Leatheran here would have heard her, and Emmott and the boy.'

'That's easily answered,' said Dr Reilly dryly. '*Because it wasn't a stranger*.'

Poirot nodded.

'Yes,' he said meditatively. 'She may have been *surprised* to see the person—but she was not *afraid*. Then, as he struck, she *may* have uttered a half-cry—too late.'

'The cry Miss Johnson heard?'

'Yes, if she *did* hear it. But on the whole I doubt it. These mud walls are thick and the windows were closed.'

He stepped up to the bed.

'You left her actually lying down?' he asked me.

I explained exactly what I had done.

'Did she mean to sleep or was she going to read?'

'I gave her two books—a light one and a volume of memoirs. She usually read for a while and then sometimes dropped off for a short sleep.'

'And she was—what shall I say—quite as usual?'

I considered.

'Yes. She seemed quite normal and in good spirits,' I said. 'Just a shade off-hand, perhaps, but I put that down to her having confided in me the day before. It makes people a little uncomfortable sometimes.'

Poirot's eyes twinkled.

'Ah, yes, indeed, me, I know that well.'

He looked round the room.

'And when you came in here after the murder, was everything as you had seen it before?'

I looked round also.

'Yes, I think so. I don't remember anything being different.'

'There was no sign of the weapon with which she was struck?'

'No.'

Poirot looked at Dr Reilly.

'What was it in your opinion?'

The doctor replied promptly:

'Something pretty powerful, of a fair size and without any sharp corners or edges. The rounded base of a statue, say—something like that. Mind you, I'm not suggesting that that *was* it. But that type of thing. The blow was delivered with great force.'

'Struck by a strong arm? A man's arm?'

'Yes—unless—'

'Unless—what?'

Dr Reilly said slowly: 'It is just possible that Mrs Leidner might have been on her knees—in which case, the blow being delivered from above with a heavy implement, the force needed would not have been so great.'

'*On her knees*,' mused Poirot. 'It is an idea—that.'

'It's only an idea, mind,' the doctor hastened to point out. 'There's absolutely nothing to indicate it.'

'But it's possible.'

Agatha Christie

'Yes. And after all, in view of the circumstances, it's not fantastic. Her fear might have led her to kneel in supplication rather than to scream when her instinct would tell her it was too late—that nobody could get there in time.'

'Yes,' said Poirot thoughtfully. 'It is an idea...'

It was a very poor one, I thought. I couldn't for one moment imagine Mrs Leidner on her knees to anyone.

Poirot made his way slowly round the room. He opened the windows, tested the bars, passed his head through and satisfied himself that by no means could his shoulders be made to follow his head.

'The windows were shut when you found her,' he said. 'Were they also shut when you left her at a quarter to one?'

'Yes, they were always shut in the afternoon. There is no gauze over these windows as there is in the living-room and dining-room. They are kept shut to keep out the flies.'

'And in any case no one could get in that way,' mused Poirot. 'And the walls are of the most solid—mud-brick—and there are no trap-doors and no sky-lights. No, there is only one way into this room—*through the door*. And there is only one way to the door *through the courtyard*. And there is only one entrance to the courtyard—*through the archway*. And outside the archway there were five people and they all tell the same story, and I do not think, me, that they are lying... No, they are not lying. They are not bribed to silence. The murderer was *here*...'

I didn't say anything. Hadn't I felt the same thing just now when we were all cooped up round the table?

Slowly Poirot prowled round the room. He took up a photograph from the chest of drawers. It was of an elderly man with a white goatee beard. He looked inquiringly at me.

'Mrs Leidner's father,' I said. 'She told me so.'

He put it down again and glanced over the articles on the dressing-table—all of plain tortoiseshell—simple but good. He looked up at a row of books on a shelf, repeating the titles aloud.

'*Who were the Greeks? Introduction to Relativity. Life of Lady Hester Stanhope. Crewe Traine. Back to Methuselah. Linda Condon.* Yes, they tell us something, perhaps. She was not a fool, your Mrs Leidner. She had a mind.'

'Oh! she was a *very* clever woman,' I said eagerly. 'Very well read and up in everything. She wasn't a bit ordinary.'

He smiled as he looked over at me.

'No,' he said. 'I've already realized that.'

He passed on. He stood for some moments at the washstand, where there was a big array of bottles and toilet creams.

Then, suddenly, he dropped on his knees and examined the rug.

Dr Reilly and I came quickly to join him. He was examining a small dark brown stain, almost invisible on the brown of the rug. In fact it was only just noticeable where it impinged on one of the white stripes.

'What do you say, doctor?' he said. 'Is that blood?'

Dr Reilly knelt down.

'Might be,' he said. 'I'll make sure if you like?'

'If you would be so amiable.'

Mr Poirot examined the jug and basin. The jug was standing on the side of the washstand. The basin was empty, but beside the washstand there was an empty kerosene tin containing slop water.

He turned to me.

'Do you remember, nurse? Was this jug *out* of the basin or *in* it when you left Mrs Leidner at a quarter to one?'

'I can't be sure,' I said after a minute or two. 'I rather think it was standing in the basin.'

'Ah?'

'But you see,' I said hastily, 'I only think so because it usually was. The boys leave it like that after lunch. I just feel that if it hadn't been in I should have noticed it.'

He nodded quite appreciatively.

'Yes. I understand that. It is your hospital training. If everything had not been just so in the room, you would quite unconsciously have set it to rights hardly noticing what you were doing. And after the murder? Was it like it is now?'

I shook my head.

'I didn't notice then,' I said. 'All I looked for was whether there was any place anyone could be hidden or if there was anything the murderer had left behind him.'

'It's blood all right,' said Dr Reilly, rising from his knees. 'Is it important?'

Poirot was frowning perplexedly. He flung out his hands with petulance.

'I cannot tell. How can I tell? It may mean nothing at all. I can say, if I like, that the murderer touched her—that there was blood on his hands—very little blood, but still blood—and so he came over here and washed them. Yes, it may have been like that. But I cannot jump to conclusions and say that it *was* so. That stain may be of no importance at all.'

'There would have been very little blood,' said Dr Reilly dubiously. 'None would have spurted out or anything like that. It would have just oozed a little from the wound. Of course, if he'd probed it at all...'

I gave a shiver. A nasty sort of picture came up in my mind. The vision of somebody—perhaps that nice pig-faced photographic boy, striking down that lovely woman and then bending over her probing the wound with his finger in an awful gloating fashion and his face, perhaps, quite different...all fierce and mad...

Dr Reilly noticed my shiver.

'What's the matter, nurse?' he said.

'Nothing—just goose-flesh,' I said. 'A goose walking over my grave.'

Mr Poirot turned round and looked at me.

'I know what you need,' he said. 'Presently when we have finished here and I go back with the doctor to Hassanieh we will take you with us. You will give Nurse Leatheran tea, will you not, doctor?'

'Delighted.'

'Oh, no doctor,' I protested. 'I couldn't think of such a thing.'

M. Poirot gave me a little friendly tap on the shoulder. Quite an English tap, not a foreign one.

'You, *ma soeur*, will do as you are told,' he said. 'Besides, it will be of advantage to me. There is a good deal more that I want to discuss, and I cannot do it here where one must

Agatha Christie

preserve the decencies. The good Dr Leidner he worshipped his wife and he is sure—oh, so sure—that everybody else felt the same about her! But that, in my opinion, would not be human nature! No, we want to discuss Mrs Leidner with—how do you say?—the gloves removed. That is settled then. When we have finished here, we take you with us to Hassanieh.'

'I suppose,' I said doubtfully, 'that I ought to be leaving anyway. It's rather awkward.'

'Do nothing for a day or two,' said Dr Reilly. 'You can't very well go until after the funeral.'

'That's all very well,' I said. 'And supposing *I* get murdered too, doctor?'

I said it half jokingly and Dr Reilly took it in the same fashion and would, I think, have made some jocular response.

But M. Poirot, to my astonishment, stood stock-still in the middle of the floor and clasped his hands to his head.

'Ah! if that were possible,' he murmured. 'It is a danger—yes—a great danger—and what can one do? How can one guard against it?'

'Why, M. Poirot,' I said, 'I was only joking! Who'd want to murder me, I should like to know?'

'You—or another,' he said, and I didn't like the way he said it at all. Positively creepy.

'But why?' I persisted.

He looked at me very straight then.

'I joke, mademoiselle,' he said, 'and I laugh. *But there are some things that are no joke.* There are things that my profession has taught me. And one of these things, the most terrible thing, is this: *Murder is a habit...*'

CHAPTER 18

Tea at Dr Reilly's

Before leaving, Poirot made a round of the expedition house and the outbuildings. He also asked a few questions of the servants at second hand—that is to say, Dr Reilly translated the questions and answers from English to Arabic and *vice versa*.

These questions dealt mainly with the appearance of the stranger Mrs Leidner and I had seen looking through the window and to whom Father Lavigny had been talking on the following day.

'Do you really think that fellow had anything to do with it?' asked Dr Reilly when we were bumping along in his car on our way to Hassanieh.

'I like all the information there is,' was Poirot's reply.

And really, that described his methods very well. I found later that there wasn't anything—no small scrap of insignificant gossip—in which he wasn't interested. Men aren't usually so gossipy.

I must confess I was glad of my cup of tea when we got

Agatha Christie

to Dr Reilly's house. M. Poirot, I noticed, put five lumps of sugar in his.

Stirring it carefully with his teaspoon he said: 'And now we can talk, can we not? We can make up our minds who is likely to have committed the crime.'

'Lavigny, Mercado, Emmott or Reiter?' asked Dr Reilly.

'No, no—that was theory number three. I wish to concentrate now on theory number two—leaving aside all question of a mysterious husband or brother-in-law turning up from the past. Let us discuss now quite simply which member of the expedition had the means and opportunity to kill Mrs Leidner, and who is likely to have done so.'

'I thought you didn't think much of that theory.'

'Not at all. But I have some natural delicacy,' said Poirot reproachfully. 'Can I discuss in the presence of Dr Leidner the motives likely to lead to the murder of his wife by a member of the expedition? That would not have been delicate at all. I had to sustain the fiction that his wife was adorable and that everyone adored her!

'But naturally it was not like that at all. Now we can be brutal and impersonal and say what we think. We have no longer to consider people's feelings. And that is where Nurse Leatheran is going to help us. She is, I am sure, a very good observer.'

'Oh, I don't know about that,' I said.

Dr Reilly handed me a plate of hot scones—'To fortify yourself,' he said. They were very good scones.

'Come now,' said M. Poirot in a friendly, chatty way. 'You shall tell me, *ma soeur*, exactly what each member of the expedition felt towards Mrs Leidner.'

'I was only there a week, M. Poirot,' I said.

'Quite long enough for one of your intelligence. A nurse sums up quickly. She makes her judgments and abides by them. Come, let us make a beginning. Father Lavigny, for instance?'

'Well, there now, I really couldn't say. He and Mrs Leidner seemed to like talking together. But they usually spoke French and I'm not very good at French myself though I learnt it as a girl at school. I've an idea they talked mainly about books.'

'They were, as you might say, companionable together—yes?'

'Well, yes, you might put it that way. But, all the same, I think Father Lavigny was puzzled by her and—well—almost annoyed by being puzzled, if you know what I mean.'

And I told him of the conversation I had had with him out on the dig that first day when he had called Mrs Leidner a 'dangerous woman'.

'Now that is very interesting,' M. Poirot said. 'And she—what do you think she thought of him?'

'That's rather difficult to say, too. It wasn't easy to know what Mrs Leidner thought of people. Sometimes, I fancy, *he* puzzled *her*. I remember her saying to Dr Leidner that he was unlike any priest she had ever known.'

'A length of hemp to be ordered for Father Lavigny,' said Dr Reilly facetiously.

'My dear friend,' said Poirot. 'Have you not, perhaps, some patients to attend? I would not for the world detain you from your professional duties.'

Agatha Christie

'I've got a whole hospital of them,' said Dr Reilly.

And he got up and said a wink was as good as a nod to a blind horse, and went out laughing.

'That is better,' said Poirot. 'We will have now an interesting conversation *tête-à-tête*. But you must not forget to eat your tea.'

He passed me a plate of sandwiches and suggested my having a second cup of tea. He really had very pleasant, attentive manners.

'And now,' he said, 'let us continue with your impressions. Who was there who in your opinion did *not* like Mrs Leidner?'

'Well,' I said, 'it's only my opinion and I don't want it repeated as coming from me.'

'Naturally not.'

'But in my opinion little Mrs Mercado fairly hated her!'

'Ah! And Mr Mercado?'

'He was a bit soft on her,' I said. 'I shouldn't think women, apart from his wife, had ever taken much notice of him. And Mrs Leidner had a nice kind way of being interested in people and the things they told her. It rather went to the poor man's head, I fancy.'

'And Mrs Mercado—she was not pleased?'

'She was just plain jealous—that's the truth of it. You've got to be very careful when there's a husband and wife about, and that's a fact. I could tell you some surprising things. You've no idea the extraordinary things women get into their heads when it's a question of their husbands.'

'I do not doubt the truth of what you say. So Mrs Mercado was jealous? And she hated Mrs Leidner?'

146

'I've seen her look at her as though she'd have liked to kill her—oh, gracious!' I pulled myself up. 'Indeed, M. Poirot, I didn't mean to say—I mean, that is, not for one moment—'

'No, no. I quite understand. The phrase slipped out. A very convenient one. And Mrs Leidner, was she worried by this animosity of Mrs Mercado's?'

'Well,' I said, reflecting, 'I don't really think she was worried at all. In fact, I don't even know whether she noticed it. I thought once of just giving her a hint—but I didn't like to. Least said soonest mended. That's what I say.'

'You are doubtless wise. Can you give me any instances of how Mrs Mercado showed her feelings?'

I told him about our conversation on the roof.

'So she mentioned Mrs Leidner's first marriage,' said Poirot thoughtfully. 'Can you remember—in mentioning it—did she look at you as though she wondered whether you had heard a different version?'

'You think she may have known the truth about it?'

'It is a possibility. She may have written those letters—and engineered a tapping hand and all the rest of it.'

'I wondered something of the same kind myself. It seemed the kind of petty revengeful thing she might do.'

'Yes. A cruel streak, I should say. But hardly the temperament for cold-blooded, brutal murder unless, of course—'

He paused and then said: 'It is odd, that curious thing she said to you. "*I know why you are here.*" What did she mean by it?'

'I can't imagine,' I said frankly.

'She thought you were there for some ulterior reason apart from the declared one. What reason? And why should she be so concerned in the matter. Odd, too, the way you tell me she stared at you all through tea the day you arrived.'

'Well, she's not a lady, M. Poirot,' I said primly.

'That, *ma soeur*, is an excuse but not an explanation.'

I wasn't quite sure for the minute what he meant. But he went on quickly.

'And the other members of the staff?'

I considered.

'I don't think Miss Johnson liked Mrs Leidner either very much. But she was quite open and above-board about it. She as good as admitted she was prejudiced. You see, she's very devoted to Dr Leidner and had worked with him for years. And of course, marriage does change things—there's no denying it.'

'Yes,' said Poirot. 'And from Miss Johnson's point of view it would be an unsuitable marriage. It would really have been much more suitable if Dr Leidner had married *her*.'

'It would really,' I agreed. 'But there, that's a man all over. Not one in a hundred considers suitability. And one can't really blame Dr Leidner. Miss Johnson, poor soul, isn't so much to look at. Now Mrs Leidner was really beautiful—not young, of course—but oh! I wish you'd known her. There was something about her... I remember Mr Coleman saying she was like a thingummyjig that came to lure people into marshes. That wasn't a very good way of putting it, but—oh, well—you'll laugh at me, but there *was* something about her that was—well—unearthly.'

'She could cast a spell—yes, I understand,' said Poirot.

'Then I don't think she and Mr Carey got on very well either,' I went on. 'I've an idea *he* was jealous just like Miss Johnson. He was always very stiff with her and so was she with him. You know—she passed him things and was very polite and called him Mr Carey rather formally. He was an old friend of her husband's of course, and some women can't stand their husband's old friends. They don't like to think that anyone knew them before they did—at least that's rather a muddled way of putting it—'

'I quite understand. And the three young men? Coleman, you say, was inclined to be poetic about her.'

I couldn't help laughing.

'It was funny, M. Poirot,' I said. 'He's such a matter-of-fact young man.'

'And the other two?'

'I don't really know about Mr Emmott. He's always so quiet and never says much. She was very nice to him always. You know—friendly—called him David and used to tease him about Miss Reilly and things like that.'

'Ah, really? And did he enjoy that?'

'I don't quite know,' I said doubtfully. 'He'd just look at her. Rather funnily. You couldn't tell what he was thinking.'

'And Mr Reiter?'

'She wasn't always very kind to him,' I said slowly. 'I think he got on her nerves. She used to say quite sarcastic things to him.'

'And did he mind?'

Agatha Christie

'He used to get very pink, poor boy. Of course, she didn't *mean* to be unkind.'

And then suddenly, from feeling a little sorry for the boy, it came over me that he was very likely a cold-blooded murderer and had been playing a part all the time.

'Oh, M. Poirot,' I exclaimed. 'What do you think *really* happened?'

He shook his head slowly and thoughtfully.

'Tell me,' he said. 'You are not afraid to go back there tonight?'

'Oh *no*,' I said. 'Of course, I remember what you said, but who would want to murder *me*?'

'I do not think that anyone could,' he said slowly. 'That is partly why I have been so anxious to hear all you could tell me. No, I think—I am sure—you are quite safe.'

'If anyone had told me in Baghdad—' I began and stopped.

'Did you hear any gossip about the Leidners and the expedition before you came here?' he asked.

I told him about Mrs Leidner's nickname and just a little of what Mrs Kelsey had said about her.

In the middle of it the door opened and Miss Reilly came in. She had been playing tennis and had her racquet in her hand.

I gathered Poirot had already met her when he arrived in Hassanieh.

She said how-do-you-do to me in her usual off-hand manner and picked up a sandwich.

'Well, M. Poirot,' she said. 'How are you getting on with our local mystery?'

Murder in Mesopotamia

'Not very fast, mademoiselle.'

'I see you've rescued nurse from the wreck.'

'Nurse Leatheran has been giving me valuable information about the various members of the expedition. Incidentally I have learnt a good deal—about the victim. And the victim, mademoiselle, is very often the clue to the mystery.'

Miss Reilly said: 'That's rather clever of you, M. Poirot. It's certainly true that if ever a woman deserved to be murdered Mrs Leidner was that woman!'

'Miss Reilly!' I cried, scandalized.

She laughed, a short, nasty laugh.

'Ah!' she said. 'I thought you hadn't been hearing quite the truth. Nurse Leatheran, I'm afraid, was quite taken in, like many other people. Do you know, M. Poirot, I rather hope that this case isn't going to be one of your successes. I'd quite like the murderer of Louise Leidner to get away with it. In fact, I wouldn't much have objected to putting her out of the way myself.'

I was simply disgusted with the girl. M. Poirot, I must say, didn't turn a hair. He just bowed and said quite pleasantly:

'I hope, then, that you have an alibi for yesterday afternoon?'

There was a moment's silence and Miss Reilly's racquet went clattering down on to the floor. She didn't bother to pick it up. Slack and untidy like all her sort! She said in a rather breathless voice: 'Oh, yes, I was playing tennis at the club. But, seriously, M. Poirot, I wonder if you know anything at all about Mrs Leidner and the kind of woman she was?'

Again he made a funny little bow and said: 'You shall inform me, mademoiselle.'

Agatha Christie

She hesitated a minute and then spoke with a callousness and lack of decency that really sickened me.

'There's a convention that one doesn't speak ill of the dead. That's stupid, I think. The truth's always the truth. On the whole it's better to keep your mouth shut about living people. You might conceivably injure them. The dead are past that. But the harm they've done lives after them sometimes. Not quite a quotation from Shakespeare but very nearly! Has nurse told you of the queer atmosphere there was at Tell Yarimjah? Has she told you how jumpy they all were? And how they all used to glare at each other like enemies? That was Louise Leidner's doing. When I was a kid out here three years ago they were the happiest, jolliest lot imaginable. Even last year they were pretty well all right. But this year there was a blight over them—and it was *her* doing. She was the kind of woman who won't let anybody else be happy! There *are* women like that and she was one of them! She wanted to break up things always. Just for fun—or for the sense of power—or perhaps just because she was made that way. And she was the kind of woman who had to get hold of every male creature within reach!'

'Miss Reilly,' I cried, 'I don't think that's true. In fact I *know* it isn't.'

She went on without taking the least notice of me.

'It wasn't enough for her to have her husband adore her. She had to make a fool of that long-legged shambling idiot of a Mercado. Then she got hold of Bill. Bill's a sensible cove, but she was getting him all mazed and bewildered. Carl

Reiter she just amused herself by tormenting. It was easy. He's a sensitive boy. And she had a jolly good go at David.

'David was better sport to her because he put up a fight. He felt her charm—but he wasn't having any. I think because he'd got sense enough to know that she didn't really care a damn. And that's why I hate her so. She's not sensual. She doesn't *want* affairs. It's just cold-blooded experiment on her part and the fun of stirring people up and setting them against each other. She dabbled in that too. She's the sort of woman who's never had a row with anyone in her life—but rows always happen where she is! She *makes* them happen. She's a kind of female Iago. She *must* have drama. But she doesn't want to be involved *herself*. She's always outside pulling strings—looking on—enjoying it. Oh, do you see *at all* what I mean?'

'I see, perhaps, more than you know, mademoiselle,' said Poirot.

I couldn't make his voice out. He didn't sound indignant. He sounded—oh, well, I can't explain it.

Sheila Reilly seemed to understand, for she flushed all over her face.

'You can think what you choose,' she said. 'But I'm right about her. She was a clever woman and she was bored and she experimented—with people—like other people experiment with chemicals. She enjoyed working on poor old Johnson's feelings and seeing her bite on the bullet and control herself like the old sport she is. She liked goading little Mercado into a white-hot frenzy. She liked flicking *me* on the raw—and she could do it too, every time! She liked

Agatha Christie

finding out things about people and holding it over them. Oh, I don't mean crude blackmail—I mean just letting them know that she *knew*—and leaving them uncertain what she meant to do about it. My God, though, that woman was an artist! There was nothing crude about *her* methods!'

'And her husband?' asked Poirot.

'She never wanted to hurt him,' said Miss Reilly slowly. 'I've never known her anything but sweet to him. I suppose she was fond of him. He's a dear—wrapped up in his own world—his digging and his theories. And he worshipped her and thought her perfection. That might have annoyed some women. It didn't annoy her. In a sense he lived in a fool's paradise—and yet it wasn't a fool's paradise because to him she was what he thought her. Though it's hard to reconcile that with—'

She stopped.

'Go on, mademoiselle,' said Poirot.

She turned suddenly on me.

'What have you said about Richard Carey?'

'About Mr Carey?' I asked, astonished.

'About her and Carey?'

'Well,' I said, 'I've mentioned that they didn't hit it off very well—'

To my surprise she broke into a fit of laughter.

'Didn't hit it off very well! You fool! He's head over ears in love with her. And it's tearing him to pieces—because he worships Leidner too. He's been his friend for years. That would be enough for her, of course. She's made it her business to come between them. But all the same I've fancied—'

'*Eh bien?*'

She was frowning, absorbed in thought.

'I've fancied that she'd gone too far for once—that she was not only biter but bit! Carey's attractive. He's as attractive as hell... She was a cold devil—but I believe she could have lost her coldness with him...'

'I think it's just scandalous what you're saying,' I cried. 'Why, they hardly spoke to each other!'

'Oh, didn't they?' She turned on me. 'A hell of a lot you know about it. It was "Mr Carey" and "Mrs Leidner" in the house, but they used to meet outside. She'd walk down the path to the river. And he'd leave the dig for an hour at a time. They used to meet among the fruit trees.

'I saw him once just leaving her, striding back to the dig, and she was standing looking after him. I was a female cad, I suppose. I had some glasses with me and I took them out and had a good look at her face. If you ask me, I believe she cared like hell for Richard Carey...'

She broke off and looked at Poirot.

'Excuse my butting in on your case,' she said with a sudden rather twisted grin, 'but I thought you'd like to have the local colour correct.'

And she marched out of the room.

'M. Poirot,' I cried. 'I don't believe one word of it all!'

He looked at me and he smiled, and he said (very queerly I thought): 'You can't deny, nurse, that Miss Reilly has shed a certain—illumination on the case.'

CHAPTER 19

A New Suspicion

We couldn't say any more just then because Dr Reilly came in, saying jokingly that he'd killed off the most tiresome of his patients.

He and M. Poirot settled down to a more or less medical discussion of the psychology and mental state of an anonymous letter-writer. The doctor cited cases that he had known professionally, and M. Poirot told various stories from his own experience.

'It is not so simple as it seems,' he ended. 'There is the desire for power and very often a strong inferiority complex.'

Dr Reilly nodded.

'That's why you often find that the author of anonymous letters is the last person in the place to be suspected. Some quiet inoffensive little soul who apparently can't say Bo to a goose—all sweetness and Christian meekness on the outside—and seething with all the fury of hell underneath!'

Poirot said thoughtfully: 'Should you say Mrs Leidner had any tendency to an inferiority complex?'

Dr Reilly scraped out his pipe with a chuckle.

'Last woman on earth I'd describe that way. No repressions about her. Life, life and more life—that's what she wanted—and got, too!'

'Do you consider it a possibility, psychologically speaking, that she wrote those letters?'

'Yes, I do. But if she did, the reason arose out of her instinct to dramatize herself. Mrs Leidner was a bit of a film star in private life! She *had* to be the centre of things—in the limelight. By the law of opposites she married Leidner, who's about the most retiring and modest man I know. He adored her—but adoration by the fireside wasn't enough for her. She had to be the persecuted heroine as well.'

'In fact,' said Poirot, smiling, 'you don't subscribe to his theory that she wrote them and retained no memory of her act?'

'No, I don't. I didn't turn down the idea in front of him. You can't very well say to a man who's just lost a dearly loved wife that that same wife was a shameless exhibitionist, and that she drove him nearly crazy with anxiety to satisfy her sense of the dramatic. As a matter of fact it wouldn't be safe to tell any man the truth about his wife! Funnily enough, I'd trust most women with the truth about their husbands. Women can accept the fact that a man is a rotter, a swindler, a drug-taker, a confirmed liar, and a general swine without batting an eyelash and without its impairing their affection for the brute in the least! Women are wonderful realists.'

'Frankly, Dr Reilly, what *was* your exact opinion of Mrs Leidner?'

Agatha Christie

Dr Reilly lay back in his chair and puffed slowly at his pipe.

'Frankly—it's hard to say! I didn't know her well enough. She'd got charm—any amount of it. Brains, sympathy... What else? She hadn't any of the ordinary unpleasant vices. She wasn't sensual or lazy or even particularly vain. She was, I've always thought (but I've no proofs of it), a most accomplished liar. What I don't know (and what I'd like to know) is whether she lied to herself or only to other people. I'm rather partial to liars myself. A woman who doesn't lie is a woman without imagination and without sympathy. I don't think she was really a man-hunter—she just liked the sport of bringing them down "with my bow and arrow." If you get my daughter on the subject—'

'We have had that pleasure,' said Poirot with a slight smile.

'H'm,' said Dr Reilly. 'She hasn't wasted much time! Shoved her knife into her pretty thoroughly, I should imagine! The younger generation has no sentiment towards the dead. It's a pity all young people are prigs! They condemn the "old morality" and then proceed to set up a much more hard-and-fast code of their own. If Mrs Leidner had had half a dozen affairs Sheila would probably have approved of her as "living her life fully"—or "obeying her blood instincts". What she doesn't see is that Mrs Leidner was acting true to type—*her* type. The cat *is* obeying its blood instinct when it plays with the mouse! It's made that way. Men aren't little boys to be shielded and protected. They've got to meet cat women—and faithful spaniel, yours-till-death adoring

Murder in Mesopotamia

women, and hen-pecking nagging bird women—and all the rest of it! Life's a battlefield—not a picnic! I'd like to see Sheila honest enough to come off her high horse and admit that she hated Mrs Leidner for good old thorough-going personal reasons. Sheila's about the only young girl in this place and she naturally assumes that she ought to have it all her own way with the young things in trousers. Naturally it annoys her when a woman, who in her view is middle-aged and who has already two husbands to her credit, comes along and licks her on her own ground. Sheila's a nice child, healthy and reasonably good-looking and attractive to the other sex as she should be. But Mrs Leidner was something out of the ordinary in that line. She'd got just that sort of calamitous magic that plays the deuce with things—a kind of Belle Dame sans Merci.'

I jumped in my chair. What a coincidence his saying that!

'Your daughter—I am not indiscreet—she has perhaps a *tendresse* for one of the young men out there?'

'Oh, I don't suppose so. She's had Emmott and Coleman dancing attendance on her as a matter of course. I don't know that she cares for one more than the other. There are a couple of young Air Force chaps too. I fancy all's fish that comes to her net at present. No, I think it's age daring to defeat youth that annoys her so much! She doesn't know as much of the world as I do. It's when you get to my age that you really appreciate a schoolgirl complexion and a clear eye and a firmly knit young body. But a woman over thirty can listen with rapt attention and throw in a word here and there to show the talker what a fine fellow he is—and few young men can resist that! Sheila's a pretty girl—but Louise Leidner was beautiful. Glorious eyes and that amazing golden fairness. Yes, she was a beautiful woman.'

Yes, I thought to myself, he's right. Beauty's a wonderful thing. She *had* been beautiful. It wasn't the kind of looks you were jealous of—you just sat back and admired. I felt that first day I met her that I'd do *anything* for Mrs Leidner!

All the same, that night as I was being driven back to Tell Yarimjah (Dr Reilly made me stay for an early dinner) one or two things came back to my mind and made me rather uncomfortable. At the time I hadn't believed a word of all Sheila Reilly's outpouring. I'd taken it for sheer spite and malice.

But now I suddenly remembered the way Mrs Leidner had insisted on going for a stroll by herself that afternoon and wouldn't hear of me coming with her. I couldn't help wondering if perhaps, after all, she *had* been going to meet Mr Carey... And of course, it *was* a little odd, really, the way he and she spoke to each other so formally. Most of the others she called by their Christian names.

He never seemed to look at her, I remembered. That might be because he disliked her—or it might be just the opposite...

I gave myself a little shake. Here I was fancying and imagining all sorts of things—all because of a girl's spiteful outburst! It just showed how unkind and dangerous it was to go about saying that kind of thing.

Mrs Leidner *hadn't* been like that at all...

Of course, she *hadn't* liked Sheila Reilly. She'd really been—almost catty about her that day at lunch to Mr Emmott.

Funny, the way he'd looked at her. The sort of way that you couldn't possibly tell what he was thinking. You never could tell what Mr Emmott was thinking. He was so quiet. But very nice. A nice dependable person.

Now Mr Coleman was a foolish young man if there ever was one!

I'd got to that point in my meditations when we arrived. It was just on nine o'clock and the big door was closed and barred.

Ibrahim came running with his great key to let me in.

We all went to bed early at Tell Yarimjah. There weren't any lights showing in the living-room. There was a light in the drawing-office and one in Dr Leidner's office, but nearly all the other windows were dark. Everyone must have gone to bed even earlier than usual.

As I passed the drawing-office to go to my room I looked in. Mr Carey was in his shirt sleeves working over his big plan.

Terribly ill, he looked, I thought. So strained and worn. It gave me quite a pang. I don't know what there was about Mr Carey—it wasn't what he *said* because he hardly said anything—and that of the most ordinary nature, and it wasn't what he *did*, for that didn't amount to much either—and yet you just couldn't help noticing him, and everything about him seemed to matter more than it would have about anyone else. He just *counted*, if you know what I mean.

He turned his head and saw me. He removed his pipe from his mouth and said: 'Well, nurse, back from Hassanieh?'

'Yes, Mr Carey. You're up working late. Everybody else seems to have gone to bed.'

Agatha Christie

'I thought I might as well get on with things,' he said.

'I was a bit behind-hand. And I shall be out on the dig all tomorrow. We're starting digging again.'

'Already?' I asked, shocked.

He looked at me rather queerly.

'It's the best thing, I think. I put it up to Leidner. He'll be in Hassanieh most of tomorrow seeing to things. But the rest of us will carry on here. You know it's not too easy all sitting round and looking at each other as things are.'

He was right there, of course. Especially in the nervy, jumpy state everyone was in.

'Well, of course you're right in a way,' I said. 'It takes one's mind off if one's got something to do.'

The funeral, I knew, was to be the day after tomorrow.

He had bent over his plan again. I don't know why, but my heart just ached for him. I felt certain that he wasn't going to get any sleep.

'If you'd like a sleeping draught, Mr Carey?' I said hesitatingly.

He shook his head with a smile.

'I'll carry on, nurse. Bad habit, sleeping draughts.'

'Well, good night, Mr Carey,' I said. 'If there's anything I can do—'

'Don't think so, thank you, nurse. Good night.'

'I'm terribly sorry,' I said, rather too impulsively I suppose.

'Sorry?' He looked surprised.

'For—for everybody. It's all so dreadful. But especially for you.'

'For me? Why for me?'

'Well, you're such an old friend of them both.'

'I'm an old friend of Leidner's. I wasn't a friend of hers particularly.'

He spoke as though he had actually disliked her. Really, I wished Miss Reilly could have heard him!

'Well, good night,' I said and hurried along to my room.

I fussed around a bit in my room before undressing. Washed out some handkerchiefs and a pair of wash-leather gloves and wrote up my diary. I just looked out of my door again before I really started to get ready for bed. The lights were still on in the drawing-office and in the south building.

I suppose Dr Leidner was still up and working in his office. I wondered whether I ought to go and say goodnight to him. I hesitated about it—I didn't want to seem officious. He might be busy and not want to be disturbed. In the end, however, a sort of uneasiness drove me on. After all, it couldn't do any harm. I'd just say goodnight, ask if there was anything I could do and come away.

But Dr Leidner wasn't there. The office itself was lit up but there was no one in it except Miss Johnson. She had her head down on the table and was crying as though her heart would break.

It gave me quite a turn. She was such a quiet, self-controlled woman. It was pitiful to see her.

'Whatever is it, my dear?' I cried. I put my arm round her and patted her. 'Now, now, this won't do at all... You mustn't sit here crying all by yourself.'

She didn't answer and I felt the dreadful shuddering sobs that were racking her.

Agatha Christie

'Don't, my dear, don't,' I said. 'Take a hold on yourself. I'll go and make you a cup of nice hot tea.'

She raised her head and said: 'No, no, its all right, nurse. I'm being a fool.'

'What's upset you, my dear?' I asked.

She didn't answer at once, then she said: 'It's all too awful…'

'Now don't start thinking of it,' I told her. 'What's happened has happened and can't be mended. It's no use fretting.'

She sat up straight and began to pat her hair.

'I'm making rather a fool of myself,' she said in her gruff voice. 'I've been clearing up and tidying the office. Thought it was best to *do* something. And then—it all came over me suddenly—'

'Yes, yes,' I said hastily. 'I know. A nice strong cup of tea and a hot-water bottle in your bed is what you want,' I said.

And she had them too. I didn't listen to any protests.

'Thank you, nurse,' she said when I'd settled her in bed, and she was sipping her tea and the hot-water bottle was in. 'You're a nice kind sensible woman. It's not often I make such a fool of myself.'

'Oh, anybody's liable to do that at a time like this,' I said. 'What with one thing and another. The strain and the shock and the police here, there and everywhere. Why, I'm quite jumpy myself.'

She said slowly in rather a queer voice: 'What you said in there is true. What's happened has happened and can't be mended…'

She was silent for a minute or two and then said—rather oddly, I thought: 'She was never a nice woman!'

Well, I didn't argue the point. I'd always felt it was quite natural for Miss Johnson and Mrs Leidner not to hit it off.

I wondered if, perhaps, Miss Johnson had secretly had a feeling that she was pleased Mrs Leidner was dead, and had then been ashamed of herself for the thought.

I said: 'Now you go to sleep and don't worry about anything.'

I just picked up a few things and set the room to rights. Stockings over the back of the chair and coat and skirt on a hanger. There was a little ball of crumpled paper on the floor where it must have fallen out of a pocket.

I was just smoothing it out to see whether I could safely throw it away when she quite startled me.

'Give that to me!'

I did so—rather taken aback. She'd called out so peremptorily. She snatched it from me—fairly snatched it—and then held it in the candle flame till it was burnt to ashes.

As I say, I was startled—and I just stared at her.

I hadn't had time to see what the paper was—she'd snatched it so quick. But funnily enough, as it burned it curled over towards me and I just saw that there were words written in ink on the paper.

It wasn't till I was getting into bed that I realized why they'd looked sort of familiar to me.

It was the same handwriting as that of the anonymous letters.

Was *that* why Miss Johnson had given way to a fit of remorse? Had it been her all along who had written those anonymous letters?

CHAPTER 20

Miss Johnson, Mrs Mercado, Mr Reiter

I don't mind confessing that the idea came as a complete shock to me. I'd never thought of associating *Miss Johnson* with the letters. Mrs Mercado, perhaps. But Miss Johnson was a real lady, and so self-controlled and sensible.

But I reflected, remembering the conversation I had listened to that evening between M. Poirot and Dr Reilly, that that might be just *why*.

If it were Miss Johnson who had written the letters it explained a lot. Mind you, I didn't think for a minute Miss Johnson had had anything to do with the murder. But I *did* see that her dislike of Mrs Leidner might have made her succumb to the temptation of, well—putting the wind up her—to put it vulgarly.

She might have hoped to frighten away Mrs Leidner from the dig.

But then Mrs Leidner had been murdered and Miss Johnson had felt terrible pangs of remorse—first for her cruel trick and also, perhaps, because she realized that those letters were acting as a very good shield to the actual murderer. No wonder she had broken down so utterly. She was, I was sure, a decent soul at heart. And it explained, too, why she had caught so eagerly at my consolation of 'what's happened's happened and can't be mended.'

And then her cryptic remark—her vindication of herself—'she was never a nice woman!'

The question was, what was *I* to do about it?

I tossed and turned for a good while and in the end decided I'd let M. Poirot know about it at the first opportunity.

He came out next day, but I didn't get a chance of speaking to him what you might call privately.

We had just a minute alone together and before I could collect myself to know how to begin, he had come close to me and was whispering instructions in my ear.

'Me, I shall talk to Miss Johnson—and others, perhaps, in the living-room. You have the key of Mrs Leidner's room still?'

'Yes,' I said.

'*Très bien*. Go there, shut the door behind you and give a cry—not a scream—a cry. You understand what I mean—it is alarm—surprise that I want you to express —not mad terror. As for the excuse if you are heard—I leave that to you—the stepped toe or what you will.'

At that moment Miss Johnson came out into the court-yard and there was no time for more.

I understood well enough what M. Poirot was after. As soon as he and Miss Johnson had gone into the living-room

Agatha Christie

I went across to Mrs Leidner's room and, unlocking the door, went in and pulled the door to behind me.

I can't say I didn't feel a bit of a fool standing up in an empty room and giving a yelp all for nothing at all. Besides, it wasn't so easy to know just how loud to do it. I gave a pretty loud 'Oh' and then tried it a bit higher and a bit lower.

Then I came out again and prepared my excuse of a stepped (stubbed I *suppose* he meant!) toe.

But it soon appeared that no excuse would be needed. Poirot and Miss Johnson were talking together earnestly and there had clearly been no interruption.

'Well,' I thought, 'that settles that. Either Miss Johnson imagined that cry she heard or else it was something quite different.'

I didn't like to go in and interrupt them. There was a deck-chair on the porch so I sat down there. Their voices floated out to me.

'The position is delicate, you understand,' Poirot was saying. 'Dr Leidner—obviously he adored his wife—'

'He worshipped her,' said Miss Johnson.

'He tells me, naturally, how fond all his staff was of her! As for them, what can they say? Naturally they say the same thing. It is politeness. It is decency. It *may* also be the truth! But also it may *not*! And I am convinced, mademoiselle, that the key to this enigma lies in a complete understanding of Mrs Leidner's character. If I could get the opinion—the honest opinion—of every member of the staff, I might, from the whole, build up a picture. Frankly, that is why I am here today. I knew Dr Leidner would be in Hassanieh. That makes it easy for me to have an interview with each of you here in turn, and beg your help.'

'That's all very well,' began Miss Johnson and stopped.

'Do not make me the British *clichés*,' Poirot begged. 'Do not say it is not the cricket or the football, that to speak anything but well of the dead is not done—that—*enfin*—there is loyalty! Loyalty it is a pestilential thing in crime. Again and again it obscures the truth.'

'I've no particular loyalty to Mrs Leidner,' said Miss Johnson dryly. There was indeed a sharp and acid tone in her voice. 'Dr Leidner's a different matter. And, after all, she was his wife.'

'Precisely—precisely. I understand that you would not wish to speak against your chief's wife. But this is not a question of a testimonial. It is a question of sudden and mysterious death. If I am to believe that it is a martyred angel who has been killed it does not add to the easiness of my task.'

'I certainly shouldn't call her an angel,' said Miss Johnson and the acid tone was even more in evidence.

'Tell me your opinion, frankly, of Mrs Leidner—as a woman.'

'H'm! To begin with, M. Poirot, I'll give you this warning. I'm prejudiced. I am—we all were—devoted to Dr Leidner. And, I suppose, when Mrs Leidner came along, we were jealous. We resented the demands she made on his time and attention. The devotion he showed her irritated us. I'm being truthful, M. Poirot, and it isn't very pleasant for me.

Agatha Christie

I resented her presence here—yes, I did, though, of course, I tried never to show it. It made a difference to us, you see.'

'Us? You say us?'

'I mean Mr Carey and myself. We're the two old-timers, you see. And we didn't much care for the new order of things. I suppose that's natural, though perhaps it was rather petty of us. But it *did* make a difference.'

'What kind of a difference?'

'Oh! to everything. We used to have such a happy time. A good deal of fun, you know, and rather silly jokes, like people do who work together. Dr Leidner was quite light-hearted—just like a boy.'

'And when Mrs Leidner came she changed all that?'

'Well, I suppose it wasn't her *fault*. It wasn't so bad last year. And please believe, M. Poirot, that it wasn't anything she *did*. She's always been charming to me—quite charming. That's why I've felt ashamed sometimes. It wasn't her fault that little things she said and did seemed to rub me up the wrong way. Really, nobody could be nicer than she was.'

'But nevertheless things were changed this season? There was a different atmosphere.'

'Oh, entirely. Really. I don't know what it was. Everything seemed to go wrong—not with the work—I mean with us—our tempers and our nerves. All on edge. Almost the sort of feeling you get when there is a thunderstorm coming.'

'And you put that down to Mrs Leidner's influence?'

'Well, it was never like that before she came,' said Miss Johnson dryly. 'Oh! I'm a cross-grained, complaining old dog. Conservative—liking things always the same. You really mustn't take any notice of me, M. Poirot.'

'How would you describe to me Mrs Leidner's character and temperament?'

Miss Johnson hesitated for a moment. Then she said slowly: 'Well, of course, she was temperamental. A lot of ups and downs. Nice to people one day and perhaps wouldn't speak to them the next. She was very kind, I think. And very thoughtful for others. All the same you could see she had been thoroughly spoilt all her life. She took Dr Leidner's waiting on her hand and foot as perfectly natural. And I don't think she ever really appreciated what a very remarkable—what a really great—man she had married. That used to annoy me sometimes. And of course she was terribly highly strung and nervous. The things she used to imagine and the states she used to get into! I was thankful when Dr Leidner brought Nurse Leatheran here. It was too much for him having to cope both with his work and with his wife's fears.'

'What is your own opinion of these anonymous letters she received?'

I had to do it. I leaned forward in my chair till I could just catch sight of Miss Johnson's profile turned to Poirot in answer to his question.

She was looking perfectly cool and collected.

'I think someone in America had a spite against her and was trying to frighten or annoy her.'

'*Pas plus sérieux que ça?*'

'That's my opinion. She was a very handsome woman, you know, and might easily have had enemies. I think, those

Agatha Christie

letters were written by some spiteful woman. Mrs Leidner being of a nervous temperament took them seriously.'

'She certainly did that,' said Poirot. 'But remember—the last of them arrived by hand.'

'Well, I suppose that *could* have been managed if anyone had given their minds to it. Women will take a lot of trouble to gratify their spite, M. Poirot.'

They will indeed, I thought to myself!

'Perhaps you are right, mademoiselle. As you say, Mrs Leidner was handsome. By the way, you know Miss Reilly, the doctor's daughter?'

'Sheila Reilly? Yes, of course.'

Poirot adopted a very confidential, gossipy tone.

'I have heard a rumour (naturally I do not like to ask the doctor) that there was a *tendresse* between her and one of the members of Dr Leidner's staff. Is that so, do you know?'

Miss Johnson appeared rather amused.

'Oh, young Coleman and David Emmott were both inclined to dance attendance. I believe there was some rivalry as to who was to be her partner in some event at the club. Both the boys went in on Saturday evenings to the club as a general rule. But I don't know that there was anything in it on her side. She's the only young creature in the place, you know, and so she's by way of being the belle of it. She's got the Air Force dancing attendance on her as well.'

'So you think there is nothing in it?'

'Well—I don't know.' Miss Johnson became thoughtful. 'It is true that she comes out this way fairly often. Up to the dig and all that. In fact, Mrs Leidner was chaffing

David Emmott about it the other day—saying the girl was running after him. Which was rather a catty thing to say, I thought, and I don't think he liked it... Yes, she was here a good deal. I saw her riding towards the dig on that awful afternoon.' She nodded her head towards the open window. 'But neither David Emmott nor Coleman were on duty that afternoon. Richard Carey was in charge. Yes, perhaps she *is* attracted to one of the boys—but she's such a modern unsentimental young woman that one doesn't know quite how seriously to take her. I'm sure I don't know which of them it is. Bill's a nice boy, and not nearly such a fool as he pretends to be. David Emmott is a dear—and there's a lot to him. He is the deep, quiet kind.'

Then she looked quizzically at Poirot and said: 'But has this any bearing on the crime, M. Poirot?'

M. Poirot threw up his hands in a very French fashion.

'You make me blush, mademoiselle,' he said. 'You expose me as a mere gossip. But what will you, I am interested always in the love affairs of young people.'

'Yes,' said Miss Johnson with a little sigh. 'It's nice when the course of true love runs smooth.'

Poirot gave an answering sigh. I wondered if Miss Johnson was thinking of some love affair of her own when she was a girl. And I wondered if M. Poirot had a wife, and if he went on in the way you always hear foreigners do, with mistresses and things like that. He looks so comic I couldn't imagine it.

'Sheila Reilly has a lot of character,' said Miss Johnson. 'She's young and she's crude, but she's the right sort.'

'I take your word for it, mademoiselle,' said Poirot.

He got up and said, 'Are there any other members of the staff in the house?'

'Marie Mercado is somewhere about. All the men are up on the dig today. I think they wanted to get out of the house. I don't blame them. If you'd like to go up to the dig—'

She came out on the verandah and said, smiling to me: 'Nurse Leatheran won't mind taking you, I dare say.'

'Oh, certainly, Miss Johnson,' I said.

'And you'll come back to lunch, won't you, M. Poirot?'

'Enchanted, mademoiselle.'

Miss Johnson went back into the living-room where she was engaged in cataloguing.

'Mrs Mercado's on the roof,' I said. 'Do you want to see her first?'

'It would be as well, I think. Let us go up.'

As we went up the stairs I said: 'I did what you told me. Did you hear anything?'

'Not a sound.'

'That will be a weight off Miss Johnson's mind at any rate,' I said. 'She's been worrying that she might have done something about it.'

Mrs Mercado was sitting on the parapet, her head bent down, and she was so deep in thought that she never heard us till Poirot halted opposite her and bade her good morning.

Then she looked up with a start.

She looked ill this morning, I thought, her small face pinched and wizened and great dark circles under her eyes.

'*Encore moi*,' said Poirot. 'I come today with a special object.'

And he went on much in the same way as he had done to Miss Johnson, explaining how necessary it was that he should get a true picture of Mrs Leidner.

Mrs Mercado, however, wasn't as honest as Miss Johnson had been. She burst into fulsome praise which, I was pretty sure, was quite far removed from her real feelings.

'Dear, *dear* Louise! It's so hard to explain her to someone who didn't know her. She was such an *exotic* creature. Quite different from anyone else. You felt that, I'm sure, nurse? A martyr to nerves, of course, and full of fancies, but one put up with things in her one wouldn't from anyone else. And she was so *sweet* to us all, wasn't she, nurse? And so *humble* about herself—I mean she didn't know anything about archaeology, and she was so eager to learn. Always asking my husband about the chemical processes for treating the metal objects and helping Miss Johnson to mend pottery. Oh, we were all *devoted* to her.'

'Then it is not true, madame, what I have heard, that there was a certain tenseness—an uncomfortable atmosphere—here?'

Mrs Mercado opened her opaque black eyes very wide.

'Oh! who *can* have been telling you that? Nurse? Dr Leidner? I'm sure *he* would never notice anything, poor man.'

And she shot a thoroughly unfriendly glance at me.

Poirot smiled easily.

'I have my spies, madame,' he declared gaily. And just for a minute I saw her eyelids quiver and blink.

'Don't you think,' asked Mrs Mercado with an air of great sweetness, 'that after an event of this kind, everyone always pretends a lot of things that never were? You know—tension, atmosphere, a "feeling that something was going to happen"? I think people just *make up* these things afterwards.'

'There is a lot in what you say, madame,' said Poirot.

'And it really *wasn't* true! We were a thoroughly happy family here.'

'That woman is one of the most utter liars I've ever known,' I said indignantly, when M. Poirot and I were clear of the house and walking along the path to the dig. 'I'm sure she simply hated Mrs Leidner really!'

'She is hardly the type to whom one would go for the truth,' Poirot agreed.

'Waste of time talking to her,' I snapped.

'Hardly that—hardly that. If a person tells you lies with her lips she is sometimes telling you truth with her eyes. What is she afraid of, little Madame Mercado? I saw fear in her eyes. Yes—decidedly she is afraid of something. It is very interesting.'

'I've got something to tell you, M. Poirot,' I said.

Then I told him all about my return the night before and my strong belief that Miss Johnson was the writer of the anonymous letters.

'So *she's* a liar too!' I said. 'The cool way she answered you this morning about these same letters!'

'Yes,' said Poirot. 'It was interesting, that. *For she let out the fact she knew all about those letters*. So far they have not been spoken of in the presence of the staff. Of course, it is quite possible that Dr Leidner told her about them yesterday. They are old friends, he and she. But if he did not—well—then it is curious and interesting, is it not?'

My respect for him went up. It was clever the way he had tricked her into mentioning the letters.

'Are you going to tackle her about them?' I asked.

M. Poirot seemed quite shocked by the idea.

'No, no, indeed. Always it is unwise to parade one's knowledge. Until the last minute I keep everything here,' he tapped his forehead. 'At the right moment—I make the spring—like the panther—and, *mon Dieu!* the consternation!'

I couldn't help laughing to myself at little M. Poirot in the role of a panther.

We had just reached the dig. The first person we saw was Mr Reiter, who was busy photographing some walling.

It's my opinion that the men who were digging just hacked out walls wherever they wanted them. That's what it looked like anyway. Mr Carey explained to me that you could feel the difference at once with a pick, and he tried to show me—but I never saw. When the man said '*Libn*'—mud-brick—it was just ordinary dirt and mud as far as I could see.

Mr Reiter finished his photographs and handed over the camera and the plates to his boy and told him to take them back to the house.

Poirot asked him one or two questions about exposures and film packs and so on which he answered very readily. He seemed pleased to be asked about his work.

He was just tendering his excuses for leaving us when Poirot plunged once more into his set speech. As a matter of fact it wasn't quite a set speech because he varied it a little

Agatha Christie

each time to suit the person he was talking to. But I'm not going to write it all down every time. With sensible people like Miss Johnson he went straight to the point, and with some of the others he had to beat about the bush a bit more. But it came to the same in the end.

'Yes, yes, I see what you mean,' said Mr Reiter. 'But indeed, I do not see that I can be much help to you. I am new here this season and I did not speak much with Mrs Leidner. I regret, but indeed I can tell you nothing.'

There was something a little stiff and foreign in the way he spoke, though, of course, he hadn't got any accent—except an American one, I mean.

'You can at least tell me whether you liked or disliked her?' said Poirot with a smile.

Mr Reiter got quite red and stammered: 'She was a charming person—most charming. And intellectual. She had a very fine brain—yes.'

'*Bien!* You liked her. And she liked you?'

Mr Reiter got redder still.

'Oh, I—I don't know that she noticed me much. And I was unfortunate once or twice. I was always unlucky when I tried to do anything for her. I'm afraid I annoyed her by my clumsiness. It was quite unintentional... I would have done *any*thing—'

Poirot took pity on his flounderings.

'Perfectly—perfectly. Let us pass to another matter. Was it a happy atmosphere in the house?'

'Please?'

'Were you all happy together? Did you laugh and talk?'

'No—no, not exactly that. There was a little—stiffness.'

He paused, struggling with himself, and then said: 'You see, I am not very good in company. I am clumsy. I am shy. Dr Leidner always he has been most kind to me. But—it is stupid—I cannot overcome my shyness. I say always the wrong thing. I upset water jugs. I am unlucky.'

He really looked like a large awkward child.

'We all do these things when we are young,' said Poirot, smiling. 'The poise, the *savoir faire*, it comes later.'

Then with a word of farewell we walked on.

He said: 'That, *ma soeur*, is either an extremely simple young man or a very remarkable actor.'

I didn't answer. I was caught up once more by the fantastic notion that one of these people was a dangerous and cold-blooded murderer. Somehow, on this beautiful still sunny morning it seemed impossible.

CHAPTER 21

Mr Mercado, Richard Carey

'They work in two separate places, I see,' said Poirot, halting.

Mr Reiter had been doing his photography on an outlying portion of the main excavation. A little distance away from us a second swarm of men were coming and going with baskets.

'That's what they call the deep cut,' I explained. 'They don't find much there, nothing but rubbishy broken pottery, but Dr Leidner always says it's very interesting, so I suppose it must be.'

'Let us go there.'

We walked together slowly, for the sun was hot.

Mr Mercado was in command. We saw him below us talking to the foreman, an old man like a tortoise who wore a tweed coat over his long striped cotton gown.

It was a little difficult to get down to them as there was only a narrow path or stair and basket-boys were going up and down it constantly, and they always seemed to be as blind as bats and never to think of getting out of the way.

As I followed Poirot down he said suddenly over his shoulder: 'Is Mr Mercado right-handed or left-handed?'

Now that was an extraordinary question if you like!

I thought a minute, then: 'Right-handed,' I said decisively.

Poirot didn't condescend to explain. He just went on and I followed him.

Mr Mercado seemed rather pleased to see us.

His long melancholy face lit up.

M. Poirot pretended to an interest in archaeology that I'm sure he couldn't have really felt, but Mr Mercado responded at once.

He explained that they had already cut down through twelve levels of house occupation.

'We are now definitely in the fourth millennium,' he said with enthusiasm.

I always thought a millennium was in the future—the time when everything comes right.

Mr Mercado pointed out belts of ashes (how his hand did shake! I wondered if he might possibly have malaria) and he explained how the pottery changed in character, and about burials—and how they had had one level almost entirely composed of infant burials —poor little things—and about flexed position and orientation, which seemed to mean the way the bones were lying.

And then suddenly, just as he was stooping down to pick up a kind of flint knife that was lying with some pots in a corner, he leapt into the air with a wild yell.

He spun round to find me and Poirot staring at him in astonishment.

He clapped his hand to his left arm.

'Something stung me—like a red-hot needle.'

Immediately Poirot was galvanized into energy.

'Quick, *mon cher*, let us see. Nurse Leatheran!'

I came forward.

He seized Mr Mercado's arm and deftly rolled back the sleeve of his khaki shirt to the shoulder.

'There,' said Mr Mercado pointing.

About three inches below the shoulder there was a minute prick from which the blood was oozing.

'Curious,' said Poirot. He peered into the rolled-up sleeve. 'I can see nothing. It was an ant, perhaps?'

'Better put on a little iodine,' I said.

I always carry an iodine pencil with me, and I whipped it out and applied it. But I was a little absentminded as I did so, for my attention had been caught by something quite different. Mr Mercado's arm, all the way up the forearm to the elbow, was marked all over by tiny punctures. I knew well enough what *they were—the marks of a hypodermic needle*.

Mr Mercado rolled down his sleeve again and recommenced his explanations. Mr Poirot listened, but didn't try to bring the conversation round to the Leidners. In fact, he didn't ask Mr Mercado anything at all.

Presently we said goodbye to Mr Mercado and climbed up the path again.

'It was neat that, did you not think so?' my companion asked.

'Neat?' I asked.

M. Poirot took something from behind the lapel of his coat and surveyed it affectionately. To my surprise I saw that it was a long sharp darning needle with a blob of sealing wax making it into a pin.

'M. Poirot,' I cried, 'did *you* do that?'

'I was the stinging insect—yes. And very neatly I did it, too, do you not think so? You did not see me.'

That was true enough. *I* never saw him do it. And I'm sure Mr Mercado hadn't suspected. He must have been quick as lightning.

'But, M. Poirot, why?' I asked.

He answered me by another question.

'Did you notice anything, sister?' he asked.

I nodded my head slowly.

'Hypodermic marks,' I said.

'So now we know something about Mr Mercado,' said Poirot. 'I suspected—but I did not *know*. It is always necessary to *know*.'

'And you don't care how you set about it!' I thought, but didn't say.

Poirot suddenly clapped his hand to his pocket.

'Alas, I have dropped my handkerchief down there. I concealed the pin in it.'

'I'll get it for you,' I said and hurried back.

I'd got the feeling, you see, by this time, that M. Poirot and I were the doctor and nurse in charge of a case. At least, it was more like an operation and he was the surgeon. Perhaps I oughtn't to say so, but in a queer way I was beginning to enjoy myself.

Agatha Christie

I remember just after I'd finished my training, I went to a case in a private house and the need for an immediate operation arose, and the patient's husband was cranky about nursing homes. He just wouldn't hear of his wife being taken to one. Said it had to be done in the house.

Well, of course it was just splendid for me! Nobody else to have a look in! I was in charge of everything. Of course, I was terribly nervous—I thought of everything conceivable that doctor could want, but even then I was afraid I might have forgotten something. You never know with doctors. They ask for absolutely anything sometimes! But everything went splendidly! I had each thing ready as he asked for it, and he actually told me I'd done first-rate after it was over—and that's a thing most doctors wouldn't bother to do! The G.P. was very nice too. And I ran the whole thing myself!

The patient recovered, too, so everybody was happy.

Well, I felt rather the same now. In a way M. Poirot reminded me of that surgeon. *He* was a little man, too. Ugly little man with a face like a monkey, but a wonderful surgeon. He knew instinctively just where to go. I've seen a lot of surgeons and I know what a lot of difference there is.

Gradually I'd been growing a kind of confidence M. Poirot. I felt that he, too, knew exactly what he was doing. And I was getting to feel that it was my job to help him—as you might say—to have the forceps and the swabs and all handy just when he wanted them. That's why it seemed just as natural for me to run off and look for his handkerchief as it would have been to pick up a towel that a doctor had thrown on the floor.

When I'd found it and got back I couldn't see him at first. But at last I caught sight of him. He was sitting a little way from the mound talking to Mr Carey. Mr Carey's boy was standing near with that great big rod thing with metres marked on it, but just at that moment he said something to the boy and the boy took it away. It seemed he had finished with it for the time being.

I'd like to get this next bit quite clear. You see, I wasn't quite sure what M. Poirot did or didn't want me to do. He might, I mean, have sent me back for that handkerchief *on purpose*. To get me out of the way.

It was just like an operation over again. You've got to be careful to hand the doctor just what he wants and not what he *doesn't* want. I mean, suppose you gave him the artery forceps at the wrong moment, and were late with them at the right moment! Thank goodness I know my work in the theatre well enough. I'm not likely to make mistakes there. But in this business I was really the rawest of raw little probationers. And so I had to be particularly careful not to make any silly mistakes.

Of course, I didn't for one moment imagine that M. Poirot didn't want me to hear what he and Mr Carey were saying. But he might have thought he'd get Mr Carey to talk better if I wasn't there.

Now I don't want anybody to get it in to their heads that I'm the kind of woman who goes about eavesdropping on private conversations. I wouldn't do such a thing. Not for a moment. Not however much I wanted to.

And what I mean is if it *had* been a private conversation I wouldn't for a moment have done what, as a matter of fact, I actually did do.

As I looked at it I was in a privileged position. After all, you hear many a thing when a patient's coming round after an anaesthetic. The patient wouldn't want you to hear it—and usually has no idea you *have* heard it—but the fact remains you *do* hear it. I just took it that Mr Carey was the patient. He'd be none the worse for what he didn't know about. And if you think that I was just curious, well, I'll admit that I *was* curious. I didn't want to miss anything I could help.

All this is just leading up to the fact that I turned aside and went by a round about way up behind the big dump until I was a foot from where they were, but concealed from them by the corner of the dump. And if anyone says it was dishonourable I just beg to disagree. *Nothing* ought to be hidden from the nurse in charge of the case, though, of course, it's for the doctor to say what shall be *done*.

I don't know, of course, what M. Poirot's line of approach had been, but by the time I'd got there he was aiming straight for the bull's eye, so to speak.

'Nobody appreciates Dr Leidner's devotion to his wife more than I do,' he was saying. 'But it is often the case that one learns more about a person from their enemies than from their friends.'

'You suggest that their faults are more important than their virtues?' said Mr Carey. His tone was dry and ironic.

'Undoubtedly—when it comes to murder. It seems odd that as far as I know nobody has yet been murdered for having too perfect a character! And yet perfection is undoubtedly an irritating thing.'

'I'm afraid I'm hardly the right person to help you,' said Mr Carey. 'To be perfectly honest, Mrs Leidner and I didn't hit it off particularly well. I don't mean that we were in any sense of the word enemies, but we were not exactly friends. Mrs Leidner was, perhaps, a shade jealous of my old friendship with her husband. I, for my part, although I admired her very much and thought she was an extremely attractive woman, was just a shade resentful of her influence over Leidner. As a result we were quite polite to each other, but not intimate.'

'Admirably explained,' said Poirot.

I could just see their heads, and I saw Mr Carey's turn sharply as though something in M. Poirot's detached tone struck him disagreeably.

M. Poirot went on: 'Was not Dr Leidner distressed that you and his wife did not get on together better?'

Carey hesitated a minute before saying: 'Really—I'm not sure. He never said anything. I always hoped he didn't notice it. He was very wrapped up in his work, you know.'

'So the truth, according to you, is that you did not really like Mrs Leidner?'

Carey shrugged his shoulders.

'I should probably have liked her very much if she hadn't been Leidner's wife.'

He laughed as though amused by his own statement.

Agatha Christie

Poirot was arranging a little heap of broken potsherds. He said in a dreamy, far-away voice: 'I talked to Miss Johnson this morning. She admitted that she was prejudiced against Mrs Leidner and did not like her very much, although she hastened to add that Mrs Leidner had always been charming to her.'

'All quite true, I should say,' said Carey.

'So I believed. Then I had a conversation with Mrs Mercado. She told me at great length how devoted she had been to Mrs Leidner and how much she had admired her.'

Carey made no answer to this, and after waiting a minute or two Poirot went on: 'That—I did not believe! Then I come to you and that which you tell me—well, again—*I do not believe...*'

Carey stiffened. I could hear the anger—repressed anger—in his voice.

'I really cannot help your beliefs—or your disbeliefs, M. Poirot. You've heard the truth and you can take it or leave it as far as I am concerned.'

Poirot did not grow angry. Instead he sounded particularly meek and depressed.

'Is it my fault what I do—or do not believe? I have a sensitive ear, you know. And then—there are always plenty of stories going about—rumours floating in the air. One listens—and perhaps—one learns something! Yes, there *are* stories...'

Carey sprang to his feet. I could see clearly a little pulse that beat in his temple. He looked simply splendid! So lean and so brown—and that wonderful jaw, hard and square. I don't wonder women fell for that man.

'What stories?' he asked savagely.

Poirot looked sideways at him.

'Perhaps you can guess. The usual sort of story—about you and Mrs Leidner.'

'What foul minds people have!'

'*N'est-ce pas?* They are like dogs. However deep you bury an unpleasantness a dog will always root it up again.'

'And you believe these stories?'

'I am willing to be convinced—of the truth,' said Poirot gravely.

'I doubt if you'd know the truth if you heard it,' Carey laughed rudely.

'Try me and see,' said Poirot, watching him.

'I will then! You shall have the truth! I hated Louise Leidner—there's the truth for you! I hated her like hell!'

CHAPTER 22

David Emmott, Father Lavigny and a Discovery

Turning abruptly away, Carey strode off with long, angry strides.

Poirot sat looking after him and presently he murmured: 'Yes—I see...'

Without turning his head he said in a slightly louder voice: 'Do not come round the corner for a minute, nurse. In case he turns his head. Now it is all right. You have my handkerchief? Many thanks. You are most amiable.'

He didn't say anything at all about my having been listening—and how he knew I *was* listening I can't think. He'd never once looked in that direction. I was rather relieved he didn't say anything. I mean, I felt all right with *myself* about it, but it might have been a little awkward explaining to him. So it was a good thing he didn't seem to want explanations.

'Do you think he did hate her, M. Poirot?' I asked.

Nodding his head slowly with a curious expression on his face, Poirot answered.

'Yes—I think he did.'

Then he got up briskly and began to walk to where the men were working on the top of the mound. I followed him. We couldn't see anyone but Arabs at first, but we finally found Mr Emmott lying face downwards blowing dust off a skeleton that had just been uncovered.

He gave his pleasant, grave smile when he saw us.

'Have you come to see round?' he asked. 'I'll be free in a minute.'

He sat up, took his knife and began daintily cutting the earth away from round the bones, stopping every now and then to use either a bellows or his own breath. A very insanitary proceeding the latter, I thought.

'You'll get all sorts of nasty germs in your mouth, Mr Emmott,' I protested.

'Nasty germs are my daily diet, nurse,' he said gravely. 'Germs can't do anything to an archaeologist—they just get naturally discouraged trying.'

He scraped a little more away round the thigh bone. Then he spoke to the foreman at his side, directing him exactly what he wanted done.

'There,' he said, rising to his feet. 'That's ready for Reiter to photograph after lunch. Rather nice stuff she had in with her.'

He showed us a little verdigrissy copper bowl and some pins. And a lot of gold and blue things that had been her necklace of beads.

The bones and all the objects were brushed and cleaned with a knife and kept in position ready to be photographed.

'Who is she?' asked Poirot.

'First millennium. A lady of some consequence perhaps. Skull looks rather odd—I must get Mercado to look at it. It suggests death by foul play.'

'A Mrs Leidner of two thousand odd years ago?' said Poirot.

'Perhaps,' said Mr Emmott.

Bill Coleman was doing something with a pick to a wall face.

David Emmott called something to him which I didn't catch and then started showing M. Poirot round.

When the short explanatory tour was over, Emmott looked at his watch.

'We knock off in ten minutes,' he said. 'Shall we walk back to the house?'

'That will suit me excellently,' said Poirot.

We walked slowly along the well-worn path.

'I expect you are all glad to get back to work again,' said Poirot.

Emmott replied gravely: 'Yes, it's much the best thing. It's not been any too easy loafing about the house and making conversation.'

'Knowing all the time *that one of you was a murderer*.'

Emmott did not answer. He made no gesture of dissent. I knew now that he had had a suspicion of the truth from the very first when he had questioned the house-boys.

After a few minutes he asked quietly: 'Are you getting anywhere, M. Poirot?'

Poirot said gravely: 'Will you help me to get somewhere?'

'Why, naturally.'

Watching him closely, Poirot said: 'The hub of the case is Mrs Leidner. I want to know about Mrs Leidner.'

David Emmott said slowly: 'What do you mean by know about her?'

'I do not mean where she came from and what her maiden name was. I do not mean the shape of her face and the colour of her eyes. I mean her—herself.'

'You think that counts in the case?'

'I am quite sure of it.'

Emmott was silent for a moment or two, then he said: 'Maybe you're right.'

'And that is where you can help me. You can tell me what sort of a woman she was.'

'Can I? I've often wondered about it myself.'

'Didn't you make up your mind on the subject?'

'I think I did in the end.'

'*Eh bien?*'

But Mr Emmott was silent for some minutes, then he said: 'What did nurse think of her? Women are said to sum up other women quickly enough, and a nurse has a wide experience of types.'

Poirot didn't give me any chance of speaking even if I had wanted to. He said quickly: 'What I want to know is what a *man* thought of her?'

Emmott smiled a little.

'I expect they'd all be much the same.' He paused and said, 'She wasn't young, but I think she was about the most beautiful woman I've ever come across.'

'That's hardly an answer, Mr Emmott.'

'It's not so far off one, M. Poirot.'

He was silent a minute or two and then he went on:

Agatha Christie

'There used to be a fairy story I read when I was a kid. A Northern fairy story about the Snow Queen and Little Kay. I guess Mrs Leidner was rather like that—always taking Little Kay for a ride.'

'Ah yes, a tale of Hans Andersen, is it not? And there was a girl in it. Little Gerda, was that her name?'

'Maybe. I don't remember much of it.'

'Can't you go a little further, Mr Emmott?'

David Emmott shook his head.

'I don't even know if I've summed her up correctly. She wasn't easy to read. She'd do a devilish thing one day, and a really fine one the next. But I think you're about right when you say that she's the hub of the case. That's what she always wanted to be—*at the centre of things*. And she liked to get *at* other people—I mean, she wasn't just satisfied with being passed the toast and the peanut butter, she wanted you to turn your mind and soul inside out for her to look at it.'

'And if one did not give her that satisfaction?' asked Poirot.

'Then she could turn ugly!'

I saw his lips close resolutely and his jaw set.

'I suppose, Mr Emmott, you would not care to express a plain unofficial opinion as to who murdered her?'

'I don't know,' said Emmott. 'I really haven't the slightest idea. I rather think that, if I'd been Carl—Carl Reiter, I mean—I would have had a shot at murdering her. She was a pretty fair devil to him. But, of course, he asks for it by being so darned sensitive. Just invites you to give him a kick in the pants.'

'And did Mrs Leidner give him—a kick in the pants?' inquired Poirot.

Emmott gave a sudden grin.

'No. Pretty little jabs with an embroidery needle—that was her method. He *was* irritating, of course. Just like some blubbering, poor-spirited kid. But a needle's a painful weapon.'

I stole a glance at Poirot and thought I detected a slight quiver of his lips.

'But you don't really believe that Carl Reiter killed her?' he asked.

'No. I don't believe you'd kill a woman because she persistently made you look a fool at every meal.'

Poirot shook his head thoughtfully.

Of course, Mr Emmott made Mrs Leidner sound quite inhuman. There was something to be said on the other side too.

There had been something terribly irritating about Mr Reiter's attitude. He jumped when she spoke to him, and did idiotic things like passing her the marmalade again and again when he knew she never ate it. I'd have felt inclined to snap at him a bit myself.

Men don't understand how their mannerisms can get on women's nerves so that you feel you just have to snap.

I thought I'd just mention that to Mr Poirot some time.

We had arrived back now and Mr Emmott offered Poirot a wash and took him into his room.

I hurried across the courtyard to mine.

I came out again about the same time they did and we were all making for the dining-room when Father Lavigny appeared in the doorway of his room and invited Poirot in.

Mr Emmott came on round and he and I went into the dining-room together. Miss Johnson and Mrs Mercado were

Agatha Christie

there already, and after a few minutes Mr Mercado, Mr Reiter and Bill Coleman joined us.

We were just sitting down and Mercado had told the Arab boy to tell Father Lavigny lunch was ready when we were all startled by a faint, muffled cry.

I suppose our nerves weren't very good yet, for we all jumped, and Miss Johnson got quite pale and said: '*What was that?* What's happened?'

Mrs Mercado stared at her and said: 'My dear, what *is* the matter with you? It's some noise outside in the fields.'

But at that minute Poirot and Father Lavigny came in.

'We thought someone was hurt,' Miss Johnson said.

'A thousand pardons, mademoiselle,' cried Poirot. 'The fault is mine. Father Lavigny, he explains to me some tablets, and I take one to the window to see better—and, *ma foi*, not looking where I was going, I steb the toe, and the pain is sharp for the moment and I cry out.'

'We thought it was another murder,' said Mrs Mercado, laughing.

'Marie!' said her husband.

His tone was reproachful and she flushed and bit her lip.

Miss Johnson hastily turned the conversation to the dig and what objects of interest had turned up that morning. Conversation all through lunch was sternly archaeological.

I think we all felt it was the safest thing.

After we had had coffee we adjourned to the living-room. Then the men, with the exception of Father Lavigny, went off to the dig again.

Father Lavigny took Poirot through into the antika-room and I went with them. I was getting to know the things pretty well by now and I felt a thrill of pride—almost as though it were my own property—when Father Lavigny took down the gold cup and I heard Poirot's exclamation of admiration and pleasure.

'How beautiful! What a work of art!'

Father Lavigny agreed eagerly and began to point out its beauties with real enthusiasm and knowledge.

'No wax on it today,' I said.

'Wax?' Poirot stared at me.

'Wax?' So did Father Lavigny.

I explained my remark.

'Ah, *je comprends*,' said Father Lavigny. 'Yes, yes, candle grease.'

That led direct to the subject of the midnight visitor. Forgetting my presence they both dropped into French, and I left them together and went back into the living-room.

Mrs Mercado was darning her husband's socks and Miss Johnson was reading a book. Rather an unusual thing for her. She usually seemed to have something to work at.

After a while Father Lavigny and Poirot came out, and the former excused himself on the score of work. Poirot sat down with us.

'A most interesting man,' he said, and asked how much work there had been for Father Lavigny to do so far.

Miss Johnson explained that tablets had been scarce and that there had been very few inscribed bricks or cylinder

Agatha Christie

seals. Father Lavigny, however, had done his share of work on the dig and was picking up colloquial Arabic very fast.

That led the talk to cylinder seals, and presently Miss Johnson fetched from a cupboard a sheet of impressions made by rolling them out on plasticine.

I realized as we bent over them, admiring the spirited designs, that these must be what she had been working at on that fatal afternoon.

As we talked I noticed that Poirot was rolling and kneading a little ball of plasticine between his fingers.

'You use a lot of plasticine, mademoiselle?' he asked.

'A fair amount. We seem to have got through a lot already this year—though I can't imagine how. But half our supply seems to have gone.'

'Where is it kept, mademoiselle?'

'Here—in this cupboard.'

As she replaced the sheet of impressions she showed him the shelf with rolls of plasticine, Durofix, photographic paste and other stationery supplies.

Poirot stooped down.

'And this—what is this, mademoiselle?'

He had slipped his hand right to the back and had brought out a curious crumpled object.

As he straightened it out we could see that it was a kind of mask, with eyes and mouth crudely painted on it in Indian ink and the whole thing roughly smeared with plasticine.

'How perfectly extraordinary!' cried Miss Johnson. 'I've never seen it before. How did it get there? And what is it?'

'As to how it got there, well, one hiding-place is as good

as another, and I presume that this cupboard would not have been turned out till the end of the season. As to what it *is*—that, too, I think, is not difficult to say. *We have here the face that Mrs Leidner described.* The ghostly face seen in the semi-dusk outside her window—without body attached.'

Mrs Mercado gave a little shriek.

Miss Johnson was white to the lips. She murmured: 'Then it was *not* fancy. It was a trick—a wicked trick! But who played it?'

'Yes,' cried Mrs Mercado. 'Who could have done such a wicked, wicked thing?'

Poirot did not attempt a reply. His face was very grim as he went into the next room, returned with an empty cardboard box in his hand and put the crumpled mask into it.

'The police must see this,' he explained.

'It's horrible,' said Miss Johnson in a low voice. 'Horrible!'

'Do you think everything's hidden here somewhere?' cried Mrs Mercado shrilly. 'Do you think perhaps the weapon—the club she was killed with—all covered with blood still, perhaps... Oh! I'm frightened—I'm frightened...'

Miss Johnson gripped her by the shoulder.

'Be quiet,' she said fiercely. 'Here's Dr Leidner. We mustn't upset him.'

Indeed, at that very moment the car had driven into the courtyard. Dr Leidner got out of it and came straight across and in at the living-room door. His face was set in lines of fatigue and he looked twice the age he had three days ago.

He said in a quiet voice: 'The funeral will be at eleven o'clock tomorrow. Major Deane will read the service.'

Mrs Mercado faltered something, then slipped out of the room.

Dr Leidner said to Miss Johnson: 'You'll come, Anne?'

And she answered: 'Of course, my dear, we'll all come. Naturally.'

She didn't say anything else, but her face must have expressed what her tongue was powerless to do, for his face lightened up with affection and a momentary ease.

'Dear Anne,' he said. 'You are such a wonderful comfort and help to me. My dear old friend.'

He laid his hand on her arm and I saw the red colour creep up in her face as she muttered, gruff as ever: 'That's all right.'

But I just caught a glimpse of her expression and knew that, for one short moment, Anne Johnson was a perfectly happy woman.

And another idea flashed across my mind. Perhaps soon, in the natural course of things, turning to his old friend for sympathy, a new and happy state of things might come about.

Not that I'm really a matchmaker, and of course it was indecent to think of such a thing before the funeral even. But after all, it *would* be a happy solution. He was very fond of her, and there was no doubt she was absolutely devoted to him and would be perfectly happy devoting the rest of her life to him. That is, if she could bear to hear Louise's perfections sung all the time. But women can put up with a lot when they've got what they want.

Dr Leidner then greeted Poirot, asking him if he had made any progress.

Miss Johnson was standing behind Dr Leidner and she looked hard at the box in Poirot's hand and shook her head, and I realized that she was pleading with Poirot not to tell him about the mask. She felt, I was sure, that he had enough to bear for one day.

Poirot fell in with her wish.

'These things march slowly, monsieur,' he said.

Then, after a few desultory words, he took his leave.

I accompanied him out to his car.

There were half a dozen things I wanted to ask him, but somehow, when he turned and looked at me, I didn't ask anything after all. I'd as soon have asked a surgeon if he thought he'd made a good job of an operation. I just stood meekly waiting for instructions.

Rather to my surprise he said: 'Take care of yourself, my child.'

And then he added: 'I wonder if it is well for you to remain here?'

'I must speak to Dr Leidner about leaving,' I said. 'But I thought I'd wait until after the funeral.'

He nodded in approval.

'In the meantime,' he said, 'do not try to find out too much. You understand, I do not want you to be clever!' And he added with a smile, 'It is for you to hold the swabs and for me to do the operation.'

Wasn't it funny, his actually saying that?

Then he said quite irrelevantly: 'An interesting man, that Father Lavigny.'

'A monk being an archaeologist seems odd to me,' I said.

'Ah, yes, you are a Protestant. Me, I am a good Catholic. I know something of priests and monks.'

He frowned, seemed to hesitate, then said: 'Remember, he is quite clever enough to turn you inside out if he likes.'

If he was warning me against gossiping I felt that I didn't need any such warning!

It annoyed me, and though I didn't like to ask him any of the things I really wanted to know, I didn't see why I shouldn't at any rate say one thing.

'You'll excuse me, M. Poirot,' I said. 'But it's "stubbed your toe", not *stepped* or *stebbed*.'

'Ah! Thank you, *ma soeur*.'

'Don't mention it. But it's just as well to get a phrase right.'

'I will remember,' he said—quite meekly for him.

And he got in the car and was driven away, and I went slowly back across the courtyard wondering about a lot of things.

About the hypodermic marks on Mr Mercado's arm, and what drug it was he took. And about that horrid yellow smeared mask. And how odd it was that Poirot and Miss Johnson hadn't heard my cry in the living-room that morning, whereas we had all heard Poirot perfectly well in the dining-room at lunch-time—and yet Father Lavigny's room and Mrs Leidner's were just the same distance from the living-room and the dining-room respectively.

And then I felt rather pleased that I'd taught *Doctor* Poirot one English phrase correctly!

Even if he *was* a great detective he'd realize he *didn't* know *everything*!

CHAPTER 23

I Go Psychic

The funeral was, I thought, a very affecting affair. As well as ourselves, all the English people in Hassanieh attended it. Even Sheila Reilly was there, looking quiet and subdued in a dark coat and skirt. I hoped that she was feeling a little remorseful for all the unkind things she had said.

When we got back to the house I followed Dr Leidner into the office and broached the subject of my departure. He was very nice about it, thanked me for what I had done (Done! I had been worse than useless) and insisted on my accepting an extra week's salary.

I protested because really I felt I'd done nothing to earn it.

'Indeed, Dr Leidner, I'd rather not have any salary at all. If you'd just refund me my travelling expenses, that's all I want.'

But he wouldn't hear of that.

'You see,' I said, 'I don't feel I deserve it, Dr Leidner. I mean, I've—well, I've failed. She—my coming didn't save her.'

'Now don't get that idea into your head, nurse,' he said earnestly. 'After all, I didn't engage you as a female detective.

I never dreamt my wife's life was in danger. I was convinced it was all nerves and that she'd worked herself up into a rather curious mental state. You did all anyone could do. She liked and trusted you. And I think in her last days she felt happier and safer because of your being here. There's nothing for you to reproach yourself with.'

His voice quivered a little and I knew what he was thinking. *He* was the one to blame for not having taken Mrs Leidner's fears seriously.

'Dr Leidner,' I said curiously. 'Have you ever come to any conclusion about those anonymous letters?'

He said with a sigh: 'I don't know what to believe. Has M. Poirot come to any definite conclusion?'

'He hadn't yesterday,' I said, steering rather neatly, I thought, between truth and fiction. After all, he hadn't until I told him about Miss Johnson.

It was on my mind that I'd like to give Dr Leidner a hint and see if he reacted. In the pleasure of seeing him and Miss Johnson together the day before, and his affection and reliance on her, I'd forgotten all about the letters. Even now I felt it was perhaps rather mean of me to bring it up. Even if she had written them, she had had a bad time after Mrs Leidner's death. Yet I did want to see whether that particular possibility had ever entered Dr Leidner's head.

'Anonymous letters are usually the work of a woman,' I said. I wanted to see how he'd take it.

'I suppose they are,' he said with a sigh. 'But you seem to forget, nurse, that these may be genuine. They may actually be written by Frederick Bosner.'

'No, I haven't forgotten,' I said. 'But I can't believe somehow that that's the real explanation.'

'I do,' he said. 'It's all nonsense, his being one of the expedition staff. That is just an ingenious theory of M. Poirot's. I believe that the truth is much simpler. The man is a madman, of course. He's been hanging round the place—perhaps in disguise of some kind. And somehow or other he got in on that fatal afternoon. The servants may be lying—they may have been bribed.'

'I suppose it's possible,' I said doubtfully.

Dr Leidner went on with a trace of irritability.

'It is all very well for M. Poirot to suspect the members of my expedition. I am perfectly certain *none* of them have anything to do with it! I have worked with them. I *know* them!'

He stopped suddenly, then he said: 'Is that your experience, nurse? That anonymous letters are usually written by women?'

'It isn't always the case,' I said. 'But there's a certain type of feminine spitefulness that finds relief that way.'

'I suppose you are thinking of Mrs Mercado?' he said. Then he shook his head.

'Even if she were malicious enough to wish to hurt Louise she would hardly have the necessary knowledge,' he said.

I remembered the earlier letters in the attaché-case.

If Mrs Leidner had left that unlocked and Mrs Mercado had been alone in the house one day pottering about, she might easily have found them and read them. Men never seem to think of the simplest possibilities!

Agatha Christie

'And apart from her there is only Miss Johnson,' I said, watching him.

'That would be quite ridiculous!'

The little smile with which he said it was quite conclusive. The idea of Miss Johnson being the author of the letters had never entered his head! I hesitated just for a minute—but I didn't say anything. One doesn't like giving away a fellow woman, and besides, I had been a witness of Miss Johnson's genuine and moving remorse. What was done was done. Why expose Dr Leidner to a fresh disillusion on top of all his other troubles?

It was arranged that I should leave on the following day, and I had arranged through Dr Reilly to stay for a day or two with the matron of the hospital whilst I made arrangements for returning to England either via Baghdad or direct via Nissibin by car and train.

Dr Leidner was kind enough to say that he would like me to choose a memento from amongst his wife's things.

'Oh, no, really, Dr Leidner,' I said. 'I couldn't. It's much too kind of you.'

He insisted.

'But I should like you to have something. And Louise, I am sure, would have wished it.'

Then he went on to suggest that I should have her tortoiseshell toilet set!

'Oh, no, Dr Leidner! Why, that's a most *expensive* set. I couldn't, really.'

'She had no sisters, you know—no one who wants these things. There is no one else to have them.'

I could quite imagine that he wouldn't want them to fall into Mrs Mercado's greedy little hands. And I didn't think he'd want to offer them to Miss Johnson.

He went on kindly: 'You just think it over. By the way, here is the key of Louise's jewel case. Perhaps you will find something there you would rather have. And I should be very grateful if you would pack up—all her clothes. I daresay Reilly can find a use for them amongst some of the poor Christian families in Hassanieh.'

I was very glad to be able to do that for him, and I expressed my willingness.

I set about it at once.

Mrs Leidner had only had a very simple wardrobe with her and it was soon sorted and packed up into a couple of suitcases. All her papers had been in the small attaché-case. The jewel case contained a few simple trinkets—a pearl ring, a diamond brooch, a small string of pearls, and one or two plain gold bar brooches of the safety-pin type, and a string of large amber beads.

Naturally I wasn't going to take the pearls or the diamonds, but I hesitated a bit between the amber beads and the toilet set. In the end, however, I didn't see why I shouldn't take the latter. It was a kindly thought on Dr Leidner's part, and I was sure there wasn't any patronage about it. I'd take it in the spirit it had been offered, without any false pride. After all, I *had* been fond of her.

Well, that was all done and finished with. The suitcases packed, the jewel case locked up again and put separate to give to Dr Leidner with the photograph of

Mrs Leidner's father and one or two other personal little odds and ends.

The room looked bare and forlorn emptied of all its accoutrements, when I'd finished. There was nothing more for me to do—and yet somehow or other I shrank from leaving the room. It seemed as though there was something still to do there—something I ought to *see*—or something I ought to have *known*.

I'm not superstitious, but the idea *did* pop into my head that perhaps Mrs Leidner's spirit was hanging about the room and trying to get in touch with me.

I remember once at the hospital some of us girls got a planchette and really it wrote some very remarkable things.

Perhaps, although I'd never thought of such a thing, I might be mediumistic.

As I say, one gets all worked up to imagine all sorts of foolishness sometimes.

I prowled round the room uneasily, touching this and that. But, of course, there wasn't anything in the room but bare furniture. There was nothing slipped behind drawers or tucked away. I couldn't hope for anything of that kind.

In the end (it sounds rather batty, but as I say, one gets worked up) I did rather a queer thing.

I went and lay down in the bed and closed my eyes.

I deliberately tried to forget who and what I was. I tried to think myself back to that fatal afternoon. I was Mrs Leidner lying here resting, peaceful and unsuspicious.

It's extraordinary how you *can* work yourself up.

I'm a perfectly normal matter-of-fact individual—not the least bit spooky, but I tell you that after I'd lain there about five minutes I began to *feel* spooky.

I didn't try to resist. I deliberately encouraged the feeling.

I said to myself: 'I'm Mrs Leidner. I'm Mrs Leidner. I'm lying here—half asleep. Presently—very soon now—the door's going to open.'

I kept on saying that—as though I were hypnotizing myself.

'It's just about half-past one...it's just about the time... The door is going to open...*the door is going to open*... I shall see who comes in...'

I kept my eyes glued on that door. Presently it was going to open. I should *see* it open. And I should see *the person who opened it*.

I must have been a little over-wrought that afternoon to imagine I could solve the mystery that way.

But I did believe it. A sort of chill passed down my back and settled in my legs. They felt numb—paralysed.

'You're going into a trance,' I said. 'And in that trance you'll see...'

And once again I repeated monotonously again and again:

'The door is going to open—the door is going to open...'

The cold numbed feeling grew more intense.

And then, slowly, *I saw the door just beginning to open.*

It was horrible.

I've never known anything so horrible before or since.

I was paralysed—chilled through and through. I couldn't move. For the life of me I couldn't have moved.

Agatha Christie

And I was terrified. Sick and blind and dumb with terror.

That slowly opening door.

So noiseless.

In a minute I should see…

Slowly—slowly—wider and wider.

Bill Coleman came quietly in.

He must have had the shock of his life!

I bounded off the bed with a scream of terror and hurled myself across the room.

He stood stock-still, his blunt pink face pinker and his mouth opened wide with surprise.

'Hallo-allo-allo,' he said. 'What's up, nurse?'

I came back to reality with a crash.

'Goodness, Mr Coleman,' I said. 'How you startled me!'

'Sorry,' he said with a momentary grin.

I saw then that he was holding a little bunch of scarlet ranunculus in his hand. They were pretty little flowers and they grew wild on the sides of the Tell. Mrs Leidner had been fond of them.

He blushed and got rather red as he said: 'One can't get any flowers or things in Hassanieh. Seemed rather rotten not to have any flowers for the grave. I thought I'd just nip in here and put a little posy in that little pot thing she always had flowers in on her table. Sort of show she wasn't forgotten—eh? A bit asinine, I know, but—well—I mean to say.'

I thought it was very nice of him. He was all pink with embarrassment like Englishmen are when they've done anything sentimental. I thought it was a very sweet thought.

'Why, I think that's a very nice idea, Mr Coleman,' I said.

And I picked up the little pot and went and got some water in it and we put the flowers in.

I really thought much more of Mr Coleman for this idea of his. It showed he had a heart and nice feelings about things.

He didn't ask me again what made me let out such a squeal and I'm thankful he didn't. I should have felt a fool explaining.

'Stick to common sense in future, woman,' I said to myself as I settled my cuffs and smoothed my apron. 'You're not cut out for this psychic stuff.'

I bustled about doing my own packing and kept myself busy for the rest of the day.

Father Lavigny was kind enough to express great distress at my leaving. He said my cheerfulness and common sense had been such a help to everybody. Common sense! I'm glad he didn't know about my idiotic behaviour in Mrs Leidner's room.

'We have not seen M. Poirot today,' he remarked.

I told him that Poirot had said he was going to be busy all day sending off telegrams.

Father Lavigny raised his eyebrows.

'Telegrams? To America?'

'I suppose so. He said, "All over the world!" but I think that was rather a foreign exaggeration.'

And then I got rather red, remembering that Father Lavigny was a foreigner himself.

He didn't seem offended though, just laughed quite pleasantly and asked me if there were any news of the man with the squint.

Agatha Christie

I said I didn't know but I hadn't heard of any.

Father Lavigny asked me again about the time Mrs Leidner and I had noticed the man and how he had seemed to be standing on tiptoe and peering through the window.

'It seems clear the man had some overwhelming interest in Mrs Leidner,' he said thoughtfully. 'I have wondered since whether the man could possibly have been a European got up to look like an Iraqi?'

That was a new idea to me and I considered it carefully. I had taken it for granted that the man was a native, but of course when I came to think of it, I was really going by the cut of his clothes and the yellowness of his skin.

Father Lavigny declared his intention of going round outside the house to the place where Mrs Leidner and I had seen the man standing.

'You never know, he might have dropped something. In the detective stories the criminal always does.'

'I expect in real life criminals are more careful,' I said.

I fetched some socks I had just finished darning and put them on the table in the living-room for the men to sort out when they came in, and then, as there was nothing much more to do, I went up on the roof.

Miss Johnson was standing there but she didn't hear me. I got right up to her before she noticed me.

But long before that I'd seen that there was something very wrong.

She was standing in the middle of the roof staring straight in front of her, and there was the most awful look on her face. As though she'd seen something she couldn't possibly believe.

Murder in Mesopotamia

It gave me quite a shock.

Mind you, I'd seen her upset the other evening, but this was quite different.

'My dear,' I said, hurrying to her, 'whatever's the matter?'

She turned her head at that and stood looking at me—almost as if she didn't see me.

'What is it?' I persisted.

She made a queer sort of grimace—as though she were trying to swallow but her throat were too dry. She said hoarsely: 'I've just seen something.'

'What have you seen? Tell me. Whatever can it be? You look all in.'

She gave an effort to pull herself together, but she still looked pretty dreadful.

She said, still in that same dreadful choked voice: '*I've seen how someone could come in from outside—and no one would ever guess.*'

I followed the direction of her eyes but I couldn't see anything.

Mr Reiter was standing in the door of the photographic-room and Father Lavigny was just crossing the courtyard—but there was nothing else.

I turned back puzzled and found her eyes fixed on mine with the strangest expression in them.

'Really,' I said, 'I don't see what you mean. Won't you explain?'

But she shook her head.

'Not now. Later. We *ought* to have seen. Oh, we ought to have seen!'

Agatha Christie

'If you'd only tell me—'
But she shook her head.
'I've got to think it out first.'
And pushing past me, she went stumbling down the stairs.

I didn't follow her as she obviously didn't want me with her. Instead I sat down on the parapet and tried to puzzle things out. But I didn't get anywhere. There was only the one way into the courtyard—through the big arch. Just outside it I could see the water-boy and his horse and the Indian cook talking to him. Nobody could have passed them and come in without their seeing him.

I shook my head in perplexity and went downstairs again.

CHAPTER 24

Murder is a Habit

We all went to bed early that night. Miss Johnson had appeared at dinner and had behaved more or less as usual. She had, however, a sort of dazed look, and once or twice quite failed to take in what other people said to her.

It wasn't somehow a very comfortable sort of meal. You'd say, I suppose, that that was natural enough in a house where there'd been a funeral that day. But I know what I mean.

Lately our meals had been hushed and subdued, but for all that there had been a feeling of comradeship. There had been sympathy with Dr Leidner in his grief and a fellow feeling of being all in the same boat amongst the others.

But tonight I was reminded of my first meal there—when Mrs Mercado had watched me and there had been that curious feeling as though something might snap any minute.

I'd felt the same thing—only very much intensified—when we'd sat round the dining-room table with Poirot at the head of it.

Agatha Christie

Tonight it was particularly strong. Everyone was on edge—jumpy—on tenterhooks. If anyone had dropped something I'm sure somebody would have screamed.

As I say, we all separated early afterwards. I went to bed almost at once. The last thing I heard as I was dropping off to sleep was Mrs Mercado's voice saying goodnight to Miss Johnson just outside my door.

I dropped off to sleep at once—tired by my exertions and even more by my silly experience in Mrs Leidner's room. I slept heavily and dreamlessly for several hours.

I awoke when I did awake with a start and a feeling of impending catastrophe. Some sound had woken me, and as I sat up in bed listening I heard it again.

An awful sort of agonized choking groan.

I had lit my candle and was out of bed in a twinkling. I snatched up a torch, too, in case the candle should blow out. I came out of my door and stood listening. I knew the sound wasn't far away. It came again—from the room immediately next to mine—Miss Johnson's room.

I hurried in. Miss Johnson was lying in bed, her whole body contorted in agony. As I set down the candle and bent over her, her lips moved and she tried to speak—but only an awful hoarse whisper came. I saw that the corners of her mouth and the skin of her chin were burnt a kind of greyish white.

Her eyes went from me to a glass that lay on the floor evidently where it had dropped from her hand. The light rug was stained a bright red where it had fallen. I picked it up and ran a finger over the inside, drawing back my hand with a sharp exclamation. Then I examined the inside of the poor woman's mouth.

There wasn't the least doubt what was the matter. Somehow or other, intentionally or otherwise, she'd swallowed a quantity of corrosive acid—oxalic or hydrochloric, I suspected.

I ran out and called to Dr Leidner and he woke the others, and we worked over her for all we were worth, but all the time I had an awful feeling it was no good. We tried a strong solution of carbonate of soda—and followed it with olive oil. To ease the pain I gave her a hypodermic of morphine sulphate.

David Emmott had gone off to Hassanieh to fetch Dr Reilly, but before he came it was over.

I won't dwell on the details. Poisoning by a strong solution of hydrochloric acid (which is what it proved to be) is one of the most painful deaths possible.

It was when I was bending over her to give her the morphia that she made one ghastly effort to speak. It was only a horrible strangled whisper when it came.

'*The window...*' she said. '*Nurse...the window...*'

But that was all—she couldn't go on. She collapsed completely.

I shall never forget that night. The arrival of Dr Reilly. The arrival of Captain Maitland. And finally with the dawn, Hercule Poirot.

He it was who took me gently by the arm and steered me into the dining-room, where he made me sit down and have a cup of good strong tea.

Agatha Christie

'There, *mon enfant*,' he said, 'that is better. You are worn out.'

Upon that, I burst into tears.

'It's too awful,' I sobbed. 'It's been like a nightmare. Such awful suffering. And her eyes... Oh, M. Poirot—her eyes...'

He patted me on the shoulder. A woman couldn't have been kinder.

'Yes, yes—do not think of it. You did all you could.'

'It was one of the corrosive acids.'

'It was a strong solution of hydrochloric acid.'

'The stuff they use on the pots?'

'Yes. Miss Johnson probably drank it off before she was fully awake. That is—unless she took it on purpose.'

'Oh, M. Poirot, what an awful idea!'

'It is a possibility, after all. What do you think?'

I considered for a moment and then shook my head decisively.

'I don't believe it. No, I don't believe it for a moment.' I hesitated and then said, 'I think she found out something yesterday afternoon.'

'What is that you say? She found out something?'

I repeated to him the curious conversation we had had together.

Poirot gave a low soft whistle.

'*La pauvre femme!*' he said. 'She said she wanted to think it over—eh? That is what signed her death warrant. If she had only spoken out—then—at once.'

He said: 'Tell me again her exact words.'

I repeated them.

'She saw how someone could have come in from outside without any of you knowing? Come, *ma soeur*, let us go up to the roof and you shall show me just where she was standing.'

We went up to the roof together and I showed Poirot the exact spot where Miss Johnson had stood.

'Like this?' said Poirot. 'Now what do I see? I see half the courtyard—and the archway—and the doors of the drawing-office and the photographic-room and the laboratory. Was there anyone in the courtyard?'

'Father Lavigny was just going towards the archway and Mr Reiter was standing in the door of the photographic-room.'

'And still I do not see in the least how anyone could come in from outside and none of you know about it... But *she* saw...'

He gave it up at last, shaking his head.

'*Sacré nom d'un chien—va!* What *did* she see?'

The sun was just rising. The whole eastern sky was a riot of rose and orange and pale, pearly grey.

'What a beautiful sunrise!' said Poirot gently.

The river wound away to our left and the Tell stood up outlined in gold colour. To the south were the blossoming trees and the peaceful cultivation. The water-wheel groaned in the distance—a faint unearthly sound. In the north were the slender minarets and the clustering fairy whiteness of Hassanieh.

It was incredibly beautiful.

And then, close at my elbow, I heard Poirot give a long deep sigh.

'Fool that I have been,' he murmured. 'When the truth is so clear—so clear.'

CHAPTER 25

Suicide or Murder?

I hadn't time to ask Poirot what he meant, for Captain Maitland was calling up to us and asking us to come down.

We hurried down the stairs.

'Look here, Poirot,' he said. 'Here's another complication. The monk fellow is missing.'

'Father Lavigny?'

'Yes. Nobody noticed it till just now. Then it dawned on somebody that he was the only one of the party not around, and we went to his room. His bed's not been slept in and there's no sign of him.'

The whole thing was like a bad dream. First Miss Johnson's death and then the disappearance of Father Lavigny.

The servants were called and questioned, but they couldn't throw any light on the mystery. He had last been seen at about eight o'clock the night before. Then he had said he was going out for a stroll before going to bed.

Nobody had seen him come back from that stroll.

The big doors had been closed and barred at nine o'clock as usual. Nobody, however, remembered unbarring them in the morning. The two house-boys each thought the other one must have done the unfastening.

Had Father Lavigny ever returned the night before? Had he, in the course of his earlier walk, discovered anything of a suspicious nature, gone out to investigate it later, and perhaps fallen a third victim?

Captain Maitland swung round as Dr Reilly came up with Mr Mercado behind him.

'Hallo, Reilly. Got anything?'

'Yes. The stuff came from the laboratory here. I've just been checking up the quantities with Mercado. It's H.C.L. from the lab.'

'The laboratory—eh? Was it locked up?'

Mr Mercado shook his head. His hands were shaking and his face was twitching. He looked a wreck of a man.

'It's never been the custom,' he stammered. 'You see—just now—we're using it all the time. I—nobody ever dreamt—'

'Is the place locked up at night?'

'Yes—all the rooms are locked. The keys are hung up just inside the living-room.'

'So if anyone had a key to that they could get the lot.'

'Yes.'

'And it's a perfectly ordinary key, I suppose?'

'Oh, yes.'

'Nothing to show whether she took it herself from the laboratory?' asked Captain Maitland.

'She didn't,' I said loudly and positively.

I felt a warning touch on my arm. Poirot was standing close behind me.

And then something rather ghastly happened.

Not ghastly in itself—in fact it was just the incongruousness that made it seem worse than anything else.

A car drove into the courtyard and a little man jumped out. He was wearing a sun helmet and a short thick trench coat.

He came straight to Dr Leidner, who was standing by Dr Reilly, and shook him warmly by the hand.

'*Vous voilà, mon cher*,' he cried. 'Delighted to see you. I passed this way on Saturday afternoon—en route to the Italians at Fugima. I went to the dig but there wasn't a single European about and alas! I cannot speak Arabic. I had not time to come to the house. This morning I leave Fugima at five—two hours here with you—and then I catch the convoy on. *Eh bien*, and how is the season going?'

It was ghastly.

The cheery voice, the matter-of-fact manner, all the pleasant sanity of an everyday world now left far behind. He just bustled in, knowing nothing and noticing nothing—full of cheerful bonhomie.

No wonder Dr Leidner gave an inarticulate gasp and looked in mute appeal at Dr Reilly.

The doctor rose to the occasion.

He took the little man (he was a French archaeologist called Verrier who dug in the Greek islands, I heard later) aside and explained to him what had occurred.

Verrier was horrified. He himself had been staying at an Italian dig right away from civilization for the last few days and had heard nothing.

He was profuse in condolences and apologies, finally striding over to Dr Leidner and clasping him warmly by both hands.

'What a tragedy! My God, what a tragedy! I have no words. *Mon pauvre collègue.*'

And shaking his head in one last ineffectual effort to express his feelings, the little man climbed into his car and left us.

As I say, that momentary introduction of comic relief into tragedy seemed really more gruesome than anything else that had happened.

'The next thing,' said Dr Reilly firmly, 'is breakfast. Yes, I insist. Come, Leidner, you must eat.'

Poor Dr Leidner was almost a complete wreck. He came with us to the dining-room and there a funereal meal was served. I think the hot coffee and fried eggs did us all good, though no one actually felt they wanted to eat. Dr Leidner drank some coffee and sat twiddling his bread. His face was grey, drawn with pain and bewilderment.

After breakfast, Captain Maitland got down to things.

I explained how I had woken up, heard a queer sound and had gone into Miss Johnson's room.

'You say there was a glass on the floor?'

'Yes. She must have dropped it after drinking.'

'Was it broken?'

'No, it had fallen on the rug. (I'm afraid the acid's ruined the rug, by the way.) I picked the glass up and put it back on the table.'

'I'm glad you've told us that. There are only two sets of fingerprints on it, and one set is certainly Miss Johnson's own. The other must be yours.'

He was silent for a moment, then he said: 'Please go on.'

I described carefully what I'd done and the methods I had tried, looking rather anxiously at Dr Reilly for approval. He gave it with a nod.

'You tried everything that could possibly have done any good,' he said. And though I was pretty sure I had done so, it was a relief to have my belief confirmed.

'Did you know exactly what she had taken?' Captain Maitland asked.

'No—but I could see, of course, that it was a corrosive acid.'

Captain Maitland asked gravely: 'Is it your opinion, nurse, that Miss Johnson deliberately administered this stuff to herself?'

'Oh, no,' I exclaimed. 'I never thought of such a thing!'

I don't know why I was so sure. Partly, I think, because of M. Poirot's hints. His 'murder is a habit' had impressed itself on my mind. And then one doesn't readily believe that anyone's going to commit suicide in such a terribly painful way.

I said as much and Captain Maitland nodded thoughtfully. 'I agree that it isn't what one would choose,' he said. 'But if anyone were in great distress of mind and this stuff were easily available it might be taken for that reason.'

'*Was* she in great distress of mind?' I asked doubtfully.

'Mrs Mercado says so. She says that Miss Johnson was quite unlike herself at dinner last night—that she hardly replied to anything that was said to her. Mrs Mercado is quite sure that Miss Johnson was in terrible distress over something and that the idea of making away with herself had already occurred to her.'

'Well, I don't believe it for a moment,' I said bluntly.

Mrs Mercado indeed! Nasty slinking little cat!

'Then what *do* you think?'

'I think she was murdered,' I said bluntly.

He rapped out his next question sharply. I felt rather that I was in the orderly room.

'Any reasons?'

'It seems to me by far and away the most possible solution.'

'That's just your private opinion. There was no reason why the lady should be murdered?'

'Excuse me,' I said, 'there was. She found out something.'

'Found out something? What did she find out?'

I repeated our conversation on the roof word for word.

'She refused to tell you what her discovery was?'

'Yes. She said she must have time to think it over.'

'But she was very excited by it?'

'Yes.'

'*A way of getting in from outside.*' Captain Maitland puzzled over it, his brows knit. 'Had you no idea at all of what she was driving at?'

'Not in the least. I puzzled and puzzled over it but I couldn't even get a glimmering.'

Captain Maitland said: 'What do you think, M. Poirot?'

Poirot said: 'I think you have there a possible motive.'

'For murder?'

'For murder.'

Captain Maitland frowned.

'She wasn't able to speak before she died?'

'Yes, she just managed to get out two words.'

'What were they?'

'*The window...*'

'The window?' repeated Captain Maitland. 'Did you understand to what she was referring?'

I shook my head.

'How many windows were there in her bedroom?'

'Just the one.'

'Giving on the courtyard?'

'Yes.'

'Was it open or shut? Open, I seem to remember. But perhaps one of you opened it?'

'No, it was open all the time. I wondered—'

I stopped.

'Go on, nurse.'

'I examined the window, of course, but I couldn't see anything unusual about it. I wondered whether, perhaps, somebody changed the glasses that way.'

'Changed the glasses?'

'Yes. You see, Miss Johnson always takes a glass of water to bed with her. I think that glass must have been tampered with and a glass of acid put in its place.'

'What do you say, Reilly?'

'If it's murder, that was probably the way it was done,' said Dr Reilly promptly. 'No ordinary moderately observant human being would drink a glass of acid in mistake for one of water—if they were in full possession of their waking faculties. But if anyone's accustomed to drinking off a glass of water in the middle of the night, that person might easily stretch out an arm, find the glass in the accustomed place, and still half asleep, toss off enough of the stuff to be fatal before realizing what had happened.'

Captain Maitland reflected a minute.

'I'll have to go back and look at that window. How far is it from the head of the bed?'

I thought.

'With a very long stretch you could just reach the little table that stands by the head of the bed.'

'The table on which the glass of water was?'

'Yes.'

'Was the door locked?'

'No.'

'So whoever it was could have come in that way and made the substitution?'

'Oh, yes.'

'There would be more risk that way,' said Dr Reilly. 'A person who is sleeping quite soundly will often wake up at the sound of a footfall. If the table could be reached from the window it would be the safer way.'

'I'm not only thinking of the glass,' said Captain Maitland absent-mindedly.

Rousing himself, he addressed me once again.

'It's your opinion that when the poor lady felt she was dying she was anxious to let you know that somebody had substituted acid for water through the open window? Surely the person's *name* would have been more to the point?'

'She mayn't have known the name,' I pointed out.

'Or it would have been more to the point if she'd managed to hint what it was that she had discovered the day before?'

Dr Reilly said: 'When you're dying, Maitland, you haven't always got a sense of proportion. One particular fact very likely obsesses your mind. That a murderous hand had come through the window may have been the principal fact obsessing her at the minute. It may have seemed to her important that she should let people know that. In my opinion she wasn't far wrong either. It *was* important! She probably jumped to the fact that you'd think it was suicide. If she could have used her tongue freely, she'd probably have said "It wasn't suicide. I didn't take it myself. Somebody else must have put it near my bed *through the window*."'

Captain Maitland drummed with his fingers for a minute or two without replying. Then he said:

'There are certainly two ways of looking at it. It's either suicide or murder. Which do you think, Dr Leidner?'

Dr Leidner was silent for a minute or two, then he said quietly and decisively: 'Murder. Anne Johnson wasn't the sort of woman to kill herself.'

'No,' allowed Captain Maitland. 'Not in the normal run of things. But there might be circumstances in which it would be quite a natural thing to do.'

'Such as?'

Captain Maitland stooped to a bundle which I had previously noticed him place by the side of his chair. He swung it on to the table with something of an effort.

'There's something here that none of you know about,' he said. 'We found it under her bed.'

He fumbled with the knot of the covering, then threw it back, revealing a heavy great quern or grinder.

That was nothing in itself—there were a dozen or so already found in the course of the excavations.

What riveted our attention on this particular specimen was a dull, dark stain and a fragment of something that looked like hair.

'That'll be your job, Reilly,' said Captain Maitland. 'But I shouldn't say that there's much doubt about this being the instrument with which Mrs Leidner was killed!'

CHAPTER 26

Next It Will Be Me!

It was rather horrible. Dr Leidner looked as though he were going to faint and I felt a bit sick myself.

Dr Reilly examined it with professional gusto.

'No fingerprints, I presume?' he threw out.

'No fingerprints.'

Dr Reilly took out a pair of forceps and investigated delicately.

'H'm—a fragment of human tissue—and hair—fair blonde hair. That's the unofficial verdict. Of course, I'll have to make a proper test, blood group, etc., but there's not much doubt. Found under Miss Johnson's bed? Well, well—so *that's* the big idea. She did the murder, and then, God rest her, remorse came to her and she finished herself off. It's a theory—a pretty theory.'

Dr Leidner could only shake his head helplessly.

'Not Anne—not Anne,' he murmured.

'I don't know where she hid this to begin with,' said Captain Maitland. 'Every room was searched after the first crime.'

Something jumped into my mind and I thought, 'In the stationery cupboard,' but I didn't say anything.

'Wherever it was, she became dissatisfied with its hiding-place and took it into her own room, which had been searched with all the rest. Or perhaps she did that after making up her mind to commit suicide.'

'I don't believe it,' I said aloud.

And I couldn't somehow believe that kind nice Miss Johnson had battered out Mrs Leidner's brains. I just couldn't *see* it happening! And yet it *did* fit in with some things—her fit of weeping that night, for instance. After all, I'd said 'remorse' myself—only I'd never thought it was remorse for anything but the smaller, more insignificant crime.

'I don't know what to believe,' said Captain Maitland. 'There's the French Father's disappearance to be cleared up too. My men are out hunting around in case he's been knocked on the head and his body rolled into a convenient irrigation ditch.'

'Oh! I remember now—' I began.

Everyone looked towards me inquiringly.

'It was yesterday afternoon,' I said. 'He'd been cross-questioning me about the man with a squint who was looking in at the window that day. He asked me just where he'd stood on the path and then he said he was going out to have a look round. He said in detective stories the criminal always dropped a convenient clue.'

'Damned if any of my criminals ever do,' said Captain Maitland. 'So that's what he was after, was it? By Jove, I wonder if he *did* find anything. A bit of a coincidence if both he and Miss Johnson discovered a clue to the identity of the murderer at practically the same time.'

He added irritably, 'Man with a squint? Man with a squint? There's more in this tale of that fellow with a squint than meets the eye. I don't know why the devil my fellows can't lay hold of him!'

'Probably because he hasn't got a squint,' said Poirot quietly.

'Do you mean he faked it? Didn't know you could fake an actual squint.'

Poirot merely said: 'A squint can be a very useful thing.'

'The devil it can! I'd give a lot to know where that fellow is now, squint or no squint!'

'At a guess,' said Poirot, 'he has already passed the Syrian frontier.'

'We've warned Tell Kotchek and Abu Kemal—all the frontier posts, in fact.'

'I should imagine that he took the route through the hills. The route lorries sometimes take when running contraband.'

Captain Maitland grunted.

'Then we'd better telegraph Deir ez Zor?'

'I did so yesterday—warning them to look out for a car with two men in it whose passports will be in the most impeccable order.'

Captain Maitland favoured him with a stare.

'*You* did, did you? Two men—eh?'

Poirot nodded.

'There are two men in this.'

'It strikes me, M. Poirot, that you've been keeping quite a lot of things up your sleeve.'

Poirot shook his head.

'No,' he said. 'Not really. The truth came to me only this morning when I was watching the sunrise. A very beautiful sunrise.'

I don't think that any of us had noticed that Mrs Mercado was in the room. She must have crept in when we were all taken aback by the production of that horrible great bloodstained stone.

But now, without the least warning, she set up a noise like a pig having its throat cut.

'Oh, my God!' she cried. 'I see it all. I see it all now. *It was Father Lavigny*. He's mad—religious mania. He thinks women are sinful. *He's killing them all.* First Mrs Leidner—then Miss Johnson. And next it will be *me...*'

With a scream of frenzy she flung herself across the room and clutched Dr Reilly's coat.

'I won't stay here, I tell you! I won't stay here a day longer. There's danger. There's danger all round. He's hiding somewhere—waiting his time. He'll spring out on me!'

Her mouth opened and she began screaming again.

I hurried over to Dr Reilly, who had caught her by the wrists. I gave her a sharp slap on each cheek and with Dr Reilly's help I sat her down in a chair.

'Nobody's going to kill you,' I said. 'We'll see to that. Sit down and behave yourself.'

She didn't scream any more. Her mouth closed and she sat looking at me with startled, stupid eyes.

Agatha Christie

Then there was another interruption. The door opened and Sheila Reilly came in.

Her face was pale and serious. She came straight to Poirot.

'I was at the post office early, M. Poirot,' she said, 'and there was a telegram there for you—so I brought it along.'

'Thank you, mademoiselle.'

He took it from her and tore it open while she watched his face.

It did not change, that face. He read the telegram, smoothed it out, folded it up neatly and put it in his pocket.

Mrs Mercado was watching him. She said in a choked voice: 'Is that—from America?'

'No, madame,' he said. 'It is from Tunis.'

She stared at him for a moment as though she did not understand, then with a long sigh, she leant back in her seat.

'Father Lavigny,' she said. 'I *was* right. I've always thought there was something queer about him. He said things to me once—I suppose he's mad...' She paused and then said, 'I'll be quiet. But I *must* leave this place. Joseph and I can go in and sleep at the Rest House.'

'Patience, madame,' said Poirot. 'I will explain everything.'

Captain Maitland was looking at him curiously.

'Do you consider you've definitely got the hang of this business?' he demanded.

Poirot bowed.

It was a most theatrical bow. I think it rather annoyed Captain Maitland.

'Well,' he barked. 'Out with it, man.'

But that wasn't the way Hercule Poirot did things. I saw perfectly well that he meant to make a song and dance of it. I wondered if he really *did* know the truth, or if he was just showing off.

He turned to Dr Reilly.

'Will you be so good, Dr Reilly, as to summon the others?'

Dr Reilly jumped up and went off obligingly. In a minute or two the other members of the expedition began to file into the room. First Reiter and Emmott. Then Bill Coleman. Then Richard Carey and finally Mr Mercado.

Poor man, he really looked like death. I suppose he was mortally afraid that he'd get hauled over the coals for carelessness in leaving dangerous chemicals about.

Everyone seated themselves round the table very much as we had done on the day M. Poirot arrived. Both Bill Coleman and David Emmott hesitated before they sat down, glancing towards Sheila Reilly. She had her back to them and was standing looking out of the window.

'Chair, Sheila?' said Bill.

David Emmott said in his low pleasant drawl, 'Won't you sit down?'

She turned then and stood for a minute looking at them. Each was indicating a chair, pushing it forward. I wondered whose chair she would accept.

In the end she accepted neither.

'I'll sit here,' she said brusquely. And she sat down on the edge of a table quite close to the window.

Agatha Christie

'That is,' she added, 'if Captain Maitland doesn't mind my staying?'

I'm not quite sure what Captain Maitland would have said. Poirot forestalled him.

'Stay by all means, mademoiselle,' he said. 'It is, indeed, necessary that you should.'

She raised her eyebrows.

'Necessary?'

'That is the word I used, mademoiselle. There are some questions I shall have to ask you.'

Again her eyebrows went up but she said nothing further. She turned her face to the window as though determined to ignore what went on in the room behind her.

'And now,' said Captain Maitland, 'perhaps we shall get at the truth!'

He spoke rather impatiently. He was essentially a man of action. At this very moment I felt sure that he was fretting to be out and doing things—directing the search for Father Lavigny's body, or alternatively sending out parties for his capture and arrest.

He looked at Poirot with something akin to dislike.

'If the beggar's got anything to say, why doesn't he say it?'

I could see the words on the tip of his tongue.

Poirot gave a slow appraising glance at us all, then rose to his feet.

I don't know what I expected him to say—something dramatic certainly. He was that kind of person.

But I certainly didn't expect him to start off with a phrase in Arabic.

236

Yet that is what happened. He said the words slowly and solemnly—and really quite religiously, if you know what I mean.

'Bismillahi ar rahman ar rahim.'

And then he gave the translation in English.

'In the name of Allah, the Merciful, the Compassionate.'

CHAPTER 27

Beginning of a Journey

'*Bismillahi ar rahman ar rahim*. That is the Arab phrase used before starting out on a journey. *Eh bien*, we too start on a journey. A journey into the past. A journey into the strange places of the human soul.'

I don't think that up till that moment I'd ever felt any of the so-called 'glamour of the East'. Frankly, what had struck me was the *mess* everywhere. But suddenly, with M. Poirot's words, a queer sort of vision seemed to grow up before my eyes. I thought of words like Samarkand and Ispahan—and of merchants with long beards—and kneeling camels—and staggering porters carrying great bales on their backs held by a rope round the forehead—and women with henna-stained hair and tattooed faces kneeling by the Tigris and washing clothes, and I heard their queer wailing chants and the far-off groaning of the water-wheel.

They were mostly things I'd seen and heard and thought nothing much of. But now, somehow they seemed *different*—like a piece of fusty old stuff you take into the light and suddenly see the rich colours of an old embroidery...

Then I looked round the room we were sitting in and I got a queer feeling that what M. Poirot said was true—we *were* all starting on a journey. We were here together now, but we were all going our different ways.

And I looked at everyone as though, in a sort of way, I were seeing them for the first time—*and* for the last time—which sounds stupid, but it was what I felt all the same.

Mr Mercado was twisting his fingers nervously—his queer light eyes with their dilated pupils were staring at Poirot. Mrs Mercado was looking at her husband. She had a strange watchful look like a tigress waiting to spring. Dr Leidner seemed to have shrunk in some curious fashion. This last blow had just crumpled him up. You might almost say he wasn't in the room at all. He was somewhere far away in a place of his own. Mr Coleman was looking straight at Poirot. His mouth was slightly open and his eyes protruded. He looked almost idiotic. Mr Emmott was looking down at his feet and I couldn't see his face properly. Mr Reiter looked bewildered. His mouth was pushed out in a pout and that made him look more like a nice clean pig than ever. Miss Reilly was looking steadily out of the window. I don't know what she was thinking or feeling. Then I looked at Mr Carey, and somehow his face hurt me and I looked away. There we were, all of us. And somehow I felt that when M. Poirot had finished we'd all be somewhere quite different...

Agatha Christie

It was a queer feeling...

Poirot's voice went quietly on. It was like a river running evenly between its banks...running to the sea...

'From the very beginning I have felt that to understand this case one must seek not for external signs or clues, but for the truer clues of the clash of personalities and the secrets of the heart.

'And I may say that though I have now arrived at what I believe to be the true solution of the case, *I have no material proof of it*. I *know* it is so, because it *must* be so, because *in no other way* can every single fact fit into its ordered and recognized place.

'And that, to my mind, is the most satisfying solution there can be.'

He paused and then went on:

'I will start my journey at the moment when I myself was brought into the case—when I had it presented to me as an accomplished happening. Now, every case, in my opinion, has a definite *shape* and *form*. The pattern of this case, to my mind, all revolved round the personality of Mrs Leidner. Until I knew *exactly what kind of a woman Mrs Leidner was* I should not be able to know why she was murdered and who murdered her.

'That, then, was my starting point—the personality of Mrs Leidner.

'There was also one other psychological point of interest— the curious state of tension described as existing amongst the members of the expedition. This was attested to by several different witnesses—some of them outsiders—and I

Murder in Mesopotamia

made a note that although hardly a starting point, it should nevertheless be borne in mind during my investigations.

'The accepted idea seemed to be that it was directly the result of Mrs Leidner's influence on the members of the expedition, but for reasons which I will outline to you later this did not seem to me entirely acceptable.

'To start with, as I say, I concentrated solely and entirely on the personality of Mrs Leidner. I had various means of assessing that personality. There were the reactions she produced in a number of people, all varying widely in character and temperament, and there was what I could glean by my own observation. The scope of the latter was naturally limited. But I *did* learn certain facts.

'Mrs Leidner's tastes were simple and even on the austere side. She was clearly not a luxurious woman. On the other hand, some embroidery she had been doing was of an extreme fineness and beauty. That indicated a woman of fastidious and artistic taste. From the observation of the books in her bedroom I formed a further estimate. She had brains, and I also fancied that she was, essentially, an egoist.

'It had been suggested to me that Mrs Leidner was a woman whose main preoccupation was to attract the opposite sex—that she was, in fact, a sensual woman. This I did not believe to be the case.

'In her bedroom I noticed the following books on a shelf: *Who were the Greeks?*, *Introduction to Relativity*, *Life of Lady Hester Stanhope*, *Back to Methuselah*, *Linda Condon*, *Crewe Train*.

Agatha Christie

'She had, to begin with, an interest in culture and in modern science—that is, a distinct intellectual side. Of the novels, *Linda Condon*, and in a lesser degree *Crewe Train*, seemed to show that Mrs Leidner had a sympathy and interest in the independent woman—unencumbered or entrapped by man. She was also obviously interested by the personality of Lady Hester Stanhope. *Linda Condon* is an exquisite study of the worship of her own beauty by a woman. *Crewe Train* is a study of a passionate individualist, *Back to Methuselah* is in sympathy with the intellectual rather than the emotional attitude to life. I felt that I was beginning to understand the dead woman.

'I next studied the reactions of those who had formed Mrs Leidner's immediate circle—and my picture of the dead woman grew more and more complete.

'It was quite clear to me from the accounts of Dr Reilly and others that Mrs Leidner was one of those women who are endowed by Nature not only with beauty but with the kind of calamitous magic which sometimes accompanies beauty and can, indeed, exist independently of it. Such women usually leave a trail of violent happenings behind them. They bring disaster—sometimes on others—sometimes on themselves.

'I was convinced that Mrs Leidner was a woman who essentially worshipped *herself* and who enjoyed more than anything else the sense of *power*. Wherever she was, she *must* be the centre of the universe. And everyone round her, man or woman, had got to acknowledge her sway. With some people that was easy. Nurse Leatheran, for instance,

Murder in Mesopotamia

a generous-natured woman with a romantic imagination, was captured instantly and gave in ungrudging manner full appreciation. But there was a second way in which Mrs Leidner exercised her sway—the way of fear. Where conquest was too easy she indulged a more cruel side to her nature—but I wish to reiterate emphatically that it was not what you might call *conscious* cruelty. It was as natural and unthinking as is the conduct of a cat with a mouse. Where consciousness came in, she was essentially kind and would often go out of her way to do kind and thoughtful actions for other people.

'Now of course the first and most important problem to solve was the problem of the anonymous letters. Who had written them and why? I asked myself: Had Mrs Leidner written them *herself*?

'To answer this problem it was necessary to go back a long way—to go back, in fact, to the date of Mrs Leidner's first marriage. It is here we start on our journey proper. The journey of Mrs Leidner's life.

'First of all we must realize that the Louise Leidner of all those years ago is essentially the same Louise Leidner of the present time.

'She was young then, of remarkable beauty—that same haunting beauty that affects a man's spirit and senses as no mere material beauty can—and she was already essentially an egoist.

'Such women naturally revolt from the idea of marriage. They may be attracted by men, but they prefer to belong to themselves. They are truly *La Belle Dame sans Merci* of the legend. Nevertheless Mrs Leidner *did* marry—and we can assume, I think, that her husband must have been a man of a certain force of character.

'Then the revelation of his traitorous activities occurs and Mrs Leidner acts in the way she told Nurse Leatheran. She gave information to the Government.

'Now I submit that there was a psychological significance in her action. She told Nurse Leatheran that she was a very patriotic idealistic girl and that that feeling was the cause of her action. But it is a well-known fact that we all tend to deceive ourselves as to the motives for our own actions. Instinctively we select the best-sounding motive! Mrs Leidner may have believed herself that it was patriotism that inspired her action, but I believe myself that it was really the outcome of an unacknowledged desire to get rid of her husband! She disliked domination—she disliked the feeling of belonging to someone else—in fact she disliked playing second fiddle. She took a patriotic way of regaining her freedom.

'But underneath her consciousness was a gnawing sense of guilt which was to play its part in her future destiny.

'We now come directly to the question of the letters. Mrs Leidner was highly attractive to the male sex. On several occasions she was attracted by them—but in each case a threatening letter played its part and the affair came to nothing.

'Who wrote those letters? Frederick Bosner or his brother William or *Mrs Leidner herself*?

'There is a perfectly good case for either theory. It seems clear to me that Mrs Leidner was one of those women who

Murder in Mesopotamia

do inspire devouring devotions in men, the type of devotion which can become an obsession. I find it quite possible to believe in a Frederick Bosner to whom Louise, his wife, mattered more than anything in the world! She had betrayed him once and he dared not approach her openly, but he was determined at least that she should be his or no one's. He preferred her death to her belonging to another man.

'On the other hand, if Mrs Leidner had, deep down, a dislike of entering into the marriage bond, it is possible that she took this way of extricating herself from difficult positions. She was a huntress who, the prey once attained, had no further use for it! Craving drama in her life, she invented a highly satisfactory drama—a resurrected husband forbidding the banns! It satisfied her deepest instincts. It made her a romantic figure, a tragic heroine, and it enabled her not to marry again.

'This state of affairs continued over a number of years. Every time there was any likelihood of marriage—a threatening letter arrived.

'*But now we come to a really interesting point.* Dr Leidner came upon the scene—and no forbidding letter arrived! Nothing stood in the way of her becoming Mrs Leidner. Not until *after* her marriage did a letter arrive.

'At once we ask ourselves—why?

'Let us take each theory in turn.

'*If* Mrs Leidner wrote the letters herself the problem is easily explained. Mrs Leidner really *wanted* to marry Dr Leidner. And so she *did* marry him. But in that case, *why did she write herself a letter afterwards?* Was her craving

Agatha Christie

for drama too strong to be suppressed? And why only those two letters? After that no other letter was received until a year and a half later.

'Now take the other theory, that the letters were written by her first husband, Frederick Bosner (or his brother). Why did the threatening letter arrive *after* the marriage? Presumably Frederick could not have *wanted* her to marry Leidner. Why, then, did he not stop the marriage? He had done so successfully on former occasions. And why, *having waited till the marriage had taken place*, did he then resume his threats?

'The answer, an unsatisfactory one, is that he was somehow or other unable to protest sooner. He may have been in prison or he may have been abroad.

'There is next the attempted gas poisoning to consider. It seems extremely unlikely that it was brought about by an outside agency. The likely persons to have staged it were Dr and Mrs Leidner themselves. There seems no conceivable reason why *Dr* Leidner should do such a thing, so we are brought to the conclusion that *Mrs* Leidner planned and carried it out herself.

'Why? More drama?

'After that Dr and Mrs Leidner go abroad and for eighteen months they lead a happy, peaceful life with no threats of death to disturb it. They put that down to having successfully covered their traces, but such an explanation is quite absurd. In these days going abroad is quite inadequate for that purpose. And especially was that so in the case of the Leidners. He was the director of a museum expedition. By inquiry at the museum, Frederick Bosner could at once have obtained his correct address. Even granting that he was in too reduced circumstances to pursue the couple himself there would be no bar to his continuing his threatening letters. And it seems to me that a man with his obsession would certainly have done so.

'Instead nothing is heard of him until nearly two years later when the letters are resumed.

'*Why* were the letters resumed?

'A very difficult question—most easily answered by saying that Mrs Leidner was bored and wanted more drama. But I was not quite satisfied with that. This particular form of drama seemed to me a shade too vulgar and too crude to accord well with her fastidious personality.

'The only thing to do was to keep an open mind on the question.

'There were three definite possibilities: (1) the letters were written by Mrs Leidner herself; (2) they were written by Frederick Bosner (or young William Bosner); (3) they might have been written *originally* by either Mrs Leidner or her first husband, but they were now *forgeries*—that is, they were being written by a *third* person who was aware of the earlier letters.

'I now come to direct consideration of Mrs Leidner's entourage.

'I examined first the actual opportunities that each member of the staff had had for committing the murder.

'Roughly, on the face of it, *anyone* might have committed it (as far as opportunity went), with the exception of three persons.

'Dr Leidner, by overwhelming testimony, had never left the roof. Mr Carey was on duty at the mound. Mr Coleman was in Hassanieh.

'But those alibis, my friends, were not *quite* as good as they looked. I except Dr Leidner's. There is absolutely no doubt that he was on the roof all the time and did not come down until quite an hour and a quarter after the murder had happened.

'But was it *quite* certain that Mr Carey was on the mound all the time?

'And had Mr Coleman *actually been in Hassanieh* at the time the murder took place?'

Bill Coleman reddened, opened his mouth, shut it and looked round uneasily.

Mr Carey's expression did not change.

Poirot went on smoothly.

'I also considered one other person who, I satisfied myself, would be perfectly capable of committing murder *if she felt strongly enough*. Miss Reilly has courage and brains and a certain quality of ruthlessness. When Miss Reilly was speaking to me on the subject of the dead woman, I said to her, jokingly, that I hoped she had an alibi. I think Miss Reilly was conscious then that she had had in her heart the desire, at least, to kill. At any rate she immediately uttered a very silly and purposeless lie. She said she had been playing tennis on that afternoon. The next day I learned from a casual conversation with Miss Johnson that far from playing tennis, Miss Reilly *had actually been near this house at the time of the murder*. It occurred to me that

Murder in Mesopotamia

Miss Reilly, if not guilty of the crime, might be able to tell me something useful.'

He stopped and then said quietly: 'Will you tell us, Miss Reilly, what you *did* see that afternoon?'

The girl did not answer at once. She still looked out of the window without turning her head, and when she spoke it was in a detached and measured voice.

'I rode out to the dig after lunch. It must have been about a quarter to two when I got there.'

'Did you find any of your friends on the dig?'

'No, there seemed to be no one there but the Arab foreman.'

'You did not see Mr Carey?'

'No.'

'Curious,' said Poirot. 'No more did M. Verrier when he went there that same afternoon.'

He looked invitingly at Carey, but the latter neither moved nor spoke.

'Have you any explanation, Mr Carey?'

'I went for a walk. There was nothing of interest turning up.'

'In which direction did you go for a walk?'

'Down by the river.'

'Not back towards the house?'

'No.'

'I suppose,' said Miss Reilly, 'that you were waiting for someone who didn't come.'

He looked at her but didn't answer.

Poirot did not press the point. He spoke once more to the girl.

Agatha Christie

'Did you see anything else, mademoiselle?'

'Yes. I was not far from the expedition house when I noticed the expedition lorry drawn up in a wadi. I thought it was rather queer. Then I saw Mr Coleman. He was walking along with his head down as though he were searching for something.'

'Look here,' burst out Mr Coleman, 'I—'

Poirot stopped him with an authoritative gesture.

'Wait. Did you speak to him, Miss Reilly?'

'No. I didn't.'

'Why?'

The girl said slowly: 'Because, from time to time, he started and looked round with an extraordinary furtive look. It—gave me an unpleasant feeling. I turned my horse's head and rode away. I don't think he saw me. I was not very near and he was absorbed in what he was doing.'

'Look here,' Mr Coleman was not to be hushed any longer. 'I've got a perfectly good explanation for what—I admit—looks a bit fishy. As a matter of fact, the day before I had slipped a jolly fine cylinder seal into my coat pocket instead of putting it in the antika-room—forgot all about it. And then I discovered I'd been and lost it out of my pocket—dropped it somewhere. I didn't want to get into a row about it so I decided I'd have a jolly good search on the quiet. I was pretty sure I'd dropped it on the way to or from the dig. I rushed over my business in Hassanieh. Sent a walad to do some of the shopping and got back early. I stuck the bus where it wouldn't show and had a jolly good hunt for over an hour. And didn't find the damned thing at that! Then I got into the bus and drove on to the house. Naturally, everyone thought I'd just got back.'

'And you did not undeceive them?' asked Poirot sweetly.

'Well, that was pretty natural under the circumstances, don't you think?'

'I hardly agree,' said Poirot.

'Oh, come now—don't go looking for trouble—that's *my* motto! But you can't fasten anything on me. I never went into the courtyard, and you can't find anyone who'll say I did.'

'That, of course, has been the difficulty,' said Poirot. 'The evidence of the servants that *no one entered the courtyard from outside*. But it occurred to me, upon reflection, that that was really *not* what they had said. They had sworn that *no stranger* had entered the premises. They had not been asked *if a member of the expedition* had done so.'

'Well, you ask them,' said Coleman. 'I'll eat my hat if they saw me or Carey either.'

'Ah! but that raises rather an interesting question. They would notice *a stranger* undoubtedly—but would they have even *noticed* a member of the expedition? The members of the staff are passing in and out all day. The servants would hardly notice their going and coming. It is possible, I think, that either Mr Carey or Mr Coleman *might* have entered and the servants' minds would have no remembrance of such an event.'

'Bunkum!' said Mr Coleman.

Poirot went on calmly: 'Of the two, I think Mr Carey was the least likely to be noticed going or coming. Mr

Agatha Christie

Coleman had started to Hassanieh in the car that morning and he would be expected to return in it. His arrival on foot would therefore be noticeable.'

'Of course it would!' said Coleman.

Richard Carey raised his head. His deep-blue eyes looked straight at Poirot.

'Are you accusing me of murder, M. Poirot?' he asked.

His manner was quite quiet but his voice had a dangerous undertone.

Poirot bowed to him.

'As yet I am only taking you all on a journey—my journey towards the truth. I had now established one fact—that all the members of the expedition staff, and also Nurse Leatheran, could in actual *fact* have committed the murder. That there was very little likelihood of some of them having committed it was a secondary matter.

'I had examined *means* and *opportunity*. I next passed to *motive*. I discovered that *one and all of you could be credited with a motive*!'

'Oh! M. Poirot,' I cried. 'Not *me*! Why, I was a stranger. I'd only just come.'

'*Eh bien, ma soeur*, and was not that *just what Mrs Leidner had been fearing*? A *stranger* from *outside*?'

'But—but—Why, Dr Reilly knew all about me! He suggested my coming!'

'How much did he really know about you? *Mostly what you yourself had told him*. Imposters have passed themselves off as hospital nurses before now.'

'You can write to St. Christopher's,' I began.

'For the moment will you silence yourself. Impossible to proceed while you conduct this argument. I do not say I suspect you *now*. All I say is that, keeping the open mind, you might quite easily be someone other than you pretended to be. There are many successful female impersonators, you know. Young William Bosner might be something of that kind.'

I was about to give him a further piece of my mind. Female impersonator indeed! But he raised his voice and hurried on with such an air of determination that I thought better of it.

'I am going now to be frank—brutally so. It is necessary. I am going to lay bare the underlying structure of this place.

'I examined and considered every single soul here. To begin with Dr Leidner, I soon convinced myself that his love for his wife was the mainspring of his existence. He was a man torn and ravaged with grief. Nurse Leatheran I have already mentioned. If she were a female impersonator she was a most amazingly successful one, and I inclined to the belief that she was exactly what she said she was—a thoroughly competent hospital nurse.'

'Thank you for nothing,' I interposed.

'My attention was immediately attracted towards Mr and Mrs Mercado, who were both of them clearly in a state of great agitation and unrest. I considered first Mrs Mercado. Was she capable of murder, and if so for what reasons?

'Mrs Mercado's physique was frail. At first sight it did not seem possible that she could have had the physical strength to strike down a woman like Mrs Leidner with a heavy stone implement. If, however, Mrs Leidner had been on her knees at the time, the thing would at least be *physically possible*. There are ways in which one woman can induce another to go down on her knees. Oh! not emotional ways! For instance, a woman might be turning up the hem of a skirt and ask another woman to put in the pins for her. The second woman would kneel on the ground quite unsuspectingly.

'But the motive? Nurse Leatheran had told me of the angry glances she had seen Mrs Mercado direct at Mrs Leidner. Mr Mercado had evidently succumbed easily to Mrs Leidner's spell. But I did not think the solution was to be found in mere jealousy. I was sure Mrs Leidner was not in the least interested really in Mr Mercado—and doubtless Mrs Mercado was aware of the fact. She might be furious with her for the moment, but for *murder* there would have to be greater provocation. But Mrs Mercado was essentially a fiercely maternal type. From the way she looked at her husband I realized, not only that she loved him, but that she would fight for him tooth and nail—and more than that—*that she envisaged the possibility of having to do so*. She was constantly on her guard and uneasy. The uneasiness was for him—not for herself. And when I studied Mr Mercado I could make a fairly easy guess at what the trouble was. I took means to assure myself of the truth of my guess. Mr Mercado was a drug addict—in an advanced stage of the craving.

'Now I need probably not tell you all that the taking of drugs over a long period has the result of considerably blunting the moral sense.

'Under the influence of drugs a man commits actions that he would not have dreamed of committing a few years earlier before he began the practice. In some cases a man has committed murder—and it has been difficult to say whether he was wholly responsible for his actions or not. The law of different countries varies slightly on that point. The chief characteristic of the drug-fiend criminal is overweening confidence in his own cleverness.

'I thought it possible that there was some discreditable incident, perhaps a criminal incident, in Mr Mercado's past which his wife had somehow or other succeeded in hushing up. Nevertheless his career hung on a thread. If anything of this past incident were bruited about, Mr Mercado would be ruined. His wife was always on the watch. But there was Mrs Leidner to be reckoned with. She had a sharp intelligence and a love of power. She might even induce the wretched man to confide in her. It would just have suited her peculiar temperament to feel she knew a secret which she could reveal at any minute with disastrous effects.

'Here, then, was a possible motive for murder on the part of the Mercados. To protect her mate, Mrs Mercado, I felt sure, would stick at nothing! Both she and her husband had had the opportunity—during that ten minutes when the courtyard was empty.'

Mrs Mercado cried out, 'It's not *true*!'

Poirot paid no attention.

'I next considered Miss Johnson. Was *she* capable of murder?

Agatha Christie

'I thought she was. She was a person of strong will and iron self-control. Such people are constantly repressing themselves—and one day the dam bursts! But if Miss Johnson had committed the crime it could only be for some reason connected with Dr Leidner. If in any way she felt convinced that Mrs Leidner was spoiling her husband's life, then the deep unacknowledged jealousy far down in her would leap at the chance of a plausible motive and give itself full rein.

'Yes, Miss Johnson was distinctly a possibility.

'Then there were the three young men.

'First Carl Reiter. If, by any chance, one of the expedition staff was William Bosner, then Reiter was by far the most likely person. But if he *was* William Bosner, then he was certainly a most accomplished actor! If he were merely *himself*, had he any reason for murder?

'Regarded from Mrs Leidner's point of view, Carl Reiter was far too easy a victim for good sport. He was prepared to fall on his face and worship immediately. Mrs Leidner despised undiscriminating adoration—and the door-mat attitude nearly always brings out the worst side of a woman. In her treatment of Carl Reiter Mrs Leidner displayed really deliberate cruelty. She inserted a gibe here—a prick there. She made the poor young man's life a hell to him.'

Poirot broke off suddenly and addressed the young man in a personal, highly confidential manner.

'*Mon ami*, let this be a lesson to you. You are a *man*. Behave, then, like a *man*! It is against Nature for a man to grovel. Women and Nature have almost exactly the same reactions! Remember it is better to take the largest plate within reach and fling it at a woman's head than it is to wriggle like a worm whenever she looks at you!'

He dropped his private manner and reverted to his lecture style.

'Could Carl Reiter have been goaded to such a pitch of torment that he turned on his tormentor and killed her? Suffering does queer things to a man. I could not be *sure* that it was *not* so!

'Next William Coleman. His behaviour, as reported by Miss Reilly, is certainly suspicious. If he was the criminal it could only be because his cheerful personality concealed the hidden one of William Bosner. I do not think William Coleman, as William Coleman, has the temperament of a murderer. His faults might lie in another direction. Ah! perhaps Nurse Leatheran can guess what they would be?'

How *did* the man do it? I'm sure I didn't look as though I was thinking anything at all.

'It's nothing really,' I said, hesitating. 'Only if it's to be all truth, Mr Coleman *did* say once himself that he would have made a good forger.'

'A good point,' said Poirot. 'Therefore if he had come across some of the old threatening letters, he could have copied them without difficulty.'

'Oy, oy, oy!' called out Mr Coleman. 'This is what they call a frame-up.'

Poirot swept on.

'As to his being or not being William Bosner, such a matter is difficult of verification. But Mr Coleman has spoken of a *guardian*—not of a father—and there is nothing definitely to veto the idea.'

'Tommyrot,' said Mr Coleman. 'Why all of you listen to this chap beats me.'

'Of the three young men there remains Mr Emmott,' went on Poirot. 'He again might be a possible shield for the identity of William Bosner. Whatever *personal reasons* he might have for the removal of Mrs Leidner I soon realized that I should have no means of learning them from him. He could keep his own counsel remarkably well, and there was not the least chance of provoking him nor of tricking him into betraying himself on any point. Of all the expedition he seemed to be the best and most dispassionate judge of Mrs Leidner's personality. I think that he always knew her for exactly what she was—but what impression her personality made on him I was unable to discover. I fancy that Mrs Leidner herself must have been provoked and angered by his attitude.

'I may say that of all the expedition, *as far as character and capacity were concerned*, Mr Emmott seemed to me the most fitted to bring a clever and well-timed crime off satisfactorily.'

For the first time, Mr Emmott raised his eyes from the toes of his boots.

'Thank you,' he said.

There seemed to be just a trace of amusement in his voice.

'The last two people on my list were Richard Carey and Father Lavigny.

'According to the testimony of Nurse Leatheran and others, Mr Carey and Mrs Leidner disliked each other. They were both civil with an effort. Another person, Miss Reilly, propounded a totally different theory to account for their attitude of frigid politeness.

'I soon had very little doubt that Miss Reilly's explanation was the correct one. I acquired my certitude by the simple expedient of provoking Mr Carey into reckless and unguarded speech. It was not difficult. As I soon saw, he was in a state of high nervous tension. In fact he was—and is—very near a complete nervous breakdown. A man who is suffering up to the limit of his capacity can seldom put up much of a fight.

'Mr Carey's barriers came down almost immediately. He told me, with a sincerity that I did not for a moment doubt, that he hated Mrs Leidner.

'And he was undoubtedly speaking the truth. He *did* hate Mrs Leidner. But *why* did he hate her?

'I have spoken of women who have a calamitous magic. But men have that magic too. There are men who are able without the least effort to attract women. What they call in these days *le sex appeal*! Mr Carey had this quality very strongly. He was to begin with devoted to his friend and employer, and indifferent to his employer's wife. That did not suit Mrs Leidner. She *must* dominate—and she set herself out to capture Richard Carey. But here, I believe, something entirely unforeseen took place. She herself for perhaps the first time in her life, fell a victim to an overmastering passion. She fell in love—really in love—with Richard Carey.

'And he—was unable to resist her. Here is the truth of the terrible state of nervous tension that he has been enduring.

Agatha Christie

He has been a man torn by two opposing passions. He loved Louise Leidner—yes, but he also hated her. He hated her for undermining his loyalty to his friend. There is no hatred so great as that of a man who has been made to love a woman against his will.

'I had here all the motive that I needed. I was convinced that *at certain moments* the most natural thing for Richard Carey to do would have been to strike with all the force of his arm at the beautiful face that had cast a spell over him.

'All along I had felt sure that the murder of Louise Leidner was a *crime passionnel*. In Mr Carey I had found an ideal murderer for that type of crime.

'There remains one other candidate for the title of murderer—Father Lavigny. My attention was attracted to the good Father straightaway by a certain discrepancy between his description of the strange man who had been seen peering in at the window and the one given by Nurse Leatheran. In all accounts given by different witnesses there is usually *some* discrepancy, but this was absolutely glaring. Moreover, Father Lavigny insisted on a certain characteristic—a squint—which ought to make identification much easier.

'But very soon it became apparent that *while Nurse Leatheran's description was substantially accurate*, Father Lavigny's was *nothing of the kind*. It looked almost as though Father Lavigny was deliberately misleading us—as though he did *not want the man caught*.

'But in that case *he must know something about this curious person*. He had been seen talking to the man but we had only his word for what they had been talking about.

'What had the Iraqi been doing when Nurse Leatheran and Mrs Leidner saw him? Trying to peer through the window—Mrs Leidner's window, so they thought, but I realized when I went and stood where they had been, that it might equally have been the *antika-room window*.

'The night after that an alarm was given. Someone was in the antika-room. Nothing proved to have been taken, however. The interesting point to me is that when Dr Leidner got there he found *Father Lavigny there before him*. Father Lavigny tells his story of seeing a light. *But again we have only his word for it.*

'I begin to get curious about Father Lavigny. The other day when I make the suggestion that Father Lavigny may be Frederick Bosner, Dr Leidner pooh-poohs the suggestion. He says Father Lavigny is a well-known man. I advance the supposition that Frederick Bosner, who has had nearly twenty years to make a career for himself, under a new name, may very possibly *be* a well-known man by this time! All the same, I do not think that he has spent the intervening time in a religious community. A very much simpler solution presents itself.

'Did anyone at the expedition know Father Lavigny by sight before he came? Apparently not. Why then should not it be *someone impersonating the good Father*? I found out that a telegram had been sent to Carthage on the sudden illness of Dr Byrd, who was to have accompanied the expedition. To intercept a telegram, what could be easier? As to the work, there was no other epigraphist attached to the expedition. With a smattering of knowledge a clever

Agatha Christie

man *might* bluff his way through. There had been very few tablets and inscriptions so far, and already I gathered that Father Lavigny's pronouncements had been felt to be somewhat unusual.

'It looked very much as though Father Lavigny were an *imposter*.

'But was he Frederick Bosner?

'Somehow, affairs did not seem to be shaping themselves that way. The truth seemed likely to lie in quite a different direction.

'I had a lengthy conversation with Father Lavigny. I am a practising Catholic and I know many priests and members of religious communities. Father Lavigny struck me as not ringing quite true to his role. But he struck me, on the other hand, as familiar in quite a different capacity. I *had* met men of his type quite frequently—but they were not members of a religious community. Far from it!

'I began to send off telegrams.

'And then, unwittingly, Nurse Leatheran gave me a valuable clue. We were examining the gold ornaments in the antika-room and she mentioned a trace of wax having been found adhering to a gold cup. Me, I say, "Wax?" and Father Lavigny, he said "Wax?" and his tone was enough! I knew in a flash exactly what he was doing here.'

Poirot paused and addressed himself directly to Dr Leidner.

'I regret to tell you, monsieur, that the gold cup in the antika-room, the gold dagger, the hair ornaments and several other things *are not the genuine articles found by you*. They are very clever electrotypes. Father Lavigny, I have just learned by this last answer to my telegrams, is none other than Raoul Menier, one of the cleverest thieves known to the French police. He specializes in thefts from museums of *objets d'art* and such like. Associated with him is Ali Yusuf, a semi-Turk, who is a first-class working jeweller. Our first knowledge of Menier was when certain objects in the Louvre were found not to be genuine—in every case it was discovered that a distinguished archaeologist *not known previously by sight to the director* had recently had the handling of the spurious articles when paying a visit to the Louvre. On inquiry all these distinguished gentlemen denied having paid a visit to the Louvre at the times stated!

'I have learned that Menier was in Tunis preparing the way for a theft from the Holy Fathers when your telegram arrived. Father Lavigny, who was in ill-health, was forced to refuse, but Menier managed to get hold of the telegram and substitute one of acceptance. He was quite safe in doing so. Even if the monks should read in some paper (in itself an unlikely thing) that Father Lavigny was in Iraq they would only think that the newspapers had got hold of a half-truth as so often happens.

'Menier and his accomplice arrived. The latter is seen when he is reconnoitring the antika-room from outside. The plan is for Father Lavigny to take wax impressions. Ali then makes clever duplicates. There are always certain collectors who are willing to pay a good price for genuine antiques and will ask no embarrassing questions. Father

Agatha Christie

Lavigny will effect the substitution of the fake for the genuine article—preferably at night.

'And that is doubtless what he was doing when Mrs Leidner heard him and gave the alarm. What can he do? He hurriedly makes up a story of having seen a light in the antika-room.

'That "went down", as you say, very well. But Mrs Leidner was no fool. She may have remembered the trace of wax she had noticed and then put two and two together. And if she did, what will she do then? Would it not be *dans son caractère* to do nothing at once, but to enjoy herself by letting hints slip to the discomfiture of Father Lavigny? She will let him see that she suspects—but not that she *knows*. It is, perhaps, a dangerous game, but she enjoys a dangerous game.

'And perhaps she plays that game too long. Father Lavigny sees the truth, and strikes before she realizes what he means to do.

'Father Lavigny is Raoul Menier—a thief. Is he also—a *murderer*?'

Poirot paced the room. He took out a handkerchief, wiped his forehead and went on: 'That was my position this morning. There were eight distinct possibilities and I did not know which of these possibilities was the right one. I still did not know *who was the murderer*.

'But murder is a habit. The man or woman who kills once will kill again.

'And by the second murder, the murderer was delivered into my hands.

'All along it was ever present in the back of my mind that some one of these people might have knowledge that they had kept back—knowledge incriminating the murderer.

'If so, that person would be in danger.

'My solicitude was mainly on account of Nurse Leatheran. She had an energetic personality and a brisk inquisitive mind. I was terrified of her finding out more than it was safe for her to know.

'As you all know, a second murder did take place. But the victim was not Nurse Leatheran—it was Miss Johnson.

'I like to think that I should have reached the correct solution anyway by pure reasoning, but it is certain that Miss Johnson's murder helped me to it much quicker.

'To begin with, one suspect was eliminated—Miss Johnson herself—for I did not for a moment entertain the theory of suicide.

'Let us examine now the facts of this second murder.

'Fact One: On Sunday evening Nurse Leatheran finds Miss Johnson in tears, and that same evening Miss Johnson burns a fragment of a letter which nurse believes to be in the same handwriting as that of the anonymous letters.

'Fact Two: The evening before her death Miss Johnson is found by Nurse Leatheran standing on the roof in a state that nurse describes as one of incredulous horror. When nurse questions her she says, "I've seen how someone could come in from outside—and no one would ever guess." She won't say any more. Father Lavigny is crossing the courtyard and Mr Reiter is at the door of the photographic-room.

'Fact Three: Miss Johnson is found dying. The only words she can manage to articulate are "the window—the window—"

'Those are the facts, and these are the problems with which we are faced:

'What is the truth of the letters?

'What did Miss Johnson see from the roof?

'What did she mean by "the window—the window"?

'*Eh bien*, let us take the second problem first as the easiest of solution. I went up with Nurse Leatheran and I stood where Miss Johnson had stood. From there she could see the courtyard and the archway and the north side of the building and two members of the staff. Had her words anything to do with either Mr Reiter or Father Lavigny?

'Almost at once a possible explanation leaped to my brain. If a stranger came in from *outside* he could only do so in *disguise*. And there was only *one* person whose general appearance lent itself to such an impersonation. Father Lavigny! With a sun helmet, sun glasses, black beard and a monk's long woollen robe, a stranger could pass in without the servants *realising* that a stranger had entered.

'Was *that* Miss Johnson's meaning? Or had she gone further? Did she realize that Father Lavigny's whole *personality* was a disguise? That he was someone other than he pretended to be?

'Knowing what I did know about Father Lavigny, I was inclined to call the mystery solved. Raoul Menier was the murderer. He had killed Mrs Leidner to silence her before she could give him away. Now *another person lets him see that she has penetrated his secret*. She, too, must be removed.

'And so everything is explained! The second murder. Father Lavigny's flight—minus robe and beard. (He and his friend are doubtless careering through Syria with excellent passports as two commercial travellers.) His action in placing the blood-stained quern under Miss Johnson's bed.

'As I say, I was almost satisfied—but not quite. For the perfect solution must explain *everything*—and this does not do so.

'It does not explain, for instance, why Miss Johnson should say "the window—the window", as she was dying. It does not explain her fit of weeping over the letter. It does not explain her mental attitude on the roof—her incredulous horror and her refusal to tell Nurse Leatheran what it was that *she now suspected or knew*.

'It was a solution that fitted the *outer* facts, but it did not satisfy the *psychological* requirements.

'And then, as I stood on the roof, going over in my mind those three points: the letters, the roof, the window, I *saw*—just as Miss Johnson had seen!

'*And this time what I saw explained everything!*'

CHAPTER 28

Journey's End

Poirot looked round. Every eye was now fixed upon him. There had been a certain relaxation—a slackening of tension. Now the tension suddenly returned.

There was something coming…something…

Poirot's voice, quiet and unimpassioned, went on: 'The letters, the roof, "the window"… Yes, everything was explained—everything fell into place.

'I said just now that three men had alibis for the time of the crime. Two of those alibis I have shown to be worthless. I saw now my great—my amazing mistake. The third alibi was worthless too. Not only *could* Dr Leidner have committed the murder—but I was convinced that he *had* committed it.'

There was a silence, a bewildered, uncomprehending silence. Dr Leidner said nothing. He seemed lost in his faraway world still. David Emmott, however, stirred uneasily and spoke.

'I don't know what you mean to imply, M. Poirot. I told you that Dr Leidner never left the roof until at least a quarter to three. That is the absolute truth. I swear it solemnly. I am not lying. And it would have been quite impossible for him to have done so without my seeing him.'

Poirot nodded.

'Oh, I believe you. *Dr Leidner did not leave the roof.* That is an undisputed fact. But what I saw—and what Miss Johnson had seen—was *that Dr Leidner could murder his wife from the roof without leaving it.*'

We all stared.

'The *window*,' cried Poirot. '*Her* window! That is what I realized—just as Miss Johnson realized it. Her window was directly underneath, on the side away from the courtyard. And Dr Leidner was alone up there with no one to witness his actions. And those heavy stone querns and grinders were up there all ready to his hand. So simple, so very simple, granted one thing—*that the murderer had the opportunity to move the body before anyone else saw it*... Oh, it is beautiful—of an unbelievable simplicity!

'Listen—it went like this:

'Dr Leidner is on the roof working with the pottery. He calls you up, Mr Emmott, and while he holds you in talk he notices that, as usually happens, the small boy takes advantage of your absence to leave his work and go outside the courtyard. He keeps you with him ten minutes, then he lets you go and as soon as you are down below shouting to the boy he sets his plan in operation.

'He takes from his pocket the plasticine-smeared mask with which he has already scared his wife on a former

Agatha Christie

occasion and dangles it over the edge of the parapet till it taps on his wife's window.

'That, remember, is the window giving on the countryside facing the opposite direction to the courtyard.

'Mrs Leidner is lying on her bed half asleep. She is peaceful and happy. Suddenly the mask begins tapping on the window and attracts her attention. But it is not dusk now—it is broad daylight—there is nothing terrifying about it. She recognizes it for what it is—a crude form of trickery! She is not frightened but indignant. She does what any other woman would do in her place. Jumps off the bed, opens the window, passes her head through the bars and turns her face upward to see who is playing the trick on her.

'Dr Leidner is waiting. He has in his hands, poised and ready, a heavy quern. At the psychological moment *he drops it...*

'With a faint cry (heard by Miss Johnson) Mrs Leidner collapses on the rug underneath the window.

'Now there is a hole in this quern, and through that Dr Leidner had previously passed a cord. He has now only to haul in the cord and bring up the quern. He replaces the latter neatly, bloodstained side down, amongst the other objects of that kind on the roof.

'Then he continues his work for an hour or more till he judges the moment has come for the second act. He descends the stairs, speaks to Mr Emmott and Nurse Leatheran, crosses the courtyard and enters his wife's room. This is the explanation he himself gives of his movements there:

'"*I saw my wife's body in a heap by the bed. For a moment or two I felt paralysed as though I couldn't move.*

Then at last I went and knelt down by her and lifted up her head. I saw she was dead... At last I got up. I felt dazed and as though I were drunk. I managed to get to the door and call out."

'A perfectly possible account of the actions of a grief-dazed man. Now listen to what I believe to be the truth. Dr Leidner enters the room, hurries to the window, and, having pulled on a pair of gloves, closes and fastens it, then picks up his wife's body and transports it to a position between the bed and the door. Then he notices a slight stain on the window-side rug. He cannot change it with the other rug, they are a different size, but he does the next best thing. He puts the stained rug in front of the washstand and the rug from the washstand under the window. *If* the stain is noticed, it will be connected with the *washstand*—not with the *window*—a very important point. There must be no suggestion that the window played any part in the business. Then he comes to the door and acts the part of the overcome husband, and that, I imagine, is not difficult. For he *did* love his wife.'

'My good man,' cried Dr Reilly impatiently, 'if he loved her, why did he kill her? Where's the motive? Can't you speak, Leidner? Tell him he's mad.'

Dr Leidner neither spoke nor moved.

Poirot said: 'Did I not tell you all along that this was a *crime passionnel*? Why did her first husband, Frederick Bosner, threaten to kill her? Because he loved her... And in the end, you see, he made his boast good...

'*Mais oui—mais oui—once I realize that it is Dr Leidner who did the killing*, everything falls into place...

Agatha Christie

'For the second time, I recommence my journey from the beginning—Mrs Leidner's first marriage—the threatening letters—her second marriage. The letters prevented her marrying any other man—but they did not prevent her marrying Dr Leidner. How simple that is—*if Dr Leidner is actually Frederick Bosner*.

'Once more let us start our journey—from the point of view this time of young Frederick Bosner.

'To begin with, he loves his wife Louise with an overpowering passion such as only a woman of her kind can evoke. She betrays him. He is sentenced to death. He escapes. He is involved in a railway accident but he manages to emerge with a second personality—*that of a young Swedish archaeologist, Eric Leidner*, whose body is badly disfigured and who will be conveniently buried as Frederick Bosner.

'What is the new Eric Leidner's attitude to the woman who was willing to send him to his death? First and most important, *he still loves her*. He sets to work to build up his new life. He is a man of great ability, his profession is congenial to him and he makes a success of it. *But he never forgets the ruling passion of his life*. He keeps himself informed of his wife's movements. Of one thing he is cold-bloodedly determined (remember Mrs Leidner's own description of him to Nurse Leatheran—gentle and kind but ruthless), *she shall belong to no other man*. Whenever he judges it necessary he despatches a letter. He imitates some of the peculiarities of her handwriting in case she should think of taking his letters to the police. Women who write sensational anonymous letters to themselves are such a common phenomenon that the police will be sure to jump to that solution given the likeness of the handwriting. At the same time he leaves her in doubt as to whether he is really alive or not.

'At last, after many years, he judges that the time has arrived; he re-enters her life. All goes well. His wife never dreams of his real identity. He is a well-known man. The upstanding, good-looking young fellow is now a middle-aged man with a beard and stooping shoulders. And so we see history repeating itself. As before, Frederick is able to dominate Louise. For the second time she consents to marry him. *And no letter comes to forbid the banns.*

'But *afterwards* a letter *does* come. Why?

'I think that Dr Leidner was taking no chances. The intimacy of marriage *might* awaken a memory. He wishes to impress on his wife, once and for all, *that Eric Leidner and Frederick Bosner are two different people.* So much so that a threatening letter comes from the former on account of the latter. The rather puerile gas poisoning business follows—arranged by Dr Leidner, of course. Still with the same object in view.

'After that he is satisfied. No more letters need come. They can settle down to happy married life together.

'And then, after nearly two years, *the letters recommence.*

'*Why? Eh bien*, I think I know. *Because the threat underlying the letters was always a genuine threat.* (That is why Mrs Leidner has always been frightened. She *knew* her Frederick's gentle but ruthless nature.) *If she belongs to any other man but him he would kill her. And she has given herself to Richard Carey.*

Agatha Christie

'And so, having discovered this, cold-bloodedly, calmly, Dr Leidner prepares the scene for murder.

'You see now the important part played by Nurse Leatheran? Dr Leidner's rather curious conduct (it puzzled me at the very first) in securing her services for his wife is explained. It was vital that a reliable professional witness should be able to state incontrovertibly that Mrs Leidner had been dead *over an hour* when her body was found—that is, that she had been killed at a time when *everybody could swear her husband was on the roof*. A suspicion *might* have arisen that he had killed her when he entered the room and found the body—but that was out of the question when a trained hospital nurse would assert positively that she had already been dead an hour.

'Another thing that is explained is the curious state of tension and strain that had come over the expedition this year. I never from the first thought that that could be attributed solely to *Mrs* Leidner's influence. For several years this particular expedition had had a reputation for happy good-fellowship. In my opinion, the state of mind of a community is always directly due to the influence of the man at the top. Dr Leidner, quiet though he was, was a man of great personality. It was due to his tact, to his judgment, to his sympathetic manipulation of human beings that the atmosphere had always been such a happy one.

'If there was a change, therefore, the change must be due to the man at the top—in other words, to Dr Leidner. It was *Dr* Leidner, not Mrs Leidner, who was responsible for the tension and uneasiness. No wonder the staff felt the change without understanding it. The kindly, genial Dr Leidner, outwardly the same, was only playing the part of himself. The real man was an obsessed fanatic plotting to kill.

'And now we will pass on to the second murder—that of Miss Johnson. In tidying up Dr Leidner's papers in the office (a job she took on herself unasked, craving for something to do) she must have come on some unfinished draft of one of the anonymous letters.

'It must have been both incomprehensible and extremely upsetting to her! Dr Leidner has been deliberately terrorizing his wife! She cannot understand it—but it upsets her badly. It is in this mood that Nurse Leatheran discovers her crying.

'I do not think at the moment that she suspected Dr Leidner of being the murderer, but my experiments with sounds in Mrs Leidner's and Father Lavigny's rooms are not lost upon her. She realizes that if it *was* Mrs Leidner's cry she heard, *the window in her room must have been open, not shut*. At the moment that conveys nothing vital to her, *but she remembers it.*

'Her mind goes on working—ferreting its way towards the truth. Perhaps she makes some reference to the letters which Dr Leidner understands and his manner changes. She may see that he is, suddenly, afraid.

'But Dr Leidner *cannot* have killed his wife! He was on the *roof* all the time.

'And then, one evening, as she herself is on the roof puzzling about it, the truth comes to her in a flash. Mrs Leidner has been killed from up *here*, through the open window.

'It was at that minute that Nurse Leatheran found her.

'And immediately, her old affection reasserting itself, she puts up a quick camouflage. Nurse Leatheran must not guess the horrifying discovery she has just made.

'She looks deliberately in the opposite direction (towards the courtyard) and makes a remark suggested to her by Father Lavigny's appearance as he crosses the courtyard.

'She refuses to say more. She has got to "think things out".

'And Dr Leidner, who has been watching her anxiously, *realizes that she knows the truth*. She is not the kind of woman to conceal her horror and distress from him.

'It is true that as yet she has not given him away—but how long can he depend upon her?

'Murder is a habit. That night he substitutes a glass of acid for her glass of water. There is just a chance she may be believed to have deliberately poisoned herself. There is even a chance she may be considered to have done the first murder and has now been overcome with remorse. To strengthen the latter idea he takes the quern from the roof and puts it under her bed.

'No wonder that poor Miss Johnson, in her death agony, could only try desperately to impart her hard-won information. Through "the window," *that* is how Mrs Leidner was killed, *not* through the door—through the *window*...

'And so thus, everything is explained, everything falls into place... Psychologically perfect.

'But there is no proof... No proof at all...'

None of us spoke. We were lost in a sea of horror... Yes, and not only horror. Pity, too.

Dr Leidner had neither moved nor spoken. He sat just as he had done all along. A tired, worn elderly man.

At last he stirred slightly and looked at Poirot with gentle, tired eyes.

'No,' he said, 'there is no proof. But that does not matter. You knew that I would not deny truth... I have never denied truth... I think—really—I am rather glad... I'm so tired...'

Then he said simply: 'I'm sorry about Anne. That was bad—senseless—it wasn't *me*! And she suffered, too, poor soul. Yes, that wasn't me. It was fear...'

A little smile just hovered on his pain-twisted lips.

'You would have made a good archaeologist, M. Poirot. You have the gift of re-creating the past.

'It was all very much as you said.

'I loved Louise and I killed her...if you'd known Louise you'd have understood... No, I think you understand anyway...'

CHAPTER 29

L'Envoi

There isn't really any more to say about things.

They got 'Father' Lavigny and the other man just as they were going to board a steamer at Beyrouth.

Sheila Reilly married young Emmott. I think that will be good for her. He's no door-mat—he'll keep her in her place. She'd have ridden roughshod over poor Bill Coleman.

I nursed him, by the way, when he had appendicitis a year ago. I got quite fond of him. His people were sending him out to farm in South Africa.

I've never been out East again. It's funny—sometimes I wish I could. I think of the noise the water-wheel made and the women washing, and that queer haughty look that camels give you—and I get quite a homesick feeling. After all, perhaps dirt isn't really so unhealthy as one is brought up to believe!

Dr Reilly usually looks me up when he's in England, and as I said, it's he who's got me into this. 'Take it or leave it,' I said to him. 'I know the grammar's all wrong and it's not properly written or anything like that—but there it is.'

And he took it. Made no bones about it. It will give me a queer feeling if it's ever printed.

M. Poirot went back to Syria and about a week later he went home on the Orient Express and got himself mixed up in another murder. He was clever, I don't deny it, but I shan't forgive him in a hurry for pulling my leg the way he did. Pretending to think I might be mixed up in the crime and not a real hospital nurse at all!

Doctors are like that sometimes. Will have their joke, some of them will, and never think of *your* feelings!

I've thought and thought about Mrs Leidner and what she was really like... Sometimes it seems to me she was just a terrible woman—and other times I remember how nice she was to me and how soft her voice was—and her lovely fair hair and everything—and I feel that perhaps, after all, she was more to be pitied than blamed...

And I can't help but pity Dr Leidner. I know he was a murderer twice over, but it doesn't seem to make any difference. He was so dreadfully fond of her. It's awful to be fond of anyone like that.

Somehow, the more I get older, and the more I see of people and sadness and illness and everything, the sorrier I get for everyone. Sometimes, I declare, I don't know what's becoming of the good, strict principles my aunt brought me up with. A very religious woman she was, and most particular. There wasn't one of our neighbours whose faults she didn't know backwards and forwards...

Oh, dear, it's quite true what Dr Reilly said. How does one stop writing? If I could find a really good telling phrase.

I must ask Dr Reilly for some Arab one.
Like the one M. Poirot used.
In the name of Allah, the Merciful, the Compassionate...
Something like that.